GREAT SEA NOVELS

GREAT SEA NOVELS

including
WRECKERS MUST BREATHE
THE WHITE SOUTH
THE MARY DEARE
ATLANTIC FURY
THE STRODE VENTURER

by

Hammond Innes

COLLINS
St James's Place, London
1978

William Collins Sons & Co Ltd
London · Glasgow · Sydney · Auckland
Toronto · Johannesburg

First published 1978
© Hammond Innes 1940, 1949, 1956, 1962, 1965
ISBN 0 00 243328 1
Set in Baskerville
Made and Printed in Great Britain by
William Collins Sons & Co Ltd Glasgow

CONTENTS

WRECKERS MUST BREATHE   11
THE WHITE SOUTH   165
THE MARY DEARE   395
ATLANTIC FURY   601
THE STRODE VENTURER   827

INTRODUCTION

That my publishers should offer five of my sea novels in one volume seemed at first like the work of a lunatic chef serving dishes of one flavour only when there were many to choose from. But it does have this advantage. Those of my readers who share with me an almost obsessive fascination for the sea now hold in their hands four at any rate of the best of my sea stories.

And though the background to all these novels is the same, the setting is not and the stories are vastly different, so that each is an entirely separate world. Three of them are set in the seas around the British Isles, which I think is right, for these are some of the most dangerous and varied waters to be found anywhere. The other two – *The White South* and *The Strode Venturer* – are nearer to the main body of my work, reaching out across the world to areas remote as the Antarctic and the Maldives.

The books are presented chronologically, in the order in which they were written, beginning with *Wreckers Must Breathe*. This was included at my request because it is an example of my early work, being the first published book I am willing to acknowledge and the start of my long association with Collins. It was written just before World War II. I was a journalist then, and happening to be in Cornwall at the time of the Munich crisis, its basis is an imaginative leap in the dark to the U-boat pens that were to come after the fall of France three years later. Inevitably it is a very different sort of book to the last in this volume which was written more than a quarter of a century later.

It was the war and service in the Mediterranean that turned my mind to remote and unusual settings. As a result, I have never been short of subjects, and it is to this, probably, more than to the writing that I owe the translation of my books into so many different languages. Also perhaps to the fact that they are all based on personal observation and experience

The opening of *The Mary Deare*, for instance, did not come to me by accident. It was based on something that really happened as I sat at the helm one dark night off the Cherbourg peninsula. We were waiting for the dawn so that we could enter the little French bolthole of Omonville-la-Rogue, and this ship came at us out of the fog; no sound of engines, just a green transluscence that hardened abruptly into the pinpoint green of a navigation light. It was so startling, so like a ghost ship, that in the instant of its passing close astern of us I saw it in my imagination as a rogue tramp steamer, deserted and with nobody on the bridge.

Both this book and *The White South* were made into films. And though *The White South* is important to me as marking a transition, the development not so much of a new style as a different form, the book I am most glad to have written is *Atlantic Fury*. All the knowledge and experience gained sailing my own boat is written in this one book.

Nobody can write sensibly about the sea without first-hand experience. It is a subject of great complexity and professionalism. I have been fortunate in that the international interest in my books has enabled me to gain that experience. Writing has not allowed me time to sail across oceans, but, with my wife Dorothy, I have navigated all the coasts of Europe from Scandinavia to Turkey, and in sixteen years of sailing we have spent in total three years of our lives at sea.

It is this that has enabled me to handle the subject with a degree of confidence I would not otherwise have had. Indeed, as a result, the sea tends to infiltrate most of my novels. But it is in the creation and development of the last four stories in this volume (and in two others that are not included) that I believe I have managed to capture something of the power and infinite variety of an element that has shaped the character of my own people.

Kersey,
Suffolk

WRECKERS MUST
BREATHE

PART ONE

THE DISAPPEARANCE OF WALTER CRAIG

I

INTERRUPTED HOLIDAY

CORNWALL is a wrecker's coast. But when I left for my holiday I thought of the wrecker as a picturesque ruffian of several centuries ago who lured ships to their destruction with false beacons and waded out into the angry seas to knife the crew and unload the cargo as the vessel broke up. I did not think of Cornwall as being still a wrecker's coast, and I knew nothing of the modern wreckers I was to find havened beneath the shadow of those grim cliffs. I had intended going to the Lakes, but fate decreed that the gathering storm of the Polish crisis should keep my companion at his desk in the newsroom and that I should pick on the Lizard for my holiday.

I stayed at Church Cove, where white, thatched cottages, massed with flowers, straggled down a valley to the dark cleft of the cove with the round capstan house on its shingle beach rotting because no boats came. The Kerrises' cottage, where I stayed, was at the upper end of the village and backed on to a farm.

The cottage was really two cottages thrown into one to make a guest house. Kerris, who had done the knocking together himself, was very proud of the result. Before I had been there half an hour he was taking me over the place, showing me with his toothless mouth agrin all the pieces he had obtained from the *Clan Malcolm* which had been wrecked that winter. He had relaid the floors throughout the cottage during the winter and as far as I could gather the work had all been done with wood from the *Clan Malcolm*. There were brass doorsteps, chairs and ship's lamps, all from the same luckless ship. He was a great wrecker, was Kerris. When I expressed my amazement at the amount of stuff he had collected from that one ship, he shook his head with a rueful smile. 'Ar, she were a grand wreck,' he said. 'We'll never see the like o' her again, sir – never. She came ashore this side of the Lizard. Caught on the rocks, she was, and broke her back. She was no use for salvage purposes, so Lloyd's told the Cadgwith

13

people that if they liked to go out and salvage what they could and put it up for auction in the village they might collect a percentage of the proceeds.' He shook his head again. 'Ar, she were a grand wreck, sir. If we had one like that every winter, we'd not have to work.'

I spent five days there in a pleasant haze of bathing, lazing, pubs and Cornish cream. Then Thursday dawned, and with it the shock of a newspaper placard at the Lizard – Soviet-German Non-Agression Pact. I stopped the car and stared at it unbelievingly. Groups of holidaymakers stood about outside the newsagents' reading the papers and talking in low tones. Europe, Hitler, the whole world-fear of Nazism seemed suddenly to have enveloped the place like a sea mist. I jumped out of the car and bought a copy of my own paper, the *Daily Recorder*. It was true enough, and, what was more, Britain was calling up reserves and there were reports of mobilization in France.

I tossed the paper into the back of the car and drove on to Gunwalloe Church Cove, the other side of Mullion. What was the use of spoiling a holiday by getting upset about the international situation? Wasn't this what I had expected – the usual autumn crisis? But I had not expected a Soviet-German Non-Aggresion Pact and I knew that it might well throw all calculations out of gear. The fear of a war on two fronts removed, the German High Command might well decide to make a lightning thrust against Poland and then, if necessary, fight it out with the democracies on the Western Front.

I thought it all out as I drove across the Goonhilly Downs with the warm heavy scent of sun after rain in my nostrils, and by the time I had convinced myself that the pact was not as serious as it had at first seemed, it was twelve o'clock, and I was at Gunwalloe Church Cove. Two day ago there had been at least three hundred cars in the park. I counted a bare fifty. The beach seemed empty. Yet it was a glorious day. I had a bathe and then strolled along the beach. A tubby little man in grey flannels with a panama stuck squarely on his head nodded to mc. 'Things look pretty bad this morning, don't they?' he said.

'Not too good,' I replied. 'But it's a fine day.'

'Aye,' he said, 'that's raight, it is. And we'd best make the most of 'em. Two men in our hotel have been called oop. Wired for last night.'

Five minutes' conversation with this gentleman left me with a feeling of utter depression. I had lunch and tried to settle down to read, but my mind would not concentrate and I was conscious all the time of the emptiness of the beach. I had my third bathe of the day and went home to tea to find the cottage empty of visitors. The two couples had gone; one of the men was in the emergency reserve of officers and the other had received a telegram from his office.

And yet, as I had driven back, I had seen the harvest being gathered in and had passed cows being driven to the farms to be milked. It had only touched Cornwall through the visitors. It had not touched the real Cornwall. The everlasting struggle of man to extract from the soil and sea a winter's living went on just as before. That was reality. While that other life of diplomacy, propaganda, machines and herded populations tense and fearful with the sense of impending catastrophe was artificial, a complicated nightmare conjured by civilization. I sat for a while over my tea, wrapped in the horror of it. Before my mind's eye swept fragmentary pictures of the last war. I had been at school, but it had not passed me by entirely. I remembered the cadet corps, the boys who left never to return, the dark nights in London and the searchlights flickering like pencils across the sky; the troop trains and the hospital trains; Summerdown Camp, Eastbourne. And then I remembered the books and the plays that had followed – Sheriff's *Journey's End*, Remarque's *All Quiet*, now banned in Germany, and Henri Barbusse's *Under Fire*. It could not happen again. But I knew it could. A new generation and the horror is lost in the glory that is cried to the rooftops by a ruthless propaganda machine, and from the rooftops echoes back to a nation steeped in Wagnerian idolatry.

The radio interrupted my thought and the bland voice of the announcer gave me the weather forecasts. I waited, fascinated, yet wanting to get away from the damned thing and enjoy my holiday. More incidents on the Polish frontier. Berlin report of ten German soldiers shot on their own side of the frontier. Polish customs officials seized in Danzig. Mobilization in France. More British reservists called up. I got up and went out into the quiet of the evening. The announcer's voice followed me down the street. I made for the cove and then struck away to the left towards Cadgwith.

I reached the top of the cliffs and paused for a moment to look down at the calm leaden sea that heaved gently against the rock-bound coast. The cry of the gulls was balm to the turmoil of my thoughts. That high screaming cry had always been synonymous with holidays to me, for from my earliest childhood I had always spent them on the rocky coastlands. There was peace here and quiet. I looked back at the little group of cottages huddling down the valley to the cove. It was satisfying to think that whatever happened this coast and the cottages would remain to bring peace of mind to those who lived on and to other generations. Two gannets swung effortlessly down the coast, their black wing-tips showing clearly in the slanting rays of the sun. The air was still and breathless. Not a ripple stirred the burnished surface of the sea and the white streaks of the currents setting from the Lizard were plainly visible. Every now and then a little patch of dark troubled water showed as a shoal of mackerel or pilchards broke the surface in their evening play.

I went on with the ache of a great beauty and a great peace in my heart. The other world that was mirrored like a monstrous nightmare in the pages of the newspapers seemed even more unreal. Being a dramatic critic, I think I had become infected with a characteristic which I have often noticed in actors – I was unable to apprehend reality. Probably because their brains and senses are so accustomed to reacting to stimuli which are imaginatively but not factually true, actors envisage the situation more vividly than the next man, but once envisaged, it is done with. They have difficulty in accepting it as actual, irrevocable. There is an instinctive feeling that at the appointed hour the curtain will come down and one can go home to supper. I think I suffered now from this limitation – or if you like this blessed ability. However grim the drama, I felt there must still be an alternative world outside it. Thus I alternated between moods of blank despair and moods of refreshing, almost gay normality.

Twenty minutes' walking brought me to the Devil's Frying Pan. I skirted that huge circular inlet with its archway of grass-grown rock to the sea and, passing through a farmyard, obtained my first glimpse of Cadgwith. They say it is the only real fishing village left in Cornwall. Certainly the little fleet of blue boats drawn up side by side on the beach and the wheeling screaming gulls dominate the huddle of white thatched cottages. The noise of the gulls is incessant and the boats and the smell of fish testify to the industry of the villagers. And yet the place looked sleepy.

I went down the steep road to the village itself. There were cars drawn up by the shingle. One, backed close against the lifeboat, had a string of mackerel tied to its bonnet. Opposite the cars, on an old spar which did service as a bench, fishermen were sitting, smoking. I went on to the pub. The place was dark and thick with tobacco smoke and there was the airless warmth that men love who lead an open-air life. On the wall was a painting of the village. It was by a local artist, I discovered later, but it missed something. It took me some time to realize what it was. The village dominated the boats. If I had been painting the village, I should have done it so that it reeked of fish.

I ordered a bitter and sat down next to a big man in a fisherman's jersey. He had a small beard and this increased the Slav effect of his high cheekbones and small nose. A heated discussion was in progress. I caught the word spongecakes several times. An old fisherman was thumping the table angrily, but I could make no sense of what the whole room was arguing about. I asked the man with the beard. 'Oh, they've bet him five bob he can't eat a dozen spongecakes straight off. You know, the old game – it looks easy, but after you've had about four your mouth gets so dry you can barely swallow.'

'I tell you it's easy,' the old man roared, and the whole room laughed knowingly.

At that moment a young fellow in dungarees came in. His plimsoles were sopping wet and his hair curled with salt water. He went straight over to two lads seated at a table in the corner drinking from pint glass tankards. 'What luck?' they asked.

For answer he tossed a telegram on to the table. 'I'm afraid you'll have to count me out tomorrow. I've got to join my ship at Devonport. I'm leaving right away.'

Their conversation was drowned in a sudden flood of talk. 'It's been the same hall of the bloody day,' the old man who had wanted to eat the spongecakes said. 'The visitors hare going back and some of hour lads have been called up for the naval reserve.'

'Did ye see the fleet going down the Channel?' somebody asked.

'They've been going down the whole ruddy day,' said a young round-faced man. 'I seen 'em from my boat. They bin going down all day, 'aven't they, Mr Morgan?' he asked the coastguard, who was sitting smoking quietly with his back against the bar and his white-rimmed hat on the back of his head.

He nodded. 'That's right, Jim – all day.'

'Did ye see how many there was, Joe?'

'Ar, I didn't count,' replied the coastguard, his voice quiet but firm.

War had invaded the snug friendliness of the bar. The older men began to talk of the last one. The man next to me said, 'I counted upwards of fifty. That'll fix Italy all right.'

I felt somehow annoyed that talk of war had obtruded even into the warm seclusion of this pub. 'To hell with the war,' I said. 'I'm trying to enjoy a holiday.'

'What's wrong with a war?' he demanded with a twinkle in his grey eyes. 'A war would see us nicely through the winter. It's either that or steamboating.'

I looked at him. Behind the twinkle in his eyes was a certain seriousness.

'Yes,' I said, 'it must hit you pretty bad coming two years in succession and right on the holiday season.'

'Well, it wasn't so bad last year – it came later.' There was a trace of a brogue in his voice, but otherwise it was devoid of any local accent. 'Even then,' he said, finishing his beer, 'I had to do six voyages. It'll be worse this year. You can't make enough out of fishing nowadays to carry you through the winter. And the Government doesn't give any help, sir – though they want us badly enough when it comes to war.'

'Can't you do any fishing in the winter?' I asked.

He shrugged his shoulders. 'We go out when we can, but mostly the sea is pretty big outside. And then we've got all our gear to make. We're running two hundred pots a boat here, as well as nets. And there's not so much fish as there used to be. They change their grounds. Something to do with the Gulf Stream, I suppose. I tell you, sir, this is a dying industry. There's only three thousand of us left on these coasts now.'

I said, 'Yes, I know. Down at Mullion, for instance, all the young men are going off to work in the towns.'

'Ar, but you won't find that here. We're not afraid of work. The young 'uns, they're not afraid of work either. Now, in the summer, we're out at five with the pots. And then when I come in, I'm taking parties out for the rest of the day. Sometimes I take out three parties a day. That's pretty long hours.'

I nodded and ordered two beers. He took out a pouch and rolled a cigarette. 'Have one?' he asked. We lit up and sat drinking in silence for a while. It gave me an opportunity of studying him. He was a man of tremendous physique. He was over six feet with broad shoulders and a deep chest. The beard completed the picture. With his Slav features and shock of dark brown hair he looked a real buccaneer.

His eyes met mine. 'You're thinking that all I need is the gold earrings,' he said unexpectedly.

I felt extremely awkward until I saw the twinkle in his eyes. Then I suddenly laughed. 'Well, as a matter of fact,' I said, 'that's just what I was thinking.'

'Well, you must remember that some of the Armada was

wrecked on those coasts. There's Spanish blood in most of us. There's Irish too. When the fishing industry was at its height down here girls would come from Ireland to do the packing.' He turned to the bar and tossed a florin on to it. 'Two halves of six,' he ordered.

'No, I'm paying for this,' I said.

'You're not,' he replied. 'It's already ordered.'

'Think of the winter,' I said. 'I'm on holiday. It doesn't matter to me what I spend.'

He grinned. 'You're drinking with me,' he said. 'We're an independent lot of folk down here. We don't sponge on visitors if we like them. Our independence is all we've got. We each have our own boat. And though you can come out mackerel fishing with us and we'll take your money for it, we'll not take you out if we don't like you.'

'Anyway,' I said glancing at my watch, 'I ought to be starting back. I shall be late for my supper as it is. I walked over from Church Cove.'

'Church Cove,' he said, as he placed a stein of beer in front of me. 'I'll run you back in the boat.'

'That's very kind of you. But it won't take me long to walk it and you certainly don't want another trip in your boat when you've been out in it all day.'

'I would. It's a lovely evening. I'd like a quiet run along the coast. The boat's out at her moorings. It won't take me ten minutes.'

I thanked him again and drank my beer. 'Why did you call this a half of six?' I asked. 'What beer is it?'

'It's Devenish's. There are three grades – fourpence, sixpence, and eightpence a pint. If you come here in the autumn you'd only be offered four.'

I nodded. 'Do you like steamboating?'

'Oh, it's not so bad. It would be all right if I could take Cadgwith along with me. I hate leaving this place. I did six voyages to the West Indies last winter. You can always pick up a berth at Falmouth. This time I think I'll try a tanker on the Aden route. If there's a war, of course, we'll be needed for the minesweepers or on coastal patrol.'

I offered him another beer, but he refused and we left the pub. It was not until we were walking down the village street in the pale evening light that I fully realized the size of the man. He was like a great bear with his rolling gait and shaggy head, and the similarity was even more marked when he had put on his big sea boots, for they gave him an ungainly shambling walk.

I enjoyed the short run back to Church Cove. For one thing, it gave me my first glimpse of the coast from the sea. For another, I got to know my friend better, and the more I knew of him the more I liked him – and the more I was intrigued. In that short run we covered a multitude of subjects – international situation, bird life on Spitzbergen, stocks and shares, Bloomsbury, Cadgwith. My impression of him was of a rolling stone that always and inevitably returned homesick to Cadgwith. But though he had obviously gathered no moss – he lived in a little hut on the slopes above Cadgwith – he had certainly gathered a wide knowledge of life, and that knowledge showed in his eyes, which were shrewd and constantly twinkling with the humour that bubbled beneath the stolid exterior of the man. His nature was Irish and his features Slav, and the mixture was something new to me.

Once I expressed surprise, for he told me that War Loan had risen $\frac{7}{8}$ to $89\frac{3}{8}$ on the previous day and suggested that, since the Stock Exchange was apparently taking quite an optimistic view of the situation, war did not seem likely.

I could not help it. I said, 'What do you know of stocks and shares?'

He grinned at my surprise. 'I could tell you the prices of quite a number of the leaders,' he said. 'I always read the City page of the paper.'

'Well, it's the first time I ever heard of a fisherman reading the City page of a paper,' I said. 'Whatever do you read it for?'

'I'm in a capitalist country, running a luxury business. Stock and share prices are the barometer of my summer earnings. When prices were going up in 1935 and 1936, I did pretty well. Since then there's been a slump and I have to go steamboating in the winter.' He looked at me with that twinkle in his eyes. 'I read a lot of things you probably wouldn't expect a fisherman to read. There's a free library over to Lizard Town. You can even get plays there. I used to be very fond of plays when I was in London.'

I explained that plays were my life and asked him what he had done in London. 'I was in a shipping office for a time,' he said. 'But I soon got bored with that and turned to stevedoring. I was with the River Police for a time. You know, you meet people down here, quite important people, on holiday. And they say you're wasting your time in Cadgwith. It's not difficult to get the offer of a job in London or to pull strings when you're there. But London is no life for a man. After a few months, Cadgwith calls to me again, and I come back.'

That I suppose was why he spoke so well. Talking to me, his voice had no trace of the sluggish Cornwall accent. Yet I had noticed that the local accent came readily enough to his lips when he spoke to the villagers.

Interspersed with our conversation, he pointed out interesting parts of the coastline as we went along. He showed me the seaward entrance to the Devil's Frying Pan with its magnificent arch of rock. He also pointed out Dollar Ogo to me. The cave did not look particularly impressive from the outside, but he told me that students from the 'varsity had come down and explored it for five hundred yards. 'They had to swim most of the way,' he said, 'pushing biscuit tins with lighted candles in front of them.'

'How far can you get up it by boat?' I asked. I was thinking that it would give me such an excellent opportunity of examining the various rock formations. Geology was one of my hobbies. But his reply was, 'Not very far.'

When we arrived at Church Cove, I said, 'I must come out mackerel fishing with you some time.'

'Any time you like, sir,' he said as he carried me pick-a-back ashore. 'Any of the boys will tell you where I am.'

'Who shall I ask for?' I enquired.

'Ask for Big Logan,' he replied, as he shoved the boat off and scrambled on board. 'That's what they all call me.'

'After the Logan Rock?' I asked with a grin.

He looked at me quite seriously and nodded. 'Quite right, sir,' he said. 'After the Logan Rock.'

That was the last I saw of Big Logan for a whole week. When I got back to the cottage I found a letter waiting for me. It was from my editor. He was not recalling me, but he wanted me to do a series of articles on how the international situation was affecting the country.

Kerris came in to see me after supper. He had seen that the letter was from my paper and he wanted to know whether I was leaving or not. I explained the position and said that I might be away a night or two, it depended how far afield I found it necessary to go for material, 'By the way,' I said, 'do you know Big Logan of Cadgwith?'

'Surely,' he said, 'Why?'

'He brought me back here from Cadgwith this evening by boat. Nice fellow, isn't he?'

'Ar, very nice fellow to speak to,' was his reply. 'To speak to, mind you.' He looked at me for a moment and the temptation to gossip was too much for him. 'But no good,' he said, shaking his head. 'Not worth that plate. Comes of a good family, too – his mother was a lady at one of the big houses over to Helford.'

'And his father?' I asked.

'One of the fishermen at Cadgwith.'

And then I understood why it was that he had been named Logan. It explained so much of his complex character. 'He was born at a house near the Logan Rock, wasn't he?' I asked.

'Ar, it was at the farm up there.' He shook his head. 'But he's no good,' he said. 'He's proved that. He married a Birmingham girl who was here on holiday. She had money and she built a house over to Flushing in Gillan. She were a lovely garl. But he didn't know when he was well off. He played around with the local garls and she's divorced him now and gone back to Birmingham. Now he lives alone in a little shack in Cadgwith.' He shook his head again. 'He's no good is Big Logan,' he said as he went out of the room.

I smiled to myself at that. Generations of wreckers in Kerris, I felt, spoke that condemnation of Big Logan. I felt sure that it wasn't because he had fooled around with the local girls that he thought Big Logan no good, but because, having got on to a good thing, Big Logan had let it go as Kerris never could have done. Big Logan's parentage explained so much.

That evening I settled down by the light of the oil lamp and wrote the first of my articles. The other two, however, were not so easily written and required a good deal of travelling, including an excursion into Devon, where I spent a night at Post Bridge in the midst of Dartmoor. Cornwall was much more affected by the crisis than Devon, for in general it was the departure of the visitors that brought it home to the country districts at that time. Not until later were the farmers inundated with schemes for growing more food. It is true that in the towns and even in the villages men were being called up, but this hardly touched Dartmoor and the more agricultural areas of Devon. In South Devon and in South Cornwall, however, I found the atmosphere very tense around the big towns. I had a look at Falmouth, Devonport and Plymouth, and in none of these ports was a warship to be seen. 'Most of them left last Thursday,' I was told. It was this departure of the fleet that brought it home to them. That and the appearance of sand-bags, tin helmets and gas masks.

Back at the Lizard again I found things much the same. There were fewer visitors and the villagers spoke of cancelled bookings. But visitors still came and gradually everything was slipping back towards normality. Most of the tourists I spoke to were trying desperately hard to ignore the news and enjoy their holidays. 'God knows when we'll get another,' was their justification. But they read the newspapers just the same and still hoped against hope.

Then on Thursday, 31 August, came the news that the children were to be evacuated and I had to re-write my final article, for Cornwall was a reception area and this brought the crisis right home to even the remoter farms and villages. On Friday I spent the day lazing and bathing, determined to forget the war scare. But when I got back I was just in time to see the first bus-load of Midlands children arrive with their teachers at Lizard Town. They looked tired, but happy. I stopped and spoke to them. They thought it a grand adventure. I found one little boy with a gas mask that seemed larger than himself who had never been outside Birmingham streets. There were many who had never seen the sea. I went home to be met by Kerris in a state of some excitement. 'Have you heard the news, Mr Craig?' he asked. 'Germany has marched into Poland. It came through on the news midday. And we've got three little boys billeted on us. Fair bastards they be. Still, mustn't grumble. Government pays us eight-and-sixpence each for them.'

My stomach felt suddenly hollow within me. So it was war after all. Somehow, I had always felt that Hitler must climb down if we called his bluff. 'Well, at least the tension is over,' I said dully. 'We know the worst.'

When I had finished my tea I went out for a walk, taking the path along the cliffs towards Cadgwith. The peace of the coast closed in around me, but it was a bitter balm. The fact that this would remain, whatever happened to my generation, no longer afforded me the satisfaction it had done a week earlier. Rather, I hated it for its aloofness and felt that it had no right to be so serene and beautiful when all Europe was to be subjected to the torture of war. I found myself even longing for the appeasement of the previous September. But it was the cry of emotion rather than reason. I knew that it could not be this time. We were not simply tied to Poland by a treaty. We were faced with the forces of oppression and brute force and we had to tread them under-foot before they ran riot over all Europe and had outgrown the strength of democracy.

I found myself suddenly looking down upon Cadgwith without any knowledge of the walk there. It was just the same as before, the boats drawn up on the beach, the gulls wheeling and screaming, the little white cottages and the smell of fish. That men were dying in a desperate fight for freedom against a mechanized army that had no thought but those instilled into its soldiers by a vast propaganda machine, left this little fishing village untouched. And the probability was that it never would be touched. I shrugged my shoulders. War or no war, there was no reason why I should not get an evening's fishing. I went down into the village and found Big Logan operating the donkey engine that hauled the boats up. While the wire hawser was being hitched on to the next boat I had time to arrange for two hours fishing on the following day at six in the evening. I went to the pub where I heard that five destroyers had been seen going down the Channel. The rumour was that they were going to pick up the *Bremen* now two days out from New York after the hold-up by the American authorities. And I spoke to a man who said that the coastguard had seen a submarine about six miles off the coast moving westward. 'That will be a bloody U-boat,' my informant told me.

Like all the other people still on holiday, I tried hard to treat the following day as a normal one. Only when actually in the water, however, did I forget the atmosphere of tension that gripped me. On the beach, I felt moody and depressed. I could not settle down to enjoy the sunshine and the temptation to go back to the cottage to listen to the news bulletins which were broadcast with disturbing frequency was too much for me. Automatically I listened to broadcast after broadcast that were no more than a repetition of the previous ones, in most cases not even worded differently. There was nothing new – no ultimatum, no outbreak of hostilities on the Western Front; only the rapid progress of German troops into Poland. By the time I left for Cadgwith I was heartily sick of the news.

With a pair of lines over the side of the boat and the gentle chug-chug of the engine, I was at last able to forget that the country was living under the threat of war. And soon my whole mind was occupied with the task of landing mackerel. Big Logan stood facing me at the tiller, whistling softly through his teeth. He hardly spoke a word, except when I hauled a line in and he looked astern for the darting strip of silver that would tell him there was a mackerel on it.

We went as far as Dinas Head. As we headed back the wind began to freshen from the sou'west and little scuds of cloud appeared, flying low across the sky. By seven-thirty the light was beginning to go. 'Looks like a bad night,' I said.

'Ar, it's going to rain all right.' He rolled himself a cigarette and put the boat in towards the cliffs. 'We might have a try for pollock,' he said.

The sea was getting up and away on the starboard bow I could see the waves swirling white round a submerged rock. 'You want to know this coast pretty well,' I said.

'You're right there. It's a wicked bit of coast this – submerged rocks everywhere. And they're not rounded like they are over to Land's End, but all jagged. See the Gav Rocks over to Kennack here?' He pointed across the bows to the jagged reef, now half-submerged, that curved out across Kennack Sands. 'A Dutch barge went aground there – oh, it must have been four winters back. In three days there was nothing of her left except an iron stern post that's there to this day, wedged among the rocks.'

'Have you had any wrecks recently?' I asked. 'There was the *Clan Malcolm*, I know – but since then?'

'Not just round here. There was one over to St Ives.' He lit his cigarette. 'Now the *Clan Malcolm*, she was a lovely wreck – a real Cornishman's wreck.' He shook his head over it. 'If we had a wreck like that every year we wouldn't need to worry about the winter.' He put the tiller down and edged the boat along the shore. We were very close in now and the sea was making it difficult for me to stand. 'You might get at pollock here,' he said, taking over my other line.

But, though we circled for more than ten minutes around the spot, all I got was a snide – a cross between a baby swordfish and an eel that made the bottom of the boat abominably slimy and got thoroughly tied up in the line. At length Big Logan headed the boat out to sea again. 'You ought to get a few mackerel on the way back,' he said. At that time I had caught just on forty. The sea was getting very jumpy, and every now and then I had to sit down on the thwart for fear of losing my balance. The movement of the boat did not seem to worry Logan. With feet spread slightly apart his great hulk seemed to tread the planks and almost to steady the boat.

We were level with Caerleon Cove and about half a mile out when I got my next bite. I felt one sharp tug and then the line went quiet. I pulled it in. It was a mackerel all right. They always seemed to lie quiet after they had been hooked. I left Logan to deal with it and went over to the other line. As soon as I felt it I knew it was shoal mackerel for there was one on this line too. I began to pull it in. Suddenly there was a flash of broken water in the trough of a wave. I caught sight of it out of the corner of my eye. Something solid went streaking through the water beside the boat. The sea swirled and eddied, and before I had time to see what it was the line went tight in my hand and I was whipped overboard.

Instead of bobbing to the surface immediately, I seemed to be sucked down into the sea. I was seized with a sudden panic. My breath escaped in a rush of bubbles and with my lungs suddenly emptied, I found myself as near to drowning as I have ever been. I fought my way upwards with a horrible feeling of constriction across the chest. And when I thought I could not restrain my lungs from functioning normally any longer, I came to the surface and trod water, gasping for breath.

Almost immediately Big Logan hailed me from the boat, which had now circled and was making towards me. A moment later he had hauled me on board and I lay panting on the bottom of the boat. A fish flapped unhappily on the boards beside my head. I rolled over and found myself face to face with the mackerel that I had left Big Logan to deal with. It's plight was so similar to what mine had been an instant ago that I scooped it up in my hand and threw it back into the sea. Then I sat up and looked at Big Logan. 'What was it?' I asked.

He shook his head and tugged at his beard. 'I'd just got the mackerel off your line,' he said, 'and had dropped the weight back into the water, when suddenly the whole boat was rocking like hell and you were overboard. I looked up just in time to see your feet disappearing over the side. The line was tight in your hand, I could see that. Something pretty big must have got hold of it. It not only jerked you overboard so violently that your feet did not even touch the gun'l, but it snapped the line as clean as though it had been cut with a knife.'

The boat was now headed back towards Cadgwith, and I scrambled to my feet.

'How are you feeling?' he asked.

'Unpleasantly wet, but otherwise all right.' But I was a bit shaken and had to sit on the thwart. 'Does this sort of thing often happen?' I asked him. I glanced up and surprised a rather puzzled look on his face.

'Never known it to happen afore, sir,' he replied.

'What was it?' I persisted. 'An outsize in pollock, a tunny fish, a shark – or what?'

'Well, it might have been a tunny or a shark,' he said, a trifle doubtfully I thought. 'You had a mackerel on that line, didn't you?'

I nodded. 'And I saw something break the surface of the water just beside the boat,' I said. 'It was in the trough of a wave and moving fast in the direction of the mackerel. Would it have been the fin of a shark, do you think? Do you get sharks round this coast?'

'Sometimes. You get 'em on most coasts.' He shook his head. 'It must have been a pretty big one,' he murmured. 'You should have seen the state of the sea after you'd taken your header. It was as though a whale had submerged.'

He rolled a cigarette for me and we fell silent, smoking thoughtfully. I was beginning to feel pretty cold by the time we reached Cadgwith. As soon as we had landed he took me straight up to the pub, where I was introduced to the landlord, given a pair of old trousers and a jersey, and my wet clothes hung up to dry. I ordered a hot rum and lemon. Big Logan and the landlord joined me with whiskies and then fell to an interminable discussion of the whole business. I had already decided it was a shark and I was not interested. Sitting in front of the warm kitchen range I soon began to feel sleepy.

Big Logan had to shake me awake in order to tell me that he would take me back to Church Cove by boat. I could hear the wind howling in the chimney and I shook my head. 'I'll walk,' I said.

'Your clothes aren't dry yet and you're tired,' he said. 'Much better let me run you back. There's still a little light left and the sea isn't too bad yet.'

But I shook my head. 'Honestly, I'd like the walk,' I told him. 'It'll warm me up. That is, if you don't mind my hanging on to these clothes until tomorrow?' I asked the landlord.

'That's all right,' he said. 'You're welcome. And if you'll come over tomorrow we'll have your own clothes dry for you by then.'

I thanked him and got to my feet. I tried to pay Big Logan for the fishing trip, but he said he didn't accept money for nearly drowning people. And when I tried to insist, he thrust the pound note back into the pocket of my jacket, which I had put on, wet though it was, because it contained my wallet and my keys. He even offered to accompany me along the cliffs, but by this time I was feeling sufficiently wide awake and buoyed up by the drink to insist that I should enjoy the walk.

As he came out of the pub with me, he called to two fellows in the bar to come and help him in with his boat. The evening light was still sufficient for me to be able to see it bobbing about at its moorings. The wind was rising still and already the waves were beginning to sound noisily on the shingle beach as they tumbled into the inlet. I climbed the roadway to the cliffs and met the full force of the growing gale. I was more than ever glad then that I had not accepted Logan's offer to run me back to Church Cove.

The heat of exertion made the jersey and the rough serge trousers most uncomfortable. I had nothing on underneath them and my skin was sensitive to the rough material. Moreover, my shoes, which were still wet, squelched at every step. I found the farmyard, and climbing the stone stile, reached the path that skirted the Devil's Frying Pan. The flashing of the Lizard light was plainly visible along the coast. There was still a slight glow in the sky ahead, but despite this I found it very difficult to see the path and every now and then I was reduced literally to feeling my way along for fear I should strike out towards the edge of the cliffs.

I passed the big white house on the headland and in a little while came to a part-wooden bungalow that did service as a café. Half of a window still showed light through orange curtains, but the other half was already blacked out with brown paper. I suddenly remembered that for more than three hours I had forgotten all about the crisis. The rum seemed to recede all at once from my brain and leave me wretchedly depressed. I climbed another stone stile and followed the path inland as it circled a long indent. I followed it automatically, for my mind was entirely wrapped in a mental picture of the Western Front. And I suddenly felt that, having come so near to death that night, a merciful God should have finished the job rather than spare me to rot in a stinking trench.

I was possessed of the cowardice that is the heritage of an imaginative mind. It is anticipation and not the pain itself that breeds fear. I singled myself out for a horrible death as I trod that cliff path. In fact, from the way in which I regarded my death as inevitable one would have thought that it was for that sole purpose that Hitler had regimented Germany for six years. And when I almost stumbled into a man standing, a vague blur, on the path in front of me, I recoiled involuntarily with a little cry.

'I am sorry. I am afraid I frightened you,' he said.

'Oh, no,' I said. 'You startled me a bit, that's all. I was thinking about something else.'

'I was hoping you could direct me to a cottage called Carillon that lies back from the cliffs somewhere near here.'

'Carillon?' I murmured. Suddenly I remembered where I had seen the name. 'Is it above Church Cove?' I asked.

'That is right,' he said. His speech was so precise and impersonal that I felt he must be a BBC announcer on holiday.

'If you care to come with me,' I said, 'I think I can find it for you. It lies just back from this path about half a mile further on.'

He thanked me and fell into place behind me. As I went past him I found that the rather stiff looking waterproof he wore was soaked practically to the waist.

'You're wet,' I said.

There was a moment's pause, and then he said, 'Yes, I have been out in a boat and had some trouble getting ashore. The sea is getting quite rough.'

'Funny!' I said. 'I've just got wet through too.' And I told him about my little adventure.

Somehow I got the impression that he was rather impressed by what had happened. 'And what do you think it was?' he asked, when I had finished.

I told him I thought it must have been a shark. He had drawn level with me as the path widened, and I saw him nod. 'They are to be seen about these western coasts. It went for the mackerel.' He then referred to the crisis and asked me whether there were any fresh developments. Then he asked if I had seen anything of the fleet. I told him it had passed down the Channel a week ago and that not a single naval vessel had been seen off the coast since then, except for five destroyers and one submarine of unknown nationality.

He sighed. 'I am afraid it will be war,' he said.

I nodded. 'Oh, well,' I said, 'it's no more than one expected. But it's a bit of a shock when it comes.' I sensed that he too was depressed. 'Will you be called up?' I asked.

'I expect so.'

'What branch?'

'Navy.'

'It's better than most,' I consoled him. 'Better than the trenches.'

'Maybe,' he said, but he did not sound very enthusiastic.

For a time we walked in silence. Then to take our minds off morbid thoughts I began to talk of the coast, the submerged rocks and the wrecks. 'The fisherman I was out with today told me of a Dutch barge that was completely broken up on the Gav Rocks at Kennack in three days,' I said.

'Yes, I have been here before,' he said. 'It is a bad coast.'

I nodded. 'It is,' I agreed. 'And they say that quite a lot of the submerged rocks aren't even charted and are only known by the local fisherman.'

'I know,' was his reply. 'There is a great reef out off Cadgwith that is not properly charted. It is the worst bit of coast I think I have ever seen.'

'Of course, these fishermen know it all,' I said. 'They know just where to find a sand bottom among the rocks. I suppose the knowledge of the rock formations on the bed of the sea is handed down from father to son and grows with the knowledge gained by each new generation.' We had reached the top of a headland and a path branched off to the right, skirting a field. 'You go up there,' I said. 'The cottage is on the right.'

He thanked me and we parted, his slim erect figure merging into the gloom. I went on down into Church Cove.

2

SUSPICION

'WILL listeners please stand by for an important announcement which will be made at nine-fifteen.' It was early Sunday morning and even the announcer's voice sounded strained and unfamiliar. I sat in the Kerrises' kitchen, smoking cigarettes and waiting. So we heard of the final two-hour ultimatum delivered by Sir Neville Henderson. Later came the news that the Prime Minister would broadcast at eleven-fifteen. Rather than hang about waiting for what I knew to be inevitable, I got the car out and drove over to Cadgwith with the clothes the landlord had lent me.

When I returned to the car, with my own clothes dried and neatly done up in brown paper, I met Big Logan coming up from the beach. 'You don't mean to say you've been out with the boats this morning?' I said. There was quite a sea running, though the wind had dropped and it was a fine morning.

He laughed. 'War or no war we've still got to earn our living,' he said. 'I hope you're none the worse for your bathe last night?'

'Not a bit,' I replied, as I threw the bundle of clothes into the back of the car. 'Funny thing was,' I added, shutting the door, 'I met a fellow on my way back to Church Cove who had also got pretty wet landing from a boat.'

'Landing from a boat?' He looked puzzled. 'Where did he land?' he asked.

I shrugged my shoulders. 'I don't know. Somewhere round

here, I suppose. I met him on the path just past that little café on the cliff.'

'No boat came in here. We were the last in.'

'Well, he probably landed somewhere along the coast,' I suggested.

'Why should he do that? Nobody would think of landing anywhere between here and Church Cove with the sea as jumpy as it was last night – unless of course he had to. How wet was he?'

'I should say he had been up to his waist in water. Anyway, what does it matter?' I demanded. I was a trifle annoyed at his persistence.

He hesitated. His feet were placed slightly apart and his hands rested on the leather belt around his waist. At length he said, 'Well, I've been thinking. That business last night – how do we know it was a fish?'

'What else could it have been?' I asked impatiently.

He looked at me, and once again I was impressed by the shrewdness of his small eyes. 'It might have been a submarine,' he said.

I stared at him. 'A submarine?' Then I suddenly laughed. 'But why should a submarine jump half out of the water and pounce upon a poor inoffensive mackerel? Submarines don't have to feed. Anyway, it would be dangerous to come so close in without surfacing.'

'Did it jump half out of the water?' he asked, and I saw that he was perfectly serious. 'Are you certain it was after the mackerel?'

'Perhaps jumping half out of the water is an exaggeration,' I admitted, 'but at least I saw a fin or something streak through the water in the trough of a wave.'

'Or something,' he said. 'Mightn't it have been a periscope?'

I thought about this for a moment. 'I suppose it might,' I agreed. 'But why should it take my line?'

'The line might have got caught up in the submarine.'

'But it's absurd,' I said.

'You didn't see the water after you'd taken that header. It boiled as though a bloody whale had gone down. The disturbance was too much for a shark. Anyway, that's what I think.'

'But, whatever would it be doing so close in?' I asked.

'That's what's been puzzling me,' he said. 'But you mentioning that fellow you met having got so wet has given me an idea. They might have wanted to land someone.'

I thought this over for a moment. It was not altogether fantastic. And yet it seemed incredible. Looking back, I think that what seemed so incredible to me was not the presence of the submarine, but the fact that I had become involved in its presence. I am not accustomed to being caught up in violent adventures. My job is to comment on drama, not take part in it, and I felt somehow a little sceptical of my being knocked overboard by a submarine.

'Did the fellow you met say anything to you?' Big Logan asked.

'Yes, he asked me the way to a cottage called Carillon, which stands back from the cliffs above Church Cove.' It was then that I remembered his perfect English, and suddenly it seemed to me that it was almost too perfect. Word for word, as far as I could remember it, I repeated my conversion with the man.

The conversation seemed harmless enough. But Big Logan was plainly excited. 'How did he know there was a hidden reef off Cadgwith?' he demanded.

'He'd been down here before,' I pointed out. 'It may have been you yourself who told him. He probably went out fishing.'

'Then can you tell me how he knew it wasn't properly charted?'

I couldn't, but at the same time I was by no means convinced that this made the man a spy. Nevertheless, I was glad Big Logan had not realized that in conversation with this stranger I had given him important information concerning the movement of the fleet. Anyway, I consoled myself, if he were a spy he would have the information soon enough.

'I suggest we go along and have a word with Joe,' Logan said. 'He knows everybody around these parts. He'll be able to tell us about the people who own this cottage.'

I followed him back into the pub. We found the landlord in the bar. He had been going over his stock and he had the radio on. He put his fingers to his lips as we went in. Two of his visitors were sitting listening.

'This morning the British Ambassador in Berlin handed the German Government a final note stating that unless we heard from them by eleven o'clock that they are prepared at once to withdraw their troops from Poland a state of war would exist between us. I have to tell you that no such undertaking has been received and that consequently this country is at war with Germany.'

The voice was Chamberlain's. The fact of war came as no great shock to me. It had been a certainty for the past twenty-four hours. Yet my stomach turned over within me at the actuality of it.

The Premier's speech was followed by announcements, commencing with details of the sounding of air raid sirens. The two visitors got up and left the bar, one saying that he was going to telephone his brother. When they had gone, Big Logan turned to the landlord. 'Do you know who lives at Carillon now, Joe? It must be over two years since Mrs Bloy died.'

'Nearer three,' replied the landlord. 'Old man of the name of Cutner has owned it ever since. Retired bank manager, I think. What do you want to know for?'

Big Logan hesitated, and then said, 'Oh, nothing – this gentleman wanted to know, that's all.' He caught me looking at him in some surprise and glanced hurriedly away. 'Know whether he has many visitors?'

'How should I know?' The landlord was looking at him curiously.

'No, of course you wouldn't. I was only – ' He stopped short. The three of us glanced round the room uneasily, aware of a sudden change. I think we all realized what it was at the same moment, for we turned and stared at the radio set at the far end of the bar. The current was still on and we could hear it crackling, but the air had gone dead. At the same moment the visitor who had gone out to phone his brother came in with an anxious look on his face to say that the local exchange could get no answer from London.

He and I were the only ones who leaped immediately to the obvious conclusion. I thought of Bloomsbury with its old houses. They would be absolute death traps. And the trees and the Georgian houses in Mecklenburg Square – should I see those again as I had known them? 'If it is a raid,' I said, 'it's quick work.'

'Perhaps it's only a test,' he said.

'Or just a coincidence,' I murmured. 'The BBC is working under emergency conditions and London is probably inundated with calls.'

'Yes, that's probably it.' His voice did not carry much conviction. Later, of course, we heard that an air raid warning had been sounded, but the possibility of both radio and telephone systems having broken down at the same time enabled us to continue our conversation while the visitor went back to the phone to try again.

Big Logan steered off the subject of the owner of Carillon without any explanation as to why he had been interested in the man. We had a drink on the house and, after discussing the war for a while, we left the pub.

Outside, Big Logan said, 'We'd best go up and have a talk with Ted Morgan.' Morgan was one of the coastguards and it was plain that my companion was not feeling too sure of himself. He had not told the landlord about his suspicions, and had thus prevented the story from circulating throughout the village. Clearly he now wanted confirmation of the conclusion he had arrived at. The coastguard was the sort of father of all wisdom in the village.

But when I was introduced to him in the Board of Trade hut on the cliffs, I doubted whether he was as shrewd as Big Logan. In their relations with the Government, however, the fishermen of the village always turned to Morgan, since he understood the regulations and knew all about the forms they had to fill in. The habit had stuck.

Big Logan told him the whole story. With his feet thrust slightly apart and his thumbs in his leather waistbelt, he seemed to fill the whole hut, his head wagging up and down as he spoke. By comparison, the little Welshman, seated at the desk before the telescope, seemed very small indeed. When Logan had finished I sensed that Morgan was sceptical. He put his head on one side like a bird and drummed with his fingers on the desk. 'It is possible, of course,' he conceded, and he darted a glance at the big fisherman. 'It is possible. I saw what I think was a U-boat about six miles off the coast only yesterday.' He leaned forward in his chair. 'But where would he have landed?'

'What about the Devil's Frying Pan?' suggested Logan.

'Yes, indeed – but it was very choppy last night. The boat would have been stove in.'

'They have collapsible boats,' replied Logan. 'They're made of rubber.'

'Well, supposing it was possible to land a man safely from a submarine at the Frying Pan, why should the Germans want to? Surely they would have all their spies in the country by now?'

It was a very reasonable point. Logan shrugged his great shoulders. 'I'm not responsible for their actions,' he said. 'Maybe this man Cutner is a spy and one of the officers of the U-boat was sent ashore to collect important information from him.'

The coastguard considered this for a moment whilst he explored his small discoloured teeth with a toothpick. At length he shook his head and said, 'You know, there are sharks on this coast.'

'Good God Almighty!' exclaimed Big Logan with sudden exasperation. 'Do you think I don't know a bloody shark when I see one? This wasn't a shark. The displacement of water was too great. It was either a submarine or a whale. And if you think you've ever seen a whale from this little perch of yours, you'd better put in for your discharge right now.'

This outburst apparently left the little coastguard unmoved. He

34

continued to drum with his fingers on his desk and to pick his teeth with the toothpick. In the end he turned to me and said, 'What do you think about it, Mr Craig?'

His question put me in an awkward situation. I was not at all convinced that Logan was right. It seemed much too fantastic. On the other hand, I did not want to offend him. I said, 'I think the matter ought to be investigated.'

The coastguard then turned to Logan. 'What would you like me to do about it? Get on to the police?'

'What the hell's the good of the police?' demanded Logan. 'Either get on to the Admiralty, or phone Scotland Yard and tell them to pass the information on to M.I.5.' It was only then that I realized that he must be old enough to have been through the last war. Generally the inhabitants of English country districts call it the secret service. 'If you don't feel like doing either of these,' he continued, 'I suggest we settle the matter locally.'

'How?'

'Well, figure it out this way,' he said. 'You're probably right when you say a spy wouldn't be landed by submarine – certainly not on this part of the coast. If he is a German, then he'll have been landed to collect information. And if he's been landed to collect information, he's still got to get it back to the submarine. Our job is to see that he doesn't.'

'He may have rejoined his boat already,' I said.

'What – last night?' Big Logan shook his head. 'The sea was rising fast. By the time he'd reached the cottage and got back to the shore again it would have been absolutely impossible to get a boat in anywhere along the cliffs there. It would have been pretty bad landing at Cadgwith even. What I suggest is, we lie in wait for him on the cliffs above the Frying Pan tonight. If he doesn't come – well then, we can consider what's best to be done.'

The coastguard considered this. Then he said, 'All right, Big Logan. You and Mr Craig here wait for him on the cliffs. I'll take two of the boys and keep watch by the head there.' He nodded through the window to the opposite headland that guarded the entrance to Cadgwith from the south west. 'I suppose we can take your boat?'

Big Logan nodded. 'Surely. And take that old service revolver of yours, Ted – you may need it.'

The coastguard pulled open a drawer and, routing among a pile of government forms and other papers, produced a revolver. He turned it over reflectively in his hand as though it brought back old memories. Then he shook his head. 'It's early for spy

35

scares. Still, it won't do any harm to take it along.'

So it was that at nine-thirty that evening Big Logan and I met on the path above the Devil's Frying Pan. By that time I had heard the news of the sinking of the *Athenia* and was suffering from that indefinable desire to express my horror in action. This, I think, is the most deadly moral effect of war. As I had walked along the path from Church Cove my mind had evolved all sorts of wild schemes by which I could bring about the destruction of the submarine. It wasn't until I had settled down to the long vigil on the cliff-top that I gave a thought for the men in the boat itself. Then all the horror of the *Thetis* disaster flooded back into my mind. Journalism and the theatre foster the growth of an imagination. And in war an imagination is a definite handicap. I could not help – despite the sinking of the *Athenia* – a sudden feeling of deep sympathy for men of the German submarine service scattered about the high seas, cooped up in their steel shells, facing a horrible and almost inevitable death.

But after all, there was no question of destroying the submarine. Somehow I felt thankful that Big Logan had not felt sure enough of himself to insist upon the Admiralty being notified. I could picture the torpedo boat waiting under the shelter of the headland and then dashing out, as the U-boat submerged, to drop depth charges that would blow her back to the surface and destroy her utterly. But there was only Big Logan's boat waiting, with no bigger armaments than the coastguard's revolver, and the two of us sitting on top of the cliffs. Anyway, there probably was no U-boat.

That belief grew as the hours slipped monotonously by. We could neither smoke nor talk. We sat on a great rock on the westward side of the Frying Pan, watching the sea until everything merged into the blackness of a tunnel. There were no stars, no moon – the night was like a pit. I had brought some chocolate. We ate that, spinning it out as long as possible, for it gave us something to do. At length I began to feel drowsy. It was then nearly two. I was cold and stiff. For a time I felt angry with Big Logan for assuming that I would accompany him on this damfool errand. The belief that he did not know a shark when he saw one had grown to a certainty by the time I fell asleep.

It seemed but a second later that I was being shaken out of my sleep. I opened my mouth to speak, but a rough hand closed over it and Big Logan's voice whispered in my ear, 'Keep quiet and watch the sea.'

I felt suddenly tense. The night was as black as ever and, as I stared out into it, I felt that I might just as well be blind. Then suddenly a light showed out there on the water. I saw its reflection for an instant in the sea. Then it was gone, and the night was as dark as ever, so that I felt it must have been my imagination. Big Logan did not move. I sensed the rigidity of his body. His head, only a few feet away from my own, was just visible. It was tilted slightly to one side as he listened, his eyes fixed on the spot where I supposed the water must flow into the Frying Pan. At length he rose. And I scrambled to my feet too, though I had heard nothing. He took my arm and together we moved with great care back on to the path. There we waited, huddled against the wall of the big white house that lay back from the Frying Pan. 'The boat has arrived,' he whispered in my car. 'It's down in the Frying Pan now. And I saw the flash of your friend's torch away along the cliff as he signalled the submarine.'

It seemed hours before we heard the sound of footsteps on the path. Actually I suppose it was only a few minutes. They drew nearer. I felt Logan tense for the spring. Then they ceased. Almost at the same time there was the flash of a torch reddened by a screening hand. And in that flash the slim waterproof-clad figure stood out quite clearly. He had left the path and had reached almost the exact spot where we had been sitting. He was descending the steep shoulder of the Frying Pan towards the archway.

For all his bulk, Logan moved swiftly. He was down the slope, a vague blur in the darkness, almost before I had crossed the path. As I scrambled down the shoulder I saw him pounce. It was so dark that it was difficult to distinguish what happened, but I think the man turned just before the attack. My one fear had been that he would have a revolver. But if he had, he got no chance to use it. Logan had the advantage of the slope and his own huge bulk. They went down together, and when I reached them Logan had his man pinioned to the ground, his hand across his mouth. 'Search him,' he said.

I ran my hands over his body and felt the outline of an automatic in the pocket of his waterproof. I was on the point of removing it when the whole scene was suddenly illuminated by a torch. I looked up and was almost blinded by its light. I have a vivid mental picture of Big Logan's bearded head in silhouette against that dazzling light. The light came steadily nearer. A tall man in uniform was standing over us. His arms rose and fell, and as it fell in front of the torch I saw that his hand grasped a big service revolver by the barrel. There was a sickening thud, and Big Logan slumped forward. The man in the waterproof thrust

37

Logan's body away from him and scrambled to his feet. Something cold and hard was pressed against my head. I knew what it was and I thought my last hour had come. The man had not switched off his torch and I could see Big Logan's head hanging loosely over a rock and blood was trickling down from his scalp into his beard. I thought the blow had killed him.

'Wir werden sie beide mitnehmen.' It was the man in the waterproof speaking. I was never so thankful for a knowledge of German. Their decision to take us along was presumably due to a desire to leave no evidence of the fact that they had landed and to safeguard, as far as possible, the owner of Carillon.

The man in the waterproof turned to me. 'You must regard yourself as our prisoner,' he said in his precise English. 'You will walk two paces in front. Any attempt to escape or to attract attention and you will be shot.' He motioned me forward with his automatic, and then he and the other German each took hold of one of Logan's arms. The torch was switched off and in the sudden darkness I could hardly see where I was going. I could hear Logan's feet dragging along the ground behind me as I went down the slope to the bottom of the Frying Pan. The Germans frequently had to pause in order to adjust Logan's wieght between them and the sound of their breathing became louder.

It grew darker than ever as we descended and I almost stumbled into the arms of a man waiting at the water's edge. He challenged us in German. 'Schon gut, Karl,' answered the man in the waterproof. 'Sehen Sie, dass die Leute ins Boot kommen.'

'Zu Befehl, Herr Kapitaenleutnant.'

So Logan had been right. It was the commander of the U-boat that had been landed. I began to wonder what it was that he had come ashore for. It must have been something of considerable importance for him to run that risk at the outbreak of war. We ought to have realized that one of the boat's crew might come up to meet him. Our only hope now lay in the coastguard, waiting off the headland – or had they already dealt with him? Was that what had put them on their guard?

The boat was dragged in closer. It was a collapsible affair with two oars, and by the time Logan's inert body had been placed in it, there seemed no prospect of it holding four more men. However, it did, though it sat very low in the water as a result. The commander sat facing me with his automatic ready, while the other two men took an oar each.

Silently we slid beneath the great archway that had originally formed the entrance to the cave before it had collapsed to make the Frying Pan. It was lighter as soon as we got out into the open sea and it was possible to distinguish the dim outline of the cliffs towering above us. Soon, however, even this landmark merged and was lost in the night. It seemed impossible to believe that we should find the submarine in the dark until, turning my head, I saw the merest pinprick of a light showing straight over our bows.

I looked back at the commander. He was watching me, the automatic gripped in his hand, its barrel pointed at me. Big Logan lay inert between us. There was no sign of the coastguard's boat. Then I began to think of the information that the U-boat commander had presumably obtained. What was it – movements of merchant ships, fleet dispositions, transport sailings? It might mean the loss of hundreds of lives if he were allowed to reach the submarine with it. I shifted my position. The boat rocked dangerously. 'Still!' Though the commander spoke English, his voice was not English. There was something cold about it, and I sat rigid, the automatic thrust a few inches nearer.

But it was my life and possibly Big Logan's against the lives of many others. On me lay the responsibility for action. I hesitated. Then suddenly I made up my mind. I would jump on the side of the boat. It was bound to capsize. Then anything might happen. I tensed my muscles for the spring.

And at that moment I heard the roar of a powerful engine. A searchlight suddenly stretched out a white pencil of light across the water. It swept round in a short arc and came to rest on the rubber boat, blinding us completely. The drone of the engines grew louder and then came the rattle of machine gun fire. Little spouts of water flew up all round us. One of the men at the oars slumped into the bottom of the boat, almost capsizing it.

The searchlight bore rapidly down on us. The boat's intention was obvious. It was going to ram us. Close behind us came a sudden ear-splitting explosion. A huge spout of water flew up white in the searchlight. Another flung spray right over the advancing boat. It veered away and I saw the grey lines of a British torpedo boat flash past our stern, the water swirling up from its bows. Before I had time to do anything the steel bows of a submarine nosed alongside.

The Commander jumped out on to the deck, which was half awash. In an instant I found myself hauled out of the boat and bundled towards the conning tower. I passed the for'ard gun just as it fired again and my ears went completely deaf. As I was thrust down the conning tower hatch I saw the torpedo boat swing in a great arc. Its searchlight suddenly went out and everything was black. The commander dropped down beside me, shouting a string of orders so fast that I could not understand them. Immediately the submarine's engines came to life and she began to swing sharply to port. I knew then that the commander was afraid of being torpedoed and I felt a sudden emptiness inside me.

Logan's great body, still unconscious, was thrust down the hatch almost on top of me. We were pushed out of the way and the crew scrambled down, two carrying the man who had been hit. The hatch closed with a bang. The sound of the engines immediately seemed like a great throbbing pulse. It was very warm and there was a strong smell of oil. We were bundled into two bunks out of the way. Every man was at his action station.

The boat seemed to shudder as she gathered way. A bell sounded, and a few seconds later the floor took a decided tilt. We were diving. It was a crash dive and the roar of the electric motors took the place of the diesels. We were no sooner on an even keel than I sensed rather than actually felt the boat turning. I had read enough about submarine experiences in the Great War to know what the commander was trying to avoid. The muscles of my face contracted in anticipation and my hands were clenched so tight that the nails bit into the palms.

A second later it came – a terrific crash. The U-boat bucked as though it had hit a rock and there was the sound of breaking crockery. The lights went out and, with the fuses blown, the motors stopped. There was a sudden deathly stillness. And in that stillness it was just possible to hear the drone of the torpedo boat's propellers on the surface of the sea above us. The emergency lighting came on. The shock of the depth charge had rolled Logan out of his bunk into the gangway. He picked himself up, fully conscious now. Then he saw me and said, 'My head feels bloody. There are sort of explosions going on inside it. It feels as though it will burst.'

I was about to enlighten him when a second depth charge exploded. It was not so near as the other, but even so the U-boat rocked violently for the trim was bad. The bows seemed to dip and then there was an ominous jar for'ard. Logan took one look round the place and understood. He was like a drunkard that has suddenly sobered up by danger. His eyes cleared and he was instantly alert.

The commander shouted some order. Two seamen dashed down the gangway, pushing Logan to one side. They were followed by the man who had knocked Logan out. He was the first-lieutenant. For a moment everything seemed pandemonium.

Orders were shouted and men rushed aft. Then there was quiet. Water was flooding in from the control room. The crew were on the hand gear for everything to save noise. The only sound was a gramophone playing 'Deutschland, Deutschland über Alles.' For the second time that night I found myself thinking of the *Thetis* disaster, but there was little comfort in Professor Haldane's assurance at the enquiry that the men would not have suffered greatly.

The regulating tank had been flooded and the submarine was now on an even keel. I found I had scrambled out of my bunk. The Number One came back along the gangway shouting, 'Die Kammer achtern ist unter Wasser, und Wasser dringt in den Maschinenraum.'

'Do you understand what he said?' asked Logan.

'He said the stern compartment is flooded and water is coming into the engine room,' I told him.

Then there was a report of water coming in for'ard. But by this time the leak in the control room had been stopped. Two more depth charges boomed in the distance. The commander came out of the control room and was met by the engineer officer. He reported engine room leak stopped, but port motor damaged. One of the watchkeepers who was down with 'flu walked dazedly past along the gangway in his pyjamas. 'What's happened?' he asked.

'Plenty – your temperature is a hundred and two,' came the answer. 'Report to your bunk.' Then to the engineer officer, the commander said, 'What about the starboard motor?'

'Propeller shaft fractured.'

'Well, see if you can get the port motor working.'

The commander then had a long talk with his second. Part of it I could not catch. But the gist of the second's remarks gave me some idea of what had happened following the first depth charge. The explosion had apparently blown open the engine-room hatch allowing a huge volume of water to enter. Then the pressure of water from outside had sealed the hatch completely. Moreover, it appeared that the boat was now far too heavy and bobbing about between fifty and sixty feet. 'We'll have to empty the bilges,' the commander decided suddenly, 'even if the oil does give our position away.'

The second gave the order, and soon even a layman like myself could realize that the boat was lighter and more manageable. Then the second and the commander bent over a chart. I could just see them from where I was seated on my bunk. I think the commander must have sensed me watching him, for he looked up and his gaze swung from me to Logan. Then he strode down the gangway. He was still dressed in civilian clothes and wearing his stiff military-looking waterproof though the interior of the submarine was getting extremely hot. He stopped opposite Logan. 'You are a fisherman, are you not?' he asked.

Logan looked up and nodded.

'Well, I do not expect you want to die any more than we do,' the commander said. 'I should be glad if you would help us. We are lying at about fifty feet. The motors are out of action and that torpedo boat of yours is somewhere up above waiting for us. We dare not surface. But we do not know the drift so close to the shore. If we stay down we may pile ourselves up on the rocks. I calculate that at the moment we are less than a quarter of a mile off the entrance to Cadgwith.'

Big Logan stroked his beard and looked across at me. I felt a sudden excitement. It was almost exultation. I think he sensed it, for he turned to the commander, grinning all over his face. 'You're given me a crack on the head and dragged me on board this blasted tin fish of yours,' he said, 'and now you want me to get you out of the mess you've got yourself into.'

'Pardon me, but it was you who got us into this mess – or rather your friend here. We did not arrange for a British torpedo boat to be waiting for us.'

'Torpedo boat, was it?' Big Logan suddenly clicked his fingers. 'Well, I'm damned,' he said. 'So Ted Morgan took my word for it after all. And he wanted me to believe it was a shark.' He poked a large forefinger into the U-boat commander's ribs. 'It wasn't this gentleman – ' he indicated me – 'that gave you away. It was your bloody submarine coming up right under my boat when he and I were out after mackerel last night. A shark! Well, I'm damned!' And suddenly he began to laugh. He laughed until the tears ran down his cheeks. The crew gathered round, staring at him. I think they thought he had gone off his head with fright.

At length, weak with laughter, he said, 'And here you are, like a lot of stuck pigs, just because you interfered with this gentleman's fishing.' I thought he was going off into another paroxysm of laughter. But suddenly he sobered up. 'Know what I'll do?' he said. 'I'll make a bargain with you – the papers you got from your friend at Carillon for information about the currents.'

I thought the commander would strike him. He was a young man and Logan had made him furious. He was a nice looking lad, very slim and erect, but he had the Prussian features and the Prussian lack of any sense of humour. The joke was on him and he could not see it. 'You are a prisoner,' he said. His voice was cold and precise. 'You will do as you are told.'

'I'll see you on the Gav Rocks first,' was Big Logan's reply. And he began to bellow with laughter again.

The commander's hand came up instantly and smacked Logan first on one cheek and then on the other. Logan's answer was instantaneous. He laid the commander out with one blow of his huge fist.

The second immediately drew his revolver. I read Logan's death sentence in his eyes and at the same time one of the crew seized me from behind. But as the second raised the gun it was struck out of his hand by another officer who had appeared behind him. It was the navigating officer. 'Don't be a fool,' he said in German. 'He's our only chance of getting out of this alive.'

Then he turned to Logan and said in broken English, 'Eet ees the lifes of you and dese other gentleman who ees at stake, as well as our own. Will you not help us? The torpedo boat, she will wait all night for us. Eef we could drift half a mile down the coast without wrecking ourselfs we could surface. Then we should be all right.'

Logan's reply was, 'I've told this officer' – he indicated the inert figure of the commander – 'what my terms for helping you are. I've lived by the sea all my life and I'm not afraid to die by it, even if it is in a glorified sardine tin.'

'And that goes for me too,' I said. It was a heroic little gesture for my stomach felt queasy at the thought of death by suffocation. I suppose most people with any imagination possess a mild form of claustrophobia, but I must say that Logan's phrase about a glorified sardine tin struck home.

The navigating officer, whom I guessed to be a far more human individual and consequently a much better reader of character, immediately took Logan at his word and set reviving the commander. This took several minutes, for Logan's whole weight had been behind the punch.

The man eventually staggered to his feet, but he was so dazed by the blow that it was several minutes before the navigating officer could make him understand the position. When he did he blazed up in a fury. 'You have the audacity to try to make terms with me,' he cried turning on Logan. But he kept his distance this time. 'You came aboard this ship as a prisoner, you behave like a lunatic, strike the commander and then expect to barter information which you possess on fantastic terms.' He gave an order to the crew. Three of them closed in on Logan. Logan remained calm and impassive, but his little grey eyes roamed the narrow gangway, guaging distances and possibilities. It looked like a real scrap.

The navigating officer, however, continued to talk in low tones with the commander. The two men were of completely contrasting types. The navigating officer was small in height and rather stocky, with a round ruddy face that spoke of years at sea. The commander, on the other hand, was a typical Nazi – excitable, overbearing and cold-blooded. However, the navigating officer apparently got his way, for the commander turned to Logan and said, 'If you help us, we will land you and your companion on shore as soon as it is safe to do so.'

I pictured the surface of the sea, the towering cliffs, Cadgwith and the green fields beyond. What a relief it would be to get out of this little nightmare world of machinery that reeked of oil and was so hot and stuffy. A word or two from Logan and we were safe. He glanced at me. Something stubborn and perverse seemed to rise up within me. I shook my head. He nodded and smiled. 'We want the papers,' he said.

The commander swung round on him. 'Well, you won't get them – understand that.'

'Then neither will your superiors,' Logan answered quietly.

When the fury of a man's emotions gets the better of him and he is at the same time baffled, it is not a pretty sight. I wondered how long his nerves would hold out against the incessant tension of service in U-boats. The strain had been too great for a number of submarine commanders in the last war.

At last he mastered himself sufficiently to say, 'Very well, we'll stay down for half an hour.'

'And send youself and your crew to certain death?' asked Logan. He looked at me. 'That serves our purpose just as well, eh?'

I had to agree with him, though I felt like being sick.

The commander tried to bluster for a moment. 'You are bluffing,' he shouted angrily.

Logan shrugged his shoulders. 'You'd best call my bluff, if you think so.'

The man's uneasiness, however, got the better of him. He stood watching Logan for some seconds and then he said, 'All right. I'll get you the papers.' He turned and strode down the gangway to the officers' quarters.

I looked at Logan, wondering what good it would do to get hold of the papers since the man might very well have a copy or have memorized them. 'Why don't you keep silent and let them run on the rocks?' I asked in a whisper.

44

'Because,' he replied, 'the drift of the current here is seaward. They're as safe as houses, if they only knew it. If we can't get an undertaking from them to wireless the information through to Fort Blockhouse, then we'll have to try and scare them into surfacing and hope that the torpedo boat will still be around.'

The prospect seemed pretty grim.

It was some time before the commander returned. He held in his hand a single sheet of paper. This he handed to the navigating officer, who passed it on to Logan. 'Now step up here and explain the drift on the chart,' the commander said.

Logan glanced at the sheet of paper and then held it out so that I could also read it. I cannot remember all the details of it. But it gave the position, longitude and latitude, of a rendezvous for three separate squadrons of British ships – one from Gibraltar, one from the Atlantic and one from Portsmouth. Logan explained to me that the rendezvous was about thirty miles south of the Shambles Light – that is off Portland. Those coming from Gibraltar and the Atlantic were largely capital ships. Those coming from Portsmouth were mainly destroyers and mine-sweepers.

Logan placed his big forefinger on the list of those coming from the Atlantic. 'They're short of destroyers,' he said. 'Until they meet up with the Portsmouth boats those four battleships will be sufficiently screened. What a chance for the U-boats!'

There were certainly not nearly so many destroyers and torpedo boats with this squadron as with that coming up from Gibraltar. My eyes travelled on down the paper. The rendezvous was for Monday, 18 September at 13.30 hours. The object of the gathering was to sweep up the Channel, pass through the Downs and carry out a raid on the Kiel Canal. Blockships were to be waiting in the Downs and these were to be sunk in the canal if it proved possible to silence the shore batteries. Raids by Bomber Command of the R.A.F. were to accompany the attack and three fighter squadrons would co-operate in preventing enemy aircraft from harassing the raiding fleet.

As I grasped the magnitude and daring of the plan, I could not help being amazed at the ability of the German secret service to obtain information of such a vitally secret nature. 'Have they got a chance of sinking those four battleships?' I asked.

'Quite a good chance, I should say,' Logan replied. 'And if there are enough U-boats in this vicinity they might have a shot at the main gathering.'

Our conversation was interrupted by the commander. 'Stop

that whispering,' he ordered, 'and let us have the information we require.'

Logan strode down the gangway towards the control room. 'Certainly,' he said, 'if you'll transmit a message to Fort Block-house, Portsmouth.'

The commander's eyes narrowed. 'You have the information I obtained. Keep your side of the bargain.'

'You know my purpose in requiring this information before directing you to safety,' Logan answered. 'My intention was to prevent its use by the enemies of my country. If you have a copy of this or if you have memorized – '

'I have neither copied it nor memorized it,' the other cut in.

'In that case there is no objection to your sending my message to the Admiralty.'

The commander moved forward. There was something stealthy, almost cat-like in the way he moved. 'I will not be called a liar in my own ship – certainly not by a verflucht Britisher. You have the insolence to demand that this ship's radio be used to transmit messages to the British Naval authorities. I'll see you in hell first.'

'Then, you won't have long to wait,' was Logan's reply.

The navigating officer, who had been following the conversation intently, said, 'Eet will be your lifes as well as ours.'

'If these ships meet as arranged,' Logan replied, tapping the paper in his hand, 'it may mean the loss of hundreds of lives. It's our lives against theirs. We prefer that it should be two and not several hundred British lives that are lost. So it's Davy Jones for you if you don't give me a solemn pledge to radio my warning to the authorities as soon as I have got you out of this mess and you have a chance to dry off your aerials.'

'As you wish,' said the commander. There was something of a sneer in his voice. I think he thought we might crack up under the strain, for after he had barked out an order in German he stood watching us. The hiss of the compressed air entering the tanks of the submarine, forcing the water out, was incredibly loud. It seemed to fill my ears.

'Now do you still withhold the information we need? If you do, I am going to surface and take a chance with this torpedo boat of yours.' And when neither of us answered, the commander shrugged his shoulders. 'Gun crews stand by!' he ordered in German. Then he disappeared up into the conning tower.

The next few minutes were some of the most unpleasant I have ever experienced. It was not difficult to sense the tension in the submarine. The atmosphere was by now getting very heavy and I was sweating like a pig with the heat of the place. The hiss of the compressed air gradually lessened. The second officer adjusted the trim. The submarine had risen on an even keel and was now, I presumed, lying at periscope depth while the commander watched the torpedo boat and chose his time. I wondered whether the port diesel had been affected or not. If it had, then we were for it.

The commander's voice suddenly called out, 'Blow all tanks! Surface!' The compressed air hissed in the tanks and the boat shot up so quickly that I could hear the sea water flooding back from the deck. 'Geschuetzmannschaften auf Bereitschaft!' The gun crews swarmed like monkeys into the conning tower. The hatch slammed back and feet sounded over our heads. Then the one diesel engine began to throb and the ship shuddered as the bows bit into the waves.

The gun crews would be at their stations now. I could hear the swirl of the water overhead and I presumed we were travelling with decks awash in order to keep the boat steady. The U-boat's surface speed of 18 knots was reduced, Big Logan reckoned, to about 9 or 10 as a result of the damage to the starboard propeller shaft. The speed of the torpedo, on the other hand, was well over 40 knots. We had not long to wait. A bell sounded in the engine room. The pulsing of the single engine grew more and more frenzied. The whole ship seemed to be shaking and rattling. The din was incredible. Then suddenly there was a sharp detonation and we were almost thrown off our feet. For a moment I though we had been hit by a torpedo. But I had barely recovered my balance when the explosion was repeated and I realized that it was the after gun being fired. So the torpedo boat had spotted us and we were in action!

To analyse my hopes during the minutes that followed is quite impossible. I was torn between the desire for self-preservation and what I sensed to be my duty. The two were completely ir-reconcilable. I have, however, a vivid recollection of growing horror at the idea of being imprisoned and suffocated in that infernal U-boat, and towards the end of the action I must admit that that was my dominating thought. I must have been in a pitiable state of funk by the end for I remember nothing about it except that I babbled incoherent nonsense whilst Logan shook me till my teeth rattled in order to prevent me from going completely off my head.

It was a most unpleasant experience, and as an exhibition it must have been disgusting. Strangely enough, it did not make it impossible for me afterwards to go in a submarine again. In fact, those twenty minutes seemed to sweat all terror of death by suffocation out of me. Logan, on the other hand, preserved that same calm throughout the engagement, though he informed me afterwards that he had never actually been in a submarine before. All his experience of submarine warfare in the last war had been gained on minesweepers and coastal patrols, and later on 'Q' ships.

I do not remember much about that engagement. All that remains vivid in my mind is the throb of the engines, which seemed to pulse right through me, the draught from the open conning tower hatch, the incessant gunfire and my own terror. I remember that a few minutes from the outset the after gun crew ceased firing. But they remained at their stations and some ten minutes later the for'ard gun opened fire and at the same time the commander ordered an eight point turn to starboard – eight points represent a right-angle. I think it was this order that really finished me, for I was pretty certain that it meant a torpedo had been launched at us.

Later, I learned from listening to the conversation of the officers and men that we had surfaced about half a mile out off Caerleon Cove, which lies just east of Cadgwith. The torpedo boat was still off Cadgwith, but within a few seconds her searchlight had picked up the U-boat. The torpedo boat had immediately extinguished her searchlight. The commander, explaining the action to the navigating officer later, said that the drone of the torpedo boat's engines was plainly audible from the conning tower even above the sound of the U-boat's own engine. The order had been given for the U-boat's searchlight to be switched on and as soon as it had picked out the attacking craft the after gun crew had opened fire.

The U-boat was then travelling almost due east with the torpedo boat dead astern. Shortly afterwards the gun crew scored what looked like a direct hit and the torpedo boat swerved off its course and was lost to sight. The U-boat then made a turn of sixteen points and doubled back in the hope of shaking off the torpedo boat if it were still in action.

What actually happened I have pieced together from a talk I had some months later with the coastguard who was on board the torpedo boat. After getting out of range of the U-boat's searchlight, the boat had hove-to and listened for the sound of the submarine's engine. As they had expected, the U-boat's searchlight was extinguished and it began to double back. By this time the clouds had thinned and a rather pale young moon had appeared. As the U-boat approached they got under way with their engines just ticking over and moved up between the shore and the U-boat, endeavouring to merge their craft into the background of the cliffs. This proved so successful that they had actually manœuvred into position and fired their torpedo before they were sighted. In actual fact, it was the torpedo, and not the torpedo boat, that the U-boat commander first sighted, for the wake of the torpedo showed like a streak of silver in the moonlight. It was then that the order for an eight point turn was made. At the same time our own searchlight picked out the torpedo boat and the for'ard gun opened fire. As the submarine swung on to her new course the after gun crew took up the fire. The torpedo apparently almost scraped the U-boat's side.

The gun crew had the range almost immediately this time and their third shot hit the sea just behind the torpedo boat, seriously damaging the engines and injuring one man. At the same time our port look-out reported a ship on the port bow. All he had seen was the white bow wave. But through his glasses the commander picked out the shape of a destroyer coming at full tilt to the scene of action.

Down in the bowels of the U-boat we heard orders being shouted and then the clatter of sea boots on the deck plates above our heads. The men came tumbling down through the conning tower, the hatch cover slammed to and in a few seconds I was experiencing my second crash dive of the evening.

This time, however, we were far enough out for the commander to have complete confidence in the charts. There was apparently a sand bottom and the dive was straightened out, the boat trimmed and we settled slowly on to the bed of the sea. For nearly an hour we could hear the ugly boom of depth charges in the distance. None came very near us, however, and we settled down to a long vigil.

I think it was this long vigil that really cured me of my terror. Time dulls the senses and in the end I settled down to a game of cards. That we were allowed, as prisoners, to indulge in a game of cards by a commander who obviously could not regard us in too friendly a light may seem surprising. I think my own exhibition of terror was the cause. Fear is catching, and fear in a submarine at a time of emergency is to be avoided at all costs.

That game of poker must constitute something of a record. It started at three o'clock in the morning and it went on, subject to various interruptions, until nearly midnight the following night. We sat or reclined on the bunks and for a table we had a packing case from the store chamber. The light, which was directly above us, threw the interior of the bunks into complete darkness, so that it was impossible to see anyone's features, and even when they leaned forward to put their cards down it only shone on the tops of their heads. The contrast between Logan's head and those of the Germans who played with us remains very vivid in my mind. His hair stood up like a great mop, which together with his beard, gave him a very wild look. The Germans, on the other hand, had close-cropped heads and even those whose overalls were blackened with oil still managed to look quite smart.

The navigation officer played with us most of the time, acting as interpreter. At Logan's suggestion I pretended that I did not understand a word of German, a pretence which was to stand us in good stead later. Different members of the crew joined us at various times. They gave us the benefit of the tourist rate of exchange for our money. Nobody seemed to feel like sleep until well into the next day.

I began to feel drowsy, however, quite soon after breakfast, which was an excellent meal of pressed ham and hard boiled eggs. For a time I played more or less automatically. Big Logan, on the other hand, seemed to remain quite fresh. Despite the language bar, he seemed to get on the best of terms with those he played with, laughing and joking, so that it was difficult to realize that we were in imminent danger of our lives. In fact, the atmosphere became so friendly that, with the sound of Big Logan's voice booming in my ears, I found it difficult to believe in my drowsy state that I was not back in the pub at Cadgwith.

By midday the air was beginning to get pretty bad and most of us lay down and tried to sleep. Throughout the whole time we were submerged the engineers were working on the port electric motor. Twice it was started up, but each time there was an awful clanking sound. By lunch-time they had given it up, and in the afternoon they also turned in.

The only man who did not seem to sleep at all was the commander. I did not like him. He was the personification of the effects of Nazism upon the youth of Germany. He was cold-blooded, brutal and very ready to sneer. But he was efficient. He could not have been more than about twenty-five, yet his men had complete confidence in him. His coolness when actually in action had the quality of a machine, and I could not help thinking that if the German army were officered by a sufficiency of young men of his calibre it must be a very powerful machine.

But like so many Germans, especially those of Prussian stock, he lacked any understanding of the importance of psychology. He formed his opinion of men and expected them to act thereafter according to a formula. As far as the men under his command were concerned this seemed to work out well – he knew how each one would react in given circumstances. But like so many Germans he had no understanding of the English. Whether we are a much more complex race than the Germans I do not know – perhaps we are. At any rate, I had several verbal clashes with him, for when I told him I was a journalist he began to question me about the reasons Britain had entered into the war. He simply could not understand that we had entered purely and simply because we hated the precepts of Nazism and refused to live indefinitely under the threat of aggression. He spoke sneeringly of imperialistic aims and honestly believed that the whole thing had been engineered by Churchill and Eden.

As regards myself, too, he revealed himself as having not the slightest understanding of the complex psychological reactions that go on in the mind of a man accustomed to living an entirely individualistic life. Because I had been terrified when the action with the torpedo boat had been in progress, he thought I was a coward. And the more he implied that I was a coward, the more determined he made me to prove, as opportunity offered, that I was not a coward.

We remained on the bottom until shortly after midnight. By the time the order was given to blow the tanks, the atmosphere was so thick that it was really painful to breathe. Certainly by then I was cured of any fear of being cooped up in an air-tight vessel. Haldane is perfectly right. You gradually reach a condition in which your senses become so dulled that the prospect of death is by no means unpleasant.

We stopped at periscope depth. The commander reported all clear and at long last we rose to the surface. The conning tower hatch was thrown back and a sudden waft of cool air entered the submarine. I never realized till then how lovely it was to actually feel yourself breathing good life-giving air. Each man was allowed a few minutes out on the conning tower platform and I don't think I have ever enjoyed a few minutes fresh sea air so much. The submarine was travelling at about 8 knots with her decks awash and the water creaming up white over the bows. It was a fine sight to see the vague outline of her slipping steadily through the long Atlantic swell. The night was cloudy, but there was a faint luminosity from the moon.

'We're travelling due west,' Logan whispered.

'How do you know?' I asked.

'The moon, for one thing,' he said.

'What are they going west for?' I asked. 'Surely with a fractured propeller shaft and one of the motors out of action they'll have to return to Germany for repairs?'

'They wouldn't stand much chance of getting through the Straits now that they can't travel under water. Maybe they're going to try and get round the north of Scotland. Or perhaps they have a base in Spain or somewhere like that.'

Our guards, who kept very close to us in case we attempted to jump into the sea, indicated that our spell of fresh air was over. With the boat rolling heavily, I found the descent of the conning tower ladder something of a feat. We went back to the bunks that had been allotted to us, and for the first time since we had come on board I really slept. I think it was the drone of the engine that did it. The incessant rhythmic throbbing lulled my senses.

When I woke up the engine had stopped. There was considerable activity for'ard. I leant out over the edge of my bunk and peered into the one below where Logan lay. 'What happened?' I asked.

'I don't know,' he replied. And then in a whisper, he added, 'I reckon we're not far off the North Cornish coast.'

'How do you know?' I asked.

For answer he moved his arm so that I could see he held in the palm of his hand a big silver watch that he always carried in his trouser pocket. It was turned face downward and the flap at the back was open revealing a luminous compass. 'It's now just after four,' he said. 'We moved off from Cadgwith shortly after midnight. Then for nearly two hours our course was practically due west. At two-twenty we bore away to the north – presumably rounding Land's End. By three-fifteen our course was practically north nor'east. We hove-to about five minutes ago.'

'What's the idea, do you think?' I asked. 'Perhaps the commander is passing on the information he received to another boat?'

Logan did not reply, but turned his watch the right way up. The flap at the back closed with a snap. I looked up to find that our guard had risen from his seat on a bunk a little way down the gangway and was watching us warily. The conning tower hatch was still open. If we could rush the guard, get hold of his revolver and reach the controls of the tanks we might be able to submerge the U-boat. Death would come quickly with the conning tower hatch open. But even as I pondered the idea, trying to remember all the controls I had seen being used, there came the sound of feet on the deck plates above our heads and the members of the crew who had been up above began to tumble in through the conning tower hatch. The commander was last down and the hatch closed with a bang. I cursed myself for not having thought of the scheme sooner.

The order was given to submerge and the inrush of water into the tanks was plainly audible. There was a grating noise for'ard that I did not quite understand and the U-boat slowly submerged. Then there was silence. The commander, who had now left the conning tower, picked up an earphone that hung from a hook in the control room and began speaking into it. His voice was subdued, but I caught the words 'motors' and 'fixed.' Almost immediately the grating sound was resumed.

'We're facing sou'east,' Logan whispered.

'Then if you've worked out our bearings right,' I said, 'we are facing in to the coast.'

He nodded.

Twice the submarine seemed to bump the bed of the sea. I became convinced that we were moving forward, though the motors were silent. There was suddenly a horrible grating sound against the hull just behind our bunks, then another bump and the movement of the boat ceased. The tanks were then blown and we rose slightly.

The commander put down the earphone and moved out into the gangway. 'All right, boys,' he said, 'we've arrived.'

The burst of cheering that followed this announcement was almost deafening in that enclosed space. The men came hurrying from their stations, pushing past our guard in a sort of mad race for the conning tower. In a few seconds, it seemed, the boat was empty. Our guard motioned us forward with his revolver. We scrambled out of our bunks and went along the gangway and up through the conning tower.

I cannot describe my amazement as I came out on to the bridge of the U-boat. I had presumed that we had been brought alongside a ship. Several ideas had occurred to me. I knew that supply ships were essential if repeated and hazardous returns to bases were to be avoided and I thought it possible that the Germans had produced some sort of vessel with a false bottom into which the submarine rose. That, I felt, would account for the fact that we had had to submerge first. What in fact I found was something much more sensational.

3

THE GESTAPO

THE U-boat was lying in a colossal cave. From end to end this cave was nearly a hundred yards long. The width, however, was only about forty or fifty feet. The roof, which was arched like a huge tunnel and about forty feet high, was strengthened by huge steel girders. The whole place was lit by brilliant arc lights and echoed to the hum of giant machinery. I know it must sound fantastic. I was myself utterly astonished when I saw it. The U-boat commander realized this, as he stood beside me on the bridge, and there was a sort of smug satisfaction in the way he said, 'The world has yet to understand – and the English in particular – that Germany does not go to war unprepared. Already we are sweeping your shipping from the high seas. Your papers will be reassuring your people that Germany cannot do this for long as her submarines will have to return to Germany for munitions and supplies. This is the answer. It is a complete naval submarine base. We even have our own foundry.'

As he spoke my eyes took in the whole scene. The crew of the U-boat, some sixty men in all, were crowding the deck for'ard. Right at the bows three men were working to cast off a big cylindrical buoy to which the submarine was moored. The buoy itself was attached to a big chain which ran round a powerful-looking donkey-engine and dropped back into the water. I gathered that it was by this chain that the submarine had been dragged through the underwater entrance and guided to the surface.

'You'd be in an awkward fix if the British secret service discovered your hide-out,' I said. 'With only that one exit you'd be caught like rats in a trap.'

He laughed. 'Strange to say, that thought had already occurred to us.' He took a step towards me. 'And don't think you're going to be the little hero that takes word to the authorities. Or you either,' he added, swinging round on Logan. 'You'll earn your keep with hard work and you'll not leave here alive till Germany has won the war.'

'Then it looks as though we're doomed to die here,' said Logan with a twinkle in his eyes.

The muscles on the back of the commander's neck tightened. I waited for the inevitable. But he thought better of it and went down from the bridge on to the deck.

'I'm afraid you're getting the wrong side of him,' I said.

Logan shrugged his shoulders. 'What's it matter,' he said. 'He's not in charge of this place, and as soon as his ship is repaired he'll put to sea again.'

'Well, at least try and keep on the right side of the man who is in charge,' I said. 'Somehow we've got to get out of here.'

At that moment the cave echoed to the fussy chug-chug of a small boat which appeared from one of the archways leading off the main cave. In several of these archways I could see the dark grey sterns of submarines. The buoy had by now been cast off. A hawser was paid off to the boat, which did service as a diminutive tug. As soon as the hawser had been made fast the boat took the submarine in tow.

At the far end, the cave suddenly widened out into a big semi-circle. Radiating from this semi-circle were no less than seven caves. Each of these was wide enough to take one submarine and leave a reasonably broad dockside. Each cave was numbered. U 34 which was our boat, was taken into No 5 berth. A number of the men had small boat hooks with which they fended the submarine off the rough-hewn rock sides of the dock. As the conning tower passed the entrance I saw the top of a metre guage sticking up out of the water, while folded back against the sides of the dock were strong gates. The tide was apparently at the high. When the tide was low, the water could then be drained out of each basin and the gates closed to constitute a dry dock. The ingenuity of the whole place was incredible.

As soon as the submarine had been moored, we were led along the dockside and up a slope to a gallery that ran along the ends of the docks. We turned right, past docks 6 and 7 and up a long sloping ramp that curved to the left. This brought us to the first of two upper galleries. Here were sleeping quarters for hundreds of men, with rest rooms, which included billiard tables and equipment for all sorts of other games. There were also kitchens and lavatories, and the whole place was air-conditioned and kept free from the damp, that was so noticeable in the galleries at dock level, by means of double doors. The walls, floors and ceilings of these galleries were all cemented so that, though here and there trickles of moisture were to be seen, they were in general remarkably dry.

The crew of the submarine were each allotted a little cubicle which contained a camp bed. Logan and I were handed over to the watch. This was in reality a guard. We were taken to the upper level galleries and into the guard-room where we were introduced to a little man in civilian clothes who smoked endless cigarettes. He had a square head, a rather heavy jowl and little blue eyes placed too close together. He was quite pleasant to us, but I did not like him. Later, I discovered that he was a member of the Gestapo. Apparently even in the submarine service the Nazis do not trust their men, for there were four agents at this base, and I learned later that in each submarine there was always one man in the pay of the Gestapo. The four men at the base, though they were ostensibly there to deal with any prisoners like ourselves that were brought in, divided the day into eight-hour watches, and were in fact the watchdogs of the base, wielding practically unlimited power. I was to observe this power later to our disadvantage.

A few routine questions were put to us, and then we were marched down to the dock-level gallery. We turned off this opposite No. 6 dock into what I believe miners would call a crosscut. Here several small caves had been hollowed out of the rock and fitted with steel grills across the entrance. We were both put into one of these. I had more immediate needs than sleep, but as I turned to explain the matter, the grill clanged to, the key grated in the lock and the guard marched off.

The only furniture in the cells was two camp beds with three blankets at the foot of each. I wondered how long the blankets had been there, for the rock floor sparkled with water and the place was chill with damp. The naked electric light bulb in the gallery outside remained on and though it was manifestly absurd that there could be any movement of air, a sort of chill draught rose from the docks where the U-boats lay. The sloping tunnel leading down to No. 6 dock was just visible from the corner of the cell.

I got little sleep that night. I suppose it was past five by the time we were under out blankets. But the unfamiliarity of the place combined with the chill and glare of the light to keep me awake. When at last I did get off to sleep it was to be woken up almost immediately by the clatter of electric welders and the roar and bustle of what sounded like a huge steelworks, for every sound was magnified a hundredfold by the caves and galleries. Sounds mingled so extraordinarily that, except for the welders, I could not identify a single noise. Every sound was made hollow and reverberating by the echo, so that it was as though it were being amplified by an old-fashioned loudspeaker with the tone control set to pick out the drums.

I looked at my watch. It was nine-thirty. Logan, his feet sticking out over the bottom of the bed, was sound asleep. Above the general roar I could just hear the snoring intake of his breath. I lay half awake for some time in that uncomfortable state of reluctance to get up that is induced by an insufficiency of bed-clothes. I felt chilled to the bone, yet I had not the strength of will to climb out from beneath my inadequate covering.

At ten o'clock sharp a guard of three men appeared – a petty officer and two ratings. They were equipped with side arms and revolvers. We were marched to the washrooms. But though we were allowed to wash, we were not given any razors, and even after a thorough clean-up I could hardly recognize my own features in the glass. My rather long face was rounded by the beginnings of quite a healthy-looking beard. My eyes were sunken and red-rimmed. In fact, I looked a proper ruffian. I said so to Logan. 'That's nothing,' he replied with a bitter laugh. 'You wait till these bastards have been at you for a week. If the naval authorities here had control of the prisoners it wouldn't be so bad. But you're in the hands of the Gestapo. We're going to have a helluva time.'

He was right, of course – I knew that. But I felt he might have been a little more optimistic. As soon as we had completed our toilet, we were marched off to the guard-room, where we were introduced to another Gestapo agent who was presumably on the day turn. He was a little man with a large head and a sharp face. I liked him no better than the first. He picked up a green-coloured form from his desk, glanced through it and then led us down a narrow gallery that led off the guard-room and into the office of the commandant of the base. This was Commodore Thepe. He was a short thick-set man with greying hair and a fine head. He impressed me quite favourably and I recalled Big Logan's words in the washroom.

The Gestapo man conferred with the commodore for a time in low tones while we stood between our guards at the door. At length the commodore ordered us to approach his desk. 'You know the Cornish coast – is that so?' he asked Logan. He had a quiet precise way of speaking, but his English was not as good as that of the U-boat commander.

Logan nodded, but said nothing.

'We are in possession of charts detailing all coastal information,' he went on. 'We have not, on the contrary, the fullest information about the rock formation and currents close in to the shore. This we require and you can give it to us, yes?'

Logan shook his head slowly. He had a puzzled look, rather like a dog that has been refused a bone. 'I don't know,' he said. 'You don't know? Why?' The commodore glanced at the form before him and then at Logan. 'You are a fisherman, yes?' Logan was still looking puzzled. 'Yes,' he said hesitantly. 'I believe so – I don't know.' I glanced at him, wondering what had come over him. I thought at first he was playing some deep game. But he had his hand to his head and he was rubbing his eyes as though he had just been woken from a deep sleep.

The commodore looked at him closely. 'You are a prisoner. You understand that?'

Logan nodded. 'Yes, your honour.'

'As a prisoner you must answer questions.' The commodore spoke kindly as though to a child.

'Yes.'

'Then come over here.' The commodore led him over to a glass-topped cabinet in the corner. Beneath the glass was a chart. He slid this out and replaced it with one of the west Cornish coast from the files which filled the cabinet. 'Here is Cadgwith,' said the commodore, indicating a point on the map with his finger. 'Now are all the submerged rocks charted?'

Logan did not answer, but just stood staring at the chart in a dazed kind of way.

'Are they or are they not?' demanded the commodore, getting impatient.

'They may be,' murmured Logan, lapsing into the slurred syllables of the Cornish dialect.

'Answer the Commodore's question,' ordered the Gestapo man, coming up behind Logan. He had a sharp penetrating voice and spoke English fluently.

Logan looked round furtively, like a trapped beast. 'I can't,' he said. And for a moment I thought he was going to burst into tears, his face was so puckered.

'Explain yourself,' snapped the Gestapo man.

'I – I just can't. That's all. I don't remember.' And Logan suddenly turned and went blindly towards the door like a child in a panic. His breath was coming in great sobs as he passed me and I could see the tears running down into his beard. To see a grown man crying is always rather pitiful. But to see Logan crying was so unexpected that it shocked me profoundly.

The guards turned him back and for a moment he staggered round in a circle. Then he stood still, his face buried in his hands. His sobs gradually lessened.

I saw that both the commodore and the Gestapo agent were puzzled. Well they might be. I was puzzled enough myself. They talked together for a moment in low tones, and then the commodore turned to Logan and said, 'Come here.'

Logan approached the desk at which the commodore had resumed his seat. When he had reached it the commodore said not unkindly, 'I fear you have had an uncomfortable time on the submarine. I am sorry. But this information I require urgently. Either you take hold of yourself or else we shall be forced to make you talk. Is that chart correct for your area?'

Logan's great fist descended with a crash on the desk. 'Don't keep asking me questions,' he roared, and his voice was almost unrecognizable it was so high-pitched and hysterical. 'Can't you see I don't remember. I don't remember anything. My mind is blank. It's horrible.'

I don't think I have ever seen two men more surprised than those Germans. Until that moment I think they had regarded Logan as either a half-wit or a prisoner bent on playing them up.

Logan looked at them with what can only be described as compassion. There was something extraordinarily animal-like about him. 'I'm sorry,' he said. 'I have frightened you. I didn't mean to. It was just – just that I didn't remember anything. I was afraid.' His hands fluttering uncertainly, were surprisingly expressive.

The commodore glanced at me then. 'What is the matter with your friend?' he asked.

I had to admit that I did not know. 'He seemed all right in the submarine,' I said. 'But last night he became rather morose.' Then suddenly I remembered. 'When we were captured,' I said, 'he was clubbed with the butt of a revolver. That may be the trouble. Later, in the submarine, he got a bit excited.'

The commodore pondered this information for a moment. Then he ordered one of the guard to go and fetch the U-boat commander and the doctor.

The doctor was the first to arrive. He examined Logan's head and reported that, though the scalp was cut and rather swollen, there were no signs of any fracture. Whether or not Logan was suffering from concussion he would not say. He thought it unlikely, but pointed out that it was impossible to be sure.

The U-boat commander, when he arrived, testified to the fact that Logan had had a severe blow from the butt end of a revolver and to the fact that, though he had seemed to have all his wits about him when in the submarine, he had at the same time behaved as though he were a little unbalanced. He explained how Logan had roared with laughter when he had been asked for information that would have saved the U-boat from disaster, but he made no mention of that part of the episode in which he had been knocked down.

In the end, we were returned to our cell. As we went out I heard the commodore giving instructions to the doctor to keep an eye on Logan. As soon as we were alone I said, 'Look here, Logan, are you playing them up or are you really ill?'

He looked at me apathetically.

'Is this some deep game you're playing?' I persisted.

'Would you call it a game if your mind were a complete blank and you were fighting all the time to remember things?' he asked.

Even then I could not believe that he had really lost his memory. 'You seemed all right this morning,' I said.

'Maybe,' he said, as he lay down on his bed. 'It wasn't until they began questioning me that I realized what had happened.'

But it was not until I had seen him refuse his lunch, his tea and his supper that I really began to regard the matter as serious. Throughout the day he lay on his bed, mostly with his head buried in his arms. Sometimes he groaned as though the effort of trying to remember something were too great. Once or twice he suddenly started to beat the pillow in a frenzy of frustration.

When he refused his supper I asked the guard to leave it with me. Bit by bit I coaxed him to eat it. It was like getting a sick child to eat. When the guard came in for the tray I asked if he could fetch the doctor. He understood the word 'doctor.' By that time I was really worried.

About half an hour later the doctor arrived. Logan was lying face downwards on the bed. But he was not asleep. I explained that I was worried because he had refused his food and seemed so abjectly unhappy. Fortunately the doctor understood English, though he could not speak it very well, so that I was still able to keep up my pretence of not being able to speak German. When I had explained, he told me not to worry. He pointed out that it was quite natural for a man who had lost his memory to be un-happy. 'Would you not veel onhappy?' He spoke very broken English and often had to pause for a word. 'He ees among strangers – a preesoner. He fears what will 'appen to 'im. And 'e cannot remember what 'e was before. He can remember nothing. Eet ees very sad. You must 'elp 'im. Tell 'im about 'is home, 'is village – perhaps 'e remember later, yes?'

He gave me two sleeping tablets to give Logan in some cocoa he would have sent down. I thanked him. He was a kindly man. As he left he pulled a packet of cigarettes from the pocket of his mess jacket. 'These may 'elp,' he said. The packet was nearly full. Later two steaming cups of very excellent-smelling cocoa arrived. As the man who had brought it placed it on the floor between our beds the guard outside sprang to attention. A tall slim rather elegant man appeared at the entrance to our cell. He was quite obviously a member of the Prussian officer class, the type that would have worn a monocle in the days of the Kaiser. 'What's this?' he barked in German, indicating the cups of cocoa.

The man who had brought them explained that the doctor had ordered them to be sent down to the prisoners. He dismissed the man and turned his attention to us. 'Stand up!' He spoke a thick guttural English. I got to my feet. But Logan remained lying full length on the bed. 'Stand up, do you hear!' he thundered. Then, as Logan made no move, he drew the bayonet of the guard standing beside him and stepping deliberately on to the tray containing the cups of cocoa, dug the point of the bayonet sharply into Logan's buttocks. I saw the pleasure that act gave him mirrored in his little grey eyes.

Logan jumped to his feet with a cry. I feared for a moment that he would strike the man, and I could see by the look on the other man's face that he was hoping he would. Then as Logan stood sullenly in front of him, he said, 'So you have lost your memory?' There was no attempt to veil the sneer.

Logan said nothing. He looked very unhappy.

'Well, we'll soon get it back for you,' the other continued. 'Tomorrow you'll go to work – both of you. We'll soon sweat this insolence out of you.'

I said, 'The man is ill.'

He swung round on me. 'Speak when you're spoken to.' He turned to the man who had accompanied him. It was the little Gestapo agent who had taken us in to see the commodore that morning. 'Put them to work on the hull of U 39 tomorrow,' he said in German. As he moved to go, he turned to me and said, 'I should advise you to see that your friend finds his memory.'

I said nothing, but my eyes fell to the two cups of cocoa now lying on their sides, the cocoa still steaming as it mingled with the water on the floor. I knew it was no use asking for more. The grill clanged to.

'Who was he?' asked Logan dully.

'Senior agent for the Gestapo at the base, I should imagine,' I said.

'What is the Gestapo?' he asked.

I was puzzled. 'You understood what the Gestapo was earlier today,' I said. But there is no accounting for the effect of loss of memory upon a man's brain. 'Never mind,' I said. 'The doctor has given me two sleeping tablets for you. They'll help you to remember things. Don't worry about the Gestapo.' I got him to lie down again and then I collected a sufficiency of water in the least broken of the two cups from a little trickle that ran down the wall at the head of my bed. I crushed the tablets into this and gave it to him. He drank it without question like a child. 'The doctor gave us something else, too,' I said, and showed him the packet of cigarettes. I gave him one and he smiled happily. Then I found that we had no matches. Our clothes had been taken from us together with all the possessions in their pockets, and we had been issued with a pair of coarse dungarees each.

I went to the grill and attracted the attention of the guard. I indicated by signs that I wanted a match. There were two men on guard and they both shook their heads. 'Verboten,' said one. I nodded, but pointed to my companion. 'He is ill,' I said. 'It would help him.' They did not speak English, but they seemed to understand, for after glancing hurriedly up and down the gallery one of them passed me a box of Swedish matches with the drawing of a sailing ship on it through the bars.

I lit our cigarettes. As I passed the matches back to the guard I asked who the officer was. He understood the word 'officer.' 'Herr Fulke?' he asked. 'Er ist in der Geheimen Staatspolizei.' Having said this he turned away. He did not wish to talk. I went back and got into bed. I smoked my cigarette slowly and with great relish and watched a tiny fresh-water shrimp slip slowly down the wall in a little rivulet of water. The guard was changed at nine. By that time Logan was fast asleep. I tucked the bedclothes round him and went back to my own bed, drawing the blankets right over my head in order to keep out the light. It was a long time before I could get to sleep. I was not accustomed to sleeping in my clothes and I found the rough blankets very irritating to the skin of my neck. They had a peculiar stuffy smell similar to British army blankets and took me back to my schooldays and camp.

And as I lay there listening to the sounds of footsteps and voices from the galleries above, made hollow by the echo and barely distinguishable above the incessant hum of the dynamos, I felt more miserable than I think I had ever felt before. I had that lost feeling that one has as a new boy in a big school. Had Logan been all right, I think I should have been able to keep my spirits up.

But in his present state he only contributed to my dejection. It was not only a question of loss of memory. It seemed to me that his brain had been rendered defective. He had become so childlike that I felt responsible for him, and I was fearful of what the Gestapo might do to him if they were not quickly convinced that he was really ill. I was under no delusion as to the sympathy he might expect from these men. I had spoken to too many who had suffered agonies in German concentration camps to be in any doubt as to what we might expect. The only consolation was that neither of us looked in the least like Jews.

The next day we were woken at six and set to work on the hull of U 39, which stood up, stained and dirty, like a stranded fish in the empty dock. I gathered from the conversation of the men working with us that she had docked the night before our own boat after a cruise on the north Atlantic trade routes. This accounted for the fact that her hull was coated thick with sea grass. Our job was to scrape it clean.

Our guard had been changed at three in the morning. It was changed again at nine. The petty officer of this guard was a real slave driver. To give him his due he had probably received instructions to see that we worked at full pressure all the time, but by the way he watched us and yelled at us as soon as we slowed down I knew he enjoyed the job.

Logan seemed to like the work. Perhaps it took his thoughts off the blankness of his mind. At any rate he went steadily forward with the work, never flagging and doing about ten square feet to my four. My muscles were soft with years of sedentary work and I quickly tired. By eleven the guard was making use of a bayonet to keep me at it. But the stab of the point in my buttocks was as nothing to the ache in my arms and back. We were allowed a twenty minutes break for lunch at twelve. Then we had to set to again. The sweat streamed off me and my arms got so tired that I could hardly raise them and at the same time hold the scraper in my shaking fingers.

Sheer dogged determination, induced I think more by a desire not to make myself conspicuous rather than by fear, kept me going. But about two hours after lunch I blacked out. Fortunately I was only standing on the lower rungs of the ladder and the fall did not injure me. I came to with an unpleasant sensation of pain in my ribs. I looked up. The hull of the U-boat bulged over me, whilst very far away, it seemed, the petty officer was telling me to get up and at the same time kicking me in the ribs.

Then Logan's huge body came into my line of sight. He

stepped down off his ladder and with quiet deliberation knocked the petty officer flying with a terrific punch to the jaw. Then, before the guard had time to do anything, he had climbed back on to his ladder and resumed his work.

I scrambled painfully to my feet. The guard was looking bewildered. Quite a number of men had witnessed the affair and they were making humorous comments to the guard. 'Why don't you call the police?' asked one, and there was a howl of laughter. There was no doubt that Logan had made something of a hit with the men. From their tone I gathered that the petty officer was not popular.

As the petty officer remained quite motionless where the force of Logan's blow had flung him, one of the guards at length announced that he was going for the doctor. Logan continued with his work as if nothing had happened. It was not that he was trying to pretend that he had nothing to do with the business. He seemed completely oblivious to the fact that he had knocked a German petty officer cold. A crowd had gathered on the dockside above us. Everyone seemed to be talking at once and the sound merged into a low roar that almost drowned the roar of machinery. Men were attracted from other docks, and I could see that the crowd was growing every minute because the ones in front had to strain backwards in order to avoid being pushed over the edge of the dock. Some of them had jumped on to the submarine itself in order to see what was happening.

Nobody seemed to think of going to the assistance of the petty officer, so I went over to where he lay crumpled up against the side of the dock in a pool of water. His clothes were already wet through. I felt his heart, fearful that Logan might have killed him. But it was beating faintly and there seemed nothing the matter with him except for the punch on the jaw he had received. In falling against the side of the dock his head seemed to have been protected by his upflung arm.

I made him as comfortable as I could, and by that time the guard had returned with the doctor. The electric arc lights glinted on his pince-nez as he climbed down the steel ladder into the dock.

His examination of the man was brief. 'He's all right,' he said in German, and ordered two men to take him to his bunk. As the petty officer was hauled up to the top of the dock, the doctor turned to me. 'Vat 'appened?' he demanded. I told him. He nodded. 'Your friend vill be in troble,' he said.

A sudden hush fell over the men on the dockside. I looked up.

64

The Gestapo man – Fulke – had arrived. Like shadows the men seemed to melt away. He descended to the bottom of the dock. 'I hear that man – ' he indicated Logan – 'has knocked down an officer of the guard. Is that right?' He spoke in German, and there was a kind of eagerness in his eyes that it was impossible to mistake. The man was a sadist.

'That is true,' the doctor replied. 'But he did it because – '

'The reason does not interest me,' snapped Fulke. He turned to the guard. 'Take that man to the guardroom. Strap him to the triangle. I'll teach prisoners to knock down officers of the Fuehrer's navy. Get Lodermann. He is to use the steel-cored whip. I will be along in a few minutes. And take this man with you.' He nodded in my direction. 'It will doubtless be instructive for him to see how we maintain discipline.'

The guard saluted and turned away, at the same time indicating that I was to follow him. They took Big Logan from his work and marched him along the dock gallery and up the ramp to the guard-room. I went with them, a horrible empty sickness in the pit of my stomach. Behind me, as I left the dock, I heard the doctor saying, 'You're not going to have that man flogged with a steel-cored whip, surely? He's not well, mentally? Anyway, his action was not unjustified.' There followed a sharp altercation between the two, but I was by then too far away to hear what was said. In that moment I was thankful to know that there was one man in the place with some human understanding.

But I knew it was useless to expect that he would be able to prevent the flogging. The Gestapo's commands were law, and I was convinced that his man Fulke wanted to see Logan flogged. I had heard tales from refugees of floggings in concentration camps with this same steel-cored whip. It cut a man's back to ribbons and he seldom survived the full number of strokes to which he was sentenced. Something seemed to cry out with agony inside me. As I watched them strip Big Logan and tie him to the heavy iron triangle in the guard-room, I think I went through almost as much mental agony as Logan would go through physical agony later. I felt entirely responsible for what had happened, and it was pitiful to see Logan's docility. He did not seem to understand what was happening. Stripped, his terrific physique was even more evident. I felt that if he cared to let himself go, he could have killed every member of the guard with his bare hands, and I longed to call out to him to do so. But what was the use?

A big powerful seaman had taken the steel-cored whip from an oblong box. He had removed his coat and rolled up his sleeves.

The bristles on the back of his thick neck gleamed in the electric light. He adjusted the position of the triangle so that the whip, which was short and knotted, would not catch the walls. The guard had been augmented to six men. The little Gestapo man whom we had first met had taken control. There was a deathly stillness in the room as the man with the whip made his dispositions. The clock on the wall ticked monotonously on as we waited for Fulke.

At length he arrived. 'Close the door!' he ordered. Then he crossed the room and took up a position on the other side of the triangle. His narrow face shone with sweat and his eyes had a glassy stare. 'Why did you strike an officer of the guard?' he asked in English.

Logan made no reply. It was as though he had not heard.

Fulke's hand shot out and he slapped Logan across the face. He did it with the back of his hand, so that a gold ring set with diamonds which he wore on his right hand scored Logan's cheek. 'Answer me, you dog!' he shouted.

Logan's face remained completely vacant.

'Geben Sie ihm eins mit der Peitsche, das wird ihn aufwecken,' he ordered.

The seaman measured his distance. Involuntarily I closed my eyes. The steel-cored thongs sang through the air and cracked down with a thud. Three red lines immediately showed on Logan's brown back. They broadened and merged together into trickles of blood that ran down his hairy buttocks.

'Now will you answer me? Why did you hit the officer of the guard?'

Still Logan made no reply. In sickening anticipation I waited for the order to give the next stroke. But at that moment the door of the guard-room opened and the commodore came in, accompanied by the doctor.

'Who gave the order for this man to be flogged?' demanded the commodore. There was an ominous ring in his voice that no one could mistake. A sudden feeling of excitement gripped me.

'I did,' replied Fulke, stepping forward to meet the other. 'Do you challenge it?' There was a veiled sneer in the way he put the question. He seemed very sure of his ground.

The commodore's only answer was to order the guard to release Logan from the triangle. Fulke advanced a step. For a moment I thought he was going to hit the commodore. A vein on his temple was throbbing violently. 'He has struck the officer of his guard,' he said. 'He is to be flogged. Order and discipline are to be preserved in this base. Heil Hitler!' He raised his right hand.

The commodore seemed quite unmoved by this display. He did not answer the Nazi salute. 'I am in command here.' He spoke quietly but firmly. Then to the guard, 'Take that man down.'

'My instructions are that this man be flogged,' Fulke almost shrieked.

The commodore ignored him. 'Take that man down,' he thundered, as the guard hesitated. At that the men jumped to it. In an instant Logan had been released from the triangle.

'You exceed yourself, Herr Commodore.' Fulke was almost beside himself with rage. 'That man is to be flogged. If you persist in your attitude my next report will be most unfavourable. You know what that means?'

The commodore turned and faced Fulke. He was completely unruffled. 'You forget, Herr Fulke – we are now at war,' he said. 'For three months you have bounced around this base, over-riding my orders, undermining the morale of my men by your schoolboy ideas of discipline. This is the submarine service, not a Jewish concentration camp. For three months I have borne with you because you had the power to hinder my work. Now we are at war. We have work to do – men's work. No reports, except my own will leave this base.'

'You will regret your attitude, Herr Commodore,' snarled Fulke.

'I think not.'

'I'll have you removed from your post. I'll have you discharged the service. You will be sent to a concentration camp. I will see to it that – '

'You will not have the opportunity. In any case, Herr Fulke, you must realize that men with long experience in the services are indispensable in wartime. On the other hand, the Gestapo is not indispensable. For instance, I cannot think of one useful thing that you can do. Doubtless we can teach you to cook. You will report on board U 24 which leaves for the Canary Islands tomorrow. You will replace their cook, who is ill.'

Fulke's hand went to his revolver. The commodore did not hesitate. His fist shot out and laid the Gestapo agent out with a lovely right to the jaw. I do not know how old the commodore was – at least fifty I should have said – but there was plenty of force behind that punch. His hand was raw after it, where the skin had split at the knuckles. 'Guard! Arrest that man!' he ordered. The two nearest men jumped forward. He turned to the other Gestapo agent. 'You are under arrest, Herr Strasser. Disarm him!'

When both men were disarmed, he turned to his orderly. 'Fetch Commander Brisek here! You'll find him in the mess.'

The orderly disappeared. The commodore rubbed his knuckles gently. There was the beginning of a smile on his ruddy face. 'I don't know when I've enjoyed myself so much,' I heard him whisper to the doctor. Aloud he said to the doctor, 'You'll look after the prisoner?' He indicated Logan. 'Have them both transferred to quarters on the other side of this gallery.' He stroked his chin gently, and there was a twinkle in his eye. 'I think we might put Fulke and his friends in the wet cells that he insisted on having constructed. I wonder how they'll take to the U-boat service – do you think they'll be frightened?'

'I have an idea they will,' replied the doctor with no attempt to conceal his smile. 'What I know of psychology prompts me to the view that Fulke at any rate will be very frightened.'

The commodore nodded. 'I will give Varndt instructions to stand no nonsense.'

The door swung open and a naval officer entered followed by the orderly.

'Ah, Heinrich, I have a little commission for you which I think you will enjoy. I have placed these men' – he indicated the two Gestapo agents – 'under protective arrest. Take a guard and arrest the other two.'

'Very good, Herr Commodore.' Commander Brisek marched out with three men of the guard.

The commodore turned and went out of the room, followed by his orderly. The doctor went over to Logan and took him by the arm. As he led him towards the door, he nodded to me. I followed him. He took us to a small but comfortable little cell on the other side of the gallery, almost directly opposite the door of the guard room. He sent a man for his bag and in a very short while he was easing the pain of the cuts on Logan's back. Almost immediately afterwards our evening meal was brought to us. It was six o'clock.

When the doctor had finished and had left us, I said to Logan, 'Well, thank God for that! I didn't think it would end as comfortably as this. How are you feeling?'

'My back is bloody painful,' he said.

'I'm sorry,' I said. 'But you're lucky to get away with nothing worse.' I felt this was ungracious so I said, 'Many thanks for doing what you did. I owe it to you that my ribs are still intact. But it was a dangerous thing to do.'

'Ar,' he said, 'but it was a real pleasure.'

I looked at him closely. His eyes were shut and he was grinning happily. There was something very Irish and a little unbalanced about him. I said, 'Well, for God's sake leave me to get out of my own scrapes. If you knock any more officers out you'll be for it.'

'Is that why they were going to whip me?'

'Of course. What did you think?'

'I don't know,' he said. 'I thought it might be their idea of fun.' He turned over so that he was facing the wall. 'Good-night,' he said.

I stared at him. He just did not seem to grasp things. The old alertness was gone. He seemed dull and slow-witted. I put the light out and climbed into my bed. 'Good-night,' I said.

The warmth of the cell and the darkness were wonderfully comforting after the wet cells in the dock gallery. But even so I found it difficult to get to sleep. My brain was too full of thoughts to be still. The fantastic events of the last few hours ran through and through my mind. I had keyed myself up to see Logan whipped to death before my eyes for something that he had done for me. Miraculously he had been saved from that and now he did not seem to realize what had happened. It was pitiful. But gradually the relief of the changed circumstances – no cold damp cell – no Gestapo – lulled me into a state of coma. I kept on seeing Fulke's face, shiny with sweat, as he realized what the commodore's words meant, the loose twist of his normally set lips, his sudden dive for the revolver. In how many sections of the German war machine were service men suddenly throwing off the yoke of the Gestapo? I had seen the relish in the commodore's eyes as he had hit Fulke. Then his words to the doctor – 'I don't know when I have enjoyed myself so much.' If the services felt like this towards the watchdogs of the Nazi Party, how did the German people feel? Was there hope in this for a short war, or merely food for thought? Questions, questions, questions – but no answers.

4

U-BOAT BASE

It was breakfast at seven next morning and then we were set to work on the hull of U 39 again. Logan worked stripped to the waist because his clothes rubbed against the wounds on his back. But though he moved rather stiffly, he worked with the same methodical speed that he had done on the previous day. My own muscles soon lost their stiffness, and I found the work required less effort.

So morning ran into evening and evening into morning again with only the routine of the place to distinguish night from day. We worked a ten-hour day, from seven-thirty in the morning until six in the evening with a half-hour break for lunch. Hull scraping only occurred when a submarine came in from a lengthy cruise. If it were a rush job a whole party of ratings was put on to it with us and it only took a few hours. Otherwise, we had the work to ourselves and it took nearly two days. When there was no hull scraping, we worked in the canteen, washing up, peeling potatoes. Sometimes, when a submarine was due to go out we had to help carry provisions from the store-rooms and load them on to the submarine. Every morning, whatever else we had to do, we cleaned out the latrines, which were of the bucket type.

Now that we were no longer under the control of the Gestapo we had less supervision. So long as we did our job and kept to the times laid down for us, chief of which were to rise at seven in the morning and return to our cell at seven in the evening, there was little fear of trouble. But we remained under a guard. The officer of the day was responsible for us. He was in charge of fatigue parties. Fatigue parties were provided as required by the submarines in the base, so many men being detailed from each boat. No man went on fatigue more than once until every other rating from his own boat had also done his turn. The whole point of the base, so far as the crews of the U-boats were concerned, was to provide the maximum relaxation – a thing that was very difficult to achieve in view of the cramped quarters which were really very little different from quarters in a U-boat. The main trouble, of course, was that the men never saw the light of day in the base. It was all underground, and, with the constant sound of machinery and the queer echoes, the place was apt to get on men's nerves.

These fatigue parties worked on more or less the same basis as we did, though they were free to do what they liked when they came off duty at six. Like ourselves, however, they had to hold themselves ready for duty when a submarine was coming into the base or leaving it. This meant that the fatigue parties were often called out in the middle of the night as it was only during the hours of darkness that the boats could get in or out of the base.

Thus it was that I was present when U 24 left the base. This gave me great joy for it enabled me to watch Fulke's arrival in charge of two guards. Until then I do not think I had ever seen real panic in a man's eyes. He was struggling like a madman and I was certain he would prove quite useless as a cook and be an infernal nuisance to every one on board. The crew lined up to watch him come on board and there were broad grins on their faces. It was plain that the men of the German submarine service had no use for the Gestapo. It is not altogether surprising. Fulke demanded complete and absolute obedience to every petty and arbitrary rule he made. This may be all right in the army and possibly in the big ship navy, but it does not work in submarines.

The submarine service is probably much the same in all countries. It differs from every other branch of the services because of its danger. It is not a question of tradition or the honour of the service. To be of the service is in itself to be a hero. And a hero is above discipline. Throughout the service stress is laid on efficiency – nothing else. It is a question of existence. Each man has in his hands the fate of the whole ship. In these circumstances discipline is automatic. But when they return to base, especially a base like this, the crews want to relax, not to be pestered by petty disciplinary regulations.

And so Fulke was given a warm welcome by the crew of U 24. I don't know what the man had originally been. Some thought he was one of the Munich Putsch crowd. I doubt it. But at any rate, he had apparently been with the Party since 1933 and had wielded for a sufficient length of time the power of life and death to have become completely callous to his victims' feelings. And now he was scared. I heard one man on the dockside say that he had been in the submarine that had brought Fulke to the base. 'He looked pretty scared then,' he said. 'And he'd been drinking heavily before he came on board. He's a coward – no doubt of that.' And he spat. Then in a whisper he added, 'I wouldn't wonder if most of the Gestapo aren't afraid as soon as they get the wrong end of the lash.'

Perhaps they did Fulke an injustice. Perhaps he had second sight. At any rate, U 24 was sunk by a seaplane in the Bay of Biscay two days later.

Before U 24 went out the commodore walked down with her commander, Varndt. Whatever time of the night a submarine left he always accompanied the commander to his boat. It was a ritual. I saw Varndt's face as he went on board. It was set, but cheerful. Before descending the conning tower, he saluted, then waved his hand. They were all the same, these U-boat commanders – their men, too, for that matter. Most of them were young. They knew what they faced. The chances of death at that time were only two-to-one against every time they went out. The odds were short enough. They had responsibilities thrust upon them at which much older men would have blenched in peace-time. Yet they accepted these responsibilities and the danger without question, and with set faces and sublime cheerfulness went out to almost certain death.

Before I had been in the base more than a few days my admiration for the German submarine service was immense. And I was filled with a great sense of depression. These men were mostly young. They faced death and accepted their responsibilities without question. They were the pick of Germany's seamen. And they were being thrown away to fulfil the destinies of a man whose boundless ambition spelt ruin for his country, himself and half the civilized world. More, they were given orders the execution of which brought universal opprobrium upon them and their Service. In the first days of the war, it was in fact for German youth that my soul cried out against that fanatic, who had diagnosed his country's and the world's disease correctly, yet attempted a cure that had been tried before and had been found only to increase the suffering of the masses.

As far as Logan and I were concerned life was not unpleasant. We worked hard, it is true, and the air was not too good despite a system of ventilation. But in the evenings, when we retired to our own quarters, there were German magazines to read. There was a plentiful supply of these available and I would surreptitiously read stories to Logan. He enjoyed this, but though I talked to him endlessly of Cadgwith and South Cornwall, his mind seemed quite blank. He had loved the place. It had been, I think, his only permanent love. Yet he showed no interest in it and never at any time asked me to tell him about it or describe it to him in greater detail. Much of his time he spent fashioning pieces of wood into models of boats with an ordinary table knife. I suppose it was some sort of subconscious manifestation of the life he could no longer remember. No one seemed to object. In fact the doctor encouraged it. He said he thought it might help him to remember. Sometimes Logan would spend hours carving his name on the wooden legs of his camp-bed as though he were afraid of forgetting that, too.

As time went on, we were allowed to mix more and more freely with the men. They took to Logan very quickly. They made fun of him, but he did not seem to mind. His great bulk and terrific strength seemed to fascinate them. And as it became quite obvious that he was not only rather simple, but also quite harmless, they would take him into the mess of an evening and stand him drinks and put him through his tricks. His tricks were largely a matter of strength. He could lift two average size sailors up on to the bar by the seat of their pants. This, and the fact that a very few drinks now seemed to go to his head and make him fuddled and rather amusing, made him popular. Big Logan had become something of a buffoon, and I found the spectacle somehow rather revolting.

Meanwhile, I learned my way about the base. Generally speaking, we had the freedom of the three galleries, but not the docks nor the repair and munition depots. There were grave penalties for entering these other than when ordered to do so. Nevertheless, in the course of my duties I eventually penetrated to even the most remote sections of the base, and gradually I was able to build up a plan of the place in my mind's eye. When I had a complete picture of it clear in my mind, I made a rough plan, and this, with a few comments added later, I have reproduced.

I have always credited the Germans with a greater eye for detail than any other race. But it was not until I had a working knowledge of that U-boat base that I fully understood what the thoroughness of the German mind meant. It was incredible. Later I was to learn that it had taken two years to build and had cost the equivalent of about £5,000,000. Moreover, all equipment, or the raw materials to manufacture the equipment on the spot, had been brought into the base by a submersible barge. I have already explained the dock sections, the long cave into which the submarines rose, the heavy haulage gear and the seven docks radiating off from the slightly wider section of the main cave.

I should perhaps explain the haulage gear more thoroughly, though here again I did not discover the details of its working until later. First, no U-boat was allowed to enter the base in any circumstances during the hours of daylight or in moonlight. The haulage gear itself ran out through the underwater mouth of the cave and round a pylon fixed to the bed of the sea about a hundred yards or so off the shore. In suitable conditions, a glass ball of a type used by fishermen for their nets was floated up from the pylon. This ball was coated with mildly phosphorescent paint, and was attached to the pylon by ordinary rope. This in turn was connected electrically with the shore. Any sharp tug on the glass ball – the buoyancy of the ball was not sufficient – started a buzzer in the haulage gear control room. A submarine commander desiring to enter the base had to give in morse by tugs on the ball the number of his boat and his own name. If any unauthorized person attempted to haul it up it was immediately released.

When a U-boat had given the correct signal, a small buoy was released in which there was a telephone. Communication was thus possible between the base and the incoming submarine. When required the main buoy was released, the submarine was coupled to it by a grappling hook at the bows and the U-boat then submerged. Care was necessary to submerge in the correct position, namely at right angles to the shore, or two points south of due west. The reason for this was that the submarine had to come to rest on an iron cradle which ran on a line laid from the cliffs out along the seabed. This, I understand, was the most difficult of all the tasks that confronted the German engineers. The sea-bed was mostly rock and rails were the only means of preventing the submarine being injured while being hauled into the base.

The base itself had three galleries. The first was at dock level. The wet cells were situated on this level. This gallery ran in a semi-circle round the ends of the submarine docks. Opposite each dock was a tunnel leading down into relatively large caves. These were the store-rooms. They were guarded by steel doors. At each end the gallery cut sharply back from the docks into really big caves strengthened by girders. In the cave near the ramp leading to the upper galleries were the dynamos run by diesel engines, and farther back a complete foundry with electric furnaces. And still farther in were the workshops where there were lathes and machine tools capable of producing every component of a submarine. The big cave at the other end of the curved gallery was a gigantic fuel and munition store. The fuel was in great tanks that resembled the tanks on petrol trucks. There were also stocks of copper, steel ingots, lead, zinc, manganese and other vital materials.

The upper two galleries ran straight, one on top of the other. These were the men's quarters. At a pinch there was accommodation for nearly seven hundred men. The personnel of the base itself numbered over a hundred, while most of the U-boats using the base were of the deep-sea type and had a crew of sixty or more.

These galleries were all cemented to avoid damp and leading off them were big food store-rooms.

The time required to complete the construction of this colossal undertaking and the huge quantities of material which would have had to be brought in through the under-sea entrance made me convinced that Logan's belief that we were on the north coast of Cornwall was incorrect. True, he had appeared to be all right when following the submarine's course with his compass, but in a mental case appearances were, I knew, often deceptive, and I was by no means sure that at that time his mental faculties were quite sound. My own belief was that the direction of the submarine's change of course had been southerly and not northerly, and that, in fact, the base was somewhere on the north Spanish coast.

Though I did not at that time know precisely how long it had taken to build the base. I knew that it must have been a considerable time. This tied up with the fact that the Spanish civil war began in July, 1936. Germany came into it from the start, and one of the reasons she did this was to obtain air and submarine bases in that country. The more I thought about it the more convinced I became that Logan had not been in a fit mental state to plot a course at the time U 34 was making for the base. And yet he was quite capable of thinking things out for himself. He could do a job of work as well and as thoroughly as any one. It was mainly in his conversation, or rather his lack of it, that he revealed his mental state. He very seldom spoke, and even when asked a direct question would as often as not reply with a non-committal, 'Ar!' I had two conversations with the doctor about him, and found him frankly puzzled. On each occasion, he stressed that he was not a mental specialist. 'I do not onderstand vat ees the matter vith him,' he said on the second occasion.

This depressed me and so did the atmosphere of the base, for as the days passed there was an almost imperceptible change in the spirit of the men. The reason for this was the score boards. At the end of each of the big canteens were large blackboards. On the left hand side were the numbers of all U-boats operating from the base. In all there were seventeen, their numbers ranging from 15 to 62. As and when opportunity offered the boats radioed their sinkings in code to the base. Such communication was often delayed owing to the necessity of surfacing and drying off the aerials before communication could be established. However, experience showed that in general boats reported at least every other day, and there was a standing order that they should endeavour to do this, if possible, in order that the commodore should be able to replace as early as possible boats stationed on particular trade routes which were believed lost.

Information regarding sinkings was chalked up on the boards opposite the number of the submarine responsible. Wherever possible the tonnage as well as the name of the ship was given. One of the first to be marked up was the *Athenia*. This was marked up the day before our arrival at the base. I did not see the boards

until after we had been at the base three days. But from the conversation of the men I gathered that they were very jubilant about
it. They were not so jubilant, however, when those who understood English and listened in to American broadcasts realized the
heavy loss of life and the tone of the American press. Moreover, the
attitude of the German High Command towards this sinking was
not encouraging. The base was notified of their attitude through
the English broadcasts. The base had no wireless transmitter and
there was no attempt to keep in direct wireless contact with
Germany. Moreover, the base had no separate wavelength for
receiving instructions from Germany. Instructions were given to
the base by way of an ingenious code worked into the broadcasts
in English. It was only by accident that I learned this – my
unrevealed knowledge of German was the cause. All communications to the base were included in announcements about
U-boats. How the code worked I do not know, but the idea of it
was clever, for no one would look for coded instructions in
German propaganda broadcasts.

Whenever the wireless-room orderly entered the canteen to
chalk up sinkings there was great excitement among the men at the
base, for quite heavy bets were constantly being made either on
the basis of the submarines with the greatest tonnage of sinkings or
on the basis of the number sunk. But by the end of the first week
four boats had not reported a sinking for three days. After ten
days, there were seven boats that had not reported for three days
or more. Moreover, four days after our arrival at the base, U 47
had come in with her after deck ripped open as a result of being
rammed. She was leaking badly and had eight men killed. Three
days later, on the Sunday that was, U 21 docked with her bridge
twisted to ribbons and her for'ard gun and both AA guns wrecked
– total killed, twelve, nine wounded. Including our own boat, U
34, there were three boats in for heavy repairs.

That was the reason for the change of atmosphere. I do not
believe that the German naval authorities had reckoned with
losses on this scale. Every man in the service knew that the losses
in modern warfare would be heavy. But seven in two weeks and
three badly damaged out of a total of seventeen, was something
that brought death very near to every U-boat man. On 14
September the boards were taken down. Every man in the base
knew what that meant. Losses were, in the official view, becoming
so heavy that they were likely to affect the morale of the men.

It was only then, I think, that I really understood how it was
possible for the commodore of the base to take such drastic action

against the Gestapo as Commodore Thepe had done. It could never have happened in Kiel or even at a base in the South Atlantic. What had made it possible here was the cramped quarters. The commodore had been thrown into too close contact with Fulke for over three months. Moreover, as in the removed-from-the-world atmosphere of a school, the commodore had come to regard the base as his whole world. Germany and the Gestapo were no longer real to him.

Throughout the day following the removal of the score boards the whole base radiated an atmosphere of tension. And just before U 41 went out, shortly after midnight, I thought the men would refuse to go. They came down to the dock looking haggard and dejected, and some of them seemed definitely mutinous. Once fear gets hold of a man there is no buoyancy in him. But the commander was a tough little bow-legged man, and he came down as cheery as I've ever seen a man who was going to his death. He came down with the commodore full of jokes about what he'd do when he met the British Atlantic fleet. The crew went aboard all grins. A week later U 41 was rammed and sunk by a British destroyer convoying a fleet of tankers from the Gulf of Mexico.

U 41 was the last boat to leave the base for some time. Thereafter, boats were laid up as they came in and the crews told to take a rest. By that I knew some big operation was pending and I remembered the paper that the commander of U 34 had given Logan. The date for the meeting of those units of the British fleet was 18 September. It was now 14 September. We had three days in which to do something.

This sounds rather as though I had only just remembered this aspect of the affair. That is not strictly true. It had loomed in the back of my mind as something which had to be faced sooner or later. I had certainly not forgotten about it. After all, it was the cause of our presence at the base. But the many little everyday problems of life as a prisoner and the life itself combined to drive it into the background. Only when I saw the U-boats being held back at the base and heard the vague rumours circulating of a big action pending, did I realize that the responsibility for endeavouring to prevent the loss of many British lives rested entirely on my shoulders.

It was up to me to think out some scheme whereby the U-boats could be prevented from leaving the base. And that brought me face to face with another problem – the sacrifice of my own life. I don't suppose I am any more of a coward than the average person.

After all, I had been willing to sacrifice my life when on board the U-boat. But it is one thing to accept the line of action decided upon by someone else and quite another to settle down in cold blood deliberately to plot one's own death. But this is what I had to do. I could not imagine any possibility that might achieve my purpose that would not mean my own death and Logan's.

I don't believe I slept at all that night. Interminable hours I lay there in the dark, thinking. I heard the guard changed at three. I was feeling tired but determined to think out a scheme. I wanted to talk the matter over with Logan, but he was snoring peacefully and anyway I was convinced that he would be quite incapable, in his present state, of assisting in the evolution of a workable scheme, and also I feared he might not be discreet. At the same time, I was certain I could count on his help – he did everything I told him like a child.

Not unnaturally my thoughts centred around high explosive, of which there was a big store in the base, if only one could get at it. There seemed, on the face of it, two possible schemes. One was the complete destruction of the base by detonating the munitions store. The other was the blocking of the entrance by means of some sort of explosive charge. Of the two I favoured the latter. It at least gave us a chance of escape, slender though it was. At the same time the submarines were left intact. At the back of my mind I think I had a vague picture of myself presenting the First Lord with half a dozen submarines as my contribution to Britain's war effort. It was the sort of grandiose fantastic vision that revolves in one's brain when one is on the verge of sleep.

I suppose I must have then slept, for the next thing I remember is being woken up by the guard. 'Fatigue!' We tumbled out of bed. I glanced at my watch. It was five o'clock. When we got down to the docks we found that it was the submersible barge that was coming in. It was the first time I had seen it. In appearance it looked like a small tramp steamer – the sort of coastal barges that you see carrying oil fuel up the Thames. She plied between Dublin and Lisbon, calling at the base on each journey and always arriving empty at these two ports. Her papers were faked, I suppose.

We were back in our cell again just before six. As I lay in bed I could hear the rattle of cups in the guard-room. They were always served with coffee at six. I lay awake, thinking. A depth charge would, of course, be the most satisfactory method of blocking the entrance to the base. But there were no depth charges available and anyway I didn't know how to handle them. Another idea was to fire the after torpedo of U 21 which was lying in No. 4 dock. This dock was the centre one of the seven and the submarine's stern would be facing straight down the main cave so that the torpedo would strike that part of the cave which was directly above the under-sea exit. Even if the fall was only slight, it would take a diver some time to clear it away for the cradle to run out smoothly on its rails. The rails themselves might even get bent and have to be relaid.

The only snag was that I knew nothing about torpedoes and felt certain that they were highly complicated. Moreover, the dock gates would have to be open and the submarine floating. At present she was sitting high and dry in a dock that had been emptied of water. There remained only the guns. The after six inch gun of U 21 was in working order. But I was not quite sure what impression a six inch shell would make on the rock. In addition, of course, I had not the faintest idea how it worked or how I could get hold of the ammunition. And then there was the question of my own guard.

The key grated in the lock of our door and a petty officer poked his head in. 'Aufstehen!' he said. I dressed myself quite automatically, ate my breakfast and started my daily chores with my mind full of the wildest and most fantastic schemes for getting control of the after gun of U 21. I now considered this the only practical means of achieving my aim of blocking the exit. It was now Friday, 15 September. The rendezvous was for 1.30 p.m. on Monday, 18 September. That meant that the U-boats would leave the base on Sunday night. Between now and Sunday evening I had got to find out how the gun worked and think out all the details of the plan. It was a horrible responsibility, and, because my mind was elsewhere, I was reprimanded several times for slacking.

Throughout the whole of the morning we did service as stevedores, unloading the store barge and piling cases of provisions on trolleys which were then dragged off to the various store-rooms of the base. Some went to the store-room opposite each dock to provision submarines. Others went to the stores in the upper galleries and were for consumption in the base. There were in all about fifty men working on the barge or busy storing the cargo in the various store-rooms.

After lunch, however, I had a bit of luck. We were taken to No. 4 dock where men were working with a mobile automatic drill. We were given shovels and a barrow with which to remove the debris. What was happening was that it had been found necessary to remove the for'ard gun of the U-boat *en bloc* from the deck so that the deck-plates, which had been buckled, could be renewed while the gun itself was repaired on the dockside by the workshop engineers. When we arrived, the gun had been unbolted from its mounting, but in order to sling it on to the dockside it was necessary to erect a derrick. One leg of the derrick could be braced against the opposite side of the dock, but it had been found necessary to drill holes to steady the two shorter legs on the dock itself.

The first little pocket took about ten minutes to drill. The granite was extremely hard and splinters kept on flying from the point of the drill. But the other one proved quite simple owing to a fault in the rock and to the appearance of a much softer strata. This, as soon as I began to shovel up the broken chunks, I found to be limestone. It was an interesting discovery for any one who studied geological formations. I looked at the stone closely. It was carboniferous limestone of the type that predominates in North Cornwall from Tintagel to Hartland Point. My immediate interest was in the fact that a fault of carboniferous limestone should occur in rock that was, as far as I had been able to see, entirely igneous. Igneous rock is the oldest of the pre-cambrian group, whereas limestone belongs to the palæzoic group, which occurred much later in the evolution of the world. It suggested that there must have been some movement of the granite formation long after it had been thrown up.

And then another thought occurred to me. Here was a fault of carboniferous limestone, a rock that covers practically the entire north of Cornwall. And the fault was in igneous rock which, though comparatively rare, certainly occurs in the mining districts of Cornwall. Perhaps Logan had been right after all. On the other hand, the north-west corner of Spain has much the same rock formations, with limestone and igneous rock in close proximity. Brittany also has a similar formation. I decided in the end that I was no further forward at all and having, as a matter of interest, traced the fault right back to the main gallery and into the store gallery opposite, widening all the way, I transferred my attention to the gun. Our two guards seemed quite content, after watching over our removal of the debris, to stay and see the gun manœuvred on to the dockside.

It was swung across by lengthening the long leg of the derrick, and as it was lowered on the ratchet chain it descended slowly on to the dockside only a few feet from me. I had ample opportunity to examine the weapon. But though I could understand the breech mechanism and guess at the handgear for sighting it, I did not see how the thing was fired and I certainly could not imagine how I was to get hold of the necessary shells. The magazine, I knew, was somewhere beneath the gun, but how the lift worked I did not know.

I suddenly remembered that Logan had been on a 'Q' ship in the last war. 'Do you know how these things work?' I asked.

He looked at me quickly. Then he frowned. 'I feel I should,' he said slowly. 'But I don't know.' He shook his head from side to side. He did not seem really interested.

It was up to me to learn for myself. I watched them dismantle the barrel, saw the breech opened and shut and the firing position altered by the handgear, but still I did not see how it was fired. However, if I did not discover the workings of the gun, at least I learned something from the conversation of the men who were working on it. The U 47, which had got so badly damaged by being rammed, had been patched up and was leaving for Germany by way of the Irish Sea and the Hebrides that night. This was only an operating base capable of keeping submarines supplied and effecting light repairs. U 47 had apparently taken such a beating that the engineers considered that nothing short of a general overhaul and refit would make her properly seaworthy. So, patched as well as the base could do it, she was to make a bid for Kiel and the old Germania yard. Apparently she made it, for she was later, I heard, sunk in the South Atlantic. This left only four boats in the base. Among them was our own boat, U 34, now ready for sea again. Two more boats were apparently expected in that night. That made a submarine fleet of six boats, provided the U 21 were ready in time. It was not a pleasant prospect. If they got out it might mean the end of all four of the capital ships in the Atlantic squadron and possibly the loss of some of the Mediterranean squadron at the rendezvous.

At that moment there was a sudden shout of 'Wache!' Our two guards looked uncertainly at each other. The men at work on the gun paused and listened. The sound of heavy boots on rock echoed down the galleries. Men were running. More men joined them. Doors slammed. The call was repeated – 'Wache!' Then through the galleries rang the clamour of a bell. 'The emergency alarm!' exclaimed one of the engineers at the gun. And another said, 'Yes, that means action stations.' At that they all went running down the dockside and into the gallery at the end. One of our guards began to follow them. The other hesitated and shouted something, indicating us. Then the one who had been so anxious about us remained whilst the other dashed off to see what had happened.

It was the chance of a lifetime. I looked at Logan, but he seemed quite unconscious of anything unusual. Our guard was watching the gallery at the end of the dock rather than us and his senses were centred on the medley of sounds coming from the upper galleries in an effort to discover what had happened. I heard the ring of rifle butts against rock and rapid shouts of command. The tramp of feet began to resound through the base. I glanced at the guard. He was still watching the end of the dock. Slowly I began to edge away towards the gangway that led on to the submarine. I had almost made it when he caught sight of my movement out of the corner of his eyes and in the same instant his revolver was covering me. 'Ruhe!'

Was it just luck that Logan was now directly behind him? For one wild moment I thought that Logan was going to lay him out. Then the sound of feet marching in the gallery that ran past the end of our dock drew my eyes. A double file of ratings came marching on to the dock. Others marched on to the farther docks. The guard relaxed. The chance was gone.

The ratings were fully armed and under the command of their officers. They were the crew of U 21. Apparently as soon as the alarm sounds each man has to report with arms outside his quarters. They are then marched to the dock in which their submarine lies and there await instruction. Ten men in each submarine are attached to the base guard as emergency watch. These report to the guard-room immediately on the sounding of the alarm. It is their job to defend the base until the last U-boat has got clear. When all the boats are away, and that may be several hours because of the necessity of waiting for the tide to flood the docks, they have to destroy the base and any submarine that has not been in a fit condition to escape. Then, and then only, are they allowed to surrender. The chances of being alive after the destruction of several hundred tons of high explosive and a large quantity of fuel oil are, of course, not very great.

I could not help wondering at that time why it was necessary in an underground base of this type to have emergency regulations for its defence. Clearly, nothing could attack the base from the sea except by shelling the cliffs above the underwater entrance. It is possible that naval vessels might locate and sink submarines as they left the base, but the U-boats were attached to the buoy on the haulage gear by an automatic coupling that could be released without surfacing. The tricky surface work was only necessary on entering the base. In any case, there was a look-out, the entrance to which led off the cliff side of the upper gallery just near our own cell. This look-out made it possible for U-boat commanders to be notified of any craft in the vicinity when ready to go out.

Presumably, therefore, they feared an attack from the land. And if there were a way of getting into the base from the landward side, then there must be a way of getting out. The thought sent a thrill of hope through me. This sudden sense of exultation was followed almost immediately by a mood of complete and utter despair. What chance was there of discovering this bolt-hole of theirs, let alone escaping through it?

I was brought back to a sense of the immediate happenings by the arrival of our other guard. 'We are to take them to their cell,' he said. He was flushed with running and his words came in short gasps.

'What's happened?' demanded the one who had stayed with us.

'I don't know – nothing yet. The emergency alarm went in the guard-room a few minutes ago. Eight men were sent out to reconnoitre. Come on! We're to put these men in their cell and report to the guard-room. The emergency guard has been called out and every one is standing by.'

We were told to march. By this time the dockside was empty. The crew of U 21 had gone to their stations. The tide was at the high and I could hear the gurgle of water as the dock was flooded. The commander and his Number One were standing on the bridge. The boat was not ready for sea, yet they were prepared to take her out and risk it if necessary rather than leave her to be destroyed. It was the gesture of a proud service. As we marched down the gallery and climbed the ramp to the next level our two guards continued their conversation:

First Guard: 'Are we being attacked?'

Second Guard: 'I don't know.'

First Guard: 'Well, what are they doing about it? Who sounded the warning?'

Second Guard: 'They don't know yet. But they've sent out a reconnoitring party.'

First Guard: 'Maybe it's a false alarm.'

Second Guard: 'Maybe.'

First Guard: 'Suppose we're being attacked – what do we do?'

Second Guard: 'Who do you think I am – Commodore Thepe? I don't know.'

First Guard: 'Well, I do. We blow up the exit galleries and

then we're caught like rats in a trap. We're marines. We don't belong to the submarine service. But the only chance we'll have of getting out of this base will be by submarine – and the hell of a bloody chance that will be!'

As far as I was concerned the conversation ended there, for we were bundled into our cell and the key turned in the lock. I heard the clatter of the guards' boots as they went into the guard-room opposite. And then an unearthly stillness descended on the place. I had never heard it so silent. All the machinery, even the dynamos, had been stopped. I felt a sense of frustration. Something exciting was happening. Something that might vitally affect our lives. Yet here we were cooped up in a cell with no means of knowing what was taking place. It was complete anti-climax.

I glanced at Logan, who was sitting placidly on his bed. He was listening, too. He sensed I was watching him and he looked up at me. 'What's happening?' he asked. I said I didn't know. I began pacing the cell, but it was so small that I eventually sat down on my bed again. We sat there, listening to the silence, while quarter of an hour slipped by.

I began to imagine things. Somewhere at the back of the base were underground workings. Perhaps even now the guard was fighting an enemy whilst the U-boats slipped out of the base. It did not matter that it was daylight for the exit. How long would it be before they were all clear? Five boats and the barge – that might take between three and four hours. Then what? Would they destroy the base? The silence and my own enforced inactivity began to get on my nerves.

Then suddenly there were voices, the clang of a door and silence again. Ten more minutes passed, and then the sound of the guard-room door being opened and the scuffle of service boots running down the gallery. Within a few minutes came the murmur of many voices and the clatter of boots. Then the gentle soothing hum of the dynamos was resumed. Life at the base was normal again.

'I wonder what all that was about,' I said. I felt almost exhausted by my own curiosity. 'Perhaps it was a false alarm,' I suggested. 'Or just a test.'

Logan made no reply, but I could see him listening intently. I began to talk to him again and then stopped, realizing that it was pointless. I sat on my bed and waited, watching the minutes tick slowly by on my wrist-watch, which I had been allowed to keep. Shortly after four-thirty the grill opened and I just caught a glimpse of the nose and eyes of a man looking in at us before it clanged to again. Then there was the sound of boots on the rock outside and the door of the cell to the right of ours opened and then closed. I could hear the faint murmur of voices, but the rock walls were too thick to distinguish what language was being spoken. The cell door beyond closed with a bang and the grate of a key in the lock. Then the guard-room door slammed to and there was silence again.

Another quarter of an hour passed. Logan was getting more and more restive. Once he tried to pace up and down the cell as I had done, but it was too small for him and he resumed his seat on the bed. I was beginning now to think in terms of mutiny. After all it was not impossible. The men were by no means happy. I remembered the departure of U 41. The commander had only just saved the situation then. The only thing against the possibility of mutiny was the fact that the morale had been better during the past few days – in fact, ever since the word had gone round that something big was pending. It is inactivity more than fear that undermines morale, and now that they had something big to look forward to, I could not quite see a mutiny.

I had just arrived at this conclusion when there came a dull explosion that seemed to shake the very rock out of which the cell was hewn. It was followed almost immediately by a second. And then silence again. Both of us had automatically jumped to our feet. Were they scrapping the U-boats? The thought flashed through my mind. But I knew that it was out of the question. If they had blown up two of the boats the explosions would have been terrific, and they certainly hadn't exploded the munitions store. These explosions were muffled and far away. Perhaps the entrance to the base was being shelled from the sea.

The door of the guard-room opened, footsteps sounded and then the door of the cell to the left of us was opened. There was the murmur of voices. Then the door of the cell was closed and locked, and the footsteps returned once more to the guard-room. Silence again. The tension was making me over-wrought. I forced myself to sit down on the bed again, and I tried desperately to control my excitement. But I could not keep my hands still.

Logan had taken up his stand by the door. I looked up at him. He was standing quite still, his huge body leaning against the door. But for once his face seemed alive and I realized that he was listening. I strained my senses. I could hear nothing. Logan went over to his bed and set his ear to the wall. I did likewise, but I could hear nothing. I went back to my own bed. I found myself wondering how much more of this tension would break Logan's brain completely and transform him into a raving lunatic.

I picked up a magazine and began to read a story. But I could not concentrate. I kept on catching sight of Logan listening at the wall. At length I put the magazine down. 'Can you hear anything?' I asked.

'No, can you?'

As a conversation piece it was not brilliant. I gave it up and for the next five minutes my mind chased the story about the man who asked a lunatic who had his ear to the ground that same question. Someone knocked on the door. I looked up. Logan was standing there, beating a tattoo with his fist on it. Footsteps sounded in the gallery outside. He ceased. But as soon as the guard-room door had shut again, he resumed his knocking.

'Look, suppose I read you a story?' I suggested. I picked up the magazine again.

He did not reply, but stretched out his hand and picked up the spoon from his plate which was still lying on the bed. With this he began to strike the iron bars of the grill. It was getting on my nerves. 'Come and sit down,' I said.

He turned and looked at me, and he was grinning broadly. 'What is the name of your paper?' he asked.

'The *Daily Recorder*,' I said. 'Why?'

But he had begun tapping again, this time much slower. Then he stopped and listened with his head tilted slightly on one side like a dog's. I was getting a little nervous. It would be more than two hours before our evening meal was brought to us and that would probably be my first chance of getting hold of the doctor.

Then suddenly Logan turned to me. 'Here's a pencil,' he said. He drew the half-chewed stub of one out of the pocket of his dungarees and tossed it over to me. 'Put this down on something.' He began tapping again with his spoon. Then he stopped and listened. 'I,' he said, '-c-a-m-e break h-e-r-e break – ' He was spelling the words out letter by letter very slowly, sometimes with quite long intervals between each letter. 'W-i-t-h break t-p-l-e-e break.' He tapped with his spoon on the iron grill again. And then went on, 'C-a-n-c-e-l break t-h-r-e-e break m-i-n-e-r-s.'

AT this stage it is necessary to digress in order to recount the experiences of Maureen Weston, the novelist, which had such an important bearing on later events. She very kindly offered to allow me to lift *en bloc* the story as she told it in her book *Groundbait for death*. I should like to take this opportunity of thanking her for her kindness. I have, however, refrained from taking advantage of her offer because I feel that the bare facts as she gives them in her communications to Charles Patterson, news editor of the *Daily Recorder*, together with various other communications which complete the picture, are more suitable to a straight forward narrative of this type. I should state that I am also indebted to the authorities at Scotland Yard for their kind assistance in supplying me with copies of a number of official communications.

PART TWO

THE DISAPPEARANCE OF MAUREEN WESTON

Wire from the news editor of the Daily Recorder to Maureen Weston, Sea Breezes, St Mawes, dispatched from Fleet Street at 12.15 p.m. on September 4:

Note story in *Telegraph* seven two stop Can you cover disappearance Walter Craig query Still a member Recorder staff stop Full details obtainable Cadgwith – Patterson.

The following story appeared under a D head in the Telegraph of September 4, page seven, column two:

U-BOAT ATTEMPTS LANDING

BELIEVED SUNK BY TORPEDO BOAT

From Our Own Correspondent

Somewhere on the Coast of England – Sept. 3: A daring attempt was made this evening to effect a landing from a German U-boat. It is believed that the intention was to land a spy in this country. Thanks to the British Secret Service, however, the U-boat's intention was known beforehand and the naval authorities at Falmouth notified.

As a result, a British torpedo boat was waiting for the U-boat. As soon as the U-boat surfaced it put off a boat. The torpedo boat attempted to ram this and at the same time opened fire on the U-boat.

The submarine replied and a smart engagement followed. The boat was not rammed and its crew escaped on to the submarine again. The torpedo boat then fired a torpedo at the U-boat, but failed to register a hit. The U-boat then submerged. The torpedo boat immediately dashed to the spot and dropped depth charges. The first of these brought a quantity of oil to the surface and this encourages the belief that the U-boat was destroyed.

Two men, who were watching for the U-boat from the shore are reported to be missing. One was a local fisherman named Logan and the other, Walter Craig, the well-known dramatic critic.

Wire from Maureen Weston to Charles Patterson of the Daily Recorder dispatched from St Mawes at 2.55 p.m. on September 4:

Busy on new book stop Walter untype involved scrape – Maureen.

Wire from Charles Patterson of the Daily Recorder to Maureen Weston dispatched from Fleet Street at 4.5 p.m. on September 4:

Damn book stop Yard asking questions stop Convinced story stop Cannot spare any one investigate from this end stop Relying on you stop Writing hotel Cadgwith stop Suggest five pound daily retainer expenses plus space – Patterson.

Wire from Maureen Weston to Charles Patterson of the Daily Recorder dispatched from St Mawes at 6.20 p.m. on Spetember 4:
Okay stop God help if wild-goose chase – Maureen.

Letter from Charles Patterson of the Daily Recorder to Maureen Weston at the hotel Cadgwith, dated September 4:

DEAR MAUREEN,
    Officers from Scotland Yard questioned me about Walter Craig yesterday morning. There is apparently not the slightest doubt that he and this man Logan have disappeared.
    In some respects the story in the *Telegraph* is not quite accurate. For one thing the U-boat was not landing any one, but taking off a man who had been landed the previous night. I gathered from the detectives that Craig met this man shortly after he had been landed and that later he became suspicious. The coastguard is mixed up in it somewhere. It was he who warned the naval authorities at Falmouth. I believe Craig and this fellow Logan lay in wait for the German above the cliffs. The police seem to think that both were captured and taken on board the submarine. There is some doubt as to whether it was destroyed.
    The question is – why did the submarine land this German? Who did he contact on shore, and why? It must have been something urgent for them to have taken that risk.
    I am sorry to have dragged you out of your book. I tried to get you on the phone in order to explain the situation, but every business in London has moved out to the West Country and it is quite impossible to get a call through. At the moment I dare not spare any one from this end, for though we are running a smaller

paper and half the staff is hanging about doing nothing, at any moment a rush of war news may come through. At the same time local men are no good for a job of this sort.

What I am hoping for is a first-class spy story. Good hunting, and very many thanks for helping me out.

Yours sincerely,

CHARLES PATTERSON.

Transcript of a code wire from Detective-inspector Fuller to Superintendent McGlade at Scotland Yard and dispatched from Cadgwith at 4.15 p.m. on September 5. The wire was decoded and sent by special messenger to M.I.5:

Enquiries about disappearances being made by Maureen Weston stop Description height about five-two black hair parted left waved brown eyes slim nails painted young attractive stop Arrived hotel about seven last night in green Hillman ten number FGY 537 stop Has contacted Morgan and now walking over cliffs inspect Carillon stop Keeping contact pending instructions – Fuller.

Transcript of a code wire from Superintendent McGlade to Detective-inspector Fuller at the police station at Lizard Town and sent on by hand to Mr Fuller's lodgings at Mrs Forster Williams', arriving shortly after 7 p.m. on September 5:

Maureen Weston was a reporter on *Daily Recorder* until year ago when retired to St Mawes to write stop Now acting for *Recorder* again stop Editor concerned as to whereabouts of Walter Craig stop Have no power to prevent her conducting own enquiries stop Suggest you help and facilitate disinterest – McGlade.

Typescript of a phone call by Charles Patterson of the Daily Recorder from Maureen Weston just before 5 p.m. on September 6 and taken down in shorthand by his secretary:

I have been shown the spot where the submarine's boat landed. I have talked to the coastguard and have walked over to Carillon, the cottage inquired for by the man landed from the submarine. But I am no further forward.

However, this much I have got. It gives the background. Walter Craig went out after mackerel with a man known locally as Big Logan and came back soaking wet. Big Logan, by the way, is a bit of a character – apparently he is very large and bearded, about forty, tough and fond of the girls. Well, apparently Walter had got pulled into the sea by what he thought was a shark which went for a mackerel he had just hooked. Logan thinks this over and decides it isn't a shark but a submarine. Then, when Walter comes down on the Sunday and begins talking of a fellow he met on the cliffs going home the previous night who had just come in by boat, Logan gets properly suspicious, for his boat was apparently the last one in at Cadgwith. The man Walter met asked the way to a cottage called Carillon on the cliffs above Church Cove.

Logan asks the landlord at the local who the owner of Carillon is. That is as far as they go with the landlord. After that they trot off to the coastguard. I could not get much out of Morgan even though he is Welsh. He is in bed suffering from shock and feeling rather sorry for himself. Apparently the U-boat came very near to sinking the torpedo boat. He says that he is not allowed to say anything about it – not even to get his picture in the papers.

A Mr Fuller introduced himself to me this morning. He seemed to know all about me and why I was in Cadgwith. I began to get suspicious. And when he told me he was from Scotland Yard I was quite certain I had found the master spy. However, it turns out that he is from the Yard and he helps quite a bit. Here's the low down.

It was arranged that Walter and Logan should wait on the cliffs whilst the coastguard and two other fishermen lay in wait just around the headland in Logan's boat. It appears, however, that the coastguard, on thinking the matter over, decided to notify Falmouth, and the naval authorities dispatched a torpedo boat to intercept the submarine. The action was much as the *Telegraph* account describes it. The U-boat is believed damaged, but it is by no means certain that it was destroyed. Fuller told me that the police had found marks on the slopes above the place where the landing was made which indicate a struggle. Their theory is that both Walter and Logan were taken prisoner. Incidentally, the boat made the submarine. It was a collapsible rubber boat and was picked up farther down the coast the next day. On it was painted the letters U 34.

The owner of Carillon was arrested that night. His name is George Cutner. He had been at Carillon just over two years. I gather that he paid frequent visits to London and other places. Nobody down here seems to know much about him. To them he was a foreigner and regarded much as the summer visitors. Any one is a foreigner down here who was not born in the district. He was very fond of fishing, though he seldom went out in a boat. He was often with a rod at a picked spot called the Bass Rock at the extremity of one of the headlands. There was nothing in the least unusual about his appearance. He was about fifty-five, short and rather bald – in fact, much like the retired bank manager he was meant to be. There is a police guard on the cottage and I cannot find out where the man has been removed to. Moreover, friend Fuller seemed to expect me to be satisfied with what he had told me and clear out, so perhaps I had better. I shall take up the search with the agents from whom Cutner purchased Carillon.

I don't know whether you will be able to get a story out of this. However, I will hope to get something really hot in due course. Incidentally, this is the last time I try and get you on the phone. I waited two and a half hours for this call. I'll wire in future.

Cutting from the front page of the September 7 issue of the Daily Recorder:

RECORDER MAN EXPOSES

GERMAN SPY

AND BECOMES FIRST BRITISH

WAR CAPTIVE

NOW PRISONER ON BOARD DAMAGED U-BOAT

Walter Craig, the *Recorder's* theatre critic, is the man responsible for the exposure of the first German spy to be captured since the outbreak of war. His action has cost him his freedom and possibly his life. He is now a captive on board a German U-boat, which is known to have been damaged and may well have been destroyed.

The spy was posing as a retired bank manager at a little coastal village. For reasons of national importance names and localities cannot be given. His capture was the result of a remarkable piece of deductive work on the part of Walter Craig.

Here is the story as told by one of his colleagues who went down to the place where he had disappeared in an endeavour to discover whether he was alive or dead.

Every detail of Maureen Weston's story that could be got past the Censor was included in this splash. The story was taken up by the evening papers and caused something of a sensation in the Street.

A cutting from the Daily Recorder of Friday, September 8. It appeared in the form of a box on the front page and was based on nothing more hopeful than a wire dispatched from Penzance at 4.45 p.m. the previous day and reading:

Agents not very helpful but looking around – Maureen.
The box read as follows:

RECORDER SPY HUNT

Following Walter Craig's brilliant exposure of the first German spy to be captured since the beginning of the war, the *Daily Recorder* has sent one of its star reporters to take the hunt where Walter Craig was forced to lay it down.

The *Daily Recorder* is convinced that Walter Craig's brilliant work opens the way to the exposure of a whole network of German espionage in England. This must not be regarded by readers as being in the nature of a spy scare. It is nothing of the sort. But it would be foolish to imagine that Germany, which has been preparing for this war for over five years, will not have perfected an intelligence system of the greatest efficiency in this country. This will have been facilitated by the influx of refugees into this country since Nazism first began to spread terror in Europe.

This does not mean that you should regard all your neighbours, especially those with foreign names, with suspicion. But you would be wise to remember not to discuss in public the little pieces of information, military and civil, that you glean in the course of your business or through conversation with friends. Remember – Walls have ears. In the meantime the *Daily Recorder* is investigating this menace.

Wire from Maureen Weston to Charles Patterson of the Daily Recorder dispatched from Falmouth at 4.45 p.m. on September 8:

Cutner imprisoned here stop Local force succumbed but Cutner unhelpful stop Declares visitor was commander U-boat and he gave him envelope contents unknown stop Insists he was purely an intermediary stop Discussion with estate agents at Penzance unhelpful – Maureen.

Letter from Maureen Weston at the hotel, Cadgwith, dated September 10

and received by Charles Patterson of the Daily Recorder on the morning of
Monday, September 11:

DEAR CHARLIE,

It's not for the recipient of a £5 daily retainer to doubt a news
editor's wisdom in continuing it, but I must admit that you don't
seem to be getting your money's worth. Needless to say, I'm doing
my best, but it doesn't seem to be leading any place. Either I'm
no good as an investigator or else Cutner was just what he said he
was – an intermediary. The only objection to this theory is that his
identity was rather elaborately faked – at least that my opinion.

I stayed the Friday night at Falmouth and on the Saturday
morning received an answer to a wire I had sent to the local paper
at Gloucester the previous night. Gloucester was where Cutner
was supposed to have been a bank manager and I had asked for
full details as to appearance, interests, visits abroad if any and
present whereabouts. The description given in the reply tallied
with Cutner in every detail. Interests were given as golf and bridge
– golf handicap was four! He was a widower and, following his
retirement in June, 1936, he had embarked on an extensive tour of
Europe. Present whereabouts was given as Carillon, Church Cove,
near Lizard Town, Cornwall.

I then presented myself once more at the local police station.
But the law had become unpleasantly official overnight. Exit
your glamorous investigator, baffled, to meet friend Fuller on the
doorstep. He did not seem in the least surprised to see me and
frankly admitted that he was responsible for the attitude of the
local force. So I weighed in with a few questions: What were the
countries visited by Cutner in his European tour? Was Germany
one of then? Did he play golf? If so what was the handicap and
had they found out whether he really could play? And so on.

When I had finished, Fuller said, 'So you've got that far, have
you, Miss Weston.' I said, 'What do you mean – that far?' He
said, 'Never mind.' We then discussed the weather and left it at
that. He was not inclined to be helpful.

Deductions, my dear Watson – lucky I write detective stories,
isn't it? – are as follows, Cutner vanished in Germany. His passport, clothes, and in fact, his whole personality were taken over
lock, stock, and barrel by the gentleman now in prison. This
gentleman returned, and, with Cutner's background to fall back
on if questioned, purchased Carillon from the executors of the
deceased Mrs Bloy. This all sounds rather like an excerpt from
one of my books, but I am quite convinced that if only I could get

this man Cutner on to a golf course I could prove it. The average German isn't very interested in golf and I doubt whether the man would know one end of a club from another.

However, the net result of this was to send me posthaste back to Cadgwith in an attempt to pick up the threads from that end. But nothing doing. The man had few visitors and no one seems to know anything about them. The police have withdrawn from the cottage and last night I went over it. Not a smell. The police will almost certainly have removed anything they thought might be interesting. But I doubt whether Cutner was the man to leave anything about. When I saw him in the cell at Falmouth he struck me as a secretive little man. He looked like a bank manager. His whole appearance shrieked figures, routine and a methodical mind. I doubt whether he ever had an affair in his life. Incredible the sort of people who will go in for intelligence work! There's not an ounce of romance or adventure about him. If he is a master spy, he's a damned dull one. But there you are, that's just the sort of man you want for a spy.

The point I am leading up to is this. I am no further forward on this business than when I started. I don't mean I've discovered nothing. But I have not discovered anything that would lead me to a big spy network or even to suggest that such a network existed. From your point of view I'm a washout, and after this letter I'm quite expecting you to wire me to get back to my book. The only trouble is I've got interested in this business. The way I look at it is this. Presuming my deduction to be right, why did the German Intelligence go to such pains to plant at Cadgwith a man who was to be no more than an intermediary? It doesn't make sense. Any one would have done for the job of intermediary.

Now I have a proposition to put forward. I continue this investigation and the *Recorder* pays me expenses. I'll chuck it as soon as I realize I'm getting no further. And if I chuck it you'll only be out of pocket to the extent of my expenses. If, on the other hand, I get on to something that is really worth while you can pay me my daily retainer for the period and for whatever you are able to print. Let me know what you think.

Yours,
MAUREEN WESTON.

Wire from Charles Patterson of the Daily Recorder to Maureen Weston at the hotel, Cadgwith, dispatched from Fleet Street at 11.10 a.m. on September 11:

Okay go ahead stop Good luck – Patterson.

Letter from Maureen Weston at the Red Lion Hotel, Redruth, dated September 12 and received by Charles Patterson of the Daily Recorder on the morning of Wednesday, September 13:

DEAR CHARLIE,

Believe we may be getting somewhere, but God knows where. Am leaving here early tomorrow for St Just near Land's End. It's a long shot and can't for the life of me think why I am feeling suddenly optimistic.

My last letter, if I remember rightly, was written on Sunday evening at the hotel in Cadgwith. On Monday morning I ran over to Penzance and had another talk to the agents who sold Carillon to Cutner. I don't know whether it was a sort of hunch or just that, having drawn blank at Church Cove, I turned in desperation to the agents as the one possible link between Cutner and the others.

The agents were Messrs Gribble, Tolworth and Fickle – incredible, isn't it? Previously I had only spoken with the chief clerk. This time I demanded to see the senior partner. This was Mr Fickle, the other two being dead! He was a pompous little Scotsman and vera vera careful. The police had apparently been at him and he was beginning to fear for his reputation. When I told him that I represented the *Recorder*, I feared he was going to throw me out. However, we played the old game and I said it would look as though he were concealing something if he was not prepared to discuss the matter openly with a representative of the press. In the end he told me everything I wanted to know, and it wasn't much at that.

Cutner had purchased the cottage on February 2, 1937. He paid for it with a cheque on the branch at Gloucester where he had been manager – ergo, if my reasoning is correct, this makes him a passable forger as well. He had looked at a number of cottages before choosing Carillon. Several of these were inland, but Fickle seems to have been left with the impression that what Cutner was really interested in was one on the coast. An interesting point is that he offered him one at Sennen Cove, which was in every way ideal and much more suited to his stated requirements than Carillon, but he turned it down without even bothering to go and look at it. For some reason it had to be in South Cornwall. In all, Cutner spent the better part of a week in Penzance, motoring out daily in various directions to have a look at properties. An entry in the register at the Wheatsheaf Hotel, Penzance, where I stayed the night, shows that he was there from January 27 to February 1, 1937. He instructed his purchase agreement to be sent to his hotel at Torquay. He was resident at that hotel from December 4, 1936, to January 26, 1937, and again from February 2 to February 28, 1937, when he took up his residence at Carillon.

All this is getting nowhere, you'll say. Quite right, but it shows that I'm being thorough. Now here we come to the little sequence of coincidence which is sending me scuttling down to St Just. The hall porter at the Wheatsheaf remembers Mr Cutner. And the reason he remembers him is that he tipped him with a dud ten shilling note. I know what you're going to say. That dud ten shilling note shows, Miss Weston, that your reasoning is all wrong. Cutner was not ingeniously smuggled into this country by Germany. He is just a petty criminal passing dud notes and ready to take on anything, even a little espionage work, to keep himself in funds. But wait a minute. This man paid his bill by cheque, and it was honoured. He paid in two cheques at his Torquay hotel and both were honoured. As far as I can find out this was the one and only dud note that he passed. My conclusion is that it was just one of those things. But it has served my purpose, for to this day the hall porter remembers all about Mr George Cutner. He remembers that he wore brown boots with a dark grey suit and that he kept a big gold watch, which he would frequently consult, in his waistcoat pocket. And that during his stay at the hotel he had a visitor. This visitor was a man of the name of Robertson – short and thick-set, with rimless glasses, heavy cheeks and a way of puffing as he moved as though he were perpetually short of breath.

Using the office of Gribble, Tolworth and Fickle as a poste restante I wired this description to Cutner's Torquay hotel and to Detective-inspector Fuller at the Falmouth police station. The reply from the Torquay hotel was not long delayed. It read – 'Man answering description visited Cutner several times stop Name Jones.' I waited at the estate agents for some time, hoping for a reply from Fuller. In the end I gave it up and went along to see the editor of the local paper. Here I drew blank. No one in the office knew any one of the name of either Jones or Robertson who answered to the description. In fact, no one knew any one at all who answered to that description.

So back to the hotel and further talks with the porter. A genuine ten shilling note changes hands – this will be included in expenses – and from the depths of the remote past this worthy individual, who has needless to say the acquisitive nature of the Cornish wrecker well developed, conjures the memory of a telephone call from said Mr Robertson to Cutner when the latter was out. Later Mr Robertson rings through again and as Cutner is still out leaves a message. The message is to the effect that Cutner is to meet him in Redruth that evening. When the porter asks where and at what time, this Robertson says, 'Seven o'clock. He knows where.'

So then I get the car out and start for Redruth. And as the estate agents is on the way I stop off to see whether Fuller has answered my wire. I should have been warned by the sleek black roadster that is drawn up at the curb. Detective-inspector Fuller is waiting for me inside with a whole heap of questions. How did I get to know about this man? Who had seen him? Where did I get my description from?

'So you recognize the description, do you?' I asked.

And he said, 'Like hell I do. I've been trying to trace this man ever since Cutner was arrested.'

'Well, isn't that a coincidence,' I said, 'I'm trying to trace him too.'

And then we start the questions all over again. But I get the answer to my wire. This fellow Robertson had visited Carillon several times. So I say good-afternoon and thank him for being so kind as to come all the way over to Penzance in order to reply to my wire. He thinks I think I've made rather a hit and that makes him very embarrassed. Even so he sticks to the point and keeps on with the questions. We both get rather hot under the collar and in the end he takes himself off to go the round of the hotels and through the whole gamut of investigation that I've just been through, while I go on to Redruth.

And here everything tumbles right into my lap. The editor of the local paper listens to my description and says, 'Sounds like Tubby Wilson. Started up the old Wheal Garth mine and packed up about a year back.' Then he gets down two bound volumes of the paper and after about ten minutes search produces a photograph of a fat little man standing with feet apart, his thumbs in his waistcoat pockets and a broad grin on his moon-like face. The man has a battered trilby on the back of his head and I can see a faint mark on his waistcoat that looks like a watch chain. The photograph appeared in the issue of March 2, 1937 – that is shortly after he had had these meetings with Cutner. And the reason the photograph is in the paper is that he has just floated a small private company called Cornish Coastal Wilson Mines Ltd. Then in the issue of March 16 of that year appears the announcement of the purchase of the Wheal Garth tin mine near St Just.

Eighteen months later the mine closed down. But it evidently had good backing for there was no question of bankruptcy – all the creditors were paid in full and the mine is still the property of this now very nebulous company. Well, that's the low down on Tubby Wilson. By the time you get this letter I shall be on my way to have a look at his mine and talk to people in the neighbourhood of St Just who worked there – that is if friend Tubby is the man I think he is. I obtained two back numbers of the issue in which his photograph appeared. One cutting I have sent to my friend, the hotel porter, with a request to wire me in the morning if he recognizes it as Robertson. The other I am keeping myself for identification purposes. In the meantime I am trying to ferret out Tubby's antecedents and history. The editor of the local paper, a jovial old boy who regards me as something of an *enfante terrible*, is taking me to the local mineowners' club tonight. I threatened to go on my own, but apparently he didn't think that would be quite, quite. In the meantime, could you have someone go along to Bush House and look up Tubby's ancestors? If you have any luck wire me at the St Just post office.

I suggest you keep these interminable reports and publish them under the title of 'Letters of a Special Investigator to her Employer.'

Yours,
SHERLOCK WESTON.

Wire from Maureen Weston to Charles Patterson of the Daily Recorder dispatched from Hayle at 10.5 a.m. on September 13:

Porter corroborates identity stop John Desmond Wilson known in Redruth prior flotation stop Something of rolling stone been prospecting various goldfields also tin Malay stop Writing arrival Saint Just – Maureen.

Wire from Charles Patterson of the Daily Recorder to Maureen Weston at the Post Office, St Just, dispatched from Fleet Street at 11.15 a.m. on September 13:

Born Düsseldorf ninety four naturalized British twenty two stop Keep going – Patterson.

Letter from Maureen Weston, c/o Mrs Davies, Cap View, Pendeen, Cornwall, dated September 13 and received by Charles Patterson of the Daily Recorder on the afternoon of September 14:

DEAR CHARLIE,

I'm feeling a little scared. Your special investigator is going down the mine tomorrow morning, and she's not the least bit keen. This is the most God-awful place. I've never seen these Cornish mining villages before – they're even worse than the Welsh. They're so drab and the coastal scenery is so colourful. Today, for instance, as I pottered around the cliffs looking at the mines, the sea was a brilliant turquoise blue with a white edge where it creamed against the cliffs. It reminded me of the Mediterranean, except that the coast here is much more ragged and deadly looking than anything I have seen before. From this I came back to Pendeen to make inquiries as to who had worked in Wheal Garth, and by comparison this little huddle of grey stone cottages is unbelievably squalid.

However, I have been quite lucky. I am installed in a little cottage half-way between Pendeen and Trewellard and clear of the depressing atmosphere of a mining village. But there is no opportunity to forget that I am in the mining district of Cornwall. There is open ground on the other side of the road and it is dotted with grass-grown slag heaps, piles of stones which were once miners' houses and ruined chimneys that acted as flues for the ventilation shafts of the mines. This is what I look out on from my bedroom window. And, believe me, when it rained this evening it looked a scene of utter desolation. It is getting dark now and I'm writing this by the light of an oil lamp. A sea mist has come up and the lighthouse at Pendeen Watch is moaning dismally. However, when it's fine it is possible to see right across to the cliffs, and I can just see the top of Cape Cornwall, which I gather is why the cottage is called Cap View. I feed in the kitchen with the family – mother, father, daughter aged seven, and an evacuee, male, aged five. And from the window there you look up the slope of the moors to the huge pyramid heaps of the china clay pits.

So much for the local colour. Now to the result of my labours. First thing I did on arrival was to locate the mine. Refer to your collection of Ward, Lock, and in the West Cornwall volume you will find it given as lying between mines Botallack and Levant, both now defunct. I have had quite an interesting prowl round. There is the remains of what looks like a miniature railway running for the better part of half a mile along the very edge of the cliffs. There is just the cutting left and an occasional wooden sleeper. In fact, but for the wooden sleepers, I should have said it was a water duct, for it is a definite cutting all the way. Maybe what I think are sleepers are old slats of wood that formed the framework for the wooden trough in which the water ran. Whatever it is, I think it once belonged to Wheal Garth. What I take to be the main shaft of the mine is about a hundred yards in from the cliff edge. There's a high stone wall round it that looks fairly recent. I climbed over and had a look down, lying flat on my stomach. There's a sheer drop of about a hundred feet to a lot of old pit props, and there's the sound of water dripping – most unpleasant! The cliffs here are simply pitted with these shafts. Each has its stone wall, but that is the only protection. Others have been filled, some have fallen in, and the scars of diggings and the mounds of old slag heaps are everywhere.

Your acquisitive little Maureen was seen making for the local with several small-sized boulders clasped to her bosom. Some of the stones on the slag heaps are beautifully coloured, but actually what I had got were several pieces of greenish rock flecked with gold. Optimism outran intelligence and I pictured myself opening up Wheal Garth as a gold mine.

At the pub I find a most admirable and intelligent landlord. Note the style of Pepys! I order a gin and lime, dump my little pieces of rock on the bar and ask if the bright stuff is gold. Whereupon my drink is delivered to me with a huge guffaw and a smell of stale beer. 'Aye, that's raight foonny!' he says. He hails from the North in case you hadn't noticed my spelling. 'That's moondic, that is. Arsenic deposit. Ee, we allus gets a laff oot o' t' visitors wi' moondic. They arl think it's gold.' He produced a piece of rock from the back of the bar that shone like solid gold only the look of it was rather more metallic. This was a lovely example of mundic. Then he showed me a piece of what they call mother tin from a new lode that had just been struck at Geevor. The whole village, incidentally, now seems to live on Geevor. It's the only mine for miles around that is still working.

I know what you're muttering to yourself – when is this so-and-so woman coming to the point? Well, here it is. The landlord recognized the picture of Tubby. As soon as he sees it, he says, 'Ee, 'a knaw 'im raight enoof. That's Toobby Wilson, that is.' Then over a pint of mild and bitter he gives me the low down on the mine.

Wheal Garth is what they call a wet mine, or rather it was in the old days. Its hey-day appears to have been about 1927-28. Tin was around £240 a ton at the time and they were working on a three-foot wide seam of mother tin. Profits of Wheal Garth for 1928 were something like £200,000. This was on a capital of some £60,000, the mine having been bought for a song in 1925. That's the way with these Cornish mines, derelict one year and then some small speculating prospector strikes a seam and a fortune is made. Apparently this seam ran out under the sea. That was why it was a wet mine. It resulted in very bad silicosis. In the words of the landlord, 'Nae boogger laiked t' place.'

Then in November, 1928, the undersea workings collapsed and a whole shift – thirty-two men – were trapped and killed. It was, I understand, one of the worst disasters in the history of Cornish mining. An inquiry was held and it was found that a huge under-water cavern, which ran into the face of the cliff immediately above the galleries leading into the undersea workings, extended much deeper than had been thought. Thus, instead of having, as they thought, some twenty feet of solid rock above the under-water galleries, there had only been some three feet. The cave was known of course to the engineers and divers sent down when the galleries were first cut in 1916. But the sand that filled the bottom of the cave had proved deceptive. Frankly I doubt whether the engineers took full precautions. Owners are notoriously free with the lives of miners, and 1916 was a year in which every effort was being made by the Cornish mines to meet the demands of the war machine. There might be a story in that for you later – How Corn-wall is Feeding the Tinplate Industry. As far as I can gather no effort was made by the company that took over in 1925 to check the safety of these galleries. They were in fact safe enough at the time. It was only when they came to widen them in order to lay a small railway and so increase the output of the mine that they collapsed.

You are probably wondering at my preoccupation with the mine rather than with Tubby Wilson. I must admit that when I last wrote you my idea in coming down here was simply to check up on the man and see if I could find out whether any other suspicious persons had contacted him at the mine. What decided me to pay close attention to the mine itself was the talk I heard at the mineowners' club in Redruth last night. Apparently Tubby Wilson and his activities at Wheal Garth had always been some-thing of an enigma to some members. The point to remember is that these boys have been in the business for years. They know how to run a mine. They know what to look for and what to go out for without involving themselves in terrific costs. When Noye, the local editor, collected a few of his particular cronies – big men in the tin business, as he told me – round the bar and explained that I worked for the *Recorder* and wanted information about Wilson, they were only too ready to discuss the business. When Tubby

Wilson floated his company and opened up Wheal Garth, the price of tin was falling sharply. And they naturally thought that what he was going to do was drive another shaft and run fresh galleries out to pick up the undersea lode beyond the spot where the old workings had ceased, so by-passing the danger area. The only thing was, they thought his capital insufficient for the job. They told him this, but he throws a wide guy act and says he's got other ideas. Well, these other ideas are apparently to go for the shore end of the lode. Now this is a bum idea and they tell him so. The lode was discovered only about twenty feet from the sea and some thirty feet below sea level. The shoreward end was worked out before ever they started on the undersea section. Moreover, prospecting work was carried out over a wide area at the shoreward end in a fruitless effort to discover the continuation of a lode. The boys at the club told him he'd be throwing his money away if he started looking for that end of the lode. His reply was that he had an idea. Well, his idea was to sink a new shaft about a hundred yards back from the cliffs dead in a line with the cave, then he throws new galleries out until he meets the cave which apparently extends some two hundred yards inland. Then he begins to cast about in a big semi-circle with broad adits running off every few yards into the cave. Then he casts inland in two great drives at each end of his main gallery. Then he runs adits off opposite the ones he has run into the cave. Then he tries a higher level. Then a higher level still. Then he goes bust and the mine closes down.

The boys I spoke to thought he must have spent in all four times the nominal capital of the company. He employed forty men on the job and an engineer who came down from London and didn't know a thing about Cornish tin mining. They think he was nuts. What do you think?

Anyway, that's why I'm fussing over the mine. I'm also interested in this engineer from London – long lean fellow with horn-rimmed spectacles, thinning hair and what is thought to have been the makings of a Scotch accent. The name is Jesse Maclean. See what you can get?

It was the landlord who put me on to Alf Davies. Davies is a Welshman, whatever, and was foreman of the Wheal Garth under Maclean. I thanked him and asked whether it would be possible to have a look over the mine. He said it was closed, but that Alf Davies would be able to tell me all about it.

Davies is a proper little Welsh miner, short and broad, a bundle of muscle and vitality, with false teeth and a sour glum-looking face beaten brown by the wind. But for all his glumness, he's got a sense of humour and smiles sometimes. When I asked him after tea this afternoon whether he could take me down Wheal Garth he said, 'Indeed and I'd like to, but look you the mine is closed.' I said there must surely be some way in and offered him a fiver for his trouble – please note for expenses! I saw him hesitate, for he is on the dole now, and then he said, 'Well, if you're so anxious that it's worth that much to you to go down a lousy mine like Wheal Garth I can't stop you. But there's no dependence on the old workings whatever and it's rough going, by damn it is.' I said I didn't mind, so it's all fixed up. In due course I'll let you know what happens. I must admit I haven't the faintest idea what I'm expecting to find. It's just that I'm curious.

Yours,
MAUREEN.

Transcript of code wire from Detective-inspector Fuller to Superintendent McGlade at Scotland Yard, dispatched from Penzance at 3.15 p.m. on September 13:

All information John Desmond Wilson mine owner and gold prospector please stop Formed Cornish Coastal Wilson Mines Ltd April thirty seven – Fuller.

Transcript of a code wire from Superintendent McGlade to Detective-inspector Fuller at police station, Penzance, dispatched at 5.55 p.m. on September 13:

Wilson born Düsseldorf ninety four naturalized British twenty two stop No police record stop *Daily Recorder* made similar inquiries today stop Intelligence officer meeting you in morning – McGlade.

Letter from Maureen Weston posted at Penzance on the evening of September 14 and received by Charles Patterson of the Daily Recorder on the Friday afternoon:

DEAR CHARLIE,
Further to my report of September 13, I have examined the mine and quite frankly the experience was not a pleasant one. For one thing, you've no idea how eerie the place was. It reeked of water and the air was pretty stale. For another, my guide seemed to become rather uneasy when we reached the lower levels. I know that must sound silly – it does to me now I am sitting writing

about it in the cosy warmth of my little bedroom. But, believe me, it is unpleasant enough going down a discarded Cornish tin mine without your guide getting scared. Perhaps 'scared' isn't quite the right word. 'Puzzled' might be better – and yet he was more than just puzzled. He was quite confident when we started. After all, it was his mine, so to speak. But there are all sorts of funny noises in those empty galleries. The drip of water echoes and is magnified. There are strange creaking sounds where old props are taking a strain, queer glimpses of pale light where old shafts come down, the sound of falling stones, the weird echo of one's own footsteps going up one gallery and coming back at one down another, and at the lower levels a faint roar as of water falling. I didn't worry much about all these weird sounds until I sensed that Alf was uneasy. Then these sounds became so magnified in my imagination that at times I could have sworn we were being followed and at other times that the roof of the gallery was coming down.

This probably reads rather like the hysterical blathering of a woman who has been thoroughly frightened by her first experience of going down a mine, so I had better begin at the beginning. To start with, I'll go over my conversation with Alf Davies on the previous night in greater detail. When I asked him whether he could take me over the mine and he hesitated at the suggestion of a fiver, he told me one or two things. First, that so far as he knew the mine had not been entered since it had closed down in 1937. Second, that the new main shaft had been blocked at the bottom. Third, that the only possible means of getting into the mine was the way they had got into it when they opened it up in 1937. Fourth, that this entrance meant going through the old workings which were not particularly safe, and that to get into them necessitated climbing down an old half-ruined shaft with the aid of a rope. I must admit the prospect was not exactly encouraging, but I had made up my mind to have a look at the mine, so I put the best face I could on it and said I adored climbing down unsafe shafts on the end of a rope.

Well, we left at eight-thirty this morning equipped with a coil of rope, a pair of electric torches and a packet of sandwiches apiece. Fortunately I had had the sense to bring a pair of old corduroy trousers with me on this assignment of yours so that I looked reasonably business-like. We walked for about a quarter of a mile through the waste of old mine workings opposite the cottage and then went through a gate and crossed a field. Thence through another gate on to the sort of heath that runs to the cliff edge. There were no mine chimneys here, but grass mounds and barrows pointed to old workings, and here and there were the small circular walls that marked a shaft. We struck away to the left along the wall that circled the field, pushing our way through a tangle of briars. We then came to a vague fork in the path and bore right, away from the wall. The ground here was covered with briar and heather – or heath, I never know which.

I don't think I've ever seen such a frighteningly desolate spot. The ground about us was pock-marked with old workings, all overgrown and ruined. Some of the shafts had only pieces of rotting timber across them with a few lumps of rock thrown carelessly on top. One or two we passed were practically unprotected, with ferns growing out of the sides and very wet. Alf told me that the cattle quite often fall down these shafts. 'Quite a good place for a murder,' I said, wondering whether to make this the setting for my next book. But Alf – I'd told him what I did for a living – said, 'Yes, indeed, it is creepy enough, but you would not get away with it.' Apparently as soon as a carcase that has fallen down a shaft begins to rot the birds gather over it in clouds. That was the moment he chose to introduce me to the entrance to the old workings of Wheal Garth and I had an immediate vision of ravens and gulls and choughs wheeling in a monotonous screaming symphony of black and white over our decaying bodies.

A more evil looking spot than the entrance to those workings I cannot imagine. Out of a tangle of briars rose an old lichen-covered wall that was rapidly disintegrating. It was circular, like all the rest, and about twelve feet in diameter. And when I looked over, it was to peer down into a black wet pit surrounded by ferns and water-weed. 'Do I have to go down that?' I asked. At that he grinned. 'Indeed and ye don't have to, miss, it's your own party.'

I smiled a little weakly. He was right – I didn't have to. Quite frankly I nearly walked out on him. However, I asked him whether he thought it was all right, and he said, 'Yes, indeed, why not?' And he seemed so confident about it and so matter-of-fact that I said nothing when he began looking around for a suitable rock to which he could secure the rope.

By the way, I think I owe you an apology for writing you such long screeds when from your point of view there is very little news in them. But I am regarding these daily reports to you as a sort of diary, and whatever material you don't use I shall probably incorporate in a book.

Well, he secured the rope to a good-sized rock, clambered over the wall and dropped the other end of it down the shaft. He then asked me whether I thought I was capable of climbing down the rope or if it would be better for him to lower me down. When I discovered that if he lowered me it would necessitate my going down first and waiting at the bottom alone, I decided to risk the climb. The depth of the shaft was apparently only a matter of thirty or forty feet. As he lowered his legs into the shaft he looked up at me and said, 'Don't ye mind about anything else but the rope.' I asked him what he meant and he grinned and quoted, 'Fra' ghoulies and ghosties and long-leggety beasties. I'm not saying there mayn't be a bat or two down here,' he explained. 'Just you remember to hang on to the rope.' Then he caught hold of the rope and disappeared. It was a good start.

I could hear his feet scrabbling against the uneven stone sides of the shaft, and several times stones clattered down into the depths, making a hollow unreal sound. Then the rope went slack and his voice came up the shaft, deep and cavernous. I climbed over the wall and sat down with my legs dangling over the edge of the shaft. And there I remained for what seemed an age. I suppose it was, in fact, only a few seconds, but I thought I should be rooted there for ever. There were large ferns in the shaft and the stone sides were all slimy with water. And there were little noises that I could not recognize.

The feeling I had sitting on top of that shaft was horribly primitive. It's funny. I wouldn't have minded going down a new shaft. In fact, I shouldn't have hesitated. We're quite accustomed to going underground. We do it every day in London. But when the shaft leading underground is shorn of its civilized trappings you suddenly realize that when you descend you will be going *under ground*.

Then Alf's voice came floating up to me again, and I knew it was very little different from the first bathe of the season and that the sooner I got on with it the better. So, before I could change my mind and start panicking again, I had swung my legs over, gripped the rope with my feet and was lowering away. Strange as it may seem, it wasn't as unpleasant as I had expected, chiefly, I imagine, because my whole attention was concentrated on the task of keeping hold of the rope. I thought my arms would never stand it. I couldn't come down gripping the rope with my feet because it swung close to the wall and was apt to rub my nose against the slimy water-weed. I had to let my arms take the strain and brace my feet against the many crevices that I found in the side. There were quite a number of cobwebs and I'm sure that I should have hated it if I'd had a torch. But as soon as I had got about ten feet down it was quite impossible to see a thing except the glaring white circle of daylight at the top, and this gradually diminished in size. Once, I did encounter a bat, but by that time I was too concerned about whether or not I should ever last out till the bottom to worry about it. It fluttered about for a few moments and then settled again. I think it was dark enough for it to see me and avoid me. What I should have done if it had flown in my face I don't know.

Just as I thought my arms would be wrenched from their sockets, I felt Alf's hand grip me and I stepped down on to the level floor of the shaft. 'Ye ought to come to Wales and do some real climbing,' he said. It was a compliment which I felt I had deserved. I moved my feet and immediately there was a dry rattle. I flashed my torch and stared a little uncomfortably at the skeleton of what I presumed had once been a cow.

Alf switched his torch on and disappeared along a wet stale-smelling tunnel that gradually sloped at a steeper and steeper angle. I followed him. It was rather like exploring a long cave. There was little to show that the walls had been cut by human hands. They were rough and not hewn to any definite shape. Here and there were slight falls that had to be negotiated, some-times with considerable difficulty, and the floor was irregular and strewn with stones that made it treacherous. In places it was like the bed of a stream. Alf told me that he believed these particular workings dated back more than two centuries. I could well believe it. But the thought that they had stood for that long comforted me. In one part, however, there had been a particular bad fall and for a time we thought we should not be able to get through. But by removing one or two rocks we were able to crawl under it on our hands and knees. Alf spent some time examining this fall, and when I asked him what he was up to, he said he was just wondering what had caused it.

After about half an hour's very uncomfortable travelling, mostly down a sharp incline, we suddenly struck the level and the roof rose so that we could walk upright. We had reached the more recent workings. My back ached abominably. However, from then onwards the going was much less difficult.

Now this is what I want to impress upon you. The unpleasant part was over. We had left the old workings. The workings we were in now were quite safe – that is as mines go down this part of the world. Yet we hadn't progressed more than a hundred yards into these new workings before I began to feel uneasy. That sounds daft, I know. But the fact remains that throughout our scramble through the old workings it had seemed rather fun – an adventure. Now I didn't like it.

The reason, I am convinced, was Alf. He was the guide and he had been so assured coming through the old workings that I had complete confidence in him. It was his mine and I felt he ought to know his way about it like his own house. But my reliance on him made me very susceptible to his mood, and I was not slow in sensing what I think was a certain bewilderment – the sort of feeling one has if one is not sure of the way out. Its effect on me was to produce an immediate sense of uneasiness. I became jittery and all the unfamiliar little sounds about me – the drip of water, the rattle of stones and the echo of our movements – became magnified in the stillness.

I didn't get as frightened as all that at once. It was cumulative. It started when we came to a point in the more recent workings where the water that ran down from the old workings, and it was deep enough now to be over our ankles in places, was diverted from what I believe is known as a winze. This is a sharp slope going down from one level to the next, and a little wall of stones had been erected across it and cemented together so that the water continued along the level on which we stood. Alf examined this artificial barrier for a moment in the light of his torch. He even bent down and felt the cement with his hand. Then we splashed on along the level and heard the sound of falling water. It was a faint splashy sound, and suddenly we came to the end of the level.

At this point the gallery was wide enough for us to walk abreast and I got rather an unpleasant shock when in the light of the torch I saw that the floor level simply vanished. We could hear the splash of water on rock many feet below. There was no ceiling either. In fact the level ran out into an old shaft that was blocked at the top.

I don't know why the discovery that the level just ended in a sheer drop should have upset me so much. I think there must always be something very unpleasant about finding a sheer drop underground. Probably it is the immediate and involuntary feeling that if one had no torch and stumbled on it in the dark one would now be lying at the bottom where the water was splashing. I felt rather foolish really, because quite automatically I had clutched at Alf's arm – and as a one-time Fleet Street woman I pride myself on being tougher than most females. I mean, damn it, one knows quite well that mine shafts are put down and levels cut at various depths.

We retraced our steps and went down the winze into the next level. At the bottom we turned left until we came to what Alf described as a cross-cut. We took this and at the end turned right. By this time I was feeling an uncomfortable desire to cling on to his arm. With all these bewildering turns and the memory of that drop into the old shaft, I was terrified of being separated from him. I remembered all sorts of ghoulish stories about the catacombs of Rome, and pictured myself wandering alone in the place till I either died of starvation or killed myself by falling down a shaft in the dark. It was from this point, I think, that I began to get really frightened of the dark. It seemed to press in on us from every side as though endeavouring to muffle our torches. The air was warm and stale and damp, and the echo of our footsteps had an unpleasant habit of coming back at us down the disused galleries long after we had moved.

Quite often now Alf would pause and listen, with his head cocked on one side. I asked him once whether he was listening for ghosts, thinking of the miners who had been trapped. But he didn't smile. His round craggy face was set and taciturn. Every time we paused we could hear that faint roar, as of an underground waterfall, and the echo of footsteps came whispering back at us. It was then I began to feel that we were being followed. I no longer felt sure it was the echo of our own footsteps. Again I remembered the men who had lost their lives in that disaster ten years ago. We were nearing that section of the mine and I began to see in every shadow the ghost of a dead miner. Once I cried out at my own shadow cast against a wall of rock ahead of me. I tell you, I was really frightened.

By this time we had descended another winze and Alf announced in a whisper that we had reached the lowest level in this section of the mine. And a second later down the gallery behind came the whisper – 'the lowest level in this section of the mine' – with the sibilants all magnified. It was uncanny. There was a good deal of timber in this section, not all of it sound. Much of it was green and beginning to rot. Once I stumbled on a piece of rock and clutched at a prop to save myself from falling. The outer surface of the wood crumbled in my hand, all wet and sloppy.

Then we came to the bricked up foot of the new shaft. We bore away to the left along a gallery in which the timber was still grey and sound. The gallery sloped downwards and curved away to the right. Sections of rail still lay along the floor and the roar of distant water was much louder. The sound was peculiar and distorted, more like a hum, as though a rushing cataract were pouring through a narrow gorge. Remembering the disaster, I felt that at any moment we might be overwhelmed by a wall of water, though Alf assured me we were still well above sea level. My nerves were completely gone.

At length the gallery flattened out and branched into three. Alf hesitated, and then took the right-hand branch. The sound of water became even louder. The gallery here was very well built. It was about seven feet wide and the same high, and in places it was cemented to keep out the water. Then suddenly we rounded a bend and came face to face with the most ghastly-looking fall. The whole of the roof had simply caved in and the gallery was blocked by great chunks or rock that looked as though they might have been part of Stonehenge. It suddenly made me realize that it is possible to get trapped in even the soundest-seeming galleries.

Alf played his torch over the debris and at length we turned back and retraced our steps to where the main gallery had branched. We took the next branch, and before we had gone more than forty feet we came up against another huge fall. I began to have a feeling that the whole place must be unsafe. All I wanted to do was to get out of it before it caved in on top of us.

Alf spent even longer examining this fall. But at length he led me back and down the next branch. It was the same thing. Thirty feet or so down the gallery we were stopped by a fall. I guessed then that there must be a serious fault in the whole rock formation at this point. I said as much to Alf, but he only grunted and continued to poke about amongst the debris. Then he began to examine the walls.

At last I could stand it no longer. 'I'm getting out of this,' I said.

He nodded. 'All right, miss,' he said. But he made no move. He simply stood there with his head on one side, listening. Involuntarily I began to listen too. I could hear the hum of the water somewhere beyond the falls and occasionally there was the creak of a pit prop.

I suddenly clutched his arm. 'I can't stand this,' I said. 'What are you listening for? What's the matter with the place?' He seemed a little put out by my questions. 'You're uneasy, aren't you?' I went on. 'I've felt it ever since we left the old workings. For God's sake tell me what it is. Have we lost our way, is somebody following us – what? I don't mind so long as you tell me what it is.'

Then he told me. 'Somebody has been in this mine since it was closed down,' he said. He told me not to be alarmed. Then he said, 'Remember that fall we had to scramble through in the old workings?' I nodded. 'That was what first made me uneasy,' he went on. Then he explained that he thought the fall unnatural. 'Do you suppose it would have been done to discourage people from entering the mine?' he asked. Then he pointed out that the watercourse had been diverted. Normally it would have run through these workings and out beyond into the cave. And what about these falls, he asked. He took my hand and showed me clean-cut flakes on the walls and marks as though the rock had been blackened. 'These falls are not natural,' he said. He spoke fast and excited in his musical Welsh voice. 'The rock has been blasted. Those marks are the marks of dynamite. Someone has blocked off the new workings.' He swung round on me. 'Why is that?' he asked. 'Indeed, and can you tell me why you wanted to come down this mine?'

I explained that I had reason to be suspicious of the last owner. He looked at me with his head on one side. 'Mr Wilson was not a good man,' he said. 'But I did not think him dishonest.'

He took my arm and led me back up the gallery. 'Tomorrow we will come down with two friends of mine. I believe we may be able to find a way through this fall.'

And that is how things stand at the moment. We got out of the mine shortly after one. I felt pretty near exhausted and very dirty. Since then I have had a wash, a meal and a rest. I don't know what to think. I had a hunch that the mine would be worth looking at. Now I've been down it and am informed that someone has tampered with it since it was closed – in fact, that someone has deliberately produced four falls of rock. But we were able to get through the first fall – the one in the old workings. Was that design or inefficiency? Was I mistaken when I had that unpleasant feeling that we were being followed? And the three big falls – what was on the other side? What is that faint roar of water? Alf says it doesn't sound like water. Is somebody drilling? The whole thing is so fantastic. Do you remember Conan Doyle's *Tales of Horror and Mystery*? Well, I feel as though I'm writing the diary in one of his tales of horror that will be found after I am dead and from which others will draw the wildest conjectures. Suppose there is an underground race and they are coming to the surface to conquer us? Stupid! But when you are deep in the bowels of the earth anything seems possible. Quite frankly I'm not looking forward to tomorrow.

Your scared investigator,
MAUREEN.

P.S. Since writing this I have heard rather a peculiar thing. I went down to the local as Alf's guest. They're a tough crowd at Pendeen, but very friendly. I met Alf's pals who are coming on tomorrow's expedition. One's tall and the other's short, and they both look very tough indeed. They're out of work, like Alf. Both worked in Wheal Garth under Maclean. What I wanted to tell you, however, is a curious little story that is drifting around. They are very superstitious in this neighbourhood and apparently there has been talk recently of the miners who were killed in that disaster lying uneasy. They say that the white skull of a dead miner can be seen on dark nights floating in the sea just off Wheal Garth right over the spot where they were trapped.

Now the talk was going on about this when an old boy in the corner of the pub gives tongue and says that his son that keeps a bar over to St Ives told him a fisherman coming back late the other night picked up a glass net float that was bobbing up and down in the water and shining like a little full moon. It was apparently covered with phosphorous. 'That's what you see,' the old man said. 'That flawt were drifting and a phawsphorescent fish rubbed itself against it. The skull of a dead miner!' He laughed.

I thought about this as Alf and I were walking home. 'What do you think?' I asked. He shrugged his shoulders. 'Miners are superstitious folk,' he said. It was a dark night. 'I've got a pair of binoculars in the car,' I said. 'Would you care to walk with me as far as the cliffs?' He agreed, so we fetched the glasses and walked over to the cliffs. Well, it was there all right. At first I could see absolutely nothing. It was so dark that, looking through the glasses, it was as though I had covered the lenses with my hands. And then suddenly I saw a faint little point of light bobbing about like a will-o'-the-wisp. Alf saw it too. It was so faint that it was barely visible. But it was there all right.

Now what do you make of that? I hear there's a boat to be hired at Cape Cornwall. Tomorrow night, if I get back from the mine in time, I'm going out to have a look at the skull of that miner if I can get someone to come with me. Alf was very silent as we walked back. I don't know whether he, too, is superstitious, or if he was just trying to reason things out. I must admit that I don't feel too happy myself. It's easy to be matter-of-fact in a newspaper office and pour verbal ridicule upon country superstitions. But down here there seems a bit more to it. After all, there are thirty odd men lying dead under the bed of the sea there. I think I'm going to have nightmares tonight. Now I must go out and post this endless screed. I'll report developments tomorrow. I wonder how long it will take us to get through one of those falls? – M.W.

Wire from Charles Patterson of the Daily Recorder to Maureen Weston at Cap View, Pendeen, dispatched from Fleet Street at 3.25 p.m. on Friday, September 15:

Jesse Maclean British now directing mining work of national importance for Supply Ministry stop No police record nothing against him – Patterson.

Wire from Charles Patterson of the Daily Recorder to Maureen Weston at Cap View, Pendeen, dispatched from Fleet Street at 6.10 p.m. on Friday, September 15:

Letter received grand work stop Wire results days operations – Patterson.

Wire from Charles Patterson of the Daily Recorder to Maureen Weston at Cap View, Pendeen, dispatched from Fleet Street at 10.5 a.m. on Saturday, September 16:

Report at once results yesterdays activities – Patterson.

Wire from Charles Patterson of the Daily Recorder to Davies at Cap View, Pendeen, dispatched from Fleet Street at 12.35 p.m. on Saturday, September 16 and carrying with it a reply-paid form:

Please inform whereabouts of Maureen Weston residing with you – Patterson.

Pre-paid wire from Mrs Alf Davies to Charles Patterson of the Daily Recorder dispatched from Pendeen at 2.40 p.m. on Saturday, September 16:

Miss Weston and my husband visited Wheal Garth mine yesterday and have not returned stop Search party organized – Davies.

Transcript of a code wire from Detective-inspector Fuller to Superintendent McGlade at Scotland Yard dispatched from Pendeen at 2.50 p.m. on Saturday, September 16:

Maureen Weston and three local miners missing stop Went down

Wheal Garth mine yesterday following visit previous day stop **Am** convinced she had discovered something stop Mine reported to be unsafe stop Two falls heard late yesterday afternoon stop Locals fear they are trapped stop Rescue parties have opened up new shaft and are working desperately to clear falls stop Advise detention of Jesse Arthur Maclean late engineer to mine for questioning stop Description tall lean dark hair thinning glasses Scotch stop Also locate and detain Wilson – Fuller.

Record of a phone call put through by Superintendent McGlade of Scotland Yard to Chief-inspector Saviour of Durham at 3.45 p.m. on Saturday, September 16:

I want you to detain Jesse Arthur Maclean, engineer in charge of the mining work at the munitions dump at Dutton. You can do it under the Emergency Powers (Defence) Act – I've nothing against him so far.

Note from Superintendent McGlade to Colonel Blank at M.I.5. and dispatched by a special messenger at 5.30 p.m. on Saturday, September 16:

For your information I enclose copies of a number of letters and telegrams sent from a Miss Maureen Weston to Charles Patterson, news editor of the *Daily Recorder*. They may be of interest to you. You will remember she was investigating the disappearance of Walter Craig in the Cadgwith U-boat incident for her paper. I am detaining the man Maclean mentioned in her letters who is now working on a munitions dump and am endeavouring to discover the whereabouts of Tubby Wilson.

This file of communications received by Patterson from Miss Weston was handed to me this afternoon by Patterson himself after he had learned that the girl had not returned from an expedition into the Wheal Garth mine.

I should be glad to hear what you think of them.

Yours.
McGLADE.

Memorandum from the Naval Intelligence Department of the Admiralty to Colonel Blank of M.I.5 dispatched by special messenger at 8.45 p.m. on Saturday September 16:

Here are details of reports of U-boats in the vicinity of the Cornish coast received since the outbreak of war from coastal patrols of the Navy and the Fleet Air Arm:

September 4, 51.12 north 51.48 west. September 6, 49.54 north 5.5 west. September 9, 49.51 north 3.36 west. September 10, 49. 11 north 2.24 west. September 10, 51.8 north 5.21 west. September 13, 52.3 north 5.48 west. September 14, 50. 17 north 5.54 west. September 15, 49.45 north 6.35 west. September 15, 50.25 north 5.31 west.

In most cases depth charges or bombs were released, but only in two cases has the destruction of the U-boat been definitely achieved. Hope this is what you wanted – F.E.

Communiques dispatched from the War Office and the Admiralty shortly after 9.30 p.m. on Saturday, September 16, as a result of phone calls from M.I.5:

From the War Office to officer commanding H.M. Forces encamped at Trereen, Cornwall:

Dispatch immediately two companies of infantry to Pendeen. One company is to mount guard on all exits of the Wheal Garth mine. If one company proves insufficient further troops must be dispatched. The second company is to enter the mine. Contact Detective-inspector Fuller of Scotland Yard who will be awaiting your arrival at the inn. He will provide guides to the mine and will inform you of the position.

From the Admiralty to commanders of destroyers EH 4 and EH 5 stationed at Newlyn:

Proceed immediately to 50 degrees 23 minutes north 5 degrees 43 minutes west and patrol West Cornish coast from Botallack Head to Pendeen Watch.

PART THREE

THE WHEAL GARTH CLOSES DOWN

I

PLANS

WITH a sudden thrill of excitement I realized what Logan was doing. He was carrying on a conversation in morse. But was it a conversation? Was he making it up? I looked at what I had written down. It read: 'I came here with three miners. Progress into new workings blocked by falls. Had removed part of lightest fall and found way through when met by armed Germans. What is this place?'

I looked up at Logan. His face was intent on the movements of the spoon against the iron bars of the grill. Heavy tap, pause, four light taps, pause, tap tap, pause, tap tap tap, long pause, short short, pause, short short short, long pause, short short short, short short long – and so it went on. I did not understand morse, but I presumed he was replying to the question.

I looked down again at what I had written. It made sense. It suggested that this was part of a mine. That tied up with the idea of the base being either in Cornwall or in Spain. It certainly did not read like the imaginings of a man who was mentally sick. I got up and went over to the door. Logan had finished tapping. Faintly I heard a metallic click, then two more, louder and close together. Then short short short short, pause, dash dash dash. There was no doubt about it. Someone was morsing from the next cell. 'Who is it?' I asked Logan.

'That's just what he's asked us,' he replied. 'One of the first things he said when we established contact was that he represented the *Daily Recorder*. Evidently they sent someone out to look for you.' He resumed his tapping with the spoon. I waited. So Logan remembered his morse, did he?

He stopped tapping and listened. Then he took my pencil and wrote down slowly in block letters – IS CRAIG REALLY THERE THIS IS MAUREEN WESTON. 'Good God, it's a woman!' said Logan. Then he wrote: PATTERSON SENT ME TO INVESTIGATE YOUR DISAPPEARANCE.

I was amazed. 'Ask her how she found us,' I said.

The spoon went tap-tap again and presently Logan began writing the reply: 'Worked back from the spy at Carillon. This led me to phoney mine owner. And this is the mine. It lies four miles north of Saint Just.'

'So you were right,' I said. 'This base is in Cornwall. Ask her whether any one knows where she is.'

Back came the reply: 'Please repeat slower. I am working the code from a diary.'

Logan wielded the spoon again with longer pauses between each letter. Then came the reply: 'Yes. But the Germans have blown up galleries in old workings so that it will look as though we have been trapped by a fall. Have you any plans?'

Heavy, light, pause, heavy heavy heavy went the tapping of Logan's spoon. It was so short that I knew what that must be. Then we were interrupted by the opening of the guard-room door. Shortly afterwards our evening meal was brought to us.

When we were alone again I said: 'You know, we've only got till Sunday evening at the latest?'

He nodded with his mouth full of potato stew and contrived to grin at the same time.

I looked at him closely. 'Do you remember who the owner of Carillon was?' I asked.

'Ar, his name was Cutner – is that right?'

'Your memory is not so bad after all,' I said. 'I suppose it's all come back to you?'

'That's right.' He nodded and grinned, and there was that twinkle in his eyes that I had not seen since Cadgwith.

I was still not altogether convinced. It seemed incredible that the man could have put an act over on me so completely. After all, I had been his constant companion for nearly two weeks. Anyway, I failed to see the necessity of it. I tried him with another question. 'Can you tell me the name of the coastguard at Cadgwith?' I asked, and there was a trace of anxiety in my voice, for I was desperately anxious for someone to share with me the responsibility of immobilizing the base.

'Let me see,' he hesitated, his Slav features puckered with amusement. 'It wouldn't be Ted Morgan, now, would it?'

I felt a sudden great relief. 'Thank God for that,' I breathed. 'But why the devil didn't you tell me you were only shamming?'

'I would have,' he said, 'but I figured it out that I'd have a better chance of putting it across if you thought I was going balmy too. Anyway, I'm no actor. I knew the only thing was to make myself believe I was balmy. I tell you, at times I was afraid I really was.'

I gave a short laugh. 'That's what most actors have discovered,' I said. 'But what was the idea?'

'I wanted to avoid giving them the information they were after. And also I thought it might help.'

'Well, it doesn't seem to have,' I said.

'Hasn't it?' He beckoned me across to his bed. 'Here's the result of my carving,' he said. He bent down and tilted the bed up so that he could get hold of the leg nearest the wall and farthest from the door. With the help of his knife he began to prise very carefully at one of the letters of his name which he had cut on the inside of the leg, low down. And in a second the whole section with his name had come away, and in a hollow cut below it was a key fitted snugly into the wood.

He put the section back and tapped it carefully into position. It fitted perfectly and very tightly. Unless any one were looking for it, it was unlikely to be discovered. 'What key is it?' I asked.

'The key to this cell.'

'But how did you get hold of it?'

He returned to his stew. 'There are four cells along here,' he said, 'and the locks are all the same. Remember those ratings that were put in the other cells to cool off after a brawl last Monday? The guards used the same key for all the cells. And I noticed another thing. The guards were sometimes careless. They left the keys in the cell doors instead of returning them to the guard-room. So I started my craze for modelling and hollowed out my little hiding-place. Because I was supposed to be daft I got away with it. And two days after I had finished it I had the chance of lifting a key from the lock of the neighbouring cell. It was missed about two hours later. You remember we were searched on Wednesday night and the whole cell turned upside down by the guard? But by then it was safely tucked away.'

'I wonder they haven't put bolts on the door,' I said.

'Probably the guard didn't report the loss.'

I sat down on my bed again and considered the matter. It was certainly a step forward. We had the means of getting out of our cell at any time of the night. But having got out, what then? The various stores were all locked and we hadn't the key to any of these. That meant we could not get at either the fuel or the munitions. And the guards went the rounds every hour. Moreover, the arrival of Maureen Weston and her three miners complicated matters in that any plan to destroy the whole base meant the loss of their lives as well as ours.

The same thought seemed to have crossed Big Logan's mind, for he said: 'What's this Maureen Weston like?'

I cast my mind back to the time when she had been on the staff of the *Recorder*. 'She's small and dark and very attractive,' I said. 'She has Irish blood in her and as women go she's pretty tough.' I suddenly remembered that big men like small women. 'She's just your type if you're feeling repressed.'

He grinned. 'Sounds interesting,' he said. 'But just at the moment I was thinking out some way of destroying her and every one else in this base.'

'So was I,' I said. 'But how arc we going to do it?'

'We should be able to deal with the guard. There are only two who actually do the rounds. All we have to do is to get the keys off them, go into the munitions store and blow the place up.'

'It sounds easy, put like that,' I said. 'But suppose we aren't able to deal with the guards silently and they rouse the base?'

'We'll have to take the chance. Even if they were able to give the alarm we'd still have plenty of time.'

'True,' I nodded, 'but, on the other hand, we can't afford to take chances. Can't we manage it without attacking the guards? What I've been thinking about is those six-inch guns on the submarines. You know how to handle them, don't you? The after gun on U 21 is in working order and the boat lies with its stern facing straight down the main cave. One shot with that could surely be sufficient to block the underwater entrance. That would stop the submarines leaving without destroying them.'

He shook his head. 'We must destroy the submarines,' he said. 'They might blast their way out through the cliff. And the only way to destroy the boats is to blow the place up. Your scheme would only work if we could get out of the place ourselves and warn the naval authorities.

'Listen!' I said. The relief of being able to discuss the position with someone instead of just lying and racking my brains had made me somewhat excited. 'Maureen has brought three miners with her. If we could release them and, after firing the gun, get into the landward exit with picks and so on, we might be able to get through the falls they have made this afternoon.'

At that he laughed. 'Do you know what a bad fall of rock in a Cornish tin mine is like?' he demanded. 'There's maybe a hundred feet of roof brought down along our exit gallery. And the blockage will be caused by huge chunks of granite. And you suggest three miners get through it with picks!'

'Well, there are mobile drills in the base,' I said, a trifle put out. At that he stopped grinning and said: 'So there are.' He sat silent for a moment, stroking his beard. 'The trouble is they'd guess where we had gone. As soon as they had searched the base, they'd be after us, and we shouldn't have a dog's chance.'

'I'm not so sure,' I said. 'In the first place they would probably be too worried about other things to come after us for some time, and by then we could have partially blocked the exit gallery behind us. For another, we could lay for the guards and if successful, arm ourselves at the expense of the base. What I mean is that, though I think it rather risky to be dependent upon a successful attack on the guards for our means of destroying the base, I think we might deal with the guards as well as man the gun. If we succeeded with the guards we should have about ten minutes, maybe quarter of an hour, in which to ransack the base for the equipment and weapons we required. If we didn't succeed, then we'd be no worse off. With the gun loaded and sighted, it would only be a matter of an instant to fire.'

Logan snapped his fingers. 'Sure and I believe you've got it,' he said. 'The next thing to do is to get in touch with this Weston girl again and find out what part of the base she came out into.'

At that moment we were interrupted by the arrival of the guard to collect our empty stew cans. 'You'd better get some sleep,' he said in German, pointing to our beds and laying his hands against his cheek to indicate what he meant. 'Two submarines are coming in tonight.' He held up two fingers in front of my face and said: 'Boats.'

I thanked him and he departed smiling. He was one of the nicest of our guards, a large fellow with a frank open face and a ridiculous little moustache. I passed the information on to Logan. 'Thank God, they're both coming in tonight,' I said. 'That leaves tomorrow night free. Unless of course U 47 doesn't leave tonight, as planned.'

He got up and went over to the door. In his hand he held the knife he had used to hollow out the leg of his bed. But there seemed much more activity than usual in the gallery. In fact, it was not until nearly ten o'clock that he was able to establish contact with Maureen Weston. Movement in the gallery outside remained remarkably active, and as a result he was not able to keep up a sustained conversation. What he learned was very damping to our spirits. The mine gallery by which she and her companions had reached the base entered it by way of a recess in the guard-room. Moreover, the mine gallery was practically blocked about two hundred feet from the base.

This meant that the possibility of getting anything like a mobile drill through was small and in any case the chances of ever having the opportunity of entering the mine by way of the guard-room seemed somewhat remote. I understood now the cause of the activity in the gallery outside and the continual movement of men in and out of the guard-room opposite. It was from the guard-room that they were prepared to meet an attack. Probably they had machine-guns ready mounted in the mine galleries in case miners cleared the falls.

But this activity did not explain the faint but persistent clatter of electric welders and the muffled roar of machinery. Usually at this time of night the base was comparatively quiet, save for the hum of the dynamos and the murmur of voices. But for the fact that my watch said it was ten-twenty I should have said it was daytime. It could mean only one thing. 'They're rushing the repairs to U 21,' I said.

Logan nodded. 'I'm afraid they are,' he agreed. 'Which means that they're going to send the boats out tomorrow night and not Sunday.'

'Maybe they'll get some away tonight.'

'Hell! I wish I hadn't left it so late.'

'Why did you?' I asked. 'For the same reason that I did?'

'What was that?'

'Oh, just that I put it off until I couldn't put it off any longer.'

'Perhaps,' he said. 'Also I wanted to get the maximum number of boats in the base. Your friend Maureen doesn't seem to have helped us much.'

'Except in so far as her disappearance may make people suspicious about this mine. Patterson is no fool.'

'But why should they suspect that there is something wrong with the mine? The girl goes down with three miners to look over it and doesn't appear again. Two deep rumbling sounds are heard – an explosion or a fall? A search party is organized. They find the workings blocked by a big fall. Every one is then satisfied as to the reason why she and her companions never got back.'

'That depends on Patterson,' I said. 'Ask her how often she was reporting to Patterson and how much she has told him about the mine.'

But to get a message through now took some time owing to the activity outside. In all I think it was nearly half an hour before we got the full reply. It came through bit by bit as opportunity offered. It read: 'Patterson has no idea mine is submarine base.

All he knows is that I was suspicious of it and that on the first occasion I went down I found falls that should not have been there and that looked unnatural.'

'And that's that,' said Logan, returning to his bed.

'Patterson is no fool,' I reiterated. 'And he's got the sharpest nose for news of any man I know. I think he'll move heaven and earth to get the mine opened up.'

'Ar, that may be so, but who is going to do the opening up? To clear a big fall of rock takes time and costs a deal of money. Who is going to pay for it – not the paper, I know.'

'Well, it's our only hope,' I said, 'if they send the boats out tomorrow night.'

At that moment the key grated in the lock and one of the guards came in. The first of the two U-boats was coming in and we were marched down to the docks.

We had a wait of more than fifteen minutes in the cold damp atmosphere of No. 3 dock with the constant chugging of the donkey engine echoing from the main cave. In the course of this time I gained several pieces of interesting information. All work had been suspended on U 47 and she would not be ready to go out until Sunday night at the earliest. The whole engineering effort of the base was bing concentrated on U 21 and the word had apparently gone out that she must be ready for active service by tomorrow afternoon – that was Saturday. This confirmed my belief that the whole fleet would go out on the Saturday and not the Sunday night. There was a rumour that the boat coming in now was the one that had sunk the *Athenia*. And there was also talk that the second boat was already waiting to come in. That meant that in a few hours' time there would be no less than six of Germany's largest ocean-going U-boats in the base, as well as the store barge.

I passed on the information to Logan. But I did not hear his comment for there was a sudden swirl of water in the dock and a large wave slid quietly along it overflowing on to the dockside and thoroughly wetting our feet. There was much seething of water in the main cave, then the slam of metal against metal, followed by prolonged cheers. The first of the two U-boats had arrived.

The diminutive diesel-engined tug fussed noisily about the main cave and in a few minutes the bows of the U-boat appeared opposite No. 3 dock. A rope was tossed on to the dockside and we passed it from hand to hand. As soon as it was fully manned the order was given to heave and we dug our heels into the uneven rock floor and strained at the rope. Slowly the boat slid into the dock, the ratings that lined her decks fending her off from the sides with boat-hooks.

You seldom realize how wide a submarine is below the surface until you see one manœuvred into a confined space. Empty, the dock presented quite a wide surface of water, oily and glinting in the electric light. But the U-boat filled it from side to side, and her conning tower almost touched the roof of the cave. I could not help feeling then how entirely insulated this base was from the outside world. It was, in fact, a world of its own. And after a fortnight there it seemed to me quite possible that no other world existed, that my memories of green fields, of huddles of white cottages among the Cornish cliffs, of Piccadilly, of factories and ships were all a dream, and that this was the only reality. And now here was this U-boat come from that other world with probably Kiel as its last port of call.

As soon as the boat had been made fast the crew were assembled and marched off to their quarters. Normally we should have then been taken back to our cells. But on this occasion we were taken to the next dock, No. 4, where the U 21 lay. Men were required to assist in moving the for'ard six-inch gun from the electric trolley on which it had been taken to the foundry, back on to the deck of the submarine. Repairs to the gun had been completed.

There was ten minutes' back-breaking work as it was lifted on pulleys attached to the steel derrick and swung, largely by brute force, into position. It was while this was happening that a slight accident occurred which had a wholly disproportionate influence on what happened later. The commander of U 21 had come down to welcome the Number One of the boat that had just come in, U 27, who was apparently a particular friend. And having seen him to his quarters, he came down to see how the engineers were getting on with his own boat. He was smoking a cigarette. This was strictly against regulations, but no one seemed inclined to point that out to him. There came a moment in the hoisting of the gun when every man was required to strain his utmost to keep the mountings from swinging against the side of the submarine. The commander did not hesitate, but threw his weight in with the rest. It reminded me of a scrum down. We were all pushing against each other with our heads down until at last the mounting was clear of the deck and was allowed to swing slowly inwards.

We were just straightening our aching backs and getting our breath back when suddenly somebody said: 'There's something burning.' The acrid smell of smouldering rags seemed all around us. Then something flared up by one of the legs of the derrick. For a split second every one stood motionless and my mind recorded a vivid impression as though I were looking at a still from a film. Then one of the engineers dived at the flames and began stamping them out with his feet. What had happened was that the commander had thrown the stub of his cigarette away before helping with the gun, and it had set fire to a mass of oil-sodden rags. Probably they were impregnated with petrol as well. Before the engineer could muffle them the flames had caught at his overalls and the oil in them was burning.

The U-boat commander ripped off his jacket and flung it round the man's burning legs. For a second every one seemed to forget about the fire itself, which was now flaring noisily and causing some to move back on account of the heat of it. Moreover, the dockside itself, impregnated with oil, was alight in places. Having settled the engineer's trousers, the commander flung his jacket on to the flames and stamped them under with his feet.

By this time we were all coughing with the smoke, which was very heavy now that the flames themselves were muffled. As he stamped with his feet the commander kept coughing. I could see the sweat gathering in beads on his forehead. Then suddenly his knees seemed to sag under him and he collapsed. One man pulled him clear of the smouldering pile of rags, while two others finished the job of extinguishing the fire.

The doctor was sent for, but it was some time before the commander came round and every one who had been standing near the fire seemed to be feeling queer. One man actually fainted, but recovered as soon as he had been laid out a little farther down the dock. I myself found difficulty in breathing and my head reeled as though I were a little drunk. Logan, too, complained of feeling peculiar.

Then the order was given to get over to No. 1 dock as the second submarine was coming in. It was shouted by the officer in charge of the fatigue from the end of the dock. Some men obeyed, but the majority were too busy getting their breath back or arguing as to the cause of the trouble. The order was repeated. But instead of obeying it Logan swung himself on to U 21 and joined the engineers in their struggle to lower the gun into its correct position. I followed him. We had lost touch with our guards. The gun was eased into its mountings. The operation took about three minutes and gave us ample opportunity to look around. But the result was most discouraging. Even ready-use ammunition was stowed below deck and it was quite impossible to get at the armoured ammunition truck.

Our guard then re-established contact with us. As we climbed down on to the dockside I saw that the commander was now on his feet again, looking very white and his clothes in a filthy state. He still seemed a bit short of breath. The doctor said something about asphyxiation, but I couldn't hear the whole sentence. We were marched down to No. 1 dock. The fatigue party had already manned the hawser and I could see the dark pointed bows of the submarine nosing into the dock. As we took our place, Logan said: 'What was the matter with him?'

'Asphyxiation of some sort,' I said.

'Yes, but why did we all suffer from it? What caused it?'

I said I didn't know, but presumed it was something to do with the burning waste. Our conversation was interrupted by the order to heave. As soon as the submarine had been made fast, the fatigue party was dismissed and we were taken back to our cell. When the door was closed Logan said: 'This is a helluva mess. Your idea of manning the after gun of U 21 is quite hopeless.'

'You mean we can't get hold of the ammunition?' I said.

'Not only that. There's the guard. It wasn't until I saw the one on the bridge that I remembered they mount two guards on every submarine in the base day and night. The other was in the bows.'

I nodded. I was feeling very despondent. When I had discovered that Logan was as alive as I was to the situation, I had for some reason felt that success was assured. His great bulk gave one confidence where it was a question of action.

Not only were the guns out of the question, but we had only twenty-four hours in which to carry out any plan. And throughout that time the base would be a hive of activity. It was, as Logan put it – a hell of a mess. Failure would mean the loss of hundreds of British lives. Moreover, it would mean a severe blow to British prestige, and might as a result seriously affect the course of the war, for neutral opinion was a vital factor in the initial stages. I had a sudden picture of those four great ships of the Atlantic squadron wallowing up the Channel, of periscopes cutting the water inside the screening destroyers, of sudden explosions and the sterns of those proud ships lifting as they sank. It was not to be thought of. Something had to be done.

'Well?' Logan said.

I began removing my wet shoes and socks. 'Looks as though we make a desperate attack on the guard,' I said.

'When?' he asked. 'Tonight?' His tone was sarcastic. He had taken off his dungarees and was climbing into bed. 'I'm going to sleep on it,' he announced.

'But, good God, man,' I said, 'this is the last full night we've got in which to do something.'

'And the base full of men repairing things. Did you see No. 3 dock after we had berthed that last submarine? The stores department were already at work replenishing the supplies. They'll be at it all night – food, water, munitions. U 21 has got to be finished by tomorrow afternoon. You told me so yourself. And every other boat in the base will have to be ready for sea by then. We'll have to wait. If we left this cell now every one we met would wonder what we were up to. But if we left it in the daytime – say, when we were having tea – no one would pay any attention to us. They'd just think we were on fatigue. They're used to seeing us around the base in the daytime.'

'I see your point,' I said, and put the light out and climbed into bed. He was right, of course, but at the same time it made it a rather last-minute job. The truth was that now zero-hour had been definitely fixed my whole soul revolted against it. It is extraordinary how powerful the will to live is in the average human being. If it had been a question of immediate action, I could have faced it. Subconsciously, I suppose, I had keyed myself to expect action that night. I had felt that it was tonight or never as soon as I knew for certain that the boats were going out the following night. And I honestly believe that if it had been a question of instantaneous action, I would have walked out of that cell and blown the whole place up quite calmly. But to plan such and action sixteen hours in advance somehow revolted me.

Sleep was out of the question. I simply lay in the darkness and thought and thought till plans went round in my head without meaning. And as I became more and more mentally tired, my plans gained in phantasy until they had no relation to reality whatsoever. Schemes for blasting a way out through the cliff by firing a six-inch gun like a machine-gun, for escaping through the main entrance in diving suits, for constructing all sorts of Heath Robinson contrivances to blow the base up without killing myself rattled round my brain. I even remembered the strata of limestone I had discovered and thought of drilling through that to the main shaft of the mine or burning piles of oil-impregnate cotton waste in order to asphyxiate Fulke.

And then for some reason I was awake. It did not take me long to discover the reason. My subconscious schemes were still clear in my head and I realized that my mind had connected the limestone strata and the burning waste and I was back in my schooldays listening to a rather portly man with a mortarboard and horn-rimmed spectacles initiating myself and about fifteen others into the mysteries of chemistry.

I leant over and shook Big Logan. Instantly it seemed he was wide awake. I heard him sit up in his bed. 'What is it?' he asked. 'Listen!' I said, I was excited. 'Do you know what happens to limestone when it's heated? It gives off carbon dioxide and leaves calcium oxide, which is quick lime. If I remember rightly the equation is – $CaCo_3 = CaO + CO_2$.'

'How does that help?' he asked.

'Well, don't you see? Carbon dioxide is poisonous when it replaces air – lack of oxygen causes suffocation. That's what happened to the commander of U 21 tonight. There's a strata of limestone running down No. 4 dock and across into the storage cave opposite, and it broadens out to a width of about five feet at the entrance to the store. That burning waste was lying on this strata of limestone and was giving off CO_2. The commander passed out through lack of oxygen and we were all affected slightly. Now, suppose we could get a really big fire going on the limestone.'

'And then ask the commander of the base to hold a scouts' jamboree round it,' suggested Logan.

'I'm serious,' I said.

'I know you are,' he said. 'You've been lying awake thinking up all sorts of impossible schemes to avoid being killed yourself.'

It was a direct accusation of cowardice and I resented it, largely because I knew it to be true. 'I was only trying to think out a scheme that had a chance,' I said. 'I'm not afraid of dying.'

'Well, I am, if it's unnecessary,' he replied.

'Then think up something better,' I said, and turned over.

He did not reply, and when I had recovered from my resentment at his attitude, I began to consider the scheme in detail. Certainly the bald outline I had given did not sound particularly convincing. Several questions immediately leapt to my mind. First, how were we to make the necessary fire without it being put out before it had got to work on the limestone? Second, how were we to immunize ourselves? Third, what about Maureen and her companions? And fourth, was the ventilation system so good that it would be impossible to get sufficient CO_2 into the base to render every one unconscious?

I began to consider these questions one by one. The first, of course, depended upon circumstances. It was a matter for action when the opportunity offered. Tanks of oil and petrol were often being trundled round the base when a submarine was being refuelled. I had a box of matches in the pocket of my dungarees. A drum would have to be broached and some of its contents poured over the limestone strata. The flames would then have to be fed. A mixture of oil and petrol would be best. Then we should want picks and shovels to break up the limestone and build it round the flames. Moreover,, the flames must not be allowed to spread – there was a good deal of oil on the docksides and in the dock gallery. What we really ought to do was to build a little circle of broken limestone and pour petrol and oil into the centre. Then there was the question of our own immunization. I began to see the reason for Logan's sarcasm.

At that moment Logan turned over towards me and said: 'What exactly is the effect of carbon dioxide? Does it kill a person?'

'It's not exactly poisonous, like coal gas,' I said. 'It just uses up the oxygen in the atmosphere. You saw the effects this evening. A man gets dizzy and then passes out. Put him in the fresh air and he comes round again. But I believe it can be lethal if it goes on long enough.'

Then he began asking all the questions that I had been asking myself. And the more we discussed it the more elaborate and impossible the whole thing seemed. To immunize ourselves we needed an oxygen cylinder. How were we to get hold of one? True, there were plenty in the base, but would one be around just when we wanted it? Then there was the question of the four other prisoners. Logan said: 'They would have to take their chance. In a locked cell they might not come off too badly and you say we can revive them with oxygen.' As to the air conditioning, Logan pointed out that fresh air was brought in through a hole drilled in the cliff above the underwater entrance and the stale air was driven out through the look-out hole, the entrance to which led off the upper galleries. 'That means the carbon dioxide would circulate through the entire base,' he said.

But though this seemed to help, I must admit I had by then come to the conclusion that the scheme was unworkable. And after we had talked it over for some time, I said: 'For heaven's sake try to think out some scheme by which we can get at the munitions store and blow the place up.' I was by then tired and discouraged. We discussed various plans for dealing with our guards at a time when the munitions store was open, getting into it and using one of the many mines stored there to explode the place. But Logan kept reverting to my own scheme and asking questions. I suppose my brain must have been tired out, for my answers became more and more vague, and the next thing I remember is being shaken by the guard and told to get up. I looked at my watch. It was seven o'clock and my breakfast of porridge, bread and jam and tea was lying on the floor beside me.

2

ACTION

LOGAN was already seated on his bed, eating his porridge. As the door closed behind the guard, I said: 'Well, have you decided on any plan of action?'

He shook his head and continued eating. 'We'll have to take advantage of any opportunities that offer,' he said. He made no mention of my own scheme, and frankly, when I came to consider it with the prospect of putting it into action within the next few hours, it did not seem practicable. There were so many snags. I felt nervous and depressed. We had no plan, and yet we had to do something within the next twelve hours.

When he had finished his porridge, Logan knelt down on the floor and removed the key from its hiding-place. 'What do you want that for?' I asked, as he slipped it inside one of his socks and began putting on his shoes, which were still wet from the previous night.

'We may need it,' he said.

Even then, though I knew he had no plan, he gave me confidence. It wasn't just a question of his strength. There was something solid about the man, and I thanked God that his brain was all right and that I had not got to carry out some desperate plan on my own. At that moment I wished that my experience on the *Daily Recorder* had been as a reporter and not as dramatic critic. I could think of one or two men in the news-room who would have revelled in a situation like this, men who had lived on their wits and knocked about the world all their lives. I had never had to use my wits as a means of livelihood in that sense. How much Big Logan had had to use his wits, as opposed to brute force, I did not know, but his swift adaptation to circumstances on the cliffs above the Devil's Frying Pan and later in the U-boat was encouraging.

Almost before we had finished breakfast, the guard was back again. But instead of beginning the morning's work in the latrines and kitchens, we were taken straight down to the docks and set to work carrying stores from the store-rooms to U 54, which was the boat that had come into No. 1 dock the previous night. This seemed promising, for No. 1 dock was the nearest to the munitions store. And I felt a distinct zero-hour feeling within me.

We obtained the stores from No. 1 store-room, directly opposite the dock. That meant crossing the main gallery and entering an electrically-lit tunnel, protected by sheet metal doors, that led to the store itself. These doors now stood open and the key was in the lock. It would take only a matter of a second to close the doors and lock them. That would look after the provisioning officer of U 54 and the four men who were working under him in the store. The trouble was that, though our own two guards did not present much difficulty since they had become accustomed to us and regarded us as quite harmless – it must be remembered that Logan was still a mental defective to all who knew him in the base – there were the customary two guards on the U-boat itself, one standing on the bridge and the other near the bows, as well as several men lifting the stores from the deck, where we placed them, and passing them into the submarine through an after-hatch. Even supposing we were able to deal with all these, there was still the problem of the guards to the munitions store. I had never been into this store. Only certain men were allowed in. But I had been as far as the entrance. A huge steel bulkhead had been built across the entrance in an effort to protect the base from any mishap. The door through this bulkhead was only just wide enough to take a munitions trolley. The guards were stationed one on either side of the tunnel that led off the main dock gallery just beyond No. 1 dock.

The prospect seemed hopeless. But at least we were near the munitions dump, and I was keyed up ready for a desperate attempt. But Logan made no move, even when we were joined by three more men, dressed in dungarees like ourselves. They were under a guard of two ratings and a petty officer, and were presumably Maureen Weston's miners. The guard complicated the position, for, unlike our own guards, they were watchful of the new-comers. But the miners did represent an addition to our force, especially as they looked to me about the toughest trio I had ever set eyes on. One, who seemed to be their leader, was short and bow-legged, and had a Welsh accent. The other two were undoubtedly Cornish. Whether Logan thought that their usefulness was cancelled out by the guard they had brought, I do not know, but when I asked him in a whisper if he was going to make a move, he replied: 'Not yet.'

Once we had to go to the foundry, which was right at the other end of the dock gallery, to collect the conning tower hatch, which had been fitted with a new rubber jointing ring. The activity along the whole gallery and in most of the docks was terrific, especially in docks 3 and 4. When we passed No. 4, fresh water was being run into U 21 from a mobile tank and torpedoes were being hoisted aboard from a munitions truck. Riveting had ceased, but engineers were still at work on one of the AA guns. The boat that had come into No. 3 dock the night before was being provisioned and fuelled.

Listening to the talk of the men, I found there were only two topics of conversation – the coming action and the rumour of a woman in the base. No statement had been issued about the previous day's alarm, but it seemed to be generally known that certain prisoners had arrived in the base, including a woman. Doubtless the emergency guards had passed on the information to their friends. What interested me was the effect that the unseen presence of a woman in this monastic place had on different men. Those who had been stationed on the Atlantic trade routes and at the base long before war broke out had not seen a woman now for some months. Some became sentimental and talked of their sweethearts and wives. But the majority seemed to take it as a great joke and already obscene stories, based on Maureen's presence in the base, were going the rounds. It seemed strange that I should see this stock theatrical situation actually happening in real life, especially against such a novel background.

But though a girl's presence in the base was something of a sensation, the coming action was the main topic of conversation. I realized then how similar must be the feelings of these men to my own at that moment. Zero-hour for them was somewhere about midnight. At present they were safe enough, if somewhat bored. But tonight they were leaving the safety of the base for the un-known. The chances of ever returning were not great, they knew that. And like me, probably their best chance of remaining alive rested in failure.

About eleven o'clock, when we had completed the piling of the necessary stores on the after deck of U 54, Logan and I were marched off to our usual job of emptying the latrines. Death has its compensations! When we had finished we were marched back to the docks, and joined the three new prisoners at carrying stores to U 21. The dockside seemed littered with stores of various kinds. There were cases of margarine and jam, tins of biscuits, cardboard cases full of tinned foods and packets of coffee, sugar, salt, and all sorts of other foodstuffs. The three miners had carried all this from No. 4 store and were piling it on the dockside, opposite the after-hatch. Mines were being loaded into the after-mine-laying compartments and a huge tank of oil had been brought on to the dock on a trolley. There was also a smaller tank of petrol. But refuelling operations had not yet begun.

We stood about for a time, and then several of the crew, together with the cook, arrived. The after-hatch was opened and they descended into the bowels of the submarine. We then brought a small gangway and laid it from the dockside to the submarine. Our job was to carry the stores from the dock to the submarine and lower them through the after-hatch on a rope.

It was now nearly twelve – first lunch. There were two lunch times – twelve and twelve-thirty. This made it easier for the kitchen staff when there were a large number in the base, as there were now, and at the same time enabled any rush work to be carried on without any complete stoppage for the midday meal.

We had not been carrying on this work long when, just as I was lowering a case of margarine down the hatch, I saw Logan time his arrival at a pile of cases at the same moment as the little leader of the miners arrived with the next load. I could not be sure, but I felt convinced that Logan said something to the man. I did not get an opportunity to speak to Logan for some time, but I noticed that the miners, instead of putting the cases down anyhow, were piling them on top of one another, so that they made a sort of wall of cases across the dockside.

Convinced that something was afoot, I gradually speeded up my work so that, instead of alternating with Logan, I was bringing my cases up just behind him. At last I managed it so that I put my case down on the deck of the submarine at the same time as he put his down. I had just opened my mouth to question him when he whispered: 'Stand by.'

A few minutes later orders were suddenly shouted from the main gallery. I glanced at my watch. It was midday. I looked down the length of the submarine. Men in their white uniforms were passing along the gallery in the direction of the ramp leading to the upper galleries. The docks were much quieter now and there was far less movement of men up and down the gallery at the end of the dock.

I took a quick look round at the disposition of the guards as I walked off the submarine. Our own two guards were standing chatting beside the pile of cases. One was actually leaning on them. The U-boat guard was now reduced to one and he was standing on the deck for'ard of the conning tower. The other guard was on duty inside the submarine as base personnel were now storing munitions. A munitions trolley loaded with shells was standing on the dockside. Another gangway had been thrown from the dockside to the deck of the submarine and these shells were being carried in through the for'ard hatch. At the moment the trolley, with upwards of twenty shells on it, was standing deserted on the dockside, the personnel having gone to first lunch. There remained only the miners' guard of a petty officer and two ratings.

I was now following close behind Logan and feeling uncomfortably self-conscious. Our guards were deep in conversation, with their backs half-turned to us. As we approached the pile of cases, one of them looked round. I could not believe he would not notice the air of expectation about me. We each took hold of a case of canned goods. The guard turned to answer a question the other had put. Logan carefully replaced his case. Then he straightened up. Until then I don't think I had realized how enormous his hands were. He stretched them out and took each of the guards by the throat. His body seemed to brace itself and the muscles of his arms swelled as he forced those two men silently to the ground behind the barrier of packing cases. They seemed to lose consciousness without even a kick.

'Get into his uniform,' he said, pointing to the smaller of the two men.

I did not hesitate. The die was cast now. We could not go back. And strangely enough, now that I had something to do, I did not feel in the least nervous.

Logan glanced over the boxes and then picked up a case and took it on to the deck of the submarine. Feverishly I worked at the uniform of the guard, afraid that at any moment he might become conscious again or that the miners' guard would reappear. By the time Logan was back I had got the uniform off the man. One by one he banged their heads sharply against the rock floor. I thought he had smashed their skulls, but he must have seen my look of horror, for he said: 'It's all right. Only making certain that they stay out.'

It was a matter of seconds for me to slip into the man's uniform. Logan glanced once more round the store boxes. Then he dragged the man whose uniform I had borrowed to one side and covered him with cases. Then he said: 'Step out on to the deck and call to the petty officer of the guard. His name is Kammel. Just call his name and beckon to him.'

I did as he told me. I stepped out from behind the cases. 'Herr Kammel!' I called. 'Here!' And I nodded to him with my head. He came at once and I stepped back behind the cases. Logan told me to kneel down and pretend to be examining the unconscious guard. I knelt down and supported the man's head with my arm.

The footsteps of the petty officer rang sharply on the rock as he approached. I never saw the blow, but I heard it. It was a low dull thud and was accompanied by the sound of splintering bone. I felt slightly sick as I looked up and saw Big Logan holding the man by the scruff of his neck like a puppy as he lowered his unconscious body beside the other. The man's mouth was hanging open. The jaw had obviously been broken.

There remained the two ratings. And then there was the guard still standing serenely on the deck of the submarine just in front of the conning tower. Looking over the cases, I could just see part of his uniform and his right hand. The three miners had just appeared out of the store at the end of the dock and were being escorted towards us by their guard. 'What do we do now?' I asked Logan.

'Get the guard,' he said, and bending down he removed the petty officer's revolver from its holster. 'When they come up to the cases, you be bending down over the petty officer and tell them to get hold of his legs and shoulders. Make your voice sound as though it were urgent. I'll do the rest.' He pushed the unconscious guard, who had acted as decoy for the petty officer, under the cases with his mate, and then waited, the revolver behind his back.

I bent down and lifted the petty officer's head. I waited until I heard the sound of cases being stacked and then I called out in German to the two ratings. 'The petty officer has fainted,' I said. 'Come and help me lift him.' I heard their boots on the rock behind me. I did not dare look up. It was a nasty moment. I was dressed as a rating and consequently could not give them an order.

'What's the matter with him?' asked one. He spoke with a soft Bavarian accent.

'I don't know,' I said. 'You take his feet.'

Out of the tail of my eye I saw him take hold of the petty officer's feet. But the other man remained standing, obviously expecting me to take hold of the arms. 'You take his arms,' I said, and began to unbutton the petty officer's tunic and loosen his collar.

There was a moment's hesitation, and then the man bent down and slipped his hands beneath the officer's armpits. I remember noticing that his nails were unpleasantly bitten. 'Ready?' I said. And at the same moment came the sickening thud of metal on bone. As the man holding the petty officer's feet collapsed, I straightened up and covered the other with my revolver. He was too surprised to cry out. He looked from the fallen man to me with his mouth agape, and in that second strong hands gripped him by the throat. I looked round as the man slid unconscious to the floor. The little bow-legged miner was standing over him. I got to my feet. It had all happened in a flash. When I looked over the barricade of cases, I could see no one on the dockside. The guard on the U-boat was still standing just for'ard of the conning tower.

'Get into these uniforms as quick as you can,' Logan told the three miners. 'And if any of them come round, you know what to do.' Then he nodded to me and lifted one of the cases. I followed him up the gangway, my revolver swinging from its lanyard. He lowered the case through the hatch. Then we moved quickly for'ard, the grey curved bulk of the conning tower between us and the last remaining guard.

We stopped at the after gun. 'Get him round here,' Logan whispered. 'Pretend you've discovered something wrong with the gun. Keep your face turned away from the light.'

I nodded. 'Wache!' I called. Then I repeated it. 'Wache!' There was the sound of boots on hollow steel and the ring of a rifle. Unlike our own guards, who were armed with revolvers, the ratings that provided the U-boat guards were equipped with rifles and had bayonets fixed. I pointed to the telescopic sights at the side of the gun. 'Someone seems to have broken this,' I said.

It was simple. He peered at the sight. The next second I had caught hold of him as he fell. He never made a sound as Logan hit him. We laid him out on the deck. 'Quick!' said Logan. He ran to the ladder leading to the bridge. I followed him. At the top he paused. Someone was passing along the gallery at the end of the dock. I glanced back. Our miners were now struggling into the uniforms. I looked up at Logan. He seemed very different from the friendly Cornish fisherman I had known – and very different indeed from the friendly half-wit the base had known. His face had an intent purposeful look and that huge bulk that had been a harmless spectacle to the German ratings now seemed most sinister. It seemed to me scarcely credible that the man should have dealt so silently and so swiftly with no less than four armed guards.

Logan waited until the man had passed the end of the gallery and then, in a flash, he was on the bridge, had tumbled down the conning tower hatch. I followed him. We passed the control room and moved silently forward. Both of us had our revolvers ready. Then Logan hesitated and nodded to me to go forward. We had reached a bulkhead. Beyond it I could see our last guard. He was leaning against a rack of rifles, humming to himself. I went in, my hand on my revolver. At the sound of my footsteps, he sprang to attention, thinking I was an officer. The butt of his rifle rang on the steel floor plates. 'Give me that rifle,' I said in German. And I stepped forward and grabbed hold of it. His first instinct was to obey the order, and before he had realized that Big Logan was covering him with a revolver, the weapon was in my hands.

'March him aft,' Logan said.

I gave the order and we went clattering down the gangway past the control room and the ward-room and into the storage chamber. Here three men and an officer were busy dealing with the cases that we had lowered through the hatch. They turned as we entered. They were unarmed and could do nothing.

'Tell them that I'll shoot the first man that utters a sound,' Logan said.

I told them.

'Now get up through that hatch and have all our late guards dropped down here,' Logan said to me.

I ran up that little ladder and out on to the deck again. As soon as I had signalled to the three men on the dockside to bring the bodies on board I ran for'ard and got hold of the guard we had knocked out by the after gun. When we had lowered the bodies we closed the hatch. Almost immediately the men inside were attempting to force it open. I sent two of the miners to bring the heaviest articles they could find on the dockside with which to pin it down. The largest of them, whose uniform incidentally was much too small for him, stood with me on the hatch and held it down. In a few seconds the other two returned, struggling with a small portable forge, which is part of the equipment of every submarine. It had been left against the wall of the dock and weighed several hundredweight. It was a most effective weight and we placed it on the hatch. Then the miner I had detailed to mount guard went for'ard.

By this time I was beginning to get anxious about Logan, who had not yet reappeared. I felt at any moment men might come on to the dock. Moreover, there was the possibility that the men in the store-room at the end of the dock might get curious as to why the prisoners were no longer collecting the cases. I hurried for'ard to the conning tower. As I climbed the ladder to the bridge, Logan's head appeared in the hatch. He carried a light machine-gun and several magazines. 'Get that trolley alongside the gun,' he said.

'Are they the right shells?' I asked.

'I don't know,' was his reply. 'We'll have to see.'

I signalled to the men aft and jumped on to the dockside. I walked down to where the munitions trolley stood. The little bow-legged miner seemed intelligent, for he appeared to understand what I was up to, and he and his companion, the big man who had helped me hold the hatch down, brought the gangway along. The iron wheels of the trolley clattered noisily as I dragged it along the dock.

Suddenly there was a shout from behind me and I spun round, my hand moving automatically to my revolver. A man was standing in the doorway of the store-room. 'What have you done with those damned prisoners?' he shouted. Someone passing along the gallery stopped to see what the trouble was.

I thought we were for it. 'The lieutenant wants them to clear this pile of cases off the dock before they bring any more,' I shouted back to him in German. 'And he wants these shells got off the dock.'

The man hesitated, and then shrugged his shoulders. 'Well, hurry up,' he grumbled. 'It's nearly lunchtime.' He went back into the store-room and the man who had paused in the gallery continued on his way. I thanked God for my knowledge of German and dragged the trolley level with the gun.

By this time the two miners had placed the gangway in position and we each took a shell up on to the deck of the submarine. Big Logan was already bending over the gun. As I climbed up on the deck, I saw the muzzle of it slowly falling as Logan sighted it on the far end of the main cave. As I reached him he flung the breech open. I slipped the shell in. It fitted perfectly. He closed the breech and straightened his back. 'There we are,' he said. 'Everything ship-shape and ready to fire. All you have to do now is pull that lanyard.' He pointed to the trigger lanyard. 'Then you fling open the breech – so. The used shell falls out, in with the next and fire.'

The two miners put their shells down beneath the gun.

'Do you know how to fire a machine-gun?' Logan asked them.

'We were both in the last war,' replied the little bow-legged one, whom I later discovered to be Alf Davies, one-time foreman at the Wheal Garth.

'All right.' Logan turned to me. 'Will you take charge?' he

said. 'There are rifles, hand-grenades and any other weapons you fancy in the submarine where we found that guard. Get what you want. Fire the gun only when there is no chance of holding the dock any longer. But it must be fired. I'm going to collect that girl.'

I said: 'Don't be a fool, Logan. You haven't a hope.'

'I've got the key,' he said. 'I'm still daft, remember. I think I'll get away with it.'

'Anyway, what's the good of bringing her down here?' I demanded. 'It's certain death.'

'That's where you're wrong,' he said. 'There's just a chance. I found three engineers in the engine-room and I've shut them in. All we've got to do is flood the dock and float the submarine out stern first. The tide is only about an hour on the turn. If we hurry we'll just be able to do it. Once out in the main cave we submerge and get out through the undersea entrance under our own power.'

'Good God, what a chance!' I exclaimed, thinking of the masses of complicated machinery with which the boat was filled. 'There isn't a hope.'

'Maybe not, but can you suggest anything else?' he asked. 'The mine is blocked, remember.'

I couldn't, and he jumped on to the dockside. I watched him walk down it, apparently quite calm, and disappear into the gallery. I told Alf Davies to man the gun and took the big miner up on to the bridge and down through the conning tower hatch. Well, I thought to myself, I suppose we're lucky to have any sort of a chance at all. After all, I had been expecting to try to blow myself and every one else into the next world. But I must say I did not relish the idea of trying to manœuvre the submarine out through the underwater mouth of the cave under her own power with only three men on board who knew anything about the works, and unwilling men at that. Our only hope was that they were not all the heroic type.

I led the way for'ard to the magazine room. It was the hand-grenades I was after. I had the germ of an idea at the back of my mind. At that moment I don't think it was conscious. But it was sufficiently strong to direct me towards the grenades. We took up four each in our pockets, two rifles and a box of ammunition between us. We brought our haul out and laid it on the deck beside the gun. Then I looked at my watch. It was one-twenty-five. Another five minutes and first lunch would be over. Surely Logan ought to be back by now? But he had to get up to the top gallery. If the guard-room door were open he might have to bide his time.

At that moment there was a shout from the end of the dock. 'Wache! Send those bastards down here to collect these cases.' I poked my head round the conning tower. The same man was standing in the tunnel leading down to the store-room. 'They'll come as soon as they've packed the stuff away up here,' I replied. Then my heart sank. An officer had appeared, and I recognized him as the commander of U 21. He stopped and spoke to the man in the entrance to the store. The fellow pointed to the pile of cases on the deck and shrugged his shoulders. The commander nodded and came striding down the dockside. 'Get behind that gun,' I said. I dragged the rifles and the machine-gun out of sight. Then the two miners and myself crouched down, waiting.

The commander paused by the gangway. He looked up at the man mounting guard just for'ard of the conning tower, who had not moved a muscle, and then back at the gangway. I could just see his face between the mountings of the gun. He was puzzled by the position of the gangway. At length he stepped aboard and went aft. I picked up a rifle which I had loaded. I pushed forward the safety catch with my thumb. We were for it now. He would see the forge lying over the hatch. I left my hiding-place and moved quickly after him, my rifle ready. He bent over the forge. Then he began to shift it. I was about fifty feet from him. I put one knee to the deck and raised the rifle to my shoulder. 'You're covered,' I said in German. 'Put your hands behind your back and keep still.'

He swung round, and without a second's hesitation his hand went to his revolver. The choice was his. I pulled the trigger. The explosion in that confined space seemed deafening. His hand suddenly checked as it touched his holster, then his knees began to sag. I did not wait to see if he were dead. But as I raced for'ard I heard him slump to the deck. 'Man that gun,' I ordered.

Davies took his place beside the gun as I ran up. 'Hand-grenades,' I panted to the other miner. 'You look after No. 3 dock. I'll look after No. 5. We've got to block the gallery both sides.' He dived for the grenades, and despite his bulk had jumped on to the dock in a flash.

I picked up three grenades and followed him. I had dropped my rifle, but my revolver was still hanging round my neck by its lanyard. As we raced along the dock several men came running down the gallery. Two went past in the direction of No. 5 dock. But three more paused and came running to meet us. Fortunately they were ratings and therefore not armed. I fired, and though I had not aimed at any of them, they broke and ran. I was not accustomed to a revolver and I found the kick unexpectedly powerful.

Men had by now appeared in the entrance to the store-room. But they, too, were unarmed and drew back into the tunnel. We had almost reached the end of the dock now and I had drawn level with my miner. And at that moment I saw that one of the guards from No. 3 dock had appeared. But he held his rifle uncertainly, put out by our uniforms. 'Get back!' I yelled in German. 'Guard your own dock. It's mutiny.'

He did as I had ordered. But when we came to the gallery itself we found that he and two other guards were now standing across the gallery leading to No. 3 dock with their rifles at the ready. 'Okay,' I said to my companions. 'Out with the pins and let 'em have it.' I left him to look after the three guards whilst I took the gallery between our own and No. 5 dock. I could see men coming from the other docks and out of the store-rooms farther along the gallery. I think we both tossed our grenades into the gallery at about the same time, for we were both running together with bullets singing past our ears and shrieking as they ricocheted off the walls.

Then came a terrific roar. And then another. The ground shook under our feet and a blast of hot air sent us both sprawling. My face hit the rocky surface of the dockside only half-protected by my upflung arm and I felt the blood warm in my nose. There was a horrible splitting noise as the rock began to crack. We clambered to our feet and staggered forward. And at the same moment there was a splitting and a rumbling behind us. I turned to see the whole roof of the gallery between our dock and No. 3 collapse. One moment I could see the white uniforms of the guards as they turned to run, and the next instant there was just a tumbled heap of rocks half-invisible in a cloud of dust.

My companion stumbled to his feet. There was a nasty cut across his left eye. The dust was beginning to clear now and I could see that the gallery leading to No. 3 dock was completely blocked. But I could not see what had happened to the right, between our own dock and No. 5, except that a whole lot of debris had spilled on to the floor of the gallery where it passed the end of our dock.

I ran back down the dock, a hand-grenade ready in my hand. The force of the explosion had broken most of the electric-light bulbs. But in the half-dark I was just able to see the white uniform of an officer, as he appeared up the tunnel from the store-room. The beam of a torch almost blinded me. 'What's happened?' he asked, mistaking me for one of the base guards. Then I suppose he saw the grenade in my hand, for he said: 'What are you up to?' I had no alternative. I pulled the pin out, threw it into the tunnel in which he stood and ducked sideways. The bullet from his revolver sang past my head. A second later there was a flash and a great rumbling explosion. By one of those freak chances his torch remained alight and as it fell, it showed up for an instant the tunnel. The whole roof seemed to crumble. For an instant it actually hung suspended with small pieces of rock pouring from it. Then it came rumbling down and the whole scene went black.

I pulled the emergency torch that the guards always carried from my pocket and switched it on. The place was an absolute ruin. The whole of the end of the dock was just a pile of split and broken rock. Most of it was limestone, and it was then that I consciously realized why I had wanted the grenades. I had the limestone and there on the dock, behind me, was the oil storage tank and the smaller petrol tank. There was no chance of any one attacking us from this end for some time. I knew we had nothing to fear from the direction of No. 3 dock. Probably in all there were not more than twenty or thirty men working on docks 1, 2 and 3, including those in the munitions and fuel stores. They were trapped there, and the only means they had of rejoining the main body of the base was by swimming across the open ends of the docks. The danger would come from the direction of No. 5 dock. If only I had been able to block the ramp leading from the upper galleries! But I hadn't, and the whole personnel of the base would now be streaming into docks 5, 6 and 7. I listened. Between the intermittent sound of crumbling rock I could hear shouts and the murmur of voices coming from the open end of the dock. I clambered over the debris of rock and examined the fall between our own and No. 5 dock in the light of my torch. Where the gallery had been was solid rock from floor to ceiling. I reckoned that it would take them several hours to clear it sufficiently to attack us from this side, even using mobile drills to break down the large pieces of rock.

Having satisfied myself that we could not be taken in the rear, I scrambled back over the debris and rejoined the big miner. In an endeavour to wipe the blood from his eyes he had smeared his whole face with it. 'Come on!' I said, 'we've got to move the machine-gun up to the stern of the submarine.' My orders were entirely automatic. I had been over the whole thing so many

times in my own mind that I knew exactly what to do. But I had
lost all sense of reality. I had involuntarily slipped into the war
mentality. When I had thrown the grenade at the stores officer he
had been just a target, not a human being. It was the first time I
had killed a man.

We ran back to the gangway and rejoined Davies and the other
miner. They were both standing by the gun. Davies I told to
remain with the gun. Briefly I explained the necessity of its being
fired before we were overwhelmed. Then I and the big miner,
whose name was Kevan, picked up the light machine-gun and
carried it aft. The third miner, Trevors, followed with the
magazines, a rifle and several grenades.

We rigged the gun up in the stern of the U-boat and stacked
round it several cases of canned goods to act as a barricade. Then
Trevors, who had been a machine-gunner in the last war, got
down and fired a burst to make certain that the gun was in
working order. It was. The clatter of it seemed to fill the cave.
What is more, he hit his mark, which had been the top of the
haulage gear buoy floating in the main cave. The bullets made a
hollow sound as they struck the huge round cylinder and then
ricocheted off to finish with a dull thwack against the sides of the
cave.

As soon as I was certain that he could handle the gun satisfactorily, I took Kevan and ran back along the submarine to the
conning tower. My aim was to get sufficient arms to ensure that
we should be able to hold the end of the dock long enough for me
to carry out my plan. It was the only chance – flimsy though it
was – of our re-establishing contact with Logan and Maureen and
of getting out of the base. There was no chance now of slipping out
on the high tide and attempting to run the submarine through the
undersea exit on her engines. As soon as we were out in the main
cave we should be under the fire of the other submarines in the
base and, before we had a chance to submerge, we should be
sunk. True, that would probably achieve our object of blocking
the undersea exit. But the plan I had in mind would achieve that
and at the same time give us all a chance of escape.

Altogether we made four trips to the magazine of the submarine.
The first thing we brought up was another light machine-gun,
four magazines and some more hand-grenades. These we carried
aft. Before going back for further arms, I made Trevors experiment with the changing of the magazines. It didn't take him long
to find out how they worked and after seeing him fire a test burst
from his gun, we returned to the submarine. Thereafter we

brought up another light machine-gun, which we placed beside Davies at his post by the gun, four automatic rifles together with the necessary magazines and a further supply of grenades.

As we came up with the last load the soft chug-chug of the little diesel-engined tug could be heard. We raced aft, and at the same moment Trevors opened fire with his machine-gun. We had covered about half the distance when I saw a small dark object hurtle through the air. It dropped into the water just abaft the stern of U 21, and almost immediately a big column of water was thrown up and was followed by a muffled roar.

We flung ourselves down behind the packing cases and Kevan took over the spare machine-gun. I picked up an automatic rifle. The deck was very wet and Trevors was soaked. It was clear what they had tried to do. If they could cause a heavy fall of rock at the entrance to the dock they could trap us completely. Their difficulty was that they could not hit the entrance to the dock without exposing themselves to our fire. Nevertheless, the underwater explosion of the grenade they had thrown had apparently damaged the flood gates of the dock, for I could hear the water gurgling below us as it entered the dock. As far as I could tell the tide was about an hour beyond the high.

The engine of the tug sounded very close now. The boat was in fact off the entrance to No. 5 dock and was only protected by the buttress of rock that separated the two docks. The tug's engines seemed suddenly to rev up. Trevors reached for a grenade. He had the pin out the instant the boat's nose showed beyond the buttress. I knelt on one knee and raised my automatic rifle, sighting it over the top of our protecting pile of packing cases. The boat, with its propeller threshing the water into a foam at its stern, seemed to shoot out from the cover of the buttress.

I sighted my rifle and pulled the trigger. It was like holding a pneumatic drill to one's shoulder as it pumped out a steady stream of bullets. I heard the clatter of Kevan's machine-gun at my side and sensed rather than saw Trevor's arm swing as he threw the grenade. The man at the wheel of the boat collapsed under our fire and another in the bows stopped dead in the act of throwing a grenade and crumpled up in the bottom of the boat. Almost immediately there was a terrific explosion and the boat seemed to split in half. It sank instantly, leaving a mass of wreckage, oil and three dead bodies on the surface of the water.

It was not a pleasant sight. Kevan said: 'Good for you, Steve.' But Trevors shook his head. 'Mine fell short,' he said. 'It was one of you two shooting that fellow in the bows that done it. He had the pin out when you hit him and the grenade exploded right in the bottom of the boat.'

At that moment we came under machine-gun fire from dock No. 7 But the shooting was wild, the reason being that the last explosion had put the remaining lights in our dock out. Shortly afterwards, however, they rigged up a searchlight. We then moved farther back into the dock. It was the only thing to do. They might risk casualties, but we daren't. We built a second barricade of packing cases, this time in a complete semi-circle across the deck, for we were being worried by the ricochet of bullets from the side of the cave. The trouble was that because the seven docks branched off fan-shape from the main cave, it was possible for the Germans operating from No. 7 to cover the mouth of our own dock.

I called up Davies to the shelter of our new barricade and we held a council of war. Then I explained my plan. 'It may work or it may not,' I said. 'We'll just have to risk it. Unless any of you have any other ideas?' But none of them had. We were trapped and it was only a matter of time before we would be overwhelmed. We were four against at least six hundred, and if we surrendered we should be shot. 'We can't hold this dock a minute if they float a submarine out before the tide falls,' I said. 'One shot from a six-inch gun at the mouth of this dock will trap us if it doesn't kill us. If they miss the tide, however, we may be able to hold out for as long as ten hours.'

'Whatever happens,' I went on, 'we've got to block the entrance to this base.' I then told them of the plan to attack a squadron of British capital ships which it was known would be for a time insufficiently screened by destroyers. I said: 'I suggest we proceed straight away with the demolition of the underwater entrance.'

To this they agreed. Even if they missed the tide I was afraid that under cover of fire from No. 7 dock they might try to block the entrance of our dock with grenades thrown from the collapsible rubber boats that the U-boats carried. I explained this and Trevors volunteered to go aft again and extinguish the light of the search-light with machine-gun fire. But I said: 'Wait until we've fired this gun.'

3

SURPRISE

I LEFT Davies to operate the gun and climbed up to the bridge of U 21. I switched on the U-boat's searchlight and swung it round, so that its brilliant beam was shining straight aft and illuminating the whole of the main cave. Towards the seaward end the roof sloped down until it disappeared below the level of the water, which showed black and oily in the bright light.

'Is it sighted correctly?' I asked.

'All correct,' replied Davies.

I braced myself against the rail of the bridge. 'Fire!' I said.

I saw Davies pull the trigger lanyard. Instantly there was a terrific explosion. I was practically thrown off my feet and I heard the hull plates of the U-boat grate most horribly on the rock of the empty dock. Almost simultaneously there was a blinding flash in the roof of the main cave, just where it disappeared below the water, and an explosion that seemed, in that confined space, to numb my whole body. A great wind of hot air struck my face and, in the light of the searchlight, I saw the whole far end of the cave collapse in a deep rumbling roar.

As a sight it was terrific. I had not fully realized the explosive power of a six-inch shell. The dock in which the U 21 lay was at least a hundred and fifty yards from the spot where the shell struck. Yet I could feel the whole of the rock round me tremble and vibrate, and quite large pieces of rock fell from the roof of our dock, making a hollow sound as they struck the submarine's deck. At least thirty yards of the main cave had collapsed. Huge masses of rock fell into the water, and as they fell a great wave rose in the basin. I yelled out to the others to hold tight. I don't think they heard, but they saw it coming – a great wall of water that surged down the main cave and swept up into the dock. It must have been a good ten feet high, for it swept into the empty dock almost at deck height. The submarine reared up on it like a horse as it suddenly floated. I had fallen flat on the bridge of the conning tower, and as the submarine lifted, I heard the rail strike the roof just above my head and the searchlight went out. Then the bows jarred violently against the end of the dock.

At any moment I expected to be crushed to death. But after bucking up and down for a moment, grating sickeningly against the sides of the dock, the submarine settled down again, this time afloat. Through my singing ears I heard the water running out through the damaged flood gates of the dock. I scrambled to my feet. The place was as dark as pitch and I could hear shouts and cries. 'Are you all right, Mr Craig?' someone called out from the direction of the gun.

'Yes,' I replied. 'Are you?' And without waiting for his reply I hurried down the conning tower ladder. I paused at the bottom in order to accustom my eyes to the dark. There was a faint luminosity at the end of the dock. Presumably not all the lights of the base had been extinguished by the explosion. Around me everything was black with darkness, but where the dock ran out into the main cave there was a half-circle of indefinite light. Against this I could just make out the dark bulk of the gun and figures moving about it.

I suddenly remembered my torch. I pulled it out of my pocket and switched it on. The faces of the there miners looked white as they faced the light. But they seemed all right. Fortunately the water had not swept over the deck, so that, though they were all soaked with the water that had slopped up between the submarine and the dock walls, the machine-gun, rifles and ammunition were still beside the gun.

Armed with automatic rifles we went aft. The forge was still in position over the after hatch, but the water had swept right over the stern of the submarine and our barricades of packing cases had been swept away. The deck seemed strewn with tins and lumps of rock, and the dockside, which was still awash, was dotted with packing cases.

One of the machine-guns had fetched up against the deck stanchions. We retrieved this. The other was missing. The magazines were where we had left them and we were able to retrieve one of the automatic rifles from the dockside. Hastily we rebuilt our barricade of packing cases. This was not an easy task as both gangways had been smashed to pieces and most of the cases had to be passed up from the dockside and dragged up the sloping sides of the submarine by rope.

However, ten minutes' work saw our barricade complete again. All the grenades appeared to have rolled overboard, so I paid another visit to the magazine of the submarine. It was whilst I was getting the grenades from their racks that I noticed the crew's escape apparatus. It was much the same as the Davis equipment

147

used in British submarines and they were stacked in a large rack of their own. I picked up one of them. It had a face mask and a large air bag which strapped round the waist. A small cylinder of oxygen completed the equipment. It was in fact just what I required.

I hurried on deck with the grenades to find the main cave brilliantly lit. The submarine in No. 6 dock had switched on its searchlight. Then I understood the reason for the cries and shouts. On the black oily surface of the water that was still slopping about in the main cave bobbed three collapsible rubber boats, two of them floating upside down.

'They were just going to launch an attack when we fired that gun,' I said, nodding in the direction of the boats, as I put the grenades down on the deck behind the packing cases.

Kevan said: 'Ar, we'll be able to hawld this place faw sawm tame naw.'

'How do you mean?' I asked.

'They'll nawt be able to get the bawts awt naw. Dawn't ye feel us grainding on the bottom of the dawck?'

He was right. I had been too busy to notice it. Though the water had flooded the dock, the tide had receded sufficiently for the hull of the submarine to be just touching the bottom.

'Thank God for that!' I said. They had lost their chance. Our worst danger had been postponed. We had ten hours' grace so far as attack from another submarine went. Then and there I decided that, if the worst came to the worst and my own scheme failed, we would try to get our own boat out before the others and go down fighting rather than face a firing squad. It seemed easy to face death now that we were in action. I wondered what had happened to Logan.

Having completed our barricade, I left Davies and Trevors to hold the end of the dock and took Kevan down on to the dockside. The water had receded now. By the wall we found picks and shovels that had been used the previous day for erecting the derrick. We took these to the end of the dock, where the gallery had been blocked, and set to work to clear a space in the midst of the debris. We kept our automatic rifles handy in case the open end of the dock should be attacked.

Mostly we did the work with our hands, advancing steadily into the debris and piling the rocks behind us. It was a gigantic task and I was thankful that the work I had had to do in the fortnight I had been at the base had hardened my muscles. Even so, I found that Kevan, despite the fact that he had been unemployed for a considerable time, worked just about twice as fast as I was able to.

Half an hour passed and the basin I was trying to hollow out in the debris was beginning to take shape. We worked in silence and without pause. The constant stooping to throw out great lumps of limestone soon made my back ache abominably. We had climbed high on to the pile of fallen rock and were tossing the broken lumps out behind us so that the rim of the basin behind gradually rose. It was slow and hard work. Not only did my back and arms ache, but we were both constantly coughing with the rock dust.

At the end of half an hour, as though by common consent, we straightened our backs, and took a breather. I looked at my watch. It was just past three. I was standing now behind a huge circular rampart of rock. The roof, all jagged and looking very unsafe, was about ten feet above my head. On three sides of us the broken limestone was piled right to the roof. Only in the direction of the docks did the rock fall away, and here we were piling it up in order to make a kind of rock tank. This rampart had grown by now practically as tall as ourselves. I looked over it and along to the open end of the dock. The searchlight was still flooding the main cave and the light from it glistened on the wet walls of the dock and threw the conning tower of the submarine into black silhouette. The great dark shape of the boat seemed to fill the whole cave, and at the far end I could see our barricade of packing cases. I could see no sign of Davies and Trevors, however, for they lay in the shadow cast by the cases.

As I bent to resume my work, I saw Kevan standing tense at my side, listening. There was the sound of slipping rock, and then voices. It came from behind the fall that blocked the gallery between ourselves and No. 5 dock. Then came the unmistakable ring of metal on stone. 'They're trying to clear the fall,' said Kevan.

'How long will it take?' I asked.

He looked at the fall. The whole gallery had been blocked. 'Depends on the depth,' he said. 'I reckon it'll take them all of a good hour.'

'Good!' I said. 'By then we'll have finished this. Then we'll wait for them to come through. The draught will help.'

We resumed our work. But about ten minutes later the whole place suddenly resounded to the clatter of machine-gun fire. It came from the open end of the dock. In an instant we were over the rampart of stone we had been piling up, had collected our automatic rifles and were running as hard as we could along the dockside.

There was a muffled explosion and a column of water shot up just abaft the stern of the submarine. We clambered on to the deck of the submarine and as I ran down it, I saw a figure half-rise from behind the barricade of packing cases and an instant later there was a loud roar and lumps of rock fell from the roof of the main cave into the water. At the same instant the searchlight was switched off.

We threw ourselves down behind the packing cases, our rifles ready. 'What's happened?' I panted.

'They had rigged up a raft,' replied Davies. 'There were several of them protected by packing cases. They had automatic rifles and one of them was flinging grenades. But Trevors got them with one of his grenades. Blew the whole raft apart.'

'Good work!' I said. 'Do you think you could hold them off for another half-hour, Trevors?' I asked.

There was no reply.

I put out my hand to where he lay behind his machine-gun. My hand touched his face. It was resting against one of the packing cases and it was warm and sticky. I screened my torch with my hands and switched it on. His muscular little body was crumpled up beside his gun, the back of his head resting on the protruding corner of a packing case. His blue unshaven jaw hung open, and his jacket was sodden with blood. A bullet had caught him in the throat.

I felt a sudden sickening sensation inside me. One out of four. There were only three of us now. Trevors had stood up in order to make sure of his aim. At the sacrifice of his own life he had demolished the raft. But there would be another raft and another. I said: 'We've got to get on with that job quickly. Can you finish off that basin, Kevan? It wants to be at least three feet deeper. I'll stay here with Davies and hold the fort.'

I heard him scramble to his feet. 'Give me a shout,' I said, 'when it's complete.' I gave him my torch and saw his big figure outlined against its light hurry back down the deck of the submarine.

Then Davies and I and the dead Trevors settled down to wait for the next attack. The searchlight had been switched on again and in its light I saw a German rating dive into the oily waters of the main cave and rescue a man who was injured and drowning. He was the sole survivor of the crew of the raft. Swimming steadily on his back and holding the injured man's head between his hands, the German disappeared into the neighbouring dock. Then the searchlight was switched off again. Three pools of light marked the entrances to docks 5, 6 and 7. Then one by one these were extinguished. To the left of our own dock everything was in complete darkness. To the right, however, docks 1, 2 and 3 still showed a faint glow of light.

Suddenly a voice shouted in German: 'Put those lights out over there.' The order was repeated several times. Then one by one the lights of these three docks were switched off. We were plunged into total darkness. It seemed to press down on us like a curtain. We could see nothing, not even the cases in front of us.

'They are going to try attacking in the dark,' whispered Davies.

'We'll just have to listen for them,' I said.

'Why wait for Kevan to deepen the basin?' he asked. 'Why not get on with your scheme right away?'

'It's no use doing it by halves,' I said. 'Once we get it going there's no possibility of feeding the fire.'

So we lay there in the dark and the minutes slipped slowly by. Gradually my ears accustomed themselves to all the various sounds in the docks. It was difficult to distinguish them, for they merged into each other to form a peculiar bustling murmuring sound. But occasionally I could pick out words of comamnd and the sound of boots on rock, and from No. 5 dock came the persistent sound of tumbling rock as they worked to clear the fall and get through into our own dock.

It was an eerie business, lying there waiting for heaven knew what. I kept on mistaking the movement of the water for the sound of a raft being paddled towards us. I found myself praying desperately that Kevan would finish the work before the attack was launched. But I knew it must take him a full half-hour working on his own, and as I lay watching the luminous dial of my wristwatch the minutes seemed to tick by incredibly slowly. A quarter of an hour passed by. Once I raised my rifle and was on the point of firing. But it was nothing. The darkness was absolutely impenetrable. Twenty minutes. Then we heard a new sound, a sound of hammering.

'They're making another raft,' whispered Davies.

At that moment my eyes were attracted by the flickering of a torch from the far end of our own dock. Kevan wanted me. 'I shan't be long,' I said to Davies, and screening a torch, which I had removed from Trevors, I hurried along the deck of the submarine. As soon as I could, I jumped down on to the dock and began to run.

Kevan met me by the oil tank. He said: 'They're almost through the fall.' I could hear the sound of shifting rocks quite clearly.

'Okay,' I said, 'let's pump the oil in.'

There was no time to see whether the basin in the limestone was sufficiently deep. We took hold of the oil tank and dragged it on its trolley to the edge of the debris. Then, while Kevan took the canvas pipe across the debris and laid it over the rampart of rocks so that the nozzle hung down into the basin, I ran back for the smaller petrol tank. Each tank was fitted with a hand pump, and Kevan was already pumping the oil into the basin by the time I had got the pipe of the petrol tank into position. In the light of my torch I could see the black crude oil pouring down amongst the rocks. At the same time I was uncomfortably aware of the sound of voices and falling rocks in the direction of No. 5 dock. At any moment I expected the Germans to break through.

I scrambled back to the petrol tank and began pumping, thankful to have my automatic rifle beside me. When the guage told me I had half-emptied the tank, I went over to help Kevan. The oil tank was still nearly three-quarters full.

I found that Kevan had no need of my assistance, so I looked around and found a length of iron piping and some rags. I tied the rags round one end of the piping and then dipped them first in oil and then petrol. The resultant torch I put down on top of the oil tank. By this time the sound of the Germans coming through the fall was becoming much louder, until by the murmur of their voices I was quite certain that they had broached it.

Kevan straightened his back. The oil tank was empty. I played my torch over the rampart of rock. It seemed to be holding the oil quite satisfactorily. Then, quite distinctly, I heard an exclamation in German. Evidently they had seen the light. Kevan had started the pump of the petrol tank. I could hear the liquid pouring out into the basin. I raised my automatic rifle to cover the spot where the Germans would emerge.

At that moment there was a burst of machine-gun fire from the open end of the dock. I glanced round. Was it another attack? There was no light at all. After the one burst there was silence. Perhaps Davies had made a mistake? Then, faintly, came the sound of Davies's voice speaking. I could not hear what he said, but I was convinced he was speaking to the Germans in the next dock. 'Hurry!' I said to Kevan.

'Nearly finished,' he replied.

Then echoing down the dock came Davies's voice. 'Mr Craig!

Mr Craig!' There was a note of urgency in it.

I took the matches from my pocket and thrust them into Kevan's hand. 'Light the torch and throw it into the basin as soon as you're ready,' I said. 'But for God's sake don't let them get through first.'

'Ar, I'll see to it.' He took the matches, never pausing in his pumping, and I ran down the dock as hard as I could.

'Mr Craig!' Davies's voice again. I clambered on to the deck of the submarine. My shoes rang hollow on the steel plates. At last I put out my torch and felt my way forward to the packing cases. 'What is it?' I asked as I threw myself down beside Davies.

'They've got Miss Weston and your friend Logan.'

'Well?'

'They say they've got them bound and are going to use them as a shield for a machine-gunner unless we surrender. I asked them to wait so that I could consult you.'

At that moment the searchlight of the submarine in the next dock was switched on. Then I understood. Floating just off the entrance to No. 5 dock was a raft, and strapped to it in a kneeling position were Maureen Weston and Big Logan. They were kneeling side by side, and between them poked the muzzle of a machine-gun. It was quite impossible for us to fire at the gunner behind without hitting them. I saw Big Logan's huge body rigid with the effort of trying to tear himself clear of his bonds. The sweat was glistening on his broad forehead and his long brown hair was lank. Maureen looked quite fresh, but the position in which she was held was obviously most uncomfortable. The raft was slowly moving towards us, propelled, I imagine, by at least two ratings swimming in the rear.

'Will you surrender? Or will you risk the lives of your friends?' I recognized the voice as that of Commodore Thepe.

'What are the conditions?' I asked to gain time.

'There will be no conditions,' was the sharp reply.

'Don't be a bloody fool,' said Logan. 'They're going to shoot you.' I saw an arm move from behind him and his body jerked at the sudden pain of a jab from a bayonet.

'You stick to your guns, Walter,' Maureen said. 'Don't worry about us. We'll be shot anyway.'

At that moment I heard the sound of a shot from the dock behind me. I turned to see the distant figure of Kevan stagger, the torch I had left with him blazing in his hand. In the light of it I could just see the figure of a German high up on the rocks above the basin. Then Kevan's arm swung and the blazing torch sailed in a perfect arc into the rock basin. There was an instantaneous flash that lit up the whole dock as the petrol lying on top of the crude oil ignited. Then the whole of the end of the dock seemed suddenly ablaze. What happened to the Germans coming through over the fall from No. 5 dock I cannot imagine. The heat must have been terrific, and the flames were immediately drawn through the gap by the draught. The sound of the flames came down the dock like the roar of a mighty wind. And against their intense light I could see the big ungainly figure of Kevan come stumbling down the dockside, his shadow flickering along the wall of the dock in front of him.

And at that moment the machine-gunner on the raft opened fire on us. I told Davies to make a dash for it. He hesitated an instant, crouching behind the packing cases. Then he darted out and ran as hard as he could down the deck of the submarine. I heard his boots ringing on the deck plates as I opened fire with our own machine-gun. I aimed to the side of the raft, well clear of Maureen and Logan, but it was sufficient to keep the gunner's attention from Davies long enough for him to get into the dock, out of the line of fire.

Almost consciously I forced myself not to think of the possibilities I faced. I had to get for'ard to the conning tower. I bunched my legs up under me and then jumped to my feet and started running as hard as I could down the deck. The light of the flames made it quite easy to see my way without a torch. I remember consciously thinking how little time had passed, for, as I started to run, I saw Kevan's figure still running towards us along the dockside.

Bullets began to whistle to the left of me and I was uncomfortably aware of the persistent clatter of the machine-gun behind me. The gunner had been prepared for my dash and he had swung his gun on me almost before I had broken cover.

I learned later from Maureen that I owed my life at this moment to Logan. As I rose from behind the packing cases he made a superhuman effort to shift himself sufficiently to upset the aim of the gun. He just managed to touch the gun with his elbow and so shift it out of alignment. This occurred, I suppose, just as the gunner swung his gun towards me, for I had not run more than a few yards when I received what felt like a violent kick in the left arm, accompanied immediately by a sharp pain. After that the bullets went wide, and in a few seconds I passed out of the gunner's line of sight.

I saw Kevan struggling on to the deck of the submarine. He

seemed unable to use his right arm, and by the dancing light of the flames I could see the sweat glistening on his face. Davies was standing irresolute at the foot of the conning tower. 'Get inside,' I yelled. He began to swarm up the ladder to the bridge. Kevan reached it just before I did. I followed him up, but when I tried to grasp the rails of the ladder I cried out with the sudden pain in my left arm. The forearm was broken just above the wrist and was bleeding fast.

With my right arm I pulled myself up the ladder. From the bridge of the conning tower I took one brief glance round. In the lurid light, I could just make out a corner of the raft as it slowly approached the end of the dock. At the other end, our improvised tank of oil and petrol was burning furiously. Then I tumbled down the conning tower hatch and closed it after me, fastening it on the inside.

Coming down from the conning tower, I found Davies bandaging Kevan's shoulder. There was a nasty wound just near the arm joint. I ran quickly aft to the store-room bulkhead. I dragged the bulkhead back. The imprisoned Germans were sitting on the packing cases. They sprang up as the door opened. I covered them with my revolver. 'Put your hands above your heads,' I said in German. I backed down the gangway, keeping them covered. 'Follow me!' I backed as far as the engine-room hatch. 'Open that!' I ordered the officer.

He turned back the lever and pulled the hatch open. 'Now get down there – all of you,' I ordered. I saw the officer hesitate, weighing up his chances. 'Wache!' I called. Then I said: 'Get down there.' My call for the guard seemed to settle him, for he went through the hatch and the other followed him. I closed it and fastened it. Then I went back into the store-room. As I climbed the ladder to the hatch I heard the sound of boots moving stealthy along the deck above my head. I fastened the hatch. Then I went for'ard to see about the hatch through which the munitions had been lowered. By the time I had climbed up and fastened this I was feeling pretty faint. Walking back along the gangway, I found myself following a trail of my own blood.

I arrived back in the control room to find Kevan just easing his shoulder into his jacket. 'Better?' I asked. Davies turned at the sound of my voice and then exclaimed: 'Good God in heaven, Mr Craig! Whatever is the matter with you?'

I pointed to my left arm. 'Do you think you can manage a tourniquet?'

'Why, yes, indeed.'

He took my coat off, rolled my sleeve back and then with a strip of material torn from his shirt, he bound my arm just above the elbow. 'You'll want a splint too,' he said, and broke a heavy chart ruler in half. I then spent a most painful five minutes. The force of the bullet had pushed the bone out of place so that splinters were showing through the mess of blood and broken skin. I think I passed out twice whilst Davies was resetting it. 'Lucky it is you are with a miner, Mr Craig,' Davies said, as he bandaged it into place against the splints. 'It's not every one that knows how to set a broken limb properly, is it now?'

I agreed that it wasn't, and sat down on the chart table, feeling rather uncertain of my legs. 'What do we do now?' asked Davies.

'Wait. Just wait,' I said. 'And pray that they don't get into the submarine before the fire had got properly to work on the lime-stone.'

We stayed in the control room for some time, listening to the sound of footsteps overhead. I could imagine the puzzlement of the Germans. What would they think? One minute we are holding the dock, and the next a huge fire is blazing and we have disappeared inside the submarine. I could imagine the raft plying to and fro between our dock and No. 5 bringing more and more men on to the scene. What would they do about the fire? Would they try to put it out? Even if they had been able to get their fire-fighting equipment into our dock, they hadn't a hope of ex-tinguishing it.

'Let's examine the oxygen supply,' I said. I was feeling a little better now. But the submarine was getting very hot. I could imagine the terrific heat of that fire reddening the bow plates. If we were forced to stay in the submarine any length of time it would become a death trap – a positive oven.

We found the oxygen supply equipment. Davies seemed to know how it worked. It looked very complicated to me. Footsteps kept running backwards and forwards over our heads. It was very eerie in that submarine. All movements on deck came to us as hollow sounds. Very faintly we could hear the sound of voices. The air was already beginning to get stale. I knew we could not have already used up the available air, so I presumed that some of the CO_2 given off by the fire in the limestone basin was begin-ning to seep into the submarine. The hatches were only fully air-tight when subjected to pressure from water outside. Davies switched on the oxygen supply.

I went along the gangway and through the magazine to the spot where I had seen the escape apparatus. From the rack I took five sets of equipment. They consisted of a mask, which clipped over the head and covered the nose and mouth, an air bag which was strapped round the body and a small cylinder of oxygen. To my great relief I discovered that the oxygen cylinders were filled.

As I joined the others I heard a muffled hissing noise coming from the direction of the conning tower. We went into the control room. It was louder there and coming from the hatch. 'Sounds like an oxy-acetylene cutter,' said Davies.

'I'm afraid so,' I said. 'Better stand by to repel boarders.' We found a revolver for Kevan. Davies was the only one capable of using an automatic rifle. As we stood staring up at the conning tower hatch we saw the metal of it suddenly redden at one point. It glowed like a cigarette in the half-darkness, then broadened and whitened. An instant later molten metal was dripping down at our feet and the flame of the cutter had appeared.

We watched the brilliant white flame slowly cutting through the metal. There was a sort of horrible fascination about it. It was a race between the cutter and the gas given off by the fire. Or had the fire been put out? I did not think so for the submarine was so hot. But my mind was so hazy that I could not be certain of anything. Anyway, I was so exhausted that it didn't seem to matter one way or the other.

A large part of the hatch now showed a dull red. The white line of cut metal grew until it showed as a definite segment of a circle. Very slowly I could see the cutting flame moving through the metal. The sound of it was now much louder. Soon the segment had grown to a semi-circle. 'What do we do – fight or surrender?' asked Kevan.

'We'd better take a vote on it,' I said. I was feeling very depressed. My mind kept groping over the formula – $CaCO_3 = CaO + CO_2$. Surely that was right? Or had I made a mistake?

Then suddenly I saw that the cutting flame was no longer moving. 'He's stopped,' I said. We watched. The whiteness of the metal where it had been cut was dimming. It was reddening, and the hatch cover as a whole was becoming black again. Gradually the hiss of the oxy-acetylene blower dwindled until it had stopped altogether.

'Thank God!' I breathed. 'Listen!' Not a sound. I walked down the length of the submarine and back again. There was not a sound from the deck overhead. When I rejoined the others in the control room I said: 'Davies – you and I will go out and bring in Logan and Miss Weston.'

Kevan helped us into the escape apparatus. We blew the air

bags up and switched on the oxygen. Then, wearing a pair of gloves, Davies unfastened the hatch and threw it back. I carried two spare oxygen equipments. We clambered out, breathing through our masks. The fire was still roaring, the flames flickering redly on the rock walls of the dock. Quickly we slammed the hatch back to conserve the pure air in the submarine. As we did so the body of the acetylene cutter rolled face upwards. It was a horrible sight. He had collapsed on to the flame of the blower and his face was burned out of all recognition.

The deck of the submarine presented a most amazing sight. There must have been at least twenty Germans lying huddled where they had collapsed. We hurried to the stern where we found two collapsible rubber boats moored. In one there was a German seated at the oars. He was looking dazed, but was not properly unconscious. But even as we climbed into the other boat, which was empty, he collapsed.

I cast off and Davies rowed quickly round to dock No. 5. Here the sight was even more amazing. The whole dock seemed strewn with the bodies of German sailors. It was like rowing in some fantastic crypt filled with the dead. I looked at Davies, pulling steadily on the oars, his face obscured by the awful futurist mask. So one might depict a modern Charon rowing a new-comer to Hades across the river Styx.

We moored to the flood gates of No. 5 dock and Davies scrambled up on to the dockside. I remained in the boat. In a very short while he returned, dragging Big Logan's unconscious body. I thought I should never be able to get him into the boat safely. But, rocking precariously, I lowered it into the bottom of the boat. Maureen's slight figure was easier to handle. Within less than three minutes of landing we were rowing back to No. 4 dock. Whilst Davies rowed, I fitted the escape apparatus first on to Logan and then on to Maureen. Then I untied their remaining bonds, not an easy procedure since I could use only one hand. Almost as soon as he began to breathe the oxygenized air, Logan showed signs of life. The first thing he did when he recovered consciousness was to try to tear the mask from his face. This I managed to prevent him from doing, and by the time we had reached our own dock, he had recovered sufficiently to lift himself on to the submarine. By that time Maureen had also recovered consciousness, but she needed assistance in climbing up on the deck of the submarine.

Back in the interior of the submarine, we removed their masks and our own. Kevan had plugged the circular cut in the conning tower hatch, and the oxygenized air in the submarine was good to breathe after the mask, which was not at all comfortable. The place was getting very hot indeed, however, and I did not think we should be able to stay there much longer. Kevan had also found a flask of brandy. He passed it first to Maureen. Then on to Logan and so to myself.

Soon after the brandy Maureen lost her dazed look and asked conventionally where she was. I explained what had happened, and she giggled a little uncertainly. 'I never thought I should live to be rescued by you, Walter,' she said. I didn't know quite how to take this, so remained silent. Her dark hair was hanging over her eyes, and flushed with newly regained consciousness, she looked startingly provocative. I saw Logan watching her.

I said: 'I'm afraid you've had rather an unpleasant time.'

But she shook her head. 'No, it wasn't too bad. As soon as Dan here saw the fire he told me what you were up to. You put us to sleep quite comfortably, didn't he?' She turned to Logan.

'Is your name Dan?' I asked.

Logan grinned. 'Yes, they even gave me a Christian name,' he said. 'Where's Trevors?' he added.

'Dead,' I said.

There was a long silence.

By this time every one seemed sufficiently recovered, so I suggested that we started out for the back exit of the base. We put on our oxygen apparatus and each of us took a spare. Also we took one of the submarine's oxygen cylinders, just in case. We had no idea how long our apparatus would keep us going. Then I sent Kevan aft to place a packing case or something fairly heavy over the engine-room hatch and unfasten it. I did not want the men down there to be trapped in this oven.

When we tied up at No. 5 dock and clambered up on to the dockside I was once again conscious of the eeriness of the place. There were men everywhere, but not a soul stirred. It was like a place of the dead. And we five masked figures looked like five horrible ghouls picking our way amongst the dead. The Germans seemed to have been struck down without warning. One still knelt before a piece of wood he had been sawing, kept upright by the saw. It was difficult to believe that they were only unconscious as yet, not dead.

At the end of the dock we found one of the mobile drills. They had been using it to get through the fall that blocked the gallery into our own dock. We then found two more cylinders of oxygen and several picks and placed them on top of the drill. We passed the ends of docks 6 and 7 and then dragged the drill up to the upper galleries. On the ramp and in the galleries we had to skirt unconscious bodies and sometimes they lay so thick that we had to move them in order to get the drill through.

At last we arrived at the guard-room and the cells we knew so well. Logan and Davies, who were armed with automatic rifles, went in front. They threw open the door, their rifles raised in case the gas had not penetrated the closed door. But the guard-room was empty. Davies went straight across to the other side where a rack of rifles stood. He pushed it sideways. A whole section of the cemented wall slid back on rollers to reveal a black cavity in the rock behind.

We hesitated, each looking questioningly from one to the other. Were we to risk everything in a desperate attempt to get through the falls in the mine? That meant blowing up the guard-room and imprisoning ourselves in the mine, for it was impossible to say how long the fire would last and once the men in the base regained consciousness they could come after us in order to prevent us making contact with the outside world. I remembered what Logan had said about falls in tin mines. It seemed pretty hopeless.

'Isn't there some sort of a lookout?' Maureen's voice was muffled by her mask.

'Yes,' I replied, 'but it's like a periscope – just a piece of steel piping thrust through the rock. We'd never get through.'

'Ventilation?'

I shook my head. 'What do you say, Logan?'

'This is our only chance,' was his reply.

'I agree,' I said. 'First, we need some food. And keep that door shut. We don't want to lose any good air there is in the mine.'

Davies pushed the section of wall back across the opening and he and Kevan remained in the guard-room, whilst Logan, Maureen and I went in search of food. In the nearest kitchen we found two of the cooks sprawled across the table and another had burned himself on the stove and slipped to the floor in front of it. We collected enough provisions for a week in a big packing case and a large can of water and dragged them along to the guard-room. We loaded them on to the drill trolley, and after providing ourselves with torches, some spare batteries, an automatic rifle each and magazines, together with several grenades, we went through into the mine.

I think we all felt somewhat chilled at leaving the lighted guard-room for this dark damp tunnel. It was like stepping straight from the warmth and comfort of civilization into some aged vault. To me it was like walking into one's grave, for I was not hopeful for our being able to break through the falls. There were only two of us properly able-bodied, and I was afraid that lack of ventilation would kill us long before our food gave out.

As soon as the section of the guard-room wall had been pushed back behind us we took off our masks. The air smelt damp and stale. By the light of a torch we walked steadily along the gallery, the drill trolley, now badly overloaded, jolting on the uneven floor. After we had gone about two hundred yards we came to a fall. This was the one that Maureen and her companions had worked their way through. She pointed to something. It was a piece of wire that led to one of the larger rocks. Evidently that was what had give the alarm. The gap they had made was not large and it proved quite impossible to get the trolley through. We debated whether to try to widen it or not. I was all for leaving the trolley. I had suddenly remembered that its engine would pollute the air. Anyway, it could be brought along later. The others agreed to this, so we unloaded it and passed all the various articles which we had loaded on to it through the narrow gap in the fall. It was a fearful struggle, and by the time everything we wanted had been transferred I felt completely exhausted. What little I had done had caused my arm to start bleeding again and I was conscious of the warm blood trickling down the splints on to my hand.

As soon as everything had been transferred to the farther side of the fall, I asked Davies if he would go back and demolish the gaurd-room. 'A few grenades will do the trick,' I said. 'But see that you leave yourself time to get clear. And keep the door into the mine as near shut as possible and hold your breath whilst you're in the guard-room.'

We wished him good luck and he climbed back through the fall. Gradually the sound of his footsteps died away. Then faintly we heard the door to the guard-room being slid back. Silence for a moment. Then the faint rumble of the door sliding to again and the sound of footsteps running towards us down the mine gallery. We braced ourselves for the explosion. It came a few seconds later, a terrific muffled roar that shook the rock in which the gallery was cut and seemed to rumble through our very bodies. It was not one explosion, but several very close together, and the roar of them and the crash of falling rock was continuous. Pieces of rock fell from the roof of the gallery round us and I felt the fall shift slightly.

Gradually silence descended on us again. We listened. Not a sound. We called out, but Davies did not answer. 'I'll go back for him,' said Logan.

'No, I will,' I said. I felt sick for fear I had sent the man to his death.

But before I could move Logan was already scrambling over the rocks of the fall. He had to shift great lumps of dislodged rock before he could get through the gap. Again we waited. Two or three minutes later we heard him coming back up the gallery. 'It's all right,' he called from the other side of the fall. 'He got laid out by a lump of rock.'

I felt greatly relieved. And shortly afterwards Davies himself climbed back through the gap in the fall. He had a nasty scalp wound, but otherwise seemed all right. 'The force of it knocked me over,' he said. 'Then a bloody great rock hit me on the side of the head.'

'I went back and had a look at the damage,' Logan said as he climbed through. 'The gallery is completely blocked some yards from the entrance to the guard-room.'

We had burned our boats. I think we all had that sinking feeling. There was no going back. Whatever falls lay ahead, we just had to get through them. Each carrying as much as he could, we went on along the gallery. It sloped gradually upward and bore to the left. There were the remains of sleepers and here and there old lengths of rail on the floor of the gallery. Suddenly it broadened out and we found ourselves emerging from the farthest right of three branches off a main gallery. Logan, who was leading, glanced back at Davies. 'The main gallery,' said the Welshman. 'The other branches are no use whatever. They end in falls, and if you worked through them you'd most likely find yourself back with the submarines.'

So we pushed on up the main gallery. But we had not gone more than a hundred yards or so before we found the gallery completely blocked with rock. 'This is the fall they made yesterday,' said Davies.

'Looks pretty hopeless,' said Maureen rather dully.

'Depends how deep it goes,' was Davies's reply.

We put our things down and set to work immediately. Maureen tried to get Kevan and myself to rest. But I knew the value of time and though we could each use only one arm we were better than nothing.

Davies wielded a pick and the rest of us attacked the fall with our bare hands, pulling the loosened rocks down and piling them up behind us. When we started on it the time was just on four. But after that time had no meaning for me. It was dust and rocks and straining and heaving and sweating. Pain, too, for the exertion brought the blood pumping into my wound. Time went on and I really had no idea what progress we were making. I was just automatically pushing behind me rocks that were thrust at me from above. We took it in turns to rest. Sometimes we had water, sometimes some food, and days seemed to pass.

Nothing seemed real except my intense longing to rest. As in a dream I heard Logan say: 'Listen!' I listened, but I could hear nothing but the pumping of the blood against my ear drums. But still as in a dream I saw the others getting wildly excited and setting to work furiously on the fall again. Once more I began automatically shifting the rocks that were thrust at me. Then I heard faint picking sounds beyond the fall and later I remember Maureen saying: 'It's all right, Walter, they're coming for us.'

I think it was then that I passed out, and I remember nothing until I woke to the lovely cold feel of fresh night air on my face. I had not felt fresh air for a fortnight. I breahted it in – sweet cool stuff smelling of grass and little rock plants. And then I opened my eyes and saw stars and a great round moon floating high in the velvet night. I closed my eyes again and slept.

The following is the report of Captain Marchant, which was forwarded to the War Office by the commanding officer at Trereen:

I proceeded to Pendeen with two companies, arriving there at 22.10 hours. Detective-Inspector Fuller was awaiting my arrrival at the inn, together with an officer of the Intelligence. The latter informed me that the Wheal Garth mine was believed to be occupied and to have some connection with U-boats. A woman reporter and three miners had failed to return from the mine after a visit the previous day.

There were three possible exits at the mine. I detailed a section to guard each of these exits. The fourth section I detailed to watch the cliffs above the mine. Lieutenant Myers took charge of these operations and each section was allotted a local miner as a guide.

With 'B' company I proceeded to the most recent shaft of the mine, which had been opened up by a rescue party. Detective-Inspector Fuller informed me that he had had plant brought over from Wheal Geevor and that thirty miners were working in relays to clear the fall.

We then proceeded down the shaft by rope ladder and through several galleries to the fall. It was then 23.30 hours. At 2.20 hours sounds were heard from the other side of the fall. A way was cleared through and the woman reporter and two of the three miners who had gone down with her were discovered. With them were two men – Craig and Logan – who had disappeared after the landing of a U-boat commander near Cadgwith recently. They reported a complete submarine base with seven docks and accommodation for more than six hundred men. They had fought their way out largely by the ingenious method of causing a fire in a limestone fall and so immobilizing the base with CO_2. They had blocked the gallery behind them.

We proceeded to this fall, and by 5.40 hours had cleared a passage into the base. The gas had cleared and many of the Germans had regained consciousness. But they put up a weak resistance. By 6.50 hours we were in control of the whole base.

Our casualties were two dead – Sgt. Welter and Pte. Gates – and three wounded – Ptes. Morgan, Chapman and Regal. The enemy lost four dead and six wounded in action against us. There were also a further forty-six dead by asphyxiation or by other means. Many were seriously ill as a result of the effects of the gas. A fall in the main gallery by the docks prevented those who resisted from getting at the munition stores and blowing up the whole base. One submarine was, however, destroyed by explosives.

Altogether five ocean-going U-boats have been captured intact and one destroyed, as mentioned above. Also one submarine store ship and a large quantity of war material fell into our hands. Prisoners taken totalled five hundred and sixty-five.

Signed,
MARCHANT.

Following a report by the intelligence officer to M.I.5 the proposed action against Kiel was postponed, it being feared that information concerning this plan might have been transmitted to Germany by a submarine.

After the capture of the base the area of sea immediately off the entrance was closely mined and a phosphorescent float moored in the usual position. By this means four more U-boats were destroyed.

THE WHITE
SOUTH

DISASTER IN THE ANTARCTIC

DAWN was breaking as the first news of the disaster reached London. It was 10 February and the rattle of milk bottles was the only sound in the black, frost-bound streets. Up in the City, Covent Garden and Billingsgate were halfway through the day's work and the pubs were open. In nearby Fleet Street a Reuter's operator was handed a news flash and his fingers ran automatically over the keys of his machine as he transmitted the message to subscribers. Two blocks away, in the office of a big London daily, a sleepy sub-editor heard the clack of the message as it came through on the teleprinter. He watched it as the carriage of the machine jerked back and forth. Then the yellow tongue of paper was thrust through the slit in the glass top. He tore it off and stood there reading it:

CAPE TOWN FEB 10 REUTER: SOS RECEIVED FROM FACTORY SHIP SOUTHERN CROSS. SHIP IS CAUGHT IN ICE IN WEDDELL SEA AND IN DANGER OF BEING CRUSHED. NORWEGIAN FACTORY SHIP HAAKON 400 MILES FROM POSITION OF SOUTHERN CROSS GOING TO RESCUE.

REUTER 0713

The sub-editor yawned, tossed the sheet of paper into the news basket and returned to the work of subbing a feature page article. In a big office block in Fenchurch Street, the telephone rang incessantly on the third floor. These were the offices of the South Antarctic Whaling Company and only the cleaners were there. The telephone went unanswered. In Whitehall, at the Admiralty, a messenger hurried along the empty, echoing corridors. He handed a message to the duty officer. The duty officer rubbed the sleep out of his eyes, read the message through, placed it in a basket marked 'for immediate attention' and enquired about tea. High up above Queen Victoria Street an operator at one of the switchboards in Faraday Buildings noted the urgency of an incoming call from Cape Town and searched the telephone directory. Then she switched the call from the offices of the South Antarctic Whaling Company to the flat of Albert Jenssen in South Kensington.

Albert Jenssen was still in bed. The telephone woke him and he was half asleep as he groped for the receiver and lifted it to his ear. A moment later and he was sitting up in bed, wide awake and speaking rapidly into the phone. When he had finished, he replaced the receiver automatically and sat there for a moment, regardless of the cold air that blew in through the open windows, a dazed expression on his face. Then he fell upon the telephone and call after call went out from the flat in South Kensington: cables to Durban, the Falkland Islands and the whaling stations of South Georgia; calls to Sandefjord and Tönsberg in Norway, to Leith in Scotland, to the BBC, to a Cabinet Minister and finally to the Admiralty. The duty officer at the Admiralty was forced to abandon his second cup of tea and interrupt an admiral in the midst of shaving.

And by eight o'clock messages were pouring over the ether: Admiralty to C-in-C. American West Indies; Admiralty to HM Sloop *Walrus*, at Port Stanley in the Falklands; Director South African Naval Forces, Cape Town, to Admiralty, London; British Broadcasting Corporation to Australian Broadcasting Commission. And as the official messages increased in a desperate effort to avert disaster, the news agencies joined in and the tempo grew – Reuter's Correspondent, Cape Town, to Reuter's, London; U.P. to New York; Tass to Moscow; Havas to –

By midday more than 150 million people knew that a ship of 22,000 tons belonging to a British whaling company was locked in the grip of the Antarctic ice and was being slowly crushed. As they sat at their desks or worked in their factories they were secretly thrilled at the thought of over 400 men face to face with death in the pitiless, frozen wastes of the Antarctic.

The Admiralty ordered the sloop, *Walrus*, to proceed to South Georgia, refuel and then make an attempt to reach the *Southern Cross*. A South African naval corvette was despatched from Cape Town, also with orders to refuel at South Georgia. The Board of Trade diverted a tanker, unloading in Durban, to South Georgia to fuel search vessels. *Det Norske Hvalselskab* of Sandefjord, Norway, announced that their factory ship, *Haakon*, which had steered for the *Southern Cross* within half an hour of receiving the first S O S at 03.18 hours, was now within 200 miles of the ship's last position. The United States government offered the services of the aircraft carrier *Ohio* then cruising off the River Plate.

Meanwhile events moved fast in the Antarctic. An early report that the *Southern Cross* had dynamited an area of clear water and was being warped round, was followed by the news that the way out of the ice was blocked by several icebergs which were charging into the pack. The tanker, *Josephine*, and the refrigerator ship, *South*, were standing by on the edge of the pack, together with the rest of the South Antarctic Company's fleet, unable to do anything. By midday the whole of the starboard side of the *Southern Cross* was buckling under pressure of the ice, and at 14.17 hours Captain Eide, the master, gave the order to abandon ship. In a final message before unloading the radio equipment on to the ice, Eide warned the *Haakon* not to enter the ice beyond the line of icebergs. That was the last message received from the *Southern Cross*.

All that night the lights blazed in the South Antarctic Whaling Company's offices in Fenchurch Street. But no message came through from the survivors. Utter silence had closed down on the abandoned ship and it was clear that this was the worst sea disaster in peacetime since the *Titanic* went down in 1912.

The most detailed picture of the events leading up to the disaster available on the morning of the 11th was contained in a feature article in London's largest daily. The writer's main sources of information were Jenssen, London manager of the South Antarctic Whaling Company, the company's agent in Cape Town, the Admiralty, *Det Norske Hvalselskab* and the files of his office library. The article gave the full story of the South Antarctic Company's whaling expedition. It was headed – DISASTER IN THE ANTARCTIC – and read:

'The *Southern Cross* left the Clyde on 16 October last with a total of 411 men and boys. In charge of the expedition was Bernt Nordahl, factory manager. Hans Eide was master and as assistant manager was Erik Bland, son of the chairman of the South Antarctic Whaling Company. About 78 per cent of those on board were Norwegians, mainly from Sandefjord and Tönsberg. The rest were British. With her sailed an ex-Admiralty corvette, converted to act as a whale-towing vessel, and the refrigerator ship, *South*.

'The *Southern Cross* arrived at Capetown on 14 November where her catchers and a tanker were waiting for her. The expedition sailed on 23 November. The fleet then consisted of the factory ship, a vessel of 22,160 tons, 10 whale catchers, each of under 300 tons, two buoy boats (catchers used for towing), three ex-naval corvettes for towing whale, one refrigerator ship, one tanker, and an old whaler to transfer the meat to the refrigerator ship. One of the towing vessels was later sent back to Cape Town to pick up electric harpoon equipment. The company intended to experiment during the season with the electrocution of whales, a method of killing that was in its infancy prior to the war.

'The whaling season in the Antarctic is of four months' duration – December, January, February, March. These are the summer months and whaling expeditions are limited to a certain period by international agreement in an attempt to preserve the whale and allow uninterrupted breeding. Unrestricted killing during the last century in the Arctic resulted in the complete extermination of whale in the Northern Hemisphere for many years. The present season for fin whale opened on 9 December. But prior to that, operations are permitted against the sperm whale. Most expeditions avail themselves of this in order to test equipment. This season, apart from the South Antarctic Company's expedition, there were eighteen others – ten Norwegian, four British, one Dutch, one Russian and two Japanese.

'On 29 November the *Southern Cross* sighted South Georgia and was in radio-telephone communication with the shore-based whaling stations on this island. They reported unprecedentedly bad conditions. Temperatures were much lower than normal with pack ice still piled against the western and southern shores of the island. Their catchers, operating in a 200-mile radius, spoke of heavy drift ice with bergs much more frequent and much bigger than usual. On 2 December the *Southern Cross* commenced operations, her catchers killing 36 sperm whale in seven days, despite low temperatures and severe gales. On 9 December she began full-scale operations. She was then about 200 miles west of South Thule, the most southerly of the Sandwich Group, and steaming southwest. Reports of both Nordahl, the factory manager, and Captain Eide, the master, to the London office all spoke of violent and incessant gales, low temperatures, loose pack ice and an unusually large number of gigantic icebergs.

'Whale seemed very scarce by comparison with the previous bumper season and on Boxing Day Nordahl reported trouble with the men. This is almost unheard of in Norwegian or British whaling fleets where the men have a financial interest in the catch. But when Jenssen was pressed for fuller details he said he had no statement to make on the matter.

'The matter must have been serious, however, for Colonel Bland, chairman of the company, left London Airport on 2 January for Cape Town in a privately chartered plane. He undertook the journey against the advice of his doctors. He had been seriously ill for some time with heart trouble. With him went his daughter-in-law, a German technical adviser on the electrical harpoon and Aldo Bonomi, the well-known photographer. His daughter-in-law, Mrs Judie Bland, is the daughter of Bernt Nordahl. On 3 January news was received at the London office that Nordahl, the leader of the expedition, had disappeared the previous night, presumed lost overboard.

'Colonel Bland arrived at Cape Town early on the 6th and left the same night, together with Nordahl's daughter, in the towing boat which had been dispatched to collect the new harpoon equipment. On reaching the *Southern Cross* on the 17th Colonel Bland assumed control of the expedition. Only 127 whale had been caught at that time against a previous season's total of 214. In a week of bad gales the ten catchers had only brought in 6 whale. Bland sent his catchers out in a wide search. They found heavy pack ice to the south and south-east and one of the catchers had difficulty in extricating itself from the ice. All catchers reported few whale. Meanwhile radio contact had been established with the *Haakon*, 600 miles to the south-west. The Norwegian ship reported whale in plenty. Colonel Bland decided on the 18th to steam south. A great deal of loose pack was encountered, but on the 23rd the vessels were in open sea in Lat. 66.01 S., Long. 35.62 W. with an abundance of whale.

'Operations from the 23 January to 5 February produced 167 whale. On the 6th and 7th there was a bad storm and on the night of the 7th one of the catchers, which had run into the ice for shelter, damaged its rudder on a floe. When the wind had died down a catcher and a corvette were sent to its assistance. But in the early hours of the 8th these two vessels were in collision in the ice, one of them being sunk and the other set on fire. The mishap occurred about 120 miles south-east of the *Southern Cross* and within sight of the catcher they had come to rescue. Both crews were reported safe on the ice with the loss of two men.

'Another corvette was sent to the assistance of the three vessels. Meanwhile, the *Southern Cross*, which had already refuelled from the tanker, completed the transfer of whale oil to this ship. On the night of the 8th the corvette reported that heavy pack ice was preventing her from approaching nearer than 20 miles to the damaged catchers. No further news had been received from these vessels.

'The wind had risen again to gale force. But despite this the *Southern Cross* herself went to the assistance of the catchers. At 6.30 p.m. on the 9th she sighted the corvette, which had run into loose pack in order to shelter from the heavy seas. The whole fleet was then together with the exception of the three missing catchers, for owing to the bad conditions no catchers had been sent out after whale. A conference was held on the *Southern Cross* and it was decided to steam into the pack ice, following leads which ran east and west in the direction of the damaged vessels.

'It is not difficult to picture the scene. The *Southern Cross*, big and squat like an enormous tanker with her fat funnels aft, steaming into the ice, the sea slopping about in the stern hole through which the whales are drawn up on to the after-plan. There is a gale blowing and the *Southern Cross* is steaming into it, steaming against the whole weight of the pack ice thrust westwards by the howling fury of the wind. All round her is loose pack – a flat, broken plain of white, glimmering in that peculiar twilight that is night in a region where the sun never sets. The loose pack draws closer and closer together until it is solid pack ice. There are icebergs now and they are smashing into the pack. And the great ship steams steadily on along a lead of black water that winds deeper and deeper into the ice, past the icebergs, right into the heart of the danger area.

'Was it madness to go on, risking all for a handful of lives? That factory ship represented nearly £3,000,000 of money and on board were over 400 lives. What drove Colonel Bland on? What made him take the risk? What about his officers – didn't they warn him? A ship like that, of 22,000 tons, with specially strengthened bows, can smash through ice 12 feet thick. But if those jagged edges once grip her thin steel plates, they can smash her in no time. Didn't he realize the danger? Or was the lead so narrow that once they were in it they couldn't turn back, but had to go on?

'The truth of the matter we may never know. All we know at the moment is that at 03.18 hours on 10 February the *Southern Cross* was firmly beset by the ice and she was sending out an SOS. Sometime during the night that lead must have come to an end. The westward-driven pack ice closed round her and in a matter of hours she was gone.

'That a ship of 22,000 tons should be crushed so easily may seem strange to those who remember that Filchner and Shackleton, beset in much smaller vessels in this same Weddell Sea, existed for months in the ice and saved themselves in the end. But these men were explorers. Their ships were specially built for the ice. The sheer sides of the *Southern Cross* were never designed to withstand the huge lateral thrust of ice piled up into pressure ridges by the battering force of giant icebergs.

'For the full story of what happened we must await the reports of survivors. In the meantime, it is to be hoped that the Government and other whaling companies will do all in their power to speed the rescue of these men. They probably have good stores of whalemeat and blubber on the ice with them. But their equipment is unlikely to be very good and they clearly cannot survive a winter in the Antarctic.'

So much for the story of the *Southern Cross* disaster, as the public knew it then. It was a nine days' wonder that ousted everything else from the headlines of the world's newspapers. Then, as the rescue attempts dragged on without success, it quietly faded out. Interest revived momentarily when the United States aircraft carrier, *Ohio*, arrived on the scene and flew its first sorties. But bad weather hindered the search. And since the failure of protracted rescue attempts is not news and public interest wanes rapidly in the face of negative results, the fact that well over 400 men were marooned somewhere in Weddell Sea was forgotten.

By the middle of March winter was setting in. Conditions became very cold with new ice beginning to form. By the 22nd all search vessels had turned back. They refuelled at Grytviken in South Georgia and proceeded to their bases. By 15 April Jan Eriksen, factory manager of the *Nord Hvalstasjon*, Grytviken, reported to his company: *All search vessels have now left Grytviken. Haakon and rest of Det Norske Hvalselskab fleet passed within 100 miles South Georgia yesterday on their way back to Cape Town. There are now no vessels in the area of the tragedy. Winter is closing in. If any survivors are still alive, God help them – for no man can until summer. I am preparing to close down the station.*

That report wrote *finis* to all attempts to rescue any possible survivors of the *Southern Cross*. It was dispatched to the offices of the *Nord Syd Georgia Hvalselskab* in Oslo and Erikson began the work of closing the whaling station at Grytviken as the Antarctic winter closed in on the ice-capped island of South Georgia.

But the story doesn't end there, for on 21 April, two days before he sailed with his men for Cape Town, Eriksen radioed a message that set linotypes and presses the world over rolling out the name *Southern Cross* in great, flaring headlines. For, on the 21 April –

But this is Duncan Craig's story. Let him tell it.

DUNCAN CRAIG'S STORY

*of the loss of the 'Southern Cross',
the Camp on the Iceberg, and the Trek
that followed*

I

I DID not actually join the *Southern Cross* until 17 January, only three weeks before the disaster occurred. Indeed, a month before that date, I was unaware of the existence of the ship or of the South Antarctic Whaling Company. I am not a whaler, and apart from a season's work in Greenland with a university exploration club, I had never before been in high latitudes. I wish to make this point clear at the outset so that those who have long experience of Antarctic conditions and of whaling in particular will understand that what is familiar to them came to me with the impact of complete novelty. The reason I have been asked to set down a full account of all that occurred is due to the fact that, through circumstances largely outside my control, I was in close association with the personalities concerned in the disaster and know probably more about the real cause of what happened than anyone now living.

My connection with the events that led up to the loss of the *Southern Cross* began with the New Year. I was emigrating to South Africa and on the night of 1 January I was waiting in the offices of a private charter company at London Airport in the hopes of hitching a ride to Cape Town. The decision to emigrate had been made on the spur of the moment. And if I'd known then where it was going to lead me, I'd have turned right back, pocketed my pride and resumed the routine of a clerk's life in the offices of Messrs Bridewell & Faber, tobacco importers of Mark Lane.

The flight was scheduled for 01.00 hours. The plane had been chartered by the South Antarctic Whaling Company for a Colonel Bland. There were five seats available and Bland's party numbered three. That was all I knew. Tim Bartlett, the pilot of the aircraft, had tipped me off at a New Year's Eve party the night before. As far as he was concerned it was okay. He'd take me. But it was up to me to talk my way into one of the two spare seats.

Bland arrived at twelve-thirty. He came into the terminal offices, stamping and blowing through his cheeks. 'Is the plane ready?' he asked the clerk. [His manner was peremptory. He had the air of a man always in a hurry. There were three other people with him – two men and a girl. A blast of cold air blew in through the open door and outside I saw a big limousine, its lights glistening on the wet tarmac. A uniformed chauffeur brought in their baggage. 'The pilot's waiting,' the clerk said. 'If you'll just sign these forms, Colonel Bland. And here's a cable – arrived about half an hour ago.'

I watched his thick fingers rip at the cable envelope. He pushed his horn-rimmed glasses up on to his forehead and held the cable closer to the light. His eyes were hard under the tufty brows and his bluish jowls quivered slightly as he read. Then he swung round abruptly. 'Here, read this,' he said to the girl. He held the flimsy cable sheet out and it shook slightly in his thick, hairy hand.

The girl came forward and took it. She was dressed in a pair of old slacks and a green woollen jersey. A lovely mink coat was draped carelessly over her shoulders. She looked tired and her face was pale under its make up. She read it through and then looked at Bland, her lips compressed into a thin line, her eyes blank.

'Well?' Bland's voice was almost violet. She didn't say anything. She just looked at him and I saw she was trembling slightly. 'Well?' he barked again. And then the violence inside him seemed to explode. 'First you and now your father. What have you got against the boy?' His fist suddenly crashed down on the desk top. 'I'll not recall him. Do you hear? Your father had better learn to get along with him. Any more ultimatums like that and I'll accept your father's resignation. He's not the only leader available.'

'He's the only one that can get you the results you've been accustomed to,' she answered defiantly, a flush of anger colouring her cheeks.

Bland was about to reply, but then he saw me and stopped. He turned abruptly and seized the forms that the clerk had thrust towards him. His hand shook as he signed them. And as I watched him Cape Town seemed to recede. I'd met his type before. He was the aggressive, self-made business man, even to the black hat and black overcoat with astrakhan collar. He was as hard as a lump of granite. And he looked as though he were on the verge of a nervous breakdown. To ask him for a lift in his plane would be like asking for the loan of a gold brick from the Bank of England. And the hell of it was that I'd burned my boats. I'd given up my rooms, requested my bank to transfer what little money I possessed to Cape Town and the letter throwing up my job had been posted that afternoon.

As though he sensed that I was watching him, he suddenly turned and stared at me. His small blue eyes were distorted by the thick lenses of his glasses. 'Are you just waiting for a plane, sir – or do you want to speak to me?' he demanded aggressively.

'I'm waiting for a plane,' I said.

He grunted, but didn't take his eyes off me.

'Whether I get it depends on you,' I went on. 'My name's Craig – Duncan Craig. The pilot of your plane is a friend of mine. He told me there might be a spare seat and I was wondering whether you'd be – '

'You're trying to scrounge a lift?'

The way he put it made me curl. But I kept a tight hold on my temper and said, 'I'd very much like to come with you to Cape Town.'

'Well, you can't.'

And suddenly I didn't care. Perhaps it was his manner – perhaps it was the way he'd spoken to the girl. 'There's no need to be offensive, Colonel Bland,' I said angrily. 'All I asked for was a lift.' And I reached down for my bags.

'Just a minute,' he said. The violence seemed to have died out of him. As I looked up, he was leaning against the desk, his thick fingers tugging at the lobe of his left ear. 'There are some two hundred thousand people waiting to get to South Africa. Why should I take you more than any of the others?'

'It happens that I'm the one that asked you. They didn't.' I had picked up my bags now. 'Forget it,' I said and moved towards the door.

'All right, Craig,' he said. 'As it happens there is a spare seat. If the pilot vouches for you and you're through the formalities in time, you can have it.'

He seemed to mean it. 'Thanks,' I said and made for the door to the airfield.

'Check your bags and sign the papers,' he said. The abruptness was back in his voice.

'I've done all that,' I said. 'I did it in advance – just in case.' I didn't want him to think that I'd taken it for granted I'd get the lift.

His thick brows dragged down over his eyes and his jowls

quivered. Then he suddenly laughed. 'Where did you learn efficiency – in business or in the services?'

'In the services,' I replied.

'Which – the Army?'

'No. The Navy.'

That seemed to exhaust his interest in me. He turned and watched the baggage being weighed. Tim Bartlett came through from the flight office with his co-pilot, a man called Fenton. He glanced at me with a lift to his eyebrows. I nodded and he grinned. He introduced himself and Fenton to Bland and asked the clerk for the passenger details. As he glanced through the papers he said to Bland, 'I see you've increased your party from three to four?'

'Yes. Mrs Bland wanted to come.' He nodded in the direction of the girl.

Tim Bartlett's brows lifted and he nodded. 'Which is Weiner?' he asked. One of the two men standing in the shadows by the door came forward slowly into the light. 'I am Weiner,' he said. His voice was a gutteral whisper and he moved like a marionet, as though jerked along against his will by invisible strings. He was a Jew and his clothes were several sizes too large for his shrunken body. He had a bald head, thin, emaciated features and a tubercular cough. 'Do you wish to see my papers?' he asked in that same wretched whisper.

'No, that's all right,' Tim said.

'And I am Bonomi – Aldo Bonomi.' It was the fourth member of the party. He stepped out of the shadows into the light with the swagger and bounce of an opera singer. He wore a camel-hair coat with padded shoulders and tie-on belt and round his neck was a silk scarf of peacock blue with little yellow designs. Gold rings flashed as he seized Tim's hand and pumped it up and down. 'I am so pleased to know that we shall be in such good hands. You are an artist. I can see that. I, too, am an artist. I go to take pictures for *El Colonnello*.' He paused for breath and peered anxiously up into Tim's face. 'But I hope you are a careful driver. Last time I fly the driver he make play with the airplane and I am very seek.'

Tim got his hand back from the Italian and said, 'It's all right. You needn't worry, Mr Bonomi. It will all be very dull, I hope.' And we went out to the airfield.

The rest of us followed as soon as Bland's party had had their passports checked and been through the customs. We piled into the plane. The luggage was strapped down, the doors closed. Fenton came through from the cockpit and told us to fix our safety belts. The engines roared into life and the plan taxied out on to the tarmac. The lights of the airport glittered frostily. We made the end of the runway and waited there for the okay from the control tower. My stomach suddenly felt hollow. It always does before a take-off. That uninsurable half minute! I don't know anyone who's really got over it.

I looked round at the others. Their bodies were self-consciously relaxed, the muscles under the surface rigid against the possibility of a crash. Nobody spoke. Bland had closed his eyes. The girl had her hands thrust deep in the pockets of her fur coat. Her grey eyes were wide and stared straight in front of her. Little curls of fair hair had escaped from beneath the silk scarf that covered her head. Bonomi wriggled in his seat. He couldn't keep still. He was like a rubber ball, his head darting about, one moment peering forward out of the window, the next twisted round to examine the inside of the plane. Only Weiner seemed completely relaxed. He lay slumped in his seat like a bundle of old clothes. A nerve twitched at the side of his mouth, but his expression was one of complete apathy. His hands were held against his stomach, the long, nervous fingers plucking at the locking device of his safety belt.

The engines suddenly roared. The plane rocked and vibrated. Then the brakes were off and we were gathering speed down the runway. I braced myself automatically and peered out of the window, where the lights of the plane showed the concrete streaming by. The rear end of the fuselage bumped twice and then lifted. The lights of the control tower showed through the darkness moving slowly away from us. Then suddenly we were riding air, smooth and steady, the note of the engines changing to a solid drone, the seat pressing my body upwards. The control tower was a rapidly receding pinpont of light now. Headlights cut swathes along the narrow ribbon of the road bordering the airport. Then we banked and the lights of London stretched away to the darkness of the horizon. Clear in my mind, like a montage, was the notice I'd pasted on my office desk – *Gone to South Africa*. Was it only yesterday evening I'd put it there? I thought of Mr Bridewell standing there, staring at it, uneasy, suspecting a leg-pull, completely unable to comprehend why I had left. Even my letter wouldn't explain that to him.

I undid my safety belt. Now I was actually on my way, I wanted to sing, shout, do something to show how I felt. Across the gangway, the little Jew was still twining his fingers round the lock of his belt. Behind me Bland suddenly said, 'Judie. Change places with Franz. I want to discuss this electrical killing gear with him.'

I half turned in my seat. Nobody seemed to notice my surprise. The girl said, 'Don't you think you ought to rest?'

'I'm all right,' Bland replied gruffly.

'Doctor Wilber said – '

'Damn Doctor Wilber!'

'If you're not careful you'll kill yourself.'

'I'll take a lot of killing.' He stared at her for a second. 'Where's that cable? I gave it to you.'

The girl felt in the pocket of her fur coat and brought out the crumpled cable flimsy. I heard him smoothing it out on his brief-case. Then he snorted. 'Bernt's no right to cable me like this.' Anger was catching hold of him again. 'He's not giving the boy a chance.' I heard the cable crushed in the sudden clenching of his fist. Then: 'The trouble is that only Erik stands between him and full control of the company when I'm gone.' His voice was a deep, angry rumble.

'That's not fair.' The girl's voice blazed.

'Not fair, eh? What the hell am I to think? They weren't a week out of Cape Town before there was trouble between them.'

'And whose fault do you suppose that was?' the girl demanded angrily.

'Bernt was playing on his lack of experience.'

'That's Erik's story.'

'What of that? Do you expect me not to believe my own son?'

'Yes, but you don't know him very well, do you? You were in London all through the war and since then – '

'I know when a boy's being victimized,' Bland snapped back. 'Why, Bernt even had the nerve to cable that he was causing trouble among the Tönsberg men. There's never any trouble with whalers. They're far too interested in the success of the expedition.'

'If Bernt said he was causing trouble among the Tönsberg men, then he was.' The girl's voice steadied. 'He's never thought of anything but the interests of the company. You know that.'

'Then why does he send me this ultimatum? Why does he demand Erik's recall?'

'Because he's seen through him.'

'Seen through him? That's a fine way to talk of your husband.'

'I don't care. You may as well know the truth about him.'

'Shut up!' Bland's voice vibrated like a plucked string.

'I won't shut up,' the girl rushed on. 'It's time you knew the truth. Erik's – '

'Shut up!' Bland's voice was thunderous. 'Don't talk like that. I can see what's happening to him now. You undermining him at home and your father undermining him out there. His confidence in himself is being sapped by the pair of you. No wonder he needs – '

'His confidence!' The girl's tone was half contemptuous, half hysterical. 'You don't know him at all, do you? You still think of him as the gay, reckless boy of ten years ago – sailing his boat, winning ski jump championships. You think that's all he wants. Well, it isn't. He likes to control things – men, machines, an organization. He wants power. Power, I tell you. He wants control of the company. And he's got his mother – '

'How dare you talk like that!'

'God! Do you think I don't know Erik by now?' She was leaning forward across the gangway, her body rigid, her face a white mask. 'I've been meaning to tell you this for some time – ever since that first cable. But you were too ill. Now, if you're well enough to travel, you're well enough to know what – '

'I refuse to listen.' Bland was trying to keep down his anger. 'You're hysterical.'

'You've got to listen. I'm not hysterical. I'm telling you what I should have told you – '

'I tell you I won't listen. Damn it – the boy's your husband.'

'Do you think I don't know that?' Her voice sounded frighteningly bitter. 'Do you think he hasn't made me aware of that every hour of every day we've been married?'

Bland was peering at her through his thick glasses. 'Don't you still love him?' he asked.

'Love him!' she cried. 'I hate him. I hate him, I tell you.' She was crying wildly now. 'Oh, why did you agree to send him out as second-in-command?'

'You seem to forget he's my son.' Bland's voice was ominously quiet.

'I haven't forgotten that. But it's time you knew the truth.'

'Then wait till we're alone.'

The girl glanced at me and saw that I was watching her. 'All right,' she said in a low voice.

'Franz!' The man next to me jerked in his seat. 'Come and sit back here. Change places with Franz,' he ordered the girl. 'And try to calm down.'

She got up heavily and changed places with the German. I watched her as she settled in the seat across the gangway from me. Her face was tense, her small hands clenched so tight the knuckles showed white. She sat there, quite still and rigid, as though frozen.

I sat back and stared out of my window at the red glow of the port navigation light. The Kent coast was sliding from under us. Ahead, the corrugated surface of the Channel was lit by a crescent moon. And above the drone of the engines I caught snatches of Bland's conversation.

'The equipment has arrived . . . cable two days ago from the Cape . . . *Tauer III* is picking it up . . . I've ordered Sudmann to wait for. us . . . all prepared for test.'

I think I was too excited to sleep. In the end I got up and went through into the pilot's cockpit. Fenton was at the controls. Tim was pouring coffee from a Thermos. 'Well, there's the last you'll see of England for a bit,' he said, nodding through the side window. 'Should begin to get warmer tomorrow. Getting on all right with Bland's party?'

'I've hardly spoken to them,' I said. 'Bland and the girl have just had a hell of a row. Now he's talking to Weiner about some new equipment or something. Weiner's German, isn't he?'

'That's right. He's an expert on electrical harpoons. He's on loan to Bland from one of the big Ruhr companies. Poor devil! Think of it. Four months in the Antarctic. Flying over the Alps is quite cold enough for me.'

'Is Bland going out to the Antarctic, too?'

'Yes, they're all going as far as I know. There's a boat waiting for them at the Cape to take them out to the factory ship. I gather there's some sort of trouble on board the *Southern Cross*. Anyway, Bland sounded as though he were in a hell of a hurry to get out there.'

'Do you mean to say the girl's going, as well?' I asked.

He shrugged his shoulders. 'Don't know about her,' he answered. 'She only joined the party at the last moment. According to her papers, she's Norwegian by birth and South African by marriage. Looks rather a poppet.'

'She doesn't behave like one,' I answered. 'More like a wild cat. And she's all tensed up over something. It's an odd set-up.'

'You should worry. You got your ride, didn't you? If you want company, go and talk to Aldo Bonomi. There must be something behind the bounce, for he's one of the world's best photographers. Like some coffee?'

'No, thanks,' I said. 'I'll sleep better without it.'

He set down the flask. 'That reminds me. I'd better hand out some blankets. You might give me a hand, will you, Duncan.'

Back in the main body of the plane everything was just as I'd left it. Bland and Weiner were poring over sheets of figures. The girl sat staring out of the window. She didn't look up as we came through. It seemed as though she hadn't moved since I went through into the cockpit. Bonomi, however, had fallen asleep, his mouth slightly open, his snores lost in the sound of the engines. We handed round the blankets. 'Breakfast at Treviso,' Tim said as he went for'ard. I settled in my seat across the gangway from the girl. She had wrapped her blankets round her, but she still sat tense and wide-eyed. My thoughts drifted to South Africa and the new world that lay ahead. I still had a sense of excitement about it. It wasn't real yet. I thought of Table Mountain as I'd seen it once before in a vivid dawn from the bridge of my corvette as I convoyed reinforcements for Egypt and the Sicilian campaign. What sort of a job would Kramer find me when I got there? The drone of the engines gradually lulled me to sleep.

A frozen dawn showed us the Alps as a wild barrier of snow-capped peaks with the crevassed glacier ice tumbling down through giant clefts. Then we were over the flat expanse of the Lombardy plain and setting down at Treviso for breakfast.

I was right behind Bonomi as we went into the canteen. I was curious about Bland and I thought Bonomi the most likely of the four to gratify my curiosity. He picked a table away from the others and I seated myself opposite him. 'I gather you're a photographer, Mr Bonomi,' I said.

'But of course. You have heard of Aldo Bonomi, no?'

'Er – yes, of course,' I murmured quickly.

The corners of his mouth dragged down and he spread his hands in a little gesture of despair. 'You do not fool me. You have not heard of Aldo Bonomi. Where do you leev, Mistair Craig?' His brown eyes gazed at me pityingly.

I thought of the people I met at the office and at my rooms. I was right out of his world. 'And you're going to take pictures of whaling in the Antarctic?' I said.

'*Si, si.*' The waiter came and he ordered, speaking fast in Italian. 'May I order for you, Mistair Craig? I think I get you something good.'

'Thanks,' I said. And when the waiter had gone I asked him whether he liked the idea of going to the Antarctic.

He gave a little shrug to his shoulders. 'It is business, you understand.'

'But it's a rather unusual assignment, isn't it?'

'Unusual? Per'aps. But my business is often unusual. One day

I take pictures of a zoo, another day I am photographing the Rand mines. Then again I am with the Canadian Railways.'

'You travel quite a bit then?'

'But, of course. Oh, you do not understand. I am Aldo Bonomi. Everyone wish for my photographs. One week I am in America, next I am in Paris. Travel, travel, travel, – I am always in trains or aeroplanes.'

'And now you're going to the Antarctic with Colonel Bland. Tell me – what do you think of him? You heard the row he had with his daughter-in-law? Is there something wrong on board the factory ship?'

His hand fingered his little green and red bow tie. 'Mistair Craig – I never talk about my clients. It is not good for business, you understand.' The flash of white teeth in his swarthy face was half ingratiating, half apologetic. He smoothed his hand over the shining surface of his black hair. 'Let us talk about you,' he said. The waiter came with our breakfast. As he poured the coffee, Bonomi said, 'You emigrate to South Africa, yes?'

I nodded.

'That is very exciting. You throw up everything. You go to another country and you start again. That is the big adventure. You have no job, but you go all the same. That needs guts, eh? You are a man with guts. I like men with guts. You like a drink with your coffee?' And as I half shook my head, he said, 'Just a leetle one, so I can drink your health. Besides, I like to drink with my breakfast.' He turned to the waiter. '*Due cognaci.*'

'What makes you think I haven't got a job?' I asked as the waiter disappeared.

'If you have a job, then you do not need to ask for a ride. It is all fixed by your company. I know because I am always working for some company. But tell me – what makes you leave England?'

I shrugged my shoulders. 'I don't know,' I said. 'I just got fed up.'

'But something make you decide very quick, eh? Oh, I do not mean something serious, you understand. Life, she is not like that. Always it is the little things that make up our minds for us.'

I laughed at that. 'You're right there.' And suddenly I was talking to him, telling him the whole thing. He was conceited, effeminate-looking and full of his own importance, but he was easy to talk to. 'I suppose I've been feeling a sense of frustration ever since the war ended,' I explained. 'I went straight from Oxford into the Navy. When I came out I had a queer idea that my country owed me a living. Then I found that commanding a corvette didn't qualify me to run a business. I finished up as a clerk with a firm of tobacco importers.'

'That is not so much after commanding a ship, eh?' He nodded sympathetically. The waiter came with the cognac. '*Salute!*' he said as he raised his glass. 'I wish you *buona ventura*, Mistair Craig. And what is the little thing that brings your frustration to a head, eh?'

'A fiver,' I said. 'Mr Bridewell, the man who ran the business, gave us each a fiver on New Year's Eve. But the fool had to make a speech about it.'

'And you do not like this Mistair Bridewell?'

'No. It wasn't that. He's a decent little man. And it was a decent gesture. But I couldn't stomach the lecture. I thought it was a hard way to earn a fiver. I went out and got drunk with it. And during the course of the evening I ran into Bartlett, the pilot of our plane. He told me he was flying to South Africa with two spare seats and I decided to chance it.'

'I understand. But do you know what conditions are like now in South Africa?'

'Oh, I know the post-war boom is over, the same as it is in England. But a fellow I met during the war said he could always find me a job if I came out.'

'Ah, yes – a fellow you meet during the war.' He shrugged his shoulders and stared at his drink. At length he gave a little sign and said, 'Well, I wish you luck. I hope the job he have for you is a very good one.'

Tim Bartlett came in then and said it was time to leave. We finished our drinks and walked out to the plane. But as we roared down the runway and swung into the blue of the Italian skies, South Africa seemed suddenly less exciting. I should have contacted Kramer about that job first. I'd known it all along. But I'd pushed the thought into the back of my mind. Now, as South Africa became a reality – and a rapidly nearing reality – the problem of that job loomed more and more important.

The trip over the Med was bumpy; the sea very blue, but flecked with white. The Western Desert looked cold and drab. Cairo came up at us marked by the geometrical square of the pyramid at Giza. An icy wind blew dust across the airport. Tim told us there'd be a six-hour stop there. We'd start again at ten. Bonomi went off with a journalist friend who'd arrived in a BOAC plane. Bland decided to rest. His big face was pale and sweaty. He looked ill and exhausted. Weiner was suffering from air sickness. I stood around, wondering what to do with the time on my hands. Cairo wasn't one of the places I'd got to during the war. I'd just made up my mind to go and find some place to get a drink when a voice behind me said, 'Mr Craig.'

I turned. It was the girl. She looked cold and pale. 'Could you – would you mind taking me into Cairo – for a drink or something?' Her grey eyes were wide and her mouth trembled slightly. I think she was on the verge of tears. She was all wound up like something that's tied too tight and ready to burst.

'Come on,' I said, and took her arm. I could feel the tightness inside her. She wasn't trembling, but it was there like a charge of electricity. We found a taxi and I ordered the driver to take us to Shepheard's Hotel.

There was a long silence as the taxi rattled out through the airport gates. I didn't hurry her. I knew it would come. She suddenly said, 'I'm sorry.'

'Why?' I asked.

'Inflicting myself on you like this. I – I don't think I'll be very good company.'

'Don't worry,' I said. 'Just relax.'

'I'll try,' she said and closed her eyes.

At Shepheard's I took her to a table in a corner. 'What'll you have?' I asked.

'Whisky,' she said.

I ordered doubles. We tried a little small talk. It didn't work. When the drinks came, she drank in silence. I gave her a cigarette. She dragged at it as though her nerves were screaming out for a sedative. 'Wouldn't it help to tell me about it?' I suggested.

'Perhaps,' she said.

'It'll help spread the load,' I added. 'It always does. And it's not likely we'll meet again.'

She didn't say anything. It was as though she hadn't heard. She was gazing at a noisy group at a nearby table. But she didn't see them. God knows what she saw. For a girl who couldn't be more than twenty-five, her face looked almost haggard. Suddenly she said, 'I'm scared about my father. I don't know why I'm scared, but I am. It came over me last night in the plane. It was as though – ' She put her elbows on the table and rested her head in her hands. 'Oh, God!' she said in a choking voice. 'It all seems such a mess.'

I wanted to do something to comfort her. But there was nothing I could do. I lit another cigarette and waited.

At length she raised her head. 'All last night,' she said, 'I was thinking about my father and Erik – down there in the Antarctic.'

'Erik is your husband, is he?' I asked.

'Erik Bland. Yes.' She nodded.

'And your father's there, too?'

'Yes. He's the manager of the factory. He's also leader of the expedition.' Her fingers were clutching her glass so hard that the knuckles showed white. 'If only Erik weren't there,' she whispered. And then with sudden violence, 'If only he'd been killed during the war.' She looked at me sadly. 'But it's always the wrong ones that get killed, isn't it?' And I wondered whether there was somebody she'd been fond of. She looked down at her glass again.

'I'm frightened,' she said. 'Erik's been working for this for two years. Through his mother, who's Norwegian, he's got a lot of Sandefjord men of his own choosing into the crew. And now, this season, he's persuaded Colonel Bland to let him go out as assistant manager. They weren't a fortnight out of Cape Town before he was cabling that my father was turning the Tönsberg men against him. There were other cables and then finally one which said: *Nordahl openly saying he will have control of the company soon.* My father would never say a thing like that – not in front of the men. I know he wouldn't. It's all part of a plan to drive a wedge between him and Colonel Bland.'

'Is Nordahl your father?' I asked.

'Bernt Nordahl – yes. He's a wonderful person.' Her eyes came alive for the first time since I'd met her. 'Nineteen seasons he's been out in the Antarctic. He's as tough and – ' She checked herself and her tone flattened as she said, 'You see, Bland's just had a stroke. It's heart trouble. He knows he hasn't got long to live. That's why he finally agreed to Erik going out this season. Normally he wouldn't. He knows he hasn't sufficient experience. But he wants Erik to follow him in the company. It's natural. Any father would. But he doesn't know him. He doesn't know what he's like.'

'And your father does?' I suggested.

She nodded. 'Yes.' She hesitated and then said, 'That cable Bland received at the airport last night – it was from my father. It said either Erik must be recalled or he would resign.'

I looked at her, trying to understand why she had married Erik Bland. She wasn't beautiful. She was a little too stockily built for that, and that ridiculous little up-tilted nose gave her face a snubbed appearance. But she had grace. She had strength, too, and a bubbling vitality that showed even through the blank misery of her present mood. She'd been brought up on skis and long treks through the mountains. I'd been at the landings at

Aandalsnes in 1940. I knew the country and to me she was all Norway with that lovely golden hair, creamy skin and wide, generous mouth. She was the sort of girl that's born to fight for the right to live alongside her man. And from what I'd heard on the plane it was clear she'd made a wrong choice.

'Mind if I ask you a personal question?' I said.

Her grey eyes were suddenly on the defensive. 'Go ahead,' she said.

'Why did you marry Erik Bland?'

She shrugged her shoulders. 'Why does any girl marry the man she does?' she answered slowly. 'It was in 1938. Erik was very attractive. He's tall and fair and very boyish. He's a fine skier, dances beautifully and keeps a lovely little yacht at the Dronningen. Everybody thought I was very lucky.'

'And he was a sham?'

'Yes.'

'When did you discover that?'

'During the war. We grew up during the war, didn't we? Before, all I thought about was having a good time. I studied in England and in Paris. But it was the parties and the ski-ing and the sailing that I lived for. Then the Germans came.' Her eyes which had sparkled for a moment, clouded now. 'All the boys I knew disappeared from Oslo. They went North to join the fighting. And when that was over, they were back, some of them, for a little time. But one by one they drifted away, some across the North Sea to join the Norwegian forces, some through Finland and Russia, others up into the mountains to continue the fight.' She stopped then, her lips pressed tight together.

'But Erik didn't go,' I finished for her.

'No.' There was sudden violence in her tone. 'You see, he liked the Germans. He liked the Nazi way of life. It fascinated him. It satisfied a sort of – it's difficult to put into words – a craving for self-expression. Do you understand?'

I thought of the mother who adored him and the father whose personality and achievement had dominated his whole life, leaving him nothing to strive for. I could understand. I nodded.

'It meant nothing to him that Norway was fighting for her existence,' she went on. 'He didn't seem to understand – ' Her voice trailed away. When she spoke again it was in a softer tone. 'Perhaps it wasn't altogether his fault. Life had been made too easy for him.'

'But why wasn't he interned?' I asked. 'He's English, isn't he?'

'Well – South African. He claimed Boer descent on his father's side, and of course his mother's Norwegian. Their police checked on him periodically, that was all.'

'Was Colonel Bland over in Norway during the war?'

'No. London. But Erik's mother remained at Sandefjord. She'd plenty of money, so it didn't make much difference to him.' She hesitated, and then said, 'We began to have rows. I refused to go out with him. There were Germans at most of the parties he went to. He took them ski-ing, even out in his yacht. He just couldn't see my point of view. Then the Resistance got going. I tried to make him join. I thought if I could only get him to mix with the boys who were going on with the fight he'd wake up to understanding what it was all about. I kept at him until at last he agreed to join. They thought he might be useful because of his German contacts. We forgot that the Germans might think him useful because of his Norwegian contacts. He went up into the hills for one of the drops. A week later the same dropping ground was used. The Resistance Troup collecting on that drop was practically wiped out. Nobody suspected.'

'Except you,' I said as she stopped, her teeth biting into her lip.

She nodded slowly. 'Yes. I got it out of him one night when he was drunk. He actually – he actually boasted about it. Said it served them right, that they were on the wrong side anyway. It was horrible. I hadn't the nerve to tell the Resistance. He knew that and he – ' She glanced up at me quickly. 'Nobody knows what I have just told you,' she said. 'So please – ' She tossed the request aside as unnecessary. 'It doesn't matter though.' Her tone was suddenly bitter. 'No one would believe it. He's so devilishly charming. That's the hell of it – to know what he is and see him keeping up his front of popularity. His father – ' She spread her hands helplessly and sighed.

'You've never told him about the Resistance business, of course?' I said.

'No,' she said. 'I wouldn't want to tell any father that about his son – not unless I had to.'

There was a long silence after that. There was nothing I could say. She stared past me, her mind far away, out there in the white wastes of the Antarctic where she was going. Suddenly she finished her drink. It was a quick, decisive movement, like the ringing down of the curtain. 'I can hear dance music,' she said with a sudden hard brightness. 'Let's go and dance.' As I rose, she put her hand on mine. 'Thank you,' she said, 'for being – so nice.'

I don't know how she managed it, but we had a lovely evening.

Perhaps it was reaction. Maybe it was sheer effort of will. But her gaiety, which was forced and brittle as we went on to the floor, became quite natural as we danced. She danced with her body very close to mine. She seemed to want to dance with complete abandon, and she danced divinely. Once she murmured, 'You said we'd never meet again.' Her lips were almost touching my ear. In the taxi going back to the airport, she snuggled close to me and let me kiss her.

But when the taxi swung in through the gates of the airport she straightened up. As she made up her face, I saw the worried look was back in her eyes. She caught my glance and made a wry face. 'Cinderella's home again,' she said, and her voice was flat. Then with a sudden rush of warmth she took my hand in hers. 'It's been a wonderful evening,' she said softly. 'Perhaps if I'd met somebody like you – ' She stopped there. 'But there'd have to have been a war first, wouldn't there? You see I was a spoilt little bitch myself.'

It was just on eleven. The others were waiting for us. We went straight out to the plane. Ten minutes later the lights of Cairo were vanishing below us and the black of the desert night stretched ahead. We settled down to sleep.

It must have been about four in the morning that Tim came through from the cockpit. The sound of the door sliding back woke me up. He had a slip of paper in his hand. He went past me and stopped at Bland, shaking him awake. 'Urgent message for you, Colonel Bland,' he said, speaking softly. Bland grunted and there was a rustle of paper.

I turned in my seat. Bland's face was white and puffy. He was staring down at the slip of paper that trembled in his hand. He swallowed twice and then glanced across at Judie, who was fast asleep.

'Is there any message to be sent?' Tim asked him.

'No. No, there's no reply.' Bland's voice was barely audible. It was as though he'd been belted in the stomach and all the breath had been knocked out of him.

'Sorry to bring you bad news at this time of the morning.' Tim went back to the cockpit. I tried to get back to sleep. But I couldn't. I kept on wondering what was in that message. Somehow I was certain it had some connection with Judie. Twice I turned round. Each time Bland failed to notice my movement. He wasn't asleep. He was sitting there, slumped in his seat, his eyes open and staring at the message.

Dawn came and with it a glimpse of Mount Elgon on the starboard beam. Shortly afterwards the snow-covered peak of Kilima Njaro was above the horizon and we were landing at Nairobi for breakfast. We all sat at the same table. Bland didn't eat anything. I thought at first that he was suffering from air sickness. The last part of the flight had been pretty bumpy. But then I saw he kept on glancing at Judie. He looked almost scared.

Bonomi, who was sitting next to me, suddenly leaned closer and said, 'What is the trouble with Colonel Bland? He looks as though he is very seek about somethings.'

'I don't know,' I said. 'But he got a message during the night.'

When we got up from the meal I saw Bland motion for Judie to join him outside. He wasn't gone long, and when he came back he was alone. 'Where's Mrs Bland?' I asked. 'Is anything wrong?'

'No,' he answered. 'Nothing.' His tone made it clear it was none of my business.

I lit a cigarette and went outside. I thought maybe Judie had gone to powder her nose. But as I turned the corner of the building I saw her walking alone across the airfield. She was walking aimlessly, as though she'd no idea where she was going and didn't care anyway. I called to her. But she didn't answer. She just kept on walking, following her feet, changing her course like a ship without a rudder.

I ran after her then. 'Judie?' I called. 'Judie!' She stopped then and half turned, waiting for me to come up with her. Her face was quite blank. 'What's happened?' I asked. Her eyes were empty, her whole being withdrawn inside itself. She didn't answer. I caught hold of her hand. It was cold as ice. 'Come on,' I said. 'Tell me. It's the message your father-in-law received during the night, isn't it?' She nodded bleakly. 'What did it say?' For answer she opened her other hand. I took the crumpled ball of paper and spread it out.

It was from the South Antarctic Company, dispatched at 21.30 hours. It read: *Eide reports Manager Nordahl lost overboard from factory ship stop further information later signed Jenssen.*

Her father dead! I read the message through again, wondering what I could possibly say to her. She'd worshipped him. I knew that from the way she had talked about him in Cairo. *He's a wonderful person.* I remembered the way her eyes had lit up when she had said that. The message didn't say how it had happened; didn't even say if there'd been a storm. It just said – *lost overboard.* 'Who is Eide?' I asked.

'The captain of the *Southern Cross*.' Her voice sounded numbed.

I took her arm and we walked on slowly for a while in silence.

Then suddenly the pent-up emotion inside her broke out. 'How did it happen?' she cried wildly. 'He couldn't have just fallen overboard. He's been on ships all his life. Something's wrong down there. Something's wrong. I know it is.' She began to cry then, her whole body shaking, her head buried against me like a puppy that's lost its mother. I remember thinking then that if Erik Bland had had any decency he'd have cabled her himself.

2

IT was summer in Cape Town. As we swung down towards the airport the scene was like a colour plate – the houses all white and Table Mountain a mass of brown rock against the brilliant blue of the sky. My stomach felt hollow inside me. Somewhere down there my future was waiting for me – if I could find it. I was excited and nervous all in one. It was the start of a new life. The very fact that the sun was shining in a clear sky gave me a wonderful sense of freedom. I'd left winter behind. As we touched down on the long ribbon of the runway I wanted to sing. Then I glanced across at Judie and the mood was gone. She was slumped in her seat, staring tensely out of the window the way she had been all the way from Mombassa. I remembered the ride in the taxi in Cairo. And then I remembered that moment on the airfield at Nairobi when she had broken down with her grief. I wished there was something I could do. But there wasn't.

At the airport buildings I thanked Bland for the trip. He shook my hand. His grip was like iron, but his face was white. 'Glad we could give you a lift.' He mumbled conventional good wishes automatically and then went out with Weiner at his heels. I said goodbye to Tim Bartlett and then Bonomi popped up like a jack-in-the-box, smiling and shaking my hand. 'If South Africa is no good, Mistair Craig, you go to Australia,' he said. 'Here is the name of a man in Sydney who is useful. Tell him Aldo Bonomi send you.' He handed me a piece of paper on which he had scribbled an address. I thanked him and wished him luck in the frozen south. He pulled a face. 'I prefer to stay 'ere, I think.' Then he shrugged his shoulders and grinned. 'But I sacrifice everyt'ing for my art – even my comfort.'

Then Judie was coming towards me. 'Well, this is goodbye, Duncan,' she said, and held out her hand. She even managed a little smile. Her fingers were warm and firm in my hand. 'Just two ships . . .' she said. 'Are you going to a hotel?'

'Yes,' I said. 'I'll go to the Splendide. I'll probably end up in some dingy boarding-house, but just for a few days I'm going to pretend I'm important.' She nodded and smiled. 'Where are you staying?' I asked her.

But she shook her head. 'We part here,' she said. 'We shall probably go straight on board. Everything is arranged. In an hour's time we'll be sailing out of Table Bay.'

I hesitated. I didn't know quite what to say. But I had to say something. 'I hope you – you – ' I just couldn't put it into words.

She smiled. 'I know. And thanks.' Then suddenly on a higher pitch: 'If only I knew what had happened. If only Eide or Erik had cabled details. But there's nothing at the airport – nothing.' Her fingers squeezed my hand. 'I'm sorry. You've got problems of your own. Good luck. And thank you for being so sweet.' She reached up then and kissed me on the lips. And before I could say anything she had turned and her heels were tap-tapping across the concrete floor as she went out to the car that was waiting for her. She didn't look back.

That should have been the end of it. I should have got myself a job and they should have sailed for the Antarctic. But it didn't work out that way.

I got myself fixed up at the Splendide and then rang Kramer. He was down in the book as a mining consultant. His secretary told me he wouldn't be in till after lunch. In the end I didn't get him till almost tea time. He sounded pleased to hear from me until I mentioned why I was in Cape Town. 'You should have written me, old man,' he said. 'Then I could have warned you. This isn't the moment to come out here looking for a job, not when you haven't any technical qualifications.'

'But you said you could get me a job any time,' I reminded.

'Good God!' he said. 'That was during the war. Things have changed since then. They've changed a lot in the past year. And you couldn't have picked a worse moment than this. It's sticky – very sticky, old man. Right now there's a scare on and everyone's got cold feet.'

'What's the trouble?'

'One of these West Rand outfits – a company known as "Words" – has turned out a stumer. It's only a small company, but everyone's panicky – afraid the whole field may turn out the same way.

But I'm throwing a little party out at my place tonight. Come along. May be able to fix you up with something.' He gave me the address and rang off.

I put the phone down and sat staring out of the window. The sunshine suddenly seemed a brittle sham. I went and had a bath. And whilst I was lying there thinking it out the phone bell rang. I flung a towel round me and went through into the bedroom. Had Kramer found me a job after all? I picked up the receiver. 'Is that Craig?' It was a man's voice, abrupt and solid. 'Craig speaking,' I said.

'Oh, Bland here,' said the voice and my spirits sagged again. 'My daughter-in-law tells me you commanded a corvette during the war.'

'That's right,' I said.

'Where and how long for?'

I didn't see what he was driving at, but I said, 'Pretty well everywhere. I took command of her in '44 and had her for the rest of the war.'

'Good.' There was a slight pause and then he said, 'I'd like to have a word with you. Can you come down to Room 23?'

'You mean here – in the hotel?'

'Yes.'

'I thought you were sailing right away?'

'I'm staying here the night.' The tone was suddenly abrupt. 'When can you come down?'

'I'm just having a bath,' I told him. 'But I'll be down as soon as I've dressed.'

'Fine.' And he rang off.

I didn't hurry over my dressing. I needed time to think it out. I'd got a damn-fool idea in my mind that I couldn't shake off. It was that question of Bland's about my being in command of a corvette during the war.

But at last I was dressed and couldn't put it off any longer. I went out and took the lift down to the second floor. I knocked at the door of Number 23. Bland answered it himself. 'Come in, Craig,' he said. He took me into a big room facing Adderley Street. 'What would you like? A whisky?'

'That'll do fine,' I said.

I watched him as he poured it. His hands shook slightly. His movements were heavy and slow. He gave me a cigar with the drink. 'Sit down,' he said. 'Now then, suppose you face facts, young man. You haven't got a job and you've found that the prospects here aren't too good.'

'Oh, I don't know,' I said defensively, 'I haven't started to look – '

'I said, let's face facts,' he cut in with the imperturbability of a man accustomed to being listened to. 'I know a lot of people here. I've interests in South Africa, too. There's a gold scare on and things aren't going to be easy for a newcomer.'

He settled his big bulk carefully into a chair. I waited. He sat for a moment staring at me impersonally. Suddenly he heaved himself farther back into the chair. 'I'm prepared to offer you a job with the South Antarctic Whaling Company,' he said.

'What sort of a job?' I asked.

'I want you to take command of *Tauer III* – that's the towing ship that's waiting to take me out to the *Southern Cross*. Sudmann, her skipper, and the second mate were involved in a car crash last night. They're both in hospital.'

'What about his first mate?' I asked.

'He's not on board. He was taken ill before *Tauer III* left the factory ship. I gather you know that Nordahl, the manager of the *Southern Cross*, is dead. It's essential that I get out there as soon as possible. I've spent all day looking for a man to take command of *Tauer III*. But I can't find anyone suitable. Those that are suitable don't want to spend four months out in the Antarctic. It was only this evening that my daughter-in-law told me you had commanded a corvette during the war. These towing boats are ex-Naval corvettes, converted. I rang you straight away.'

'But I haven't the necessary papers,' I said. 'I couldn't just walk on to the bridge of – '

He waved his thick hand. 'I'll fix all that. You can leave that to me. I take it there's no technical problem? You can remember how to handle them, eh? You haven't forgotten your navigation?'

'No. But I've never taken a ship into the Antarctic. I don't know that – '

'That doesn't matter. Now then, as regards terms. You'll get the same pay as Sudmann – that's £50 a month plus bonus. You'll sign on for the season with the option of being landed at the Cape or taken back to England. You understand that your command of *Tauer III* will be a temporary one covering the trip from here to the factory ship. You'll hand over to the senior mate in the catcher fleet. I can't engage you over their heads. But we'll find you something interesting to do. And you'll have the same pay as if you were in command of the boat. Now what do you say?'

'I don't know,' I said. 'I'd like to think it over.'

'There isn't time.' His voice had sharpened. 'I want to know now. I must get out there and find out what's happened.'

'Have you no further news about how Nordahl met his death?' I asked.

'Yes,' he answered. 'A message came through just after lunch. Nordahl disappeared. That's all. There wasn't any storm. No reason for it at all. He just vanished. That's why I want to get out there.'

In the silence that followed I tried to shake my thoughts into some sort of order. I'd be away nearly four months. And then the search for a job would start again. Whilst, who knows, Kramer might have talked to somebody so that I'd get the offer of a job at this party. 'I'll need to think this over,' I said. 'I'm seeing a friend this evening. I'll let you know after that.'

His cheeks quivered slightly. 'I want your answer now,' he said.

I got to my feet. 'I'm sorry, sir. I appreciate you're making me this offer. But you must give me a few hours.'

He was about to make some violent retort. But then he thought better of it. For a moment he sat, regarding the end of his cigar. Then he gave a grunt and levered himself up out of the chair. 'All right,' he said. 'Ring me when you've made up your mind. I'll wait for your call.'

I had a drink or two at the bar downstairs, hoping to see something of Judie. In the end I got the hall porter to call me a cab. All the way out to Kramer's place the thought of Judie and her father's mysterious death occupied my thoughts. I felt as though I were destined to be mixed up in the business. I'd felt like that ever since Bland had phoned me. And something inside of me had kept saying: *Give yourself this one chance to get clear of it. Give yourself this one chance.* But as soon as I reached the party I knew that it wasn't going to be any good. I was destined for the Antarctic.

Kramer's house was built on the lines of a Dutch farm. A lot of money had been spent on it. A good deal more had been spent on the interior. The party was in full swing. There was plenty of liquor about. The males were mostly business men. There were a lot of young women. Kramer greeted me with warmth, but the way he talked I might have come out there just to get an introduction to one or two of the 'gurls' as he called them. He left me in the clutches of a pretty little thing who proved a salacious gossip. I passed her on to a man in the hardware industry and went to the bar.

A group of men were discussing the latest mining gossip. One of them said, 'But suppose the mine wasn't salted?'

'Of course, it was salted,' another replied. 'If it weren't absolutely certain, they'd never have dared go as far as arresting Vynberg. I thought all along the assays were too good to be true.'

'Sure it was salted,' said the third, a stout American with a lot of gold fillings. 'But Vynberg's only the front, poor devil. There's others behind him.'

'Who?'

'I've heard three names mentioned. Vynberg's and two guys I never heard of before – Bland and Fisher. They were unloading for all they were worth twenty-four hours before the thing broke.'

'Excuse me.' I was bored, standing there by myself – or perhaps it was the association of the name Bland. 'Everybody I meet talks about the effect of the "Words" crash on the financial situation out here. Just exactly what is "Words"?' The three pairs of eyes fastened on me and were instantly hostile. 'I only arrived out here from England this morning,' I explained quickly.

'You mean to say you don't know what "Words" is?' the American asked me.

'I know nothing about finance,' I said.

I sensed their instant relief. 'Well, I'll be damned!' said the American. 'It's a real pleasure to meet somebody who hasn't got his fingers burned. "Words" is the market name for Wyks Odendaal Rust Development Securities. The abbreviation has turned out remarkably apt. The ten shilling shares have risen from nineteen shillings to just over five pounds in the last four months on development reports showing high values at comparatively low depths. Now the whole game's bust wide open. The managing director's been arrested. They've stopped dealings in the shares on the stock exchange. I don't reckon you could give 'em away right now. And they're too thick to be used for bumph,' he added crudely. 'I've had some myself.'

'Who's this man Bland?' I asked almost without thinking. 'You mentioned – '

'Young fellow, I mentioned nobody of the name of Bland. And if I had it's a common enough name. And I don't like people listening to what I'm saying.' His fishlike eyes were staring at me coldly. I glanced at the others. The hostility was back in their eyes, too.

I turned away and picked up my drink. When I had finished it I slipped quietly out and strolled down through the velvet-soft shadows to the lights of Cape Town. It was beautiful. The air smelt of blossom and the cool of evening after hot sun.

Down where the lights began I got a taxi back to the hotel. As I went towards the desk to get my key, a girl got up from a corner of the entrance hall and came towards me. It was Judie. I scarcely recognized her. She had on an off-the-shoulder evening gown and she was wearing little high-heeled silver slippers. She looked much taller and more graceful. A fur cape was flung round her shoulders. 'I've been waiting for you,' she said. Her face was very pale in the gold frame of her hair.

'For me?' I said. 'Why?'

'Have you made up your mind yet? Will you take command of *Tauer III*?' Her eyes pleaded as they stared at me.

'Yes,' I said.

'Thank God!' she breathed. 'If you hadn't it would have meant waiting for them to fly a man out from England. I couldn't have waited that long.'

'I'm sorry,' I said, realizing what a wait of even a few hours had meant to her.

She took me straight up to Bland's room. He nodded when he heard my decision. 'Everything's fixed,' he said. 'I guessed what your decision would be.' He picked up the phone, ordered a taxi to stand by and arranged for our luggage to be brought down. 'Yes, Mr Bonomi and Mr Weiner will be leaving, too. Also Mr Craig, Room 404.' He turned to me as he replaced the receiver. 'Get yourself packed up, Craig,' he said. 'We're leaving tonight.'

Tauer III lay in the inner basin of the harbour. Picked out in the dock lights as she chafed the concrete, she didn't look much like a corvette. She was dressed in black and grey paint, the bows had been built up for smashing through the ice and all the armament that gives the jagged look to a warship's profile had been cleared out of her. Her line was quite smooth now, though still basically the corvette line with the low after-deck. She looked what she was, a narrow-built, very fast, very powerful tug. Two seamen came down the gangway for our bags. They were big, bearded men. They said, '*God dag*,' as they passed us.

The deck hands were all Norwegian. But by the grace of God the chief engineer was a Scot. There was a knock at the door of my cabin and there he was. 'Me name's McPhee,' he said. He was a little man with thin, sandy hair. He held out an oily hand.

'I'm Craig. I'm taking over from Sudmann.'

His face lighted up and he seized hold of my hand. 'God-Christ, mon,' he cried. 'Anither Scot. There's no another Scot walking his ane bridge in the whole fleet. Ye're the one and only.

The rest of 'em is all Norwegians.'

'The appointment's temporary,' I said. But I couldn't help smiling at his excitement. 'I hope you've got some Scotch on board to celebrate with?'

'Och, aye, Ah've got a wee drap tucked away.' He peered up at me quickly. 'Tell me, mon, do ye know anything aboot these tin cans? I hope to Christ ye do, for she's an ex-corvette and a mean cow in a big sea when she's got some ice on her.'

'You needn't worry, McPhee,' I said. 'I was brought up in corvettes.'

'Och now, that's a relief, sur. Me, Ah was on the big ships.'

'Then we'll have plenty to talk about,' I said. 'Now, what about fuel and water?'

'Tanks all full.'

'Steam up?'

'Aye, we've been standing-by, ready to sail, since this morning.'

'Fine,' I said. 'As soon as we get the okay from Colonel Bland, we'll be moving out. Any of the Norwegian hands speak English?'

'Most of them speak a word or two.'

'Then send the brightest linguist up to the bridge, will you?'

'Aye, aye, sur.'

As he turned to go, I stopped him. 'McPhee. When was this ship last cleaned down. She smells dirty.'

He grinned. 'Och, that's whale,' he said. 'Ye'll no worry aboot it once you get alongside o' the factory ship.'

'It's not very pleasant,' I said.

'Wait till ye've got four rotten carcases alongside. Ye'll remember what ye're smelling noo as the pure odour of carbolic.'

When he'd gone I went up on to the bridge. It had been rebuilt together with the accommodation. I looked aft along the slim length of the ship. The paint was beginning to show rust marks and she was dirty. Over everything hung the indefinable, sickly smell of whale – like a mixture of oil and death on a light breeze. But warps were neatly coiled and everything was greased and cared for. It might not be Navy fashion, but it was workmanlike.

One of the crew tapped me on the arm. 'The *hr. direktör*,' he said. Bland was coming up the gangway. I watched him lumber for'ard along the deck and then he was heaving himself up on to the bridge. 'Find your way about all right?' he enquired.

'Yes, thanks,' I answered.

'Come into the chartroom then and I'll give you the position of the *Southern Cross*.' He found the chart he wanted. 'She's about there,' he said, stabbing his finger at a point roughly three hundred miles west sou'west of the Sandwich Group. I marked the spot with a pencil. 'She's working her way south. Eide says there's a good deal of ice about and the weather's thickening. We'll get their exact position tomorrow.' He turned and rushed through the door on to the bridge. 'Met the Chief yet?' he asked. 'He's a Scot.'

'Yes, I've just been talking to him.'

'Engines all right?'

'Yes,' I said.

He nodded. 'Our agents here have fixed everything. I've got all the necessary papers with me. You can get going as soon as you're ready. Do you need a tug?'

'I've never had to be towed out of port yet,' I said.

His big hand gripped my arm. 'You and I are going to get on fine,' he said, and levered his bulk down the ladder to the deck below.

I stood for a moment, looking out across the litter of cranes to the star-filled warmth of the night over Table Bay. The palms of my hands were sweating. I was nervous. A strange ship and a strange crew. And out there, way, way south, pack ice and a fleet of ships whose operations I didn't understand.

Footsteps sounded on the ladder to the bridge. I turned. It was one of the crew. '*Kaptein* Craig?' He pronounced it Krieg. 'McPhee speaks me to come here.'

'Good,' I said. 'I want somebody to translate my orders for me.'

'*Ja.*' He nodded his big, bearded head. His eyes glinted below the greasy peak of his cap. 'I speak *Engelsk* good. I am two years on American ships. I speak okay.'

'All right,' I said. 'You stand by me and repeat my orders in Norwegian. What's your name?'

'Peer,' he said, 'Peer Solheim.'

I told him to get hold of the coxs'n and arrange for a man to take over the wheel. The coxs'n was short and broad. He rolled for'ard like a small, purposeful barrel. 'Okay, *Kaptein*,' he called up to me, and I saw that he had placed men at the warps and at the fenders. The gangway had already been brought on board. 'Let go for'ard,' I ordered. Solheim repeated the order. The heavy warp was hauled inboard. My mouth felt dry. It was a long time since I'd done this. 'Slow ahead!' The engine-room telegraph rang before Solheim had repeated the order. The helmsman understood. 'Let go aft!' I watched the warp come in, heard their report of all clear in Norwegian as the gap between ship and quay widened. I ordered starboard helm and watched the bow come round. The stern didn't even graze the concrete of the wharf. The men with the fenders stood there watching the concrete slide by, and then they glanced up towards the bridge. I felt suddenly at home. 'Steady as she goes,' I ordered as the bow swung to the mouth of the basin. 'Half ahead!' The engine pulsed steadily. The bridge plates vibrated gently under my feet. The concrete arms of the basin mouth slid towards us out of the warm night. We passed through into Table Bay.

A voice at my elbow said, 'It's good to see the Navy at work.' I turned to find Judie standing behind me, muffled in her fur coat. She smiled. I thought of all the times I'd manoeuvred my old corvette in and out of harbours. I'd have traded a year's pay then for the compliment and the smile and the presence of a pretty girl on the bridge. Out of the corner of my eye I saw Bland's bulky figure turn abruptly on the deck aft of the bridge and make for his cabin. 'We were both a little scared you might have trouble getting out of the basin,' Judie said.

I grinned at her. 'You thought I might run into something?' I accused her.

'Well, we'd only your word for it that you could handle a corvette.' She smiled. 'But now I am requested to inform you that the company has the greatest confidence in your ability to sail the ship.'

'Thanks,' I said. 'Is this Bland speaking or you?'

She laughed then. 'I'm only a daughter of the company, so to speak. It's the chairman who has confidence in you. In a flash of inspiration he thought the message would be more appreciated if delivered by me.'

I glanced quickly down into her eyes. 'What about you?' I asked.

'A wise girl reserves judgement,' she said with a little laugh. And then suddenly, as though she knew the thought that was in my mind, she turned and left the bridge with a quick, 'Good night.'

I stood for a moment, gazing at the stars, identifying the blazing constellation of the Southern Cross. Table Mountain was a dark shadow crouched above the lights of the city, a shadow that blocked out the night sky. I was suddenly conscious of the helmsman. 'Okay Kaptein?' he asked, nodding towards the binnacle. He was steering S.50 W.

'Okay,' I said and clapped him on the shoulder. When I laid off the course I found the man was correct to within 3 degrees.

All next day we steamed sou'west at a steady thirteen knots

through blazing summer sun and a blue, windless sea. I wasn't a whaler and I couldn't adapt myself to their free and easy ways. I ran the ship the only way I knew, the way I'd learned in the Navy. I took the coxs'n with me in the morning on an inspection of the ship and was surprised to find that the decks had been hosed down, mess tables scrubbed, the galley shining and the men practically springing to attention, all grins, whenever I spoke to them. When I reached the engine-room I said to McPhee, 'It's almost like being back in the Navy.'

He grinned and wiped a greasy hand across his freshly-shaven jaw. 'Dinna fool yourself, sur,' he said. 'This is a whale towing ship, not a corvette. But they'll play your game for a day or two. The word got round you were a Navy officer and not a whaler. A lot of 'em were in the Navy during the war. They were tickled to death when they heard there was to be an inspection.'

I felt the blood mounting to my face. 'There'll be no more inspections then,' I said curtly.

'Och, dinna spoil their fun, sur. It'll be the talk of the fleet when we reach the *Southern Cross* – how they had a British Navy officer for the trip and stood to attention and were inspected.' He winked. 'Dinna spoil their bit o' fun,' he repeated. And then anxiously: 'Ye're no offended because Ah've put ye wise to it's all being a wee bit of a game?'

'Of course not,' I said.

Looking over the list of the crew later in the day I found a name that didn't seem to fit in – Doctor Walter Howe. I was on the bridge at the time and I got McPhee on the blower. 'Who's this Doctor Howe and why haven't I seen him?' I asked. 'Presumably he messes with the officers?'

'Aye, but it's no verra often we see him for breakfast,' McPhee's voice replied up the pipe. 'He's the biggest soak in the whole whaling fleet. And that's saying something. He also kens more aboot what makes a whale tick than anyone else. He's a scientist. He's worked for the South Antarctic Company since the war. He's a wee bit o' a nuisance at times, but he's no a bad sort when ye get to know him.'

I got to know the doctor that night. I had had coffee and sandwiches up on the bridge and when the coxs'n relieved me, I went down to my cabin, put on a pair of slippers and relaxed with the assistance of a bottle of Scotch from Sudmann's locker. Then the door opened and Doctor Howe came in.

He didn't knock. He just came straight in. 'My name's Howe.' He stood, swaying slightly in the doorway, looking at me uncertainly out of rather bulging, bloodshot eyes as though he expected me to deny that that was his name. He was a tall lath of a man with a pronounced stoop and an oddly shaped head that was all forehead and no chin. He had a prominent Adam's apple which jerked up and down convulsively as though he were continually trying to swallow something. His eyes dropped to the whisky bottle. 'Do you mind pouring me a drink?' He moved forward into the cabin and I saw that the sole of his left shoe was built up. He wasn't lame, but that slight shortness of one leg gave him an awkward, rather crab-like way of walking and he swung his right arm out wide as though to balance himself.

He sat down on my bunk and fingered his frayed and dirty collar as though it were too tight for him. I poured him a drink and passed it to him. He absorbed it as the desert absorbs rain. 'A-ah, that's better,' he said and lit a cigarette. Then he saw I was looking at him and his thick rubbery lips twisted into a quick impish smile. 'I'm ugly, aren't I?' he said. And then as I turned quickly to my drink: 'Oh, you needn't be embarrassed. It amuses me – when I'm drunk.' He paused and then added, 'And mostly I'm drunk.'

He leaned forward, suddenly tense. 'Ugly duckling. That's what my sisters used to call me. God damn their eyes! That's a hell of a way to start a kid brother out in life. Fortunately my mother was sorry for me, and she had money of her own. I started drinking at the age of puberty.' He gave a harsh laugh and put his feet up on the bunk, lying back and closing his eyes. His clothes were dirty and looked as though he slept in them.

'What's your job with the company?' I asked.

'My job?' He opened his eyes, screwing them up as he stared at the ceiling. 'My job is to tell 'em where the whales go in the summer time. I'm biologist, oceanographist, meteorologist, all rolled into one. It's the same as fortune-telling. Only I use *plankton* instead of a crystal and I'm called a scientist. Any of the old *skytters* manage just as well by intuition. Only don't tell Bland that. I've held this job ever since the war and it suits me.'

To stop him sneering at himself I said, 'I don't know anything about whaling, as you've probably gathered. What's *plankton*, and who are the *skytters*?'

He laughed. It was a gobbling sound that jerked at his Adam's apple. The ungainly head slewed round and grinned at me like a gargoyle. '*Plankton* is sea food. The stuff the fin whales feed on. Oh God – now we're off.' He sat up and knocked back the rest of his drink, pushing the empty glass towards me in an unmistakable manner. I filled it up. 'There's two main types of cetacean,' he said, assuming a mock school-masterly voice. 'Those with teeth and those with finners. Whale like the spermacetti, have teeth and live on large squids from the ocean bed. The fin whale has a mouthful of finners and lives on *plankton*, which is like a very tiny shrimp. He gulps twenty ton or so of water into his mouth and then forces it out through the fins, which act as a sieve. The water goes out, the *plankton* remains. It needs an awful lot of *plankton* to keep an eighty-ton whale alive,' he added. 'Mostly we catch fin whales. So if you know where their food is – well, that's what I try to do, forecast by water temperature, currents, weather and so on where the *plankton* is.'

'And *skytters*?' I asked as he paused.

'*Skytter* is the Danish origin of the English word shooter, and it's pronounced the same way. The *skytters* are the catcher skippers. It's always the skipper who operates the harpoon gun. Sometimes we call them gunners.'

He lay back as though exhausted by this brief dissemination of information. The silence must have lasted over a minute whilst I racked my brain for something in common that we could talk about. 'Queer about Nordahl,' he said suddenly. I only just caught what he said. He seemed to be talking to himself. 'He was a wonderful man.'

I could hear Judie's voice saying exactly the same. 'That's what his daughter thinks,' I said.

'To hell with his daughter,' he cried angrily, thrusting himself up on to one elbow. 'A little bitch that falls for a tyke like Erik Bland shouldn't be able to call Bernt Nordahl her father.'

'Don't shout,' I said. 'Bland might hear you.'

'Do Bland good to know what his son is really like,' he stormed angrily.

'What's wrong with him?' I asked.

He sat up, swinging his feet off the bunk. 'Nothing,' he said, 'except the way he's been brought up and the way his mind works.' His voice was bitter. 'Bland's a fool to think he can make his son fit to take over the business by sending him out for one season. All Bland thinks about is finance. It's Bernt Nordahl who handles the whaling side. He was the best *skytter* in Norway. Then after the war he and Bland floated the South Antarctic Company. Nordahl took over management of the factory ship. In some out-fits it's the Master of the factory ship who's in charge of operations. In our case it's the Manager. And in the four seasons we've been operating, we've got more whale than any other outfit. Why?

Because I know where the *plankton* is? Because the *skytters* have good intuition? No. Because old Bernt Nordahl can smell whale. And the whales went through the factory ship cheaper, faster and with less waste than on any other factory ship. And that's because the men would do anything Nordahl says – they worshipped him. Or rather the old crowd did – the Tönsberg men.' He gulped down the rest of his drink. 'And now he's dead. Lost overboard. Nobody knows how or why.' He shook his head. 'I don't know what to think. He'd been on ships all his life.' The very words Judie had used. 'He was as much at home in these frozen seas as we'd be in London. He couldn't just vanish like that. By Christ!' he added violently. 'I'll ferret out the truth of what happened if it takes me the rest of the voyage.'

I think it was then that I got the first premonition of trouble ahead. Howe had buried his head in his hands and was rocking gently to and fro. 'I'd like to know what was in his mind that night he died,' he murmured.

'What are you thinking of?' I asked. 'Suicide?'

'Suicide?' His head jerked up as though I'd hit him. 'No,' he said angrily. 'No, he'd never have done that.' He shook his head. 'You don't know him, of course. He was a small man, but he had great energy and a sense of humour. His eyes were always twinkling. He was a happy man. The thought of suicide would never enter his head. He enjoyed life.'

'But if Bland were planning to hand control of the company to his son – surely that might be grounds for suicide?' I suggested.

Howe gave a quick laugh – a jackal laugh, half bark. 'Bland pinched his girl once,' he said. 'Bernt Nordahl didn't commit suicide then. No, he went and consoled himself with a married woman.' He smiled as though at some secret joke. 'No. Whatever happened, he didn't commit suicide.' His fingers had tightened on his empty tumbler so that I thought he'd crush the glass. Then he leaned forward and picked up the bottle, automatically filling the tumbler to the brim with neat whisky.

'Why is Bland in such a hurry to hand over the business to his son?' I asked.

'Because every man dreams of a son to carry on where he leaves off,' he snarled. And I understood then why he needed to stay drunk.

'But why the hurry?' I asked.

'Why, why, why?' – his voice had risen again. 'You're as full of questions as a damned school kid. I was a schoolmaster once,' he added irrelevantly. 'Taught science.' He took another gulp at his drink. 'You want to know why Bland is in a hurry? All right, I'll tell you. He's in a hurry because he's going to die. And he knows it. He's had two strokes already. And as far as I'm concerned the sooner he's dead the better. He's a financial crook with about as much sense of – ' His voice jerked to a stop. His mouth stayed open, the jaw slack. He was gazing at the cabin door.

I twisted round in my seat. The door was open as it had been all along. And framed in it was Bland's heavy bulk. He came in and I saw that his face was mottled with the pressure of his anger. 'Get to your cabin, Howe,' he said in a terrible, controlled voice. 'And stay there. You're drunk.' Behind him, in the passage I caught a glimpse of Judie's pale face.

Howe cringed away from him as though he expected to be struck. Then his long neck jerked out. 'I'm glad you heard,' he breathed. 'I wanted you to hear.' His voice steadied. It was unnaturally quiet as he said, 'I wish you were dead. I wish you'd died before you ever left South Africa and came to Norway and met Anna Halvorsen.' His hands clenched and he stared vacantly into space. 'I wish I'd never been born,' he whispered.

'Craig. Get him to his cabin.' Bland's voice shook.

I nodded. 'Come on,' I said to Howe.

The man staggered to his feet, swaying slightly. He still had the vacant look, but he turned his head and focused slowly on Bland. His hands clenched again and he thrust out his head like a tortoise, peering into Bland's eyes. 'If you killed him,' he hissed, 'God help you.' His face was twisted with venom. Hate blazed in his eyes.

Bland's big hands caught hold of him. 'What do you mean by that?' He looked as though he was on the point of battering Howe's ugly face to pulp.

Howe seemed to relax slightly. His thick lips drew back from his teeth in a smile. It was as though he suddenly dominated Bland, as though the other were afraid of him and he knew it. 'If Uriah, the Hittite, had lived,' he said softly, 'what would have happened the next time?'

'Don't talk to me in riddles,' Bland snapped.

'Then have it in plain words,' Howe shouted. 'You tricked Bernt out of the woman he loved. And now you've been trying to trick him out of his interest in the company. For all I know you've done worse than that. But don't worry, Bland. I'll find out the truth about his death. And if you're the cause of it – ' he stooped his head down so that his eyes were looking straight into Bland's – 'I'll kill you,' he said.

He turned then, swaying slightly and reached the door, his

body inclined as though leaning against a strong wind. Bland found his voice again. 'As from today, you cease to be in the employ of the company,' he said abruptly.

Howe turned, smiling slily. 'I shouldn't do that, Bland,' he said. 'Wouldn't look good – first Bernt, then me. Too much like making a clean sweep.' He was face to face with Judie now in the doorway. I saw her shrink back. Her eyes were very wide, her face a pale mask. Howe stopped and stared at her a moment. Then he laughed, and still laughing, staggered along the passage to his cabin.

Judie watched him go, her lips a tight-drawn gash of red against the white of her face. She didn't say anything. Bland turned to me. He gave an apologetic shrug of his shoulders. 'I'm sorry you should have been witness to such a melodramatic scene,' he said. 'The man's not right in the head, I'm afraid. I'd never have employed him but for Nordahl. But until this moment I didn't know he knew certain personal things. It gives his warped mind the sense of a grudge. I'd be glad if you'd keep the matter to yourself.'

'Of course,' I said.

The man looked terribly shaken. His face had a bluish tinge and his heavy cheeks quivered. 'Goodnight,' he muttered.

'Goodnight,' I replied.

He closed the door behind him. I poured another drink and sat there wondering what the hell I'd got myself into.

3

NEXT day the sun had gone. The sea was grey and flecked with whitecaps. A southerly wind drove ragged wisps of cloud across the sky. In a night's sailing we seemed to have left summer behind us. The wind was cold and I began to think of the miles of ice-infested seas that lay ahead. The deck heaved as *Tauer III* lurched over the waves like a drunkard. Things were different this morning. The crew stood about in little groups, talking furtively. There was a sullen, brooding air about the ship.

There were no friendly grins as I inspected the ship that morning. And later in the day an ugly fight broke out between two

of the men. The coxs'n wouldn't let me interfere, so I got McPhee
up on to the bridge and asked him what the trouble was.
'Weel.' He fingered his jaw the way he had. 'It's no exactly
easy to explain. Ye see, this is a Nordahl boat. The men are all
from Tönsberg. And noo that they know Nordahl is dead – '
'How did they find that out?'
'Ye canna have a row like there was between Bland and Howe
last night wi'oot it getting aroond the ship. Ye'd be surprised,
but the men are fond of Howe, the same way they were fond of
Nordahl.'
'But they don't have to fight about it.'
'Och, that was just their way of blowing off steam. The cox'n
was quite right to stop ye from interfeering. Ye see, there's no
love lost between Tönsberg and Sandefjord men, and it's a
Sandefjord man got hurt.'
'Sandefjord's one of the whaling towns of Norway, isn't it?' I
asked.
'Aye. The biggest. And Tönsberg's another whaling toun.'
'But they don't have to fight, just because there's rivalry
between the two towns.'
'Och, ye don't understand. It's this way. Nordahl was a
Tönsberg man. When he and Colonel Bland started the company
after the war, Nordahl had a free hand wi' the signing on of the
crews. Naturally he signed on Tönsberg men. But Mrs Bland –
she's Norwegian ye ken – she comes from Sandefjord. Och, it's
maybe joost gossip, but they say she fancies herself as a wee bittie
queen of the place. Whatever the cause of it, Sandefjord men were
included in the crews last season. An' this season the proportion's
aboot fifty-fifty. Weel, it dinna make for smooth-running. There's
a natural resentment amongst the Tönsberg men.'
'So they took it out of this poor devil from Sandefjord?'
'Aye, that's aboot it. They're in an angry and soospicious
mood – angry because they weren't told aboot Nordahl's death –
soospicious . . . Weel, there's one or two persons they would'na
mind shoving overboard.'
'Meaning – who?' I asked.
But he shook his head. 'Ah'm no saying anither worrd.'
'Do you mean Bland and his son?' I asked him.
'Ah'm no saying anither worrd,' he repeated. But I saw by the
glint in his eye that I'd hit the nail on the head.
'Well, I hope they don't do anything foolish,' I said. 'It's
coming up dirty.'
He cocked his eye at the sky to windward and nodded. 'Aye, it'll

be a dirrty nicht, Ah'm thinking. But they'll sail the ship all reet. Ye dinna ha' to fash yerself aboot that.'

'And the Sandefjord man?'

'He'll be all reet noo.' He hesitated, shuffling his feet awkwardly. 'Ye'll no pass on what Ah said jist noo aboot they're wanting to get rid o' one or two pairsons?'

'Of course not.'

He suddenly grinned. 'It's the de'il when ye've got factions like this an' they're cooped oop togither in a God-forsaken place like the Antarctic for moonths on end. It's no so bad on the catchers and the towing ships. Each ship is either Tönsberg or Sandefjord, wi' a smattering of Scots in the engine-rooms. The Sandefjord laddie is only on board here because he was held in Capetown for hospital treatment. But I tell ye, it's no sa gude on the factory ship.'

'You mean they've a mixed crew on the *Southern Cross*?' I asked him.

'Aye. An' it isna only the crew that's mixed. It's the flensers and lemmers and labourers, that's mixed, too. And they're a violent bluidy bunch o' bastards.' He shook his head gloomily and turned to go.

'Perhaps you'd care to have a drink with me later,' I suggested.

His face relaxed into a dour smile. 'Aye, Ah would that.' And he slid down the ladder to the deck below, leaving me with a welter of half-digested thoughts in my head.

I paced up and down for a time, my mind saturated with conjecture. Perhaps Bland sensed this. It's the only explanation I can give for the sudden intimacy of his conversation. I hadn't seen him all day. He'd kept to his cabin. But about seven o'clock he pulled himself up on to the bridge. He was muffled up in coats and scarves and he looked even broader than usual. His face was blue and puffy, the bloodvessels showing through the skin in a mottled web. 'Has the *Southern Cross* given you her position yet?' he asked.

'Yes,' I said. 'I got a message from Captain Eide this morning.'

'Good.' He peered over the helmsman's shoulder at the compass and then stared out to windward, screwing his eyes up behind his thick-lensed glasses. 'Hear there was a fight,' he said.

'Yes. Sandefjord versus Tönsberg. Tönsberg won,' I added. I don't know quite why I put it like that. I suppose I wanted him to talk.

He gave me a quick glance and then leaned his heavy bulk against the windbreaker. 'Women are the devil,' he muttered. I think he was speaking to himself, but I was to leeward of him and the wind flung the words at me. 'You married?' he asked, turning abruptly towards me.

'No,' I said.

He nodded slowly. It was as though he were saying – *You're lucky.* 'A man's no match for a woman,' he said, looking straight at me. 'A man's mind and interests range. A woman's narrow. They've a queer, distorted love of power – and they're fonder of their sons than they are of their husbands.' He turned his head away and stared down at the sea where it was beginning to break inboard over our plunging bow.

I didn't say anything. For a moment I thought the sudden intimacy had been broken. But then he said, 'Human relationships are queer. Have you ever thought what a thin veneer our civilization is? It's little more than a code of manners, concealing the primitive.'

'Human nature doesn't change,' I said.

He nodded. 'It becomes cribbed by the regulations and hoodoos of society. But I agree, it doesn't change. Once let slip the leash of organized society . . .' He didn't finish the sentence, but stood with his face to the wind as though to cool the inflamed blood-vessels that webbed it.

'What exactly are you trying to tell me?' I asked bluntly.

He looked round at me then, peering up at me through his glasses. 'I don't know,' he said. 'But you're intelligent – and you're outside it all. A man must have somebody to talk to when things are getting too much for him.' He turned his head back to the sea again, hunching it into the fur collar of his topcoat. He was like a big bull-frog squatting there against the windbreaker. 'Howe told you I was dying?' It was a statement rather than a question.

'He said something about you having had a couple of strokes,' I told him.

'Well, I'm dying.' He said it matter-of-factly as though he were informing a group of shareholders that the company had traded at a deficit.

'We're all doing that,' I said.

He grunted. 'Of course. But we're not usually given a time limit. The best man in Harley Street gives me a year at most.' His hand gripped the canvas of the windbreaker and jerked at it as though he wanted to tear it in little shreds. 'A year's not long,' he said hoarsely. 'It's twelve months – three hundred and sixty-five days. And at any moment I may get another stroke, and that'll finish me.' He suddenly laughed. It was a bitter, violent sound.

'When you're told that, it changes your approach to life. Things which seemed important before cease to be important. Others loom larger.' His hand relaxed on the windbreaker. 'When we reach the *Southern Cross*,' he said, 'get to know my son. I want your opinion of him.' He turned abruptly then and went ponderously down the ladder to the deck below. I watched him go, wishing I'd been able to hold him just a little longer. There were questions I'd like to have asked him.

In the middle of our meal that night, the radio operator brought Bland a message. His heavy brows dragged down as he read it. Then he got to his feet. 'A word with you, Craig,' he growled.

I followed him to his cabin. He closed the door and handed me the message. 'Read that,' he said.

I took the message to the light. It read: *Eide to Bland. Men demanding enquiry Nordahl's death. Erik Bland has rejected demand. Please confirm rejection. Mood of Tönsberg men dangerous. Whale very scarce. Position 57.98 S. 34.62 W. Pack ice heavy.*

I handed the message back to him. He crumpled it up in his big fist. 'The damned fool!' he growled. 'It'll be all over the ship that he's not happy about Erik's decision. And Erik's quite right to reject a demand like that. It's a matter for the officers to decide.' He paced up and down for a moment, tugging at the lobe of his ear. 'What worries me is that they should be demanding an enquiry at all. If the circumstances warranted an enquiry, then Erik should have ordered it right away instead of waiting for the men to demand it. And I don't like Eide's use of the word *dangerous*,' he added. 'He wouldn't use it unless the situation was bad.' He swung round on me. 'What's the earliest we can expect to reach the *Southern Cross*?'

'Eight days at least,' I answered.

He nodded gloomily. 'A lot can happen in eight days. The worst news in that message is that they're getting few whales. When men are busy they haven't the energy to brood. But when no whales are coming in – I've seen men change from smiles to hatred in the twinkling of an eye when the whales have been lost. And they'll link it in their minds with Nordahl's death, damn them. They're a supersittious lot, and Nordahl had a nose for whale.'

'What are you scared of?' I asked. 'You're not suggesting that the men would mutiny, are you? Presumably a factory ship comes under normal British maritime laws. It takes a lot to drive men to mutiny.'

'Of course I'm not suggesting they'd mutiny. But they can make things damned awkward without going as far as mutiny. There's three million pounds invested in that outfit. To make money on a capital outlay as big as that in a four month season everything has got to move with clock-like precision.' He began tugging at the lobe of his ear again. 'Erik can't handle a thing like this. He hasn't the experience.'

'Then put somebody else in charge,' I suggested. 'Captain Eide, for instance.'

He looked up at me quickly. His small eyes were narrowed. I could see the battle going on inside him – pride against prudence. 'No,' he said. 'No. He must learn to handle things himself.'

He paced up and down. He didn't say anything. The silence in the cabin was the sort of silence that is audible. I could see the conflict working in the man. With sudden decision he went to the door. 'I'll have Eide report independently,' he threw over his shoulder.

I went up on to the bridge. The sea was a heaving mass in the dreary half light. I stood there for a moment, watching the heavy weight of water surging white across the bow every time the little ship plunged. An albatross wheeled over the mast. Its huge wings were still as it planed into the wind. The air was bitterly cold. A thin film of ice was spreading on the windbreaker so that the canvas was stiff and smooth to the touch. I went into the wheelhouse and looked at the barometer. 'No good,' said the bearded Norwegian at the wheel. He was right. The glass was very low and still falling. 'The sommer she do not kom, eh?' His bearded face opened in a grin. But there was no answering humour in his blue eyes.

The door flung back and Judie entered, the wind blowing her in with a swirl of sleet. She shut the door with difficulty. 'The weather looks bad,' she said. Her face was pinched and cold.

'We're getting into high latitudes,' I reminded her.

She nodded bleakly. I offered her a cigarette. She took it, and as I struck a match to light it for her I saw that her hand was trembling slightly. She gulped in a lungful of smoke and then asked, 'Was that message from Eide?'

'Yes,' I said.

'What did it say?'

I told her.

She turned and stared out through the window. The sea was cold and grey, a tumbled mass of water, barely visible, yet seeming to crowd its menace right into the wheelhouse. She didn't speak for some time, and when she did she startled me by saying, 'I feel scared.'

'It's just the weather,' I said.

She dropped her cigarette and ground it out violently with her heel. 'No. It's not the weather. It – it's something I don't understand.' She turned and faced me. 'I should just be feeling wretched because he's dead. It should end there – with sorrow. But it doesn't.' And then she said again, 'I'm scared.'

I stepped forward and took her hand. It was cold as ice. 'It's rotten for you,' I said. 'But there's no need for you to worry. Things will sort themselves out when we reach the *Southern Cross*.'

'I don't know,' she said. 'I feel as though that's just the beginning.' She looked up at me. Her grey eyes were deeply troubled. 'Walter knows something – knows something that we don't.' Her voice trembled. She was overwrought.

'Why should Howe know anything we don't?' I said. 'You're imagining things.'

'I'm not imagining things,' she answered violently. 'I'm seeing things for the first time.'

I didn't say anything and we stood there for some time, quite silent. She didn't attempt to withdraw her hand from mine. But there was no contact between us. Then she suddenly jerked her hand away, pulled a packet of cigarettes out of her pocket and offered me one. 'Is this the farthest south you've ever been?' she asked, her voice controlled and a little abrupt.

'Yes,' I said and raised my other hand to show I was still smoking. 'But I'm not new to ice. When I was twenty I went on a university expedition to South East Greenland.'

'So. You are an explorer?' She took one of her cigarettes and I lit it for her. 'But you'll find it very different down here. The land mass of the South Pole makes it much colder.'

She took a long pull at the cigarette and added, 'But it's unusual for the pack to be so far north at this time of the year. It's like it was in the summer of 1914 when Shackleton came down here in the *Endurance*.'

'I was in Oslo just after the war,' I said. 'I went over to Bygdoy and saw the *Fram*. I think that must be the best exhibition of Polar exploration in the world.'

'Yes. I like it, too. We are very proud of the *Fram*.'

The conversation languished there, so I said, 'I suppose this is your first trip into the Antarctic?'

'No,' she replied. 'Not my first. When I was eight years old my father brought me with him to South Georgia. My mother had just died and we had no home. Bernt was one of the *skytters* at Grytviken. I was there about two months. Then he sent me to friends in New Zealand. He said it was time I learnt English. I learned my English in Auckland. I was there a year and then he took me back with him at the end of the next season.'

'Is Grytviken in South Georgia?' I asked.

'Yes. There are shore stations there. I made three or four trips with my father in his catcher.'

'Then you're quite an experienced whaler,' I kidded her.

'No,' she said. 'I'm not like Gerda Petersen.'

'Who's she?' I asked.

'Gerda is the daughter of Olaf Petersen,' she answered. 'Olaf was once mate on my father's catcher when he was at Grytviken. Gerda and I are the same age. We used to play together when we were at Grytviken. But she's tough. She's more like a man. This is her second season with our company. Her father says he'll make her the first woman *skytter* in Norway.'

'She must be tough,' I said.

She laughed. 'Poor Gerda. She's not very beautiful, you know. She ought to have been born a boy. She's passed all her exams. She could be master of a ship, like women are in Russia. But she prefers to come south as her father's mate. His men worship her. She may not be very beautiful, but I think she's very happy.'

A sudden gust of wind hit the wheelhouse. The ship heeled and dipped violently. I caught a glimpse of the white sheet of spray flung up by the bows as they crashed into a wave, felt the whole ship tremble. The door burst open and the coxs'n came in. Judie said, 'I think I'll go below now.'

'I'll come with you,' I said. 'I want to get some sleep before the storm breaks.' I told the coxs'n to wake me if it got worse and took Judie below. I saw her to her cabin. Below decks the movement of the ship seemed much more violent. I was very conscious that the worst was yet to come. 'I'll introduce you to Gerda,' Judie said as I held the door of her cabin open for her. 'She's very fat and very jolly – and you'll like her.' She gave me a quick smile. 'I hope you'll have enough clothing,' she said. 'It'll be cold up on the bridge when dawn comes.'

'Fortunately Sudmann and I are about the same size,' I said. I wished her good night and closed the door. Back in my own cabin, I took off my boots and climbed into my bunk with my clothes on.

For a long time I lay awake, listening to the straining of the ship, sensing the growing pressure of the wind and seas, and all the time wondering about the factory ship still two thousand miles sou'west of us.

The full force of the storm hit us just after four in the morning. I woke to sudden consciousness, feeling the weight of the water holding us down. The struggle of the ship against the fury of the elements was there in every sound of her – in the creaking of the cabin furniture, in the jerk and shudder of the engine, in the staggering movement of her as she plunged and climbed, plunged and climbed. I could feel the steel of the cabin walls bending under the strain. She was like a live thing fighting for breath.

I rolled out of my bunk and fumbled for my sea boots. The coxs'n came in as I was dragging on my oilskins. He didn't say anything. He just nodded and went out again. Outside the full force of the wind hit me, thrusting me against the rail, taking my breath away. Seas rolled green over the after-deck. I hauled myself up to the bridge. The short night was over. But the dawn was a grey half darkness. The coxs'n had headed her up into the wind. The waves seemed mountains high, their tops a hissing whirl of spindrift. And the sleet drove parallel with the wavetops, a wild, driven curtain of darkness.

I won't attempt to describe those next eight days. They were eight days of unrelieved hell for everyone on board. Sometimes it rained. More often it just blew. The weight of the wind varied, but I doubt whether it ever dropped below Force 6. It was from the south-west, varying about two points either side. The sea was like a mountain range on the move. There wasn't a dry place in the ship. Nearly everyone was seasick. In all those eight days we only saw the sun once, and that was a watery gleam that flashed out for a few minutes through a vent in the storm wrack. I ceased to think about the object of our journey, or about the *Southern Cross*; I ceased to think about anything but the ship. My mind was a blank of sleeplessness in which the safety of the ship was the only tangible idea.

I saw hardly anything of the others. I was up on the bridge most of the time. Bland came up twice, his heavy features blue with cold and the exhaustion of seasickness. Each time he asked for our position. The man had a driving purpose which was accentuated by the knowledge of his illness. His interest in life had narrowed down to an urgent desire to reach the *Southern Cross* as soon as possible. He was impatient at our slow progress, impotently angry at the elements. I remember him standing there on the bridge and shaking his fist at the sea and shouting, 'Damn you! Damn you!' as though curses could subdue the wind. Some ice had formed on the rungs of the bridge ladder. He slipped as he went down, and a wave, bursting against the side of the ship, nearly swept him overboard. He was wet through and badly shaken. He didn't come up to the bridge again.

Judie came up once and I was angry with her, telling her to keep to her cabin. I think I threw some bad language at her. I was too wrought up to know what I said. It had the desired effect and she didn't come up again. But after that every morning one of the crew brought up a flask of brandy. 'Fra fru Bland.' I was grateful to her for that.

Bonomi was the only one of the passengers who was a daily visitor on the bridge. He was suffering badly from seasickness, but he'd struggle up each day with his camera, regardless of the danger, and take pictures of the storm. His greeting was invariably the same: 'It is turn out nice again – yes?' And his monkey-like face, green under the olive tan, would crack in a wide grin. Once I asked him about Doctor Howe. 'Is he sick?' I asked.

'He is sick, of course,' he answered. 'But what is sickness to a man who drink two bottles of whisky a day? He is incredible, that man!'

In a way the storm was a good thing. There was no more trouble with the Sandefjord man. The crew were fully occupied with the weather. This, according to the old hands, was quite unprecedented. It was much colder that it should have been and the gale prolonged itself out of all expectation. But by the 14th we were in 53.42 S. 24.65 W. some 500 miles east of South Georgia. Daylight was now virtually continuous throughout the twenty-four hours. Visibility fortunately was not too bad for on the 15th we sighted our first iceberg. And shortly after the evening meal the masthead lookout reported land on the port beam. This was the first of the Sandwich Group. It was the only glimpse we got of it as the storm clouds closed in and heavy, icy rain reduced visibility to a few miles.

Our course was still S. 47° W. and we began to sight icebergs regularly, some of them big, towering masses of ice, pinnacled and ramparted like floating forts. One we passed must have been fully three miles long with a completely flat top except for one steep and sudden mass like the superstructure of a ship. It bore, in fact, a striking resemblance to a monstrous aircraft carrier coated in ice.

I was constantly up on the bridge now for we were closing the last position we had received from the *Southern Cross*. We should have been in radio telephone communication – the R/T sets had a radius of 400 miles or more. But early in the storm our aerials had been brought down and it had been impossible to re-rig.

On the night of the 16th the gale got worse than ever. Heavy, freezing rain brought visibility down to almost zero and in the half light around midnight I reduced speed. Shortly afterwards the lookout called down, '*Isen.*' I rang for slow ahead and a few moments later caught the white glimmer of ice ahead. It wasn't a berg. It was our first taste of loose pack. The floes were small and broken – the thawing fringe broken from the pack ice farther south and flung north-eastward by the storm. The coxs'n shook his head gloomily. 'Nefer haf I seen the ice up here in sommer.'

I turned the ship westward and remained at slow ahead. Early that morning the wind suddenly veered to the south and died away to a gentle breeze. The clouds drifted away astern and we saw the sun clearly for the first time in eight days. It was low on the horizon and had little warmth. But it was wonderful just to see it. The sky was blue and the world looked suddenly cheerful. But the sea remained a mountainous, heaving mass and despite the blue of the sky it had a peculiar, cold green colour. Away to the south a glimmer of white showed the fringe of the loose pack ice. Through bleary eyes I watched the sun climb quickly up the sky. Soon everything was steaming.

Then gradually the sun's light paled. The warmth died out of it and the blue gradually faded from the sky. A damp cold gripped the ship. The horizon faded. The distant line of white that marked the ice became blurred and then vanished, merging into what looked like a low strata of cloud at sea level. Then the sun vanished altogether. The colour drained out of everything. The scene became a flat black and white picture. It was cold, like an etching. Then the sharpness of it faded as the fog rolled over us, enveloping us in its chill, soundless blanket.

We kept at slow ahead with lookouts in the bow and at the masthead. I was taking no chances with icebergs, though in that brief glimpse of the ice-littered sea to the south I had seen no sign of any.

Shortly after ten Bland himself came up on to the bridge. Eight days of enforced idleness and little food had made a great difference to him. His face was leaner. The bluish tinge had gone and the mottled veining of his skin was not so noticeable. His movements were quicker too, and his eyes more alert. 'What's our position?' he asked. His tone was crisp. The personality that had driven the man to the top in his own world was there in his voice.

'Fifty-eight south, thirty-three west,' I told him. I took him into the wheelhouse and showed him the position on the chart – roughly 200 miles west of South Thule the southernmost point of the Sandwich Group.

'We ought to be able to get the *Southern Cross* on the R/T,' he said.

'Sparks is rigging a new aerial now,' I told him. 'I'll let you know as soon as he makes contact.'

He nodded and went out on to the bridge. He stood for a while, staring out into the fog. He stood like that for several minutes, his big hands, encased in fur gloves, gripping the ice-stiff canvas of the windbreaker. Suddenly he swung round on me. 'I've been mixed up in whaling for the last twenty-five years,' he said. 'I've never heard of summer conditions as bad as this.'

I made the same remark that Judie had made eight days before – that it was the sort of conditions that Shackleton experienced in the *Endurance* in 1914. He gave a grunt. 'This isn't a damned polar expedition,' he growled. 'This is business. See any whale this morning?'

'None,' I said.

'Where's Howe?'

'I haven't seen him since the storm started,' I replied.

He turned and barked an order in Norwegian to one of the crew.

The man looked at him. It wasn't exactly insolence. But the man's manner was sullen as he said, '*Ja*,' and crossed the bridge to the ladder.

Bland spoke to him sharply. The man's face darkened. '*Ja – hr. direktor*,' he muttered and slid down the ladder to the deck below. Bland said something violent under his breath and walked to the starboard wing of the bridge. He stood there alone peering out over the side, until Howe appeared.

Howe looked thin as a wraith beside the squat bulk of the company's chairman. He had a weak growth of beard that looked untidy on his queer face and his eyes were bloodshot. But he was sober. Standing in front of Bland he seemed nervous as though, without liquor inside him, he found it difficult to face the man. 'For the last four years Nordahl has employed you as a scientist,' Bland rumbled, his small eyes looking the other up and down with marked distaste. 'Now it's up to you to justify that appointment.

Conditions out here this summer are abnormal. The last report we had from the *Southern Cross* spoke of few whales. We've seen none. By tomorrow morning I want a report from you on the probable movement of whale in these conditions.'

'I understood you to say I was no longer employed by the company.' Howe's voice had developed a slight stutter. His Adam's apple jerked up and down under his scrubby beard.

'Forget it,' Bland said. 'You were drunk. I shall assume you didn't know what you were saying. Your continued employment will depend on your usefulness to the company. Now get to work. I want a full report first thing tomorrow morning.'

Bland turned on his heel. Howe hesitated. I knew what he wanted to say. He wanted to tell Bland that it was unfair to expect the impossible, that the very abnormality of the conditions made it so. He was being blackmailed and he knew it. Bland wanted whales. Howe was to produce them, like a conjurer, or be sacked. His Adam's apple jerked violently once or twice. His mouth opened and then suddenly closed. He turned and stumbled past me to the bridge ladder.

Shortly afterwards Bland went below. An hour later, Bonomi called up to me to say that the radio was working. I left the coxs'n on the bridge and stumbled wearily down to the deck below. My eyes were bleary with lack of sleep and the strain of staring into days of wind and sleet and the morning's impenetrable blanket of fog. Bland and Judie were both in the wireless room. Judie had dark circles of strain under her eyes. But her smile of greeting was warm and friendly. 'You must be dead,' she said.

'The daily flask of brandy was a great help,' I said.

She looked away quickly as though she hadn't wanted to be thanked. Bland turned his big head towards me. He had taken off the little fur cap with the ear flaps that he'd been wearing and his mane of white hair was rumpled. He looked like a rather surprised owl. 'Just trying to get the *Southern Cross* on the R/T,' he said. 'We've been speaking to the *Haakon* – one of the Sandefjord factory ships. She's got eight whale in the last ten days. Now she's steaming south towards the Weddell Sea. Hanssen, the master, says he's never known conditions like this. He's about three hundred miles west-sou'west of us.'

The radio crackled. Then clear and distinct came a voice speaking in Norwegian. I guessed it must be the *Southern Cross*, for Bland stiffened and his head jerked round towards the receiver. The radio operator leaned down towards the mike. "*Ullo-ullo-ullo – Syd Korset. Tauer III anroper Syd Korset.*' There was a quick exchange in Norwegian and then he turned to Bland. 'I have Captain Eide for you,' he said, and passed the microphone across to him. The chairman's thick fingers closed round the bakelite grip. 'Bland here. Is that Captain Eide?'

'*Ja, hr. direktor.* This is Eide.' The voice crackled in sing-song English faintly reminiscent of a Welsh accent.

'What's your position?' I nodded for Sparks to take it down. Fifty-eight point three four south, thirty-four point five six west. I made a swift mental calculation. Bland's eyebrows lifted in my direction. 'That's about forty miles west of us,' I said. He nodded, and resumed his conversation, this time in Norwegian. I didn't listen. I couldn't concentrate enough to pluck the sense out of it from the few words I'd managed to pick up. The warmth of the cabin was enveloping me. My eyelids became unbearably heavy. Sleep rolled my head against the wood panelling of the cabin wall.

Then suddenly I was awake again. A new voice was talking over the radio, talking in English. 'They're holding out for an enquiry. I've told them there isn't going to be any enquiry. It's a waste of time. There's nothing to enquire into. Nordahl's gone, and that's all there is to it.' It was an easy, cultured voice – smooth like an expensive car. But it was just a veneer. It revealed nothing of its owner. 'The real trouble is that the season's been terrible. Even the Sandefjord men are grumbling. As for the Tönsberg crowd – they're more nuisance than they're worth. If you hadn't been coming out I'd have sent the whole lot home.'

'We'll talk about that when I see you, Erik,' Bland cut in, his voice an angry rumble. 'How many whale have you caught so far?'

'Fin whale? A hundred and twenty-seven – that's all. The fog's just beginning to lift now. Perhaps the luck will change. But there's pack ice to the south-east of us and the men don't like it. They say conditions are abnormal.'

'I know all about that,' said Bland. 'What are your plans?'

'We're cruising east now along the northern edge of the pack. We'll just have to hope for the best.'

'Hope for the best!' Bland's cheeks quivered. 'You get out and find whale – and find 'em damn quick, boy. Every day without whale is a disaster. Do you understand?'

'If you think you can find them when I can't – well, you're welcome to come and try.' The voice sounded sharp and resentful.

Bland gave an angry grunt. 'If Nordahl were alive – '

'Don't you start throwing Nordahl at me,' his son interrupted in a tone of sudden violence. 'I'm sick of hearing about him. He's dead, and the mere mention of his name, as though it were a sort of talisman, won't produce whale.'

'We'll be with you in a few hours now,' Bland said soothingly. 'We'll talk about it then. Put Eide back on.' Eide's voice was comfortingly calm. He spoke in Norwegian and Bland was answering him in the same language. There was a pause. Then suddenly his voice was back in the cabin again, shouting. '*Hval! Hval! En av hval-baatene har sett hval!*' Bland's face relaxed. He was smiling. Everybody in the cabin was smiling.

I looked at Judie. She leaned towards me, and I saw that even she was excited. 'They've sighted whale.' She turned her head to the radio again and then added, 'They have seen several *pods*. They are all going south – into the ice.'

'How many whales to a *pod*?' I asked.

She laughed. 'Depends on the sort of whale. Only one or two in the case of the blue whale. But three to five for the fin whale.' She shook her head. 'But it's bad for them to be going south.'

The skipper of the *Southern Cross* signed off and Bland turned to me. 'You got their position?' he asked.

I nodded and got stiffly to my feet. Sparks handed me a slip of paper on which he'd written the present position and course of the *Southern Cross*. I climbed up to the bridge and laid our course to meet up with the factory ship. *Tauer III* turned, heeling slightly as the helmsman swung her on to the new bearing. I told the coxs'n to wake me in four hours' time and went below for the first real sleep I'd had in eight days.

But I didn't get my full four hours. The messboy woke me just after midday and I dragged myself up to the bridge. The coxs'n was there, sniffing the air. 'You smell something, *ja*?' He was grinning. I smelt it at once – a queer, heavy smell like a coal by-product. 'Now you smell money,' he said. 'That is whale.'

'The *Southern Cross*?'

'*Ja.*'

'How far away?'

'Fifteen – maybe twenty mile.'

'Good God!' I said. I was imagining what the smell must be like close to. I ordered the helmsman to point the ship up into the light southerly wind. An hour later the fog began to lift and I ordered full speed. Slowly the fog cleared, revealing a bleak, ice-green sea heaving morosely under a low layer of cloud. Away to the southeast I got my first sight of the ice blink. This was the light striking up from close pack ice, its surface mirrored in the cloud. The effect was one of brilliant whiteness, criss-crossed with dark seams. The dark seams were the water lanes cutting through between the floes, all faithfully mapped out in the cloud mirror above it.

Bonomi was up on the bridge with his camera. When I'd worked out our position and sent a lookout to the masthead, he came across to me. 'You feel good now, eh? Everything is fine.' He grinned. His cheerfulness added to the sense of depression that had been growing up inside me. I wasn't looking forward to closing with the *Southern Cross*. For one thing, it meant the end of my temporary command. For another – well, all I can say is that I had developed an uneasy feeling about the *Southern Cross*.

'Bland is saying we must go south into the Weddell Sea,' Bonomi babbled on. 'I 'ope so. He says that after Nordahl, Hanssen is the best whaler in Norway, and if he take the *Haakon* south, then we shall go too. In the Weddell Sea I think I get very good pictures. You will see.'

He was getting on my nerves and I was too dead with lack of sleep to have any hold over my tongue. 'Don't you think of anything else but your bloody pictures?' I said.

He looked up at me with a sort of shocked surprise. 'But what else should I think of?' He peered up at me as though gauging my temper. 'Do not worry about losing the ship. I find a nice job for you, eh – carrying my camera?'

We were both laughing at his little joke when there was a cry of Ship ahoy! from the masthead. Ten minutes later a thick blur of smoke, fine on the starboard bow, was visible from the bridge. Bland, Judie, Weiner – they all came up, gazing excitedly at that first glimpse of the factory ship. 'Trying out by the look of it,' Bland said. I glanced at him quickly. His small eyes gleamed behind their glasses. For him the smoke meant money. For Judie it meant something different and her gaze was clouded. Bonomi was excited. He positively bounced up and down and insisted on shaking everybody by the hand. Weiner looked at it with the apathy of a man to whom nothing has a sense of reality. Howe also came up on to the bridge and stood, a little removed from the rest, gazing out towards the smoke. I wished I could read his thoughts. I saw him glance covertly at Bland and then back again towards the smoke on the horizon. And in that instant I felt a tingle run up my spine.

Judie caught my eye. 'I hope the whales – ' She didn't finish the sentence, but stared at me, her mouth slightly open, caught in the utterance of the next word. I think she knew that Howe worried me.

Bland went aft to the wireless room then. The others followed. Howe was the last to go. He stood, gripping the windbreaker with his bony hands. Conscious of my gaze, he turned and looked at me. Then he swung away and stared for a moment south, towards the ice blink. I watched him, fascinated. His glance went once more to the factory ship, and then back to the mirrored brightness of the pack ice. He stared at it for a long time. Then he turned quickly. 'I must go and prepare my report,' he said and there was a curiously sly lift to the corners of his mouth as he said this.

Once I went down to the wireless room. It was a babel of sound. Norwegian voices boomed out of the R/T receiver; catchers to the factory ship, the factory ship to the buoy boats and tow-ers – everyone was talking on the air at once. I gathered the whales were plentiful. Bland was smiling. And in intervals between communications he was discussing the new electrical equipment with Weiner, sometimes in English, sometimes in German.

It was a strange and rather wonderful sight as we closed the *Southern Cross*. It wasn't just a factory ship. It was a whole fleet of ships. I examined them through my glasses. There were five catchers strung out in a line behind the *Southern Cross*. They appeared to be idle. Another catcher was almost alongside. There were two towing ships. I recognized them by their corvette lines. There were also two old-type catchers that I was told were buoy boats – that is to say, they were towing vessels that could be used to supplement the catcher fleet if required. Behind these was an old whaling ship which ferried the meat to the refrigerator ship, a vessel of about 6000 tons which was lying astern of the others. Near this was a large tanker and more catchers were scurrying about on the horizon. To see all those ships gathered together in these hostile southern seas fired the imagination. It was such a gigantic operation – a litter of masts that reminded me of D-Day.

Bonomi gripped my arm and pointed across the port bow. A spout of vapour rose not two cables' length away from us, and the water boiled as a smooth, sleek shape, like a submarine, dived. There was a snort almost alongside and another spout thrust ten or fifteen feet into the air, so close that the wind whipped some of the water on to our decks. It was our first sight of whale. Bonomi dived for his camera. We were in the midst of a *pod*.

I brought the ship round in a wide circle to come up parallel

with the *Southern Cross*. In doing so we passed right through the
black, oily smoke that drifted to leeward of her. The thick,
noisome smell closed down on us like a blanket. It was heavy, oily,
all-pervading smell. It seemed to weigh down on the senses, thick
and cloying and penetrating.

As we emerged from it, I could hear the sound of voices on the
factory ship and the clank of winches. The stern was open, like a
dark cavern, and a whale was being hauled up through it to the
after-plan. The ship was big – about twenty thousand tons. Her
steel sides, already rusting, towered above us as we glided alongside. Up on the bridge a man in a fur cap held a megaphone to
his lips and called down to us. It was Eide. I caught the name.
That was all. The rest was in Norwegian. Judie said, 'He's
lowering a boat and coming over to us himself.' Her face looked
puzzled. 'I wonder why?' she added.

I glanced across at Bland. He was standing in the port wing of
the bridge, gazing aft to where the catchers were strung out in
a line. His brows were dragged down and his face had a thunderous look.

We were all there on the bridge when Eide arrived. He was a
gaunt, bony man with hatchet-like features and a trick of continually chewing on a matchstick which he slipped to the corner
of his mouth when he spoke. He was wearing a thick polo-necked
sweater and his gabardine trousers were secured by a wide leather
belt with a silver buckle. 'Well?' Bland barked at him. 'What's
the trouble? Why aren't all the catchers out?'

Eide looked quickly. 'I will speak in English,' he said, noticing
that the man at the helm was watching him. 'There is trouble.
Half the men in the ship have struck. Also the men on five
catchers and one towing ship.'

'The Tönsberg men?' Bland asked.

'*Ja*. They have threatened to stop the others working. But they
have not yet made any trouble.'

'They're waiting to see what I do. Is that it?'

Eide nodded.

Bland's fist thudded on the bridge rail. 'You've not much more
than a hundred whales to show for six weeks' work.' He was
almost shouting. 'And now, when we are right in the midst of
whale, they strike. Why? What's their complaint?'

'They want an enquiry into Nordahl's death.' Eide hesitated
and then said, 'Also they wish your son to be removed from the
position of acting manager.'

'Who's behind all this?'

'Kaptein Larvik, I think. He speaks for the others. As you know he was a great friend of Nordahl. It is he, I think, who start this idea of an enquiry. But they are all of them in it now – Larvik, Petersen, Korsvold, Schnelle, Strand and Jensen.'

Bland's hand clenched into a fist. Then it relaxed. He took off his glasses and wiped them slowly. His heavy jaw was set, his small eyes steely. I watched his mouth spread into a tight-lipped smile. Then he put his glasses on again. 'Very well,' he said quietly. 'If that's the way they want it – ' He glanced quickly at Eide. 'Who do they want as factory manager instead of my son?'

'Kaptein Petersen,' Eide replied. 'He is a good leader and he manage one of the South Georgia stations for three seasons. He returns to catching because he likes the active life.'

'All right, Captain Eide. You will signal for the captains of those five catchers and the towing ship to come on board for a conference with me. I shall then give them an ultimatum – either get on with the job or they are relieved of their commands.'

'Perhaps they will refuse to come.' Eide's voice sounded embarrassed.

'Good God!' Bland exploded. 'If things have been allowed to get as out of hand as that, then there are other methods of dealing with them. How will they get on in the Antarctic without oil and supplies from the factory ship? Come, pull yourself together, Eide. We can be just as tough. Get down to the wireless room and instruct them to come on board the *Southern Cross* right away.' His jaw thrust out suddenly. 'And if they try to make conditions, tell them they'd better not aggravate me further. Whilst you're doing that, we'll get our things into the boat. Craig,' he said, turning to me, 'you'll come with us. The coxs'n can take temporary command here. Before you know where you are you'll be in charge of a catcher.' He was almost grinning now. He was the sort of man who thrived on a fight. But I must say I didn't much fancy the roll of strike-breaker amongst a lot of Norwegians whose feuds I didn't fully understand.

Eide was leaving the bridge now, but Bland stopped him. 'Why didn't Erik come to report this himself?' he demanded.

The skipper of the factory ship hesitated. Then he said, 'He is on the fore-plan. He could not come.'

Bland grunted. 'He's got assistants, hasn't he?' he growled.

I must say that at that moment I felt some sympathy for Erik Bland. Whatever the man's nature, he'd certainly been handed a a tough job, and I didn't blame him for staying up on the fore-plan. I looked at Judie to see whether she was feeling sympathy for her husband's position. But she was staring up at the towering, ugly bulk of the *Southern Cross* and I realized that her thoughts were on her father.

4

I WASN'T present at the meeting between Bland and the skippers of the Tönsberg catchers. But I saw them leave and I got the impression that Bland had given them something to think about. There were five of them – tough, bearded men with fur caps on their heads, thick jerseys under their windbreakers and feet encased in knee-length boots. They stopped at the head of the gangway, talking together in a little bunch. They were joined almost immediately by two other men. One was short and stout with a jolly, wrinkled face and the appearance of a seal. The other was a big man with a jagged scar on his cheek over which his beard refused to grow. They stood a little apart from the others for a moment, talking earnestly in low voices. As I passed them I heard the man with the scar say, '*Ja, Kaptein Larvik.*' Then he turned away and the other joined the group at the head of the gangway.

I was being conducted round the ship at the time. Captain Eide had allocated me a bunk in the second officer's cabin and had detailed one of his officers, a Scot from Leith, to show me round.

My guide had taken me first to the flensing decks. This is the centre of activity in a factory ship when the whales are coming in. There are two flensing decks – the fore-plan and the after-plan. And both looked the sort of charnel house you might dream up in a nightmare. Men waded knee-deep in the bulging intestines of the whales, their long-handled, curved-bladed flensing knives slashing at the bleeding hunks of meat exposed by the removal of the blubber casing. The winches clattered incessantly. The steam saws buzzed as they ripped into the backbone, carving it into star-shaped sections still festooned with ragged strands of red meat. Men with huge iron hooks dragged blubber, meat and bone to the chutes that took it to the boilers to be tried out and the precious oil extracted. The noise and the smell were indescribable. And the work went on unceasingly as whale after whale was dragged up the slipway, the men working like demons and the decks slippery with blood and grease.

I followed one whale as it came up through the cavity in the stern. It was eighty feet long and weighed nearly a hundred tons. The men on the after-plan fell on it when it was still being winched along the deck. The flensers cut flaps of blubber from around its jaws, hawser shackle was rigged in holes cut in these flaps and in a moment the winches were ripping the blubber off the huge carcase, the flensers cutting it clear of the meat as it was rolled back. To clear the blubber from the belly, they winched the whale over on to its back, and as it thudded over on the deck urine poured out of its stomach in a wave and the pink mass of the tongue flopped over like a huge jelly. Stripped of its blubber it was winched to the fore-plan. The meat was cut away from the backbone and then the bone itself was cut up and sent to the pots. In just over an hour that hundred-ton monster had been worked up and absorbed by the factory ship.

I want to give a clear impression of this ship, because only then is it possible to appreciate the shock of what happened later. She was a floating factory – a belching, stinking, muck-heap of activity two thousand miles from civilization. Her upper works were black with grease and filth from the cloud of smoke that rolled out of her trying out funnel. And over everything hung the awful smell of whale. It was like a pall. It was the smell of decaying flesh, mingled with oil and fish, and lying on the air, thick and cloying, like an inescapable fog. But though her decks might present the appearance of some gargantuan slaughter-house, below all was neat and ordered as in a factory. There were the long lines of boilers, hissing gently with the steam that was being injected into them and with gutters bubbling with the hot oil. There was the refrigeration plant and machinery for cutting and packing and dehydrating the meat. There were crushing machines for converting the bone to fertilizer. There were laboratories and workshops, sick bays, mess rooms, living quarters, store rooms, electric generating plant – everything. The *Southern Cross* was a well-stocked, well-populated factory town.

When we got up on deck again, the five catchers that had been lying idle astern of us had already scattered in search of whale. Four carcases were lying alongside, gashed to prevent decay through the internal heat of the mass of dead flesh, and horribly bloated through being inflated with air to keep them afloat. One of the towing ships was bringing in five more.

The whole fleet was in action now with whales spouting all round us. It was an incredible sight. Standing there on the deck of the factory ship we could hear the dull double thud of the harpoon guns in action. I saw one catcher quite close. The *skytter* was running down the catwalk that connected the bridge with the gun platform perched precariously on the high bows. He seized the gun, his legs braced apart, waiting for the moment to strike. Twice the catcher drove the whale under. Then suddenly the spout was right under the catcher's bow. I saw the sharp-ended point of the harpoon dip as the gun was aimed. Then it flew out – a hundred and fifty pound javelin-like projectile with a light forerunner snaking after it. There was the sharp crack of the gun and then the duller boom of the warhead exploding inside the whale as it sounded. Next moment the line was taut, dragging at the masthead shackles and accumulator springs as the heavy line ran out and the winch brakes screamed. The whole thing took on the proportions of a naval operation.

But by this time my stomach was in open revolt. I thanked my guide hurriedly and staggered off to my cabin. Maybe if I hadn't been so tired, my stomach could have stood it. But the gale and sleepless days had weakened my resistance to that insidious, filthy smell. I gave up all I had to the cabin basin and, cold with sweat, fell into an exhausted sleep on my bunk. I didn't wake up until Kyrre, the second officer, came in. He grinned at me as I opened my eyes. 'You are ill, yes?' The corners of his eyes creased in a thousand wrinkles and he roared with laughter. He was a big, blond fellow with a beard and gold fillings to his teeth. 'Soon you are better,' he added. 'No more whale.'

'You mean you've finished catching for the day?' I struggled up on to my elbow. I felt weak, but my stomach was all right now.

'Finish for the day. *Ja.*' His eyes suddenly lost their laughter. 'Finish for altogether, I think,' he said. 'The whale go south. It is what you say the migration.' He shook his big head. 'I do not know,' he muttered. 'It is very funny, this season. I have been four times to the Antarctic. But it was never like this before.' He scratched at his beard with a great, dirty paw of a hand. 'Maybe we have to go south, too.'

'That means going through the pack ice, doesn't it?' I said, putting my feet over the side of the bunk.

'*Ja,*' he said and his eyes looked troubled. '*Ja* – through the pack ice. It is bad, this season. The *Haakon* she is going south already. We go also I think.' Then suddenly he grinned and clapped me on the back. 'Come, my friend. We go to have some food, eh? But first, you try some *aquavit*. That is good for the stomach.' He produced a bottle and glasses. 'This is good stuff – real Line *aquavit*.' He thrust the bottle in front of me so that I could see through the colourless spirit the back of the label on which was printed the name of the ship in which the liquor had crossed the Line.

'*Skaal!*' he said when he'd filled the glasses. He knocked it straight back. I did the same. It was like fire in my throat. 'God!' I said. 'Real firewater.'

'Firewater!' He roared with laughter. '*Ja*. That is good. Firewater! Now we eat, eh?'

The officers' mess was plain and well scrubbed, the predominating note bleak cleanliness. Most of the men wore beards. They didn't talk. I don't imagine they ever talked much once the food was served. But a sense of tension brooded over the table. Covert glances were cast at Bland where he sat with Judie on one side of him and Eide on the other. Judie was toying with her soup. Her eyes were blank. She might have been alone. The man next to her made some remark. She ignored it.

'Which is Erik Bland?' I asked my companion.

It was as I had guessed. The man sitting next to Judie was her husband. He was taller and much slimmer than his father but he had the same round head and short, thick neck. Stripped of his beard, the features might have been those of Bland thirty or forty years ago. But there wasn't the same strength. There was no violent set of the jaw, no dragging down of the brows from a wide forehead. Instead there was a sort of arrogance.

I drank my soup and watched him as he talked to the secretary who was sitting on the other side of him. His manner suggested there was more of his mother than his father in his make-up. Nevertheless, with his fair hair and blue eyes, he looked a fair example of clean-limbed Norwegian youth.

The soup was followed by plates piled high with slabs of meat covered in a thick gravy. I was hungry and though it was a little too highly spiced, I was enjoying it until somebody said, 'Now you are eating whalemeat. It is good, eh?' My mind conjured up an immediate picture of the charnel house of the flensing decks and I pushed the plate away from me. This brought a roar of laughter. 'If you do not eat whalemeat,' Captain Eide said, 'I think you will starve on the *Southern Cross*.' Another gust of laughter shook the room and I realized that they were all glad of something to laugh at.

'Well, I'll stick to bread and cheese this evening,' I said. It was good rye-bread, freshly baked.

The laughter evaporated. A gloomy silence invaded the room again. When the meal was over Eide asked me to have a drink with him. He took me to his cabin and we talked about the war. He had commanded a Norwegian destroyer and I found he'd been with several convoys that I had been attached to. At length I brought the conversation round to Nordahl's disappearance. But all he'd say was: 'It's a complete mystery. I don't understand it at all.'

'What's your opinion of Erik Bland?' I asked, purposely putting the question so bluntly that he couldn't evade answering it without appearing rude.

'How do you mean?' he asked guardedly.

'I gathered he'd been causing trouble with the Tönsberg men.'

Eide's brows lifted. 'On the contrary. He's done everything to smooth things over. He's young, of course, and inexperienced. But that's not his fault. He'll learn. And a lot of the men like him.'

'But he didn't get on with Nordahl, did he?'

Eide hesitated. 'You've seen the messages to Colonel Bland, eh?' I nodded. 'Well,' he said, 'Nordahl wasn't an easy man to get on with. I'm not saying he wasn't a good leader. He was. But he expected people to accept his views without question. He was impatient of opposition and wasn't open to suggestion. That suits the mentality of the *skytters* whose job it is to act and not to think. But it made the day-to-day management of the factory ship difficult.'

'There must have been more to it than that for Nordahl to send that ultimatum to Colonel Bland,' I suggested.

There was a short, embarrassed silence and then Eide said, 'If you do not mind, I would prefer not to discuss this matter with you. You understand – there are politics in every company and it is better not to talk about them.'

'Of course,' I said, 'I understand. You're not by any chance from Sandefjord, are you?'

He looked at me and his lips spread into a brief smile. 'My home is in Kristiansand,' he said. 'I am master of the *Southern Cross* this trip because Andersen, who was a Tönsberg man, has retired.'

After that I switched the conversation back to the war. About half an hour later I excused myself and went down to my cabin.

I was still very tired and I slept as though I'd been drugged.

At breakfast the next morning there was soup and more whale-meat and a *koldtbord* of pressed whale beef, tinned fish and brown Norwegian goats' cheese. The pressed whale beef was good. Shortly after breakfast I was told that Bland wanted to see me in his cabin. I didn't know it then, but this was the morning of the fatal decision. I'd already been up on deck. The wind had sprung up again, a roaring blast of bitterly cold air out of the sou'west. The clouds were low and threatening. To the south the prevailing grey was turned to brilliant white by the ice blink. It was as though the moon were about to rise. The catchers were scattered, searching for whale. Thick smoke continued to belch from the trying-out stack, but the clatter of winches had ceased and the smell of whale was less noticeable.

Eide and Erik Bland were in the cabin when I entered. Bland himself was seated in a swivel chair, his elbow resting on the desk. The man's face was pallid. He was wiping his glasses and I noticed that there were thick pouches under his eyes. 'Craig – I want you to meet my son,' he said. 'Erik. This is Commander Craig.'

Erik Bland came over and shook my hand. 'Glad to have you with us,' he said. His manner was friendly. 'My father thinks you're a fine sailor.'

'If I am,' I said, 'the credit's due to the British Navy.' My antagonism was already melting. His manner was easy and natural. He might not have the drive and pugnacity of his father, but his manners were better and he had confidence in himself. I suddenly began to wonder how much of Judie's reactions were due to a father complex.

Bland swung round in his chair so that he faced me. 'Sit down, Craig,' he said. 'I've got a job for you.' He put his glasses on and began fingering the lobe of his ear. 'For some reason that I don't understand the Tönsberg men have got the idea that Nordahl's death wasn't accidental. The man behind the whole thing is Larvik. But that's neither here nor there. I'm not interested in the logic of their suspicions. I'm interested only in the fact that they are suspicious and that until their suspicions are settled one way or the other it interferes with the working of the ship and the catchers. I've told them that an enquiry will be held. And since they seem to have an idea that in some way I or my son are involved, neither of us will be on the committee of enquiry. The committee will consist of three people. The two members will be Captain Eide here and my daughter-in-law.'

'Good God!' I said. 'You're not going to make her go through the agony of examining all the men who had conversation with Nordahl just before he vanished? Surely you must understand her feelings in the –'

'I'm not interested in her feelings,' he growled at me. 'My problem is that a lot of damned suspicious nonsense has got into the heads of some of the men. With Judie on the committee they'll accept the findings, whatever they are. In fact, Larvik has already agreed.'

'Have you spoken to her about it?' I asked.

'Not yet.'

'But surely she has some –'

'I'm not prepared to argue.' His little eyes glared at me. 'Her husband agrees.'

'That's no answer,' I replied hotly.

'Do you think you have a better right to speak for her than her husband?' he asked. His voice was suddenly violent.

I didn't say anything.

'Very well,' he said, relaxing. 'Now then – the reason I've asked you up here is this. I want you to act as chairman of this committee. You're entirely outside any company politics. With you, Eide and Judie on the committee, the men will be satisfied. Well?'

I hestitated. I didn't want to be drawn into it.

'I said I'd find you an interesting job,' he added. 'And this is it.'

The point he was making was obvious. I was being paid by the company and if I didn't know enough to operate one of the whaling ships, it was up to me to take on anything I was given. Whether it was this that decided me or the fact that Judie was on the committee and I wanted to lessen the pain of it for her, I don't know. But I heard myself say, 'All right. I'll act as chairman.'

'Good!' He shifted more easily in his chair. 'Get down to it right away. The sooner the job's completed the better.' There was a knock at the door. 'Come in,' he called.

It was Howe. He had a sheaf of papers in his hand. His face was slightly flushed and there was a queer excitement in his eyes. 'Ah, come in, Howe,' Bland said. 'Have you got that report for me?'

Howe nodded. He didn't seem able to trust himself to speak. He came across the cabin with that awkward, crab-like walk and handed Bland the papers. Bland didn't look at them. He looked at Howe instead. 'Well?' he said. 'What are your conclusions? Where's the best place to hunt for whale in a season like this?'

Howe swallowed nervously. 'Come on, man. You know very well not a catcher has reported whale all morning though conditions have been ideal. The *skytters* all say we just caught the tail end of a migratory movement. Where do you think we'll find whale? Do we go east or west? Back towards South Georgia or down into the Weddell Sea? Well?'

Howe's Adam's apple gave one final jerk. 'Through the pack,' he said. 'Through the pack into the Weddell Sea.' His mouth had a sly twist to it and his watery eyes gleamed. I suddenly had the feeling that the man's report was based on nothing more substantial than the fact that he wanted Bland to go south.

And the strange thing was that Bland himself seemed to want to go south, too. 'Good, good,' he said. 'Did you know Hanssen was taking the *Haakon* into the pack?'

'No.' The Adam's apple jerked again.

'Apparently he thinks the same. So do Petersen and Larvik – and after Nordahl they're the most experienced men we have.' I glanced quickly at Erik Bland as his father mentioned the name Nordahl, but it produced no reaction.

Bland had got up and was staring out of the porthole. Suddenly he swung round. 'Very well, Captain Eide,' he said. His tone was abrupt, decisive. 'Recall the catchers. As soon as they have all come in, get the gunners aboard for a conference. My view is that we should go south right away. We've only just over two months left and to make up for lost time we need plenty of whale. Have we enough meat to give the refrigerator ship a full cargo?'

'No,' Eide replied and looked across at Erik Bland, who added, 'The *South* is only one-third full.'

'She must come with us then. Now go and recall the catchers.' He dismissed his son with a nod and turned to me. 'I want the findings of that enquiry completed whilst the catchers are assembling – before we start south. Captain Eide has agreed to release the second officer from all duties to assist you in deciding who you wish to come before you to give evidence. He's a Tönsberg man, he speaks English and he was on watch the night Nordahl vanished.' He nodded to us. 'That's all then, gentlemen. Tomorrow we will enter the pack ice.'

The imminence of our entry into the pack ice gave me little enough time to hold the enquiry. Immediately after the conference in Bland's cabin the ship turned its bow towards the ice blink. She was travelling at half speed. As soon as all the catchers were assembled, and they couldn't be more than a few hours' steaming away, all speed would be made to the south. Once in the pack I realized that it would be difficult to continue the enquiry. Captain Eide, for one, would not be available, nor would Kyrre. I was glad I'd had some experience of enquiries whilst in the Navy.

Kyrre had already received instructions and was waiting for me in our cabin. I got from him a brief account of Nordahl's movements on the night he'd disappeared and drew up a list of men to be interviewed. Bland sent down copies of a typewritten notice annoucing the enquiry. The officers' smokeroom had been set aside for it and there was a blank against the time for me to fill in. It asked any man who thought he might have information relevant to the factory manager's disappearance to come before the committee. I found Eide on the bridge and fixed for the enquiry to begin at eleven. Then I went down to Judie's cabin. She was sitting on her bunk, very still, very scared looking.

'You've been told about this enquiry?' I asked. I made my voice sound as matter-of-fact as possible.

She nodded.

'I've fixed it for eleven,' I said. 'That's in just over half an hour. That all right for you?'

'Yes.' Her tone was almost harsh as though she were bracing herself for the ordeal.

I turned to go. Then I stopped. 'It's a rotten job for you,' I said.

'I'll be all right.' She gave me a wan smile.

At eleven o'clock there were five men, besides the ones we'd called, scuffling their feet outside the door of the smokeroom. As I passed through them with Judie there was a muttered *'God dag.'* One man said, *'God dag, frøken Nordahl.'* Not *fru Bland,* but *frøken Nordahl.* Kyrre was already there. Eide came in as we were seating ourselves.

'Right,' I said. 'Let's have the men we've called first – in the order we agreed, Kyrre.'

It took us two hours to get the story of that night out of them. But it was quite straightforward. There was nothing in any of the evidence to prepare us for the labyrinth of ill feeling and suspicion we were to plough our way through later. On the evening of the 2 January Nordahl had joined the other officers for the evening meal as usual. He hadn't talked much. But he wasn't any more silent that night than he had been since the ship left Cape Town. He seemed to have had a premonition that the season was going to be a bad one. The secretary, who saw a lot of him, said that he was increasingly concerned about the absence of whale. Nordahl had a very considerable financial interest in the company. Judie couldn't say exactly what the figure was, but thought it might be as high as thirty or thirty-five per cent.

After the meal Nordahl had had a few drinks and then worked for half an hour in the office. A good deal of his time was spent in the office – not only was it necessary for him to supervise the checking of stores and the supply of fuel, stores and equipment to the catchers and towing ships, but also to keep an eye on the entry of whale brought in and handled, since all the men got a share, over and above their pay. The outfit was run on what amounted to a co-partnership basis. Young Bland wasn't much help to him here as he had insufficient knowledge. In fact, Nordahl bore the whole weight of management, both as regards policy and detail. The secretary said that he was very tired at the end of the day. He was sixty-two years old and the burden of decision and administrative detail must have been considerable.

After leaving the office, Nordahl went up on to the bridge. He stayed there for a short time, talking to the officer of the watch. The half light of the Antarctic summer night had fallen. But shortly after Nordahl left the bridge a bank of fog rolled up.

Leaving the bridge, Nordahl had gone as far as was known straight to Eide's cabin. There he'd had two drinks – that made about half a dozen he'd had during the evening, and he was a man with a big capacity for liquor.

Captain Eide, who then gave evidence, said that he had seemed perfectly normal. 'But he was tired, you know,' he added. 'There had been trouble between him and Erik Bland. I must say it – since it may have a bearing on his state of mind – Bland did not know enough about the job. On the other hand, the trouble was not by any means all Bland's fault. Nordahl did not like him and he took no trouble to conceal his dislike. Also he was impatient. He made no allowance for Bland's inexperience.'

'Was there open trouble between them?' I asked.

Captain Eide shook his head. 'I do not think so. Bland always treated the manager with the respect that was his due – even when he was provoked. But there were those messages to Colonel Bland. Things like that have a way of getting round a ship. The Tönsberg men supported Nordahl and most of the Sandefjord men sided with Bland. It did not make for smooth running.'

'And Nordahl took most of Bland's work on his own shoulders?' I suggested.

'*Ja.* That is so.'

'And you think this was too much for him? He was overtired?'

Eide nodded.

After leaving Eide's cabin Nordahl had gone to the wireless room. He was there talking to the Chief Wireless Officer till shortly after midnight.

I then called Kyrre, who had been officer of the watch during the period Nordahl must have disappeared. He had come on watch at midnight. The ship was stationary and blanketed in fog. The navigation lights of the ships riding astern of her were not visible. Nothing unusual happened throughout his watch. After he had been on watch about half an hour the fog suddenly lifted and visibility increased to several miles. I asked him whether he had heard a cry or a splash. No, he had noticed nothing unusual. Had he seen Nordahl or anyone that might possibly have been Nordahl up on the deck? But he'd seen nothing. 'The fog, she was very thick. I could see nothing beyond the bridge.'

'And about twelve-thirty the fog lifted and visibility was good?'

'*Ja.*'

'If Nordahl had gone overboard then he would have been seen?'

'That is so. I was out on the bridge all watch, and there was the lookout.'

It was clear, therefore, that Nordahl must have gone overboard between the time he had left the wireless room and just after twelve-thirty when the fog lifted.

Finally I called Erik Bland. I nodded to a chair and he sat down. He was frowning slightly and his eyes were screwed up so that they were small, like his father's. I was conscious again of the similarity in appearance and the dissimilarity in character. He seemed nervous. 'There's only one question I want to ask you, Bland,' I said. 'Nordahl left Captain Eide's cabin shortly after ten-thirty on the night of 2 January. Did he visit you at all?'

'No. I had a few words with him during the evening meal.' His eyes flicked towards Judie and he gave a slight shrug of his shoulders. 'I never saw him again.'

'Had you had a row with him?' It was Judie who put the question, and I remember the feeling of shock caused by the blunt way she put the question and the hardness of her voice.

Bland hesitated. 'Do I have to answer that question?' he asked me.

It was clear he was trying to save her unnecessary pain, but I had no alternative. 'I'm afraid so,' I said.

He looked at her then and said, 'Yes. You know as well as I do we couldn't get on together. It wasn't the first row we'd had.'

'What was it about?' Judie's voice was drained of any emotion.
'Nothing. Just a difference of opinion about the promotion of a
certain man.'

'As assistant manager your duty surely was to assist my father,
not to obstruct him?'

'I wasn't obstructing him.' His voice was pitched a shade
higher. 'Listen, Judie – your father and I didn't get on. Leave it at
that, can't you? I had nothing to do with his death.'

'Nobody is suggesting you had,' I said.

He looked at me quickly. His face was paler now and there
were beads of sweat on his forehead. 'No? Then what is she driving
at? And she's not the only one. Larvik and Petersen are spreading
the idea through the ship – and the Tönsberg men will believe
anything they say. Everyone on the ship knows Nordahl and I
couldn't get on together. What they don't know is the reason.' He
turned back to Judie. 'Your father did everything he could to make
things difficult for me. I was new to the job, yet he couldn't have
been more impatient with me over my mistakes if I'd been on as
many expeditions as he had.'

'I don't believe it.' Judie's voice was sharp and uncompromising.

'Whether you believe it or not, it's true. He wanted to put me in
a position where I'd be forced to ask my father to recall me.'

'Why?' I asked.

'Why? Because he wanted to control the company after my
father's death. He wanted me out of the way.'

'This is getting us nowhere,' I cut in. 'Have you any suggestions
to make concerning Nordahl's death?'

'No,' he said. 'I've no more idea how it happened than you
have. The only explanation I can think of is that he had financial
troubles.'

'Financial troubles?' Eide repeated. 'What sort of financial
troubles?'

'He was gambling – ' But Bland stopped short there. 'It's his
affair,' he murmured.

'I don't believe that,' Judie said quietly. 'Father never gambled.
He couldn't possibly have had financial troubles. He was interested
only in whale.'

'He would like to have controlled the company, though,
wouldn't he?' There was a suggestion of spite in his tone. Then
he gave a quick shrug to his shoulders. 'I'm sorry, gentlemen. I'd
rather not say any more about it.'

'But he had financial worries,' I said, 'and you think this may have had some bearing on his death?'

'Perhaps.'

'And you saw nothing of him after he left the officers' mess?'

'I told you – no.'

'Very well,' I said. 'I think that's all.' I glanced at the others. Eide nodded to indicate that he was satisfied. Judie was sitting, very pale, staring at her husband. Her hands were clenched where they lay in her lap. She didn't say anything so I nodded to Bland. 'Thank you,' I said. He got up quickly. I could see he was relieved. I didn't know what to think. There was clearly something behind his statement that Nordahl had been in financial difficulties, but just what I didn't know and Judie either couldn't or wouldn't enlighten me.

The last witness I called was the officers' messboy who had brought tea to Nordahl's cabin as usual at six in the morning. He told how he'd found the cabin empty, the bunk not slept in. Finally Eide detailed the steps he had taken as Captain to discover what had happened. His enquiries had told him no more than we'd discovered that morning. 'There are many men on this ship who do not like Erik Bland,' he added. 'So much I discover. You will hear this after *middag* when we see the men who wish to give evidence. There will be talk of much bad feeling. But there will be nothing definite.' He shrugged his shoulders. 'I think there is no doubt what happens.'

'You're suggesting my father committed suicide, aren't you?' Judie's voice trembled as she said this. Neither Eide nor I said anything. I must admit it was the conclusion that I had come to. Nordahl was clearly over-worked. He may even have had personal worries that we knew nothing of. Tired and worried, his mind had become over-wrought. 'Captain Eide – you knew him quite well,' she went on in a more controlled voice. 'Was he, in your opinion, the sort of man to take his own life?'

Eide hesitated, rubbing his beard with his fingers. 'No,' he said. 'Not in normal circumstances. But – '

'Please,' she interrupted. 'I knew him better than anyone. He was my father. Please believe me when I say – it would never occur to him to take his own life.'

I said, 'We'll adjourn now. After lunch we'll see the men who want to give evidence.'

We broke up then. But all through *middag* Judie sat silent and pale. She hardly ate anything. I saw Erik Bland glance at her once or twice, and I thought there was something half-pleading, half-scared, in the way he looked at her. Bland himself only once referred to the enquiry. He asked me when I'd be through. 'Some time this afternoon,' I said. 'We only have to take the evidence of those who have volunteered to make statements.'

'Hurry it,' he said. 'There are two more catchers to come in – that's all – and I want to start south as soon as I've had a talk with the gunners.'

But by the end of the afternoon we were still sitting. The men who had volunteered to give information were Tönsberg men, all of them, and their evidence put a different complexion on the whole business. Even allowing for exaggeration, it became clear that the trouble between Nordahl and Erik Bland was much more serious than we'd been led to believe.

The trouble, it appeared, had started a week after the ship had left Cape Town. Certain rations essential for the prevention of scurvy had been withdrawn. When a deputation headed by one of the boiler-cleaners had raised the matter with Erik Bland, who had given the instructions to the chief cook, instead of admitting his mistake, he had enforced his decision. Nordahl had reversed it. A few days later a similar thing had happened over the issue of certain essential clothing. Bland had accused Nordahl in front of the slop-chest manager of toadying to the men. The first day they handled whale, a winch hawser had snapped and one of the lemmers had been seriously injured. Nordahl had found that the equipment had not been properly inspected. Bland had told Nordahl he wasn't going to be the scapegoat for everything that went wrong on the ship. He ignored the fact that he had been given the job of inspecting all equipment before use. They had had a bitter row on the after-plan in front of the men. But the worst row appeared to have been over an error in the figures for whale brought in by *Hval 4*. Petersen, skipper of *Hval 4*, had queried the figures. The mistake was Bland's. He had reported these whale to the secretary as being brought in by *Hval 8*, one of the Sandefjord catchers. Petersen, who had come on board to right the matter, called the plan foreman to substantiate his claim. It was this man who volunteered an account of what had happened in the office.

Bland had refused to admit his mistake. White-faced, he had accused Nordahl of concocting the whole thing between Petersen and the foreman. 'I know what it is,' he had shouted; 'you're trying to get rid of me. You're trying to get rid of my father, too. You want to control the whole company.'

Nordahl had asked him what he meant by that, and he had answered, 'I know what you're up to. You crawl to me for financial advice. You thought you'd make enough out of it to buy control. Do you think I don't know what you were up to whilst you were in Cape Town. Well, you wait till the crash comes. If I didn't know it was coming, I'd – I'd – ' He hadn't finished, but had flung out of the office.

I recalled the secretary and asked him why he hadn't given us this piece of evidence. He replied that he hadn't thought it relevant. But I could see that his real reason was that he was scared of losing his job now that Bland was manager and his father was on board. Pressed by me, however, the secretary confirmed every word of the foreman's evidence.

There was another row in Nordahl's cabin, which was over-heard by one of the winch-boys. All he heard as he passed was Bland saying, 'I refuse to resign. Fire me if you like. But see what my father has to say when he arrives.' And Nordahl had answered wearily, 'Your father can do what he likes. I'm not going to be saddled with a rat like you and I'll see that the company isn't either.'

There had been the sound of a blow then. And just as the boy, who had been listening outside, was slipping away, Bland had burst out of the cabin, his face white and his mouth working with anger. 'He looked as though he were about to burst into tears,' the boy added.

I looked at Eide, remembering his support of Bland. It was clear somebody had been pulling the wool over his eyes. And that could only have been Erik Bland himself. He'd almost fooled me too.

Next came the evidence that all this had gradually been working up to. The witness was a big man with a scar on his cheek over which his beard had refused to grow. I recognized him at once. It was the man who had accompanied Captain Larvik to the gang-way that first afternoon just after I'd come aboard.

His evidence was that he'd been up on deck shortly after mid-night on the night of 2/3 January. He had gone aft and had seen Nordahl smoking a cigar near one of the boats. The Manager had been pacing up and down in a rather agitated manner. The man had seen his face in the glow of the cigar. When he went for'ard again, Nordahl was still there. A few paces farther on he met Erik Bland going towards Nordahl. He had stopped then, wondering whether there was any fresh trouble between them. He had heard the beginnings of an altercation. No, he couldn't say what was said. He was too far away. The men's voices grew angry. There was a sudden cry. Then silence. He saw Bland come back. His face was very white. Then he had gone aft to the point where Nordahl had been. Nordahl was no longer there.

'Did Bland see you?' I asked through Kyrre.

'No. I was beside one of the ventilators and there was the fog.'

I had been watching the man closely whilst he gave his evidence. He had a habit of nervously fingering the clean stretch of skin where the scar was. He kept his eyes fixed all the time on the table at which we were sitting. He spoke in a monotone. There was no feeling or interest behind his words. I got the idea that he didn't see the scene he was describing.

'And you say Bland's face was white?' I asked.

'*Ja*.'

'Yet it was so foggy he didn't see you standing beside a ventilator?'

'He was very much upset.'

Eide stirred. 'Why didn't you give me this information when I was enquiring into hr. Nordahl's disappearance?' he asked.

The man hesitated. 'I was scared,' he said.

He didn't look the sort of man who was easily scared.

'What's your job on this ship?' I asked.

'Seaman,' he answered, frowning in puzzlement at the question.

'Ever crewed on one of the catchers?'

He nodded.

'On Captain Larvik's catcher?'

I saw the quick shift of his eyes as they glanced at me and then away again. He didn't answer.

I said, 'I don't believe a word of your evidence.' His eyes looked suddenly shifty. 'Who put you up to this? Was it Captain Larvik? Come on, man,' I shouted at him as though I were back on the bridge of my corvette. 'Let's have the truth now. It was Captain Larvik, wasn't it? Yesterday when he and the others came on board to see Colonel Bland. He told you to give this evidence.'

The man fidgeted awkwardly.

'All right,' I snapped. 'You can go.'

I looked across at Eide. There was no doubt in my mind. Captain Larvik had primed the fellow. 'Why?' I asked, voicing my own thoughts.

Eide was fingering his beard. 'I think we should call *Kaptein* Larvik.'

I turned to Judie for her agreement. She nodded. Her face was set, chin slightly thrust out where it rested on the knuckles of her two hands. 'I think he knows something,' she said quietly. 'Peer Larvik is a great friend of my father.'

We had a break then whilst Captain Eide sent for Larvik, whose catcher had just rejoined the *Southern Cross*. Up on deck the air was cold. I took Judie down to my cabin and got one of the messboys to bring us tea. It was the first opportunity I'd had of talking to her alone since we had begun the enquiry. 'Look, Judie,' I said when the tea had arrived, 'is there anything you can tell us that would help to discover what really did happen?' Put like that it sounded ponderous. But I felt awkward. I knew what a strain the whole enquiry was on her.

She stirred her cup for a moment. Then she said, 'No. I don't think I can.' Her voice trembled slightly. 'All I know for certain, deep down in my heart, is that he did not commit suicide.'

'Do you believe the evidence of that man with scar – Ulvik?'

'No,' she replied. 'No, you showed quite clearly that he was lying.'

'You agree that Captain Larvik put him up to it?'

'Yes.'

'But why?' I asked.

She looked up at me then. And there was something in her eyes that disturbed me. 'He had a reason,' she said. Her voice was suddenly beyond her control. It was harsh and violent. 'The man was saying what he'd been told to say. But it's what Peer Larvik believed happened.'

I hesitated. But I had to put it to her. 'Do you believe your husband murdered your father?' She didn't answer and I added, 'Is that what you believe?' My voice sounded peremptory.

Her grey eyes were wide as saucers as she looked up at me. Then suddenly something inside her snapped and she buried her head in her hands. 'I don't know what to think.' She was sobbing violently. 'It's horrible – horrible.' Her shoulders shook with the sudden pent-up force of her emotions breaking out.

I went over and put my hands on her arms. 'Stop crying,' I said. 'You're a member of a committee of enquiry, not a school-girl.' I shook her. It was the only thing to do. She was on the verge of hysterics. My violence and lack of sympathy checked her. 'Stop blubbering and try to reason it out,' I said, forcing her to meet my gaze. 'Either your father committed suicide, or your husband's a murderer.' She gasped. But I could see her mind was suddenly facing up to the facts that she had been trying to avoid.

There was a knock at the door. It was a message from Eide to say that Larvik was on board. 'I'm sorry, Judie,' I said. 'Don't think I don't realize how rotten this is for you. But we've got to find out what was in Larvik's mind. Will you question him?'

She nodded and reached for her handbag. When she had made up her face again we went down and joined Captain Eide. 'Mrs Bland will put the questions,' I said. I nodded to Kyrre to fetch in Captain Larvik.

At close quarters the whaling skipper looked even broader and even more like a seal. He sat down awkwardly on the edge of a chair. He was nervous. He didn't look at Eide or myself. His small, immensely blue eyes were fixed on Judie. Was it sympathy, or was there something else in the expression of his eyes? I had an uncanny feeling that those blue eyes were trying to tell her something. '*Kaptein* Larvik,' she said. 'Yesterday, when you were on board the *Southern Cross*, you spoke with one of the crew – a man named Ulvik.' She spoke carefully in English.

'*Ja.* That is so,' Larvik replied in the same language. He was a Bergenske and he spoke English with a Germanic guttural accent, relic of the days when the Hanseatic League ruled the Bergen shipping trade.

'We have heard Ulvik's evidence,' she added, and outlined briefly what he had told us. 'Commander Craig here takes the view that that evidence is unreliable. In fact, he thinks you instructed the man to give false evidence.'

'And you, fru Bland – what do you think?'

She hesitated for a fraction of a second and then said, 'I think so too.'

Larvik shrugged his shoulders. He didn't say anything. He just sat there, staring at her.

'Why, Kaptein Larvik?' Judie asked him. 'Why did you tell him to say that Erik and my father had a row up there on the deck in the fog the night my father – disappeared.'

His big hands waved awkwardly like a pair of flippers. 'I do not wish to hurt you more than you have been hurt already,' he said. His voice was kindly, as though he were talking to a child or a dog of which he was fond. 'But it is what I believe happens.'

'You are accusing my husband of being a murderer,' she said, and Larvik winced at the bluntness of her tongue. 'Of murdering my father,' she added. 'Why didn't you come to us directly or to Captain Eide and make this statement yourself? To present your suspicions in this roundabout way, getting Ulvik to make a statement you and he knew to be false, is horrible. Erik didn't see my father at all that night – after the evening meal.'

'How do you know?' Larvik's voice was gruff. Sudden anger

showed in his eyes.

'Erik made that statement in evidence before this enquiry.'

'Then he's lying,' Larvik growled.

Judie stared at him as though she'd been silenced with a blow. I could see she believed this fat, bearded whaler. I thought: *Larvik and her father are old friends. This man probably played with her as a child. She accepts him – everything he is and everything he says – in the same way that she would accept her father and anything he said.* I saw her lips tremble. Her body seemed to sag. 'Oh, God,' she breathed. She was shaking uncontrollably, her eyes quite blank. She wasn't crying. She was past that.

'How do you know Bland is lying?' I demanded angrily. If the man couldn't substantiate his statement, then why in God's name had he made it?

I saw Larvik steady himself. His eyes were full of sudden pity. His hands flapped awkwardly. But beneath the beard his lips clamped into a tight line. 'I have nothing more to say,' he growled. And then added, 'That is what I believe happened. I wished for the enquiry to know that and act on it.'

'But what makes you so sure that Erik Bland saw Nordahl later that night?' I demanded. 'You say Bland is lying?'

'*Ja.*'

'How do you know?'

'That is what I believe,' he answered stubbornly.

'But good God, man!' I shouted at him. 'You must have some reason for your suspicions?'

But all he replied was, 'Ask Bland.'

I looked at Eide. I could see that he thought the same as I did – that we should get no further with Larvik. It was no good asking Judie if she had any further questions to ask. She was staring at Larvik, dry-eyed, with a sort of dawning horror mirrored on her white face. 'All right,' I said to Larvik. 'We've no further questions to put to you. I would only like to add that I consider your conduct in this matter disgraceful. You have made a very dangerous accusation which you are not prepared to substantiate. I trust your attitude will be more helpful and less underhand when the police interview you.' I glanced at Eide, who nodded in support of my remarks.

But I could see that they had had no effect on Larvik. His eyes were fixed on Judie. They were full of pain. He was sharing the hell that she was going through. 'Please return to your ship, Captain Larvik,' I said.

He got up then, standing awkwardly in front of the table, still looking at Judie. Once he cleared his throat as though about to say something. Then he turned abruptly on his heel and left the room.

I looked at Eide. 'I think we should have Bland back again,' I whispered. He agreed. I turned to Judie. She hadn't moved. I put my hand on hers. 'Are you prepared to face your husband now,' I said, 'or shall we adjourn for a bit?'

She swallowed quickly. 'Please – now,' she said. She wanted to get it over.

'All right,' I said, and phoned the radio officer on duty to put out a call on the public address system for Erik Bland to attend the enquiry again. I did it that way to scare him. We waited in silence. Faintly we heard the amplifiers sounding Bland's name through the ship. The silence in the room seemed to cry out.

When Bland came in he was breathing heavily as though he'd been hurrying. And it was a different Bland to the disarmingly helpful young man who had faced us earlier in the day – or so it seemed to me. His face looked puffy. His eyes darted about the room, crossing, but not meeting, our gaze. I motioned him to a chair. He sat down quickly. The tension of the room was enveloping him. I let it work on him. 'Well?' he asked, unable to bear the silence any longer. 'What do you want to ask me now?' The abruptness of his tone was startlingly different to his previous ease of manner.

'We have just heard the evidence of one of the men,' I said. I let that sink in for a moment. If I handled it right, whatever it was he was scared of would come out. 'Do you still persist in your statement that you didn't see Nordahl after the evening meal on the night he disappeared?'

His eyes flicked up at me and back to the floor. 'Yes,' he said. 'Yes I do.' Then his hands caught hold of the arms of the chair. 'You've had Larvik on board. You've interviewed him, haven't you?' So that was what had got him worried. 'He's trying to fix it on me.' His voice was uncontrolled. Something was gnawing at his mind. Something he was scared of. 'It isn't one of the men who's been talking to you. It's Larvik. He's always hated me. He's a friend of Nordahl's. He's using Nordahl's death to get at me. He's lying. He's lying, I tell you.'

'He says you're lying,' I said.

'It's my word against his.' Bland's voice was wild. 'He's guessing. That's all he's doing.'

I said, 'Wait a minute, Bland. We're not dealing with Larvik's evidence. We're dealing with the evidence of one of the men. He says that at about midnight Nordahl was standing by one of the boats.' I knew the man's statement was false. I had no right to use it to force Bland's hand. But I had to find out the truth. I justified myself on the grounds that if Bland were hiding anything it would force him into the open. 'Nordahl was smoking a cigar,' I went on. 'As the man passed him on his way for'ard again he met you. He says you were going towards where Nordahl was standing.' Bland's face was ashen. He seemed to be holding his breath. 'Well?' I said. 'Did you go towards Nordahl as he stood there by one of the boats, smoking a cigar?' I emphasized the details. I emphasized every point of the picture.

'No,' he cried. 'No.'

'The man said he then stopped by one of the ventilators,' I went on. 'He heard the beginnings of an altercation. There was a cry. And then silence.'

'No. It isn't true.'

'He said that a moment later you passed him, going for'ard. Your face was very white. You didn't see him because of the fog and the fact that he was hidden behind the ventilator cowl. He then went back to the spot where he had seen Nordahl.' I hesitated. Bland was staring at me, fascinated. 'Nordahl wasn't there any more.'

Bland opened his mouth. But nothing came out. He seemed to be gasping for breath. Then he suddenly said, 'All right. I was up there. I did see Nordahl. We did have a row. But that was all. That was all, I tell you.'

'What was the row about?' I asked.

'What was the row – about?' He seemed dazed for the moment. His eyes shifted quickly round the room as though searching for some way of escape from the three of us sitting there behind the plain deal table. He moistened his lips with his tongue and then said, 'He accused my father of ruining him.'

'On what grounds?' I asked.

He looked at me then. And his eyes held my gaze as though he wanted to batter the information he had to give me into my brain. 'Nordahl wanted control of the company,' he said. 'He wanted to run it his own way. He wanted all the men to be from Tönsberg. He liked to think of himself as an important figure in Tönsberg.'

'That is not true,' Judie said. The denial seemed to be torn out of her, it was so violent.

Bland ignored her. 'He didn't want me on the ship. He did everything he could to make it difficult for me. He even altered figures in the catchers' books so that the Tönsberg men should be able to bring complaints. He was afraid my father when he died would make me chairman over his head.'

'Come to the point,' I said, as he paused. 'Why did he accuse your father of ruining him?'

'He needed money,' Bland answered. 'He was making a desperate bid to get control of the company. He badgered my father until he let him in on a deal he was planning in South African mines. He put everything he'd got into it. The crash came two weeks after we left Cape Town.'

'What was the name of the company he invested in?' I asked. 'Was it Wyks Odensdaal Rust Development?'

'Yes,' he said, and his voice sounded surprised.

The plan foreman in his evidence had suggested that it was from Erik Bland, not his father, that Nordahl had obtained financial advice. I hesitated. But there was no point in raising the matter. 'In your opinion Nordahl was broke then?'

'Yes. He'd mortgaged everything – all his holdings in the South Antarctic Company – in a desperate effort to cash in.'

'Then he was going to buy out the other people interested in the company?'

'Yes. That was his idea.'

'When he'd done that, would he have thrown your father out?' Again Bland hesitated. 'I don't know,' he said.

'What you were really afraid of,' I said, 'was that he'd throw you out. Isn't that it?'

He ignored the point. 'The case didn't arise,' he said. 'My father was too smart to be caught like that. I tell you, Nordahl was broke – finished. And he knew it. He cursed me there on the deck.'

'Why did he cry out?' I asked quickly.

Again that momentary hesitation. 'He didn't cry out,' he answered. 'I think perhaps it was I who cried out. I don't know. All I know is that he hit me. I left him then. I didn't want to hit back at an older man, especially as he was wrought up over his losses.'

'Do you remember an altercation you had with Nordahl in his cabin?' I asked. 'One of the crew overheard it. Nordahl demanded your resignation. You refused it. You said – "See what my father does when he arrives." ' I looked down at my notes. 'Nordahl then said – "Your father can do what he likes. I'm not going to be saddled with a rat like you and I'll see that the company isn't, either." ' I looked across at Bland's white face. 'You didn't baulk at striking an older man then,' I said. 'Are you sure it was Nordahl who struck you?'

'Yes,' he said. 'Nordahl struck me and I left him then.'

'The man whose evidence has produced all this,' I said slowly, 'went straight back to the spot where Nordahl had been standing. Nordahl wasn't there.'

'I tell you, he knew he was ruined.' Bland's face was tense. He was fighting to make us see it his way. 'He was finished. He could never face Tönsberg again. He took the only way out.'

'My father never took an easy way out in his life.' Judie's voice was clear-cut and distinct. It was like a douche of cold water on the heat of Erik Bland's argument.

'Well, he took it this time.' There was something almost truculent in the way he said it.

I looked at Eide. 'Any more questions?' I asked. He shook his head. I turned to Judie. Her lips were compressed. She was staring at Erik Bland with a sort of horror in her eyes. 'All right, Bland,' I said. 'That's all.'

He got up slowly as though he didn't want to be released like that. He started to say something, but then his eyes met Judie's and he turned quickly and went out. I realized then that whatever he had once meant to her it was finished now. And I was suddenly, unaccountably glad about that.

As the door closed behind him, I said, 'Well, do we need to call anybody else?' I was thinking: *It's a matter for the police now. Either Bland killed him, or Nordahl committed suicide. Those were the only two possible alternatives. Judie said he would never commit suicide. She ought to know if anyone did. She was his daughter. But who could possibly tell how a man would react when all he's lived for and worked for is shattered in the wreckage of a wild gamble? He'd played his hand and lost. He'd tried his hand at Bland's game – finance – and failed. How could she know what he would do in those circumstances?*

It was Judie who interrupted my thoughts. 'I would like to call Doctor Howe,' she said in a small, bleak voice. It was drained of all emotion – empty, toneless.

I looked at her in surprise. 'Doctor Howe? Why?' I asked. 'He wasn't even on the *Southern Cross*. He was in Cape Town, waiting for us.'

'I think he might be able to tell us something,' was all she said.

'All right,' I agreed and nodded to Kyrre.

Howe was pale and nervous when he came in. It was as though he'd been nerving himself for this moment. Judie said, 'Walter, we want some information about father's affairs.' His Adam's apple gave a leap, but his hands were steady and his gaze was direct as he looked at Judie. 'Was he involved in Wyks Odensdaal Rust Development?' she asked him.

Howe nodded. 'Yes,' he said.

'And he'd mortaged everything he had – all his holdings in the South Antarctic Company – for this gamble?'

'Yes.'

'I see,' she said quietly. 'And he acted on Colonel Bland's advice?'

'I don't know whose advice he was acting on.'

She nodded. 'Thank you. That perhaps explains it.' Her voice was barely audible.

I nodded for Howe to go. He hesitated, looking at Judie's bent head. He wanted to help her. I saw it in his eyes. His face didn't look ugly in that moment. Then he was gone and I heard myself saying in a matter-of-fact voice, 'Why is it that Howe knows so much about your father's affairs?'

'Bernt and Walter were very close,' she answered quietly.

'You're satisfied your father was gambling in South African mines?' I asked.

She nodded.

'You can call Colonel Bland himself if you like,' I said.

'It's not necessary. Walter wouldn't lie to me.'

I glanced at Eide. 'You satisfied, too, Captain?' I asked him. '*Ja*. I am satisfied.'

'Very well then,' I said. 'It only remains to agree on our findings.' I glanced at Judie. Her thoughts were far away. 'Judie,' I said. 'Can I have your views?'

'I will agree to whatever you think,' she said. Her voice was vague. She sounded as though she were far away.

The telephone rang and I picked it up. It was Bland. He wanted to know whether we were through. 'In about five minutes,' I said. 'We're just deciding on our findings.'

'Good. As soon as you're through I want you and Eide to come down to the saloon. The gunners are all here.'

When I put the receiver back Judie had risen. 'You must wait until we have agreed on our findings,' I said gently.

'I don't want to wait,' she answered. 'I don't wish to talk about it any more. Please – I will agree with your verdict.' She went out then and I looked at Eide. He was massaging the side of his beard. 'Bland wants us both up in the saloon,' I said. 'Can I have your views?'

'*Ja.* I think it is a matter for the police. As far as we can discover it is Erik Bland who sees him last. It is either – murder, or suicide.'

'Fine,' I said. 'That's what I think. In the circumstances I think we should refuse to reach any conclusions. This committee of enquiry has no legal standing. We should merely file the evidence and hand it over to assist the police in their investigations.' Eide nodded. His gaunt, hatchet face was set in the lines beaten into it by years of violent weather. 'Bland will not like it,' he said. 'It is bad for the men that we do not reach some conclusion. But we cannot. I agree. So.' He pulled himself to his feet. 'We had better go to the conference now.'

I gathered up the sheets of evidence I had so laboriously taken down, clipping them together and stuffing them into my pocket. Up on deck Eide paused, gazing south towards the ice blink. The white, mirrored on the under-surface of the low cloud, was streaked with wide, dark lines. 'See,' he said. 'There are many wide leads – and they all run south. That is good.' It was like looking at a map of the ice below.

The saloon was full of smoke when we entered. Bland was sitting in a big chair. The skippers of the catchers were grouped round him in a circle. Charts littered the floor. Erik Bland was also there. He was sitting close to his father. 'Well, Captain Eide,' Bland said as we sat down, 'the others agree with me – that we should go south through the pack. The *Haakon* has reached open sea 600 miles south of us. She reports plenty of whale.'

'Then we also must go south,' Eide said. 'There are good leads and the weather is fine.'

'Good. Then it's settled.' Bland rang for the messboy and ordered drinks. Then he got up and came over to me. 'A word with you, Craig,' he said. I followed him out of the saloon and along the corridor to his cabin. 'Now,' he said, as I closed the door. 'What are your findings?' His voice was hard and his small eyes had narrowed.

I pulled the sheets of evidence out of my pocket and handed them to him. He put them down on the desk. 'Your findings?' he repeated. 'Come on, man,' he added impatiently as I hesitated. 'You must have reached some conclusion.'

'Yes,' I said. 'But I don't think you'll like it. In our opinion Nordahl's disappearance is a matter for police investigation.'

He blew his cheeks out like a grampus. It was as though he'd been holding his breath. 'Why?' he asked sharply.

'There are two possibilities,' I said. 'Either Nordahl committed suicide or he was – murdered.'

'Go on.'

'As this enquiry has no legal standing, we take the view that it would not be right for it to attempt to reach any conclusion. The evidence, which I have now passed on to you, should be handed over to the police on our return to port.'

'I see. You and Captain Eide and my daughter-in-law all take the view it is either suicide or murder.'

'That is my view and Captain Eide's. Mrs Bland was too upset to consider the findings.'

'And – is my son involved in any way?'

'Yes,' I said. 'He was the last person to see Nordahl alive. In his first evidence he denied seeing Nordahl at all after the evening meal. Later he admitted that he had had a row with him up on the deck. That was shortly after midnight. At twelve thirty-five the fog cleared. It was only possible for Nordahl to have gone overboard unobserved during the intervening twenty minutes.'

'I see.' Bland slowly sank into a chair. 'But it could be suicide.'

'His daughter doesn't think so. She says he wasn't a quitter, that suicide would never enter his head.'

'But you think it is a possibility. Why?'

'You should know,' I answered.

'What do you mean by that?'

'Weren't you in on the Wyks Odensdaal Rust Development racket?' I countered.

Bland turned on me with a quick oath. 'How do you know – ' He stopped then. 'Well?'

'Nordahl came to you and asked to be put on to something good in the financial world. He mortgaged all his holding in the South Antarctic Company and invested everything he had in Wyks Odensdaal Rust Development.'

'If he did, then it's the first I've heard of it,' Bland barked. 'He never asked me for financial advice in his life. And I wouldn't have given it to him if he had. He knew nothing about finance and I'm old enough to know that to give financial advice is the quickest way of making enemies.'

So it was Erik Bland who had advised Nordahl. 'Well,' I said, 'that's what your son says.'

'I see.' He stood by the porthole a moment, drumming with his fingers on the top of the toilet cabinet. At length he turned and faced me. He looked tired and somehow older. He didn't say anything, but sat down at the desk and began running through the sheets of evidence. Then for a long time he sat staring at one single page. At last he pushed the papers into a drawer and got to his feet. 'Very well, Craig,' he said heavily. 'I agree. It is a matter for the police. Some changes must be made now.' He went to the door and I followed him back to the saloon.

One of the *skytters* gave me a drink and I knocked it back. I needed it badly. Bland had sat down again. Something in his manner silenced the room. He watched them, his heavy brows dragged down, his face set in its solid, imperturbable rolls. 'I have some changes in command to announce,' he said. 'Nordahl's death has left us without an experienced leader. As I am here, and intend to stay out during the whole season, I shall direct operations personally. Petersen, you will take over from my son as manager of the *Southern Cross*.' There was a murmur of surprise and a quickening of interest at this announcement. 'Commander Craig, you are posted to command of *Hval 4* in Petersen's place.'

I saw the eldest of the whaling skippers stir in his seat and lean forward. 'Excuse me, sir,' I said quickly, 'I don't wish to query your orders. But I would like to remind you that I've no experience as a gunner.'

'I'm well aware of that, Craig,' he answered. 'But you will take command of *Hval 4*.' He rounded on Petersen before the old *skytter* could begin to argue. 'I know what you're going to say, Petersen. But I won't have a girl in charge of a catcher. Not down here. Craig will command the boat. Your daughter will remain in her present position as mate. But in addition she will act as gunner. Some adjustment will be made financially in her terms of employment. Does that satisfy you?'

The old skytter relaxed. '*Ja*, hr. Bland. I am satisfied.'

'Good. Erik. You will take command of *Tauer III*. The ship is without deck officers at the moment. You can choose your own mates.' He turned to Petersen again. 'I shall rely on you to see that there is no more trouble between the Sandefjord and Tönsberg men. More than six weeks have passed and we've only just over a hundred whales. In the next two months the leeway has got to be – '

But I wasn't listening. I was staring at Erik Bland. His face seemed to have crumpled up on hearing his father's decision. But it wasn't his face so much as his eyes that held my gaze. There was something violent, almost vicious, about those small blue slits between the creases of fat.

I was brought back to the conference again with a jolt. It was Captain Larvik. 'Has the enquiry into Nordahl's death been completed yet, hr. Bland?' he asked.

'Yes,' replied the chairman, and glanced quickly at me.

'Can we have the findings of the committee then?'

'They have not been typed yet,' Bland answered. 'They will be published tomorrow.'

Again I was conscious of a quick glance in my direction and then he was hurrying on into details of organization for the journey through the pack. Finally he said, 'Well, gentlemen, I think that's all. We will start as soon as you have rejoined your ships.' He was as casual as if he were terminating a rather dull board meeting. The *skytters* got to their feet. There was no argument, no indication that only just over twenty-four hours before several of them had refused to operate. Bland sat, squat and solid in his chair, smiling genially, dominating them. There was something implacable in the calm assuredness of the man. I thought: *Money is power and he's had that all his life. He's had it because that's what he's fought for and in doing so he's learned to beat down all opposition. They know that. They know that it's no good fighting him. So they do what he says.* I didn't like Bland. But I couldn't help admiring him. Out of chaos and a tricky situation, he had produced order – and obedience.

The whalers were leaving now. Bland motioned me over to him. His son was still hunched angrily in his chair, waiting to speak to his father. 'Craig,' Bland said quietly as I approached him, 'I want you to understand that the interests of the expedition must come first. I am referring to the committee of enquiry. Your attitude in the matter is quite correct. But the safety of the *Southern Cross* and the catcher fleet depend on the morale of the men. For the moment that must be my sole consideration. But privately I wish you to know that the whole matter of Nordahl's disappearance, together with the evidence you have taken, will be handed over to the police at the earliest opportunity. In the meantime, anything I may do in the matter will be done with Captain Eide's full knowledge. Do you understand?'

'Yes, sir,' I said.

As I turned to go his son rose from his seat. 'Does that include posting me to command of a towing ship?' His tone was pitched a shade high. I got the impression that he was scared of his father. But something stronger was driving him now.

Bland looked at him. 'It does,' he said.

'But Nordahl committed suicide. He must have done. It – it's the only logical explanation. He was finished. He'd ruined himself in that mad gamble. That's why he killed himself. I tried to make Craig understand that. He'd lost everything he had. He'd nothing to live for. Why didn't you tell the *skytters* the truth – that Nordahl was a ruined man?'

'I'm doing what I think best, boy.' Bland's voice was a deep, angry rumble.

'You're being weak.' Erik Bland was trembling, his eyes fever-bright and his mouth twitching. 'You're discarding me like you do everyone when it suits you.'

'Talk to me like that again, Erik, and I'll send you back to the Cape in irons.' Bland took off his glasses and wiped them carefully. He was trembling with anger. He had calmed down a little by the time he'd put his glasses on again. He took out his wallet and extracted a piece of paper. 'Read that,' he said, passing it across to his son.

'*Cargo unloaded as per instructions,*' Erik Bland read aloud and his brow puckered.

'It's a copy of a radio message received by Nordahl on Christmas Eve. It was sent by Howe from Cape Town.'

'What's it mean?'

'I'll leave you to think about what it means for a moment.' Bland turned to me. 'You'll please regard what has passed between Erik and myself here as confidential, Craig. You have my assurance that, whatever I put out for the benefit of the men in present circumstances, all the evidence you have taken at the committee of enquiry will be handed to the police immediately on our return to port. Now I suggest you join your ship.'

I nodded and turned to go. But he stopped me. 'I shall be sending Doctor Howe over to join you. I think it would be better if he didn't remain on the factory ship. He is excitable and when drunk he might – ' He shrugged his shoulders. 'Bernt Nordahl,' he began, and then hesitated. He seemed to have difficulty in finding the right words, 'Nordahl was his father,' he finished abruptly.

'His father?' I echoed in surprise. And I saw a shocked, almost dazed look on Erik Bland's face.

'Yes,' Bland said. 'He is Nordahl's natural son by a Mrs Howe of Newcastle. That is why I think it would be better if he were on one of the catchers.' He nodded for me to go and then added, 'You will find Gerda Petersen not very beautiful, but a good first mate.'

That he should be capable of this little flash of dry humour at that moment made me wonder whether Nordahl's death meant anything to him. I remember thinking that a man who was involved in the Wyks Odensdaal Rust business might not stop at other things. As I walked away from the saloon I heard the door opened and then closed. It was as though they had suspected me of listening in the corridor.

I went straight to my cabin. Judie was there, sitting on my bunk. Howe was pacing up and down. They both turned to face me as I came in. 'Shut the door, Craig,' Howe said. He was agitated, almost excited. Judie sat very tense, her eyes dark shadows in the tightness of her face. She was beyond tears – near the breaking point.

I shut the door. 'Something happened?' I asked.

Judie nodded. 'Tell him, Walter.' Her voice was barely audible.

'All right.' Howe swung round on me. 'But understand this, Craig – not a word of what I'm going to tell you must be passed on to anyone. Understand?' I nodded. 'Promise?'

'I promise,' I said.

He peered at me quickly. 'I don't know you well enough to be certain you can be trusted.' He hesitated and then shrugged his shoulders. 'However, Judie wants me to tell you, so – ' He started pacing the cabin again without finishing his sentence. There was a sort of incredible violence about the man. I sat very still, watching him. It was like waiting for an animal to make up its mind whether it regards you as a friend.

At length he stopped his pacing and came and stood right in front of me. 'Erik Bland said Nordahl was ruined, didn't he?'

I nodded.

'That's the basis for thinking Nordahl's death might be suicide?'

Again I nodded.

'The only basis?'

'Yes,' I said.

'If Nordahl weren't ruined, it would mean that Erik Bland killed him?'

'On the evidence we have at the moment it would be reasonable to suppose that,' I said, cautiously, wondering what the hell he was driving at.

Howe nodded excitedly. 'That's what I told Judie. If Nordahl were a rich man then Erik Bland killed him, pushed him overboard in the fog.'

'What are you getting at?' I demanded.

'Why do you suppose I was left in Cape Town?'

'I thought you'd been ill.'

'That was only an excuse. I stayed in Cape Town to look after Nordahl's interests. Erik Bland was quite right – as far as he went. Nordahl invested everything he had in Wyks Odensdaal Rust Development, even to mortgaging his interest in the South Antarctic Company. Erik Bland got the whole of his father's plan for the boosting of these shares from his mother. He passed it on to Nordahl as a straight tip, forgetting to mention that it was a racket, that the mine was to be salted and at a certain moment Bland was going to go on the bear tack. Nordahl had never dabbled much in finance. But he was an astute man. He saw through the reason for Erik Bland giving him the tip and he saw in it a chance to prevent Erik Bland from becoming head of the firm on his father's death. He got an introduction to one of the sharpest brokers in the business, and dealt through them. And when the *Southern Cross* sailed from Cape Town I stayed behind with his power of attorney. On Christmas Eve I cabled the *Southern Cross* that I'd sold all the shares.'

'Cargo unloaded as per instructions,' I said. I was beginning to understand.

Howe looked at me sharply. 'How did you know the wording?'

I told him about Bland handing the copy of the cable to his son.

'So the old man knows, eh?' He chuckled to himself. 'It must have shaken him – reading the evidence and knowing that.' He caught hold of my arm. 'Nordahl was a rich man when he died. A very rich man.'

I stared at him. I don't think I made any comment. I only remember the shock of realizing what must have happened, that Erik Bland had killed him.

'Don't you see,' Howe rushed on. 'Up there on the boat deck, Erik Bland told Nordahl what had happened, told him he was a ruined man. You can imagine how sympathetically he broke the news. And then Nordahl told him the truth – that he'd sold out, that he was rich. He probably told him that he'd see he never again set foot on one of the company's ships. And then Bland pushed him.'

'It could have been an accident,' Judie whispered. 'He may have struck Bernt without realizing – in the fog – ' Her voice trailed away.

Howe laughed. It was a derisive sound. 'You don't really believe that,' he said.

'Why didn't you tell this to the committee of enquiry?' I asked him.

'Why? Because it would have given my hand away. And don't forget your promise, Craig. Nothing I've told you must be repeated to anyone. I don't think the old man knew what his son was up to. But he knows now. And he's not the sort of man to regard justice as applicable to himself or his.' He stooped down suddenly. 'I hear he refused to give the findings of the enquiry to the *skytters* – said they weren't typed. Did he by any chance mentioned something to you about morale and the exigencies of the moment?'

I nodded. 'But he has assured me that all the evidence will be handed to the police on our return to port.'

Howe gave that derisive, barking laugh again. 'You wait. Vital witnesses will be sent home in another ship, Eide and the secretary will be persuaded that it's not in the interest of the company to incur unprofitable publicity, and the whole thing will quietly fizzle out. That's why I wasn't coming out into the open. And I've still got something up my sleeve.'

But I wasn't listening to him any longer. I was staring at Judie. I remember thinking: *My God! She knows.* And realizing what hell it must be for her.

5

HALF an hour later I was up on deck with my things packed. The wind had freshened and ugly whitecaps were beginning to fleck the marching lines of cold grey water. Howe was waiting for me at the head of the gangway. 'Well, skipper,' he said, 'all the problem children being evacuated.'

'Bland's right all the same,' I said. 'There's two months of the season still to go.'

'I see you're one of the reasonable sort.' He smiled at me crookedly. 'You haven't had much to do with the Blands of this world, have you?'

'How do you mean?'

'In your world, right is right and wrong is wrong. But there's another world where it's a free-for-all and devil take the hindermost. You're in that other world now – Bland's world.'

'Why not relax?' I said. Up there on the deck my sense of proportion had reasserted itself. We were going south into the Antarctic and I'd been given command of one of the catchers. That was quite enough without having Howe on board behaving like a maniac. 'There's nothing you can do about Nordahl's death now,' I added. 'Wait until we get back to –'

'You fool,' he hissed. 'Don't you understand Judie's a rich woman? She holds the key to the control of the company. When Erik Bland knows that – ' He paused and then added, 'A man who's prepared to commit murder to get what he wants won't stop at that. Just now he's probably scared. But sooner or later – ' He shrugged his shoulders. And then in a matter-of-fact voice he said, 'If we stand here talking all day we'll get wet going over to the catcher.'

I started down the gangway. But then I stopped. There were three boats at the bottom of the gangway and one of them was just pushing off. In the stern sat Judie. She was sitting next to Larvik and her face was tense.

'Why's she going over to Larvik's catcher?' I asked. 'Did Bland send her?'

'No,' Howe answered. 'She sent herself. Bland doesn't know she's gone yet.'

'But why?'

'Because I advised her to. She's safer there than on the *Southern Cross*.'

'But Good God!' I said. 'You don't think anything would happen – '

'This is the Antarctic,' he reminded me, 'not suburbia.' He went down the gangway then. As he dumped his kit aboard the boat I caught the chink of bottles. He grinned as he saw that I'd heard. 'Always believe in being self-sufficient,' he said. It was incredible how the man's mood could change. 'You've got to be if you want to drink. Officially all these ships are dry.' He sent the two seamen up to bring down his instruments whilst we held the boat to the ship's side. A few minutes later we had pushed off and were bobbing up and down past the yawning cavity of the *Southern Cross*'s stern. The clean, ice-fresh air blew the events of the past twenty-four hours from my brain. Ahead of me lay *Hval 4*, a battered little toy of a boat with a saucy rake to her up-tilted bows. The harpoon gun, loaded and with the tip of the harpoon pointed downwards, was a grim reminder of her job as a killer. The knowledge that this was my new command gradually took hold of me as we approached her through the rising anger of the sea and drove every other thought out of my head.

Olaf Petersen met us as we clambered aboard. He was a big, bluff man with sharp eyes and a queer way of looking around him with a swaying motion of the head, rather like a polar bear. 'I am happy to welcome you on my ship.' His English was heavy and solid, like the creaking of something little used. The grip of his hand was the clutch of a bear's paw. 'You haf not meet my daughter.' His head lunged round. 'Gerda. Here is Commander Craig.'

I shouldn't have known she was a girl but for the breadth of her hips, the bulkiness of her chest and the fact that she was clean shaven. She was dressed in a heavy seaman's jersey, blue serge trousers and wore a fur cap on her head. The only spot of colour was a rather dirty-looking yellow silk scarf half hidden under her jacket. Her hand was rough as it gripped mine. I glanced at her quickly. She had large, very brown eyes. Her face was tanned and smooth, a chubby, friendly face with a lot of fat flesh round the eyes and a nose that was almost flattened as though the Maker had forgotten about it until the last moment and then as an after-thought slapped on a little button of flesh without any bone. There was no resentment as she met my gaze, only amusement. Her eyes twinkled in the creases of fat as though at any moment they would burst out laughing. 'I do not expect you have women as officers in your Navy,' she said.

'Only ashore,' I said with a grin.

'Ah, yes. A woman's place is ashore.' The laughter gurgled up from her throat, warm and happy. 'And then you call them Wrens, eh – little birds!'

Her father's big paw slapped my shoulder so that I nearly lost my balance. 'You will haf to get used to Gerda,' he boomed. 'Always she make mock of people. Even me – her father – I am to be made mock of. Always since she was so high and learn to speak English she call me *landlubber*. Me – *landlubber*.' His great laugh seemed to rattle round the ship, and he slapped me on the back again. But I was prepared for it this time and braced myself for the impact.

'Come,' Gerda Petersen said. 'I show you to your cabin. Walter, you come too. What's in that box – whisky?'

Howe grinned. He seemed relaxed for the first time since I'd met him. And when he grinned like that, it was strange, but he didn't look ugly any more. 'No,' he said. 'That's my instruments. The drink's in the bag here.' He kicked it and laughed when she scowled at the clinking sound of the bottles. 'That means you have not brought enough clothes and we must raid the slop-chest for you.' She glanced quickly at me and added, 'For you also, skipper. You look' – she hesitated, her eyes bubbling with laughter – 'you look as though you have borrow your clothes from all the crew of the *Southern Cross*.'

'Gerda!' Petersen's tone was half amused, half serious. 'You

will not get in the good books of your new captain if you make fun
of him. What must you think, Commander Craig? You will think
I have brought up my daughter badly and there is no discipline on
my ship. Well, by God there is.'

His daughter laughed. 'Take no notice of him,' she whispered.
'He is a big bear and he think he is important now he is to be
manager of the factory ship.'

Her father shrugged his shoulders in mock despair.

'I'll be only too glad to borrow from your slop-chest,' I said.

'Fine. Then come and take a look at your new command. I
hear you are the devil for spit and polish.' She grinned at me slily
over her shoulder. 'Well, I can tell you, this ship need some
polishing. That dirty man has made a pigsty of her.' With this
parting shot at her father she pulled herself up the ladder that led
to the bridge accommodation.

The catcher was a good deal smaller than *Tauer III*. The
captain's cabin was directly below the bridge, a part of the for'ard
deckhouse. 'I am sorry,' Gerda said, 'but we have not the
accommodation of a factory ship. You will have to share your
cabin with Walter Howe. Do you mind?'

'That's all right,' I said. 'Provided he's willing to share his
Scotch with me.'

She laughed. 'Do not worry. I will see that he is not dog-in-the-
manger with his drink. I, too, get thirsty.' Her eyes twinkled.
'You must excuse me for my rotten English. It is vair rusty.'
Howe staggered in then with his box of instruments. 'Walter, you
will share the skipper's cabin and he is to share your whisky.
Okay?'

Howe's eyebrows lifted. 'He'll have to drink fast,' he said, 'if he
is to get the same share of my drink that I get of his cabin.'

They both laughed. They seemed to understand each other.
'This ought to be the wireless room,' Gerda said, leading me to
the next cabin. 'But because I am Olaf Petersen's daughter, he
make a little adjustment. This is my cabin and the wireless is aft
in the second mate's berth. That is the only concession he make,'
she added quickly.

She took me on a brief tour of the ship then, introducing me to
the crew. 'Do not trouble to remember their names,' she said as
she noticed my concentration. 'You will soon have sort them out.'

The ship was rather like a small Fleet sweeper in appearance
with its high bow and high bridge and a long, low after-deck. She
was narrow in the beam, built for speed and power. She was
capable of about $13\frac{1}{2}$ knots and looked a very seaworthy little ship,

though I guessed she'd be extremely lively in heavy weather. Perched on a platform on the bow was the harpoon gun, a deadly-looking weapon with a three and a quarter inch breech and firing a harpoon weighing around a hundredweight. The gun platform was connected to the bridge by a catwalk. Aft of the chain locker was a hold containing two 500-fathom coils of 2-inch manila. These whale lines ran up to the winches on deck. Each winch had two drums and the line ran three times round each drum and thence up to masthead blocks and so out through a fairlead in the bow. The masthead blocks were connected to huge springs – accumulators – with a pressure of twenty tons. The springs performed the same function as the whip in a fishing-rod, allowing the whale to be played on the winches without the sudden movements of the vessel in a seaway parting the line.

Aft of the hold was the engine-room. Then came the crew's quarters – cabins with bunks for two or four – and finally the tiller flat. Below the captain's cabin in the bridge accommodation was the galley and the mess-room.

By the time I had completed the round of the ship Captain Petersen was ready to leave. 'Well, I hope you will like *Hval 4*,' he said, gripping my hand as though trying to squeeze the flesh out from between the bones. '*Ja*. I hope so. I hope also Gerda behave herself, no? There is one good thing about a woman as first mate – if she do not behave herself you can always put her across your knee. She has a vair big bottom. You cannot miss, even if you are drunk, eh?' And he went down the ladder to the deck below roaring with laughter.

'You have only the nerve to say that because you are leaving,' the girl answered, two angry little spots of colour showing on the dark tan of her cheeks.

'Because I am leaving, eh? *Ja*. That is good. When I am skipper here my life she is not worthing living. It is Olaf this and Olaf that all day long. I tell you, Commander Craig, it is worse than being married to have a daughter on board.' He turned and looked up at us, his fat face creased in laughter. 'One thing I do not haf to worry about. My daughter is safe with any man. She is a nice girl – but ugly as a fat leetle pig, eh?'

Gerda made a face at him and put out her tongue. Still laughing, he climbed over the side into the boat that had been sent across from the factory ship. We watched it bobbing across the waves towards the *Southern Cross*. '*Mange hval*,' Petersen roared across at us and with a final wave of his big hand seated himself in the stern.

'I am afraid all this talk will have made you think this is a play-ship,' Gerda said, her voice suddenly serious. 'But that is just our fun.'

'I like it,' I said. 'I feel at home already. I think the ship must be a very happy one.'

'*Ja*, I think so too.' She wrinkled her nose. It was a habitual gesture, half serious, half humorous. 'You are nice,' she said. 'My father and I have been three seasons together out here. We are not bad whalers. We work well together. Last season we are second only to Peer Larvik in the number of whales we have caught. This time we lead all the fleet – though that is not much. We have twenty-two whales so far.'

'I hope we manage to hold the lead,' I said.

She patted me on the shoulder. It was a gesture copied from her father, but I was glad to find it hadn't the same weight behind it. 'I think we get on fine, skipper. But I am not so good a *skytter* as Olaf. And you will have to learn how to control the ship for me.' She glanced at me quickly. 'I know what you are thinking. You are thinking the Antarctic is no place for a girl. But you must remember one thing. We can stand the cold well – I have much fat, eh?' And she tapped her bosom and laughed. I was thinking of the Eskimo women I had met on that Greenland expedition. They had stood the cold as well as the men. Looking at Gerda Petersen, I wondered if there wasn't some Eskimo or Lapland blood in her – she had the flattened face and narrow, fat-creased eyes of the northern Slav. Later I discovered her mother was a Finn from the Aaland Islands.

As we stood there on the deck a boat came across from *Tauer III.* It was McPhee. Bland had agreed to his transfer. I watched the Chief Engineer of *Hval 4* as he climbed down into the boat. It was clear that he didn't want to leave his own ship. But I'd had to have one officer that I knew. And McPhee was glad to come with me. I could see that in the dour way he said, 'Och, ye dinna ha' to fash yoursel' aboot me leaving me ane engine-room. Ah'll soon have this ane as smart as the ither.'

At eight thirty-five there was a series of whoops on the factory ship's siren. The sea boiled under the ugly cavity of her stern. I order Half Ahead, and as the engine-room telegraph rang, the deck plates began to vibrate to the rising hum of the engine as we swung into position astern of the *Southern Cross.* The other ships took up station and the whole fleet, strung out in a long line behind the mother ship, headed south into the ice.

The sky cleared about eleven that night. The sun was almost

due south, a flaming yellow ball, its lower edge just above the horizon. A towering iceberg loomed up to starboard, catching the sunlight and flashing fire like an enormous pink diamond. Fragments of ice began to drift past us – tiny 'growlers,' almost completely submerged. And ahead of us the loose pack ice stretched like an unending, broken plain of pink straight into the sun. It was an incredible sight.

Gerda, who was standing between Howe and myself on the bridge, caught hold of my arm and said, 'It is beautiful, yes? I bet you do not ever see anything so beautiful as this. You are glad we go south?'

I nodded. But I was looking at Howe. I was thinking – *He doesn't see the beauty of it. But he's exultant. The ice means something else to him.* He was standing quite still, his long neck thrust out and his hand clenched on the canvas windbreaker. His face looked almost ferocious. Again I had that sense of being afraid of him – the feeling that I'd had on *Tauer III* when Bland had ordered him to prepare that report. It was as though the man were part of the destiny of things. After all he was Bernt Nordahl's son and I remembered Judie saying – *Bernt and Walter were very close.*

'Howe!' The unconscious peremptoriness of my tone jerked him away from his contemplation of the ice ahead. 'That report you did for Bland. Why did you come to the conclusion that we must go south into the Weddell Sea?'

He started at me for a moment and the corners of his mouth lifted in that sly smile of his. He didn't attempt to justify his findings with a lot of technicalities. He just shrugged his shoulders and said, 'I wanted Bland to go south – that's all.'

'Why?'

Again the slight shrug. 'Why? God knows why. I just wanted him to go south – away from civilization.'

'But why?' I asked again.

He let go of the windbreaker than and caught hold of my arm in a grip that hurt, it was so violent. 'Because if he's given enough rope – ' He stopped there and gave a quick laugh. 'Just leave it at that.' And he turned away and went quickly down to the cabin.

'You find Walter a little queer perhaps?' Gerda said with a laugh that sounded unnatural. 'Poor man – he has not had an easy life. And he worshipped Bernt Nordahl.'

'And you' – I said – 'what did you think of Nordahl?'

'I think he is a big loss to the company – to all of us who work with him. He was a fine man.'

McPhee came up on to the bridge then to discuss a defect in one of the winches and the conversation was never resumed. By midnight, with the sun lipping the southern horizon, we had entered the ice, following a broad lead and steaming south at about ten knots. The lead was more than a mile wide and the water in it looked black by comparison with the shimmering iridescence of the ice on either side. On our port quarter was a large, flat-topped berg. Apart from this we were surrounded by loose pack – a flat expanse of ice tinged with pink and criss-crossed with innumerable black lines that marked the division between one floe and another. And as the sun climbed and circled northwards towards midday, the colours drained out of the scene and the ice became a blinding sheet of white, very painful to the eyes. Even with dark glasses I found it tiring.

There was nothing dangerous about the ice. The weather remained fair and we were able to observe a steady shipboard routine of watch and watch about. Sometimes the lead was so broad we might have been in the open sea but for the glare. At other times it narrowed down to a dark highway winding between occasional icebergs and surrounded by that unending plain of loose pack. Only once it petered out and then the *Southern Cross* thrust into the pack, parting the floes in great sheets that layered one on top of the other until we were in a new lead.

Occasionally we sighted whale. Once a big spermacetti came up to blow almost alongside. They were all headed south. There were plenty of the smaller killer whales hunting for seals among the icefloes. One morning a whole string of these ugly brutes passed across our bows. Their high triangular fins stood about five feet out of the water and the whole line of them rose and fell as they cut through the water, blowing steadily. Gerda and Howe were on the bridge with me at the time and she said, 'Ugh, those devils!'

'*Orca Gladiator*,' Howe said. 'That's the official terminology.'

'*Gladiators!*' Gerda's voice was almost angry. 'For once your official terminology, as you call it, is right. That's exactly what they are – gladiators. Have you ever seen one close to?' she asked me.

I shook my head. 'I've never seen them before.'

'Well, I do not advise it. Once I see one close up, and it is enough, I think. When he is full grown the killer is perhaps thirty feet long, his mouth is about four feet wide and he has ugly eyes and uglier teeth. I was hunting for seal with my father. It was near Grytviken and we had left our boat and were on a small icefloe. This killer whale, he start snorting and blowing all round us. Then suddenly he push his nose over the edge of the floe and look straight at us. Then he start to turn the floe over with his weight. Fortunately my father have his gun and he shoot. But it is a very near thing and it is a long time before I go for the seal again.' Later I was to remember this story and wish she had never told it to me.

She was, in fact, a mine of information on the Antarctic and she would talk for hours about whales and ships and hunting expeditions on the ice in the same matter-of-fact way that most women would talk about a shopping expedition in Oxford Street. It was she who picked out a sea-leopard for me in the glasses so that I was able to watch the great spotted brute rushing across the ice with an undulating, snake-like movement as it charged a group of seals. She pointed out to me the small Adelie penguins, and one evening she showed me a little group of Emperor penguins clustered on an ice-ledge, where they bowed and chattered to each other with the distant dignity of foreign diplomats at an Embassy social.

On the morning of the fourth day in the ice the sky to the south became very black and louring. There was a lot of low cloud and at first I thought a storm was coming up. But Gerda shook her head. 'It is the open sea. It always look dark when you are in the ice blink.' She was right. The lead we were following gradually opened out. The floes became looser and more scattered. And early on the 23 January we were in open sea in 66.01 S., 35.62 W. with the ice blink behind us.

Almost immediately *Hval 1* and *Hval 3* ahead of us peeled off. Gerda had ordered a lookout to the *tonne*, which is the barrel crow's-nest and a few minutes later came the cry of '*Blaast! Blaast!*'

'*Hvor er den?*' Gerda called up.

'*Paa styrbord side.*'

We picked it up almost immediately. I ordered starboard helm and emergency full ahead and we were off on our first whale hunt. I've heard people say that there's no longer any excitement in whaling, that Sven Foynd's invention of the explosive harpoon took all the adventure out of it. Don't you believe it. Whaling is still the biggest of all big-game hunting and only the arm-chair whalers make statements like that.

I must admit that as we swung away at full speed on that cry of *Blaast* I was under the impression that the work of a catcher was just the shooting down of the whale. I hadn't realized the chase that was involved. Almost immediately the whale sounded and Gerda suggested we reduce to half speed. All eyes were scanning the sea ahead, waiting for the next sight of the thin plume of vapour as the whale surfaced again to blow. I found myself nervous and excited as I stared into the heaving, slate-grey waste of water. Gerda plucked at my sleeve. 'You have not done this before, so perhaps if you take the wheel and I give directions – ' She hesitated. 'It is very difficult to get so that we can shoot him. We must drive him under again and again until he is blown. You understand?'

'Of course,' I said. She didn't wish to embarrass me, but at the same time she wanted our first whale hunt to be successful. I think we were both a little excited and a little awkward at sharing the command.

I took the wheel and almost immediately one of the hands gave a shout and Gerda ordered full speed. The whale was wallowing on the surface about two cables' length ahead of us. We were on top of him almost immediately and the sleek, grey back curved as it sounded.

Gerda ordered 'Stop!' and the vibration of the engine died as we drifted forward. When next he broke surface he was away on the port beam and we heeled over as I turned the catcher in pursuit. Five times we drove the whale under, and each time we were closer to him. Now we were driving him under almost before he had time to blow and all my nervousness was gone in the excitement of the chase. 'Now I think we have him,' Gerda shouted to me as it wallowed in the trough of a wave so close that we could hear the snort of the water being expelled from the huge body. Her eyes were alight with excitement. She thrust open the door of the bridge and ran down the catwalk to the gun platform. From there she directed me by hand signals which we had rehearsed beforehand.

We were steaming at slow ahead and turning to port. She had taken hold of the slender butt of the gun. She signalled for half speed and I saw the whale surface right ahead of us, not fifty feet away, as I jerked the engine-room telegraph. The catcher gathered speed. Gerda braced her legs apart and swung the harpoon gun. We were right on top of the whale now. I lost sight of it under the high bows and braced myself for the shock of our bows ripping into it. There was a flash, the sharp crack of an explosion and I saw the harpoon fly down into the water, the light forerunner snaking after it. There was another, duller explosion, a terrible flurry of spray and then the winch drums were screaming and the masthead block dragging down as the heavy two-inch whale line went roaring out through the fairlead in the bow.

Gerda came running back to the bridge. 'My shot is no good,' she said. 'I tell you I am not so good a *skytter* as Olaf. The harpoon, he explode outside. I do not hit the backbone. Slow now please.'

The whale had sounded and the line was still roaring out with the block dragged down to the danger mark. I watched one, two splices run through the block. Each splice meant 120 fathoms of line gone out. Altogether there were four lengths – three splices. Just when the third splice was reeling through the block we saw the whale surface half a mile ahead.

Gerda was gripping the windbreaker in a frenzy. This was her first whale independent of her father. It meant a lot to her. The last splice went through the fairlead. She ordered full speed. And just as I rang the engine-room telegraph, I saw the block start to rise up the mast. 'We win,' she cried. 'We win.' McPhee at the winch was braking now. I could hear the scream of the brake drums above the hum of the engines. Then suddenly the line was slack. Gerda ordered stop and the winch began to clatter as McPhee took in line. We drifted and the line continued to come in slack.

The suddenly it was taut again, stretched so tight that from a diameter of two inches it was shrunk to half an inch. It was like a violin string. I thought it must break. The block was down the mast again and the whole ship was being dragged through the water at about 6 knots. McPhee paid out line on the winches. It lasted like that for perhaps a minute – maybe only thirty seconds. It seemed like years. Then it was over. It was the whale's last bid for freedom. We began to winch in. It was still lashing the water with its huge tail as we hauled up to it and Gerda ran down to the gun platform and fired another harpoon into it. There was a sudden spout of blood and then the great brute was motionless, lying alongside us like a half-submerged submarine.

'Next time I shoot better I hope,' Gerda said and took me down to the bows to superintend the pumping of air into the whale. As one of the hands thrust the lance with the air pipe in it, there was a cry of '*Blaast!*' *Blaast!* from the *tonne*. The air hissed as it went into the huge carcase. The harpoon holes were plugged, a long steel rod with a flag was thrust deep into the animal and a moment later we were back on the bridge and off after our next whale, two men working furiously to reload the harpoon gun and rig a new fore-runner as we went.

I have given this detailed account of our first whale hunt to show the degree of concentration the work entailed. It occupied all our waking thoughts and energies and when we fell into our bunks we were so tired we slept like the dead. For whale were plentiful and when we had killed one, another was sighted almost immediately. The cry of *Blaast! Blaast!* echoed almost unceasingly from the *tonne* and the crack of the harpoon gun slamming its deadly weight of metal into the whale sounded all day and on through the unending daylight of the night. When we'd flagged three or four whale we'd put through a call on the R/T for one of the towing vessels or a buoy boat and go on to the next kill whilst they picked up our catch and towed it back to the factory ship. All around us, through good weather and bad, the rest of the catcher fleet was working in the same frantic haste. The only occasions on which we returned to the *Southern Cross* were to refuel and take on provisions and a new supply of harpoons straightened out in the blacksmith's shop. I had neither the time nor the energy to think about Nordahl's disappearance and though I wondered sometimes how Judie was getting on in Larvik's catcher, my mind was so tired that the image it sketched of her was blurred as though she were a girl I'm met years ago.

Even the announcement over the R/T that the committee of enquiry over which I had presided had found that Nordahl had committed suicide whilst the balance of his mind was affected by financial worries made little impression in the fatigue induced by hard and constant work. Bland had said that he must consider the morale of the men in any announcement he made and I must say I agreed with him. Whatever Howe might say, I had no reason to suppose that he would not carry out his promise to hand over the evidence to the police on our return to Cape Town. And if he failed in this I could always notify the police myself. Howe's reactions was, of course, very different. 'I told you what would happen,' he shouted at me. 'I told you they'd try to hush it up. But I can wait. I can wait. And sooner or later – ' But I was too tired to listen to his railing. Too many things demanded my attention for him to be able to corner me for more than a moment at a time. And when I wasn't on duty I was asleep and then not all the angels of wrath calling for vengeance could have got an answer out of me.

In two weeks we chased and killed forty-six whale. Most of these were shot by Gerda for I felt it was unfair on the men to assume the role of gunner except at the end of a good day's hunting. They had a financial interest in the whale we caught.

However, by the end of that fortnight I was becoming quite a fair *skytter* and the men, who were a good crowd, would ask me to go down and see if I could get one, laying small bets against each other as to whether I'd be successful or not with my first shot. They were very proud of their ship and I think they were unwilling to accept the idea of a skipper that wasn't also a *skytter*.

Towards the end of this period of intense activity an incident occurred which brought the whole question of Nordahl's disappearance back into my mind. We'd had a good day and after our fourth kill we radioed for a towing vessel to pick up the catch. As it happened it was *Tauer III* that answered our call. We were quartering the sea on the line of her approach and as she neared us she swung off her course and made straight for us, her sharp bows cleaving the water at a steady 14 knots. She came round in a wide circle and steamed up almost alongside. Erik Bland was on the bridge and he called to me on the loud-hailer, asking permission to come aboard and have a word with me.

Before I could reply, Howe came pell-mell up the ladder to the bridge. He was breathless and his face was working. He caught hold of my arm, forcing the megaphone away from my lips. 'Don't let him come on board.' His eyes looked wild and the grip of his fingers of my arm was like a vice.

'Why?' I asked.

'Why?' He shook me. 'You ask me why?' His voice was trembling. 'If that bastard sets foot on board this ship, I'll kill him. That's why. I'll kill him. I swear it.'

I stared at him for a second in amazement. His violence had taken me by surprise. Yet the strange thing is, I never doubted that he meant it. We hadn't seen much of him during the last few days. He'd kept to the cabin mostly, working on what he'd told me was a treatise on whaling. He'd been drinking hardly anything. I realized suddenly that what he'd been doing was brooding. 'All right,' I said, and raised the megaphone to my lips. 'Ahoy there! I – will – come – over – to – you.'

The two vessels were steaming parallel only twenty feet or so apart. Bland waved his hand to signify he'd heard and I ordered the engine stopped and a boat swung out. As my men rowed me across the long swell to the waiting corvette I had time to wonder what it was Bland wanted to see me about. And in those few minutes I thought more about the antagonism between him and Nordahl that we'd unearthed at the enquiry than I'd had time to do in the past few days.

He met me at the head of the ladder they'd thrown over for

me, and I was astonished at the change in the man. His face was almost haggard and there was a nervous twitch at the corner of his mouth. The small eyes seemed to have sunk farther into his head. He took me straight to his cabin without a word and poured me a drink with hands that shook. '*Skaal!*'

I didn't say anything, but raised my glass and drank.

'Well,' he said. 'Don't you want to know why I asked to see you?'

'It would help,' I said. 'You're supposed to be picking up our catch and we're supposed to be searching for more whale.'

He toyed with his glass, running the yellow liquid round the inside and watching it as though it were a crystal. Suddenly he leaned forward, staring at me. 'You think I killed Nordahl, don't you?' And when I didn't say anything, he repeated – 'Don't you?' His voice was savage.

'I've no views on the matter,' I said. 'I took evidence at a committee of enquiry. The rest is for the police to decide.'

'What if there was a row?' he cried. 'What if it did come to blows and he fell overboard. That doesn't make me a murderer, does it?'

I didn't know what to say. The man seemed to me on the very edge of sanity and I wished I hadn't come on board. 'A court will have to decide that.'

He peered at me, measuring my mood, his hands clenching and unclenching. 'There's Judie,' he said quietly.

'What's Judie got to do with it?'

'She's Nordahl's daughter – and she's my wife.' He hesitated, and then said suddenly, 'You're in love with her, aren't you?'

I stared at him in shocked surprise. The unexpectedness of the question put everything else out of my mind. Put bluntly like that I realized that it was a question I'd been asking myself.

He sat back, suddenly relaxing. His face had a cunning look. 'You wouldn't want her dragged through an ordeal like that – her husband accused of murdering her father. Picture it in the English newspapers – the Sunday ones. And I'll swear that she was your mistress here on board *Tauer III*.'

I went for him then, I was so angry. But he caught my arm and flung me back into a chair. He was a big man and pretty powerful. 'Oh no,' he said. 'Oh no you don't. This isn't a matter to fight over. You just sit there and listen to me. I'm in a jam and I'm not having a rope put round my neck by you or anyone else, do you understand? Now listen. Only four people know the whole of the evidence taken by the committee of enquiry over which you presided. My father holds that evidence. He'll die soon, anyway. But I can handle him and I can handle Eide. Judie can't give evidence against me. She's my wife. There remains you.'

'There's also Howe,' I reminded him. After all that cable must have shown him Howe's part in the business.

'Ah, yes. The illegitimate doctor.' The sneer in his voice made it clear that he didn't take Howe very seriously. 'I can look after him too. If you were to keep your mouth shut, then the whole thing could be hushed up. Will you do that?'

'The answer is No,' I said.

He nodded as though he'd expected that. 'All right then. I'll make a bargain with you. Keep your mouth shut and I'll let Judie divorce me.'

'You must be mad to think I'd do such a thing,' I answered hotly.

He shrugged his shoulders. 'Then I'd remind you again that Judie is my wife. If you go through with this I'll make her life hell. Whether I'm convicted or not, I'll see she curses the day she was born. I'll show her up as a common tart. I'll represent that the row with Nordahl was about her. Oh, you needn't worry. That sort of dirt sticks, and there's always enough evidence if used in the right way to sway the minds of a jury. And when I'm acquitted, I'll still be her husband. And I'll see she lives with me. She'll get no grounds for divorce and if she tries to divorce me I'll oppose it and cite you for one as co-respondent.'

'You must be mad,' I said. I'd got to my feet. I didn't want to stay there another minute.

But he jumped between me and the door and said, "Well, which is it? Do you keep your mouth shut or – ' He left the sentence unfinished. 'Look, Craig,' he said. 'You've no alternative. Nordahl's dead. Trying to hang me for what was no more than an accident won't bring him to life again. You've a choice between Judie and revenge for something that happened to a man you didn't even know. Come on now. Be reasonable.' His manner was suddenly boyish as though he were asking me to keep quiet about some indiscreet prank.

I said, 'If you don't mind, I'll go to my ship now. You're lucky that you're a more powerful man than I am, or I'd thrash you within an inch of your life.'

He stood aside and his smile was almost friendly, as though I'd paid him a social call. 'All right,' he said. 'But think it over. And don't forget. I can break Judie mentally so that in two years you won't even recognize her.'

I stopped then. A wave of uncontrollable anger engulfed me. But there was nothing I could do. 'Watch out somebody doesn't kill you before we get back to Cape Town,' I said. And then I went quickly past him through the door. If I'd had a gun on me I swear I'd have shot him.

Outside on the deck the air was cold, the sea slate-grey and a mile away a flag stood out of the water marking a dead whale. The scene was just as it had been when I'd come on board. I could hardly believe the conversation in that cabin had really taken place. It seemed so horribly unreal. Yet when I glanced back, there was Erik Bland watching me with that vicious little smile on his lips.

I climbed down into the boat and was rowed in silence back to my ship. Howe was there on the deck, waiting for me. 'Well, what did he say?' he asked. But I brushed by him and went straight to my cabin. There I paced up and down, my mind a bewildering turmoil of half-formed ideas. On only one thing was I really clear. It was there in my mind like a flash of light. Bland was right. I *was* in love with Judie. And in no circumstances could I let her go through the hell he'd planned for her.

At length there was a tap on the door and Gerda came in. 'We have sighted another whale,' she said. 'I think you should be on the bridge.' No questions. No desire to peer into my mind. Just – *I think you should be on the bridge.* I could have hugged her for that. It was something practical for my mind to grasp and cling to.

But with Howe it was different. When I came down that night to get some sleep, he was sitting at the desk, his papers spread out in front of him, waiting for me. I was tired out. All I wanted was to lie down on my bunk and sleep. But I'd hardly got my boots off when he said, 'Craig. Suppose you tell me what Erik Bland said to you.' His voice was tense.

'It's none of your business,' I told him and rolled over on to the bunk.

'Anything to do with Bernt Nordahl is my business,' he answered in a flat, obstinate voice. 'What did he say about Nordahl's disappearance?' He was leaning slightly forward now. 'That's what he wanted to talk to you about, wasn't it?'

'For God's sake,' I said wearily, 'get on with your damned book, can't you – or go to bed. I'm tired.'

'I'm going to sit here asking you questions until I find out what happened,' he answered obstinately.

'The conversation was private. It was between Bland and myself.' I closed my eyes.

'But it was about Nordahl's disappearance, wasn't it?' He hesitated and then said, 'You know I've a right to know. You'll probably be surprised at this. But I'm related to Bernt Nordahl.'

'Yes, I know,' I answered. 'But my conversation – '

'You know?' he interrupted on a note of sudden anger. 'How do you know? Who told you?'

'Colonel Bland.'

'He would.' He sounded bitter. He was silent for a moment. Then he got up and began rummaging in one of his bags. 'And knowing I'm his son, you still won't tell me what Bland said?'

'No,' I answered. I was thinking that if I told him what Bland had said, I would no longer be a free agent. I'd no longer be able to make a bargain with Bland if I wanted to. And my mind stopped with a jolt on that thought. I realized suddenly that I was in fact seriously considering the proposition he'd made. My sense of justice wouldn't accept that. And yet there was Judie. I was no longer tired now. I was wide-awake, my mind facing up to the problem, thinking of Judie and what the future would be for her if Bland was brought to trial.

'Perhaps this may help you to decide.' I looked up to find Howe standing over me. He had a gun in his hand. I sat up quickly and he laughed. 'It's all right, Craig. I'm not threatening you.' He sat down, turning the gleaming nickel of the pistol over and over in his hand. 'Life doesn't mean very much to me,' he said quietly, and the sudden steadiness of his voice compelled attention. 'I've nothing much to lose, you see. And this – ' he held up the pistol – 'this could be a way out. I know why Erik Bland wanted to see you. It's just as I said. They think they can hush the whole thing up provided they square you. What did he do – threaten you through Judie?'

'How did you guess?' I asked in surprise.

'Because I know the sort of bastard Erik Bland is.' The word *bastard* had a violence on his lips that I'd never noticed in it before. 'I suppose he offered to trade Judie for your silence?'

I didn't answer.

He laughed suddenly. 'If he knew the whole story nothing would induce him to part with Judie.'

'How do you mean?' I asked.

'Because Judie is the South Antarctic Whaling Company. She controls it now – not Bland. My job in Cape Town wasn't only to sell Nordahl's South African holdings on a certain day. With the profits I was to buy out three of the larger shareholders in the South Antarctic Company. Before we left Cape Town, Nordahl held 57 per cent of the shares in the company. They don't know that – yet.' And he chuckled quietly to himself. Then suddenly he was silent, his eyes searching my face. 'You like Judie, don't you?'

He didn't put it as bluntly as Bland had done, but I knew what he meant. I think I hesitated. But I'd no longer any doubts on the matter. 'Yes,' I said. 'I'm very fond of her.'

He nodded slowly as though it confirmed something that he was already satisfied about. 'If Erik Bland were dead, would you marry her?'

I stared at him then, trying to read his mind. 'The situation doesn't arise,' I said and my voice sounded harsh.

'It could arise,' he said, tapping the gun against the palm of his hand. 'Well. Would you?'

'I can't answer that,' I said.

'But you'd want to?'

'Yes,' I said.

He nodded. 'And that was the threat Bland held over you, wasn't it?' His head had jerked forward and he was gazing at me intently. 'Judie's happiness against your silence?'

I didn't answer and he suddenly got up. 'All right,' he said. 'I just wanted to know what the situation was. Thank God I persuaded her to go across to *Hval 5*.' He stood then, looking down at me for a moment, then he turned away, slipping the gun into his pocket. 'Bernt Nordahl's interest in life was the South Antarctic Whaling Company.' He walked slowly across to the door. 'He'd have liked you, Craig. Good night.' And he was gone, closing the door behind him.

I lit a cigarette and lay there in the half light that filtered in through the porthole, trying to understand the mind of the man. He wasn't mad. Of that I was certain. There was a cold, relentless sanity about him. And he wasn't entirely sane either.

In the next few days he worked steadily at his book. He no longer brooded. He worked all day and far into the night as though he had not too much time in which to complete it. And he was more natural, more cheerful than I'd seen him at any time since I'd known him. Occasionally he'd come up on to the bridge for a breath of air and stand there, cracking jokes with Gerda and watching everything with the excited interest of a small boy. Gerda reacted strangely, like a mother given an ugly duckling to rear. In a rough, good-natured way she fussed over him. I even found her mending a tear in one of his shirts on the day we had to put back to the factory ship to refuel. I made some crack about it being unusual for the mate of a catcher to take up darning in her spare time and she flew into a temper and told me to mind my own business. It was the only time I ever saw her put out. Afterwards she was sweetness itself to me, but I didn't make the same mistake again when I saw her mending a pair of socks that I knew weren't her own.

It was on the 6 February that we refuelled. Whale had suddenly become scarce. The catchers were out in a wide sweep, some of them as much as 200 miles away from the *Southern Cross*. *Hval 5* had just reported a *pod* 150 miles to the north-east and we were directed to steam in that direction. Early on the 7th we got two about 100 miles away from the factory ship and radioed for a towing ship. *Tauer III* answered our call. The clouds had come down very low. They were dirty, ragged wisps driving before a rising sou'wester. The glass was rapidly falling and visibility was reduced to little more than a mile.

Throughout the rest of the day we steamed slowly north-eastwards, searching. But a cold, stinging rain was driving across the ship, and this, combined with the spray driven from the breaking wavetops, made it impossible for us to see the spout of a whale even if there were any about. The cry of *Isen* came more and more often from the wretched lookout, perched in the *tonne* at the bucking masthead. Sometimes it was an iceberg. More often it was a floe half-hidden in the breaking waves. Gerda ordered a lookout in the bows as well and her foresight was justified when we narrowly missed a 'growler' – a large platform of ice almost submerged. 'I think we must find shelter,' she shouted to me. 'It is very bad.'

I nodded. The movement of the ship was becoming more and more violent as the wind rose to gale force. I realized the necessity of having a lookout in the bows. But I was getting concerned for the man's safety. He had lashed himself to the end of the catwalk, but the bows were buried at times so deep in the waves that he seemed to be up to his waist in water. I felt the catwalk itself might be torn out of the ship.

'*Isen*.' There it came again, that frightening cry from the *tonne*. We peered through the murk of a rain squall, waiting. And then suddenly it emerged out of the storm wrack – a great wall of ice with breakers flinging water into the driven clouds. The helmsman swung the wheel before my order had even reached him. The catcher turned and we ran parallel to the ice wall, where it stood out of the raging sea on the edge of visibility. 'I think we find shelter here,' Gerda shrieked to me.

The berg was a huge one. We must have gone nearly two miles before we turned the edge of it. But it was quite narrow and in a few minutes we had turned north-westward and were cruising along in comparatively calm water. I ordered stop, and the sudden cessation of the engine was noticeable only in the absence of vibration. We drifted quietly, the wall of ice just visible to port, the little ship lifting and dropping away again as the long swell of the gale rolled under her. It was queer, there in the lee of the iceberg – an unnatural calm in the midst of chaos. There was hardly any wind, yet we could hear the gale screaming over our heads and in the intervals between rain squalls we saw the ragged clouds driving pell-mell towards the north-east. And over and above the howling fury of the wind we could hear a deep rumble like a heavy artillery barrage – giant waves battering at the farther side of the iceberg. 'I hope she do not capsize,' Gerda said to me. 'It has been known in a gale. If she is top heavy and the wind get hold of her – ' She didn't finish, but I could imagine the roaring tidal wave of water that would be set up by that huge mass, as large as Lundy Island, rolling over in the sea.

It was in these conditions, an hour later, that we received the SOS. I climbed out of deep sleep like a drowning man coming to the surface to find Gerda shaking me violently.

'You must get up please, Duncan. There is an SOS. One of the catchers is in difficulties.' Her face looked white and strained. 'I think we are the nearest ship.'

I swung myself off the bunk. 'What catcher is it?' I asked.

'*Hval 5.*'

'My God!' I said and pulled on my boots. 'Have they given their position?'

'*Ja.*'

'Get the chart then. Bring it to the wireless room. I'll be there. What's happened to her?' I asked.

'Damaged her rudder – possibly her propeller,' she answered as she hurried out.

I put on my oilskins and slid down the ladder to the after-deck. I was thinking of Judie. A catcher with rudder and screw damaged would be at the mercy of the storm. When I reached the second mate's cabin, I found Raadal huddled over the radio. 'The operator on the *Southern Cross* tell all vessels east and north of the factory ship they must stand by their radios,' he said in his thick English. 'It is Gerda who hear the SOS. She is on watch and she listen as always at the hour.' I glanced at the clock above his bunk. It was five past one.

The door flung back and Gerda came in. Howe was close behind her. 'I have work him out,' she said, spreading the chart across Raadal's bunk. 'This is their position – 66.25 S., 33.48 W. And we are about here. We are not more than forty miles distant.'

'Have you given the *Southern Cross* our position?'

'*Ja*. They have the positions of all the ships in this area.'

I turned to the door, my mind suddenly made up. 'Raadal. When the *Southern Cross* comes on the air again, tell them that we are going to the assistance of *Hval 5*.'

He nodded. '*Ja hr. Kaptein.*' I was half out of the door when he called me back. The radio was crackling and a voice was saying – '*Ullo-ullo-ullo, Syd Korset. Hval Fem anroper Syd Korset.*'

I saw Howe stiffen and lean forward. Gerda, too, was straining forward, a set expression on her face.

'What is it?' I asked. 'What's happened?'

Howe silenced me with an impatient movement of his hand. A spate of Norwegian was pouring out of the radio. All of them – Raadal, too – were listening intently. Finally came three quick whistles and the radio went dead as the speaker signed off.

'What was he saying?' I demanded.

But no one seemed to hear me. Howe was staring at Gerda. She turned to Raadal. 'Send Kaptein Craig's message, Hans,' she ordered. 'We must go there immediately.'

I caught hold of her shoulder and spun her round. 'Do you mind telling me what's happened?' I demanded.

'They have been driven on to some ice. Kaptein Larvik is injured. They are afraid the ship will not last long.'

I seized the chart from the bunk. 'You stay by the radio, Raadal.' I slammed out of the cabin, leaving Gerda and Howe staring at each other and ran to the bridge. 'Half ahead!' I ordered the helmsman. 'Steer north-east.' I dived down the ladder to my cabin and worked out the course. Back on the bridge again I ordered N.55E. and sent a lookout to the bow. Gerda joined me then. She still seemed dazed. She said something, but it was lost in the wind. We were moving out of the shelter of the iceberg now and sheets of stinging spray were lashing across the bridge as we ran before the full force of the gale.

Death seemed suddenly very close to us. As I stared out into the rain-driven murk, all I saw was Judie's face and *Hval 5* being hammered against a wall of ice. And I shouted ugly words into the wind because I didn't dare order more than half speed.

6

'Isen! *Isen!*' The cry was from the masthead. The lookout at the end of the catwalk signalled to starboard. The helmsman swung the wheel. The flat surface of a floe slid by, glimmering grey in the half light. Then the messboy came hurrying along the after-deck clinging like a monkey to the life-line that had been rigged. He reported that *Hval 5* was still afloat but in danger of being trapped between two icefloes.

Shortly afterwards Howe came up. 'They're all right so far,' he shouted to me. 'I've been talking to Dahle, the first mate. He says they've been holed by the ice, but he thinks the pumps can handle it for a time at any rate. Eide has just been on the radio. He confirms your decision to go to *Hval 5*. We're the nearest boat. *Tauer III* has been ordered to stand by at her present position. But she hasn't acknowledged the order.

'Do you think they're in trouble, too?' I asked.

He shrugged his shoulders.

'*Isen! Isen!*' Another change of course. Another floe. Gerda tugged at Howe's sleeve. 'Walter! Do you think we shall reach them in time?' She screamed the question at him, yet her voice barely reached me.

'Yes,' he shouted back. But I wasn't so sure. It depended on how much ice lay between them and us. I was feeling pretty scared. I'd never taken a ship into ice before. I cursed Bland for putting me in command of a catcher and in the same breath thanked God that I'd be the one to reach Judie first.

'*Isen! Isen!*' I reduced speed to slow ahead. The ice was all round us now. A sudden jar ran through the ship and there were a number of sharp, staccato cracks and then the grinding of ice along the sides. I stopped the engine, peering into the glimmer of white ahead. Then a squall came. It was sleet this time, not rain, and it blotted out everything. We lay there, drifting slowly forward, ice all round us. The sea was much less now. As though she read my thoughts Gerda said, 'There is much ice, I think. It is holding down the sea.'

Half an hour went by whilst we lay there, waiting for the sleet to pass. The water froze on our oilskins. It was bitterly cold and every now and then there was the horrible grating sound of ice against the steel sides of the catcher. But the weight of the wind was lessening. The sleet no longer drove horizontal with stinging violence. It came down in straight lines, making the dull gleam of the deck plates dance. Then suddenly all was quiet. And with the passing of the sleet, an immense silence seemed to brood over us, as though we had drifted into a vacuum. 'It is getting lighter,' Gerda said, and her voice, raised against the wind that was no longer there, seemed unnaturally loud.

Visibility was increasing and we could see that we'd fallen foul of a small huddle of icefloes. We watched the black rearguard of the rain sweep north-eastward and as it went it showed us more and more ice. Behind us the low clouds were dark and louring as though heralding another storm. But ahead they were a dazzling white, their torn bellies mirroring the ice below, picking it up in a blinding light. I backed the catcher carefully out of the icefloes and headed her at half speed into the ice blink. A little group of Emperor penguins huddled on a floe watched us go, bowing sedately as though to hide the joy they felt at our departure in diplomatic etiquette.

The ice blink was criss-crossed by dark lines and we scanned it, reading it like a map, searching for the most suitable lead. As we approached the loose pack the ice blink mapped for us a narrow lead like a long tendril that ended at the broad line of a much wider lead running north-east, and we headed for this. The ice closed round us, a flat, broken plain of dazzling white that heaved to the swell like ground moving under the impact of an earthquake. In the distance a large berg towered like a small mountain. Another, smaller one, showed against the dark background of the clouds behind us. It looked like a sailing ship, hull down and driving under every stitch of canvas.

I didn't dare move from the bridge now. Gerda or Howe were constantly in Raadal's cabin and they kept me informed of all radio messages. *Hval 5* reported the propeller shaft cracked and rudder almost ripped from its seating. They were attempting to clear it and rig a jury rudder. With the passing of the storm they were no longer in imminent danger of being crushed. They reported a wide lead running sou'west and passing within half a mile of their position.

'I hope to God that's the lead we're making for,' I said to Howe, who had brought me this piece of information. The lead we were following was narrowing rapidly now. Another mile and it had petered out into a litter of small floes. I took the wheel myself and at slow ahead twisted and turned through the narrow channels. From the bridge we could no longer see the lead we were making for. I had to work on the instructions of the masthead lookout.

The channels were becoming narrower and narrower. Sometimes I had to stop the engine altogether, the ship's sides practically scraping the ice. Fortunately the edges of the floes were fairly smooth. The comparative warmth of the sea at that time of the year had smoothed off the sides except where they had been broken up in the storm. At times I had barely steerage way on the ship.

Soon we could see the broad lead from the bridge. But between us and it the pack seemed to huddle closer in a protective bank. I turned the edge of a floe into a narrow gap and jerked at the engine-room telegraph. I had turned into a cul-de-sac. The gap just petered out. And there, not two hundreds yards ahead of us, was the dark water of the lead. As we drifted towards the flat sheet of ice that barred our progress, I went to the side of the bridge and leaned out, gazing aft along the length of the ship. The gap we had come up had almost closed behind us, the floes on either side having been sucked together by the movement of the ship. There was no question of going astern. We should have damaged our rudder, possibly sheered the blades off our propeller.

'Ram it,' Howe said. 'It's not thick. Only, for God's sake, shut your engine off before you hit, otherwise you'll damage it.'

I nodded. 'Send word round the ship – everyone to lie flat on the deck. Don't forget the engine-room.'

He clattered down the ladder and I stood there, waiting, my hands on the wheel, the engine-room telegraph at my elbow. I stared at the ice that barred our path, trying to gauge its thickness. It couldn't be more than a foot or two. The edge of it was scarcely above the water. I wondered how strongly built the catcher's bows were. The sides, I knew, were like tin when it came to meeting ice, but surely they'd have given the bows some strength. Anyway, there was no alternative. *Hval 5* was holed. I didn't dare wait in the hopes that a gap would be opened out by the swell. It might just as easily start grinding the ice up against us. Also the glass was still very low, and I didn't want to be caught here in a resumption of the gale. It was a risk, but it had to be taken. I sent one of the crew to close the for'ard bulkheads and then with a lookout aft, I rang for slow astern and backed down the cut until we reached the limit of clear water.

Howe came to the bridge and reported that everyone had been warned. I waited until the man I'd sent to close the bulkheads had returned to the bridge, then I stretched out my hand to the engine-room telegraph and rang for emergency full ahead. The ship shuddered as the screw lashed the water. Above the hum of the engine I heard the froth of the sea under our stern. I braced myself against the wheel. The catcher gathered speed. The heaving ice raced past, sometimes grazing our plates.

We had nearly a quarter of a mile of clear water and as my hand reached for the handle of the telegraph we must have been doing six or seven knots. The unbroken sheet of ice seemed to hurl itself towards us. I braced myself against the wheel and slammed the telegraph handle down. There was a sudden deathly silence as the sound of the engine dropped and the bridge became dead under my feet. There was an awful period of waiting – waiting in complete silence save for the soft hum of engines running free and the sound of water thrust back from our bows.

Then there was a crash. The ship seemed to stop dead. I was flung against the wheel, all the breath knocked out of me. The bridge swayed forward. A sound like rifle fire crackled ahead of us and then was lost in the grinding crunch of ice on steel. The whole ship was staggering and the noise of the ice attacking the steel plates was overwhelming.

Then we were driving slowly forward and a great crack was opening up in front of us.

I rang for slow ahead and, with the ice still grinding against our sides, we thrust like a wedge into the gap, the swell that was running helping us to break through. In a matter of moments it seemed we had thrust right through the thin barrier of ice and were in the open water of the lead.

I gave two whoops on the siren to tell the crew we were through. Then Gerda came running along the deck and up the ladder to the bridge. 'We're through,' I told her.

'I know,' she said. 'Well done.'

'*Isen! Isen!*' Another half-submerged floe. I sent Gerda to sound the well and make certain that we had suffered no damage in ramming our way through the ice.

Howe came and stood at my side. We stared silently into the frozen waste of black and white that lay ahead.

'I wonder what Bland's up to?' he said suddenly.

'How do you mean?' I asked.

'*Tauer III* never acknowledged that order to stand by.'

'Perhaps she didn't get it,' I suggested. 'Maybe their radio's out of action.'

'Perhaps.' He was silent for a moment, and then he said, 'Craig. You realize you and I are the only people that have the evidence to convict him?'

'What are you getting at?' I demanded.

'I don't know. That's the hell of it – I don't know. But I've got a feeling. Here we are going into the pack and there's not another boat within a hundred miles except *Tauer III*.'

'You're crazy,' I said. Actually I thought he was getting scared. It was pretty frightening standing on the bridge there, driving into the world of ice. It gave one a horrible sense of loneliness.

'I don't think I'm crazy,' he said slowly. 'If Bland could get you and me out of the way at one blow he'd be safe.'

'What about Judie, Eide, Larvik, and there are probably others?'

'He doesn't think they're important, otherwise he wouldn't have tried to make a bargain with you.' He began stamping his feet. 'He can handle Eide. No man's going to risk a new command by trying to incriminate the chairman's son the first season he's out with the company. Judie can't give evidence anyway.'

'And Larvik?' I asked. 'He knows something. I'm certain.'

'Larvik knows nothing – nothing definite,' he replied. 'I had a talk with him after you'd had him up for cross-examination.'

'Then how could he give such an accurate description of Bland's last meeting with Nordahl?' I asked. 'Bland himself confirmed it. It was correct in every detail, even to the cigar. He couldn't have made it up and got it so accurate.'

'He didn't make it up.' He stopped stamping his feet and turned to me. 'Apart from Erik Bland, Larvik was the last person to see Nordahl alive. He was with him up on the deck. He left him just after twelve. They decided the fog was going to lift and Larvik went to arrange for a boat to take him back to *Hval 5*. The fog lifted a quarter of an hour later.'

'Then why didn't he tell us he was one of the last people to see Nordahl alive?'

'Because he knew his evidence would be regarded as prejudiced,' Howe answered. 'He didn't see it happen. He only guessed at what happened. But he knew where Nordahl was at the time he disappeared. If you'd told Bland the information had come from Larvik you'd never have got him to admit he'd had a row with Nordahl up there by the boats. Peer Larvik never made any secret of the fact that he loathed Bland's guts.'

'I see.'

'Anyway,' Howe added, 'Judie and Larvik are on *Hval 5*. If we don't reach them for some reason, then Bland would be ordered to try. And if he said conditions were impossible, they might never be rescued.'

'What the devil are you suggesting then?' I demanded.

Howe slammed his fist against the windbreaker and a shower of ice tinkled on to the winches below. 'I'm not suggesting anything,' he said. 'I'm just wondering. Bland would never get an opportunity as good as this. That's all I know.' His voice was agitated and I felt as though he were wound up like a clock. 'Something's driving him. Something that's bigger than himself, bigger than life. And Judie, the little fool, hasn't made a will.'

He caught hold of my arm then. 'I know a good deal about psychology. It doesn't help me solve my own problems. But I can understand other people's. Erik Bland was brought up by his mother. He's always had money. Anything he wanted, it was there. He'd only got to ask for it – boats, parties, cars, girl-friends. But power – you can't buy that, can you? All his life he's been dwarfed by his father. I think that's what's driving him – a sense of impotence – an inferiority complex if you like. He's no real sense of values or morals. He's never given a thought for anyone but himself. That's what makes him dangerous. His sense of frustration is like a load of dynamite inside him.' Then, as though he'd revealed too much of himself, he added quickly, 'I'm just guessing. Forget it.' He turned towards the bridge ladder and then paused. 'Only, for God's sake, make all the speed you can.' With that he left and went below.

I thought of *Tauer III* somewhere astern of us. Suppose Howe were right? It was fantastic. But though I tried to dismiss it, the idea kept coming back. If Erik Bland would commit a murder . . . Well, a murderer doesn't always stop at one crime, and certainly Howe's diagnosis of the man's mental state seemed reasonable enough. It fitted his actions. But surely the man had shot his bolt. I remembered the scene in his cabin on board *Tauer III*. Fear had driven him then – fear of a rope round his neck. He'd been badly scared. Another squall enveloped us and the icy cascade of sleet washed all thought of Erik Bland out of my mind.

And with the squall came the wind. It seemed to materialize out of nowhere like a howling demon coming up out of the ice. This time it was from the north-east and it lashed the sleet in a stinging sheet against our faces. Visibility was cut in a moment to a few hundred yards. I didn't reduce speed. I just huddled my chin into my oilskins and kept on, peering into the watery murk, my face numb with the bite of wind and sleet.

We were in constant communication with *Hval 5* now. Gerda kept me in touch with the reports. Two miles south-west of the damaged ship there was a large iceberg with a flat top like Table Mountain except for a tall pinnacle of ice at its southern end. This was our mark.

We reached what I thought was the approximate position of *Hval 5* shortly after nine. That was on the morning of 8 February. Visibility was very poor. There was no possibility of our sighting the ice mark and I hove to, waiting for the weather to clear. We were then in open water with no ice in sight. The wind was rising to gale force and there was a lumpy sea that caused us to pitch a lot. Above the howl of the wind we could hear the ugly sound of icefloes crashing against each other. Behind this was a deeper, more violent sound which Gerda told me was a pressure ridge building up amongst a solid area of pack.

That wait seemed endless. I had a horrible feeling of being trapped. I couldn't see it, but I knew there was ice all round us, and I felt as though it were closing in. We could hear it, and in that twilight of driven sleet it grew like a barrier between us and safety. The only thing that gave me courage was the thought that Judie was somewhere quite close and that I was there to bring her out of the ice.

Then Gerda came up to say that we were no longer in radio contact with *Hval 5*. 'It was quite sudden – in the middle of a message.' Her face looked scared.

The loneliness of the Antarctic seemed to have moved a step nearer. 'What was the message?'

'He said, "The ice is very thick now. We are getting – " And that was all. I thought I heard someone shout. I am afraid – ' She didn't finish, but stared at me round-eyed.

'Get Raadal to call them,' I ordered.

'He is doing that.'

'Tell him to go on trying.'

She nodded and clattered quickly down the ladder.

Howe came up shortly afterwards. When I questioned him he shook his head. 'We keep calling, but there's no reply.' I listened to the grumbling of the ice out there beyond the grey curtain of the sleet, and the cold seemed to eat right into me.

'We must do something,' Howe shouted at me. 'Start the engine. We must find them.'

My hand reached for the telegraph. Anything rather than this enforced inactivity. But the rigid discipline of six years in the Navy stopped me. I shook my head. 'No good until visibility improves. We've the lives of our crew to consider.'

He opened his mouth to argue, then stopped and nodded. After that he paced up and down the bridge, with his awkward, crab-like shuffle till every turn he made jarred on my nerves. And I just stood there, staring into the driving murk and praying for the sleet to lift.

Shortly after ten the weather began to show signs of improving. The sleet slackened and gradually visibility lengthened out and the atmosphere became full of light. Gerda came out on to the after-deck and sniffed at the wind. Then she hurried to the bridge. 'It is better, *ja*?' Her voice sounded thick and guttural.

I nodded, peering into the light that was beginning to hurt my eyes. 'Any news?' I asked.

'Nothing. They do not answer.'

A moment later the sleet lifted like a curtain and we could see the dark water of the lead with the ice all round it. It was like a black waterway in a dead, white plain. And as the rain rolled south-westward, a mercurial flash of sunlight showed an iceberg on our port quarter, flat like Table Mountain, with the pinnacle at its southern end glistening like a spearhead.

I ordered half ahead and starboard helm. As the catcher swung round, the flash of sunlight vanished and the world was grey and cold, a frozen etching across which torn wisps of cloud scurried before the wind. 'There is more sleet to come – maybe snow,' Gerda said, gazing at the sky to windward, where the clouds were gradually darkening again.

I nodded. Every moment was important now. The break might last only a few minutes. I searched the area just north-east of the berg with my glasses. The ice looked a solid mass, torn like ground after an earthquake where the floes had been layered by the pressure ridge that had been built up against the massive bulk of the iceberg. Then suddenly I saw it. A black patch in the torn surface of the ice. Through the glasses it resolved itself into the upper works of a catcher. The masts and funnel slanted so sharply that it looked as though it were lying on its side. I gave several blasts on the siren. Then I called the lookout down and climbed to his place in the *tonne*.

From the masthead I could see it quite plainly. It was not more than a mile away and appeared to be in the grip of two floes which were layering under the pressure of the ice thrusting against the berg. I could see tiny figures moving about on the ice, and as far as

I could tell, with the mast swaying and dipping, they were unloading stores on to the ice. I swept the area between the broad lead we were in and the ship. The shortest distance was about half a mile. Several leads thrust out towards the stricken ship like crooked lines drawn in charcoal. The sudden tingle of sleet on my face made me look at the sky. The weather was closing in again from the north-east. The clouds were black and heavy. The wind seemed driving the clouds down on to the ice.

I turned my attention back to *Hval 5* and the lines of open water between the floes, trying to memorize them. The crew were up on deck, leaning over the rail, talking excitedly. I clambered down on to the bridge and took a bearing. I had barely finished before the sleet closed in on us.

Howe clutched my arm. 'Isn't that a ship – coming up the lead towards us?' He was pointing away from *Hval 5*, straight over our bows. But even as I followed the line of his finger the atmosphere seemed to thicken and congeal into a solid wall of grey that blotted out sight.

'I didn't see anything,' I said. 'It couldn't have been.'

He hesitated as though about to argue. Then he shrugged his shoulders. 'I could have sworn I saw the outline of a ship steaming towards us.'

'The light plays tricks,' I said.

He nodded. 'Yes. I suppose that's it. I was thinking about *Hval 5*.'

I took over the wheel now and at slow head we felt our way down the northern edge of the lead until I saw what I thought was the opening we wanted. Cautiously I turned into the gap and we began to thrust our way between the floes on a general course of N.55° W. Ahead of us we could hear the gunfire sounds of the pressure ridge building up towards the iceberg. Every 30 seconds I gave three blasts on the siren, hoping that *Hval 5* would still have steam up and be able to reply.

For perhaps ten minutes we forced our way deeper and deeper into the loose litter of icefloes, sounding our siren. We strained our ears, listening for the answering call. But there was no sound except the wind's howl in the rigging and the sizzle of the sleet as it lashed the decks. Beyond these sounds we could hear the sharp thundercracks of splitting ice. The floes gradually thickened, packing tighter until at last we could go no farther. I stopped the engine and we lay there, heaving to the storm waves which were blanketed by miles of ice into a long, heavy swell. All we could do was keep sounding the siren and continue to listen. But there wasn't even an echo. Its moan went off in a wisp of steam at the funnel top and was instantly whipped away by the wind and lost in the grey void that surrounded us. It was like being buried alive. I thought of the *Flying Dutchman* and all the other mysteries of the sea. It was so easy to imagine ourselves lost for ever as we lay there in that waste of ice and storm with the floes grinding against our sides.

And it was at this moment that Howe gripped my arm and shouted, pointing over the port quarter. A vague shape drifted on the edge of visibility. I lost it and rubbed my eyes, thinking I must have imagined it. But a moment later it was there again. A ship! I could see the faint outline of funnel as well as bows. It was like a ghost ship – faint and indistinct, one moment visible, and the next, lost behind that curtain of sleet.

'Is it *Hval 5*?' Howe shouted to me.

I shook my head. I had lost it again. But I knew it wasn't *Hval 5*. It was bigger than a catcher and it was headed into the ice just as we were. It reminded me of a warship. Could a vessel have been lost down here in the ice during the war? But I could have sworn I'd seen smoke coming from its stack. I pulled myself together and ordered slow astern. There was a lead of clear water running towards the spot where we'd seen the ship and I decided to investigate.

I continued sounding our siren and with lookouts fore and aft began to manoeuvre into the lead. But I'd barely ordered slow ahead when there as a sudden shout from the lookout in the bows and Gerda screamed for full ahead. The telegraph jangled as the curtain of the mist to port seemed thrust aside by the knife-edged bows of a ship bearing straight down on us.

There was no time to do anything and yet the moment of waiting seemed like eternity. I seized the cord of the siren and kept it at full blast. But the ship that bore down on us seemed to gather speed. I could hear the hum of her engine and see the water creaming up in a cold green wave at her bow. Howe shouted something and jumped for the catwalk. It was only as he ran for the harpoon gun that I realized what he'd said; just one word – *Bland*. And immediately I recognized those warship lines, that sharp, deadly-looking bow. It was a corvette. And now I could see the name white against her black paint, *Tauer III*.

I awoke then to full realization of what was going to happen. 'All hands on deck,' I shouted. I rang for the engine to be stopped and seized hold of the engine-room communication pipe and ordered McPhee to get his men up as fast as he could. As I dropped the tube I saw Howe down on the gun platform, swinging the harpoon gun towards the oncoming ship.

One man stood alone on the corvette's bridge. Against the grey back-cloth of cloud he stood out clear like an etching. His oilskins were a dark gleam in the hissing sleet, his black Norwegian sou'wester framed his white face. His hands were braced on the wheel, his whole body hunched over it like a rider driving his horse at a jump. It was Erik Bland.

Then everything seemed to happen at once. There was the violent crack of an explosion from our bows as Howe fired. The harpoon rose in a wide arc, passing over Bland's shoulder and crashing down behind the bridge, the thin forerunner snaking after it. And in the same instant a man flung himself on to the bridge, swept Bland aside and swung the wheel over. The bows began to turn. The ship heeled. The engine-room telegraph clanged, loud and clear above the wind. But it was too late.

I can see it now as vividly as when it happened. It's like a strip of film running through my mind. Yet it all happened in a second or so. The bows were no longer driving straight at me. They were swinging away towards our stern. But they were right on top of us now. And as they drove through the last few yards of the gap, they seemed to grow bigger and sharper. I remember a patch of flaking paint just below the hawse-hole and a streak of rust that had almost obliterated the letter E of the name. I remember the way our bulwarks buckled in like tin sheet under the impact – the shriek of tortured metal.

She struck us just aft of the engine-room, smashing the port boat and ploughing up the deck plates. Men were coming out on to our after-deck as the bows broke into our thin sides. There was the heavy shock of impact and an awful grinding, tearing sound as metal was ripped and torn open. Men fell sprawling on the deck. And in the same instant I was flung sideways and fetched up against the wooden side of the bridge with a jolt that drove all the breath out of me. The grinding and ripping of the metal seemed to go on unendingly.

Then suddenly all was still. Nothing seemed to move. The wind howled and beyond its howl was the rumbling gunfire of the ice. I gulped air and caught my breath at the pain in my side. Slowly the scene round me came to life. Gerda picked herself up from the corner of the bridge where she'd been flung. Men were staggering to their feet on the after-deck. The bows of the corvette stood like a huge wedge in the twisted steel of the after-deck. Our funnel was bent over with the impact. A plume of steam was escaping from the engine-room.

Somebody moved on the bridge of *Tauer III*. It was the man who'd tried to take the wheel. Bland was cursing him, ordering him for'ard. His voice came to me on the wind as an angry scream. As the man left the bridge, Bland turned. His teeth were bared and he had a wild look about him. His hand reached out towards the engine-room telegraph. I yelled at him not to go astern. My wits were so dulled by the disaster that I don't think I'd really grasped that it had been intentional. I know he heard me yelling, for he raised his hand. It was a gesture of farewell. And then the engine-room telegraph rang.

I understood then and I gripped the canvas of the windbreaker in a sort of dazed fascination. I'd never seen a man coolly murdering a ship's crew. I'd heard of U-boat commanders doing it during the war. But I'd never seen it happen.

The engine of the corvette began to hum. The black water at her stern was churned to an icy green and she began to back away from us. Our stern swung slowly with her. Then with a horrible tearing sound the bows wrenched free of us and she began to pull clear of the wreckage of our stern. Howe was screaming from the gun platform – screaming for them to stop. The fore-runner of the harpoon lifted from the water in a slack loop, unwound slowly and as slowly tightened. And as it became taut there was a dull, muffled explosion from somewhere deep inside the corvette.

It's queer, but whilst I have that vivid mental picture of the actual ramming, I have only a confused recollection of what followed immediately after. I remember standing there for a second, watching the corvette draw away and stop, seeing Bland turn at the sound of the explosion, rage darkening his face, and hearing a confused medley of shouts and orders and the ugly roar of escaping steam from somewhere in the bowels of the ship. Then I was down from the bridge, running aft, shouting orders.

A quick examination of the damage made it clear we couldn't stay afloat for long. The after-bulkhead doors were damaged and water was pouring into the engine-room. The crew's quarters aft had borne the brunt of the collision. Raadal was dead – crushed beyond recognition. Another man had been pinned against his bunk by a jagged strip of metal. It had gone through his stomach. He was unconscious and there was nothing we could do for him. Two other men were injured – one with a broken arm, another with broken ribs. The radio had been completely wrecked. As for the gap in the little vessel's side, there was no question of patching it up. It was a great, ragged hole about eight feet wide and as many deep. It ran from deck to keel.

I sent McPhee down to the engine-room to see if he could get way on the ship and I ordered one of the men to the bridge with instructions that if the engine could be got going he was to steer into the ice. Gerda I ordered to get the remaining boat swung out and to collect all the stores she could, in case we had to camp on the ice. Then I ran up to the bridge and hailed *Tauer III* through a megaphone. The ship was lying-to about twenty yards from us, her bows slightly crumpled and steam and smoke pouring out of her engine-room hatches. A man came running down to the bows. He looked scared. 'Can you come alongside and take us off?' I shouted to him.

But he shook his head. '*Nei, nei*. We have damage in the engine-room and fire.'

My stomach seemed suddenly empty. I looked back along the length of the catcher. Her stern was already badly down. 'You must take us off,' I shouted. 'We will help you fight the fire.'

The man hesitated uncertainly. He glanced behind him as though trying to decide whether his ship was in better case than ours. And as he did so a great tongue of flame leapt out from amidships. Almost instantly there was a heavy roar of steam and the whole ship was enveloped in a white cloud against which her battered bows stood out black and sharp. Then the white of the steam darkened, became black and turned to great billowing clouds of smoke. I knew what that meant. The oil was alight inside her. I turned on Howe, who was standing beside me, staring with open mouth at the belching column of smoke. 'You bloody fool! You bloody, silly fool!' It wasn't any good cursing him. I knew that. His damned harpoon was fired now. But I went on cursing him. I went on cursing him because I was scared. *Tauer III* had been our one chance. I felt sure the men wouldn't have abandoned us even if that was what Bland had intended.

It was Gerda who pulled me out of my senseless mouthings. 'We must begin landing stores,' she called up. McPhee was standing beside her and the expression on his face told me that he'd failed to do anything with the engine. Fortunately the starboard boat was intact. 'Clear the boat and start loading,' I ordered.

I sent Gerda with the first boatload to choose a good stretch of ice. I remained on board, working to bring up the sort of stores we would need – food, clothing, canvas, petrol, oil, matches, instruments, charts, rifles and ammunition. My mind went back to that Greenland expedition, visualizing the things we'd needed then and on the basis of that trying to imagine our requirements now.

Tobacco. I remembered that, and lighters. I could recall how short we had got of matches. The food stores I packed in wooden boxes. I got up every packing case we could lay our hands on. Wood was always useful. Two drums of oil. Blankets to make into sleeping-bags. Needles and thread. Cooking utensils. Nails. Tools. It was the little things that could so easily be overlooked. The after-deck was almost awash now. We hadn't much time. And once she went there would be no going back for anything that had been forgotten.

The boat returned, was loaded with stores and men, and was sent back to the ice, McPhee in charge. Gerda remained on board, her woman's mind quick to think of things I had forgotten: mending things, medical supplies, tins of fat, some personal stores of her father's, including some brandy, leather ripped from chairs and seats, spare bootlaces. The boat came back again and this time we loaded the heavy stuff – frozen whale-meat, the two oil drums, coils of wire, steel stanchions cut from the ship for tent supports, a roll of canvas, packing cases filled with flour, axes, saws, guns, a block and tackle with four 60-fathom lengths of forerunner (my idea for hauling the boat if necessary) and a whole pile of junk that had been flung down by men acting on their own initiative as to what would be necessary. We piled it all in and sent the boat back.

It was a risk. There were still seven of us on the ship and she was very low. But I was determined that if we were to be forced to live on the ice then we should have everything that was necessary. To occupy the men I sent them to comb the ship – or what was left above water – for anything else of use. Then I went over to the port side and looked at *Tauer III*. I suppose in all about half an hour had passed since I had last looked at her. My whole effort had been concentrated in getting the stores together and ferrying them to the ice. Now I was amazed at the sight that met my eyes. The corvette was enveloped in a cloud of black smoke. Her bows were still clear of it. But aft of the bridge she was a roaring inferno with flames licking up to funnel height. A group of men were dragging stores up on to a floe beyond the ship. They were just black figures against the white of the ice that disappeared into the grey curtain of the sleet. The boat was being pulled back to the ship. I watched it come alongside. More stores were being lowered. And then my eyes went back to the corvette's bridge where something had moved and I realized with a shock that Bland was still standing there. I picked up my glasses, which were lying on a pile of my own personal things, and focused them on him. He was no longer grinning. He seemed dazed, his face white and his lips moving as though he were muttering to himself.

And then Gerda tugged at my arm. 'I brought this down, Duncan,' she said. It was the radio from my cabin. 'It is a portable in case of emergencies. My father always say it is good to hear even if you cannot send.'

I cursed myself for having forgotten it and started to rack my brains again in case there was anything else I had overlooked. 'I wonder if *Tauer III* managed to send a message?' I said.

She shrugged her shoulders. 'We shall know when we join up on the ice. I think they will have radioed the *Southern Cross*. You see their R/T is below the bridge and that is still clear of the fire.'

The catcher gave an ugly little wriggle then. I glanced quickly aft. We were very low now. The bows seemed higher. I dived for the rail. The boat was on its way back. 'Quick!' I shouted. The men bent to their oars. 'Just drop everything in,' I ordered the others. 'Then follow quickly. We haven't much time.'

The boat slid alongside. I felt another tremble run through the ship. I had a horrible feeling that the bows were rising higher and higher. The deck seemed to be slanting away to the stern like a water chute. And as the men tumbled over the side the water slid quietly over my ankles. The catcher was beginning to sink stern first. Gerda heaved herself over the rail. I dropped the radio into someone's lap and flung myself in after her. 'Row like the devil,' I shouted.

But they didn't need any urging. The oars bent under the thrust of the rowers. The heavily laden boat thrust away from the catcher. And as we pulled away *Hval 4* gave a violet shudder. Her tottering stack shook free of its mountings and fell with a crash. And as though that were the last straw, the little vessel slid quietly stern first into the sea, the sharp bows pointing higher and higher as she went and the harpoon gun swinging aimlessly. She disappeared with barely a ripple, mast tip and gun the last to go. And where she had been the icy water swirled in black whorls for a moment and then settled as though there had never been a vessel there.

It was the first time I'd lost a ship. I had no sense of personal loss. She hadn't been my ship in the way my corvette had been. But I felt an awful sense of emptiness, as though I had been suddenly disarmed in mortal combat. It took all the courage out of me. I glanced at Gerda and saw she was crying. Her brown eyes were staring almost unbelievingly at the spot where *Hval 4* had been and big tears rolled down her cheeks. For her it was different. The catcher had been her home. I lent forward to pat her hand. Then I saw that Howe was gripping her arm, staring into her face, his eyes looking hurt as though he felt the loss through her.

I looked about me, taking stock of my surroundings. From the deck of *Hval 4*, even though she had been sinking, I'd felt a sense of security as though the storm and the ice and the black, heaving sea were all slightly unreal – something apart. Now the ship had gone and from the slender freeboard of an overloaded boat the scene looked frighteningly real. I think in all that followed I never felt lower in spirits than at that moment. There was just the group of men huddled round the stores on the ice, another group farther away and the burning hulk of the corvette. And the icy sleet swept over everything – cold and wet and dismal. Behind it was the wind and beyond that still the staccato cracking of the ice.

The boat touched the ice, crunching into the thin edge of it, and we climbed out on to the floe. We were up to our ankles in a soft slush of half-melted ice. My first thought was for the stores, particularly the flour. Everything was just heaped there in the rotten ice with the sleet streaming off it. The floe was a big one, jammed in against other floes. It rocked gently to the swell that ran under it and its edges ground against the others. A little to the north of us one floe had layered on another so that the ice was higher and slightly sloping. I floundered through the slush towards it. Once I slipped and found myself up to my knees in water. For a moment I thought I was falling between two floes. But it was only a weak patch that had filled with a morass of half-melted ice. I reached the floe that had layered and climbed up on to it. The ice was hard here and clear of slush. I found a way back that avoided the hole I had stumbled into and ordered all the stores to be moved up to the new site. Tarpaulins were laid on the ice, and when all the stores were piled on to them, others were placed over the top. Then we set to work to construct tents and I ordered the steward to try and produce some sort of a stew.

There were fourteen of us on the ice and two of those were injured. As soon as there was any sort of shelter, Gerda and I went to work, first on Jacobsen's broken arm and then on Grieg's ribs. The arm we set in splints and we must have done a pretty fair job on it, for it mended fine. But though we didn't know it then, Grieg's ribs were not a simple fracture. Only an X-ray could have shown us the extent of the damage and it was to be a constant source of worry to us. It was whilst we were strapping him up that I became conscious again of the pain in my chest that I'd felt when I lay against the side of the bridge gasping for breath. Association of ideas, I suppose. Maybe I'd strained a muscle. Possibly I did have a slight fracture of one of the ribs. It went off in the end, but it gave me a lot of pain during the next few days, particularly when I was lifting anything.

We had just finished strapping Grieg up when McPhee called to me that a boat was coming alongside. We ducked out of the canvas shelter to find the sleet easing off and *Tauer III*'s boat running in towards our floe. Four men were rowing it and in the stern sat a big, bearded man with a flattened nose and sharp, close-set little eyes. 'Who's that?' I asked Gerda.

'It is Vaksdal,' she said. 'He is made first mate on *Tauer III*. He is a Sandefjord man. He is a good whaler, but I hear he have a bad temper.'

The man certainly looked an ugly customer. Howe came up beside me as I watched the boat pull in to our floe. 'I wonder what sort of a story Bland has thought up,' he said, and his voice trembled slightly.

That was the first time any of us had commented on the cause of our predicament. We'd been too busy to think about it. We'd accepted the situation and concentrated wholly on endeavouring to cope with it. But seeing Vaksdal's set face and the purposeful way he came towards us, I knew why he'd come. I think Howe knew, too.

'You Kaptein Craig?' he asked. The gentle lilt of Eastern Norway was entirely swallowed by the violence of his tone. The man was tense with anger.

'Yes,' I said. 'What do you want?'

'Did you order that harpoon to be fired?'

'No,' I said.

But he didn't wait for my reply. He went straight on: 'That harpoon explode in our engine-room. That is what cause the fire. That is what put us in this damn mess.' His little eyes fastened on Howe. 'You fire that harpoon.' He hunched forward slightly, his hands clenching as he moved in purposely on Howe.

'Just a moment,' I said.

But Gerda brushed past me and faced the man. 'What do you expect us to do, you fool?' she said, her eyes blazing. 'You wish us to sit still and be murdered? You go back to your Erik Bland and ask him why he ram us?'

The man had stopped. 'It was an accident,' he said. And his hand stretched out to push her aside.

'Don't you dare put your hands on me, Vaksdal,' she said angrily. 'And you listen to what I tell you. That was no accident. Bland meant to ram us. There are people on this ship that he must kill if he is not to hang for the murder of Bernt Nordahl. Why do you think he bring *Tauer III* here when he is ordered to stand by at his earlier position?'

'Who say we are to remain in our old position?' Vaksdal demanded. 'And what is all this about murder? It is suicide.'

'It was murder,' Gerda snapped back at him. 'And it is Kaptein Eide who ordered you to stand by. Don't you listen to your radio?' The man hesitated and she added, 'Ask your radio operator.'

'He is injured by the fire when he send the SOS.'

'Well, somebody must have listen to the radio.'

'It was out of action for a little while.'

'So. Now you think. Was Bland near the radio when it go out of action?'

Vaksdal looked surprised. 'Yes, but – '

'And when did the radio work again?' she cut in. 'Not till Bland go down to the wireless room, I bet.' She suddenly stepped right up to him. 'Was Bland alone on the bridge when he rammed us?'

'When the accident happen – '

'Was he alone – just tell me that?'

'Yes.'

'Then you go back and ask him why he send the helmsman below at that moment. You go back and make a few enquiries before you bring your anger over to us. I think you find much to be angry about over there. Now go. And see you do not have trouble with your men. It is bad to have trouble with the men on the ice. They are from Tönsberg. And if you do not make enquiries, they will.'

He turned away then, a baffled look on his face. It was clear he resented being out-faced by a woman. But it was clearer still that he was puzzled about something. 'Just a minute, Vaksdal,' I said. 'Have you got your radio ashore?'

He half turned and shook his head. 'The fire has consume everything. But we have send a message to the *Syd Korset*.'

'With our position?'

'Ja.'

'And it was acknowledged?'

'*Ja.*'

'One more question,' I said as he turned again. 'Is Bland still on *Tauer III*?'

'*Nei*. The ship, she is on fire all over. Everyone is on the ice. Kaptein Bland is very sad man. He feel he is reponsible for the accident.'

'Accident!' Howe screamed. 'It wasn't an accident. He rammed us. He rammed us deliberately.' He was moving forward impetuously, his skinny neck thrust out, his arms sawing the air in his excitement. 'Take me across to Bland. Take me to him. I said I'd kill him – and by God I will.'

'You have done enough, I think, already,' Vaksdal said.

'Enough? Do you realize what he's done? He's murdered us all. We'll never get out of this ice alive. Nor will Larvik or any of the people on *Hval 5*. He's killed us all as surely as if he'd mowed us down with a machine-gun.'

Howe's voice had risen to a high-pitched cry as he ran forward, flailing the air, mouthing threats about what he'd do to Bland. Vaksdal watched him come up. 'I think you *sinnsvak*,' he said.

'I'm not crazy,' Howe shrieked. 'Take me across to Bland. Take me over to him.'

Vaksdal flung him back and turned on his heel. 'You will hear some more about this,' he said over his shoulder.

Howe, sprawling in the slush of wet ice, watched the big mate step into the boat. He was trying to speak, but he couldn't. His whole body was shuddering in his effort to speak. The boat pushed off and the oar blades dipped into the ice green sea. Beyond it a great tongue of flame licked up from the bowels of the corvette, a red glare against the dark water sky to the west. Gerda ran forward and pulled Howe to his feet and they stood there, in silhouette against the flames, watching the boat row back to the dark huddle of men on the ice about a mile away.

7

THAT night the sleet turned to snow. It was bitterly cold now that
we no longer had the protection of our ship. Out there on the ice
we were exposed to the full force of the wind. It seemed to blow
right through our makeshift tents. Our food was cold almost before
we had time to swallow the first mouthful. Even with the whole
party huddled together in two small tents the temperature inside
was well below freezing. And a few hundred yards away the
blazing wreck of *Tauer III* consumed as much stored-up heat in an
hour as would have kept us warm for a whole year. We turned in
about eight. Everyone was very tired and I wanted them to be
fresh should the weather improve. The boat was moored to the
floe by an anchor dug into the ice. Watches were of two hours'
duration with two men on duty.

When I turned in the wind had backed to the sou'west and it
was sleeting. Gerda and I had the radio between us and for a
while we lay smoking and listening to the monotonous calling of
the *Southern Cross*. Her operator would call *Hval 5*, then us, then
finally *Tauer III*. There would be a five-minute pause. Then he'd
start calling all over again. At length I switched off, not wishing to
waste the battery. With my blankets wrapped tightly round me I
tried to work up the warmth necessary to sleep. But the ground
was wet and the wind blew under the canvas in an icy draught.
The grinding of the floes seemed to run right through my body.
Every tremor of the ice communicated itself to us as we lay in our
tents.

When I did finally get to sleep I was roused almost instantly
by loud shouts and the grinding clash of floes. I scrambled out of
the tent to find myself in a grey-white world of driven snow in
which men appeared like ghostly shadows leaning against the
bitter wind. A voice shouted out of the void: '*Her! Kvikk! Til
baaten.*' I staggered towards the voice. The grinding of the floes was
very loud. The ice shook under my feet as though it were being
battered by a huge steam hammer. And then in the half light I
saw the reason for the lookout's cry. The open water where we'd
anchored the boat was gone. There was only a narrow gap and

this was fast closing as another floe swung in on us. I got out my whistle and blew on it till the men came stumbling towards me out of the murk of snow. We hauled on the painter and lifted the bows of the boat on to the ice. One man missed his footing and would have slithered into the sea but for Gerda, who caught hold of him by his collar. As it was he got wet to the waist. We dragged the boat clear of the water and right on up to our camp. When I went back to see that nothing had been left behind, I was just in time to see the gap close with a snap, the edges of the two floes grinding like a giant gnashing his teeth. I began to realize then how watchful we should have to be if we were to come alive out of this hell of ice.

As I turned back to the camp the snow slackened. The orange glow of the blazing ship showed for an instant in the weird light and was gone again. Before turning in I gave my whistle to one of the men on watch. It was a sharper and more penetrating warning than the human voice. I think the exertion in the middle of the night made us all very hungry. I know that I felt so ravenous that I could hardly sleep. But I also felt warm and I think I soon dozed off. I awoke stiff with cold, the shrill blast of the whistle sounding urgently in my ears and the floes clashing together like thunderclaps. When I went out the snow had stopped and the wind was dropping. For a moment I stood there, dazed, staring at the man blowing frantically on the whistle. The floe was covered in a white carpet of snow. But it had stopped falling. The camp with its tents and the men staggering sleepily out of them looked clear-cut and black against the snow. I saw no reason for the alarm. Then there was a splintering crash. The ice trembled under my feet and the man with the whistle pointed behind the tents. A dark line ran zigzagging through the snow. It broadened and then closed with the snap of a shark biting. Another crash, more trembling, and the line opened again. And this time it stayed open – a widening crevasse that wavered right across the floe.

There was no more rest for us that night. The boat was on one side of the crack, the camp on the other. We got the boat across the gap just in time. It widened out under the pressure of the other floes until we could see the sea. It became a sort of creek and widened till it was a river with sheer, ice-green banks. Tents and stores were right on the edge of it and everything had to be moved back to the middle of what was now quite a small floe. We were being battered by the ice from all sides. We huddled in the re-erected tents, drinking hot tea laced with rum, and waiting for the floe to crack again.

Gerda said suddenly, 'I wonder what sort of a night it is for the men of *Tauer III*?'

'I'm more concerned about *Hval 5*,' I said. I was thinking of Judie.

She put her hand on my shoulder. 'I understand,' she said. 'But you must not be angry with the men of *Tauer III*, Duncan. They are from Tönsberg. I know them all. They are good men. It is not their fault this happen.'

'What's more to the point,' Howe said, 'what is Bland up to?'

'Bland?' I remembered the dazed look on his face as he stood there alone on the bridge whilst the men worked at unloading. 'I don't think Bland will bother us any more. His men will have realized the truth by now. He's finished, whatever happens. Either he dies out here on the ice or he faces a charge of murder.'

'That's what makes him dangerous.'

'No,' I said. 'He's shot his bolt this time. You didn't see the dazed look on his face. I had a look at him through my glasses when he was alone on the bridge. He was numb with the shock of what had happened.'

'The numbness will wear off,' Howe said. 'And when it does he'll realize he's still got a chance. If he can get out alone – if he's the sole survivor and all the rest of us die, then he's achieved his purpose.'

'He still wouldn't control the company,' I reminded him.

'He doesn't know that,' Howe's voice replied out of the darkness. 'And anyway, if Bernt Nordahl's estate passes to Judie and Judie dies, the probability is he'll inherit it.'

'Anyway,' I said, 'the thing's impossible. He couldn't hope to get out on his own. That harpoon of yours finished him. He's hoist with his own petard and – '

'What is petard?' Gerda asked.

I spent some time trying to explain the quotation to Gerda and eventually we drowsed off.

The shuddering and grinding of the ice had gradually lessened. Sometime in the night it must have ceased altogether, for when I went out at five everything was quite still. The air was clear and frosty and the light from the new-fallen snow was blinding. There wasn't a cloud to be seen. The sun had huge circles of light round it with lines of gold radiating from the centre. At one part of the circle the light was intensified to produce a mock-sun of gold shot with prismatic colours. All about us the ice had a faint sheen of colour and towards the south and west columns of black smoke rose – frost-smoke caused by warm air from the sea lanes rising into the frozen atmosphere. It was breathtakingly beautiful and for a moment I just stood there, seeing the scene as a panorama without absorbing the detail. Then I saw the burnt-out hulk of *Tauer III* that had blazed at me so startlingly in the night. There were no flames now and only a thin column of smoke rose straight up into the incredible sky. Mast, funnel, bridge – everything except the hull – were gone. She was completely gutted. Her crew were moving about on the ice, handling stores. Several floes had layered near them and it was clear that they, too, had experienced trouble from the movement of the ice during the night.

Our own situation might have been worse. The gap that had opened during the night had closed again. There were narrow sea lanes to the south and west of us, dividing us from the *Tauer III* camp. But to the north-east the ice seemed solid – a jagged, broken plain, with small, lumpy hills like rock outcrops, covered with snow, and broken edges where floes had been up-ended. The horizon was a trembling blur, constantly moving as though I were looking at it through water. There were some big icebergs there as far as I could see, but they were for ever changing shape in the distorting mirror of the atmosphere.

On the face of it we looked secure. But the snow covered all the flaws and a thing that worried me was the grumbling thunder of ice movement to the east. It hadn't been there the previous day. And now I got the impression of a tremendous weight of ice thrusting towards us from the heart of the pack.

My main object was to link up with the survivors of *Hval 5*. Amongst the things Gerda had brought off the catcher were skis belonging to herself and her father. After breakfast I took Kalstad, one of the hands who was reckoned the best skier, and roped together with one of the harpoon forerunners, we made for a floe-berg that stood up about a quarter of a mile to the north of us. The snow was crisp and the going quite good. We were glad of the rope, however, for in several places the ice was so honeycombed by the summer thaw as to be rotten and only our skis saved us from going right down into the water. It took us an hour to do that quarter of a mile, and with the sun getting stronger every minute it was warm work.

The floe-berg was perhaps twenty feet high. I imagine it was originally pack ice that had layered. From the top of it we could look across to the black blob of *Hval 5*. It was very difficult to see it clearly through the glasses because of the shimmering of the light off the snow. The vessel was lying almost on its side, jammed up against a small floe-berg by a whole series of layered floes. There were figures moving about on the ice and some form of shelter or a dump of stores had been set on a ledge of the berg. Between us and the ship was nearly a mile of ice thrust up in ridges and giant creases as though it had been compressed. Even as I stared at the scene through the glasses I saw movement in the ice. At first I thought it was a trick of the light that made the white mass beyond the ship heave and writhe. Then I saw great blocks of ice as big as houses being thrown into the air as they were ejected between the jaws of grinding floes. Faintly through the still air came the rumble and crack of the pressure ridges building up towards the table-topped iceberg beyond.

I got a mirror out of my pocket that I had borrowed from Gerda, and after experimenting with Kalstad, managed to focus the sun glare roughly on the ship. For about a quarter of an hour I endeavoured to make contact by this primitive heliograph with no result. I was just putting the mirror back in my pocket when I caught the glint of an answering flash. It was intermittent and I could make nothing of their morse. Probably neither I nor they had succeeded in focusing the flash accurately. For some time we tried ineffectually to get a message across. In the end I gave it up. Before turning back to our camp I made a close examination of the ice between us and *Hval 5*. But without actually reconnoitring, it was impossible to decide whether we could link up.

The return journey took much longer and was much more hazardous. The snow was beginning to thaw and the going was sticky. More and more often our skis broke through the surface on rotten ice. We kept to the ridges as much as possible. When not actually on a ridge our field of vision was reduced to a few yards. It gave one the sensation of being hemmed in by a forest of ice. We made camp in the end, wet to the waist and actually sweating with heat. Gerda met me with a serious face. 'The pressure, she is increasing,' she said. 'Also there are several icebergs coming up from the south-west which I do not like.'

I stood by the camp, listening to the groaning and rumbling away to the east. It certainly seemed louder. And there was a faint and almost constant trembling of the ice under us. Occasionally the low artillery rumble would be broken by a nearer and sharper sound like a signal gun where a section of the pack had suddenly split across. She took my arm and pointed to the sou'west. Clouds of white vapour lay along the horizon. They had no form, but were constantly changing like jets of steam in a gusty wind. They would flatten out into layers, then plume upwards, blossoming like atomic explosions. Once they looked like castles of ice upside down in the sky. 'Icebergs,' she said. 'I see them this morning. Now I think they are nearer.'

I nodded and cocked my ear again to the growl of the ice to the east. 'I don't like it,' I said.

'There is a storm there,' Gerda said. 'It is driving the ice down on us. But I think there is an eastward drift and that is what bring the icebergs up.'

'Suppose the two meet?' I asked.

She shrugged her shoulders and grinned with a slight down-dragging of the corners of her mouth. 'Then I think it is not very nice. We must find stronger ice.'

I looked back to the floe-berg from which Kalstad and I had tried to signal to *Hval 5*. It looked solid enough. But then I thought of the way the ice had heaved and thrown up huge blocks over towards the table-topped iceberg. I felt suddenly as though there was no future in struggling against the giant forces that faced us. 'Any news from the *Southern Cross*?'

'*Ja*. She has dispatched *Tauer I* in answer to *Tauer III*'s SOS. Larsen, her *kaptein*, say he is approaching several icebergs about twenty miles from the position given by *Tauer III*.'

'Twenty miles!' I glanced back to the south-west. There was no open water visible at all. Perhaps there were leads and we couldn't see them. But the burnt-out hulk of *Tauer III* was entirely beset with floes and the ice ran uninterrupted to the horizon. A corvette wouldn't have a chance of breaking through. 'If only we had our R/T,' I murmured. 'It's useless sending one of the towing vessels.'

'Per'aps.' Gerda shrugged her shoulders again. 'But it is all we will get. They will not risk the *Southern Cross*.'

'Why not?' I asked.

'It is too much – too much value, too many lives – for the sake of even three of the catcher fleet. We must be content with a towing boat, or at best the tanker.'

'A corvette won't get through,' I said. 'And I doubt whether the tanker could.' I suddenly made up my mind. 'Better start trying to shift camp to that floe-berg. Divide the stores into two equal lots. We'll shift one lot today.'

We knocked up two makeshift sledges out of packing cases. Then we split into two watches – one watch to rest and look after the camp whilst the other made the journey to the floe-berg. I took the starboard watch out on the first run, blazing the trail ahead of them on ski. It was back-breaking work. Where I could travel on skis, the men very often sank to their waists in rotten ice. Several times the leading sledge broke through. The snow was wet, and the going was very heavy. It took three hours to reach our goal. We had a half-hour rest and then went back, following almost the same route. The return journey took us an hour and a half. Gerda, who was in charge of the other watch, came out to meet us on skis. She was excited. I could see it in the reckless way she swooped towards us across the treacherous ice. She brought up in front of me with a jump Christi that sent the wet snow spattering over us. 'The *Southern Cross* is coming herself,' she cried.

'Coming into the ice?' I asked.

She shook her head. 'That I cannot say. But just after you have left Kaptein Larsen come on the radio. He say he is held up by the ice and can find no way through. Eide tell him to try again. But he fail. He say there is no way. Colonel Bland speak with him then. He tell him he damn well got to find a way. But an hour later he come on again to say the pack is too close. He has patrolled it for ten miles, trying every lead, but it is no good. So then Bland say he come up with the *Southern Cross*. Maybe the *Southern Cross* try to break through, eh?' Her voice trailed away uncertainly.

'You said yourself they'd never risk the factory ship,' I reminded her. I wanted no false optimism.

She nodded. '*Ja*. I think perhaps they do not come, except to look.' She stood there fiddling with her ski-sticks, staring out across the ice.

I knew she had something on her mind, so I got the party moving again and slid alongside her on my ski. 'Well,' I said. 'What else did Colonel Bland say?'

She looked up at me quickly. 'It was not Bland. It was Larsen. He say there is a whole line of icebergs – five or six; some of them big ones – and they are drifting into the pack. He say already the ice is being built up into pressure ridges along a wide front. It is packing the ice in tight and he think it will get worse.'

'Are these the bergs we thought we saw this morning?' I asked her.

She nodded. 'Wait till you are at the camp and can stand on the boxes. You can see them quite distinctly now. You can also hear the ice. They are much nearer, I think.'

I didn't say anything, but pressed on into the camp. Gerda was quite right. The bergs were nearer. Standing on the packing cases I got a clear view to the west. I counted seven of them in a long line – and I was no longer looking at their reflections in the atmosphere, but at the bergs themselves. Probably they had calved from the barrier ice somewhere along the Caird Coast or Luitpold Land at roughly the same time and had been kept together by the current that had swept them down into our latitudes. They looked like a fleet of sailing ships in line ahead. 'I think there is a very big storm somewhere,' Gerda said. 'The pressure on the ice is increasing. The floes are being packed closer together all the time.'

'Well, there's nothing we can do about it,' I answered sharply, and sent her off with the second load of stores.

There was nothing to do but lie in our tents and smoke and listen to the radio. The men were excited, full of optimism. They talked and laughed. And when the *Southern Cross* ordered *Tauer I* to stand by and herself turned into the ice, I think they felt they were as good as rescued. One man produced a bottle of whisky, a smuggled piece of personal property, and offered drinks all round. Another produced a pack of cards and four of them settled down to a game of bridge as unconcernedly as though they were waiting for a train. I sat sucking an empty pipe and wondering what had made Colonel Bland decide to risk the *Southern Cross* in the ice.

The factory ship was quite capable of crashing through the sort of ice we had come into the previous day. Her 22,000 tons and reinforced bows could smash a way through ice 12 feet thick. If conditions had been the same as yesterday she'd have had no difficulty in reaching us. But from where I sat at the entrance of the tent I could see across the smouldering hull of *Tauer III* to the icebergs on the horizon. I could feel the trembling of the ice under me. It ran like a quiver up my spine. And I could hear the distant growl of the floes piling up under the eastward thrust of the distant storm. Bland knew nothing of this. I wished we were in radio contact so that we could warn him. But at least he could see the icebergs. He'd pass quite close to them, maybe through them. He was in a better position than we were to estimate the danger. And I began wondering again what it was that had decided him to risk the lives of over 400 men, quite apart from the ship, in an attempt to get through to us. Was it because of his son? Or was it because of Bernt Nordahl and what had happened? Or was it because he knew he was dying and didn't care anyway?

I tried to picture him, sitting there in his big cabin, making the decision. The man was quite ruthless. The lives of others wouldn't enter into his reckonings. Money, yes – but money was no longer important to him. Money couldn't buy him an extra minute of life now. He could afford to throw it away in some magnificent gesture. He'd always had to fight and now he was face to face with the elements. He'd risk the ship and every man in it if he decided to fight the ice. His decision might well be a queer mixture of quixotish bravado and a desire to purchase from his conscience an easy passage through the eye of a needle. It was tough on the men of the *Southern Cross*, that was all.

Shortly after eight the operator on the *Southern Cross* began calling us, first in Norwegian, then in English. He went on calling for half an hour. Then there was a pause. When he came on again it was with a message. '*At 21.00 hours we are going to make smoke. I repeat, at 21.00 hours we are going to make smoke. As soon as you sight our smoke make signals by whatever means possible. Southern Cross to catchers, Hval –* ' And he went on repeating it. I had one of our barrels of oil tapped and arranged a drip on to a bundle of clothes. We piled packing cases on top of each other until we had a lookout post fully ten feet high. And just before nine I sent one of the younger hands up aloft as lookout. We were all pretty excited. None of us felt like staying in the tents and I had the radio brought out on to the ice.

At nine o'clock the *Southern Cross* operator came through with another message: '*We are now making smoke. We are three miles east of a line of icebergs, having passed between the second and third berg counting from the north. Signal to us if you can.*'

We were all watching the lookout now. His eyes were screwed up against the glare of the sun which was slanting down to the west and south. The man blinked and several times rubbed his hand across his eyes. I wished we had got sun goggles. Then suddenly he stiffened and pointed. '*Der er'n.*' The men cheered. Two of them began to dance, jigging from foot to foot. The ice trembled under us as a floe cracked under pressure with a noise like a thunderclap. If only *Tauer III* were still burning!

I gave the order to light the oil-soaked clothes and then stopped the man just as he was about to strike the match. The lookout was rubbing his eyes and shaking his head. The two men stopped dancing. We all looked at him as he peered into the sun. Then he was pointing again. But the direction of his hand seemed farther to the south. I climbed up beside him, the packing cases wobbling under our combined weight. There was smoke there all right. But it was too near and in the wrong place. Even as I watched it broadened out into a great black streak. I couldn't see the icebergs now because of the glare. But I knew it was to the south of them. 'I think it's frost-smoke,' I said and the men were silent, staring westward. It was as though the cold hand of death had touched their spirits. I screwed up my eyes and tried to pierce the glare in the direction the *Southern Cross* must lie. But it was impossible to make anything out clearly. The whole atmosphere seemed constantly shifting. It was as though I were seeing everything through a film of water. A delicate, iridescent colour tinged the ice – prismatic and ephemeral. It was like a canvas full of beautiful pastel shades done by an impressionist portraying the coldness of beauty without the detail. Nothing had substance. As well try to see an object in a kaleidoscope as look for the smoke of the *Southern Cross* in that shot-silk curtain of blinding light.

The growl of the ice moved nearer, thundering at the floes and shaking our perch so violently that I jumped down on to the ice again. Somebody shouted and there, not a mile away, just beyond *Tauer III*, a floe turned on end, stood there for a moment and then slid back into the sea. A gap was opening out. We could see a stretch of water. It showed as a dark gash against the white of the surrounding ice. The air seemed to thicken and congeal like a gauze curtain. The gap widened. The air became solid and black. The frost-smoke rose like a fog, darkening everything, screening the sun. It wiped out the glare and drained the colour out of the ice. The world was suddenly white and cold. I felt a chill creep through me. I tried to buck the men up by telling them that the frost-smoke was a better marker than any smoke we could make. But it didn't comfort them. That cold, black curtain stood between them and sight of rescue. I ordered the steward to brew some coffee. The four who had been playing bridge returned to their game. I posted two lookouts and took the radio back to my tent. The ice shook under us. I began to wonder how long the thin layer on which we were camping would stand this battering from the east. I felt shut in and depressed. The growing pressure of the ice and that black curtain of frost-smoke were overwhelming reminders of the forces we were up against. The chill of fear was in my stomach and not even the hot coffee warmed me.

'*We can see patches of frost-smoke, but no signals. You must try and signal to us. The ice is getting very thick. We do not know how long we can go on.*' For half an hour the *Southern Cross* went on imploring us to signal our position. Once Olaf Petersen came on, speaking direct to Gerda, trying to encourage her and us. Colonel Bland, however, made no attempt to contact his son. The messages became more urgent. Finally the *Southern Cross* operator radioed:

'*We are now making very slow progress. The icebergs are ploughing into the ice behind us. Unless we can pick up your signals soon we may have to abandon the attempt to reach you.*' Previous messages had been in both English and Norwegian. But this was broadcast only in English, probably with the idea of not disheartening the crews. But even those that didn't understand English read the sense of the message in the faces of those that could. One of the men began cursing in Norwegian.

If only that frost-smoke hadn't appeared! If only we could see! At least we should then have been able to occupy ourselves with searching the glare for the factory ship's smoke.

There was a sudden shout from one of the lookouts and I dived out of the tent. 'Somebody is coming on skis,' he said.

'*Frøken Petersen?*' I asked.

'*Nei, nei. Fra Tauer III.*' And he pointed towards the black curtain of frost-smoke.

I followed the direction of his arm. But I could see nothing except the cold, white shape of the ice. '*Der er'n. Der er'n.*' I caught a glimpse of something black moving on a ridge of ice and then it was hidden again. A moment later it reappeared not a hundred yards away. It was the figure of a man all right. He was covered in snow and ice. He waved a ski stick and called to us, then staggered and came on, thrusting himself forward with his sticks.

I don't know whom I expected – either Bland or Vaksdal, I think. I know I debated whether to go back to my tent for a rifle. I felt naked and helpless out there on the snow. And yet I didn't want to admit I was afraid by going back for my gun. So I stood my ground and waited, wondering whether I had to deal with a maniac or only a man with a violent temper. As the man approached I saw he was too short for Vaksdal. He suddenly got on to some hard ice and with a flip of his sticks he came towards me in a rush. He brought up with a quick Christi and a '*Salute, Capitano!*' And I found myself shaking Bonomi by the hand. 'Oh, it is so good to see you, Craig. You have no idea.'

'Why? What's the trouble?'

'Trouble? What is the trouble? My God!' His arms were waving so excitedly I was in danger of being hit by his ski sticks. 'You ask what is the trouble. It is that there is no order there. The men, they will do nothing for Bland, or the mates Vaksdal and Keller. They do not trust their officers and they are very bitter. At first Bland is very angry. He strike one of them. After that the men camp on their own. They are sullen and they go their own way. I tell you, Mistair Craig, they cannot exist in this cold that way. There is no order, no direction. I think there is danger, so I take the skis and come 'ere.'

'Have they got stores?'

'*Si, si*. When we abandon ship everything go fine. The trouble, she do not begin till later. Oh, but that journey across the ice. It is not more than per'aps a kilometre, but never have I made such a journey. And I am a vair good ski-er. Look, I show you. Come on to these cases. I will show you how I come.'

'There is no time – '

But he cut me short and dragged me up to our lookout post. 'There. You can see the camp. First everything is fine. Then suddenly the ice is not there and I am to the waist in water. Look. I am very wet, am I not? Then there is much bad ice with many honeycombs. Also there is a gap filled with – how do you say – loose pieces of ice?'

'Brash?'

'*Si, si*. Brash. That is it. I ski across that.' His little chest was puffed out and his eyes glowed. 'You do not believe me, eh? But I am here – that is the proof, yes? Never am I so afeared. But I do it. I go very fast and I ski straight over this brush. Then – ' He spread his hands and laughed. 'But there are so many bad places, I do not remember them all. Many times I think I give up and return. But then I remember that brush and I cannot face it and I go on. And so, here I am.'

'You shouldn't have done it on your own,' I said. 'Crossing brash is all very well, but you should have a companion, just in case.'

He was staring at me open-mouthed. 'Has – has anyone crossed this brash before. I thought that I would be the first to have dared this thing?'

I almost laughed. But instead I patted his arm. 'It has been done before, but not often. Only by experienced polar explorers who were desperate.'

'Ah, *si, si*. Of course, the polar explorers. That is different.' His teeth showed white against the black stubble. 'Now tell me – what is the news? Have you a radio? Over there' – he nodded to the *Tauer III* – 'they have no radio.'

'We've a portable,' I said. 'We can receive, but we can't send.'

'Then you will know what is happening, yes?'

'The *Southern Cross* herself has entered the ice and is asking us to signal to her.'

'Ah. That is wonderful.' He beamed. 'Then I can have a bath.

307

I am so dirty I think I must smell like a whale. I shall lie and wallow for an hour. Now I will rest a little.'

He was apparently not in the least interested in how we were going to signal to the *Southern Cross* through that black fog of frost-smoke. In fact, I doubt whether he even realized it presented any difficulty. The *Southern Cross* was coming into the ice to rescue us. He would get his bath. It was as easy as that. I almost envied him his sublime acceptance of the certainty of rescue.

I was beginning to be worried now about Gerda and her party. They had been away five hours. I waited half an hour and then got my skis out. But I'd hardly gone a hundred yards along the sledge trail when the lookout called to me that they were coming. I climbed an ice hillock and watched them winding like a black snake through the sunless white of our frozen world. Gerda saw me and waved and came on ahead on her skis. I told her the news. 'Then they must be quick,' was her comment. 'The ice is getting very bad. Over to *Hval 5* it is terrible. The table-top iceberg of theirs is nearer, you know. Whole floes are being tossed about under the pressure. The journey back was bad, too. The ice round us is beginning to move.'

I nodded and told her how the gap from which the frost smoke was rising had suddenly opened out.

'*Ja.* Soon we have trouble, I think. But it is colder now. Perhaps the sea freeze in the gap. Then maybe we see the *Southern Cross* and can make a signal.'

When we got into the camp I stopped for a minute to look at the stores. A whole day's work and the pile still looked just as big. We'd shifted barely a quarter of it. Bonomi seized on Gerda as a fresh audience and throughout the evening meal, which the steward served as soon as the whole party were in, we had Bonomi's great trek across the ice. I'd barely finished the last mouthful and was just lighting my pipe when there was a shout from the lookout. The frost-smoke was going. By the time we'd tumbled out it was no more than a faint grey curtain. It was gone almost immediately. Colour came back to relieve the deadness of the eternal white. The sun was low to the south, slanting rays right across the sky and making the ice gleam with soft colour like the inside of an oyster shell. The scene was so soft and satiny that it was difficult not to believe that you could stretch out your hand and stroke it. But our eyes were on the lookout, standing on the packing cases and gazing westward. At length he shook his head. 'No *Southern Cross*,' he said to me. 'But the icebergs, they are nearer, I think.'

I climbed up beside him and the pair of us stared westward through screwed-up eyes. But there was nothing – not even a column of frost-smoke to mistake for the factory ship. The steward called me to the tent. His face was serious. 'It is the radio, Kaptein Craig. Listen! There is a message.' His voice was trembling slightly.

'. . . *repeat that in English. We have now ceased making smoke. If you are trying to signal us, do not continue. Do not waste your materials. We are temporarily held up by the ice which is much thicker here. I shall radio again at 22.30 hours.*'

There was a stunned silence when I broke the news to the men. 'It must be bad to hold the *Southern Cross* up,' one man said, and he cocked his ear, listening to the thunder of the pressure ridges. The others, too, were listening. It was as though they were suddenly awake to the fact that the sound might well be the forerunner of death for all of us.

'I do not understand,' Bonomi said suddenly. 'How can the *Southern Cross* be held up? She is a big ship and the ice is quite thin. We came through it yesterday. It is only of a thickness when it is an iceberg. But they do not have to go through the icebergs. They can go round them. Craig. What do you say? What is the trouble?'

I shrugged my shoulders. 'How the hell should I know?' I answered a little abruptly.

At ten-thirty the *Southern Cross* operator announced that they were still held up and that he would broadcast at half-hourly intervals. I set the watches and ordered the men to turn in. But I don't think anyone slept. At broadcasting times I turned the radio up so that they could hear it in the other tent even above the noise of the ice. The message was always the same – nothing further to report. I could feel despondency growing in our little camp. It wasn't only the broadcasts. The thunder of the ice movement to the east seemed to grow and grow. The floe trembled under us, sometimes so violently that it seemed as though we were being actually shaken. It was like trying to rest on top of an earthquake. But I was very tired and drowsed occasionally. I'd drowse a bit and then jerk awake, numb with cold, and look at my watch. At the hour and the half-hour I'd switch on the radio. It was comforting just to hear the voice of the operator. It gave us a false sense of security to be in touch with the outside world. The man's voice was so quiet and natural. I felt as though I had only to wait a little and he'd walk into the tent to tell us the *Southern Cross* had arrived to pick us up. I thought of the warmth of the cabin I'd shared and the good food and the sense of mastery over the elements that the huge ship had given.

I must have fallen asleep, for suddenly Gerda was shaking me. 'I think there is something wrong with the radio,' she whispered. 'It is past three and I can get nothing.'

I sat up and fumbled with the tuning knobs. There was a faint crackling, but I could pick up nothing on our R/T wavelength. I switched over to the next waveband and almost immediately picked up music from a shore station. 'Nothing wrong with the radio,' I said. 'Sure you didn't alter the tuning knob?'

'No. I switched on just before three. There was nothing. Then I look at the tuning. It is quite okay. I think they do not broadcast.' Her voice trembled slightly.

'But they must have done,' I told her. 'They know how anxiously we'll be following their broadcasts. They'd never just miss out one. I'll try again at three-thirty.'

I glanced at my watch. It was ten past three. I lit my pipe and sat there, waiting for the next broadcasting time. And as I sat there, listening to the thunder of the pressure ridges and the crunch of the man on watch pacing up and down outside, an awful thought crossed my mind. Suppose the operator were too busy to broadcast to us! I tried to put the thought out of my mind. But it persisted. It persisted and grew with the groaning and crashing of the ice and the sudden, deathly periods of silence. They'd never forget to broadcast. If Gerda were right and they had failed to broadcast, then there must have been a reason. And there could be only one reason – more important traffic. I glanced at my watch. It was fourteen minutes past three. I looked across at Gerda. She was lying down, breathing quietly. Twice in the hour, for three minutes, there is a period of radio silence. From 15 minutes to 18 minutes past the hour and from 45 minutes to 48 minutes past the hour every operator in every ship in the world listens on a Watch wave of 500 k.c. for emergency calls. I just had to set my mind at rest. I leaned quickly forward, switched the set on and tuned to the Watch wave. The radio crackled. I gazed at the luminous dial of my wrist-watch, and as the minute hand touched the quarter I was sweating despite the cold. The radio crackled. That was all. Relief flooded through me. I told myself I'd been a fool. And then, so faint that I could not catch the words, the voice of an operator crackled out of the set.

I leaned forward quickly and fingered the tuning knob. The name *Southern Cross* was repeated twice. Then I was on the wavelength and the operator's voice was echoing through the tent: '*We*

are beset by ice in 66.21 S. 34.06 W. Southern Cross calling all shipping. SOS. SOS. Can you hear me? We are beset by ice in 66.21 S. 34.06 W. Southern Cross calling all ships. SOS. SOS . . .'
It went on like that unendingly. The operator's tone never varied. It was unemotional, ordinary. He might have been making a weather statement. But the monotonous repetition of the words drummed at my brain and I sat there, quite regardless of the cold, seeing nothing, hearing nothing beyond that voice, completely stunned.

There was movement in the tent round me. Gerda caught at my arm. She was thinking of her father. Nobody spoke, but I knew they were all awake and listening. Sometimes the operator sent in English sometimes in Norwegian. Always the message was the same. Then a new voice was on the air. *'Haakon to Southern Cross. Haakon to Southern Cross. Repeat your position. Over.'*

The position was repeated. There was silence for perhaps five minutes. Then the Norwegian factory ship was back on the air. *'Haakon to Southern Cross. Proceeding to your assistance. Our position is now 64 S. 44 W. We should be with you at about 20.00 hours. Report fully on your present circumstances.'* And the operator gave an R/T wavelength.

After I had tuned to him, Eide himself came on the air. *'We passed between two icebergs in a wide lead at 17.30 hours yesterday, going to the assistance of three of our catcher fleet damaged in the ice. At about 19.00 hours the lead came to an end and we entered the ice which was loose pack and not thick. At 21.45 hours we were held up by a mass of very heavy pack. We tried to back out of this, but the icebergs we had passed through were piling the pack up across our line of retreat. It appears that there is a strong eastward drift here. The icebergs are moving with the drift. But to the east there is a storm thrusting the ice westward. We are being caught between these two forces. When you reach the ice you will find there are seven icebergs in a row. Do not try to proceed beyond this line. I repeat, do not try to proceed beyond this line. We will keep you informed of all developments.'*

'Haakon to Southern Cross. Thank you for your warning. We will do all we can.'

'It is not believable,' Gerda whispered.

I didn't say anything. I felt utterly crushed. I think I prayed. I don't know. My mind was a sort of blank in which I could think of nothing but the fact that I needn't have been here. I wasn't a whaler. I wasn't a part of this Antarctic organization. If only I hadn't been so damned foolish about that fiver Bridewell had given us as a New Year present! Or if only I'd had the sense to

confirm that Kramer could get me a job in Cape Town! It was as
though Fate had organized it all. I felt bitter and lonely.

'*Capitano*.' Bonomi's voice trembled in the dark corner of the
tent where he lay. 'You will get us out of here, yes? You can
navigate. You have been on a polar expedition. You can get us –'

'It wasn't a polar expedition,' I snapped at him. 'It was only to
Greenland.'

'What is the difference? You understand how to travel on the
ice. Tell me, please – it is possible to get out of the ice, eh?'

'In Greenland we had dogs.'

'Yes. But we have a boat.'

'Would you like to drag a boat through twenty miles of the
conditions through which you ski-ed this evening?'

'No. But I must get back. When I complete these whaling
pictures, I am to go to the Rand to work for some goldmining
companies. Oh, you people, you do not understand. You are not
artists. For me my work is everything. I must get back. I cannot
be snuffed out here like any common photographer. I have much
fine work yet to do.'

'Oh, shut up,' I said. But the way he'd talked made me realize
that there were fifteen people right here on the ice with me who
expected me to save them. The responsibility wrapped itself round
me and lay like a heavy mantle on my shoulders. Gerda touched
my hand. 'You must not worry, you know. God will help us.'

Bonomi heard her and said, 'God?' Though I couldn't see him,
I could picture the down-droop of his mouth and the upward roll
of his eyes. 'God has done too much for us already, I think.
Madonna mia! We must do for ourselves now.'

The refrigerator ship, *South*, and the tanker, *Josephine*, were
now on the air. They were ordered to close, but to stand off, clear
of the ice.

All night the *Southern Cross* issued reports – to her own ships and
to the *Haakon*. But they showed no improvement until shortly after
six when our hopes were raised by the news that she had dynamited
a patch large enough for her to be warped round. I felt then that
there was a chance. She was facing out of the ice and a powerful
ship of that size ought to be able to batter her way clear along the
route by which she had entered. Everybody was cheerful at
breakfast. But a broadcast shortly after eight-thirty shattered our
hopes. The icebergs were charging into the pack and building it
up into huge pressure ridges. The way out was blocked. Though
we couldn't see the *Southern Cross* because of the glare, we could
see the icebergs. And to do this we no longer had to climb to our

lookout. They were much nearer and plainly visible from the tents.

Shortly after nine, Colonel Bland himself came on the air instructing the *Josephine* to refuel all catchers and towing vessels and escort them to South Georgia. This, more than anything else, brought home to us the seriousness of the situation. To give such an order it was clear that the officers on board the *Southern Cross* considered there was no chance of their being able to resume operations that season.

There is no need for me to record here in detail what everyone knows. By ten o'clock the *Southern Cross* was reporting damage due to the pressure of the ice, though the pumps were still holding the water. But an hour later the whole starboard side of the factory ship was buckling under the constant attack from the ice. By eleven-thirty she was pierced in several places and the crew were off-loading stores and equipment. Oil was being pumped out to be ignited later as a guiding beacon.

Gerda took me aside then. 'Duncan. I think we must begin to carry more stores to the floe-berg. I am not happy here. If we get caught between those icebergs and the pack ice to the east we may lose everything.'

I nodded. 'You're right,' I said, and gave the order for my party to get ready. The men were reluctant. They didn't argue, but I could see it in their faces. The morbid fascination of listening to the reports from the *Southern Cross* had gripped them. The sky to the east of us changed as we began to load the sledges. The opaque, iridescent light faded out of it till it was a dead, white glare. Wisps of cloud drifted across the sun and thickened like a fog. The last spark of comparative warmth vanished and the world was a cold etching in black and white. Then the first flurry of snow scattered like a handful of confetti through the camp. With the snow came the wind. At first it was just a cold breath of air out of the east. But in a moment a gust hit us, whipping at the end of one of the tarpaulins. It died away again and then suddenly it was blowing hard and the snow had thickened to a driving blanket. It was a thick cloud of black specks against the ice, but where it settled it produced a carpet of clear white. We secured the stores, pegging down the ends of the tarpaulins, and crawled into our tents.

From the clear sunlight of the morning, it had changed to a world of howling chaos. The wind moaned and screamed and the snow drove like a biting shroud across the ice. We sat and smoked. Nobody said anything. The only voice was the voice of the operator on the *Southern Cross*. The blizzard was making it difficult to unload their stores and they could no longer estimate the extent of their danger.

I shall always remember that morning. I think it was the longest I have ever spent. It was very dark in the tent. The other occupants were vague humps huddled under their blankets for warmth. The only thing that was unchanged was the steady voice coming out of the radio.

I think we all felt that the end was inevitable. Yet I remembered the profound shock the announcement caused. It was at seventeen minutes past two. Eide was speaking to the *Haakon*, which had now sighted the *Josephine* and the rest of the catchers. His voice was trembling slightly as he announced: '*The ship is pierced in several places. The pumps are no longer holding the water. She is sinking and I have given the order to abandon ship.*' At 15.53 hours the operator on the *Southern Cross* announced: '*All the crew safely on the ice, together with a reasonable quantity of stores. The ship is very low. Owing to the blizzard our camp is not very satisfactory and the movement of the ice is threatening. We are right in the path of the icebergs and unless the westward thrust of the storm eases soon our position will be dangerous. Captain Eide is about to leave the ship and I shall now remove the radio equipment to the ice. I will radio again as soon as I have set up the equipment.*'

That was the last message we received from the *Southern Cross*. We sat there for hours in the semi-darkness of the tents, the crackle of radio barely audible above the sound of the storm, but no message came from the *Southern Cross* survivors. At six o'clock in the evening the *Haakon* began calling the *Southern Cross*. The voice of the *Haakon* operator went on and on, a monotonous drone that gradually got on our nerves. There was no reply and at length I switched the radio off. The voice was too much like someone trying to call the dead. We lay there in the shadowy gloom of our tents and wondered what had happened. And with each minute that passed the sound of the wind seemed to encroach upon our refuge till it dominated us all with its syren scream of warning. We were alone, without hope of rescue, and I think we felt our smallness and were afraid.

8

To wake up on an icefloe with a blizzard blowing and realize
that you are responsible for the lives of thirteen men, a girl and a
young boy, is not pleasant. I knew I had got to get them out, but
in the moment of waking I was so dazed that I don't think I
realized the full extent of the disaster that had occurred. I lay in the
shadowed darkness of the tent, listening to the blizzard and trying
to measure our distance from the main centre of pressure by the
trembling of the ice under me. And as I lay there it slowly came
back to me – how the *Southern Cross* was gone and there was no
prospect of help from the outside world and how a line of icebergs
was driving towards us through the ice. At least the floe hadn't
split up in the night. That was something. I climbed out of the
tent into a screaming world of wind and stinging snow. The two
men on watch were white ghosts against the dirty grey backcloth
of the storm.

I got one of them to help me brew some tea and took it to the
men myself. The only one of them who said anything was McPhee.
'Mon, ye'd make a bonnie waitress,' he grinned as I handed him
his mug. 'Do ye ken if they charge extra for tea in bed at this
hotel.'

'The tea's free,' I said, 'and so's the weather.'

'Weel, thanks for the tea, anyway.'

Howe stirred at his side. 'And you can thank God for the
weather.' He sounded bitter.

'Ye'll do no gude blaming the Almighty,' McPhee admonished
him. 'Better to get doon on your knees and pray to Him for
guidance.'

Tempers were short and the hours passed slowly in that bitter
cold. It was too dark to read or to play bridge. I found a notebook
in my pocket, tore out all the used pages and started a log. The
first entry is a queer scribble, written more or less blind: *11 Feb.
The Southern Cross was abandoned yesterday. Still no message from the
survivors. Blizzard blowing outside, but party all safe in the tents. No
prospect of being rescued. Morale low. Movement of ice becoming violent.
As soon as the storm ceases intend to move to nearby floe-berg.* I then listed

the names of all the party, including Bonomi, and the names of the two men who were killed in the collision.

I was sitting there, wondering morbidly who would eventually read the log and whether it was worth entering the reasons for the collision, when the ice quivered violently under me. There was a shout and a report like a pistol shot. I felt the tent moving. I put out my hand to support myself and fell on my side. The floor of the tent was no longer there. In the dim light a dark gash was opening under us. The canvas of the tent began to rip. I flung myself towards the entrance, dragging Gerda with me. Bonomi gave a shout. Howe was slipping, but somebody had caught hold of his legs. Hans, the deckboy, was in the gap, clawing at the edge and screaming. He was all tied up in his blankets. McPhee pulled him out. We got to our feet and fought our way out of the tent, the men outside pulling the canvas clear of us.

The sight that met my gaze as I flung the last fold clear of my face was pretty frightening. A crack was opening right across the floe. Fortunately it missed the stores and the other tent. But it had cut our own sleeping quarters clean in half. Our sleeping positions were moulded in the ice by the warmth of our bodies. The shapes of our heads and shoulders were on the far side of the gap, our hips and legs on the near side. If the floe had split during the night, when we were asleep, nothing could have saved us. Even as I stared at it, the gap closed with an ugly snap. It did this several times – opening out to about three or four feet and then closing again with a clash of ice on ice. Finally it stayed closed and we could hear the broken edges grinding together under the pressure.

I knew we ought to move to the floe-berg. But it was impossible in that weather. We could not have made it and in any case we had no idea what was happening to the ice along the sledge route. We re-erected our tent as best we could and crawled inside. It was only then that we realized we hadn't got the radio. I went outside to look for it. The others joined me, searching anxiously in the snow. But it was gone. And then Hans said he saw it fall into the gap as he was being pulled out. Questioned by Gerda, he admitted that he had grabbed at it to hold himself and had pulled it in. After that we knew it had gone and we went disconsolately back to the tent.

You can't imagine what a difference the loss of the radio made. Whilst we'd had it we at least had the illusion of contact with the outside world. Now we were completely cut off. Its loss produced temporarily a mood of despair in all of us. But it also brought us face to face with reality. I don't think the men, or even I myself, had fully faced up to our position until then. As long as there was a voice on the radio telling us every move on the part of the rescue ships, bringing right into our tent the voices of men straining every nerve to do what they could to reach us, I think we felt unconsciously perhaps that we needn't exert ourselves, that we had but to stay put and everything would be all right. Now we were out of touch. We'd no means of knowing what the rescue ships were doing or what they planned to do. One thing we did know, however, and that was that our plight was now lost in the far greater disaster of the *Southern Cross*. There were over four hundred men out there on the ice somewhere, and their rescue would be the first objective.

McPhee put it into words when he said, 'Ah dinna think the radio is much o' a loss. There's nobody will save us noo except oorselves.'

All that day the snow continued and the wind blew like a raging monster out of the east. The cold was numbing and we lay huddled in our tents, waiting with fear in our hearts for the floe to open up again. Nobody spoke much and the cards lay forgotten, though it became just light enough to see. I cut watches to half an hour and that was quite long enough out there in that hell. Once one of the men on watch went a few yards from the camp to investigate a noise that sounded as though the floe were cracking again. We were shouting and blowing on my whistle for three-quarters of an hour before he stumbled into the camp again, utterly exhausted. You had only to go a few yards and the camp was lost to sight under its canopy of snow. It was only by luck that he'd found it again. After that I gave orders for the watch to remain close to the tents and within sight of each other.

At five the next morning the snow ceased. The wind remained, but we were no longer hemmed in by the blanket of the snowstorm. We could see, and the sight that met our eyes was truly terrifying. The icebergs were not six miles away and they were bearing down upon us, churning the ice up before them like giant bulldozers. I gave the order to load the sledges. I had biscuit tins broken up and the tin nailed to the outside of the boat round the bows. This was to save the woodwork from being pierced or damaged by sharp edges of ice, for I was determined to take the boat with me. The boat was our only hope of safety. Without the boat we were doomed.

Whilst these preparations were going on Gerda and I went out on skis to reconnoitre the route to the floe-berg. The snow was deep and crisp. Our skis slid easily along the surface of it. It took us only a few minutes to reach the floe-berg – a journey that had taken Kalstad and I over an hour the day before. It was incredible. It seemed no distance at all. But though the snow was all right on skis, I wondered how it would be for the men on foot. The smooth carpet of white covered everything – all the flaws and honey-combs and areas of rotten ice. I was afraid the weight of the boat would soon find the bad patches.

When we got back the steward had breakfast ready. It was the best meal we had. I had told him to use anything he liked from the stores we were leaving behind. We were ready to leave shortly after ten. Bonomi bustled about taking pictures. 'I must have pictures of everything,' he said. 'The camp of the disaster, the trek, the boat, everything. When we are back, everyone will say, "Bravo! Bravo! Aldo Bonomi, he has done it again." '

That was how we came to call the place Disaster Camp. The man was unbelievable. He had come across to us with a rucksack on his back and his camera slung round his neck. Do you think that rucksack contained so much as a change of socks? Not a bit of it. It was full of unused film for his camera.

Before we started he insisted on taking a group picture, all of us standing in front of the stores we were abandoning. It was just as he was taking this photograph that Howe seized my arm and pointed towards *Tauer III*. A line of figures was winding slowly through the broken contours of the ice. Somebody raised a cheer and in an instant the men were all shouting and waving excitedly. The fools thought it was a rescue party from the *Southern Cross*. I counted seventeen men – seventeen black dots moving against the dead white of the snow. I turned on my crew and shouted at them to be quiet. 'It is the crew of *Tauer III*.' The cheering wavered and died. I saw the light of hope leave their eyes. Their faces looked suddenly white and pinched under their beards. The deckboy, Hans, began to cry. The dry sobs that shook him were audible, even above the howl of the wind – it was as though the sudden fear in the men's hearts had been translated into sound. Gerda went to him and put her arm around him, comforting him. We waited like men frozen by the cold as the crew of *Tauer III* approached.

They were dragging improvised sledges piled with stores. But they had no boat with them. I searched the long, straggling line with my glasses. Vaksdal was leading. His big, Viking figure was unmistakeable. With only one man to help him, he was pulling one of the sledges. I searched down along the line, peering at each man's face. Most of them I could recognize from the brief period I had been in command of them. But I was searching for one face and I did not find it. The full complement of a towing vessel was sixteen men and two deckboys. There were only seventeen. Erik Bland was not with them.

As they reached our camp, Vaksdal came towards me. His eyes avoided mine. 'The men wish to be under your command, Kaptein Craig,' he said harshly.

I ordered my steward to get the stove alight and prepare hot food for them. Then I turned to Vaksdal. 'Where's Bland?' I asked him.

'He remain with the stores,' he answered. He was shifting uneasily on his big feet.

'Why?' He did not answer me and I added, 'Why have you abandoned him?'

'Because the men wish it,' he answered. His voice was sullen and angry.

'The men wish to abandon their captain?'

'*Ja*. Also he do not wish to come with the men. He wish to stay. He ask Keller and me to stay, too.'

'Why didn't you?'

'Because the men wish to leave.'

'And you left Bland to die in the ice alone?'

The man's face was sullen. 'He would not come. He wish to be left.'

'You're the first mate, are you?' I asked him.

'*Ja*.'

'You assumed command?'

He nodded.

'Why?'

'Because the men refuse to do what Bland tell them. They say it is Bland's fault, that it is not an accident. They are angry and they do not obey orders. They are Tönsberg men.' He said it as though that explained everything.

'Did you take the view that Bland deliberately rammed my boat?'

'No. He would not do that, not here in the ice. No whaler would do a thing like that. It is true what Frø Petersen say, that he send the helmsman below, but it is for some cocoa. It is also true that our radio is mysteriously out of order. These are things that will have to be cleared up at the enquiry when we get back to the *Southern Cross*. But I do not –'

'The *Southern Cross* is gone,' I interrupted him.

'Gone? I do not understand.'

'She got caught in the ice in an attempt to reach us. She is sunk.'
I looked round at the ring of faces, listening open-mouthed. They looked scared and disheartened. 'Gerda,' I said. 'Get these men to work. I want all the sledges lashed together, nose to tail.' Then I turned back to Vaksdal. 'So you are in command of these men?'

'*Ja.*'

'When did you assume command?'

'When it is clear to me that the men will not obey Kaptein Bland.'

'Then it was your decision to abandon Bland.'

'That is not true. The men wish to leave Bland, and also Bland wish to stay.'

'But you say you were in command?'

'*Ja.*' His voice was sullen and his tongue flicked across his lips.

'Who is your second mate?'

'Keller.' He nodded to a short, stout man with a woollen cap. I called him over. 'Do you speak English?' I asked him.

'*Ja, hr. Kaptein.*'

'Why did your abandon Bland?'

'The men demand that we – '

'Damn the men!' I shouted at him. 'The two of you were in command, yet you did exactly what the men wanted. You are forthwith relieved of your commands and revert to ordinary seamen, both of you.'

Vaksdal took a step towards me. 'You cannot do this,' he growled.

'I can and I will,' I answered him. 'You're neither of you fit to command.'

Vaksdal's eyes blazed. 'You dare to say that!' he shouted. 'You who have not served one season in the Antarctic. You know nothing and you tell us what we should and should not do. I have been eight voyages to the Antarctic. I know what is right.'

'You know what is right, do you?' I said. 'You assume command of a crew cut off in the ice, and you abandon your boats. How do you think you're going to get to safety without your boats?'

'I did not know the *Southern Cross* is sunk.' He was looking at the ground, shuffling his feet angrily in the snow.

'Did it never occur to you that the *Southern Cross* might not be able to reach us? Were you planning to just sit on your bottoms and wait to be rescued? Abandoning your captain when you believed him innocent of the men's charges is tantamount to mutiny. Abandoning your boats shows that you're not fit to command in these circumstances, either of you. You are now relieved of your commands. If you have anything to say, hold it for the enquiry when we get back.' I turned on my heels then and went over to Gerda. 'Get all the men together. I want to talk to them.'

'But Duncan, it is too cold for talk now,' she said.

'They'll be colder if they die out here,' I answered. 'And that's what will happen if we don't scotch this trouble right at the start. I want another mate – one of the *Hval 4* men. Who do you suggest?'

'Kalstad.'

'Good.'

She paraded the men then and I spoke first to the men of *Tauer III.* I told them that what they'd done was equivalent to mutiny. That unless they obeyed their officers they would never get out of the ice alive. I told them what had happened to the *Southern Cross,* that we were now entirely on our own. I then appointed Kalstad a mate, in command of the *Tauer III* crew, and announced that I had relieved Vaksdal and Keller of their commands.

One of the men interrupted me. He was the coxs'n of *Tauer III* and he started on a denunciation of Bland.

'That is no reason for abandoning him,' I answered. 'He will stand trial when we get back. You have no right to take the law into your own hands, which is what you have done in abandoning him. Moreover, you have abandoned your boats, too. And without them you have no chance of reaching safety.' I then asked for volunteers from the *Hval 4* crew to go back and bring in Bland and the two boats.

Every man of them volunteered – even the two injured men and the boy, Hans. I was proud of them and I remember that my voice felt choky at this display of confidence in me. The coxs'n of *Tauer III* stepped forward a little shamefacedly then and asked if his men might not volunteer.

But I shook my head. 'You've done one trek today. My men are fresh.' I ordered Gerda to get the sledges moving as soon as the *Tauer III* men had fed. 'When you have set up the new camp and the men are rested come back with a dozen volunteers to help us bring in the boats.'

Gerda nodded and began running out ropes from the sledges. I felt a tug at my sleeve. It was Howe. 'Bring back the boats,

Craig,' he said. 'But for God's sake leave Bland there.'

'I can't do that,' I said.

'He's a murderer,' he said. 'You know that. Bring him back and you give him a second chance. Let him find his own way out – if he can without any boats.'

But I shook my head. 'I can't do that,' I repeated.

'My God!' Howe said. 'If you bring him back I'll have to kill him. I've sworn I will. I've sworn to avenge my father. But I don't want to do it – not now. You see, there's Gerda – ' He hesitated awkwardly and then said, 'Why not let the ice do it? Please. To bring him back will make so much unhappiness. Gerda is already frightened for her father. And if I kill Bland – '

'No,' I said. 'And you're not going to kill Bland either. When I've brought him back and if these icebergs don't finish us, I'll try him by a summary court here on the ice, and if he's convicted of deliberately ramming us, he'll be put to work as an ordinary seaman pending trial when we get back to civilization.'

Howe stared at me. 'You damned fool!' he said. He was almost crying, he was so worked up. 'You're not in the Navy now. This is the Antarctic. That man's killed my father. He's caused the loss of three ships and endangered the lives of over four hundred men. Can't you realize that he's better dead? If you bring him back he'll fight to kill us all and get out alone. You heard what Vaksdal said. He wanted to be left there. Well, if he wants to be left – '

'If he wants to be left,' I said, 'then I'll not force him to come. There, will that satisfy you?'

He opened his mouth to speak, but Gerda came up then. 'Everything is ready for us to go,' she said.

'Fine,' I replied. 'And don't forget to come back for us. It's going to be a hard trek with two boats.'

'I won't.'

'Good luck then.'

'Thank you. And be careful, Duncan,' she added. 'You are a nice man and it would not be good if we lose you.' And with that she stretched up and kissed me.

I collected my volunteers, leaving only the two injured men and Hans and Howe of the *Hval 4* crew with Gerda, and we set out west along the sledge tracks that led towards the black hulk of *Tauer III*.

You may think it odd in that setting and amongst a bunch of tough men of whom she was in command, that Gerda should have kissed me. Perhaps the feminine element is out of place in the Antarctic. It certainly seems so as I write and I was tempted to leave it out. But I am setting down everything as it happened. Gerda was a mate in charge of men. But that did not mean that she hid the woman in her. Her method of handling men was quite different from a man's method. Yet all I can say is that if ever I am in as tough a position again, I'd give my right hand to have Gerda as my second-in-command. Her endurance was a constant spur to the rest. She'd shame them and coax them all in one and under her leadership they could achieve the impossible. As for the kiss – it was an open expression of her wish that we should return safely and accepted as such by the men. In fact, I not only had her kiss on my lips to encourage me but a cheer from the men of *Tauer III*. Only Vaksdal watched us sullenly as we left the camp and I hoped I had not made a permanent enemy of him, for he was a man I thought would prove useful.

We took with us three of the harpoon forerunners, our boat anchor and block and tackle. The snow had been packed down by the *Tauer III* sledges and the going was good, with the exception of one bad patch of honeycombed ice round which I managed to find a way. With the wind on our backs we made the trip in just over half an hour.

The camp itself was completely obliterated by snow. Only the sledge tracks running up to it and ceasing marked its position for us. As we neared the camp we could see the ice grinding at the wreck of *Tauer III*. The rusty sides of the ship stood up black and sheer above the floes, blotched here and there with white patches of snow. The ice was riding up on the farther side, and though we could not hear it, we could see that the steel plates were being broken under the stress. Beyond the ship the ice seemed in constant motion. It would lie dormant for a while, a lumpy plain of white, then suddenly a floe would heave up, showing jagged green teeth, or a great slab of ice would pop out of the snow as though ejected as indigestible by some giant sea monster.

From an ice hillock I looked beyond *Tauer III* to the line of icebergs. The nearest was not three miles away – a huge, wedge-shaped cliff of ice ploughing into the pack, turning it up on either side like the bow wave of a huge battleship held motionless in the still of a camera picture. But it was only motionless if you glanced at it quickly. I stood there for a moment, staring at it, and saw that it was moving all the time. Thick floes were being crushed and churned back. I thought of the survivors of the *Southern Cross*. The icebergs must have ploughed their way right across the position where the factory ship had foundered.

There was a chill in my stomach as I slid down into a trough of the ice on my skis, glad to have the sight blotted from my view. I felt there was no hope. Strive how we might, we were doomed to the same death as the men of the *Southern Cross*. The advance of the icebergs was slow but inevitable, like the Day of Judgement. I tried to grin cheerfully at the men, but my lips seemed frozen. I made some crack about the ice – I don't remember what, but it seemed a hollow mockery. The men laughed and I thought – *My God, they've got guts.* I found myself praying God to give me strength. In that illimitable waste of storm-swept ice I felt the smallness of man and He seemed nearer to me then than ever before, nearer even than that time when I'd steamed away from the convoy in my corvette, one of a screen of tiny ships thrown out to halt the *Bismark*.

As my skis slid along the sledge tracks into the *Tauer III* camp, Erik Bland emerged from a sail-cloth tent pitched in the lee of some packing cases. 'It's you, Craig, is it?' he said as I stopped just short of him. His voice was thick and he was swaying slightly. 'What do you want?'

I was well ahead of the men and for the moment we were alone. 'I've come for you,' I said. 'I think you know why.'

'I suppose you think I rammed you deliberately?' His eyes had a glazed look and his face was white and mean under the dark stubble of his beard. He was very drunk. 'Well, what if I did? You can't prove it. You can't prove anything. If that bloody little bastard Howe hadn't fired that harpoon – '

'You'd be out of the ice by now, reporting that there was no way through. Is that it?'

'You think you're clever, don't you?' he sneered. 'Well, I'll beat you yet – all of you.'

'Better get your things together, Bland,' I said. 'You're coming back with me.'

'To have you rig another little court of enquiry?' He laughed. 'Oh, no. I'm staying here.'

'You're not taking the easy way out like that,' I told him. 'You're coming back with me to stand trial. If we ever get out of the ice I think you're going to find yourself responsible for a lot of deaths.'

'I'm not responsible for what the ice does,' he answered. 'You can't prove anything. It was an accident. And don't imagine I'm going to die. I'm not taking the easy way – ' He stopped then, peering out across the snow. He'd seen the men. 'So you're so damned scared of me you bring a dozen men with you.' His eyes were suddenly narrowed. He was fighting to sober himself up.

'I didn't bring the men in order to persuade you to come back with me,' I said. 'I brought them because I've come for the boats Vaksdal was fool enough to leave behind.'

'The boats! You leave the boats alone!' He stared at me a second and then swung round and lunged into the tent. Like an idiot, it never occurred to me what he was after until he came out carrying a gun. 'You leave the boats alone!' he screamed at me. He was tugging at the bolt, which was jammed with frozen snow. 'As long as I have the boats, I've got a chance.'

I drove my sticks hard into the snow and charged him on my skis. I drove into him head first and we collapsed in a tangled heap. He was quicker on to his feet than I was, encumbered by my skis. But I had the gun and the bolt was free. I got up carefully, watching him all the time. I'd misjudged his motive in staying behind. I could see now that one of the boats had already been partly decked-in with pieces of packing cases. It was just as Howe had said. He wanted to be the only man out of the ice alive. Only his nerve had failed him when he was alone and he'd had to get drunk. 'How the hell do you think you'd get away in one of those boats without a crew?' I demanded angrily.

'I've sailed boats single-handed all my life,' he answered sullenly. 'If that berg missed the camp, I'd have got back to the *Southern Cross* somehow.'

'You damned fool!' I shouted at him. 'You don't realize the half of what you've done. The *Southern Cross* came into the ice after us. She was beset and smashed.'

He stared at me. His mouth hung slackly open. 'I don't believe it,' he cried. 'It isn't true.' And then as I didn't say anything, he added, 'How do you know? Your radio went down with your ship.'

'We had a portable,' I said.

The men were coming into the camp now. I ordered them to start breaking the first boat out. Then I slipped the bolt out of the rifle and threw the weapon into the tent. 'Better get to work, Bland,' I said. 'You're going to help us run these boats back to the camp.'

He didn't say anything. He just stood there. It was as though he couldn't realize the truth of what I'd told him. I went over to help the men. They were hitching the ropes to the first boat and running them out to block and tackle fixed to the anchor bedded in the ice. Bland lumbered across to me and caught hold of my arm.

'Is she sunk?' he demanded hoarsely. The steam of his breath in the cold air smelt of whisky.

'Yes,' I answered.

'Any survivors?'

'We don't know yet. We've had no message since they abandoned ship.'

He suddenly laughed. It was an ugly sound, half drunken, half menacing. 'Nobody will dare come into the ice to rescue us now. We're alone. Alone, out here in the ice. An' it's a damn good thing, too. Damn good thing.'

'Doesn't the loss of that ship mean anything to you?' I demanded angrily.

'Why should it? The insurance people will pay.' He was grinning almost happily.

I fought down a sudden desire to strike him, knock him down and kick him till he understood what he'd done. 'Your father was on that ship,' I reminded him.

'Why should I care about my father? I hardly knew him.' His gaze wandered to the men straining on the rope to break the boat out. He lurched towards them and caught hold of the rope. 'Come on, damn you – pull!' He was like a man suddenly possessed of a devil. 'Come on, Craig,' he shouted. 'Don't stand there gaping. Lend a hand.'

He was like that for perhaps ten minutes whilst we broke both boats out from where they were frozen in. Then the drink died in him and he became morose and sullen. We ran the two boats out of the camp. There were eleven of us with Bland. But though we could shift them all right, it was exhausting work. With the aid of my skis I was able to put my full weight on the rope without breaking through the snow. But the others went through, sometimes up to the waist. It was hopeless. I spliced the forerunners together, ran them out to the anchor with block and tackle, and that's how we got the boats back to Disaster Camp. It was slow work. But it was the only way.

We reached the camp just before ten that night, utterly exhausted. The pain in my side was like the stab of a knife. Gerda had left one tent still standing. We cooked a meal and lay down. No watch was set, for I knew not one of us could stand even half an hour out there in the biting wind.

Three hours later I woke to find Gerda shaking me. 'You must come quickly, Duncan,' she said. Her voice was urgent. 'The icebergs are not more than two miles away and the ice is breaking up.'

I was so tired I did not care if an iceberg crushed the tent with us in it. It seemed easier to die than to go on. I was weak and numbed with cold and pain. The ice was shuddering under me, yet my heavy eyelids closed and the movement of the ice merged into Gerda shaking me violently. Then my face was being slapped and I was dragged out into the freezing wind. I staggered to my feet then and stood swaying weakly, staring unbelievingly at the cold, ice-clad scene. *Tauer III* was gone. There was no sign of it. And along the trail we'd dragged the boats the ice was heaving like a frozen sea. An iceberg with a tall, jagged spire, like the Pillar Rock, was driving towards us, icy chaos running out ahead of it.

The others were being pulled out of the tent. 'Hurry! Hurry!' Gerda called to them. She had a dozen men with her. They began to move out of the camp, dragging the men from the tent with them.

'Wait!' I called. 'We must take the boats.'

'No,' Gerda shouted at me above the wind. 'We must go quickly or we shall be too late.'

I stared at the iceberg. There seemed little hope whether we stayed here or reached the floe-berg. I pulled myself together. 'Get your men on to the boats,' I ordered her.

She started to argue, but I stopped her. 'With the two crews there are over thirty of us. We need all three boats. If we do escape destruction and we lose these boats, then we are doomed anyway. Better to die with the boats.' I called the men together and there in the ice with the wind driving right through us, we knelt down and I prayed that we might be delivered from the disaster that threatened. After that the men took up the ropes of the first boat without a word.

I shall never cease to marvel at man's determination to cheat death. It wasn't love of life that drove them out there on the ice. Life wasn't lovely to them then – it was days and days of cold and hunger and exertion stretching ahead of them unendingly. It was their determination not to die. Call it fear if you like. But whatever it was it gave them strength – incredible, fantastic strength – and courage.

With all twenty-two of us tugging on the ropes we'd take one boat in a rush a hundred yards, sometimes two hundred. Then we'd come back and do the same with the other boat. The ice was splitting all round us, the cracks opening like bursts of machine-gun firing. Yet they never hesitated to go back for the second boat and I never had to drive them. Twice men were only saved by the ropes from the opening jaws of the ice. Once we had to rush the second boat across a gap that was half a boat's length in width. But we did it in the end. And as we dragged the second boat to the foot of the floe-berg, a whole crowd of men came down and took the boats with a rush to the top of the berg. I remember a vague impression of new faces, of soft hands, of another voice taking command in Norwegian, then I had slipped into oblivion.

My return to consciousness was like the slow drag to the surface of a drowning man. I lay still, panting as though I'd run a race, and listened to the deathly stillness that seemed to surround me. I was stiff and numb. The cold struck through to the very core of me and the pain gripped me every time I breathed. There was a sudden grating roar. It rose till it filled all the place with sound, and terminated in one splitting crash. Was this death? Was this what Milton had tried to portray? The world-shaking sound did not roll on ponderously like thunder. It ceased abruptly. There was no echo. The stillness filled my ears, shutting me in upon my own thoughts. And yet I wasn't alone. There were others near me. I could hear their breathing, feel their faint stirrings. I could smell them, too – the sour odour of men's sweat. I opened my eyes. I was in a world of sepia glory with huddled shapes packed close beside me.

Then I suddenly wanted to laugh. The sepia glory was the sun slanting through brown sail canvas. The men around me were not dead. They were sleeping. I sat up and then I didn't want to laugh any more. I wanted to be sick.

I crawled out of the tent, staggered to my feet in the snow and stood there, retching. The wind was gone. The air was still and all the white, incredible snow-scape steamed in the sun so that the atmosphere was iridescent, impermanent – a water mirror in which nothing was real and every changing form of ice writhed and shimmered in mutability. The sweat broke cold on my forehead. I had nothing to bring up. The retching stopped. And in that moment the dragon's roar of sound that had invaded the stillness of the tent came again, terrifyingly loud, like a clarion call of the Four Horsemen galloping through Hell's gates. The crash that followed seemed like an atom split. I straightened my aching side and searched the blinding, gold-tinted ice for the source of the sound. And I stared unbelievingly as a block of ice that seemed as big as the Crystal Palace I'd known as a kid emerged out of the ice. It opened up like a flower and then fell crashing, shattered into a million fragments, each prismatic, each an enormous diamond throwing forth sparks of eye-blinding light. The sound of its fall was like the end of the world. But no mountain crags sent the sound reverberating round the heavens. It was a noise that split the ear-drums and then ceased – ceased as though there

328

had never been any noise. Stillness shut down on the ice again and a hand touched my arm.

'Feeling better?'

I swung round at the voice. The sound of it was as loud as blasphemy in the stillness of a cathedral. It was Howe who had spoken. His face was white and his hand trembled as it held my arm. He was scared. 'Feeling better?' he repeated. And then as I nodded dumbly he produced a flask. 'Take a swig at this,' he said. 'It's brandy. Do you good.' I took a pull at the flask. 'You were all pretty exhausted when you got in last night.'

I didn't say anything. I was trying to remember what had happened. Of course, we'd brought the boats to the floe-berg. There they were, black against the frozen snow. Four boats and a litter of stores, tents and make-shift sledges. Somebody had stuck a Norwegian flag on an up-ended oar outside one of the tents. The triangle of red with the blue cross hung dejectedly. A splintering shivered the frosty air and behind it sounded the deep, artillery rumble of ice pounded to rubble. Beyond the floe-berg the ice stretched westward in crumpled, jagged folds. And beyond that ploughed-up field of ice was a huge berg. It was a fairy crag, a gigantic, prismatic skyscraper citadel of ice, one pinnacle reaching like the torch of the Statue of Liberty into the gold-shot rainbow of the sky. At its base the ice was moving, turning back on itself, splintering and folding as the wedged cut-water ploughed into the floes. To the north of it was another, and to the south another and another – great masses of shimmering ice.

I shivered and handed Howe back his flask. 'Thanks,' I said. 'Not much future for us, is there?'

'I've worked it out that at its present rate of drift that one over there will be ploughing right through the camp at about midday tomorrow.' His voice was the voice of science, quite unemotional.

'There wasn't much point in shifting our camp, then,' I said wearily.

He shrugged his shoulders. 'If it were just one – ' he began and then again he shrugged his shoulders as though it wasn't any good talking about it. He didn't speak for a moment and when he did his voice was bitter. 'Why couldn't you leave well alone?'

'How do you mean?' I asked.

'Why couldn't you leave him to die in the *Tauer III* camp? I told you not to bring him back.'

'And I told you I'd only abandon him if that was what he wanted.' I felt very tired. 'He didn't want to be left – not when he knew I'd come for the boats.'

'What was he planning to do?'

'The fool thought he'd got a chance of getting away alone in one of the boats. He'd got one of them half decked-in before he started drinking.'

'What happened? Did he lose his nerve?'

'Maybe,' I said. 'Any man would lose his nerve on his own out here, watching those icebergs ploughing into the ice towards him.'

'Why the hell do you waste your sympathy on him?' Howe demanded.

'I'm not wasting my sympathy on him,' I replied wearily. 'I'm just explaining what happened. Where is he now?'

'Over there.' He nodded towards one of the tents. 'Talking to Vaksdal and Keller.' His gloved hand caught hold of my arm. 'Don't you realize what you've done?' His voice was hoarse. 'We're in a bad enough fix without having Bland here. He's a murderer. He knows it and he knows that we know it, too. It's not only Nordahl. There's Raadal and that other poor devil. And all these men here' – he waved his hand round the camp – 'they're all going to die. We're all as good as dead – you and me; Gerda and Judie, too. And why?' His voice was unsteady, almost out of control. 'Because of Bland. But for him we'd have got the crew of *Hval 5* out. Instead we're all locked in the ice and the men of the *Southern Cross* as well. Gerda's beside herself. She's scared for her father. She loved him. And you go and bring Bland back and Gerda has to be a party to his rescue. God, I could have throttled you to see you going out like a bloody little Sir Galahad to rescue a man who's responsible for the killing of nearly five hundred men.'

'I went for the boats,' I reminded him.

'What good are the boats to us?' He stared out across the ice, his hands clenching and unclenching. 'We're going to die and you've forced on me the choice of killing a man or dying with him without doing what I swore I would do.' He paused and then said, 'And if we do get clear of this iceberg, we're going to have trouble with Bland. He's lost his nerve for the moment. But if he can do something to get back his self-confidence, then he'll be dangerous. I'm going to have a word with Peer Larvik.'

'Larvik!' I swung round, not hearing what he replied, seeing four boats where there should only have been three and the Norwegian flag drooping from the upended oar. I seized hold of him, shaking him in my sudden excitement. 'Is Larvik here? Have the *Hval 5* crew joined up with us?'

He nodded and I hesitated, steadying myself, conscious of the pulse-beat in my body. 'Judie? Is she all right? Is she here, too?'

He stared at me, astonished. 'Good God! Don't you remember? You collapsed into her arms last night.'

I stood there for a moment, cursing the ice that made our time so short, cursing myself for bringing her husband back. 'Where is she?' My voice sounded hoarse and unnatural.

'Over there – in Larvik's tent.'

I stood there without moving for quite a while. I was thinking that perhaps it was as well for both of us that we had only a few hours left of life. I bent down and scooped up a handful of snow, rubbing it over my face. I no longer felt weak. I felt strong – strong enough to cheat death and to fight my way out of the ice. And yet it was better this way. I knew that. I walked slowly over to the tent where the Norwegian flag hung and called to her.

In a moment she was out there in the glory of that iridescent sunshine, holding my hands, looking up into my face and smiling and laughing all in one, her eyes gleaming like frosted diamonds. We just stood and looked at each other and laughed with happiness. And then without a word we turned and walked through the powdery snow to the farther edge of the floe-berg and stood and watched the towering cliffs of ice tearing up the floes, not seeing them as death any more, but dominating their terror with our sense of life, so that they were just something exciting to watch. It was as though our love could exorcise the devil of fear. And that's a funny thing. We never had to ask each other about our love – the truth was there in our eyes.

But our moment alone together was very short. Kalstad came up. His round, rather Slavonic face looked worried. 'What's the trouble, Kalstad?' I asked, as he coughed awkwardly.

'It's Vaksdal and Keller,' he said. 'The men do not want them in their tents. They are Sandefjord men, both of them.'

'Good God!' I exclaimed. 'This is no time to worry about whether a man comes from Sandefjord or Tönsberg.'

'Also these two men will not do what I order,' Kalstad added woodenly.

'Then make them.'

'I have tried, but – ' Kalstad shrugged his shoulders. 'Vaksdal is a big man and it is no time to fight, I think. Also he is very angry because he is no longer mate.'

'I see. What about Keller?'

'Keller will do what Vaksdal do.'

'All right, bring Vaksdal here.'

Vaksdal was in an ugly mood. I could see that by the morose way he slouched towards me. When he stood in front of me he was a good head taller. 'Kalstad informs me you refuse to obey his orders?' I said.

'*Ja*. It is not right he should give me orders.'

'Did you hear me appoint him mate yesterday?'

'*Ja*.'

'And I reduced you to ordinary seaman for abandoning your boats.'

'Kaptein Bland say you have not the authority to – '

'Damn Bland!' I shouted. 'Bland is – ' I stopped then. I was seething with anger. 'You come and talk to Captain Larvik.'

'No.' Judie's hand was on my arm. 'You must not worry Peer Larvik with this, Duncan.'

'It's his responsibility,' I said. 'He's in charge now.'

But she shook her head. 'No. You're in command. Larvik is very ill. His ribs are crushed, and his legs. He got caught between the side of *Hval 5* and the ice. I was just going back to him. I don't think – ' She hesitated and there were tears in her eyes. 'I don't think he'll live very long. You must handle this yourself.' She turned then and walked towards the tent where the Norwegian flag hung. I felt suddenly very tired again. So the responsibility was still on my shoulders. I looked up at Vaksdal. 'Have you ever thought what it's like to die?' I asked him.

He looked puzzled. 'No,' he said. 'I do not think about such things.'

'You've never looked death in the face.' I turned him round so that he faced the slow, inevitable advance of the iceberg. 'You are looking at death now,' I said. 'I don't think we have much hope. But so long as we're alive there's still a chance. So long as we're alive and working together. This is no time to cause trouble, is it?'

'I do not begin it,' he growled. 'It is the men who begin it. They are Tönsberg men. Me and Keller, we are from Sandefjord.'

'All right,' I said. 'I'll have a word with the men later. In the meantime have the sense to accept orders. If, when this iceberg has passed, there are any of us alive, then I'll discuss the question of my authority to act as I have done.'

He stared down at me for a moment and then I saw his eyes drawn to the towering bulk of the iceberg, as though it were a magnet. 'All right,' he growled, and turned quickly and went back to Keller who had been standing by the tents watching us.

I crossed the top of the floe-berg where the stores and boats were lashed down and reached the tent with the flag outside. The flap was drawn back and Judie was bent over a figure lying in a huddle of blankets. There was blood on the trodden snow and the man's head that showed in the sunlight over Judie's shoulder was unrecognizable. The blue eyes were sunk deep in their sockets and the lower lip showed red and bloody in the stubble of his beard where the bared teeth had bitten into the flesh with the pain.

Judie looked up as my shadow fell across her. 'Is he conscious?' I asked.

She nodded. 'I was just coming to fetch you,' she said. 'He wants to speak to you.' She crawled out of the tent and stood up. 'Don't let him talk for long. He's very weak.'

I bent down and sat myself in the doorway of the tent. 'Judie says you want to see me,' I said.

'Craig?' The voice was very faint.

'Yes,' I said.

'Come nearer, please.' I slithered into the tent, and then I knew he was going to die. The tent smelt of rotting flesh, even with the tent flap pulled back and the cold air circulating. It was gangrene. 'You can smell my legs, eh?' There was no fear in his voice and his eyes were quite steady. 'Judie has done her best, but it will not be long now.' He said something else, but it was lost in a crash of splintering ice so loud that it seemed just outside the tent. His hand came out from under the blankets and fastened on my shoulder. It was grey and the veins and knotted muscles stood out like cords in the wasted flesh. 'You are in command now. You must get them out of the ice. There is not much hope, but – ' He gnawed at his lip, fighting the pain. 'What are you going to do?' he asked at length.

'We could start trekking,' I said. 'Now the wind has dropped, the westward thrust of the ice seems to be lessening. If we left now, we might be able to keep ahead of this iceberg.'

He shook his head slowly. 'No good,' he said. 'If you leave here, how do you live? How do you finally escape without the boats? I hear what you do yesterday. Gerda tell me. You know that there is only hope so long as you have the boats.' For a while he lay still without speaking, staring out through the open tent to the scintillating mass of the berg grinding its way towards us. 'If it is only one berg, per'aps south or north. But here it is a line. Also it is not good to retreat. It is not good for morale.' He turned his head towards me and I saw that his eyes were excited. 'I think you must advance, eh? That will have better appeal to the men, you know.'

I suppose my face must have shown that I was mystified, for his grip tightened on my shoulder. 'All morning I am lying here with nothing to do but look out of the tent. Look!' He nodded through the open tent flap. 'Do you not see something, on the berg to the south? There is a ledge there. It slope up like a ramp. I have look at him through the glasses. If you can transfer the camp to that ledge – '

'But it's impossible,' I said.

He shrugged his shoulders. 'It is difficult. But nothing is impossible. As you say, the rate of advance of the iceberg is becoming more slow. Already it is breaking the ice up more gently. Our camp here is a small berg. The icefloes round us will be broken up. We shall be thrown about, but perhaps we do not break entirely. Perhaps we are for a little while close to the ledge. With God's help we may get there. You are a sensible man. You think to bring forerunners and tackle. I also bring my forerunners. I think we have a chance. It is a very small chance, but it is the only one.' He looked at me quickly. 'You agree?'

I didn't say anything for a moment. I stared at the foot of the iceberg where it ploughed into the floes. It was less than a mile away now. I'd once seen lava engulfing a village – that was when my corvette was in the Bay of Naples and Vesuvius was in eruption. The iceberg was advancing at about the same speed and though it was as cold as the lava had been hot, it had the same slow, ponderous inevitability of destruction about it. It was advancing at the rate of about two hundred yards an hour directly towards us. For a mile or more to right and left of it the ice was in a state of chaos, the floes being splintered, broken up and layered. The outer fringe of this area of chaos was the worst, for there the chaos of one iceberg met the chaos of the next and all was a confusion of up-ended floes and great slabs of ice tossed in the air like snowballs. Nowhere could I see a floe-berg as substantial as the one we were on, and as the chaos was worse at the sides of the iceberg than in front of it, there seemed just the barest chance, for we were in the direct path of its advance. At least the idea of riding the source of the destruction appealed to me in its daring. I nodded. 'At any rate it gives us something to try for.'

'Something to try for.' Larvik nodded slowly. He looked drained of life and I realized that I'd let him exhaust himself.

'Something to try for,' he said again, his voice scarcely audible. Then he seemed to rally. He patted my arm. 'When you are on his back, he will be your horse and you can laugh when he charge the ice. Perhaps he – break a way out for you.' He closed his eyes. I stayed there beside him for a little longer, then as he still lay motionless with his eyes closed, I began to slide out of the tent. But his hand moved on my arm. 'Is Bland there?' he asked. His voice was thick as though his throat were clogged with blood.

'Yes,' I said. 'Do you want to speak to him?'

He didn't answer for a moment. Then he said, 'No. I do not think I am strong enough to say what I should wish.' He coughed and writhed in agony. I held his hand till he was quiet again. 'Whatever I may think of Old Bland, he is a man. This pup of his has gone wrong. He is dangerous, Craig. Judie is now the biggest shareholder in the company. Bernt Nordahl leave her everything. I know because I witness the will. Look after her, my friend. And see that Erik Bland does not get out of the ice alive. You understand?' His sunken eyes stared at me. 'Promise you – ' His voice was too faint for me to hear the rest. His eyes were gazing urgently into mine.

I knew what he wanted. But I couldn't promise that, so I slid quietly out of the tent. Judie was waiting for me. 'You've been a long time,' she said. 'Is he all right?'

'He's very weak,' I told her.

Her face looked small and unhappy. 'I am afraid he will not last the night.' She crawled into the tent then and I turned and stared at the giant iceberg, searching that ledge. It started right at the base of the berg and sloped gently up till it merged into the cliff of ice that formed the side about fifty feet above the surrounding pack. There was just a chance, I felt. Just the slightest chance. And I prayed that Larvik, who had given us this chance, would live to reach that ledge.

I got the men together then and told them the plan.

It appealed to them. Anything positive would have appealed to them and they threw themselves into the work of preparation with an enthusiasm that was derived as much from a desire to blot out the fear that was in them as from any sense of hope. Forerunners were thawed of ice and spliced together in lone lines. Anchor stakes were prepared and sliding tackle rigged. Boat slings were fitted. Stores were packed and secured in bundles, for the idea was that boats and stores should be run out to the ledge on the iceberg on the life-line and bos'n's chair principle. But as the day wore on and the iceberg came nearer and nearer to our camp, I noticed the men glancing over their shoulders at it with a scared look in their faces.

By evening the work was done. Only the tents and immediate stores were left unpacked. After the evening meal there was nothing for the men to do. No one felt like sleep and they stood about on the ice in groups, gazing with awe at the towering mass of ice. It loomed over the camp like death in visible form. The noise of the floes being crushed and thrust aside as it advanced was incessant – a grinding rumble, penetrated by sharp, splintering cracks. Wonderful golden bars radiated from the sun's gleaming centre of light low to the south and from a fabulous mock sun much higher in the sky. The light glistened on crags of ice a hundred feet and more high. In the shadows, the naked ice, sheer in places like a glass wall, was a cold green or colder blue. But where the sun-bars struck it, its surface gleamed like burnished metal, mirroring the prismatic and uncertain lights of the sky.

Our camp became as cold as death. The men's eyes shied at the blinding scintillation of the sunny side of the berg and turned more and more often to the green and blue of the shadows where glacial jaws gaped black and the spilling wave-crests of ice were cold and remote. They'd stand and gaze at the shadowed flank for a moment, their mouths agape and their faces awestruck. Then they'd turn with a shiver of cold and slink into the tents for warmth. But no one could sleep and soon they'd be out again to stare, fascinated by the inevitability of the end.

Bland kept mostly to his tent. Vaksdal and Keller had erected one against some packing cases and he had moved in with them. I suppose I should have discouraged his association with his two mates, but there seemed no point. On the few occasions I saw him outside the tent, he was alone. He seemed to have withdrawn into a sullen, brooding mood so that he scarcely noticed anyone around him. I can't really recall how much the men knew or had been told about his part in the business. Our own men at any rate must have suspected that he'd rammed us deliberately. In other circumstances they might have killed him. As it was, the iceberg and the approach of death dominated everything. Only once did any incident occur.

It was in one of the rare moments when Judie wasn't looking after Larvik. We were sitting together on the edge of one of the boats. Gerda and Howe were standing at the edge of the floeberg gazing towards the sun. They were holding each other's hand. As they turned back towards the camp, Bland came out of his tent. Howe stopped at the sight of him. His face was tense. Then he let go Gerda's hand and went towards Bland.

He passed right by us. He was crying and there was a strange desperate look of longing on his face. Bland saw his coming and stopped, his eyes narrowing and his body stiffening. Judie's hand tightened on my arm. Howe looked so puny as he faced Bland. I got up. Howe might have a gun. He might have screwed up his courage to kill him. And if he hadn't, then I could see him being hurt. Bland could break him as easily as he could snap a twig.

But as I rose, Gerda ran past me. She caught Howe by the arm and dragged him away from Bland. As she brought him back, leading him by the hand, his face was horribly convulsed and there was an air of bitterness and frustration about him that was quite frightening.

Judie's hand slipped into mine. 'He is tearing himself apart,' she whispered. 'Oh, how I wish they could live!'

I glanced down at her. 'Do you think they would be happy?' I asked.

'Yes, I think perhaps they might,' she answered. She sighed and gave a little shrug. 'Poor Gerda – it's the maternal instinct with her. With Walter it's different. He's in love. I think he's found happiness for the first time in his life. That's what is tearing him apart. He wants to live – and kill.' She sighed again and added, 'I think it might have worked out very well.'

'Why the devil doesn't he just enjoy the fact that he's alive and Gerda is with him?' I said.

She was silent for a moment. Then she said, 'If we ever reach that ledge, Duncan, you must have a trial at once. The men must know the truth. I wish you hadn't – ' She stopped short and I said: 'Hadn't what?'

'No,' she answered. 'I must not wish that. But he frightens me.'

I knew that what she was wishing was that I hadn't brought Bland back from the *Tauer III* camp. She wanted her husband dead and I could understand how she felt. I remember thinking: *Well, we'll all be dead soon. It doesn't matter.* I'd no real hope of our getting across that litter of broken ice on to the ledge. The mere sight of it appalled me, knowing that sooner or later I had got to attempt to cross it.

'But it doesn't matter now,' Judie said suddenly. 'Nothing matters now except that we are together – for a little.'

Judie had all the realism of her sex. She was not buoyed up by any preposterous illusion of hope. She saw the inevitable and accepted it. She made no attempt to bolster up her courage with the idea that we could cheat the death that stared us in the face from those glass-hard cliffs of ice. Her attitude affected me in a strange way. Instead of being scared, I, too, felt acceptance of the inevitable. And I almost welcomed it. To go like this – loving someone and loved by someone; it was sublime. In that bitter cold there was no suggestion of passion. I can't explain it quite – but if we have souls then it was the merging of our two souls. In that twilight evening of death our love was out of this world. We were two people wanting to pass over into the beyond together.

I have often wondered since what Bland's feelings about Judie really were. The fact that he threatened me through her that time I went across to *Tauer III* is no indication. And anyway love and hate are never far apart. But I remember one occasion that evening when the man's feelings blazed through the sullen façade he'd erected as a barrier between himself and the people round him. It does not answer the question, but I think I should record it and the reaction it produced in Judie.

It was towards midnight and she and I were watching the sun sweep low in the egg-shell pale sky to the south. Standing there I was suddenly conscious of being watched. Judie must have felt it, too, because she turned as I did. Bland was standing outside his tent. He was standing quite still about twenty yards from us. His face was heavy and brooding. There was something in his features, in the way he stood, that reminded me of his father. Our eyes met and I remember I was shocked to see such a violence of hatred. I have never, thank God, had a man look at me like that before or since. It was the look of the lone wolf – the rogue male – barred from the pack and bitter with the thought of what others enjoyed. It was bitterness and frustration turned to hate. But whether it indicated a depth of feeling for Judie that she was unaware of I do not know.

But I do know that she saw it and recognized it, for her fingers caught at my arm and as we turned back towards the sun her face looked white. 'You must be careful,' she said, and her voice trembled. She glanced quickly over her shoulder. Bland had gone back to his tent. 'Erik is dangerous,' she added. And then, 'I must go and see my patient.' She turned quickly away towards Larvik's tent.

The cold became intense that night. A very slight breath of air came out of the west and the thermometer fell as it brought into the camp the chill ice temperature of the berg. The hours passed vaguely as in a dream. The camp was restless and for the first time since we'd abandoned ship the men on watch had company.

There is a strange fascination about death. No one likes it to

338

catch him unawares. And inside the tents the noise and the quaking of the ice seemed magnified so that one lay in a sort of tense expectancy of fear, the berg growing in one's imagination to undreamed-of heights and toppling down on the flimsy sepia curtain of canvas. It was a relief then to go out and see the real height of the berg and mark how slowly it ground its way towards us.

But though it might come slowly when we watched it, when we ignored it for a moment and looked again, we'd realize with horror how swift in terms of the future that advance was. The ledge on the south side gleamed clear and bright like a ramp leading to heaven in some super colossal colour-film monstrosity. But I don't think any of us had any hope of reaching it. Between us and that ledge was a slowly closing gap of moving ice. There were great crevasses that opened and closed with a snap, floes that stood on end, all jagged, and then sank slowly beneath the heaving mass, and huge blocks of ice that were spewed up and fell crashing on to the floes. And where the sheer prow of the iceberg crushed its way through the pack there was a moving wave of ice that looked like powdered glass, and along the flanks of the berg ran a black line in which water splashed, catching the sun on its green crests.

I wasn't scared. At least it didn't seem like fear to me then. The scene was so stupendous as to seem remote and unreal. I felt like a spectator. And I knew I should go on feeling like a spectator until the moment when I had to cross the gap and the ice overwhelmed me.

9

Most of you who read this will have faced death at one time or another. You'll know how it feels. The car coming at you on the wrong side of the road produces the same reaction as high explosive whistling down at you from the sky. There is the tensing of the nerves, the sudden photographic clarity of vision. But no fear. That comes later when nerves stretched beyond endurance relax, leaving you shivering with the reaction. It is the same, only more prolonged, with the man going into battle. He is tensed up, ready for it – and when it comes he conquers fear. And afterwards he is limp, exhausted. But when death comes slowly and inevitably, then the nervous tension cannot be sustained. That's when men crack. It's like battle exhaustion. Men can't go on facing death indefinitely. If the period is too sustained then the nervous reaction sets in before the moment of impact. Then comes fear – naked, uncontrolled fear.

That's what happened at our camp the morning the iceberg reached us.

Just after six Judie crawled into my tent. Her eyes were very large and dark-ringed. She looked exhausted. 'Duncan. Will you come, please. I think he's gone.'

I followed her to Larvik's tent. There was no sun that morning. A grey wrack of cloud had drifted up and the wind was rising out of the sou'west. It was gloomy in the tent and I could hardly see Larvik's bearded face. His body was cold and when I became accustomed to the gloom I saw that his eyes were glazed. I pulled a blanket over him.

Outside the tent I saw that many of the men had come out of their tents. They were watching us furtively and there was an air of tension over the camp. It was as though they had sensed death. 'How shall we bury him?' Judie asked.

'Leave him where he is,' I said.

'But we must have a service for him.'

'No,' I answered harshly. She started to argue and I said, 'Look at the men. They're scared enough as it is without knowing that Larvik is dead.'

She turned and looked round the camp. I could see there were tears in her eyes. 'For God's sake don't cry,' I said sharply. 'They mustn't know. Do you understand?'

I saw her bite her lip. Then she looked at me and nodded. 'Yes. I understand. I think he will understand, too.'

I turned away then and shouted for the stewards to get a meal ready.

That meal was the best they could devise. But the men were silent and tense as they ate in their tents. And when it was finished they were out again in the open, staring at the crumbling ice.

It is frightful to think that you have had your last meal. The advance of the berg was as inevitable as the hangman's rope after the final breakfast. There was nothing I could give the men to do. They stood around in little groups staring at the berg, and occasionally their eyes wandered to Larvik's tent where the

Norwegian flag still flew.

The prow of the iceberg was not three hundred yards from us now. And behind the prow the ice towered up and up in sheer crags of blue and green, cold and still, until it lost itself in the clouds. Losing its top like that in the clouds made it far more terrifying. It added to its stature.

The noise of the shattering ice was so loud that we had to shout if we wanted to make ourselves heard. The floe-berg was quivering. It was like being on a ship battered by giant seas. We could actually see the ice shaking. The boats rocked and the packing cases tied together rolled over. Our floe was like an island in the midst of chaos. All round us the ice was breaking up now. We were right in the thick of what we had been watching for so long. And in a little while I should be down in that maelstrom, fighting to get a rope across to the ledge. I felt fear gripping at me.

The moment of panic came when a floe between us and the berg split across with an earsplitting crackle. The half nearest us reared up, turning slowly on to its back. For a moment it seemed poised above us, forty or fifty feet high. Then it came crashing down. Its edge splintered on the forward ledge of our refuge. A piece of ice as large as a barn door knocked one of the *Hval 5* men flying. A great chunk was torn off our floe-berg. For a moment the sea boiled black. Then the gap closed, the floes rushing together, grinding and tearing at each other in their effort to get relief from the frightful pressure. It was a stampede of ice.

No one moved for a moment. We were stunned by the terrible power of the forces at work. Then Hans suddenly screamed. It was a high-pitched, rabbit scream. The boy turned like a hunted hare and began to run. The men watched him for a second, immobile, fascinated. Then one of them also began to run, and in a second half the crews were following the boy.

I started forward to stop them, but Vaksdal was before me. He caught the first man and knocked him cold with one blow of his huge fist. And he got Hans – scooped the boy up with one hand and turned to face the break. The men stopped. They were breathing heavily. They stood watching him for a moment like cattle that have been headed. Then they turned and shuffled shame-facedly back towards the camp.

I met them as they came back. I realized that it was now or never. If I waited any longer their morale would be too low to make the effort. I couldn't talk to them because of the noise of the splintering ice. But I gathered them all round me and knelt down on the ice. They knelt down, all of them, and every man as he knelt turned so that he faced the advance of the berg. And as we knelt there I felt that comforting sense of oneness develop in us – oneness of purpose in adversity. I stared at the two-hundred-yard gap of jagged, surging ice that I'd have to cross, and then I looked at Judie. Her eyes met mine and smiled. And I felt sure of myself again. I could face it, whatever it was to be.

I got up from the ice and called out to the men that the moment for action had come, that now we were going to attack the berg itself. Judie was close beside me and I heard her say, 'Who makes the first attempt?'

'Vaksdal and I,' I answered.

I looked at her quickly. She nodded as though she had braced herself for that. I shouted to Kalstad and he brought the ropes. I don't know whether Bland knelt in prayer with the rest. I don't remember seeing him. But he was there with the crews as they pressed round me. I remember his eyes were feverishly bright, a brightness that seemed a queer mixture of fear and excitement.

The ropes were coiled down on the ice at the side of the camp nearest the berg. I took the two ends and shouted for Vaksdal. He came forward sullenly. I handed him the end of one of the ropes. He hesitated. His eyes were angry. For a moment I thought he was going to refuse. 'Because of the boats,' I shouted at him. I don't know whether it was because he recognized the justice of my choice or because he was afraid of being regarded as a coward, but he took the rope and began to tie it round his body. I took the other rope and we went to the edge of the floe where the ice dropped in a steep slide to the quivering pack. Judie came up to me and kissed me. Then she took the rope and began to tie it round my body.

But as she started to tie it, there was a sudden surge in the crowd and she was swept aside. The rope was whipped away from me and Erik Bland slipped over the edge on to the pack ice below. He held the rope in his hand and I can see him now as he looked up at me with a sort of crazy grin, tying the rope round his waist and calling to Vaksdal to come. I seized hold of the rope to haul him back. Whatever relief I automatically might feel was swallowed in my instant realization of the danger of such an indisciplined action. But as I reached for the rope, Howe gripped my arm. 'Let him go!' he shouted. 'Let him go, I tell you!' The scream of his voice was loud in a sudden, unnerving silence. As I hesitated, I saw relief and satisfaction in his eyes. He was convinced that whoever tried to make the crossing would die.

In that instant of hesitation I lost my one chance of stopping

Bland, for as I reached for the rope again I saw it uncoiling steadily. Down on the ice Vaksdal and Bland were going forward together. And then I saw that Bland was wearing crampons. Where he'd got them from I don't know. But the fact that he was wearing them made it clear that his action wasn't done on the spur of the moment. This was what he'd planned to do. I looked round at the men. They were watching him intently and in some of their eyes I caught a glint of admiration. McPhee and Kalstad were paying out line. Bonomi was moving excitedly from one position to another taking photographs.

Down on the pack the two men were moving into the broken ice. Trailing the slender lines, they climbed out on to the edge of a floe that was slowly being tilted. They dropped from view. The floe rose almost vertical, hiding them. Then it broke across and subsided into the ice, showing us Vaksdal leaping in great bounds from one precarious foothold to another. Bland was lying flat, clinging to the edge of a floe which was slowly being ground to powder. I thought for a moment he was injured. But he pulled the rope into a coil beside him, gathered himself together and leapt for a block of ice no bigger than one of our boats. He was up and following Vaksdal now from one foothold to another.

They got to within twenty feet or so of the ledge and there they paused, facing a gap full of powdered ice in which the sea sometimes showed. Vaksdal coiled his rope and leapt. For a moment I thought he'd made it. But the ice received his weight like a bog. In an instant he was up to his knees. Then he was floundering full length, with only the upper half of his body visible. He was within two yards of the ledge, but it might have been two miles for all the chance he had of reaching it. He was rolled over in the grey stream. His mouth was a dark gap in the blond of his beard as he cried out something or screamed with pain. We could hear nothing but the splitting and grinding of the ice.

Bland hesitated, staring at Vaksdal and coiling his rope. Then he backed away and started to run. Judie's fingers dug into my arm. Whatever she might think of him now, Erik Bland was after all a part of her life. Instead of jumping, he flung himself full length in a beautiful flying tackle. His impetus carried him half across the gap, his body sliding on the surface of the ice. Then he was clawing forward, his arms working like a swimmer doing the crawl. His body didn't sink, and foot by foot his arms dragged him across.

Then at last he was standing on the ledge itself and was hauling Vaksdal up after him. The men cheered wildly as the two men stood together on the ledge. They were symbols of renewed hope. They represented Life. Bland looked across at the cheering men. My eyes, weakened by the constant glare of the past few days, couldn't make out the expression of his face. But it looked as though he were grinning. Well, he'd a right to grin. And the men were right to cheer. He'd done a pretty brave thing. But Howe was screaming in my ear, 'He's laughing at us. He's on his own now. That's what he wanted.'

I brushed him aside, shouting to Dahle, first mate of *Hval 5*, whom I'd put in charge of loading, to get tools and anchors across. The men tied them to the rope and as they were hauled across the two-hundred-yard gap Howe was pulling at my sleeve and yelling, 'He'll abandon us, I tell you.'

'Don't be a fool,' I snapped. 'He can't do anything without boats and stores.'

'Well, get across yourself with the first batch of men.'

I shook my head angrily. The loading plan was all arranged – one boat, stores, then a dozen men. The process to be repeated until boats, stores and men had all been transported to the ledge. And now that Bland had done the job of getting the ropes across, as leader I was bound to be the last man to leave the camp.

Vaksdal and Bland were working like mad to fix the anchors firmly. As soon as this was done and the rope set up, the first boat was run across. Owing to the movement of the berg towards us, the rope sagged and we had to have men constantly swigging on it. About the middle the boat was bumping dangerously on the ice, and just before it reached the ledge one of the two anchors broke out. Fortunately the other anchor held and the boat was got safely to the ledge. But this and the constant slackening of the rope made me realize that more men were required on the ledge at once and that it was there that the major difficulties would be experienced. As the slings were hauled back I gave the order for the first batch of men to go, instead of stores, which were next on the loading table.

Gerda came across to me as the men were getting into the slings. 'I think you should be there, Duncan,' she shouted. 'It is important nothing go wrong at that end.'

I didn't like the idea of being one of the first across, but I had already reached the conclusion that I should be there. I ordered Dahle to assume command of the rear party and took the place of one of the men in the slings. We also hitched on the two remaining anchors.

It was a strange experience crossing that surging gap of ice supported only by a single sagging rope. The lines, as I have said, could not be kept sufficiently taut, and when we reached the centre the sag was so great that our feet were dancing on the moving surface of the ice. This would have been all right except that a floe split open as we were crossing it and rose on end so that for a moment it completely overtopped us and looked as though it would carry away the ropes and ourselves with it. However, it slid back under the ice and we made the ledge with nothing worse than sore buttocks where the rope slings had cut into our flesh.

With the extra personnel and anchors, we soon had both lines set up securely and began to ferry the stores across. I had arranged the order of transhipment very carefully, so that should the ice split the party at any time, each section would have its proper complement of boats and stores.

It was whilst we were hauling the second boat across that the movement of the old camp on the floe in relation to the iceberg first became really noticeable. We were using both ropes for the boats now, for greater safety. As we started to haul across, these ropes, instead of sagging, seemed to get tauter, till they were stretched like slender threads. We brought the boat over with a rush and slackened off. We were only just in time. Another minute and the lines would have carried away. What had happened was that the floe-berg had been caught in a sort of eddying out-thrust of ice and was moving steadily outwards, away from the berg.

With the arrival of the next party, I hacked a bollard out of a block of ice nearby and had the ends of the rope run through blocks and round this ice-bollard with men tagging on the ends. It meant a delay, but I was glad I had done it, for when we resumed operations it became clear at once that the floe-berg was beginning to show considerable movement. It was now no longer on the starboard bow of the iceberg, so to speak. It was abeam of the ledge and beginning to feel the bow-wave effect of the ice being thrown about by the berg's advance. One moment the men on the ropes would be right close to the bollard; the next they would be hauling back up the slope of the ledge. Then again, they'd be coming down and letting out rope. They acted like the accumulators in a catcher, moving back and forth along the slope according to the strain on the lines.

At length we were hauling in the last boat. As it came in to the ledge the men on the ropes came down with a run, paying out line as fast as they could let it through their hands. We swung the boat down on to the ledge. Somebody shouted to me. A rope-end went trailing over the edge. I glanced quickly across at the huddle of dark figures in the ice. They were standing, staring towards us, quite motionless. All the stores had been cleared. There was just the rearguard – Dahle and five of the *Hval 5* crew. The floe on which they stood was being whirled away from us, caught in a gigantic surge of the ice. We flung our weight on the last remaining rope. But it was no good. It was dragged from our hands by forces that were far beyond our puny strength. The end of it trailed over on to the ice and we could do nothing but stand and watch that little group of figures alone in a heaving chaos.

I put my arm round Judie's shoulders. She was standing very tense, her face quite white and her whole body trembling. Her lips moved in agitated prayer. The floe-berg on which Dahle and his companions were marooned was turning slowly round and round, as though it were at the very centre of a revolving whirlpool in the ice. Then it seemed to rise up, caught between opposing forces. A moment later it split. The noise was like a battery of heavies firing and was clearly audible above the thunder of sound all round us. One or two of the men abandoned their shattered ice island and began floundering towards us across the churning ice. But their starting point in relation to the iceberg was very different to what it had been when Bland and Vaksdal had made the crossing. They were right in the broken ice now. They hadn't a chance.

Through my glasses I could see only three men standing near where our camp had been. One was Dahle. The remains of the floe-berg, now a block no bigger than a large house, began to roll. The three men scrambled and clawed their way across the ice, fighting to keep on the uppermost side.

It was horrible, standing there watching them go like that, especially as I should have been one of them. The *Hval 5* men had volunteered to be in the rear party. But I felt very upset, all the same. Judie must have understood my mood, for her hand gripped my arm as I stood staring out across the ice. 'It's not your fault,' she said.

'If we'd been quicker,' I answered. 'If we'd started on the job a few minutes earlier.' Three or four minutes more would have seen those six men with us on the ledge. I turned away angrily. No good brooding over it. There was work to be done and I set about the task of organizing the new camp.

I detailed a dozen men to cut a way through the jagged ice of the ledge and drag the boats up as far as possible. Then I turned to get the stores secured and the tents pitched. And as I turned Bland came towards me. I hadn't really noticed him since reaching the ledge. There had been too much to do. But now, as he approached me, he seemed to have an air of truculence, and there was something about his eyes – a queer sort of confidence, something like a sneer. He was somehow different. He'd lost the dazed look. He came right over to me and stopped in front of me. 'I want a word with you, Craig,' he said. There was a sudden authority in his tone that stopped me in my tracks. He had spoken loudly and I saw several of the men stop work to watch us.

'Well?' I asked.

'In future you'll keep away from my wife,' he said.

'That's for her to decide,' I answered, trying to keep the anger I felt out of my voice.

'It's an order,' he said.

I stared at him. 'The hell it is,' I said. 'Get to work on the boats, Bland.'

He shook his head, grinning. I saw the fever of excitement in his eyes. 'You don't give orders here.' And then in a moment of quiet he said, 'Mister Craig. Please understand that, now that Larvik is dead, I am in command.' He swung round on the men, who were all watching us now. 'In the absence of my father I shall, of course, take command here as his deputy. As commander I brought the ropes across. Craig, as second-in-command, should have remained with the rear party as I instructed, but – ' He shrugged his shoulders. 'As a newcomer to the company,' he said to me, 'you will realize that you are too inexperienced to have any sort of command in a situation like this.' He turned abruptly and strode towards the men. There was almost a swagger in the way he walked.

I just stood there for a moment without moving. I was too amazed by the absurdity of the thing to make a move. I remember thinking: *Howe was right. He's got back his confidence. Nordahl's death, the ramming – he's forgotten it all.* And I cursed myself for not realizing he was dangerous.

He began shouting orders at the men. I saw the amazement I felt written on their faces. But they were overawed by the terror of their surroundings. They would follow any leader, so long as he led. I started forward, and as I came up to Bland I heard him announce the reinstatement of Vaksdal and Keller as mates. He gave an order. The men hesitated. Their eyes shifted to me. Bland turned. The sneer was gone now. But the truculence was still there. I ordered him to pick up one of the packing cases. His eyes shifted quickly from me to the men. Another instant and he'd believe what he wanted to believe – that he was not responsible for the predicament we were in. That mad scramble across the ice had almost wiped any sense of guilt from his mind. And as he didn't move when I repeated the order, I knew there was only one thing to do. 'McPhee. Kalstad.' The two *Hval 4* men moved forward. 'Arrest that man,' I ordered. And then, turning quickly to Bland, I said, 'Erik Bland, you are charged with the murder of Bernt Nordahl and also with the deliberate ramming of *Hval 4*, an action which caused the immediate death of two men and which may be responsible for all our deaths. You will be held and committed for trial when and if we ever reach civilization.'

I was watching his eyes all the time as I spoke. For a moment they had a wild, almost hunted look. Then he laughed. 'You can't get away with this, Craig,' he shouted. 'First you try to steal my wife, now you try to get control of the company through her.'

I called to two or three of the *Hval 4* men and with Kalstad and McPhee moved in to get him. I knew just what he was capable of now and I was taking no more chances. I wanted him secured. He watched us approach and I thought for a moment he was going to fight. His face was very white under his brown beard and his eyes shifted uneasily from side to side.

Then suddenly he turned and slithered down the ice of the ledge. A man-hunt wasn't going to be good for morale, but I was determined to get him. I sent Kalstad and the rest after him. He had stopped at one of the packing cases that had apparently been burst open with a pick. I thought we'd mastered him without the sordid business of a fight. I had turned back to speak with the men, when Howe gave a shout of warning. As I swung round, Bland was lifting a rifle out of the broken packing case.

Kalstad started to run towards him. Then he and the men behind him checked suddenly. Bland had the gun cocked and levelled straight at them. He was laughing at them. A shot rang out close behind me. I turned to find Vaksdal struggling with Howe. Vaksdal had hold of his arm, and as he twisted it back the gloved fingers released the weapon. It fell to the ice. For a moment there was a glint of nickel-plating slithering down the ramp, then it disappeared over the edge.

Bland was coming up the ledge now, and he was driving the *Hval 4* men back at the point of his gun. He was immensely pleased with himself. You could see it by the gleam in his eyes and the way he walked. He bunched all the survivors together. None of us hesitated to obey. His eyes were narrowed and cold, and his manner and the way he held the rifle made it clear that he would not hesitate to use it.

He called Vaksdal and Keller over to him. They hesitated uncertainly. Bland as the son of the chairman of the company was one thing. Bland with a gun another. But they went down to him all the same. Then he called on the rest of the men to join him. He spoke in Norwegian. They looked at me and then began muttering amongst themselves. 'He tell them it is safe to have only one leader,' Gerda translated for me. 'That he is in command and that it is mutiny if they do not obey him.'

The thing had got to be stopped at once. I called out to the men. And then Judie's hands were tugging at my arm. Bland was yelling at me to shut up. He had the gun to his shoulder and was aiming straight at me. 'Keep quiet, Duncan,' Judie pleaded. 'He will shoot. There is plenty of time.'

Howe, just behind me, said, 'We've got to get his gun.'

As we hesitated, one or two of the men moved down the slope of the ledge towards Bland. In an instant they would all go. They needed a leader. Bland had a gun and the will to use it. It seems incredible now. But out there on that ledge in that chaotic wilderness of ice it didn't seem so incredible. The law of the wild holds good when it comes to pitting your puny strength against the violence of nature. If we could stop the men, isolate Bland and his two mates, then the sheer threat of our numbers would wear him down. I started forward. If I got killed – well, it was just too bad. In the moment of horror the men might rush him then.

But just as I moved out to stop what had begun to look like a general movement towards Bland, Gerda rushed past me. She stopped, facing the men with her back to Bland. Her small, bulky figure blocked their way down the ledge and she poured a flood of Norwegian at them, her eyes bright, her face flushed. The men stopped. I heard Nordahl's name and *Hval 4* mentioned repeatedly. She was telling them the truth now and the men growled angrily.

I glanced at Bland. He had lowered the gun. He was sane enough to realize that if he shot her the men would kill him. But he was coming up the slope, his face white and convulsed with rage. I called to Gerda to look out. But she kept on speaking. Bland struck her from behind, stunning her with one blow of his hand across the nape of her neck. Howe gave an inarticulate cry and ran forward. Judie clutched at him, but too late. He flung himself shrieking on Bland, who met him with a jab of the rifle barrel to his stomach. And as Howe folded up, he brought his knee up sharply so that his head jerked back. Bland caught him as he slipped to the ice. I heard him shout something about wanting to do it for a long time, and he smashed his fist into the wretched man's face. Howe's face looked dazed and a gush of blood shone very crimson against the white of the snow. His knees gave and suddenly he was a crumpled bundle of clothing lying on the ice. Bland kicked at him viciously, his gun ready, waiting for the first man to break and rush at him. He was grinning all the time.

I felt Judie stiffen beside me. This was the real Bland. This was the Bland she knew – the man who admired the Nazis and their methods. And seeing him kicking at Howe's senseless body, I knew that none of us would get out of the ice alive; not unless we killed Bland first. God! How I wished I'd never gone back to the *Tauer III* camp for the boats.

For a moment he was lost to everything but the pleasure of taking it out of Howe. We might have rushed him then. But I think we were all too astonished at the sudden display of violence. And by the time we had started to move in on him, the moment was gone. He checked us with the gun. And then he began talking to the men. And as he talked to them I realized how he had been able to pull the wool over Eide's eyes. It was impossible to believe that a moment before he'd been kicking a senseless man. With the gun in his hand and the memory of that dash across the ice to the ledge, he had complete confidence in himself. His manner was a queer mixture of the arrogance of the leader and the almost boyish excitement of the adventurer.

'He's trying to persuade the men to desert us,' Judie said.

I'd already realized that. 'You must do something,' she added. 'They may follow him if we don't do something to stop them.'

But it was no good my talking to them. The weakness of my position was that I was an outsider. And though I didn't understand what Bland was saying, I knew from the contemptuous way in which he mentioned my name that he was using that fact to sway the men. 'You talk to them,' I said. 'They're all of them Tönsberg men. Talk to them about your father.'

She stared at me in surprise. And then very reluctantly, as she saw I wouldn't move, she stepped forward. Her face was very white. It was hard for her. The man was her husband and she had to tell the men that he'd murdered her father. She began to speak, her voice clear even above the growl and thunder of the ice. For a moment she and Bland were talking at the same time. Then the attention of the men became riveted on her. Bland hesitated and then stopped speaking. The boyish arrogance gradually slipped from his manner. His eyes shifted uneasily from the men to Judie and back again to the men. His grip on his gun tightened as an angry murmur rose from them.

Then suddenly he shouted an order. His voice was crisp and hard. He was calling on the men to follow him. They talked uncertainly among themselves for a moment. Then they were silent. He called to them again. But no one moved. 'All right,' he shouted at them in English. 'Have it your own way then. Stay with Craig and see where it lands you.' He turned to me. 'They're your responsibility now, Craig.' He drew a line with the heel of his boot across the ice of the ledge. 'You'll camp above this line. Any mutineer that crosses this line will be shot. Understand? You'll be issued with tents and stores. Once a day, at midday, you'll send two men to collect rations. Bonomi.'

The little Italian started. '*Si, signore*.'

'Can you cook?'

'A leetle. But I am not – '

'You'll cook for the officers then. Go down and report to Vaksdal. The rest of you get back up the ledge. Go on. Get moving.' He made a threatening gesture with the gun. '*Go an. Go an*.' I could almost hear the Nazi *Raus! Raus!* echoing the violence of his voice.

'What about the boats?' I asked.

Bland looked at me. He was breathing heavily and his eyes were bright. He no longer looked in the least boyish. He had the mean look of something that's been cornered. 'The boats will remain with me. I'll look after them for you.' He turned to Judie then and said, 'You'd better stay with your boy-friend.'

Judie turned without answering him. He watched her and there was a strange look in his eyes. It wasn't remorse. I think perhaps it was regret – a sudden sense of sadness for what might have been. Gerda had recovered consciousness and was staggering to her feet. I got two of the men and we picked Howe up. He was just beginning to come round. His upper lip was swollen and pulpy and his right arm was bruised, otherwise he seemed all right. The rest of the crews had already moved up the slope of the ice ledge. We followed.

Bland took no chances with the men. He got right on with the issuing of tents and stores. I imagine he picked the best of everything for himself and his companions, but there was still plenty for us. I set the men to levelling platforms for the tents and cutting into the ice wall at the back of the ledge to provide extra shelter, for when it began to blow again it would be terribly exposed up there on that ledge.

As the day wore on, Judie's attitude began to worry me. Only once did she speak to me and then it was to upbraid me for not doing something about Bland when he'd faced us with his gun. When I tried to explain to her that there was nothing I could have done, she turned away angrily. Her face was pale and tense. She seemed bitter and resentful. It was almost as though she were blaming me for what had happened.

She and Gerda were given a tent to themselves. As soon as it was erected, Judie crawled into it. And that was the last I saw of her that day. Once when I passed I heard the sound of sobbing. I hesitated, wondering whether to go in and try to comfort her. But someone called to me and I passed on. Setting up camp on that ledge was a job that occupied all my attention. I had no time to worry about her.

That night, after the evening meal, as I lay in my tent talking to Howe and McPhee and Kalstad who shared it, Gerda crawled in. 'What are you going to do, Duncan?' she asked.

'Nothing,' I said.

'But you must do something.'

'Not yet,' I answered. She was sitting close to Howe and I saw her hand was holding his. It made me think of Judie. I asked Gerda whether she were all right.

'*Ja.* I think so. But she is not very happy.' She peered at me uncertainly in the half light. 'It is not very nice her position, I think. Also she feel you must do something. You make her speak to the men. She have to bare her soul in front of them all, so that they will follow you and not Bland. Now she think you must – ' She stopped uncertainly.

'Must what?' I asked.

'Please do not be offended, Duncan. It is so difficult, not in my own language. But she feel – that you must justify the men's faith, that you must take control. It – it is not that she do not believe in you. I am sure of that. But – you must try to understand. It is terrible for her, this position.'

'What does she expect me to do?' I asked harshly. I was very tired.

'I do not know. She is not clear in her mind, I think. You see it is all a terrible muddle for her. Bland is her husband. She know he murder her father. She is in love with you, and Bland, whom you save from dying alone, now controls everything.'

'Gerda's right,' Howe said, his words blurred through his thickened lips. 'They're both right. We've got to do something.'

That was what he had been saying before she came in. 'Yes, but what?' I demanded irritably. 'We've no weapons. Altogether Bland has three rifles and about a thousand rounds of ammunition. Also, he's not afraid to use them. There's no period of darkness in which we can surprise him. As for the men, they're well fed and for the first time for days they feel secure. When supplies get short and they get desperate, then maybe we can rush Bland.'

'Perhaps it is too late then,' Gerda said. 'This berg may break out of the pack in the next storm. Then Bland will get away in one of the boats and stove in the rest. His one chance is to be the sole survivor.' It was almost as though Howe were speaking through her, but he remained huddled in his blankets, sucking at his swollen lips.

'We'll just have to wait,' I answered stubbornly. 'Don't worry. Time and the ice will wear him down. Anyway, I'm not risking anyone's life, my own included, in some premature attempt to regain control of the stores. I suggest you all get some sleep now.' And I rolled over in my blankets. Gerda stayed talking to Howe for some time. Then she left and there was silence in the tent, a silence that was dominated all the time by the grinding and crashing of the berg's advance through the pack, a violent pandemonium of sound that was paralleled by a constant quivering of the berg itself, a quivering that was felt through the whole body as one lay on the ice floor of the ledge. And then Howe produced an iron stanchion and with a file began working away at the tip of it. The rasp of the file and grinding of the ice seemed to tear at my nerves as I fell asleep.

I won't attempt to give a day-to-day account of our sojourn on the iceberg. One day was very much like another, varying only in the intensity of cold and the strength and direction of the wind. For myself it was a period of loneliness and waiting. Technically I was in command. But it was not an easy command. The men of *Hval 4* were all right. I held them through Gerda. But with the others it was different. Even to the *Tauer III* men, whom I had commanded on the run out from Cape Town, I was an outsider. Only the fact that they were Tönsberg men and believed what Judie had told them about her father's death kept them with us. Tempering every decision was the fear that some of these men might break away and join Bland. This became increasingly a source of worry as Bland's ration issue became less and the monotony of our existence grew. Bland had the boats and the stores. They represented hope and a full belly. The men knew from Bonomi that in Bland's camp food and tobacco were plentiful. And once the men started to break away, it would become a stampede. Orders became little more than requests and all the time Judie kept to her tent and refused to speak to me.

I worried about Judie a lot. I worried about Howe, too. He took no interest in the work of the camp and made no effort to help. He hardly stirred from the tent. He was morose and silent, seemingly occupied with his own thoughts. And all the time he whittled away at the iron, working the end to a point with a double edge like a spear. The grating of the file seemed to rasp at my nerves till I could stand it no longer. 'For God's sake,' I snapped at him, 'stop it – do you hear?'

He stared at me sullenly and went on working at the tip of it. McPhee rolled over in his blankets, snatched the stanchion from him and flung it out of the tent. 'Noo, will ye let us get some sleep, ye crazy loon.'

Howe said nothing, but later that night I woke to the rasp of the file. I cursed him then, spending all my pent-up anger on him. He let me go on shouting at him and when I had finished he said quietly, 'What would you do if Bland had killed your father?' And then, as though he'd been bottling it all up inside him, he started to tell me about Nordahl, how he'd come to see him at Newcastle, how he'd bought him a boat when he was twenty-one, how he'd taken him out to Grytviken for a season. 'If I'd been his legitimate son he couldn't have done more for me. And then after the war he gave me this job. Do you think I don't know what I have to do? And I'd have done it, too. I'd have done it by now if it hadn't been for Vaksdal. I'd have shot him dead here on this ledge. But Vaksdal had to interfere, damn his bloody hide. Why did he have to stop me? Why didn't he let me do it then?' His voice had risen now. 'I had him. I'd only to pull the trigger. Bland would have been dead by now if it hadn't been for Vaksdal. Vaksdal deserves to die. If I can't kill Bland without Vaksdal, then I'll – '

There was a muttered curse and McPhee sat up. 'Will ye shut up, for Christ's sake.'

'I tell you, I'll kill them both if I have to. I'll kill them all if they – '

'Shut up, do ye hear!'

But Howe's voice went on and on, talking about killing, eternally talking about killing. I fell asleep to the drone of his voice and woke in the morning to the rasp of the file. It was enough to drive a man crazy.

I told Gerda what he was up to, but whenever she came into

the tent he hid the stanchion under his blankets. When she asked about it, his face puckered up like a kid about to cry. He hadn't wanted her to know. I saw that at once, saw the struggle going on inside him between his love of her and the need to justify his existence by avenging the one man he'd loved. He wasn't really sane. Every flicker of emotion was mirrored instantly in his features. And when Gerda took the wretched thing away from him, he behaved like a kid whose favourite toy has been confiscated. He had it back by evening and was filing at it with desperate energy, till the rasp of it drove us nearly crazy and McPhee tore the iron out of his hands and flung it out over the ledge on to the ice below. Howe burst into tears then. But by next day he was at work on another stanchion. By then we were too tired to care and the rasp of the file seemed to merge with the grinding of the ice as we fell asleep in a coma of exhaustion.

It was on the 17th February that we established ourselves on the iceberg. A period of fairly good weather followed and to keep the men constructively occupied and to give them some constant glimmer of hope, however slight, I set them to work cutting steps in the side of the berg.

We maintained a constant watch, and each day this lookout was posted higher and higher as we laboriously cut our way upwards, until at last our lookout post was on the flat top of the berg. This was at about 120 feet above the pack. We did not attempt to climb the pinnacle which rose another fifty feet. It would have been of little use to us had we done so, for we experienced almost constant low cloud and more often than not the pinnacle was lost in a swirling mist.

On 23 February shortly before midday I was dragged from my tent by an excited lookout. 'There is smoke, *hr. Kaptein*,' he said.

'Where?' I asked.

'*Vestover*,' was his reply.

I climbed the hundred and forty-seven steps to the lookout and there, just to the south of west, was a great column of smoke. It could have been frost-smoke. But the sea was freezing over now wherever it was exposed to the atmosphere for any length of time, and all day the column of smoke continued to rise from the same spot. And that night, when the sun dipped just below the horizon, we could see a red glow under the smoke. The whole camp was in an uproar of excitement. The sudden thought of rescue was in everyone's mind. It was a hard thing for me to have to tell them that the only thing it could possibly be was the crew of the *Southern Cross* igniting the oil they had pumped out of the ship as a

guiding beacon to the rescue ships. But even that didn't damp
their spirits. If the survivors of the *Southern Cross* had decided to
make a signal, then it must surely mean that there were rescue
ships in the vicinity.

For two days everyone was cheerful and the talk was all of
rescue. Then the gale hit us. It came up out of the south-west and
flung itself on us with a banshee howl that drowned the constant
thunder of the breaking ice, seeming to pin us by its very weight to
the ice walls of the berg.

When the storm broke, our ledge was facing straight into it.
Our situation would have been bad enough down on the ice. But
up there, on an exposed ledge, we got the full force of the wind.
And with the wind came sleet and snow. It was terrifying – the
bitter cold and the constant noise, the inability to breathe outside
our tents and the lack of hot food. It sapped our strength and
damped our spirits.

No one spoke of rescue any more. In fact we hardly spoke at all.
We were glued to the face of the berg, by the weight of the wind,
like flies on a flypaper, and the snow piled up round us and
froze, so that there was no longer a ledge. Drawing rations from
Bland each day became a major expedition.

We lost a man during this storm. He went out with two others
and never returned. They were *Tauer III* men, all of them, and
though I questioned them later, I never really got to the bottom
of it. They admitted to going down to the lower camp to scrounge
extra rations from Bland, but they wouldn't say any more. I think
what really happened was that they went down there with the
intention of deserting our camp for Bland's only to find that
Bland didn't want them. That one of them disappeared over the
edge was, I believe, an accident. It was easy enough to slip over in
those conditions and whenever a party went down to draw rations
I insisted on them being roped. At any rate, the two who came
back suddenly became violently anti-Bland and infected their
whole tent.

For six days we lay in a coma of cold and hunger, hardly daring
to go out, the tents overcrowded, insanitary and wholly covered
by a mixture of snow and ice. On the sixth day all was suddenly
quiet. The wind had gone. And on that day the men, led by the
two survivors of that trip to the lower camp, complained to me
about the amount of rations Bland had issued. They were getting
desperate. Bonomi had told them that food was still plentiful in
the lower camp. I said I'd go down and talk to Bland himself.

Howe dragged me aside then. 'This is what we've been waiting for,' he said.

But I knew what that would mean. 'If we led them amok like that,' I said, 'they'd pillage the stores. Three men eating well doesn't make much of a hole in rations being doled out for over forty.'

'It's the chance we've been waiting for,' he insisted. His eyes were sunk deep in their sockets and feverishly bright.

'No,' I said.

I went down the ledge before he could argue further. Bonomi was standing by the barricade of frozen snow that marked the boundary between the two camps. I called to him. 'I want to speak to Bland,' I said.

He put his finger to his lips. 'I wish to speak with you.'

'Well, what is it?' I asked. I didn't want to talk to him. I felt he was a toady and he looked sleek and well fed by comparison with the wraith-like figures who had crowded round me a moment ago demanding more food.

'I wish you to know that Bland is becoming frightened,' he said. 'All the time I am telling him how the men are getting desperate and how they believe he killed Nordahl and rammed your ship. At first he would tell me to shut up. Once he strike me in anger. Now he sits morose and uneasy and all the time I am telling him how desperate the men are become. I do not think he sleep well any more.'

'Is this true, Bonomi?' I demanded.

'*Madonna mia!* Do I trouble to tell it to you if it is not true? I tell you, he is becoming desperate. He is hoping all the time that the iceberg break out of the pack. The storm makes him hopeful. But now he no longer have any hope of that. I think he abandon the camp soon. There is only twenty-five more days of food left and he does not dare to reduce the rations any more.'

'Go and tell him I want a word with him,' I ordered.

He hesistated, looking a little crestfallen. I think he had expected me to congratulate him on his Machiavellian campaign.

Perhaps I should have, for when Bland came up the slope towards me I saw his confidence was broken. He looked well fed, but his eyes were sunk in their sockets and his body seemed slack. His gaze did not easily meet mine. 'Well?' he said, with an attempt at self-assurance.

'The men are complaining about the rations,' I said.

'Let them complain,' he said.

'There's no rationing, I believe, down in your camp,' I accused him angrily.

'Why should there be?' he answered. 'They made the choice.'

'They're getting desperate,' I told him. 'If you're not careful they'll rush the stores. You know what that means, don't you, Bland?'

He passed his tongue quickly over his chapped lips. 'I'll shoot anyone who attempts to rush us. Tell them that, Craig. And tell them also that it's not my fault we're short of food.'

'They'll believe that when they know that you're on the same scale of rations as they are,' I answered. 'How many days' supply is left? Bonomi says only twenty-five.'

'Damn that little bastard,' he muttered. 'He talks too much.'

'Is that correct, Bland?'

'Yes. They'll get the present scale of rations for twenty-five more days. That's all. Tell them that.'

I made a quick mental calculation of the quantity of food four men, unrationed, would consume in that period. 'I want thirty days' rations for my men, three boats together with our full share of stores and navigating equipment by nightfall,' I said.

He stared at me and I saw he was scared at my tone. 'If you're not careful, Craig, I'll cut off rations completely.'

'If what I've asked for isn't ready at this barrier by 18.00 hours tonight, I won't answer for the consequences. That's an ultimatum,' I added, and left him to think over what I'd said. If Bonomi had told the truth, and it certainly looked like it from Bland's manner, then he'd do as I'd demanded.

I told the men what I'd done. For the first time in days I saw them grinning. 'But it doesn't mean the end of rationing,' I warned them. 'It just means that we shall control our own rationing.'

The men gathered in hungry groups at the snow barrier. I saw Bland watching them uneasily. Just after midday the men cheered. Down in the lower camp Bland's two mates and Bonomi had started humping stores. Bland himself kept guard with his rifle. We broke down the snow barrier and boats and stores were run into the upper camp. I put McPhee in charge of stores and Gerda in charge of food. Without Gerda, I think the men would have broken into the food in one glorious orgy. We were all desperately hungry.

The end of the month came and went with only the entries in my log to mark the passage of time. There was a period of darkness at night now, and each day this period lengthened with amazing rapidity. But though the weather was calmer, in ten days I only managed to shoot the sun once. My calculations gave me a position of 63.31 S. 31.06 W., just about 230 miles nor'nor'east of the position at which we had abandoned *Hval 4*. It gives some idea of the rate of drift.

All this time Howe had been working away at his stanchion, working secretly for fear that McPhee would send it flying over the edge after the other one. Every time either of us or Gerda came into the tent he hid it from us and lay there, feeling it with his hand, watching us with a guilty smile on his face.

Apart from this and our general situation, Judie was a source of worry. Her attitude was an additional weight on my mind, so that I found it very hard to shake off the increasing periods of depression. She hadn't spoken to me since the day we had reached the ledge. She seemed to have withdrawn into herself, into a state of more or less blank misery. Gerda told me that she sometimes woke up in the night to find her crying and murmuring her father's name.

'You must do something,' Gerda said to me one day. 'If you do not, I think she will just fade away.' That was on 8 March. I went to Judie's tent and tried to speak to her. She looked very pale and thin and her eyes were huge in their sunken sockets. She stared at me without a word as though she didn't recognize me. I told Gerda to feed her some of the precious meat extract that had been included amongst the rations Bland had handed over to us. I left the tent in a mood of utter despair.

That was the day the aircraft flew over us. It was an American plane, the star markings plainly visible as it passed over at about 500 feet. We had nothing to signal with, and half blanketed in snow on the sheer flank of the iceberg it was hardly surprising that they did not see us. We piled inflammable stores together and kept constant watch in a fever of excitement and renewed hope. Two days later we saw another plane, away to the south. I picked it up in the glasses, but it was too far for our smoke to be visible and I would not give the order to ignite our precious reserves of fuel.

Sleet and snow followed and we never saw another glimpse of the search planes. The monotony of hunger, cold, and dying hope settled on the camp.

Once in the middle of the night I was woken by one of the lookouts who told me Howe had passed him without a word making for the lower camp. We found him halfway down the ledge, standing there quite still, the spear-sharp stanchion gripped in his hand. He didn't move as I came up to him. He seemed lost in his own thoughts and in the cold light of the stars I saw the conflict inside him written on his face. He must have been standing there for some time, for he was so stiff with cold that he could hardly move. He let me take the weapon from him and as I led him back he was crying. He would have done no good anyway, for I saw a movement down in the lower camp and knew that a guard was posted. I called Gerda and left him with her.

There were no storms now. Just the everlasting glare of low cloud and the nights lengthening with the increasing cold. The steadily falling temperature was magnified by lack of food and our decreasing resistance. Life became a monotony of waiting for the end, without hope. The men no longer looked hungrily at the lower camp, for through Bonomi we knew that their ration scale was as low as ours. Daily I checked the stores and watched our meagre reserves of food dwindle. The lookout no longer searched the sky for planes, but peered at the ice through eyes inflamed by the constant glare, searching for some sign of life – seal or penguin, anything that would do for food. The movement of the berg through the ice gradually slowed. Everything was much quieter; the silence of death seemed to be settling over us. No pressure ridges sent their roaring battle challenge thundering over our precarious perch. All round us stretched a silent, lifeless waste. Our fuel was almost finished. Soon we should have nothing hot. Without any hot drinks, life would quickly desert us.

The 19 March carries the following entry in my log: *Reduced rations still further. Grieg dead. Broken rib probably pierced lung. Has been weakening for a long time. Slipped his body over the edge as though burying at sea, none of us having the strength to cut a grave in the snow, which is hard like ice. Very cold. Wind has dropped and iceberg now stationary in pack. No hope now of breaking out to open sea.*

I knew it was time for the last desperate effort I had been planning. Gerda apparently had the same thought. She came to my tent next morning. As she sat there in the dim light I was surprised to see how much weight she had lost. She was almost slim. Howe was with her, thin as a wraith under the bulk of his clothes, his ugliness lost in the aesthetic sunken appearance of his features. He reminded me somehow of a modern artist's impression of Christ on the cross.

'Duncan. It is time we do something,' Gerda said. 'We cannot just stay here, waiting for death.'

I nodded. 'I've been thinking the same thing,' I said.

'Anything is better than to die without effort. I think soon I go to join my father.' She paused and then said, 'It is quiet now.

We can go down on to the ice. The *Southern Cross* was per'aps fifteen, not more than twenty miles from us when she sink. Per'aps my father is alive. I do not know. But I must go and see.'

'You realize we've drifted nearly 250 miles from the place where the *Southern Cross* went down?'

'*Ja, ja.* But they also will have drifted. I think perhaps we do not find them. But I must try.'

'Don't forget we've been on this iceberg,' I said. 'We've been moving steadily through the pack for days. Suppose there are some survivors, they'll be a lot more than twenty miles away. You'd never make it. You're too weak.'

She shrugged her shoulders. 'I also think they will be a long way away. Also, we cannot be sure in what direction they now are. But I must go. Per'aps I am too weak, as you say. But it is the spirit that is important. My spirit is strong. I shall go to search for my father.'

There was no point in arguing. I could see she had made up her mind. 'And Howe?' I asked.

Her face betrayed no emotion. She knew it meant his death. He would die first and she would have to watch him die. But she never flinched. She just said, 'Walter comes with me.'

I could see they had been over this together. Their minds were made up. In their faces was a sort of glow of exaltation. I almost loved Howe's ugliness in that moment, for he wasn't ugly – he was beautiful. His spirit, purged of all bitterness and cynicism by Gerda's love, shone through his features and transformed them.

I lay back, not saying anything, but going over in my mind something that had been there for a long time. At length I sat up. I was looking at Howe, wondering how he'd take it, hating myself for having to do it. 'Walter,' I said, using his Christian name for the first time. 'You're not strong – physically. Whatever your strength of will, you know you will die before you reach the position where the *Southern Cross* survivors might be. You know that, don't you?'

His eyes clouded. The glow died out of him. He knew the drift of my words. He nodded slowly, and there was a queer resignation in his face. It was as though I'd killed his spirit. 'You think I should say goodbye to Gerda here?'

'Are you prepared to if it would give her a chance of reaching her father – and give us all just a chance of preserving life a little longer?'

'Yes,' he said, his voice scarcely audible.

I got up then and crawled out of the tent, Gerda clutching

frantically at me, pleading to know what I intended to do. I think she was a little scared at the thought of making the journey without Howe. He was now the source of her strength. I said, 'Wait,' and called the men together, those that could still crawl out of the tents. The air was cold and still as they assembled round me.

'You know there is food for only a few days more?' I said.

They nodded.

'I checked the stores this morning,' I went on. 'On our present rations there is food for seventeen more days. That is all. After that there is nothing. We have seen no sign of any living thing in all this time. Unless we get food and fuel we shall die.' They stood there, dumb – stunned by having what they all knew put bluntly to them in words.

'Gerda Peterson wishes to try to reach the position of the *Southern Cross*,' I went on. 'She wishes to know whether her father is alive. She has the right to go, if anyone does.' They growled agreement, waiting for me to continue.

I then told them what I planned to do. 'The *Southern Cross* unloaded stores on the ice before she went down,' I said. 'She had a big cargo of whale-meat. This and blubber would have been transferred to the ice. If there are any survivors, then they will have meat and fuel. I intend to try and reach them. It is a desperate chance, and you must decide whether you agree to my going. We have no hope of reaching them in our present condition. The party, which should consist of three, must be properly fed for at least two days. That and the rations they will have to take with them will cut your own food supplies by about three days. It is up to you to decide whether you wish to take this chance.'

The men nodded and began to talk amongst themselves. Gerda stepped forward and said, 'Whatever you decide I must go. I do not need your food.'

The men stared at her. Then one old man from her father's ship said, 'We will not let you go without food. *Hval 4* will give you part of their rations.'

The men of her own crew nodded agreement, their eyes kindled – not by hope, but by their sacrifice for something they thought right and good.

McPhee stepped forward and said, 'Will ye tell us, sir, who ye'll be taking with ye?'

'Yes,' I said. 'Kalstad, if he agrees to come.' And then I added, 'Before you decide, let me warn you that there is little hope in this and we shall almost certainly die on the way. But it is a chance, and we should take that chance, however slight, before we are too weak to attempt it.'

'I will kom,' said Kalstad.

'Good,' I said, and asked the men for their decision. They didn't say anything, but I saw one of the stewards had gone to prepare a meal. They were all grinning excitedly like children. They made of their sacrifice a sort of festival. They crowded round the cook-pot, advising, offering more food. Gerda was crying, her eyes starry, and she went amongst them, thanking them, kissing them in her excitement and her sense of their innate kindness. She thought that they were doing it for her, and not for any desperate hope of relief – and I'm not at all sure she wasn't right. Rough men have a way of showing their love with inordinate sacrifice, and there wasn't a man who hadn't gained strength and courage from her indomitable cheerfulness.

So it was arranged and for two days the three of us fed like fighting cocks. I could literally feel the strength flowing back into me. It coursed with the blood through my veins. Depression was thrown off. I even had some hope. And the cold receded. Kalstad grew taller and more cheerful. And as we were fed up, the rest of the men seemed to shrink into sunken-eyed ghosts by comparison. The air of cheerfulness was kept up at a forced and artificial level as the men crowded round us to watch us eat, trying desperately to hide the hunger fever in their eyes and the saliva that drooled from their lips at the sight of so much food.

On the evening of the first day on full rations, something happened which should have warned me what Bland was planning. Bonomi came into our camp and asked to speak to me. He looked shrunken and cold and very frightened. He pleaded to come and join our camp. 'They eat everything,' he cried wildly. He was almost in tears of self-pity. 'They will give me nothing, and they eat and eat. Soon there is nothing left. I am 'ungry and I do not wish to be cook to them no more.'

'That's a matter for you to sort out with Bland,' I said. 'You've done pretty well out of being their cook so far.'

'Si, si. But now they will give me nothing. Nothing, I tell you.'

'Better go and talk to Bland. He holds your rations.'

'But he will give me nothing.'

'It's a matter between you and Bland,' I repeated. 'Go and sort it out with him.'

I am afraid I was rather brusque. My mind was on more vital things than Bonomi's rations. That morning we completed the building of a really good light sledge. We turned in at midday and the evening meal was served to us in our blanket sleeping-bags. One more day at Iceberg Camp and then we should be out on our own, trekking across illimitable wastes of ice searching for the *Southern Cross* Camp. We didn't know where it was. We didn't even know whether it existed. We should just have to go on and on until the end came. It was a frightening thought – more frightening now that our bellies were full and we had the energy to hope. The three of us were together now in my tent and we talked interminably of the best possible route, little knowing that the route would be chosen for us.

I was wakened very early the following morning by somebody shaking me and calling my name. For a moment I thought it was time for us to leave. But then I realized that it was not until the next day, the 22nd, that we were starting out. I opened my eyes to find Bonomi bending over me. '*Capitano, Capitano*. They 'ave gone. They 'ave gone and they 'ave leave me nothing. Nothing at all.' He was excited and scared.

I sat up. 'Who's gone? What are you talking about?' I demanded.

'Bland,' he cried. 'Bland is gone and he take all the rations, everything. He is down on the ice – he and Vaksdal and Keller. Come and see if you do not believe.'

I crawled out of my tent and stood in the cold stillness of the ledge, shielding my eyes from the glare and trying to see what Bonomi was pointing to. It was an incredible morning. The sun was a blood-red orange away to the north-east, the sky a sort of greeny blue and all the ice was tinged with silken pink, like a damask quilt. 'There. Do you see?'

I followed Bonomi's pointing finger and saw three figures moving across the ice – three tiny figures dragging a sledge. They had their backs to the sun and they were headed towards the position where the *Southern Cross* might be expected to be. I ought to have realized what it had meant when Bonomi had said that Bland and the two mates were eating full rations. Bland had finally despaired of the iceberg breaking through to the open sea and had started westward in search of the *Southern Cross* Camp or the rescue ships which might still be searching on the edge of the pack.

Bonomi's excitement had roused the camp. One by one the men stumbled out into that satin-pink morning and stared at the three figures moving slowly across the ice below. I remember one man said, 'I think perhaps you do not go now, Kaptein. They have had more food, those three. If anyone reach the *Southern Cross* Camp they will. There is good hope now.'

Howe heard him and he said, 'If Bland reaches the *Southern Cross* Camp, no rescue party will come here. He's gambling on being the sole survivor. That's the only way he can save himself from being hanged for murder.' He turned to me. 'Craig,' he said 'you've just got to get there. Don't let him beat you on the last stretch. You and Gerda have got to reach the *Southern Cross* Camp.'

It meant that we should have to follow Bland's tracks. I had no illusions about the man. Somewhere along the route he would abandon Vaksdal and Keller. And if he did reach the *Southern Cross* Camp and we didn't, then there'd be no rescue party for the survivors on the iceberg.

The three of us remained in the tent all day, conserving our energies and eating enormously. We'd talk over our prospects, possible routes, what would happen if we caught up with Bland; then we'd drowse, only to start talking about the same things as soon as we woke. Lying there, warm and well fed, the iceberg assumed the friendliness of a home. In contrast, the trek that was to begin next day seemed more and more frightening.

That night, shortly after our evening meal, the flap of the tent was pulled back and Judie's voice, very low, almost scared, said, 'Can I come in a moment, Duncan?'

She crawled in, caught hold of my hand and fell, sobbing, into my arms, her cold cheek against mine, her body trembling. At length she said, 'I have been so stupid. All this time – I have wasted it, lying in my tent being miserable. And now – ' She kissed me and lay close against me, quietly crying. It was as though Bland's departure had freed her from the thing that had lain so heavy on her mind.

At length she said, 'You must sleep now. I shan't watch you leave tomorrow. I'll say goodbye here.' She kissed me, her fingers caressing my beard. Then she said, 'I don't think we shall meet again, Duncan – not in this world. Will you please remember that I – love you – always. And I'll be with you out there – if it helps.' She stretched her hand across to Gerda. 'Goodbye, Gerda,' she said. 'I wish I were coming with you to find *my* father.' She kissed Gerda. Then she kissed me again. The flap of the tent dropped back. She was gone and I'd only the salt of her tears on my face to remind me she had been in the tent.

Gerda touched my hand. 'You must get through, Duncan – for

her. You must go on, whatever happens. You understand?'

I didn't say anything. I understood what she meant. Decisions like that couldn't be taken in the comfort of a full stomach and a warm tent. That was for the next day and the days and days of weary ice that lay ahead.

10

NEXT morning, as soon as it was light, we started out. We carried food for six days, a little tobacco, a pair of skis, one length of rope, a small primus with a little fuel, tent, blanket sleeping-bags and a change of clothes. All this was piled on one sledge. The morning was very still and our breath hung round us like a cloud of steam. The sun came up as we went down the ledge and the world turned gold with an orange band along the horizon. Most of the men turned out to see us off. They came with us as far as the bottom of the ledge and a ragged cheer went up as we lowered ourselves on to the broken surface of the pack ice. Our sledge was lowered after us and then McPhee, who had climbed down with us to help get the sledge on to the ice, gripped my hand. 'Good luck, sir,' he said.

'We'll be back with whale-meat within a fortnight,' I said. I spoke loudly and with a confidence I did not feel in order to encourage the men. 'If we're not back by then,' I said to him privately, 'do the best you can.' Poor devil, it was a rotten job I'd given him. Gerda said I should have put Mueller, the second mate of *Hval 5*, in charge. But I didn't know Mueller. I did know McPhee. He was an engineer, not a whaler, but he had all the tenacity of the Scot and I knew he could be relied on to the bitter end.

'Och, ye'll find 'em,' he said. 'Dinna worry aboot us. Maybe the berg will break out into the open sea yet.'

I clapped him on the shoulder and picked up the sledge ropes. Gerda was saying a last farewell to Howe, who'd scrambled down beside us. Kalstad and I started out with the sledge along the track that Bland and his party had blazed. Howe called after me: 'Craig, you've got to get through. If Bland gets through alone . . .' He didn't finish, but I knew what was in his mind.

I waved my hand in acknowledgement and Kalstad and I began to wind our way through the hummocks of snow-covered ice. Gerda caught us up, and in a moment the three of us were swallowed into a strange world of ice – an iridescent fairyland of golden silence.

As we wound our way through the great humps of ice we caught occasional glimpses of the iceberg with dark figures moving back up the ledge to the tents that showed black against the green of ice as yet untouched by the sun. Once I saw a figure I thought was Judie waving to me. I waved back and then turned my face resolutely to the west. It was surprising how quickly the iceberg was lost to view in that broken plain.

I am familiar, as I've no doubt you are, with the great ice treks of Polar exploration; Peary's sledge run to the North Pole, Scott and Shackleton's desperate struggles and Amundsen's great dash to the South. In execution and design our trek across the ice was in no way comparable. I realize that. But in fairness to my companions – both of whom are dead – I must make it clear that what we suffered was little short of what the great explorers suffered in the most desperate of their journeys. We had no dogs, no special equipment, no finely designed sledges or proper clothing – not even real tents. And we were weakened by exposure and starvation before we started. We weren't explorers, and, therefore, we had no great goal to lift our morale and keep us struggling forward. We were shipwrecked sailors with shipboard clothes, and sledges made out of bits of packing cases, an old piece of canvas for a tent and short rations. Our only goal was to save our own lives and those of the men we'd left behind on the iceberg. We were going to try and find the survivors of a ship. We weren't sure whether there were any survivors and we weren't sure of the position in which it had gone down. In fact we were on a forlorn hope – a last desperate bid for life in which I don't think any of us really believed.

Finally, there were none of the smooth miles of snow to be found on the Ross Barrier or the high land in towards the South Pole. True it was not so cold and the blizzards not so severe, but winter was coming on and it was cold enough in our weakened condition. And the area across which we were trekking was the area through which our own iceberg had smashed its way, leaving chaos in its wake – an area of jumbled, broken, jagged ice in which every step forward was a struggle. The skis were useless. We trekked on foot, one of the party path-finding, the two others following, dragging the sledge.

But though we had soon lost sight of the iceberg owing to the broken nature of the pack, I remember the bitter disappointment I felt when on pitching camp that night I climbed to the top of an ice hummock and saw berg and ledge picked out clearly in the pink of the setting sun. It was like a fairy castle and seemed so near that I had only to stretch out my hand to touch it. I could even see the camp and figures moving about it. Gerda had some sort of a hot stew ready by the time I returned to the tent. We ate it hurriedly and turned in, taking our boots into our sleeping-bags with us to prevent them from becoming frozen.

In four days, trekking fourteen hours a day, we made about thirty miles. It doesn't sound much, but though the weather was good, the going was incredibly bad. We were trekking back over the pack through which the icebergs had ploughed their way. It was as though an earthquake had thrown the floes in all directions. In addition, the snow which half covered this fantastic litter of ice was partly thawed, particularly at midday, and time and again the pathfinder was only saved by the rope. Also, of course, we were weak after our long period of malnutrition, exposure and inactivity. I doubt whether we would have made thirty miles in four days if we hadn't been following the tracks of Bland's sledge.

It was strange, those sledge tracks. At first, we had regarded Bland as the enemy, something to be beaten in addition to the ice. We followed the sledge tracks for convenience, knowing we could leave them when it suited us or when our planned route lay away from his. But as we trekked on and on, those tracks gradually ceased to be hostile. We'd no gun. If we caught up with Bland he could kill us if he wanted to – and if there was any chance of reaching the *Southern Cross* survivors or being rescued by the search ships, I knew that that was what he would do, just as he would have to get rid of his two companions. And yet, though we never actually mentioned it, I'm certain none of us, after the first few days, would have thought of turning aside from the tracks and striking out on our own. With hard frosts and clear skies the tracks remained as sharp and clear as when they were made. And as exhaustion gripped us, they became our only friends in that white wilderness. Those two lines ran out endlessly ahead of us, our only contact with other human beings. Soon we were following them blindly, not caring where they led, buoyed up by the constant hope that somewhere ahead of us, round the next ice hillock, over the next limit of our horizon, they would connect us with the outside world.

On the fourth day Gerda began to show signs of weakening.

Kalstad was limping from a swollen ankle and I was beginning to feel the stabbing pain in my chest again. We made little more than two miles that day, the snow having softened with the result that we sank through the honey-combed ice. We nearly lost the sledge in a crevasse. In a strange land of cold green caverns draped with almost golden icicles we pitched camp. Up to that time, I think we had been going faster than Bland, for early that morning we had passed his fourth camp site. It makes a lot of difference in the conditions we were experiencing if someone has blazed the trail for you. But we were pretty depressed that night. The only thing that encouraged us was that from the top of an upturned floe we had seen a dark line along the western horizon that looked as though it might be a water-sky, indicating open sea ahead. But how far ahead? It might be forty miles, and we knew we could not do very much more.

Next day Gerda was weaker. She showed signs of dysentery. Kalstad and I were also suffering from diarrhoea and beginning to weaken. Also the constant glare without sun goggles was inflaming our eyes, so that it was difficult to see. The snow held crisp that day and we pressed on fast, using up in savage effort the last reserves of energy. It was the first day of good going and we had to take advantage of it.

By midday I think we had made as much as ten or eleven miles. I know that when I climbed to the top of a hillock of snow-covered ice and looked back I could only just see the tips of the icebergs on the horizon to the east of us. They were tall ships sailing in line on the horizon's glare, insubstantial mirages that came and went, now expanding, now contracting. Only by taking a bearing could I decide which was our own berg.

After eating a biscuit and two pieces of sugar each we pushed on. The sun became a pale disc shining wanly through a curtain of mist. The air became colder and the world we moved through lost its colour. It was less painful to the eyes, but it was also less friendly. I think we must have gone on to the limit of endurance. And then suddenly we knew we could go no farther and we pitched camp.

In the stillness of early evening I thought I heard voices. Imagination plays hellish tricks. That night as we lay in the tent Gerda whispered, 'Duncan. It is no good. You must leave me behind.'

I remember experiencing a terrible sense of shock. I hadn't realized how near the limit of endurance the day's trek had brought her. I remember I shook my head angrily. 'We'll go on together,' I said.

She caught hold of my arm. 'Please,' she whispered. Her voice, though weak, was urgent. 'It was selfish of me to come. I should have known I have not a man's strength. It is your duty to go on without me. I shall hinder you and always you must think of all those peoples on the iceberg.'

'We'll talk about it in the morning,' I said. And I got close against her, so that if she moved I should know. I was afraid she might walk out into the snow.

For a long time I lay half awake, thinking over what she had said, arguing against what I knew was inevitable. And at length I shifted my body away from hers and went to sleep. It was horrible. But I knew that she was right. Too many lives depended on us. The fittest must always push on until the very end.

Some time in the night the wind rose and by morning it was blowing a blizzard. I looked out of the corner of the tent into a grey, swirling void. Then I turned quickly to see if Gerda was still there. She was, thank God, for we could not move, and the enforced rest might enable her to make another day's march.

For three days the blizzard continued, and in those three days we finished all our food with the exception of five biscuits and fifteen lumps of sugar. The tent was in perpetual darkness. It was like being buried alive. We used an old biscuit tin as a bed-pan and just lay listlessly in our sleeping-bags, never stirring except to turn over to relieve the aching stiffness of our limbs.

The night it stopped snowing we smoked our last cigarette. In the grey light of morning I wrote in my log: *There is now no hope and no reason to go on. The others, I think, realize this now. I shall not abandon Gerda. There is no point.*

We made an early start, wishing to take full advantage of what little energy we had been able to store up by lying still. For the first time there were no sledge tracks running out ahead of us. The snow was feet deep. I made Gerda put on the skis. The snow was crisp and fairly firm and we moved off with a feeling almost of cheerfulness. And round the first snow hillock we came upon the trampled snow of a camp. It had been evacuated that morning, for beyond the camp, sledge and ski tracks marked the new snow, stretching out ahead of us again and disappearing round a cornice of blue, snow-free ice. 'Bland?' Gerda asked as she stopped beside me.

I nodded. So I really had heard voices that night the blizzard started. It was incredible. For three days we'd been camped within a hundred yards of Bland and his party and not known it. 'They're probably not more than an hour ahead of us,' I said.

'What will happen when we catch them up?'

'I don't know,' I answered her. 'I don't think it matters much.' I didn't think there was much chance of our catching up with them. There were three of them to pull the sledge, and both Bland and Vaksdal were big men.

'Perhaps we should strike away from their tracks,' she suggested. But I shook my head. 'They're travelling roughly in the direction we decided on. The going is easier for us if we follow their tracks.'

So we went on, following the sledge marks through the fresh snow. Kalstad and I pulled the sledge and Gerda kept up with us easily on the skis. For two or three hours we made good progress. But about midday the sun came through. The glare was frightful and soon the snow began to soften and the going became harder as our boots broke through the surface crust. In some of the drifts we struggled forward through sifting snow that was well over our knees and had the consistency of rice grain. It took too much of our small reserve of energy and I made camp.

When darkness fell the stars came out in a clear, frozen night. It was terribly cold and none of us slept very well. The cold seemed to eat into our under-nourished bodies. Gerda suffered agonies of pain in her stomach and Kalstad complained of frost-bite due to the fact that his boots, worn by the ice, were no longer water-tight.

The next morning was cold and cheerless with low cloud and a biting wind out of the south. We were late in starting. Gerda had no energy, no desire to move. Also, she had left her boots outside her sleeping-bag and they were frozen stiff, so that she could not put them on until we had softened the leather over the primus. When we did start we made good progress, for the cold wind had frozen the thawed snow of the previous day into an ice-hard crust. Ahead of us Bland's sledge tracks unwound steadily like a snaking line meandering through the snow hills of the churned-up pack.

'Soon we kom to their camp, I think, *ja*?'

Kalstad was right. The snow hills gradually flattened out until finally we emerged into an almost flat desert of white where the pack had had time to settle before becoming frozen solid. And in this dead plain we saw the sledge tracks running straight, like parallel lines drawn by a ruler to a black patch. 'That is their camp,' Kalstad shouted to me. 'And they are still there. I see some peoples moving.'

I screwed up my eyes, trying to concentrate sufficiently on my vision to produce a clear picture. But the throbbing pain at the back of my eyeballs obscured my sight. All I could see was a dark patch in the virgin white of the snow, a patch that danced and wavered. I don't know why we pressed on so hard then. We didn't really want to join up with Bland. It wouldn't help us. And yet the mere thought of contact with other human beings in that grim waste of frozen snow spurred us forward. 'Your eyes are better than mine, Kalstad,' I said. 'Are they striking camp?'

'I think so,' he replied. '*Ja*. There is no tent.' And a moment later, he said in a puzzled tone, 'I do not see more than two people.'

'Only two?' I screwed up my eyes in an agony of concentration. The dark patch in the snow wavered and separated into two figures. There seemed to be nothing else but those two men. We threw ourselves on the sledge ropes. I think we were both in a panic that it would prove to be a mirage, that the two dots that looked so like human beings would vanish and the snow demons would laugh at us in the howl of the wind. And then faint across the frozen waste came a hail in Norwegian. We could see the two figures waving to us now. We shouted back and ran, slithering on the ice-hard snow towards them. Kalstad was limping badly, yet for a brief spell we must have been going forward at a good three miles an hour.

'It is Vaksdal and Keller,' Kalstad gasped.

'No sign of Bland?' I asked him.

'*Nei, nei*. Only Vaksdal and Keller.'

They came out to meet us, shouting and cheering and waving their arms. But when they were about a hundred yards from us, they stopped and were suddenly silent. We dragged the sledge up to them, exhausted, gasping for breath. They made no move to help us. They just stood and stared at us dumbly. Vaksdal looked thinner and gaunter and he had no boots on. Keller also had no boots. He had a knife and a piece of leather in his hand. 'Where's Bland?' I gasped, dropping the sledge rope and staggering slightly now that the impetus of moving forward no longer held me in a straight line.

'Bland?' Vaksdal's eyes suddenly blazed from their deep sockets. 'He is gone on. We thought you were a rescue party who have found our sledge tracks. How much food do you have?'

'None,' I said. 'A few pieces of sugar and a biscuit or two.' I sat down on the sledge. Now that I'd stopped exhaustion was taking hold of me. I just wanted to lie down and sleep. God, how sleepy I was! And the cold drove right through me. 'What did you say about Bland?' I asked, trying to concentrate my mind.

'He is gone.' Vaksdal's voice was angry. 'You are right, *hr*.

Kaptein. You are all right and Keller and I are fools. He is left us. This morning we wake to find the wind blowing on us and Bland pulling the sledge out of the camp with the tent thrown on top of it. We shout to him and he just laugh at us. We start to follow. But he has take our boots. My gun is gone, but Keller has his inside his blankets. He try to shoot then. But Bland is too far. We have nothing; no tent, no food, no boots, nothing. The bastard have left us to die.'

So it had happened, just as Howe had said it would. He'd used them as pack mules, and when they were nearly fifty miles from the iceberg and there was a chance of reaching open water and rescue, he'd abandoned them. He'd chosen a lone death just as he had when he'd stayed behind at the *Tauer III* Camp in order to have the faint chance of coming out alive as the sole survivor. 'How much food had he?' I asked Vaksdal.

'For one man – perhaps three or four days. But very little, you understand.'

'And he's weak?'

'*Ja.* Too weak to pull the sledge alone for very far.'

'All right,' I said. 'Start pitching camp, Kalstad.' The skis; that was the answer. I turned to speak to Gerda. But she wasn't there. I looked back along the line of the sledge track. Gerda was lying in the snow several hundred yards behind us. I unstrapped our gear and cleared it from the sledge. Then Kalstad and I started back. I don't think I knew how exhausted we were until I turned back for Gerda. It was only about three hundred yards, but it seemed miles that we dragged that empty sledge before we reached her crumpled figure lying face down in the snow.

She was alive. I could see that by the way her breath had thawed the snow around her nostrils. But she was quite unconscious. It was as much as the two of us could manage to lift her body on to the sledge. Her weight made a vast difference and I thought we'd never reach the spot where I'd off-loaded our gear. I don't think we'd have got her there, but for the fact that Vaksdal and Keller came out to help us.

We set up camp then and got some water boiling and made some beef tea. Gerda's return to consciousness was slow. The beef tea she retched up. But I managed to get a little of our precious brandy down her throat. And when she could speak, she kept on saying, 'You must leave me now, Duncan. You must go on. You must go on.' Her voice was so urgent that she exhausted herself. To keep her quiet I told her how Bland had abandoned his two companions and gone on alone with all their stores. She didn't say anything when I'd finished, but just lay with her eyes closed, her face grey and puffy. I thought she hadn't heard. Then her hand touched my arm. 'One of you must go on,' she whispered faintly. 'Take the skis and go on. He must not get out alone. There are all those men on the iceberg.'

I said, 'Don't worry. One of us will go on.'

She seemed to relax then and I think she went to sleep. Kalstad pulled at my arm. 'Her spirit has outrun her body, I think,' he said. 'She is like a horse who is too willing.'

He was telling me she was going to die. I felt the tears at the back of my eyes. I should have known how terribly driven she had been to keep up with us and not be a burden. And still she had had energy to think of us and of those others back on that ledge. I crawled out of the tent. One of us must go after Bland. I thought immediately of Vaksdal. He was the strongest. And he could be trusted, now that he knew the sort of man Bland was. Anger at being abandoned to die like that would spur him on. But when I began to organize the thing, I soon discovered that in removing their boots, Bland had as effectually stopped them following him as if he'd shot them down as they lay in the snow. Whoever went after Bland must go on ski, and that meant well-fitting boots. Kalstad's feet and mine were much smaller than Vaksdal's or Keller's. To loan them our boots was, therefore, out of the question. The choice lay then between Kalstad and myself and Kalstad was suffering from frost-bite.

There was nothing for it. I should have to take what little rations remained and go on myself. 'Get your rifle, Keller,' I said, 'and some ammunition.' I packed a rucksack, and when I was all ready to go I crawled into the tent. I don't know whether Gerda was asleep or unconscious. She was quite still and her eyes were closed. I bent and kissed her. She moved slightly. Perhaps she knew I'd kissed her. At any rate, I'm glad I did and I hope she knew – knew that I was saluting a very brave woman.

I went out into the biting cold of the wind then. Kalstad helped me to fix the skis. I slung Keller's rifle over my shoulder. Then Kalstad lifted the rucksack on to my shoulders, the rucksack that contained for him all that was left of life. I was leaving them nothing but the remains of the beef extract and the primus with the last of the fuel. He clapped me on the back and said, 'Good luck, *hr. Kaptein.*' I gripped his hand. Vaksdal and Keller looked on, sullen and morose. Since the discovery that we were not a rescue party and had virtually no food they had been in a state of miserable despair. Not even the fact that I was going out after

Bland had stirred them.

'You are in command now, Kalstad,' I said. 'Look after Gerda Petersen.'

I turned then and set out along the track of Bland's sledge. I didn't look back. I didn't want to be reminded of the pathetic loneliness of that last camp. Gerda and the rest would die there. And somewhere out along the sledge track I was following, I, too, should die. I kept my eyes on those ruler-straight tracks and concentrated on the thought of vengeance.

Christian teaching would say it is a bad thing to go out to your death with only the thought of vengeance in your mind. I can only say this, that it was through that thought of vengeance that I achieved the strength to go on. It gave me a purpose. I no longer had any hope of finding the *Southern Cross* Camp, or even any hope that there was such a camp. I was going out to kill the man who had brought about all our deaths, who had killed Judie's father, rammed my ship and abandoned his two companions. I didn't stop to think that if there was no chance of him being rescued, then the ice and snow would do the job for me. I just knew I had to kill Bland with my own hands. That alone in my mind would justify my existence in that moment. And that alone gave me strength.

It was surprising how much easier and quicker I found it travelling on ski. The surface of the snow was crisp and firm. The skis slid forward with a crunching hiss, and only the constant driving of arms on sticks was tiring. And the going was over flat, snow-covered ice. In places it was ridged like the sea and here I had difficulty until I learnt to control my legs, for it's extraordinary how, in the unending white of limitless snow, it is impossible for the eyes to differentiate between an undulating and a flat surface.

Bland had, I reckoned, a three-hour start of me. I had left the others shortly after midday. Presuming that I could travel twice as fast as a man dragging a sledge, I should be up with him about three in the afternoon. I had, therefore, only a few hours' margin of daylight. If I wasn't in possession of Bland's tent by nightfall, then I should never see another day. A night in the open would kill me. I don't think I really thought about this. But it was there at the back of my mind, a spur to my body, for I knew that if I were to achieve my purpose, it must be done before nightfall.

Ahead of me the sky was dark, like the beginning of night. In contrast the low cloud behind me seemed dazzlingly white. The world was flat – flat like the Western Desert, but white; blindingly, eye-searingly white. And as I slid through this unending world of snow, the surface began to change. There were crevasses, under the surface. Without the skis I could not have gone a mile. The snow bridged innumerable gaps and I heard it crumble as I slid across. Then I was in an area of open fissures, gaps too wide for the snow to bridge. The sledge tracks began to wind between these crevasses and in one place I saw Bland had had trouble getting his sledge across where the snow had crumbled into a gap.

It was shortly after two that I saw the first open water in weeks. It was like a black lake and clotted thick with brash ice. I pressed on faster now, drawing on my last reserves of energy. Darkness was not far off and the patches of open water that were beginning to appear suggested we were nearing the edge of the pack. Bland had food for four days. There was still just a chance. And this ray of hope seemed to revitalize me.

I wasn't far out in my reckonings, for it was just after three when I sighted a small, black dot moving ahead of me. For some time the sledge tracks had been winding amongst black pools of half-frozen brash towards a small berg caught in the pack, and it was against the sheer green slope of this berg that the figure showed like a small dot dancing in the white void. It was painful to try and keep my eyes on it, and dangerous because it tended to make me lose my balance. After I'd had one fall through not watching my skis and had got up again with great difficulty, I ceased to worry about the mark ahead and concentrated on ski-ing as fast as possible.

When I looked again the berg was much nearer, but there was no sign of Bland. Presumably he'd passed behind it. Or had he seen me? Was he lying in wait? I left his tracks and circled away to the north of the berg. I soon caught sight of him then, not half a mile away and moving along the flank of the berg, which was a long one. Between us the snow lay flat, like a sheet of white. I drove my sticks into it, thrusting forward on a line that would converge with Bland.

He had almost reached the end of the berg when he saw me. He stopped and then his voice reached me on the cold wind. He was shouting to me and waving his sticks. Just as his companions had done, he thought I was part of a rescue party.

I unslung my rifle then, cocked it and slithered forward with the ski sticks looped over one wrist. Now that the moment had come I found my heart hammering wildly. I fought to steady myself as I went forward.

Something in the way I moved towards him must have warned

him, for he suddenly stopped shouting and stood quite still, staring at me as I advanced on him. I was getting close now, and though the snow-glare made it difficult for me to see, he was outlined against the final shoulder of the berg and a good target. But I was taking no chances. I closed him steadily, just as I would have done an enemy ship.

'Who are you?' His hail came to me quite clearly and I realized I was getting into the shelter of the berg.

'Craig,' I yelled back, and there was an exultant feeling inside me and I saw him stare at me for a moment and then dive for the sledge and his gun. But he didn't get up again and a moment later the thin crack of a shot sounded across the snow. He was firing from the shelter of the sledge. I turned then and circled to the west of him, cutting off his line of advance and reaching the shelter of the western end of the berg. He fired at me several times before I was out of sight, but I was a moving target and his bullets vanished into space.

The snow was heaped in fantastic shapes round the berg and I moved steadily through the sheltering hummocks towards the final shoulder. And here, round the corner of a hollowed cliff that gaped with green jaws filled with the white teeth of icicles, I saw Bland's sledge deserted in the snow. He was in the cover of the broken ice close in to the berg's flank. I crept slowly forward. There was the crack of a shot and a puff of ice in my face. I felt blood flowing from a cut. I brushed it away and raised my gun. I could see him now, peering from behind a fluted column of ice, his gun raised. I was just about to fire when I saw something moving behind him. It was travelling fast across the snow with a strange undulating movement like a well-sprung sleigh. It was a big, ungainly animal, tawny-coloured with brown spots, and although I'd never seen one before, I knew what it was. It was a sea-leopard, after the killer whale the most dangerous inhabitant of the Antarctic.

Bland must have seen it at the same time, for his gun swung away from me, and I heard the sharp crack-crack as he fired. The huge beast did not check. He fired once more, at point-blank range, and then it was on him. He staggered as he was born back and then he fell with the beast on top of him.

I went towards him as quickly as I could over the uneven surface. Blood was staining the snow crimson at his side. I saw the beast move, jerking as though injured. From a range of a few yards I pumped a whole magazine into it. I went forward then. The beast was quite still, lying across Bland's legs. I saw Bland move, trying to free himself. He still had his rifle gripped in his hands and he was trying to work the bolt. I tore it from his grasp and threw it clear of us. Then I saw that the huge brute's jaws were dripping bloood and there was a terrible wound in Bland's side. He started to say something. Then he lost consciousness.

Looking down at him, with the big carcase of the sea-leopard stretched across his legs, I suddenly realized what this meant. It was the end of Bland, and for us new hope. Here, stretched dead at my feet, was thousands of pounds of fresh meat and blubber. Here was life for Gerda – and hope for the future. Somehow I'd got to go back, go back along those weary miles loaded with meat and fat.

I got Bland's sledge and dragged it up close to his body. As soon as I had erected the tent, I dug Bland's legs out from under the sea-leopard and got him into it. Then, when I had bandaged him as best as I could, I got to work with my knife and soon I had a blubber stove warming the tent and big steaks of juicy meat grilling in the smoke. Bland couldn't eat, but I managed to feed him some of the hot blood. Meantime I ate more in a few minutes than I'd eaten in as many days. The blood seemed to give Bland strength for once he shifted his position and asked who had left the iceberg with me. When I told him, he grinned and said, 'Now we can all die in the snow together.' He seemed to relapse into unconsciousness then and I lay wrapped in a blanket, unable to sleep for the gripping pains in my stomach caused by unaccustomed food.

In the darkness of the night I awoke suddenly with a feeling of being choked. I sat up, gasping for breath and racked by violent coughing. I didn't know what had happened for a moment. Then I realized that the tent was filled with smoke. I turned towards Bland and found he wasn't there. Through streaming eyes I saw an orange glow against the canvas of the tent. I crawled out. Flames were leaping up out of the snow, licking over the body of the sea-leopard, reaching out with wind-fanned fingers towards the fabric of the tent which was already blackened and charred at one side. Bland lay in the middle of the flames, his face buried in the smouldering carcase, the snow steaming and beginning to form in crimson pools.

I pulled Bland clear and scooped up armfuls of snow, throwing it on the flames till they were completely smothered under a white drift. At first I thought Bland had tried to stop the fire. But as I was smothering it, I saw an empty kerosene container and the primus with the stopper of its tank unscrewed lying in the snow.

I knew then that he'd started the fire, started it in order to burn the carcase, burn the tent with me in it. Both pairs of skis had been thrust well into the blaze and had been badly charred.

When the fire was out at last I crawled exhausted back into the tent. To this day I don't know whether Bland was dead when I dragged him clear of the fire he'd made. All I know is that he was dead and frozen stiff when I went outside the tent in the morning. For all I know I killed him by leaving him out there. But I don't care. I only know I was glad to find him dead.

Fortunately I'd saved the skis in time. They were charred, but they were still usable. I cooked myself a meal. Then I covered Bland with some snow, and leaving the tent all standing, set out on the journey back, carrying Bland's skis and enough meat and blubber to give the rest of the party a good meal.

The wind had swung round to the west and was blowing hard. And as I started out I was conscious of a slight movement of the ice under me. However, the going remained good, and though a fine drift of snow had sifted across the sledge tracks, they were still visible and I reached the other camp without mishap just after midday.

It was then that I received the most bitter blow of all that ghastly period. Gerda was dead. She had died in the night, never having regained consciousness since my departure. Kalstad showed me the mound of snow where they had buried her, and I stood there in the wind and cried like a child. Lying there, three hours' journey away, was the means of giving her strength. Her death seemed so unnecessary. Why is it always the nicest people that go? 'She look very happy when we bury her,' Kalstad said. 'I think per'aps she find her father. If he is also dead, then it is per'aps best. She love her father very much.'

Kalstad had trekked out along the sledge route the previous day and found where Bland had buried his companions' boots in the snow. We were able, therefore, to start out for the new camp as soon as we had had a meal. We all suffered from terrible pains at the unaccustomed food. Kalstad was sick and weakened rapidly. We were trekking straight into the wind, which was rising to gale force and gradually obliterating the tracks. It was a nightmare journey. The ice was heaving under us, breaking into fissures and growling as the broken edges of floes ground together under their covering of snow.

But for the iceberg I don't think we should ever have found the sea-leopard again, for by three o'clock we were struggling across a plain of virgin white, all traces of my ski tracks made only

379

that morning having vanished. I saw the iceberg black against the pale circle of the westering sun and within an hour we were snug in two tents with a blubber stove going and meat cooking.

At the time I blamed Fate for what happened. But it was really my own fault. I should have remembered that there had been stretches of open water the previous day and realized how thin the ice was. We should have camped on the berg. But then I don't know that any of us had the strength to drag tent and stores and sledges up on to the higher ground.

All that night the wind howled with demoniac force. I slept fitfully, racked with pain and conscious all the time of the increasing movement of the ice and the rising sound of the grinding floes. Towards morning I must have fallen into a heavy sleep, for I was woken by the ice splitting with the crackle of rifle fire. I crawled to the entrance of the tent, but it was dark and I could see nothing. I lay back and dozed off again to the sound of lapping water.

In the grey light of early dawn I was horrified to see water slopping in at the tent entrance. My feet were numb and the bottom of my sleeping-bag was frozen stiff. It was as though I were lying with my feet in a block of ice. I put my head out of the tent. The scene had changed completely. In place of the flat white expanse of snow-covered ice, I found myself looking across a black expanse of brash-filled water. All round us the ice had broken up into separate floes which drove against each other under the lash of the wind. As I leaned forward on my hands and knees the ice tipped slowly under me. I gazed with fascination as the water lapped the edge and slopped over my hands. When I drew back into the tent the water receded. I fought down a feeling of panic and pulled back the canvas at the other end of the tent.

I knew why the water had lapped over the edge as I'd leaned forward, of course, but it wasn't nice to have that knowledge confirmed. The two tents were floating on a raft of ice not more than forty feet across and we were in the middle of the open channel of water. The jagged edge of our floe fitted like a piece of a jig-saw puzzle to the main floe from which it had calved. The spot was marked by our sledge and the carcase of the sea-leopard. It was hard to see us drifting slowly away from all that meat. We had three or four pounds of the meat in the tent which we were keeping thawed. But it wouldn't last long. We were drifting away from the only source of life and strength we had.

I was just putting back the canvas to exclude the cold when I saw something – a fin moving stealthily through the water, slipping along like a black dhow sail, making scarcely a ripple. It was a killer whale. As though attracted by my gaze it turned quickly and came straight towards our floe. The high dorsal fin passed out of my view and a moment later I heard the great beast snorting on the other side of the canvas. It was an ugly, pig-like sound – and deadly sinister. I waited, scarcely daring to breathe. The floe trembled as the monster skimmed beneath it. More snorting. I put back the canvas and lay down, rigid and trembling, waiting, tense, for the moment when the whale would see us and tip the floe over.

That was what Gerda had said they did – peered over the edge of a floe and then tipped it up with their weight. How long ago that seemed now! I remember how she'd teased her father that day I had come aboard *Hval 4*. I remembered other things she'd done and said – her indomitable cheerfulness, her guts, the way she handled the men. And I was comforted by the thought that at least she'd been spared an end like this.

The snorting was close beside me now. I lay still, not waking the others. Better that they should not know till it happened. It would be over quicker for them that way.

The snorting went on for what seemed eternity. Once the floe tilted, rocked violently, and I tensed, waiting for the sudden flurry of water, the cold and the snapping jaws. But the snorting died away. The floe rocked gently to the movement of the water. I relaxed slowly and with relaxation came sleep, a queer half coma of things remembered and things imagined.

I woke suddenly to the soft grinding of ice on ice and a knocking, juddering under the floe. For a moment I thought it was the killer whale back again. Then the soft griding of the ice told its tale and I peered out, praying that we'd fetched up the same side of the channel as our meat.

But fortune was against us. About a quarter of a mile of water separated us from the sledge and the sea-leopard. Still, at least we had fetched up against a big, solid-looking floe. I woke the others and got them on to firm ice. There we repitched the tents and cooked a meal. And whilst we ate I racked my brains for a means of getting across the water to the sea-leopard meat.

But it was impossible. The wind had swung to the south and the gap between us and our old camp was widening all the time. I didn't know whether to push on or wait in the hopes that the gap would freeze over or the wind change. The break-up of the ice might mean we were nearing the edge of the pack. But when I mentioned this to the others, Vaksdal shook his head gloomily and pointed to the west. 'The ice-blink,' he said. 'I think there are many miles of pack yet.' It was true. There was no longer a water-sky to the west of us. Ice and cloud were merged together in a void of blinding white. Anyway, Kalstad was delirious and seemed too weak to move, and I decided to remain in the hope of being able to reach the carcase of the sea-leopard the following morning.

At some point during that timeless day, Kalstad woke me. His eyes were very big and his face quite white. He wasn't delirious any more, but he was shaking slightly and seemed possessed of some sort of a fever. 'You must go on, hr. *Kaptein*,' he said. His voice was very faint.

I shook my head. I knew what he meant. His voice was merged with the memory of Gerda's. 'There's no point,' I said.

'The others,' he whispered. 'I shall die here. You must leave me and go on.'

'You're not going to die,' I told him. But I didn't believe it. I knew we were all going to die.

As night came on we made a blubber fire, and though we practically choked ourselves with the acrid fumes, we managed to cook the rest of the meat. Kalstad refused to have any. Shortly after that I went to sleep. For the first time for days I slept like a log without dreams or any disturbance. It was more a coma than sleep, for I was numb all over with no feeling whatever in my feet.

When I woke it was clear and sunny. A channel two miles wide separated us from the iceberg where the sea-leopard lay. To the north and west the pack seemed to have closed again in a solid mass. When I crawled back into the tent again I saw that Kalstad was dead. The skin of his forehead was waxen under the dirt. His mouth was slightly open in the stiff mat of his beard and his eyes stared at me sightlessly. I felt his hands. They were rigid and quite cold.

I roused the others, and we buried him there in the snow. For him the struggle was over. 'Now we go on, *ja*?' Vaksdal had seen the wide channel of water. He accepted the loss of the sea-leopard and the inevitability of going forward until we dropped. His eyes were running and horribly inflamed, so that they seemed rimmed by raw flesh. His long beard looked dirty against the transparent pallor of his gaunt face. Both he and Keller were suffering from the beginnings of frost-bite due to walking in the snow after Bland had taken their boots. Yet they were willing to go on. They were tougher than I was. I just wanted to crawl into my tent and die as

Kalstad had died.

But somewhere there is always a last flicker of energy. We took one tent, our sleeping-bags and the rifle. Everything had to be carried. Before leaving, we ate the blubber off the stove over which we'd cooked the last of the meat the night before. Then I got out the compass, set our course and we started off, leaving Kalstad to his lonely vigil in the ice, just as we had left Gerda.

We were all very weak. We took it in turns to use the skis. But soon we had to discard them, for we hadn't the strength to hold our balance, and the extra weight on our legs when we had to lift them over broken outcrops of clear ice was too much. The food we'd had caused us great pain. So did our feet. We were all suffering from frost-bite now. Keller weakened rapidly and only the fact that I refused to give in until the two Norwegians were beaten kept me going.

Our progress was painfully slow. Constant detours had to be made round patches of open water. But the ice was fairly flat. By midday we had made something like two miles, but by then Keller had to be supported between the two of us. The glare was like a red-hot needle against my eyeballs. I began to see things that weren't there. At times the landscape vanished into a blur of blinding white. It was the beginning of snow blindness.

If we'd only had some definite goal it would have given an impetus to our struggle. But there was no goal, only a vague hope that none of us believed in. There was no point in going on. I found myself dogged by an overwhelming desire to drop in the snow and let the relief of death steal over me. The longing for death became an obsession that completely replaced any hope of finding survivors from the *Southern Cross* or the store of whalemeat the crew had landed. It was a thing that had to be fought together with exhaustion, the griping pains of hunger and the aching stab of my eyes.

That night Keller wanted to be left behind. He said he was too weak to go on. But we couldn't leave him. There was only the one tent. We had to go on together or stop and die together. Vaksdal told him he was a coward. He didn't deserve to be called that, but it had its effect and he came on with us. There is an entry in my log made that morning which reads: *14th Day. We are going on. But this is the last day we can hope to move. Those on the iceberg will run out of food today. God help them.*

Barely able to stand up for weakness, we made about a mile that morning. My eyes had become so bad that I could hardly see to lay a course. Keller was barely conscious as he stumbled on with his arms about our necks. At times he was actually delirious as he walked, babbling incoherently in Norwegian. Vaksdal and I were in little better case.

Shortly after midday we pitched our tent for the last time. It was whilst we were doing this that Vaksdal seized my arm and pointed into the snow-glare. 'Pingvin,' he croaked. Penguins? That meant food. I followed the line of his arm, screwing up my eyes against the glare. Several dark dots hovered in the mirage of the ice, waving their flippers. I picked up the rifle. God give me strength to shoot straight. The gun was incredibly heavy. The barrel wavered. I could not get the sights to stay for a second on the target. I told Vaksdal to kneel in the snow and I rested the barrel on his shoulder. The penguins were waving their flippers over their heads and vaguely, like sounds in a dream, I heard shouts. The trigger was heavy. I couldn't see the sights properly and the shouts kept ringing in my ears.

Then suddenly I knew they weren't penguins. Penguins didn't wave their flippers over their heads. Those shouts were real. I dropped the gun and started forward. The figures melted, lost in a mirage of light that wavered uncontrollably. It was all a dream. There was no substance in those dark dots against the snow. I was delirious and imagining things. I knew this was the end even as I stumbled forward at a ridiculous, wobbly run. I heard hoarse raven croaks coming from my throat. Then I stumbled and pitched forward. The snow was soft. A wonderful lethargy stole through me. I knew I must struggle to my feet. But I hadn't strength. And I didn't want to. I didn't want to struggle any more. I remember I thought for a moment of Judie, dying of starvation up there on the ledge of the iceberg. But there was nothing I could do about it – nothing. I was finished. And slowly – luxuriously – unconsciousness came like a blanket to cover me.

I woke to warmth and the smell of food. A spoon was pushed between my cracked lips. My gorge rose as I tried to swallow the hot liquid. I opened my eyes. Pain flamed at the back of my eyeballs. Captain Eide was bending over me. I couldn't believe it at first. I was convinced that I was dead. But then he was forcing hot liquid between my teeth again and I knew that I was alive and that I'd linked up with the survivors of the *Southern Cross*. His face came and went in front of me and I heard a croaking sound that was my own voice. There were things I had to tell him. But I kept losing the drift of what I wanted to say as I slipped back into unconsciousness.

I'm told I slept for sixteen hours. When I finally got my eyes open I found Kyrre, the second officer of the *Southern Cross*, in the tent beside me. The things I'd been trying to tell them rushed to the forefront of my mind. 'They have no food,' I croaked.

Kyrre put out his hand to steady me. The violent urgency of my voice must have shaken him. 'It is all right, Craig,' he soothed me. 'Lie down and rest. Kaptein Eide left yesterday, you know, with nine men. We are to follow.'

'But he doesn't realize the urgency,' I cried excitedly. 'He doesn't know they are – '

He smiled and patted my arm as though I were a child. 'He knows everything. You have been delirious. For hours you say nothing else but that they have no food and will die soon if no one reaches them. You are still telling us that long after Eide has left. He has two sledges and a week's meat for them and he is making forced marches. He tell me to say – do not worry. He will get there.'

'But the gap,' I cried. 'He does not know there is a channel of water a quarter of a mile wide only a few miles to the east of us.'

'You tell us that also – many times.' Kyrre's hand pressed me back. 'You must rest, for soon we must start. We have sledges piled with whale-meat and soon we must start.'

I thought of the long trek back over that frightful road to the iceberg. I knew I couldn't make it. 'Give us one man as guide and some food. We will go on to the *Southern Cross* Camp. We shall only hinder you.'

But he shook his head. 'You did not hear what Eide tell you last night. The *Southern Cross* Camp is abandoned. You see, though we have an enormous quantity of meat and blubber, we have no boats. They were destroyed. So we go where the boats are. Each day we make a journey with half the sledges and then return for the other half. When we are too weak for this we make a dump of half the sledges and go on with the others.'

'How many men have you?' I asked as I lay back.

'Forty-six including those who have gone forward with Kaptein Eide.'

'The boats will not hold them,' I said. And added, 'Even supposing we ever find open water to launch them in.'

'That is so. But we are agreed that everyone must be together. While the ice holds we shall continue to make journeys until all the meat is with the boats. So we may perhaps survive the winter, if we must. Sometime the iceberg must drift out of the pack. Then the fittest will try to reach South Georgia, as Shackleton did, and bring relief. It is our only hope.'

'Is Colonel Bland with him?' I asked.

But he shook his head. 'Colonel Bland is dead. It was his heart. He died soon after Dahle reach us.'

'Dahle?' I stared at him. Do you mean the mate of *Hval 5*?'

He nodded. 'He is gone on with Eide now to the iceberg. He and two other men reach us early last month.'

'But – how?'

'It seems they were swept away from you in the ice. They are on a floe-berg. When it is quiet they find the *Tauer III* Camp. Then – '

'You mean the *Tauer III* Camp was still there?' I interrupted him.

He nodded.

So Erik Bland had been right. The icebergs would have missed him there. If he'd stayed he'd have had a chance of getting out alone. 'Go on,' I said.

'There is not much to tell. They get food and shelter there and survive the storm. Then, with the weather clear, they see the oil smoke with which we try to signal to aircraft and they join us. They are five days without food and journey is terrible, I think. But they are all right.'

'What about you? What happened after the *Southern Cross* went down?'

'We lose our radio so we cannot talk with the rescue ships. Then we were caught by one of the icebergs, as you were. Only a few survive. Olaf Petersen and the others are dead. Then Dahle tell us how you are on a ledge on an iceberg with four boats, and Eide start out with volunteers to reach you. But they are caught in a blizzard and have to turn back. We were beginning a second attempt with all the men when we are lucky enough to find you.'

I was beginning to feel tired again. Behind Kyrre I could just make out the grotesque, emaciated features of Weiner. As I went off to sleep again I remember thinking: *He's just like all D.P.s. You can't kill them. They're indestructible. It's always someone else that saves them, always someone else that dies.* And I thought how Gerda had gone and Peer Larvik and Olaf Petersen. The good ones, the fighters – they're always the ones that are sacrificed. I thought of Dunkirk and Salerno and Anzio and the ships that had gone down in convoys I'd escorted. It was always the fighters.

Next morning, after an early meal, all the tents but the one in which Vaksdal, Keller and I lay were struck and Kyrre set out with his men and the first convoy of sledges loaded with whale-meat. One man was left behind to help us. We were to lie in for a bit and then come on in our own time. We should have nothing to carry and only a single journey to make to the new camp, whilst the rest made three journeys over the same ground.

The trek east, back along the trail we had come, was painfully slow. For the first three days we just made the single journey from camp to camp. We carried nothing and could take our time, for Kyrre's men, when they'd pitched the next camp, had to go back for the second lot of sledges. The open water where we'd been parted from the sea-leopard couldn't have been very extensive. We made a slight detour to the south and saw no sign of it. For all I know the ice may have closed up again, or perhaps it had frozen over, for the air was very still and there would have been little movement of the water to break up new ice. On the fourth day Vaksdal and I were sufficiently recovered to pull our weight on the single journey. Keller was still weak. But next day he, too, was pulling the single journey, whilst we had progressed to the full three trips between camps. With an abundance of regular food my strength quickly returned, only the deadness in my feet and the pain in my side remained.

Slowly the line of icebergs came up over the horizon. I began to dread their approach, for when we reached them I should have to tell Howe about Gerda's death. And I didn't want to do that. Eide would have broken it to him. But he would still want to hear how it happened from my own lips. The thought of that meeting weighed on my spirits like the depression one gets after flu. It was going to knock him for six. I remembered how embittered he'd been as he soaked up liquor like a sponge on the trip out from Cape Town. And then the change that had come over him whilst he was with Gerda. What could I possibly say to him? I remembered that scene on the ledge when he'd renounced his right to accompany Gerda. He'd committed her to my charge. I was responsible for her - not only to him, but to myself. The fact that we were without hope, certain we were going to die, did not help now. Only one thing consoled me; that was that she died without knowing that her father had been killed. But that wouldn't help me with Howe.

I could see his features quite distinctly as I trudged through the ice, leaning my weight on the sledge ropes. I could see the bitter look coming back into his face. And when we got back - if we got back - he'd start drinking again. Drink was all that was left to him. It would kill him in the end, and somehow I didn't want him to go like that.

At last we could see the whole of our own iceberg. The sky was black behind it – a water-sky – and against that backcloth the berg stood out white like a giant pillar of salt. The pinnacle of ice on the top stood up free of cloud with all the sublime upthrust of hope that belongs to a church spire in a flat plain. With my inflamed eyes I looked through Kyrre's glasses and saw the ledge on which our camp should be. Perhaps we were too far away, but my heart sank as I saw no sign of life, no dark smudge that could be the boats and stores.

But at midday the following day – that is, on 9 April – we saw figures coming towards us across the snow. I thought: *My God! It's Eide coming back. They're all dead.* I wasn't worrying about Howe then. I was thinking of Judie and there was an awful ache in my heart. Then the figures were waving to us and shouting. My stabbing eyeballs couldn't recognize them. I dropped the sledge ropes and broke into a stumbling run towards them.

There were about half a dozen of them and the first one I recognized was Eide. I was sure then that the others were dead. He caught hold of my arm, grinning and slapping me on the shoulder. Then he pulled one of the others forward and the next instant Judie was sobbing and laughing in my arms.

And when I looked at her, she was no longer thin and emaciated. She looked well fed and fit, except for the tears that ran down her cheeks. 'I thought you were dead,' she said through sobs of laughter. 'Then Captain Eide came and told us you were all right. Oh, Duncan – I didn't want to go on without you. I couldn't have faced it without you.'

I had my arms tight round her. She was trembling. The cold air seemed suddenly warmer and I no longer felt tired. 'The others?' I asked. 'Are they all right?'

'Yes,' she said. 'Yes, everyone's fine. Except Walter.'

'Except Walter?' I stared at her. 'What do you mean?'

'Two days after you left,' she said. 'Only two days – and thousands of penguins appeared on the ice round the berg. Migrating, or something. We killed over two hundred in one day and more the next. We were rolling in food. We tried to make signals. But you didn't see. Then Walter went after you. He went in the night without telling anyone. In the morning we could see him going out along the trail of your sledge. Eide says he didn't find you?'

'No,' I said. A great weight seemed to have been taken off my mind. Howe was dead. He was safe from the bitterness of life. He was dead and I didn't have to tell him about Gerda.

'There's open sea within five miles of us.'

I was thinking about Howe and I didn't take that in until she repeated it. 'We're drifting north and the ice is breaking up. If there's a gale the iceberg may break through the pack in a matter of days.'

I turned to Eide. 'Is this true?' I asked incredulously. 'Is there a chance of the iceberg breaking out?'

'Not only a chance,' Eide answered. 'It's a certainty. We'll be able to launch the boats inside a week.'

'And then?' I said, glancing round at the *Southern Cross* survivors.

He caught the drift of my thoughts. 'And then we split up. We have four boats. Four chances of getting help. The rest must camp on the iceberg. One of the boats will surely get through.'

I turned and stared at the iceberg. It looked solid enough, but the open sea was different to the pack. It wasn't going to be pleasant marooned on an island of ice swept by gales and the piled-up waves of the South Atlantic. And those tiny boats! Winter was closing in. There'd be gale after gale. This area was noted for them. An almost constant holocaust of wind. What chance had they? The thought made me shudder. I thought again of the trip I'd just made – the futility of it. We had gone in the wild hope of bringing back meat, and two days after we'd left they'd had meat in abundance. Gerda and Howe need never have died, and Eide would have joined up with us anyway. But we hadn't known that. Just as now, we didn't know whether or not a rescue boat would sight us on the iceberg if we stayed there. And because we didn't know, we'd have to attempt the impossible and sail those flimsy lifeboats to South Georgia.

I put my arm round Judie's shoulders and pressed her to me. It was worth it for her sake. But – 'I hope to God Fate doesn't play us any more dirty tricks.'

She looked up at me quickly and I realized I'd spoken aloud. Then he said, 'You're thinking of Gerda, aren't you?'

I nodded.

'She was a lovely person. But, you know, she wouldn't have been happy without her father. Walter couldn't fill his place in her life.' And then she looked up and smiled. 'I think we are all right now. Everything is going to work out.'

The sledges were moving forward again and we turned our faces towards the great castle of ice ahead of us – and the future. Behind the ice was the black cloud-scape that marked the open sea. And beyond was South Georgia. One of the men began to sing. It was a Norwegian song I'd heard them singing on board ship, something about going home. In an instant it was taken up by the rest of the men and the sledges slid forward to the swelling of men's voices, breaking the eternal silence of the ice with their challenge of hope and longing. The sound was thin in the limitless plain of pack ice, but it was indomitable and it sent a thrill of pride and courage through me. Judie was singing, too – singing for me, with her grey eyes laughing and her young body flung forward, straining on the ropes. And her words echoed in my ears – *I think we are all right now. Everything is going to work out.*

THE SURVIVORS

On the 21st April a radio message from South Georgia put the name of the *Southern Cross* back in the headlines of the world's newspapers. It was from Jan Eriksen, manager of the whaling station at Grytviken, to the offices of his company in Oslo, and read: *Two boats containing survivors of the* Southern Cross *arrived Grytviken.*

Two hours later a further message was received containing the first news that there were survivors marooned on an iceberg in the Antarctic. This read: *Two boats each carried six survivors. Commanders: Hans Eide, Einar Vaksdal. List of crews to follow. Two further boats (Kyrre and Dahle) not yet arrived. Sixty-seven persons, including Mrs Judie Bland, marooned on iceberg in open water, position 62.58 S. 30.46 W. Four catchers dispatched to search for missing boats. On arrival station relief ship, Pingvin, I will attempt to rescue survivors marooned on iceberg.*

Winter was closing in on the ice-capped island of South Georgia. In two days the whaling station would have been closed and the place deserted. Eide had made it with just two days to spare. It was an incredible story.

The iceberg had broken out of the pack in a gale on 10 April. The ledge on which their camp was situated then faced straight into the wind. Swept by icy spray from the waves that thundered against the berg, they clung precariously to life for twenty-four hours. Then the berg swung round so that their ledge was sheltered from the wind. They had already decked-in the boats with pieces of packing cases and canvas. They now re-cut the ledge, and on the afternoon of the 11th when the gale had begun to subside they ran the boats down the ice slipway with the crews in them, letting them take the water like lifeboats being launched from a shore station.

In the mountainous waves and the almost continual gloom, the four boats were soon swept apart and separated. For ten days they drove northwards towards South Georgia, their scraps of sail driving them pell-mell through the water on the crests of the waves and hanging slack for lack of wind in the troughs.

Eide, in his radioed report of the boat journey, said: 'I have never experienced such hardship during my thirty-two years at sea. There was a crew of six to each boat. There was no place to sleep. We were constantly bailing for our lives and chipping away the ice that coated the boat and threatened to sink her. Only once was I able to shoot the sun and check my navigation. It was so cold that men froze stiff as boards at the tiller and could not move their limbs until they had been well rubbed to restore the circulation. By the fifth day we were suffering badly from exposure and there were cases of frost-bite. The fear that I should make an error in navigation, miss South Georgia and drive on into the Atlantic was constantly with me.'

They experienced one bad gale. And then late on the tenth day they sighted the south-eastern tip of South Georgia, and in the morning, as they sailed up the northern side of the island, they saw Vaskdal's boat following about a mile behind them.

These were, in fact, the only two boats to get through. What happened to the others we shall never know. Maybe they missed South Georgia and drove on into the Atlantic. Maybe they were swamped or the men became too weakened to chip the ice off and they just capsized. The catchers sent out from Grytviken to search for them reported nothing, not even wreckage.

Meanwhile messages were pouring in to the *Nord Hvalstasjon*. The attention of the whole world had suddenly become focused on this lonely whaling outpost. Eide found himself with offers of assistance from a dozen different countries. But they were all useless. Within a few weeks the pack ice would have moved north with the winter and the iceberg would be beset again. There would be no hope of rescue then until next summer, and he knew that those on the iceberg could not survive the winter. His only hope was the *Pingvin*.

This little vessel arrived at Grytviken on the 22nd and began refuelling at once. It left in the early hours of the 23rd with Eide and Eriksen on board. Before he left, Eide had radioed a full account of the disaster and the names of the survivors marooned on the iceberg. This was the first intimation we had that an Englishman, Duncan Craig, was in command of the survivors.

There followed an anxious period of waiting. The catchers searching for the two missing boats were forced by heavy storms to return to Grytviken. No messages were received from the *Pingvin*. The ship was held up by loose pack and heavy seas, and though we didn't know it at the time, Jacobsen, the captain, insisted on turning back early on the 26th. Only the pleading of Eide and Eirksen persuaded him to to risk his ship and his men a few more hours in those terrible seas.

On the evening of that same day came the first piece of good news. A radio message from Grytviken reported: *Pingvin has sighted iceberg. Pack is heavy and weather conditions bad.*

After that – nothing. For over twenty-four hours Grytviken had nothing to report. Newspapers began running gloomy accounts of conditions in the Antarctic in late April, and as the hours of waiting passed and still there was no news, fears grew that the rescue attempt would fail.

Then, just after midday on the 28th, the teleprinters began clacking out the news for which the public had been waiting:

ICEBERG SURVIVORS RESCUED. OSLO 28 APRIL REUTER: MESSAGE RECEIVED FROM STATION RELIEF SHIP PINGVIN STATES ALL SURVIVORS OF SOUTHERN CROSS MAROONED ON ICEBERG NOW SAFE. PACK ICE AND HEAVY SEAS DELAYED RESCUE OPERATIONS. SURVIVORS SAY CONDITIONS VERY BAD ON ICEBERG IN OPEN WATER OWING TO HEAVY SEAS BREAKING OVER LEDGE CAMP AND FREEZING.

REUTER 1317

Well, that is the end of the story of the *Southern Cross* disaster. There is little more to add, except that now, just over a year after it all happened, a new *Southern Cross* is building at Belfast. It is to cost over £2,500,000 and is expected to be ready for next season. The South Antarctic Whaling Company still has its offices in Fenchurch Street. Only the list of directors has changed. Sir Frederick Sands, well-known financier, is the new chairman, and Duncan Craig is on the board.

Judie Bland is now Judie Craig. They were married in Cape Town on their way back from South Georgia, and according to Craig most of South Africa turned out for the wedding. Besides being a director of the company, Duncan Craig sails as master of *Southern Cross II* when the South Antarctic's next expedition leaves in October. Eide, who was cleared of all blame for the disaster, is already in the Antarctic as master of another factory ship.

It is unlikely that Judie Craig will make another trip to the White South. Already she is a mother and they have a charming house looking out over the Falmouth estuary, where they spend the summer months sailing. There is nothing now to remind them of the terrible hardships they suffered except for a series of beautiful ice studies presented to them by Aldo Bonomi. And – most treasured of all – a picture of Gerda Petersen taken just before the start of the trek across the ice. It faces you in the wide entrance hall as you go in, so that no one can enter their house without meeting her.

THE MARY DEARE

PART ONE

I

I was tired and very cold; a little scared, too. The red and green navigation lights cast a weird glow over the sails. Beyond was nothing, a void of utter darkness in which the sea made little rushing noises. I eased my cramped legs, sucking on a piece of barley sugar. Above me the sails swung in a ghostly arc, slatting back and forth as *Sea Witch* rolled and plunged. There was scarcely wind enough to move the boat through the water, yet the swell kicked up by the March gales ran as strong as ever and my numbed brain was conscious all the time that this was only a lull. The weather forecast at six o'clock had been ominous. Winds of gale force were reported imminent in sea areas Rockall, Shannon, Sole and Finisterre. Beyond the binnacle light the shadowy outline of the boat stretched ahead of me, merging into the clammy blackness of the night. I had dreamed of this moment so often. But it was March and now, after fifteen hours at sea in the Channel, the excitement of owning our own boat was gone, eaten up by the cold. The glimmer of a breaking wave appeared out of the darkness and slapped against the counter, flinging spray in my face and sidling off into the blackness astern with a hiss of white water. God! It was cold! Cold and clammy – and not a star anywhere.

The door of the charthouse slammed back to give me a glimpse of the lit saloon and against it loomed Mike Duncan's oilskin-padded bulk, holding a steaming mug in either hand. The door slammed to again, shutting out the lit world below, and the darkness and the sea crowded in again. 'Soup?' Mike's cheerful, freckled face appeared abruptly out of the night, hanging disembodied in the light from the binnacle. He smiled at me from the folds of his balaclava as he handed me a mug. 'Nice and fresh up here after the galley,' he said. And then the smile was wiped from his face. 'What the hell's that?' He was staring past my left shoulder, staring at something astern of us on the port quarter. 'Can't be the moon, can it?'

I swung round. A cold, green translucence showed at the edge of visibility, a sort of spectral light that made me catch my breath in a sudden panic with all the old seamen's tales of weird and frightful things seen at sea rushing through my mind.

The light grew steadily brighter, phosphorescent and unearthly – a ghastly brilliance like a bloated glow-worm. And then suddenly it condensed and hardened into a green pin-point, and I yelled at Mike: 'The Aldis – quick!' It was the starboard navigation light of a big steamer, and it was bearing straight down on us. Her deck lights were appearing now, misted and yellow; and gently, like the muffled beat of a tom-tom, the sound of her engines reached out to us in a low, pulsating throb.

The beam of the Aldis lamp stabbed the night, blinding us with the reflected glare from a thick blanket of mist that engulfed us. It was a sea mist that had crept up on me in the dark without my knowing it. The white of a bow wave showed dimly in the brilliance, and then the shadowy outline of the bows themselves took shape. In an instant I could see the whole for'ard half of the ship. It was like a ghost ship emerging out of the mist, and the blunt bows were already towering over us as I swung the wheel.

It seemed an age that I watched *Sea Witch* turn, waiting for the jib to fill on the other tack and bring her head round, and all the time I could hear the surge of that bow wave coming nearer. 'She's going to hit us! Christ! She's going to hit us!' I can still hear Mike's cry, high and strident in the night. He was blinking the Aldis, directing the beam straight at her bridge. The whole superstructure was lit up, the light reflecting back in flashes from the glass windows. And the towering mass of the steamer kept on coming, thundering down on us at a good eight knots without a check, without any alteration of course.

The main and mizzen booms swung over with a crash. The jib was aback now. I left it like that for a moment, watching her head pay off. Every detail of *Sea Witch*, from the tip of her long bowsprit to the top of her mainmast, was lit by the green glow of the steamer's starboard light now high above us. I let go the port jib sheet, hauling in on the starboard sheet, saw the sail fill, and then Mike screamed, 'Look out! Hold on!' There was a great roaring sound and a wall of white water hit us. It swept over the cockpit, lifting me out of my seat, tugging at my grip on the wheel. The sails swung in a crazy arc; they swung so far that the boom and part of the mainsail were buried for a moment in the back of a wave whilst tons of water spilled across our decks; and close alongside the steamer slid by like a cliff.

Slowly *Sea Witch* righted herself as the water poured off her in a white foam. I still had hold of the wheel and Mike was clutching the backstay runner, shouting obscenities at the top of his voice. His words came to me as a frail sound against the solid thumping of the ship's engines. And then another sound emerged out of the night – the steady thrashing of a propeller partly clear of the water.

I shouted to Mike, but he had already realized the danger and had switched the Aldis on again. Its brilliant light showed us plates pitted deep with rust and a weed-grown Plimsoll mark high above the water. Then the plates curved up to the stern and we could see the propeller blades slashing at the waves, thumping the water into a swirling froth. *Sea Witch* trembled, sails slack. Then she slid off the back of a wave into that mill race and the blades were whirling close along our port side, churning white water over the cabin top, flinging it up into the mainsail.

It was like that for a moment and then they flailed off into the darkness beyond the bowsprit and we were left pitching in the broken water of the ship's wake. The Aldis beam picked out her name – *MARY DEARE* – *Southampton*. We stared dazedly at her rust-streaked lettering whilst the stern became shadowy and then vanished abruptly. Only the beat of her engines remained then, throbbing gently and gradually dying away into the night. A faint smell of burning lingered on for a while in the damp air. 'Bastards!' Mike shouted, suddenly finding his voice. 'Bastards!' He kept on repeating the word.

The door of the charthouse slid back, and a figure emerged. It was Hal. 'Are you boys all right?' His voice – a little too calm, a little too cheerful – shook slightly.

'Didn't you see what happened?' Mike cried.

'Yes, I saw,' he replied.

'They must have seen us. I was shining the Aldis straight at the bridge. If they'd been keeping a lookout – '

'I don't think they were keeping a lookout. In fact, I don't think there was anybody on the bridge.' It was said so quietly that for a moment I didn't realize the implication.

'How do you mean – nobody on the bridge?' I asked.

He came out on to the deck then. 'It was just before the bow wave hit us. I knew something was wrong and I'd got as far as the charthouse. I found myself looking out through the window along the beam of the Aldis lamp. It was shining right on to the bridge. I don't think there was anybody there. I couldn't see anybody.'

'But good God!' I said. 'Do you realize what you're saying?'

'Yes, of course, I do.' His tone was peremptory, a little military. 'It's odd, isn't it?'

He wasn't the sort of man to make up a thing like that. H. A.

Lowden – Hal to all his friends – was an ex-Gunner, a Colonel retired, who spent most of the summer months ocean racing. He had a lot of experience of the sea.

'Do you mean to say you think there was nobody in control of that ship?' Mike's tone was incredulous.

'I don't know,' Hal answered. 'It seems incredible. But all I can say is that I had a clear view of the interior of the bridge for an instant and, as far as I could see, there was nobody there.'

We didn't say anything for a moment. I think we were all too astonished. The idea of a big ship ploughing her way through the rock-infested seas so close to the French coast without anybody at the helm . . . It was absurd.

Mike's voice, suddenly practical, broke the silence. 'What happened to those mugs of soup?' The beam of the Aldis lamp clicked on, revealing the mugs lying in a foot of water at the bottom of the cockpit. 'I'd better go and make another brew.' And then to Hal who was standing, half-dressed, his body braced against the charthouse: 'What about you, Colonel? You'd like some soup, wouldn't you?'

Hal nodded. 'I never refuse an offer of soup.' He watched Mike until he had gone below and then he turned to me. 'I don't mind admitting it now that we're alone,' he said, 'but that was a very unpleasant moment. How did we come to be right across her bows like that?'

I explained that the ship had been down-wind from us and we hadn't heard the beat of her engines. 'The first we saw of her was the green of her starboard navigation light coming at us out of the mist.'

'No fog signal?'

'We didn't hear it, anyway.'

'Odd!' He stood for a moment, his long body outlined against the port light, and then he came aft and seated himself beside me on the cockpit coaming. 'Had a look at the barometer during your watch?' he asked.

'No,' I said. 'What's it doing?'

'Going down.' He had his long arms wrapped round his body, hugging his seaman's jersey. 'Dropped quite a bit since I went below.' He hesitated and then said, 'You know, this gale could come up on us pretty quickly.' I didn't say anything and he pulled his pipe out and began to suck on it. 'I tell you frankly, John, I don't like it.' The quietness of his voice added strength to his opinion. 'If the forecast turns out right and the wind backs north-westerly, then we'll be on a lee shore. I don't like gales and I don't like lee shores, particularly when the lee shore is the Channel Islands.'

I thought he wanted me to put back to the French coast and I didn't say anything; just sat there staring at the compass card, feeling obstinate and a little scared.

'It's a pity about the kicker,' he murmured. 'If the kicker hadn't packed up – '

'Why bring that up?' It was the only thing that had gone wrong with the boat. 'You've always said you despise engines.'

His blue eyes, caught in the light of the binnacle, stared at me fixedly. 'I was only going to say,' he put in mildly, 'that if the kicker hadn't packed up we'd be halfway across the Channel by now and the situation would be entirely different.'

'Well, I'm not putting back.'

He took his pipe out of his mouth as though to say something and then put it back and sat there, staring at me with those unwinking blue eyes of his.

'The real trouble is that you're not used to sailing in a boat that hasn't been kept up to ocean racing pitch.' I hadn't meant to say that, but I was angry and my nerves were still tense from the steamer incident.

An awkward silence fell between us. At length he stopped sucking on his pipe. 'It's only that I like to arrive,' he said quietly. 'The rigging is rusty, the ropes rotten and the sails – '

'We went over all that in Morlaix,' I said tersely. 'Plenty of yachts cross the Channel in worse shape than *Sea Witch*.'

'Not in March with a gale warning. And not without an engine.' He got up and went for'ard as far as the mast, bending down and hauling at something. There was the sound of splintering wood and then he came back and tossed a section of the bulwarks into the cockpit at my feet. 'The bow wave did that.' He sat down beside me again. 'It isn't good enough, John. The boat hasn't been surveyed and for all you know the hull may be as rotten as the gear after lying for two years on a French mud bank.'

'The hull's all right,' I told him. I was calmer now. 'There are a couple of planks to be replaced and she needs restopping. But that's all. I went over every inch of her with a knife before I bought her. The wood is absolutely sound.'

'And what about the fastenings?' His right eyebrow lifted slightly. 'Only a surveyor could tell you whether the fastenings – '

'I told you, I'm having her surveyed as soon as we reach Lymington.'

'Yes, but that doesn't help us now. If this gale comes up on us suddenly . . . I'm a prudent mariner,' he added. 'I like the sea, but it's not a creature I want to take liberties with.'

'Well, I can't afford to be prudent,' I said. 'Not right now.' Mike and I had just formed a small salvage company and every day we delayed getting the boat to England for conversion was a day lost out of our diving season. He knew that.

'I'm only suggesting you steer a point off your direct course,' he said. 'Close-hauled we can just about lay for Hanois on Guernsey Island. We'll then be in a position to take advantage of the wind when it backs and run for shelter to Peter Port.'

Of course . . . I rubbed my hand over my eyes. I should have known what he was driving at. But I was tired and the steamer incident had left me badly shaken. It was queer the way the vessel had sailed right through us like that.

'It won't help your salvage venture if you smash the boat up.' Hal's voice cut across my thoughts. He had taken my silence for refusal. 'Apart from the gear, we're not very strongly crewed.'

That was true enough. There were only the three of us. The fourth member of the crew, Ian Baird, had been sea-sick from the time we had left Morlaix. And she was a biggish boat for three to handle – a forty-tonner. 'Very well,' I said. 'We'll head for Guernsey.'

He nodded as though he'd known it all along. 'You'll need to steer North 65° East then.'

I turned the wheel, giving her starboard helm, and watched the compass card swing to the new course. He must have been working out the course in the charthouse just before the steamer came up on us. 'I take it you worked out the distance, too?'

'Fifty-four miles. And at this rate,' he added, 'it'll be daylight long before we get there.'

An uneasy silence settled between us. I could hear him sucking at his empty pipe, but I kept my eyes on the compass and didn't look at him. Damn it, I should have thought of Peter Port for myself! But there'd been so much to do at Morlaix getting the boat ready . . . I'd just about worked myself to a standstill before ever we put to sea.

'That ship.' His voice came out of the darkness at my side, a little hesitant, bridging the gap of my silence. 'Damned queer,' he murmured. 'You know, if there really was nobody on board . . .' He checked and then added, half-jokingly, 'That would have been a piece of salvage that would have set you up for life.' I thought I sensed a serious note underlying his words, but when I glanced at him he shrugged his shoulders and laughed. 'Well, I think I'll turn in again now.' He got up and his 'good night' floated back to me from the dark gap of the charthouse.

Shortly afterwards Mike brought me a mug of hot soup. He stayed and talked to me whilst I drank it, speculating wildly about the *Mary Deare*. Then he, too, turned in and the blackness of the night closed round me. Could there really have been nobody on the bridge? It was too fantastic – an empty ship driving pell mell up the Channel. And yet, cold and alone, with the pale glimmer of the sails swooping above me and the dismal dripping of mist condensed on the canvas, anything seemed possible.

At three Hal relieved me and for two hours I slept, dreaming of blunt, rusted bows hanging over us, toppling slowly, everlastingly. I woke in a panic, cold with sweat, and lay for a moment thinking about what Hal had said. It would be queer if we salvaged a ship, just like that, before we'd even . . . But I was asleep again before the idea had more than flickered through my mind. And in an instant I was being shaken and was stumbling out to the helm in the brain-numbing hour before the dawn, all recollection of the *Mary Deare* blurred and hazed by the bitter cold.

Daylight came slowly, a reluctant dawn that showed a drab, sullen sea heaving gently, the steepness flattened out of the swell. The wind was northerly now, but still light; and some time during the night we had gone over on to the other tack.

At ten to seven Hal and I were in the charthouse for the weather report. It started with gale warnings for the western approaches of the Channel; the forecast for our own area of Portland was: *Wind light, northerly at first, backing north-westerly later and increasing strong to gale.* Hal glanced at me, but said nothing. There was no need. I checked our position and then gave Mike the course to steer for Peter Port.

It was a queer morning. There was a lot of scud about and by the time we had finished breakfast it was moving across the sky quite fast. Yet at sea level there was scarcely any wind so that, with full main and mizzen set and the big yankee jib, we were creeping through the water at a bare three knots, rolling sluggishly. There was still a mist of sorts and visibility wasn't much more than two miles.

We didn't talk much. I think we were all three of us too conscious of the sea's menace. Peter Port was still thirty miles away. The silence and the lack of wind was oppressive. 'I'll go and check our position again,' I said. Hal nodded as though the thought had been in his mind, too.

But poring over the chart didn't help. As far as I could tell we were six miles north-north-west of the Roches Douvres, that huddle of rocks and submerged reefs that is the western outpost of the Channel Islands. But I couldn't be certain; my dead reckoning depended too much on tide and leeway.

And then Mike knocked the bottom out of my calculations. 'There's a rock about two points on the starboard bow,' he called to me. 'A big one sticking up out of the water.'

I grabbed the glasses and flung out of the charthouse. 'Where?' My mouth was suddenly harsh and dry. If it were the Roches Douvres, then we must have been set down a good deal further than I thought. And it couldn't be anything else; it was all open sea between Roches Douvres and Guernsey. 'Where?' I repeated.

'Over there!' Mike was pointing.

I screwed up my eyes. But I couldn't see anything. The clouds had thinned momentarily and a queer sun-glow was reflected on the oily surface of the sea, merging it with the moisture-laden atmosphere. There was no horizon; at the edge of visibility sea and air became one. I searched through the glasses. 'I can't see it,' I said. 'How far away?'

'I don't know. I've lost it now. But it wasn't more than a mile.'

'You're sure it was a rock?'

'Yes, I think so. What else could it be?' He was staring into the distance, his eyes narrowed against the luminous glare of the haze. 'It was a big rock with some sort of tower or pinnacle in the middle of it.'

The Roches Douvres light! I glanced at Hal seated behind the wheel. 'We'd better alter course,' I said. 'The tide is setting us down at about two knots.' My voice sounded tense. If it was the Roches Douvres and the wind fell any lighter, we could be swept right down on to the reef.

He nodded and swung the wheel. 'That would put you out by five miles in your dead reckoning.'

'Yes.'

He frowned. He had taken his sou'wester off and his grey hair, standing on end, gave his face a surprised, puckish look. 'I think you're under-rating yourself as a navigator, but you're the boss. How much do you want me to bear up?'

'Two points at least.'

'There's an old saying,' he murmured: 'The prudent mariner, when in doubt, should assume his dead reckoning to be correct.' He looked at me with a quizzical lift to his bushy eyebrows. 'We don't want to miss Guernsey, you know.'

A mood of indecision took hold of me. Maybe it was just the strain of the long night, but I wasn't sure what to do for the best. 'Did you see it?' I asked him.

'No.'

I turned to Mike and asked him again whether he was sure it was rock he'd seen.

'You can't be sure of anything in this light.'

'But you definitely saw something?'

'Yes. I'm certain of that. And I think it had some sort of a tower on it.'

A gleam of watery sunlight filtered through the damp atmosphere, giving a furtive brightness to the cockpit. 'Then it must be the Roches Douvres,' I murmured.

'Look!' Mike cried. 'There it is – over there.'

I followed the line of his outstretched arm. On the edge of visibility, lit by the sun's pale gleam, was the outline of a flattish rock with a light tower in the middle. I had the glasses on it immediately, but it was no more than a vague, misty shape – a reddish tint glimmering through the golden haze. I dived into the charthouse and snatched up the chart, staring at the shape of the Roches Douvres reef. It marked drying rock outcrops for a full mile north-west of the 92-foot light tower. We must be right on the fringe of those outcrops. 'Steer north,' I shouted to Hal, 'and sail her clear just as fast as you can.'

'Aye, aye, skipper.' He swung the wheel, calling to Mike to trim the sheets. He was looking over his shoulder at the Roches Douvres light as I came out of the charthouse. 'You know,' he said, 'there's something odd here. I've never actually seen the Roches Douvres, but I know the Channel Islands pretty well and I've never seen any rock that showed up red like that.'

I steadied myself against the charthouse and focused the glasses on it again. The gleam of sunlight had become more positive. Visibility was improving all the time. I saw it clearly then and I was almost laughing with relief. 'It's not a rock,' I said. 'It's a ship.' There was no doubt about it now. The rusty hull was no longer blurred, but stood out clear and sharp, and what I had taken to be a light tower was its single funnel.

We were all of us laughing with the sense of relief as we turned back on to the course. 'Hove-to by the look of it,' Mike said as he stopped hauling in on the main-sheet and began to coil it down.

It certainly looked like it, for now that we were back on course her position didn't seem to have altered at all. She was lying broadside on to us as though held there by the wind and, as we closed with her and her outline became clearer, I could see that she was stationary, wallowing in the swell. Our course would leave her about half a mile to starboard. I reached for the glasses. There was something about the ship . . . something about her shape and her rusty hull and the way she seemed a little down at the bows.

'Probably pumping out her bilges,' Hal said, his voice hesitant as though he, too, were puzzled.

I focused the glasses and the outline of the vessel leaped towards me. She was an old boat with straight bows and a clean sweep to her sheer. She had an old-fashioned counter stern, an untidy clutter of derricks round her masts, and too much superstructure. Her single smoke stack, like her masts, was almost vertical. At one time she had been painted black, but now she had a rusty, uncared-for look. There was a sort of lifelessness about her that held me with the glasses to my eyes. And then I saw the lifeboat. 'Steer straight for her, will you, Hal,' I said.

'Anything wrong?' he asked, reacting immediately to the note of urgency in my voice.

'Yes. One of the lifeboats is hanging vertically from its davits.' It was more than that. The other davits were empty. I passed him the glasses. 'Take a look at the for'ard davits,' I told him and my voice trembled slightly, the birth of a strange feeling of excitement.

Soon we could see the empty davits with the naked eye and the single lifeboat hanging from the falls. 'Looks deserted,' Mike said. 'And she's quite a bit down by the bows. Do you think – ' He left the sentence unfinished. The same thought was in all our minds.

We came down on her amidships. The name at her bow was so broken up with rust streaks that we couldn't read it. Close-to she looked in wretched shape. Her rusty bow plates were out of true, her superstructure was damaged and she was definitely down by the bows, her stern standing high so that we could see the top of her screw. A festoon of wires hung from her mast derricks. She was a cargo ship and she looked as though she'd taken a hell of a hammering.

We went about within a cable's length of her and I hailed her through our megaphone. My voice lost itself in the silence of the sea. There was no answer. The only sound was the sloshing of the swell against her sides. We ran down on her quickly then, Hal steering to pass close under her stern. I think we were all of us watching for her name. And then suddenly there it was in rust-streaked lettering high above our heads just as it had been during the night: *MARY DEARE* – *Southampton*.

She was quite a big boat, at least 6000 tons. Abandoned like that she should have had a salvage tug in attendance, ships standing by. But there wasn't another vessel in sight. She was alone and lifeless within twenty miles of the French coast. I glanced up along her starboard side as we came out from under her stern. Both davits were empty, the lifeboats gone.

'You were right then,' Mike said, turning to Hal, his voice tense. 'There wasn't anybody on the bridge last night.'

We stared up at her in silence as we slipped away from her, awed by the sense of mystery. The rope falls hung forlornly from the empty davits. A thin trailer of smoke emerged incongruously from her funnel. That was the only sign of life. 'They must have abandoned ship just before they nearly ran us down,' I said.

'But she was steaming at full ahead,' Hal said, speaking more to himself than to us. 'You don't abandon ship with the engines going full ahead. And why didn't she radio for help?'

I was thinking of what Hal had said half-jokingly last night. If there was really nobody on board . . . I stood there, my hands braced on the guardrail, my body tense as I stared at her, searching for some sign of life. But there was nothing; nothing but that thin wisp of smoke trailing from the funnel. Salvage! A ship of 6000 tons, drifting and abandoned. It was unbelievable. And if we could bring her into port under her own steam . . . I turned to Hal. 'Do you think you could lay *Sea Witch* alongside her, close enough for me to get hold of one of those falls?'

'Don't be a fool,' he said. 'There's still quite a swell running. You may damage the boat, and if this gale – '

But I was in no mood for caution now. 'Ready about!' I called. And then, 'Lee ho!' We came about on to the other tack and I sent Mike below to get Ian out of his bunk. 'We'll jog up to her close-hauled,' I told Hal. 'I'll jump for the ropes as you go about.'

'It's crazy,' he said. 'You've a hell of a height to climb to the deck. And supposing the wind pipes up. I may not be able to get you – '

'Oh, to hell with the wind!' I cried. 'Do you think I'm going to pass up a chance like this? Whatever happened to the poor devils who abandoned her, this is the chance of a lifetime for Mike and myself.'

He stared at me for a moment, and then he nodded. 'Okay. It's your boat.' We were headed back for the ship now. 'When we get under her lee,' Hal said, 'we'll be pretty well blanketed. I may have some difficulty – ' He stopped there and glanced up at the burgee.

I had done the same, for there was a different feel about the boat now. She was surging along with a noise of water from her bows and spray wetting the foredeck. The burgee was streamed out to starboard. I checked with the compass. 'You'll have no difficulty standing off from her,' I said. 'The wind's north-westerly now.'

He nodded, his eyes lifting to the sails. 'You're still determined to go on board?'

'Yes.'

'Well, you'd better not stay long. There's some weight in the wind now.'

'I'll be as quick as I can,' I said. 'If you want to recall me in a hurry signal on the fog-horn.' We were doing all of four knots now and the ship was coming up fast. I went to the charthouse door and yelled to Mike. He came almost immediately. Ian was behind him, white-faced and still sweaty-looking from his bunk. I gave him the boat-hook and told him to stand by in the bows ready to shove off. 'We'll go about just before we get to her. That'll take the way off her and you'll be all set to stand-off again.' I was stripping off my oilskins. Already the rusty sides of the *Mary Deare* were towering above us. It looked a hell of a height to climb. 'Ready about?' I asked.

'Ready about,' Hal said. And then he swung the wheel. *Sea Witch* began to pay off, slowly, very slowly. For a moment it looked as though she was going to poke her long bowsprit through the steamer's rusty plates. Then she was round and I made up the starboard runner as the boom swung over. There was little wind now that we were close under the *Mary Deare*. The sails flapped lazily. The cross-trees were almost scraping the steamer's sides as we rolled in the swell. I grabbed a torch and ran to the mast, climbed the starboard rail and stood there, poised, my feet on the bulwarks, my hands gripping the shrouds. Her way carried me past the for'ard davit falls. There was still a gap of several yards between me and the ship's side. Hal closed it slowly. Leaning out I watched the after davit falls slide towards me. There was a jar as the tip of our cross-trees rammed the plates above my head. The first of the falls came abreast of me. I leaned right out, but they were a good foot beyond my reach. 'This time!' Hal shouted. The cross-trees jarred again. I felt the jolt of it through the shroud I was clinging to. And then my hand closed on the ropes and I let go, falling heavily against the ship's side, the lift of a swell wetting me to my knees. 'Okay!' I yelled.

Hal was shouting to Ian to shove off. I could see him thrusting wildly with the boat-hook. Then the end of the boom hit me between the shoulder-blades, the jar of it almost making me lose my hold. I hauled myself upwards with desperate urgency, afraid that the stern might swing and crush my legs against the ship's side. There was the slam of wood just below my feet and then I saw *Sea Witch* was clear and standing out away from the ship. 'Don't be long,' Hal shouted.

Sea Witch was already heeling to the wind, the water creaming back from her bows and a white wake showing at her stern as she gathered speed. 'I'll be as quick as I can,' I called back to him, and then I began to climb.

That climb seemed endless. The *Mary Deare* was rolling all the time, so that one minute I'd be swung out over the sea and the next slammed against the iron plates of her side. There were moments when I thought I'd never make it. And when, finally, I reached the upper-deck, *Sea Witch* was already half a mile away, though Hal had her pointed up into the wind and was pinching her so that her sails were all a-shiver.

The sea was no longer oil-smooth. Little waves were forming on the tops of the swell, making patterns of white as they broke. I knew I hadn't much time. I cupped my hands round my mouth and shouted: '*Mary Deare!* Ahoy! Is there anybody on board?' A gull shifted his stance uneasily on one of the ventilators, watching me with a beady eye. There was no answer, no sound except the door to the after deck-house slatting back and forth, regular as a metronome, and the bump of the lifeboat against the port side. It was obvious that she was deserted. All the evidence of abandonment was there on the deck – the empty falls, the stray pieces of clothing, a loaf lying in the scuppers, a hunk of cheese trampled into the deck, a half-open suitcase spilling nylons and cigarettes, a pair of sea boots; they had left her in a hurry and at night.

But why?

A sense of unease held me for a moment – a deserted ship with all its secrets, all its death-in-life stillness – I felt like an intruder and glanced quickly back towards *Sea Witch*. She was no bigger than a toy now in the leaden immensity of sea and sky, and the wind was beginning to moan through the empty ship – hurry! hurry!

A quick search and then the decision would have to be made. I ran for'ard and swung myself up the ladder to the bridge. The wheelhouse was empty. It's odd, but it came as a shock to me. Everything was so very normal there; a couple of dirty cups on a ledge, a pipe carefully laid down in an ash-tray, the binoculars set down on the seat of the Captain's chair – and the engine-room telegraph set to *Full Ahead*. It was as though at any moment the helmsman might return to take his place at the wheel.

But outside there was evidence in plenty of heavy weather. All the port wing of the bridge had been stove in, the ladder buckled and twisted, and down on the well-deck the seas had practically stripped the covering from the for'ard holds and a wire hawser was lying uncoiled in loops like dannert wire. And yet that in itself didn't account for her being abandoned; another tarpaulin hatch cover had been partly rigged and fresh timbering lay around as though the watch on deck had just knocked off for a cup of tea.

The chartroom at the back of the wheelhouse shed no light on the mystery; in fact, the reverse, for there was the log book open at the last entry: *20.46 hours – Les Heaux Light bearing 114°, approximately 12 miles. Wind south-east – Force 2. Sea Moderate. Visibility good. Altered course for the Needles – north 33° east.* The date was 18 March, and the time showed that this entry had been made just an hour and three-quarters before the *Mary Deare* had almost run us down. Entries in the log were made every hour so that whatever it was that had made them abandon ship had occurred between nine and ten the previous night, probably just as the mist was closing in.

Checking back through the log I found nothing to suggest that the ship would have to be abandoned. There had been constant gales and they had taken a bad beating. But that was all. *Hove-to on account of dangerous seas, waves sometimes breaking against bridge. Making water in No. 1 hold. Pumps not holding their own.* That entry for 16 March was the worst. Wind strength was given as Force 11 for twelve solid hours. And before then, ever since they had left the Mediterranean through the Straits, the wind had never fallen below Force 7, which is moderate gale, and was several times recorded as Force 10, whole gale. The pumps had been kept going all the time.

If they had abandoned ship in the gale of 16 March it would have been understandable. But the log showed that they had rounded Ushant on the morning of 18 March in clear weather with seas moderate and the wind Force 3. There was even a note – *Pumps making good headway. Clearing wreckage and repairing Number One hatch cover.*

It didn't make sense.

A companion-way led to the upper or boat-deck level. The door to the Captain's cabin was open. The room was neat and tidy, everything in its place; no sign of hurried departure. From the desk a girl's face in a big silver frame smiled at me, her fair hair catching the light, and across the bottom of the picture she had scrawled: *For Daddy – Bons voyages, and come back soon. Love – Janet.* There was coal dust on the frame and more of it on the desk and smudged over a file of papers that proved to be the cargo manifest, showing that the *Mary Deare* had loaded cotton at Rangoon on 13 January and was bound for Antwerp. On top of a filing tray filled with papers were several air mail letter-cards slit open with a knife. They were English letter-cards post-marked London and they were addressed to Captain James Taggart, *s.s. Mary Deare* at Aden, addressed in the same uneven, rather rounded hand that had scrawled across the bottom of the photograph. And below the letters, amongst the mass of papers, I found report sheets written in a small, neat hand and signed James Taggart. But they only covered the voyage from Rangoon to Aden. On the desk beside the tray was a sealed letter addressed to Miss Janet Taggart, University College, Gower Street, London, W.C.1. It was in a different hand and the envelope was unstamped.

All those little things, those little homely details . . . I don't know how to express it – they added up to something, something I didn't like. There was that cabin, so quiet, with all the decisions that had driven the ship throughout her life still there in the atmosphere of it – and the ship herself silent as the grave. And then I saw the raincoats hanging on the door, two blue Merchant Navy officers' raincoats hanging side by side, the one much bigger than the other.

I went out and slammed the door behind me, as though by closing it I could shut away my sudden, unreasoned fear. 'Ahoy! Is there anyone on board?' My voice, high and hoarse, echoed through the vaults of the ship. The wind moaned at me from the deck. Hurry! I must hurry. All I had to do was check the engines now, decide whether we could get her under way.

I stumbled down the dark well of a companion-way, following the beam of my torch, flashing it through the open doorway of the saloon where I had a glimpse of places still laid and chairs pushed hastily back. A faint smell of burning lingered on the musty air. But it didn't come from the pantry – the fire was out, the stove cold. My torch focused on a half-empty tin of bully lying on the table. There was butter, cheese, a loaf of bread with the crust all covered in coal dust; coal dust on the handle of the knife that had been used to cut it, coal dust on the floor.

'Is there anybody about?' I yelled. 'Ahoy! Anyone there?' No answer. I went back to the 'tween-decks alley-way that ran the length of the port-hand midships section. It was as silent and as black as the adit of a mine. I started down it, and then I stopped. There it was again – a sound I had been conscious of, but had not thought about; a sound like the shifting of gravel. It echoed within the ship's hull as though somewhere the steel plates were shifting on the bottom of the sea. It was a strange, uncanny sound, and it stopped abruptly as I walked on down the alley-way so that, in the vacuum of abrupt silence, I heard the wind's howl again.

The door at the end of the alley-way swung open to the roll of the ship, letting in a glimmer of daylight. I started towards it, conscious that the acrid smell of burning had increased until it quite overlaid the fusty mixture of hot oil, stale cooking and sea water dampness that permeates the 'tween-decks of all cargo ships. A fire hose, fixed to a hydrant near the engine-room door, snaked aft through pools of water and disappeared through the open door, out on to the well-deck beyond. I followed it. Out in the daylight I saw that Number Three hatch was burned and blackened, eaten half away by fire, and Number Four had been partly opened up. Fire hoses curled round the deck, disappearing into the open inspection hatch of Number Three hold. I went a few rungs down the vertical ladder, flashing my torch. But there was no smoke, no lurid glow, and the acrid fumes of the fire had a stale, washed-out smell, mixed with the pungent odour of chemicals. An empty foam extinguisher toppled on its side, clattering against the steel of the bulkhead plating. My torch showed the black pit of the hold piled high with charred and sodden bales of cotton and there was the sound of water slopping about.

The fire was out – dead – not even a wisp of smoke. And yet the ship had been abandoned. It didn't make sense. I was thinking of last night, how the smell of burning had lingered in the mist after the ship had gone past us. And there was the coal dust on the captain's desk and in the galley. Somebody must have put that fire out. I ran back to the engine-room door, remembering the grating sound of gravel shifting. Could it have been coal? Was there somebody down in the stokehold? Somewhere in the ship a hatch slammed, or maybe it was a door. I went in, on to the cat-walk that hung over the black abyss of the engine-room, criss-crossed with the steel gratings and vertical ladders. 'Ahoy!' I yelled. 'Ahoy there!'

No answer. My torch showed a glint of polished brass and the duller gleam of burnished steel amidst the shadowy shapes of the engines. No movement either . . . only the sound of water that made little rushing noises as it slopped about to the roll of the ship.

I hesitated, wondering whether to go down to the stokehold, held there by a sort of fear. And it was then that I heard the foot-steps.

They went slowly along the starboard alley-way – boots clang-ing hollow against the steel flooring; a heavy, dragging tread that passed the engine-room door, going for'ard towards the bridge. The sound of the footsteps gradually faded away and was lost in the slapping of the water in the bilges far below me.

It couldn't have been more than twenty seconds that I remained there, paralysed, and then I had flung myself at the door, dragged it open and dived out into the alley-way, tripping over the step in my haste, dropping my torch and fetching up against the further wall with a force that almost stunned me. The torch had fallen into a pool of rusty water and lay there, shining like a glow-worm in the darkness. I stooped and picked it up and shone it down the passage.

There was nobody there. The beam reached the whole shadowy length as far as the ladder to the deck, and the corridor was empty. I shouted, but nobody answered. The ship rolled with a creak of wood and the slosh of water, and above me, muffled, I heard the rhythmic slamming of the door to the after deck-house. And then a faint, far-distant sound reached me, a sound that had a note of urgency in it. It was *Sea Witch*'s fog-horn signalling me to return.

I stumbled for'ard and as I neared the ladder to the deck, the fog-horn's moan was mingled with the noise of the wind soughing through the superstructure. Hurry! Hurry! There was a greater urgency in it now; urgency in the noise of the wind, in the fog-horn's blare.

I reached the ladder, was starting up – when I saw him. He was outlined for an instant in the swinging beam of my torch, a shadowy figure standing motionless in the recess of a doorway, black with a gleam of white to his eyes.

I checked, shocked into immobility – all the silence, all the ghostly silence of that dead ship clutching at my throat. And then I turned the beam of the torch full on him. He was a big man, dressed in reefer and sea boots, and black with coal dust. Sweat had seamed his face, making grime-streaked runnels as though he had wept big tears and the bone of his forehead glistened. All the right side of his jaw was bruised and clotted with blood.

He moved suddenly with great rapidity, came down on me

413

with a rush. The torch was knocked from my hand and I smelt the stale smell of sweat and coal dust as his powerful fingers gripped my shoulders, turning me like a child, twisting my head to the cold daylight that came down the ladder. 'What do you want?' he demanded in a harsh, rasping voice. 'What are you doing here? Who are you?' He shook me violently as though by shaking me he'd get at the truth.

'I'm Sands,' I gasped out. 'John Sands. I came to see – '

'How did you get on board?' There was a note of authority, as well as violence, in the rasp of his voice.

'By the falls,' I said. 'We sighted the *Mary Deare* drifting and when we saw the lifeboats gone, we came alongside to investigate.'

'Investigate!' He glared at me. 'There's nothing to investigate.' And then quickly, still gripping hold of me: 'Is Higgins with you? Did you pick him up? Is that why you're here?'

'Higgins?' I stared at him.

'Yes, Higgins.' There was a sort of desperate violence in the way he said the man's name. 'But for him I'd have got her safe to Southampton by now. If you've got Higgins with you . . .' He stopped suddenly, his head on one side, listening. The sound of the fog-horn was nearer now and Mike's voice was hailing me. 'They're calling you.' His grip tightened convulsively on my shoulders. 'What's your boat?' he demanded. 'What sort of boat is it?'

'A yacht.' And I added inconsequentially: 'You nearly ran us down last night.'

'A yacht!' He let go of me then with a little gasp like a sigh of relief. 'Well, you'd better get back to it. Wind's getting up.'

'Yes,' I said. 'We'll have to hurry – both of us.'

'Both of us?' He frowned.

'Of course,' I said. 'We'll take you off and when we reach Peter Port . . .'

'No!' The word exploded from his lips. 'No. I'm staying with my ship.'

'You're the Captain, are you?'

'Yes.' He stooped and picked up my torch and handed it to me. Mike's voice came to us faintly, a strangely disembodied shout from the outside world. The wind was a low-pitched, whining note. 'Better hurry,' he said.

'Come on then,' I said. I couldn't believe he'd be fool enough to stay. There was nothing he could do.

'No. I'm not leaving.' And then a little wildy, as though I were a foreigner who had to be shouted at: 'I'm not leaving, I tell you.'

'Don't be a fool,' I said. 'You can't do any good here – not alone. We're bound for Peter Port. We can get you there in a few hours and then you'll be able to – '

He shook his head, like an animal at bay, and then waved an arm at me as though signalling me to go.

'There's a gale coming up.'

'I know that,' he said.

'Then for God's sake, man . . . it's your one chance to get clear.' And because he was the Captain and obviously thinking about his ship, I added, 'It's the one hope for the ship, too. If you don't get a tug out to her soon she'll be blown right on to the Channel Islands. You can do far more good – '

'Get off my ship!' He was suddenly trembling. 'Get off her, do you hear? I know what I have to do.'

His voice was wild, his manner suddenly menacing. I stood my ground for a moment longer. 'You've got help coming then?' I asked. And when he didn't seem to understand, I said, 'You've radioed for help?'

There was a moment's hesitation and then he said, 'Yes, yes, I've radioed for help. Now go.'

I hesitated. But there was nothing else I could say, and if he wouldn't come . . . I paused halfway up the ladder. 'Surely to God you'll change your mind?' I said. His face showed in the darkness below me – a strong, hard face, still young but with deep-bitten lines in it, made deeper by exhaustion. He looked desperate, and at the same time oddly pathetic. 'Come on, man – whilst you've got the chance.'

But he didn't answer; just turned away and left me there. And I went on up the ladder to meet the weight of the wind howling along the deck and find the sea a mass of whitecaps with *Sea Witch* pitching violently two cables off.

2

I HAD stayed too long. I knew that as soon as *Sea Witch* turned to pick me up. She came roaring down-wind, the big yankee jib burying her bows deep into the wind-whipped waters, her long bowsprit thrusting into the backs of the waves, spearing them and coming out in a welter of spray. Hal had been right. I should never have boarded the ship. I ran to the falls, damning the crazy madman who'd refused to be taken off. If he had come with me, there would have been some point.

Sea Witch heeled over in a gust as Hal fought the wheel, bringing her round through the wind, all her sails flogging madly. The big yankee filled with a crack like a pistol shot, heeling the boat over till all the weed-grown boot-topping showed in the trough of a wave; and then the big sail split across and in an instant was blown to tatters. The wind was strong to gale in the gusts and she should have been reefed by now, but they hadn't a hope of reefing, just the three of them. It was madness for them to attempt to come alongside. I had never seen a sea whipped up so quickly. But Mike was waving to me, signalling downwards with his hand, and Hal was braced at the wheel, edging her up towards the ship's side, mainsail shivering, barely filled, the remnants of the yankee fluttering in streamers from the forestay. I caught hold of one of the falls then and swung myself out over the side, slithering down hand over hand until the surge of a wave soaked me to the waist and I looked up and saw that the rusty plates stood above me, high as a cliff.

I could hear *Sea Witch* now, hear the slap of her bows as she hit a wave and the solid, surging noise of her passage through the water. There were shouts and over my shoulder I saw her coming up into the wind, very close now, her head unwilling to pay off, the bowsprit almost touching the steamer's side. A gust of wind buffeted me, the main boom slammed over, sails filling suddenly, and she went surging past me a good twenty yards out from where I clung, swinging sickeningly in mid-air. Hal was shouting at me. 'The wind . . . strong . . . the ship turning round.' That was all I caught and yet he was so close I could see the water dripping off his oilskins, could see his blue eyes wide and startled-looking under his sou'wester.

Mike eased the sheets and the boat roared off down-wind. Hanging there, soaked with sea water thrown up from the wave tops breaking against the ship's side, I felt the weight of the wind pressing me in towards the rusty hull. At each roll I had to brace myself to meet the shock of my body being flung against her. Gradually I realized what had happened. The wind was swinging the *Mary Deare* broadside on; and I was on the windward side, exposed to the full force of the rising gale.

Sea Witch went about again and I wanted to shout to Hal not to be a fool, that it was no good. Now that the *Mary Deare* had swung, it was dangerous to come alongisde with the wind pressing the yacht down on to the ship. But all I did was pray that he'd make it, for I knew I couldn't hang there much longer. The ropes were getting slippery with water and it was bitterly cold.

I don't know how Hal managed it, but despite the lack of head-sails to bring her bow round, he got her about with almost no way on her a short stone's throw from where I was clinging. Then he let her drift down-wind. It was a superb piece of seamanship. There was a moment when her stern was almost within my reach. I think I might have made it, but at that moment the roll of the *Mary Deare* swung me against her sides and I was held fast against the wet chill of her hull, whilst the familiar counter of my boat slid away as Hal got her moving again to prevent her from being battered to pieces against the ship. 'No good . . . daren't . . . too dangerous . . . Peter Port.' The ragged snatches of Hal's shouts reached me through the wind as I was freed from the ship's side and swung out over the water, right over the spot where *Sea Witch*'s stern had been only a few seconds before. I wanted to shout to him to try again, just once more. But I knew it was risking the boat and their lives as well. 'Okay,' I yelled. 'Make Peter Port. Good luck!'

He shouted something back, but I couldn't hear what it was. *Sea Witch* was already disappearing beyond the steamer's bows, going fast with all her sheets eased and the wind driving at the great spread of her mainsail. I glanced up quickly at the towering wall of iron above my head and then I began to climb whilst I still had some strength left.

But each time the ship rolled I was flung against the side. It gave me extra purchase, flattened hard against the rusty plates, but it battered me, knocking the wind out of me. And each time I was swung clear the loss of purchase almost flung me off, for my fingers were numbed with cold and my arms and knees trembled with the strain of clinging there too long. The waves broke, engulfing me in ice-cold spray, and sometimes green water sloshed up the side of the ship and gripped me about the waist, plucking at me as it subsided.

I made only a few feet, and then I was finally halted. I could climb no further. Flattened against the ship's side, I gripped the rope with my shaking legs and, letting go with one hand, hauled up the free end, pulling it up between my legs and wrapping it over my shoulder. It took the strain off my arms. But it didn't get me back on to the ship's deck. I began to shout then, but the sound of my voice was whipped away by the wind. I knew the man couldn't possibly hear me, but I still went on shouting, praying that he'd come. He was my only hope. And then I stopped shouting, for I had no breath left – jarred and bruised, swung one moment out over the tumbled waters, the next slammed against the ship's side, it came to me slowly that this was the end.

It is difficult to be scared of something that is inevitable. You accept it, and that is that. But I remember thinking how ironical it was; the sea was to me a liquid, quiet, unruffled world through which to glide down green corridors to the darker depths, down tall reef walls with the fish, all brilliant colours in the surface dazzle, down to the shadowy shapes of barnacle-crusted wrecks. Now it was a raging fury of a giant, rearing up towards me, clutching at me, foaming and angry.

And then hope came suddenly in the graze of my hand against the rusty plates. Blood oozed in droplets from my knuckles, to be washed away by a blinding sheet of spray, and I stared, fascinated, as a flake of rust was peeled off by the upward scrape of my body. I didn't look up. I didn't move for fear I had imagined that I was being hauled up. But when the sea no longer reached me as it burst against the ship's side, I knew it was true. I looked up then and saw that the davits had been hauled in-board, saw the ropes move, taut, across the rail-capping.

Slowly, a foot at a time, I was hauled up, until at last my head came level with the deck and I looked into the haggard face and the wild, dark eyes of the *Mary Deare*'s captain. He dragged me over the side and I collapsed on to the deck. I never knew till then how comfortable iron deck plates could be. 'Better get some dry clothes,' he said.

He pulled me to my feet and I stood there, trying to thank him. But I was too exhausted, too numbed with cold. My teeth chattered. He got my arm round his neck and half dragged me along the deck and down to one of the officers' cabins. 'Help yourself to what you want,' he said as he lowered me on to the bunk. 'Rice was about your height.' He stood over me for a moment, frowning at me as though I were some sort of a problem that had to be worked out. Then he left me.

I lay back, exhaustion weighting my eyelids, drowning consciousness. But my body had no warmth left in it and the cold cling of sodden clothes dragged me up off the bunk, to strip and towel myself down. I found dry clothes in a drawer and put them on; woollen underwear, a shirt, a pair of trousers and a sweater. A glow spread through me and my teeth stopped chattering. I took a cigarette from a packet on the desk and lit it, lying back again on the bunk, my eyes closed, drawing on it luxuriously. I felt better then – not worried about myself, only about *Sea Witch*. I hoped to God she'd get safe to Peter Port.

I was drowsy with the sudden warmth; the cabin was airless and smelt of stale sweat. The cigarette kept slipping from my fingers. And then a voice from a great distance off was saying: 'Sit up and drink this.' I opened my eyes and he was standing over me again with a steaming mug in his hand. It was tea laced with rum. I started to thank him, but he cut me short with a quick, angry movement of his hand. He didn't say anything; just stood there, watching me drink it, his face in shadow. There was a strange hostility in his silence.

The ship was rolling heavily now and through the open door came the sound of the wind howling along the deck. The *Mary Deare* would be a difficult tow if it blew a gale. They might not even be able to get a tow-line across to us. I was remembering what Hal had said about the Channel Islands as a lee shore. The warmth of the drink was putting new life into me; enough for me to consider what faced me, now that I was marooned on board the *Mary Deare*.

I looked up at the man standing over me, wondering why he had refused to leave the ship. 'How long before you expect help to reach us?' I asked him.

'There won't be any help. No call went out.' He leaned suddenly down towards me, his hands clenched and his jaw, thrust into the grey light coming in through the porthole, showing hard and knotted. 'Why the hell didn't you stay on your yacht?' And then he turned abruptly and made for the door.

He was halfway through it when I called after him. 'Taggart!' I swung my legs off the bunk.

He spun round on his heels as though I'd punched him in the

back. 'I'm not Taggart.' He came back through the doorway. 'What made you think I was Taggart?'

'You said you were the captain.'

'So I am. But my name's Patch.' He was standing over me again, a dark shadow against the light. 'How did you know about Taggart? Are you something to do with the owners? Is that why you were out there . . .' The wildness went out of his voice and he wiped his hand across the coal dust grime of his face. 'No. It couldn't be that.' He stared at me for a moment and then he shrugged his shoulders. 'We'll talk about it later. We've plenty of time. All the time in the world. Better get some sleep now.' He turned then and went quickly out.

Sleep! Five minutes ago that was what I'd wanted most in the world. But now I was wide awake. I won't say I was scared; not then. Just uneasy. That the man should behave oddly was not surprising. He had been twelve hours alone on the ship. He'd put out a fire single-handed and he'd stoked furnaces till he was on the brink of exhaustion. Twelve hours of hell; enough to unbalance any man. But if he was the captain, why wasn't he Taggart? And why hadn't the ship radioed for assistance?

I got up stiffly off the bunk, pulled on a pair of sea boots that were lying under the desk and staggered out into the corridor. There was a lot of movement on the ship now. Lying broadside to the seas, she was rolling heavily. A rush of cold air brought with it the battering noise of the wind. I went straight up to the bridge. It was raining and visibility was down to less than a mile; the whole sea was a dirty white of breaking water with the spray smoking from the crests and streaming away before the wind. It was already blowing gale force in the gusts.

The compass showed the ship lying with her bows to the north. The wind had backed into the west then; almost a dead run to Peter Port. I stood there working it out, listening to the thundering of the gale, staring out at that bleak waste of tumbled water. If Hal made it – if he got under the lee of Guernsey and made Peter Port . . . But it would take him several hours and he wouldn't realize at first that no distress signal had been sent out. Even when he did, the lifeboat would have to fight the gale to reach us; it would take them six hours at least, and by then it would be dark. They'd never find us in the dark in this sort of weather.

I turned abruptly and went through into the chartroom. A new position had been marked on the chart; a small cross two miles north-east of the Roches Douvres with 11.06 pencilled against it. It was now eleven-fifteen. I laid off the line of our drift with the parallel rule. If the wind held westerly we should drive straight on to the Plateau des Minquiers. He had discovered that, too, for a faint pencil line had been drawn in and there was a smudge of dirt across the area of the reefs where his fingers had rested.

Well, at least he was sane enough to appreciate the danger! I stood, staring at the chart, thinking about what it meant. It wasn't a pleasant thought. To be driven ashore on the rocky cliffs of Jersey would have been bad enough, but the Plateau des Minquiers . . .

I reached out to the bookshelf above the chart table, searching for Part II of the Channel Pilot. But it wasn't there. Not that it mattered. I knew them by reputation: a fearful area of rocks and reefs that we call The Minkies.

I was thinking about the Minkies and how it would feel to be on board a ship being pounded to pieces in such a maelstrom of submerged rocks when I noticed the door at the back of the chart-room with W/T stencilled on it. There was a steep ladder with no door at the top and as soon as I entered the radio shack I knew why no distress call had been sent out. The place had been gutted by fire.

The shock of it halted me in the doorway. The fire in the hold, and now this! But this was an old fire. There was no smell of burning, and planks of new wood had been nailed over the charred gaps that the fire had burned in roof and walls. No attempt had been made to clear the debris. The emergency accumulators had come through the burned-out roof and lay on the floor where they had fallen; one had smashed down on the fire-blackened table and had crushed the half-melted remains of the transmitter. Bunk and chair were scarcely recognizable, skeletons of blackened wood, and the radio equipment fixed to the walls was distorted beyond recognition and festooned with metal stalactites where solder had dripped and congealed; more equipment lay on the floor, black, twisted pieces of metal in the debris of charred wood. Whatever had caused the fire, it had burned with extraordinary ferocity. Water had seeped in through the gaps in the walls, streaking the blackened wood. The wind stirred the sodden ashes, shaking the rotten structure as it howled round the bridge.

I went slowly back down the ladder to the chartroom. Maybe the log book would tell me something. But it was no longer open on the table. I went through to the wheelhouse and was halted momentarily by the sight of a shaggy comber rearing up out of the murk on the port bow, spindrift streaming from its crest. It crashed down on to the iron bulwarks, and then the whole fore part of the ship, all except the mast and derricks, disappeared beneath a welter of white water. It seemed an age before the shape of the bows appeared again, a faint outline of bulwarks rising sluggishly, reluctantly out of the sea.

I hurried down the companion-way and made straight for the captain's cabin. But he wasn't there. I tried the saloon and the galley, and then I knew he must be down in the stokehold again. There was no doubt in my mind what had to be done. The pumps had to be got going. But there was no light in the engine-room, no sound of coal being shovelled into the furnaces. I shouted from the catwalk, but there was no answer; only the echo of my voice, a small sound lost in the pounding of the waves against the outside of the hull and the swirl of water in the bilges.

I felt a sudden sense of loss, a quite childish sense of loneliness. I didn't want to be alone in that empty ship. I hurried back to his cabin, the need to find him becoming more and more urgent. It was empty, as it had been before. A clang of metal aft sent me pushing through the door to the boat deck, and then I saw him. He was coming towards me, staggering with exhaustion, his eyes staring and his face dead white where he had wiped it clean of sweat and coal dust. All his clothes were black with coal and behind him a shovel slid across the deck. 'Where have you been?' I cried. 'I couldn't find you. What have you been doing all this time?'

'That's my business,' he muttered, his voice slurred with fatigue, and he pushed past me and went into his cabin.

I followed him in. 'What's the position?' I asked. 'How much water are we making? The seas are breaking right across the bows.'

He nodded. 'It'll go on like that – all the time now – until the hatch cover goes. And then there'll only be the shored-up bulkhead between us and the sea bed.' It was said flatly, without intonation. He didn't seem to care, or else he was resigned.

'But if we get the pumps going . . .' His lack of interest checked me. 'Damn it, man,' I said. 'That was what you were doing when I came aboard, wasn't it?'

'How do you know what I'd been doing?' He suddenly seemed to blaze up, his eyes hard and angry and wild. He seized hold of my arm. 'How do you know?' he repeated.

'There was a wisp of smoke coming from the funnel,' I said quickly. 'And then all that coal dust; you were covered with it.' I didn't know what had roused him. 'You must have been down in the stokehold.'

'The stokehold?' He nodded slowly. 'Yes, of course.' He let go of my arm, his body gradually losing its tautness, relaxing.

'If the pumps could keep her afloat coming up through the Bay . . .' I said.

'We had a crew then, a full head of steam.' His shoulders drooped. 'Besides, there wasn't so much water in the for'ard hold then.'

'Is she holed? I asked. 'Is that the trouble?'

'Holed?' He stared at me. 'What made you . . .' He pushed his hand up through his hair and then down across his face. His skin was sallow under the grime; sallow and sweaty and tired-looking. The ship lurched and quivered to the onslaught of another wave. I saw his muscles tense as though it were his own body that was being battered. 'It can't last long.'

I felt suddenly sick and empty inside. The man had given up hope. I could see it in the sag of his shoulders, hear it in the flatness of his voice. He was tired beyond caring. 'You mean the hatch cover?' He nodded. 'And what happens then?' I asked. 'Will she float with that hold full of water?'

'Probably. Until the boiler-room bulkhead goes.' His tone was cold-blooded and without emotion. That hold had been flooded a long time. The ship had been down by the bows when we had sighted her through the mist. And last night . . . I was remembering the draught marks high out of the water at her stern and the blades of the propeller thrashing at the wave tops. He had had time to get used to the idea.

But I was damned if I was going to sit down and wait for the end. 'How long would it take to get steam up – enough to drive the pumps?' I asked. But he didn't seem to hear me. He was leaning against the deck, his eyes half-closed. I caught hold of his arm and shook him as though I were waking him out of a trance. 'The pumps!' I shouted at him. 'If you show me what to do, I'll stoke.'

His eyes flicked open and he stared at me. He didn't say anything.

'You're just about all in,' I told him. 'You ought to get some sleep. But first you must show me how to operate the furnace.'

He seemed to hesitate, and then he shrugged his shoulders. 'All right,' he said, and he pulled himself together and went out and down the companion ladder to the main deck. The weight of the wind was heeling the ship, giving her a permanent list to starboard. Like that she rolled sluggishly with an odd, uneven motion that was occasionally violent. His feet dragged along the dark,

423

echoing alley-way; at times he seemed uncertain of his balance, almost dazed.

We turned in through the engine-room door, crossed the cat-walk and descended an iron ladder into the dark pit of the engine-room, the beams of our torches giving momentary glimpses of vast shadowy machinery, all still and lifeless. Our footsteps rang hollow and metallic on the iron gratings as we made our way for'ard through a litter of smaller machinery. There was a sound of water moving in little rushes and heavy thuds echoed up the tunnel of the propeller shaft.

We passed the main controls with the bridge telegraph repeaters and then we reached the doors leading in to the boiler-room. Both doors were open, and beyond, the shapes of the boilers loomed bulky and majestic, without heat.

He hesitated a moment, and then moved forward again. 'It's this one,' he said pointing to the port-hand of the three boilers. A dull red glow rimmed the furnace door. 'And there's the coal.' He swung the beam of his torch over the black heap that had spilled out of the coal-box opening. He had half-turned back towards the furnace, when he checked and stood staring at the coal as though fascinated, slowly lifting the beam of his torch so that the white circle of it shone on plate after plate, all black with dust, as though he were tracing the line of the coal coming down from the bunkering hatch at deck level. 'We'll work two-hour shifts,' he said quickly, glancing at his watch. 'It's nearly twelve now. I'll relieve you at two.' He seemed suddenly in a hurry to go.

'Just a minute,' I said. 'How do you operate the furnace?'

He glanced impatiently back at the boiler with its temperature gauge and the levers below that operated the furnace doors and the dampers. 'It's quite simple. You'll get the hang of it easily enough.' He was already turning away again. 'I'm going to get some sleep,' he muttered. And with that he left me.

I opened my mouth to call him back. But there seemed no point. I should probably find out easily enough and he needed sleep badly. For a moment, as he passed through the stoke-hold doors, his body was sharply etched against the light of his torch. I stood there listening to the sound of his feet on the steel ladders of the engine-room, seeing the faint reflection of his torch limning the open doorway. Then it was gone and I was alone, conscious suddenly of the odd noises about me – the murmur of water, the queer booming of waves breaking against the ship's hull and the sudden little rushes of coal tipping in the chutes as she rolled;

conscious, too, of a sense of claustrophobia, of being shut in down there below the waterline. Beyond the boilers were the baulks of timber shoring the bulkhead, and beyond the rusty plates was water. I could see it trickling down the seams.

I stripped off my borrowed jersey, rolled up my sleeves and went over to the furnace. It was barely warm. I could put my hands on the casing of it. I found the lever and flung open the furnace door. A pile of ash glowed red. There was no rush of flame, no sign of it having been stoked in hours. I picked up one of the crowbar-like slices that lay about and prodded the glowing mass. It was all ash.

I had a look at the other two furnaces then, but their draught vents were all wide open, the fires burned out, the boilers cold. There was just that one furnace still alive, and it was alive because the dampers were shut right down. I remembered then how his footsteps had dragged past the engine-room door that first time I had stood on the catwalk calling into the abyss below. He hadn't been down here – then or at any time. Yet he was covered in coal dust. I stood there, leaning on my shovel, thinking about it until the noise of the waves booming against the hollow hull reminded me that there were other, more urgent matters, and I began shovelling in coal.

I piled it in until it was heaped black inside the furnace. Then I shut the door and opened all the dampers. In a few minutes the furnace was roaring, the bright light of flames showing round the edges of the door and lighting the stoke-hold with a warm glow, so that the shapes of the boilers emerged, dim and shadowy, from the darkness that surrounded me. I opened the door again and began shovelling hard, the shovel and the black coal lit by the lurid glow. Soon I was stripped to the waist and the sweat was rolling off me so that my arms and body glistened through their coating of coal dust.

I don't know how long I was down there. It seemed like hours that I shovelled and sweated in the cavernous inferno of the stoke-hold. The furnace roared and blazed with heat, yet it was a long while before I noticed any change in the pressure gauge. Then slowly the needle began to rise. I was standing, leaning on my shovel, watching the needle, when faint above the furnace roar I heard the slam of metal against metal and turned.

He was standing in the rectangle of the stoke-hold doors. He didn't move for a moment and then he advanced towards me, reeling drunkenly to the movement of the ship. But it wasn't the rolling that made him stagger. It was exhaustion. I watched him as he came towards me with a sort of fascination. The furnace door was open and in the glow I saw his face sweating and haggard, the eyes sunk into shadowed sockets.

He stopped as he saw me staring at him. 'What's the matter?' he asked. There was a nervous pitch to his voice, and his eyes, turned now to catch the furnace glow, had a wild look in them. 'What are you staring at?'

'You,' I said. 'Where have you been?'

He didn't answer.

'You haven't been to sleep at all.' I caught hold of his arm. 'Where have you been?' I shouted at him.

He shook me off. 'Mind your own damn' business!' He was staring at me wildly. Then he reached for the shovel. 'Give me that.' He snatched it out of my hand and began to feed coal in through the open furnace door. But he was so exhausted he could hardly balance himself to the roll of the ship. His movements became slower and slower. 'Don't stand there watching me,' he shouted. 'Go and get some sleep.'

'It's you who need sleep,' I told him.

'I said we'd take it in two-hour shifts.' His voice was flat, his tone final. Coal spilled suddenly out of the chute, piling over his feet to a heavy roll. He stared at it with a sort of crazy fascination. 'Get out of here,' he said. And then, shouting: 'Get out! Do you hear?' He was leaning on the shovel, still staring down at the coal spilling out of the chute. His body seemed to sag and he brushed his arm across his sweaty face. 'Go and get some sleep, for God's sake. Leave me here.' The last almost a whisper. And then he added, as though it were a connected thought: 'It's blowing full gale now.'

I hesitated, but he looked half-crazed in that weird light and I picked up my jersey and started for the door. I checked once, in the doorway. He was still watching me, the furnace-glow shining full on his haggard face and casting the enormous shadow of his body on the coal chute behind him.

Clambering up through the gloom of the engine-room I heard the scrape of the shovel and had one last glimpse of him through the open door; he was working at the coal, shovelling it into the furnace as though it were some sort of enemy to be attacked and destroyed with the last reserves of his energy.

The sounds of the gale changed as I climbed up through the ship; instead of the pounding of the waves against the hull, solid and resonant, there was the high-pitched note of the wind and the hissing, tearing sound of the sea. Cold, rushing air hit me in a blast

426

as I stepped out into the corridor and made my way for'ard to my borrowed cabin. I had a wash and then lay back on the bunk, exhausted.

But though I was tired and closed my eyes, I couldn't sleep. There was something queer about the man – about the ship, too; those two fires and the half-flooded hold and the way they had abandoned her.

I must have dozed off, for, when I opened my eyes again, I was suddenly tense, staring at the dim-lit unfamiliarity of the cabin, wondering where I was. And then I was thinking of the atmosphere in that other cabin and, in the odd way one's mind clings to a detail, I remembered the two raincoats hanging on the door, the two raincoats that must belong to two different men. I sat up, feeling stale and sweaty and dirty. It was then just after two. I swung my feet off the bunk and sat there staring dazedly at the desk.

Rice! That was the name of the man. Less than twenty-four hours ago he had been on board, here in his cabin, perhaps seated at that desk. And here was I, dressed in his clothes, occupying his cabin – and the ship still afloat.

I pulled myself up and went over to the desk, drawn by a sort of fellow-feeling for the poor devil, wondering whether he was still tossing about on the sea in one of the lifeboats. Or had he got safe ashore? Maybe he was drowned. Idly I opened the desk top. There were books on navigation; he'd been an orderly man with a sense of property for he had written his name on the fly-leaf of each – John Rice, in the same small, crabbed hand that had made most of the entries in the bridge log book. There were paperbacks, too, mostly detective fiction, exercise books full of trigonometrical calculations, a slide rule, some loose sheets of graph paper.

It was under these that I found the brand-new leather writing case, the gift note still inside – *To John. Write me often, darling. Love – Maggie.* Wife or sweetheart? I didn't know, but staring up at me was the last letter he had written her. *My darling Maggie* it began, and my eyes were caught and held by the opening of the second paragraph: *Now that the worst is over, I don't mind telling you, darling, this has been a trip and no mistake. Nothing has gone right.*

The skipper had died and they had buried him in the Med. And out in the Atlantic they had run into heavy weather. On 16 March they were hove-to – *a real buster* – the pumps unable to hold their own, Numbers One and Two holds flooded, and a fire in the radio shack whilst they were trying to shore up the boiler-room bulkhead, with the crew near panic *because that bastard*

Higgins, had told them that explosives formed part of the cargo, whatever the manifest said. A Mr Dellimare, whom he referred to as *the owner*, had been lost overboard that same night.

Patch he described as having joined the ship at Aden as first officer in place of *old Adams who was sick.* And he added this: *Thank God he did or I don't think I'd be writing this to you. A good seaman, whatever they say about his having run the* BELLE ISLE *on the rocks a few years back.* And then this final paragraph: *Now Higgins is first officer and honestly, Maggie, I don't know. I've told you how he's been riding me ever since we left Yokohama. But it isn't only that. He's too thick with some of the crew – the worst of them. And then there's the ship. Sometimes I think the old girl knows she's bound for the knacker's yard. There's some ships when it comes to breaking up . . .*

The letter ended abruptly like that. What had happened? Was it the shout of Fire? There were questions racing through my mind, questions that only Patch could answer. I thrust the letter into my pocket and hurried down to the stoke-hold.

I had got as far as the engine-room before I stopped to think about the man I was going to question. He'd been alone on the ship. They'd all abandoned her, except him. And Taggart was dead – the owner, too. A cold shiver ran through me, and on the lower catwalk I stopped and listened, straining my ears – hearing all the sounds of the ship struggling with the seas, all magnified by the resonance of that gloomy cavern, but unable to hear the sound I was listening for, the sound of a shovel scraping coal from the iron floors.

I went down slowly then, a step at a time, listening – listening for the scrape of that shovel. But I couldn't hear it and when I finally reached the door to the stoke-hold, there was the shovel lying on the coal.

I shouted to him, but all I got was the echo of my own voice, sounding thin against the pounding of the seas. And when I flung open the furnace door, I wondered whether he existed at all outside of my imagination. The fire was a heap of white-hot ash. It looked as though it hadn't been stoked since I had left it.

In a frenzy, I seized the shovel and piled on coal, trying to smother my fears in physical exertion, in satisfaction at the sound of the coal spilling out of the chute, at the roar of the furnace.

But you can't just blot out fear like that. It was there inside me. I suddenly dropped the shovel, slammed the furnace door shut and went rushing up through the ship. I had to find him. I had to convince myself that he existed.

You must remember I was very tired.

He wasn't on the bridge. But there were pencil marks on the chart, a new position. And the sight of the seas steadied me. They were real enough anyway. God! they were real! I clung to the ledge below the glass panels of the wheelhouse and stared, fascinated, as a wave built up to port, broke and burst against the ship's side, flinging up a great column of smoking water that crashed down on the foredeck, blotting everything out. The sea rolled green over the bows. And when the outline of the bulwarks showed again and she struggled up with thousands of tons of water spilling off her, I saw that the for'ard hatch was a gaping rectangle in the deck.

There was no litter of matchwood. The deck was swept clear of all trace of the hatch covers. They had been gone some time. I watched the water spilling out of the hold as the ship rolled. But as fast as it spilled, the angry seas filled it up again. The bows were practically under water. The ship felt heavy and sluggish under my feet. She didn't feel as though she could last much longer.

I glanced round the bridge, rooted to the spot by the strange emptiness of it and the sudden certainty that the ship was going to go down. The spokes of the wheel were flung out in a forlorn circle. The brass of the binnacle gleamed. The telegraph pointers still stood at Full Ahead. The emptiness of it all . . . I turned and went down to the captain's cabin. He was there, lying back in the arm-chair, his body relaxed, his eyes closed. A half-empty bottle of rum stood on the desk at his elbow. The glass was on the floor, spilling a brown wet stain across the carpet. Sleep had smoothed out the lines of his face. Like that he seemed younger, less tough; but he still looked haggard and his right hand twitched nervously where it lay against the dark leather arm of the chair. The two blue raincoats still hung incongruously side-by-side on the back of the door. The girl still smiled at me sunnily from her silver frame.

A big sea broke against the ship's side, darkening the portholes with upflung water. His eyelids flicked back. 'What is it?' He seemed instantly wide awake, though his face was still puffed with sleep, flushed with the liquor he'd drunk.

'The for'ard hatch covers have gone,' I said. I felt a strange sense of relief. He was real and it was his responsibility, not mine. I wasn't alone after all.

'I know that.' He sat up, pushing his hand across his face and up through his black hair. 'What do you expect me to do about it – go out and rig new ones?' His voice was a little slurred. 'We did that once.' He pulled himself up out of the chair and went over to the porthole and stood there, looking at the sea. His back was towards me, his shoulders slightly hunched, hands thrust into his pockets. 'It was like this all the way up through the Bay – heavy seas and the ship making water all the time.' The daylight filtering through the porthole shone cold and hard on his exhausted features. 'And then that storm! God! What a night!' He stared out through the porthole.

'You'd better get some more sleep,' I said.

'Sleep?' His hand went to his eyes, rubbing them, and then pushing up through his hair again. 'Mabye you're right.' His forehead wrinkled in a frown and he smiled so that his face had a surprised look. 'You know, I can't remember when I last slept.' And then he added: 'There was something . . .' He was frowning. 'God! I can't remember. Something I was going to look up.' He stared down at the chart and books that lay on the floor beside the arm-chair. The chart was Number 2100, the large-scale chart of the Minkies. And then he was looking at me again and in an odd voice he said, 'Who exactly are you?' He was a little drunk.

'I told you that earlier,' I replied. 'My name is – '

'To hell with your name,' he shouted impatiently. 'What were you doing out there in that yacht? What made you board the ship?' And then before I had time to say anything, he added, 'Are you something to do with the Company?'

'What company?'

'The Dellimare Trading and Shipping Company – the people who own the *Mary Deare*.' He hesitated. 'Were you out there, waiting to see if – ' But then he shook his head. 'No, it couldn't have been that. We weren't steaming to schedule.'

'I'd never heard of the *Mary Deare* until last night,' I told him. And I explained how we'd almost been run down. 'What happened?' I asked him. 'How was it that the crew abandoned her with the engines still running and you on board? Was it the fire?'

He stared at me, swaying a little on his feet. And then he said, 'She was never meant to make the Channel.' He said it with a sort of smile, and when I asked him what he meant, he shrugged his shoulders and turned back to the porthole, staring out at the sea. 'I thought we were in the clear when I'd got her round Ushant,' he murmured. 'God damn it! I thought I'd taken all the knocks a man could in the course of a single voyage. And then that fire.' He turned and faced me again then. He seemed suddenly to want to talk. 'It was the fire that beat me. It happened about nine-thirty last night. Rice rushed in here to say that Number Three hold was ablaze and the crew were panicking. I got the hoses run out and part of Number Four hatch cleared so that we could play water on the bulkhead. And then I went down the inspection ladder into Number Four to check. That's how they got me.' He pointed to the bloodied gash on his jaw.

'You mean somebody hit you – one of the crew?' I asked in astonishment.

He nodded, smiling. It wasn't a pleasant smile. 'They battened the inspection hatch down on top of me when I was unconscious and then they drove the crew in panic to the boats.'

'And left you there?'

'Yes. The only thing that saved me was that they forgot we'd cleared part of the hatch cover. By piling bales of cotton up – '

'But that's mutiny – murder. Are you suggesting Higgins . . .'

He lurched towards me then, sudden violence in his face. 'Higgins! How did you know it was Higgins?'

I started to explain about the letter Rice had written, but he interrupted me. 'What else did he say?' he demanded. 'Anything about Dellimare?'

'The owner? No. Only that he'd been lost overboard.' And I added, 'The Captain died, too, I gather.'

'Yes, damn his eyes!' He turned away from me and his foot struck the overturned glass. He picked it up and poured himself a drink, his hands shaking slightly. 'You having one?' He didn't wait for me to reply, but pulled open a drawer of the desk and produced a glass, filling it almost to the brim. 'I buried him at sea on the first Tuesday in March,' he said, handing the drink to me. 'And glad I was to see the last of him.' He shook his head slowly. 'I was glad at the time, anyway.'

'What did he die of?' I asked.

'Die of?' He looked up at me quickly from under his dark brows, suddenly suspicious again. 'Who the hell cares what he died of?' he said with sudden truculence. 'He died and left me to face the whole . . .' He made a vague gesture with the hand that held his glass. And then he seemed suddenly to notice me again, for he said abruptly: 'What the hell were you doing out there in that yacht of yours last night?'

I started to tell him how we'd bought *Sea Witch* in Morlaix and were sailing her back to England for conversion into a diving tender, but he didn't seem to be listening. His mind was away on some thought of his own and all at once he said: 'And I thought it was decent of the old bastard to get out and make room for a younger man.' He was laughing again as though at some joke. 'Well, it's all the same now. That bulkhead will go soon.' And he looked at me and added, 'Do you know how old this ship is? Over forty years old! She's been torpedoed three times, wrecked twice. She's been rotting in Far Eastern ports for twenty years. Christ! She might have been waiting for me.' And he grinned, not pleasantly, but with his lips drawn back from his teeth.

A sea crashed against the ship's side and the shudder of the impact seemed to bring him back to the present. 'Do you know the Minkies?' He lunged forward and came up with a book which he tossed across to me. 'Page three hundred and eight, if you're interested in reading the details of your own graveyard.' It was the Channel Pilot, Part II.

I found the page and read: *PLATEAU DES MINQUIERS. – Buoyage. – Caution. – Plateau des Minquiers consists of an extensive group of above-water and sunken rocks and reefs, together with numerous banks of shingle, gravel and sand . . . The highest rock, Maîtresse Île, 31 feet high, on which stand several houses, is situated near the middle of the plateau . . .* There were details that showed the whole extent of the reefs to be about $17\frac{1}{2}$ miles long by 8 miles deep, and paragraph after paragraph dealt with major rock outcrops and buoyage.

'I should warn you that the so-called houses on Maîtresse Île are nothing but deserted stone shacks.' He had spread the chart out on the desk and was bending over it, his head in his hands.

'What about tide?' I asked.

'Tide?' He suddenly seemed excited. 'Yes, that was it. Something to do with the tide. I was going to look it up.' He turned and searched the floor again, swaying slightly, balanced automatically to the roll of the ship. 'Well, it doesn't matter much.' He downed the rest of his drink and poured himself another. 'Help yourself.' He pushed the bottle towards me.

I shook my head. The liquor had done nothing to the chill emptiness inside me – a momentary trickle of warmth, that was all. I was cold with weariness and the knowledge of how it would end. And yet there had to be something we could do. If the man were fresh; if he'd had food and sleep . . . 'When did you feed last?' I asked him.

'Oh, I had some bully. Sometime this morning it must have been.' And then with sudden concern that took me by surprise, he said, 'Why, are you hungry?'

It seemed absurd to admit to hunger when the ship might go down at any moment, but the mere thought of food was enough. 'Yes,' I said. 'I am.' Anyway, it might get him away from the bottle, put something inside him besides liquor.

432

'All right. Let's go and feed.' He took me down to the pantry, holding his glass delicately and balancing himself to the sluggish roll. We found a tin of ham – bread, butter, pickles. 'Coffee?' He lit a Primus stove he'd found and put a kettle on. We ate ravenously by the light of a single, guttering candle; not talking, just stuffing food into our empty bellies. The noise of the storm was remote down there in the pantry, overlaid by the roar of the Primus.

It's surprising how quickly food is converted into energy and gives a man back that desperate urge to live. 'What are our chances?' I asked.

He shrugged his shoulders. 'Depends on the wind and the sea and that bulkhead. If the bulkhead holds, then we'll be driven on to the Minkies sometime during the night.' The kettle had boiled and he was busy making the coffee. Now that the Primus was out, the pantry seemed full of the noise of the gale and the straining of the ship.

'Suppose we got the pumps working, couldn't we clear that for'ard hold of water? There was a good deal of pressure in the boiler when I was down there and I stoked before I left.'

'You know damn' well we can't clear that hold with the hatch cover gone.'

'Not if we ran her off before the wind. If we got the engines going . . .'

'Look,' he said. 'This old ship will be weeping water at every plate joint throughout her whole length now. If we ran the pumps flat out, they'd do no more than hold the water that's seeping into her, let alone clear Number One hold. Anyway, how much steam do you think you need to run the engines and the pumps as well?'

'I don't know,' I said. 'Do you?'

'No. But I'm damn' sure it would need more than one boiler; two at least. And if you think we could keep two boilers fired . . .' He poured the coffee into tin mugs and stirred sugar in. 'With one boiler we could have the engines going intermittently.' He seemed to consider it, and then shook his head. 'There wouldn't be any point in it.' He passed me one of the mugs. It was scalding hot.

'Why not?' I asked.

'For one thing the wind's westerly. Keeping her stern to the wind would mean every turn of the screw would be driving her straight towards the Minkies. Besides . . .' His voice checked, ceased abruptly. He seemed to lose himself in some dark thought of his own, his black brows furrowed, his mouth a hard, bitter line. 'Oh, to hell with it,' he muttered and poured the rest of his rum into his coffee. 'I know where there's some more liquor on board. We can get tight, and then who the hell cares?'

I stared at him, my bowels suddenly hot with anger. 'Is that what happened last time? Did you just give up? Is that what it was?'

'Last time?' He was frozen to sudden immobility, the mug of coffee halfway to his lips. 'What do you mean – last time?'

'The *Belle Isle*,' I said. 'Did she go down because . . .' I stopped there, checked by the sudden, blazing fury in his eyes.

'So you know about the *Belle Isle*. What else do you know about me?' His voice was shrill, uncontrolled and violent. 'Do you know I was on the beach for damn' near a year? A year in Aden! And this . . . The first ship in a year, and it has to be the *Mary Deare*, a floating bloody scrap-heap with a drunken skipper who goes and dies on me and an owner . . .' He pushed his hand up through his hair, staring through me, back into the past. 'Fate can play dirty tricks, once she's got her claws into you.' And then, after a pause: 'If I could keep this old tramp afloat . . .' He shook his head. 'You wouldn't think it would happen to a man twice, would you,' he murmured. 'Twice! I was too young and green to know what they were up to when I got command of the *Belle Isle*. But I knew the smell of it this time. Well, they got the wrong man.' He gave a bitter laugh. 'A lot of good it did me, being honest. I got her up through the Bay. God knows how I did it, but I did. And round Ushant I headed for Southampton.' His eyes focused on me again and he said, 'Well, now I don't care any more. You can't go on fighting a thing. This gale has finished me. I know when I'm licked.'

I didn't say anything, for there wasn't anything I could say. It had to come from him. I couldn't drive him. I knew that. I just sat there and waited and the silence tightened between us. He finished his coffee and put the mug down and wiped his mouth with the back of his hand. The silence became unbearable, full of the death-struggle sounds of the ship. 'Better come and have a drink,' he said, his voice tense.

I didn't move. I didn't say anything either.

'It's tough on you, but you didn't have to come on board, did you?' He stared at me angrily. 'What the hell do you think I can do?'

'I don't know,' I said. 'You're the captain. It's for you to give the orders.'

'Captain!' He laughed without mirth. 'Master of the *Mary Deare!*' He rolled it round his tongue, sneeringly. 'Well, at least I'll have gone down with the ship this time. They said she was jinxed, some of them.' He seemed to be speaking to himself. 'They were convinced she'd never make it. But we're all jinxed when times get hard; and she's been kicked around the world for a good many years. She must have been a crack cargo liner in her day, but now she's just a rusty old hulk making her last voyage. We'd a cargo for Antwerp, and then we were taking her across the North Sea to Newcastle to be broken up.' He was silent after that, his head on one side, listening. He was listening to the sounds of the ship being pounded by the waves. 'What a thing it would be – to steam into Southampton with no crew and the ship half-full of water.' He laughed. It was the drink in him talking, and he knew it. 'Let's see,' he said, still speaking to himself. 'The tide will be turning against us in a few hours. Wind over tide. Still, if we could hold her stern-on to the wind, maybe we could keep her afloat a little longer. Anything could happen. The wind might shift; the gale might blow itself out.' But there was no conviction in the way he said it. He glanced at his watch. 'Barely twelve hours from now the tide will be carrying us down on to the rocks and it'll still be dark. If visibility is all right, we should be able to see the buoys; at least we'll know – ' His voice checked abruptly. 'The buoys! That's what I was thinking about before I went to sleep. I was looking at the chart . . .' His voice had become animated, his eyes suddenly bright with excitement. And then his fist crashed against the palm of his hand and he jumped to his feet. 'That's it! If we were to hit the tide just right . . .' He pushed by me and I heard his feet take the steps of the ladder leading to the bridge two at a time.

I followed him up and found him in the chartroom, poring over a big book of Admiralty tide-tables. He looked up and for the first time I saw him as a leader, all the fatigue wiped out, the drink evaporated. 'There's just a chance,' he said. 'If we can keep her afloat, we might do it. It means working down in that stoke-hold – working like you've never worked in your life before; turn-and-turn about – the stoke-hold and the wheelhouse.' He seized hold of my arm. 'Come on! Let's see if we've got sufficient head of steam to move the engines.' A wave hit the side of the ship. Sheets of water fell with a crash, sluicing into the wheelhouse through the broken doorway leading to the port wing of the bridge. Out of the tail of my eye I saw water thundering green across the half-submerged bows. And then I was following him

down the ladder again into the body of the ship and he was shouting: 'By God, man, I might cheat them yet.' And his face, caught
in the light of my torch as it was turned momentarily up to me,
was filled with a sort of crazy vitality.

3

THE DARKNESS of the engine-room was warm with the smell of hot
oil and there was the hissing sound of steam escaping, so that the
place seemed no longer dead. In my haste I let go at the bottom
of the last ladder and was pitched a dozen feet across the engine-
room deck, fetching up against a steel rail. There was a prolonged
hiss of steam as I stood there, gasping for breath, and the pistons
moved, thrusting their arms against the gleaming metal of the
crankshaft, turning it – slowly at first, and then faster and faster so
that all the metal parts gleamed in the light of my torch and the
engines took on that steady, reassuring thump-thump of vitality
and power. The hum of a dynamo started and the lights began to
glow. The humming became louder, the lights brighter, and then
abruptly they snapped full on. Brass and steelwork gleamed. The
whole lit cavern of the engine-room was alive with sound.

Patch was standing on the engineer officer's control platform.
I staggered down the catwalk between the two big reciprocators.
'The engines!' I shouted at him. 'The engines are going!' I was
beside myself with excitement. For that one moment I thought
we could steam straight into a port.

But he was already shutting off the steam, and the beat of the
engines slowed and then stopped with a final hiss. 'Don't stand
there,' he said to me. 'Start stoking. We want all the steam we
can get.' For the first time he looked like a man in control of the
situation.

But stoking was more difficult now; dangerous, too. The
movements of the ship were unpredictable. One moment I would
be flinging a shovelful of coal high up against the thrust of gravity,
the next I would be pitched towards the flaming mouth of the
furnace and the coal would seem to have no weight in it at all as it
left the shovel.

I don't know how long I was working there alone before he

joined me. It seemed a long time. I didn't see him enter. All my mind was concentrated on the coal and that gaping furnace door, concentrated on gauging the pitch of the ship, avoiding being flung against the red-hot fire. I felt a hand on my arm and I looked up to find him standing over me. I straightened up and faced him, panting, with the sweat pouring off my body. 'I've got the pumps going,' he said.

I nodded, too short of breath to waste it in speech.

'I've just been up on the bridge,' he went on. 'Half the time the bows are right under. Any moment that bulkhead may go. Do you think you could hear the engine-room telegraph from in here?'

'I don't know,' I said. 'I expect so.'

He took me through into the engine-room then and showed me the engine controls and the voice pipe that connected with the bridge. 'I'll go up to the bridge now,' he said. 'You go back to the boiler-room and start stoking. I'll give you a ring on the engine-room telegraph. If you don't hear it after two minutes come to the voice pipe. Okay?'

I nodded and he went clambering up the ladder, whilst I returned to the stoke-hold. Even in that short time my arms and back had stiffened. I had to force myself to start shovelling again. I was beginning to get very tired and I wondered how long we could keep this up. Faint above the roar of the furnace and the sounds of the engine-room came the jangling of the bridge telegraph. I flung the furnace door to and went through to the engineer's control platform. The pointer stood at Full Ahead. I spun the control wheel, opening up the steam valves, and for the first time I understood the thrill and pride an engineer officer must feel; the hiss of steam, the pistons moving and the engines taking up a steady, pulsating beat, vibrant with power. The heart of the ship had come alive, and it was I who had made it alive. It was satisfying.

Back in the stoke-hold the shovel felt strangely light. I barely noticed the aching of my arms. Confidence and the will to fight back had returned. I was suddenly full of energy.

It worked out that about every ten minutes or so the engines had to be run; it took about three minutes to get her stern-on again. Those three minutes produced a big drop in the pressure gauge. Only by keeping the furnace full and roaring could that pressure be built up again in time to meet the next demand from the bridge.

At 15.30 he called me up to take over the wheel. 'Watch the

spindrift,' he said. 'That will tell you the wind direction. Lay her exactly along the direction of the wind. If you're a fraction out the stern will swing almost immediately. And have full rudder on from the moment you order me to start the engines – and don't forget she'll carry way for a good five minutes after the engines have stopped.' He left me then and I was alone at the wheel.

It was a welcome relief to be able to stand there with nothing heavier than the wheel to shift. But whereas in the stoke-hold, with the roar of the furnace and the periodic sound of the engines, there had been a sense of security and normality, here I was face to face with the reality of the situation. A grim half light showed the bows so badly down in the water that they barely lifted above the marching wave tops even when running dead before the wind, and, as soon as the ship swung and I had to use the engines, the whole deck for'ard of the bridge became a seething welter of water. The sweat cooled on my body, an ice-cold, clammy coating to my skin, and I began to shiver. I found a duffle coat in the chartroom and put it on. A new position had been marked in on the chart. We were lying just about halfway between the Roches Douvres and the Minkies. The congested areas of submerged reefs was looming rapidly nearer.

At 16.30 he relieved me. He stood for a moment looking out across the bows into the faded daylight of that wretched, gale-swept scene. His face and neck glistened with sweat and his eyes were deep-sunk in their sockets, all the bone formation of his face standing out hard and sharp. 'Come through into the chartroom a minute,' he said, taking hold of my arm – whether out of a need for the companionship of physical contact or to steady himself against the roll of the ship, I don't know. 'The wind is westerly now,' he said, pointing to our position on the chart. 'It will probably back further into the south-west. If we're not careful we're going to be driven slap into the middle of the Minkies. What we've got to do now is to inch our way to the south'ard. Every time we run the engines we've got to make full use of them.'

I nodded. 'Where are you heading for – St Malo?'

He looked at me. 'I'm not heading anywhere,' he said. 'I'm just trying to keep afloat.' He hesitated and then added, 'In four hours the tide will start running against us. It'll be wind over tide then and throughout most of the night. It'll kick up a hell of a sea.'

I glanced out of the chartroom window and my heart sank, for it didn't seem possible that the sea could be worse than it was now. I watched him work out the dead reckoning and mark in another cross about five miles west and a little south of the other. 'We can't have moved that much in an hour,' I protested.

He flung down the pencil. 'Work it out for yourself if you don't believe me,' he said. 'The tide's running south-easterly three knots. Allow two miles for wind and engines, and there you are.'

I stared at the chart. The Minkies were getting very close. 'And in the next two hours?' I asked.

'In the next two hours the tide slacks off considerably. But my reckoning is that we'll be within a mile or so of the south-west Minkies buoy. And there we'll stay for the first half of the night. And when the tide turns . . .' He shrugged his shoulders and went back again into the wheelhouse. 'Depends whether we've managed to edge south at all.'

With this cheerful prospect I went below again, back to the familiar, aching grind and blazing heat of the stoke-hold. One hour in the stoke-hold; one on the bridge. Turn and turn about; it became a routine. Dazed with tiredness we did it automatically, unconsciously adjusting ourselves to the greater movement of the bridge and then readjusting ourselves to the quicker, less predictable and much more dangerous motion of the stokehold.

I remember being at the wheel when darkness fell. It seemed to steal up on us almost imperceptibly. And then suddenly I couldn't see the bows, couldn't tell where the wind was because I couldn't see the spume flying off the wave tops. All I could see was darkness shot with the white-tumbling wave tops. The deck sloped forward under my feet and, with broken water all round the ship, it was as though we were running the rapids of a giant river, slipping downhill at tremendous speed. I steered by the compass and the feel of the ship then, all the time pushing her towards the south with every burst of the engines.

At the helm just after midnight a glimmer of light showed for an instant in the rushing, wind-torn darkness beyond the bows. I hoped to God I had imagined it. I was very tired by then and it had just been a momentary gleam, indistinct and ephemeral. But a little later I saw it again, a flash of light about two points off the starboard bow. It showed intermittently, often obscured by the backs of the waves.

By the end of my watch it was possible to identify it as group-flashing two. The chart showed the south-west Minkies buoy as Gp.fl.(2). 'About what we expected,' Patch said when he relieved me. His voice showed no lift of interest; it was flat and slurred with weariness, his face gaunt in the light of the binnacle.

And after that the light was always with us, getting a little nearer, a little clearer until it began to fade with the first grey glimmer of dawn as I took over the wheel at five-thirty in the morning. I was almost dead with exhaustion then, hardly able to stand, my knees trembling. The night in the stoke-hold had been hell, the last hour almost unendurable, shovelling coal with rivulets of water spilling across the floor and spitting steam as they swirled round the hot base of the furnace.

The tide had turned now and the double flash of the Minkies buoy began to come down on us fast, and on the wrong side of us. Soon, as the daylight strengthened, I could see the buoy itself, one of those huge pillar buoys that the French use, and, even above the wind, I thought now and then I could catch the mournful, funeral note of its whistle. We were going to pass at least half a mile inside it. I had a look at the chart and then got Patch on the voice pipe and told him to come up.

It seemed a long time before he appeared on the bridge, and when he came he moved slowly, his feet dragging as though he were just out of a sick bed. Changing watches during the night, he had been just a shadowy shape in the pale, reflected glow of the binnacle light. Now, seeing him suddenly in the cold light of day, I was shocked. He looked ghastly. 'You're just about out on your feet,' I said.

He stared at me as though he hadn't understood. I suppose I looked pretty bad myself. 'What is it?' he asked.

I pointed to the Minkies buoy, now almost four points on the starboard bow. 'We're passing too far inside it,' I said. 'At any moment we may hit the Brisants du Sud rocks.'

He went into the chartroom and I waited, expecting him to send me running below to get the engines going. He was gone a long time. Once I shouted to him, afraid that he must have gone to sleep. But he answered immediately that he was watching the buoy through the window and working something out. The tide had got a firm hold of us now. I watched the bearing of the buoy altering rapidly. It was almost abeam of us before he emerged from the chartroom. 'It's all right,' he said. 'There's water enough at this stage of the tide.' His voice was quite calm.

The wind had caught our stern now and we were swinging. Not two cables' length away an eddy marked a submerged rock and the heavy overfalls broke against each other in violent collision, sending up great gouts of water. And beyond was a cataract of broken water where the waves spilled in tumbled confusion, raging acres of surf. A big sea hit us, thudding against the ship's side and rolling in a white tide across the foredeck. Tons o water crashed down on the bridge. The whole ship shuddered. 'Aren't you going to get the engines started?' I demanded.

He was standing with his back to me, staring out to starboard. He hadn't heard me. 'For God's sake!' I cried. 'We're being carried right on to the Minkies.'

'We're all right for the moment.' He said it quietly, as though to soothe me.

But I didn't believe him. How could we be all right? All ahead of us was nothing but reefs with the seas pouring white across miles of submerged rock. Once we struck . . . 'We've got to do something,' I said desperately.

He didn't answer . He was staring through the glasses out beyond the starboard bow, his legs straddled against the sickening lunges of the ship.

I didn't know what to do. He seemed calm and in control of the situation, and yet I knew that he had gone physically beyond the limits of endurance – mentally, too, perhaps. 'We've got to get clear of the Minkies,' I told him. 'Once we're clear of the Minkies we're all right.' I let go of the wheel and started for the companion ladder. 'I'm going to start the engines.'

But he grabbed hold of my arm as I passed him. 'Don't you understand?' he said. 'We're sinking.' His face was as stony as the gaze of his dark eyes. 'I didn't tell you before, but water is flooding through that bulkhead. I had a look at it just before I relieved you.' He let go of my arm then and stared through the glasses again, searching for something in the grey, scud-filled dawn.

'How long – ' I hesitated, unwilling to put it into words. 'How long before she goes down?'

'I don't know. A few minutes, an hour, maybe two.' He lowered the glasses with a little grunt of satisfaction. 'Well, it's a slender chance, but . . .' He turned and stared at me as though assessing my worth. 'I want pressure in that boiler for ten to fifteen minutes' steaming. Are you prepared to go below and continue stoking?' He paused and then added, 'I should warn you that you'll stand no chance at all if that bulkhead goes whilst you're down there.'

I hesitated. 'For how long?'

'An hour and a half I should say.' He glanced quickly away to starboard, half nodded his head and then caught hold of my arm. 'Come on,' he said. 'I'll give you a hand for the first hour.'

'What about the ship?' I asked. 'If she strikes on one of these reefs . . .'

'She won't strike,' he answered. 'We're drifting down just

about a mile inside the buoys.'

Down in the stoke-hold there was a strange sense of remoteness from danger. The warmth and the furnace glow and the blaze of the lights were comfortingly normal. Now that I could no longer see the seas thundering over the reefs I was enveloped in a false sense of security. Only the boom of the waves crashing against the hollow sides of the ship and the bright rivulets of water streaming from the started rivet holes reminded us of the danger we were in; that and the forward slant of the decks and the water sluicing up out of the bilges, black with coal dust, filthy with oil.

We stoked like madmen, shoulder-to-shoulder, flinging coal into the furnace with utter disregard of exhaustion. It seemed an eternity, but the bulkhead held and finally Patch looked at his watch and flung his shovel down. 'I'm going up to the bridge,' he said. 'You'll be on your own now. Keep on stoking until I ring for full speed. Then, when you've got the engines going, come straight up to the bridge. All right?'

I nodded, not trusting myself to speak. He was pulling his clothes on and I watched him as he staggered through to the engine-room and disappeared. The sound of the waves thundering against the hull seemed louder now. I looked down at my wrist watch. It was twenty past seven. I started to shovel coal again, conscious all the time of the hull plates towering above me and of the slope of the decks; conscious that at any moment this lit world might plunge below the seas. Water was sloshing about in the bilges, spilling over on to the plates and swirling round my feet.

Half-past seven! Quarter to eight! Would he never ring for the engines? Once I paused, leaning on my shovel, certain that the deck below my feet was at a steeper angle, watching that streaming bulkhead and wondering what the hell he was doing up there on the bridge. What was this slender chance he had talked of? Exhausted, my nerves strung taut with fear and the long wait, I suddenly wasn't sure of him any more. What did I know about him? My first impressions – of a man unbalanced by circumstances – returned, stronger now because more dangerous.

And then suddenly, faint above the booming of the waves, came the jangle of the telegraph. It was almost eight o'clock. I flung my shovel down, slammed the furnace door shut and, with my clothes in my hand, staggered quickly through into the engine-room. The telegraph indicator was at Full Ahead. I turned the steam full on and as I raced up the ladders, the whole steel-traceried vault of the engine-room became alive with the pounding of the engines.

He was standing at the wheel, steering the ship, as I panted up the ladder on to the bridge. 'Are we clear of the Minkies yet?' I gasped.

He didn't answer. His hands were gripped tight on the wheel, his whole body tense as he stared out ahead. The ship heeled in a long agonizing roll and I staggered down the slope of the bridge-deck to the starboard windows. A buoy, painted red and white, was sliding past us. The bows were completely submerged.

'Almost there now.' His voice was taut, barely audible. His eyes looked out of their sunken sockets, staring fixedly. And then he shifted the balance of his feet and the wheel spun under his hands. I couldn't believe it for a moment. He was turning the wheel to port. He was turning the ship to port, turning her in towards the rock outcrops of the Minkies. 'Are you crazy?' I shouted at him. 'Turn to starboard! To starboard, for God's sake!' And I flung myself at the wheel, gripping the spokes, trying to turn it against the pressure of his hands.

He shouted something at me, but it was lost in the noise of a big sea crashing against the bridge. I wouldn't have heard him any-way. St Malo was only twenty miles away and the beat of the engines throbbed through the deck plates, beating a message of hope against the soles of my feet. We had to turn to starboard – away from the Minkies, towards St Malo. 'For Christ's sake!' I screamed at him.

Fingers gripped my hair, forcing my head back. He was shout-ing at me to let go of the wheel, and my eyes, half-closed with pain, caught a glimpse of his face, set and hard and shining with sweat, the lips drawn back from his teeth and the muscles of his jaw knotted. 'It's our only chance.' His voice was barely audible above the roar of the seas. And then the muscles of my neck cracked as he flung me back and I was caught on a downward plunge and fetched up against the window ledge with such force that all the breath was knocked out of me. A patch of broken water slid past on the port side and almost ahead of us the sea flung a curling wave-top round a little huddle of rocks that were just showing their teeth. I felt suddenly sick.

'Will you take the wheel now?' His voice was distant, quite cool. I stared at him, dazed and not understanding. 'Quick, man,' he said. 'Take the wheel.' He was on his own bridge, giving an order, expecting it to be obeyed. The acceptance of obedience was implicit in his tone. I dragged myself to my feet and he handed over to me. 'Steer north ten degrees east.' He fetched the hand-bearing compass from the chartroom and went out with it on to the starboard wing of the bridge. For a long time he stood there, quite motionless, occasionally raising the compass to his eye and taking a bearing on some object behind us.

And all the time I stood there at the wheel, holding the ship to ten degrees east of north and wondering what in God's name we were doing sailing straight in towards the reefs like this. I was dizzy, still a little sick, too scared now to do anything but hold on to the course I had been told, for I knew we must be in among the rocks and to try to turn the ship would mean certain disaster. And through the windows, out in that maelstrom of white water that filled all my horizon, there gradually emerged the shapes of more rocks, whole masses of rocks, getting nearer and nearer every minute.

'Steer due north now.' His voice was still calm. Yet all ahead of us was nothing but waves tumbling and falling and cascading on the half-exposed reefs. There was one lone island of rock nearer than the rest and, as the ship drove towards it, he was back at my side. 'I'll take her now.' There was a gentleness in the way he spoke and I let him have the wheel, not saying anything, not asking any questions, for his face had a strange, set look as though he were withdrawn inside himself, out of the reach of any human.

And then we struck – not suddenly with an impact, but slowly, gently, a long grinding to a halt that sent me staggering forward until I was brought up against the window ledge. The ship checked, her keel making a noise that was felt in vibration rather than heard above the roar of the storm. For a moment she seemed to tear herself loose and go reeling on through the water; then she struck again and ground to a sudden, sickening halt. The engines continued without pause as though the heart of her had refused to recognize death.

It was a queer moment. Patch was still standing there at the wheel, still staring out ahead with set face and the knuckles of his hands white with the violence of his grip on the wheel spokes. The wheelhouse looked exactly the same, and for'ard, through the glass windows, the bows remained submerged with the waves rolling across them. The deck under my feet still pulsed with life. Nothing had changed; only that we were now motionless and at rest.

Trembling, I wiped the cold sweat from my forehead with my hand. We were aground on the Minkies now. I felt a sense of finality. I turned and looked at him. He seemed dazed. His face, where it had been wiped clear of coal dust, was chalk-white, his dark eyes staring. He was gazing out across the tumbled waste of the sea. 'I did what I could,' he breathed. And then again, louder: 'God in heaven, I did what I could.' There was no blasphemy in the way he said it; only the sense of a man in torment. And finally his hands dropped slackly from the spokes of the wheel as though relinquishing at last his command of the ship and he turned away and walked, slowly and deliberately in the manner of a sleep-walker, through into the chartroom.

I pulled myself together then and followed him.

He was bent over the chart and he didn't look up. A wave crashed against the ship's side, throwing a solid mass of water against the chartroom window, momentarily blocking out the daylight. As it fell away he pulled the log book towards him and, picking up the pencil, began to write. When he had finished, he closed the book and straightened up, as though he had written *Finis* to that section of his life. His eyes came slowly round and met mine. 'I'm sorry,' he said. 'I should have explained what I was going to do.' He was like a man woken from a dream and suddenly rational. 'It was a question of hitting the tide just right.'

'But we should have headed towards St Malo.' I was still dazed, a little stupid – I didn't understand.

'In just over two hours, if we'd lasted that long, the tide would have turned and driven us north across the reefs.' He slid the chart along the table towards me. 'See for yourself,' he said. 'The only chance was to beach her here.' And he put his pencil on the spot where the ship was lying.

It was about a mile south of the main body of the reefs in an area showing $2\frac{1}{4}$ fathoms depth at low water. 'That rock away on the port bow is Grune à Croc,' he said. It was marked as drying 36 ft. 'And you'll probably find the Maîtress Île just visible away to starboard.' His pencil point rested for a moment on the high point to the east of the main reefs. 'At low water it should be reasonably sheltered in here.' He threw the pencil down and straightened up, stretching himself and rubbing his eyes. 'Well, that's that.' There was finality and the acceptance of disaster in the way he said it. 'I'm going to get some sleep.' He went past me then without another word, through into the wheelhouse. I heard his feet on the companion ladder descending to the deck below. I hadn't said anything or tried to stop him. I was too tired to question him now. My head throbbed painfully and the mention of sleep had produced in me an intense desire to close my eyes and slide into oblivion.

I paused on my way through the wheelhouse and stood looking out on the grey, desolate sea-scape of rock and broken water. It was queer to stand there by the wheel with the feel of the engines under my feet, knowing all the time that we were hard aground on the worst reef in the English Channel. Everything in the wheelhouse seemed so normal. It was only when I looked out through the windows and saw the rocks emerging from the tide and the ship's bows no more than a vague outline below the creaming break of the waves that I was able to comprehend what had happened.

But for six hours or more we should be safe; until the rising tide exposed us again to the full force of the seas. I turned and made my way below, moving as though in a dream, like a sleep-walker. Everything seemed vague and a little remote and I staggered slightly, still balancing automatically to the roll of a ship which was now as steady as a rock. As I reached my cabin I felt the beat of the engines slow and stop. Either we had exhausted the steam or else he had gone below and stopped the engines himself. It didn't seem to matter either way. We shouldn't be wanting the engines again, or the pumps. Nothing seemed to matter to me then but sleep.

That sleep should have been possible in those circumstances may seem incredible, but having thought him mad and then found him, not only sane, but capable of an extraordinary feat of seamanship, I had confidence in his statement that we should be sheltered as the tide fell. In any case, there was nothing I could do – nothing either of us could do; we had no boats, no hope of rescue in the midst of those reefs, and the gale was at its height.

I woke to complete darkness with water running like a dark river down the corridor outside my cabin. It came from a broken porthole in the saloon – probably from other places, too. The seas were battering against the ship's side and every now and then there was a grumbling, tearing sound as she shifted her bottom on the shingle bed. I moved up to Patch's cabin then. He was lying on his bunk, fully clothed, and even when I shone my torch on him he didn't stir, though he had been asleep for over twelve hours. I made two trips below to the galley for food and water and the Primus stove, and it was on the second of these that I noticed the little white rectangle of a card pinned to the mahogany of the door just aft of the captain's cabin. It was a business card: *J. C. B. Dellimare*, and underneath – *The Dellimare Trading and Shipping Company Ltd*. The address was St Mary Axe in the City of London. I tried the door, but it was locked.

It was daylight when I woke again. The wind had died down and the seas no longer crashed against the ship's side. A gleam of watery sunlight filtered in through the salt-encrusted glass of the porthole. Patch was still asleep, but he had taken off his boots and some of his clothes and a blanket was pulled round his body. The companion ladder leading to the saloon and the deck below was a black well of still water in which things floated. Up on the bridge, the sight that met my eyes was one of utter desolation. The tide was low and the rocks stood up all round us like the stumps of rotten teeth, grey and jagged with bases blackened with weed growth. The wind was no more than Force 5 or 6 and, though I could see the seas breaking in white cascades over the further rocks that formed my horizon, the water around was relatively quiet, the broken patches smoothed out as though exhausted by their passage across the reefs.

I stood there for a long time watching the aftermath of the storm whirl ragged wisps of thin grey cloud across the sun, staring at the chaos of rocks that surrounded us, at the seas breaking in the distance. I felt a deep, satisfying joy at the mere fact that I was still alive, still able to look at sunlight glittering on water, see the sky and feel the wind on my face. But the davits were empty arms of iron uplifted over the ship's side and the boat that had been hanging by one of its falls was a broken piece of splintered wood trailing in the sea at the end of a frayed rope.

Patch came up and joined me. He didn't look at the sea or the the sky or the surrounding rocks. He stood for a moment gazing down at the bows which now stood clear of the sea, the gaping hole of the hatch black and full of water. And then he went out to the battered port wing and stood looking back along the length of the ship. He had washed his face and it was white and drawn in the brittle sunlight, the line of his jaw hard where the muscles had tightened, and his hands were clenched on the mahogany rail-capping.

I felt I ought to say something – tell him it was bad luck, that at least he could be proud of an incredible piece of seamanship in beaching her here. But the starkness of his features checked me. And in the end I went below, leaving him alone on the bridge.

He was there for a long time and when he did come down he only said, 'Better get some food inside you. We'll be able to leave in an hour or two.' I didn't ask him how he expected to leave with all the boats smashed. It was obvious that he didn't want to talk. He went and sat on his bunk, his shoulders hunched, going through his personal belongings in a sort of daze, his mind lost in its own thoughts.

I got the Primus going and put the kettle on whilst he wandered over to the desk, opening and shutting drawers, stuffing papers into a yellow oilskin bag. He hesitated, looking at the photograph, and then he took that, too. The tea was made by the time he had finished and I opened a tin of bully. We breakfasted in silence, and all the time I was wondering what we were going to do, how we were going to construct a boat. 'It's no good waiting to be taken off,' I said at length. 'They'll never find the *Mary Deare* here.'

He stared at me as though surprised that anybody should speak to him in the dead stillness of the ship. 'No, it'll be some time before they find her.' He nodded his head slowly, still lost in his own thoughts.

'We'll have to build some sort of a boat.'

'A boat?' He seemed surprised. 'Oh, we've got a boat.'

'Where?'

'In the next cabin. An inflatable rubber dinghy.'

'A rubber dinghy – in Dellimare's cabin?'

He nodded. 'That's right. Odd, isn't it? He had it there – just in case.' He was laughing quietly to himself. 'And now we're going to use it.'

The man was dead and I saw nothing funny about his not being here to use his dinghy. 'You find that amusing?' I asked angrily.

He didn't answer, but went to the desk and got some keys, and then he went out and I heard him unlock the door of the next cabin. There was a scrape of heavy baggage being moved and I went to give him a hand. The door was opened and, inside, the cabin looked as though a madman had looted it – drawers pulled out, suitcases forced open, their hasps ripped off, their contents strewn over the floor; clothes and papers strewn everywhere. Only the bed remained aloof from the chaos, still neatly made-up, un-slept-in, the pillows stained with the man's hair oil.

He had the keys. He must have searched the cabin himself. 'What were you looking for?' I asked.

He stared at me for a moment without saying anything. Then he shifted the big cabin trunk out of the way, toppling it on to its side with a crash. It lay there, a slab of coloured hotel labels – Tokyo, Yokohama, Singapore, Rangoon. 'Catch hold of this!' He had hold of a big brown canvas bundle and we hauled it out into the corridor and through the door to the open deck. He went back then and I heard him lock the door of Dellimare's cabin. When he returned he brought a knife with him. We cut the canvas straps, got the yellow dinghy out of its wrappings and inflated it.

The thing was about twelve feet long and five feet broad; it had paddles and a rudder and a tubular telescopic mast with nylon rigging and a small nylon sail. It even had fishing tackle. 'Was he a nervous sort of man?' I asked. For a shipowner to pack a collapsible dinghy on board one of his own ships seemed odd behaviour – almost as though he suffered from the premonition that the sea would get him.

But all Patch said was, 'It's time we got moving.'

I stared at him, startled at the thought of leaving the comparative security of the ship for the frailty of the rubber dinghy. 'The seas will be pretty big once we get clear of the reefs. Hadn't we better wait for the wind to drop a bit more?'

'We need the wind,. He sniffed at it, feeling for its direction with his face. 'It's veered a point or two already. With luck it will go round into the north-west.' He glanced at his watch. 'Come on,' he said. 'There's four hours of tide with us.'

I tried to tell him it would be better to wait for the next tide and get the whole six hours of it, but he wouldn't listen. 'It would be almost dark then. And suppose the wind changed? You can't beat to windward in this sort of craft. And,' he added, 'there may be another depression following on behind this one. You don't want to be caught out here in another gale. I don't know what would happen at high water. The whole bridge deck might get carried away.'

He was right, of course, and we hurriedly collected the things we needed – food, charts, a hand-bearing compass, all the clothes we could clamber into. We had sou'westers and sea boots, but no oilskins. We took the two raincoats from the cabin door.

It was nine forty-five when we launched the dinghy from the for'ard well-deck. We paddled her clear of the ship and then hoisted sail. The sun had disappeared by then and everything was grey in a mist of driving rain, the rocks appearing further away, vague battlement shapes on the edge of visibility; many of them were already covered. We headed for Les Sauvages and in a little while the flashing buoy that marked the rocks emerged out of the murk. By then the *Mary Deare* was no more than a vague blur, low down in the water. We lost her completely as we passed Les Sauvages.

There was still a big sea running and, once we cleared the shelter of the Minkies, we encountered the towering swell left by

449

the gale. It marched up behind us in wall upon wall of steep-fronted, toppling water, and in the wet, swooping chill of that grey day I lost all sense of time.

For just over four hours we were tumbled about in the aftermath of the storm, soaked to the skin, crammed into the narrow space between the fat, yellow rolls of the dinghy's sides, with only an occasional glimpse of Cap Frehel to guide us. And then, shortly after midday, we were picked up by the cross-Channel packet coming in from Peter Port. They were on the look-out for survivors, otherwise they would never have sighted us, for they were passing a good half mile to the west of us. And then the packet suddenly altered course, coming down on us fast, the bows almost hidden by spray flung up by the waves. She hove-to a little up-wind of us, rolling heavily, and as she drifted down on to us rope ladders were thrown over the side and men came down to help us up, quiet, English voices offering words of encouragement, hands reaching down to pull us up.

People crowded us on the deck – passengers and crew, asking questions, pressing cigarettes and chocolate on us. Then an officer took us to his quarters and the packet got into her stride again, engines throbbing gently, effortlessly. As we went below I caught a glimpse of the dinghy, a patch of yellow in the white of the ship's wake as it rode up the steep face of a wave.

4

A HOT shower, dry clothes and then we were taken into the officers' saloon and a steward was bustling about, pouring tea, bringing us plates of bacon and eggs. The normality of it – the incredible normality of it! It was like waking from a nightmare. The *Mary Deare* and the gale and the tooth-edged rocks of the Minkies seemed part of another life, utterly divorced from the present. And then the Captain came in. 'So you're survivors from the *Mary Deare*.' He stood, looking from one to the other of us. 'Is either of you the owner of the yacht *Sea Witch*?'

'Yes,' I said. 'I'm John Sands.'

'Good. I'm Captain Fraser. I'll have a radio message sent to

Peter Port right away. A Colonel Lowden brought her in. He was very worried about you. He and Duncan were on board yesterday, listening to the radio reports of the search. They had planes out looking for you.' He turned to Patch. 'I take it you're one of the *Mary Deare*'s officers?' His voice was harder, the Scots accent more pronounced.

Patch had risen. 'Yes. I'm the master of the *Mary Deare*. Captain Patch.' He held out his hand. 'I'm most grateful to you for picking us up.'

'Better thank my first officer. It was he who spotted you.' He was staring at Patch, small blue eyes looking out of a craggy face. 'You say your name is Patch?'

'Yes.'

'And you're the master of the *Mary Deare*?'

'Yes.'

The iron-grey brows lifted slightly and then settled in a frown. 'I understood that a Captain Taggart was master of the *Mary Deare*.'

'Yes, he was. But he died.'

'When was that?' There was a sharpness in the way the question was put.

'Just after we cleared Port Said – early this month.'

'I see.' Fraser stared at him stonily. And then, consciously relaxing: 'Well, don't let me interrupt your meal. You must be hungry. Sit down. Sit down, both of you.' He glanced at his watch and then called to the steward to bring another cup. 'I've just time before we go into St Malo.' He sat down, leaning his elbows on the table, his little blue eyes staring at us, full of curiosity. 'Well, now, what happened, Captain Patch? The air has been thick with messages about the *Mary Deare* for the last twenty-four hours.' He hesitated, waiting. 'You'll be glad to know that a boatload of survivors was washed up on Île de Brehat yesterday afternoon.' Patch still said nothing. 'Oh, come; you can't expect me not to be curious.' His tone was friendly. 'The survivors report that there was a fire and you ordered the crew to abandon ship. That was Thursday night and yet Lowden told me – '

'I ordered them to abandon ship?' Patch was staring at him. 'Is that what they say?'

'According to a French report, yes. They abandoned ship shortly after 22.30 hours. Yet at 09.30 the following morning Lowden saw the *Mary Deare* . . .' He hesitated, silenced by Patch's

451

hard, uncompromising stare. 'Damn it, man!' he said in sudden exasperation. 'What happened? Is the *Mary Deare* afloat or sunk or what?'

Patch didn't say anything for a moment. He seemed to be thinking it out. Finally he said, 'A full statement will be made to the proper authorities. Until then – ' He was still staring at Fraser. 'Until then you'll excuse me if I don't talk about it.'

Fraser hesitated, unwilling to let it go at that. Then he glanced at his watch again, drank up his tea and rose to his feet. 'Very proper of you, Captain,' he said, his voice formal, a little huffed. 'Now I must go. We're just coming into St Malo. Meantime, please accept the hospitality of my ship. Anything you want, ask the steward.' As he went out, he paused in the doorway. 'I think I should tell you, Captain, that we have a young lady on board – a Miss Taggart. She's Captain Taggart's daughter. She flew out to Peter Port yesterday, and when she heard survivors had come ashore on the coast of France, she came on with us.' He paused, and then came back a few steps into the saloon. 'She doesn't know her father is dead. She's hoping he's amongst the survivors.' Again a slight hesitation. 'I presume you notified the owners?'

'Of course.'

'I see. Well, it's a pity they didn't see fit to inform his next-of-kin.' He said it angrily. 'I'll have my steward bring her to you.' And then in a softer tone: 'Break it to her gently, man. She's a nice wee thing and she obviously adored her father.' He left then and a silence descended on the room. Patch was eating with the concentration of a man shovelling energy back into his body. There was nothing relaxed about him.

'Well, what did he die of?' I asked him.

'Who?' He looked at me with a quick frown.

'Taggart.'

'Oh, Taggart. He died of drink.' He resumed his eating, as though dismissing the matter from his mind.

'Good God!' I said. 'You can't tell her that.'

'No, of course not,' he said impatiently. 'I'll just tell her he died of heart failure. That was probably the medical cause anyway.'

'She'll want to know details.'

'Well, she can't have them.' I thought he was being callous and got up and went over to the porthole. The engines had been slowed. We were coming into the *Rade* and I could see the tourist hotels of Dinard climbing the hill from the quay, deserted and forlorn in the rain. 'He was running around the ship, screaming

like a soul in torment.' He pushed his plate away from him. 'I had
to lock him in his cabin, and in the morning he was dead.' He
pulled out the packet of cigarettes he had been given and opened
it with trembling fingers, tearing at it viciously. His face was
deathly pale in the flare of the match.

'DTs?' I said.

'No, not DTs. I only discovered afterwards . . .' He dragged
on his cigarette, pushing his hand up through his hair. 'Well, it
doesn't matter now.' He pulled himself to his feet. 'We're nearly
in, aren't we?'

The ship was moving very slowly now. Lock gates glided past.
Boots rang on the deck overhead and there was the clatter of a
donkey engine. 'I think we're going into the basin now,' I told
him.

'You're lucky,' he said. 'You're through with the *Mary Deare*
now.' He had started pacing restlessly up and down. 'God! I
almost wish I'd gone down with the ship.'

I stared at him. 'It's true then . . . You did order the crew to
take to the boats. That story about your being knocked out – '

He turned on me, his face livid. 'Of course, I didn't order them
to take to the boats. But if they stick to that story . . .' He flung
away towards the other porthole, staring out at the grey daylight.

'But why should they?' I demanded. 'If it isn't true – '

'What's truth got to do with it?' He stared at me angrily. 'The
bastards panicked and now they're saying I ordered them to
abandon ship because they've got to cover themselves somehow.
A bunch of damned cowards – they'll cling together. You'll see.
When it comes to the Formal Enquiry . . .' He gave a little shrug
of his shoulders. 'I've been through all this before.' He said it
slowly, half to himself, his head turned away, staring out through
the porthole again at the waste ground with the rusty railway
wagons. He muttered something about it being a strange coincidence, and then a door slammed and there was the sound of
voices, a medley of French and English. He swung round, staring
at the door and said, 'You will, of course, confine yourself to a
statement of the reasons for your presence on board the *Mary
Deare*.' He spoke quickly, nervously. 'You are in the position of a
passenger and any comments – ' The door opened and he half
turned, facing it.

It was Captain Fraser, and with him were two French officials.
Smiles, bows, a torrent of French, and then the shorter of the two
said in English: 'I regret, Monsieur le Capitaine, I have bad

news for you. Since half an hour I have heard on the radio that some bodies have been washed ashore on Les Heaux. Also some wreckage.'

'From the *Mary Deare*?' Patch asked.

'Mais oui.' He gave a little shrug. 'The lighthouse men on Les Heaux have not identified them, but there is no other ship in distress.'

'Les Heaux is an island just north of the Île de Brehat – about forty miles west of here,' Fraser said.

'I know that.' Patch moved a step towards the official. 'The survivors,' he said. 'Was there a man called Higgins amongst them?'

The officer shrugged. 'I do not know. No official list of survivors is yet completed.' He hesitated. 'Monsieur le Capitaine, if you will come to the Bureau with me it will assist me greatly. Also it will be more simple. The formalities, you understand . . .' He said it apologetically, but it was clear he had made up his mind.

'Of course,' Patch said, but I could see he didn't like it. His eyes glanced quickly from one to the other of them, and then he went across the room and passed through the lane they opened out for him to the door.

The official turned to follow him, but then stopped and looked back at me. 'Monsieur Sands?' he enquired.

I nodded.

'I understand your boat is waiting for you in Saint Peter Port. If you will give my friend here the necessary particulars and your address in England, I do not think we need detain you at all.' He gave me a quick, friendly smile. 'Bon voyage, mon ami.'

'Au revoir, monsieur,' I said. 'Et merci, mille fois.'

His assistant took the particulars, asked a few questions and then he, too, departed. I was alone, and I sat there in a sort of coma, conscious of the bustle and hubbub of passengers descending to the quay, yet not sure that it was real. I must have dozed off for the next thing I knew the steward was shaking me. 'Sorry to wake you, sir, but I've brought Miss Taggart. Captain's orders, sir.'

She was standing just inside the door; a small, neat girl, her hair catching the light from the porthole just the way it had done in that photograph. 'You're Mr Sands, aren't you?'

I nodded and got to my feet. 'You want Captain Patch.' I started to explain that he had gone ashore, but she interrupted. 'What happened to my father, please?'

I didn't know what to say. She should have been asking Patch, not me. 'Captain Patch will be back soon,' I said.

'Was my father on the *Mary Deare* when you boarded her?' She stood there, very straight and boyish, and quite determined.

'No,' I said.

She took that in slowly, her eyes fixed steadfastly on mine. They were grey eyes, flecked with green; wide and startled-looking. 'And this Captain Patch was in command?' I nodded. She stared at me for a long time, her lip trembling slightly. 'My father would never have abandoned his ship.' She said it softly and I knew she had guessed the truth, was bracing herself for it. And then: 'He's dead – is that it?'

'Yes,' I said.

She took it, dry-eyed, standing there, stiff and small in front of me. 'And the cause of death?' She tried to keep it formal, impersonal, but as I hesitated, she made a sudden, small feminine movement, coming towards me: 'Please, I must know what happened. How did he die? Was he ill?'

'I think it was a heart attack,' I said. And then I added, 'You must understand, Miss Taggart, I wasn't there. I am only passing on what Captain Patch told me.'

'When did it happen?'

'Early this month.'

'And this Captain Patch?'

'He was the first mate.'

She frowned. 'My father didn't mention him. He wrote me from Singapore and Rangoon and the only officers he mentioned were Rice and Adams and a man named Higgins.'

'Patch joined at Aden.'

'Aden?' She shook her head, huddling her coat close to her as though she were cold. 'My father always wrote me from every port he stopped at – every port in the world.' And then she added, 'But I got no letter from Aden.' Tears started to her eyes and she turned away, fumbling for a chair. I didn't move and after a moment she said, 'I'm sorry. It's just the shock.' She looked up at me, not bothering to wipe away the tears. 'Daddy was away so much. It shouldn't hurt like this. I haven't seen him for five years.' And then in a rush: 'But he was such a wonderful person. I know that now. You see, my mother died . . .' She hesitated and then said, 'He was always coming back to England to see me. But he never did. And this time he'd promised. That's what makes it so hard. He was coming back. And now – ' She caught her breath and I saw her bite her lip to stop it trembling.

'Would you like some tea?' I asked.

She nodded. She had her handkerchief out and her face was turned away from me. I hesitated, feeling there ought to be something I could do. But there was nothing and I went in search of the steward. To give her time to recover, I waited whilst he made the tea and brought it back to her myself. She was composed now and though her face still looked white and pinched, she had got back some of the vitality that there had been in that photograph. She began asking me questions and to keep her mind off her father's death I started to tell her what had happened after I boarded the *Mary Deare*.

And then Patch came in. He didn't see her at first. 'I've got to leave,' he said. 'A question of identification. They've picked up twelve bodies.' His voice was hard and urgent, his face strained. 'Rice is dead. The only one I could rely on – '

'This is Miss Taggart,' I said.

He stared at her. For a second he didn't know her, didn't connect her name; his mind was concentrated entirely on his own affairs. And then the hardness slowly left his face and he came forward, hesitantly, almost nervously. 'Of course. Your face . . .' He paused as though at a loss for words. 'It – it was there on his desk. I never removed it.' And then, still looking at her, as though fascinated, he added almost to himself: 'You were with me through many bad moments.'

'I understand my father is dead?'

The forthright way in which she put it seemed to shock him, for his eyes widened slightly as though at a blow. 'Yes.'

'Mr Sands said you thought it was a heart attack?'

'Yes. Yes, that's right – a heart attack.' He said it automatically, not thinking about the words, all his mind concentrated in his eyes, drinking her in as though she were some apparition that had suddenly come to life.

There was an awkward pause. 'What happened? Please tell me what happened?' She was standing facing him now and there was a tightness in her voice that betrayed her nervousness. I suddenly felt that she was afraid of him. A sort of tension stretched between them. 'I want to know what happened,' she repeated and her voice sounded almost brittle in the silence.

'Nothing happened,' he answered slowly. 'He died. That's all.' His voice was flat, without feeling.

'But how? When? Surely you can give me some details?'

He pushed his hand up through his hair. 'Yes. Yes, of course. I'm sorry. It was 2nd March. We were in the Med. then.' He hesitated as though searching in his mind for the words he wanted.

'He didn't come up to the bridge that morning. And then the steward called me. He was lying in his bunk.' Again a pause and then he added, 'We buried him that afternoon, at sea.'

'He died in his sleep then?'

'Yes. That's right. He died in his sleep.'

There was a long silence. She wanted to believe him, wanted to desperately. But she didn't. Her eyes were very big and her hands were pressed tightly together. 'Did you know him well?' she asked. 'Had you sailed with him before?'

'No.'

'Had he been ill at all – during the voyage, or before you joined the ship at Aden?'

Again the slight hesitation. 'No. He hadn't been ill.' He seemed to pull himself together then. 'I gather the owners didn't inform you of his death. I'm sorry about that. I notified them by radio immediately, but I received no reply. They should have notified you.' He said it without any hope that they would have done so.

'What did he look like – before his death? Tell me about him please. You see, I hadn't seen him – ' The pleading sound of her voice trailed away. And then suddenly in a firmer voice she said, 'Can you describe him to me?'

He frowned slightly. 'Yes, if you want me to.' His tone was reluctant. 'I — don't quite know what you want me to tell you.'

'Just what he looked like. That's all.'

'I see. Well, I'll try. He was small, very small – there was almost nothing of him at all. His face was red – sun-burned. He was bald, you know, but when he had his cap on and was up on the bridge he looked much younger than – '

'Bald?' Her voice sounded shocked.

'Oh, he still had some white hair.' Patch sounded awkward. 'You must understand, Miss Taggart, he wasn't a young man and he'd been a long time in the tropics.'

'He had fair hair,' she said almost desperately. 'A lot of fair hair.' She was clinging to a five-year-old picture of him. 'You're making him out to be an old man.'

'You asked me to describe him,' Patch said defensively.

'I can't believe it.' There was a break in her voice. and then she was looking at him again, her chin up, her face white. 'There's something more, isn't there – something you haven't told me?'

'No, I assure you,' Patch murmured unhappily.

'Yes, there is. I know there is.' Her voice had suddenly risen on a note of hysteria. 'Why didn't he write to me from Aden?

He always wrote me . . . every port . . . and then dying like that and the ship going down . . . He'd never lost a ship in his life.'

Patch was staring at her, his face suddenly hard and angry. Then abruptly he turned to me. 'I've got to go now.' He didn't look at the girl again as he turned on his heels and walked quickly out.

She looked round at the sound of the door closing, staring at the blankness of it with wide, tear-filled eyes. And then suddenly she slumped down into her chair and buried her head in her arms, her whole body racked by a paroxysm of sobs. I waited, wondering what I could do to help her. Gradually her shoulders ceased to shake. 'Five years is a long time,' I said gently. 'He could only tell you what he knew.'

'It wasn't that,' she said wildly. 'All the time he was here I felt – ' She stopped there. She had her handkerchief out and she began dabbing at her face. 'I'm sorry,' she whispered. 'It was silly of me. I – I was just a schoolgirl when I last saw my father. My impression of him is probably a bit romantic.'

I put my hand on her shoulder. 'Just remember him as you last saw him,' I said.

She nodded dumbly.

'Shall I pour you some more tea?'

'No. No, thanks.' She stood up. 'I must go now.'

'Is there anything I can do?' I asked. She seemed so lost.

'No. Nothing.' She gave me a smile that was a mere conventional movement of her lips. She was more than dazed; she was raw and hurt inside. 'I must go – somewhere, by myself.' It was said fugitively and in a rush, her hand held out to me automatically. 'Good-bye. Thank you.' Our hands touched, and she was gone. For a moment her footsteps sounded on the bare wood of the deck outside, and then I was alone with the sounds of the ship and the dock. Through the porthole I saw the bare, grey walls of St Malo glistening wet in a fleeting gleam of sunlight – the old walls of the city and above them the new stone and roofing of buildings faithfully copied to replace the shattered wreckage that the Germans had left. She was walking across the cobbled roadway, walking quickly, not seeing the passengers or the French or the sombre, fortress-like beauty of the ancient city; a small, neat figure whose mind clung to a girl's memories of a dead father.

I turned away and lit a cigarette, slumping wearily into a chair. The crane, the gangway, the passengers in their raincoats and the French dock men in their blue smocks and trousers; it all seemed so ordinary – the Minkies and the *Mary Deare* were a vague dream.

And then Captain Fraser came in. 'Well,' he said, 'what *did* happen? Do you know?' The curiosity in his blue eyes was unveiled now. 'The crew say that he ordered them to abandon ship.' He waited and when I didn't say anything, he added, 'Not just one of them; it's what they all say.'

I remembered then what Patch had said: *They'll cling together . . . because they've got to cover themselves somehow.* Who was right – Patch or the crew? My mind went back to that moment when we had grounded, when he had relinquished the wheel from the grip of his hands in the midst of that waste of sea and rock.

'You must have some idea what really happened.'

I was conscious of Fraser again and was suddenly and for the first time fully aware of the ordeal that Patch now faced. I pulled myself stiffly up out of the chair. 'I've no idea,' I said. And then, because I sensed in the man a sort of hostility towards Patch, I added quickly, 'But I'm quite certain he never ordered the crew to take to the boats.' It was an instinctive rather than a reasoned statement. I told him I was going ashore then to find a hotel, but he wouldn't hear of it and insisted on my accepting the hospitality of his ship, ringing for the steward and putting a cabin at my disposal.

I saw Patch once more before I took the plane for Guernsey. It was at Paimpol, twenty or thirty miles to the west of St Malo, in a little office down by the *bassin*. There were fishing vessels there, packed two and three-deep along the walls – tubby wooden bottoms, all bitumen-black, nudging each other like charladies, with mast-tops nodding, gay with paint – and the water of the *bassin* was poppled with little hissing waves, for it was blowing half a gale again. As the police car that had brought me from St Malo drew up I saw Patch framed in the fly-blown office window; just his face, disembodied and white as a ghost, looking out like a prisoner on to the world of the sea.

'This way plees, monsieur.'

There was an outer office that served as a waiting-room with benches round the wall and a dozen men were seated there, dumb, apathetic and listless – flotsam washed in by the sea. I knew instinctively that they were all that remained of the *Mary Deare*'s crew. Their borrowed clothes breathed shipwreck and they huddled close together, like a bunch of frightened, bewildered sheep; some that were clearly English, others that might be any race under the sun. One man, and one man alone, stood out from the motley bunch. He was a great hunk of a brute with a bull's neck and a bull's head, all hard bone and folds of flesh. He stood with his legs spread wide, solid as a piece of sculpture on the pedestal of his feet, his huge, meaty hands thrust inside his trousers, which were fastened with a broad leather belt that was stained white with a crust of salt and had a big square brass buckle that had turned almost green. He held his hands there as though trying to prevent the great roll of fat, like a rubber tyre, that was his belly escaping entirely from the belt. His clothes were borrowed – a blue shirt that was too small for him and blue trousers that were too short. His thighs and legs tapered away like a bull terrier's hind quarters so that they looked on the verge of buckling under the weight of that great barrel of a body.

He started forward as though to bar my way. Tiny eyes, hard as flint, stared at me unwinking over heavy pouches of flesh. I half-checked, thinking he was going to speak to me, but he didn't; then the gendarme opened the door to the inner office and I went in.

Patch turned from the window as I entered. I couldn't see his expression. His head and shoulders were outlined against the window's square of daylight and all I could see was the people in the road outside and the fishing boats moving restlessly in the *bassin* beyond. There were filing cabinets ranged against the walls under faded charts of the harbour, a big, old-fashioned safe in one corner, and, seated at an untidy desk facing the light, was a ferrety little man with twinkling eyes and thinning hair. 'Monsieur Sands?' He held out a thin, pale hand. He didn't rise to greet me and I was conscious of the crutch propped against the wooden arm of his chair. 'You will excuse me please for the journey you make, but it is necessary.' He waved me to a seat. 'Alors, monsieur.' He was staring at the sheet of foolscap in front of him that was covered with neat, copper-plate writing. 'You go on board the *Mary Deare* from your yacht. C'est ça?'

'Oui, monsieur.' I nodded.

'And the name of your yacht, monsieur?'

'*Sea Witch.*'

He began to write slowly and with meticulous care, frowning slightly and biting softly at his underlip as the steel nib scratched across the surface of the paper. 'And your name – your full name?'

'John Henry Sands.' I spelt it for him.

'And your address?'

I gave him the name and address of my bank.

'Eh bien. Now, you boarded the *Mary Deare* how long after the crew had abandoned the ship?'

'Ten or eleven hours after.'

'And Monsieur le Capitaine?' He glanced at Patch. 'He was still on the ship, eh?'

I nodded.

The official leaned forward. 'Alors, monsieur. It is this that I have to ask you. In your opinion, did Monsieur le Capitaine order the crew to abandon ship or did he not?'

I looked across at Patch, but he was still just a silhouette framed in the window. 'I can't say, monsieur,' I replied. 'I wasn't there.'

'Of course. I understand that. But in your opinion. I want your opinion, monsieur. You must know what had happened. He must have talked about it with you. You were on that ship through many desperate hours. It must have occurred to you both that you might die. Did he not say anything that would enable you to form some opinion as to what really happened?'

'No,' I said. 'We didn't talk very much. There wasn't time.' And then, because it must seem extraordinary to him that we hadn't had time to talk in all the hours we had been on board together, I explained exactly what we had had to do.

He kept on nodding his small head whilst I was talking, a little impatiently as though he weren't listening. And as soon as I had finished, he said, 'And now, monsieur, your opinion. That is what I want.'

By then I had had time to make up my mind. 'Very well,' I said. 'I am quite convinced that Captain Patch never ordered his crew to abandon ship.' And I went on to explain that it was impossible to believe that he had done so since he himself had remained on board and, single-handed, had put out the fire in the after hold. All the time I was talking the steel pen scratched across the surface of the paper, and when I had finished the official read it through carefully and then turned the sheet towards me. 'You read French, monsieur?' I nodded. 'Then please to read what is written there and sign the deposition.' He handed me the pen.

'You understand,' I said, when I had read it through and signed it, 'that I wasn't there. I do not *know* what happened.'

'Of course.' He was looking across at Patch. 'You wish to add anything to the statement you have made?' he asked him. And when Patch merely shook his head, he leaned forward, 'You understand, Monsieur le Capitaine, that it is a very serious charge

that you make against your crew – your officers also. Monsieur
'Iggins has sworn that you gave the order to him, and the man at
the wheel – Yules – has confirmed that he heard you give the
order.' Patch made no comment. 'I think perhaps it will be best if
we have Monsieur 'Iggins and the other man in here so that I
can – '

'No!' Patch's voice trembled with sudden violence.

'But, monsieur.' The official's voice was mild. 'I must understand what – '

'By Christ! I tell you, no!' Patch had come forward to the
desk in two strides, was leaning down over it. 'I won't have my
statement queried in front of those two.'

'But there must be some reason – '

'No, I tell you!' Patch's fist crashed down on the desk. 'You
have my statement and that's that. In due course there will be an
Enquiry. Until then neither you nor anybody else is going to
cross-examine me in front of the crew.'

'But, Monsieur le Capitaine, do you understand what it is you
accuse them of?'

'Of course, I do.'

'Then I must ask you – '

'No. Do you hear me? No!' His fist slammed the desk again.
And then he turned abruptly to me. 'For God's sake, let's go
and have a drink. I've been in this wretched little office . . .'
He caught hold of my arm. 'Come on. I need a drink.'

I glanced at the official. He merely shrugged his shoulders,
spreading his hands out palm upwards in a little gesture of despair.
Patch pulled open the door and strode through the outer office,
not glancing to left or right, walking straight through the men
gathered there as though they didn't exist. But when I started to
follow him, the big man blocked my path. 'Well, wot did you
tell 'em?' he demanded in a throaty voice that was like steam
wheezing up from the great pot of his belly. 'I suppose you told
'em that he never ordered us to abandon ship. Is that wot you
said?'

I tried to push past him, but one of his great paws shot out and
gripped me by the arm. 'Come on. Let's have it. Is that wot you
told 'em?'

'Yes,' I said.

He let go of me then. 'God Almighty!' he growled. 'Wot the
hell do you know about it, eh? You were there I s'pose when we
took to the boats?' He was grinning, truculent, and the stubble
mat of his face, thrust close to mine, was still grey with salt and

dirt. For a man who had been shipwrecked he looked oddly pleased with himself. He oozed self-confidence like a barrel oozes lard and his small, blood-shot eyes glittered moistly, like a pair of oysters, as he said again, 'You were there, eh?' And he guffawed at his own heavy humour.

'No,' I told him. 'Of course I wasn't there. But I don't – '

'Well, we was there.' His voice was raised and his small eyes darted to the half-open door behind me. 'We was there an' we know dam' well wot orders were given.' He was saying it for the benefit of the French official in the inner office. 'It was the right order, too, with the ship half full of explosives and a fire on board. That's wot we felt at the time – me and Rice and the old Chief . . . everybody.'

'If it was the right order,' I said, 'how was it possible for Captain Patch to put the fire out on his own?'

'Ah. You'd better ask him that.' And he turned and looked at Patch.

Patch came slowly back from the street door. 'What exactly do you mean by that, Higgins?' he demanded. His voice was quiet, but it trembled slightly and his hands were clenched.

'Wot a man's done once, he'll do again,' Higgins said, and there was a little gleam of triumph in his eyes.

I thought Patch was going to hit him. So did Higgins, for he stepped back, measuring the distance between them. But Patch didn't hit him. Instead, he said, 'You deserve to be strung up for murder. You killed Rice and those others as surely as if you'd taken a gun to them and shot them down in cold blood.' He said it through clenched teeth and then turned abruptly to walk out.

And Higgins, stung, shouted hoarsely after him: 'You won't get away with it at the Enquiry – not with your record.'

Patch swung round, his face white, and he was trembling as he looked at the pitiful little gathering, his eyes passing from face to face. 'Mr Burrows.' He had picked on a tall, thin man with a sour, dissipated face. 'You know damn' well I never gave any orders to abandon ship.'

The man shifted his feet nervously, not looking at Patch. 'I only know what was passed down to me on the blower,' he muttered. They were all nervous, doubtful, their eyes on the floor.

'Yules.' Patch's gaze had switched to an under-sized little runt of a man with a peaked, sweaty face and shifty eyes. 'You were at the wheel. You heard what orders I gave up there on the bridge. What were they?'

The man hesitated, glancing at Higgins. 'You ordered the boats swung out and the men to stand by to abandon ship,' he whispered.

'You damned little liar!' Patch started to move towards him, but Higgins stepped forward. And Yules said, 'I don't know what you mean.' His voice was high-pitched on a note of sudden spite.

Patch stared at him a moment, breathing heavily. And then he turned and went out quickly. I followed him and found him waiting for me on the pavement outside. His whole body was shaking and he looked utterly drained. 'You need some sleep,' I said.

'I need a drink.'

We walked in silence up to the square and sat at a little *bistro* that advertised *crêpes* as a speciality. 'Have you any money?' he asked. And when I told him Fraser had lent me some, he nodded and said, 'I'm a distressed seaman and a charge on the Consul. It doesn't run to drinks.' There was a note of bitterness in his voice. And then, when we had ordered cognac, he suddenly said, 'The last body wasn't brought in until two o'clock this morning.' His face looked haggard as it had done on the *Mary Deare*, the bruise along his jaw even more livid against the clean-shaven pallor of his face.

I gave him a cigarette and he lit it with trembling hands. 'They got caught in the tide-rip off the entrance to Lezardrieux.' The drinks came and he knocked his back and ordered two more. 'Why the hell did it have to be Rice's boat?' The palm of his hand slapped viciously against the table. 'If it had been Higgins . . .' He sighed and relapsed into silence.

I didn't break it. I felt he needed that silence. He lingered over his second drink and every now and then he looked at me as though trying to make up his mind about something. The little square bustled with life, full of the noise of cars hooting and the quick, excited chatter of French people as they hurried along the pavement outside. It was wonderful just to sit there and drink cognac and know that I was alive. But my mind couldn't shake itself free of the *Mary Deare*, and watching Patch as he sat, staring down at his drink, I wondered what had really happened on that ship before I boarded her. And that little huddle of survivors in the office overlooking the *bassin* . . . 'What did Higgins mean – about your record?' I asked. 'Was he referring to the *Belle Isle*?'

He nodded, not looking up.

'What happened to her?'

'Oh, she ran aground and broke her back . . . and people talked. That's all. There was a lot of money involved. It's not important.'

But I knew it was. He'd kept on talking about it, saying you wouldn't think it could happen to the same man twice. 'What's the connection between the *Belle Isle* and the *Mary Deare*?' I asked.

He looked up at me quickly. 'How do you mean?'

'Well . . .' It wasn't easy to put it into words with him staring at me like that. 'It's a pretty strange story, you know – the crew saying you ordered them to abandon ship and you saying you didn't. And there's Taggart's death,' I added. 'Dellimare, too.'

'Dellimare?' The sudden violence of his voice shook me. 'What's Dellimare got to do with it?'

'Nothing,' I said. 'But . . .'

'Well, go on. What else are you thinking?'

It was a question that had been in my mind for a long time. 'That fire . . .' I said.

'Are you suggesting I started it?'

The question took me by surprise. 'Good God, no.'

'What are you suggesting then?' His eyes were angry and suspicious.

I hesitated, wondering whether he wasn't too exhausted to answer rationally. 'It's just that I can't understand why you put the fire out and yet didn't bother to get the pumps going. I thought you'd been stoking that boiler. But it hadn't been touched.' I paused there, a little uncertain because of the strange look on his face. 'What had you been doing?'

'God damn you!' His eyes suddenly blazed. 'What's it got to do with you?'

'Nothing,' I said. 'Only . . .'

'Only what? What are you getting at?'

'It was just the coal dust. You were covered with it and I wondered . . .' I saw his hand clench and I added quickly, 'You can't expect me not to be curious.'

His body relaxed slowly. 'No. No, I suppose not.' He stared down at his empty glass. 'I'm sorry. I'm a little tired, that's all.'

'Would you like another drink?'

He nodded, sunk in silence again.

He didn't speak until the drinks came, and then he said, 'I'm going to be quite honest with you, Sands. I'm in a hell of a spot.' He wasn't looking at me. He was looking down at his glass, watching the liquor cling to the sides of it as he swirled it gently round and round.

'Because of Higgins?'

He nodded. 'Partly. Higgins is a liar and a blackguard. But I can't prove it. He was in this thing right from the start, but I can't prove that either.' He looked at me suddenly. 'I've got to get out to her again.'

'To the *Mary Deare*?' It seemed odd that he should think that it was his responsibility. 'Why?' I asked. 'Surely the owners will arrange – '

'The owners!' He gave a contemptuous little laugh. 'If the owners knew she was on the Minkies . . .' And then abruptly he changed the subject and began questioning me about my own plans. 'You said something about being interested in salvage and converting that yacht of yours into a diving tender.' That had been up in his cabin when he'd been half-doped with liquor and exhaustion. I was surprised he remembered it. 'You've got all the equipment, have you – air pumps and diving suits?'

'We're aqualung divers,' I said. His sudden interest had switched my mind to the problems that lay ahead – the conversion, the fitting out, all the business of starting on our first professional salvage operation.

'I've been thinking . . .' He was drumming nervously on the marble-topped table. 'That boat of yours – how long will it take to convert her?'

'Oh, about a month,' I said. And then it dawned on me. 'You aren't suggesting that we take you out to the *Mary Deare*, are you?'

He turned to me then. 'I've got to get back to her,' he said.

'But, good God – why?' I asked. 'The owners will arrange for the salvage – '

'Damn the owners!' he snarled. 'They don't know she's there yet.' He leaned urgently towards me. 'I tell you, I've got to get out to her.'

'But why?'

His eyes gradually dropped from my face. 'I can't tell you that,' he muttered. And then he said, 'Listen, Sands. I'm not a salvage man. But I'm a seaman, and I know that ship can be refloated.'

'Nonsense,' I said. 'Another gale and she'll be flooded – she'll probably break up.'

'I don't think so. She'll have water in her, but she won't be flooded. It isn't as though she's sunk,' he added. 'At low water you could get pumps operating from her deck and, with all the apertures sealed up . . .' He hesitated. 'I'm trying to put it to you as a business proposition. That ship is lying out there and you and I are the only people who know she's there.'

'Oh, for God's sake!' I said. The effrontery of the proposition staggered me. He didn't seem to understand that there were laws of salvage, that even if it were possible to refloat the *Mary Deare*, it involved agreement between the owners, the insurance people, the shippers – everybody.

'Think it over,' he said urgently. 'It may be weeks before some fisherman finds her there.' He gripped hold of my arm. 'I need your help, Sands. I've got to get into that for'ard hold. I've got to see for myself.'

'See what?'

'That hold didn't flood because the ship was unseaworthy. At least,' he added, 'that's what I believe. But I've got to have proof.'

I didn't say anything, and he leaned towards me across the table, his eyes on mine, hard and urgent. 'If you won't do it . . .' His voice was hoarse. 'I've nobody else who'll help me. Damn it, man! I saved your life. You were dangling at the end of that rope. Remember? I helped you then. Now I'm asking you to help me.'

I looked away towards the square, feeling a little embarrassed, not understanding what it was that he was so worried about. And then the police car that had brought me to Paimpol drew up at the curb and I watched with relief as the gendarme got out and came into the *bistro*.

'Monsieur – if you wish to catch your aeroplane . . .' He nodded towards the car.

'Yes, of course.' I got to my feet. 'I'm sorry. I've got to go now.'

Patch was staring up at me. 'What's your address in England?' he asked.

I gave him the name of the boatyard at Lymington. He nodded, frowning, and looked down at his empty glass. I wished him luck then and turned to go.

'Just a minute,' he said. 'You've got a bank, I suppose?' And when I nodded, he reached into his pocket and pulled out a package and tossed it on to the table. 'Would you have them lock that up for me?'

'What is it?' I asked as I picked it up.

He moved his hand in a vague, impatient gesture. 'Just some personal papers. Afraid they may get lost.' And then, without looking up at me, he added, 'I'll collect them when I see you.'

I hesitated, wanting to tell him it was no good his coming to see me. But he was sitting there, slumped in his chair, lost apparently in his own thoughts. He looked drawn and haggard and ghastly tired. 'You better get some sleep,' I said, and my words took me back again to the *Mary Deare*. He didn't answer, didn't look up. I slipped the package into my pocket and went out to the car. He was still sitting there slumped over the table as I was driven away.

Two hours later I was in the air, high up over the sea. It was like a corrugated sheet of lead and out beyond the starboard wing-tip was an area all flecked with white.

The Frenchman in the next seat leaned across me to peer out. 'Regardez, regardez, monsieur,' he whispered eagerly. 'C'est le Plateau des Minquiers.' And then, realizing I was English, he smiled apologetically and said, 'You will not understand, of course. But there are rocks down there – many, many rocks. Trés formidable! I think it better we travel by air. Look, monsieur!' He produced a French paper. 'You 'ave not seen, no?' He thrust it into my hands. 'It is terrible! Terrible!'

It was opened at a page of pictures – pictures of Patch, of Higgins and the rest of the survivors, of a dead body lying in the sea, and of officials searching a pile of wreckage washed up on some rocks. Bold black type across the top announced: MYS-TÈRE DE VAISSEAU BRITANNIQUE ABANDONNÉ.

'Interesting, is it not, monsieur? I think it is also a very strange story. And all those men . . .' He clicked his tongue sympathetically. 'You do not understand how terrible is this region of the sea. Terrible, monsieur!'

I smiled, overwhelmed by a desire to laugh – to tell him what it had been like down there in the Minkies. But by now I was reading the statement made to the authorities by *le Capitaine Gideon Patch*, and suddenly it was borne in on me that he had not stated the *Mary Deare*'s position. He hadn't even mentioned that the ship was stranded and not sunk. '. . . *and you and I are the only people who know she's there.*' His words came back to me and I sat, staring down at the paper, knowing suddenly that this wasn't going to be the end of the *Mary Deare*.

'A strange affair, is it not, monsieur?'

I nodded, not smiling now. 'Yes,' I said. 'Very strange.'

PART TWO

I

THE FORMAL ENQUIRY into the loss of the *Mary Deare* was finally fixed for Monday, 3 May, at Southampton. For a Ministry of Transport Enquiry, this must be considered unusually expeditious, but I learned later that the date had been brought forward at the urgent request of the insurance companies. The sum involved was a very large one and right from the start it was the question of insurance that was the vital factor.

In fact, we had only been in Lymington a few days when I had a visit from a Mr F. T. Snetterton representing the H. B. & K. M. Insurance Corporation of San Francisco. It was that section of the cargo consigned by the Hsu Trading Corporation of Singapore that interested him. Could I testify as to the nature of it? Had I been down into any of the holds? Had Patch talked to me about it?

There was a devil of a racket going on. *Sea Witch* had just been slipped and the yard men were drawing keel bolts for inspection and Mike and I were stripping the old engine out of her. I took him down to the waterfront, where we could talk in peace.

'You understand, Mr Sands,' he explained earnestly, 'I have to be sure that the cargo was exactly what the Hsu Trading Corporation claim. I have to establish the manifest, as it were. Now surely you must have seen something that would enable you to give an opinion as to the nature of the cargo? Think, sir. Think.' He was leaning forward, blinking in the bright sunshine, quite over-wrought by the urgency of his problem.

I told him I had been down the inspection hatch of Number Three hold. I described the charred bales to him. 'Please, Mr Sands.' He shook his head impatiently. 'It's the aero engines I am interested in. Only the aero engines.'

That was the first time anyone had mentioned aero engines to me. 'I heard she had a cargo of explosives.'

'No, no – aero engines.' He sat down on the railing of one of the pontoons where the boats were laid up, a neat, dapper man dressed in black with a brief-case. He looked entirely out of place. 'The ship herself,' he said in his precise way, 'is not important –

twice the break-up value, that's all. And the cotton was insured by a Calcutta firm. No, it's the aero engines we're worried about. There were a hundred and forty-eight of them – surplus American stores from the Korean war – and they were insured for £296,000. I must be certain that they were on board at the time the ship went down.'

'What makes you think they weren't?' I asked him.

He looked at me quickly, hesitating and fidgeting with his brief-case. 'It's a little difficult,' he murmured. 'But perhaps – since you're not an interested party . . . perhaps if I explain, it may help you to remember something – some little thing . . . an unguarded word, perhaps.' He looked at me again, and then said, 'Shortly after the claim was filed, we heard from our agent in Aden that a man named Adams had been talking about the *Mary Deare* and her cargo in a Steamer Point bar. He was reported to have given it as his opinion that she contained nothing but bales of cotton at the time she went down.' And he added hastily, 'You understand, sir, this is in the strictest confidence.' And then he asked me again whether I couldn't remember some little detail that would help him. 'Surely if you were on that ship for forty-eight hours you must have learned something about the cargo?'

'There was a gale blowing,' I said. 'The ship was sinking.'

'Yes, yes, of course. But you must have talked with Mr Patch. You were with him through a critical period. A man will often say things in those circumstances that he would be reluctant . . .' He let the sentence go, staring at me all the time through his glasses. 'You're sure he said nothing about the cargo?'

'Quite sure.'

'A pity!' he murmured. 'I had thought . . .' He shrugged his shoulders and stood up. I asked him then how he thought it was possible for a cargo consigned to a ship not to be on board her at a later date? He looked at me. 'All things are possible, Mr Sands, where a great deal of money is involved.' I remembered Patch saying the same thing about the loss of the *Belle Isle*. And then he suddenly asked me whether Patch had mentioned the name of another boat whilst we were together on the *Mary Deare*?

'I don't think so,' I said quickly. If Snetterton wanted to find out about the *Belle Isle*, he could find it out from somebody else.

But he wasn't to be put off so easily. 'You don't think so?' He was peering at me. 'I want you to be quite certain about this, Mr Sands. It may be vitally important.'

'I am quite certain,' I said irritably.

'Mr Patch never mentioned the name of another ship to you?'

Damn it, the man had no right to come here questioning me about what Patch had said. No, I told him. And I added that if he wanted to find out what ships Patch had been connected with why the devil didn't he go and ask him.

He stared at me. 'This isn't a ship that Mr Patch ever sailed in.'

'Well, what ship is it then?'

'The *Torre Annunziata*. Now please think back very carefully. Did Mr Patch ever mention the name *Torre Annunziata* to you?'

'No,' I said. 'Definitely not.' I felt relieved and angry. 'What's the *Torre Annunziata* got to do with it?'

He hesitated. 'It's a little delicate, you understand . . . so much supposition . . .' Then he suddenly made up his mind and said, 'The Dellimare Company owned only two ships – the *Mary Deare* and the *Torre Annunziata*. The *Torre Annunziata* was in the Rangoon River at the same time that the *Mary Deare* put in to load her cotton cargo.' He glanced at his watch and then rose to his feet. 'Well, sir, I won't trouble you any further for the moment.'

He turned then and began to walk back towards the slip, and as we negotiated the wooden duck-boards of the pontoons, he said, 'I'll be quite honest with you. This is a matter that might in certain circumstances . . .' He hesitated there and seemed to change his mind. 'I am waiting for a report now from our agent in Rangoon. But . . .' He shook his head. 'It is all very disturbing, Mr Sands. The *Torre Annunziata* has been sold to the Chinese. She has vanished behind what I believe is called the Bamboo Curtain – not only the ship, but her crew as well. And Adams has disappeared, too. We are almost certain that he shipped out in a dhow bound for Zanzibar. It may be weeks before we can contact him. And then there are these two fires on the *Mary Deare* and the loss of Mr Dellimare. A fire in the radio room is most unusual, and Mr Dellimare had been in the Navy. The possibility of suicide . . . small firm, you know . . . might be in difficulties . . .' He tucked his brief-case more firmly under his arm. 'You see what I mean, Mr Sands. Little things in themselves, but together . . .' He glanced at me significantly. And then he added, 'The trouble is the time factor. The H. B. & K. M. are making great efforts to increase their business in the Pacific. And Mr Hsu is a big man in Singapore – considerable influence in Eastern ports. They feel it calls for prompt settlement of the claim unless . . .' He shrugged.

We had reached the slip and he paused for a moment to admire

Sea Witch's lines, asking questions about our diving plans, the aqualungs we were using and the depths at which we could work. He seemed genuinely interested and I explained how we had financed ourselves by salvaging bits and pieces from the wreck of a tanker in the Mediterranean and that we were now going to work on the wreck of an LCT in Worbarrow Bay off the Dorset coast. He wished us luck and gave me his card. 'Think about what I've said, Mr Sands. If you remember anything – well, you have my card, sir.'

It was only after Snetterton had gone – when I had had time to think over what he had told me – that I began to understand what the loss of the *Mary Deare* was going to lead to. There would be other people besides Snetterton coming to ask me questions. He was just the breeze before the storm. The newspaper reports I had read had all taken it for granted that the ship was sunk – so had Snetterton and the two reporters who had come to see me when I had arrived with *Sea Witch*. Everybody thought she was sunk. But sooner or later they would start probing, and before then I had to see Patch and find out his reasons for concealing her position.

I thought it must be connected in some way with his past record and when I was in London two days later to sign our salvage contract with the underwriters, I made a few enquiries about the *Belle Isle*. She had been wrecked on the Anambas Islands north-east of Singapore nearly ten years ago, and she was entered in the records as a 'total loss'. Her master was given as Gideon S. Patch. An Enquiry had been held in Singapore and the Court had found the stranding to be due to default of the Master and had suspended his Certificate for a period of five years. That was all. There were no details. But, discussing it with one of my friends in the marine section of Lloyd's, who specialized in the Far East, I learned that some ugly rumours had got about afterwards to the effect that the stranding had been a put-up job. The ship had been very heavily insured.

I was very close to St Mary Axe and I decided to have a look at the Dellimare Company office. It was partly that I was curious to see the sort of company it was, and also I wanted to find out where I could contact Patch. Their offices were at the Houndsditch end, on the fourth floor of a dingy building full of small trading businesses. I found myself in a poky little room with a desk and a gas fire and some filing cabinets. The single typewriter had its cover on and dirt-grimed windows looked out across a litter of chimney pots to the white-tiled rear of a big office block. There was a bell on the counter and amongst a litter of papers was some Dellimare Company notepaper. It gave the directors as J. C. B. Dellimare, Hans Gundersen and A. Petrie. When I rang the bell, the door of an inner office was opened and a full-bosomed, fleshy-looking woman appeared, dressed in black with a lot of cheap jewellery and blonde hair that was startling because it was clearly natural.

When I gave her my name, she said, 'Oh, are you the Mr Sands who was on board the *Mary Deare*? Then perhaps you can help me.' She took me through into the other office. It was a much brighter room with cream walls and a red carpet and a big green and chromium steel desk that was littered with press clippings, mostly from French newspapers. 'I'm trying to find out what really happened to him,' she said. 'To Mr Dellimare, that is.' And she glanced involuntarily at a big photograph in an ornate silver frame that stood beside her on the desk. It was a head and shoulders portrait, showing a rather hard, deeply-lined face with a small, straight mouth under the thin pencil-line of a moustache.

'You knew him well?' I asked.

'Oh, yes. We formed the Company. Of course, after Mr Gundersen joined, it was all different. Our main office became Singapore. Mr Dellimare and I just looked after the London end.' There was something entirely personal about the way she said 'Mr Dellimare and I', and after that she began asking me questions. Had Captain Patch said anything to me about how Mr Dellimare had been lost? Did I go into his cabin? Had I talked to any of the survivors? 'He had been in the Navy. He couldn't just have gone overboard like that?' Her voice trembled slightly.

But when she realized I could tell her nothing that she didn't already know, she lost interest in me. I asked her then for Patch's address, but she hadn't got it. 'He came in about three days ago to deliver his report,' she said. 'He's coming back on Friday, when he'll be able to see Mr Gundersen.' I gave her the address of the boatyard and asked her to tell Patch to contact me, and then I left. She came with me to the door. 'I'll tell Mr Gundersen you've been,' she said with a quick, brittle smile. 'I'm sure he'll be interested.'

Mr Gundersen! Perhaps it was the inflection of her voice, but I got the impression that she was a little nervous of him, as though he were entirely remote from the Dellimare Company office that she knew with its silver-framed photograph and its view over the chimneys.

It never occurred to me that I should meet Gundersen, but on

473

Friday afternoon the boy from the yard's office came down to the slip to say that a Mrs Petrie was calling me from London. I recognized the slightly husky voice at once. Mr Gundersen had just arrived by plane from Singapore and would like to have a talk with me. He was coming down to Southampton tomorrow, would it be convenient for him to call on me at the yard at eleven o'clock?

I couldn't refuse. The man had come all the way from Singapore and he was entitled to find out all he could about the loss of the Company's ship. But, remembering the things Snetterton had hinted at, I had a feeling of uneasiness. Also, my time and all my energies were concentrated on the conversion of *Sea Witch* and I resented anything which took my mind off the work that Mike and I had planned and struggled for over years of wreck-hunting. I was worried, too, about what I was going to tell him. How was I to explain to him that nobody had been notified of the position of the wreck?

And then early next morning Patch came on the phone from London. No, they hadn't given him any message from me. I thought then that he was ringing me about the package I had brought over for him and which I realized was still on board, locked away in my brief-case. But it wasn't that. It was about Gundersen. Had Gundersen been to see me? And when I told him that I was expecting him at eleven o'clock, he said, 'Thank God! I tried to get you last night – to warn you.' And then he added, 'You haven't told anybody where the *Mary Deare* is lying, have you?'

'No,' I said. 'Not yet.' I hadn't told anybody, not even Mike.

'Has a man called Snetterton been to see you – a marine insurance agent?'

'Yes.'

'You didn't tell him?'

'No,' I said. 'He didn't ask me. He presumed the ship was sunk.' And then I said, 'Haven't you notified the authorities yet? If you haven't, I think it's time – '

'Listen,' he said. 'I can't come down now. I've got to see somebody. And on Monday I've got to go to the Ministry of Transport. But I'll be able to come down and see you on Tuesday. Will you promise to say nothing until then?'

'But why?' I said. 'What's the point in concealing her position?'

'I'll explain when I see you.'

'And what about Gundersen? What am I to say to him?'

'Say anything you like. But for God's sake don't tell him where she is. Don't tell anybody. I ask you as a favour, Sands.'

'All right,' I said doubtfully.

He thanked me then and rang off.

An hour later Gundersen arrived. The boy came down to say that he was waiting for me in the yard manager's office. A big chauffeur-driven limousine stood outside and I went in to find Gundersen seated on the edge of the desk smoking a cigarette and the manager standing in front of him in uneasy silence. 'You're Mr Sands, are you?' Gundersen asked. He didn't offer me his hand or get up or make any move. The manager gave us the use of his office and slipped out. As soon as the door was shut Gundersen said, 'You know why I'm here, I imagine?' He waited until I had nodded and then said, 'I saw Mr Patch yesterday. I understand you were with him during the last forty-eight hours on the *Mary Deare*. Naturally I wanted to hear your version of what happened on our ship.' He asked me then to go through the whole sequence of events. 'I want every detail, please, Mr Sands.'

I went through the whole story for him, leaving out only the details about Patch's behaviour and what had happened at the end. He listened in complete silence, not interrupting once. His long, immobile face, tanned by the sun, showed no flicker of expression, and his eyes, behind their horn-rimmed glasses, watched me all the time I was talking.

Afterwards he asked me a series of questions – straightforward, practical questions concerning course and wind strength and the length of time we had run the engines. The ordeal we had gone through seemed to mean nothing to him and I got the impression of a cold personality.

Finally, he said, 'I don't think you have yet understood, Mr Sands, what it is I wish to know.' His slight accent was more noticeable now. 'I want to discover the exact position in which the ship went down.'

'You don't seem to realize the conditions prevailing at the time,' I said. 'All I can tell you is that she was close to the Roches Douvres at the time I boarded her.'

He got up then. He was very tall and he wore a light-coloured suit of smooth material draped in the American fashion. 'You are not being very helpful, Mr Sands.' A signet ring on his finger flashed in the pale April sunlight. 'It seems odd that neither you nor Patch can say where the ship was at the time you abandoned her.' He waited, and then he said, 'I have also talked to Higgins. He may not have a Master's Certificate, but he's an experienced seaman. You may be interested to know that his calculations, based

475

on wind strength, probable drift and tide, put the *Mary Deare*'s final position a good deal to the east of where you and Patch seem to think you were. Have you any comment to make?' He stood facing me, his back to the window.

'None,' I said, nettled and a little angry at his manner. And then, because he was still staring at me, waiting, I said, 'I'd remind you, Mr Gundersen, that I am not concerned in this. I was on board your ship by accident.'

He didn't answer for a moment. Finally he said, 'That remains, perhaps, to be seen.' And he added, 'Well, at least I have got something out of you. Now that we have some idea of the length of time the engines were running and the course steered whilst they were in use, it should be possible to arrive at an approximation of the position.' He paused again. 'Is there anything further you would care to add to what you have already told me, Mr Sands?'

'No,' I said. 'Nothing.'

'Very well.' He picked up his hat. And then he paused. 'The manager here tells me that you're interested in salvage. You've formed a company – Sands, Duncan & Company, Ltd.' He stared at me. 'I think I should warn you that this man Patch has a bad record. Unfortunately our Mr Dellimare was inexperienced in matters connected with shipping. He employed this man when nobody else would, and the result has proved disastrous.'

'He did his best to save the ship,' I said angrily.

For the first time his face moved. An eyebrow lifted. 'After he had caused the crew to panic and take to the boats. I have yet to discover his precise motives, but if you're mixed up in this, Mr Sands . . .' He put his hat on. 'You can contact me at the Savoy Hotel if you should find you have some further information to give me.' He went out of the office then and I watched him drive away with an uneasy feeling that I was getting myself dangerously involved.

This feeling persisted, and it came between me and my work so that I was not in a particularly sympathetic mood when Patch finally arrived. We were living on board *Sea Witch* by then, which was fortunate because he didn't arrive until the evening. I had expected him to look rested, the lines in his face smoothed out. It came as a shock to me to find him looking just as haggard. We had only one light on board, an inspection lamp clamped to a half-erected bulkhead, and in its harsh glare he looked ghastly, his face quite white and a nervous tic at the corner of his mouth.

We cleared the saloon table of tools and wood-shavings, and I sat him down and gave him a drink and a cigarette and introduced him to Mike. It was neat rum I gave him and he knocked it straight back, and he drew on his cigarette as though it were the first he'd had in days. His suit was old and frayed and I remember wondering whether the Dellimare Company had paid him. Oddly enough, he accepted Mike at once and, without attempting to get me alone, asked straight out what Gundersen had wanted, what he had said.

I told him, and when I had finished, I said, 'Gundersen suspects something. He hinted as much.' I paused, waiting for the explanation he had promised me. But all he said was, 'I'd forgotten that Higgins might work it out.' He was speaking to himself.

'What about that explanation?' I asked him.

'Explanation?' He stared at me blankly.

'You surely don't imagine,' I said, 'that I can be a party to a piece of deception that involves the owners, the insurance people, everybody with a financial interest in the ship, unless I know that there is some good reason?' I told him I considered that my duty was clear. 'Either you explain why you've withheld this vital information or I go to the authorities.' An obstinate, shut look had come over his face. 'Why pretend the ship went down, when at any moment she may be sighted lying there in the middle of the Minkies?'

'She could have been carried there by the tides,' he murmured.

'She could have been, but she wasn't.' I lit a cigarette and sat down opposite him. He looked so desperately tired of it all. 'Listen,' I said more gently. 'I've been trained in marine insurance. I know the procedure after the loss of a ship. Any moment now the Receiver of Wreck will start taking depositions under oath from everybody connected with the loss. And under oath I've no alternative but to give the full – '

'You won't be called on to make a deposition,' he said quickly. 'You weren't connected with the ship.'

'No, but I was on board.'

'By accident.' He pushed his hand up through his hair in a gesture that brought it all back to me. 'It's not for you to make any comment.'

'No, but if I have to make a statement under oath . . .' I leaned across the table towards him. 'Try and see it from my point of view,' I said. 'You made me a certain proposition that day in Paimpol. A proposition which, in the light of your failure to notify the owners of the present whereabouts of the ship, was entirely crooked. And Gundersen is beginning to think – '

'Crooked?' He began laughing and there was a note of hysteria in his voice. 'Do you know what cargo the *Mary Deare* carried?'

'Yes,' I said. 'Aero engines. Snetterton told me.'

'And did he tell you that the other Dellimare ship was moored next to the *Mary Deare* for four days in the Rangoon River? Those aero engines are in China now – sold to the Chinks for a mint of money.'

The positiveness of his accusation took me by surprise. 'How can you be certain?' I asked him.

He looked at me, hesitating for a moment. 'All right. I'll tell you. Because Dellimare offered me five thousand quid to wreck the *Mary Deare*. Cash – in fivers.'

In the sudden silence I could hear the lapping of the water at the bottom of the slip. 'Dellimare? Are you serious?' I asked.

'Yes, Dellimare.' His voice was angry and bitter. 'It was after old Taggart died. Dellimare was desperate then. He had to improvise. And, by the luck of the devil, I was on board. He knew my record. He thought he could buy me.' He leaned back and lit another cigarette, his hands shaking. 'Sometimes I wish to God I'd accepted his offer.'

I poured him another drink. And then I said, 'But I still don't understand why you should conceal the *Mary Deare*'s position. Why haven't you told all this to the authorities?'

He turned and looked at me. 'Because if Gundersen knows where she is, he'll go out there and destroy her.'

That was nonsense, of course. You can't destroy a 6000-ton ship just like that. I told him so. He'd only got to go to the authorities, demand an examination of the vessel and the whole thing would be decided. But he shook his head. 'I have to go back myself – with somebody like you that I can trust.'

'You mean you're not sure about what you just told me – about the cargo?'

He didn't say anything for a moment, but just sat there, hunched over his drink, smoking. You could feel his nerves in the stillness of the cabin. 'I want you to take me out there,' he said finally. 'You and Duncan.' He turned, leaning towards us. 'You've been in marine insurance, haven't you, Sands? You know how to fix up a salvage contract. Now listen. When will your boat be ready?'

'Not till the end of the month,' Mike said, and the way he said it was a warning to me that he didn't want to have anything to do with it.

'All right. The end of the month. I'll come back then. Have you got an underwater camera?' And when I nodded, he leaned forward earnestly. 'You could take a picture then of the damage to the for'ard holds. The insurance people would give you a lot of money for that – and for pictures of the cargo.' And then he added, 'And if I'm wrong, then there's quarter of a million pounds' worth of aero engines – enough salvage to set you up in a big way. Well?' His eyes moved quickly, nervously, from one to the other of us.

'You know very well I can't agree to a proposition like that,' I said. And Mike added, 'I think you should put the whole matter in the hands of the authorities.'

'No. No, I can't do that.'

'Why not?' I asked.

'Because I can't.' The tension was building up in him again. 'Because I'm up against a company. I've a record behind me and they'll twist things . . . I've been through all this before.' Sweat was shining in beads on his forehead. 'And there's Higgins and the crew. Everything is against me.'

'But if the Receiver of Wreck made an examination – '

'I tell you, No. I'm not having the Receiver of Wreck out there – or anybody.' He was staring at me wildly. 'Can't you understand – I've got to go back there myself.'

'No, I can't,' I said. 'If you refused Dellimare's offer, you've nothing to worry about. Why conceal the fact that you beached her on the Minkies?' And when he didn't answer, I said, 'Why do you have to go back? What the devil is there on that ship that you've got to go back for?'

'Nothing. Nothing.' His voice quivered in tune with his nerves.

'Yes there is,' I said. 'There's something drawing you back to her as though – '

'There's nothing,' he shouted at me.

'Then why not tell the authorities where she is? What is it you're afraid of?'

His fist crashed down on the table top. 'Stop it! Questions . . . questions . . . nothing but questions. I've had enough of it, do you hear?' He got abruptly to his feet and stood, staring down at us. He was trembling all over.

I think he was on the verge of telling us something. I think he wanted to tell us. But instead he seemed to get a grip of himself. 'Then you won't take me out there?' There was a note of resignation in his voice.

'No,' I said.

He seemed to accept that and he stood there, his body slack, staring down at the table. I got him to sit down again and gave him another drink. He stayed on to supper. He was very quiet and he didn't talk much. I didn't get anything more out of him. He seemed shut away inside himself. When he left he gave me his address. He was in lodgings in London. He said he'd come down at the end of the month and see if we'd changed our minds. I saw him out across the darkened yard and then walked slowly back through the dark shapes of the slipped boats.

'Poor devil!' Mike said, as I went below again. 'Do you think Dellimare really offered him five thousand to wreck the ship?'

'God knows!' I said. I didn't know what to think. It seemed to me that perhaps Patch might be a psychological case – a man whose balance had been destroyed because of the ship he had lost before. 'I know almost nothing about the man,' I murmured. But that wasn't true. You can't live through what we'd lived through together without knowing a good deal about a man. He was tough. He had great reserves. And I admired him. I almost wished I'd agreed to take him out to the Minkies – just to discover the truth.

I told Mike the whole story then, all the little details I'd left out when I rejoined *Sea Witch* in Peter Port. And after I had finished, he said, 'It's a hell of a situation for him if the cargo really has been switched.'

I knew what he meant. He was thinking of the insurance companies, and, having worked for seven years in the marine section of Lloyd's, I knew very well that once they got their teeth into a claim, they'd never let go.

I worried a lot about this during the fitting out. But a few days after Patch had visited us, I received notification of the date of the Formal Investigation and I comforted myself with the thought that it would all be resolved then.

Sea Witch was ready sooner than we had dared to hope. We sailed on Tuesday, 27 April, motoring down to the Solent and then heading westwards under full canvas with a light northerly wind. I hadn't seen Patch again, but I couldn't help thinking that the wind was fair for the Channel Islands. Twenty-four hours' sailing would have taken us to the Minkies, and the forecast couldn't have been better – continental weather with a belt of high pressure over the Azores. We had Mike's old diving friend, Ian Baird, with us again, and with three of us working we could have got into the *Mary Deare*'s holds and checked that cargo and still got back for the Investigation. And as *Sea Witch* leaned to the breeze, her new sails gleaming white in the sunlight, I felt none of the elation that I should have felt at the start of this venture that Mike and I had dreamed about for so long.

The devil of it was that, now I was at sea, I remembered things I had forgotten in the bustle of fitting out. Patch had saved my life and, though he hadn't referred to it that night he had come to see us at Lymington, I could remember the desperation that had prompted him to remind me of it in Paimpol. I had the sense of a debt owed, but not paid.

It wasn't only that I felt I had failed in an obligation. Sitting there, with my hands on the wheel, feeling the ship lift to the swell and hearing the water creaming past, I wondered whether it wasn't fear that was directing my course west towards Worbarrow Bay, instead of south to the Minkies. I had seen the Plateau des Minquiers in bad conditions, and deep down in my heart I knew I was scared of the place.

And the irony of it was that for four days we dived in Worbarrow Bay in conditions that were as perfect as I have ever seen them in the Channel – clear blue skies and a calm sea ruffled by only the slightest of breezes. The only limiting factor was the coldness of the water which affected us after a time, even though we were using our heaviest foam rubber suits. In those four days we located and buoyed the wreck of the LCT, cut through into the engine-room and cleared the way for lifting out the main engines, work that we had feared might take anything up to a month.

In the same time, if I had had the nerve to take the gamble, we could have cut our way into each of the *Mary Deare*'s holds. I thought about it sometimes as I worked down in the green depths with *Sea Witch*'s hull a dark shape in the translucent sea above me, and at night the tally of the day's work seemed a reproach and I turned into my bunk in a mood of depression.

It was almost with relief that I woke on the Sunday to a grey dawn misted with rain and a forecast that announced a deep depression over the Atlantic moving eastwards. By midday the seas were beginning to break; we got the anchors up and plugged it on the engine against a strong westerly wind for the shelter of Lulworth Cove.

I left early next morning for Southampton. It was stormy, and the downland hills, that crooked chalk fingers round the natural lagoon of the cove, were a gloomy green, shrouded in curtains of driving rain. Big seas piled up in the narrow entrance, filling the cove with an ugly swell, which broke in a roar on the shingle beach. Gusts of wind funnelled into the cove from the tops of the downs, flattening the water in sudden, violent swirls. Nobody was about. The whole chalk basin – so regular in its circle that it might have been the flooded crater of an extinct volcano – was deserted. There was only *Sea Witch*, rolling heavily, and the gulls, like scraps of paper, whirled about by the wind.

'Better set an anchor watch if it gets any worse,' I told Mike as he rowed me ashore. 'It's not very good holding ground here.'

He nodded, his face unnaturally solemn under his sou'wester. 'What are you going to do if things go against him at this Enquiry?' he asked.

'Nothing,' I replied and my voice sounded peevish against the blatter of the wind. I was tired. I think we were both pretty tired. We had been diving hard for four days. 'If I'd been going to do anything,' I added, 'the time to do it was last week, when we sailed from Lymington. The worst that can happen to him is that they'll cancel his Master's Certificate again.' Mike didn't say anything. His yellow oilskins gleamed with water in the grey light as he moved rhythmically back and forth to the swing of the oars, and over his shoulders the houses of Lulworth stood silent, with a grey, shut look, on the flank of the hill.

The dinghy grounded with a sudden jar and Mike jumped out into the backwash of a wave and hauled it up so that I could step out dry-footed in my shore-going clothes. We stood there in the rain for a moment, talking about ordinary, mundane things, things that had to be done around the boat. And then, as I turned to climb the beach, he checked me. I just want you to know, John . . .' He hesitated, and then said, 'As far as I'm concerned you're free to make any decision you like – whatever the risk.'

'It's very decent of you, Mike,' I said. 'But I don't think – '

'It's not a question of being decent.' He was grinning. 'I just don't like working with a man who's got something on his mind.' He left me then and pushed out in the dinghy, and I climbed the steep slope of the beach to the road where the bus was waiting for me.

IT WAS almost eleven when I reached the court. I was late and the corridor leading to the courtroom was almost empty. The letter requesting my attendance gave me the guidance of one of the officials and as we reached a small door leading into the court, it opened and Snetterton came out. 'Ah, Mr Sands.' He blinked at me. 'Come to see the fun, eh?'

'I'm here as a witness,' I said.

'Yes, yes, of course. Pity to drag you away from your diving. Heard you had started work on that wreck in Worbarrow Bay.' He hesitated and then said, 'You know, we seriously considered approaching you over the question of the *Mary Deare*. We were going to try an asdic search. But then some new information came up and it became unnecessary.'

'What new information?' I was wondering whether the *Mary Deare* had been found. The weather had been bad during most of April, but there was always the chance . . .

'You'll see, Mr Sands. Interesting case, most interesting . . .' And he hurried off down the corridor.

The official opened the door for me then and I went into the court. 'The seats for witnesses are on the right, sir,' he whispered. There was no need for him to have whispered. The room was full of the murmur of voices. I stood there in the doorway, a little dazed. There were many more people than I had expected. The whole court seemed crammed to overflowing; only in the public gallery was there any vacant space. The witnesses were crowded into the seats usually occupied by jurymen called but not serving and some of them had spilled over into the jury box itself. Patch I saw at once, sitting well down towards the front, his face pale and taut, but harder now, like a man who knows what is coming and has nerved himself to meet it. Behind him, and to the right, the crew were clustered in a little hard knot round Higgins's solid bulk. They looked awkward and ill-at-ease, a little exotic in their new shore-going clothes. Fraser, the captain of the Channel packet that had picked us up, was there, too, and sitting beside him was Janet Taggart. She gave me a quick smile, tight-lipped and a little wan, and I wondered why the devil they needed to drag her in as a witness.

And then somebody was signalling me from just behind her and, as he craned his neck up, I saw it was Hal. I pushed my way down the row and squeezed in beside him. 'I didn't expect to find you here,' I whispered.

'Very important witness,' he said. 'Don't forget that it was I who first reported the ship as a derelict hulk containing the person of my erstwhile and somewhat foolhardy skipper.' He smiled at me out of the corners of his eyes. 'Anyway, I wouldn't have missed it for the world. Going to be a damned interesting case if you ask me.'

At the time I had entered, men in various parts of the court, but chiefly on the side across from me, were standing up to give their names and state their business and who they represented. There were a surprising number of them, for, besides the insurance companies and the owners, the builders of the *Mary Deare* were represented, the Marine Officers' Association, the Radio Operators' Association, the various unions; there was even a solicitor appearing for the relatives of Captain Taggart deceased.

The atmosphere was very informal by comparison with a court of law – no wigs, no gowns, no police, no jury. Even the judge and his three assessors wore lounge suits. Across the court from where I sat the desks were occupied by the various counsel appearing for interested parties. They were very crowded. The witness box nearby stood empty and beyond was the Press desk with two reporters at it. On our side of the court the desks were occupied by the Treasury counsel and his junior and the Treasury solicitors and assistants.

Hal leaned towards me. 'Do you know who's representing the insurance people?' he whispered.

I shook my head. I had no information about the legal representatives. All I knew was that a Mr Bowen-Lodge QC was chairman of the Enquiry.

'Sir Lionel Falcett. About the most expensive man they could have got.' His blue eyes darted me a quick glance. 'Significant, eh?'

I glanced down at Patch. And then I was remembering that I, too, might have to go into the witness box, and all the counsel had the right to cross-examine.

A hush slowly spread through the room. The Chairman, who had been engaged in earnest discussion with his assessors, had turned and faced the court. As soon as there was complete silence he began his opening address. 'Gentlemen. This Court meets here today, as you are well aware, to investigate the loss of the steamship *Mary Deare*. It will be the duty of the Court to examine, not only the circumstances of the loss itself, but all the relevant factors that may possibly have contributed to that loss. The scope of this investigation, therefore, covers the state of the ship at the time she started on her ill-fated voyage from Yokohama, her seaworthiness, the condition of her machinery, the nature of her cargo and the manner of its stowage, and, in particular, the state of her fire-fighting equipment. It covers also the behaviour and conduct of all those concerned in the running of the vessel to the extent that they may or may not have contributed to the disaster.

'For disaster it was, gentlemen. Out of a total crew of thirty-two, no less than twelve men – over a third of the ship's complement – lost their lives. Moreover, the captain died during the voyage and a director of the company owning the vessel is reported missing. It is a sad business that we are investigating and it is possible that relatives of men who lost their lives may be present in this courtroom today. I, therefore, consider it my duty to remind you that this is a Formal Enquiry to determine the cause of this disaster and, whilst I am anxious that proper respect should be paid to the dead and that no advantage should be taken of men who, through death, are unable to testify, I would impress upon you that we are here to investigate this whole terrible business thoroughly and impartially.' Bowen-Lodge leaned a little forward. 'I will now call on Mr Holland to open proceedings on behalf of the Ministry of Transport.'

Holland might have been a banker or perhaps a stockbroker. Whereas the judge, despite his sour, dyspeptic-looking features, had comprehended the tragedy that lay behind the Enquiry and had filled the court with the drama of it, this tall, smooth-faced barrister with the sleek head of black hair had a cold-blooded urbanity of manner that suggested an interest in figures rather than the frailties of human behaviour

'Mr Learned Chairman.' He had risen and was facing the judge and the three assessors, his hands thrust into the pockets of his jacket. 'I think I should bring to your notice at the outset that the Receiver of Wreck, in his report to the Minister, stressed that in several particulars the evidence of the survivors was conflicting. As you know, in cases of this nature, the Receiver of Wreck prepares his report on the basis of depositions in writing. These depositions are made under oath. I do not propose, therefore, to outline in detail the events leading up to the disaster or the disaster itself. I will confine myself to a brief statement of the established facts concerning the voyage and leave the details – the story as it were – to emerge from the evidence of the various witnesses.'

He paused and glanced down at his notes. Then he faced the courtroom itself and in a smooth, rather bored voice summarized the events of the voyage.

The *Mary Deare* had been purchased by the Dellimare Trading and Shipping Company in June of the previous year. She had belonged to a Burmese company and for two years had been laid-up in a creek near Yokohama. On completion of the purchase she had been towed into Yokohama for a complete overhaul. On 18 November she had been granted a seaworthy certificate to cover a single voyage to Antwerp and thence to England where she was to be broken up. On 2 December she completed coaling. On 4 December she began loading her cargo. This consisted of 148 war surplus aircraft engines of American manufacture, including 56 jet engines for a particular fighter in use with NATO forces. In addition to this cargo, which was destined for Antwerp and was distributed fairly equally over the four holds, a large quantity of Japanese cotton and rayon goods were loaded. This part of the cargo was destined for Rangoon and was, therefore, loaded on top of the aircraft engines. The whole of the cargo, including the engines, was the property of the Hsu Trading Corporation, a very large and influential Chinese merchanting organization in Singapore.

The *Mary Deare* sailed from Yokohama on 8 December. On 6 January she reached Rangoon and off-loaded her cargo of Japanese goods. A cargo of raw cotton for England, also the property of the Hsu Corporation, was not ready at the docks for loading. The ship, therefore, proceeded to bunker and then moved out into the river, where she moored to a buoy already occupied by the *Torre Annunziata*, another of the Dellimare Company ships. Four days later she moved into the docks again and loaded her cargo of cotton, the bulk of it in Numbers Two and Three holds.

She sailed from Rangoon on 15 January, reaching Aden on 4 February. There she landed Mr Adams, the first officer, who was sick. Mr Patch was accepted to fill this vacancy. The ship sailed on 6 February. On 2 March, the Master, Captain James Taggart, died, and Mr Patch assumed command of the ship. The *Mary Deare* was then in the Mediterranean, four days out from Port Said. On 9 March she passed through the Straits of

Gibraltar, out into the Atlantic. Almost immediately she ran into heavy weather. She was making a certain amount of water and the pumps were kept going intermittently. On 16 March conditions worsened and it blew full gale.

'And now,' Holland said, his voice lifting slightly from the smooth monotone in which he had been addressing the Court – 'Now we come to the series of incidents – mysteries you might almost call them – that are the subject of this Investigation.'

Briefly he enumerated them: the damage sustained by the ship in the for'ard holds, the water making headway against the pumps, the shoring of the stoke-hold bulkhead, the fire in the radio shack, the disappearance of Dellimare; and then, after rounding Ushant, the fire in Number Three hold, the abandonment of the ship by all except the captain, the discovery of the ship still afloat the following morning, her final abandonment. He punched these events home to the packed courtroom one after another in terse, hard sentences, so that the effect of them was cumulative.

'Twelve men went to their death, gentlemen,' he added, after a pause, his voice now very quiet. 'Went to their death in a mad scramble to get away from a ship that, in point of fact, was in no immediate danger of sinking. That in itself is significant.' He had turned and was facing the Chairman of the Court. 'It is not for me to attempt to influence the Court in any way, merely to present the facts. But I am entitled to draw your attention to certain points, and the points, Mr Learned Chairman, to which I wish to draw the attention of the Court are – firstly, the succession of incidents affecting the safety and sea-keeping ability of the ship, and secondly, the abandonment of a ship that was to stay afloat in gale conditions for more than 48 hours. I submit that this is one of the most extraordinary cases to come before a Formal Enquiry and one that may, as a result of your decision, have far-reaching consequences for one or more of the people here in this courtroom today.'

In making that pronouncement his eyes had roved the room – to the lawyers representing the various interested parties across the floor of the court, to the public gallery, and, finally, he had turned his body round and had stared at the witnesses. His gaze was cold and hard and accusing.

Still facing the witnesses, he went on: 'I have referred to a lack of consistency in the evidence given on oath in depositions made by the various witnesses. Those same witnesses, and some others, will be giving evidence on oath before this Court. But here there is a difference; you can be cross-examined on your evidence in the witness box by myself or by any or all of the representatives of the interested parties.' He paused and then added, 'I would remind you that perjury is a serious offence.'

There was complete silence as he stared at us, and some of the *Mary Deare*'s crew shifted uneasily in their seats. Abruptly, he sat down. For perhaps thirty seconds he let the silence his speech had produced hang over the court, and then he got slowly to his feet again and called 'Gideon Patch'.

Patch was sitting quite still, his eyes fixed across the court – fixed on nothing – and he didn't move. I thought for a moment that he hadn't heard his name called. But then he turned his head and looked at Holland, and quietly, like a man who cannot believe that the moment has finally come, he got to his feet. He seemed to brace himself to meet the situation and, with a firm, decisive tread, he crossed the floor of the court and took his stand in the witness box.

The movement released the tension in the court so that there was a sudden murmur of voices and shifting of feet that continued whilst the oath was being administered and then gradually died away as Holland began his questions, Patch answering them in a voice that was barely audible.

His name was Gideon Stephen Patch. He had been educated at Pangbourne, joined the Merchant Service as a cadet in 1935, Mate's Certificate 1941, Master's Certificate 1944, first command 1945, the *Belle Isle* incident, the years on the beach; the wasted, frustrated years – Holland took him through it all, fact after fact in that same bored voice as though he were tracing the history of a parcel sent through the post. And then the technical details: Did he consider the *Mary Deare* seaworthy? Had he examined the fire-fighting equipment? Had he inspected the boats himself? Did he regard the crew as efficient? Were the officers, in his opinion, competent?

And Patch, once over the hurdle of the *Belle Isle* sinking and the suspension of his Master's Certificate, began noticeably to relax and to gain confidence. It was all so impersonal. Yes, the boats were all right, he had inspected them personally. The crew were average – he had sailed with worse. The officers? He would rather not comment. Some were good, some were not.

'And the captain?' The question was put in the same flat, bored voice.

Patch hesitated, and then said, 'I imagine he was a good seaman.'

'You imagine?' Holland's dark brows lifted slightly.

'Captain Taggart was a sick man, sir.'

'Then why was he not put ashore?'

'I don't know.'

'The first officer, Adams, was put ashore because he was sick. Why wasn't Captain Taggart put ashore, if he was also sick?'

'I imagine the owners thought him fit enough to complete the voyage.'

'By the owners you mean Mr Dellimare?'

'Yes.'

'Tell me, what was the nature of Captain Taggart's illness?'

Patch had clearly been expecting that question, and, now it had come, he looked unhappy about it and for a moment his eyes glanced towards the waiting witnesses. He was looking towards Janet Taggart. And then he was facing Holland again. 'I'm sorry, sir, but I do not think I can answer that.'

Holland made a little impatient gesture. It was obvious that he intended to press the point, but the Chairman intervened. 'Mr Holland.' He was leaning forward. 'It seems hardly necessary for us to pursue this matter. I do not feel that the nature of Captain Taggart's illness can have any bearing on the subject of this Investigation.'

Holland had turned and was facing the judge's chair, his hands gripping the lapels of his jacket as though he were, in fact, wearing a gown. 'I submit, Mr Learned Chairman, that everything connected with the *Mary Deare* is relevant to your Investigation. I am endeavouring to present a complete picture. To do so I must give you the facts – all the facts.'

'Quite so, Mr Holland.' Bowen-Lodge's mouth was a trap-shut line. 'But I see here' – and he glanced at his papers – 'that Miss Taggart is amongst the witnesses in this court. I would ask you to bear that in mind, Mr Holland, and, in your references to her father, to avoid as far as possible giving her any further cause for pain.'

'Unfortunately . . .' But Holland checked himself before Bowen-Lodge's cold, official stare, and then turned to face Patch. 'I will content myself at the moment with asking you whether, in fact, you knew what was wrong with Captain Taggart?'

'Yes, I knew,' Patch answered. And then added quickly, 'But I had no idea that it would prove fatal.'

'Quite so.' Holland turned to the cargo then. 'As first officer you would assume responsibility for the state of loading of the holds. Did you examine the holds yourself?'

'I satisfied myself they were properly loaded.'

'All four holds?'

'Yes.'

'You actually went into each of the holds yourself?'

'Numbers One and Four holds, yes. The other two were full of cargo, but I was able to get some idea of the stowage by looking in through the inspection hatches.'

'Before or after sailing from Aden?'

'Before.'

'Would you tell the Court exactly how these holds were loaded.'

Patch started with Number One hold and worked aft. He gave the dimensions of each – they ran the full width of the ship throughout their depth. The floor of each hold was covered by cases. He gave the approximate dimensions of the cases and the USAAF code numbering painted on them.

'You knew that those cases contained aero engines?' Mr Holland asked.

'Yes, I did.'

'From personal observation? By that I mean, did you at any time examine the contents of one of those cases yourself?'

'No. I had no occasion to. In any case, it would have been very difficult to get one opened – they were tightly packed and, except in Numbers One and Four holds, the cotton cargo completely covered them.'

'I see. So that when you say you knew the cases contained aero engines, you are really saying that that was how the contents were described on the manifest?' Patch nodded. 'Did Captain Taggart show you the manifest before you made your inspection of the holds?'

'I had a look at the manifest before I made my inspection.'

Holland stared at him. 'That wasn't what I asked you. Did Captain Taggart show you the manifest before you made your inspection?'

Patch hesitated and then said, 'No.'

'Had you seen Captain Taggart at that time?'

'Yes.'

'Did you ask him for the manifest?'

'No.'

'Why not? Surely if you were going to inspect the holds – '

'Captain Taggart wasn't well, sir.'

Holland hesitated. Then he half-shrugged his shoulders and turned to the ship herself. There followed nearly half an hour of technical details – her dimensions, construction, date of building, repairs, alterations, characteristics and behaviour, and her history.

She had been built on the Clyde in 1910 for the Atlantic trade. Patch had got her history from some old notebook he had found on board. He had even discovered the origin of her name; the result of some long-dead chairman's dry sense of humour, his wife being called Mary and his own second name being Deare. The ship had been torpedoed twice in the first World War, patched up and kept at sea in convoy after convoy, and then in 1922 she had hit a growler off the Gulf of St Lawrence and after that she'd been sold and for ten years had tramped the seas. The Depression caught her in a Far Eastern port where she lay rotting until the shadow of another war raised shipping freights and she changed hands again and was put to work in the Indian Ocean and the China Seas. She was torpedoed again in 1941, just outside Singapore, packed with troops. She limped into Rangoon, was patched up and sailed to San Francisco. There she had the only decent overhaul in twenty years and went back to work again in the Far Eastern theatre. And then in the last days of the Japanese war, she was stranded on a coral reef under shell-fire. Half her bottom was torn out, her keel permanently kinked, part of her superstructure shot away.

'Any modern ship would have broken her back,' Patch said, and there was a sort of pride in the way he said it.

He went on to tell how she had changed hands again in 1947 – a Burmese owner this time; how she had gone on struggling from port to port throughout the Far East with a twisted back and botched-up repairs until she had been discarded in Yokohama, four years later, and left there to rot until the Dellimare Company purchased her.

In telling her story, he somehow invested the *Mary Deare* with personality. If he had laid stress on the fact that she was a broken-down old hulk on her way to the scrap-heap he could have demonstrated his ability as a seaman and as a Master in bringing her up through the Bay in one of the worst storms of the year. Instead, he told the Court that she was a fine ship, easy to handle, and explained that it was only the repairs, carried out in poorly-equipped Far Eastern ports, that caused her to leak. His loyalty to the ship was impressive, but it lost him the sympathy he might so easily have had.

After that Holland was taking him over the details of the voyage – up through the Red Sea and the Suez Canal and into the

491

Mediterranean; and all the time he questioned him about the crew, the officers, the relations between Dellimare and Taggart; and the picture that emerged was not a pleasant one – the crew ill-disciplined, the chief engineer incompetent, a poker addict, gambling indiscriminately with crew and officers, the captain keeping to his cabin, never on the bridge, and Dellimare roaming restlessly round the ship, feeding alone in his cabin, occasionally with Higgins, and sometimes shut up with the captain for hours on end.

The court was very still as Holland reached the point at which Patch had assumed command. 'According to your entry in the ship's log, Captain Taggart died some time in the early hours of 2nd March. Is that correct?'

'Yes.'

'You had no doctor on board?'

'No.'

Janet Taggart was leaning forward, her face very pale, the knuckles of her hands white as they gripped the back of the seat in front of her.

'Did you treat Captain Taggart yourself?'

'I did what I could.'

'And what was that?'

'I got him to bed. I tried to get him to take a sedative, but he wouldn't.' Patch's voice trailed off and he glanced quickly across the court at Janet Taggart.

'Did you lock him in his cabin?'

'Yes.' His voice was scarcely above a whisper.

'Why?'

Patch did not reply.

'You state in the log that, in your opinion, Captain Taggart died of heart failure. Would you please explain to the Court what it was that caused his heart – if it was his heart – to fail?'

'Mr Holland.' Bowen-Lodge's voice cut in, sharp and high. 'I must remind you of what I said before. I do not consider this relevant or necessary.'

But Holland was obstinate this time. 'With all due deference, Mr Learned Chairman, I consider it highly relevant. The witness is showing commendable restraint regarding the nature of Captain Taggart's illness. That illness, however, has a consider-able bearing on the efficiency of the command he inherited and in fairness to him the Court must be informed.' And, without waiting for permission, he swung round on Patch and said, 'Now that you know the reason for the question, perhaps you will answer it.

What was the basic cause of death?'

Patch stood there, obstinately silent, and Holland became suddenly impatient. 'The man died locked in his cabin. Isn't that correct?'

It was brutally put and there was a shocked look on Patch's face as he nodded dumbly.

'Why did you lock him in his cabin?' And when Patch didn't answer, Holland put a leading question. 'Is it true that you locked him in his cabin because he was raving?'

'He was delirious, yes,' Patch murmured.

'He was upsetting the crew?'

'Yes.'

'Making wild accusations?'

'Yes.'

'What accusations?'

Patch glanced unhappily round the court, and then said, 'He was accusing the officers of stealing liquor from his cabin.'

'Now, will you please answer this question.' Holland was leaning forward. 'What was the basic cause, as far as you know, of Captain Taggart's death?'

Patch might have remained obstinate on this point, but Bowen-Lodge's voice cut in from high up on the judge's seat. 'Witness will kindly answer the question put to him by Counsel. I will repeat it for his benefit – what was the basic cause of death?'

Patch hesitated. 'Drink, sir,' he said reluctantly.

'Drink? Do you mean he died of drink?'

'Because of it – yes.'

The stunned silence that enveloped the court was broken by a girl's voice. It was shrill and high and quavering as she cried out, 'That's not true. How can you say a thing like that – when he's dead?'

'Please, Miss Taggart.' Holland's voice was gentle, almost fatherly. 'The witness is under oath.'

'I don't care whether he's under oath or not, he's lying,' she sobbed wildly. Patch's face had gone very white. Fraser was trying to pull her back into her seat. But she had turned towards the Chairman. 'Please stop him,' she sobbed. And then, flinging up her head, she declared. 'My father was a fine man, a man anybody here would be proud to have known.'

'I understand, Miss Taggart.' Bowen-Lodge's voice was very quiet and soft. 'But I must remind you that this Court is investigating a disaster in which many men lost their lives. The witness is under oath. Moreover, he is not the only witness. You may rest assured that this accusation will be probed and the truth revealed. Will you please be seated now. Or if you prefer it, you may leave the court and wait outside until you are called to give evidence.'

'I'll stay,' she answered in a small, tight voice. 'I'm sorry.' She sat down slowly, her face completely white, her hands fumbling for a handkerchief.

Holland cleared his throat. 'Only one more question on this subject and then we will leave it. About how much liquor was Captain Taggart in the habit of consuming each day?'

'I cannot answer that. I don't know.' Patch's voice was scarcely audible.

'You mean you didn't actually see him consume any set quantity?'

Patch nodded.

'But you must have some idea. What was it he habitually drank – whisky?'

'Yes.'

'Anything else?'

'Sometimes a bottle of cognac. Occasionally rum.'

'How much?'

'I don't know.'

'Had this been going on ever since the start of the voyage?'

'Yes, I think so.'

'Then, since it affected you directly as first officer, you must have made enquiries as to how much he drank. How much did you gather he consumed each day?'

Patch hesitated, and then reluctantly: 'The steward said a bottle, a bottle and a half – sometimes two.' The court gasped.

'I see.' The sound of suppressed sobbing was distinctly audible in the stillness of the court. 'So that he was completely incapable as the Master of the ship?'

'Oh, no.' Patch shook his head. 'Towards the end of the day he would become a little fuddled. But otherwise I would say he was reasonably in command of the situation.'

'You mean to say' – Bowen-Lodge was leaning forward ' – that he was in full command of his faculties when he was steadily drinking one or two bottles a day?'

'Yes, sir. That is to say, most of the time.'

'But you admitted that he was raving and you had to lock him in his cabin. If he was raving, then surely . . .' the Chairman's brows lifted in a question.

494

'He wasn't raving because he was drunk,' Patch answered slowly.

'Then why was he raving?'

'He had run out of liquor.'

A shocked silence gripped the court. Janet Taggart had stopped sobbing. She was sitting quite rigid, staring at Patch with a sort of fascinated horror.

'I would like to get this point perfectly clear before we go any further,' Bowen-Lodge said in a quiet, controlled voice. 'What you're suggesting is that Captain Taggart did not die of drink, but the lack of it. Is that correct?'

'Yes, sir.'

'Do you really think absence of liquor can kill a man?'

'I don't know,' Patch answered wretchedly. 'All I know is that he lived on nothing else, and when he hadn't got it, he went raving mad and died. He never seemed to have anything in the way of food.'

Bowen-Lodge considered for a moment, his pencil tracing lines on the paper in front of him. At length he looked down at Counsel. 'I think, Mr Holland, we should call medical evidence to establish the point one way or another.'

Holland nodded. 'I have already arranged for that – it seemed necessary after reading his deposition.'

'Good. Then we can leave the matter in abeyance till then.' He sounded relieved. 'Please proceed with the examination of the witness.'

The next stage of the voyage was uneventful, but Patch was taken through it in detail and the picture that emerged was of a conscientious officer doing his best to pull a ship's company together with the presence of the owner a constant irritant. The incidents that came to light under Holland's steady questioning were trivial enough in themselves – the crew's mess table uncleaned between meals, cockroaches, several men lousy, the galley dirty, a lifeboat without provisions, a man injured in a fight, the engines stopped for the replacement of a bearing that had been allowed to run hot – but together they produced an impression of a ship that was badly served by the men who ran her.

Other things emerged, too. The log was improperly kept, the wells not sounded regularly, water consumption unchecked, and as often as not it was Higgins, by then acting as first officer, who was responsible. Patch showed that he was coming to depend more and more on his second officer, John Rice, and the growing sense

495

of comradeship between the two men ran like a strong thread through the evidence.

Twice Patch referred to Dellimare. Once of his own accord, when he was dealing with the lack of supervision of the engine-room staff. 'He was encouraging Mr Burrows, my chief engineer, in his poker playing. I had to insist that he stopped entertaining Mr Burrows in his cabin. They were playing cards together till all hours of the night and it was throwing undue responsibility upon Mr Raft, the second engineer.'

'Did Mr Dellimare raise any objection?' Holland asked.

'Yes.'

'What did he say?'

'He said it was his ship and he would do what he damn' well liked and entertain any of the officers he pleased when he pleased.'

'And what did you say to that?'

'That it was endangering the safety of the ship and the morale of the engine-room and that I was the captain, not him, and the ship would be run the way I wanted it run.'

'In other words you had a row?'

'Yes.'

'And did he agree to stop playing poker with the chief engineer?'

'In the end, yes.'

'In the end? You used some persuasion?'

'Yes. I told him I had given Mr Burrows a direct order and that, if it wasn't obeyed, I should know what action to take. And I made it a direct order as far as he was concerned.'

'And he accepted that?'

'Yes.'

'Will you tell the Court what your relations with Mr Dellimare were at this stage?'

Patch hesitated. He had revealed that his relations with the owner were strained. He could in one sentence explain the reason for those strained relations and in doing so gain the sympathy of the whole court. But he let the opportunity go, merely saying, 'We did not see eye-to-eye on certain matters.' And Holland left it at that.

A further reference to Dellimare occurred almost accidentally. Patch had just assured the Court that he had personally checked all four holds as the ship ran into heavy weather off the coast of Portugal, and Holland, again being scrupulously fair to him, drew attention to the fact that he hadn't relied on his first officer's report to make sure that there could be no shifting of the cargo.

'You didn't trust him, in other words?'

'To be honest, no.'

'Did Mr Higgins, in fact, check the holds?'

'I don't know.'

'You thought so little of him that you didn't even ask whether he had checked them?'

'Yes, I suppose that is correct.'

'Did anybody, other than yourself, check the holds?'

Patch paused a moment before replying. Then he said, 'I think Mr Dellimare checked them.'

'You think he checked them?'

'Well, he was in Number One hold when I went in through the inspection hatch to check. I presumed that he was there for the same purpose as myself.'

Holland seemed to consider this for a moment. 'I see. But this was the duty of one of the ship's officers. It seems odd that the owner should find it necessary to check the cargo himself. Have you any comment to make on that?'

Patch shook his head.

'What sort of man was Mr Dellimare?' Holland asked. 'What was your impression of him?'

Now, I thought – now he'll tell them the truth about Dellimare. It was the opening he needed. But he stood there, without saying anything, his face very pale and that nerve twitching at the corner of his mouth.

'What I am trying to get at is this,' Holland went on. 'We are coming now to the night of 16 March. On that night Mr Dellimare disappeared – lost overboard. Did you know that Mr Dellimare had been in the Navy during the war?'

Patch nodded and his lips framed the word 'Yes.'

'He served in corvettes and frigates, mainly in the Atlantic. He must have been through a great many storms.' There was a significant pause, and then Holland said, 'What was your impression of him, at this time, when you knew you were running into very heavy weather? Was he normal in every way?'

'Yes, I think so.' Patch's voice was very low.

'But you're not certain.'

'I didn't know him very well.'

'You had been on this ship with him for over a month. However much he kept to his cabin, you must have had some idea of his mental state. Would you say he was worried?'

'Yes, I think you could say that.'

'Business worries or private worries?'

'I don't know.'

'I'll put it quite bluntly. When you found him checking the cargo, what interpretation did you put on his action?'

'I didn't put any interpretation on it.' Patch had found his voice again and was answering factually and clearly.

'What did you say to him?'

'I told him to stay out of the holds.'

'Why?'

'He shouldn't have been there. The cargo wasn't his responsibility.'

'Quite. I'll put it to you another way. Would you say that his presence there indicated that he was getting scared, that his nerves were going to pieces? He had been torpedoed once during the war and was a long time in the water before being picked up. Would you say that his war experience was in any way affecting him?'

'No, I would . . . I don't know.'

Holland hesitated and then he gave a little shrug. He had been a man seeking after the truth, using the depositions already made as a base from which to probe. But now he changed his tactics and was content to let Patch tell the story of the night the *Mary Deare* was hove-to in the wind-spun waters of the Bay of Biscay, not questioning, not interrupting – just letting it run.

And Patch told it well, gaining from the rapt silence of the court, telling it in hard, factual sentences. And the *Mary Deare* floated into that court, rusty and battered, with the seas bursting like gunfire against the submerged reef of her bows. I watched his face as he told it straight, man-to-man – from the witness box to the Court – and I had the odd feeling that all the time he was skating round something. I looked up at the Chairman. He was sitting slightly forward with his chin cupped in his right hand, listening with a shut, tight-lipped, judicial face that told me nothing of his reactions.

The facts, as Patch presented them, were straightforward enough: the glass falling steadily, the seas rising, the wind increasing, the ship rolling, rolling steady and slow, but gradually rolling her bulwarks under as the mountains of water lifted her on to their streaming crests and tumbled her down into the valleys between. He had been on the bridge since dusk. Rice had been there, too. Just the two of them and the helmsman and a lookout. It had happened about 23.20 hours – a slight explosion, a sort of shudder. It had sounded like another wave breaking and slamming against the bows, except that there was no white water at that particular moment and the ship did not stagger. She was down in a trough and rising slowly. The break of the wave came later and, with it, the hesitation, the crash of the impact, and the sudden blur of white hiding all the fore part of the ship.

Nothing had been said for a moment, and then Rice's voice had cut through the gale's roar as he shouted, 'Did we hit something, sir?' And then he had sent Rice to sound the wells and back had come the report – making water in both the for'ard holds, particularly in Number One. He had ordered the pumps to be started in both Number One and Number Two holds, and he had stood on the bridge and watched the bows become heavy and the seas start to break green over all the for'ard part of the ship. And then Dellimare had come on to the bridge, white-faced and scared-looking. Higgins, too. They were talking about abandoning ship. They seemed to think she was going down. And Rice came back to say the crew were panicking.

He had left the bridge to Higgins then and had gone out on to the upper-deck with Rice. Four men in life-jackets were starting to clear Number Three boat. They were scared and he had to hit one man before they would leave the boat and go back to their duties. He had taken all the men he could find, some ten of them, and had set them to work under the bos'n and the third engineer to shore up the bulkhead between Number Two hold and the boiler-room just in case. And it was whilst he was supervising this that the helmsman had reported to the engine-room that the bridge was full of smoke.

He had taken half a dozen men and when he reached the bridge there was only the helmsman there, his eyes streaming, racked with coughing, as he clung to the wheel, nursing the ship through the crowding storm-breakers, the whole place filled with a fog of acrid smoke.

The fire had been in the radio shack, a little above and behind the bridge. No, he had no idea how it had started. The radio operator had gone below to get his life-jacket. He had stayed below to relieve himself and to have a mug of cocoa. Higgins had gone aft to inspect the steering which seemed slack. No, he didn't know where Dellimare was. He regretted that the helmsman was not among the survivors.

They had used foam extinguishers on the fire. But the heat had been so intense that they hadn't been able to get inside the room. What had finally put the fire out was the partial collapse of the roof, which had allowed the water from a breaking wave to engulf the flames.

The wind was now Force 12 in the gusts – hurricane force. He had hove-to then, putting the ship's bows into the wind with the engines at slow ahead, just holding her there, and praying to God that the seas, piling down in white cascades of water on to the bows, wouldn't smash the for'ard hatch covers. They had stayed hove-to like that, in imminent danger of their lives, for fourteen hours, the pumps just holding their own, and all the time he and Rice had kept moving constantly through the ship, to see that the bulkhead – which was leaking where the weight of water was bulging it, low down near its base – was properly shored, to keep the crew from panicking, to see that they kept to their stations and helped the ship in its struggle against the sea.

About 06.00 hours, after twenty-two hours without sleep, he had retired to his cabin. The wind was dropping by then and the glass beginning to rise. He had gone to sleep fully clothed and two hours later had been woken by Samuel King, the Jamaican steward, with the news that Mr Dellimare could not be found.

The whole ship had been searched, but without success. The man had vanished. 'I could only presume that he had been washed overboard,' Patch said, and then he stood silent, as though waiting for Holland to question him, and Holland asked him if he had held any sort of enquiry.

'Yes. I had every member of the crew make a statement before Mr Higgins, Mr Rice and myself. As far as we could determine, the last man to see Mr Dellimare alive was the steward. He had seen him leave his cabin and go out through the door on to the upper-deck leading aft. That was at about 04.30 hours.'

'And nobody saw him after that?'

Patch hesitated, and then said, 'As far as anybody could find out – no.'

'The upper-deck was the boat-deck?'

'Yes.'

'Was there any danger in going out on to that deck?'

'I don't know. I was on the bridge dealing with the fire.'

'Yes, but in your opinion – was there danger in crossing that deck?'

'No, I don't think so. It's difficult to say. Spray and some seas were sweeping right across all the decks.'

'Right aft?'

'Yes.'

'And Mr Dellimare was going aft?'

'So King said.'

Holland paused and then he asked, 'Have you any idea where

Mr Dellimare was going?'

'No.'

'In view of what you have told us before, would it be reasonable to assume that he might be going aft to check that the hatches of the after-holds were still secure?'

'Possibly. But there was no need. I had checked them myself.'

'But if he had gone to check those hatches, it would have meant going down on to the after well-deck?'

'He could have seen the state of the hatches from the after end of the upper-deck.'

'But if he had gone down, would it have been dangerous?'

'Yes. Yes, I think so. Both well-decks were being swept by the seas.'

'I see. And that was the last anyone saw of him?' The court was very still. The old ship, with her water-logged bows pointed into the gale and a man's body tossed among the spindrift out there in the raging seas; there wasn't anybody in the room who couldn't see it for himself. The puzzle of it, the mystery of it – it held them all enthralled. And behind me somebody was crying.

Then Patch's voice was going on with his story, nervous and jerky, in tune with the sense of tragedy that was seen only in the imagination and not in the cleansing, healing atmosphere of salt wind and spray.

The wind had fallen, and the sea with it, and at 12.43 hours, according to the entry in the log, he had rung for half-ahead on the engines and had resumed course. As soon as it was practicable he had ordered the hand pumps manned, and, as the bows slowly emerged from the sea, he had set a working party under Rice to repair the damage to the for'ard hatches.

He had considered putting into Brest. But, with the weather improving and the pumps holding their own, he had finally decided to hold his course, and had rounded Ushant early on the morning of the 18th. By then he had increased the engine revolutions to economical speed. There was still a big swell running, but the sea was quiet, almost dead calm, with very little wind. Nevertheless, he had hugged the French coast just in case there was some sudden change in the state of the for'ard holds. Île de Batz was abeam at 13.34, Triagoz light at 16.12, Sept Îles at 17.21. He read these times out to the Court from the log. At 19.46 the group occulting light on Les Heaux was just visible through a light mist four points on the starb'd bow. He had then altered course to North 33 East. This would take him outside the Barnouic and Roches Douvres reefs and leave Les Hanois, the light on the south-western tip of Guernsey, about four miles to starb'd. After altering course he had informed his officers that he had decided to take the ship into Southampton for inspection and repairs.

At approximately 21.20, when the steward was clearing his evening meal, which he had taken, as usual, alone in his cabin, he had heard shouts, and then Rice had rushed in to say that the after hold was on fire and that the crew were in a state of panic.

'Any particular reason for their panic?' Holland asked.

'Well, I think they thought the ship was jinxed,' Patch answered. 'In the last two days I had heard that word often.'

'And what did you think? Did you think the ship was jinxed?'

Patch faced the Chairman and the assessors. 'No,' he said. 'I thought there had been a deliberate attempt to wreck her.'

There was a stir of interest throughout the courtroom. But he didn't punch it home with any direct accusation. He just said: 'It was too coincidental – the damage to the holds and then the fire in the radio shack.'

'You were convinced that there had been some sort of explosion in Number One hold?' Holland asked.

Patch hesitated. 'Yes. Yes, I think so.'

'And the radio shack?'

'If it was an explosion, then the radio shack had to be put out of action – it was my means of communication with the rest of the world.'

'I see.' Holland paused, and then he said, 'What you are saying, in fact, is that there was somebody on board who was trying to destroy the ship.'

'Yes.'

'And when you heard that Number Three hold was on fire – did you immediately think that this was another attempt to destroy the ship?'

'Yes, I did.'

'And is that still your opinion?'

Patch nodded. 'Yes.'

'You realize that this is a very serious accusation you are making?'

'Yes, I realize that.'

Holland held the court in utter silence for a moment. And then he said, 'There were thirty-one men on board the *Mary Deare*. If the fire were deliberately started, it endangered all those lives. It was tantamount to murder.'

'Yes.'

'And you still say that the fire was started deliberately?'

'Yes, I do.'

The next question was inevitable. 'Who did you suspect of starting it?' Holland asked, and Patch hesitated. To produce the story of Dellimare's offer now was pointless. Dellimare was dead. He couldn't have started that fire, and all Patch could say was that he hadn't had much time for formulating suspicions – he had been too busy trying to save the ship.

'But you must have thought about it since?'

'Yes, I have.' Patch was facing the judge and the assessors. 'But I think that is a matter for the Court to decide.'

Bowen-Lodge nodded his agreement and Holland then got Patch back to the events following the outbreak of the fire. He and Rice had organized a fire-fighting party. No, Higgins wasn't there. It was his watch. But the second engineer was there and the radio operator and the bos'n. They ran out hoses and got them playing on to the flames through the inspection hatch whilst they cleared part of the main hatch cover. They also cleared a section of Number Four hatch cover in case it was necessary to play the hoses on the bulkhead between the two holds. He had then gone down into Number Four hold through the inspection hatch.

'Why did you do that?'

'I wanted to see how hot the bulkhead plates had become. I didn't want the fire to spread aft. Also, because that hold was only partly filled with cargo, I hoped to be able to tell from the heat of the plates just how serious the fire was – what hold it had got.'

'And what did you discover?'

'It had clearly only just broken out. The bulkhead wasn't even hot. But I didn't discover that until later.'

'How do you mean?'

He explained then how he had been knocked unconscious just as he had reached the bottom of the vertical ladder. He told it in the same words that he had told it to me in his cabin on the *Mary Deare* and when he had finished Holland said, 'You're sure it wasn't an accident – that you didn't slip?'

'Quite sure,' Patch answered.

'Perhaps something fell on you – a loose piece of metal?'

But Patch pointed to his jaw where the scar still showed, maintaining that it was quite impossible for it to have happened accidentally.

'And when you came to, was there any sort of weapon near you that your assailant might have used?'

'No, I don't think so. But I couldn't be certain. The place was

503

full of smoke and I was dazed, half-asphyxiated.'

'I put it to you that one of the crew – a man, say, who had a grudge against you – could have followed you down . . . hit you perhaps with his fist?'

'He would have had to be a very powerful man.' Patch was looking across at Higgins. And then he went on to describe how, when he had come to, he could still hear the men shouting as they got the boats away. He had crawled back up the vertical ladder to the inspection hatch, but the cover had been closed and clamped down. What saved him was the fact that the main hatch had been cleared at one corner and after a long time he had managed to stack enough bales of cotton up to be able to reach this opening and crawl out on to the deck. He had found Number Three boat hanging from its bow falls, the other davits empty. The engines were still running, the pumps still working and the hoses were still pouring water into Number Three hold. But not a single member of the crew remained on board.

It was an incredible, almost unbelievable story. And he went on to tell how, alone and unaided, he had put the fire out. And then in the morning he had found a complete stranger wandering about the ship.

'That would be Mr Sands, from the yacht *Sea Witch*?'

'Yes.'

'Would you explain why you didn't accept his offer to take you off?'

'I saw no reason to abandon ship. She was badly down by the bows, but she wasn't in imminent danger. I thought he would notify the authorities and that it would help the salvage tug if I were on board to organize the tow.'

He told them then how he had seen me fail to regain my yacht, how he had pulled me on to the deck, and then he was telling them of our efforts to save the ship in the teeth of the rising gale, how we had got the engines going and the pumps working and kept her stern to the wind. But he made no mention of the Minkies. According to him, we had finally abandoned the ship in a rubber dinghy taken from Dellimare's cabin when she was on the verge of sinking. No, he couldn't say exactly what the position was, but it was somewhere to the east of the Roches Douvres. No, we hadn't seen her go down. The rubber dinghy? Well, yes, it did seem to indicate that Dellimare had been nervous, had not trusted the boats or the seaworthiness of the ship.

'Two final questions,' Holland said. 'And they are very important questions for you and for everybody connected with the ship.' He paused and then said, 'On reflection, are you quite convinced that it was an explosion that caused the flooding in Number One hold? I put it to you that in the conditions prevailing it was almost impossible to be certain that it wasn't some submerged object that you hit or a wave breaking against the bows.'

Patch hesitated, glancing round the court. 'It definitely wasn't a sea breaking,' he said quietly. 'It was afterwards that the next sea broke over the bows. As to whether we hit something or an explosive charge was set off, only an inspection of the actual damage could prove it one way or the other.'

'Quite. But since the ship is probably lying in at least twenty fathoms of water and we don't know quite where, inspection of the damage is out of the question. I want your opinion.'

'I don't think I can say any more than I have. I can't be certain.'

'But you think it was an explosion?' Holland waited, but getting no reply, he added, 'Having regard to the fire in the radio shack and, later, the fire in the after hold – taking them all together, you incline to the theory that it was an explosion?'

'If you put it that way – yes.'

'Thank you.' Holland sat down and even then nobody moved. There was no whispering, no shuffling of feet. The whole court was held in the spell of the evidence.

And then Sir Lionel Falcett rose. 'Mr Learned Chairman, I would be glad if you would put one or two additional questions to the witness.' He was a small man with thinning hair and a high forehead, a very ordinary-seeming man except for his voice, which had great depth of tone and was vibrant, so that one was conscious of the power of great energy and vitality behind it. It was his voice, not the man, that instantly dominated the court. 'Witness has made it clear that he is convinced, in his own mind, that some attempt was made to wreck the *Mary Deare*. And indeed, the incidents he has related to the Court, in the absence of any natural explanation, would appear to support this conclusion. I would, however, point out to the Court that the value of the ship herself was not such as to justify so elaborate a plot and that we must, therefore, presume that, if such a plot existed, it was directed towards fraudulently obtaining the insurance value of the cargo. I would respectfully point out to you, Mr Learned Chairman, that there would only be financial gain in such a dastardly and murderous endeavour if, in fact, the cargo had been removed prior to the loss of the ship.'

Bowen-Lodge nodded. 'I quite understand your argument,

Sir Lionel.' He glanced at the clock at the far end of the court, above the public gallery. 'What is your question?'

'It concerns the time the ship was moored alongside the *Torre Annunziata* in the Rangoon River,' Sir Lionel said. 'My information is that the *Mary Deare*'s crew were given shore leave, and that during that period the *Torre Annunziata* was a blaze of lights with all her winches in operation.' He looked across at Holland. 'I understand that a deposition to this effect will be introduced later and that it states that the official concerned was informed by the Master of the *Torre Annunziata* that he had been shifting cargo to make room for some steel tubing he was due to load.' He turned back to face Bowen-Lodge. 'I should like to know, Mr Learned Chairman, whether the witness heard any of his officers speak of this after he had joined the ship – whether, in fact, it had been the subject of some comment?'

The question was put and Patch answered that he had heard of it from Rice. He hadn't at the time attached any significance to it.

'But you do now?' Sir Lionel suggested.

Patch nodded. 'Yes.'

'Just one more question, Mr Learned Chairman. Can the witness tell us whether Mr Dellimare at any time made any reference to the cargo?'

The question was put and, when Patch answered, no, Sir Lionel said, 'You had no indication from anyone that the cargo might be other than that stated on the manifest?'

'No.'

'I will put it to you another way – a ship is a very tight little company of men, and in any enclosed community like that a thing popularly known as the grapevine operates. Did you hear any rumours about the cargo after you joined the ship?'

'Some men seemed to think that we had a cargo of explosives on board,' Patch answered. 'It was a rumour that persisted despite the fact that I posted a copy of the manifest on the crew's notice board.'

'You thought it dangerous that they should think they were sitting on top of a lot of explosives?'

'I did.'

'Having regard to the sort of crew you had?'

'Yes.'

'Would you say that this rumour would be sufficient in itself to cause panic amongst the crew as soon as they knew a fire had broken out?'

'Probably.'

'In point of fact Rice reported that they were panicking.' Sir Lionel leaned forward, staring at Patch. 'How did this extraordinary rumour get around the ship?'

Patch glanced involuntarily towards the waiting witnesses. 'I don't think Mr Higgins was ever convinced that we were carrying the cargo declared on the manifest.'

'He thought it was a cargo of explosives, eh? What gave him that idea?'

'I don't know.'

'Did you ask him?'

'Yes, I did.'

'When?'

'Just after we had rounded Ushant.'

'And what did he say?'

'He refused to answer.'

'What were his exact words when you put the question to him?'

'His exact words?'

'Yes.'

'He said I could bloody well try and get the answer out of Taggart or Dellimare and stop bothering him. They were both dead, of course.'

'Thank you.' Sir Lionel folded himself delicately into his seat. Bowen-Lodge looked at the clock again and adjourned the court. 'Two o'clock please, gentlemen.' He rose and the court rose with him, standing whilst he left by the door at the rear of the judge's chair, followed by his three assessors.

When I turned to leave I found that Mrs Petrie had been sitting right behind me. She gave me a little brief smile of recognition. Her face was puffy and pallid under her make-up and her eyes were red. Gundersen was there, too. He had been sitting beside her, but now he had moved along the row and was talking to Higgins. She went out on her own. 'Who's that woman?' Hal asked me.

'One of the Dellimare directors,' I replied, and I told him about my visit to the company's offices. 'I rather think she may have been living with Dellimare,' I told him.

Outside, the sun shone on rain-wet pavements, and it came as something of a shock to discover that there were people – ordinary people who knew nothing of the *Mary Deare* – hurrying about their everyday affairs. Patch was standing alone on the pavement's edge. He had been waiting for me and he came straight across.

'I'd like a word with you, Sands.' His voice was hoarse with talking and his face looked drained.

Hal said he would go on to the hotel where we had decided to lunch and Patch watched him go, fidgeting with the coins in his pocket. As soon as Hal was out of ear-shot, he said, 'You told me your boat wouldn't be ready until the end of the month.' He said it accusingly, anger and resentment in his voice.

'Yes,' I said. 'It was ready a week earlier than I expected.'

'Why didn't you let me know? I went down to the yard last Wednesday and you'd already gone. Why didn't you tell me?' And then he suddenly burst out, 'All I needed was one day. Just one day out there.' He stared at me, literally grinding his teeth. 'Don't you realize – one look at that hole in the ship's hull and I'd have known. I'd have been able to tell the truth then. As it is – ' his eyes were a little wild, like something brought to bay and not knowing which way to turn. 'As it is I don't know what the hell I'm saying, what God-damn pit I'm digging for myself. One day! That was all I wanted.'

'You didn't tell me that,' I said. 'In any case, you know very well that an inspection of that sort would have to be carried out by the authorities.' But I could understand how he had wanted to be certain, to prove that his suspicions were justified. 'It'll work out,' I said, patting his arm.

'I hope you're right,' he said between his teeth. 'I hope to God you're right.' He was looking at me and his eyes were bright like coals. 'All that effort . . . to put her on the Minkies . . . wasted. My God! I could – ' And there he stopped and his eyes, looking past me, widened, and I turned to find Janet Taggart coming straight towards us.

I once saw a painting entitled 'Vengeance'. I can't remember the artist's name and it doesn't matter now, because I know it wasn't any good. Vengeance should be painted the way Janet Taggart looked. She was pale as death, and in the pallor of her frozen face her eyes were enormous. She stopped just in front of him and struck out at him blindly.

I don't remember her words now – they came in a great over-whelming torrent of cutting, lacerating sentences. I saw Patch's eyes go dead as he flinched before the whip-lash of her tongue, and then I left them, walking quickly, wanting to get the picture of the two of them right out of my mind. I wondered if she knew what power she had to hurt the man.

We had a quick lunch and returned to the court, and on the stroke of two Bowen-Lodge took his place on the judge's seat.

There were five men at the Press desk now. They were gathering like vultures at the smell of news. 'With your permission, Mr Chairman,' Holland said, rising, 'I propose to proceed with the other evidence in order that the Court shall have a complete picture.'

Bowen-Lodge nodded. 'I think that a very proper course, Mr Holland. Your first witness must, however, remain in the court. Those representing the various interested parties will, I know, wish to put further questions to him.'

I had expected Higgins to be the next witness. Instead, Holland called for 'Harold Lowden' and I suddenly realized that I still hadn't made up my mind what I was going to say. Hal stood in the witness box, very erect, very much the soldier, and in short, clipped sentences told of our encounter with the *Mary Deare* and how we had found her abandoned the following morning. And when he stepped down it was my turn and I found myself automatically crossing the court and taking my stand in the witness box. I was in a cold sweat.

I repeated the oath and then Holland was facing me, smooth and urbane, asking me in that soft, bored voice of his whether I was John Henry Sands, my business and background and why I was sailing the yacht *Sea Witch* in that area of the Channel on the night of 18 March. And as I gave the answers, I could hear the nervousness in my voice. The court was very silent. Bowen-Lodge's small gimlet eyes watched me and Holland stood there in front of me, waiting to prompt me with questions, to probe if necessary.

Across the court I saw Patch, sitting a little forward, his hands clasped, his body tense and rigid. His eyes were fixed on my face. I was telling them what the *Mary Deare* had looked like that morning when I boarded her, and suddenly my mind was made up. To tell them that the ship was stranded on the Minkies would prove him a liar. It would cut the ground from under his feet. I couldn't do it. I think I had known that all along, but the strange thing was that, once I had made the decision, all nervousness left me. I knew what I was going to say and I set out to present Patch to the Court as I had seen him through those desperate hours – a man, staggering with exhaustion, who had put out a fire single-handed and could still go on fighting to save his ship.

I told them about the bruise on his jaw, about the coal dust and the smoke-blackened haggardness of his face. I told them how we'd sweated down there in the stoke-hold to raise steam on that one boiler, how we'd got the pumps going, how we'd used the engines to keep her stern to the wind and how the seas had swept across her submerged bows in thundering cataracts of white water. And I left it at that, simply saying that we had finally abandoned her on the morning of the second day.

The questions started then. Had Patch made any comments to me about the crew having abandoned ship? Could I give the Court any idea of the *Mary Deare*'s position at the time we had taken to the dinghy? Did I think that, if there had been no gale, the ship could have safely got to some port?

Sir Lionel Falcett rose to his feet and put the same questions that Snetterton had asked me – about the cargo, the holds, Patch. 'You lived with this man through a desperate forty-eight hours. You shared his fears and his hopes. Surely he must have said something, made some comment?' And I replied that we had had little opportunity for talking. I told them again of our exhaustion, the fury of the seas, the moment-to-moment fear that the ship would go down under us.

And then suddenly it was over and I walked back across the floor of the court, feeling like a rag that has been squeezed dry. Hal gripped my arm as I sat down. 'Magnificent!' he whispered. 'You've damn' near made a hero of the man. Look at the Press desk.' And I saw that it was emptying hurriedly.

'Ian Fraser!' Holland was on his feet again and Captain Fraser was making his way across the court. It was routine evidence of how he had picked us up, and then he was released and Janet Taggart was called.

She went into the witness box pale as death, but with her head up and her face a tight little defensive mask. Holland explained that he had called her at this stage in order to release her from the painful ordeal of listening to any further statements that might be made by witnesses about her father. He then took her gently through a description of her father as she had known him – his letters, coming unfailingly from every port he visited, his presents, the money to take her on from college to university, his care of her after the death of her mother when she was seven. 'I never knew how wonderful he had been as a father until these last few years, when I was old enough to understand how he must have scraped and saved and worked to give me the education I've had.' She described him as she had last seen him, and then she read the letter he had written her from Rangoon. She read it in a small, trembling voice, and his love and concern for her were there in every line of it.

It was very painful to hear her, knowing the man was dead, and when she had finished there was a murmur of men clearing their throats and shifting uneasily in their seats.

'That will be all, Miss Taggart,' Holland said with that gentleness that he had used with her throughout her evidence. But she didn't move from the witness box. She had taken a picture postcard from her bag and she stood with it clutched in her hand, looking across at Patch. And the look on her face sent a cold shiver through me as she said, 'A few days ago I received a postcard from Aden. It had been delayed in the post.' She shifted her gaze to Bowen-Lodge. 'It's from my father. May I read part of it please?'

He nodded his permission and she went on: 'My father wrote: "The owner has engaged a man called Patch to be my first officer in place of poor old Adams".' She wasn't reading it. She was staring straight at Bowen-Lodge, the postcard still gripped in her hand. She knew it by heart. ' "I do not know what will come of this. Rumour has it that he stranded a ship once, deliberately. But whatever happens I promise you it shall not be of my doing. God go with you, Janie, and think of me. If all goes well, I shall keep my promise this time and see you again at the end of the voyage".' Her voice broke on a whisper. The court held its breath. She was like a spring coiled too tight and near to breaking.

She held the card out to Holland and he took it. 'Witness is excused,' Bowen-Lodge said. But she had turned and was facing Patch across the court. Wildly she accused him of dragging her father's name in the mud to save himself. She had checked on the loss of the *Belle Isle*. She knew the truth now and she was going to see that the Court knew it. Bowen-Lodge beat on his desk with his gavel. Holland was at her side, remonstrating with her. But she ignored him, and Patch sat there, white-faced and appalled, as she blamed him for the fires, for the flooded holds, for the whole wreckage of her father's ship. 'You're a monster,' she sobbed as they dragged her from the witness box. And then she went suddenly limp and allowed herself to be hurried out of the court, her whole body convulsed with the passion of her tears.

The courtroom eased itself a little self-consciously. Nobody looked at Patch. Nobody looked anywhere until Bowen-Lodge's matter-of-fact voice lifted the tension from the room. 'Call the next witness.'

'Donald Masters!' Holland was in his place again. The Court began to get back into its stride. Technical witnesses followed, giving details of the ship and its equipment, passing judgement on its age and condition, with depositions sworn by the surveyor in Yokohama and the Lloyd's official who had issued her load-line certificate. Another by the Docks Superintendent at Rangoon giving information about the *Torre Annunziata* and the adjustments to her cargo. And then Holland called 'Angela Petrie' and the court, so predominantly male, stirred with interest as Mrs Petrie went into the witness box.

She explained that the Dellimare Trading and Shipping Company had been formed as a private limited company in 1947 with Mr Dellimare, a Mr Greenly and herself as directors. It had been entirely a trading concern, specializing in the import-export business, chiefly with India and the Far East. Later Mr Greenly had ceased to be a director and Mr Gundersen, who operated a similar type of business in Singapore, had joined the board, the capital had been increased and the business considerably expanded. She gave figures, producing them from memory with quiet efficiency.

'And the position of the Company now?' Holland asked.

'It's in process of being wound-up – a voluntary liquidation.'

'And that was arranged before Mr Dellimare's death?'

'Oh yes, it was decided some months back.'

'Any particular reason?'

She hesitated, and then said, 'There were certain tax advantages.'

A little murmur of laughter ran round the court and Holland sat down. Almost immediately Patch's lawyer was on his feet, a thin, dried-up man with a reedy voice. 'Mr Learned Chairman, I should like to ask the witness whether she is aware that Mr Dellimare was involved, just before the formation of this Company, in a case of fraudulent conversion?'

Bowen-Lodge frowned. 'I do not regard that as relevant, Mr Fenton,' he said acidly.

'I should like to answer that question.' Mrs Petrie's voice was bold and clear and vibrant. 'He was acquitted. It was a malicious accusation with no shred of evidence to support it.'

Fenton sat down a little hurriedly and Sir Lionel Falcett rose. 'Mr Learned Chairman, I should like to know from the witness whether any ships were purchased by the Company at the time of its formation?'

Bowen-Lodge put the question and Mrs Petrie answered none.

'You hadn't the capital, is that it?' Sir Lionel asked. And when she agreed, he said, 'In point of fact, it was quite a small business?'

'Yes.'

'Then why call it the Dellimare Trading and Shipping Company? Surely it was a rather unnecessarily grandiose title?'

'Oh, well, you see, Mr Dellimare was always very keen about ships, and being ex-Navy and all that, he hoped one day . . . Anyway,' she added, with a flash of pride, 'we did finish up by owning ships.'

'You had the *Mary Deare* and the *Torre Annunziata*. Any others?'

She shook her head. 'No. Just the two.'

Sir Lionel glanced down at his papers. 'The purchase of the *Mary Deare* was completed on 18 June of last year. When was the *Torre Annunziata* purchased?'

For the first time Mrs Petrie showed a slight hesitation. 'I can't remember exactly.'

'Was it in April of last year?'

'I don't remember.'

'But you are a director of the Company and this must have involved a considerable amount of finance. Do you mean to say you have no records of the transactions?' Sir Lionel's voice had sharpened slightly.

'I may have. I don't know.' And then she added quickly, 'We were expanding fast at that time and it was all fixed up at the Singapore end.'

'And you were not kept fully informed, is that it?' She nodded and he then asked, 'At what date did Mr Gundersen join the board?'

'On 2 March of last year.'

'So that these shipping transactions were a result of his joining the board?'

'Yes, I suppose so.'

Sir Lionel turned to the Chairman. 'There is just one more question I should like to put to the witness. As the Court is already aware, the *Mary Deare* was making just this one voyage and was then being sold for scrap. The *Torre Annunziata* made only two voyages and then she was sold to the Chinese. I should like to know what the margin of profit was on these transactions.'

Bowen-Lodge put the question, but she shook her head. She didn't know.

'What was the cost of acquiring these ships, then?' Sir Lionel put the question to her direct.

'No figures have yet been passed across to our office.'

'And I suppose you have no idea who put up the money?'

She shook her head. 'I'm afraid I don't know. It was all arranged at the Singapore end.'

Sir Lionel nodded and sat down. Mrs Petrie was released from the witness box and she walked back across the court. I saw that her eyes were fixed on someone just behind me, and I guessed it must be Gundersen. Her face was very white and she looked scared.

Hal leaned across to me. 'Looks as though Lionel is mounting an attack on the Company,' he whispered, and I nodded, thinking that perhaps Patch was saving his announcement of Dellimare's offer until he was questioned by Sir Lionel. It seemed reasonable. And that question by his lawyer, Fenton – it had been clumsily done, but he had made his point.

Perfume wafted over me as Mrs Petrie resumed her seat, and I heard Gundersen's voice, cold and angry, say, 'Why didn't you tell him? I gave you those figures weeks back.' And she answered him in a whisper: 'How can I think of figures now?'

And then Holland called 'Hans Gundersen.'

He described himself as a financier and company director and he made a strong impression on the Court. He was a business man and he had all his facts and figures at his finger-tips. Without any prompting from Holland he explained to the Court exactly why he had joined the Company, why they had acquired the *Mary Deare* and the *Torre Annunziata*, how the purchases had been financed and what the expected profits were.

He explained his interest in the Dellimare Company in the cold, hard language of business. He had many interests in Singapore and other ports in the Far East. It suited his interests at that time to take a hand in the affairs of this small company. He had the chance to acquire two old ships at a very low figure. He had taken the view that freight rates were on the mend and that in a year's time it would be possible to sell the ships at a handsome profit. He had chosen the Dellimare Company as the medium through which to make the purchase because he knew Mr Dellimare and discovered that he was willing to have the Company wound up at the end of the transaction. 'In my experience,' he added, 'that is much the most remunerative way of engaging in these operations.' In the case of the *Torre Annunziata* his object had been achieved. They had sold the ship to the Chinese at a figure much higher than the purchase price. The *Mary Deare*, however, had not proved such a good proposition. Her condition had been worse than he had been led to believe. The result was that he had decided that she should make one voyage and then be sold for scrap in England. Break-up price less purchase price and overhaul would have given the Dellimare Company a small margin of profit plus the profits of the voyage. He handed Holland a slip of paper. 'Those are the figures, actual and estimated,' he said.

Holland passed them up to Bowen-Lodge and then sat down. The Chairman checked through the figures, nodded and glanced towards Sir Lionel, who rose and said, 'I should like to know from the witness who financed the acquisition of these ships and how exactly he stood to gain from the deal.'

Bowen-Lodge put the question and Gundersen replied, 'Of course. I financed the operation myself. In return I was allotted all the shares of the increased capital of the Company.'

'In other words,' Sir Lionel said, 'your motive for becoming a director of this company was profit?'

'Naturally. I am a business man, sir.'

'I appreciate that.' Sir Lionel smiled drily. 'Now, about the *Mary Deare*. You have admitted that she was not in the condition you had hoped. How was it that such a valuable cargo was entrusted to her? Did Mr Dellimare arrange that?'

'No. I arranged it through my contacts in Singapore. You must understand that I am very well known in business circles there.'

'One further question. For what reason were these two ships – the *Mary Deare* and the *Torre Annunziata* – routed in such a way that they were in the Rangoon River together from 7 to 11 January?'

'I don't understand the reason for your question, sir,' Gundersen replied. 'Mr Dellimare looked after all the details of the Company management. If a ship is sailing from England to China and another from Japan to Antwerp, then they will cross somewhere.'

Sir Lionel asked him a number of further questions, but Gundersen refused to admit any responsibility for the details of ships' schedules. 'You must understand that I have many calls on my time. This was a very small business. I do not concern myself with the day-to-day management of affairs of companies I am interested in.'

'But you flew all the way from Singapore as soon as you heard what had happened to the *Mary Deare* and have remained in this country ever since.'

'Of course. I am a director of the Company and this is a serious business. When something goes wrong, then it is necessary to be on the spot. Particularly as Mr Dellimare is dead.'

'One final question; why was it necessary for Mr Dellimare to travel on the *Mary Deare* as supercargo. Surely in these days it is very unusual?'

Gundersen shrugged his shoulders. 'Mr Dellimare was in Yokohama to arrange all the details. I don't think he was a rich man, and it is cheaper to travel a long distance like that in your own ship.'

There were no further questions and Gundersen stood down. He was dressed now in a dark-grey double-breasted suit, obviously cut by a London tailor, and he looked a typical English business man – quiet, remote, competent.

More technical evidence followed, and then Bowen-Lodge adjourned the Court. 'Tomorrow at ten-thirty, gentlemen.'

As I followed Hal into the corridor, a hand plucked at my sleeve. 'You're Mr Sands, aren't you?' A little, grey-haired woman was smiling up at me a little uncertainly.

'Yes,' I said. There was something about her face that I seemed to recognize.

'I thought you were, but I'm never quite certain about people – my eyes, you know. I just wanted to tell you how glad I am he has one good friend in all this terrible business. You were splendid, Mr Sands.'

I saw the likeness then. 'You're his mother, aren't you?' I was looking round for Patch, but she said, 'Please. He doesn't know I'm here. He'd be terribly angry. When he came down to see me at Bridgwater, he didn't tell me anything about it. But I knew at once that he was in trouble.' She gave a little sigh. 'It was the first time I had seen him in seven years. That's a long time, Mr Sands, for an old body like me. I only had the one, you see – just Gideon. And now that his father's dead . . .' She smiled and patted my arm. 'But there, you don't want to hear about my troubles. I just wanted you to know that I'm glad he's got one good friend.' She looked up at me. 'It will be all right this time . . . you do think so, don't you, Mr Sands?'

'I'm sure it will,' I murmured. 'Sir Lionel Falcett is obviously concentrating on the cargo and the Company.'

'Yes. Yes, that's what I thought.'

I offered to see her to her hotel, but she wouldn't hear of it and left me with a brave little smile, moving along with the crowd. Hal joined me then and we went out to his car. I caught a glimpse of her standing, waiting for a bus. She was off-guard then, and she looked lonely and a little frightened.

Hal had offered to put me up for the night and we collected my suitcase from the station and drove down to his house at Bosham, a small, thatched place with a lawn running down to the water. I had bought an evening paper in Southampton; it was all over the front page and three columns of it inside – *Captain's Daughter Breaks Down at Enquiry; Strange Story of Loss of Mary Deare.*

It wasn't until after dinner that Hal began to ask me specific questions about Patch. At length he said, 'That day you rejoined us at Peter Port – you didn't say very much about him.' He was standing by the window, looking out across the lawn to where the water was a milky blur in the dusk. There were a couple of yachts moored out there and their masts were bobbing to the lop and the wind gusts. He turned and looked at me. 'You knew about the *Belle Isle* business then, didn't you?'

I nodded, wondering what was coming. It was very cosy in that room with its lamps and its glimmer of Eastern brass and the big tiger skins on the floor, very remote from all that I had lived with during the past two months. Even the glass of port in my hand seemed part of the illusion of being in another world.

He came and sat down opposite me. 'Look, old chap,' he said. 'I don't want to pry into what, after all, is your concern. But just how sure are you about this fellow?'

'How do you mean?'

'Well, you've got to be damn' sure about a man . . . I mean . . .' He hesitated, searching for the words he wanted. 'Well, put it this way. If Patch wrecked that ship – deliberately wrecked her – then it was murder. They may only be able to pin a charge of manslaughter on him in law, but before God he'd be guilty of murder.'

'He didn't do it,' I said.

'You're sure of that?'

'Absolutely.' And having said that, I sat back, wondering why I'd said it, why I was so certain?

'I'm glad,' Hal said. 'Because, you know, all the time you were in the witness box, I was conscious that you were defending him. You were selecting your evidence, keeping things back, and at times you were a little scared. Oh, you needn't worry. I don't think anybody else noticed it. I noticed it because I know you and because at Peter Port, when you'd had less time to think it all out, you were so obviously covering up.' He paused and sipped his port. 'Go carefully, though,' he added. 'I know Lionel Falcett. Member of my club. Seen him in action, too. Don't let him get his claws into you.'

3

IT WAS still blowing and the streets were wet as we drove to the court the following morning. Proceedings started sharp at ten-thirty with evidence about the cargo. And then a doctor was called who showed that it was quite possible for a man who lived on nothing but liquor to die for lack of it. Through all this the courtroom was restless as though waiting for something. The public gallery was packed, the Press desk crammed. And then at last Holland called 'Alfred Higgins' and, as Higgins thrust his huge bulk into the witness box, there was a sudden, expectant hush, so that the sound of a clock striking eleven was quite audible through the taking of the oath.

He was forty-three years old, Higgins told the Treasury Counsel, and, when asked for his qualifications, he explained that he'd started life on his father's barge, sailing the East Coast ports until he was fifteen; then he'd got mixed up in some smuggling racket and had stowed away on a banana boat. He'd stayed at sea after that, moving from ship to ship across the traffic lanes of the world – square-riggers, tramps and liners, tugs and coasters; he rolled the names of them out of his great barrel of a body like pages picked at random from Lloyd's Register.

He began his story back where the *Mary Deare* steamed out of Yokohama. According to him, the ship was a floating death-trap of rattling rivets and clanging plates, a piece of leaking iron-mongery taken off the junk-heap of the China Seas. Of the captain, he simply said, 'The 'ole ship knew 'e was drinking 'isself ter death.' The first mate was sickening for jaundice and the third officer, Rice, was only a kid of twenty-four on his second voyage with a watch-keeper's certificate. The implication was that he, Higgins, was the only reliable deck officer on board, and though he looked like a bull about to charge, there was something impressive about him as he stood there and gave his evidence in a throaty rumble.

Singapore, Rangoon, Aden – and then he was covering the same ground that Patch had covered, but from a different angle. He thought the crew 'not bad considerin' the moth-eaten sort o' a

518

tub she was.' Patch he regarded as 'a bit pernickity-like' and added, 'But that's ter be expected when a man wiv 'is record gets command again.'

And then up through the Bay of Biscay the Court got little glimpses of Patch, nervous, over-bearing, at odds with the owner, with his officers – 'All 'cept Rice. 'E was the white-headed boy, as the sayin' is.' And when it came to the gale itself and the ship down by the bows and the radio shack gutted by fire, Higgins didn't give it graphically as Patch had done, but baldly, factually. He had been asleep in his bunk when the hold had started to flood. He had taken over the bridge and had remained on watch until 10.00 hours the following morning – eleven solid hours. He had then organized a more thorough search for Dellimare. No, Mr Patch hadn't ordered him to. He'd done it on his own initiative, having been relieved. He couldn't believe that Dellimare 'who was Navy an' a good bloke on a ship' could have gone overboard. Altogether he had been forty-two hours without sleep.

'You liked Mr Dellimare?' Holland asked him.

'I didn't like or dislike 'im. I jus' said 'e was a good bloke, an' so 'e was.'

'Did you advise Mr Patch at one stage to abandon ship?'

'Well, yes, in a manner o' speakin'. We considered it, Mr Dellimare an' me.'

'Why?'

' 'Cos we knew the sort o' ship she was. We'd bin through two gales already comin' across from Singapore. Patch 'adn't. An' the one in the Bay was a lot worse than wot we'd gone through before.'

'And you thought an explosion had occurred in the for'ard hold?'

'I didn't think nothin' of the kind. I knew she was rotten an' we were takin' a helluva pounding. We didn't think she'd stand much more.' And then he said, 'If you're suggesting we were scared, just remember what it was like out there. Ten to one the boats wouldn't 've got launched in that sea, let alone stayed afloat. It took guts to even think 'o takin' ter the boats, pertikly fer Mr Dellimare who'd had a basinful o' that sort o' thing during the war. Later, when we 'ove-to, things was easier an' I thought maybe we had a chance.'

And then he was dealing with the night the fire had broken out in the after hold and they had abandoned ship. Yes, it had been about 21.20 hours. It was a stoker who had discovered it, a

man called West. He'd come out of the after deck-house and had
seen smoke coming from the hatch of Number Three hold. He'd
reported at once to the bridge by phone. Rice had been there at
the time and Higgins had sent him to check the report and notify
Mr Patch. Not once in his evidence did he refer to Patch as the
captain.

'And what happened then?' Holland asked him.

'I didn't hear nothin' further for about quarter of an hour. But
I knew it was fire orl right 'cos the after derrick lights was switched
on an' there was a lot of activity with men running about the
deck. Then Mr Patch comes up to the bridge lookin' very wild
and all covered in smoke grime an' says he's ordered the boats
swung out just in case. I asked him whether he'd like me ter take
charge of the fire-fighting party and he said No, Mr Rice was in
charge. He stood aba't fer a bit after that as though he couldn't
make up his mind aba't somethin'. An' after a bit Rice comes
runnin' up to the bridge in a bit of a panic an' says the fire's
getting worse. And at that Patch orders him to pass the word to
stand by to abandon ship. "You notify the engine-room, Mr
Higgins," he says. "Then take charge of the fire-fighting party.
Mr Rice, you'll have charge of the upper-deck. See there's no
panic when I give the word." An' that's the last I saw of him,'
Higgins added.

The rest was a pattern of disaster that comes from absence of
command. Higgins and his men had fought the fire for a further
fifteen minutes or so, and all the time it seemed to be gaining on
them. The men were scared. They believed the ship was jinxed,
that the cargo was explosives. Higgins sent Rice to tell Patch he
couldn't hold the men much longer and Rice came back to say he
couldn't find Patch anywhere. 'By then the men were near ter
panic. Some were already on the upper-deck, piling into Number
Three boat. There weren't nothing I could do 'cept give the order
to abandon ship.'

The order had resulted in a stampede for the boats. When he
reached the upper-deck, Higgins saw Number Three boat hanging by its bow falls with one man clinging to it. Number One
boat had also been cleared. She was empty and being battered to
pieces against the ship's side. By using his fists he'd got some sort
of order out of the chaos on deck and he and the officers had
organized the men into the two remaining boats. He had put
Rice in charge of Number Four boat and had waited to see him
safely clear. He had then lowered and released his own boat.
Owing to the speed at which the ship was travelling he had lost

contact with Rice by the time his boat hit the water and he never regained it.

'Do you mean to say,' Holland asked, 'that you took to the boats with the ship still steaming?'

'Yes. Acting on Mr Patch's instructions I had ordered the engine-room staff to stand by to take to the boats. When I gave the order to abandon, they didn't 'ave no instructions about stopping the engines an' afterwards none o' 'em would go below to do it.'

'But surely if you gave the order – '

'What the hell use were orders?' Higgins growled. 'Patch'd gone – vanished. One boat was already hanging in her davits, the men in her all tipped into the sea; another was bein' smashed up alongside. The men were panicking. Anybody who went below stood a good chance of coming up and finding the last two boats gone. It was as much as Rice an' I could do ter get those boats away orderly-like.'

'But good heavens!' Holland exclaimed. 'Surely, as an experienced officer, you had some control over your – '

But Higgins interrupted him again. 'Ain't you got no imagination?' he burst out. 'Can't you see what it was like – Patch gone and the crew in a panic and a fire raging on top of a cargo of explosives.'

'But it wasn't explosives.'

' 'Ow were we ter know?'

'You've heard the evidence proving that the cases loaded at Yokohama contained aero engines. There was no justification for believing – '

'We know now they was full of aero engines,' Higgins said quickly. 'But I'm telling you wot we thought at the time. We thought they was full of explosives.'

'But you'd seen the manifest,' Holland reminded him. 'Mr Patch even posted a copy of it on the crew's notice board.'

'What difference does that make?' Higgins demanded angrily. 'A crew don't 'ave ter believe everything that's posted on their notice board. An' let me tell you, mister, men that sail in ships like the *Mary Deare* don't go much by the manifest, pertickly in the China Seas. We may be uneddicated, but we ain't stupid. A manifest is just a piece of paper somebody's written what he wants believed on. Least, that's the way I look at it – an' I've me reasons for doin' so.'

There was no answer to that. The outburst called for a rebuke from the Chairman, but it was given mildly. Higgins was accepted for what he was, a piece of human flotsam speaking with the voice of experience. In a sense he was magnificent. He dominated that drab court. But not by the power of his personality, which was crude. He dominated it because he was different, because he was the obverse of the coin of human nature, a colourful, lawless buccaneer who didn't give a damn for authority.

'In other words,' Holland said, 'you've known a lot of strange things happen aboard ships around the world. Now, have you ever known a stranger set of circumstances than those that happened aboard the *Mary Deare*?'

Higgins pursed his lips, then shook his head. 'No, I can't say I 'ave.'

'Take the flooding of the for'ard holds. You say you didn't think it was an explosion of some sort.'

'I didn't say nuthing of the kind. I said I didn't think about it, not at the time. There was a lot of other things ter think aba't. Anyway, I wasn't on the bridge.'

'And what's your opinion now?'

Higgins shook his head. 'I don't know wot ter think.'

'And what about the fires? Were they natural outbreaks?'

'Ah, the fires – that's different.' His cunning little eyes darted a glance to where Patch sat, watching him with a tense face.

'You think they were started deliberately?'

'Yes, I reckon so.'

'You suspect somebody then?'

'I don't know about that. But,' he added, 'I knew we was in fer trouble as soon as 'e come aboard.' And he nodded his hard bollard of head towards Patch. 'Stands ter reason, a man wiv 'is record don't get the job fer nuthing – and then the skipper dying so convenient-like.'

'Are you blaming somebody for Captain Taggart's death?' There was a note of censure in Holland's voice.

'I ain't blamin' anyone. But somebody swiped the poor devil's liquor and all I say is it only did one man any good.'

An excited buzz ran round the court as Holland sat down. Fenton was immediately on his feet. It was a disgraceful allegation, made without a shred of evidence to support it. And the Chairman agreed, leaning forward and asking Higgins whether it wasn't true that Taggart had accused several of the officers. And when Higgins admitted that it was, he said, 'Yourself as well?'

'The poor devil was ravin',' Higgins declared angrily.

'So he's raving when he accuses you, but not when he accuses Mr Patch, is that it?' Bowen-Lodge's voice was icy.

'Well, it didn't do me no good, him dying,' Higgins muttered.

'I put it to you that Captain Taggart just ran out of liquor.'

But Higgins shook his head. 'There was a lot of stuff brought off to 'im by a ship's chandler in Aden. 'E couldn't 've drunk it all in the time. It weren't 'umingly possible.'

'What did you think about it at the time? Did you take his accusations seriously?'

'No, why should I? When a man's ravin' the way he was, you don't know wot ter believe.' Higgins had a baffled look as though he wasn't sure where the questions were leading. 'Mebbe 'e 'ad liquor, an' mebbe 'e didn't,' he muttered hoarsely. 'Mebbe somebody pinched it – I dunno. All I know is, we searched the 'ole bloomin' ship fer 'im, jus' ter make 'im 'appy, 'an we didn't find a single bottle wot belonged to 'im. 'Course,' he added, 'if we'd known as 'ow 'e was goin' ter die fer lack of the stuff, there's some of us, as was plannin' ter smuggle the odd bottle through the Customs, who'd 've chipped in ter 'elp 'im, as the sayin' is.'

Bowen-Lodge nodded and Fenton started to question Higgins, trying to get him to admit that Patch had never given the order to stand-by to abandon ship, trying to confuse him and break him down over little details. But Higgins was a dangerous witness to cross-examine. He made it clear with every answer that he didn't trust Patch, and he didn't budge an inch from his original testimony.

But with Sir Lionel it was different. His interest was the cargo. What had led the witness to believe that the cases loaded at Yokohama contained explosives? Had he discovered something whilst he was loading the cases? But when the Chairman put the question, Higgins said he hadn't been a member of the ship's company at the time the cases were loaded.

'When did your employment as second officer commence then?' Bowen-Lodge asked.

'The day before the ship sailed,' Higgins answered. 'By then she was all loaded up, hatches battened down an' lying out in the fairway.'

'You were shown the manifest?'

'No. I never saw the manifest, not till later.'

'Then what gave you the idea that the cargo contained explosives?'

'There was rumours around the docks.'

'And amongst the crew?'

'Yes.'

'Have you ever known explosives packed in cases clearly marked as aero engines?'

'Not exactly. But I've heard of explosives bein' packed and marked as other things, to avoid the regulations as you might say.'

'But you had no definite indication that the cases might contain other than what was stated on the manifest?'

'No.'

'And you did your utmost to scotch this rumour?'

For the first time Higgins showed uncertainty. 'Well, no, to be honest I can't say I did.'

'Why not?'

The muscles along Higgins's neck thickened. 'Well, if it comes ter that, why should I? Wasn't none of my business.'

Bowen-Lodge glanced across at Sir Lionel with one eyebrow raised. The next question concerned the four days the ship was moored in the Rangoon River. Yes, Higgins admitted, he had gone ashore with the rest. Well, why not? It wasn't every day the owners gave a ship's company forty-eight hours ashore, expenses paid. The reason? Mr Dellimare was a good bloke, that's why – knew how to treat a crew, believed in a happy ship.

'When you got back to the ship – ' Sir Lionel was now putting his questions direct to the witness again – 'did you talk to any of the officers or men of the *Torre Annunziata*?'

'Yes. The first officer, a bloke called Slade, came aboard for a drink wiv me and the Chief.'

'Did you ask them why they had been shifting cargo around?'

'No. But Slade tol' me they'd 'ad ter do it because of some clerical mess-up over the destination of the steel tubes they were due to load.'

'Did you talk to Adams about it?'

'No.'

'But you saw him when you got back on board?'

'Yes.'

'Did he suggest that the crew of the *Torre Annunziata* had been tampering with the *Mary Deare*'s cargo?'

'No.' And then he added quickly, 'An' if they 'ad, 'e'd 've known about it 'cos when I saw 'im, 'e was up an' about an' feelin' better fer 'is two days in bed.'

'Adams being sick, I take it you were in charge of the loading of the cotton cargo?' Higgins nodded and Sir Lionel then asked him, 'Did you notice any change in the disposition of the cargo?'

'No, can't say I did.'

'You're quite certain?'

' 'Course I'm certain.'

Sir Lionel's small head shot forward and his voice was suddenly crisp and hard as he said, 'How could you be? You said you joined the ship after she was loaded?'

But Higgins wasn't easily put out. His tongue passed over the dry line of his lips. But that was the only sign of uneasiness he gave. 'I may not 've bin there when she was loaded. But I was when we discharged our top cargo of Japanese cotton an' rayon goods. I took special note of 'ow the cases was stowed 'cos I guessed I'd 'ave to load the bales of raw cotton when they was ready.'

Sir Lionel nodded. 'Just one more question. You say you didn't go aboard the *Mary Deare* until the day before she sailed. How was that?'

'Well, I wasn't took on till then.'

'Who engaged you – Captain Taggart?'

'No, Mr Dellimare. Oh, Captain Taggart signed the papers. But it was Dellimare wot engaged me.'

'Why?'

Higgins frowned. ' 'Ow d'you mean?'

'I asked you why he engaged you. Were you the only man who applied for the vacancy?'

'Well, not exactly. I mean . . .' Higgins glanced round the court and again his tongue passed along his lips. 'It didn't 'appen like that.'

'You mean the job wasn't offered in the usual way? You were engaged by Mr Dellimare privately?'

'I suppose so.' Higgins sounded reluctant.

'Perhaps you would be good enough to explain to the Court how it happened.'

Higgins hesitated. 'Well, we 'appened ter meet, as you might say, an' 'e was short of a second officer an' I wanted a berth, an' that's all there was to it.'

'Where did you meet?'

'Some bar da'n by the waterfront. Don't remember the name of it.'

'By arrangement?'

Higgins's face was reddening, the muscles on his neck swelling. 'Yes, by arrangement.' He said it angrily as though challenging Sir Lionel to make something of it.

But Sir Lionel only said, 'Thank you. That was what I wanted to know.' And sat down. He had established two things: that, if the Dellimare Company were planning to wreck the *Mary Deare*, the vital shift of cargo was a possibility, and that Higgins could have been the instrument of their choice. But he had nothing definite against Higgins and that, he admitted to Hal long afterwards, was the real trouble. To justify his clients in withholding payment of the insurance claim he had to have something more positive.

It was the evidence of the other survivors that finally decided him, and the most damaging evidence was that of the helmsman, Yules, who had been on the bridge with Higgins when the fire broke out. He was timid and he gave his evidence with a slight stutter. He wasn't a very strong witness, but he clung to his statement that Patch had given the order to stand by to abandon ship with unshakeable obstinacy. He even had the words off pat, and though Patch's counsel rose to the occasion and had him so terrified that he kept on looking to Higgins for support, he never budged.

He was the last witness before lunch and I didn't need Hal to tell me that Patch would have a bad time of it when he took the stand for examination by the various counsel. The Court hadn't begun to get at the truth yet. But what was the truth? Hal asked me that over lunch and all I could say was, 'God knows.'

'Dellimare couldn't have started that fire in the hold,' he said, and I agreed. Dellimare was dead by then. It had to be Higgins. Evidently Bowen-Lodge had also considered this possibility over his lunch, for, when the Court reassembled, he had Yules recalled and questioned him closely about the movements of the officer of the watch. And Yules swore that Higgins had been on the bridge from 20.00 hours and hadn't once left it. Later, Burrows, the chief engineer officer, testified that Higgins had been playing poker with him and two members of the crew who had been drowned, from 17.00 hours to 20.00 hours with only a brief break for food.

One after the other the survivors went into the witness box, each from his different angle corroborating what had gone before – the certainty that the ship was jinxed, that she carried explosives and that she was destined to go to the bottom. It was the story of men carrying within themselves the seeds of inevitable tragedy.

And then at last Holland called 'Gideon Patch' and he was standing there in the witness box again, slightly stooped, his hands gripping the rail, knuckles as white as the pallor of his face. He looked worried sick and the twitch was there at the corner of his mouth.

Bowen-Lodge questioned him first – questioned him in minute detail about the orders he had given after the fire broke out. He had him go through the whole thing again from the moment Rice had rushed into his cabin to report the outbreak. Then, when Patch had told it exactly as he'd told it before, Bowen-Lodge gave a little shrug and Holland took up the questioning again. And all the time it was obvious that something was being kept back. You could sense it in the way the man stood there with that hunted look on his face and his body all tense and trembling. And the questions went back and forth with nobody making any sense out of it and Patch sticking to his statement that he had been knocked out and that the fire had been started deliberately.

'Yes, but by whom?' Bowen-Lodge demanded.

And Patch had answered in a flat, colourless voice, 'That is for the Court to decide.'

After that the ball had been tossed to the counsel representing the interested parties and they hounded him with questions about Taggart and Dellimare, about his handling of the crew, about the seaworthiness of the ship, and then finally the counsel for the Marine Officers' Association was on his feet, going back once again over the orders he'd given the night the ship was abandoned, and Bowen-Lodge was beginning to glance at the clock.

At last Sir Lionel rose, and his questions were all about the cargo. If Patch could have said that those cases were empty or contained something other than aero engines, that would have been that and Sir Lionel would have been satisfied. But he couldn't say it and the questions went on and on until Sir Lionel had exhausted all the possibilities. He paused then and seemed on the point of sitting down. He was bending forward, peering at some notes and he looked up over his reading glasses and said, 'Perhaps Mr Learned Chairman, you would ask the witness to tell me how he came to be on the *Mary Deare*.'

The question was put and Patch answered, quite unsuspecting, that he thought he had already explained that he had replaced Mr Adams who had been taken to hospital suffering from jaundice.

'Yes, yes, quite,' Sir Lionel said impatiently. 'What I meant was, who signed you on – Captain Taggart or Mr Dellimare?'

'Captain Taggart.'

'He came ashore and made the choice himself?'

'No.'

'Who did come ashore then and make the choice?' Sir Lionel's voice still sounded bored. He gave the impression that he was dealing with a small routine point.

'Mr Dellimare.'

'Mr Dellimare?' Sir Lionel's face was suddenly expressive of surprise. 'I see. And was it done privately, a meeting in some bar – by arrangement?' His tone carried the bite of sarcasm in it.

'No. We met at the agents'.'

'At the agents'? Then there were probably other unemployed officers there?'

'Yes. Two.'

'Why didn't Mr Dellimare choose one of them? Why did he choose you?'

'The others withdrew when they heard that the vacancy was for the *Mary Deare*.'

'But you did not withdraw. Why?' And when Patch didn't answer, Sir Lionel said, 'I want to know why?'

'Because I needed the berth.'

'How long had you been without a ship?'

'Eleven months.'

'And before that you hadn't been able to get anything better than the job of second mate on a miserable little Italian steamer called the *Apollo* working the coastal ports of East Africa. Didn't you think it strange that a man with your record should suddenly find himself first officer of a 6000-ton ocean-going ship?' And when Patch didn't say anything, Sir Lionel repeated, 'Didn't you think it strange?'

And all Patch could say, with the eyes of the whole Court on him, was, 'I never considered it.'

'You – never – considered it!' Sir Lionel stared at him – the tone of his voice, the carriage of his head all indicating that he thought him a liar. And then he turned to Bowen-Lodge. 'Perhaps, Mr Learned Chairman, you would ask the witness to give a brief resumé of the events that occurred on the night of 3rd/4th February nine years ago in the region of Singapore?'

Patch's grip on the rail in front of him tightened. His face looked ghastly – trapped. The courtroom stirred as though the first breath of a storm had rustled through it. Bowen-Lodge looked down at the questioner. 'The *Belle Isle*?' he enquired. And then, still in the same whisper of an aside, 'Do you consider that necessary, Sir Lionel?'

'Absolutely,' was the firm and categorical reply.

Bowen-Lodge glanced up at the clock again and then he put the question to Patch. And Patch, rigid, and tight-lipped, said, 'There was a report issued at the time, sir.'

Bowen-Lodge looked across at Sir Lionel, a mute question to discover whether he wished to pursue the matter. It was obvious

that he did. You could see it in the stillness with which he watched
the man in the witness box, his small head thrust a little forward as
though about to strike. 'I am well aware that there is a report
available,' he said in a cold, icy voice. 'Nevertheless, I think it
right that the Court should hear the story from your own lips.'

'It's not for me to give my views on it when a Court has already
pronounced judgement,' Patch said in a tight, restrained voice.

'I was not asking for your views. I was asking for a resumé of
the facts.'

Patch's hand hit the rail involuntarily. 'I cannot see that it has
any bearing on the loss of the *Mary Deare*.' His voice was louder,
harsher.

'That is not for you to say,' Sir Lionel snapped. And then –
needling him – 'There are certain similarities.'

'Similarities!' Patch stared at him. And then, beating with
his hand on the rail, he burst out: 'By God, there are.' He turned
to face the Chairman – still angry, goaded beyond the limits of
what a man will stand. 'You want the sordid details. Very well.
I was drunk. Dead drunk. That's what Craven said in evidence,
anyway. It was hot like the inside of an oven that day in Singapore.' He was still staring at the Chairman, but not seeing him any
more, seeing only Singapore on the day he'd smashed up his
career. 'Damp, sweaty, torrid heat,' he murmured. 'I remember
that and I remember taking the *Belle Isle* out. And after that I
don't remember a thing.'

'And were you drunk?' Bowen-Lodge asked. His voice was
modulated, almost gentle.

'Yes, I suppose so . . . in a sense. I'd had a few drinks. But not
enough,' Patch added violently. 'Not enough to put me out like a
light.' And then, after a pause, he added, 'They ran her aground
on the Anambas Islands at 02.23 hours in the morning with a
thundering surf running and she broke her back.'

'You are aware,' Sir Lionel said quietly, 'that there has been a
lot of talk since . . . suggesting that you did it for the insurance.'

Patch rounded on him. 'I could hardly be unaware of it,' he
said with wild sarcasm, 'seeing that all these years I've barely
been able to scratch a living in my own chosen profession.' He
turned back to the Chairman, gripping hold of the rail. 'They said
I ordered the course and they had the log to prove it. It was there
in my own handwriting. Craven – he was the second officer –
swore that he'd been down to my cabin to query it and that I'd
bawled him out. Later he took a fix and then came down to my
cabin to warn me again, but I was in a drunken stupor – those

were his words – and when he couldn't wake me, he went back to the bridge and altered course on his own responsibility. By then, of course, it was too late. That was his story, and he stuck to it so well that everybody believed him, even my own counsel.' He had turned his head and was looking across the courtroom at Higgins. 'By God,' he repeated, 'there are similarities.'

'What similarities?' Sir Lionel asked in a light tone of disbelief.

Patch turned to face him. It was pitiful to see how easily he was goaded. 'Just this,' he almost shouted. 'Craven was a liar. The log entry was forged. The *Belle Isle* was owned by a bunch of Greek crooks in Glasgow. They were on the verge of bankruptcy. The insurance money just about saved them. It was all in the papers six months later. That was when the rumours started.'

'And you had nothing to do with it, I suppose?' Sir Lionel asked.

'No.'

'And this man Craven had slipped a micky into your drink. Is that what you're suggesting?'

It took away from him and destroyed his defence. His muttered 'Yes' was painful anti-climax. Bowen-Lodge intervened then. 'Are you suggesting a similarity between this Greek company and the Dellimare Trading and Shipping Company?' he asked.

And Patch, fighting back, cried, 'Yes. Yes, that's exactly what I am suggesting.'

It brought the Dellimare Company's counsel on to his feet, protesting that it was a monstrous allegation, an unwarranted aspersion on a man who was dead at the time the fire broke out in the hold. And Bowen-Lodge nodded and said, 'Quite, Mr Smiles – unless there is some justification.' He turned to Patch then and said, 'Have you any reason for making such an allegation?'

Now, I thought – now he must tell them about Dellimare's offer. Whether he had evidence to support it, or not, it was the only thing for him to do. But, instead, he drove home his accusation on the basis of motive and opportunity; the Company in liquidation and the only people who would benefit by the loss of the ship. 'Why else should the owner have been on board?' he demanded. A voyage of almost five months! It was a ridiculous waste of a director's time, unless there was a reason for his being on the ship. 'And I say there was,' he declared.

Smiles jumped to his feet again, but Bowen-Lodge forestalled him. 'You seem to be forgetting the cause of the ship being abandoned and finally lost. Are you accusing Mr Dellimare of causing the fire in that after hold?'

It brought Patch up with a jolt. 'No,' he said.

'He was dead by then?'

'Yes.' Patch's voice had dropped to a whisper.

And then Smiles, still on his feet, asked what possible motive the Company could have in destroying the ship. 'She was bound for the scrap yards and in the figures Mr Gundersen has given you, Mr Learned Chairman, you will find that the scrap value was fixed at a little over £15,000. She was insured for £30,000. Is the witness suggesting that a mere £15,000 was sufficient motive to induce a company to endanger the lives of a whole ship's crew?'

'The question of motive,' Bowen-Lodge said, 'does not come within the scope of this Investigation. We are concerned solely with the facts.' He glanced towards Sir Lionel as though expecting something further from him.

'I think at this stage, Mr Learned Chairman,' Sir Lionel said, 'I should ask you to put this very serious question to the witness – Did he, or did he not, on the night of 18 March, set fire to Number Three hold of the *Mary Deare*, or cause it to be set on fire?' A sort of gasp like an eager shudder ran through the courtroom.

The eyes of the two men, Counsel and Chairman, remained fixed on each other for a moment, and then Bowen-Lodge nodded slowly and turned to face the witness. Looking down on him and speaking quietly, but with great distinctness, he said, 'I think it my duty to tell you that in my opinion this whole matter of the loss of the *Mary Deare* will be the subject of a case in another Court and to advise you that you need not answer this very direct question if you do not wish to. Having so advised you, I will now put the question.' And he repeated it.

'No, I did not,' Patch declared, and his voice was clear and firm. And then he added, turning to face Sir Lionel Falcett, 'If I'd set fire to the ship, why should I go to the trouble of putting it out?'

It was a good point, but Sir Lionel only shrugged. 'We have to consider that she might have gone aground on the nearby reefs, perhaps the coast of France, only partially burned out. The evidence would be better sunk in twenty fathoms of water. There was a gale coming up and then you had Mr Sands' arrival to consider – '

Bowen-Lodge gave a discreet little warning cough and Sir Lionel murmured his apologies. The Chairman looked up at the clock again and then leaned over and conferred with his assessors. Finally he adjourned the Court. 'Until ten-thirty tomorrow, gentlemen.'

Nobody moved for a moment, and even when they did, I sat there, stunned and angry at the injustice of it. To take a man's record and fling it in his face like that, to damn him without a shred of evidence . . . and there was Patch still standing stiff and rigid in the witness box – and Sir Lionel, picking up his papers and smiling at some little joke made by one of the other lawyers.

Patch was moving now, crossing the floor of the court. Without thinking I started forward to meet him, but Hal put his hand on my arm. 'Better leave him now,' he said. 'He needs to think it out, poor devil.'

'Think what out?' I asked angrily. I was still wrought up by the injustice of it.

'What he's going to say tomorrow,' Hal answered. And then he added, 'He hasn't told the whole story yet and Lionel Falcett knows it. He can tell it tomorrow, or he can tell it in the criminal courts! But he's got to tell it some time.'

The criminal courts. 'Yes, I suppose it will come to that,' I murmured. But before that, the truth had to be uncovered. And the truth, whatever it was, lay out on the Minkies. 'I must have a word with him,' I said. I had suddenly made up my mind and was forcing my way through the crowd towards Patch.

He didn't hear me when I called to him. He seemed oblivious to everything but the need to get out of the place. I caught hold of him, and he turned abruptly with a nervous start. 'Oh, it's you.' He was trembling. 'Well, what is it?'

I stared at him, horrified by the haggard, hunted look in his face. There were beads of sweat still on his forehead. 'Why in God's name didn't you tell them?' I said.

'Tell them what?' His eyes had suddenly gone blank of all expression.

'About Dellimare,' I said. 'Why didn't you tell them?'

His eyes flickered and slid away from me. 'How could I?' he breathed. And then, as I started to tell him that the Court had a right to the truth, he said, 'Leave it at that, can't you? Just leave it at that.' And he turned on his heel and walked quickly away towards the exit.

I went after him then. I couldn't leave it like that. I had to give him the chance he'd asked for. I pushed through a little knot of the *Mary Deare*'s crew and caught him up in the corridor outside. 'Listen,' I said. 'I'll take you out there – as soon as the Enquiry is over.'

He shook his head, still walking towards the freedom of the main doors. 'It's too late now,' he said.

His attitude exasperated me and I caught hold of his arm, checking him. 'Don't you understand? I'm offering you my boat,' I said. '*Sea Witch* is lying in Lulworth Cove. We could be over there in twenty-four hours.'

He rounded on me then. 'I tell you it's too late.' He almost snarled the words at me. And then his eyes slid past me, narrowing suddenly and blazing with anger. I felt his muscles tense, and then he had freed himself from me and was walking away. I turned to find Higgins standing there. He had Yules with him and they were both staring after Patch. All around me people were moving, whispering, watching Patch walking down the corridor, fascinated by the thought that he might be guilty of sending a lot of men to their death.

I turned to look for Hal, but Higgins caught hold of my arm, so that I was instantly conscious of the colossal brute strength of the man. 'I 'eard wot you said just then.' His throaty voice was full of the smell of stale beer as he thrust his head close to mine. 'If you think you're goin' ter take 'im a't there . . .' He checked himself quickly, his small, blood-veined eyes narrowed, and he let go of my arm. 'Wot I mean is . . . well, you steer clear of 'im,' he rasped. ' 'E's a wrong 'un – yer can take my word fer it. You'll only get yerself inter trouble.' And he turned quickly and went ploughing off down the corridor, little Yules hurrying after him.

A moment later Hal joined me. His face was serious. 'I've been talking to Lionel Falcett,' he said, as we moved off towards the entrance. 'It's as I thought. They think he's hiding something.'

'Who – Patch?' I was still shaken by what Higgins had said, wondering if he'd guessed that I'd been referring to the *Mary Deare*.

'Yes. It's only an impression, mind you. Lionel didn't say anything, but . . .' He hesitated. 'Do you know where Patch is staying?' And when I nodded, he said, 'Well, if you're absolutely certain of the chap, I'd get hold of him and tell him what the form is. It's the truth, and the whole truth now, if he wants to keep clear of trouble. That's my advice, anyway. Get hold of him tonight.'

We went into the pub across the road and had a drink. I phoned Patch from there. It was a lodging house down by the docks and the landlady told me that he'd come in, got his coat and gone out again. I phoned him later when we arrived at Bosham and once after dinner, but he still hadn't returned. It worried me and, going to bed early, I found it difficult to sleep. Rain was lashing at the window and in the twilight of half-consciousness Patch and Higgins wandered through my mind. I pictured Patch walking the streets of Southampton, walking endlessly to a decision that would justify his cry that my offer was too late and leave him just something to be identified in a mortuary.

In the morning, of course, it all seemed different. The sun was shining and there was a blackbird singing, and as we drove into Southampton, the world was going about its prosaic, everyday life – delivery vans and postmen on bicycles and kids going to school. It was ten-fifteen when we reached the court. We had arrived early so that I could have a word with Patch before the Investigation was resumed. But he hadn't arrived yet. Only a few of the witnesses were there, Higgins among them, his big body slewed round in his seat, watching the entrance.

Across the court several of the lawyers had come in and were standing together in a little knot, talking in low voices. The Press desk was filling up; the public gallery, too. Hal left me and went to his seat, and I moved out into the corridor and stood there, watching the people filing slowly in, searching for Patch amongst the faces that thronged the narrow passage-way.

'Mr Sands.' A hand touched my arm, and I turned to find Janet Taggart standing beside me, her eyes unnaturally large in the pallor of her face. 'Where is he? I can't find him.'

'Who?'

'Mr Patch. He's not in the courtroom. Do you know where he is, please?'

'No.'

She hesitated, unsure of herself. 'I'm terribly worried,' she murmured.

I stared at her, wondering how it was she had come to share my own fears. 'You should have thought of that before,' I said brutally and watched the muscles of her face contract so that the features looked small and pinched. She was different now from the sunny-smiling kid of the photograph, and the light wasn't shining on her hair any more. She looked grown up, a woman. 'He'll be here in a moment,' I said more gently, trying to calm her fears, and my own.

'Yes,' she said. 'Yes, of course.' She stood there, hesitating, her face taut. 'I went to see him last night. I didn't understand – not until I read the evidence of Higgins and the others.' She stared at me, her eyes big and scared-looking. 'He told me everything then. He was so – ' She stopped there with a little shrug, uncertain of herself and what she was saying. 'You do think he's all right, don't you?' And then, because I didn't answer, she said, 'Oh God! I could kill myself for the things I said.' But she wasn't speaking to me. She was speaking to herself.

I heard the Court rise. The corridor was empty. There was still no sign of Patch. 'We'd better go in,' I said gently.

She nodded, not saying anything more, and we went into the courtroom together and took our seats. Holland was on his feet. He had a piece of paper in his hand and he turned to face Bowen-Lodge as silence descended on the room. 'Mr Learned Chairman. I have just received information from the Receiver of Wreck to the effect that the *Mary Deare* is not sunk. The Harbour Master at St Helier, Jersey Island, has reported that the vessel lies stranded on the Plateau des Minquiers and that a French salvage company is endeavouring to refloat her.'

The gasp of surprise that greeted this news swept through the courtroom, gathering force as people gave voice to their astonishment. Men in the Press desk were on their feet. I caught sight of Higgins, sitting with a dazed look on his face. There was still no sign of Patch.

Bowen-Lodge leaned forward over his desk. 'This alters the situation entirely, Mr Holland. I take it that it means that the Receiver of Wreck will be able to make a full examination of the wreck.' And when Holland nodded, he added, 'I presume you have discussed it with him. How long before he can report to the Court?'

'He's not sure about that,' Holland answered. 'He doesn't yet know the exact position of the *Mary Deare* on the reefs nor has he any information as to the identity of the salvage company. He is making enquiries. But he informs me that the legal position may be complicated – the Minkies being part of the Channel Islands and the company concerned being French. It is a question of the Crown's rights and the rights of the salvage company. He also stated that the tides in this area, which rise and fall by over thirty feet, made the reefs particularly dangerous and, as far as the cargo was concerned, any examination might have to wait on the successful refloating of the vessel.'

'I see. Thank you, Mr Holland.' Bowen-Lodge nodded and turned to his assessors. He conferred with them, heads close together, whilst the sound of people talking broke like a wave again over the court. The Press desk was empty now. 'Well, that's that,' Hal whispered to me. 'He'll adjourn the Court now.' And then he said, 'Did you know she wasn't sunk?' And when I nodded, he said, 'Good God man! You must be daft.'

Bowen-Lodge had separated from his assessors now and he tapped with his gavel to silence the court. 'There are one or two questions, Mr Holland, arising out of the discovery that the ship is not sunk. Please recall your last witness.'

Holland nodded and called, 'Gideon Patch.'

The court was still, nobody moved.

'Gideon Patch!' And when he still didn't appear, Holland turned to the usher on the door and said, 'Call Gideon Patch.' The name was repeated, echoing in the emptiness of the corridors outside. But still nothing happened. Necks craned in the public gallery; the buzz of conversation rose again.

They waited several minutes for him, and the silence in the court was so absolute that you could almost hear the ticking of the clock. And then, after a brief discussion with the assessors, Bowen-Lodge adjourned the Court for one hour. 'At twelve o'clock please, gentlemen.' The court stood and then everybody was talking at once, and down by the jury box Higgins, Yules and Burrows stood in a little bunch with their heads close together. And then Higgins broke away from them suddenly and came lumbering towards the door. His eyes met mine for a second, and they had the dead, flat look of a man who is scared.

The wait seemed a long one. There was no news. All we could learn was that enquiries were being made at Patch's lodgings. 'A fat lot of good that will do,' was Hal's comment. 'A warrant and the police is the only thing now.' We had nothing to say to each other as we waited. He had accepted Patch's guilt as proved. Others took the same view. Scraps of comment came to me from the waiting crowd: 'Wot I say is, he's no better than a murderer . . . You can always tell, old boy. It's the eyes that give them away every time . . . And what about Dellimare and that poor Captain Taggart? . . . 'Course 'e did. Wouldn't you do a bunk if you'd killed 'alf the crew . . .' And all the time I was trying to reconcile the sort of man they thought he was with the man I had known on the *Mary Deare*.

At length the crowd began to drift back into the courtroom. As they did so a rumour ran from mouth to mouth – Patch hadn't been seen since the previous evening. Bowen-Lodge and the assessors entered and there was silence as Holland rose to say that he regretted he was not able to produce his chief witness.

'Have the police been requested to take action?' Bowen-Lodge asked.

'Yes. A search has been instituted.' There was a moment's silence as Bowen-Lodge fiddled with the papers on his desk.

'Would you care to re-examine any of the witnesses?' Holland asked.

Bowen-Lodge hesitated. He was looking over the available witnesses and for a moment I thought his cold, searching gaze was fixed on me. Finally he leaned over in conference with his assessors. I felt the shirt sticking to my body. What the hell was I going to say if he recalled me? How was I going to explain my failure to tell them the ship was on the Minkies?

The minute I was kept in suspense seemed a long time. And then Bowen-Lodge said, 'I don't think there is any point in recalling any of the witnesses now, Mr Holland.' He looked up at the court. 'In view of the fact that the *Mary Deare* has been located, the assessors and I are agreed that no further purpose can be served by continuing this Investigation, particularly as the chief witness is no longer available. I am, therefore, adjourning the Court indefinitely pending examination of the wreck. All witnesses are released. You will be notified in due course should further evidence be required of you. Thank you, gentlemen, for your attendance.'

It was over, the Chairman and assessors gone, the courtroom emptying. As I made my way towards the door, Higgins stepped forward, blocking my path. 'Where is 'e?' he demanded. 'Where's 'e gone?'

I stared at him, wondering why he should be so worked up over Patch's disappearance. He ought to have been pleased. 'What's it got to do with you?' I asked him.

Beady eyes searched my face, peering at me over sagging pouches. 'So you do know, eh? I said you would.'

'As it happens,' I said, 'I don't know. I wish I did.'

'To hell with that!' The violence inside him bubbled to the surface. 'You think I don't know what yer up to – you with your boat lyin' in Lulworth, waiting for 'im. Well, I tell yer, if that's yer game, wotch a't, that's all.' He stared at me, his small eyes narrowed, and then he turned abruptly and left us.

As we walked down the corridor, Hal said, 'You're not going to be a fool and try and slip him out of the country, are you?' He was looking at me, his face serious, a little worried.

'No,' I said. 'I don't think it ever occurred to him that that was a way out.'

He nodded, but I don't think he was convinced. He would have pressed the point further, but as we went out into the sunshine, he was greeted by a man in a reefer with a little pointed beard and greying hair. He had a high, rather strident voice, and, as I waited, I heard him say to Hal, 'Oh, not your type, Colonel – definitely not.' There was something about a motor boat, and then: '. . . rang up about an hour and a half ago. They had her on charter a month back . . . Yes, old *Griselda*. You remember. Dry rot in the keel and rolls like a bastard.' He went off with a high-pitched laugh and Hal rejoined me. Apparently the man was a yacht broker down at Bosham. 'Odd place, this, for him to do business,' Hal said. And then he added, 'I wonder if it's the Dellimare Company, chartering a boat to go out and see what the French salvage people are up to. I wouldn't be surprised.'

We started to walk to the car and he went on talking, giving me some advice about not leaving it too late. But I was thinking of Higgins. Why had Patch's disappearance scared him?

'John. You're not listening.'

'No. I'm sorry.'

'Well, that's not surprising. Nobody listens to advice.' We had reached the car. 'But if it comes to a criminal case, see that you give them the full story, just as it happened. Don't leave it to be dragged out of you in cross-examination. They'll play hell with you, and you may find yourself in real trouble.'

'All right,' I said.

We drove down to the police station then to see if there was any news of Patch. But all the sergeant at the desk could tell us was that he had been seen in a number of pubs in the dock area and had spent part of the night at an all-night café out on the Portsmouth road. He had got a lift about four in the morning in a truck headed back towards Southampton. They were now trying to trace the truck driver.

We hung around for a little, but there was no further news. 'And it's my opinion,' the sergeant added darkly, 'that there won't be any – 'cept for the finding of the body as you might say. The people at the café described him as desperate – looked like death, the report says.'

Hal drove me to the railway station then, and when he had gone I bought an evening paper. Without thinking I found myself looking at the forecast. Winds moderate, north-westerly. As I stood waiting for my train I was thinking of Higgins and the Dellimare Company and the fact that the Minkies were only a day's sail from Lulworth.

PART THREE

I

'*Sea Witch!* Ahoy! Ahoy, *Sea Witch!*'

Gulls wheeled, screaming, and my voice came back to me, a lonely shout in the drizzling rain. The yacht lay motionless in the crater of the cove, the reflection of her black topsides shattered every now and then as cat's-paws of wind riffled the mirror-surface of the water. The waves of a swell broke in the entrance and, all round, the hills loomed ghostly and grey in the mist, all colour lost, their grass slopes dropping to the dirty white of the chalk cliffs. There wasn't a soul about.

'Ahoy! *Sea Witch!*' A figure moved on the deck, a splash of yellow oilskins; the clatter of oars and then the dinghy was coming to meet me. It grounded with a crunch on the wet shingle and I climbed in and Mike rowed me out. I was relieved to find that I didn't have to tell him about the Enquiry; he had followed it all in the newspapers. But once we were on board with the dinghy made fast and my gear stowed, he began to ask questions – what had happened to Patch, why hadn't he turned up at the Court this morning? 'You know they've issued a warrant for his arrest?'

'A warrant? How do you know?' I asked. I don't know why, but it shocked me. It seemed so pointless.

'It was on the six o'clock news.'

'Did it say what the charge was?'

'No. But they've got police checks on all the roads leading out of Southampton and they're keeping watch on the ports.'

We discussed it during the meal. There were only the two of us. Ian had gone home to visit his people. Mike was to phone him as soon as we were ready to start operations again, but he hadn't done so yet because the latest forecast was wind moderate north-westerly, backing westerly later and becoming fresh, with the outlook unsettled. The thing that puzzled Mike most about the whole business was why Patch hadn't told the Court about Delli-mare's offer. Not having been present at the Enquiry, but only reading the reports, it was natural, I suppose, that he should still retain a vivid impression of Patch's visit, and over coffee he suddenly reminded me of the package I had been given at Paim-

539

pol. 'I suppose it couldn't contain some vital piece of evidence?' he said.

Until that moment I had forgotten all about it. 'If it had,' I said, 'he would have asked me to produce it.'

'Have you still got it?'

I nodded and got up and went into the after cabin. It was still there in my brief-case and I took it through into the saloon. Mike had cleared a space on the table and I reached for a knife and cut the string, feeling as I had done during the war on the occasions when I had to deal with the effects of some poor devil who'd been killed.

'Looks like a book of some sort,' Mike said. 'It couldn't be the log, could it?'

'No,' I answered. 'The log was in Court.'

Inside the brown paper wrapping was an envelope. The name *J. C. B. Dellimare* was typed on it and below, in blue pencil, was scrawled the one word *Collect*. The envelope had been ripped open, the tear crossing the stamped impress of a City bank. I had a vague hope then that perhaps Mike was right – that it was some sort of an account book belonging to Dellimare or the Company, something that would reveal a financial motive. And then I slid the contents on to the table and stared incredulously.

Lying amongst the supper things was a thick wad of five-pound notes.

Mike was gazing at the pile, open-mouthed with astonishment. He'd never seen so much cash in his life; neither of us had. I split it between us. 'Count it!' I said.

For several seconds there wasn't a sound in the saloon except the crackle of those Bank of England notes. And when we had totalled it all up, it came to exactly £5,000, and Mike looked up at me. 'No wonder he didn't want to bring it out through the Customs himself,' he said. And then, after a pause, he added, 'Do you think he accepted Dellimare's offer after all?'

But I shook my head. 'If he'd accepted, why put out the fire, why beach her on the Minkies?' I was remembering the state of that cabin when I'd gone in to help him get out the rubber dinghy. 'No, he must have taken it afterwards – after the man was dead.'

'But why?'

'God knows!' I shrugged my shoulders. There were so many things I didn't understand. I gathered the notes together and put them back in the envelope. 'If this were his payment for wrecking the ship,' I said, 'he'd have been down here to collect it the instant he landed in England.'

'Yes, that's true.' Mike took the envelope from me, frowning and turning it over in his hand. 'Odd that he should have failed to collect it. It's almost as though he'd forgotten all about it.'

I nodded slowly. And then I went up on deck and lit the riding light. It wasn't really necessary; we were the only boat in the anchorage, and nobody was likely to come in on such a reeking night. But it gave me something to do. I lit a cigarette. It was quite dark now and we lay in a little pool of light, hemmed in by the iridescent curtain of the drizzle. The wind seemed to have died away. The water was very black and still. No ripples slapped against the topsides. The only sound was the faint murmur of wavelets on the beach. I stood there, smoking in the feeble glow of the riding light and wondering what the hell I was going to do with all that money. If I took it to the authorities, I should have to account for my possession of it. Or should I send it anonymously to form the basis of a fund for the dependants of those who had lost their lives? I certainly couldn't send it to his mother, and I was damned if I was going to return it to the Dellimare Company.

I stayed there, thinking about it, until my cigarette was a sodden butt. I threw it in the water then and went below. Mike was checking over one of the aqualungs. 'Care for a drink?' I asked him.

He nodded. 'Good idea.'

I got out the bottle and the glasses.

I didn't say anything. I didn't want to talk about it. I just sat there with my drink and a cigarette, going over the whole thing in my mind. We sat for a long time in silence.

I don't know who heard it first, but we were suddenly staring at each other, listening. It came from the bows, a sort of splashing sound. 'What is it?' Mike had got to his feet. The splashing ceased and then footsteps sounded on the deck above our heads. They came slowly aft, whilst we stood waiting, frozen into immobility. They reached the hatch. The cover was slid quietly back and bare feet appeared, followed by dripping trouser legs and then the body of a man all sodden with water; he was standing suddenly at the foot of the ladder, blinking in the light, his face pale as death, his black hair plastered to his skull and water streaming from his clothes on to the grating.

'Good God!' I breathed. I was too astonished to say anything else. He was shivering a bit and his teeth were chattering, and I stood there, staring at him as though he were a ghost. 'If some-body would lend me a towel . . .' Patch began to strip off his wet clothes.

'So Higgins was right,' I said.

'Higgins?'

'He said you'd make for *Sea Witch*.' And then I added, 'What have you come here for? I thought you were dead.' God! I almost wished he were as I realized the impossible position he'd put me in. 'What the devil made you come here?'

He ignored my outburst. It was as though he hadn't heard or had shut his mind to it. Mike had found him a towel and he began to dry himself, standing naked, his hard, sinewy body still brown with the heat of Aden. He was shivering and he asked for a cigarette. I gave him one and he lit it and started to dry his hair. 'If you think we're going to slip you over to France, you're wrong,' I said. 'I won't do it.'

He looked at me then, frowning a little. 'France?' The muscles of his jaw tightened. 'It's the Minkies I want to get to,' he said. 'You promised to take me there. You offered me your boat.' A sudden urgency was in his voice.

I stared at him. Surely to God he didn't still want to go out to the Minkies? 'That was last night,' I said.

'Last night – tonight . . . what difference does it make?' The pitch of his voice had risen. He had stopped towelling himself and suddenly there was doubt in his face. It was as though he had come here in the certainty that when he had arrived everything would be all right, and suddenly he knew it wasn't.

'You probably don't know it,' I said, trying to soften the blow, 'but there's a warrant out for your arrest.'

He showed no surprise. It was as though he had expected it. 'I was walking for a long time last night,' he said, 'trying to make up my mind. In the end I knew I'd never reach the *Mary Deare* if I went into that Court this morning. So I came here. I walked from Swanage and I've been up on the hills half the day, waiting for it to get dark.'

'Have you seen a paper?' I asked him.

'No. Why?'

'The *Mary Deare* has been located and a French salvage company is endeavouring to refloat her. A full examination is to be made of the wreck, and if you think there's any point – '

'A full examination.' He seemed shocked. 'When?' And then he added, 'It was announced in Court, was it?'

'Yes.'

'Who told them where the ship was. Did Gundersen?'

'Gundersen? No. It was the Harbour Master at St Helier reporting to the Receiver of Wreck. I imagine a Jersey Island fisherman sighted the wreck. He must have seen the salvage people working on her.'

'That's all right.' He seemed relieved. 'But we'll have to hurry.' He picked up the towel. 'Have you got a drink?'

I reached into the locker and got him the rum bottle and a glass. His hands shook as he poured it out. 'I'll need some clothes, too.' He knocked the drink back at one gulp and stood gasping for breath. 'Now that they know there's going to be an official examination of the boat, we'll have to move fast.'

Mike had produced some clothes out of a locker. He put them on the table and Patch picked up a vest. 'How soon can you leave?' he asked.

I stared at him. 'Don't you understand?' I said. 'There's a warrant out for your arrest. I can't possibly take you.'

He was halfway into the vest and he stopped, his eyes fixed on me. For the first time, I think, he realized that we weren't going to take him. 'But I was relying on you.' His tone was suddenly desperate. And then he added angrily, 'It was only yesterday you offered to take me. It was the one chance and – '

'But you didn't accept it,' I said. 'You told me it was too late.'

'So it was.'

'If it was too late then,' I said, 'it's certainly too late now.'

'How could I accept your offer? They were going to arrest me. I was quite certain of that, and if I'd gone back into that Court this morning – '

'But you didn't.'

'No.'

'Why not? Can't you see you've put yourself in an impossible situation.' I leaned forward, determined to get at the truth. 'You've got the police hunting for you now – everybody against you. What in God's name made you decide to run for it?'

He pulled the vest down over his head and came to the edge of the table, leaning down over it. 'Something I learned last night – something that made me realize I had to get out to the *Mary Deare* as soon as possible.' There was silence for a moment, whilst we looked at him, waiting. And then he said, 'That salvage company – it's under contract to the Dellimare Company.'

'How do you know?' It seemed the wildest piece of guesswork. 'How can you possibly know when it's only just been announced that a salvage company is working on the wreck?'

'I'll tell you.' He began to get into the rest of Mike's clothes. 'Last night, when I got back to my rooms – I went up and got my coat. I was going for a walk – to think things over. And outside – I found Janet – Miss Taggart – waiting for me there in the street. She'd come . . .' He gave a quick shrug. 'Well, it doesn't matter, but it made a difference. I knew she believed in me then, and after that I searched the pubs all through the dock area. I was certain I'd find Burrows in one of them. He couldn't keep away from the booze so long as he had money. And he had money all right. I found him down in the old part of the town, and he told me the whole thing – drunk and truculent and full of confidence. He hated my guts. That's why he told me about the salvage company. He was gloating, knowing I'd never prove anything after they'd sunk her. And all because I'd told him he was incompetent and that I'd see to it he never had charge of an engine-room again.'

He paused and took a quick drink. The wind was rising, and in the silence the sound of it whining through the rigging was suddenly loud. Then he pulled on Mike's sweater and came and sat down opposite me. He was still shivering. 'Higgins must have worked out the course of our drift for Gundersen. Anyway, they were convinced she was on the Minkies and they chartered a boat and went over there. And when they'd found her, Gundersen signed up this French outfit to salvage her.'

'But what difference does that make to you?' Mike asked. 'It's perfectly natural for the Dellimare Company to want to salvage her.'

Patch turned on him, his lips drawn back in a smile. 'They're not going to salvage her,' he said. 'They're going to have the French pull her off and then they're going to sink her in deep water.'

I saw Mike looking at him as though he were crazy and I said, 'Do you seriously imagine they could get away with that?'

'Why not?' he demanded.

'But no salvage company – '

'It's nothing to do with the salvage company. But the contract is for refloating and towing the hulk to Southampton, and Higgins and Burrows will be on board the tow. Gundersen will insist on that. And with those two on board, it's simple. Burrows has only got to open the sea cocks and the *Mary Deare* will quietly founder at the end of her tow line. They'll wait till they're past the Casquets, I imagine, and sink her in the Hurd Deep. She'll go down in sixty fathoms or more, and everybody will think it a stroke of bad luck and put it down to the state of the hull after being pounded for a couple of months on the Minkies.' He turned and stared at me. 'Now perhaps you understand. I've got to get out to her, Sands. It's my only hope. I must have proof.'

'Of what?' Mike demanded.

He looked from one to the other of us, a quick, uncertain movement of the eyes. 'I must know for certain that there was an explosion in those for'ard holds.'

'I should have thought that was a matter for the authorities,' Mike said.

'The authorities? No. No, I must be certain.'

'But surely,' I said, 'if you went to the authorities and told them the truth . . . if you told them about Dellimare's offer – '

'I can't do that.' He was staring at me and all the vitality in his eyes seemed to have burned itself out.

'Why not?' I asked.

'Why not?' His eyes dropped and he fiddled with his glass. 'You were with me on that ship,' he whispered. 'Surely to God you must have guessed by now.' And then he added quickly. 'Don't ask me any more questions. Just take me out there. Afterwards . . .' He hesitated. 'When I know for certain – ' He didn't finish, but looked directly at me and said, 'Well? Will you take me?'

'I'm sorry,' I said. 'But you must realize it's impossible now.'

'But – ' He reached out his hand and gripped hold of my arm. 'For Christ's sake! Don't you understand? They'll refloat her and then they'll sink her out in deep water. And after that I'll never know . . .' He had a beaten look and I was sorry for him. And then a spark of anger showed in his eyes. 'I thought you'd more guts, Sands,' he said, and his voice quivered. 'I thought you'd take a chance – you and Duncan. God damn it! You said you'd take me.' He was coming up again, the muscles of his arm tightening, his body no longer sagging . . . unbelievably there was strength in his voice again as he said, 'You're not scared, are you, just because there's a warrant out for my arrest?'

'No,' I said. 'It isn't only that.'

'What is it then?'

I reached across the table for the envelope. 'This for one thing,' I said and I threw it down on the table in front of him so that the fivers spilled out of it and lay there, white and crisp, black-inked like funeral cards. 'You let me bring that back for you, not knowing what it was.' I watched him staring down at them uncomfortably and I went on, 'Now suppose you tell us the truth – why you took that money, why you didn't tell the Court about Dellimare's offer.' I hesitated, still staring at him, but he wouldn't meet my gaze. 'You took that money from his cabin after he was dead, didn't you?'

'Yes.' His voice sounded weary, exhausted.

'Why?'

'Why?' He lifted his eyes then, staring straight at me, and they were suddenly the eyes of the man I had first met on the *Mary Deare*. 'Because it was there, I suppose. I didn't reckon it belonged to him any more . . . Oh, I don't know.' He was frowning, as though trying to concentrate on something that didn't interest him. He seemed to be lost in some private hell of his own creation. 'I suppose I was a fool to take it. It was dangerous. I realized that afterwards. But at the time . . . well, I was broke, and when you know you've got to fight a company to prove you did your best to bring a ship home that they didn't want brought home . . .' He let it go at that, his mind still on something else.

'Is that why you didn't tell the Court about Dellimare's offer?' I asked.

'No.' He got suddenly to his feet. 'No, it wasn't that.' He stood for a moment looking out through the open hatch and then he came back to the table. 'Don't you understand yet?' His eyes were fixed on my face. 'I killed him.'

'Dellimare?' I stared at him in shocked silence.

'He didn't go overboard,' he said. And then, after a pause, he added, 'His body is still there on the *Mary Deare*.'

I was so staggered I could think of nothing to say. And then suddenly he began to pour out the whole story.

It had happened on the night of the gale, just after the fire in the radio shack had been reported to him. He had gone out on to the wing of the bridge, to see whether the fire could be tackled from there, and he'd seen Dellimare making his way aft along the upper-deck. 'I'd warned him I'd kill him if I found him trying to monkey with the ship. There was no reason for him to be going aft.' He had rushed down from the bridge then and had reached the after end of the deck just in time to see Dellimare disappearing through the inspection hatch of Number Four hold. 'I should have slammed the lid shut on him and left it at that.' But instead he'd followed Dellimare down into the hold and had found him crouched by the for'ard bulkhead, his arm thrust down into the gap between the top case of the cargo and the hull plates. 'I can remember his face,' he breathed. 'Startled and white as hell in the light of my torch. I believe he knew I was going to kill him.'

Patch's voice trembled now as he relived the scene that had

546

been pent-up inside him too long. Dellimare had straightened himself with a cry, holding some sort of a cylinder in his hand, and Patch had moved in with a cold, dynamic fury and had smashed his fist into the man's face, driving his head back on to the steeel of the hull, crashing it against an angle iron. 'I wanted to crush him, smash him, obliterate him. I wanted to kill him.' He was breathing heavily, standing at the end of the table, staring at us with the light shining down on his head, deepening the shadows of his face. 'There were things happening to the ship that night – the for'ard holds flooding, the fire in the radio shack, and then that little rat going down into the hold . . . and all the time a gale blowing hurricane force. My God! What would you have done? I was the Captain. The ship was in hellish danger. And he wanted her wrecked. I'd warned him . . .' He stopped abruptly and wiped his forehead.

Then he went on, more quietly, describing what had happened after Dellimare had crumpled up, lying in a heap on one of the aero engine cases with blood glistening red in his pale thin hair. He hadn't realized he'd killed him – not then. But the anger had drained out of him and somehow he had managed to get him up the vertical ladder to the deck. He had nearly been knocked down by a sea that had come surging in-board, but he had made the ladder to the upper-deck. That way he wouldn't meet any of the crew. But when he had almost reached the bridge-housing the lights shining out of the after portholes showed him Dellimare's head and he knew then that the man was dead. 'His neck was broken.' He said it flatly, without emotion.

'But surely you could have said he'd had an accident – fallen down the hold or something?' I suggested. I was remembering the coal dust and the sound of shifting coal in the bunker, knowing what was coming.

He reached for the packet and lit a cigarette. Then he sat down opposite me again. 'I panicked, I suppose,' he said. 'Poor devil, he wasn't a pretty sight – all the back of his head smashed in.' He was seeing the blood and the lolling head again, and the sweat glistened on his forehead. 'I decided to dump him over the side.'

But he had set the body down to examine it and when he bent to pick it up, he'd seen Higgins coming out through the starboard doorway from the bridge-housing. He hadn't dared carry the body to the rail then. But just beside him the hatch of the port bunkering chute stood open for some strange reason and, without thinking, he pitched the body down the chute and slammed the lid on it. 'It wasn't until hours later that I realized what I'd done.'

He took a pull at his cigarette, dragging at it, his hands trembling. 'Instead of getting shot of the man, I'd hung his body round my neck like a millstone.' His voice had fallen to a whisper and for a moment he sat in silence. Then he added, 'When you came on board, I'd slung a rope ladder down into that bunker and was in there, trying to get at the body. But by then the rolling of the ship had buried him under tons of coal.'

There was a long silence after that and I could hear the wind in the rigging, a high, singing note. The anchor chain was grating on the shingle as the boat yawed. And then, speaking to himself, his head lowered: 'I killed him, and I thought it was justice. I thought he deserved to die. I was convinced I was saving the lives of thirty-odd men, my own included.'

And then he looked at me suddenly. 'Well, I've told you the truth now.'

I nodded. I knew this was the truth. I knew now why he had to get back there, why he couldn't reveal Dellimare's offer to the Court. 'You should have gone to the police,' I said, 'as soon as you reached England.'

'The police?' He was staring at me, white-faced. 'How could I?'

'But if you'd told them about the offer Dellimare made you . . .'

'Do you think they'd have believed me? It was only my word. I'd no proof. How could I possibly justify . . .' His gaze switched to the envelope lying on the table. 'You see this money?' He reached out and grabbed up a handful of the fivers. 'He offered it to me, the whole lot. He had it there in his cabin and he spilled the whole five thousand out in front of me – out of that envelope that's lying there; and I picked it up and threw it in his face and told him I'd see him in hell before I did his dirty work for him. That's when I warned him that I'd kill him if he tried to lose me the ship.' He paused, breathing heavily. 'And then that gale and the for'ard holds suddenly making water and the fire in the radio shack . . . when I found him down in that hold – ' He was still staring at me and his features were haggard and drawn, the way I'd first seen them. 'I was so sure I was justified – at the time,' he whispered.

'But it was an accident,' Mike said. 'Damn it, you didn't mean to kill him.'

He shook his head slowly, pushing his hand up through his hair. 'No, that's not true,' he said. 'I did mean to kill him. I was mad at the thought of what he'd tried to make me do – what he was doing to the ship. The first command I'd had in ten years . . .'

He was looking down at his glass again. 'I thought when I put her on the Minkies, that I could get back to her, get rid of his body and prove that he was trying to sink her – ' He was staring at me again. 'Can't you understand, Sands . . . I had to know I was justified.'

'But it was still an accident,' I said gently. 'You could have gone to the authorities . . .' I hesitated, and then added, 'There was a time when you were prepared to – when you altered course for Southampton after rounding Ushant.'

'I still had the ship then,' he muttered, and I realized then what his ship meant to a man like Patch. So long as he'd had the *Mary Deare*'s deck under his feet and he was in command he'd still had confidence in himself, in the rightness of his actions.

He reached out his hand for the bottle. 'Mind if I have another drink?' His tone was resigned.

I watched him pour it, understanding now how desperate was his need to justify himself. I remembered how he'd reacted to the sight of the crew huddled like sheep around Higgins in the office at Paimpol. His first command in ten years and the whole thing repeating itself. It was an appalling twist of fate. 'When did you feed last?' I asked him.

'I don't know. It doesn't matter.' He swallowed some of the drink, his hand still trembling, his body slack.

'I'll get you some food.' I got up and went through into the galley. The stew was still hot in the pressure-cooker and I put some on a plate and set it in front of him. And then I asked Mike to come up on deck. The freshening wind had thinned the mist, so that the hills were dim, humped-up shapes, their shadows thrown round the cove and falling away to the narrow gap of the entrance. I stood there for a moment, wondering how I was going to persuade him. But Mike had guessed what was in my mind. 'You want *Sea Witch*, is that it, John?'

I nodded. 'For four days,' I said. 'Five at the most. That's all.'

He was looking at me, his face pale in the faint glow of the riding light. 'Surely it would be better to put the whole thing in the hands of the authorities?' I didn't say anything. I didn't know how to make him understand the way I felt. And after a while, he said, 'You believe him then – about the Dellimare Company planning to sink the ship in deep water?'

'I don't know,' I murmured. I wasn't sure. 'But if you accept that the cargo has been switched, that the whole thing was planned . . .' I hesitated, remembering how scared Higgins had been. If Higgins had started that fire and knocked Patch out and panicked the crew . . . 'Yes,' I said. 'I think I do believe him.'

Mike was silent for some time then. He had turned away from me and was staring out towards the entrance. At length he said, 'You're sure about this, John? It's a hell of a risk you're taking for the fellow.'

'I'm quite sure,' I said.

He nodded. 'Okay. Then the sooner we get under way the better.'

'You don't have to come,' I said.

He looked at me with that slow, rather serious smile of his. '*Sea Witch* and I go together,' he said. 'You don't get the one without the other.' He glanced up at the masthead. The burgee hadn't been taken down and it showed the wind westerly. 'We'll be able to sail it.' He was thinking we'd make better time under sail, for our engine was geared for power, not speed.

Down below I found Patch leaning back, the glass in his hand, smoking a cigarette. He hadn't touched the food. His eyes were half closed and his head lolled. He didn't look up as we entered.

'We're getting under way,' I told him.

He didn't move.

'Leave him,' Mike said. 'We can manage. I'll go and start the engine.' He was already pulling on a sweater.

But Patch had heard. His head came slowly round. 'Where are you making for – Southampton?' His voice had no life in it.

'No,' I said. 'We're taking you out to the Minkies.'

He stared at me. 'The Minkies.' He repeated it slowly, his fuddled mind not taking it in. 'You're going out to the *Mary Deare*?' And then he was on his feet, the glass crashing to the floor, his body jarring the table. 'You mean it?' He lurched across to me, catching hold of me with both his hands. 'You're not saying that just to keep me quiet. You mean it, don't you?'

'Yes,' I said. 'I mean it.' It was like trying to convince a child.

'My God!' he said. 'My God, I thought I was finished.' He was suddenly laughing, shaking me, gripping Mike's hand. 'I think I'd have gone mad,' he said. 'The uncertainty. Ten years and you get a ship and you're in command again, and then . . . You don't know what it's like when you suddenly lose confidence in yourself.' He pushed his hands up through his hair, his eyes alight and eager. I'd never seen him like that before. He turned and scrabbled up a whole pile of the fivers that were lying on the table. 'Here. You take them.' He thrust them into my hand. 'I don't want them. They're yours now.' He wasn't drunk, just a little crazed – the reaction of nerves strung too taut.

I pushed the notes away. 'We'll talk about that later,' I said. 'Can you navigate into the Minkies without a chart?'

His mind seemed to snap suddenly into place. He hesitated – a seaman considering a nautical problem. 'You mean from Les Sauvages to the *Mary Deare*?'

'Yes.'

He nodded slowly. He was frowning, his mind groping for the bearings. 'Yes. Yes, I'm sure I can remember. It's only a question of the tide. You've got a nautical almanac?'

I nodded and it was settled. I had charts for the Channel. All I lacked was the large-scale chart of the Minkies. 'We'll hoist sail in here, before we get the hook up,' I said. I reached for my monkey jacket and slipped it on, and then we went up on deck and got the covers off the main and mizzen. I sent Mike to get the engine going whilst Patch and I put the battens in and hoisted the mainsail, tacking it down so that the luff was set up taut. The starter whined and the engine caught, throbbing at the deck under my feet. *Sea Witch* was suddenly alive. We hoisted the dinghy on board then and the ship bustled with activity as we got her ready for sea.

It was whilst I was up for'ard, hanking the big yankee jib on to the forestay, that I heard it – the beat of an engine coming in from the sea. I stood there for a moment, listening, and then I extinguished the riding light and ran aft, shouting to Mike to get the hook up. It might be just another yacht coming in, but it wasn't the night for yachtsmen to be risking their boats, feeling their way into a place like Lulworth, and I had no desire to be caught in here with Patch on board. We were outside the law and I wanted to get clear of the cove without being seen. I switched off the lights below and sent Patch for'ard to help Mike, and then I was at the wheel and the chain was coming in with a run as I manœuvred *Sea Witch* up to her anchor on the engine.

The sound of the boat coming in was quite clear now, the beat of its engines throbbing back from the cliffs. The white of her masthead light appeared in the gap, bobbing to the swell. The green eye of a starboard light showed, and then the red as she turned in.

'Up and down,' Mike called.

'Leave it there,' I called to him. 'Hoist the yankee.'

The big jib floated up, a blur of white in the darkness. I hauled in the sheet and *Sea Witch* began to glide through the water as I swung her bows towards the gap. The in-coming boat was right in the entrance now. 'What do you think it is – the police?' Mike asked as he came back aft to help trim the sheets.

'I don't know,' I said. 'Get the mizzen hoisted.' For an instant I saw Patch's face, a white glimmer in the darkness as he stared seaward, and then he went aft to help Mike. I was keeping the engine throttled right back so that they wouldn't hear it above the noise of their own engine, hoping I could slip out without their seeing us in the darkness.

There wasn't a great deal of wind in the cove, but we were moving, steadily gathering way. The other boat came in slowly. She had a spotlight and she flashed it on the rocks by the entrance, holding a middle course between them. And then she was inside and we were bearing straight down on her. Under sail I had no chance of giving her a wide berth. I just had to hold my course and hope that she'd turn away.

But she held straight on and we passed her so close that I could see the whole shape of her, a big sea-going motor boat with flared bow and a long sloping deck-house. I even caught a glimpse of the man in the wheelhouse, a dim figure peering at us out of the night.

And then their spotlight stabbed the darkness, momentarily blinding me, picking out the triangle of our mainsail in glaring white, and a voice hailed us. I think he was asking the name of our ship, but the words were lost in the roar of the engine as I opened the throttle wide, and we went steaming out through the gap. The sails flapped wildly as we came under the lee of the cliffs and the boat heaved to the swell. Then we were through and the sails filled. *Sea Witch* heeled, the water creaming back from her bows and sliding white past the cockpit as she surged forward under the thrust of power and sail.

'She's turning,' Mike shouted down to me.

I glanced over my shoulder. The motor boat's masthead steaming light and the red and green of her navigation lights were showing in the black outline of the land behind us. She was coming out through the gap.

Mike tumbled into the cockpit, hardening in the main sheet for me as I headed south on a broad reach. With the ship blacked-out – not even a binnacle light – I sailed by the wind, my head turned every now and then over my shoulder to watch the motor boat. Her masthead light began to dance as she met the swell in the entrance, and then it was swinging steadily, rhythmically as she pitched to the sea, and the red and green of her navigation lights remained fixed on us like two eyes. Her spotlight stabbed the darkness, showing glimpses of black, lumpy water as it probed the night.

'If we'd got away half an hour earlier . . .' Patch was staring aft.

'And if we'd been five minutes later,' Mike snapped, 'you'd be under arrest.' His voice sounded on edge and I knew he didn't like it any more than I did. 'I'll go and get the anchor on board.' He disappeared for'ard and I sent Patch to help him.

It was cold in the cockpit now that we were under way. But I don't think I noticed it. I was wondering about the boat behind us. It had gained on us slightly and the spotlight, reaching out to us across the tumbled waters, lit our sails with a ghostly radiance. It didn't probe any longer, but was held on us, so that I knew they'd picked us out. The drizzle had slackened again and our white sails made us conspicuous.

Up for'ard Mike was coiling down the halyards, whilst Patch lashed the anchor. They came aft together. 'John. Hadn't we better heave-to?'

'They haven't ordered you to.' Patch's voice was hard and urgent. 'You don't have to do anything till they signal instructions.' He was back at sea again and a man doesn't easily give up in his own element. He came down into the cockpit. His face had tightened so that there was strength in it again. 'Well, are you going on or not?' It wasn't exactly a challenge, certainly not a threat, and yet the way he said it made me wonder what he'd do if I refused.

Mike jerked round, his body bunched, his quick temper flaring. 'If we want to heave-to, we will.'

The spotlight was switched off. Sudden blackness descended on us. 'I was asking Sands.' Patch's voice trembled out of the darkness.

'John and I own this boat jointly,' Mike flung out. 'We've worked and planned and slaved our guts out to have our own outfit, and we're not going to risk it all to get you out of the mess you're in.' He stepped down into the cockpit, balancing himself to the pitch of the boat. 'You've got to heave-to,' he said to me. 'That boat is gradually coming up on us and when the police find we've got Patch on board, it's going to be damned hard to prove that we weren't slipping him out of the country, especially with all that cash sculling around below.' He leaned forward, gripping hold of my shoulder. 'Do you hear me, John?' He was shouting at me above the noise of the engine. 'You've got to heave-to before that police boat comes up on us.'

'It may not be the police,' I said. I had been thinking about it all the time they'd been up for'ard. 'The police would have sent a patrol car. They wouldn't have come by boat.'

'If it's not the police, then who the hell is it?'

I glanced over my shoulder, wondering whether perhaps imagination hadn't got the better of reason. But there was the boat, still following us. The white steaming light was swaying wildly, showing the slender stick of her mast and the outline of the deck-house. 'She certainly rolls,' I murmured.

'What's that?'

I turned to him then. 'Did you get a good look at her, Mike, as we came out?'

'Yes. Why?'

'What sort of a boat was she – could you see?'

'An old Parkhurst, I should say.' Mike's training as a marine engineer had given him a quite remarkable knowledge of power craft.

'You're certain of that?'

'I think so. Yes, I'm sure she was.'

I asked him to go down below then and look up *Griselda* in Lloyd's Register. 'And if she's in the book and her description fits, then I'd like an estimate of her speed.'

He hesitated, glancing quickly from me to Patch, and then he disappeared for'ard towards the main hatch. 'And if it is *Griselda*?' Patch asked.

'Then she was chartered this morning,' I said. 'By somebody who was in that Court.'

The spotlight was on us again and he was staring at me. 'Are you sure?'

I nodded and I could see him working it out for himself. *Sea Witch* heeled to a gust of wind and I felt the drag of the prop. Spray splashed my face. And then Mike was back. 'How did you know it was *Griselda*?' he asked me.

'I was right, was I?'

'Yes – it's either *Griselda* or a sister ship. Fifty-foot over all. Built by Parkhurst in 1931.'

'And her top speed?'

'Hard to say. She's got two six-cylinder Parkhurst engines. But they're the original engines and it depends how they've been maintained. Flat out, I'd say she might do a little over eight knots.'

Sea Witch was heeling further now and the wave-tops were lopping over on to the foredeck. 'In calm water.'

'Yes, in calm water.'

The wind was rising and already the seas were beginning to break. I was thinking that in a little over two hours the tide would turn. It would be west-going then and the freshening wind would kick up a short, steep sea. It would reduce *Griselda*'s speed by at least a knot. 'I'm standing on,' I told Mike. 'We'll try and shake them off during the night.' And then I explained about the yacht broker I had met with Hal and how Higgins had warned me. 'Higgins even guessed you'd come down to Lulworth,' I said, turning to Patch.

'Higgins!' He turned and stared aft. The spotlight was on his face and there was something in the way his eyes shone – it might have been anger or fear or exultation; I couldn't tell. And then the spotlight was switched off and he was just a black shape standing there beside me.

'Well, if it's only the Dellimare Company – ' Mike's voice sounded relieved. 'They can't do anything, can they?'

Patch swung round on him. 'You don't seem to realize . . .' His voice came hard and abrupt out of the darkness, the sentence bitten off short. But I had caught his mood and I looked back over my shoulder. Was it my imagination or was the motor boat nearer now? I found myself looking all round, searching for the lights of another ship. But there was nothing – only the blackness of the night and the white of the breaking wave-tops rushing at us out of the darkness. 'Well, we go on. Is that right?' I wasn't sure what I ought to do.

'You've no alternative,' Patch said.

'Haven't we?' Mike stepped down into the cockpit. 'We could run for Poole. That boat's following us and . . . Well, I think we should turn the whole thing over to the authorities.' His voice sounded nervous.

A wave broke against the weather bow, showering spray aft, and we heeled to a gust so that our lee decks were awash. The sea was shallower here. There were overfalls and *Sea Witch* pitched violently with a short, uncomfortable motion, the screw juddering under the stern and the bows slamming into the waves so that water was sluicing across the foredeck. 'For God's sake cut that engine!' Patch shouted at me. 'Can't you feel the drag of the prop?'

Mike swung round on him. 'You don't run this boat.'

'It's stopping our speed,' Patch said.

He was right. I had been conscious of it for some time. 'Switch it off, will you, Mike?' I asked.

He hesitated and then dived into the charthouse. The noise of the engine died, leaving a stillness in which the sound of the sea seemed unnaturally loud. Under sail alone, the boat merged with the elements for which she had been designed, fitting herself to the pattern of wind and wave. The movement was easier. Waves ceased to break over the foredeck.

But though Patch had been right, Mike came back out of the charthouse in a mood of blazing anger. 'You seem bloody certain we're going to try and race that boat for you,' he said. And then, turning to me, he added, 'Take my advice, John. Turn down-wind and head for Poole.'

'Down-wind,' Patch said, 'the motor boat will be faster than you.'

'Well, head up-wind then and make for Weymouth.'

'It's a dead beat,' I said.

And Patch added, 'Either way she'll overhaul you.'

'What's that matter?' Mike demanded. 'They can't do anything. They've got the law on their side. That's all. They can't do anything.'

'God Almighty!' Patch said. 'Don't you understand yet?' He leaned forward, his face thrust close to mine. 'You tell him, Sands. You've met Gundersen. You know the set-up now.' He stared at me, and then he swung round to face Mike again. 'Listen!' he said. 'Here was a plan to clean up over a quarter of a million pounds. The cargo was switched and sold to the Chinks. That part of it went all right. But all the rest went wrong. The captain refused to play his part. They tried to sink her in a gale and they failed. Higgins was left to do the job on his own and he botched it.' His voice was pitched high in the urgency of his effort to communicate what he believed. 'Can't you see it from their point of view . . . twelve men drowned, an old man dead, possibly murdered, and the ship herself lying out there on the Minkies. They daren't let me reach the *Mary Deare*. And they daren't let you reach her either. They daren't even let you get into port now – not until they've disposed of the *Mary Deare*.'

Mike stared at him. 'But that's fantastic,' he breathed.

'Why fantastic? They must know I'm on board. And you wouldn't have sailed if you hadn't believed my story. Imagine what they face if the truth comes out.'

Mike turned to me. 'Do you believe this, John?' His face was very pale. He sounded bewildered.

'I think we'd better try and shake them off,' I said. Patch had his own reasons for driving us on. But I knew I didn't want that boat to catch up with us in the dark.

'But good God! This is the English Channel. They can't do anything to us here.' He stared at Patch and myself, waiting for us to answer him. 'Well, what the hell can they do?' And then he looked out at the blackness that surrounded us, realizing gradually that it made no difference that we were in the Channel. There were just the three of us alone in a black waste of tumbled water that spilled to white on the crests, and without another word he got the log line out of the locker and went aft to stream it astern.

'We go on then,' Patch said. The sudden relief from tension made his voice sound tired. It reminded me that he had had no sleep the night before and no food, that for days he'd been under a great strain.

Mike came back into the cockpit. 'I think we're holding them now,' he said. I glanced back at *Griselda*. Her navigation lights were masked every now and then by the marching wave-tops. 'When the tide turns,' I said, 'we'll beat up to windward and see if that will shake them off.' I got up stiffly from behind the wheel. 'Will you take the first watch, Mike?' It would have to be two hours on and four off, with one man alone at the wheel and the other two on call. We were desperately short-handed for a hard sail like this. I gave him the wheel and went through into the charthouse to enter up the log.

Patch followed me in. 'Have you thought about who will be on board that motor boat?' he asked me. I shook my head, wondering what was coming, and he added, 'It won't be Gundersen, you know.'

'Who will it be then?'

'Higgins.'

'What's it matter which of them it is?' I asked. 'What are you trying to tell me?'

'Just this,' he said earnestly. 'Gundersen is a man who would only take calculated risks. But if Higgins is in control of that boat . . .' He stared at me, watching to see whether I had understood his point.

'You mean he's desperate?'

'Yes.' Patch looked at me for a moment. 'There's no need to tell young Duncan. If Higgins doesn't stop us before we get to that salvage tug, he's done for. When he's arrested, the others will panic. Burrows, for one, will turn Queen's evidence. You understand?' He turned away then. 'I'll go and get some food inside me.' But in the doorway he hesitated. 'I'm sorry,' he said. 'I didn't mean to land you in a thing like this.'

I finished entering up the log and turned in, fully-clothed, on the charthouse bunk. But I didn't sleep much. The movement was uncomfortable, and every time I looked out through the open doorway I could see *Griselda*'s lights bobbing in the darkness astern of us, and then I would listen to the sound of the wind in the rigging, alert for the slightest indication that it was slackening. Twice Mike had to call me out to help him winch in the sheets, and at two o'clock I took over the helm.

The tide had turned and the seas were steep and breaking. We altered course to south-west, sheeting in the sails till they were almost flat as we came on to the wind. It was cold then with the wind on our faces and the spray slatting against our oilskins as *Sea Witch* beat to windward, bucking the seas and busting the wave-tops open, water cascading from her bows.

Behind us, *Griselda*'s navigation lights followed our change of course and the white of her masthead light danced crazily in the night as she wallowed and pitched and rolled in our wake. But a power boat doesn't fit herself to the pattern of the water the way a boat under sail does and gradually the red and green lights dipped more frequently below the level of the waves, until at last all we could see was her steaming light dancing like a will-o'-the-wisp on the wave-tops.

Mike's voice reached out to me through the noise of wind and sea: 'We've got them now.' He was excited. 'If we go about . . .' The rest of it was lost to me, whipped away by the wind, drowned in the crash of a wave bursting against the bows. But I knew what was in his mind. If we went on to the other tack, sailing north-west, instead of south-west, there was a good chance that they wouldn't notice our change of course, even though the night had become brilliant with stars. And once clear of them we could turn down-wind, get to the east of them and make for the Alderney Race.

There is no doubt in my mind now that Mike was right and, had I done as he suggested, the disaster for which we were headed might have been avoided. But the changed motion induced by our heading into the wind had brought Patch on deck. I could see him sitting on the main hatch, staring aft for glimpses of *Griselda*, and I wondered what his reaction would be if we went over on to the port tack, heading back towards the English coast. Also, we were over-canvassed, and when you go about there are backstays to set up as well as the sheets to handle; one slip and we could lose our mast!

'I don't like it,' I told Mike. We were short-handed and it was night. Also, of course, in those conditions, when you are tired and cold and wet, there is a great temptation to sit tight and do nothing. I thought we were drawing ahead of them.

Apparently Mike had the same thought, for, instead of pressing his point, he shrugged his shoulders and went into the charthouse to turn in. It seems extraordinary to me now that I didn't appreciate the significance of the fact that *Griselda*'s light was no longer showing astern of us, but way out on the port quarter. Had I done so, I should have known that we were not gaining on her, merely diverging from her. She was steering a more southerly course, maintaining her speed by avoiding the head-on battering of the seas. And I for my part – as so often happens at night – thought our own speed was greater than it was.

By the end of my watch it was clouding over and the wind was slackening. I called Patch and when he came up, we eased the sheets and altered course to sou'-sou'-west. We were no longer butting into the seas then, but following the lines of the waves with a wild, swooping movement. The wind was free and *Sea Witch* was going like a train.

I heated some soup then and we drank it in the cockpit, watching the dawn break. It came with a cold, bleak light and Patch stood, staring aft. But there was nothing to be seen but a waste of grey, tumbled water. 'It's all right,' I said. 'We've left them way behind.'

He nodded, not saying anything. His face looked grey. 'At this rate we'll raise the Casquets inside of two hours,' I said, and I left him then and went below to get some sleep.

An hour later Mike woke me, shouting to me to come up on deck, his voice urgent. 'Look over there, John,' he said as I emerged from the hatch. He was pointing away to port and, at first, I could see nothing. My sleep-dimmed eyes absorbed the cold daylight and the drabness of sea and sky, and then on the lift of a wave I thought I saw something, a stick maybe or a spar-buoy raised aloft out there where the march of the waves met the horizon. I screwed up my eyes, focusing them, and the next time I balanced to the upward swoop of the deck, I saw it clearly – the mast of a small ship. It lifted itself up out of the waves and behind it came the hull of the boat itself, drab white in the morning light.

'*Griselda*?' I said.

Mike nodded and passed me the glasses. She was certainly rolling. I could see the water streaming off her and every now and then a wave burst against her bows, throwing up a cloud of spray. 'If we'd gone about last night . . .'

'Well, we didn't,' I said. I glanced aft to where Patch sat

559

hunched over the wheel in borrowed oilskins. 'Does he know?' I asked.

'Yes. He saw her first.'

'What did he say?'

'Nothing. He didn't seem surprised.'

I stared at the boat through the glasses again, trying to estimate her speed. 'What are we doing?' I asked. 'Did you get a log reading at six?'

'Yes. We did eight in the last hour.'

Eight knots! I glanced up at the sails. They were wind-bellied out, tight and hard, solid tons of weight pulling at the mast, hauling the boat through the water. My God! it was hard that we hadn't shaken them off after a whole night of sailing.

'I've been thinking,' Mike said. 'If they come up with us . . .'

'Well?'

'There's not much they can do really, is there? I mean . . .' He hesitated, glancing at me uncertainly.

'I hope you're right,' I said and went into the charthouse. I was tired and I didn't want to think about it. I worked out our dead-reckoning, based on miles logged, courses sailed and tides, and found we were ten miles north-north-west of the Casquets. In two hours' time the tide would be east-going, setting us in towards Alderney and the Cherbourg Peninsula. But that damned boat lay between us and the coast, and there was no getting away from her, not in daylight.

I stayed on in the charthouse and got the forecast: wind moderating later, some fog patches locally. A depression centred over the Atlantic was moving slowly east.

Shortly after breakfast we raised the Casquets – the north-western bastion of the Channel Islands. The tide turned and began to run against us and we had the Casquets with us for a long time, a grey, spiked helmet of a rock against which the seas broke. We thrashed our way through the steamer lane that runs up-Channel from Ushant, seeing only two ships, and those hull-down on the horizon. And then we raised Guernsey Island and the traffic in the steamer lane was just smudges of smoke where sky and sea met.

All morning Patch remained on deck, taking his trick at the helm, dozing in the cockpit or sitting staring at the grey acres that separated us from *Griselda*. Sometimes he would dive into the charthouse and work frenziedly with parallel rule and dividers, checking our course and our ETA at the Minkies. Once I suggested that he went below and got some sleep, but all he said was

'Sleep? I can't sleep till I see the *Mary Deare*.' And he stayed there, grey and exhausted, existing on his nerves, as he had done all through the Enquiry.

I think he was afraid to go below – afraid that when he couldn't see her *Griselda* would somehow creep up on us. He was frighteningly tired. He kept on asking me about the tides. We had no tidal chart and it worried him. Even when the tide turned around midday, pushing us westward again, he kept on checking our bearing on the jagged outline of Guernsey Island.

I should perhaps explain that the tidal surge of six hours flood and six hours ebb that shifts the whole body of water of the English Channel builds up to an extraordinary peak in the great bight of the French coast that contains the Channel Islands. At 'springs', when the tides are greatest, it sluices in and out of the narrow gap between Alderney and the mainland at a rate of up to 7 knots. Its direction in the main body of the Channel Islands rotates throughout the twelve hours. Moreover, the rise and fall of tide is as much as from 30 to 40 feet.

I mention this to explain our preoccupation with the tide and because it has a bearing on what followed. Moreover, the whole area being strewn with submerged reefs, rock outcrops and islands, there is always a sense of tension when navigating in this section of the Channel.

Holding to our course, we were headed direct for the central mass of Guernsey. I was relying on the westward thrust of the tide to push us clear, and as we closed with the broken water that marked the submerged rocks known as Les Frettes, we were all of us watching to see what *Griselda* would do. In fact, she had no alternative, and when the rock cliffs of the island were close to port she altered course to come in astern of us.

The westernmost tip of Guernsey is marked by Les Hanois, a lighthouse set seaward on a group of rocks. We passed so close that we could see every detail of it – the cormorants standing like vultures on the rocks and the swell breaking white all along the edge; and dead astern of us *Griselda* followed in our wake, pitching and rolling with the spray flying from her bow wave. She was less than a quarter of a mile away and Patch stood with his body braced against the charthouse, staring at her through the glasses.

'Well,' I said, 'is it Higgins?' I could see a figure moving on the deck.

'Yes,' he said. 'Yes, it's Higgins all right. And Yules, too. There's another of them in the wheelhouse, but I can't see who it is.'

He handed me the glasses. I could recognize Higgins all right. He was standing by the rail, staring at us, his big body balanced to the movement of the boat. Higgins and Yules and Patch – three of the men who had sailed the *Mary Deare*! And here we were, within forty miles of where the ship was stranded.

Mike was at the wheel and he suddenly called to me. 'If we turn now, we could make Peter Port ahead of them.'

It was a straight run before the wind along the southern coast of the island. We could make St Martin's Point without their gaining on us and then a few miles under engine and we should be in Peter Port. I glanced at Patch. He had stepped down into the cockpit. 'I'll relieve you,' he said. It wasn't a suggestion. It was an order.

'No.' Mike was staring at him, anger flaring up into his eyes.

'I said I'll relieve you.' Patch reached for the wheel.

'I heard what you said.' Mike swung the wheel over, shouting to me to ease the sheets. But Patch had his hands on the wheel, too. Standing, he had more purchase and he slowly got it back, holding it there whilst Mike shouted obscenities at him. Their two faces were within a foot of each other – Patch's hard and tense, Mike's livid with rage. They were like that for a long two minutes, held immobile by the counteracting force of their muscles like two statues.

And then the moment when we had any choice of action was past. *Griselda*, clear of Les Hanois rocks, was altering course to get between us and Peter Port. Patch had seen it and he said, 'You've no choice now.' He hadn't relaxed his grip of the wheel, but the tension was out of his voice. Mike stopped cursing at him. He seemed to understand, for he turned his head and stared at the motor boat. Then he let go of the wheel and stood up. 'Since you appear to be skippering this boat, you'd better bloody well steer her. But by Christ!' he added, 'if anything happens to her . . .' He stared coldly at me, still trembling with anger, and went below.

'I'm sorry,' Patch said. He had seated himself at the wheel and his voice was weary.

'This isn't your boat,' I reminded him.

He shrugged his shoulders, looking round at *Griselda*. 'What else did you expect me to do?'

There was no point in discussing it. We were committed now to go on until we reached the *Mary Deare*. But if the wind dropped . . . 'Suppose Higgins catches up with us?' I said.

He looked at me quickly. 'He mustn't.' And then he added,

'We've got to get there first.'

'Yes, but suppose he does?' I was thinking that after all Higgins had got to keep within the law. 'He can't do very much.'

'No?' He laughed a little wildly. 'How do you know what Higgins can do? He's frightened.' He looked at me, sideways out of the corners of his eyes. 'Wouldn't you be frightened if you were Higgins?' And then he glanced up at the sails and his voice was quiet and practical again as he asked me to ease the sheets and he altered course for the north-west Minkies buoy.

After that we didn't talk any more and gradually I became conscious of the sound of the motor boat's engine. It was very faint at first, a gentle undertone to the swish of the sea going past, but it warned me that the wind was easing. The overcast had thinned and a humid glare hung over the water so that the outline of Jersey Island away to port was barely visible. I started the engine and from that moment I knew *Griselda* would overtake us.

The forecast announced that the depression over the Atlantic was deepening, moving eastwards faster. But it wouldn't help us. All the time the wind was dropping now and *Griselda* was coming up abeam of us, keeping between us and Jersey Island. The glare faded, leaving sea and sky a chill, luminous grey. There was no horizon any more. Patch went below to get some more clothes. It had suddenly become much colder and the wind was fluky, blowing in sudden puffs.

I sat at the wheel and watched *Griselda* draw steadily ahead of the beam, wallowing in the swell. I wondered what Higgins would do, what I would do in his place. I tried to think it out rationally. But it's difficult to think rationally when you're cold and tired and sitting alone, almost at water level, isolated in an opaque void. That sense of isolation! I had felt it at sea before, but never so strongly. And now it chilled me with a feeling of foreboding. The sea had an oily look as the big swells lumbered up from the west and rolled beneath us.

I didn't notice the fog at first. I was thinking of Higgins – and then suddenly a grey-white plasma was creeping towards us across the sea, shrouding and enveloping the water in its folds. Mike came up from below and I gave him the wheel, shouting for Patch to come on deck. *Griselda* had seen the fog, too, and she had turned in towards us. I watched her coming, waiting for the fog to close round us and hide us from her. 'We'll go about as soon as we lose sight of her,' I said as Patch came up through the hatch.

She wasn't more than two cables away when her outline blurred and then she vanished, swallowed abruptly. 'Lee-ho!' Mike called and spun the wheel. *Sea Witch* turned into the wind and through it, the big yankee flapping as I let go the jib sheet. And then the main boom was across and Patch and I were winching in the starboard jib sheet as we gathered way on the port tack.

We were doubling back on our tracks through a cold, dead, clammy world and I straightened up, listening to the beat of the motor boat's engines, trying to estimate her position, wondering whether the fog was thick enough for us to lose her.

But Higgins must have guessed what we'd do, or else we had lost too much time in going about, for the sound of *Griselda*'s engines was abeam of us and, just as I realized this, the shape of her reappeared. Her bows seemed to rip the curtain of fog apart and suddenly the whole of her was visible, coming straight for us.

She was coming in at right-angles, her engines running flat out and her sharp bows cutting into the swell, spray flying up past her wheelhouse. I shouted to Mike to go about again. We were heeled over, going fast and I knew that if both boats held their course we must hit. And when he didn't do anything, my throat was suddenly dry. 'Put her about!' I yelled at him. And at the same moment Patch shouted, 'Turn, man! For God's sake turn!'

But Mike stood there, his body braced against the wheel, staring at the on-coming boat with a set expression on his face. 'Let him turn,' he said through his clenched teeth. 'I'm holding on.'

Patch jumped down into the cockpit. 'He's going to ram you.'

'He wouldn't dare.' And Mike held obstinately to his course, watching *Griselda* through narrowed eyes, his face suddenly white. Out of the corner of my eye I saw Higgins lean out of his wheelhouse. He was shouting and his powerful voice reached across to us through the roar of engines – 'Stand by! I'm coming alongside.' And then *Griselda* was turning, swinging to come in on our bows and crowd us up into the wind.

Everything happened very fast then. Mike shouted at us to ease the sheets. 'I'm going to cut under her stern.' He turned the wheel and *Sea Witch* began to swing her bows in towards the motor boat. *Griselda* was halfway through her turn. There was just room for us to pass astern of her if we turned quickly.

But things went wrong. I eased out on the jib sheet, but Patch, unaccustomed to sail, failed to ease out on the main. And at the same moment we heeled to a puff of wind. It was that unlucky puff of wind that did it. With the full weight of it on the mainsail, *Sea Witch* failed to come round fast enough. And Higgins had throttled down to bring his boat alongside us. We drove straight into *Griselda*'s counter, drove straight into it with all the force of our powerful engines and tons of wind-driven canvas. We caught her on the port side just a few feet from her stern as it was swinging in towards us on the turn. There was a rending, splintering crash; our bows reared up as though to climb over her and then we stopped with a horrible, jarring shudder. I caught a glimpse of Yules, staring open-mouthed, and then I was flung forward against the charthouse. The boom jerked free of the mast and swung in towards me. I threw up my arm and it caught my shoulder a shattering blow, wrenching it from its socket and flinging me against the guardrails.

I remember clutching at the guardrails, blinded with pain, and then I was lying on the deck, my face pressed close against a metal jib sheet lead and the noise of rending wood was still there and somebody was screaming. I shifted myself and pain stabbed through me. I was looking down into the water and a man's body drifted past. It was Yules and he was thrashing wildly at the water, his face white and scared with a lock of hair washed over his eyes.

The deck vibrated under me. It was as though compressed-air drills had been put to work on the hull. I could feel the juddering all through my body. 'You all right?' Mike reached a hand down and dragged me to my feet. My teeth clenched on my lip.

'The bastard!' He was staring for'ard, his face paper-white, all the freckles showing a dull orange against his pasty skin, and his hair flaming red. 'I'll kill him.' He was shaking with anger.

I turned to see Higgins erupt from *Griselda*'s wheelhouse. He was shouting something, his great, bellowing voice audible above the noise of the engines and the continuing, rending sound of wood. The two boats were locked together and he caught hold of our bowsprit, his teeth bared like an animal, his head sunk into his bull neck and his shoulder muscles bunched as he tried to tear the boats apart with his bare hands.

Mike moved then. He had the grim, avenging look of a man who has seen something he loves and has worked for wantonly smashed up. I called to him, for the fool was running for'ard up the sloped deck, yelling at Higgins, cursing him; and he flung himself from the bowsprit, straight at the man, hitting out at him in a blind fury of rage.

The boats separated then with a tearing of wood and bubbling of water and I didn't see any more. Patch had put our engine into reverse and I staggered into the cockpit, shouting at him to stop. 'Mike is still there. You can't leave him.'

'Do you want the belly torn out of your boat?' he demanded, turning the wheel as *Sea Witch* began to go astern. 'Those props were drilling the guts out of her.' Dimly I realized that he meant *Griselda*'s props and understood what had caused the deck planks to vibrate under my body.

I turned and watched as the gap between us and the motor boat widened. *Griselda* was down by the stern with a hole torn out of her port quarter as though a battering-ram had hit her. Higgins was going back into the wheelhouse. There was nobody else on her deck. I suddenly felt sick and tired. 'What happened to him?' I asked. The sickly-sweet taste of blood was in my mouth where I'd bitten through my lip. My arm and all that side of my body was heavy and numb with pain. 'Did you see what happened?'

'He's all right,' Patch said. 'Just knocked cold.' He started to ask me about my shoulder, but I was telling him to get into forward gear and start sailing again. 'Don't lose her!' Already *Griselda*'s outlines were fading and a moment later she disappeared. Patch had put the gear lever into neutral and we could hear her engines then, racing with an ugly, grinding noise. There was a sharp report and, a little later, another. After that we couldn't hear her any more.

'Prop shafts by the sound of it,' Patch said.

Sails and mast and boat began to spin before my eyes and I sat down. Patch seemed immensely tall, standing at the wheel, and his head swung dizzily over me. I steadied myself and the roll of a swell lapped into the cockpit. I stared at it stupidly, watching the water roll back down the forward, sloping deck. And then the engine spluttered and gave out.

I shook my head, bracing myself against the dizziness that threatened to overwhelm me. There was nobody at the helm. I called to Patch and struggled to my feet. He came up out of the main hatch, his trousers dripping. 'It's up to the galley already.' And then my eyes took in the tilt of the deck, following it down to where the bowsprit was buried in the back of a wave. All the foredeck was awash. I stared at it, taking it in slowly, whilst he pushed past me into the charthouse. He came out with a jack-knife in his hand. 'She's going down,' I said. My voice sounded dead and hopeless in my ears.

'Yes,' he said. 'Not much time.' And he began slashing at the dinghy tie-ers. I watched him hoist the praam over so that she fell with her keel on the guardrails and he was able to slide her into the water.

We were still sailing, moving sluggishly through the water, and over Patch's back, as he bent to secure the dinghy painter, I caught a glimpse of *Griselda* again, a vague shape rolling sluggishly on the edge of visibility.

'Is there any food up here?' Patch was gathering up things from the charthouse and tossing them into the dinghy – blankets, duffle coats, torches, flares, even the hand-bearing compass.

'Some chocolate.' I got it from the drawer of the chart table – three small slabs and some sweets. I got life-jackets, too, from the locker aft. But my movements were slow and clumsy and by the time I had dropped them in the dinghy the whole length of the deck was awash, the mast tilted forward and the foot of the yankee below the water.

'Quick!' Patch said. 'In you get.' He was already untying the painter. I clambered in. It wasn't difficult. The dinghy rode level with the deck. He followed me and pushed off.

I never saw her go down. As we rowed away from her, she slowly disappeared into the fog, her stern a little cocked-up, the big jib and the mizzen still set, and nothing but sea for'ard of the charthouse. She looked a strange sight – like a ghost of a ship doomed everlastingly to sail herself under. I could have wept as she faded and was suddenly gone.

I turned then to look at *Griselda*. She was lying like a log, badly down by the stern and rolling slowly to the long swell – as useless as only a motor boat can be when her engines are out of action. 'Pull on your right,' I told Patch.

He stared at me, not saying anything, his body moving rhythmically to the swing of the oars. 'For God's sake pull on your right,' I said. 'You're still not headed for *Griselda*.'

'We're not going to *Griselda*.'

I didn't understand for a moment. 'But where else . . .' My voice broke off abruptly and I felt suddenly deadly scared. He had the box of the hand-bearing compass set up at his feet, the lid open. His eyes were watching it as he rowed. He was steering a compass course. 'My God!' I cried. 'You're not going to try and make it in the dinghy?'

'Why not?'

'But what about Mike?' I was suddenly desperate. I could see Higgins struggling to get his dinghy into the water. 'You can't do it.' I seized hold of his hand as he leaned forward, gripping hold of one of the oars, pain bursting like an explosive charge in my body. 'You can't do it, I tell you.'

He stared at me, his face only a foot or two from mine. 'No?' His voice grated in the stillness, and faint across the water came a cry for help – a desperate, long-drawn-out cry. He wrenched the oar free of me and began to row again. 'If you don't like it, you can get out and swim for it like that poor bastard.' He nodded across his left shoulder and at the same moment the cry came again. This time I was able to pick him out on the lift of a swell, a black head and two dripping arms thrashing their way towards us. 'H-e-lp!'

Patch rowed on, ignoring the cry. 'Are you going to leave him to drown?' I said, leaning forward, trying with my voice to touch some spark of humanity in him.

'It's Yules,' he answered. 'Let Higgins pick him up.'

'And Mike?' I said. 'What about Mike?'

'He'll be all right. That boat isn't going to sink.'

The oars dipped and rose, dipped and rose, his body swinging back and forth. And I sat there and watched him row away from the man. What else could I do? My shoulder had been driven out of its socket; he had only to touch it to send pain searing through me, and he knew it. I thought maybe he was right about the boat. It was only the stern that was damaged. All the fore part would be water-tight. And Higgins would pick Yules up. He had his dinghy launched now and was pulling away from *Griselda*. In the weird, fog-belt light he looked like a giant specimen of those insects that are called water-boatmen. Yules had seen him coming and had ceased to thrash about in the water. He was directly between us and Higgins and he lay still in the water, not crying out any more, just waiting to be picked up.

I don't know why I should have stayed, twisted round like that, in a position that gave me a lot of pain. But I felt I had to see him picked up. I had to know that there was no justification for the feeling of horror that had suddenly gripped me.

Higgins was rowing fast, a long, sweeping stroke that was full of power, and at each pull a little froth of white water showed at the dinghy's blunt bows. Every now and then he turned and looked over his shoulder, and I knew that it was at us he was looking and not at the man in the water.

We were pulling away from Yules all the time and I couldn't be sure how near Higgins was to him. But I heard Yules call out. 'Alf!' And he raised one hand. 'I'm here.' The words were distinct and very clear in the stillness of the fog. And then suddenly he was shouting and swimming with frantic desperation, his arms flailing the water, his feet kicking at the surface.

But Higgins never checked, never spoke a word to him. He left him to drown and the oars dipped and rose with terrible regularity, the water streaming from them at every stroke as he came after us.

There was one last despairing cry, and then silence. Sickened, I turned to look at Patch. 'It's a bigger dinghy than ours,' he said. He meant it as an explanation. He meant that Higgins couldn't afford to stop – not if he was to catch up with us. His face was quite white. He was rowing harder now, the sweat glistening on his forehead. His words sent a cold shiver through me, and I sat there, rigid, all pain momentarily forgotten.

After that I was conscious all the time of the dinghy behind us. I can see it still, like a deadly water-beetle crawling after us across the sea, everlastingly following us through an unreal miasma of fog; and I can hear the creak of the rowlocks, the dip and splash of the oars. And I can see Patch, too, his set face leaning towards me and then pulling back, endlessly moving back and forth as he tugged at the oars, tugged till his teeth were clenched with the pain of his blistered hands, until the blisters broke and the blood dripped on the oars – hour after wretched hour.

At one time Higgins was less than fifty yards behind us and I could see every detail of his boat. It was a gay blue metal dinghy, a little battered, with the paint flaking and dulled with age, and round the gunn'ls was a heavy canvas fend-off. The thing was meant to hold five or six people and it had bluff bows so that every time he pulled it smiled an ugly, puffy smile as the thrust piled the water up in front of it.

But he had used his brute strength recklessly and he didn't gain on us any more.

The fog thinned out as night fell until it was no more than a tattered veil through which we caught glimpses of the stars. The young moon gave it a queer luminosity so that we could still see Higgins following us, little drops of phosphoresence marking the oar blades as they lifted clear of the water.

We stopped once and Patch managed to jerk my shoulder back into its socket, and a little later I moved over to the centre thwart and took the left oar, rowing one-handed. Though I was in considerable pain, we were fairly well balanced, for by then he was very tired.

We continued like that all night, holding our course by the hand-bearing compass that stood at our feet, its card glowing faintly. The moon set and the luminosity faded. We lost sight of Higgins. A wind sprang up and waves broke on the swell, slopping water over the gunn'ls. But it died away again about four and at last the stars paled in the first glimmer of returning daylight. It was one of those cold, cloud-streaked dawns that come reluctantly. It showed a lumpy sea, full of tidal swirls, and a blanket of fog lay ahead of us, clamped down between us and the coast of France.

We breakfasted on three squares of chocolate. It was half of all we had left. The woodwork of the dinghy was beaded with dew, our clothes sodden with it. Water slopped about over the floor-boards as we pitched in the sea, and in our exhaustion it was becoming more and more difficult to row a course. 'How much further?' I gasped.

Patch looked at me, his face grey, the eyes deep-sunk. 'I don't know,' he breathed. His lips were all cracked and rimed with salt. He frowned, trying to concentrate his mind. 'Tide's west-going. Be with us in two hours.' He dipped his hand in the sea and wiped salt water over his face. 'Shouldn't be long.'

Not long! I gritted my teeth. The salt was behind my eyeballs, in my mouth; it pricked my skin. The dawn's chill gripped me. I wished to God I'd never met this gaunt stranger who rowed like death at my shoulder. My mind blurred to a vision of Mike and our plans. And now the future was dead, *Sea Witch* gone and nothing in the world to think about but the Minkies, with each stroke an agony.

The sea at dawn had been empty. I could have sworn it had been empty. I had searched it carefully – every trough, every swirl, every sudden humped-up heap of water. There had been nothing – absolutely nothing. And now, suddenly, I was looking at a speck away over Patch's shoulder. The sun was coming up in a great ball of fire and the clouds that streaked the east were glowing orange and blazing to red at their edges – and all this vivid surge of colour, imprinted in the sea, seemed designed solely to show me that speck etched black in silhouette. It was a boat with two oars and a man rowing.

Ten minutes later the fog folded its clammy blanket round us again. The speck blurred and vanished. And at that moment I thought I heard a bell, very faint to the east of us. But when we stopped rowing it was gone. There wasn't a sound, except the sea. It was all round us in our grey, boxed-in world – the wet slop of water. But a little later there was a murmuring and a sucking in the veil through which our eyes couldn't see, and almost immediately the fog darkened, became black, and a shape slid past us like the towering superstructure of a battleship. It was there for an instant, blurred and indistinct, a great mass of black rock with the swell frothing gently at its base, and then it was gone as the tide hurried us on. 'My God! We're there,' I gasped.

We had stopped rowing and all around us was the murmur of the sea. Another rock appeared out of the grey curtain of the fog, a sinister pillar of rock like a crooked finger that slid stealthily by with a froth of white water at its foot as though it were sailing past us. For a moment that damnable fog almost convinced me that I was in a geological nightmare in which the rocks steamed through the water under their own power. And then a swell came up, grew big and broke suddenly. Water surged over the gunn'l and we were thrown backwards as the dinghy hit a submerged rock. The tide swung us round and dragged us clear before the next swell broke. We were soaked, the dinghy half-full of water. It was hopeless to go on with the tide swirling us through a maze of dangerous rocks. We had reached the Minkies, but in an area of reefs almost twenty miles by ten we had no hope of getting our bearings. 'We'll have to wait till the fog clears,' Patch said. 'It's too dangerous – almost dead low water.'

In the lee of an ugly island of rock we found a little inlet where the water was still, like glass, tied the dinghy to an up-ended slab and clambered stiffly out. We stamped and moved about, but the sweat still clung to us in an icy film and we shivered under our sodden duffle coats. We ate the last of our chocolate and talked a little, grateful for the sound of our voices in that cold, dismal place.

I suppose it was inevitable that Patch should have talked about the *Mary Deare*. We were so close to her, frustrated by the fog. He talked about Rice for a bit and then he was telling me about Taggart's death. He seemed to want to talk about it. 'Poor devil!' he whispered. 'For the sake of that girl of his he'd sold his soul in every port in the Far East. He'd ruined his health and drunk himself stupid, engaging in every shady deal that would pay him more than a captain's wage. That's why they got him up from Singapore.'

'Did Gundersen engage him then?' I asked.

'Probably. I don't know.' He shrugged his shoulders. 'Whoever it was, they picked the wrong moment. The old vulture was going back home to his daughter, and he wasn't going to sink a ship on his last voyage.'

'And so Dellimare got rid of him – is that what you're suggesting?' I asked.

He shook his head. 'No, I don't think he intended to kill him. I think he just got hold of his liquor and was waiting until the old

571

man was sufficiently softened up to do what he wanted. He couldn't have known he'd die that night.' He smiled at me out of the corner of his mouth. 'But it amounts to the same thing, doesn't it?' He had sat with Taggart for several hours that night, listening to a life story told in scraps of delirium – the risks and the crookery and the shady deals . . . and then two men had been drowned. That was what had started Taggart drinking. 'Like most of us, he just wanted to forget.' And he went on, conjuring up the ghost of that dreadful old man, completely absorbed in the tragedy of it, standing there on that rock like a Trappist monk, his body shivering under the limp brown folds of his duffle coat.

He switched suddenly to the daughter . . . that photograph, what it had meant to him. Her image had been his confidante, his inspiration, a symbol of all his desperate hopes. And then the meeting in St Malo – the shock of realizing that there were things he couldn't tell her, that she knew he was hiding something from her.

'You're in love with her, aren't you?' I said. We were strangely close, alone together in the eerie stillness of the fog with the sea all round us.

'Yes.' His voice had a sudden lift to it, as though even here the thought of her could raise his spirits.

'Despite what she did to you in Court?'

'Oh, that!' He dismissed it. That last night in Southampton – she had come to apologize. And after that he had told her everything – all the things he had confided to her picture. 'I had to tell somebody,' he murmured.

He lifted his head suddenly and sniffed at a breath of wind that came to us out of the dripping void. 'Still westerly,' he said, and we talked about how soon the fog would clear. He hadn't liked the look of the dawn. 'That depression,' he muttered. 'We've got to reach the salvage ship before it starts to blow up dirty.' The words were ominous.

And shortly after that we had to go back to the dinghy. The tide had risen, covering the rocks of our inlet, and it kept us constantly on the move then. We were in a strange submarine world where everything dripped water and the floor of the sea rose steadily until the towering bastion of the rock had dwindled to a miserable little island barely two feet above the level of the sea. It was two o'clock then and the swell had increased and was showering us with spray as we sat huddled together in the dinghy.

I was barely conscious of time. The fog hung round us, very thick, so that it seemed as though nothing could exist in the whole world except that miserable strip of rock and the ugly, surging water.

We didn't talk much. We were too desperately cold. We took it in turns to sit and drift into a sort of coma. The tide went down again and the rock re-emerged like some monster lifting its dripping body out of the sea.

It was just after five that the fog began to clear. A wind sprang up and gradually the greyness lightened until it was an iridescent dazzle that hurt the eyes. Shapes began to emerge, forming themselves into rocks, and the sea stretched further and further away from us. Above our heads a patch of sky appeared, startlingly blue, and suddenly the fog was gone and the sun shone. We were in a sparkling world of blue-green water littered with rock outcrops.

We made the dinghy fast and scrambled up the barnacle-covered, weed-grown fortress of the rock. It was suddenly very warm, and from the top, which only a few hours before had been a bare, wave-worn little island, a fantastic sight met our eyes. All round us the sea was islanded with rock – mile upon mile of sinister reefs and outcrops – the Minkies at one hour before low water. Beyond the rock islands, we had glimpses of open sea – except to the south-west; to the south-west the islands became so numerous that they merged to form a solid barrier.

The beacon on Maîtresse Île, which stands 31 feet at high water, was easily identified, and from it Patch was able to get our bearings. The rock on which we stood was on the northern side of the Minkies, about a mile inside the outer bastion of the Pipette Rocks, and he reckoned that the *Mary Deare* must lie almost due south of us. I have checked since with the large-scale chart and find that he was just about right. But the three miles that separated us from our objective constituted the main body of the reefs. We didn't appreciate this at the time, nor did we fully understand the extraordinary change in configuration of the above-water reefs that could occur in the last stages of the falling tide.

The wind was blowing quite fresh and an ugly little chop was forming on the long swell that marched steadily eastwards through the reefs. Already there was a good deal of white water about, particularly in the vicinity of submerged rocks, and I think we should have been more cautious if we hadn't suddenly caught sight of Higgins. He was standing on a big rock mass not half a mile to the east of us. It was probably the Grand Vascelin, for there was a black and white beacon on it, and even as Patch pointed him out to me, I saw Higgins move and begin to scramble down to his dinghy, which we could see bobbing about at the base of the rock, its blue paint looking bright and cheerful in the sunshine.

We moved fast then, slithering and tumbling down to our own dinghy, scrambling into it and pushing off with no time to plan our route across the reefs, knowing only that the tide, which was west-going at that time, favoured Higgins and that we had to cover those three miles and reach the safety of the salvage company's vessel before he caught up with us.

Of course, we should never have shown ourselves against the skyline at the top of that rock. If we had thought about it at all, we must have known that, the instant the fog cleared, he would be standing on some vantage point watching for us. It wasn't that we had forgotten about him. You can't forget about a man when he has followed you all night through a treacherous, abandoned stretch of sea with murder in his heart. But I think the fog had so isolated us mentally that the moment it cleared we rushed to the highest point to get a sight of the world that had been hidden from us for so long. It was an instinctive reaction, and in any case we were dull-witted with cold and exhaustion.

The one sensible thing we did was to put on our life-jackets and then we pushed off from the rock that had been our perch for almost twelve hours and Patch began to row, heading south-west across the tide. Away from the lee of the rock we were conscious immediately of the weight of the wind and the way the sea was kicking up; it was a west wind, blowing over the tide, and already the waves were beginning to break. It crossed my mind that this might be the beginning of the depression. The sunshine had a brittle quality and long tongues of pale cloud, wind-blown like mares'-tails, were licking out across the sky.

The tide wasn't strong, but it carried us inexorably towards the greatest mass of the dried-out reefs. This mass is actually split by two channels, but we couldn't see that and for a time Patch attempted to make up against the tide to pass to the east of it, where we could see there was open water. But then, suddenly, he altered course. I was baling at the time, using a sou'wester, and I looked up at him enquiringly. I thought perhaps the tide had become too strong or that he felt we were shipping too much water.

But he nodded across the stern. 'Higgins,' he said, and I turned to see the big blue dinghy emerging from behind a jagged huddle of rocks. It wasn't more than two cables behind us.

We were in open water then, in the broad channel that separates the outer wall of reefs from the main fortress mass. There were no rocks to shelter us and the breaking wave-tops constantly slopped over the gunn'ls so that, though I never stopped baling, the water in the bottom of the dinghy steadily increased. I could hear Patch's breath escaping between his teeth and every time I glanced aft, it seemed that Higgins was nearer, the big metal dinghy riding higher and easier than ours. He was keeping a little to the east of us, heading us off from the open water, and all the time the outer rocks of the main reef were slowly closing in on us, the swell breaking all along their edge, the white water piling in over the black teeth of the outer fringe.

'You'll have to turn into the wind,' I shouted.

Patch glanced over his shoulder, still rowing steadily, and then nodded. The twenty-foot wall of rocks were very close now. But each time he turned, the starboard bow of the dinghy caught the full force of the breaking waves and water poured in, threatening to sink us. There was nothing for it but to hold our course, head for the rocks and hope for the best.

The tide helped us here, sliding us westwards, along the face of the rampart, into a bay where the swell built up to 4 or 5 feet and broke on outlying ledges in a cataract of foam. Every stroke of the oars carried us deeper into the bay, making escape from it more impossible. 'We'll never get out of this,' I shouted to Patch.

He said nothing. He had no breath left to talk. I glanced over the stern and saw that Higgins had closed the distance to less than two hundred yards. Patch had to go on rowing. And then, over his shoulder, I saw the rocks at the inner end of the bay draw apart and, unbelievably, there was open water between them. 'Look!' I pointed.

Patch glanced quickly over his right shoulder, saw the gap and turned the dinghy towards it. We were in the first of the two channels with the wind behind us. The dinghy rose and fell to the steep swell. We shipped hardly any water now and I was able to bale her right out so that we rode light and easy. 'We'll make it now!' Patch's voice came to me through the wind and the noise of the sea breaking along both sides of channel and it was full of confidence. He was grinning through his bared teeth, recklessly squandering his energy as he rowed with quick, straining tugs at the oars.

As soon as I had finished baling I took my place on the thwart beside him and we rowed in unison, not saying anything, just pulling and watching Higgins as he fell into the troughs of the endless waves and was borne aloft again on the next crest. The world smiled with the brittle glitter of white water. Only the rocks were ugly and their menace was oddly enhanced because the sun shone.

We reached the narrowest point of the channel, guarded by a single rock outcrop, and then it suddenly opened out into a broad area of water with a reef mass ahead, but plenty of water round it. It was protected somewhat from the wind so that, though the swells still surged across it, there were few whitecaps – just patches of broken water here and there.

But as we moved out into that broad patch of open water, a strange and terrifying change began to come over it. The first indication of something wrong was a swell that suddenly reared up behind the dinghy's stern and broke, slewing us broadside in the surf and very nearly turning us over. Patch shouted to me that we were on a reef and we pulled the dinghy clear of the danger spot. The swell was building up and breaking continuously at that point. And now, looking round, I noticed it was breaking at many other points – places where it hadn't been breaking only a few minutes before.

'The tide!' Patch yelled in my ear. 'Pull, man! Pull! It's the tide!'

I needed no urging. I would have pulled both arms out of their sockets to get out of that fearful place. All around us now were patches of white water, patches that joined up with other patches till there were irregular lines of surf breaking. What had been, only a few minutes ago, open water, was now, suddenly, transformed into a seething, roaring cauldron of broken water as the tide dropped like a lift to expose the rocks and gravel of the sea bed contained within the ramparts of the central reef mass.

I had only just grasped what was happening when a sudden wave lifted us up and crashed us down on to a rock. The jolt of it ran right up my spine like a blow to the base of the head. Water boiled all round us, white in the sunshine, glittering like soapsuds; rocks and boulders showed for an instant and then vanished as another wave of green water swept in, lifted us up and crashed us down again. And in the instant of being uplifted I have a sort of panoramic recollection of the scene: black reefs piled round that arena and the water all brittle white and boiling mad and little sections of sea bed showing – all passing before my eyes as the dinghy was swung violently round and then finally smashed down upon a little exposed hillock of grey gravel. It was a tiny oasis in the middle of chaos that came and went as the surf rolled across it.

We stumbled out, knee-deep in the spill of a wave, and, as it receded, we tipped the dinghy up, emptying it of water. But one glance told us that it was damaged beyond any repair we could effect on the spot – two planks were stove in for practically the whole length of the boat. 'Doesn't matter,' Patch shouted. 'We'd have to abandon it, anyway. Come on!' He bent down and removed the hand-bearing compass from its case. It was all he took. 'Come on!' he repeated. 'We walk and swim the rest.'

I stood and stared at him. I thought for a moment that he'd gone mad and imagined he was Christ, capable of walking the surface of that surging carpet of broken water. But he wasn't mad. He was a seaman and his mind worked quicker than mine. Already a change had come over the scene – there was less white water, and rocks and boulders and patches of gravel were appearing as the tide receded. And two hundred yards away Higgins was ploughing through water up to his knees, dragging his dinghy after him.

I bent to pick up the painter of our own dinghy and then realized it was useless. 'Come on!' Patch said again. 'We've got to be out of here before the tide comes back.' He had started to walk south and I followed, stumbling over hidden boulders, floundering into pot-holes, wet and dazed and exhausted.

The noise of the surf rolled back till it dwindled to a distant murmur, and in a moment, it seemed, all those acres that had been a roaring holocaust of tumbled water were suddenly still and quiet. No waves broke. Little raised beaches of boulder-strewn gravel shone wet in the sun and about them lay pools of water ruffled by the wind, and all round were the black rocks of the reef.

The sense of isolation, of loneliness and remoteness, was appalling. And it was enhanced by something that Higgins did, following on behind us. He came to our dinghy and, glancing back, I saw him pick it up in his two hands and smash it down against an outcrop of rock. The splintering crash of the wood breaking up was a sharp, savage sound. All the bows were stove in and my last contact with *Sea Witch* was wantonly destroyed.

And then Higgins started after us again, still dragging his dinghy. The tinny sound of it striking against the boulders was with us for a long time as we stumbled across stretches of exposed beach or waded through water that was sometimes so deep we had to swim. And at the back of my mind was the thought that we were twenty miles from the French coast, in an area that only a few local fishermen ever dared to visit. And in six short hours all this area of rock-strewn debris would be thirty feet below the sea, compressed, imprisoned, flattened by countless million tons of water. The only thing that kept me going was the thought of that salvage ship, so close now. It couldn't be more than two miles away, three at the most . . . and there'd be a bunk and dry clothes and hot soup.

I saw Patch stumble and fall. He got up and staggered on. We were halfway to the black southern bastion of the reefs, floundering over a stretch of jagged, up-ended rocks. He fell several times after that. We both did. There was no strength left in us and when a foot slipped, the muscles gave. Our sodden clothing weighed us down, tripped us up.

The sun gradually died amongst the mares'-tails. Thicker clouds came up. I didn't see them come. The sweat was in my eyes. I saw nothing but what was immediately at my feet. But rock and gravel became drab and sombre. And later, much later, there was a light drizzle on my face. The sound of the sea began to come back, but by then we were crawling amongst the great up-ended slabs of rock that lay strewn about the main outcrop.

I hadn't looked back for a long time then. I didn't know where Higgins was. I couldn't hear the sound of his dinghy any more. It was lost in the noise of the sea and the drumming of the blood in my ears. And then we were clawing our way up the final slope of weed-grown rock. I paused to see Patch up at the top, leaning against a shoulder of rock and staring southwards. 'Can you see her?' I gasped.

'No.' He shook his head.

I came out on to the top beside him and stared south. It was still the Minkies. But different. More sea. There were still rock outcrops. But they were fewer, more isolated. All ahead of us was open water, dimmed and blurred by the drizzle of rain. 'I don't see her,' I gasped.

'She's there somewhere.' His voice was flat and weary. His black hair hung wet over his eyes and his hands and face were streaked with blood where he had fallen – blood and dirt and sodden, shapeless clothing. He took my arm. 'You all right?' he asked.

'Yes,' I said. 'Yes, I'm all right.'

He stared at me and for the first time I saw an expression of concern in his eyes. He opened his mouth to say something and then thought better of it and turned his head away. 'I'm sorry,' he said, and that was all.

'How much further do you reckon?' I asked.

'About a mile.'

A mile to swim. I wondered whether we should ever make it.

He took my arm again and pointed across the litter of outcrops to a compact mass that stood higher than any of the others. 'I think that's Grune à Croc.' It stood on the edge of visibility, half hidden by the drizzle, and at the mention of its name it abruptly vanished as the rain thickened and drove across it. Somewhere beyond that rock lay the *Mary Deare.*

Behind us, the tide came licking hungrily back across the beaches, coming in from the north-west, driven by the wind and the south-going set of the stream. But Higgins was clear of it by then, rowing slowly, easily, to a nearby rock, where he moored his dinghy and sat watching us like an animal that has treed its quarry. He could afford to wait, for with each foot the tide rose the size of our rock perch was halved.

We found an over-hanging slab of rock that gave us some shelter from the wind and the rain and still enabled us to watch him, and there we crouched, huddled close together for warmth whilst the tide rose and night closed in. If only the visibility had been better; if we could have seen the *Mary Deare,* perhaps attracted the attention of the salvage people. But we could see nothing; we couldn't even hear them. All we could hear was the waves pounding on the other side of the reef mass and I wondered what it would be like at the top of the tide. Would the waves break right over these rocks? But by then we should be gone. Our plan was to slip into the water an hour before high tide and make for Grune à Croc. We were relying on a southward thrust from the tide coming through the main reef body to spill us out towards the rock, and though Patch had lost the hand-bearing compass, we thought the rock would be reasonably conspicuous, since it was the only one in the whole area to the south of us that would be exposed at high water.

Once we had decided what to do, we had nothing to occupy our minds. It was then that I became conscious of hunger pains for the first time. It wasn't only the pains that worried me, but the feeling that I had no warmth left in me, as though the rain and the bitter cold had reached the central fires on which my body depended and put them out. I fell into a sort of coma of misery and through bleared eyes I watched the rock to which Higgins had moored slowly submerge. And then he was rowing again, and gradually the tide beat him. Oddly enough it gave me no sense of pleasure. I was too tired. As the tide ran faster so he had to row harder to keep abreast of our position. And then gradually his strokes became weaker until he was forced to steer to another rock and cling to it. But the tide rose and covered that, too, and, though he started to row again, the tide carried him slowly further and further from us. Night was closing in by then and I lost him in the gathering darkness.

It meant, of course, that we shouldn't have to worry about where Higgins was when we abandoned our rock and took to the water, but when you are faced with a long swim and are afraid you may be too weak to do it, then the question of whether there may or may not be a dinghy in the way doesn't seem very important. In any case, I was slipping into unconsciousness. I was so cold, so utterly drained of warmth – I had no sense of feeling left.

It was the water that woke me. It was warmer than I was and it lapped round my legs like a tepid bath. And then it slopped into my face. That was when consciousness returned and I felt Patch stir. 'Good God!' he murmured. 'It must be just about high water.'

We stood up, stiff to the joints, forcing our bodies to unbend. Was it high water? Had the tide turned already? My numbed brain groped for the answer, knowing it was important, but not knowing why. The rain had stopped. There were stars and low-scudding clouds. A glimmer of moonlight made pale reflections on the ink-black water. 'Well, do we go? What's the time?' Patch's voice was no more than a croak. 'What's the time, for God's sake? My watch has stopped.'

Mine had stopped, too. There was no means of knowing the time, no means of knowing which way the tide was flowing. Jolted by sudden fear, the sleep cleared from my brain and I saw clearly that we had no alternative. If we stayed on that rock we should die of exposure – tomorrow perhaps or the next day, but we should die. After tonight we should never have the strength to swim that mile. And the water was warm – warmer than the sodden, icy clothes draped round our bodies, warmer than the wind and the ice-cold driving rain that would come again. Besides, we had life-jackets and, if the tide was wrong, there were other rocks to cling to and die on. 'Ready?' I said.

Patch hesitated and I suddenly realized that he wasn't sure of himself any more. He was a seaman. He was used to boats, not to the sea itself as an element in which to exist, body buoyed up by water. 'Come on,' I said. 'We're going now. Keep close to me and don't talk.'

We inflated our life-jackets fully and then together we stepped off the ledge of rock on which we had huddled. When we had first come to that ledge it had been a thirty-foot drop to the rocks below. Now we stepped off into water, warm, buoyant water, and, lying on our backs, swam slowly south, our feet to the Pole Star, glimpsed every now and then through rents in the tattered cloud-base.

We kept abreast of each other, just two arms' lengths away, moving steadily and unhurriedly. Soon we were clear of the rocks, rising and falling gently to a big swell that was rolling in across the reefs. We could hear it pounding against distant rocks – the rocks to the west of us that got the full brunt of it. 'Storm coming up,' Patch whispered.

The wind had dropped. The swell was big, but gentle-sloped with no broken water. The sea slept, heaving as it slumbered. Yet I was sure Patch was right. Though the wind was light, the clouds were hurried and torn to shreds and the pounding of that surf was ominous, like gunfire to the west. A wave suddenly reared up out of nowhere and broke, pouring surf over us, spilling us away from it. My feet touched rock for an instant. And then everything was quiet as before and we rose and fell, rose and fell to the swell. We had crossed one of those sentinel-like pillars of rock that we had seen at low water.

The rock on which we had spent half the night was disappearing now – disappearing astern of us so that I knew we were all right. We hadn't missed the tide. Patch stopped swimming, treading water. 'I can't see Grune à Croc,' he said, and his teeth chattered. 'I think we should strike more to the west.'

So we swam on with the Pole Star and the Plough to our left and I wondered how long we could last. My teeth were chattering, too, and the sea, which had felt so warm at first, was now a cold compress chilling all my stomach. We had no food inside us to generate warmth. Soon one of us would get cramp, and that would be the end.

Our sodden clothing weighed us down. The inflated life-jackets made us clumsy. Each stroke had to be powerful to drive our bodies through the water; and power meant energy – our vital, last reserves of energy. God knows how long we swam that night. We seemed to go on and on for ever. And each stroke was imperceptibly weaker than the last. And all the time I was thinking if only I were wearing a foam rubber suit or at least had my fins on my feet. It was years since I had swum in this clumsy fashion. My mind sank into a coma, a slough of pain and deep exhaustion, in which I saw myself again ploughing down to the old tanker through clear bright Mediterranean waters that glimmered with colour – the white of the sand and the silver gleam of fish; and myself, buoyant and carefree, exactly balanced, warm and breathing comfortably through my mouthpiece.

'John! John!' I opened my eyes. Black night surrounded me. I thought for an instant I was deep down, on the verge of going into a rapture of the depths. And then I saw a star and heard the surge of a wave breaking. 'John!' The voice called again out of the darkness.

'Yes. What is it?'

'There's a rock. I can just see it.' It was Patch's voice. Funny, I thought. He'd never called me John before. And then he said, 'You gave me a scare just now. I couldn't make you hear. I thought I'd lost you.'

The concern in his voice filled me with a sudden warmth for the man. 'Sorry,' I said. 'Just dreaming. That's all. Where's this rock of yours?' I turned, treading water, and there, not more than a hundred yards to my right, the dark shape of a rock stood out for an instant against the white gleam of a breaking wave. I searched the blackness beyond it. More waves were breaking out there and I thought I saw the solid mass of something.

And then it came to me that there would be lights on the *Mary Deare*. With a salvage company working on her there would have to be lights. I searched the blackness all round, each time I was lifted to the top of a swell, but there was nothing, not the faintest flicker of a light. Perhaps they were being so secret about their salvage operation that they didn't show lights. And then the thought came to me that perhaps they had lifted her already and towed her away. The cold came back into my body, more intense now, more destructive, and I felt the muscles of my left leg begin to screw themselves together in a knot.

'There's something beyond this rock' Patch croaked. 'Shall we make for that?'

'All right,' I said. It didn't seem to matter. To die in the water was better than to die of exposure on one of those God-forsaken rocks. I lay back, kicking out feebly with my legs, thrusting at water that was no longer warm, but icy cold, swimming automatically whilst my mind tangled itself up with the matter of those lights. There should have been lights. Unless we'd been swept back into the central mass of the reefs we should have seen lights right from the start. 'There should be lights,' I mumbled.

'Lights. That's it. There should be lights.' His voice sounded weak, a little scared. And then, after a bit – 'Tell them to put the lights on.' He was back on a ship, his mind wandering. 'Put those lights on, do you hear?' And then suddenly he called 'John!' His voice was very faint.

'Yes?'

'I'm sorry I landed you into this.' He muttered something about my boat. And then I heard him say, 'I should have slit my useless throat.' Silence for a moment and then: 'They booed me, that first time. Outside the Court.' Broken water slapped my face and the next thing I heard was – '. . . kick against the pricks. I should have chucked it then.' A wave broke and silenced him. He didn't speak again after that. His arms didn't move. I could just see the outline of his head, motionless.

'Are you all right?' I called out.

He didn't answer and I swam over to him. 'Are you all right?' I shouted again.

'Look! Do you see it?'

I thought his mind had gone. 'Wake up!' I shouted at him. 'We're going to swim to that rock – do you hear?'

He caught hold of my arm with the iron grip of a drowning man and, as I wrenched myself free of him, he screamed at me. 'Look, man. Look at it, damn you! Tell me I'm not dreaming!'

He had raised his arm and was pointing. I turned my head and there, against the stars, I saw the tall finger of a mast and, below it, all the black bulk of her superstructure caught for an instant in the white phosphorescent glitter of a breaking wave.

We swam then, cold and exhaustion forgotten, tugging our weary, unwieldy bodies through the water. We were coming up on her bows and they were like a reef awash: the waves rolled over them, but in the troughs their shape emerged as the sea cascaded from them. And then, beyond the bows, beyond the tall finger of the mast, the bridge deck emerged and the funnel and all the line of the decks sloping upwards to her cocked-up stern.

In the trough of a wave a hard line sprang suddenly taut, catching at my left arm so that I screamed with pain, gulping in salt water; and then it flipped me over and the top of a wave engulfed me. I swam clear of the bows then, moving painfully down the ship, just clear of the streaming bulwarks, and then swam in on her where the fo'c'stle dropped to the well-deck and Number One hatch. I came in on the top of a wave that broke as it surged over the bulwarks and then I was flung down on to the hatch coaming with a force that jarred all the torn muscles of my side and my feet scrabbled on weed-grown, slippery plating whilst the wave receded in a swirl of white water.

I fetched up in the scuppers with my hand gripped round the capping of the bulwarks, and as the next wave piled in, I fought my way aft until I was clear of the water and could reach the mast, and there I clung, shouting for Patch in a high, cracked voice, for I was scared I'd lost him. That moment of panic seemed endless. I was the better swimmer. I was trained to the sea. I should have stayed with him, seen him safe on board, and I knew I hadn't the guts to go back and search for him in the darkness; I was tired, desperately tired, with all the muscles of my body curling up with the threat of cramp. And, even more, I didn't want to be alone on that ship. It was a dead ship – dead as the rocks of the Minkies. I knew it, instinctively. I could sense that it was dead through all my body and I needed him desperately. And so I clung to the mast and screamed his name and the seas came thundering in across the bows with wicked gleams of white as the water surged and swirled and poured off them in the troughs.

I didn't see him come aboard. I was still screaming his name and he was suddenly there beside me, staggering drunkenly, an ungainly, top-heavy shape in his life-jacket caught in silhouette against the break of a wave. 'It's all right,' he gasped. 'I'm here.' He reached out and caught hold of my hand, and we clung there, gasping for breath, grateful for the sudden comfort of that touch. 'There should be lights,' he said at length. There was a sort of childish disappointment in his voice, as though the salvage company had robbed him of a pleasure to which he had been looking forward.

'They've probably closed down for the night,' I said, but without conviction. I knew the ship was dead.

'But there should be lights,' he said again. And then we staggered aft, past Number Two hatch, up the ladder to the upper-deck. The door to the deck-house stood drunkenly open, crumpled and torn from its hinges. We felt our way along the alley, past his old cabin and Dellimare's and out through the empty gap of the door beyond, out on to the upper-deck, where the twisted shapes of the empty davits stood like crooked fingers against starlit patches of the sky, and on, past the dim-seen shape of the funnel, crumpled and lying away from us at a precarious angle.

Squelching soggily on the steel of the deck, our bodies thin as paper in the cold night air, we traipsed the length of the *Mary Deare*, aft to the little deck-house on the poop and back again up the starboard side, and every now and then we shouted – 'Ahoy! Anybody there? Ahoy!' Not even an echo came back to us. The frail sound of our voices was lost in the cold, black night, buried in the noise of the waves surging over the bows.

No salvage boat lay alongside. No light suddenly flickered to guide us to the warmth of a cabin. We called and called, but nobody answered. The ship was dead, devoid of life – as dead as she had been the day we'd left her there.

'My God!' Patch breathed. 'We're the first. Nobody has been here.' There was a note of relief, almost exultation in his voice, and I knew he was thinking of the thing that lay buried amidst the coal of the port bunker. But all I cared about at that moment was that I was cold and wet and hurt and that, instead of the bunk and dry clothes, the warmth of food and drink and the companionship of human beings I had expected, there was nothing – nothing but the slime-covered, barnacle-encrusted shell of a wreck that had been battered by the seas for six long weeks.

'We'll get some dry clothes and have a sleep,' he said. 'We'll feel better then.' He had sensed my mood. But when we had staggered back to the bridge-housing and felt our way down the black iron tunnel of the alley-way to what had been his cabin, we found that the sea had been there. The door grated on sand as we forced it open and a freezing wind drove at us through portholes that stared like two luminous eyes, empty of glass. The desk had been ripped from its fastenings and lay on its side in a corner, the drawers of the bunk that contained his and Taggart's clothes were full of water and the big wall cupboard contained nothing but a sodden, gritty heap of blankets, coats and old papers.

We tried the main deck then, where the saloon and the galley were. But that was worse. The sea had swept the whole length of the alley-ways, into the officers' cabins and right aft to the crew's quarters. Everything we touched in the pitch-black darkness was sodden, filmed with slime; there wasn't a place the sea hadn't reached.

'Maybe the poop is still dry.' Patch said it wearily, without hope, and we began to move back down the port alley-way, feeling our way, bodies dead and numbed with cold, shivering uncontrollably. God, let the poop be dry! And then I staggered and hit my shoulder against the wet steel plate of the wall, thrown there by a sudden movement of the ship. I felt it through my whole body, a quiver like the first faint tremor of an earthquake. And then the ship moved again. 'Listen!' Patch's voice was urgent in the darkness. But I could hear nothing except the noise of the sea lapping at the hull. 'She's afloat,' he whispered. 'Just afloat on top of the tide.'

'How can she be?' I said.

'I don't know, but she is. Feel her!'

I felt her quiver and lift, and then she thudded back into her gravel bed. But she still went on quivering and from deep down in the bowels of her came a slow grating sound; and all the time she was trembling as though she were stirring in her sleep, struggling to free herself from the deadly reef bed on which she lay. 'It's not possible,' I murmured. The ship couldn't be afloat when her bows were submerged like a reef and the waves were rolling over them. This must be a dream. And I thought then that perhaps we had drowned out there. Did drowned men go back to their ships and dream that they shook off the reef shackles and voyaged like ghosts through dark, unnatural seas? My mind was beyond coherent thought. The ship was dead. That I knew, and beyond that, all I wanted was to lose consciousness of cold and pain, to lie down and sleep.

A hand reached out and gripped me, holding me up, and my feet trod the iron of the passage-way and climbed, without volition, up into the cold of the night air, to glimpses of stars and a drunken funnel and the unending noise of the sea. Down aft we stumbled over a steel hawser laid taut across the well-deck. It thrummed and sang to the sea's roll, and the ship moved like a drunkard, tottering its masts against the sky, as we climbed the ladder to the poop's platform and vanished into the black abyss of the little deck-house. There was clothing there in the bos'n's cabin. As I remember, it was neither wet nor dry, but it had more warmth than my own sodden clothes, and there was a dank bunk, with blankets smelling of wet like a dog's fur, and sleep – the utter oblivion of sleep, more perfect than any heaven ever dreamed of by a well-fed man seated by his own fireside.

A long time after, it seemed – many years, perhaps – the tread of a man's feet entered into that heavenly oblivion. I can't say that it woke me or even that I struggled back to consciousness. Not immediately. It was just that the tread of his feet was there; a solid, metallic sound – the ring of boots on steel plates. It was a penetrating, insistent sound. It was above my head, beside my bed, first one side, then the other, and then further away – a slow, unhurried, purposeful tread . . . the march of a dead man across the sleep of oblivion. And when it was no longer there I woke.

Daylight stabbed at my bleared eyes and a huddle of sodden blankets in the corner of the dank steel prison in which I lay, stirred and rose. It was Patch, his face ashen with fatigue. 'I thought I heard footsteps,' he said. His eyes looked wild, black marbles sunk deep in ivory sockets. 'I swear I heard somebody.'

I crawled out of the bunk, sweaty with the salt-heat of a soggy mass of blankets, but cold and stiff with a gnawing pain in my

belly and my shoulder aching like hell. It all came back to me
then, hitting me like a physical blow, and I stumbled to the door
and looked out. It was true then – not a dream. I was back on the
Mary Deare, and . . . God, she was a wreck! She was a rust-red
nightmare of a ship, smeared with a film of green slime, with a
stubble-growth of grey that was the barnacles. Her funnel lay
over at a crazy angle and all the bridge-deck was twisted and
gnarled and battered. The tide was low and, beyond the wreck of
her, the Minkies gnashed their black teeth, foam-flecked where the
stumps of rock stuck up out of the sea. No salvage ship lay anchored
off, no tug, not even a fishing boat. There was nothing – just the
ugly, familiar shape of Grune à Croc and the mass of the reefs
beyond . . . not a single sign of life, and the sky savagely grey,
with an ugly pallor that made the cloud shapes black and cold-
looking.

'My God!' I croaked. Instinctively, perhaps, I knew what we
had to face – what the pallor of the dawn meant and the savage
grey of the sky.

And Patch, sniffing the air over my shoulder, muttered,
'There's a heap of dirt coming up.'

The sky to the west of us was sombre, a black wedge of cloud
that left the horizon sharp as a line ruled between air and sea.
There wasn't much wind, but the thunder of the waves on the
exposed reefs had an ominous sound, and, even here, in the shelter
of the rocks, the swell that slopped against the *Mary Deare*'s side
was big and solid.

'Those footsteps,' I said. 'What were they?'

He shook his head, not answering, and his eyes avoided mine.
God knows what he was thinking, but a shudder ran through him,
and it crossed my mind that a lot of men had died because of this
ship. And then a strange thing happened: a little cloud of rust
rose like red steam from the well-deck bulwark as a steel hawser
ran out over the side. The bight appeared, checked on the rail,
and then fell over into the sea with a faint splash. When it was
gone, the ship was still again – no movement anywhere, and I was
conscious that Patch was gripping my arm. 'Queer,' he said, and
his voice had a hollow sound.

We stood rooted to the spot for a long time, staring along the
length of the ship. But everything was still and motionless –
nothing moved except the sea.

'There's somebody on board,' he said. His tone was uneasy and
his face was as drawn and haggard as it had been on the day I
had first met him. 'Listen!' But I could hear nothing – only the

587

slap of the waves against the ship's side and the pounding of the swell on the reefs. The wreck was as still and as quiet as the grave. A lone sea-bird drifted by, soundless on the wind and white like a piece of paper against the clouds.

Patch descended then to the well-deck and stopped to gaze at the cover of Number Four hatch. And when I joined him I saw that it wasn't the usual tarpaulin cover fixed with wooden wedges, but steel plates fresh-welded to the coaming. He had a look at the derrick winches and then we went past Number Three hatch, which was also plated over, and up the ladder to the boat deck. Here all the ventilators had been removed and lay about the deck like truncated limbs, the ventilation holes covered by rusty plating. The funnel had been cut through at the base by a blow-torch, shifted to one side and the vent plated over. The engine-room skylight was screwed down tight and the water-tight doors to the port and starboard main-deck alley-ways had been removed and the holes plated over.

There was no doubt whatever that the report of the St Helier fisherman had been correct. A salvage company had been working on the wreck. They had sealed off the whole hull of the *Mary Deare* and probably they had also repaired the leak in the for'ard holds. It explained the way she had lifted at the top of the tide and the rake of the decks to the cocked-up stern. The ship was water-tight, almost ready to float off. I found Patch standing by the port bunkering chute, his eyes riveted on the hatch cover, which had been torn from its hinges and lay abandoned on the deck. In its place a steel plate had been welded over the chute, effectively sealing the bunker off. It meant that Dellimare's body would remain there in its steel coffin until the hulk was towed into port and officials came on board with equipment to open up the ship. It meant days, possibly weeks of suspense for him, and there was despair in his face as he said, 'Well, that's that.' And he turned away, to stare aft along the length of the ship. 'They should have had a stern line out,' he said.

I wasn't following his trend of thought. I was thinking that there was all this work completed and no salvage ship. 'Why do you think they left?' I asked him.

He glanced at the sky, sniffing the breeze from the west, which was coming now in irregular puffs. 'The forecast was probably bad,' he said. 'Maybe they had a gale warning.'

I stared at the jagged reefs, remembering what it had been like before. Surely to God . . .

'What's that?' His voice came sharp and clear, and through

it, beyond the barrier of the bridge-deck, the cough of a diesel engine settled to a steady roar. I could feel the deck vibrating under my feet, and for a moment we stood, quite still, listening to the music of it. Then we were running for the bridge-deck alley-way. We came out at the head of the ladder that led down to the for'ard well-deck and there, just aft of Number Two hatch, stood a big suction pump, lashed to the deck. The engine was going full bat and the thick suction pipe was pulsating with the flow of water where it disappeared through a hole cut in an inspection hatch. Water was sluicing out of the far side of the pump, flooding across the deck and disappearing through the scuppers. And yet there was nobody there. The well-deck was empty and in all the fore part of the ship there wasn't a living soul.

It was uncanny.

'Try the bridge,' Patch said. 'Somebody started that pump.'

We dived back into the alley-way and up the ladder to the bridge. It was all so familiar, but horribly changed. The glass was gone, the doors smashed and the wind was whistling through it, pushing little rivulets of water across the sand-smeared plat-form. There was nobody there – nobody in the chartroom. And then, out on the bridge again, Patch gripped my arm and pointed. Beyond the bows a pillar-like rock stood like a bollard with the bite of a thick steel hawser round it. The hawser ran taut from rock to ship, an anchor against the pull of the tides. It was the hawser that had fouled me during the night as I swam in over the bows.

But Patch was pointing to something else – a small blue dinghy pulling out from under the *Mary Deare*'s bows. It was Higgins, and he was rowing out to the rock. The peaked cap on the bull head, the massive shoulders and the blue seaman's jersey – it was all so clear in the cold grey light. It was clear, too, what he in-tended to do. I shouted to him, but he couldn't hear me from the bridge. I dived back down the ladder, down to the well-deck and up on to the fo'c'sle. 'Higgins!' I screamed at him. 'Higgins!'

But it was blowing quite strong in the gusts now and Higgins didn't hear me. He had reached the rock and was tying the dinghy to a snag, and then he began to climb. He reached the bight of the hawser and, with an iron bar he had brought with him for the purpose, began to lever it up the rock, whilst I shouted to him, standing up in the wind, balanced right on the slippery point of the *Mary Deare*'s bows.

He had his back to me all the time and when he'd freed the loop, he pushed it up over the jagged point of the rock and the whole line of the wire that anchored the ship, right from where it ran out through the hawse-hole, went slack as it fell with a splash into the sea. Then he clambered back down the rock and got into his dinghy.

He saw me just as he'd unhitched the painter and he sat looking at me for a moment. His face was without expression and his big shoulders sagged with the effort he had made. And all the time I was shouting to him, telling him to fix the hawser back on to the rock. 'There's a gale coming,' I shouted. 'A gale!' I kept on repeating that one word, trying to din it into his thick head.

Maybe I succeeded, for Higgins suddenly let go of the rock, pivoted the dinghy on one oar and began to row back towards the *Mary Deare*. Whether he panicked and was making a desperate attempt to get back on board, or whether he was moved to unexpected pity by the desolate character of the place and was trying to take us off, I shall never know, for the tide was north-going, about three knots, and though he worked like a man possessed to drag that heavy dinghy through the water faster than the tide ran, he made not more than twenty yards' headway. He tired quickly and, after the first burst of energy, he made no further progress; and then, gradually, the tide took control and he drifted further and further away from the ship, still desperately rowing.

In the end he gave it up and steered the dinghy across the tide into the lee of Grune à Croc, and there he sat, clutching the rock, staring at the ship, his head bowed to his knees, his whole body slack with exhaustion.

The noise of the suction pump died and ceased abruptly so that I was suddenly conscious of the wind whining through the broken superstructure. Patch had switched the engine off and as I climbed down off the fore-peak he came to meet me. 'We've got to flood the ship,' he called out, his voice loud and clear. 'It's our only hope.'

But there was no way of flooding her now. Every vent and hole was sealed off and we couldn't get at the sea cocks. Even the doors of the engine-room had been welded to keep the water out. The salvage company had sealed that hull up as tight as a submarine. 'We'll just have to hope for the best,' I said.

Patch laughed. The sound had a hollow ring down there in the steel vault of the alley-way. 'A westerly gale will bring a big tide. She'll float off at high water. Bound to, with nothing to hold her. She's pumped dry, all but the two for'ard holds.' His voice sounded hoarse and cracked. 'I wouldn't mind for myself.' He was staring at me. 'But it's tough on you.' And then he shrugged his shoulders and added, 'Better see if we can find some food.'

I was appalled by his acceptance of it, and as I followed him back down the alley-way to the galley, I was thinking that if only I had woken in time. The French salvage men had had her securely moored with hawsers fore and aft, and Higgins had let them go. I couldn't hate the man. I hadn't the strength to hate. But if only I'd got up the instant I'd heard those footsteps . . . And as though he knew what was in my mind, Patch said, 'One thing – Higgins is going to have a bad time of it out there in that dinghy.'

The galley was dark and it stank. The sea had been there before us, and so had the French. There wasn't a tin of any sort in the place. There was a cupboard full of bread that was a pulped, mildewed mass and there was meat that heaved with maggots and butter thick with slime and sand. All we found was some cheese that was good in the centre, a jar of half-dried mustard, some pickles and a broken pot of marmalade. We broke our fast on that, wolfing it down, and then we searched the saloon and all through the officers' cabins and the crews' quarters. We found a sticky mass of boiled sweets and a jar of ginger and, best of all, some stoker had gone to earth with two tins of bully beef. We took our miserable haul back to the little deck-house on the poop and ate it, sitting there, shivering and listening to the rising note of the wind.

The gale came up fast with the turn of the tide and soon the waves, breaking against the side of the wreck, were reaching up to the bridge-deck and we could feel the stern beginning to move under us. Once, when I went to look out of the door, I saw the blue dinghy still bobbing in the lee of Grune à Croc.

By midday it was blowing full gale. All the forepart of the *Mary Deare* was being pounded and battered by huge seas, her bridge-deck hidden every now and then in sheets of white water, the whole hull quivering to the onslaught. Water swirled across the well-deck below us and the boom of the waves striking against the plates of her side was so shattering that I found myself holding my breath, waiting for them, as though the blows were being struck against my own body. The noise went on and on. It filled my head and left no room for any thought beyond the terrible, ever-lasting consciousness of the sea. And out beyond the sea-swept wreck of the *Mary Deare*, the stumps of the reefs dwindled as the Minkies gradually vanished in a welter of foaming surf.

I saw Higgins once more. It was about two hours before high water. The *Mary Deare* was beginning to lift and shift her bottom on the gravel bed and Grune à Croc was a grey molar stuck up out of a sea of foam with water streaming white from its sides and spray sweeping across in a low-flung cloud, driven by the wind. Higgins was moving on the back of the rock, climbing down towards the dinghy. I saw him get into it and pick up the oars. And then a squall came, blurring the shape of the rock, and I suddenly lost sight of him in a curtain of rain.

That was the last I saw of Higgins. It was the last anybody saw of him. I suppose he was trying to reach the *Mary Deare*. Or perhaps he thought he could reach the mainland in the dinghy. He had no choice, anyway; Grune à Croc would have been untenable at high water.

I stood in the doorway of our deck-house for a long time, my eyes slitted against the rain and the driving spray, watching for a glimpse of him through the squall. In the end the seas drove me in and when I told Patch how Higgins had gone, he shrugged his shoulders and said, 'Lucky bastard! He's probably dead by now.' There was no anger in his voice, only weariness.

The cabin in that deck-house was about ten feet by six, steel-walled, with a bunk, some broken furniture, a window that had no glass in it and sand on the floor. It was damp and cold, the air smoking with wind-driven spray, and it resounded like a tin box to every sound throughout the ship. We had chosen it for our refuge because it was perched high up on the stern, and it was the stern part of the ship that was afloat.

For a long time we had been conscious of movement, a rising and falling of the steel walls that coincided with the gun-fire bursts of the waves crashing against the hull below us. But now there was a shifting and a grating of the keel. It was a sound felt rather than heard, for nothing was really audible except the incredible, over-whelming noise of the sea. And then gradually it lessened. Spray ceased to come in through the window. The door blew open with a crash. The *Mary Deare* had struggled free of the sea bed and was turning head to wind.

I looked out and saw that Grune à Croc was no longer on the port bow, but away to starboard. The *Mary Deare* was afloat. The movement was easier now, the noise of the sea less terrifying. The high stern was acting as a steadying sail and she was bows-on to the breaking waves. I could hear them thundering against the bridge-deck, see them burst in a great cloud of spray, forcing water through every opening of the bridge-housing as the broken tops swept by on either side. And all the time Grune à Croc was fading away.

I shouted to Patch that we were clear and he came out from the cabin and stood looking at the incredible sight – a wreck floating with her decks streaming rivers of water and sloped down so that all the fore part of her was below the waves. 'We're clear,' I cried. 'If we clear Les Sauvages we're all right.'

He looked at me. I think he was considering leaving me in ignorance. But then he said, 'It must be very near high water.'

I nodded. 'Just about,' I said. And then it came to me: for six solid hours after high water the tide would be north and west-going – driving us back on to the Minkies, back on to the Minkies at low water with all the reefs exposed. 'God Almighty!' I breathed, and I went back into the cabin and lay down on the bunk.

The hell of it was, there was nothing we could do – not a single damn' thing we could do to help ourselves.

We struck towards dusk in a maelstrom of white water where there wasn't a single rock showing. I don't know whether I was asleep or merely lying there on the bunk in a sort of daze, but the shock of our hitting threw me to the floor. It came like the blow of a mailed fist, a fearful crash up for'ard and then a slow crunching as the plates gave and the rocks disembowelled her; and the thunder of the seas became suddenly louder, more overwhelming.

I lay quite still where I had fallen, feeling the probing teeth of the rocks through my whole body, expecting every moment that the waves would engulf us as she slid under. But nothing happened, except that a thin mist of spray touched my face as it drifted over the ship and the grinding, gut-tearing sound went on so continuously that it became a part of the general uproar of the sea.

The cabin floor was canted over and, as I got to my feet, a sudden shifting of the ship flung me through the door and I fetched up against the bulkhead with a sickening thud that wrenched at my arm and drove the breath out of my body. I saw the ship then, and the pain didn't seem to matter any more. She was lying heeled over, all the length of her clear against a boiling background of surf. Her bridge-deck was a twisted, broken mass of wreckage, the funnel gone, the fore-mast snapped off halfway up and hanging loose in a tangle of derrick wires. And over all the for'ard half of her the seas broke and rolled and tumbled incessantly.

Patch was lying, half-reclined against the steel plates of the deck-house entrance and I shouted to him: 'How long . . .' The words seemed to get caught up in my throat.

'Before she goes?'

'Yes. How long?'

'God knows.'

We didn't talk after that, but stayed there, too cold and tired and fascinated to move, watching as the first jagged points of the reef showed through the foam. The weary half-light faded very slowly into darkness. We heard the bows break off; a protracted agony of tortured metal, tearing and rending up there beyond the wreck of the bridge-deck. And then the remainder of the ship lifted slightly as it was freed of their weight, shifting across the saw-edged rocks with a terrible trembling and groaning. We could see the bows then, a black wedge out in the break of the waves to port, with cargo spilling out of a cavern of a hole where the plates had been torn open. Bales of cotton bobbed about in the white water and the waves played with the great square cases that were supposed to contain the aero engines, smashing them to matchwood on the reef.

Patch gripped my arm. 'Look!' he shouted. A case had been flung towards us and it was splitting open. The contents cascaded into the sea. God knows what it was. The light by then was very dim. But it certainly wasn't the solid lump of an aero engine.

'Did you see?' He had hold of my arm and was pointing. And then the sudden excitement left him as the wreck on which we stood split across at the after end of the upper-deck. A great crack was opening up across the whole width of the ship. It tore the port ladder leading down to the well-deck from its fastenings, twisting it slowly as though an invisible hand were squeezing it. Rivet fastenings were torn out in machine-gun bursts and steel plates were ripped like calico. The gap widened – a yard, two yards; and then it was dark and night clamped down on the *Mary Deare*. By then the falling tide had exposed the reef, the seas had receded and the wreck was still.

We went back into the cabin and lay down under our sodden blankets. We didn't talk. Maybe we slept. I don't remember. I have no recollection of that night. It is like a blank in my mind. The sea's incessant roar, the wind piping a weird note through twisted metal and the sporadic clanging of a loose plate – that is all my recollection. I didn't feel any sense of fear. I don't think I even felt cold any more. I had reached that stage of physical and mental exhaustion that is beyond feeling.

But I remembered the dawn. It filtered into the dim recesses of my mind with the sense of something strange. I was conscious of movement – a long, precipitous roll, first one way, then the other. I could hear the sea, but there was no weight in the sound. The crash and roar of mountains of water smashing down on to rocks was gone, and someone was calling me. Bright sunlight stabbed my eyeballs and a face bent over me – a face that was sweaty and flushed under the greying stubble of a beard with eyes sunk deep in hollow sockets and skin stretched taut across forehead and cheekbone. 'We're afloat!' Patch said. His cracked lips were drawn back from his teeth in a sort of grin. 'Come and look.'

I staggered weakly to the entrance and looked out on a strange scene. The reefs had disappeared. The sun shone on a heaving sea, but there wasn't a sign of a rock anywhere. And all the *Mary Deare* for'ard of the well-deck had gone, vanished. The well-deck itself was under water, but it was as Patch had said – we were afloat; just the stern section and nothing else. And the sun was shining and the gale was diminishing. I could feel Patch trembling where he stood against me. I thought it was excitement. But it wasn't. It was fever.

By midday he was too weak to move, his eyes staring, his face flushed with unnatural colour and the sweat pouring out of him. He had been too long in the East to stand up to nights of exposure in sodden clothing without food. Towards nightfall he became delirious. Much of his raving was unintelligible, but now and then the words came clear and I realized he was back on that voyage up through the Bay, giving orders, talking to Rice . . . disjointed scraps that were an appalling revelation of the strain to which he had been subjected.

Towards evening a small aircraft flew over. I watched it circling low down to the north-west, its wings glinting in the setting sun. They were searching for us on the Minkies. And then night closed in and we still floated, very low in the water. There was a young moon hanging in a clear sky full of stars and the wind had gone so that the moon carved a small silver path across a placid, kindly sea that still heaved gently like a giant resting.

That night I was almost too weak to move and Patch lay like a corpse, shivering occasionally, his face still hot and his eyes wide in the faint moon-glow. Once he started up and seized my hand, trembling all over, words tumbling from his lips, words that had no meaning. But this sudden outburst – this raving – lasted only a short while. He hadn't the strength to keep it up and he suddenly fell back exhausted. I lay close against him all the rest of the night, but I had no warmth to give and in the morning he looked like a ghost, small under the stinking blankets.

I saw the Minkies again just after the sun had risen. They were on the horizon, small, jagged points of black etched sharp against the western sky. And then, much later, I heard the sound of an aircraft's engines. I had dragged Patch out on deck to get the warmth of the sun, but he was unconscious then. The aircraft went past us. I saw the shadow of it cross the water and I pulled myself up, searching the sky for it through bleared and gritty eyes. Then I saw it turning, banking out of the sun and coming back, very low over the water. I clutched the rail for support and waved a blanket at it as it zoomed over just above my head with its engines snarling. It flew off towards the Minkies and a long time afterwards, as I lay on the warmth of the deck in a semi-coma, I heard the putter of an engine and the sound of voices.

It was the Peter Port lifeboat. They came alongside and life stirred again at the sound of friendly voices . . . strong hands helping me over the rail, a lit cigarette thrust into my mouth. They stripped us of our salt-stiff, sodden clothing, wrapped us in blankets, and then sleep came to me, the wonderful relaxed warmth of sleep. But I remember, just before I lost consciousness, a voice saying, 'Want to take a last look at your ship?' And a hand lifted me up. I shall always remember that last glimpse of what was left of her. She was stern-on to us, very low in the water so that the deck-house, in which we had lived for two nights, looked like a chicken coop floating on the surface of the water. And then, in the trough of a swell, I saw the rust-streaked lettering of her stern – *MARY DEARE* – *Southampton*.

As far as I was concerned the story of the wreck of the *Mary Deare* ended there on the edge of the Minkies. But for Patch it was different. He was more directly involved and I was reminded of this as soon as I woke in the hospital at Peter Port. I didn't know it at the time, but I had slept for more than twenty hours. I was immensely hungry, but all the nurse brought me was a small plate of steamed fish, and she told me there was somebody urgently waiting to see me. I thought perhaps it was Mike, but when the door opened it was a girl standing there.

'Who is it?' I asked. The blinds were drawn and the room all darkened.

'It's Janet Taggart.' She came to the side of my bed and I recognized her then, though she looked very tired and there were dark hollows under her eyes. 'I had to see you – as soon as you woke.'

I asked her how she'd got here and she said, 'It was in the

papers. I came at once.' And then she leaned down over me. 'Listen, Mr Sands. Please listen to me. I'm only allowed to stay a moment.' Her voice trembled with urgency. 'I had to see you before you talked to anybody.'

She hesitated then, and I said, 'Well, what is it?' I found it difficult to concentrate. There were so many things I wanted to know and my mind was still blurred.

'The police will be coming to take a statement from you soon.' She paused again. She seemed to have difficulty in putting whatever it was she wanted to say into words. 'Didn't Gideon once save your life?'

'Gideon?' She meant Patch, of course. 'Yes,' I said. 'Yes, I suppose he did.' And then I asked her how he was. 'Didn't somebody tell me he had pneumonia?' I had a vague memory of the doctor telling me that when he was examining my shoulder.

'Yes,' she said. 'He's very ill. But he passed the crisis last night. He'll be all right now, I hope.'

'Have you been with him all the time?'

'Yes, I insisted. I had to – in case he talked.' And then she went on quickly: 'Mr Sands – that man Dellimare . . . You know what happened, don't you?'

I nodded. So he'd told her that, too. 'Nobody need ever know now,' I murmured. I felt tired and very weak. 'All the for'ard part of the ship broke up on that reef.'

'Yes, I know. That's why I had to see you before you made any statement. Don't tell anybody about it, will you. Please. He's suffered enough.'

I nodded. 'No. I won't tell anybody,' I said. And then I added, 'But there's Mike. He knows.'

'Mike Duncan? I've seen him. He hasn't said anything yet – either to the Press or to the police. He said he'd do nothing about it until he'd seen you. He'll do whatever you do.'

'You've seen Mike?' I pulled myself up in the bed. 'How is he? Is he all right?'

'Yes, he's here in Peter Port.' She was leaning down over me again. 'Can I tell him you're going to forget what Gideon told you? Can I tell him you want him to keep quiet about it, too?'

'Yes,' I said. 'Yes, of course – there's no point in saying anything about it now. It's over – finished.' And then I asked her how Mike had been picked up.

'It was a fisherman from St Helier. He found the motor boat just before the storm broke. There was a man called Burrows on board, too. He was badly injured, but he made a statement to the police – about Higgins.' And then she said, 'I must leave you now. I want to see Mr Duncan and then I must be with Gideon when he wakes – to see that he doesn't talk. It's the sort of silly thing he might do.' She smiled wanly. 'I'm so grateful to you.'

'Tell Mike to come and see me,' I said. And as she reached the door, I added, 'And tell – Gideon – when he wakes that he's nothing to worry about any more . . . nothing at all.'

She smiled then – a sudden warmth that lit her whole face up; for an instant she was the girl in the photograph again. And then the door closed and I lay back and went to sleep. When I woke again it was morning and the curtains were drawn back so that the sun streamed in. The police were there and I made a statement. One of them was a plain-clothes man from Southampton, but he was uncommunicative. All he would say about Patch was that he'd no instructions at the moment to make any arrest. After that there were reporters, and then Mike arrived. The police had refused to let him see me until I had made my statement.

He was full of news. The stern section of the *Mary Deare* had gone ashore on Chausey Island. He showed me a newspaper picture of it lying on its side in a litter of rocks at low water. And yesterday Snetterton had been through Peter Port. He'd had a salvage team with him and they had left for Chausey Island in a local fishing boat. 'And I've been on to our own insurance people,' he said. 'They're meeting our claim in full. We'll have enough to build to our own design, if we want to.'

'That means losing a whole season,' I said.

He nodded, grinning. 'As it happens there's a boat for sale right here in Peter Port would suit us nicely. I had a look at her last night. Not as pretty as *Sea Witch*, of course . . .' He was full of plans – one of those irrepressible people who bounce back up as soon as they're knocked down. He was as good a tonic as I could have wished and, though he still had a piece of adhesive tape stuck across the side of his jaw where the skin was split, he seemed none the worse for his thirty hours on the water-logged wreck of that motor boat.

I was discharged from hospital next day and when Mike came up to collect me, he brought a whole pile of London papers with him. 'Altogether you've had a pretty good Press,' he said, dumping them on my bed. 'And there's a newspaper fellow flew in this morning offering you a tidy little sum for a first-hand account of what happened. He's down at the hotel now.'

Later we went and looked at the boat Mike had discovered. She was cheap and sound and we bought her on the spot. And that night Snetterton turned up at our hotel, still neat, still dapper in his pin-stripe suit, though he'd spent two days on Chausey Island. They had cut into Number Four hold at low water and opened up three of the aero engine cases. The contents consisted of concrete blocks. 'A satisfactory result, Mr Sands. Most satisfactory. I have sent a full report to Scotland Yard.'

'But your San Francisco people will still have to pay the insurance, won't they?' I asked him.

'Oh, yes. Yes, of course. But we shall recover it from the Dellimare Company. Very fortunately they have a big sum standing to their credit in a Singapore bank – the proceeds of the sale of the *Torre Annunziata* and her cargo. We were able to get it frozen pending investigation. I think,' he added thoughtfully, 'that Mr Gundersen would have been better advised to have organized the resale of the aero engines through another company. But there – the best laid schemes . . .' He smiled as he sipped his sherry. 'It was a clever idea, though. Very clever indeed. That it failed is due entirely to Mr Patch – and to you, sir,' he added, looking at me over his glass. 'I have requested the H.B. & K.M. . . . well, we shall see.'

I wasn't able to see Patch before I left Peter Port. But I saw him three weeks later when we gave evidence before the resumed Court of Enquiry. He was still very weak. The charges against him had already been dropped; Gundersen had slipped out of the country and Burrows and other members of the crew were only too willing to tell the truth now, pleading that they had supported Higgins's story because they were frightened of him. The Court found that the loss of the *Mary Deare* was due to conspiracy to defraud on the part of the owners, Patch was absolved from all blame and the whole matter was referred to the police for action.

A good deal of publicity was given to the affair at the time and, as a result of it, Patch was given command of the *Wacomo*, a 10,000-ton freighter. He and Janet were married by then, but our diving programme had prevented us from attending the wedding and I didn't see him again until September of the following year. Mike and I were in Avonmouth then, getting ready to dive for a wreck in the Bristol Channel, and the *Wacomo* came in from Singapore and moored across the dock from us. That night we dined on board with Patch.

I barely recognized him. The lines were gone from his face and, though the stoop was still there and his hair was greying at the temples, he looked young and full of confidence in his uniform with the gold stripes. On his desk stood the same photograph in its silver frame, but across the bottom Janet had written: *For my husband now – bons voyages.* And framed on the wall was a letter from the H.B. & K.M. Corporation of San Francisco.

That letter had been handed to Janet by Snetterton at their wedding reception, and with it a cheque for £5000 for her husband's part in exposing the fraud – a strangely apt figure! At the time Mike and I had been working on a wreck off the Hook of Holland, and when we got back I found a similar letter waiting for me, together with a cheque for £2500 – *as some compensation for the loss of your vessel.*

The body of Alfred Higgins was never recovered, but in August of that year a metal dinghy, with patches of blue paint still adhering to it, was found wedged in a crevice of the rocks on the south side of Alderney. It had been battered almost flat by the seas.

One final thing – an entry in the log of *Sea Witch II* made on 8 September, just after we had located and buoyed the wreck in the Bristol Channel. It reads: *11.48 – Freighter WACOMO passed us outward-bound for Singapore and Hong Kong. Signalled us: 'Captain Patch's compliments and he is not, repeat not, trying to run you down this time! Good wrecking!' She then gave us three blasts on her siren, to which we responded on the fog-horn.* A month later, with *Sea Witch II* laid up for the winter, I began this account of the loss of the *Mary Deare.*

ATLANTIC FURY

PART ONE

I

DECISION TO EVACUATE
(12–13 October)

The decision to withdraw the Unit from Laerg was taken early in October. That it was a fatal decision is now obvious. It was taken too late in the year, and in the initial phases the operation was carried out with too little sense of urgency. Whether the disastrous consequences of that decision would have been avoided if the personalities involved had been different I cannot say. Certainly personality played a part in what happened. It always does. A decision that calls for action involves men, and men cannot escape their own natures; their upbringing, their training, their basic characters. Moreover, in this particular case, a series of mishaps, unimportant in isolation, but cumulatively dangerous in combination with the colossal forces unleashed against us, led inevitably to disaster . . .

This was the opening paragraph of a statement I found among my brother's papers. It was written in his own hand, when his mind was still lucid. Intended as a refutation of the charges brought against him, the statement was never completed. Together with his notes and all his other papers, it lies before me now in the lamplight as I embark on the task of writing this account of the disaster. And the fact that I am writing of it in the solitariness of my winter isolation here on Laerg, with the same violent winds battering at the door, the same damp, salt-laden atmosphere blackening the night outside and Sgeir Mhor standing like a battlement against the Atlantic, will I hope give it a clarity not otherwise possible; that, and the fact that I was involved in it, too.

Not directly, as my brother was; and not with his burden of responsibility. Laerg was a military establishment at the time, and I am an artist, not a soldier. But for both of us it held a fatal fascination. It was in our blood, and looking back on it, our paths crossing after so many years and in such circumstances, there seems to have been something inevitable about it, as though Laerg itself were an integral part of the pattern of our lives.

There is, of course, no mention in my brother's notes of his personal reasons for wanting the Army out of Laerg, no hint of the fearful thing that drew him back to the island. And the fact that he had been so many years in the Army inhibited him in his writing. For instance, he gives no account of his interviews with Standing. He merely states the facts and leaves it at that, so that there is no indication of his relations with his Commanding Officer. Fortunately I have my own notes from which to work. These last few months I have interviewed most of the men involved in the disaster. As a result I have been able to add considerably to my personal knowledge of what happened. I have also had access to the depositions taken at the Board of Inquiry and also to the transcripts covering the first two days of the abortive Court Martial. There are still gaps, of course. So many men were killed. If I could have talked with Colonel Standing, for instance ...

However, the picture in my mind is as complete as it can ever be. And that picture is dominated, of course, by Laerg. Laerg – forbidding and mysterious, rising out of the Atlantic like the last peaks of a submerged land, its shaggy heights lost in cloud, its massive cliffs resounding to the snowflake swirl of millions of seabirds. Laerg dwarfs the men, the ships; it dominates the whole story.

Until that October I had never even seen Laerg. This may seem strange, considering my father was born there and that I'd been half in love with it since I was a kid. But Laerg isn't the sort of place you can visit at will. It lies more than eighty miles west of the Outer Hebrides, a small island group composed of Laerg itself, which with Eileann nan Shoay and Sgeir Mhor constitutes the main island; the bare rock islet of Vallay; and Fladday with its attendant stacs of Hoe and Rudha. Eighty sea miles is no great distance, but this is the North Atlantic and the seven islands of the Laerg group are a lonely cluster standing on the march of the great depressions that sweep up towards Iceland and the Barents Sea. Not only are sea conditions bad throughout the greater part of the year, but the islands, rising sheer out of the waves to a height of almost 1400 feet, breed their own peculiar brand of weather.

Oddly enough, it wasn't my father who'd made me long to go to Laerg. He seldom talked of the island. He'd gone to sea as a young man and then married a Glasgow girl and settled as a crofter on Ardnamurchan after losing his nerve in a typhoon.

It was Grandfather Ross who'd filled our heads with talk of our island ancestors.

This gnarled old man with a craggy face and huge hands had been a powerful influence in both our lives. He'd come to live with us following the evacuation of the islanders in 1930. He'd been the only man to vote against it when the Island Parliament made its decision, and to the day he died in 1936 he'd resented living on the mainland. It wasn't only that he talked endlessly of Laerg; in those six years he taught my brother Iain, and myself, everything he knew about the way to live in a world of rock and towering heights where sheep and birds were the raw materials of existence.

I'd tried to get there once a long time ago, hiding away on a trawler anchored in the bay below our croft. But that trip they hadn't gone within a hundred miles of Laerg, and then the war came and I joined Iain, working in a Glasgow factory making shell cases. A year in the Navy and ten years at sea, tramping, mainly in old Liberty ships, and then I had embarked on the thing I had always wanted to do – I began to study as a painter. It was during a winter spent in the Aegean Isles that I suddenly realized Laerg was the subject that most attracted me. It had never been painted, not the way my grandfather had described it. I'd packed up at once and returned to England, but by then Laerg had become a tracking station for the new rocket range on Harris. It was a closed island, forbidden to unauthorized civilians, and neither the Army nor Nature Conservancy, who leased it from the National Trust for Scotland, would give me permission to visit it.

That was the position until October of the following year when a man called Lane came to my studio and I was caught up in my brother's strange story and the events that led to the disaster. But first I must give the background to the Army's decision to evacuate Laerg, for without that decision the disaster would never have happened.

The future of the tracking station was discussed at a Conference held in the Permanent Under-Secretary's room at the War Office and the decision to close it was confirmed by the Director Royal Artillery at a meeting in his office four days later. In my reconstruction of the Conference I am indebted to the frankness with which the DRA described it to me. For the details of the subsequent meeting I have also had the benefit of talks with his Brigadier General Staff and with Brigadier Matthieson, the Brigadier Royal Artillery, Scottish Command. The latter, in addition, was able to recall for me in considerable detail his conversation with Braddock on the night train going north. These two senior officers both gave evidence at the Court Martial and my talks with them were supplementary to that evidence.

First then, the Conference. This was held on 7 October and in addition to the Permanent Under-Secretary for War, there were present the Director of Finance, the Director Royal Artillery, and, during the vital discussion on the fate of Laerg, a member of the staff of the Ordnance Board. The object of the conference was to review Royal Artillery expenditure for the current financial year. This was one of a series of War Office conferences necessitated by the Prime Minister's refusal to face the House with supplementaries to the original Estimates.

There were eleven items on the agenda for that afternoon, all affecting the Royal Artillery. Laerg was sixth on the list. It came up for discussion about half past three and I understand the Director of Finance had all the costings ready to hand, reading them out in a flat monotone that was barely audible above the roar of Whitehall traffic. It was a long list and when he'd finished he put it back in his brief-case and faced the DRA. 'I think you'll agree,' he said, 'that the cost of maintaining the detachment on Laerg is quite disproportionate to the contribution it makes to our guided weapons tests.' He then went on, I gather, to emphasize the point he wanted to make. 'Your firing season finishes when?'

'Some time in August,' the DRA replied.

'And it starts in May.'

'In May – yes. But we begin the build-up in April.'

'In other words, the station is dormant for at least seven months of the year. And during those seven months it requires a Detachment Commander, usually a Captain, a Medical Officer and two orderlies, cooks, drivers, a REME outfit, even seamen military, a total of anything from thirty to forty men. There are two LCTs Mark VIII involved in ferrying supplies and . . .'

'The tank landing craft don't function in the winter.'

'Quite so. But they are nevertheless committed to this operation and are merely withdrawn to Squadron Headquarters at Portsmouth for re-fit. They are replaced by an RASC trawler. Not so costly perhaps, but still pretty expensive. In addition, a helicopter is periodically required to deliver mail.'

Throughout this interchange the DRA explained to me that he was very much on the defensive. He knew the operation could not be justified on grounds of cost alone. 'It's the men,' he said. 'They feel cut off if they don't get regular mail. In any case, we've already decided to dispense with the trawler this winter and rely on Army helicopters for mail and relief of personnel. An experiment recommended by Colonel Standing, the Range Commandant. We've yet to find out how it will work. Conditions for helicopter flying are not all that good, particularly after the end of October.'

'That's merely a matter of detail,' the Director of Finance said. 'I have been into all this very carefully. Correct me if I'm wrong, but as I understand it the only maintenance required on the really vital equipment, the radar, is that it should be run once a day, mainly to warm it up. One man's work for a few hours each day. To keep him there you apparently require over thirty men . . .'

'I've reported on this to the Secretary for War more than once,' the DRA cut in. 'The tracking station cost a lot to establish. It isn't only the radar that has to be maintained. There's the camp, the vehicles, the boats; to abandon Laerg for seven months in the year would result in rapid deterioration through gales and the salt in the atmosphere. Moreover, trawlermen use Shelter Bay in the winter – Norwegians, Belgians, French, Spanish, as well as Scots. There wouldn't be much left of our installations if there were nobody there to guard them.'

At this point the Permanent Under-Secretary intervened. 'I don't think we need query the number of men involved, or the necessity for maintaining the station throughout the year in present circumstances. Presumably this was all gone into at the time and agreed as unavoidable. What we have to decide now is whether or not Laerg has become redundant in view of this new equipment we've been offered. You've had a report on it, I believe. The results of the trials were very impressive, I thought.'

The DRA didn't say anything. He was staring out of the window at the cloudless blue of the sky. From where he sat he looked across the pale stone outline of the Horseguards to the trees in St James's Park. They were still in summer leaf. It had been a mild autumn and so fine were the yellow brush strokes of the early frosts that only a painter's eye would have discerned the warning breath of winter in that green canvas. The DRA was not a painter. His hobby, he explained to me, was birdwatching and he was wishing he had been able to find time to visit Laerg during the nesting season. The room was hot and airless, full of smoke, and the sun slanted golden bars of light across the table.

'Before we finally make up our minds, perhaps we should hear what Ordnance Board have to say about it.' The Permanent Under-Secretary reached for the phone and asked for the Colonel who had conducted the trials to be sent in. The discussion that followed was technical, and as the equipment concerned was secret the DRA did not discuss it with me. He did, however, say that it was American equipment and that he had pointed out that it would be costly to install. To this the Permanent Under-Secretary had replied, 'But as they are using the range themselves they are offering it to us on a long-term credit basis.' That, the DRA told me, was the decisive factor. The matter was settled and what happened later stemmed from that moment, for the Permanent Under-Secretary was under considerable pressure. 'I'd like to be able to report to the PM,' he said, 'that you'll have your men and equipment off the island and the station closed down, say by the end of the month. Would that be possible?'

'I suppose so. It depends on the weather.'

'Naturally. But we're in for a fine spell now. I heard the forecast this morning.'

'Laerg is over six hundred miles north of here and it's getting late in the season.'

'All the more reason to hurry it.'

The DRA was not disposed to argue. He had held his appointment for less than six months, and anyway he was wondering how to handle the next item on the agenda, which was of far more importance to the Artillery than Laerg. 'I've no doubt we'll manage,' he said and made a note on his pad to instruct his Brigadier General Staff.

The BGS, questioned by the President of the Court Martial about the DRA's acceptance of that time limit, made the point that some such limit was essential in an operation of this kind. If the evacuation were not completed before the winter gales set in, there would be little likelihood of getting the men and equipment off that winter. Even a partial failure to complete it would necessitate the maintenance of the station probably until the spring, with all the attendant problems of supply aggravated by the fact that essential stores would be lacking. 'Without a time limit,' he said, 'the operation would have lacked the necessary atmosphere of urgency.'

Unfortunately, all the items on the agenda could not be dealt with that afternoon and the conference was resumed again at ten the following morning. As a result, the Brigadier General Staff received his instructions about Laerg in the form of a hurriedly dictated memo that listed some half dozen other items for his immediate attention. The BGS was a keen yachtsman, and though he had never sailed in the Hebrides, he was able to appreciate better than most people in the War Office the difficulties that could arise in an evacuation involving landing craft operating across an open beach. With the week-end imminent he decided to shelve the matter until Monday when Brigadier Matthieson was due in London. He marked it in his diary for the morning of 11 October, the final decision to be taken after discussion with the DRA. Meantime, he teleprinted Matthieson at Scottish Command ordering him to have a plan of operations prepared for the immediate withdrawal of all stores, equipment and personnel.

Having established that there was a delay of four vital days between the DRA's original agreement to the principle of evacuation and the final decision to go ahead, I should perhaps add that only exceptional circumstances would have produced speedier action, and in this case the exceptional circumstances had not arisen. The pressure at this stage was from the Permanent Under-Secretary, not from the weather; a full two weeks was to elapse before that freak meteorological brew began to ferment in the sea areas Bailey, Hebrides and Faeroes. There was, in any case, a good deal of preliminary work to be done. In particular, the agreement of the RASC to the use of the landing craft had to be obtained and the plan itself worked out. This last the DRA, Scottish Command, brought with him to London so that once it was agreed it only needed an executive order to start the thing moving.

After reading the plan and discussing it with Matthieson, the BGS took him in to see the General. It was then just after midday and again the weather was fine in London, the sun shining out of a clear sky. In describing this meeting to me, Matthieson made it clear that though the DRA was under considerable pressure at the time and obviously determined to proceed with the evacuation, he had, nevertheless, been at some pains to allay any fears his subordinates might have. 'I suppose you're worrying about the weather,' was his opening remark. 'Naturally, I raised the point myself. The Permanent Under-Secretary was not impressed. The sun was shining and it was damnably hot in his room.' He glanced towards the windows. 'The sun is still shining. Did you listen to the shipping forecast this morning?' This to the BGS. And when he admitted he hadn't, the General said, 'Well, I did. Made a special point of it. I know you sailing types. There's a high pressure system covering the British Isles and the nearest depression is down in the German Bight. As to the alternative we've been offered, the responsibility rests with Ordnance Board. I made that perfectly plain. If it doesn't work . . .'

'Oh, I expect it'll work, sir,' the BGS said.

'Well, what's worrying you then?'

'Apart from the weather – Simon Standing.'

'Standing? He's one of our best instructors.'

'That's just the trouble. He's a wizard at ballistics, but this is his first independent command and if anything went wrong . . .'

'Have you any reason to suppose that anything is going to go wrong?'

'Of course not. All I'm saying is that this operation doesn't call for the qualities that make a brilliant Instructor-in-Gunnery. It calls for a man of action.'

'Fine. It will give him some practical experience. Isn't that why you recommended him for the job? Practical experience is essential if he is to go on getting promotion at his present rate. How old is he?'

'Thirty-seven, thirty-eight.'

'That makes him just about the youngest IG with the rank of full Colonel. And he's ambitious. He'll make out all right. I seem to remember he's got Hartley as his second-in-command. Met him at Larkhill. Excellent at administration and a sound tactician. Just the man Simon needs.'

'Unfortunately he's in hospital – jaundice.'

'I see. Well, there's an adjutant presumably.'

'Young fellow by the name of Ferguson. He's not very experienced.'

'And you're not happy about him?'

'I can't say that. I don't know anything much about him. He's only twenty-six, just promoted Captain and filling in a vacancy.'

'What's wrong with him then?'

'Well . . .' I don't think the BGS wanted to go into this, but it was essential to the point he was making. 'His record shows that he volunteered for paratrooping and didn't complete the course.'

'Funked his jumps?'

'Something like that. He was posted to BAOR.'

'All right then. Get on to AG6. Have them post somebody up there temporarily just to hold Simon's hand – an older man with practical experience. The AAG ought to be able to rake up somebody to fill in for a few weeks. Anything else on your mind?'

'Only the timing. The operation has been planned on the

basis of completion by the end of the month. But nobody can possibly guarantee that. Fortunately we'd agreed to Standing's idea of cutting the size of the wintering unit and maintaining contact by helicopter. As a result one of the huts has already been dismantled. Nevertheless, I must emphasize that the maintenance of a planning schedule as tight as this depends entirely on the continuance of the present fine weather.'

'Of course. That's understood. Service Corps have already made it clear that they're not taking any chances with their landing craft. And rightly.' He turned to Matthieson. 'That satisfy you?'

Matthieson hesitated. He was well aware of the dangers. He told me he had tried to visit Laerg twice and each time had been turned back by bad weather. He had held his present post for almost two years and he knew the difficulties that must arise if conditions deteriorated and the operation became a protracted one. But this was only the second interview he had had with the DRA since the General's appointment. Doubtless he felt it wasn't the moment to voice his misgivings. My impression is that he decided to play his luck. At any rate, all he apparently said was, 'Captain Pinney, the present Detachment Commander, is pretty experienced; so is the skipper of one of the landing craft – the other was a replacement halfway through the season. Still, I think the whole thing should go off quite smoothly.' However, to cover himself, he added, 'But Laerg can be the devil if it blows up and we're getting on towards winter in the north.'

The DRA nodded. 'Well, that settles it then. We pray for fine weather and get on with the job, eh? Signal them to go ahead with the operation right away.'

And so the decision was finally agreed. Matthieson sent off the necessary signal and the BGS phoned about the temporary attachment of an officer to assist Standing.

He was immediately offered a Major George Braddock.

The reason given by the AAG for recommending this particular officer was that he wanted to be posted to the Hebrides. Not only had Braddock written twice from Cyprus, where he commanded a battery, but a few days before he had sought a personal interview with the AAG to press the matter. He had then just arrived in London on leave.

To the BGS it seemed the perfect answer to the problem. Braddock was about forty, his rank was right, and so was his record. He had an MC and two Mentions in Despatches, awarded during the last war, as well as an excellent record during the

Malayan troubles. Moreover, he was in England and immediately available. Locating him took a little time. His wife, who with her two children lived at Hertford, had apparently been separated from him for a number of years and did not know where he was. All she could say was that he liked fishing and usually went to Wales for his leave. He was eventually traced to a Country Club near Brecon. By then it was late at night and Braddock didn't reach London until the following afternoon.

That was Tuesday and as far as I can gather that was the day Ed Lane arrived in Lyons. I suppose almost every disaster requires something to trigger it off – a catalyst, as it were. *A decision that calls for action involves men, and men cannot escape their own natures . . . their basic characters.* In writing that I believe my brother was thinking of this Canadian business man from Vancouver. Lane wasn't, of course, involved in the operation. He was probing Braddock's background and to that extent he exerted a pressure on events and was, in a sense, the catalyst. He had seen Braddock in Cyprus a fortnight before and had then gone on to the Middle East on business for his firm. Now that business was finished and he was free to concentrate on his private affairs. Whilst Braddock was travelling up to the War Office, Lane was interviewing one of the few people who could help him in his inquiries.

The BGS saw Braddock just after four. In his evidence, the Brigadier simply said that the interview strengthened the favourable impression already created by his record. He was satisfied that Major Braddock was the right man for the job. He was not asked for any details, only for confirmation that he had warned Braddock about weather conditions. As a result, the Court was not aware that the Brigadier was puzzled, even a little disturbed, by the answers Braddock gave to certain rather searching questions.

In the talk I had with him later the Brigadier admitted that he had been curious to know why Braddock had applied for a posting to the Guided Weapons Establishment, particularly as his record showed that he had been one of the few survivors of the *Duart Castle*, sunk in those waters during the war. 'I should have thought your memories of that area . . .'

'That's got nothing to do with it, sir. It's just that – well, I guess it's because I spent part of my boyhood in Canada. I like cold climates. The further north the better. And I like something to get my teeth into. Malaya was all right for a bit. But Cyprus . . .'
And then with an intensity that the Brigadier found disconcerting: 'Is there any particular reason why I'm being posted to the Heb-

rides now – other than to deal with the problem of this evacuation of Laerg?'

'No, of course not. Why should there be?'

Braddock had seemed to relax then. 'I just wondered. I mean, when you apply for a posting and then suddenly get it . . .' The lined, leathery-hard face had cracked in a charming smile. 'Well, it makes you wonder what's behind it.'

'Nothing's behind it,' the Brigadier told him. 'I was simply referring to what happened to you up there in 1944.' He told me he was wishing then that he knew the man better, feeling instinctively that there was more to it than he'd admitted. 'How many of you were on that raft at the outset?' He watched the tough, poker face, saw the nerve quiver at the corner of the mouth and the eyes fixed wide in a flat, blank stare. 'No, I thought not. It's something you'd rather forget. Have you ever visited the Hebrides since?'

'No.'

'Then why do you want to be posted there now?'

But Braddock either couldn't or wouldn't answer that. 'It's just that . . . well, as I said – it sort of calls to me. I can't explain exactly.' And he'd smiled that engaging smile. 'It's a bit like Canada, I suppose.'

The Brigadier hesitated. But it was nothing to do with him and he'd let it go at that, staring down again at Braddock's record. The Normandy landings – anti-tank role – the MC for gallantry at Caen after holding a bridge with a single gun against repeated attacks by tanks – command of a troop two months later – promoted captain just before the dash for the Rhine – temporary rank of major at the end of the war . . . 'Now about this operation. Do you sail at all?'

'I've done a little.'

'Good. Then you'll have some idea what the weather means to the LCTs, particularly in view of your previous experience . . .' He had got up from his desk and turned towards the window. 'However, that isn't why I wanted to see you personally.' The sky was blue and the sun beat down on the stone ledge of the tight-shut window. 'Ever met Simon Standing?' He turned as Braddock shook his head. 'No, I didn't think your paths would have crossed. Can't imagine two people more entirely different – which may be a good thing, or again it may not. Colonel Standing is Commandant and Range Controller. He's a few years younger than you and it's his first independent command. Now this is what I want to make clear to you, and it's strictly between ourselves. Standing's up there primarily because he's an expert on ballistics and all that sort of thing. In fact, he's one of the best brains we've got in the field of guided weapons. But for a job like this . . .' He had hesitated then. 'Well, his world is figures. He's not strictly an action man, if you see what I mean.' And he went on quickly, 'Officially, of course, it's his show and you come under him as acting second-in-command. Unofficially, I want you to run the operation.' Faced with the blank stare of those black eyes he probably felt it was all damnably awkward, for he admitted to me later that he thought Braddock should have been a half-colonel at least. He had the experience and he had that indefinable something, that air of confidence denoting a born leader. He may even have wondered what had gone wrong, but at the time all he said was, 'Just keep Simon Standing in the picture and get on with the job. If you bear in mind that he's quite brilliant in his own field and . . . well, use a little tact.'

'I understand, sir.'

'I hope you do.' The Brigadier had hesitated then, feeling instinctively that a clash of temperament was inevitable. Ever since Braddock had come into his office he had been conscious of the strength of the man's personality, and something else – a tension, almost a sense of urgency. But there was nothing he could do about that now. Time was too short. 'There's a sleeper reserved for you on the night train. You'll be travelling up with the BRA, Scottish Command. He'll give you all the details.' And with a murmured 'Good luck' he had dismissed him.

He admitted later that Braddock should have been given the opportunity to discuss the operation. But throughout the interview he'd felt uncomfortable. The large hands, the dark moustache, the lined, leathery face with the heavy brows craggy above the black stare of the eyes – somehow, he said, the man seemed to fill the office, too big for it almost. So strong was this feeling that he'd been glad when the door had shut behind him.

The train left Euston at nine thirty-five and ten minutes after it pulled out Braddock visited Brigadier Matthieson in his sleeper. I suspect that Matthieson was one of those officers who joined the Royal Artillery for the riding, back in the days when the guns were horse-drawn. I don't think he had much of a brain, but he was certainly no fool and he was as good with men as he was with horses. He never forgot a face. 'Met you somewhere before, haven't I?' he said and was surprised to find this overture rejected almost fiercely. 'A long time ago, I think. Now where was it?'

'I think you've made a mistake, sir.'

But Matthieson was quite sure he hadn't. 'During the war.' He saw Braddock's face tauten, and then he had it – a tall, hard-bitten youngster in a blood-stained battledress coming back with a single gun buckled by a direct hit. 'Normandy. Autumn of forty-four. You'd been holding a bridge.' The craggy face towering above him relaxed, broke into the same charming, rather tired-looking smile. 'I remember now, sir. You were the major bivou-acked in that wood. You gave us food – the few of us that were left. A tent, too. We were just about all in.'

They'd talked about the war then, sitting on Matthieson's berth, finishing the bottle of Scotch he'd brought south with him. It was almost midnight and the bottle empty by the time they got around to discussing Laerg. Matthieson pulled out his brief-case and handed Braddock the Plan of Operations. 'The schedule's a bit tight, but that's not my fault. About ten LCT loads should do the trick. Read it through tonight. Any points we can discuss in the morning. I've a car meeting me and I'll drive you out to Renfrew Airport.'

Braddock, leafing quickly through the Plan, immediately expressed concern about the schedule. 'I have some experience of the weather up there . . .'

'On an open raft. So the BGS told me. But you're not dealing with a raft this time. These LCTs can stand quite a lot.'

'It's an open beach. If the wind's south-easterly . . .'

'You know the place, do you?'

He saw Braddock's face tighten. 'I looked it up on a map,' he said quickly, and Matthieson wondered how he'd got hold of a map with the shops closed. 'If the weather goes against us . . .'

'It's the weather you're being posted up there to deal with. The weather and that fellow Standing.' He was well aware that the schedule was too tight and he wanted to get Braddock off the subject. 'Ever met Simon Standing? Do you know anything about him?' And when the other shook his head, he went on, 'Give you a word of advice then. Don't fall out with him. War Office thinks he's wonderful. But I can tell you he's a queer fish and he's got no sense of humour.' He was very frank about the words he'd used. 'Bloody little prig, if you ask me.' I imagine he smiled then, a flash of teeth that were too white and even to be his own. 'Shouldn't be talking like this about your commanding officer, should I? But we've seen a war together. These adding machine types haven't. Probably puke if they did. A real war, I mean – blood and the stink of rotting guts, the roar of a thousand guns blazing hell out of a dawn sky. They're push-button warriors;

nothing but bloody electricians.'

He was staring down at his glass then, memories of a long-dead war merging with the future. 'Anyway, I'm getting out. In a few months' time I'll be running a stud farm near Melbourne. Australia, you know. Once I get out there they can push all the ruddy little buttons they like.' It was the drink in him talking, and because he was aware of that he said, 'Well, I'm off to bed now.'

It was then that Braddock surprised him by asking a series of questions that seemed to have very little bearing on the operation. First, he'd wanted to know whether the men on Laerg were free to roam around the island or whether their duties kept them confined to the area of Shelter Bay. When told that off-duty they could go where they liked and that many of them became enthusiastic bird-watchers, Braddock asked if they'd reported any interesting finds? 'I mean traces of . . . well, old dwellings, caves, things like that with traces of human habitation?'

Matthieson wondered what he was getting at. 'Are you a student of primitive man or are you thinking of the link between the Hebrides and Greenland? There was a link, I believe. The Vikings put the sheep on Eileann nan Shoay – Shoay or Soay is the old word for sheep, you know. They may well have been on their way west to the Greenland settlement.'

'Yes, I've read about that, but . . . Well, I just thought something fresh might have been reported.' And Braddock had stared at him with disconcerting directness, waiting for an answer.

'No, of course not,' the Brigadier replied. 'The boys are just amateurs.'

'What about civilians – naturalists and so on? Are they allowed on the island?'

Matthieson admitted he was disturbed by the other's persistence. But all he said was, 'Yes. There's usually a party of bird-watchers, a few naturalists. Students, some of them. They come in summer under the aegis of Nature Conservancy. A nuisance, but quite harmless.'

'And they've reported nothing – nothing of exceptional interest?'

'If they have, we haven't been told about it.' And he'd added, 'Anyway, you won't have time to indulge your interest. Your job is to get our boys off, and it'll be a full-time job, believe you me. You'll understand when you've had time to study that Operations Plan.' And he'd wished Braddock goodnight, wondering as the train rushed on into the night what Standing would make of his new second-in-command.

Two coaches back Braddock started going through the Operations Plan, sitting propped up in bed, the pages dancing to the sway and rattle of the train. And almost a thousand miles away another man in another sleeper was checking through the notes he'd made of his first interview with a non-Canadian survivor of the *Duart Castle*. Ed Lane was on the train to Paris, bound for London with a list of five possible names.

The night train to Glasgow got in at six-thirty in the morning. A staff car was waiting for Brigadier Matthieson at Central Station and whilst driving Braddock out to Renfrew Airport he discussed with him the details of the Operations Plan. In his evidence he made it clear that he'd allowed Major Braddock the widest possible interpretation of the evacuation orders. What, in fact, happened was that Braddock not only had a list of queries, but seemed prepared to argue that the whole conception of the Plan was at fault. It was the timing, of course, that chiefly worried him. 'I agree it doesn't give you much room for manoeuvre,' Matthieson had said. 'But that's not my fault. It's the Government that's pushing the operation.' And he'd added, 'I'm a great believer in sound planning and the chaps who handled this are very good at it. If they say it can be done, then you can take it from me that it can.'

But Braddock wasn't to be put off so easily. 'LCT so-and-so to sail on such-and-such a date, arrive Laerg about twelve hours later, loading time six hours, leave at dusk, return to base at dawn. All very nice and neat if you're sitting on your backside in an office. But there's no allowance for weather or any of the hundred-and-one things that can go wrong on an amphibious operation. It's an open beach. The equipment is pretty valuable, I gather – some of it secret. What happens if a gale blows up? Do I risk a landing craft and the equipment simply to keep to a schedule I don't believe in?'

'Damn it, man. Use your initiative. That's why you're being posted there.' And Matthieson had added, quoting, as no doubt he'd often done before, from the wartime leader he'd served under, 'I never interfere in the detailed running of things. That's my speciality. I leave it to the experts. In this case, Braddock, you're the expert. Understood?'

By that time they had arrived at Renfrew. Matthieson left him then and after a leisurely breakfast Braddock caught the ten o'clock plane. At Stornoway there was an Army helicopter waiting for him. He landed at Northton on the west coast of Harris shortly after one. There he was met by the adjutant, Captain Ferguson, who informed him that Colonel Standing was waiting for him in his office. There is no record of what happened between the two men at that first meeting. But it lasted little more than ten minutes and when they came into the Mess for lunch the atmosphere between them was already strained.

The clearest impression of Braddock's impact on the operation is contained in the deposition made by Lieutenant Field, the Education Officer. This deposition, made at the Board of Inquiry, could have had considerable influence on the subsequent Court Martial. Not only was Field much older than the other officers, but his background and experience gave weight to his judgement. The first two paragraphs are the vital ones and I give them in full:–

Major Braddock arrived at Joint Services Guided Weapons Establishment, Northton, on 13 October. I think it is right to say that his appointment came as a shock to most of the officers, not least to Colonel Standing who had only been informed of it on the phone that morning. I say 'shock' because that is how it seemed to officers accustomed to something in the nature of a winter hibernation in the Hebrides. Major Braddock was a driver. He had a very forceful personality. He was also a man of great nervous energy, great vitality. Whatever your findings, I would like to make it clear that I regard him as exactly the sort of man the operation needed at that time.

I have some knowledge of the leadership necessary in an operation that is at the mercy of the elements, and from my own observations, and from what I heard from Captain Ferguson, who was a friend of my daughter's and often visited our croft of an evening, I may say that I already had certain very definite misgivings. Not until Major Braddock's arrival was there that thrust and pressuring of officers and men, that sense of being engaged with an enemy, that is the essential prelude to exceptional human endeavour. He made them feel they were involved in a battle. Most of the youngsters got a kick out of it; the older ones, particularly some of the officers, resented it. Later, of course, they did all that any men could do in circumstances that became virtually impossible.

Before he left for London, Matthieson had had the foresight to arrange with RASC (Water Transport) for both LCTs to re-fuel, cancel all leave and stand by to sail at short notice. As a result, the position on Braddock's arrival was not unsatisfactory. One landing craft had completed its first trip and was on its way back to Laerg again; the other was just entering Leverburgh, a bare two hours behind schedule. And the weather was fine, cold and clear with a light northerly wind.

But as Field pointed out, the fine weather could not be expected to last indefinitely, nor could the men. The strains were already beginning to show; at Leverburgh where the quay was inadequate, on Laerg where the bolts securing huts and equipment were rusted solid and the men, after only two days, were tiring, moving in a sleepless daze from dismantling to loading and back to dismantling again. And whilst Braddock threw himself into the work of ensuring a faster rate of turn-round for the landing craft, Ed Lane flew into London and began checking for relatives of Albert George Piper, one-time Master-at-Arms on the *Duart Castle*.

Piper's name was the first on his list. The second was my brother's.

2

MY BROTHER, IAIN
(15 October)

It was two days later, just after ten on the morning of 15 October, that my phone rang and a man's voice, rather soft, said, 'Mr Ross? My name's Ed Lane. Are you by any chance related to a Sergeant Iain Alasdair Ross reported lost when the *Duart Castle* was torpedoed in February 1944?'

'He was my brother.'

'He was?' The voice had a vaguely American accent. 'Well, that's fine. Didn't expect to strike it that fast – you're only the fifth Ross I've telephoned. I'll be with you inside of an hour. Okay?' And he'd rung off, leaving me wondering what in the world it was all about.

I was working on another book jacket for Alec Robinson, but after that phone call I found it impossible to go back to it. I went into the little kitchenette and brewed myself some coffee. And after that I stood drinking it at the window, looking out across the rooftops, an endless vista of chimney pots and TV aerials with a distant glimpse of Tower Bridge. I was thinking of my brother, of how I'd loved him and hated him, of how there had been nobody else in my life who had made up for the loss

I'd felt at his going. And yet at the time I'd been almost glad. It had seemed better that he should die like that – in the sea, a casualty of war.

I turned away from the grubby window, glanced at the jacket design lying on the table amongst a litter of paints and brushes, and then fell to pacing my studio, wondering what this fellow Lane wanted digging up the past that was dead these twenty years and more. Surely to God they weren't going to rake over the whole wretched business again. I could still remember the shock when the Military Police had come to interview me at the factory. Did I know where Iain was, had I seen him, had he visited me? Did I realize he'd deserted? Slinging questions at me until they'd discovered my father was dead and my mother alone and ill at Ardnamurchan. 'We'll pick him up there then.' And my bursting into tears and shouting at them that whatever my brother had done it was justified and why the hell did they pick on him and not the officer. And that MP sergeant with the big ears and the broken nose – I could have drawn his face even now – snapping back at me in a grating Glaswegian voice, 'The officer was unconscious, laddie, with machine-gun bullets spraying him as he lay on the ground with a broken jaw. Aye and damn near twenty men dead who needn't have died. Justified? Christ, it was plain bluidy mur-rder.'

The jacket design stared at me, the lettering of the book title already pencilled in – THE PEACE THAT FOLLOWED. I had read it, thought it good, but now I dropped a rag over it, remembering the wartime passages, the sense of futility the writer had invoked. Sounds from the street drifted up to me, the bustle of London's East End. My studio was just an attic over a butcher's shop. It was all I could afford. Bed, table and easel took up most of the space, and the canvases stacked against the wall, all the work I'd done on Milos – there was hardly room to move. A cupboard in the corner held my clothes and above it was piled the camping equipment I'd bought from the proceeds of the only two pictures I'd sold – *Milos at Dawn Seen from a Caique* and *Greek Galley Under Water*. That was when I planned to paint on Laerg, before I'd been refused permission to go there.

I crossed to the window, thinking back over my life, back to the carefree days on Ardnamurchan and Iain in the glory of his youth fighting imaginary battles among the rocks below our croft, always in defence of Laerg with myself cast in the role of invader – a Viking, a pirate, a marauding trawlerman, anything that had recently captured his fancy. And in the evenings, sitting by the peat fire listening to the old man talking in that thick burr – tales of the Lovers' Stone, of cliff-crawling in search of puffins, of boat journeys to Fladday for the gannets which he called solan geese; wild tales of gales and ships being wrecked.

So long ago and yet so vivid, and Iain tall and handsome with his dark face, and his black hair blowing in the wind; a wild boy with a streak of melancholy and a temper that flared at a word. He could have done something with his life. I pushed up the window, leaning out to feel the warmth of the sun, thinking of my own life, stuck here in this dirty back street doing hack work for a living. I should be painting on Laerg, getting the lost world of my grandfather down on canvas. That would be something, a justification. Eleven years at sea, followed by the years learning to paint, and it all added up to this miserable little room and a few pounds in the bank.

A taxi drew up in the street below and a man got out. All I could see of him was his wide-brimmed hat and the pale sheen of his coat as he paid the driver. It crossed my mind that it was a good angle from which to paint a picture of a London street – but in the same instant I knew I wouldn't do it; nobody would buy it. He disappeared from sight and a few moments later I heard his footsteps labouring up the bare stairboards. I opened the door and ushered him in, a tubby, round-looking man with small eyes in a smooth face. His clothes were a business man's clothes, but not English. The small eyes took in the cluttered studio, scanning the walls as though in search of something. 'I guess you're an artist, Mr Ross. That right?'

'I kid myself sometimes.'

But there was no answering smile. The small eyes stared at me, cold and humourless. 'You got a picture of your brother?'

'Just why are you here?' I asked him.

He took his hat off then and sat down on the bed, a little out of breath. 'It's a long story.' Brown-stained fingers fumbled for his cigarettes. 'Smoke?' I shook my head. He flipped one out of the pack and lit it. 'It's about the *Duart Castle*. As I told you over the phone, my name's Lane. Ed Lane. I come from Vancouver. I'm over here on business – oil and gas; my company runs pipe-lines. I mention that just to show you I'm a man of some standing. The reason I've come to see you is a private one. I'm investigating something that concerns my wife's family. A matter of a Will. There's quite a lot of money involved.' He paused for breath, reached into the pocket of his light-coloured raincoat. 'I've got some photographs here.' He had come up with an envelope. But instead of producing the pictures, he sat dragging at his cigarette and staring round the room. 'An artist,' he breathed as though he'd just thought of something. 'Do you do portraits?'

'No.'

He frowned. 'You mean you can't draw heads, faces, people's features.'

'I don't paint portraits, that's all.'

He looked at the table then, twisting his head round and reaching for the rag I'd dropped over the jacket design. Behind the lettering I had already painted in the first of a series of heads representing humanity in fear. 'There you are. That's the sort of thing.' The little button eyes stared at me as though I'd purposely misled him. 'You remember your brother, do you? You haven't forgotten what he looked like?'

'Of course not. But I don't see . . .'

'You could draw me a portrait of him, couldn't you?'

'I could.'

I think he saw I was getting annoyed, for he smiled and said, 'Sure. You want to know what it's all about first.'

'You mentioned some pictures,' I said.

He nodded. 'Later,' he said. 'Later. First, there are the press-cuttings.' He pulled some clippings from the envelope, selected one and handed it to me. 'You saw that at the time, I expect.'

It was from the *Daily Telegraph*, dated 24 February 1944, the news of the sinking of the *Duart Castle* and the arrival at Donegal, Northern Ireland, of two boatloads of survivors, together with the list of their names, thirty-five in all. Pinned to it was a cutting dated 2 March giving the official account of the torpedoing and the names of those who were missing, presumed dead. Iain Alasdair Ross. There it was to bring back to me after all these years the sense of loss I'd felt at the time, the feeling of being alone in the world, all my family dead. 'I read it in the *Scotsman*,' I said and passed it back to him.

'Sure. It was in most of the papers.' He was riffling through the bunch of cuttings. 'That all you read about the *Duart Castle*?'

'That's all there was, as far as I know. Papers were small and a lot of ships were being sunk. They'd plenty of other news . . .'

'Then you didn't see this?' He handed me another clipping. 'It's from a Stornoway paper of 14 March.'

'Stornoway's in the Outer Hebrides,' I pointed out. 'I'd hardly be likely to see a copy of that.'

'Sure, it's way up north and this is a local story. No other paper seems to have printed it. You read it. Then I'll tell you why I'm interested in your brother.'

The cutting was headed: ORDEAL BY RAFT – Terrible Story of Lone Survivor: On Tuesday evening Colin McTavish, seventy-two-year-old lobster fisherman of Tobson on Great Bernera, whilst rowing out in his boat to visit his pots, came upon a Carley float lodged amongst the rocks of Geodha Cool. The figures of two men lay on the raft, both apparently lifeless. The raft belonged to the *Duart Castle*, sunk by torpedoes some five hundred miles out in the North Atlantic on 18 February. They had, therefore, been adrift on the raft for twenty-two days. Colin McTavish took the bodies into his boat and rowed back to Tobson. There it was discovered that despite the long time at sea, one of the men was still alive. His name is George Henry Braddock, 2nd-Lieutenant Royal Artillery, aged twenty. The terrible story of his ordeal cannot be told yet for a Merciful God has wiped it from his mind. He has been transferred to the hospital at Stornoway suffering from exposure and loss of memory. But we all know what he must have suffered out there in the open sea exposed to bitter cold and severe storms with no protection but the tattered remnants of a sail and his only companion dying before his eyes. The dead man is Pte. André Leroux, a French-Canadian from Montreal. He has been buried at the old cemetery above the bay at Bosta. Colin McTavish's rescue of 2nd-Lieutenant Braddock brings the total of survivors of the *Duart Castle* to thirty-six and this doubtless writes *finis* to the tragic story of a ship that was transporting Canadian reinforcements to aid the fight for freedom.

'I didn't know about it,' I said. 'But I don't see what that's got to do with my brother – or with me.'

'Your brother was on that raft when the ship sank.'

'Well, he's dead,' I said. 'What difference does it make?'

He didn't say anything; simply handed me one of the photographs from the envelope. It showed a man in a light suit walking along a street – tall, black-haired, with a dark moustache and what looked like a scar running down the centre of his forehead. It wasn't a very clear picture, just a snapshot taken in very bright sunlight. He passed me another. The same man getting out of a car. 'And here's one taken with a telephoto lens.' Head and shoulders this time, the face heavily shadowed by sunlight. 'You don't recognize him?' He was watching me closely.

'Where were they taken?'

'Famagusta in Cyprus.'

'I've never been to Famagusta,' I said.

'I asked you whether you recognized him?'

'Well, I don't. Who is he?'

He sighed and took the photographs back, sitting there, staring down at them. 'I guess they're not very clear. Not as clear as I would have liked. But . . .' He shook his head and tucked them away in the envelope together with the cuttings. 'They're pictures I took of Braddock. Major Braddock.' He looked up at me. 'You're sure they didn't strike some chord in your memory?' And when I shook my head, he said, 'They didn't remind you of your brother, for instance?'

'My brother?' I stared at him, trying to think back, remembering Iain's dark, handsome face. 'How the hell could it be my brother?' The face in those photos, lined and scarred. 'There's no resemblance at all. What are you getting at?'

'Think what he'd be like now.' The small eyes stared at me, cold and with an obstinate look.

'He's dead,' I said again, angry now, wondering what the hell this wretched little man was trying to dig up. 'And the past, that's dead, too,' I added.

'Okay, Mr Ross. If that's the way you feel. But do something for me, will you. Draw me a picture of your brother – as you think he might look now.'

'Damned if I do.' I wasn't going to help him or anyone else rake up the past. 'Why should I?'

'I'll tell you why.' His voice had a sudden bite to it. 'I don't believe the man I saw in Famagusta was Braddock.' The eyes, staring at me, still had that obstinate look. 'And if he wasn't Braddock, then who was he? That's what I want to know, and that's what I intend to find out.' He dived into his breast pocket and came out with a diary. 'I've got a list here of five names.' He turned the pages quickly, spreading the diary open on his knee. 'Five men definitely identified. That's in addition to Braddock and Leroux, the two who were still on the raft when it was washed ashore in the Outer Hebrides.' He looked up at me then. 'That makes seven we know for sure were on the raft at the time the *Duart Castle* went down. No doubt there were more, but those seven have been identified by witnesses I consider absolutely reliable. Your brother was one of them, Mr Ross.'

I didn't see what he was driving at. Whether Iain was on that raft or in the water didn't seem to make much difference. It didn't alter the fact that he was dead. 'Who told you?' I asked. 'Braddock, I suppose.'

'No, it wasn't Braddock. Braddock says he doesn't remember. What you might call a mental blackout, I guess. Very convenient.

No, your brother's name was given to me by a man I saw in Lyons on my way back from the Middle East – Tom Webster, an English textile buyer. He came ashore in one of the boats.' He closed the diary. 'I've seen altogether eight of the survivors, in addition to Braddock. The first seven were Canadians. I interviewed them before I left for Europe. Only one of them remembered seeing the float. He gave me two possible names. Webster gave me a further three, and he was very positive about them because he was thrown into the water and clung to the float for a time before swimming to the boat.' He stubbed out his cigarette. 'The three men Webster was positive about were the Master-at-Arms, the second officer – and your brother. I've checked on the first two. Neither of them had any reason to change their identity. But your brother had. Did you know he was being brought back from Canada under escort to face a number of very serious charges?'

'Yes,' I said. 'I know that. But he's listed among those lost and it's over twenty years . . .'

'He was presumed dead.' His emphasis was on the word 'presumed,' his voice flat and hard and very determined. 'There's a difference. His body was never recovered. He wasn't identified. And that brings me to the reason I'm here. The *Duart Castle* was a troopship. Most of the boys sailing in her were young Canadian conscripts. A hundred and thirty-six of them were officers, newly commissioned. Braddock was one of them.' And he went on to tell me Braddock's story.

I wanted to throw the man out. This monstrous, fantastic suggestion of his . . . But he went on talking – talking in that flat Canadian monotone. It was like a river in spate and I listened to it because I couldn't help myself, because the seed of doubt had been sown and curiosity is a universal failing.

Braddock had been born in London. His father was English, his mother Canadian. When he was two the family had moved to Vancouver. That was in 1927. In 1938 they had returned to England, the father having been appointed London representative of the Canadian firm he worked for. On the outbreak of war a year later, George Braddock, then a boy of fourteen and their only child, had been evacuated to Canada. For the next four years he'd lived with his aunt, a Mrs Evelyn Gage, on a ranch in northern BC. 'A lonely sort of a place out on the old Caribou Trail,' Lane added. 'And Evie had just lost her husband. She was alone there except for the stockman. She'd no children of her own and . . . well, I guess it's the old story. She came to regard young

George Braddock more or less as her own son, particularly after his parents were killed. They died in the bombing – a direct hit on their flat. Now this is where I come into it. When the boy went off to join the Army she made a Will leaving everything to him 'in love and affection for the boy who was like a son to me' – those are the actual words. She died last year, aged seventy-two and that Will still stands. She never made another.'

'And you're trying to break it?' Money, I thought – this smooth-faced, hard-eyed little man's whole life was money.

'Well, wouldn't you? Evie was my wife's aunt, too – by marriage; and the ranch alone is worth a hundred thousand dollars. And the boy never wrote to her, you see. All that time. It's taken lawyers six months just to trace the guy. They thought at first he was dead.'

So that was it. Because the fellow hadn't written . . . 'It doesn't occur to you, I suppose, that Braddock might not be interested in a ranch in Canada.'

'There's more to it than the ranch – around a quarter of a million dollars.' He gave me a tight little smile. 'You show me the man who'll turn down that sort of money. Unless there's some very good reason. And in Braddock's case I'm convinced there is. He's scared of it.' He got to his feet. 'Now then. You draw me a portrait of your brother and then I'll leave you. Draw it as you think he'd look now. Okay?'

I hesitated, my mind a confused mixture of thoughts.

'I'll pay you for it.' He pulled out his pocket book. 'How much?'

I damn near hit him then. What with his suspicions, the stupid allegation he'd made, and then offering me a bribe. 'Fifty dollars,' I heard myself say and even then I didn't realize why I'd decided to take his money.

I thought for a moment he was going to haggle over it. But he stopped himself in time. 'Okay, fifty it is.' He counted five ten dollar bills on to the table. 'You're a professional. I guess you're entitled to your fee.' It was as though he were excusing himself for being too open-handed.

But when I came to draw it, I found it wasn't so easy. I started the first rough in black with a brush, but it was too strong a medium; you need to have your subject clear in front of your eyes. And when I switched to pen-and-ink it required too much detail. In the end I used an ordinary pencil, and all the time he stood over me, breathing down my neck. He was a chain-smoker and his quick panting breath made it difficult to concentrate. I suppose he thought he'd be more likely to get his money's worth if he watched every pencil stroke, or maybe it just fascinated him to see the picture emerge. But my mind, going back searching for the likeness I couldn't quite capture, resented it.

It didn't take me long to realize that time had coloured my memory. Iain's features had become blurred and in that first rough I was emphasizing what I wanted to remember, discarding what I didn't. I scrapped it and started again. And halfway through something happened – it began to take on a vague, shadowy likeness to the man in those photographs. I tore that sheet up, too. But when I tried again the same thing happened – something in the shape of the head, the way the hair grew down towards the forehead, the lines round mouth and eyes, the eyes themselves, particularly the eyes. A pity he'd shown me those photographs. But I knew it wasn't that. It had been quite unconscious. I screwed the sheet up into a ball and threw it in the waste-paper basket. 'I'm sorry,' I said. 'I thought I could remember him. But I can't. Not clearly enough to draw you a true likeness.' And I picked up the fifty dollars and thrust the notes back into his hand. 'I can't help you, I'm afraid.'

'You mean you won't.'

'Have it your own way,' I said. I wanted to get rid of him, to be alone with time to think, and I thrust my hands in my pockets, for I knew they were shaking. *Donald my Donald.* How Iain's voice came back to me down the years – cruel and charming, gay and sombre, that queer Celtic mixture. And Laerg, the Laerg of our imagination that was like a Shangri-la, like a talisman – but still one thing to him, another to me. *If I go to Laerg it will be to die. Aye, Donald my Donald – death to me and life to you.* A quarter of a century and I could remember the words, still hear his voice slurred with drink in that dirty little pub. And his face, lined already, sodden that night . . . 'I'm sorry,' I said again. 'I can't do it.' And I opened the door for him, anxious to be rid of the man.

He paused, staring at me hard. 'Okay,' he said finally in that flat voice of his. I thought he was going then, but he paused in the doorway. 'If you should want to contact Braddock he's in this country.'

'I thought you said he was in Cyprus.'

'That's where I saw him on my way through to the Middle East. But he was due for leave. Now he's been posted to the Hebrides.' I didn't say anything and he added, 'You'll find him at the Guided Weapons Establishment on Harris. Just thought you'd like to know.' He was starting down the stairs when I asked him how he'd found out. 'Private inquiry agent. They've been keeping an eye on him for me.' He smiled. 'Odd, isn't it? Why should this guy Braddock get posted to the Hebrides now? And another thing, Mr Ross. I know why you wouldn't complete that drawing. I was watching your face.' He pulled his hand out of his pocket. 'I guess I'll leave these here.' He placed the dollar bills on the top step of the stairs. 'Tear them up if you like. But before you do, remember they'll just about cover your fare to the Hebrides.' And with that he left me, standing there listening to his footsteps descending the bare boards, staring down at those damned dollars.

And I thought I'd covered up. How many times in the past had I covered up for Iain when he'd acted on the spur of the moment without thought of the future? Father, the police, that poor little idiot Mavis . . . I reached down and picked up the dollar bills, feeling like Judas. But I had to know. A brother is still your brother – hate and love, the old hero-worship still there, dormant, but leaving a vacuum. And I'd no one else. No one in the world I'd really cared for. I had to know.

PART TWO

I

GUIDED WEAPONS HQ
(16–19 October)

I left for the north the following day; the night train to Mallaig, the steamer to Rodil in the extreme south of Harris. And all the way there thinking of Iain – Iain and Braddock. The rattle of the wheels, the thump of the screws; their names pounding at my brain, till the two were one. And that Canadian . . . walking up the street to the bus stop there'd been a man in an old raincoat; he'd been on the bus with me and I'd seen him at King's Cross, just behind me waiting to get his ticket. Coincidence perhaps, but if I'd been Lane . . . I pictured him sitting by the telephone in some London hotel waiting for a report, smiling gently to himself when he was told I'd left for the north. Well, to hell with that. It was natural, wasn't it – that I should want to be sure?

I'd finished that jacket design in two hours flat and Alec Robinson had liked it sufficiently to pay me cash. Fifteen guineas. It had made all the difference. Camping out I could manage for a time and I had my return ticket. Something else I'd got from Robinson, too – an introduction to Cliff Morgan, a meteorologist working at Northton five miles north of Rodil. I'd done the jacket for his book, *Airman's Weather*. It was a contact at any rate and Robinson had told me that Northton was where the Guided Weapons Establishment was.

I'd never been further north than Ardnamurchan and all up through the islands, through the Sounds of Sleat and Raasay, I was conscious of a growing sense of familiarity, a feeling almost of contentment. The sea and the islands, and the great canopy of the sky – it called to me and my spirit sang with the smell of the salt sea air and the cold wind on my face. And then the mountains of Harris, rising abruptly from the rim of the sea, piled against a leaden sky, their tops blurred by a rainstorm. Rodil proved to be nothing but a hotel and a grass-grown quay falling into decay with an old stone church on the hill behind, built on the pattern of Iona. The boatman, ferrying us from the ship to the quay, looked at my tent and said, 'If they've nae room up yonder, I could fix ye a bed maybe.' His voice was soft as the rain that was beginning to fall and when I declined his offer, he said, 'Och weel, it's yer ain business. But it'll be a tur-rible wet night I'm thinking.'

The night was both wet and cold and I went to sleep with the sound of the waves sloshing among the seaweed that clothed the rocks, and in the morning I started to walk to Northton. Just beyond the church a girl in a small estate car stopped and offered me a lift. She wore a faded green anorak with the hood pushed back and her face had the freshness of the islands; a dark, wind-browned face and bright blue eyes. 'You must have had a very uncomfortable night,' she said as we drove up the glen. Her voice was soft and that, too, belonged to the islands. 'Why didn't you come to the hotel?' Something about the way she said it, the quick, almost hostile glance she gave me – it was almost as though she resented the presence of a stranger.

But my attention was concentrated on her features, which were unusual; the dark colouring, the wide mouth below the strong, slightly beaky nose. I knew there were islands up here where Nordic blood had mixed with the Celt to produce blue eyes and dark hair and skin, and because it interested me, I said, 'You're an islander, aren't you?'

'I live here.'

'No, I meant you come from one of the islands up here.'

'My father does.' The blue eyes staring at me and again that sense of hostility. 'I'm Marjorie Field.' She said it defiantly, adding that she worked part-time at the hotel. She seemed to expect some reaction from me, and then she began asking me a lot of questions – my name, where I had come from, how long I intended to stay. At the time I put it down to the natural curiosity about strangers in an isolated community.

The fact that I was an artist seemed to surprise her. 'You mean you paint – for a living?' We were at the top of the glen then and she concentrated on her driving until the road straightened out, running down to the flat desolation of buildings scattered round marsh and loch; ugly modern dwelling houses, impermanent-looking against the misted bulk of the hills beyond. 'Artists don't come here at this time of the year,' she said quite suddenly. 'And they don't live in tents, Mr Ross – not when it's cold and wet.'

'D'you know many artists?' I asked.

'A few.' She was tight-lipped now, her manner cold, and I had a feeling she didn't believe me. We drove through Leverburgh in silence. This, according to my guide book, had been the village of Obbe until Lord Leverhulme re-named it as part of his grandiose scheme for making it the centre of the west coast trawler fleet. Beyond the village she turned to me and said, 'You're a newspaper man, aren't you?' She said it flatly, in a tone almost of resignation.

'What makes you think that?'

She hesitated, and then she said, 'My father is Charles Field.' She was watching me out of the corner of her eyes and again she seemed to expect some reaction. 'He's the Education Officer at Northton.' And then she slowed the car and turned her head. 'Please. Won't you be frank? You haven't come up here to paint. It's something else – I can feel it.'

Her reaction was disturbing, for this was something more than ordinary curiosity. We had reached the top of the next glen and there was the sea and a cloud-capped mountain, half-obscured by rain. To distract her I asked, 'Is that Toe Head?'

She nodded. 'The hill is called Chaipaval.'

It seemed bedded on sand, for the tide was out and the bay to the north was a dull, flat gleam running out to dunes. Dunes, too, formed the neck of land that made Toe Head a peninsula. But much of the sand-bunkered area had been bull-dozed flat to make a camp and a landing place for helicopters. Seaward of the camp was a wired-off enclosure with blast protection walls. The whole effect – the tarmac apron, the tight-packed ranks of the hutted camp, the flat square of the launching pad – it was raw and violent, like a razor slash on an old oil-painting. 'And that's the rocket range, I suppose?'

She nodded. 'Surprised?' She gave me a quick, rather hesitant smile. 'It always seems to surprise people. They've read about it in the papers, but when they actually see it . . .' And she added, 'Of course, being near the road, it's much more obvious than the old range down on South Uist.'

In a few minutes now we should be at the camp. 'Has a Major Braddock been posted up here?' I asked.

She nodded. 'He arrived a few days ago.' And after a moment she said, 'Is that why you're going to Northton?'

'Yes,' I said. 'I'm hoping he'll be able to get me across to Laerg.'

'Laerg? Then it isn't my father . . . You really are a painter.' She gave a quick, nervous little laugh – as though laughing at her own foolishness. 'I'm sorry, but, you see, we get so few people at Rodil – only fishermen, a few tourists, the occasional birdwatcher. Why aren't you in the Mediterranean, somewhere warm and sunny? I never knew an artist come to the Hebrides, not for the winter.' Her voice ran quickly on as though by talking she could conceal from me that the presence of an unexpected visitor had scared her. 'You're Scots, aren't you? Perhaps that explains it. But an artist wanting to go to Laerg – it's so unusual. And the birds will have flown. No gannets or puffins. They've all left now. What are you going to paint?'

'The island,' I said. 'Laerg as the islanders knew it at the worst time of the year.'

She nodded. 'I've never seen it. But Mike says it can be very beautiful, even in winter.'

We were in Northton now and I could see what it had been before the Army came, a line of small crofts clinging to an old existence in a land as old as time. It was an anachronism now, pitiful-looking against the background of the camp with its fuel dump and its MT workshops and the barrack lines of its huts. 'Where will I find Major Braddock?' I asked.

'His office is in the Admin. block. But he may not be there. He's supposed to be flying to Laerg today.' She drew up at the main gate where the model of a rocket stood and a notice board read: Joint Services Guided Weapons Establishment. 'The Admin. block is down there on the left,' she said. I thanked her and the little estate car drove off along a concrete roadway drifted with sand that led to another part of the camp.

There was no guard on the gate. I simply walked straight in. The huts stretched in two straight lines either side of a concrete road; sand everywhere and the rain driving like a thick mist. A staff car and two Land-Rovers stood parked outside the Admin. block. There was nobody about. I went in. Still nobody, and a long passage running the length of the hut with glass-panelled doors to the offices leading off it. I walked slowly down it, feeling oddly nervous, conscious of being an intruder in a completely alien world. Small wooden plaques announced the contents of each closed box of an office: RSM – W. T. Symes; Commanding Officer – Colonel S. T. Standing; 2nd-in-Command – Major G. H. Braddock, (this lettered in ink on a paper stick-on); Adjutant – Captain M. L. Ferguson.

I stood for a moment outside Braddock's door, unwilling now to face the awkwardness of this moment. Lane and his snapshots seemed a whole world away and I felt suddenly foolish to have come so far on such an errand. How could the man possibly be my brother after all these years? But I had an excuse all worked out, the excuse that I wanted to visit Laerg. He could only refuse and at least I'd know for certain then. I knocked on the door. There was no answer. I pushed it open. There was nobody inside and I had a feeling of relief at the sight of the empty desk.

There was a sliding hatch in the partition that separated this office from the adjutant's and I could hear a voice talking. But when I went into the next office Captain Ferguson was alone at his desk. He was speaking into the telephone. He wore battle-dress, a ginger-haired youngster with a square freckled face and a Scots accent that took me back to my Glasgow days. '. . . I can see it is . . . Aye, well you check with the Met. Office . . . Damned if I do. You tell him yourself. He's down at Leverburgh, but he'll be back soon. Eleven at the latest, he said, and he'll be mad as hell when he hears . . . Laddie, you haven't met the man. He'll be across to see you . . . Okay, I'll tell him.' He put the phone down and looked at me. 'Can I help you?'

'My name's Ross,' I said. 'I wanted to see Major Braddock.'

'He's out at the moment.' He glanced at his watch. 'Back in about twenty minutes. Is he expecting you?'

'No.'

'Well, I don't know whether he'll have time. He's very busy at the moment. Could you tell me what it's about?'

'A private matter,' I said. 'I'd like to talk to him personally.'

'Well, I don't know . . .' His voice was doubtful. 'Depends whether this flight's on or not.' He reached for his pad. 'Ross, you said? Aye, I'll tell him.' He made a note of it and that was that. Nothing else I could do for the moment.

'Could you tell me where I'll find Cliff Morgan?' I said. 'He's a meteorologist at Northton.'

'Either at the Met. Office or in the bachelor quarters.' He picked up the phone. 'I'll just check for you whether he's on duty this morning. Get me the Met. Office, will you.' He cupped his hand over the mouthpiece. 'There are two of them there and they work it in shifts. Hullo. That you, Cliff? Well now look, laddie, drum up a decent forecast, will you. Ronnie Adams is on his way over to see you and he doesn't like the look of the weather . . . Yes, Himself – and he'll raise hell if the flight's off. Okay. And there's a Mr Ross in my office. Wants to see you . . . Yes, Ross.'

'Donald Ross,' I said.

'Mr Donald Ross . . . Aye, I'll send him over.' He put down the phone. 'Yes, Cliff's on the morning shift. You'll find the Met. Office right opposite you as you go out of the main gate. It's below the Control Tower, facing the landing apron. And I'll tell Major Braddock you're here as soon as he gets back from Leverburgh.'

I wished then that I hadn't given my name. But it couldn't be helped. I zipped up my windbreaker, buttoning it tight across my throat. It was raining harder now and I hurried out through the gate and along the road to the hangar. Pools of rain water lay on the parking apron where an Army helicopter stood like some pond insect, dripping moisture. The bulk of Chaipaval was blotted out by a squall. Rain lashed at the glistening surface of the tarmac. I ran for the shelter of the tower, a raw concrete structure, ugly as a gun emplacement. Inside it had the same damp, musty smell. The Met. Office was on the ground floor. I knocked and went in.

It was a bleak dug-out of a room. Two steps led up to a sort of dais and a long, sloped desk that filled all the window space. The vertical backboard had a clock in the centre, wind speed and direction indicators; flanking these were schedules and code tables, routine information. The dust-blown windows, streaked with rain, filtered a cold, grey light. They faced south-west and the view was impressive because of the enormous expanse of sky. On the wall to my right were the instruments for measuring atmospheric pressure – a barograph and two mercury barometers. A Baby Belling cooker stood on a table in the corner and from a small room leading off came the clack of teleprinters.

The place was stuffy, the atmosphere stale with cigarette smoke. Two men were at the desk, their heads bent over a weather report. They looked round as I entered. One of them wore battledress trousers and an old leather flying jacket. He was thin-faced, sad-looking. His helmet and gloves lay on the desk, which was littered with forms and pencils, unwashed cups and old tobacco tin tops full of the stubbed-out butts of cigarettes. The other was a smaller man, short and black-haired, dressed in an open-necked shirt and an old cardigan. He stared at me short-sightedly through thick-lensed glasses. 'Mr Ross?' He had a ruler in his hand, holding it with fingers stained brown with nicotine. 'My publishers wrote me you would be coming.' He smiled. 'It was a good jacket design you did for my book.'

I thanked him, glad that Robinson had taken the trouble to write. It made it easier. The clack of the teleprinter ceased abruptly. 'No hurry.' I said. 'I'll wait till you've finished.'

'Sit down then, man, and make yourself comfortable.' He turned his back on me then, leaning on the tubular frame of his swivel seat to continue his briefing. '. . . Surface wind speed twenty to twenty-five knots. Gusting perhaps forty. Rain squalls. Seven-eighths cloud at five hundred . . .' His voice droned on, touched with the lilt of his native valleys.

I was glad of the chance to study him, to check what I knew of Cliff Morgan against the man himself. If I hadn't read his book I shouldn't have known there was anything unusual about him. At first glance he looked just an ordinary man doing an ordinary routine job. He was a Welshman and he obviously took too little exercise. It showed in his flabby body and in the unhealthy pallor of his face. The shirt he wore was frayed and none too clean, the grey flannels shapeless and without crease, his shoes worn at the heels. And yet, concentrated now on his briefing, there was something about him that made my fingers itch to draw. The man, the setting, the pilot leaning beside him – it all came together, and I knew this would have made a better jacket for his book than the one I'd done.

The background of his book was a strange one. He had written it in prison, pouring into it all his enthusiasm for the unseen world of air currents and temperatures, of cold and warm fronts and the global movements of great masses of the earth's atmosphere. It had been an outlet for his frustation, filled with the excitement he felt for each new weather pattern, the sense of discovery as the first pencilled circle – a fall in pressure of a single millibar perhaps reported by a ship out in the Atlantic – indicated the birth of a new storm centre. His quick, vivid turn of phrase had breathed life into the everyday meteorological reports and the fact that he was an amateur radio operator, a 'ham' in his spare time, had added to the fascination of the book, for his contacts were the weather ships, the wireless operators of distant steamers, other meteorologists, and as a result the scope of his observations was much wider than that of the ordinary airport weather man taking all his information from teleprinted bulletins.

How such a man came to be stationed in a God-forsaken little outpost like Northton needs some explanation. Though I didn't know it at the time, there was already a good deal of gossip about him. He had been up there over six months, which was plenty of time for the facts to seep through, even to that out-of-the-way place. The gossip I don't intend to repeat, but since the facts are common knowledge I will simply say this: there was apparently something in his metabolism that made him sexually an exhibitionist and attractive to women. He had become mixed up in a complex affair involving two Society women. One of them was married and a rather sordid divorce case had followed, as a result of which he had faced a criminal charge, had been found guilty and sentenced to nine months' imprisonment. He had been a meteorologist at London Airport at the time. On his release from prison the Air Ministry had posted him to Northton, where I suppose it was presumed he could do little or no harm. But a man's glands don't stop functioning because he's posted to a cold climate. Nor, thank God, do his wits – a whole ship's company were to owe their lives to the accuracy of his predictions, amounting almost to a sixth sense where weather was concerned.

The pilot was leaving now. 'Okay, Cliff, that settles it. No dice.' He picked up his helmet and his gloves. 'Pity they don't admit it's blowing like hell out there. No down-draughts, Shelter Bay calm as a mill-pond – that's the report I had from Laerg earlier this morning.'

'It's always the same when the boys are waiting for their mail.'

'That's true. But this time I'm under pressure from both ends. The mail could just as well go by LCT, but then this fellow Braddock . . .' A rain squall lashed the windows. 'Just listen to that. He should try his hand at landing a helicopter – that'd teach him to be so bloody enthusiastic. What's he want to do, commit suicide? When it's gusting forty it whams down off Tarsaval . . .' He stared angrily at the blurred panes. 'Thank God they're closing the place down. That idea of relying on a helicopter service through the winter months – who dreamed that one up?'

'Colonel Standing.'

'Well, it was bloody crazy. They'd soon have discovered the LCTs were more reliable.'

'The landing craft never operated in Scottish waters after the end of September. You know that.'

'Well, the trawler then. What was wrong with that?'

'A question of cost; that's what I heard, anyway. And there was still the problem of trans-shipping men and stores from ship to beach. They lost a lot of dories smashed up on the rocks or overturned.'

'Well, if it's a question of cost, dories are a damn sight cheaper than helicopters.' He turned up the collar of his flight jacket, huddling down into it with a jerk of the shoulders. 'Be seeing you, Cliff.' But as he turned towards the door, it was flung open and Major Braddock entered. In place of the light suit he wore battledress, but it was the same face – the face of Lane's photographs, lined and leathery, dark-tanned by the Mediterranean sun, and that scar running in a vertical line down the crease of the forehead to the nose.

'What's all this about the flight being off?' Not a glance at me, yet he knew I was there. I could feel it. And that urgent vitality, the way he leaned forward, balanced like a runner on the balls of his feet. 'Mike just told me. Is it definite?'

'''Fraid so, sir,' the pilot said. 'You see . . .'

But he had turned to me. 'You the guy that's wanting to see me?' The black eyes, staring straight at me, not a flicker of recognition, only the twitch of a muscle to reveal the nervous tension.

'Yes,' I said. 'My name's Donald Ross.'

He smiled. And in that instant I was sure. He couldn't change that smile; he'd relied too much on its charm all his life.

'A private matter,' I said.

He nodded. 'Okay, just let me deal with this . . .' He swung round on the pilot then. 'Now look here, Adams, it's all arranged. I'm staying the night there and coming back by LCT tomorrow. Just because it's a bit wet and windy . . . damn it, man, what do you expect in the Hebrides?'

'It's the down-draughts,' the pilot said unhappily. 'Being slammed down on the deck – well, you ask Cliff here. It just isn't on, not in this weather.'

And Cliff Morgan agreed, nodding to the wind speed indicator. 'Blowing twenty plus now, almost forty in the gusts. And beginning to veer already. It'll be worse out there.' He shook his head. 'The forecast's bad.'

'The immediate forecast, d'you mean?'

'Well, no. That's bad enough. But I was thinking of the next forty-eight hours. I've an idea the wind's going to veer and go on veering halfway round the clock. We could have a polar air stream with a drop in temperature of perhaps ten degrees and wind speeds as high as fifty, sixty knots.'

'When?'

'How do I know? It's just a feeling I have. It may not happen that way at all.' He indicated the wall to our left, where the big weather maps hung. 'The lower one shows the position when I came on duty at six o'clock; it relates to o-o-o-one hours this morning. The upper one is my forecast of what the pattern will look like twenty-four hours later.' This map was perspex-framed and the isobars had been drawn in with chinagraph pencil on the perspex. Here the High that had covered the British Isles for days, and which was still shown centred over Eastern Europe in the lower map, had disappeared completely, to be replaced by an intense depression moving in from the Atlantic. There was another, smaller depression behind it and a weak High over Greenland. 'A south-westerly air stream now, you see – somewhere between twenty and forty knots. But the outlook is entirely dependent upon those two depressions and what happens to that High over Greenland. My feeling is this – those depressions are going to merge, the High is going to build up. The effect would be for that depression to intensify very rapidly. By tomorrow it could be a very deep one centred over Norway and if at the same time the High builds up . . .' He shrugged. 'Wind would be north, you see, gale force at least – perhaps very strong indeed. But there's no certainty about it. Just my interpretation based on nothing more than a feeling I have.'

Braddock stared at the map. 'Well, whether you're right or wrong, the fine spell's over, eh?'

'Looks like it, Major.'

'Still, if you're right – northerlies; we'd still be able to use Shelter Bay.'

The phone rang and Cliff Morgan answered it. 'For you,' he said, handing it to Braddock.

I watched him as he took the call. The way the black brows came down and the lines deepened. The years had greatly changed him. His voice, too, harsher and more mature. '. . . Who? I see . . . badly hurt? . . . Okay, Mike, I'll tell Adams.' His eyes met mine for a moment as he put the receiver down. I thought he smiled, but it was so fleeting a movement of the mouth below the dark moustache that I couldn't be sure. He got up, went over to the pilot and stood facing him. 'Well now, that gives you a fine little problem. McGregor, the driver of the Scammell, has got himself badly smashed up. A piece of radar equipment toppled on him after he'd got it stuck on one of the bends of the High Road. His leg's crushed right up to the thigh, abdominal injuries, too.' And he stood over the wretched man, daring him to say that he still wouldn't go, just as he'd stood over me when we were kids. 'Doc says he must be flown out immediately.'

Adams licked his lips. 'What about the LCTs?'

'No good. Four-four-Double-o left Laerg at eleven-thirty last night. She should be in the South Ford by now. And Eight-six-one-o left shortly after two this morning. She's due in Leverburgh any moment. To get her unloaded . . .' He shook his head. 'It'd be almost twenty-four hours before we could get him ashore by LCT, and from what I gathered he wouldn't last that long. His life's in your hands. Either you fly him out . . .' He gave a little shrug and left it at that. And then he turned to me as though the matter were settled. 'If you're around when I get back tomorrow, we'll have that chat, eh?' He said it with his eyes staring straight at me, still not the slightest flicker and his voice so matter-of-fact I could easily have persuaded myself that he really was Braddock – just Braddock and nothing to do with me.

'I'll be here,' I said.

He nodded and went towards the door, opening it and marching straight out, leaving Adams standing there.

Cliff Morgan glanced again at the wind speed and direction indicators, pencilled a note or two on a piece of paper and passed it to the pilot. Adams took it, but he didn't look at it, nor did he look at the meteorologist. He didn't seem conscious that we were both of us watching him. He was facing the window, his eyes turned inwards, his whole mind given to the decision. I knew the answer, just as Braddock had known it. Adams knew it, too. I watched him bow to the inevitable, turning up the collar of his flight jacket and walking out without a word, the decision to fly made against his better judgement.

It was the moment that things began to go wrong, but none of us could know that, though perhaps Cliff Morgan sensed it, or again perhaps he knew his weather better than the rest of us. 'The poor bastard!' he murmured, and I knew he was referring to the pilot, not to the injured man.

He looked at me as the door shut behind Adams. 'They vary, you know,' he said. 'In temperament.' And he added, 'If it had been Bill Harrison now, he wouldn't have hesitated. A reckless devil, Bill; but he knows his own mind. He'd never have let himself be forced into it like that.' He sucked on the end of his pencil, hollowing his cheeks, and then with a quick, abrupt movement, he went into the back room, tore off the teleprint sheets and came back reading them. 'This bloody evacuation, that's what it is, man. Thinking God Almighty would arrange the weather for them whilst they got their men and equipment off the island. I warned them.'

It was the first I'd heard about the evacuation, and realizing this he began to explain as we stood by the window, watching Braddock and Adams walk out to the helicopter and climb in. But I barely took in what he was saying, for my mind had room only for one thought at that moment – the certainty that Braddock was my brother. This in itself was such a staggering revelation that it was only later that I began to consider the other factors – why, for instance, he had applied for a posting to the Hebrides, why he should have been so set on Adams making the flight?

The engine started, the rotor blades began to turn and the helicopter rose from the parking apron, drifting sideways in a gust and just clearing the hangar. Almost immediately its shape became blurred; then it vanished completely, lost in the low cloud and a squall of rain. For a moment longer the engine was faintly audible. Then that, too, was swallowed up as rain lashed at the windows.

The risk they ran in attempting that flight was something I couldn't assess; I had no experience then of the incredible malignant power of the down-draughts that come smashing down from Tarsaval and the other heights of Laerg, down into Shelter Bay. Nor was it possible for me to absorb the whole complex set-up of this military operation into the midst of which I had suddenly been pitchforked. Even when Cliff Morgan had explained to me the details of the evacuation, how Braddock had insisted on sending a detachment with towing vehicles down to the old rocket range on South Uist so that the LCTs could beach in the South Ford as an alternative to Leverburgh, the night-and-day drive to get Laerg cleared and the round-the-clock movement of landing craft, I still didn't appreciate how vulnerable the whole operation was to the weather. I had no experience of landing craft.

Nor for that matter had Cliff Morgan. But weather to him was a living thing, the atmosphere a battle-ground. He had, as I've said, a sixth sense where weather was concerned and he was very conscious of the changed pattern. 'A polar air stream now.' He said it to himself as though facing the implications for the first time. 'Jesus, man!' He lit a cigarette, staring at me over the flame. 'Know anything about weather?'

'A little,' I said, but he didn't seem to hear.

'No imagination – that's the Army for you. Look at Braddock. Up into the air and not a clue what he faces at the other end. And Standing – you'd think Standing would try to understand. He's got brains. But no imagination, you see, none at all.' He slid his bottom on to the swivel seat and drew a sheet of paper towards him. 'Look you now, I'll draw it for you. As I see it – in here.' And he tapped his forehead. 'Not the wind on my face, but a map, a chart, a picture. Imagination! But *dammo di*, they're none of them Celts. Though Braddock – ' He shook his head as though he weren't quite certain about Braddock, and then he reached for a blank sheet of paper and with his pen drew a map that included North America, Greenland, Norway – the whole North Atlantic.

On this he pencilled in the existing pattern; the Azores High bulging north towards Ireland and the two Lows driving that other High, that had been over England, east towards Russia.

'Now, the area I'm watching is down here.' His pencil stabbed the left-hand bottom edge of the map. 'That's about seven hundred miles north-east of Bermuda. It's the place where our depressions are born – the place where the cold, dry air from the north, sweeping down the east of North America, meets up with the warm, damp air of the Gulf Stream. It's the breeding place for every sort of beastliness – hurricanes bound for the States, big depressions that move across the North Atlantic at tremendous speed to give Iceland, and sometimes the Hebrides and the north of Scotland, wind speeds almost as bad as the much-publicized Coras and Ethels and Janets and what-have-yous that cause such havoc in America. Now look at this.'

He picked up a red pencil and with one curving sweep drew an arrow across to the area between Iceland and Norway. 'There! That's your Low now.' He drew it in, a deep depression centred over Norway, extending west as far as Iceland, east into Siberia. And then on the other side, over towards Greenland and Canada, more isobars drawn in with long, curving sweeps of hand and pencil. A high pressure area, and between the High and the Low, in ink, he marked in arrows pointing south and south-east. 'That's a polar air stream for you. That's a real big polar air stream, with the wind roaring out of the arctic and temperatures falling rapidly. Snow at first in the north. Then clear skies and bitter cold.'

He stared at it for a moment, an artist regarding his handi-work. 'I haven't seen that sort of weather pattern up here – not at this time of the year. But I experienced it once in Canada just after the war when I was working for the Department of Transport at Goose Bay. By Christ, man, that was something. A Low over Greenland, a High centred somewhere over the mouth of the Mackenzie River and a polar air stream pouring south across the Labrador.' He drew it for me then on another sheet of paper, adding as his red pencil circled in the pattern, 'Have you any idea what a polar air stream means up there in the Canadian North in October – to the Eskimos, the prospectors, the ships in Hudson Bay?' And when I shook my head he embarked on an explanation. I can't remember all he said; I found myself listening to the tone of his voice rather than to his actual words. It had become noticeably more Welsh, a distinct lilt that seemed to change his personality. It was his enthusiasm for the subject, I suppose, but all at once he was like a poet, painting with words on a canvas that was one quarter of the globe. I listened, fascinated; and as he talked the red pencil was constantly moving, filling in that old atmospheric battle picture until the high pressure system over north-western Canada had become a great whorl of concentric lines.

Like an artist he couldn't resist the picture as a whole, but as his pencil flew over Greenland and down as far as the Azores, it was this big High he talked about; the effect it had had on people, animals and crops – on transportation, particularly aircraft and ships. The High represented cold, heavy air; clean, crisp, dry-frozen stuff hugging the earth's surface, weighing down on thousands of square miles of ocean, thousands of square miles of pack ice. The winds around this cold mass had been clockwise and wherever they had touched the periphery of the low pressure area to the east, the movement of the cold air stream had been accelerated to hurricane force. At first those gales had been bliz-zards, thick with driving snow as damp, humid masses of air were forced into the upper atmosphere and cooled to the point of precipitation. 'When that High got really established,' he said, 'there was snow in many places that didn't expect it for another month. Blizzards in the Middle West of Canada reaching south across the border into the States, and that High was like a young giant. It went on drawing strength into itself – like a boxer in training and working himself up for the big fight.'

'You make it sound very dramatic,' I said.

'Weather is dramatic, man; indeed it is, when you've got something like that building up.' He was entirely engrossed in the picture he had drawn from memory. 'It's fluid, you see; always a shifting pattern, never still. It's a battlefield of pressures and temperatures and humidity; Highs versus Lows, with the cold fronts and the warm fronts the points of engagement. A break-through at one point can spell disaster a thousand, two thousand miles away – a ship overwhelmed, breakwaters demolished, the flooding of lowlands, the destruction of houses, death to men and livestock.'

He was being carried away again on the tide of his imagination. But then he suddenly stopped. 'It was a long time ago. But I can remember it – by God I can.' He picked up the map he'd drawn, stared at it for a moment, then crumpled it up and threw it into the biscuit tin that acted as a wastepaper basket. 'That's just one of dozens of maps I could draw you – weather I've known . . . Some of it I covered in my book. And when this High dis-

integrates or that Low fills in it's something different again.'
He turned with a quick movement of his head to stare at the map
framed on the wall, the chinagraph bright on the perspex. 'Those
two Lows coming in . . . Look at them. I'm already getting figures
that complicate the whole picture. They may behave normally.
They may remain separate entities. But somehow, I don't know
why exactly, they worry me. That's something you learn in this
game, you see – it's ninety per cent science, a matter of filling in
figures, but there's the other ten per cent . . . your instinct comes
into it then, instinct based on experience.' He gave a little laugh
and shook his head. 'Make yourself comfortable,' he said, 'whilst
I catch up on my homework.' He glanced at the clock. 'Another
fifteen minutes and then we'll go over to the Mess for lunch.
I expect you could do with a drink. I certainly could.'

I sat and watched him checking his instruments, going through
the teleprinter sheets, flying a balloon to check ceiling heights,
marking up his meteorological forms, phoning his report through
to Pitreavie, and all the time I was thinking of Iain, trying to
remember him as I had last seen him, nineteen years old and wearing battledress, the sergeant's stripes white-new on his arm. He'd
been drunk that night and within the week he'd sailed with his
unit out of the Clyde, bound for North Africa – Operation 'Torch'.
'Can I have a piece of paper?' I said, and when Morgan passed
me a scribbling pad, I began pencilling a sketch from memory.
The result was the same as when I had tried it in my studio with
that bloody little Canadian business man breathing down my
neck. I wondered what Lane was doing now – would he come up
here to bust Braddock's identity wide open?

I didn't like the thought of that. The wild streak in Iain had
always bordered on violence. That poor devil of a lieutenant, his
jaw smashed – and there had been other incidents, before that;
Big Neil McNeill knocked senseless with an oar after he'd shot
a seal. My fault that time. I hadn't wanted the seal killed and when
it was done I'd flown at Big Neil, blubbering with anger, and got
a kick in the groin that sprawled me screaming in the bottom of
the boat. And in Glasgow, at that factory – they'd called him Black
Iain – black because of his temper and his dark features and his
arrogance. They'd picked him up drunk one night and he'd
knocked out three policemen and got away. That was the night
he joined the Army.

'That's Braddock.' I looked up to find Morgan standing over
me with a puzzled look. 'Yes, Braddock,' I said. I'd have to call
him Braddock now. I'd have to think of him as Braddock. I tore

the sheet from the pad, crumpled it, and tossed it into the biscuit tin.

'You made him look much younger.'

'I was just passing the time.'

He gave me a sharp, inquiring look, nodded and went back to the desk. It was a warning. I'd have to be careful. And if Lane came north . . .

Cliff Morgan was at the barograph now. He went back to his work at the desk and, watching him again, I was conscious of a tenseness. It showed in the way he paused every now and then to stare out of the window, the quick glances at the wind speed indicator. And then the phone rang. 'All right, Mike – as soon as I'm relieved.' He slammed the receiver down. 'Can I give Colonel Standing a weather briefing? No interest in this office so long as the sun's shining, but now it's wet and blowing half a gale . . .' He shrugged. 'Have you met Colonel Standing?' And when I told him No, he added, 'I'll introduce you then. Alec Robinson said something about your wanting to get to Laerg and for that you need Standing's permission.'

Prompt at twelve Cliff Morgan's junior came dripping in out of the rain, a quiet, reserved man who gave me a fleeting smile as we were introduced. His name was Ted Sykes. 'I hear Ronnie took off. What's his ETA?'

'About twelve-thirty. Wind speed's twenty-five knots – almost a dead-noser.' Cliff Morgan pulled his jacket on and took a tie from the pocket.

'Rather him than me,' Sykes said, at the desk now, riffling through the teleprint sheets. 'Braddock with him?'

'Yes.'

'Well, I hope it keeps fine for them,' He said it sourly. It was obvious neither of them liked it. Cliff Morgan was standing at the desk, tying his tie, staring at the grey misery of the sky. Rain dribbled down the panes.

'There's a casualty to be lifted out.'

'So I heard.'

'Keep your fingers crossed then.' He turned abruptly and got his raincoat, and then we were out in the wind and the rain, hurrying through pools of water to the camp. 'Better not ask for a flight out to Laerg. It means a bloody chit, you see, and they don't like it. Landing craft's all right. I think Standing would agree to that.' His voice came to me, staccato fragments blown on the wind. 'Perhaps tomorrow. But it'll be rough. You a good sailor?' And when I told him I'd had almost eleven years at sea, he nodded. 'That's all right then. At least you'll see Laerg as it really is. Funny thing. I've never been there. Wanted to ever since I came up here. No time, and now it's being evacuated . . .' We had reached the Admin. block. 'You might offer to do some sketches of the evacuation. Standing, you see, is not a man who's very easy with strangers, but he's artistic. Paints a bit himself and I'm told he has some interesting pictures up at his house. Nudes mostly, but not sexy – the real thing.'

Standing was waiting for us in his office, tall and slightly stooped with a thin, serious face and glasses, a tight, unsmiling mouth. He looked a cold, moody man and his long-fingered hands were seldom still, nervously shifting the papers on his desk, toying with the slide-rule or gently tapping. Cliff Morgan introduced me as an artist who wanted to visit Laerg, but all I got was a nod and a cold stare. He had Ferguson with him and he was only interested in one thing, the weather. He listened to what Morgan had to say, his eyes on the window which was tight-shut against the wind. The view was depressing – the brown creosoted back of a hut, a grey waste of sky and the rain driving.

'Can Adams get the man out? That's all I want to know.' Even then he didn't look at Cliff Morgan, but sat staring at the window, drumming with his fingers.

'Only Ronnie could tell you that,' Cliff answered, and I sensed his antagonism.

'Adams isn't here. I'm asking you, Mr Morgan.'

'I'm a meteorologist. I feed the pilot information. He makes his own decisions.'

'I know that. I'm asking your opinion.'

Cliff shrugged. 'It's dicey – but then that's to be expected when you're flying to a place like Laerg.' The native lilt was stronger now.

'The decision was made in your office, I believe. Did Major Braddock order Adams to fly?'

'How could he? It's the pilot's decision – always. You know that.'

'Very well. I will put it another way. Would Captain Adams have flown if there hadn't been an injured man to bring out?'

'No.'

Colonel Standing sighed and reached for his slide-rule, running it back and forth in his hands. 'Two men's lives and an expensive machine . . .' He was staring at the slide-rule as though calculating the risk in terms of a mathematical equation. 'Captain Fairweather has all he needs, hasn't he?' This with a quick glance at his

Adjutant. 'I mean the hospital is still functioning, isn't it?'

'Aye, but it's little better than a first-aid post now, sir. And Fairweather's not a surgeon.'

'He's still a member of the medical profession. If he has to operate, then he's got the means and we can link him up with Scottish Command and give him a surgeon's guidance.' He dropped the slide-rule. 'Have them contact Adams. He's to cancel the flight and return immediately. Now what's the landing craft position? Stratton is the more experienced of the two. Where's Eight-six-one-o?'

'She passed through the Sound of Harris about nine-thirty this morning. If the tide's right, she should be beaching any moment now.'

'In the South Ford.'

'Aye. They're double-banked, you see. If you remember, sir, it was to cope with just this eventuality that Major Braddock arranged for a stand-by detachment based on the old range. Four-four-Double-o cleared from Laerg on the same tide, about three hours after Stratton. She'd have been in Leverburgh by now if it hadn't been for a wee bit of trouble with one of the oil pumps. It slowed her down for a while.'

'How far out is she – an hour, two hours?'

'Two I should think. I'll check if you like.'

'No, there's no time.' Standing's fingers were drumming gently on the desk again. 'It makes no difference anyway. She's the nearest. A pity it's Kelvedon and not Stratton. But it can't be helped. Have Signals contact him: Four-four-Double-o to turn round and make back to Laerg at full speed to pick up a casualty.'

'It'll be eight, maybe nine hours before she gets there. A falling tide then and it'll be dark.'

'They should be able to run their bows in, pick the man up and winch off again. There won't be much of a sea running in the Bay. He'll just have to do the best he can. See if you can speak to Kelvedon yourself, explain the urgency.'

Ferguson hesitated. 'You wouldn't have a word with Bob Fairweather first? Maybe the man's condition . . .'

'No, Ferguson. Captain Fairweather's concern is with the injured man. I have to consider what the position will be if Major Braddock and Captain Adams are injured, perhaps killed, and their machine written off. All right?'

'Yes, sir.'

'Contact Adams first. Then have a word with Kelvedon and

get Four-four-Double-o turned round as soon as you can.'

'She'll still be loaded.'

'Of course she will. That can't be helped. Now get moving. Every minute counts.' He watched his Adjutant leave. Then when the door was shut he turned to me. 'You've come at an awkward time.' His voice shook slightly, so did his hands; his nerves were strung taut by the decision he'd had to make.

'I didn't realize you were evacuating the island,' I said.

He was staring down at the desk. Behind him on the wall hung a six-inch to the mile map of Laerg and beside it were graphs, presumably of the past season's shooting; part of the skin of a rocket, a jagged, crumpled piece of light alloy, lay on the floor beside his chair. 'There's always somebody wanting to go to Laerg – naturalists, bird-watchers, archaeologists. They're a darned nuisance.'

'My father was born on Laerg.'

It made no impression. He wasn't interested in the island as such. Later I learned that in the year he'd been in the Hebrides, he'd only visited Laerg once – a quick trip by helicopter on a fine day. 'You're an artist, you say. Professional?'

'Yes.'

He nodded to the wall behind me. 'What do you think of that?'

It was a landscape, the mountains of Harris by the look of it, in sunlight with a glimpse of the sea. The brush-work was technically quite good, but it lacked feeling. I didn't know what to say for I knew he'd done it himself, and presumably he liked it since he'd hung it in his office.

'Well?'

I hesitated; but better to be honest. I told him it was nice but that I didn't think the artist was at home with his subject. To my surprise he nodded agreement. 'I hung it there just to remind me that the sun does shine up here sometimes. It was hot when I painted that. But you're right – I'm not at home with landscapes. If you're here for a time I'll show you some others. My wife models for me.' The phone rang on his desk. 'Standing here . . . Thinks he can make it?' He glanced at the window as the rain beat against it in a gust of wind. 'Tell Adams it's an order . . . Yes, Ferguson, an order, do you hear?' He was trembling again as he put the phone down. For a moment he just sat there, drumming with his fingers at the desk. Then, as though suddenly conscious of my presence again, he said, 'All right, Ross, we'll see what we can do. Are you any good at seascapes, ships, that sort of thing?'

'Sea and mountains and rock,' I said; 'that's what I like to paint.'

'Good. A sketch of two of the evacuation – a painting perhaps; the DRA would like that, particularly if there are some birds in it.' I pointed out that the birds wouldn't be back for another three months. 'Well, there's such a thing as artists' licence. The General likes birds.' He hesitated. Finally he nodded. 'All right. Have a word with Ferguson. He'll fix it with the Movements Officer and arrange with one of the landing craft skippers to take you out. You'll have about two days there, maybe three.'

'It'll be something just to see the island,' I said.

'So long as you don't get in Captain Pinney's way. They're under considerable pressure. Where are you staying?' And when I told him I was camping at Rodil, he said, 'We can do better than that. I'll tell Ferguson to allocate you a room for the night. We've always plenty of space in the winter months.'

I thanked him and followed Cliff Morgan out of the stuffy little office into the cold, driving rain. I was feeling in a daze. First Iain, and now Laerg . . . Laerg within reach at last. 'I didn't think it would be as easy as that,' I murmured.

'Well, they're not worried about security, you see. The place is a write-off and that makes it easier than when they were lobbing missiles into the water beside it. But you wouldn't have got there if you hadn't been an artist.' And he added, 'You never know where you are with Standing. And now that Braddock's here . . .'

He left it at that. 'What about Braddock?' I asked.

'Oh, he's all right, whatever anybody else may say. By God he's woken this place up since he arrived. Yes indeed, and he'll have a drink with you, which is more than Standing will.'

The bar was deserted when we reached the Mess. But as we stood there drinking our gin-and-tonic, the officers drifted in one by one. Major Rafferty, the Quartermaster, a big beefy man with a florid face and a Scots accent; the Movements Officer, Fred Flint – short and round with a button nose and the face of a pug, all bulging eyes and a way of dropping his aitches and watching with a glint of humour to see if it startled you; the Doc, also a captain, but younger, with the air of a man nothing can surprise any more; several lieutenants, much younger still; and finally Field – Lieutenant Field who was old enough to be their father. He had a strange hatchet face, grey hair and a mouth that drooped at the corners. His eyes were deep-socketed, tired – blue eyes that had a nervous blink and didn't look straight at you, but beyond, as though searching for some lost horizon. '. . . our Education Officer,' the ebullient Captain Flint added as he introduced us. 'Now what y'aving, Professor?'

'Oh, that's very thoughtful of you, Flinty. Let me see now. The usual, I think – a gin-and-tonic without the gin.' He smiled and the smile lit up his whole face so that it suddenly had a quality of great warmth. It was a striking face; moreover, it was a face that seemed vaguely familiar. But not in battledress; in some other rig. 'I take it the LCTs are all at sea since Movements can take time off for a lunchtime drink.'

'All at sea is just about right, Professor. Stratton's missed his tide and dropped his hook under the lee outside Loch Carnan. It'll be five hours at least before he can get her into the beaching position in the Ford, another three before the boys can start off-loading. Major B will like that – I don't think.'

'Braddock won't know anything about it. He's flown to Laerg.'

'Oh yes he will. I just met the Colonel. He's cancelled the flight. And he's turned Four-four-Double-o round fully loaded and sent her steaming back to Laerg to pick up a casualty. Proper box-up if you ask me.'

'Well, why not switch Stratton's ship to Leverburgh?' Major Rafferty suggested. 'Damn it, man, with Kelvedon turned back, the quay will be empty.'

'Tim, my boy, you're a genius. I never thought of that.' The quick grin faded. 'I did mention it, but Stratton told me to go to hell. His men needed sleep, and so does he. If Major B wants Eight-six-one-o at Leverburgh, then he'll have to give the order himself. I bet he gets the same answer, too. Those boys are just about out on their feet, and Stratton's his own master. He's not at the beck and call of anybody here – the Colonel or anybody else. I only hope,' he added, 'that Kelvedon gets there in time.' He looked down at his glass and then at Field. 'Did you know this bloke McGregor?' And when the other nodded, he said, 'Poor beggar. First blood to the new drive.' His voice sounded angry. 'And if you ask me it won't be the last. When they're tired they get careless. I told Command it needed more time when they were planning this flipping operation. But they wouldn't listen. I'm only the bloke that loads the ships. I wouldn't know.' Ferguson came in then, the freckles on his face showing up like spots in the electric light, a strained look about the eyes. 'You look shagged, my boy. I prescribe a night out with the fattest trollop you can find between the Butt of Lewis and Barra Head.'

'Aye, that'd do me fine.'

'What's the matter? Caught between the upper and the nether millstone again?'

'If by that you mean what I think you mean, then the answer is Yes and it'll cost you a Scotch for stating the obvious. The Colonel ordered Major B to turn back.'

'We know that. And he's bust the schedule wide open by converting Four-four-Double-o into a hospital ship.'

'This is going to put everyone in a good temper for the rest of the day.' Major Rafferty downed his drink and set his tankard on the bar top. 'That poor laddie, Doc – how is he?'

'He's still alive.' The MO ordered another Scotch.

'What are his chances?'

The dark eyebrows lifted. 'Now? Nil, I should say. If they'd got him out by air . . .' He shrugged. 'But I told the Colonel that. So did Bob Fairweather. McGregor had the whole of that crushing weight on top of him for almost an hour before they were able to release him.'

There was a hushed silence. 'Oh, well,' Flint said, 'let's have some lunch.' He stubbed out his cigarette and hitched up his trousers. 'And after lunch,' he added, 'I'm going to have a ziz. Four o'clock this morning, two the night before and stone the bloody crows it looks like four again tomorrow morning.' He glanced at me, his eyes popping with that irrepressible glint of Cockney humour. 'Four o'clock suit you – Captain Stratton driving and an iron bathtub slamming into a head sea fit to knock your block off?'

'For Laerg?' I asked.

'That's right – where the Jumblies live. The Colonel mentioned it to me just now. I'll fix it with Stratton; he'll give you the ride of your life . . . that is if our weather genius 'ere doesn't frighten him so as he loses his nerve.'

'Water Transport take the shipping forecasts,' Cliff said. 'They don't trust me.'

'It isn't that, Cliff. It's just that Stratton believes in continuity – likes his forecasts all the time from the same source. But shipping forecasts – hell! What I've seen of the shipping forecasts up here, they only tell you what you've got sitting on top of you, never what you're going to get – which for my money is the only thing worth a damn.' He turned to me. 'What's your view? I gather you've put in a good deal of sea time?'

It was said out of politeness to include me in the conversation, and as I stood there, sipping my drink and listening to their talk, I was conscious that this was a tight-knit, closed little world, a community not unlike a ship's company. They accepted me, as they accepted Cliff Morgan – not as one of themselves, but as an interesting specimen of the outside world, to be tolerated and treated kindly. I was even more conscious of this at lunch, which was a good meal pleasantly served by a bright little Hebridean waitress. The atmosphere was a strange mixture of democracy and paternal feudalism. It was the Navy all over again, but with a subtle difference; and the youngsters calling me 'sir' to remind me how the years had flown. 'What do you think of modern art, sir?' Picasso, Moore, Annigoni – a reproduction of Annigoni's picture of the Queen hung on the Mess wall; they knew the most publicized names and seemed eager for artistic information, so that for the moment they gave me the illusion of being a visiting genius, and I hoped to God I didn't sound pompous as I tried to answer their queries.

And then Braddock came in and the table fell suddenly silent. He sat down without a word to anyone, and I could see by the way his head was tucked down into his shoulders that he was in a blazing temper.

'Too bad you didn't make it,' Major Rafferty murmured.

The black brows came down in a frown. 'Too bad, you say?' His tone was clipped and angry. 'If Adams had had any sense he'd have unplugged his radio. We'd have made it all right.'

'Have you seen the Colonel?'

'He'd gone up to his house by the time we landed. Anyway, no point. He's made his decision.' He started in on his soup. But after a moment he glanced at the Movements Officer. 'Flint. What's the ETA for that landing craft?'

'At Laerg? Eight-thirty – nine o'clock. Maybe later. She's bucking a head sea. And that's presuming they don't have any more trouble with that oil pump.'

'Which means embarking a stretcher case from a dory in the dark.'

'Unless Kelvedon beaches her. The wind's westerly. Shelter Bay shouldn't be too . . .'

'He's not to beach her – do you understand? Stratton might do it. He's an old hand up here, but Kelvedon's new and if he gets his craft . . .' He gave a quick shrug. 'I'll have a word with him.' His eyes, shifting along the table, met mine for a moment. There was a hardness, an urgency about him. Maybe it was telepathy – I had always been able to sense his mood; I had the feeling that there was something he desperately wanted, something quite unconnected with the injured man. I was remembering the scene in the Met. Office, his determination to make that flight. And then from the files of my memory a sentence sprang: *It's the breath of life to you, isn't it, Donald? But I tell ye, man, it's death to me. That I know – deep down. Death, do ye hear, and I'll not be going there for you or anybody else.* So long ago now, but I could hear his voice still. He'd been talking of Laerg – just after that trawler had brought me back. Had he forgotten? For some reason I'd never been able to fathom, he'd been afraid of the place, as though it bore him some personal animosity; and yet at the same time he'd been fascinated – a fascination that was born of his instinctive, almost primitive fear of it. And now he was desperate to get there, had had himself posted up here to the Hebrides for that purpose; why?

The table had fallen silent, an awkward stillness. One by one the officers rose, put their napkins in the pigeon-holes on the side-table and went out into the lounge for coffee. I rose with Cliff Morgan, conscious that Braddock was watching me. 'Mr Ross.' Strange that he could call me that. His dark eyes held no glimmer of a smile, his voice no trace of the old Highland accent. 'We'll have our talk – later.'

I nodded and went out. Surely to God I couldn't be mistaken. Field handed me my coffee. 'Sugar?' I shook my head. The radio was playing softly – some jazzed-up singer mouthing of love. 'You met my daughter, Marjorie, I think.' I nodded, my mind still on Braddock. 'I thought perhaps you'd care to drop in this evening. We're not far, just beyond the church at Rodil; one of the old black houses. As a painter it might interest you. About nine o'clock. Would that suit you?'

It was kind of him, almost as though he'd known what it was like to lie alone in a small tent on the shores of a loch with a gale tearing at the nylon canopy. I felt I was very near to remembering that face then, but still the connection evaded me. In a news-paper, or a magazine, perhaps. I thanked him and added, 'But I believe I'm staying the night in the quarters here.'

He turned to Ferguson. 'Will you be along tonight, Mike? Marjorie's expecting you.'

'Yes, of course – my lords and masters permitting.'

'Then bring Mr Ross with you.'

It wasn't the sort of face you could forget, just like an axe-head, keen and sharp in the features and broadening out to the head. I was still thinking about this when Cliff Morgan said he was going over to his quarters and suggested I might like to see his radio equipment.

Outside, the rain had stopped and the overcast had lifted. 'That's the warm front – it's passed over us, you see.' The wind was still as strong, west now and colder. 'Whatever Braddock says, Colonel Standing was right to recall Adams. This is no weather for a helicopter landing on Laerg.' The quarters were only a step from the Mess. He led me down a long passage and stopped at Room Number 23. As he unlocked the door, he said, 'I don't sleep here, except when I'm calling Canada or some place that means staying up half the night. I've billeted myself out with a widow and her daughter in one of the crofts in Northton. Very irregular, but I like my comfort, you see.' He smiled and pushed open the door. There was a bed thrust close against one wall, a bureau and wardrobe huddled in a corner; all the rest of the room was taken up with his equipment. 'Since I published that book I've been able to buy all the things I couldn't afford before. It's been produced in the States and translated into German, Italian and Swedish. Now I have everything I need; very complete it is now.' He switched on, seated himself at the keyboard with his earphones. 'It's the weather I'm interested in. But you know that, of course. Now I want to find one or two ships who can tell me what it's like out to the west and north of here.' His hands, delicate as a pianist's, were fingering the dials, deftly tuning. The tall cabinet full of valves began to hum gently. And then his right hand thumbed the key and the soft buzz of his call sign sounded in the room. He was lost to me now, silent in a world of his own.

I sat on the bed, smoking a cigarette, and watching him. Time passed. I found some paper in the bureau and began to sketch him. Periodically he spoke, but to himself rather than to me: 'The *Kincaid*. An old freighter that, six thousand tons. She's outward bound for the Saguenay to pick up a cargo of aluminium. Reports wind north-easterly, force four . . . *Bismuth* – that's one of the Hastings on air reconnaissance five hundred miles west of Ireland; reporting to Bracknell.' He picked up two more ships out in the Atlantic, and then he was talking to a trawler south-east of Iceland. '*Arctic Ranger*. Wind veering northerly and a swell coming down past the east coast of Iceland. Getting quite cold up there. Temperature down to thirty-eight and flurries of snow. Wind increasing, around thirty-five knots.' He took off his earphones. 'I think I'll go up to the office now and see what Ted has on the teleprints.' He switched off.

'Worried?' I asked. I had finished my sketch and was lounging back on the bed.

'No, not worried. Uneasy, though. And if it develops as I

think it might . . .' He pushed his chair back and stood there a moment, running his hand through his thick dark hair, biting on the pencil clenched between his teeth. 'It would be unusual – so early in the season. In January now . . .' He gave that quick little shrug of his that always seemed accompanied by a sideways movement of the head, and then he was pacing up and down; half a dozen steps and then about and retrace them, back and forth with his eyes on the ground, not seeing anything but what was in his mind. He could have got the habit from his time in prison, but I thought it more likely to be the loneliness of his job. He was a solitary. Why otherwise become a meteorologist and then take to operating a 'ham' radio station as a hobby? There are countless men like Cliff Morgan – intelligent, sensitive, artists in their way. They get on all right with women, but escape from the competitive male world by burying themselves body and soul in work that is concerned with things rather than people – impersonal things. With Cliff it was the impersonal forces of the earth's atmosphere, his human contacts mostly made at one remove through the tenuous medium of the ether. I wondered what he'd do if he met opposition – direct opposition, man to man, on his own ground. I thought perhaps he could be very tricky then, perhaps behave with quite astonishing violence.

He had stopped his pacing and was standing over me, staring down at the sketch I'd drawn. 'You work pretty fast.'

'It's just a rough,' I said. 'Pencil sketch of a man who's made his work his life.'

He laughed. 'Oh, I can relax. Indeed I can – if she's pretty enough. But then there's not much difference, is there now; women and weather, they both have their moods, they can both destroy a man. That's why storms are given girls' names. Do you need that sketch? I mean, if you were just drawing to pass the time . . .'

I saw he really wanted it. 'It's your paper anyway,' I said and I handed it to him. He stood for a moment looking down at it. Then he placed it carefully on the keyboard. 'This trip to Laerg,' he said. 'Do you have to go – I mean now, tomorrow morning?'

'Of course I'm going,' I told him. 'It's what I've wanted ever since I returned to England.'

He nodded. 'Well, let's go over to the Met. Office and see what makes. But I'm telling you, man, you could have it very rough indeed.'

'No good telling me,' I said. 'Better tell the skipper of the landing craft.'

He didn't say anything, and when I glanced at him, his face was clouded, his mind concentrated on a world beyond the one in which we walked. Two big towing trucks were grinding past trundling red-painted trailers piled with stores. I don't think he even saw them, and in the Met. Office he went straight to the teleprint file and without a word to Sykes settled down at the desk to mark up a weather map.

Now that I knew something of the set-up, the Met. Office seemed somehow different – familiar ground like the bridge of a ship. The rain had stopped and it was lighter, the visibility much greater. To the left I could see the single hangar standing in the drifted sand like a stranded hulk. It was the only building in sight. Ahead, the wide windows looked out across the tarmac to a sea of dune grass rippling in the wind, humped and hollowed, as full of movement as the sea itself. And beyond the grass-grown dunes was the white blur of broken water, wind-blown waves moving in long regular lines towards the Sound of Harris.

Standing there, with the instruments of meteorology all around me, it wasn't difficult to slip into the mood of men like Cliff Morgan, to visualize the world they lived in, that great amorphous abstract world of atmosphere. I found myself thinking of Laerg, out there beyond the sea's dim horizon. I had seen photographs of it – etchings, too, by the Swedish artist, Roland Svensson. It was the etchings I was thinking of now, for I was sure Svensson had caught the mood of the wild wet world better than any photograph. Unconsciously I found my legs straddled as though to balance myself against the movement of a ship. A few hours and I should be on my way, steaming towards those sheer rock islands that for over thirty years had existed in my mind as the physical embodiment of an old man I had greatly loved.

Oddly, I felt no elation at the prospect; only a sense of awe. In my mind's eye I saw the cliffs rising sheer – black and dripping moisture. But because of my surroundings, the weather instruments and the two men working at the desk, I had also a picture of that other world comprising the moving masses of the Earth's outer skin. It was no more than the vague impression that a shipping forecast handed to the officer of the watch conjures in his mind, but it produced the same feeling of being at one with the elements, so that I found myself recapturing that sense of responsibility, of being a protagonist. The phone ringing cut across my thoughts. Sykes answered it. 'Yes, he's here.' He glanced at me. 'Okay, I'll tell him.' He put the phone down. 'Major Braddock. He'll drive you down to Rodil to pick up your things.'

'Now?'

'He'll be waiting for you outside the Admin. block.'

I had known this moment would come, but I'd have been glad to postpone it. What did you say to a man who'd spent twenty years masquerading as somebody else, and that man your brother? 'All right,' I said, and went out into the wind, wishing at that moment I'd never come north to the Hebrides. Even Laerg couldn't compensate for this.

He was sitting at the wheel of a Land-Rover, waiting for me. 'Jump in.' He didn't say anything more and we drove out through the main gate and down the sand-blown road to Northton. Neither of us spoke and yet oddly enough there was nothing awkward about the silence. It helped to bridge the years, both of us accepting the situation and adjusting ourselves to it. Side-face his true identity was more obvious – a question chiefly of the shape of the head and the way it sat on the shoulders. The profile, too; he couldn't change that. And the hair and the short, straight forehead, the shape of his hands gripping the wheel. 'Why didn't you contact me?' I said.

'You were away at sea.' He hunched his shoulders, an old, remembered gesture. 'Anyway, what was the point? When you take another man's identity – well, you'd better damn well stick to it.'

'Did you have to do that?'

'Do what?'

'Take Braddock's name?'

'I didn't have to, no. But I did.' A muscle was moving at the corner of his mouth and his voice was taut as he added, 'What would you have done? Given yourself up, I suppose. Well, I wasn't going to stand trial for busting the jaw of a man who hadn't the guts to lead his own men.'

'What happened?' I asked. 'What exactly happened out there in North Africa?'

'You really want to know?' He hesitated, frowning. 'Well . . . It was after we'd landed. The French had us pinned down. They'd got a machine-gun nest in one of those walled villas. We were all right. We were in a dried-up wadi. But it was murder for the lads on our right. They were caught in the open, a whole company of them lying out there on the bare rocks, and we had the shelter of that gully right up to the villa's walls. Instead of attacking, Moore ordered the platoon to stay put and keep their heads down. He was frightened to death. In the end I knocked him out and took command myself. It was the only way. But by then the French had got a gun in position to cover the wadi and they opened up on us when we were halfway up it. That's when I got this.' He pointed to the scar on his forehead. 'I lost eighteen men, but we took the villa. And when it was all over, I was under arrest. If I hadn't hit the little sod I'd have been all right, but that fixed me, so I got the hell out of it and back to the beach. Wasn't difficult; everything a bit chaotic. The fact that I was wounded made it dead easy. I was taken off to a troopship that was just leaving. She'd been damaged and when we were clear of the Straits she was ordered to proceed to Montreal for repairs. That was how I landed up in Canada.' He glanced at me. 'They didn't tell you that?'

'Some of it – not all.'

'I had just over a year in Canada before they picked me up. It was conscription that fixed me. I hadn't any papers, you see. And then, when the *Duart Castle* went down . . .' He gave a quick shrug. 'Well, I took a chance and it worked out.'

But looking at the deep-etched lines of his face, I wondered. He looked as though he'd been living on his nerves for a long time. There were lines running underneath the cheek-bones and down from the sides of the mouth, others puckering the scar on the forehead, radiating from the corners of the eyes; some of them so deep they might have been scored by a knife. Those lines and the harsh, almost leathery skin could simply be the marks of a hard life, but I had an uneasy feeling they were something more than that.

Through Northton he began to talk – about the Army and the life he'd led and where he'd been. It seemed to help, for he began to relax then and become more at ease; in no time at all the years had fallen away and we were on our old, easy footing, with him talking and myself listening. It had always been like that. And then suddenly he said, 'You married Mavis, did you?'

'For my sins,' I said. 'It didn't work out.'

'And the child?'

'It died.'

I thought he didn't care, for he made no comment, driving in silence again. But as we came down the hill into Leverburgh, he said, 'What was it – a boy?'

'Yes.' And I added, 'I had him christened Alasdair.'

He nodded as though he'd expected that. We were passing ugly blocks of Swedish pre-fabs and as we turned right past the loch, he murmured, 'I'm sorry.' But whether he was sorry for what he'd done to us or because the child had died I couldn't be sure. We were on a track now that led out to the quay. 'I just want to check that they're moving the stuff fast enough,' he said. 'Then I'll drive you on to Rodil to collect your gear.'

The quay looked a mess, the whole length of it littered with material brought from Laerg – piled-up sections of wooden huts, double-ended dories, trailers still loaded with stoves, radios, refrigerators, a deep-freeze, clothing, and crates full of foodstuffs, sacks of potatoes, fruit, coal; all the paraphernalia of an isolated unit being withdrawn in a hurry, and all of it soaked by the rain. One Scammell was trying to inch a trailer through the debris. Two three-ton trucks were being loaded, the men moving slowly, lethargically as though they had been doing this a long time. A single mobile crane swung its gantry lazily against the leaden dullness of the sky, and beyond the quay skerries barred the way into the Sound of Harris with here and there a light mounted on iron legs to mark the channel through the rocks.

It was a depressing sight. I wandered along the concrete edge of the quay whilst Braddock spoke to the officer in charge. 'A fine mess you'd be in,' I heard him say, 'if Four-four-Double-o had come in on schedule instead of being sent back to Laerg fully loaded.' His voice, harsh now, had a whip-lash quality.

'We're shifting it as fast as we can,' the youngster answered. 'But the men are tired. They've been at it since early this morning, and we're short of vehicles.'

'They're tired, are they? Then just think how Captain Pinney's men must be, working round the clock, crammed into only two huts, soaked to the skin. Now get moving, boy, and have this quay cleared to receive Kelvedon's ship when it comes in.'

'When will that be?'

'Dawn I should think, or a little after.' I saw him grip the young man's shoulder. 'Between now and the end of the operation this may be our one chance to catch up. See the men understand that. If Stratton's crew hadn't been dead beat you'd have had Eight-six-one-o up here by now. Make the most of this oppor-tunity, Phipps.'

'I'll do the best I can, sir.'

'Better than the best; I want miracles.' The hard face cracked in a smile. 'Okay?' He patted the lieutenant's shoulder, instilling into him some of his own urgent drive. Then he turned. 'Sergeant!' He had a word with the sergeant and then came back to the Land-Rover. 'Peacetime soldiering,' he muttered as he climbed into the driving seat. 'They don't know what it is to be beaten to their knees and still fight back. They haven't known a war. I was in

Burma.' He started the engine and yanked the wheel round. 'That was after the Normandy landings. Half these guys would get shot to bits before they'd dug a slit trench. Just because they're technicians a lot of them, they think the Army's a branch of industry – a cosy factory with set hours and plenty of recreation.'

We drove out of Leverburgh and up the glen with him talking about the evacuation and how he'd had his leave cut short to come up here and see the operation through. 'If I'd known what I know now I'd never have accepted the posting. It's drive, drive, drive, and they hate my guts most of them. But what can you do with the weather on top of you and time so short? And now we're at the critical stage. The run-down of accommodation and stores on Laerg has reached the point where the operation has got to be completed. Pinney's detachment haven't enough food and fuel left on the island to last a fortnight, let alone see the winter through. And the weather chooses this moment to break. Goddammit, the War Office should have had more sense.' He glanced at me quickly. 'What did you think of Standing?'

I hesitated, not knowing what he expected. 'I've only seen him for a few minutes.'

'Long enough to fix yourself a trip to Laerg.' There was a bite to his voice, a resentment almost, as though he disliked the thought of my going to the island. 'You were there when he cancelled that flight. How did he seem?'

'A little nervous,' I said. 'But in the circumstances . . .'

'Nervous! He's scared. Scared he'll make a wrong decision. In fact, he's scared of making any decision. Scared, too, of leaving it all to me. He's a bloody old woman with a mind like an adding machine. And his wife's one of the most beautiful women I've ever met.'

'Are you married?' I asked.

'Yes, but it didn't work out any better than yours. Lasted longer, that's all. And I'll never get shot of her. She's a Roman Catholic.' We passed the church and a moment later drew up by the hotel. He came down to the loch-side with me and helped strike the tent and carry my stuff to the Land-Rover. It only took ten minutes or so and then we were driving back. It was as we topped the rise and sighted Northton that he said, 'D'you know a man called Lane – a Canadian?' He tried to make it casual, but the tightness in his voice betrayed him.

'I've met him,' I said. 'Once.'

'And that's why you're here.'

'Partly – yes.'

He braked so suddenly that the engine stalled and I was flung forward in my seat. 'Why do you want to go to Laerg?' The tension in his voice flared to a higher pitch. 'What's behind it? What are you expecting to find there?'

'Peace. Subjects to paint.' And I added, 'I've always wanted to go to Laerg.'

'But why now? You've managed very well for over twenty years . . . Now, suddenly, you have to go there. Why? What did Lane tell you?'

'It's nothing to do with Lane.'

'Then what the hell is it?' He had gripped hold of my arm and was almost shaking it. 'As soon as I was away on that flight you went running to Standing and somehow persuaded him to ship you out on an LCT. What did you tell him?'

'Nothing about you,' I said. 'Just that my father came from Laerg and that I wanted to paint there.'

'That all?' He was staring at me, the pupils of his eyes almost black and strangely dilated. And then he let go my arm. 'You could have waited.' His voice sounded suddenly tired. 'I'd have got you to Laerg in time – if you'd asked me.'

Was he hurt that I hadn't? 'I was going to ask you,' I said. 'But you went off on that flight, and then, when I saw Colonel Standing . . .'

'Standing's not running this operation. I am. And I'm not having you or anyone else going out there and making a nuisance of themselves.' He shifted in his seat, watching me, his mouth twitching and a gleam of perspiration on his forehead. 'After all these years. Bit of a shock, isn't it?' He was smiling now, trying to recapture the old charm. But somehow the smile wasn't right. 'Be frank with me. You always were – in the old days. We never hid anything from each other.'

'I'm not hiding anything from you now.'

But he didn't seem to hear. 'What did Lane tell you? Come on now. He told you something that sent you scurrying up here with a sudden, urgent desire to get to Laerg.'

'He guessed who you were. Suspected it, anyway. He's been interviewing survivors . . .'

'I'm talking about Laerg. What did he say about Laerg?'

'Nothing,' I said. 'He's discovered you were on that raft and he's put two and two together . . .'

'Then why are you so anxious to get out to Laerg?'

There it was again. Laerg – Laerg! Why did he keep harping on Laerg? 'He never mentioned Laerg.'

'No?'

'Just listen to me, Iain,' I said. 'I came up here with one object in mind – to find out whether you were still alive or not. Having done that, I thought it was a good opportunity to see the island. I've been wanting to go to Laerg for two years now, ever since I came back from the Aegean. I want to paint there. Just to paint, that's all. Nothing else.'

But I don't think he believed me even then. His face had a stony look as though he'd shut his mind to all reason, and I had a sudden feeling there was tragedy here, a deep, wasting wound that fed on his nerves. It was a moment of intuition, I think – blood calling to blood and the sense of his desperation very strong.

'Well, you're not going.' He said it flatly, more to himself than to me. And then, as though suddenly aware of what he'd said and the need for some explanation: 'This is a military operation. The landing craft are fully committed. It's no moment for shipping tourists out to the island.'

'I'm not a tourist,' I said, resenting the implication. 'Not where Laerg is concerned.'

'You are from the Army's point of view. I'll have a word with Standing.' And he got the engine going again and we drove down into the camp, neither of us saying a word. He dropped me off at the officers' quarters. 'Room forty-two,' he said as I got my gear out of the back of the Land-Rover. 'Maybe I'll have time for a drink with you before dinner.' He was Major Braddock again and we were strangers. I watched him drive off, wishing now that I'd made more of an effort to discover what it was that was eating into his soul, for this wasn't the brother I'd known. This was quite a different man – a man driven and desperate. I had that feeling, and it scared me. Later, I said to myself. Later I'll find out.

I didn't know that there wasn't going to be a later, that time was running out and I'd missed the only chance I'd get of being alone with him before it was too late.

Room 42 was the same as Cliff Morgan's, a standard pattern with standard furniture – bed, bedside table, bureau, chair, wardrobe, all in natural oak, an armchair, wash basin and the rusted steel windows looking out on to a drab patch of coarse dune grass. I dumped my things and went for a walk, heading north from the main gate, away from the camp and the landing apron. Ten minutes and I was amongst the dunes, alone in a world that hadn't changed since the first man set foot in the Outer Hebrides. To my left Chaipaval reared heather and grass-clad slopes to the clouds. To my right the mountains of Harris stood black and sombre, their stormbound peaks shrouded in rain. I came to the last sanded bluff and ahead of me was a great stretch of sands, glistening wet, and a line of dunes standing like a breakwater between them and the sea. The island of Taransay rose misty-green beyond the dunes. There were sheep sheltering in the hollows they had worn along the edge of the bluff and below a river of water flowed towards the sea, fish marking the smooth surface with little whorls.

It was a wild wet world and I walked there until it was almost dusk, thinking of Laerg and my brother Iain, the wind on my face bringing back to me the salt taste of Ardnamurchan and my youth. The picture in my mind was of a bare, wood-lined room and the two of us, sprawled on the floor, gazing with rapt attention at the craggy, bearded face of my grandfather softened by the peat fire glow – old Alasdair Ross at the age of eighty-five or thereabouts telling two boys of the wonders of Laerg, describing the strange remote island world that had been his life and speaking all the time the Laerg brand of Gaelic he'd taught us to understand. It was a picture etched for all time in my mind. It had stood between me and the fear of death as I'd gazed down at the waxen face and the pitifully shrunken body in the big bed; it had comforted me that cold day when I stood shivering and crying bitterly beside the open grave. I could hear the rattle of the first frozen clods on the coffin lid still, but the face I remembered was the live face, vital and glowing in the firelight, the soft voice, the sea-grey eyes beneath the shaggy tufted eyebrows.

And here I stood now at the threshold of his world. In twenty-four hours I should be ashore on Laerg. Would it match my dreams, or had the old man so coloured the picture with his longing to return that he'd spoiled it for me? I wondered; wondered, too, about Iain. Was the picture the old man had painted as vivid to him as it was to me? Was that why he'd been so determined to make the flight? Or was it something else – something to do with the tension I'd sensed in him?

I had a drink with him that night in the Mess, but there were others there and I couldn't probe. In any case, his mood didn't encourage it – he had a black look on his face and was barely civil to anyone. And after dinner, Mike Ferguson drove me down to Rodil. By then the weather had closed in again, the rain slanting in the beam of the headlights. 'The forecast's not too good,' he said. 'You may be out of luck.'

I thought for a moment he was breaking it to me that permission for me to sail with the LCT had been withdrawn. But then he added, 'Stratton may decide not to go.'

'But if he does . . .?'

'Then Movements will get you on board in time. Colonel Standing's orders.' And he added, 'Major Braddock wanted him to cancel your trip. Said visitors were a damned nuisance. But the Old Man dug in his toes.' He seemed preoccupied and I didn't like to ask him what had been said. In any case, it didn't matter. It wouldn't solve the mystery of my brother's extraordinary attitude. That was something deep-buried in his past, and I sat, puzzling over it, silent as the road unwound in the headlights, my interest in Laerg more urgent than ever.

The Fields' croft was just below Rodil church. It was stone built with small windows and looked like a cow byre, the thatch curving in dim silhouette and roped against the wind, each rope-end weighted with a stone. Field met us at the door, dressed now in grey flannels and an open-necked bush shirt. 'Come in, my dear fellow.' The gentleness of his voice struck me again, strangely at odds with the hard lines of his extraordinary hatchet features. 'Marjorie's seeing to the coffee,' he told Ferguson. 'You'll find her in the kitchen.' He took me through into the living-room which was spartan and furnished only with the bare essentials. A peat fire smouldered in the grate. 'We live very simply, as you can see.' But they had electricity, and despite its bareness there was an intimacy, a cosiness about the room that made me feel instantly at home. 'Marjorie usually makes coffee about this time. Would that be all right?' There was a note of apology in his voice as though he thought I might have preferred whisky. 'I imagine this is the first time you've seen the inside of a black house?' And he went on quickly to explain that the word derived from the fact that the original Hebridean croft had virtually no windows and a peat fire in a central hearth that was never allowed to go out. 'The chimney was just a hole in the roof and smoke blackened the interior.' He smiled. 'I should know. I was born in one – not far from here, on the west coast of Lewis.' He was talking quickly, putting me at my ease, and all in the same soft, gentle voice.

He sat me down by the fire, gave me a cigarette, went on to talk about crofting, the subsidies, land disputes. The religion, too, and drunkenness, so that the impression left in my mind was one of a feckless, hard-drinking, lazy people. 'It's the climate,' he said. 'The remoteness of the islands. It's as insidious as a disease.' He smiled gently as though he himself were infected by it.

'It must be a pretty hard life,' I murmured.

'Aye, and they're the salt of the ear-rth.' There was a twinkle of humour in his eyes. 'Being one of them myself I understand them. But I've been outside the islands most of my life. It makes a difference. And coming back . . .' He shrugged. 'One would be more sympathetic if they made a greater effort to help themselves. Take this place; here's a dwelling ideally suited to the climate, the materials all ready to hand – but the status symbol up here is something constructed by a builder out of breeze-blocks. You try and paint the interior of any black house that's still occupied. They wouldn't let you across the threshold.'

'Why not?' I asked.

'Because they're ashamed of them now.' He was staring into the glowing peat, his long legs stretched half across the bearskin rug. 'Islanders should never have contact with the mainland. It's destroying them here just as it's destroyed the people of the out-islands. Laerg would never have been evacuated if the island had remained in isolation. It had a perfectly sound economy until the outside world brought to their doorsteps the illusion of an easier life. They had their sheep – the sheep the Vikings introduced a thousand years ago – and they had the birds. In its heyday Laerg supported a population of over two hundred. They salted away huge numbers of puffins each year, splitting them open like kippers and hanging them up to dry in the peat smoke. Puffins and guga – that's the young of the solan goose. They had the down of the birds for bedding, the oil for lamps. They carded their own wool, wove their own clothes. Peat was there for the digging and the wind dried it in the loose stone cleits that litter the slopes of Tarsaval. They didn't need money.'

I knew all this – from my grandfather, from the books I'd read. What I wanted to know was how much the island had been changed by the Army. 'Not a great deal,' he said. 'There's a concrete ramp built on the storm beach in Shelter Bay for the LCTs. There's the camp, of course. That's just below the village, near to the Factor's House. And there's the High Road. That's probably changed the island more than anything else. It starts at the camp, skirts the Bay just back of the storm beach, climbs Keava in three hairpins, then up the ridge to Creag Dubh where the radar station is. There's a spur, too, that runs out to the Butt of Keava overlooking Sgeir Mhor. I can show it to you on the Ordnance Survey, if you're interested.'

The door opened and Marjorie Field came in; Ferguson

followed with the coffee tray. 'Talking about Laerg,' her father said.

'Laerg?' She smiled. 'Everybody's always talking about Laerg, and I'm not allowed to go there.' She turned to me. 'I owe you an apology, don't I? You *are* a painter. I checked.'

'How?'

'With Cliff.' She turned to her father. 'Mr Ross did the jacket for Cliff's book.'

'Your daughter seemed under the impression I was a journalist.' A shadow crossed his face and he didn't smile.

'You like it black or white?' she asked me.

'Black,' I said and she handed me my coffee and then switched the conversation by asking Ferguson if there was any more news of the Russian trawlers.

'Coastal Command had a Shackleton out yesterday. They didn't see anything.'

Field shifted in his seat and reached for his coffee. 'It's just a newspaper story, Mike.'

'Not necessarily. Visibility was bad and with the cloud base down to between four and six hundred the search was very restricted. There is no doubt whatever that they do have trawlers operating in the area.'

'So have the French, the Belgians, the Portuguese. Anyway, what information could they hope to get? It would be different if the range was operating. If they could check the accuracy of fire of the various units . . .'

'That's not half so important, sir, as the fact that we're getting out of Laerg. It means we've developed some other method of pin-pointing the fall of shot – a long-range tracking service. Moscow would be very interested to know that.'

'But, my dear fellow, they wouldn't need trawlers to tell them we're getting out. Any crofter in Harris . . .' The discussion didn't concern me and I took the opportunity to examine the room which I found much more interesting. The walls were bare; no pictures, no photographs even, nothing to give a clue to Field's past. Only that bearskin rug. I wondered where that had come from. It was old, the head marked by burns. Had he shot it or was it something they'd picked up in a junk shop? The door to the kitchen had been left half open. His Service greatcoat hung there, the two pips a reminder of the incongruity of his age and rank. Below it hung a quilted jacket rather like a parka; green once, but now faded and worn and rather dirty.

My eyes turned to the daughter then; the nose, the blue eyes – I could see the likeness. But the mouth was softer, the skin darker. I wondered who her mother had been. She was perched on the arm of Mike Ferguson's chair and she looked strikingly beautiful, her face glowing in the lamplight, the skin almost nut-coloured and soft with the bloom of youth. I felt my blood stirring as it hadn't done since I'd left the Aegean. Her glance met mine and she smiled quickly, a wide-mouthed smile that had her father's warmth, lighting up her whole face. 'So you've got your wish; you're going to Laerg.'

'Yes.'

It was then that Field gave me the clue to his identity. 'Laerg,' he said, and there was a wistfulness in his voice. 'I shall miss it. One of the plums, being Education Officer here, was that I got out to Laerg once in a while. I should have been going next Saturday . . .' He shrugged. 'But I can't complain. I've had three tours.' He smiled. 'I'm envious, you see. It's an experience, particularly the first time. And, of course, the cliffs – there's some of the finest rock climbing . . .'

'It's the birds he's really interested in,' his daughter said quickly.

But she was too late. That reference to climbing. I knew who he was then, for his name had been in all the papers. Pictures of him, too. Some time in the early fifties it must have been for we were still on the Far East run and the papers had come aboard with the mail at Singapore. He'd been the leader of one of the Himalayan expeditions. I couldn't remember the details, or the name of the peak, only that he'd been brought down from somewhere near the summit just before the final assault. The official statement had simply announced that he'd been taken ill, but the newspapers had reported it in a way that made it obvious there was more to it than that. As though conscious of my thoughts, he turned away from me. 'Any news of McGregor?' he asked Ferguson.

'An emergency operation. I fixed Bob up with a link through to Command on the Military Line just before I left Camp. He's doing it under instruction.'

'How horrible for him.'

He glanced up at the girl. 'Aye, and the laddie could have been in hospital hours ago. As it is . . .' He shook his head. 'Bob's not happy about it; nobody is.'

'You think the man's going to die?' Field asked.

'Frankly, yes. I don't think he has a hope. When Bob's finished with him, the poor devil's got ten hours or more being bucketed about on a landing craft and then a flight to the mainland. If the Colonel had only left it to Ronnie Adams . . .'

'The helicopter might have crashed.'

'It might. But I doubt it. The worst the down-draughts have done to a helicopter so far is slam it on the deck so hard the rotor blades were shivered and split for about a yard from the tips. Anyway, it's for the pilot to assess the risk. That was Braddock's view, and for once I agreed with him. Not that either of them asked my views. They were too busy hammering away at each other.'

'When was this?'

'Just before dinner.'

'And you think Standing was wrong to cancel the flight?'

Mike Ferguson hesitated. 'Yes. Yes, I do; considering what was at stake – a man's life.'

Field sighed. 'Every man makes his decisions in the light of his own experience, Mike. Did you know that Colonel Standing once saw a helicopter crash? It caught fire and the chaps inside it were burned alive, right before his eyes. It makes a difference, you see.'

'And he told you about it?' Ferguson smiled. 'You've become a sort of father confessor to us all, haven't you.' There was affection as well as admiration in his voice.

'To some, yes. Not all.'

'Meaning Braddock?'

'Perhaps.' He leaned forward and poked at the fire. 'Man is a complex mechanism, each individual a solitary unit afraid of loneliness. That's something you'll discover as the years pass. Most of them seek escape from loneliness by membership of a group. The herd instinct is very strong in all of us. But there are always a few rogues – some of them men of real stature, others forced by circumstances to live solitary lives.' I thought he was speaking from experience then. The gentle voice sounded tired, weighted with weariness.

'They needn't be solitary if they're happily married,' his daughter said. And she added, 'I saw Laura this morning. She looked almost haggard.'

'Laura could never look haggard.' Her father smiled.

'Well, strained then. She knows what's going on. Ever since Major Braddock was posted up here . . .'

'Braddock's only doing his job.' Field glanced at me. 'I'm afraid Mr Ross must find this very boring.' It was a signal to close the ranks in the face of the outside world, and after that the talk was general. We left just before ten, and Ferguson drove fast, anxious to contact Laerg and get news of the LCT.

He was reluctant to talk about Field at first, but when he realized I'd already guessed his background, he admitted I was right. 'That business . . . it pretty well broke him up at the time. His whole life was climbing.'

'What did he do – afterwards?'

'Took to drink. That's why there's no liquor in the house.' And after a moment, he added, 'Maybe you can't understand it. But I can. I know how he must have felt – and it's not something you can control. It just takes charge . . .' We were on the hill above Leverburgh then and he slammed into lower gear. 'Damned shame. To escape it all he came up here, back to the islands where he was born. Then the Army arrived and that gave him the opportunity to do something useful again. He's all right now as long as Marjorie keeps an eye on him.'

I asked him then why she was so worried about newspaper men bothering him after all this time.

'Oh, it's his wife,' he said. 'He's quite a story – wartime hero, then all through the Karakoram and up into Mongolia. Now she's found out he's buried himself in the Army and she's threatening to put the Press on to him again if he doesn't go back to her. She's a bitch and no good to him – or to Marjorie.'

I thought he was referring to the girl's mother. But he said, 'No, this is his second wife I'm talking about. The first was an islander like himself. From Pabbay, I think, though he met her out in Egypt. She was a nurse in the hospital where he was sent after getting himself shot up in a Long Range Desert Group foray. Unfortunately she was killed in a plane crash. If she'd lived it might have been different. They were very happy, I believe.' And after that he was silent and we drove down into the camp.

Back in my room I found a note waiting for me. The trip to Laerg was off. *Owing to bad weather L8610 will not be sailing on the morning tide.* It was scribbled on a sheet of paper torn from a notebook and was signed Fred Flint. I had seen a light in Cliff Morgan's quarters as we drove in and I walked across.

He was seated at the keyboard and didn't look up as I entered. He had earphones clamped to his head and his mind was concentrated on another world. I sat down on the bed and lit a cigarette. He didn't notice me until he looked up to change the tuning. He started to speak, but then held up his hand, listening. After a moment he pushed up one earphone. 'You've heard the news, have you?'

'Captain Flint left a note in my quarters. Eight-six-one-o won't be sailing.'

'I wasn't referring to that. I thought as you were with Ferguson . . . He's calling him now.'

'Who?'

'Four-four-Double-o – Captain Kelvedon. He's in trouble. I picked him up on Voice about half an hour ago asking for Major Braddock. He's got himself stuck on a falling tide. Went in to pick up McGregor . . . Ah, here we are. Listen!' He switched in the loudspeaker and a metallic voice broke into the room. It was Ferguson. '. . . *ask him, but I'm quite sure he wouldn't agree to Adams attempting it in these conditions. I don't think Adams would go, anyway.*'

'*The Doc here says there isn't much time . . .*'

'That's Kelvedon,' Cliff whispered.

'*. . . and I can't get out of here for another five hours at least. We're grounded hard.*'

'*What happened?*'

'*It was the wind partly. We had it westerly, bang on the nose most of the way across. Then it suddenly backed. I'd never have attempted it, but Fairweather told me the man wouldn't live if they tried to bring him off in a dory. It was dark as hell and quite a sea running, but I thought I could edge in close enough to drop the ramp with the kedge well out astern. Maybe it was badly laid. And that sandbank. I think it must have been building up without our realizing it. The seas slewed us round and we touched the edge of it. Two hours after high water. When we came to winch off we found we were stuck fast.*'

'*I see. And what about McGregor?*'

'*He's back in his bed in the hospital hut. But Fairweather doesn't think he'll last long. The only hope is to get him out by helicopter.*'

'*Okay. I'll tell the Colonel. What about you, now? Do you want me to have the Navy stand by?*'

'*Oh Lord, no. We're pounding a bit and it's not very comfortable. But the wind's veered now. Seems all over the bloody place. But if it stays where it is, north of west, we'll get off all right on the flood.*'

'*Fine. Call me again if there's anything fresh to report. Good luck.*' And then he was calling Laerg. '*Are you there, Laerg? Base calling Laerg.*'

'*Laerg here,*' a Scots voice answered. '*Go ahead, Base.*'

'*Captain Ferguson here. Keep your set manned throughout the night. I may want to contact Captain Fairweather later.*'

'*Very good, sir.*'

'*Is Captain Pinney there?*'

There was a pause and then a new voice answered, *'Pinney here.'*

'How does the landing craft look from the shore, John?'

'Slewed off about twenty degrees and grounded on that ridge of sand. Nowhere near the ramp.'

'And the sea?'

'Moderate. Wind's getting round into the north-west, so the beach is sheltered, but there's still a biggish swell coming in. The old can's grinding a bit, but she'll be all right. It's this poor devil McGregor I'm worrying about. Just nothing but bad luck.' The voice sounded tired. *'Do what you can, will you? Have a talk with Major Braddock.'*

'He's down at Leverburgh trying to get the quay cleared.'

'Well, send a car down for him, see if he can persuade the Colonel. This boy's going to die if somebody doesn't take a chance.'

'Okay, John. Leave it with me.'

Cliff Morgan switched off and the room was suddenly dead as he reached automatically for a cigarette. He lit it, gulping a mouthful of smoke deep into his lungs, breathing it out through his nostrils. 'Not good, is it? And the wind playing tricks like that . . .' He noticed his old cigarette still burning in the ashtray at his elbow and stubbed it out. 'I don't like it when I feel like this. The number of times I've sat talking to some poor beggar riding the night sky with a load of trouble, or tapping out a message with the radio shack turning somersaults around him. I've been right too often, you see. There was that trawler, *Grampian Maid*. Nobody else could raise her and I was relaying messages until black ice turned her turtle. And a Boeing up over the Arctic – ice again and I was with him up to the moment when his messages ceased abruptly. I'm not like an ordinary "ham", you see. I've got something to give them – the weather. Ships, aircraft, they live by the weather, and if you know as much about it as I do . . .' He sighed and scratched himself under the arm, his hand burrowing inside his shirt. It was an unconscious, reflective gesture. 'You'd better go and get some sleep. And have your things packed ready.' He was leaning forward, tuning the dials of the radio again.

'You think the LCT will sail?' I asked.

'I don't know. Anything could happen . . .' He shifted in his seat, his body tense, his eyes fixed on the set as his fingers moved with the touch of a pianist, filling the room with the crackle of static. And behind the static, a man's voice, the words indecipherable. 'There they are again. Two trawlers south-east of Iceland.' He clamped both earphones tight to his head, leaning forward, his whole being concentrated in the tips of his fingers as they hovered over the dials. He'd left the loudspeaker on and a Scots voice came faintly, a voice so broad it might have been talking in a foreign tongue: '*A* dinna ken w-what it means ony mair thin ye du yersel', mon. Twa hoors ago the wind was fra the north. Noo it's roond into the sou'east an' blowing a bluidy gale.'

And the other voice barely audible through the crackle: '*Aye, an' the glass ganging doon agin.*'

'*Did ye hear that noo? A bluidy great sea reecht o'er the bows, and the fish still coming in.*'

'*Ye're on top of a shoal, are ye, Doug?*'

'*Aye, blast it. But this is no' the time to be trawling whativer the bluidy fish. It's a hell of a night. You hove-to the noo, Jock?*'

'*Aye, hove-to and wishing to God I were in me bed with the wife and a wee dram inside o' me. Ha' ye got the forecast?*'

'*Bluidy lot o' good the forecast was . . .*' The static overlaid the voices then and I couldn't decipher the rest.

After a moment Cliff Morgan pulled his earphones off. '*Arctic Ranger* talking to *Laird of Brora*. It's bad up there and I don't know quite what it means yet. There's no clear pattern, you see.' He was staring down at his notebook, drawing without thinking deep concentric rings. 'You go to bed,' he said. 'Get some sleep whilst you can.' He ran his hand up over his face, rubbing at his eyes. He looked tired.

'Are you going to stay up all night?' I asked.

'Probably. Maybe when they've stopped getting in the nets I'll be able to contact their radio operators – get some facts out of them. A pair of skippers blethering at each other. Doesn't tell you anything. I don't want to know how they feel with all hell let loose. I want to know what the barometer reads and how it compares with the reading three, four hours ago, what the weight of the wind is and whether the temperature is rising or falling.' He leaned back. 'Leave me to it, will you now. I want to see if I can raise some vessel further west. If not, I'll have a talk with the weather ships, see what they've got to say.'

'You get their reports anyway, don't you?'

He nodded. 'But it takes time. And talking to them is very different, you know, from reading the lists of figures they send in.' He put the earphones on again, leaning closer to the set as he began to tune, his fingers light as a caress on the dials. 'Those trawlers . . .' He was speaking to himself, not to me. 'On the fringe of the High and now that first depression's starting to come through. Still two of them, but very close. That would account for

671

what happened to Kelvedon – the sudden changes of wind . . .'
His voice died away, his expression suddenly intent. And then his
thumb was on the key and the buzz of morse, very rapid, filled
the room as he made contact across miles of ocean.

I watched him for a moment longer, and then I left. Back in
Room 42 I undressed, doing familiar things slowly, automatically,
smoking a cigarette and mulling over the day. It had been a
long one, so much packed into it, and London, my dismal attic
of a studio, the years of hard work to become a painter – all
seemed so far away. I was back now in a man's world of decisions
and action, involving ships and weather, my movements governed
by the sea, and I found I was glad, as though painting had been
no more than an affair with a beautiful woman and this the real
love of my life. I sat on the bed and lit a cigarette from the butt
of the old and thought about that. Was I painter or sailor, or
was this new mood that had my blood tingling the physical
reaction to the prospect of a childhood dream becoming a reality?
I didn't know. My mind was strangely confused. All I knew for
certain was that the sea was calling.

I finished my cigarette, turned the thermostat of the central
heating down to 'low' and went to bed thinking of Laerg.

2

FORBIDDEN ISLAND
(20 October)

I woke from a deep sleep with the ceiling lights blazing in my
eyes and the duty driver standing over me, shaking me by the
shoulder. 'There's a cuppa' tea for you, sir. Captain Flint said
to tell you he's leaving at four-ten.'

'What's the time now?'

'Quarter to. I'll pick you up in twenty minutes. Okay? You
are awake, aren't you, sir?'

'Yes, I'm awake, thanks.' I sat up and rubbed my eyes. Even
with the thermostat turned right down the room was suffocatingly
hot. I felt sweaty and drugged with sleep; the tea was black and
thick and sweet. I got up, washed and shaved, and then dressed
in my heaviest clothes, two sweaters and an anarak over the top.
I packed my shoes and wore my gum boots; it was the easiest

way to carry them. Outside, it was cold and windy; no sign of dawn yet, but the sky had cleared and there were stars. A half moon hung low over the camp, giving a frozen look to the un-lighted huts. A long wheel-base Land-Rover stood parked outside the Mess, torches glimmered and the muffled shapes of men stood dark in the eerie light. 'That you, Ross?' The Movements Officer took my bag and tossed it into the back of the vehicle. 'Sorry there's no coffee laid on. No time for it anyway. Is that the lot, driver?'

'Yes, sir.'

'McGregor's replacement?'

A voice from the back of the Land-Rover said, 'Here, sir. Patridge.'

'Okay. Let's get cracking then.'

We climbed in. A big, heavy-jowled man in a beret and a sheepskin jacket squeezed in beside me. Flint introduced him as Major McDermott. 'You'll be brothers in misery for the next twelve hours – that is, if Stratton decides to go. But it's by no means certain yet. Things are in such a flipping mess this morning, nothing's certain.' He sounded tired and irritable.

We drove out by the main gate and headed towards the hangar with the moon hanging over it. The helicopter was standing on the tarmac apron. The Land-Rover drew up beside it. Adams was there waiting for us, dancing up and down on the balls of his feet to keep himself warm. The wind sifted sand in a light film across the surface of the apron. I hadn't expected to be travelling by helicopter. It seemed an odd way to be joining ship, but as we settled into our seats I realized that there was no other means of getting to the landing craft. The South Ford I knew from the map was the shallow channel between Benbecula and South Uist; it was more than thirty miles away to the south with no road link because of the Sound of Harris.

The door shut and the rotors turned, gathering speed until the whole fuselage shook. And then the ground was falling away and we were slipping sideways across the hangar like a gull blown by the wind. 'Did you know we've got an LCT grounded in Shelter Bay?' Flint shouted in my ear. And when I nodded, he said, 'Stratton's standing by just in case. If the ship gets off all right, then Stratton will slip round into Carnan and land you at the quay there. If she doesn't then he'll probably have a bash at it. Even then you may land up back at Leverburgh.' He leaned across me, peering out through the window. 'Thank God I won't be with you if you do sail. My stomach doesn't like the sea.'

We were over the Sound now, the waves breaking white in the moonlight a thousand feet below us. And beyond the Sound we flew over a drowned land, all lakes, with the sea lochs reaching long, wet fingers into it. There was more water there than land. It looked wicked country in that ghostly light, and it went on and on with only a single sugarloaf hill to relieve the flat pan of its deadly monotony. At four-thirty we crossed the North Ford with the first pale glimmer of daylight showing the Isle of Skye in jagged relief on the eastern horizon. We were over Benbecula then and ten minutes later we saw the ship grounded in the South Ford with the tide creeping in over the sands; she wasn't quite afloat yet.

The helicopter dropped like a lift, turned head-to-wind and hovered just clear of her stern whilst the crew lowered the boat. Flint got up and pulled the door open. A gale of cold wind blew into the fuselage. We moved ahead then, settling gently on to the water about two hundred yards up-wind of the landing craft. As the rotors slowed and stopped a new sound invaded the cabin – the slap of waves against the floats. The buzz of an outboard motor came steadily nearer and then the dory was alongside and we were piling into it. Small waves tossed spray over the gunnel, wetting feet and baggage. A young man in a white polo-necked sweater, his fair hair blowing in the wind, jumped out on to the float. 'Flinty. You want to come aboard?'

'Not on your life. I'm going straight back to bed. Just came to see you boys were all right. What's the news?'

'Nothing yet. They're still grounded. But Captain Kelvedon was on the air about ten minutes ago to say he'd be starting to winch off any moment now.'

'Hope he makes it.'

'By God, so do I. It's going to be a dirty trip if we have to go out there in this. We're recording twenty-five knots, and we're under the lee here.'

'Stratton's made up his mind to go, has he?'

'If Four-four-Double-o doesn't get off, yes. We've got to.'

'Well, good luck, sonny.'

'Thanks, we'll need it.' He jumped off the float into the dory, balancing himself neatly. 'Wouldn't like a trip round the island, would you, Flinty?'

'Not bloody . . .' The sound of the outboard motor drowned his voice. The dory swung away, running down-wind with the steep little breaking waves. As the grey steel hull of the landing craft loomed over us I saw the helicopter lift its dripping floats from the water and go whirling away northwards in the pale light.

There was coffee waiting for us in the wardroom. It was hot in there after the raw cold outside. 'The Skipper will be along in a minute,' the fair-haired youngster told us. 'He's in the radio shack now, waiting to see what the form is. My name's Geoff Wentworth; I'm the Number One. If there's anything you want, just press the tit.' He indicated the bell-push.

I thought I had everything I wanted; hot coffee and the feel of a ship under me again – the soft, continuous hum of dynamos, the smell that is always the same, a compound of salt dampness, hot oil and stale food, the slight suggestion of movement to give life to the hard steel of deck and bulkheads. 'We're afloat, aren't we?'

'Just about,' he said, and then he left us. McDermott had removed his sheepskin jacket and I saw the insignia of the Army Medical Corps, the serpent of Aesculapius, on his battledress. He was a surgeon, he told me, and he'd left Edinburgh shortly after eleven, flown to Stornoway and then been driven right across Lewis and Harris to Northton. 'I'll be honest – I hope we don't have to go. I'm a damned bad sailor and from what I hear this boy's in a mess.' He was puffing nervously at a cigarette.

Half an hour passed. Then a door slammed, a voice gave an order, somebody shouted and rubbered feet pounded aft. The dynamos changed their note as the lights dimmed momentarily. Another piece of machinery had come into action. The door opened and Captain Stratton came in, small and dark with premature streaks of grey in his black hair and a quiet air of command. Snatched hours of sleep had left his eyes red-rimmed. 'Sorry I wasn't here to greet you. As you've probably gathered by the sounds of activity, we're getting under way.'

'I take it,' McDermott said, 'this means the LCT is still stuck out there?'

'Yes. Kelvedon's made one attempt to winch himself off. Over-eager, by the sound of it. Anyway, she didn't budge. And now he's going to wait for the top of the tide before he tries again.' And then he went on to explain his own plans. 'As we're afloat now, I thought I'd get started. We'll be bucking a head-wind up to the Sound of Harris; may take us three hours. If he gets off all right, then we'll put into Leverburgh. If he doesn't we'll be that much nearer Laerg.' He turned to me. 'I hear you have a lot of sea time. Master's ticket?' And when I nodded, he said, 'I hope you're a good sailor then.'

'I'm not sea-sick, if that's what you mean.'

He smiled. 'You may regret that statement. Have you ever been in a landing craft before?'

'No.'

'You'll find the movement a little different.' And he added, 'If you want to visit the bridge any time . . .' It was an invitation that accepted me as belonging to the brotherhood of the sea. He went out and a moment later the deck came alive under my feet as the main engines began to turn.

I watched our departure from the open door on the starboard side of the bridge housing. Dawn was breaking and the bulk of Mount Hecla sliding past was purple-brown against the fading stars. A seal raised its head snake-like from a rock, and then with a jerking movement reached the weed growth at the edge and glissaded without a splash into the water. A heron lifted itself from a grass-grown islet, ungainly in flight as it retracted its head and trailed its feet, grey wings flapping in the wild morning air. Five cormorants stood on a ledge and watched us go, curious and undisturbed. These were the only signs of life, and though the door was on the leeward side and I was sheltered from the wind, I could see it whipping at the surface of the water.

One of the crew appeared at my side hooded in his duffel coat. 'Battening down now, sir.' He pulled the steel door to and fixed the clamps. 'In a few minutes we'll be rounding Wiay Island. We'll begin to feel it then.'

The visitors' quarters were immediately aft of the wardroom pantry, a clutter of two-tier bunks with clothing scattered around and a desk littered with papers. McDermott had already turned in fully clothed. 'Seems steady enough,' he murmured.

'We're still under the lee.'

My bag had been dumped on the bunk immediately aft of his. I stripped to my vest and pants and got into it, pulling the blankets up over my head to shut out the grey light from the portholes. The time was ten to six. I must have slept, but it wasn't a deep sleep, for I was conscious all the time of the movement of the ship, the sounds, the pulsing of the engines. I knew when we turned the bottom of Wiay Island for the bunk began to heave and every now and then there was a crash as though the bows had hit a concrete wall; at each blow the vessel staggered and a shiver ran through her. Vaguely I heard McDermott stumble out to the heads. Later he was sick in his bunk.

The steward woke me shortly after eight, a teenage youngster in a khaki pullover balancing a cup of tea. 'I don't know whether you'd care for some breakfast, sir. The Skipper said to ask you.'

I told him I would, though the battering was much worse now that I was awake. 'Where are we?'

'Off Lochmaddy, sir. Half an hour and we'll be in the Sound. It'll be quieter then.'

The cabin reeked of vomit, sickly sweet and mixed with the smell of human sweat. I dressed quickly and breakfasted in solitary state, burnt sausage and fried bread with the fiddles on the table, the blue settee cushions on the floor and the framed photograph of L8610 banging at the wall. I smoked a cigarette, thinking about Laerg and the ship stuck in Shelter Bay. Lucky for them the wind was in the north. If it had come in southerly during the night . . . I got up and went along the alleyway for'ard. A curtain was drawn across the open door to the Captain's cabin. There was the sound of gentle snoring, and behind the closed door opposite I heard the buzz of the radio operator's key. I slid back the door to the wheelhouse and went in.

The deck was almost steady now. A big, heavily-built man stood at the wheel, dressed like the officers in a white polo-necked sweater. There was nobody else there, but the door to the port side wing bridge stood open and almost immediately the Number One appeared framed in the gap. 'Port ten.'

'Port ten of wheel on, sir,' the helmsman repeated.

'Steady now.'

'Steady. Steering three-o-four, sir.'

Wentworth went to the chart table, checked with his parallel rule against the compass rose. 'Steer three-one-o.'

'Three-one-o, sir.'

He straightened from the chart table and looked across at me. 'Skipper's got his head down. Did you manage to get some sleep?'

'A certain amount.' And I asked him if there was any news.

'He didn't get off.' And he added, 'The wind apparently – or so he says. It was round into the north-east and a gust caught him. Personally I think he dragged his kedge anchor when he tried that first time. Anyway, he's right up against the beach now, almost broadside-on to it.'

'You're going to Laerg then?'

He nodded. 'Going to have a shot at it, anyway. They've dispatched a Navy tug. But the Clyde's over two hundred miles away and she'll be butting straight into it. We're the only vessel that can reach Laerg by the next high water.' He glanced through the for'ard porthole and then went out on to the open wing bridge

677

again. 'Starboard five.'

The needle of the indicator half right of the helmsman swung to five as he spun the wheel. I crossed to the port side where the chart table stood, a mahogany bank of drawers. Spread out on the top of it was Chart No. 2642; it showed the Sound littered with rocks and islands, the buoyed channel very narrow. 'That's Pabbay straight ahead,' Wentworth said, leaning his elbows on the table. 'Steer two-nine six.'

'Steer two-nine-six.'

Through the porthole I looked the length of the ship. The tank hold was an empty shell with vertical walls and a flat bottom that ended abruptly at a steel half gate. Beyond the gate was the black hole of the beaching exit with the raised ramp acting as a bulkhead immediately behind the curved steel bow doors. Water sloshed in the open hold and sprung securing hooks banged in their racks. The vertical walls were topped by steel decking that ran like twin alleyways the length of the ship to finish at a small winch platform. This platform was swinging now against a backcloth of sea and islands; it steadied as the helmsman reported, 'Steering two-nine-six.' Pabbay was on the starboard bow then, a smooth hump of an island, emerald-green in a drab grey world; whilst I had slept a thin film of cloud had covered the sky.

Wentworth swung himself up the ladder to the open bridge immediately above the wheelhouse. He was back in a moment with three compass bearings which he ruled in on the chart to produce a fix. Watching him, intent, alert, entirely concentrated, I thought how young he was; a soldier in charge of a ship. That was something new to me. Later I learned that he came from a sea-faring family. Not his father, who kept a pub at Burnham Overy, but further back when every staithe along that North Norfolk coast was packed with sailing ships. He was very proud of the fact that one of his ancestors had sailed with Nelson who'd been born at the neighbouring village of Burnham Thorpe. The sea was in his blood and the fact that he was driving a ship at her maximum speed of around ten knots through a tortuous channel in a rock-infested Sound he accepted as no more than part of the day's work; accepted, too, the fact that beyond the Sound the North Atlantic waited. He ordered a slight adjustment of course and then turned to me. 'Another half hour and we'll be out of the lee of Harris. If you'd like to know what we're running into . . .' He reached across the chart table and removed a clipped sheaf of message forms from its hook. 'The synopsis makes nice reading.'

His grin was friendly, unconcerned.

The top message, scribbled in pencil, read: *Weather forecast 0645. Gale warning: Warning of N gales in operation sea areas Rockall, Bailey, Faeroes, South-East Iceland: NW gales areas Cromarty, Forties, Viking. Synopsis for 0600 GMT: a complex depression moving ENE towards Norway will affect all northern sea areas of the British Isles. This depression is likely to intensify over the next 24 hours. Another depression five hundred miles W of Ireland is almost stationary and there is a belt of high pressure over Greenland. Forecast sea area Hebrides: Winds NW or N force 7, reaching gale force 8 later. Visibility moderate to good with some rain or sleet.*

'Sounds like a pleasant trip,' I said. 'What's the barometer say?'

He pushed the chart aside and pointed to the log book. 'Nine-eight-two. Falling.' In fact, the log showed that it had dropped 2 points in the last hour, 5 since we'd sailed. Wind strength was recorded as northerly 32 knots, which is almost gale force 8 on the Beaufort scale. My eyes went involuntarily to the porthole, to the vulnerable length of that open tank deck. It wasn't difficult to imagine what it would be like with big seas breaking over the flat sides of the ship, flooding the hold with water. As though he guessed what was in my mind, he said, 'We've very powerful pumps. Last summer we were hove-to for nearly six hours in force ten with a destroyer standing by. It wasn't very comfortable, but we managed.' The Army had apparently acquired the Navy's knack of embellishment by under-statement.

The full force of the wind struck us as soon as we cleared the islands of Killegray and Ensay. There was a big swell coming in from the direction of Toe Head, now only a few miles away, and on top of the swell were steep, breaking waves. We were steaming north then, heading straight into it, and the movement was at times quite violent – a crash for'ard as we butted a wave, a shudder and then a lift and a twist as the comber went seething beneath us. Spray was whipped aft as far as the bridge. With Pabbay abeam, we altered course to almost due west, heading direct for Laerg. The motion was different then. We were no longer butting straight into it but steaming across the seas, rolling heavily with the wave crests breaking against the starboard bow. I could see the peak of Chaipaval clear of cloud and standing green against the darker Harris hills; even the camp was visible across a white waste of tumbled water.

It was whilst we were steaming out of the Sound of Harris that

Colonel Standing was faced with the difficult choice of yielding to the views of his second-in-command or adhering to the Plan of Operations. Major Braddock saw him in his office shortly after nine and what he advised was the immediate withdrawal of all personnel from Laerg. He based his argument on the weather and he had Major Rafferty with him to support his case. That he had a personal motive for wishing to hasten completion of the evacuation was not, of course, apparent to either Rafferty or Standing.

Briefly his argument was this: The weather had broken and there was a landing craft in difficulties. Even presuming that L4400 was hauled off the beach undamaged, the Squadron Commander at Portsmouth would almost certainly insist on the withdrawal of both ships from Scottish waters. The Army would then have to fall back on the RASC trawler. This vessel was anchored in the Clyde and no longer in commission. It might be a month before it was on station. The alternative would be to charter. Either way it would be expensive, and meantime the detachment on Laerg would have to be supplied by air drop.

Rafferty confirmed that the run-down of supplies on the island had reached the point where the detachment had food and fuel for less than a fortnight at full strength. He also made the point that all but one of the vital radar installations had already been shipped out. There were still four huts standing and a fair amount of equipment, clothing and stores, but the only other items of real value were the bull-dozer, two towing vehicles, about a dozen trailers loaded with gear and a Land-Rover. All these could be driven straight on to the beached landing craft in a very short time.

Braddock had been up to the Met. Office that morning and he had with him a weather map drawn for him by Cliff Morgan. It was Cliff's forecast of what the situation would be at midnight. It showed the 'complex depression' as an intense Low centred over Norway. It showed, too, the belt of high pressure over Greenland as having established itself, a massive High now extending from just west of Iceland to the Labrador coast with pressures of 1040 millibars or more at the centre. And between the High and the Low the isobars narrowed until, just east of Iceland, they were almost touching. Inked arrows indicated a strong northerly air stream.

'With northerly winds,' Braddock said, 'both landing craft could beach in safety. It may be our last chance.' And Rafferty had agreed.

If Rafferty had put the case Standing might have accepted it.

At least he might have teleprinted Command for authority to act on it. Rafferty had an Irishman's gift for winning people over to his point of view. But faced with Braddock's virtual demand for immediate evacuation, Standing reacted strongly.

'I have my orders, and so have you, Major Braddock,' he said. 'Our job is to complete evacuation according to plan.'

'But the weather . . . You can't just ignore the weather.' Braddock's voice was impatient, almost angry.

'All right. But there's no immediate hurry. We've got till this evening. We'll decide the matter then.'

It is always easier to postpone decisions and let events dictate the course of action. But in fairness it must be said that Cliff Morgan, alone of the men immediately concerned at Northton, had the weather constantly under review. It was being drummed into him all the time by the teleprinters – sheet after sheet of pressure figures. By eleven o'clock the picture had clarified to the extent that he was convinced beyond any doubt that his hunch had been right – the Hebrides lay full in the path of a polar air stream of considerable force. The magnitude and intensity of that low pressure area, combined with the Greenland High, would be drawing great masses of air south from the frozen wastes of the polar seas. This cold, dry air would be sliding in under the warmer, more humid air of the low pressure area, cooling and condensing it. Snow at first in the far north, up in the Barents Sea; sleet and rain further south, and in the Hebrides clear skies, or perhaps a film of cloud.

That would be the natural pattern. But before coming on duty that morning Cliff Morgan had re-established contact with *Arctic Ranger* and *Laird of Brora*. Both trawlers had reported a big swell still running from the north, but the wind backing westerly and the barometric pressure 2 to 3 millibars lower than the weather map indicated in that area. And now the Faeroes were reporting low cloud and rain squalls. What worried him was the original nature of that Low; the result of two depressions merging, it had the inherent weakness of all complex systems. He thought trough lines might be developing, perhaps even some more serious weakness.

Shortly after eleven o'clock he phoned the camp. Colonel Standing was not in his office. It was Mike Ferguson who took the call. He listened to what Cliff had to say and agreed to get Colonel Standing to ring him back. Meantime he passed the information to Major Braddock and it was Braddock who raised it with the Colonel immediately on his return. It is more than likely that he used Cliff Morgan's vague fears – and they were nothing more at that time – to reinforce his own argument. Almost certainly Standing rejected them. As an Air Ministry man, Cliff had no connection with the Army. Standing was under no obligation to accept the local Met. Officer's advice or even to consult him. He may well have considered that Braddock was exaggerating. At any rate, he didn't phone Cliff Morgan, deciding instead to wait for the shipping forecast which was by then due in less than two hours.

Quite a number of officers were gathered round the Mess radio at one-forty. The synopsis was much the same as before – gale warnings and the complex low pressure area intensifying to give a northerly air stream for much of the British Isles. The forecast for the Hebrides was no worse than it had been at six forty-five – winds northerly, gale force 8 increasing to 9 later; visibility good but chance of rain squalls.

As a result, Colonel Standing took no action. There was not, in fact, much he could have done at that stage, but another commander might have thought it worth walking across to the Met. Office for a local weather briefing. There may have been something personal in the fact that Standing didn't do this; he was a man of narrow moral outlook and knowing Cliff's record he probably disliked him.

I missed the one-forty shipping forecast for I was lying in my bunk at the time. I wasn't asleep. I was just lying there because it was easier to lie down than to stand up, and even flat on my back I had to hang on. The ship was lurching very violently and every now and then there was an explosion like gunfire and the whole cabin shivered. McDermott was groaning in the bunk ahead of me. The poor devil had long since brought up everything but his guts; twice he'd been thrown on to the floor.

About four in the afternoon I got up, paid a visit to the heads and had a wash. The heads were on the starboard side and from the porthole I had a windward view; it was an ugly-looking sea, made more ugly by the fact that we were passing through a squall. Daylight was obscured by the murk so that it was almost dark. Visibility was poor, the seas very big with a rolling thrust to their broken tops and the spindrift whipped in long streamers by the wind.

I went down the alleyway to the wheelhouse. Stratton had taken over. He stood braced against the chart table staring out of the for'ard porthole. He was unshaven and the stubble of his beard looked almost black in that strange half light. A sudden lurch flung me across the wheelhouse. He turned as I fetched up beside him. 'Glad to see you haven't succumbed.' He smiled, but the smile didn't reach his eyes, and his face was beginning to show the strain. 'My DR puts us about there.' He pencilled a small circle on the chart. Measuring the distance from Laerg by eye against minutes of latitude shown on the side of the chart it looked as though we still had about eighteen miles to go. But I knew his dead reckoning couldn't be exact in these conditions.

'Will you make it before dark?' I asked.

He shrugged. 'We're down to six knots. Glass falling, wind backing and increasing. It came up like a line squall. Some sort of trough, I imagine.' He passed me the log. Barometric pressure was down to 976, wind speed 40–45 knots – force 9. 'Looks as though the weather boys have slipped up.' He gave me the one-forty shipping forecast. 'If the wind increases any more before we get under the lee in Shelter Bay, we're going to have to turn and run before it.' He glanced at the radar. It was set to maximum range – 30 miles; but the sweep light showed only a speckle of dots all round the screen. The probing eye was obscured by the squall, confused by the breaking seas. 'We'll pick up Laerg soon.' It was less of a statement than an endeavour to convince himself and I had a feeling he was glad of my company. 'Ever sailed in these waters?' He switched the Decca to 15-mile range.

'No.' I said. 'But the Pacific can be quite as bad as the North Atlantic and the Indian Ocean isn't all that pleasant during the monsoon.'

'I've never commanded a proper ship,' he said. 'Always landing craft.' And after a moment he added, 'Considering what they're designed for, they're amazingly seaworthy. But they still have their limitations. They'll only take so much.' As though to underline his point a towering wall of water rose above the starboard bow, toppled and hit with a crash that staggered the ship. Water poured green over the sides, cascading like a waterfall into the well of the tank deck. I watched the pumps sucking it out through the gratings and wondered how long they would be able to cope with that sort of intake. The steward appeared with two mugs of tea. A cut on his forehead was oozing blood and there was blood on the mugs as he thrust them into our hands, balancing precariously to the surge and swoop as we plunged over that big sea.

'Everything all right below decks, Perkins?'

'Pretty fair, sir – considering.' I saw his eyes dart to the porthole and away again as though he were scared by what he saw out there. 'Will we be in Shelter Bay soon, sir?'

'Two or three hours,' Stratton's voice was calm, matter-of-fact. 'Bring coffee and sandwiches as soon as we get in. I'll be getting hungry by then.'

'Very good, sir.' And the boy fled, comforted, but glad to leave the bridge with its view of the wilderness of the elements.

The squall turned to sleet and then to hail, but the hail sounded no louder than the spray which spattered the walls of the wheelhouse with a noise like bullets. And then suddenly the squall was gone and it was lighter. The radar screen was no longer fuzzed. It still had a speckled look caused by the break of the waves, but right at the top a solid splodge of light came and went as the sweep light recorded the first emerging outline of Laerg.

It was about half an hour later that the helmsman relayed a report from the lookout on the open bridge immediately over the wheelhouse. 'Land fine on the starb'd bow, sir.'

'Tell him to give the bearing.'

The helmsman repeated the order into the voice pipe close above his head. 'Bearing Green o-five or it may be o-ten. He says there's too much movement for him to get it more accurate than that.'

Stratton glanced at the radar screen, then reached for his duffel coat and went out by the port door, leaving it open to fill the wheelhouse with violent blasts of cold air and a whirling haze of spray. He was back within the minute. 'Laerg all right – bearing o-three as far as I can tell. There's a lot of movement up there and it's blowing like hell.'

But at least visual contact had been established. I leaned against the chart table, watching as he entered it in the log, hoping to God that Shelter Bay would give us the protection we needed. It was now only two hours' steaming away. But even as my nerves were relaxing to the sense of imminent relief from this constant battering, the helmsman announced, 'Lookout reports something about weather coming through on the radio.'

Stratton glanced up quickly, but I didn't need the surprise on his face to tell me that there was something very odd about this. I had had a talk with one of the radio operators before I'd turned in and had discovered something of the set-up. There were two radio operators on board working round the clock in 12-hour watches. Their main contact was the Coastal Command net – either Rosyth or Londonderry. When not working the CCN, they kept their set tuned to 2182 kcs., which is the International

Distress frequency, and any calls on this frequency were relayed through a repeater loudspeaker to the upper bridge. 'Something about trawlers,' the helmsman reported. I think Stratton and I both had the same thought, that we were picking up a deep-sea trawler. Trawlers and some other small ships use 2182 kcs. on Voice. 'Lookout says he couldn't get all of it. There's too much noise up there.'

'Ask him whether it's a Mayday call.'

'No, sir. Definitely not Mayday. And he was calling us.'

Stratton knew better than to disturb his radio operator in the middle of receiving a message. We waited whilst the ship pounded and lurched and the outline of Laerg took clearer and more definite shape on the radar screen. At last the operator came in. 'Special weather report for you.' He steadied himself and then placed a pencilled message on the chart table. It was from Cliff Morgan. The message read: *GM3CMX to L8610. Advise weather conditions may deteriorate during night. Trawlers SE of Iceland report wind easterly now, force 9. At 0530 it was westerly their area. Suspect local disturbance. If interpretation correct could reach your area early hours tomorrow morning. This communication is unofficial. Good luck. Morgan.*

And God help you he might have added. A local disturbance on top of this lot . . . Stratton was staring down at the message, cracking the knuckles of his right hand. 'How the hell can he have contacted trawlers south-east of Iceland?'

'Morgan's a "ham" operator,' Sparks said.

'Oh yes, of course. You've mentioned him before.' He straightened up. 'Get on to Coastal Command. Check it with them.' He had to shout to make himself heard above the thunder of a breaking sea. The ship lurched, sprawling us against the chart table. There was a noise like a load of bricks coming aboard and then the roar of a cataract as water poured into the tank deck. 'A local disturbance. What the hell does he think this is?' Stratton glanced at his watch and then at the radar. The nearest point of Laerg was just touching the 10-mile circle. 'Two hours to go.' And after that he didn't say anything.

Cliff Morgan's latest contact with the trawlers had been made at 1537 hours. He took the information straight to Colonel Standing with the suggestion that L8610 be ordered to return to the shelter of the Hebrides until the weather pattern became clearer. This Standing refused to do. He had a landing craft in difficulties and an injured man to consider. Two factors were uppermost in his mind. The Navy tug, now in The Minch and headed for the Sound of Harris, had been forced to reduce speed. A message on his desk stated that it would be another twenty-four hours at least before she reached Laerg. The other factor was the position of our own ship, L8610. We were in H/F radio contact with the Movements Office at Base at two-hourly intervals and the 3 o'clock report had given our position as just over 20 miles from Laerg.

Cliff says he tried to get Standing to pass on the information. 'I warned the bloody man,' was the way he put it later. 'I warned him that if he didn't pass it on he'd be responsible if anything happened.' But Standing was undoubtedly feeling the weight of his responsibility for what had already happened. His attitude, rightly or wrongly, was that unofficial contacts such as this would only confuse Stratton. In fact, he was probably quite determined to do nothing to discourage L8610 from reaching Laerg. 'I told him,' Cliff said. 'You are taking a terrible responsibility upon yourself. You are concealing vital information from a man who has every right to it.' The fact is that Cliff lost his temper. He walked out of Standing's office and went straight to Major Braddock. My brother took the same line as Standing, though his reasons for doing so were entirely different. He wanted L8610 available in Shelter Bay to evacuate personnel. At least, that is my interpretation based on his subsequent actions. He was determined to get the Army out of the island before the whole operation ground to a halt for lack of ships.

Having failed with both Standing and Braddock, Cliff decided to send the message himself. His broadcasting installation had an output of 200 watts, giving him a range on VHF Voice of anything up to 1000 miles according to conditions. As a result his message was picked up by another trawler, the *Viking Fisher*, then about 60 miles due south of Iceland. Her first contact with him, reporting a drop of 2 millibars in the barometric pressure in that locality, was made at 1716.

Meantime, the Meteorological Office had begun to appreciate that the pattern developing in northern waters of the British Isles was becoming complicated by local troughs. The shipping forecast at 1758 hours, however, did not reflect this. The gale warnings were all for northerly winds and the phrase 'polar air stream' was used for the first time.

'So much for Morgan's forecast,' Stratton said, returning the clip of forecasts to their hook above the chart table. 'Maybe there'll be something about it on the midnight forecast. But a polar air stream . . .' He shook his head. 'If I'd known that at one-forty, I'd have turned back. Still, that means northerlies – we'll be all right when we reach Laerg.' And he leaned his elbows on the chart table, his eyes fixed on the radar screen as though willing the blur of light that represented Laerg to hasten its slow, reluctant progress to the central dot.

As daylight began to fade a rim of orange colour appeared low down along the western horizon, a lurid glow that emphasized the grey darkness of the clouds scurrying low overhead. I thought I caught a glimpse of Laerg then, a fleeting impression of black piles of rock thrust up out of the sea; then it was gone, the orange light that had momentarily revealed its silhouette snuffed out like a candle flame. Dusk descended on us, a creeping gloom that gradually hid the violence of that cold, tempestuous sea. And after that we had only the radar to guide us.

At 1857 we passed close south of Fladday, the isolated island to the east of Laerg. The two stacs of Hoe and Rudha showed up clear on the radar screen. Ahead and slightly to starboard was the whole mass of Laerg itself. For the next quarter of an hour the sea was very bad, the waves broken and confused, the crests toppling on to our starboard bow and the tank deck swilling water. The dim light from our masthead showed it cascading over the sides, torrents of water that continued to pour in almost without a break. The whole for'ard part of the ship seemed half submerged. And then, as we came under the lee of Malesgair, the eastern headland of Laerg, it became quieter, the wave crests smaller – still white beyond the steel sides, but not breaking inboard any more. The pumps sucked the tank deck dry and suddenly one could stand without clinging on to the chart table.

We had arrived. We were coming into Shelter Bay, and ahead of us were lights – the camp, the floodlights on the landing beach, and Four-four-Double-o lying there like a stranded whale. Low cloud hung like a blanket over Tarsaval and all the island heights, but below the cloud the bulk of Laerg showed dimly as a darker, more solid mass.

The home of my forebears, and to see it first at night, in a gale, coming in from the sea after a bad crossing . . . I thought that this was how it should be, and I stood there, gazing out of the porthole, fixing it in my mind, a picture that somehow I must get on to canvas – a grim, frightening, beautiful picture. In that howling night, with the wind coming down off Tarsaval and flattening the sea in sizzling, spray-torn patches, I felt strangely at peace. All my life, it seemed, had been leading up to this moment.

And then suddenly my seaman's instinct came alive and I was conscious that Stratton didn't intend to anchor. He had reduced speed, but the ship was going in, headed straight for the other landing craft. Wentworth was in the wheelhouse now. The Cox'n, too. And men were running out along the side decks, heading for the fo'c'stle platform. I caught the tail-end of Stratton's orders: '. . . heaving the lead and give the soundings in flashes on your torch. At two fathoms I'll go astern. Get the line across her then. Okay, Number One? Cox'n, you'll let go the kedge anchor when I give the word. And pay out on the hawser fast. I don't wan't that anchor to drag. Understand? We're almost at the top of the tide. We haven't much time.'

They left and Stratton swung himself up the ladder to con the ship from the square, boxed-in platform of the upper bridge. I followed him. 'Slow ahead both engines,' he ordered down the voice pipe. Their beat slowed and the ship glided, moving steadily and irrevocably nearer the beach. The stranded LCT was growing larger all the time. A spotlight had been switched on and I could see the number on her bows – L4400 painted black on grey. Wentworth and his men on the fo'c'stle were picked out in the beam's glare.

Stratton lifted a phone from its hook. 'All ready aft?' He stood, staring ahead, his eyes narrowed as he watched the approach of the shore. 'Let her go.' He replaced the phone on its hook and the ship went on with no check to show that the kedge anchor had been dropped astern. A torch stabbed five flashes from the fo'c'stle. 'Stop both engines.' The deck died under my feet. Four flashes. I could see the man heaving the lead, bracing himself against the fo'c'stle rail for the next throw. 'Slow astern together.'

Three flashes. Then two. 'Full astern both . . . Stop both.' The ship hung motionless, heaving to the swell, staggering like a drunkard in the down-draughts. The howl of the wind came and went, a thousand demons yelling murder. The sound of the rocket was thin and insubstantial, but I saw the line curve out and fall across the stern of the other LCT. Men ran to grab it and a moment later a hawser was being paid out over our bows.

Just two minutes, and as the hawser was made fast, Stratton was on the phone again giving the order to winch in. For a moment nothing seemed to be happening. Up for'ard the lead was dropped again, the torch flashed twice. Then I felt the tug astern as the anchor bit to the power of the winch hauling in. Our bows were swinging towards the shore. From the compass platform I watched the sagging line of the hawser come dripping out of the sea, rise until suddenly it was bar-taut and shivering, all the water shaken off it. Our bows stopped swinging then. A ragged cheer came to us on the wind. Men in oilskins lined the beach, standing watching just clear of the surf. It was they who had cheered.

The bows swung back towards the other craft's stern. The hawser slackened momentarily; then tightened again and I sensed that the ship was straightened out now, a direct link between stern and bow hawsers. Stratton sensed it, too. 'Slow astern both engines.' And as the screws bit, he ordered full astern. And after that we waited, tense for what would happen.

'Either she comes off now . . .' The phone buzzed and Stratton picked it up. '. . . Well, let it labour . . . All right, Cox'n. But don't let the fuses blow. Just hold her, that's all. Leave the rest to the main engines.' He put the phone down. 'The stern winch – bloody useless when you're in a jam.' His teeth were clenched tight, his face taut. 'Something's going to give soon. Breaking strain on that kedge hawser is only about forty-five tons. Not much when you're trying to hold a thousand ton vessel. And right now the Cox'n's got to control both ships, and on top of that, there's the added weight of all that sand piled up round Kelvedon's bottom.'

Time seemed to stand still with the whole ship trembling and vibrating with the effort. I left the compass platform and went aft to the port rail of the flag deck. It was dark on that side. No glimmer of light and the screws streaming a froth of water for'ard along the port side, toppling the waves so that all the surface of the water was ghostly white. I felt a sudden tremor. I thought for a moment one of the hawsers had parted. But up for'ard that single slender thread linking us to L4400 remained taut as before. A faint cheer sounded and then I saw the stern of the other ship was altering its position, swinging slowly out towards us.

Stratton joined me. 'She's coming. She's coming. Ross – do you see?' His voice was pitched high, exhilaration overlaying nervous tension. The stern swung out, the ship's profile thinning till she lay like a box end-on to us, and there she hung for a moment, still held by her bows, until suddenly we plucked her off and Stratton ordered the engines stopped for fear of over-running the stern hawser.

Ten minutes later both ships were out in the bay with their bow anchors down, manoeuvring under power to let go a second anchor. Ashore, men waded waist-deep in the surf to launch a dory. It lifted to the break of a wave and the oars flashed glistening in the floodlights. Clear of the surf, it came bobbing towards us, driven by the wind. We were at rest with both anchors down and the engines stopped by the time it came alongside. An oilskin-clad figure swung himself up the rope ladder and came dripping into the wheelhouse, a shapeless mountain of a man with tired brown eyes and a stubble growth that was almost a beard. 'Nice work,' he said. 'I was beginning to think we might be stuck here for the winter with a load of scrap iron on the beach.' He glanced round the wheelhouse. 'Where's Major McDermott? He's needed ashore.'

'I'll get him for you.' Stratton went out and the big man stood there dripping a pool of water from his oilskins, his face lifeless, dead with weariness.

'Bad trip, eh?' His voice was hoarse and very deep. The words seemed wrung out of him as though conversation were an effort.

'Pretty rough,' I said.

He nodded, briefly and without interest, his mind on something else. 'The poor bastard's been screaming for hours.' And with that he relapsed into silence until McDermott appeared, his face paper-white and walking delicately as though not sure of his legs.

'Captain Pinney? I'm ready when you are.' He looked in no shape to save a man's life.

'Can you take Mr Ross ashore this trip?' Stratton asked.

'May as well, if he's ready.' The tired eyes regarded me without enthusiasm. 'I've received instructions from Major Braddock about your visit. It's all right so long as you don't stray beyond the camp area.'

It took me only a moment to get my things. McDermott was being helped down the rope ladder as I said goodbye to Stratton. I dropped my bag to the men in the dory and climbed down the steel side of the landing craft. Hands clutched me as the boat rose to the slop of a wave and then they shoved off and we were down in a trough with the sea all round us, a wet world of broken water. The oars swung and clear of the shelter of the ship the wind hit us, driving spray in our faces.

It wasn't more than half a mile to the shore, but it took us a long time even with the outboard motor. The wind coming down off the invisible heights above was so violent that it drove the breath back into one's throat. It came in gusts, flattening the surface of the sea, flinging it in our faces. And then we reached the surf line. A wave broke, lifting the stern, flooding the dory with water. We drove in to the beach in a seething mass of foam, were caught momentarily in the backwash, and then we touched and were out of the boat, knee-deep in water, dragging it up on to the concrete slope of the loading ramp.

That was how I came to Laerg that first time, in darkness, wet to the skin, with floodlights glistening on rain-soaked rock and nothing else visible – the roar of the surf in my ears and the wind screaming. It was a night I was to remember all my life; that and the following day.

We groped our way up to the road, staggering to the buffets of the wind. A Bailey bridge, rusted and gleaming with beads of water, spanned a burn, and then we were in the remains of the hutted camp. Everywhere the debris of evacuation, dismantled hut sections and piled-up heaps of stores, and the mud shining slippery in the glimmer of the lights. The putter of a generator sounded in the brief intervals between the gusts and out in the darkness of the bay the landing craft were twin islands of light.

I was conscious then of a depressing sense of isolation, the elements pressing in on every hand – the sea, the wind, the heights above, grass and rock all streaming water. A lonely, remote island cut off from the outside world. And living conditions were bad. Already more than half the huts had been dismantled. Two more had been evacuated and officers and men were crowded together in the remaining three with the cookhouse filled with stores and equipment that would deteriorate in the open. They were living little better than the original islanders and working much harder. Everywhere men in glistening oilskins toiled in the mud and the wet and the cold, grumbling and cursing, but still cheerful, still cracking the occasional joke as they manhandled hut sections down to the loading beach or loaded trailers with stores.

Pinney took us to his office, which was no more than a type-writer and a table beside his bed in the partitioned end of a hut that was crammed with other beds. The beds were mostly un-made, with clothing and odds and ends of personal effects scattered about; the whole place told a story of men too tired to care. Pinney's bed was no tidier than the rest, a heap of blankets thrown aside as he'd tumbled out of sleep to work. The two other officers' beds were the same and they shared the end of the hut with the radio operator and his equipment. 'Cigarette?' Pinney produced a sodden packet and McDermott took one. His hands were trembling as he lit it. 'If you'd like to get cleaned up . . .' Pinney nodded vaguely to the wash basin. 'Or perhaps you'd prefer a few minutes' rest . . .'

McDermott shook his head. 'Later perhaps – if I have to operate.' His face looked shrunken, the bones staring, the skin grey and sweating. He seemed a much older man than when he'd come aboard. 'I'll have a wor-rd with Captain Fairweather now and then I'd like to have a look at the laddie.'

'There's not much of him left to look at, and what's there is barely alive.' Pinney glanced at me. 'I'll be back shortly.' They went out and I got my wet things off, towelled myself down and put on some dry underclothes. The only sound in the hut was the faint hum from the radio, the occasional scrape of the operator's chair as he shifted in his seat. He had the earphones clamped to his head, his body slouched as he read a paperback. He alone in that camp was able to pierce the storm and leap the gap that separated Laerg from the outside world.

The sound of the work parties came to me faintly through the background noise of the generator and the rattle of a loose window frame. I lit a cigarette. The hut had a musty smell, redolent of damp and stale sweat. Despite the convector heating, everything I touched was damp; a pair of shoes under Pinney's bed was furred with mould, the paper peeling from his books. A draught blew cold on my neck from a broken pane stuffed with newspaper.

I was sitting on the bed then, thinking that this was a strange homecoming to the island of my ancestors, and all I'd seen of it so far was the camp litter of the Army in retreat. They were getting out and I thought perhaps old Grandfather Ross was laughing in his grave, or was his disembodied spirit roaming the heights above, scaling the crags as he'd done in life, waiting for the island to be returned to him? Those eyes, sometimes blue and sometimes sea-grey, and the beard blowing in the wind – I could see him as clearly as if I was seated again at his feet by the peat fire. Only Iain was missing; somehow I couldn't get Iain back into that picture. Every time I thought of him it was Braddock I saw, with that twitch at the corner of his mouth and the dark eyes turned inwards.

Laerg and Alasdair Ross – they went together; they fitted this dark, wet, blustery night. But not Braddock. Braddock was afraid of Laerg and I found myself thinking of death and what Iain had once said. I got up from the bed then, not liking the way my thoughts were running, and went over to the radio operator. He was a sapper, a sharp-faced youth with rabbity teeth. 'Are you in touch with Base all the time?' I asked him.

He looked up from his paperback, pushed one of the earphones up. 'Aye.' He nodded. 'I just sit on my backside and wait for them to call me.'

'And if you want to call them?'

'Och weel, I just flick that switch to "Send" and bawl into the mike.'

As simple as that. The radio was an old Army set, the dials tuned to the net frequency. Contact with Base was through the Movements Office. There a Signals operator sat by another set of the same pattern. The only difference was that it was linked to the camp switchboard. 'You mean you can talk direct to anybody in Northton?'

'Och, ye can do more than that, sir. Ye can talk to anybody in Scotland – or in England. Ye can get the bluidy Prime Minister if you want.' They were linked through the Military Line to the GPO and could even ring up their families. 'A've heer-rd me wife speaking to me fra a call-box in Glasgie an' her voice as clear as a bell. It's no' as gude as tha' every time. A wee bit o' static sometimes, but it's no' verra often we canna get through at all.'

A small metal box full of valves and coils and condensers, and like an Aladdin's lamp you could conjure the whole world out of the ether, summoning voices to speak to you out of the black, howling night. It was extraordinary how we took wireless for granted, how we accepted it now as part of our lives. Yet fifty, sixty years ago . . . I was thinking of the islanders, how absolutely cut off they had been in my grandfather's time. There had been the Laerg Post, and that was all, the only means of getting a message through to the mainland; a sheep's inflated stomach to act as a float, two pieces of wood nailed together to contain the message, and the Gulf Stream and the wind the only way by which it could reach its destination. It had worked three or four times out of ten. At least, that's what my grandfather had said. And now this raw little Glaswegian had only to flip a switch.

The door at the end of the hut banged and Pinney came in. 'Clouds lifting. But it's still blowing like hell. Lucky for Stratton he's tucked into Shelter Bay.' He reached into his locker and passed me a plate and the necessary implements. 'Grub's up. We're calling it a day.' And as we sloshed our way through the mud to join the queue at the cookhouse, he said, 'Pity you're seeing it like this. Laerg can be very beautiful. On a still day with the sun shining and the air clean and crisp and full of birds . . . The best posting I ever had.'

The men had mess tins; it was like being back on active service. A cook ladled stew and peas and potatoes on to my plate. Another

693

handed me a hunk of bread and a mug of tea. We hurried back to the hut, trying to get inside before the wind had cooled our food. Another officer had joined us, Lieutenant McBride. We ate quickly and in silence. A sergeant came in, a small, tough-looking Irishman. 'Is it true you're wanting the generator run all through the night again, sor?'

'Not me,' Pinney answered. 'Captain Fairweather.'

'It means re-fuelling.'

'Then you'll have to re-fuel, that's all. They're going to operate.'

The sergeant sucked in his breath. 'What again? The poor divil.'

'Better see to it yourself, O'Hara. Make bloody sure no rain-water gets into the tank.'

'Very good, sor.'

He went out and Pinney, lying flat on his bed, his eyes closed, smoking a cigarette, said, 'McDermott's as white as a ghost and trembling like a leaf. He was ill coming across, I suppose.'

'Very ill,' I said.

He nodded. 'I thought so. He wouldn't have any food. Bob gave him a couple of slugs out of the medicine chest. Damned if I could operate on an empty stomach, but still . . .' His eyes flicked open, staring up at the ceiling, and he drew in a lung-full of smoke. 'What the hell am I going to say to his mother? The police will locate her sooner or later and then I'll have her on the R/T and she'll be thinking it's my fault when it was his own bloody carelessness. But you can't tell her that.' He closed his eyes again and relapsed into silence, and on the instant he was asleep. I took the burning cigarette from between his fingers and pulled a blanket over him.

McBride was already in bed, stripped to his vest and pants. 'You'll have to excuse us,' he said with a sleepy, boyish grin. 'Not very sociable, but I don't seem able to remember when we had more than four hours at a stretch. We just sleep when we can.' And he pulled the blanket up over his head. A moment later he was snoring with a whistling intake of the breath and a gurgling quiver of the nostrils. 'Och, he's awa'.' The operator showed his long front teeth in a smile. 'I mind the time when a' couldna hear a wor-rd they were saying at Base for Mr McBride lying there snoring.'

From beyond the partition the murmur of men's voices continued for perhaps five minutes, gradually dying away to silence. And after that there wasn't a sound except for the generator and the wind blasting the four corners of the hut and McBride snoring. But not everybody was asleep. Through the uncurtained window I could see a glow of light from the next hut. The shadow of a man's figure came and went against the drawn blinds, distorted and grotesque, and I knew it was McDermott . . . McDermott, who'd retched his guts out all the way across and was now trying to put together the broken pieces of another man's body.

I must have dozed off, but it could only have been for a moment. I jerked awake in my chair to see the operator shaking Pinney by the shoulder. 'Captain Pinney, sir. Captain Pinney.' There was a movement. His head came up and his eyes ungummed themselves. 'What is it, Boyd? Somebody want me?'

'Major Braddock, sir.'

'Then it's not . . '. He glanced at his watch. 'Oh well . . .' He kicked the blanket aside and swung his legs off the bed. He was obviously relieved it wasn't the call he'd been expecting. 'What's Major Braddock want?' he asked, rubbing at his eyes.

'It's urgent sir. We're evacuating.'

'Evacuating? Nonsense.' He stared at the operator in disbelief.

'Aye, it's true, sir. We're leaving right away, tonight. I hear-rd him give the order to Captain Stratton. Eight-six-one-o is coming in to beach noo.'

It was the moment of the fatal decision, the moment when the order was given that was to cost so many lives.

Pinney shook his head, forcing himself back to full consciousness. Then he was over at the set and had the earphones on, speaking into the mouthpiece. 'Pinney here.' He sat down in the chair the operator had vacated. 'Well, yes. The wind's off the shore, northerly. There shouldn't be any risk . . . What's that . . . Yes, but what about the rest of the stores? According to the schedule the landing craft should be running six more trips . . . Yes. Yes, I quite agree, but . . .' He laughed. 'No, we shan't be sorry to go. Life isn't exactly a bed of roses here. It's just that my orders . . . Yes, I gathered it was a War Office appointment. But I should have thought Colonel Standing . . .' There was a long pause, and then he said, 'All right, sir. So long as it's understood that I'm quite prepared to continue here until every piece of Army equipment has been shipped out. And so are my men . . . Fine. We'll get cracking then.' He got up and handed the earphones back to the operator. 'Remain on the set, Boyd, until you're called for boarding.' He stood there a moment looking round the room as though finding it difficult to adjust himself to the fact of leaving. Then he woke McBride and in an instant all was confusion, orders being shouted and men cursing and stumbling about as they sleep-walked into the clothes they'd only just taken off. Outside, the night was clearer, no stars, but the shadowed bulk of Tarsaval just visible. The wind was still very strong, coming in raging gusts that tore at the men's clothing, bending them double against the weight of it as they stumbled towards the beach.

An engine revved and a big six-wheeled Scammell lumbered past me. Seaward the lights of the two landing craft showed intermittently through the rain. One of them had its steaming lights on and the red and green of its navigation lights stared straight at the beach, coming steadily nearer. Orders shouted above the gale were whipped away by the wind. Pinney passed me, big in the lights of a truck stuck in the mud with its wheels spinning. 'Better get straight on board.' His voice was almost lost in a down-blast.

I was standing on the beach when Stratton brought his landing craft in towards the loading ramp. There was almost no surf now, the sea knocked flat by the wind. Bows-on the landing craft was square like a box. He came in quite fast – two knots or more, and ground to a halt with an ugly sound of boulders grating on steel, the bows lifting slightly, towering over us. Lines were flung and grabbed, steel hawsers paid out and fastened to shore anchor points, and then the bow doors swung open and the ramp came down; a stranded monster opening its mouth to suck in anything it could devour.

The bull-dozer came first, its caterpillar tracks churning sand and water. It found the edge of the ramp and lumbered, dripping, up the slope, clattering a hollow din against the double bottom as it manoeuvred to the far end of the tank hold. The Scammell followed, towing a loaded trailer, wallowing through the shallows and up the ramp where Wentworth and the Cox'n with half the crew waited to receive it. Men straggled in from the camp and they unhitched the trailer and man-handled it into position. The Scammell reversed out and by the time it was back with the next trailer, the first had been parked and bowsed down with the sprung steel securing shackles.

This went on for almost two hours; more than thirty oilskin-clad figures sweating and cursing in the loading lights and the tank deck gradually filling up. By eleven the tempo was slackening, though Pinney was still loading equipment from the camp, sending down all the small, portable, last-minute stuff.

I was working on the tank deck until about eleven-thirty. By then the Cox'n had more men than he needed. I went up to the bridge housing, took over my old bunk and cleaned myself up, and then went into the wardroom, lured by the smell of coffee. Stratton and Wentworth were there and I knew at once that something was wrong. They barely looked up as I entered, drinking their coffee in silence, their faces blank and preoccupied. 'Help yourself,' Wentworth said. Beside the coffee a plateful of bully-beef sandwiches lay untouched. 'Afraid you didn't get much of a run ashore.'

I poured myself some coffee and sat down. 'Cigarette?' I held the packet out to Stratton. He took one automatically and lit it without saying a word. Wentworth shook his head and I took one myself. A message form lay on the table close by Stratton's hand. He glanced at his watch. It was an unconscious gesture and I had the impression he knew the time already. 'Another half hour yet before low water. If we off-load – sling all this heavy stuff ashore . . .' He left the sentence unfinished, the question hanging in the air.

'And suppose nothing happens – the wind remains in the north?' Wentworth's voice was hesitant.

'Then we'll look bloody silly. But I'd rather look a fool . . .' He shook his head angrily. 'If he'd come through just two hours earlier, before we took the ground.' He pushed his hand up wearily over his eyes and took a gulp of coffee. 'Thank God there's only one of us on the beach anyway. If Kelvedon hadn't buckled a plate . . .' He lit his cigarette. 'I'd give a lot to be anchored out there in the bay with Four-four-Double-o right now.'

'It may not come to anything,' Wentworth said. 'The midnight forecast didn't say anything about it. Troughs, that's all. And the wind northerly . . .'

'Of course it didn't. This is local. Something very local.' Stratton shook his head. 'Nothing for it, I'm afraid. We'll have to unload. Empty we'll be off – what? An hour sooner?'

'Three-quarters anyway.'

'Okay. Find Pinney. Tell him what the position is. And get them started on off-loading right away.'

Wentworth gulped down the remainder of his coffee and hurried out. Stratton lay back against the cushions and closed his eyes with a sigh. The effort of reaching a decision seemed to have drained him of all energy. I was thinking of the wasted effort, all the trailers and vehicles to be got off with the men tired and exhausted. 'You've met this fellow Morgan. How good is he?' His eyes had opened again and he was staring at me. 'I think very good,' I said. And I told him something about Cliff's background and about the book he'd written.

'Pity you didn't tell me that before. I might have taken him more seriously.' And then angrily: 'But it's all so damned unofficial. Coastal Command don't know anything about it. All they could give me was what we've got right now – wind northerly, force nine, maybe more. They're checking with Bracknell. But I bet they don't know anything about it. Read that.' He reached out with his fingers and flipped the message form across to me. 'A polar air depression. That's Morgan's interpretation. And all based on contact with a single trawler whose skipper may be blind drunk for all I know.'

The message was impersonal, almost coldly factual considering the desperate information it contained: *GM3CMX to LCTs 8610 and 4400. Urgent. Suspect polar air depression Laerg area imminent. Advise you to be prepared winds hurricane force within next few hours. Probable direction between south and west. Interpretation based on contact* Viking Fisher 2347. *Trawler about 60 miles S of Iceland reports wind speed 80 knots plus, south-westerly, mountainous seas, visibility virtually nil in heavy rain and sleet. Barometric pressure 963, still falling – a drop of 16 millibars in 1 hour. Endeavouring re-establish contact. Interpretation unofficial, repeat unofficial, but I believe it to be correct. C. Morgan, Met. Officer, Northton.*

I didn't say anything for a moment. I had a mental picture of Cliff sitting in that room with his earphones glued to his head and his thumb resting on the key, and that big Icelandic trawler almost four hundred miles to the north of us being tossed about like a toy. I thought there wouldn't be much chance of re-establishing contact until the storm centre had passed over, supposing there was anything left to contact by then. A polar air depression. I'd heard of such things, but never having sailed in these waters before, I'd no experience of it. But I knew the theory. The theory was very simple.

Here was a big mass of air being funnelled through the gap between the big Low over Norway and the High over Greenland, a great streaming weight of wind thrusting southwards. And then suddenly a little weakness develops, a slightly lower pressure. The winds are sucked into it, curve right round it, are suddenly a vortex, forcing the pressure down and down, increasing the speed and size of this whirligig until it's like an enormous high speed drill, an aerial whirlpool of staggering intensity. And because it would be a part of the bigger pattern of the polar air stream itself, it was bound to come whirling its way south, and the speed of its advance would be fast, fast as the winds themselves.

'Well?' Stratton was staring at me.

'He had other contacts,' I said. 'Those two trawlers . . .'

'But nothing on the forecast. Nothing official.' He was staring at me and I could read the strain in his eyes. No fear. That might come later. But the strain. He knew what the message meant – if Cliff's interpretation was correct; knew what it would be like if that thing caught us while we were still grounded. The wind might come from any direction then. The northerly air stream from which we were so nicely sheltered might be swung through 180°. And if that happened and the wind came in from the south . . . I felt my scalp move and an icy touch on my spine. My stomach was suddenly chill and there was sweat on my forehead as I said, 'How long before you get off?'

He didn't give me an answer straight off. He worked it out for me so that I could check the timing myself. They had beached at nine forty-eight, two and three-quarter hours after high water. Next high water was at seven-twenty. Deduct two and three-quarter hours, less say half an hour to allow for the amount the ship had ridden up the beach . . . It couldn't be an exact calculation, but as far as he could estimate it we should be off shortly after five. I glanced at my watch. It was twenty minutes to one now. We still had nearly four and a half hours to wait. Four and a half solid bloody hours just sitting here, waiting for the wind to change – praying it wouldn't before we got off, knowing the ship was a dead duck if it did. 'No way of getting out earlier, I suppose?'

He shook his head.

It was a silly question really, but I didn't know much about these craft. 'There's a double bottom, isn't there? What's in between – fuel?'

'Water, too. And there are ballast tanks.'

'How much difference would it make?'

'We'll see; I should think about eighteen inches up for'ard when we've pumped it out. Geoff's checking with the ballasting and flooding board now. About cancel out the amount we ran up the beach; give us a few extra minutes, maybe.'

Sitting there in the warmth of that comfortable little wardroom with the ship quite still and solid as a rock, it was hard to imagine that in little more than four hours' time so few minutes could possibly make the difference between getting off and being battered to pieces.

'More coffee?'

I passed my cup and lit another cigarette. The radio operator came in and handed Stratton a message. 'Coastal Command just came through with the supplementary forecast you asked for.'

Stratton read it aloud. 'Winds northerly, force nine, decreasing to seven or eight. Possibility local troughs with rain squalls. Otherwise fair visibility.' He slapped the message form down on top of the others. 'Same as the midnight forecast. Nothing at all about a polar air depression; no reference to winds of hurricane force.' He turned to the radio operator. 'Anything new from Morgan?'

The operator shook his head. 'I heard him calling *Viking Fisher*, but I couldn't raise him myself.'

'Did the trawler reply?'

'No.'

'Well, see if you can get Morgan. Keep on trying, will you. I'd like to talk to him myself.' He reached for a message pad lying on the shelf below the porthole. 'And there's a message I want sent to Base. When's the next contact. One o'clock, isn't it?'

The operator nodded. 'But I can get them any time. They're standing by on our frequency.'

'Good. Give them a buzz then. Say I want to speak to Colonel Standing. And don't be fobbed off. Understand? If he's in bed, they're to get him out of it. I want to speak to him personally.' As the operator left he tossed the message pad back on to the shelf. 'Time these chaps who sit in their cosy offices issuing orders lost a little sleep on our account.'

I started in on the corned beef sandwiches then. I had a feeling this was going to be a long night. Stratton got up. 'Think I'll go and see what the wind's doing. I'll be in the wheelhouse.' Later Perkins brought some more coffee. I had a cup and then took one through to Stratton. But he wasn't there. The door was open on the port side and the wind came crowding through it in a gusty roar. The duty watch stood sheltering there, clad in sou'wester and oilskins. 'Where's Captain Stratton?' I asked him.

'On the R/T. Radio Operator just called him.'

'And the wind's still in the north, is it?'

'Aye, just aboot. Varies a wee bit, depending which side of Tarsaval it strikes.'

I went over to the porthole and looked down on to the wet steel decks gleaming under the loading lights. They'd got about a third of the tank deck clear, but the men moved slowly now, all the life gone out of them. Stratton came in then. He didn't say anything but got his duffel coat. I handed him his coffee and he gulped it down. 'Don't know what's going on at Base. Colonel Standing says he'd no idea we were evacuating. Sounded damned angry – what little I could hear. There was a lot of static.' He pulled his coat on. 'I'd better have a word with Pinney.' He turned to the duty man. 'If anybody wants me I'll be down on the loading beach.'

After he'd gone I went over to the chart table and had a look at the log. Barometer reading at midnight was given as 978, a fall of one millibar since the previous reading at eleven. I leaned over and peered at the glass itself – 977. I tapped it and the needle flickered, and when I read it again it was 976.

Time was running out; for the ship, for the men labouring on the tank deck to undo what they had done – for me, too. I could feel it in my bones, in the dryness of my tongue – a lassitude creeping through me, a feeling of indecision, of waiting. And all because a needle in a glass instrument like a clock had moved so fractionally that the movement was barely discernible. Long years at sea, standing watch on the bridges of ships, had taught me the value of that instrument, what those small changes of barometric pressure could mean translated into physical terms of weather. Somewhere in the bowels of the ship the cook would be sweating in his galley producing food to replace the energy those men on the tank deck had consumed. Deeper still the engineers would be checking their oiled and shining diesels, preparing them for the battle to come. And out there beyond the lights, beyond the invisible peaks and sheer rock cliffs of Laerg, out across the sea's tumbled chaos, the enemy was coming relentlessly nearer, ten thousand demon horsemen riding the air in a great circle, scouring the sea, flailing it into toppling ranges of water, spilling violence as they charged round that vortex pot of depressed air. Fantasy? But the mind is full of fantasy on such a night. Science is for the laboratory. Other men, who stand alone and face the elemental forces of nature, know that science as a shining, world-conquering hero, is a myth. Science lives in concrete structures full of bright factory toys, insulated from the earth's great forces. The priesthood of this new cult are seldom called upon to stand and face the onslaught.

The radio operator poked his head into the wheelhouse, interrupting my thoughts. 'Seen the Skipper? I've got that chap Morgan on the air.'

'He's doon to the beach to see Captain Pinney,' the duty man said.

Between the wheelhouse and the beach was the littered tank

deck, and Cliff Morgan wouldn't wait. 'Can I have a word with him?' I suggested.

The operator hesitated. 'Okay, I don't see why not – as one civilian to another.' He gave me a tired smile.

I followed him into the box-like cubby-hole of the radio shack. He slipped his earphones on and reached for the mike. 'L8610 calling GM3CMX. Calling GM3CMX. Do you hear me? Okay, GM3CMX. I have Mr Ross for you.' He passed me the earphones. Faint and metallic I heard Cliff's voice calling me. And when I answered him, he said, *'Now listen, man. You're on board Eight-six-one-o, are you?'* I told him I was. *'And you're beached – correct?'*

'Yes.'

'Well, you've got to get off that beach just as soon as you can. This could be very bad.'

'We're unloading now,' I said. 'To lighten the ship.'

'Tell the Captain he's got to get off – fast. If this thing hits you before you're off . . .' I lost the rest in a crackle of static.

'How long have we got?' I asked. His voice came back, but too faint for me to hear. 'How long have we got?' I repeated.

'. . . *barometric pressure?'* And then his voice came in again loud and clear. *'Repeat, what is your barometric pressure reading now?'*

'Nine-seven-six,' I told him. 'A drop of three millibars within the last hour.'

'Then it's not far away. You can expect an almost vertical fall in pressure, right down to around nine-six-o. Watch the wind. When it goes round . . .' His voice faded and I lost the rest. When I picked him up again he was saying something about seeking shelter.

'Have you made contact with that trawler again?' I asked.

'No. But somebody was calling Mayday a while ago – very faint. Now listen. I am going to try and raise the Faeroes or weather ship India. It should be passing between them, you see. And I'll phone Pitreavie. Tell the operator I'll call him on this frequency one hour from now. Good luck and Out.'

I passed the message on to the operator and went back into the wheelhouse. Nothing had changed. The duty man was still sheltering in the doorway. The barometer still read 976. Another trailer had been unloaded, that was all. And the wind still northerly. It was ten past one. Four hours to go.

3

STORM
(21–22 October)

A few minutes later Stratton came in, his duffel coat sodden.
'Raining again.' He went straight to the barometer, tapped
it and entered the reading in the log. 'And McGregor's dead.
They're bringing his body on board now.' His face was pale and
haggard-looking in the wheelhouse lights.

I passed Cliff's message on to him, but all he said was, 'We're
dried out for two-thirds the length of the ship and I can't change
the tides.' His mind was preoccupied, wound up like a clock,
waiting for zero hour. He went to his room and shortly afterwards
a macabre little procession came in through the open tunnel of
the loading doors – McDermott and the camp doctor, and behind
them two orderlies carrying a stretcher. All work stopped and
the men stood silent. A few moved to help hand the stretcher up
one of the vertical steel ladders on the port side. The body on the
stretcher was wrapped in an oiled sheet. It glistened white in the
lights. Once it slipped, sagging against the tapes that held it in
place. The orderlies stopped to re-arrange it and then the procession moved aft along the side decking. I could see their faces
then, the two officers' white and shaken, the orderlies' wooden.
They passed out of sight, moving slowly aft. They were taking
the body to the tiller flat, but I only learned that later when death
was facing us, too.

I went back into the wardroom and ten minutes later McDermott
came in followed by Captain Fairweather. They looked old and
beaten, grey-faced and their hands trembling. They didn't
speak. They had a whisky each and then McDermott went to his
bunk, Captain Fairweather back to the camp to get his kit.

By two-thirty the tank deck was clear, a wet steel expanse
emptied of all vehicles. By three the incoming tide was spilling
white surf as far as the loading ramp. The glass stood at 971,
falling. No further contact with Cliff Morgan. Nothing from
Coastal Command. And the wind still driving out of the north,
straight over the beached bows. Pinney was arguing with Stratton
in the wheelhouse. 'Christ, man, what do you think we are?

The men are dead beat. And so am I.' The decks were deserted now, all the men swallowed up in the warmth of the ship, and Stratton wanted them ashore. 'My orders were to embark my men and all the equipment I could. We got the stuff on board and then you order it to be taken off again. And when we've done that . . .'

'It's for their own good.' Stratton's voice was weary, exhausted by tension.

'Like hell it is. What they want is some sleep.'

'They won't get much sleep if this depression . . .'

'This depression! What the hell's got into you? For two hours now you've been worrying about it. The forecast doesn't mention it. You've no confirmation of it from Coastal Command, from anybody. All you've got is the word of one man, and he's guessing on the basis of a single contact with some trawler.'

'I know. But the glass is falling – '

'What do you expect it to do in this sort of weather – go sailing up? All that matters is the wind direction. And the wind's north. In just over two hours now . . .'

It went on like that, the two of them arguing back and forth, Stratton's voice slow and uncertain, Pinney's no longer coming gruff out of his big frame, but high-pitched with weariness and frustration. He was a soldier and his men came first. Stratton's concern was his ship and he had a picture in his mind, a picture conjured by the falling glass and Cliff Morgan's warning and that information I had passed on about a faint voice calling Mayday on the International Distress frequency. But even in these circumstances possession is nine-tenths of the law. Pinney's men were on board. They had their oilskins off and hammocks slung. They were dead beat and they'd take a lot of shifting. Stratton gave in. 'On your own head then, John.' And he gave the orders for the ramp to be raised and the bow doors shut.

Thirty-three men, who could have been safe ashore, were sealed into that coffin of a ship. The time was three-fourteen. Just over one and a half hours to go. Surely it would hold off for that short time. I watched figures in oilskins bent double as they forced their way for'ard and clambered down to the tank deck. The open gap, with its glimpse of the beach and the blurred shape of vehicles standing in the rain, gradually sealed itself. The clamps were checked. The half gate swung into place. Now nobody could leave the ship. And as if to underline the finality of those doors being closed, messages began to come through.

Coastal Command first: *Trawler* Viking Fisher *in distress.*

Anticipate possibility of very severe storm imminent your locality. Winds of high velocity can be expected from almost any direction. Report each hour until further notice.

Then Cliff crashed net frequency to announce contact with Faeroes and weather ship *India. Faeroes report wind southerly force 10. Barometer 968, rising. W/S India: wind north-westerly force 9 or 10. Barometer 969, falling rapidly. Very big seas.*

CCN again with a supplementary forecast from the Meteorological Office: *Sea areas Hebrides, Bailey, Faeroes, South-East Iceland – Probability that small, very intense depression may have formed to give wind speeds of hurricane force locally for short duration. Storm area will move southwards with the main northerly airstream, gradually losing intensity.*

The outside world stirring in its sleep and taking an interest in us. Stratton passed the messages to Pinney without comment, standing at the chart table in the wheelhouse. Pinney read them and then placed them on top of the log book. He didn't say anything. There wasn't anything to say. The moment for getting the men ashore was gone half an hour ago. Waves were breaking up by the bows and occasionally a tremor ran through the ship, the first awakening as the stern responded to the buoyancy of water deep enough to float her. And in the wheelhouse there was an air of expectancy, a man at the wheel and the engine-room telegraph at stand-by.

The time was twelve minutes after four.

The radio operator again. Base asking for Captain Pinney on the R/T. Pinney went out and an unnatural quiet descended on the wheelhouse, a stillness of waiting. In moments like this, when a ship is grounded and you are waiting for her to float again, all sensitivity becomes concentrated on the soles of the feet, for they are in contact with the deck, the transmitters of movement, of any untoward shock. We didn't talk because our minds were on our feet. We were listening by touch. Perhaps that's why our ears failed to register how quiet it had become.

Through my feet, through the nerves that ran up my legs, connecting them to my brain, I could feel the tremor, the faint lifting movement, the slight bump as she grounded again. It all came from the stern. But it was a movement that was changing all the time, growing stronger, so that in a moment a slight shock preceded the lift and there was a surge running the length of the ship. It was different. Definitely a change in the pattern and it puzzled me. I glanced at Stratton. He was frowning, watching a pencil on the chart table. It had begun to roll back and forth

705

at each surge. The bumps as we grounded were more noticeable now, a definite shock.

Wentworth came in. 'What is it? I told you to stay on the quarter-deck with the Bos'n.' Stratton's voice was irritable, his nerves betraying him. 'Well?'

'There's quite a swell building up.' The youngster's face looked white. 'You can see it breaking on the skerries of Sgeir Mhor. It's beginning to come into the bay. And the wind's gone round.'

'Gone round?'

'Backed into the west.'

Stratton went to the door on the port side and flung it open again. No wind came in. The air around the ship was strangely still. But we could hear it, roaring overhead. The first grey light of dawn showed broken masses of cloud pouring towards us across the high back of Keava. The moon shone through ragged gaps. It was a wild, grey-black sky, ugly and threatening. Stratton stood there for a moment, staring up at it, and then he came back into the wheelhouse, slamming the door behind him. 'When did it start backing? When did you first notice it?'

'About ten minutes ago. I wasn't certain at first. Then the swell began to . . .'

'Well, get back to the after-deck, Number One. If it goes round into the south . . .' He hesitated. 'If it does that, it'll come very quickly now. Another ten minutes, quarter of an hour. We'll know by then. And if it does – then you'll have to play her on the kedge like a tunny fish. That hawser mustn't break. Understand? I'll back her off on the engines. It'll be too much for the winch. Your job is to see she doesn't slew. Slack off when you have to. But for Christ's sake don't let her stern swing towards the beach. That's what happened to Kelvedon.'

'I'll do my best.'

Stratton nodded. 'This swell might just do the trick. If we can get her off before the wind goes right round . . .'

But Wentworth was already gone. He didn't need to be told what would happen if the wind backed southerly – wind and waves and the breaking strain on that hawser a paltry forty-five tons. And as though to underline the point, Stratton said to me, 'One of the weaknesses of these ships, that winch gear only rates about ten horse-power.' He picked up the engine-room telephone. 'Stevens? Oh, it's you, Turner. Captain here. Give me the Chief, will you.'

He began giving instructions to the engine-room and I pushed past him, out on to the wing bridge and up the steel ladder to the open deck above. The lookout was standing on the compass platform staring aft, his face a pallid oval under his sou'wester. A ragged gap in the clouds showed stars, a diamond glitter with the outline of Tarsaval sharp and black like a cut-out; a glimpse of the moon's face, and the wind tramping overhead, driving a black curtain of cloud across it. I went aft down the flag deck where the tripod structure of the mainmast stood rooted like a pylon, and a moment later Stratton joined me. 'Any change?'

'West sou'west, I think.' I couldn't be sure, but there was a definite swell. We could see it coming in out of the half-darkness and growing in the ship's lights as it met the shallows. It slid under the stern and then broke seething along the length of the sides, lifting the stern and snapping the anchor hawser taut. Across the bay we could see spray bursting against the dim, jagged shape of the skerries. The wind was definitely south of west. I could feel it sometimes on my face, though the force of it and the true direction was masked by the bulk of Keava. Raindrops spattered on my face.

But it was the swell that held us riveted, the regular grind and bump as the ship was lifted. And then one came in higher, breaking earlier. It crashed against the stern. Spray flung a glittering curtain of water that hung an instant suspended and then fell on us, a drenching cascade. But it wasn't the water so much as the ship herself that alarmed us, the sudden shock of impact, the way she lifted and slewed, the appalling snap of the hawser as it took the full weight, the thudding crash as she grounded again, grinding her bottom in the backwash.

'I hope to God he remembers to slip the winch out of gear,' Stratton murmured, speaking to himself rather than to me. 'All that weight on it . . . We've stripped the gears before now. I'd better remind him.' He turned to go, but then he stopped, his gaze turned seaward. 'Look!' He was pointing to the other LCT, a cluster of lights in the grey darkness of the bay. 'Lucky beggar.' She had her steaming lights on and was getting her anchor up; and I knew what Stratton was thinking – that he might have been out there, safe, with room to manoeuvre and freedom to do so.

A blast of air slapped rain in my face. South – south-west. Again I couldn't be sure. But into the bay; that was definite. Stratton had felt it, too. He went at once to the compass platform. I stayed an instant longer, watching the men on the after-deck immediately below me. Wentworth was standing facing the stern, with two men by the winch on the starboard quarter, their eyes fixed on him, waiting for his signal. The sea seethed back, white foam sliding away in the lights, and out of the greyness astern came a sloping heap of water that built rapidly to a sheer, curving breaker. The winch drum turned, the cable slackened; the wave broke and thudded, roaring against the stern. The men, the winch, the whole after-deck disappeared in a welter of white water. The ship lifted under me, swung and then steadied to the snap of the hawser. The thud as we hit the bottom again jarred my whole body. I saw the mast tremble like a tree whose roots are being attacked, and when I looked over the rail again, the stern was clear of water, the men picking themselves up.

The wind was on my face now. It came in gusts, and each gust seemed stronger than the last. L4400 had got her anchor; she was turning head-to-sea, steaming out of the bay.

I went for'ard to the bridge, wondering how long it would be before the hawser snapped or the men on the after-deck were swept overboard. The deck under my feet was alive now, the engine-room telegraph set to slow astern and the screws turning. Stratton was on the open side deck, trying to keep an eye on stern and bow at the same time. If only she could shake herself free. I could feel it when she lifted, the way she was held by the bows only; for just a moment, when the wave was right under her, you could almost believe she was afloat.

Pinney came up. I don't think anyone saw him come. He just seemed to materialize. 'Would you believe it? The Old Man's countermanded Braddock's orders. Said we'd no business to be pulling out ...' There was more of it, but that's all I can remember – that, and the fact that he looked tired and shaken. Nobody said anything. Nobody was listening. We had other things on our minds. Pinney must have realized this, for he caught hold of my arm and said angrily, 'What's happening? What's going on?'

'The wind,' I said. 'The wind's gone round.'

I could see it now, blowing at Stratton's hair, whipping the tops off the combers and sending the spray hurtling shorewards in flat streamers of white spindrift. We were no longer sheltered by Keava. God, how quickly that wind had shifted, blowing right into the bay now – thirty, maybe forty knots. I went down to the wheelhouse. The barometer was at 969, down another two points. *Quick fall, quick rise* – that was the old saying. But how far would it fall before it started to rise? Cliff had mentioned 960, had talked of a near vertical fall of pressure. That was what we were getting now. I hadn't seen a glass fall like that since I'd sailed into a cyclone in the Indian Ocean. I tapped it and it fell to 968.

'Full astern both engines.' Stratton's voice from the bridge above came to me over the helmsman's voice pipe. The telegraph rang and the beat of the engines increased as the stern lifted to slam down again with a deep, rending crash that jolted my body and set every movable thing in the wheelhouse rattling. 'Stop both engines.'

I was gripping hold of the chart table, every nerve taut. Gone was the silence, that brief stillness of waiting; all was noise and confusion now. 'Full astern both.' But he was too late, the stern already lifting before the screws could bite. Stop both and the jar as she grounded, the bows still held and the hawser straining. Spray hit me as I went back to the bridge. The wind was pitched high in the gusts, higher and higher until it became a scream.

The phone that linked us to the after-deck buzzed. There was nobody to answer it so I picked it up and Wentworth's voice, sounding slight and very far away, said, 'We took in half a dozen turns on the winch that time. Either the anchor's dragging . . .' I lost the rest in the crash of a wave. And then his voice again, louder this time: 'Three more turns, but we're getting badly knocked about.' I passed the information to Stratton. 'Tell him,' he shouted back, 'to take in the slack and use the brakes. I'm holding the engines at full astern. If we don't get off now . . .' A gust of wind blew the rest of his words away. The phone went dead as the ship heaved up. The crash as she grounded flung me against the conning platform.

I was clinging on to the phone wondering what was happening to those poor devils aft and trying to think at the same time. The wind was south or perhaps sou'-sou'-west; it would be anti-clockwise, whirling round the centre of that air depression and being sucked into it at the same time. I was trying to figure out where that centre would be. If it was north of us . . . But north of us should give us a westerly wind. It depended how much the air currents were being deflected in towards the centre. I was remembering Cliff's message: the Faeroes had reported baro-metric pressure 968, rising, with winds southerly, force 10. Our barometer was now showing 968. If the storm centre passed to the west of us, then this might be the worst of it. I decided not to go down and fiddle with the glass again.

'We made several yards.' Wentworth's voice was shrill in the phone. 'But the winch is smoking. The brakes. They may burn out any minute now. Keep those engines running for God's sake.'

I glanced at Stratton but I didn't need to ask him. I could feel the vibrations of the screws through my whole body. 'Engines at full astern,' I said. 'Keep winching in.'

I put the phone down and dived across the bridge to yell the information in Stratton's ear. The weight of the wind was something solid now. I felt the words sucked out of my mouth and blown away into the night. 'Christ! If the winch packs up now ... Stay on the phone, will you.' Stratton's face was white. I was lip-reading rather than hearing the words. Below him white water glistened, a seething welter of surf sucking back along the ship's side. A shaggy comber reared in the lights, curled and broke. Spray went whipping past and ectoplasmic chunks of foam suds.

The ship moved. I could feel it, a sixth sense telling me that we were momentarily afloat. And then the shuddering, jarring crash. I was back at the phone and Wentworth's voice was yelling in my ear – something about the winch gears. But his voice abruptly ceased before I could get what it was he was trying to tell me. And then Stratton grabbed the phone from my hand. 'Oil,' he said. 'There's an oil slick forming.' He pressed the buzzer, the phone to his ear. 'Hullo. Hullo there. Number One. Wentworth.' He looked at me, his face frozen. 'No answer.' There was a shudder, a soundless scraping and grating that I couldn't hear but felt through the soles of my feet. And then it was gone and I felt the bows lift for the first time. 'Winch in. Winch in.' Stratton's voice was yelling into the phone as a wave lifted the stern, running buoyant under the ship. There was no grounding thud this time as we sank into the trough and glancing for'ard I saw the bows riding high, rearing to the break of the wave. 'Wentworth. Do you hear me? Winch in. Wentworth.' His hand fell slack to his side, still holding the phone. 'There's no answer,' he said. His face was crusted with salt, a drop of moisture at the end of his slightly up-turned nose. His eyes looked bleak.

'You look after the ship,' I told him. 'I'll go aft and see what's happened.'

He nodded and I went out on to the flag deck. Clear of the bridge the full weight of the wind hit me. It was less than half an hour since I'd stood there and felt that first blast of the storm wind in my face. Now, what a difference! I had to fight my way aft, clinging to the deck rail, my eyes blinded by salt spray, the wind driving the breath back into my lungs. Fifty, sixty knots – you can't judge wind speeds when they reach storm force and over. It shook me to think that this perhaps was only the beginning.

But we'd be round Malesgair then, sheltered under its lee – I hoped. By God, I hoped as I fought my way to the after-rail and clung there, looking down to the tiny stern platform with its spare anchor and its winch gear.

Wentworth was there. He was bending over the winch. His sou'wester had gone and his fair hair was plastered to his head. He looked drowned and so did the two men with him. They were all of them bent over the winch and the drum was stationary. A broken wave-top streaming spray like smoke from its crest reared up in the lights, a shaggy, wind-blown monster, all white teeth as it slammed rolling against the stern. It buried everything, a welter of foam that subsided to the lift of the ship, water cascading over the sides, the men still gripping the winch like rocks awash. I yelled to Wentworth, but my shout was blown back into my mouth and he didn't hear me. The winch remained motionless and the hawser, running through two steel pulleys and out over the stern, just hung there, limp.

I turned and went like a leaf blown by the wind back to the open bridge and Stratton standing there, the phone in his hand and the engines still pounding at full astern. I grabbed his arm. 'The hawser,' I yelled. 'You'll over-run the hawser.'

He nodded, calm now and in full control of himself. 'Gears jammed. I've told him to cut it.' And then he said something about taking her out on radar as he put the phone down and went quickly, like a crab, down the steel ladder to the wheelhouse. It was a relief just to be out of the wind. The radar was switched on, set to the three mile-range. The screen showed us half surrounded by the mass of Laerg, the shore still very close. And when he did try to turn – what then? Broadside to that sea with the weight of the wind heeling her over, anything might happen.

But that was something else. What worried me was the thought of that hawser. I could see it clear in my mind, a great loop of wire running from the stern down through the heaving waters and under the whole length of the ship to the anchor dug into the sea bed somewhere beyond our bows now. It had only to touch one of the propeller blades – it would strip the propeller then or else it would wrap. And that wasn't the only hazard. Driving astern like this, backing into sea and wind, it might come taut at any moment. Then if it were fractionally off centre our stern would swing. Or was that what Stratton was trying to do? I glanced quickly at his face. It was quite blank, his whole mind given to the ship as he stood just behind the helmsman, watching the compass and at the same time keeping an eye on the radar.

I thought I felt a jerk, a sort of shudder. 'Stop port. Half ahead port.'

'Port engine stopped. Port engine half ahead, sir.'

Slowly the bulk of Laerg shifted its position on the radar screen. The bows were moving to starboard, swung by the screws and the pull of the anchor against the stern. The movement slowed. A wave crashed breaking against the starboard side. The ship rolled. 'Helm hard a'starboard. Stop starboard engine. Half ahead together.'

The beat changed. The ship shuddered as she rolled. The outline on the radar screen resumed its circling anti-clockwise movement. The bows were coming round again. A big sea crashed inboard, the tank deck awash. The ship reeled, heeling over so steeply that Pinney was flung across the wheelhouse. Slowly she righted, to be knocked down again and yet again, the weight of the wind holding her pinned at an angle, driving her shorewards. But the bows kept on swinging, kept on coming round. The helmsman's voice pipe whistled.

'Number One reporting anchor hawser cut,' he said.

Stratton nodded.

'He's asking permission to come for'ard.'

'Yes. Report to me in the wheelhouse.' Stratton's whole mind was fixed on the radar. Now the bulk of Laerg was on the left-hand lower side of the screen, at about eight o'clock. 'Full ahead both engines.' The telegraph rang. The shuddering was replaced by a steadier beat.

And the helmsman confirmed – 'Both at full ahead, sir.'

'Helm amidships.'

'Midships.'

We were round with Laerg at the bottom of the radar screen, the two sheltering arms running up each side, and the top all blank – the open sea for which we were headed. Steaming into it, we felt the full force of the wind now. It came in great battering gusts that shook the wheelhouse. Spray beat against the steel plates, solid as shot, and the bows reared crazily, twisting as though in agony, the steel creaking and groaning. And when they plunged the lights showed water pouring green over the sides, the tank deck filled like a swimming pool.

'Half ahead together. Ten-fifty revolutions.'

God knows what it was blowing. And it had come up so fast. I'd never known anything like this – so sudden, so violent. The seas were shaggy hills, their tops beaten flat, yet still they contrived to curve and break as they found the shallower water of the bay. They showed as a blur beyond the bows in moments when the wind whipped the porthole glass clean as polished crystal. The barometer at 965 was still falling. Hundreds of tons of water sloshed around in the tank deck and the ship was sluggish like an overladen barge.

Wentworth staggered in. He had a jagged cut above his right eye; blood on his face and on his hands, bright crimson in the lights. Beads of water stood on his oilskins, giving them a mottled effect. 'The tiller flat,' he said.

Stratton glanced at him. 'That cut – you all right?'

Wentworth dabbed it with his hand, staring at the blood as though he hadn't realized he was bleeding. 'Nothing much. Fenwick has hurt his arm.' And he added, 'They didn't secure the hatch. There's a lot of water . . .'

'What hatch?'

'The tiller flat.'

But Stratton had other things to worry about. The helmsman had been caught off balance, the wheel spinning. A figure moved and caught the spokes. 'All right, sir. I've got her.' It was the Quartermaster. A sea broke slamming on the starboard bow, but she was coming back again, swinging her bows back into the waves. God, what a sea! And I heard Stratton say, 'What's that on your oilskins – oil? It looks like oil.'

'There was a lot of it in the sea,' Wentworth answered. 'Every time a wave broke . . .'

But Stratton had pushed past me and was staring alternately at the radar screen and out through the porthole.

It was just on five-thirty then and dawn had come; a cold, grey glimmer in the murk.

Darkness would have been preferable. I would rather not have seen that storm. It was enough to hear it, to feel it in the tortured motion of the ship. The picture then was imaginary, and imagination, lacking a basis of experience, fell short of actuality. But dawn added sight to the other senses and the full majesty of the appalling chaos that surrounded us was revealed.

I had seen pictures of storms where sea and rock seemed so exaggerated that not even artistic licence could justify such violent, fantastic use of paint. But no picture I had ever seen measured up to the reality of that morning. Fortunately, the full realization of what we faced came gradually – a slow exposure taking shape, the creeping dawn imprinting it on the retina of our eyes like a developing agent working on a black and white print. There was no colour; just black through all shades of grey to white, the white predominating, all the surface of the sea streaked with it. The waves, like heaped-up ranges, were beaten down at the top and streaming spray – not smoking as in an ordinary gale, but the water whipped from their shaggy crests in flat, horizontal sheets, thin layers like razor blades cutting down-wind with indescribable force. Above these layers foam flew thick as snow, lifted from the seething tops of the broken waves and flung pell-mell through the air, flakes as big as gulls, dirty white against the uniform grey of the overcast.

Close on the starboard bow the skerry rocks of Sgeir Mhor lifted grey molars streaming water, the waves exploding against them in plumes of white like an endless succession of depth charges. And beyond Sgeir Mhor, running away to our right, the sheer cliffs of Keava were a black wall disappearing into a tearing wrack of cloud, the whole base of this rampart cascading white as wave after wave attacked and then receded to meet the next and smash it to pieces, heaping masses of water hundreds of feet into the air. Not Milton even, describing Hell, has matched in words the frightful, chaotic spectacle my eyes recorded in the dawn; the Atlantic in the full fury of a storm that had lifted the wind right to the top of the Beaufort scale.

That the landing craft wasn't immediately overwhelmed was due to the almost unbelievable velocity of the wind. The waves were torn to shreds as they broke so that their force was dissipated, their height diminished. The odd thing was I felt no fear. I remember glancing at Stratton, surprised to find his face calm, almost relaxed. His eyes met mine for an instant, cool and steady. No fear there either. Fear would come later no doubt, as a reaction when the danger had lessened. Fear requires time to infect the system, and we had had no time; it had come upon us too quickly with too much to do. And panic is an instantaneous thing, a nerve storm. Men carrying out the duties for which they have been trained, straining every nerve to meet the situation, their minds entirely concentrated on the work in hand, are seldom liable to panic.

'Have the men put their life-jackets on.' Stratton's voice was barely audible as he shouted the order to Wentworth. 'Everyone. Understand?' He turned to Pinney. 'Go with him. See that every one of your men has his life-jacket on.'

'What about the tiller flat?' Wentworth asked.

'How much water got in?'

'I don't know. It was dark down there and I couldn't see. Quite a bit, I think.'

'Did you fix the hatch?'

'Yes. But it may have got in through the rudder stock housings. It may still be . . .'

'All right, Number One. I'll have a word with Stevens. His engineers will get it pumped out.' He picked up the engine-room phone. 'And have that cut seen to.'

It was after Wentworth had left that I found my bowels reacting and felt that sick void in my guts that is the beginning of fear. If I'd been in control I wouldn't have noticed it. I'd have been too busy. But I was a spectator and what I saw both on the radar screen and through the porthole was the tip of Sgeir Mhor coming closer, a gap-toothed rock half awash and the wicked white of the seas breaking across it. Stratton was keeping the bows head-on to the waves. He had no choice. To sheer away in that sea was impossible – the head of the ship would have been flung sideways by the combined thrust of wind and water and she'd have broached-to and been rolled over. But bows-on we were headed about one-ninety degrees, sometimes nearer two hundred, for the wind was just west of south. We were slowly being forced towards the rocks that formed the western arm of Shelter Bay. Some time back Stratton had realized the danger and had ordered full ahead on both engines, but even at full ahead our progress was painfully slow, the ship labouring to make up against the almost solid wall of the elements. Yard by yard we closed Sgeir Mhor and we kept on closing it. There was no shelter behind those rocks – not enough in that force of wind; our only hope was the open sea beyond.

It was six-ten by the clock above the chart table when we came abreast of Sgeir Mhor and for a full six minutes we were butting our bows into a welter of foaming surf with the last rock showing naked in the backwash of each trough less than a hundred yards on our starboard side. Every moment I expected to feel the rending of her bottom plates as some submerged rock cut into her like a knife gutting a fish. But the echo-sounder clicking merrily away recorded nothing less than 40 fathoms, and at six-sixteen we were clear, clawing our way seaward out of reach, I thought, at last.

North-westward of us now the sheer rock coast of Laerg was opening up, a rampart wall cascading water, its top vanishing into swirling masses of cloud. We were in deeper water then and Stratton was on the phone to the engine-room again, cutting the revolutions until the ship was stationary, just holding her own against the wind. 'If the old girl can just stay in one piece,' he yelled in my ear. I didn't need to be told what he planned to do;

715

it was what I would have done in his shoes. He was reckoning that the storm centre would pass right over us and he was going to butt the wind until it did. Nothing else he could do, for he couldn't turn. When we were into the eye of the storm there would be a period of calm. He'd get the ship round then and tuck himself tight under those towering cliffs. We'd be all right then. As the centre passed, the wind would swing round into the east or north-east. We'd be under the lee of Laerg then. But how long before that happened – an hour, two hours? Out here in the deeper water the waves no longer built up in range upon range of moving hills; they lay flat cowed by the wind which seemed to be scooping the whole surface of the sea into the air. The noise was shattering, spray hitting the wheelhouse in solid sheets. Visibility was nil, except for brief glimpses of the chaos when a gust died. And then a squall blotting everything out and the Quartermaster quietly announcing that the wind had caught her and she wasn't answering.

'Full astern starboard.'

The ring of the telegraph, faint and insubstantial, the judder of the screws, and the bows steadying. She'd have come back into the wind then, but a sea caught her and she heeled over. If we'd been in the shallow waters of the bay, she'd have rolled right over, but out here it was the wind more than the waves that menaced us; it held her canted at a steep angle and the man who brought Stratton his life-jacket had to crawl on his hands and knees. Stratton tossed it into the corner by the chart table. 'Better get yours, too,' he said to me. 'Just in case.' The bows were coming round now, sluggishly. 'Full ahead both. Starboard wheel.' And then she was round with her blunt nose bucking the seas, her screws racing as they were lifted clear in the troughs.

Even head-to-wind again it was a struggle to get down the alleyway to my quarters. McDermott lay on the floor. He had tied himself with a blanket to the bunk support and he'd been sick again, all over himself and the floor. The place was a shambles. 'Was that the power steering packed in?' Wentworth asked me. He was clinging to the desk whilst Fairweather tried to stitch the cut in his head.

'We were blown off,' I said.

But he didn't seem to take that in. 'I tried to tell Stratton. They forgot to close the hatch. To the tiller flat. You remember? I told him . . .'

I did remember and my first reaction was a mental picture of McGregor's corpse being sloshed around in that small compartment above the rudders. My mind must have been sluggish for it was a moment before I realized what was worrying him. If the electric motors shorted . . . The possibility brought the sweat to my palms, a sting to the armpits that I could have sworn I smelt despite the layers of clothing. And then I remembered that the hatch was closed now and the engineers would have disposed of the water. 'They'll have pumped it out by now,' I said.

He nodded. 'Yes. Yes, of course. I remember now.' He seemed dazed, staring at me wide-eyed. 'But that oil. What do you think it was, Mr Ross?' Staring at me like that, the whites of his eyes beginning to show, I began to wonder.

'What oil?' I said.

'It was all round the stern and every time a sea broke . . . Look at my hair.' He leaned his head forward, ignoring the Doc's warning. 'See? It's oil. Diesel oil.'

'Don't worry,' I said. 'Another couple of hours . . .' I ducked out of the cabin. I wanted fresh air, the confidence that only men doing something to preserve themselves can inspire. Was Wentworth scared, or was it me? All I knew was that something like a contagious disease had touched me in that sour cabin full of the sick smell of vomit. That oil . . . I remembered when he'd first come up to the wheelhouse, how his oilskins had been mottled with it, and Stratton asking about it.

The wheelhouse steadied me. There was Stratton smoking a cigarette, the Quartermaster at the wheel, everything going on as before and the bows headed slap into the wind. The radar screen showed Sgeir Mhor dead astern of us less than a mile away. I dropped my life-jacket beside Stratton's. Should I remind him about the oil, or just forget about it? I decided to keep silent. Nothing to be done about it. What was the point? And yet . . . I lit a cigarette and saw my hand was trembling. Hell! 'What's under the tank deck?' I heard myself ask. 'Water and fuel oil, I think you said.'

'Yes, fuel oil.' Stratton's voice had an edge to it and he added, 'Something on your mind?' He was staring at me hard and I realized suddenly that he knew – knew we'd damaged the bottom plates getting off.

'No, nothing,' I said, and I left it at that, happier now that the knowledge was shared. Perhaps he was, too, for he smiled. 'Keep your fingers crossed,' he said.

But keeping your fingers crossed doesn't mend steel plates, and it doesn't prevent fuel oil seeping out through the cracks and rents in those battered plates. I stayed with him until I'd finished my cigarette and then I made some excuse and slipped out. There was only one way of finding out. I went down the companion ladder to the deck below, unclamped the steel door leading to the side deck and, leaning out, grabbed hold of the rail. I was just in time, for the force of the wind swept my legs from under me. I was left clinging there, my body flattened along the deck and my lungs filled to bursting with the pressure of air forcing its way into mouth and nostrils.

The power of that wind was demoniac. It forced my eyeballs back against the membranes with a stabbing pain. It tore at my hair and clothing. And the sheet spray flung against my face had the cutting power of sand. Raw and shaken I held on till there was a slight lull, and then I hurled myself back through the door. It took me quite a time to get it shut and the clamps in place. I was wet to the skin and panting with the effort, but I now knew – I had seen the surface of the water sheened with a film of oil, the surface spray held static by the viscosity of it.

When I got back to the wheelhouse Wentworth was there, clinging to the chart table, fresh plaster covering the cut on his forehead. Stratton glanced at me, a slight lift to his brows as he saw the state of my clothes. He knew where I'd been so I just gave a slight confirmatory nod. 'Bad?' he asked.

'Impossible to tell.'

He nodded.

'What's bad?' Wentworth asked. 'Where've you been?' His voice was slightly slurred and the whites of his eyes . . . I didn't like that tendency for the whites to show.

'I've just been sick,' I said.

He accepted that. 'So've I.' He said it quite cheerfully, the beginnings of a smile lighting up his face. He couldn't have been more than twenty-two; much too young, I thought, to face a storm like this. It was the sort of storm you only expect to face once in a lifetime, and then only if you've been all your life at sea. I wondered whether I could paint it. Could any artist get it down on canvas – this soul-destroying, brain-numbing battering, this violence that went beyond the limits of experience?

And the fact that we existed, that the ship still held her blunt bows head-to-wind, battling against the driving planes of water, made it somehow marvellous, the little oasis of the wheelhouse a miracle. In the midst of chaos, here within the tight frame of fragile steel walls, there was the reassurance of familiar things – the radar, the charts, the burly Quartermaster quite unperturbed, orders being given, messages coming in – particularly the messages.

L4400 signalling that she was under the lee of Malesgair and riding it out, safe for the moment at any rate. Coastal Command asking us whether we needed assistance, relaying to us the information that the Admiralty tug was now waiting instructions in Lochmaddy. First Braddock and then Standing asking for news of us – how many men had we embarked, what stores and equipment, obviously quite oblivious of the magnitude of the storm. The last contact with Cliff before he went on duty had given the wind locally as south, approximately fifty knots. Fifty knots, when out here it was blowing eighty, ninety, a hundred – God knows what force it was. And at six forty-five the shipping forecast: *A local depression of great intensity may affect parts of sea areas Faeroes, Hebrides . . . Winds cyclonic and temporarily reaching hurricane force* . . . I think that was the most extraordinary part of it – the sense of still being in contact with the outside world when all our own world was being blown to bits by the wind, the whole surface of the sea apparently disintegrating and being forced up into the atmosphere.

And then suddenly our little oasis of ordered security crashed about our ears. The engine-room phone had probably been buzzing for some time. But nobody had heard it. The din was too great. It was the ring of the telegraph that informed us and the Quartermaster's voice: 'Port engines losing power, sir.' The spokes of the wheel were turning under his hand, turning until he had full starboard helm on. Again he reached for the brass handle of the port telegraph, gave it two sharp rings and jammed it back at full ahead. Stratton leapt to the engine-room telephone. 'It's all right now, sir.' The Quartermaster was bringing the wheel back amidships. But I was watching Stratton. His face was white, his body rigid. '. . . Sea water, you say? . . . Yes, I knew about the leak . . . Well, can't you drain it off? . . . I see. Well, that must have happened when we were broadside on in the bay . . . All right, Stevens. Do what you can . . . Yes, we'll try. But we can't hold her any steadier. There's quite a sea . . . Well, give me warning when the other engines start cutting out.' He put the phone back on its hook. His face looked bleak.

'What is it?' Wentworth demanded. 'What's happened?'

'Main tank's leaking and we've been pumping sea water into the ready-use tank. Only the port engines affected so far, but . . .' He turned to the Quartermaster. 'Think you can hold her on starboard engines alone?'

'I'll try, sir.'

The Cox'n came in then. His flat, broad face was smeared with oil. 'Port outer engine starting to cut out, sir. Chief asked me to tell you he's afraid . . .' Something in Stratton's face stopped the breathless rush of his words. In a quieter voice he added, 'I was going round the mess decks. I could feel there was something wrong so I slipped down to the engine-room. Chief said he couldn't get you on the phone.'

'Thank you, Cox'n. I've just had a word with him. The starboard engines are all right, I gather?'

'For the moment, sir. But he's afraid the ready-use tank may be . . .'

'I've had his report on that.' Stratton's voice, quiet and controlled, stilled the suggestion of panic that had hung for a moment over the wheelhouse.

'There's another thing, sir. The tiller flat. Bilge pumps not working. Chief thinks they're choked. Anyway, there's a lot of water . . .'

'All right, Cox'n. Have some men closed up on the tiller flat, will you – just in case.'

'Very good, sir.' And as he went out Wentworth, close at my side, said, 'I had a feeling about that tiller flat. Ever since I found the hatch unfastened. We must have taken a hell of a lot of water through it when we were getting off the beach.' His manner was quite different now, almost calm, as though he'd braced himself against the urgency of the situation. He reached for the log book and began entering it up.

Everything normal again, the ship headed into the wind, the beat of the engines steady under our feet. But even with both engines at full ahead she was making little or no headway against the moving masses of air and water that seemed fused into a solid impenetrable wall. The shape of Laerg on the radar screen came and went, fuzzed by the thickness of the atmosphere. The Quartermaster shifted his stance at the wheel, gripped the spokes tighter. And in the same instant I felt it through the soles of my feet, a change of beat, a raggedness. The wheel spun. Full starboard helm and the beat steadier again, but not so strong. 'Port engines both stopped, sir.'

Stratton was already at the phone. He held it to his ear, waiting. 'Good . . . Well, if you can drain off all the sea water . . . Yes, we'll try and hold her bows-on . . . All right. Now what about the tiller flat? . . . You've got a man working on it? Fine . . . Yes, we'll just have to hope for the best.' He put the phone down, glanced at the radar screen and then at me. His lips moved stiffly in a smile. 'Hell of a time you picked to come for a sail with us.' He glanced at the helm. The wheel was amidships again. 'Answering all right, Quartermaster?' he asked.

'Pretty fair, sir.'

But we weren't making headway any longer and Sgeir Mhor a bare mile away, directly down-wind of us. Stratton produced his packet of cigarettes and we stood there, braced against the violence of the movement, smoking and watching the radar screen. And then, suddenly, the Quartermaster's voice announcing that the helm had gone dead. 'Full starboard helm and not answering, sir.'

Wentworth was already at one of the phones. 'Cox'n reports steering motors shorted. There's a lot of water . . .'

'Emergency steering.' Stratton rapped the order out and I saw the Quartermaster lean down and throw across a lever at the base of the steering pedestal.

A sea broke thundering inboard. A solid sheet of spray crashed against the wheelhouse. And as the porthole cleared I saw the bows thrown off and sagging away to leeward. It had taken a bare ten seconds to engage the hand steering, but in those ten seconds the weight of sea and wind combined had caught hold of the bows and flung them off to port.

'Emergency steering not answering, sir.'

The ship staggered to another blow and began to heel as the wind caught her on the starboard bow. She was starting to broach-to. And the Quartermaster's voice again, solid and unemotional: 'Hand steering's all right, sir. But not enough power on the engines.'

Only two engines out of four and the bows swinging fast now. Stratton was at the engine-room phone, but I could see by his face that no one was answering. 'Keep your helm hard a-starboard. You may be able to bring her up in a lull.'

But there wasn't a lull. The ship heeled further and further, and as she came broadside-on to wind and sea we were spilled like cattle down the sloping deck to fetch up half-lying along the port wall of the wheelhouse. 'Any chance,' I gasped, 'of getting the other engines going?' And Stratton looking at me, the sweat shining under the stubble of his beard: 'How can they possibly – do anything – down there?' I realized then what it must be like in the engine-room, cooped up with that mass of machinery, hot oil spilling and their cased-in world turning on its side. 'We're in God's hands now,' he breathed. And a moment later, as though God himself had heard and was denying us even that faint hope, I felt the beat of those two remaining engines stagger, felt it through my whole body as I lay against the sloped steel of the wall.

I have said that panic is a nerve storm, an instinctive, un-controllable reaction of the nervous system. I had experienced fear before, but not panic. Now, with the pulse of the engines dying, something quite uncontrollable leapt in my throat, my limbs seemed to dissolve and my whole body froze with apprehension. My mouth opened to scream a warning, but no sound came; and then, like a man fighting to stay sober after too much drink, I managed to get a grip of myself. It was a conscious effort of will and I had only just succeeded when the beat of the engines ceased altogether and I felt the ship dead under me. A glance at the radar showed the screen blank, half white, half black, as the sweep light continued to circle as if nothing had happened. We were heeled so far over that all the radar recorded was the sea below us, the sky above.

It was only the fact that we had such a weight of water on board that saved us. If the ship had been riding high, fully buoyant, she'd have turned right over. It was that and the terrific weight of the wind that held the seas flat.

The time was seven twenty-eight and Sgeir Mhor much less than a mile away now, the wind blowing us broadside towards it. Engines and steering gone. There was nothing we could do now and I watched as Stratton fought his way up the slope of the deck, struggling to reach the radio shack. In less than two minutes the operator was calling *Mayday*. But what the hell was the good of that? In those two minutes the velocity of the wind had blown us almost quarter of a mile. And it wasn't a case of the ship herself being blown – the whole surface of the sea was moving down-wind, scooped up and flung north-eastward by the pressure of the air.

Mayday, Mayday, Mayday.

I, too, had scrambled up the slope and into the alleyway. Through the open door of the radio shack I saw the operator clinging to his equipment, could hear him saying that word over and over again into the mike. And then he was in contact, reporting to the world at large that our engines had packed up and we were being driven down on to the southernmost tip of Laerg, on to the rocks of Sgeir Mhor.

The nearest ship was L4400, lying hove-to on the far side of Malesgair, a mere four miles away. But it might just as well have been four hundred miles. She didn't dare leave the shelter of those cliffs. In any case, she'd never have reached us in time. Nothing could reach us. It was pointless putting out a distress call. The ship lurched. I slipped from the supporting wall and was pitched into Stratton's cabin. I fetched up on the far side, half-sprawled across his bunk. A girl's face in a cheap frame hung on the wall at a crazy angle – dark hair and bare shoulders, calm eyes in a pretty face. She looked a million miles away. I don't know why, but I suddenly remembered Marjorie Field's eyes, blue and serious, the wide mouth smiling. And other girls in other lands . . . Would it have made any difference if there'd been only one? Did it make any difference to Stratton that he was married? When it comes to the point you're alone, aren't you, just yourself to make the passage across into the unknown?

It wasn't easy, sprawled on that bunk, to realize that in a few short minutes this cabin would be a shattered piece of wreckage tossed in the surf of breaking waves. I closed my eyes wearily. I could hear the wind and the sea, but the full blast of it was muffled, and I couldn't see it – that was the point. It made it difficult to visualize the end; flesh torn to pieces on the jagged rocks, the suffocation of drowning. And yet I knew that was the reality; disembowelment perhaps or going out quickly with the skull smashed to a pulp.

Hell! Lie here like a rat in a trap, that was no way to go. I forced myself to my feet, hauled my body up into the alley-way crowded now with men. They lay along the wall, big-chested with their life-jackets, their faces white. But no panic, just leaning there, waiting. It was all very ordinary, this moment of disaster. No orders, nobody screaming that they didn't want to die. And then it came to me that all these men saw were the steel walls of the ship. They were wrapped in ignorance. They hadn't seen the storm or the rocks. Exhausted, their senses dulled with sea-sickness, they waited for orders that would never come.

When we struck, the ship would roll over. That's what I figured, anyway. There was only one place to be then – out in the open. In the open there was just a chance. Wentworth had seen that, too. With two of the crew he was struggling to force the door to the deck open. I moved to help him, others with me, and under our combined efforts it fell back with a crash, and a blast of salt air, thick with spray, hit us. The Quartermaster was the first through. 'You next.' Wentworth pushed me through, calling to the men behind him.

Out on the side deck I saw at a glance that we were only just in time. Sgeir Mhor was very close now; grey heaps of rock with the sea slamming against them. Stratton was climbing out of the wheelhouse, the log book clutched in his hand. I shouted to him, and then I went down the ladder to the main deck, my body flattened against it by the wind. It was awkward going down that ladder, my body clumsy in the bulk of my life-jacket. I wondered when I'd put it on. I couldn't remember doing so. The Quartermaster followed me. 'Out to the bows,' he yelled in my ear, and hand over hand, clinging to the rail, we worked our way along the side of the ship. Clear of the bridge housing there would be nothing to fall on us. A big sea struck the ship and burst right over us. It tore one man from the rail and I saw him sail through the air as though he were a gull. And then we went on, working our way out above the tank deck. Only two men followed us. The rest clung in a huddle against the bridge.

Another sea and then another; two in quick succession and all the breath knocked out of me. I remember clinging there, gasping for air. I was about halfway along the ship. I can see her still, lying right over with water streaming from her decks, the sea roaring in the tilted tank hold and all her port side submerged. And broadside to her canted hull, Sgeir Mhor looming jagged and black and wet, an island of broken rock in a sea of foam with the waves breaking, curved green backs that smoked spray and crashed like gunfire exploding salt water fragments high into the air.

And then she struck. It was a light blow, a mere slap, but deep down she shuddered. Another wave lifted her. She tilted, port-side buried in foam, and Sgeir Mhor rushed towards us, lifted skywards, towering black.

I don't remember much after that – the detail is blurred in my mind. She hit with a bone-shaking impact, rolled and butted her mast against vertical rock. Like a lance it broke. Half the bridge housing was concertinaed, men flung to the waves. And then from where I clung I was looking down, not on water, but on bare rock – a spine running out like the back of a dinosaur. It split the ship across the middle; a hacksaw cutting metal couldn't have done it neater. A gap opened within feet of me, widening rapidly and separating us from all the after part of the ship. Rocks whirled by. White water opened up. For a moment we hung in the break of the waves, grating on half-submerged rocks. I thought that was the end, for the bows were smashing themselves to pieces, the steel plates beaten into fantastic shapes. But then the grating and the pounding ceased. We were clear – clear of the submerged rocks, clear of the tip of Sgeir Mhor. We were in open water, lying right over, half-submerged, but still afloat. Buoyed up by the air trapped behind the bulkheads in her sides, she was being driven across Shelter Bay, buried deep in a boiling scum of foam and spray. I didn't think of this as the end, not consciously. My brain, my body, the whole physical entity that was me, was too concentrated on the struggle to cling on. And yet something else that was also me seemed to detach itself from the rest, so that I have a picture that is still clear in my mind of my body, bulky in clothes and life-jacket, lying drowned in a turmoil of broken water, sprawled against the steel bulwarks, and of the front half of the shattered ship rolling like a log, with the sea pouring over it.

People came and went in my mind, faces I had known, the brief, ephemeral contacts of my life, giving me temporary companionship at the moment of death. And then we grounded in the shallows east of the camp, not far from the ruined Factor's House. But by then I was half-drowned, too dazed to care, mind and body beaten beyond desire for life. I just clung on to the bulwark because that was what I had been doing all the time. There was no instinct of self-preservation about it. My hands seemed locked on the cold, wet steel.

It was a long time before I realized that the wind had died away; probably because the seas, no longer flattered by its weight, were bigger then. The remains of the bows lay just where the waves were breaking. They beat upon the hollow bottom like giant fists hammering at a steel drum. Boom . . . Boom . . . Boom – and the roar of the surf. Fifty thousand express trains in the confines of a tunnel couldn't have made so great a noise.

And then that, too, began to lessen. My senses struggled back to life. The wind had gone round. That was my first conscious thought. And when I opened my eyes it was to a lurid sun glow, an orange, near-scarlet gash, like the raw slash of a wound, low down behind Sgeir Mhor. The toppling waves stood etched in chaos against it and all the cloud above me was a smoke-black pall of unbelievable density. There was no daylight on the shore of Shelter Bay, no real daylight; only darkness lit by that unearthly glow. The crofts of the Old Village, the roofless church, the cleits dotting the slopes of Tarsaval high above me – none of it was real. The light, the scene, the crazy, beat-up sea – it was all weird, a demon world.

So my mind saw it, and myself a sodden piece of flotsam washed up on that shore, too battered and exhausted to realize I was alive. That knowledge came with the sight of a fellow creature moving slowly like a spider, feeling his way down the jagged edges of what had been the tank deck.

I watched him fall into the backwash of a wave, beating at

the surf with his arms. I closed my eyes, and when I looked again, he was ashore, lying spread-eagled among the boulders.

That was when the instinct for self-preservation stirred in me at last.

I moved then, wearily, each movement a conscious effort, a desperate, aching struggle – down the jagged edges of deck plates twisted like tin-foil, down into the surf, falling into it as the other had done and fighting my way ashore, half-drowned, to lie panting and exhausted on the beach beside him.

It wasn't the Quartermaster; I don't know what had happened to him. This was a small man with a sandy moustache and tiny, frightened eyes that stared at me wildly. He'd broken his arm and every time he moved he screamed, a febrile rabbit sound that lost itself in the wind's howl. There was blood on his hair. Blood, too, on the stones where I lay, a thin bright trickle of my own blood, from a scalp wound.

'Shut up,' I said as he screamed again. 'You're alive. What more do you want?' I was thinking of all the others, the picture of the ship crushed against the rocks still vivid in my mind.

My watch had gone, torn from my wrist. How long had it been? I didn't know. Leaning up on one elbow I stared out across the bay. The orange glow had vanished and Sgeir Mhor was a shadowy outline, a grey blur masked by a rain squall. I forced myself to my feet and was immediately knocked down, beaten flat by a violent down-draught. That was when I realized the wind had gone right round. It was blowing from the other side of the island now, whipping across the Saddle between Malesgair and Tarsaval and down into Shelter Bay, cutting great swathes across it, the water boiling in its wake, a flattened, seething cauldron.

I made the grass above the beach, half crawling, and staggered past the Factor's House, up towards the Old Village and the camp. Daylight was a mockery, drab as a witch, and the wind screamed hell out of the confused masses of cloud that billowed above my head. And when I finally reached the camp I barely recognized it, the whole place laid waste and everything weighing less than a ton whirled inland and scattered across the slopes of Tarsaval. And down on the beach, the trailers we'd off-loaded in haste all gone, the trucks, too – only the bulldozer remained lying in the surf like a half-submerged rock. Wreckage was everywhere. The roof of one of the huts was gone, blown clean away, the walls sagging outwards, and where the latrines had been there was nothing but a row of closets standing bare like porcelain pots.

Pinney's hut was still intact. I turned the handle and the wind flung the door open with a crash, the walls shaking to the blast. It took the last of my strength to get it shut and in the relative peace of the hut's interior I collapsed on to the nearest bed.

How long I lay there I do not know. Time is relative, a mental calculation that measures activity. I was inactive then, my brain numbed, my mind hardly functioning. It might have been only a minute. It might have been an hour, two hours. I didn't sleep. I'm certain of that. I was conscious all the time of the shaking of the hut, of the battering, ceaseless noise of the wind; conscious, too, that there was something I had to do, some urgent intention that had forced me to struggle up from the beach. I dragged myself to my feet, staggering vaguely through the hut until I came to the radio, drawn to it by some action of my subconscious.

I realized then why I'd made the effort. The outside world. Somebody must be told. Help alerted. I slumped into the operator's chair, wondering whether there was any point, still that picture in my mind of the bridge crushed against sheer rock and the waves pounding. Could any of the crew have survived, any of those men huddled like sheep awaiting slaughter in the narrow alleyway out of which I'd clawed my way? But the wind had changed and they'd be under the lee. There was just that chance and I reached out my hand, switching on the set. I didn't touch the tuning. I just sat there waiting for the hum that would tell me the set had warmed up. But nothing happened. It was dead and it took time for my brain to work that out – the generator silent and no current coming through. There were emergency batteries below the table and by following the cables back I was able to cut them in.

The set came alive then and a voice answered almost immediately. It was thin and faint. *'We've been calling and calling. If you're still on Laerg why didn't you answer before?'* He didn't give me a chance to explain. *'I've got Glasgow on the line for you. They've found Mrs McGregor. Hold on.'* There was a click and then silence, and I sat there, helpless, the salt taste of sea water in my mouth. Fifty men battered to pieces on the rocks of Sgeir Mhor and they had to fling Mrs McGregor at me. Why couldn't they have waited for me to tell them what had happened? *'You're through.'* The police first, and then a woman's voice, soft and very Scots, asking for news of her son. I felt almost sick, remembering what had happened, the tiller flat flooded and the poor devil's body tombed up there. *'I'm sorry, Mrs McGregor. I can't tell you anything yet.'* And I cut her off, overcome by nausea, the sweat breaking out all over me and my head reeling.

When I got them again, my brother was there. Recognizing his voice I felt a flood of instant relief. 'Iain. Iain, thank God!' I was back on Ardnamurchan, crying to my elder brother for help – a rock to cling to in moments of desperation.

But this was no rock. This was a man as sick and frightened as myself. '*Major Braddock here.*' His voice, strained and uneasy, had the snap of panic in it. 'Iain,' I cried again. 'For God's sake. It's Donald.' But the appeal was wasted and his voice when it came was harsh and grating. '*Braddock here. Who's that? What's happened?*'

The time was then 0835 and Braddock had been almost six hours in the Movements Office, waiting for news. God knows what he must have been feeling. Flint said he'd paced up and down, hour after hour, grey-faced and silent, whilst the periodic reports came through from our own radio operator and from the man on L4400. Up to the moment when disaster overtook us Movements had a fairly clear picture of what was happening. And then suddenly that Mayday call, and after that silence. 'Get them,' Braddock had shouted at the Signals operator. 'Christ, man! Get them again.' But all the operator could get was L4400 announcing flatly that they were in the storm centre steaming for the shelter of the other side of the island.

'It's Eight-six-one-o I want,' Braddock had almost screamed. 'Get them, man. Keep on trying.'

He'd had far too little sleep that night and the interview he'd had with Standing at two-thirty in the morning cannot have been a pleasant one. Standing had been roused from his bed by a duty driver at twelve-forty, and Ferguson described him as literally shaking with rage when he realized what Braddock had done. The first thing he did was to speak to Stratton on the R/T and then he walked across to the quarters and saw Cliff Morgan. 'White-faced he was, man,' was the way Cliff put it. 'Calling me all sorts of names for interfering. But when I'd explained the situation, he calmed down a bit. He even thanked me. And then he went out, saying it was all Braddock's fault and if anything went wrong he'd get the bloody man slung out of the Service.'

Standing had gone straight to his office and sent for Braddock. There was nobody else present at that meeting so that there is no record of what passed between them. But immediately afterwards Braddock had teleprinted the BGS direct, giving his reasons for ordering an immediate evacuation on his own responsibility. And after that he'd remained in the Movements Office, waiting for news; and when our Mayday call went out, it was he, not Standing, who had alerted Scottish Command and set the whole emergency machinery in motion. At half past eight he'd walked over to the Met. Office. He was with Cliff Morgan for about ten minutes and it was during those ten minutes that I called Base. A relief operator had just taken over, which was why I was given the Glasgow call instead of being put straight through either to Braddock at the Met. Office or Standing, who was waiting alone in his office.

Probably if I'd got Standing his reaction would have been as slow as my brother's, for neither of them could have any idea of the appalling ferocity of that storm or the magnitude of the disaster. He didn't seem able to understand at first. '*You and one other chap . . . Is that all? Are you certain?*'

I wasn't certain of anything except the memory of the ship on her beam ends and the waves driving her against the rocks. 'If you'd seen the seas . . . It was Sgeir Mhor she hit.'

'*Jesus Christ, Donald!*' It was the first time he'd used my name and it made a deep impression. '*Jesus Christ! There must be others. There've got to be others.*'

But I didn't think there could be then. 'I've told you, the whole bridge deck was concertinaed in a matter of seconds. They can't possibly . . .'

'*Well, have a look. Go and find out.*'

'The wind,' I said wearily. 'Don't you realize? You can't stand.'

'*Then crawl, laddie – crawl. I must know. I must be certain. Surely to God it can't be as bad as you say.*' He was almost screaming at me. And then his voice dropped abruptly to a wheedling tone. '*For my sake, laddie – please. Find out whether there are any other survivors.*'

His voice. It was so strange – it was Iain's voice now, my own brother's, and the accent Scots. The years fell away . . . 'All right, Iain. I'll try.' It was Mavis all over again – Mavis and all the other times. 'I'll try,' I said again and switched the set off, going down the hut and out into a blast that whipped the door from my hand and knocked me to the ground.

I met the other fellow coming up from the beach, crawling on his hands and knees and crying with the pain of his broken arm. He called to me, but I heard no sound, only his mouth wide open and his good arm pointing seaward. But there was nothing there, nothing but the seething waters of the bay churned by the wind; all the rest was blotted out by rain and Sgeir Mhor a vague blur. 'What is it?' I yelled in his ear and I almost fell on top of him as the wind came down, a solid, breath-taking wall of air.

'The rocks, sir. Sgeir Mhor. I thought I saw . . .' I lost the rest. It was almost dark, a grey gloom with the clouds racing, and so low I could almost have reached up and touched them.

'Saw what?' I shouted. 'What did you think you saw?'

'It was clear for a moment, and there were figures – men. I could have sworn . . .' But he wasn't certain. You couldn't be certain of anything in those conditions. And your eyes played tricks.

I lay there beside him till the rain squall passed. But even then I couldn't see what he still swore he'd seen. Cloud, forced low by the down-draughts, obscured all the upper half of Sgeir Mhor. There was only one thing to do. I told him to go to the hut, and then I started out along the beach road alone. But it was impossible. The weight of the wind was too great. It caught me as I was crossing the Bailey bridge that spanned the burn and it threw me against the girders as though I were a piece of paper. The sheer weight of it was fantastic. If it hadn't been for the girders I think I should have been whirled into the air and flung into the bay. I turned back then, and when I reached the hut I collapsed on Pinney's bed and immediately lost consciousness.

How long I was out I don't know. My whole body ached and there was a pain in my side. The cut in my head had opened again and the pillow was dark with blood. Lying there with my eyes open, slowly struggling back to life, I found myself staring at Pinney's locker. Either my eyes didn't focus immediately or else it took a long time for me to realize that a pair of binoculars might save me the long walk out to Keava and up its steep grass slopes. There they were, lying on a shelf, tucked in between some books and an old khaki jersey. It was much lighter in the hut; quite bright, in fact. And the noise of the wind was less.

I picked up the binoculars and staggered stiffly to the door. And when I opened it I was looking out on to a changed world. The clouds, torn to shreds by the wind, were ragged now. And they had lifted so that all the great spine of Keava was visible and I could see the sheer gap that separated it from Sgeir Mhor, could see all the rocks and caves and patches of grass on Sgeir Mhor itself. The air was clear, washed clean by the rain. Only Tarsaval and the very top of Creag Dubh remained shrouded in gloom, the clouds clinging to their drenched slopes, billowing and swirling among the crags. Seaward, shafts of brighter light showed white water tossed in frightful confusion. I slipped into the lee of the hut and with my back braced against its sodden wall, I focused the glasses on Sgeir Mhor.

Seen suddenly at close vision, isolated like that from the rest of the island, it looked like some massive medieval fortress. All it lacked was a drawbridge spanning the narrow gut that separated it from the Butt of Keava. With the change of wind, the seas no longer exploded against it in plumes of white, but the foam of the waves that had wrecked us lay in banks like snow over all the piled-up battlements of rock. In that clean air I could see every detail and nothing moved. The place was dead; just a great heap of rock and not a living thing. How could there be? Like the cliffs of Keava, it had taken the full brunt of the storm.

I lowered the glasses. Just the two of us. All the rest dead; gone, buried, drowned under masses of water, battered to pulp, their bodies food for the fish, for the lobsters and crabs that scuttled in the holes and crevices of submarine rock terraces. Stratton, Wentworth, Pinney – all the faces I had known so very briefly on board that ship.

Can you will people alive? Was I God-given that I could stand there and pray so desperately, and then on the instant conjure movement? It seemed like that, for I looked again, hoping against hope, and there in the twin circles of magnification something stirred, a man stood for a moment etched against the luminosity of clouds thinning. Or was it my imagination? Flesh and blood amongst that waste of rock. It seemed impossible, and yet one knows the extraordinary indestructibility of the human body. Countless instances leapt to my mind – things I had read about, things I had been told, things I had actually seen during the war; all things that had really happened, and not so much the indestructibility of the human body as the unwillingness, almost the inability of the human spirit to accept defeat. And here, now, I was gazing at the impossible, and it was no figment of the imagination. This, too, was real; there was a man, off the sky-line now and crawling down the rocks, trying to reach sea level, and another following close behind him.

How many were still alive I didn't know. I didn't care. It was enough that there were survivors on Sgeir Mhor, and I rushed back into the hut and switched on the radio. Base answered my call immediately. 'Hold on.' And then a voice, not my brother's this time, asking urgently for news.

It was Colonel Standing, and when I told him I'd seen two

figures moving on Sgeir Mhor, he said '*Thank God!*' in a voice that was like a beaten man grasping at the faint hope of recovery. '*If there are two, there may be more.*' He wanted me to find out. But two or twenty – what difference did it make? The problem of rescuing them remained the same. Could I launch a boat? That was his first suggestion and I found myself laughing inanely. I was tired. God! I was tired. And he didn't understand. He'd no idea of the weight of wind that had hit the island. 'There are no boats,' I told him. 'And if there were, there's only myself and a chap with a broken arm.' It was like talking to a child. I found I had to explain in simple terms what the storm had been like – all the trailers gone and a heavy thing like the bull-dozer sucked into the sea, the camp a wreck and everything movable shattered or whirled away, the slopes of Tarsaval littered with the Army's debris. I described it all to him – the fight seaward, the engines packing up, the way she'd struck Sgeir Mhor and how the bows had stayed afloat and been driven ashore in Shelter Bay. I talked until my voice was hoarse, my mind too tired to think. Finally, I said, 'What we need is men and equipment – a boat with an out-board motor or rocket rescue apparatus to bridge the gut between Keava and Sgeir Mhor. Where's the other LCT? She could come into the bay now the wind is northerly again.'

But L4400 was twenty miles south-west of Laerg, running before a huge sea, her bridge deck stove in and her plates strained, a wreck of a boat that might or might not get back to port. Weather Ship *India* had left her station and was steaming to intercept her. The nearest ship was the Naval tug, but still twenty-four hours away in these conditions. Something my grandfather had told us came sluggishly to the surface of my mind, something about landing on Sgeir Mhor, the sheerness of the rocks. 'I don't think a boat would help,' I said. 'The only landing place on Sgeir Mhor is on the seaward side. And that's not possible except in flat calm weather.'

It took time for that to sink in. He didn't want to believe it. How did I know? Was I absolutely certain? Surely there must be rock ledges up which a skilful climber . . .'Check with my . . . with Major Braddock,' I said. 'Check with him.' This man arguing, questioning. I wished to God he'd get off the line and give me Iain again. Iain would understand. 'I'd like to have a word with Major Braddock.'

'*I'm handling this.*' The voice was curt. '*Major Braddock's caused enough trouble already.*'

'I'd still like to speak to him.'

'*Well, you can't.*'

'Why not?'

A pause. And then: '*Major Braddock is under arrest.*'

God knows what I said then. I think I cursed – but whether I cursed Standing or the circumstances, I don't know. The futility of it! The one man who could help, who had a grasp of the problem, and this stupid fool had had him arrested. 'For God's sake,' I pleaded. 'Give me Braddock. He'll know what to do.' And sharp and high-pitched over the air came his reply – unbelievable in the circumstances. '*You seem to forget, Mr Ross, that I'm the commanding officer here, and I'm perfectly capable of handling the situation.*'

'Then handle it,' I shouted at him, 'and get those men off Sgeir Mhor.' And I switched off, realizing that I was too tired now to control my temper. I just sat there then, thinking of Iain. Poor devil! It was bad enough – the loss of life, the shipwreck, but to be under arrest, sitting inactive with no part in the rescue, with nothing to do but mull over in his mind what had happened. Didn't Standing realize? Or was he a sadist? Whichever it was, the effect on Iain would be the same. The bloody, sodding swine, I thought. The cruel, stupid bastard.

'Mr Ross! Mr Ross, sir – you're talking to yourself.'

I opened my eyes, conscious of a hand shaking my shoulder. The fellow with the broken arm was standing there, staring at me with a worried frown. He no longer looked frightened. He even had a certain stature standing there proffering me a steaming mug. 'It's only Bovril,' he said. 'But I fort some'ing 'ot after our bathe . . .' He was Cockney. False teeth smiled at me out of a funny little screwed-up face. 'When you drunk it, you better change them clothes. Catch yer deaf if yer don't. Borrow off of Captain Pinney; 'e won't mind.' This little runt of a man trying to mother me and his broken arm still hanging limp. My heart warmed to him. The lights were on and a new sound – the hum of the generator audible between the gusts.

'You've got the lights going.'

He nodded. ''Ad ter – all electric 'ere, yer see. Wiv'at the generator yer can't cook. I got some bangers on and there's bacon and eggs and fried bread. That do yer?' I asked him his name then and he said, 'Alf Cooper. Come from Lunnon.' He grinned. 'Flippin' long way from Bow Bells, ain't I? Fort I 'eard 'em once or twice when we was in the flaming water, an' they weren't playin' 'ymn toons neither.'

As soon as we'd had our meal I set his arm as best I could,

and after that I showed him how to work the radio. I felt stronger now and perhaps because of that the wind seemed less appalling as I tried again to get a closer look at Sgeir Mhor. This time I was able to cross the bridge, but in the flat grassland below the old lazy beds the wind caught me and pinned me down. A bird went screaming close over my head. I crawled to the shelter of a cleit and with my back to the ruins of its dry-stone wall, I focused the glasses on Sgeir Mhor.

Visibility was better now. I could see the rocks falling sheer to the turbulence of the sea, the cracks and gullies, and a figure moving like a seal high up on a bare ledge. There were others crouched there, sheltering from the swell that still beat against the further side, covering the whole mass with spray. I counted five men lying tucked into crevices, the way sheep huddle for protection against the elements.

Five men. Perhaps there were more. I couldn't see. Just five inert bodies and only one of them showing any signs of life, and now he lay still. I started back then, keeping to the edge of the beach which rose steeply and gave me a little shelter. The burn forced me up on to the bridge and as I entered the camp a blast hit me, flung me down, and a piece of corrugated iron went scything through the air just above my head to hit the sea and go skimming across its flattened surface.

Back in the hut I called Base and was immediately put through to Colonel Standing.

4

RESCUE
(22–23 October)

Long before my first contact with Base, before even our Mayday call had gone out, all Services had been alerted and the first moves made to deal with the emergency. Coastal Command at Ballykelly had flown off a Shackleton to search for the *Viking Fisher*; the Navy had dispatched a destroyer from the Gareloch. Weather ship *India* had left her station headed for Laerg, a fishery protection vessel north-west of the Orkneys had been ordered to make for the Hebrides at full speed and a fast mine-layer was getting steam up ready to sail if required. By nine o'clock the emergency operation was being concentrated on L4400, then a battered wreck running before the storm somewhere to the west of Laerg. The destroyer was ordered to close her with all possible speed and either stand by her to take off survivors or to escort her to Leverburgh or back to the Clyde if she could make it. A second Shackleton had taken off from the Coastal Command base in Northern Ireland with orders to locate her and circle her until the destroyer arrived or until relieved by another aircraft.

That was the situation when I contacted Base with definite news of survivors from the wreck of L8610. Neither the Shackletons nor the destroyer could be of any help to the men on Sgeir Mhor. Both the fishery protection vessel and the mine-layer were too far away to be effective and conditions made the use of Northern Air Sea Rescue's helicopters out of the question. The task was allocated to the Naval tug. Not only was she a more suitable vessel than a destroyer for working close inshore among rocks, she also happened to be much nearer. She sailed from Lochmaddy at 0917 hours.

In these conditions and in these northern waters the Army was largely dependent on the other Services, and their resources were limited. Standing had to make use of what was available and in the circumstances improvisation was probably justified. When I spoke to him I think his mind was already made up. It's easy to be wise after the event and say that it was a panic decision, but considered from his point of view, he hadn't all that much choice. The tug couldn't possibly reach Laerg before nightfall. In those seas, even allowing for the fact that such a violent storm was bound to die down quickly, it would be good going if she were in Shelter Bay by dawn, and the forecast for dawn next day was not good. The depression, which had been stationary to the west of Ireland, was on the move again and expected to reach the Hebrides within twenty-four hours. Instead of a polar air stream there would then be southerly winds force 6, veering later southwest and increasing to force 7, possibly gale force 8. He had checked with Ferguson and with Field, both officers who knew Laerg well and who had climbed over Sgeir Mhor. They confirmed what I had told him, that the rocks were sheer on the side facing Shelter Bay and that the only possible landing place was on the seaward side. And since that was the side exposed to winds between south and west it was obvious that the forecast not only made it extremely unlikely that any landing could be attempted the following day, but also that there was a grave danger of the survivors being overwhelmed by the force of the waves.

That there were any survivors at all was obviously due to the change of wind direction that had occurred almost immediately after the ship had struck, and by dawn they might all be dead of exposure.

Time was, therefore, the vital factor. Moreover, both Ferguson and Field agreed that the only practical way of getting them off was to fire a line to them from the Butt of Keava and bring them over the gut by breeches buoy. That meant a rocket life-saving apparatus. The only equipment of this sort possessed by Guided Weapons had been allocated to the Laerg detachment and nobody was certain whether it had been shipped out or not. Rafferty thought not, but the Movements Officer disagreed and a squad was dispatched to search the stores heaped behind the quay at Leverburgh. Meantime, Adams had been called in. The wind at Northton was around 35 knots, gusting 40 plus. He refused point blank to fly his helicopter anywhere near Laerg. He had come to Standing's office direct from the Met. Office. He was well aware of the urgency of the situation. He also knew that the turbulence of the air around Laerg made it quite impossible for him to make a landing there.

Time was wasted contacting the two main lifeboat stations. They were standing by, but though they had breeches buoy equipment available, they were even less well placed than the tug for getting it there. There was only one answer, then, to parachute the life-saving gear in. But no Shackleton would dare fly low over the island and a high-level drop would almost certainly result in the parachutes being blown out to sea.

It was Adams who suggested a possible solution. A small aircraft owned by one of the charter companies was waiting at Stornoway for weather clearance back to the mainland. He thought the pilot, a Canadian named Rocky Fellowes who'd done a lot of bush flying in the North West Territories, might have a shot at it. And at Stornoway there was the life-saving gear they needed.

It was than that Ferguson volunteered; if the first drop were successful and the gear landed in a place that was accessible, then he'd make the jump and organize the setting up of the breeches buoy. It faced Standing with a difficult choice. He had now received my second call. He knew there were at least five men marooned on Sgeir Mhor and only seven hours of daylight left. The risk of one man's life against the almost certain death of five; rightly or wrongly, he accepted Ferguson's offer. It was then eleven forty-five. Ten minutes later Ferguson was on his way. Field went with him: also a sergeant and two men, all of whom had completed a parachute course. And while the staff car started its forty-mile dash to Stornoway, Standing got through to the airport and asked them to find Fellowes and have him ring Northton immediately. He also asked them to arrange for the life-saving apparatus to be brought to the airfield and the parachutes to be got ready. Meantime, the tug was ordered to put in to Leverburgh in the hopes that the Army's life-saving gear would be located.

This was the situation when I made my next contact with Base. I had found an alarm clock in the remains of the cookhouse and the time by this was 1253. Standing was then able to tell me that Fellowes had agreed to attempt the drop. The wind speed at Stornoway was slightly less than the reading shown by Cliff Morgan's anemometer. It was beginning to fall off and he was optimistic. I suppose I should have warned Standing. The wind speed had fallen at Laerg, too. But there is a difference between a drop from around 50 knots and a drop from the fantastic wind speeds we had been experiencing. It was still coming down off the Saddle in gusts of considerable force. Whether it would have made any difference if I had warned him, I don't know. Probably not. Nobody sitting in his office almost a hundred miles away could possibly have any idea of the battering Laerg had received and was still receiving. In any case, I was thinking of those men out on Sgeir Mhor. If the pilot was willing to try it, then it wasn't for me to discourage him. The ETA Standing gave me for the plane's arrival was 1415 approximate. In an hour's time the wind might have dropped right away. I had known it happen with storms of this intensity. And if it did, then the whole situation would be changed, and a plane overhead could make the difference between life and death to the survivors. It was up to the pilot anyway.

Standing was still talking to me, explaining about the tug and that Adams was standing by in the hope that conditions might improve sufficiently for him to fly the helicopter. Suddenly he stopped in mid-sentence and I heard him say, '*Just a minute.*' And then another voice – a voice I recognized, much fainter, but still quite audible: '*Please. I must see you. You can't do it. If you make Mike jump . . .*'

'*I'm not making him. He volunteered.*'

'*Then stop him. You've got to stop him. He'll kill himself. It's murder expecting him to jump in this wind, just to prove he can do it.'*

'For God's sake, Marjorie. Pull yourself together. He's not trying to prove anything.'

'Of course he is. You're taking advantage of him.' She was beside herself, her voice shaken with the violence of her emotions. *'It isn't fair. He'll be killed and . . .'*

I heard the clatter of the phone as he dropped it and his voice was suddenly further away: *'Look, my dear. Try to understand. This isn't just a question of Mike Ferguson. There are survivors out there and the one chance of getting them off . . .'*

'I don't care. I'm thinking of Mike.'

'Your father's with him. He'll see he doesn't do anything rash.'

But she didn't accept that. *'Daddy and Mike – they're both made the same way. You know that. They've both . . .* She hesitated, adding, *'He'll jump whatever the conditions.'* And then on a different note: *'Is it true Mr Ross is one of the survivors? Major Rafferty said something about . . .'*

'I'm just speaking to him now.' And then I heard him say, *'Marjorie!'* his voice sharp and angry. She must have grabbed hold of the phone for her voice was suddenly clear and very close to me, trembling uncontrollably so that I caught her mood, the desperate urgency of her fear. She might have been there in the hut with me. *'Mr Ross. Help me – please. Mike mustn't jump. Do you hear? You've radio. You can contact the plane.'* And then, almost with a sob: *'No, let me finish.'* But he'd got the phone away from her. *'Ross? I'll call you back at fourteen hundred hours.'* There was a click, and after that silence.

Fellowes took off from Stornoway at 1340 hours. Conditions had improved slightly with the wind easterly about 30 knots. The overcast, however, had come down again and there were rain squalls. They were in cloud before they'd reached 1000 feet and they had to climb to more than 6000 before they were above it. Field was in the co-pilot's seat; Ferguson, the sergeant and the two men back in the fuselage. The plane was an old Consul, the metal of the wings burnished bright by hail and rain, by subjection over many years to the abrasive forces of the elements. They flew for almost forty minutes in watery sunlight across a flat cotton-wool plain of cloud. Airspeed 120, the altimeter steady at 6.5 and towards the end, the pilot searching for an orographical cloud, a bulge in the overcast that would pin-point the position of Laerg. But there was no orographical cloud and at 1420 they started down through the overcast.

Fellowes' dead reckoning was based on course and speed. He had corrected for drift, but he had no means of telling whether the wind had remained constant and he was doing his sums the way the early fliers did them, his navigational aids on his knee. And all the time he was having to fly his plane in strong winds. He had spoken to me on the radio. But I couldn't even make a guess at the wind speed, for it was broken by Tarsaval and Malesgair and came down from the direction of the Saddle in violent eddies. All I could tell him was that the ceiling was under a thousand. Creag Dubh was just over the thousand and Creag Dubh was blanketed.

Coming down like that through thick cloud couldn't have been very pleasant. Field told me later that he didn't dare look at the altimeter after it had unwound to two thousand. He would like to have been able to shut his eyes, but he couldn't; they remained fixed on the grey void ahead, his body tense and strained forward against the safety belt. The engines made hardly a sound, just a gentle whispering, the wing-tips fluttering in moments of turbulence. Fellowes, too, was strained forward, eyes peering through the windshield. They were both of them waiting for that sudden darkening in the opaque film ahead that would mean hard rock and the end. Theoretically, Fellowes had overshot by five miles and was coming down over empty, unobstructed sea. But he couldn't be certain. Tarsaval was 1456 feet high.

Five minutes – one of the longest five minutes of his life, Field said. Finally, he tore his eyes away from the empty windshield and glanced at the altimeter. Eight hundred feet. The cloud darkened imperceptibly. His eyes, with nothing substantial to focus on, were playing tricks. He was on the high slopes of a great mountain again, the cloud swirling about him. And then suddenly there was a pattern – streaks of black and white, long foaming lines coming up towards them. The sea, and the long march of the waves had their tops torn from them by the wind.

The aircraft banked sharply, the wing-tip seeming almost to touch the crest of a roller that reared up, curling and then breaking in a great surge of thrusting water. They straightened out, skimming the surface, the black curtain of a rain squall ahead. Bank again to skirt it and then momentarily blinded as water beat against the windshield, driven by the force of the wind into long rivulets that were never still. And on the other side of the squall a dark wall coming to meet them, towering cliffs of black rock sliding back from the starboard wing, the glimpse of two stacs, their tops hidden in cloud. Fladday. Course 280° then and

Shelter Bay opening out ahead. Fellowes came right into it, flying at just over 500 feet, and when he turned the wind caught him and flung him like a wounded gull across the top of Sgeir Mhor.

They saw nothing that first run, but when he came in again, slower this time on a course of 020° headed straight into the wind, Field could see men standing amongst the rocks, waving to them. Through his glasses he counted eleven, and when they came in again, slightly lower this time, skimming the tops of the rocks, he made it fourteen. They stood off then, circling the open sea beyond the two arms of the bay whilst Fellowes reported to Base by radio.

Fourteen men still alive. Standing had no choice then. Nor had Ferguson. Nor had Fellowes. He yelled for the men back in the fuselage to get ready and headed back into Shelter Bay. The fuselage door was held open against the slip-stream, the two packages poised in the cold blast of the opening. Fellowes raised his hand. 'Let go.' They were flung out. The fuselage door slammed shut. The aircraft banked.

I had left the radio then and was standing in the lee of the hut. I saw the two packages fall – two black dots like bombs dropping from the side of the plane. Twin white canopies blossoming and the plane blown like a leaf towards Sgeir Mhor, losing height, its wings dipping like a bird in flight. It cleared the rocks and vanished into rain. The parachutes moved across the sky above my head, growing larger, but drifting very fast. And then first one and then the other were caught by down-draughts, the nylon canopies half-collapsed. They came down with a rush and then, just before they hit the beach, they each filled with a snap I could almost hear, were whirled upwards and then landed gently, almost gracefully, halfway up the slopes of Keava.

I saw what happened to them, but Fellowes didn't. He was too busy fighting his plane clear of Sgeir Mhor. And Field had his eyes on the rocks, not on the parachutes. All they saw when they came out of the rain squall and circled the bay were two parachutes lying side-by-side like two white mushrooms close under the first scree slope of Keava. They didn't realize it was luck not judgement that had put them there. Field signalled back to Mike Ferguson, both thumbs up, and Fellowes took the plane in again. The drill was the same. The two men held the fuselage door open. The sergeant acted as dispatcher. But this time he was dispatching a man, not two inanimate packages. Again Fellowes judged his moment, raised his hand and shouted, 'Jump!'

Whether Fellowes misjudged or whether Mike Ferguson hesitated, as the sergeant said he did, nobody will ever know. Field's impression was that he jumped immediately. But in moments like this fractions of a second count and a pilot, tensed and in control of his machine, possesses a sensitivity and a speed of reaction that is much faster than that of the ordinary man. Fellowes thought it was a long time before the sergeant called out that Ferguson was away. In view of his parachute course record it seems more than likely that Ferguson did, in fact, hesitate. If he did, it was a fatal hesitation. He may have felt in those last few moments of the run-in that he was jumping to his death. The sergeant reported that his face was very white, his lips trembling as he moved to the door. But then again, in view of his previous experience, some nervous reaction was inevitable.

In a tragedy of this sort it is pointless to try and apportion the blame. Each man is doing his best according to his lights and in any case it was the wind that was the vital factor. My back was against the hut and at the moment the plane banked and that tiny bundle of human flesh launched itself from the fuselage I felt the whole structure tremble under the onslaught of the wind. It wasn't just a gust. It came in a steady roar and it kept on blowing. I saw the parachute open, his fall suddenly checked. He was then at about 500 feet and right over my head; the plane, still banking, was being flung sideways across Sgeir Mhor.

If the wind had been a down-draught it might have collapsed his parachute momentarily. That was what had happened to the two previous parachutes. He might have landed heavily and been injured, but he would still have been alive. But it was a steady wind. It kept his parachute full. I saw him fighting the nylon cords to partially collapse it, but it was like a balloon, full to bursting and driving towards Keava at a great rate, trailing him behind it. For a moment it looked as though he would be all right. The sloped rock spine of Keava was a good 700 feet high at the point he was headed for, but as he neared it the steep slope facing Shelter Bay produced an up-draught. The parachute lifted, soaring towards the clouds. He cleared the top by several hundred feet. For a moment he was lost to sight, swallowed by the overcast. Then I saw him again, the parachute half-collapsed and falling rapidly. It was a glimpse, no more, for in the instant he was lost behind Keava.

Beyond the ridge was sheer cliff, and beyond the cliff nothing but the Atlantic and the gale-torn waves. It was all so remote that it seemed scarcely real; only imagination could associate that brief glimpse of white nylon disappearing with a man dead, drowned in a wet, suffocating world of tumbling water.

The plane stood off, circling by the entrance to the bay. It didn't come in again and nobody else jumped. I went slowly back into the hut and picked up Standing's voice on the radio. It was so shaken that I barely recognized it. He was ordering the pilot to return to Stornoway.

I was glad of that – glad that nobody else was going to be ordered to jump, glad that I didn't have to stand again outside the hut and watch another parachute blown out into the Atlantic. I found I was trembling, still with that picture in my mind of a man dangling and the white envelope coming out of the clouds, half-collapsed, and the poor fellow falling to a cold death in the Atlantic. I had liked Mike Ferguson. He'd a lot of guts to face that jump. And then I was thinking of Marjorie Field and of that interview she'd had with Colonel Standing when I had been an involuntary eavesdropper. Somebody would have to tell her and I was glad I wasn't her father. The dead have their moment of struggle, that brief moment of shock which is worse than birth because the ties with this world are stronger. But for the living, the pain does not cease with death. It remains till memory is dulled and the face that cased the loved one's personality has faded.

I was still thinking of Marjorie when Standing called me, demanding estimates of wind speed, force of down-draughts, height of ceiling. I went to the door of the hut. The wind's roar had momentarily died away. Nothing stronger now than 40 knots, I thought. My eyes went involuntarily to the sloping back of Keava. If only Mike had waited. He would have had a chance now. But it was done. He'd jumped and he was gone. The sky to the south, by the bay entrance, was empty, the plane gone.

I went back and reported to Standing. He asked particularly about down-draughts and I told him they were intermittent, that at the moment they had lost much of their force. There was a long pause and then he said they'd try and make a helicopter landing. I didn't attempt to discourage him. Those men were still on Sgeir Mhor and I was tired. Anyway, it was quieter now. How long it would last I didn't know. I just wished to God they'd flown the helicopter instead of trying to parachute men in. I wondered whether it was really Adams who had refused to fly or whether Standing's cold mathematical mind had been influenced by the high cost of these machines. That was a thought that made me angry. When you consider how the Services waste the taxpayers' money, millions stupidly spent, and here perhaps a decent man had been sent to his death for fear of risking a few thousands. 'About bloody time,' I said angrily. 'If you'd used the helicopter in the first place . . .'

I let it go at that. The poor bastard! It wasn't his fault. Decisions have to be made by the men in command and sometimes, inevitably, they're the wrong decisions. It was something that he'd tried to get help to the survivors before nightfall. I wondered what my brother would have done. With all his faults, Iain was a man of action. His behaviour in an emergency was instinctive. 'A pity you didn't leave it to Major Braddock.' I'd said it before I could stop myself. I heard his quick intake of breath. And then, in a stiff, cold voice, he said, '*We'll be with you in under the hour.*'

We! I remember thinking about that, sitting there, dazed with fatigue. Was Standing coming himself? But it didn't seem to matter – not then. The life-saving gear was up there on the slopes of Keava and all we needed were the men to collect it and set it up. Men who were fresh and full of energy. I was tired. Too tired to move, my aching body barely reacting to the orders of my brain. Nerves, muscles, every part of my anatomy cried out for rest.

I woke Cooper, told him to keep radio watch and wake me in forty minutes' time. Then I fell on to Pinney's bed, not bothering to undress, and was instantly asleep.

'Mr Ross. Wake up.' The voice went on and on, a hand shaking my shoulder. I blinked my eyes and sat up. 'Gawd Almighty! Yer didn't 'alf give me a turn. Thought you'd croaked. Honest I did.' Cooper bending over me, staring at me anxiously. 'You orl right, sir?' And then he said, 'They're on the air now. Want ter know what conditions are like. I told 'em: still blowing like 'ell, but it's clearer – only the top of Tarsaval's got cla'd on it now.'

I got up and went to the radio. The time was twelve minutes to four. Adams' voice came faint and crackling. He wanted an estimate of the wind speed, its direction, the strength of the downdraughts. I went to the door of the hut. It was certainly much clearer now; quite bright, in fact. The overcast was breaking up, torn rags of clouds hurrying across a cold blue sky and the broken water seaward shining white in patches of slanting sunlight. Keava and Malesgair, the two arms that enclosed Shelter Bay, were clear of cloud. So was Creag Dubh. For the first time I could see the Lookout where the tracking station radar had been housed. Only the summit of Tarsaval was still obscured, a giant wearing a cloth cap made shapeless by the wind. It was blowing harder, I thought, and the down-draughts were irregular. Sometimes there was a long interval in which the wind just blew. Then suddenly it would wham down off the heights, two or three gusts in quick succession.

I went back to the radio and reported to Adams. He said he could see Laerg quite plainly and estimated that he had about seven miles to go. '*I'll come in from the south at about four hundred,*' he said. '*You know where the landing ground is – down by the Factor's House. I'll watch for you there. I'm relying on you to signal me in. I'll need about sixty seconds clear of down-draughts. Okay?*' I don't think he heard my protest. At any rate, he didn't answer, and I went out, cursing him for trying to put the onus on me. Did he think I could control the down-draughts? There was no pattern about them. They came and went; one minute I was walking quite easily, the next I was knocked flat and all the breath pushed back into my throat. Damn the man! If I signalled him in it would be my responsibility if anything went wrong.

But there wasn't time to consider that. I'd barely reached the beach when I saw the helicopter, a speck low down over the water beyond the entrance to the bay. It came in fast and by the time I'd reached the Factor's House I could hear its engine, a buzz-saw drone above the suck and seethe of the surf. A down-draught hit, beating the grasses flat and whistling out over the bay, the surface boiling as though a million small fry were skittering there. It was gone almost as soon as it had come. Another and another hit the ground, flattening the long brown wisps of grass, whirling the dried seaweed into the air. They came like sand devils, spiralling down. The helicopter, caught in one, slammed down almost to sea level and then rocketed up. It was very close now and growing bigger every minute, the sound of its engine filling the air. In the sudden stillness that followed that last gust I thought I could hear the swish of its rotor blades.

No point in waiting, for every second he hovered there he was in mortal danger. I waved him in, praying to God that he'd plonk himself down in one quick rush before the next blast struck. But he didn't. He was a cautious man, which is a fine thing in a pilot; except that this was no moment for caution. He came in slowly, feeling his way, and the next gust caught him when he was still a hundred feet up. It came slam like the punch of a fist. The helicopter, flung sideways and downwards, hit the beach; the floats crumpled and at the same instant, with the rotor blades still turning, the whole machine was heaved up and flung seaward. It touched the water, tipped, foam flying from the dripping blades, and then it sank till it lay on its side, half-submerged, a broken float support sticking stiffly into the air like the leg of some bloated carcass.

Stillness then, the wind gone and everything momentarily quiet. A head bobbed up beside the floating wreck. Another and another. Three men swimming awkwardly, and then the tin carcass rolled its other splintered leg into the air and sank. Air came out of it, a single belch that lifted the surface of the water, and after that nothing; just the flat sea rippled by the wind and three dark heads floundering in to the beach.

Fortunately there was little surf. One by one they found their feet and waded ashore, drowned men gasping for air, flinging themselves down on the wet stones, suddenly exhausted as fear gripped them. I ran down to them, looking at each face. But they were men I didn't know. They were alive because they'd been in the fuselage within reach of the door. Standing had been sitting with Adams up by the controls. They'd both been trapped.

It was only minutes before, a few short minutes, that I'd been talking to Adams. It didn't seem possible. One moment the helicopter had been there, so close above my head that I'd ducked involuntarily – and now it was gone. I stood there with those three men moaning at my feet staring unbelievingly at the waters of the bay. Nothing. Nothing but the steel-bright surface exploding into spray and beneath it Standing and Adams still strapped into their seats, eyes already sightless . . . Was it my fault? I felt sick right through to my guts, utterly drained.

'Christ, man. What are you staring at?'

One of the figures, a sergeant, had staggered to his feet and was staring at me, wild-eyed, his hair plastered limp across his head.

'Nothing,' I said. It was nothing that he could see. The two dead men were in my mind and he wasn't thinking of them, only of the fact that he was alive.

'Jesus! It was cold.' He was shivering; moaning to himself. But then habit and training reasserted itself. He got his men to their feet and I took them up to the camp.

It was, I thought, the end of all hope for the survivors on Sgeir Mhor; three men killed and nothing achieved.

Standing's death had a numbing effect on the rescue operation. It was not so much the man himself as the command he represented. It left a vacuum and there was only one man in Northton with the experience to fill it; that man was lying on his bed, nursing a hatred that no longer had any point. In the midst of the flood of teleprints back and forth nobody thought of informing him that Standing was dead. He heard about it from his escorting officer who had got it from the orderly who brought them their tea. It took time for the implications to sink in and it wasn't until almost five-fifteen that he finally stirred himself, got to his feet and ordered Lieutenant Phipps to accompany him to the Movements Office. There he sent off a teleprint to Brigadier Matthieson: *In view of Colonel Standing's death presume I have your authority to take over command. Please confirm so that I can organize attempt to rescue survivors dawn tomorrow.* This was dispatched at 1723 hours.

Brigadier Matthieson, who admitted later that he considered Standing's action in placing his second-in-command under close arrest ill-advised, immediately signalled back: *Your temporary command Northton confirmed. Advise action planned for getting survivors off.*

Queen's Regulations are not very specific on the subject of an arrested officer assuming command and Matthieson's signal carefully avoided any reference to the matter. He had, in fact, very little alternative. There was no other officer at Northton competent to take control in a situation like this and to fly a replacement CO in would take time. Moreover, Braddock had the confidence of his superiors at the War Office. There was another factor, too. The Press were now alerted to what was happening up in the Outer Hebrides. The Press Officer at Scottish Command had, during the past hour or so, faced a barrage of demands for information from London as well as Scottish newspaper offices. They knew about the trawler that had disappeared. They knew that a landing craft was in difficulties to the west of Laerg. They also knew that another LCT had been shipwrecked on the island and that there were survivors. No doubt they had been briefed by amateur radio operators – either Scottish 'ham' operators monitoring my radio contacts with Base or Irish radio enthusiasts picking up the signals passing between Coastal Command and their two Shackletons.

Whatever the source of their information the effect was the same; it convinced Matthieson that this was no longer a strictly Army affair but had become something much bigger. Like a submarine disaster, it had all the dramatic qualities to capture the imagination of the British public. From tomorrow morning onwards the whole country would be waiting for news of the survivors, and if the news were bad . . . Well, he certainly didn't intend to be blamed for it, not with only a few months of his time to go. In confirming my brother as temporary Base Commander, he was clutching at a straw. If things went right then he could take some credit. And if things went wrong then he had his scapegoat. I'm convinced that that was the way his mind was working when he made the decision.

At approximately five-thirty when my brother officially took command the position was this: Two relief Shackletons had been flown off, one to continue the search for the missing trawler, the other to watch over L4400 until the destroyer, now little more than 100 miles away, reached her. W/S *India* had been ordered back on to station. The Naval tug was still snug against the quay at Leverburgh.

Apart from shore-based aircraft, there was nothing else available in the area to assist in the rescue operation. True, the destroyer would pass quite close to Laerg, but L4400 urgently needed her. The landing craft was barely afloat. Almost half her crew were casualties, the bridge deck ripped to pieces, mast and funnel gone, the tank hold full of water and the pumps barely capable of holding in check the sea pouring in through her strained and buckled plates.

And since conditions made the use of aircraft impracticable, the tug remained the only hope.

In the uncertainty that followed immediately on Standing's death, nobody had apparently thought of informing the skipper of the changed situation. That his vessel was still tied up in Leverburgh was not due to any lack of initiative on his part. He was waiting for conditions to improve, knowing that he needn't sail until six at the earliest to reach Laerg by first light.

Braddock's immediate reaction to the situation was to send out three signals in quick succession – to Command, demanding the instant dispatch of two helicopters; to Coastal Command requesting that a further Shackleton be held fuelled and ready for immediate take-off should he require it; to the destroyer urging her captain to close Sgeir Mhor on his way out to L4400 and endeavour to float off supplies to the survivors, or if that were not possible, to signal them by lamp that help was on its way. Then he went to see Cliff Morgan.

Captain Flint, who was in Movements at the time, said he personally felt a great lift when Braddock took command. If any man could get the survivors off, he thought Braddock would.

Cliff Morgan's reaction, on the other hand, was very different. Like Standing, he regarded Braddock as responsible for what had happened. He was appalled when Braddock came into his quarters – 'Bold as brass, man,' was the way he put it. '"Colonel Standing's dead and I've taken over command. Now, Morgan, let's have your ideas of the weather for the next twelve hours." Just like that. And when I told him it was a pity it was Standing who'd gone and not him he laughed in my face; told me to mind my own bloody business and stick to the weather which he thought perhaps I understood. I was in radio contact with a "ham" over in Tobermory at the time and when I started to finish the conversation, he put his big hand over the key. "You take your fat arse off that chair," he told me, "and come over to the Met. Office or I'll take you there by the scruff of your neck."'

Over in the Met. Office Cliff had given him a forecast that he admitted was enough to daunt any man planning a rescue operation on an island a hundred miles out in the Atlantic. The effect of the local depression that had caused all the havoc would die out entirely within the next hour or so – probably it had died out already. For a time then the island would come again under the influence of the polar air stream with winds northerly between thirty and forty knots. Later those winds would decrease and perhaps die out for a while as the polar air stream was gradually dominated by the new depression moving in from the Atlantic. The period of relative calm would be followed by winds of rapidly increasing strength as the depression built up and spread over the area. Southerly at first, the winds would veer south-westerly, increasing to gale force.

'When?' Braddock had asked. 'When will that happen?' And Cliff had shrugged.

'You're asking me how fast that depression is moving. I don't know.'

'Then contact somebody who does. There are more than a dozen men on that bloody rock and when this depression hits . . .' Braddock checked himself. He even patted Cliff on the shoulder. 'Just tell me when. Better still, tell me when that period of calm will be.'

Cliff says he hesitated, unwilling to commit himself. He was staring at the map he'd drawn. Sykes came in with another sheet from the teleprinter, more barometric pressure figures. He entered them in, connected them up, scoring the isobars with a red pencil. One of those figures represented a report from the Shackleton circling L4400. It showed a drop of two millibars in the past hour. 'The calm will be just about there; within the hour, at any rate.'

'Goddamit!' Braddock said. 'An hour. Are you certain?' And when Cliff nodded, he said, 'How long will it last? Listen. In an hour and a half perhaps I could have helicopters here. Say three hours by the time they're refuelled and have reached Laerg. I need four hours. Can you give me four hours?'

'No.' Cliff shook his head, quite definite now. 'You can see for yourself.' He was pointing to the red lines he'd drawn. The nearest was almost touching Laerg, coming down in a broad sweep from Iceland and running away westward just north of Ireland. 'Two hours I'd give it; no more. Two hours from now and the wind will begin blowing from the south. It must do.'

'Then God help them,' was all Braddock said and he turned and went out, walking swiftly through the fading light. Cliff called after him that there was a warm front associated with the depression. There would probably be heavy rain accompanied by low ceiling and poor visibility. Braddock didn't answer. He made no acknowledgement that he'd heard, but walked straight on, shoulders very square, head held well back on the short, thick neck – a man bracing himself for a fight, Cliff thought. And overhead the clouds gathering again, aerial cavalry of a new enemy onslaught forming themselves into dark ranks, galloping eastward and rolling up the blue-green late afternoon canopy that, though cold, had the bright promise of hope. Now hope was fallen victim to the gathering clouds and my brother, alone in the loneliness of command, had to decide what further lives, if any, should be risked to attempt to save men doomed to face a night of terror, exposed again to the fury of the elements.

Field was back when he reached the Movements Office – Charles Field, looking old and grey and stooped, the lines of his face etched deeper than ever and an uneasy, shifting light in his steel-blue eyes. He said what he had to say, adding, 'It was nobody's fault. Nobody's fault at all. I'll write a full report, of course.' He was edging towards the door. 'Think I'll go over to the Mess now.'

'The Mess?' Braddock stared at him, saw the lips twitching, the slight blink of the eyes, that shifting look. 'For a drink?'

Field nodded unhappily. 'I thought just one. Just a quick one, to steady me. A shock, you know. A most frightful shock.' And he added, justifying himself, 'I hope you realize, I don't normally drink. But on this occasion. You understand . . .'

Braddock reached him in two quick strides, seized hold of him by the arm. 'Sure. I understand. Just one, and that'll lead to another. You're the one man I want sober. So you stay here. Okay?' And he pushed him into a chair. 'You're going back to Laerg – tonight.'

'No.' Field was up from the chair, his eyes overbright. 'No. I absolutely refuse.'

'Then I'll place you under arrest and have you escorted on board.' He patted his arm as though comforting a child. 'Don't worry. I'll be with you. We're going out there together.' And he sent Phipps for the long wheel-base Land-Rover and dictated a signal to Brigadier Matthieson: *Weather forecast suggests quite impracticable attempt lift survivors out by helicopter. Am proceeding to Laerg by Naval tug. Will personally direct rescue operations on arrival dawn tomorrow.* It was sent out signed: *Braddock, Commanding Officer Guided Weapons, Northton.*

In taking Field with him my brother was instinctively seeking the support of the one man whose experience and background could help. He also took the MO, Lt Phipps, a Sergeant Wetherby and four men, all hand-picked for their toughness and their known ability in the water and on the Laerg crags. Flint went with them. It took almost half an hour to gather them and their kit and the necessary equipment – climbing ropes, inflatable dinghy, aqua-lung cylinders and frogmen's suits, everything that might possibly be of use. Meantime, radio contact had been established with the tug and the skipper requested to stand by to sail immediately they arrived on board.

They left the Base at ten to six. Unfortunately, the clothes Field needed were at his croft. It was only a few minutes' drive from Leverburgh, but Marjorie was there. For the past two hours she had been with Laura Standing. She knew what had happened. She was white-faced, on the verge of hysteria. 'Why did you let him jump?' she demanded of her father. 'Why in God's name did you let him?' And he stood there, not saying a word, because there was nothing to say, whilst his own daughter accused him of being responsible for Mike's death.

Braddock got out of the Land-Rover. 'Hurry up, Field. We've no time to waste.'

Marjorie was still pouring out a flood of words, but she stopped then, staring at the Land-Rover, the significance of it standing there full of men slowly dawning on her. She doesn't remember what she said or what she did, but Flint described it to me: 'Moments like that, when you're headed for trouble an' you don't know how bad it's going to be, you don't want a girl around then, particularly a girl who's just lost somebody she cared about. One moment she was giving her father hell, saying it was all his fault, and then all of a sudden she switched her attention to Major B. That was when she realized he was taking her father out to Laerg. "You can't do it," she said. "He's not a young man. He hasn't climbed in years." She knew what it was all about. She'd broken the news of Standing's death to his wife. She knew what had happened. She knew the sort of man Braddock was – guessed he'd stop at nothing, risk anything to get those men off. She went for him like a bitch defending her last remaining puppy, screaming at him that it was all his fault, that he'd killed Mike, killed Simon Standing; it was plain bloody murder, she said, and she wasn't going to let him kill her father. Braddock tried soothing her with logic – her father was in the Army, there was a job to do and that was that. But reasoning with a girl who's scared out of her wits, whose emotions are tearing her nerves to shreds is like pouring water on a high voltage short – it just doesn't make a damn bit of difference. In the end he slapped her. Not hard. Just twice across the face and told her to pull herself together and not disgrace her father. It shut her up, and after that she just stood there, white and trembling all over.'

It was just after six-fifteen when they boarded the tug. The warps were let go immediately and she steamed out into the Sound of Harris, heading west. We were then experiencing the lull Cliff had forecast. It was so still in the hut that I went out to see what was wrong. After hours of battering the sudden quiet seemed unnatural. Darkness was closing down on Laerg, the clouds low overhead and hanging motionless. I could see the outline of Sgeir Mhor, the sloping spine of Keava disappearing into the blanket of the overcast, but they were dim, blurred shapes. The air was heavy with humidity, and not a breath of wind.

I got a torch and signalled towards Sgeir Mhor. But there was no answering flash. It meant nothing for it was unlikely that any of the survivors had got ashore with a torch. I tried to contact Base, but there was other traffic – Rafferty talking to the destroyer, to the tug, finally to Coastal Command. And then the destroyer to me: ETA Laerg 0125 hours. Would I please stand by the radio as from 0100. Base came through immediately afterwards: The tug's ETA would be about 0430 dependent on conditions. I was requested to keep radio watch from four-thirty onwards. Roger. I had six hours in which to get some rest. I arranged with Cooper for a hot meal at one o'clock, set the alarm, undressed and tumbled into bed.

I must have recovered some of my energy, for it wasn't the

alarm that woke me. I reached out and switched on the light. A mouse was sitting up by the edge of my empty plate, sitting on its haunches on the bedside table cleaning its whiskers with its fore-paws. It was one of the breed peculiar to Laerg, a throw-back to pre-glacial life, to before the last Ice Age that covered the British Isles anything up to ten thousand years ago. It was larger than the ordinary British field-mouse, its ears were bigger, its hind-legs longer and the tail was as long as its body; the brown of its coat had a distinctly reddish tinge brightening to dull orange on the under-belly. It sat quiet still, two shiny black pin-head eyes staring at me. It seemed possessed of curiosity rather than fear, and after a moment it resumed its toilet, cleaning its whiskers with little stroking movements of its paws. The time was eleven minutes past midnight. The wind was back, beating round the corners of the hut in a steady roar that drowned the sound of the generator. And behind the wind was another, more sinister sound – one that I hadn't heard for some time; the crash and suck of waves breaking on the beach. I thought it was this sound rather than the mouse that had woken me.

There was something about that little morsel of animal life that was infinitely comforting; a sign perhaps of the indestructibility of life. The mouse in that moment meant a lot to me and I lay there watching it until it had finished its toilet and quietly disappeared. Then I got up and dressed and went to the door of the hut. It was a black night, the two lights Cooper had left on in the camp shining in isolation. The wind was from the south, about force 7. The waves, coming straight into the bay, broke with an earth-shaking thud. The sound of the surf was louder than the wind, and as my eyes became accustomed to the darkness, I could see the ghostly glimmer of white water ringing the beach; just the glimmer of it, nothing else. It was a wild, ugly night, the air much warmer so that I thought I could smell rain again, the warm front moving in.

At one o'clock I contacted the destroyer. She had Laerg clear on the radar at thirteen miles range. ETA approximately, one-thirty. Alf Cooper appeared at my side, a khaki gnome his head encased in a woollen balaclava. 'Grub up.' He put the tray down on the table beside the radio – a Thermos flask of ox-tail soup and two mess tins full of corned beef and potato hash all steaming hot. 'A night for the flippin' bears, ain't it. 'Ibernation, that's my idea o' paradise this time of the year. You reck'n that destroyer'll be able to do any good?'

'No,' I said.

He nodded, sucking at his soup. 'That's wot I fort. Ruddy waves must be breaking right over the poor bastards.' I asked him about the men from the helicopter. 'Sleepin' their ruddy 'eads orf.' he said. 'Orl right for them. They got full bellies. Me, I'm fair famished.' He reached for one of the mess tins. "Ope yer don't mind bully. Easy ter make, yer see. Fillin' too.'

At one-thirty we went out of the hut and stood in the teeth of the wind staring into the black darkness that hid Sgeir Mhor. It was drizzling, a wet, driving mist. Suddenly light blazed, the pencil stab of a searchlight that threw the blurred shape of Sgeir Mhor into black relief. It probed the mist, producing strange halos of light in the damp air. A gun flashed, a small sound against the thunder of breaking waves. The overcast glimmered with light as the star shell burst. It was a minute or two before it floated clear of the clouds over Keava; for a moment the bay and the surrounding rocks were bathed in its incandescent glare. It was an unearthly sight; the waves marching into the bay, building up till their tops curled and broke, roaring up the beach in a welter of foam, and all around the horseshoe curve of breaking water, the rocks standing piled in ghostly brilliance. Rock and cliff and sodden grass slope all looked more hellish in that macabre light. I saw the spume of waves breaking over the lower bastions of Sgeir Mhor. Then the flare touched the sea and was instantly extinguished, and after that the night was blacker, more frightening than before.

A signal lamp stabbed its pin-point of light just beyond the tip of Sgeir Mhor: *Help arriving first light. Stick it out four more hours and* . . . That was all I read for the destroyer was steaming slowly westward and the stab of her signal lamp was obscured by the rocks. The searchlight probed again, searching the far side of the rock promontory as though trying to count the survivors. And then that too went out and after that there was nothing but the pitch-black night.

I re-set the alarm and lay down again on Pinney's bed, not bothering this time to undress. Time passed slowly and I couldn't sleep. The mouse came back. I could hear its claws scratching at the aluminium of the mess tins, but I didn't switch the light on. I lay there with my eyes closed waiting for the alarm, thinking of those men out on the rocks drenched by the mist and the spray, wondering whether it would be possible to get them off.

At four-thirty I was at the radio and the tug came through prompt on schedule, my brother's voice requesting information about sea and landing conditions. I was able to tell him that the wind was now west of south. But it had also increased in strength. It was definitely blowing a gale now and it was raining heavily. However, if the wind veered further, as seemed likely, there was a chance that a landing could be made in the western curve of the bay, close under Keava where there would be some shelter. *'Okay,'* he said. *'We'll recce the lee side of Sgeir Mhor first and if that's no good, we'll anchor and attempt to make the beach on inflatable rafts.'*

It was still dark when they came into the bay and all I saw of the tug was the two steaming lights, one above the other, swinging and dipping. She came right into the bay, almost to the break of the waves, and then the lights moved apart and the distance between them increased as she turned westward. The green of her starboard navigation light showed for a while, still half-obscured by rain. And then that vanished, together with the steaming lights, and I caught glimpses of her stern light as she browsed along the western arm of the bay, a will-o'-the-wisp bounced from wave-top to wave-top. A searchlight stabbed a brilliant beam, iridescent with moisture, and the rocks of Sgeir Mhor showed ghostly grey across tumbled acres of sea; columns of spray like ostrich feather plumes waved behind it, sinking and rising with the surge of the Atlantic.

Dawn came slowly and with reluctance, a sheathed pallor stealing into the curve below the encircling hills. The tug lay close under Keava, just clear of the narrow, surf-filled gut that separated it from Sgeir Mhor. She didn't anchor, but stayed head-to-wind under power, and they came ashore in rubber dinghies where the surf was least.

I was coming along the foreshore when my brother staggered dripping out of the suck of the waves, dragging a rubber dinghy after him. He was dressed like the others in a frogman's suit and I can see him still, standing there in that twilit world that was the dawn, finned feet straddled at the surf's edge, not looking at that moment at his companions, but staring up at the cloud-hidden heights. There was a stillness about him, an immobility – he seemed for an instant petrified, a part of the landscape, his body turned to stone, statuesque like a rock.

Then the others piled in through the surf and he was a man again, moving to help them, going back into the waves to pull two more rubber dinghies ashore.

I met them on the beach. 'Thank God you made it,' I yelled to him above the wind.

He stared at me. His face looked haggard, his eyes wild. I swear he didn't recognize me.

'Iain. Are you all right, Iain?'

For a moment his face stayed blank. Then his eyes snapped. 'Ross.' He glanced quickly at Field standing at the surf's edge. Then he came towards me, gripped my shoulder. 'The name's Braddock, damn you,' he hissed, his fingers digging a warning into my flesh. His mouth had hardened and his eyes blazed black. He'd have seen me dead and drowned before he'd have admitted to his real name.

Field wiped a smear of phlegm from below his nose. 'We saw several men clinging to the rocks.' His eyes looked dead and tired, bloodshot with the salt. 'Where are the parachutes – the life-saving gear you dropped?' Braddock asked.

'Up there.' Field nodded to the heights of Keava, the long slope leading to the spine.

'Yes, up there.' I agreed. But the rain-dimmed dawn showed nothing on the slopes – only the clouds writhing in white pillars.

Their clothes, tied in plastic bundles in the dinghies, were safe and dry. They changed in the bird-oil stench of an old cleit, and then we climbed, strung out across the slopes, climbed until we met the clouds, gasping wet air. The daylight had strengthened by then and ragged gaps in the overcast showed the slopes of Keava bare to its spine and to the cliffs beyond. The parachutes had gone. Some time during the night, I suppose, a gust had filled the nylon canopies and carried them over the top and far out into the sea beyond.

Braddock shook Field's arm. 'Are you sure that's where you dropped them?'

Field nodded.

'Then they're gone.'

Field's face was set in a wooden look as he agreed they'd gone. Up there in the wind and the driving clouds, with the thunder of the waves breaking at the foot of the cliffs, he and I, we could both recall the solitary parachute lifting and sailing out into the Atlantic. 'Wasted. All wasted.' There were tears in his eyes, but it may have been the wind.

'Okay. Well, there's only one way to get a line across.'

Field nodded absently.

'We'll have to take it ourselves. Swim it across the gut, and then climb with it.'

Easy to say; not so easy to do. The drop from the Butt of Keava was possible, the 350-foot cliff went down in a series of ledges. It was the gut between and the sheer cliff beyond. The gut was 50 yards at its narrowest and the seas were breaking there in a welter of foam; the cliffs of Sgeir Mhor were black volcanic gabbro, hard as granite, smooth and unbroken for long stretches.

'Well?' Braddock stared at Field. 'I swim it, you climb it, eh?' And his face cracked in a grin. It was a dare. This was the sort of thing he loved – physical action spiced with danger. And if the other man cracked . . . Poor Field's face was ashen, his eyes staring at the smooth black panels of wet rock beyond the mael-strom of the chasm.

I think my brother had watched quite a few men crack. I don't say it gave him pleasure, but it may well have been some-thing he needed, a bolster to his own morale. His world had always been a physical one. Mentally and emotionally he was something of a child; or that was how he had often seemed to me; which was why, I suppose, our relationship, so inimical at times, had been at others so strangely close; we had each supplied what the other lacked.

Now, he didn't hesitate. He didn't even watch for Field's reaction. He caught the man's fear at a glance and overlaid it with his own determination, the quick, positiveness of his orders. He led us pell-mell back down the slope, back to the beach and the dinghies laden with rope and all the things he'd feared they might need. And then, in his frogman's kit again, up the sloping shoulders of the rocks to the wet thunder of the surf breaking through the gut.

The sergeant and I, with two men, were ordered to the top of the cliff with one end of the nylon climbing rope. Down at the bottom he and Field, together with Lieutenant Phipps and the two other men, manoeuvred one of the rubber dinghies.

Flat on my stomach at the cliff's edge I watched Iain working his way along the ledges westward through the gut. He was alone and his thick, powerful body in its black rubber suit looked like a seal's as it flattened itself against the rocks to meet each wave as it broke foaming across the ledges – a baby seal from that height, the rope around his waist and trailing white behind him like an umbilical cord. And then from the furthest point west that he could fight his way, he suddenly stood on a sheer-edged shelf of rock and dived.

He dived into the back-surge of a big wave and went deep, his fins beating furiously, drumming at the surf. It looked so easy. One moment he was diving and the next he had bobbed up on the back of a breaker on the far side, a black head with black arms paddling. A quick look round, then down again as the next comber broke, and as it spent its energy, he rode its back on to a long, sloped ledge, and pulled himself up.

Now, with the dawn light stronger, I could see two figures prone among the rocks on the far side, peering down. I thought I recognized Wentworth, but I couldn't be sure. The face was a dim blur in the rain and the flying spray.

Iain was clear of the water now, clear of the surge of even the biggest waves, curled up at the furthest end of that sloped ledge and pulling on the rope. Below me I saw Field hesitate. The rope came taut on the rush of a wave. The rubber dinghy shifted on the rocks. And then it was in the water, and he was in it, head down, hands gripping the gunnels as it was pulled across. Once I thought he was lost. The dinghy reared on a curling crest, turned half over as it broke. But then it righted itself, lifted on the backwash from the far side, and in one buoyant rush came to rest on the ledge where Iain crouched.

I saw arms wave on the cliff opposite. There were three bodies there now, all waving in the excitement of imminent rescue. But there was still that sheer cliff and the men on the top could do nothing to help. It was up to Field now. Field alone could lift the end of that rope the 300-feet that would transform it from just the tail end of a line into a connecting link, a bridge between the two masses of rock – a bridge that could act as a means of escape.

Field had crossed the gut barefooted, but in his battledress. Now, soaked to the skin, he leaned against the vertical rock and put on his climbing boots. That done, he fastened a belt round his waist that was stuffed with rock pitons like steel dogs' teeth. An ice hammer looped by its thong to his wrist, the rope fastened around his waist, and he was ready. But then he stood for a long time with his head thrown back, gazing up at the cliff above him.

He stood like that for so long that I thought he was held fast by the sheer impossibility of it. Perhaps by fear, too. And I for one wouldn't have blamed him. Those shining panels of rock, trickling water – a spider would have its work cut out to find a footing. There were ledges and crevices, it was true. There are in almost any rock. But they were so minute and spaced so far apart. And all the time the sea swirled about his legs. The din of it was incessant, the gut streaming with wind-blown spray, gusts of spume, spongy masses of it flying through the air.

At last he moved; a flick of the hand holding the rope. Iain squatted tighter into his niche, waiting, both hands on the rope. The three men on the cliff-top opposite me leaned out and waved.

757

Field saw them, for he lifted his hand. And then at last he began to climb, traversing out along a toe-hold crack that was a fractured continuation of the ledge on which he had stood.

It was fascinating to watch him. He must have been over fifty and out of practice, yet he balanced himself like an acrobat, hanging in space and moving steadily upwards, his feet doing the work, the rest of his body still and quiet. To the left at first, a long traverse, and then a quick gain of perhaps fifty or sixty feet up toe and finger holds I couldn't see; a short traverse right and then a pause. The pause lengthened out, his hands reaching occasionally and drawing back. Then for a long time he hung there quite motionless.

Had his nerve gone? I don't know. I asked him once, but he only smiled and said, 'It was an ugly place. I thought it better to start again.'

I didn't see him jump. One moment he was there, and the next he was in the sea, and Iain was hauling him back to the ledge where he lay for a while getting his breath. Then he started up again.

The same route, but a left traverse at the top and then he was hammering a piton into a crevice, snapping on a hook for the rope, and up again using pitons from the clanking string of them around his waist, one after another. He must have hammered in about two dozen of them before he reached the overhang, and there he stuck with less than fifty feet to go – a fly on wet slate with the spume curling up like smoke from the cauldron below him.

He got round it eventually by going down about half the distance he'd climbed and working another crevice line to the right. This brought him almost opposite me, and right below him then was a deadly mass of rocks awash. He looked down once and I could imagine how he felt with only the rope running now through three pitons to hold him. The last 50 feet seemed to take him almost as many minutes. The crevices were too shallow for the pitons and he was white with cold, his clothes heavy with water. But he did it.

His head came level with the cliff-top. Hands reached down and he went over the top on his belly. Then he suddenly passed out, lying there, limp. But the rope was there and that was life to those who'd survived. The tail-end, passed back down the cliff to Iain, was made fast to a heavier line, and so, with many goings back and forth to the camp, we rigged up a makeshift breeches buoy.

It took us all morning in the teeth of the gale with five of the tug's crew and the Doc and the men who had survived the heli-copter crash. Baulks of timber had to be brought up, heavy hawsers, block and tackle, and everything rigged by trial and error. Just after midday we managed to get food and clothing across to them. But it wasn't until almost 2 p.m. that we got the first man over the gut and safe on to Keava. And after that it was slow, back-breaking work, for many of them were stretcher cases, who, when they reached Keava, had to be carried down the slopes and along the beach to the camp. There was no vehicle, no means of transporting them other than by hand.

We took altogether twenty-three men off Sgeir Mhor, five of them unconscious, and several badly injured. All were suffering from exposure, their skin a leprous white from constant immersion in salt water. Wentworth was the last to come across, a different man now, burned up by the twenty-four hours he'd been in command. Stratton was dead – with the Cox'n he'd been getting the men out of the mess deck when the whole bridge structure had been crushed like a biscuit tin; and Pinney, who'd thought Laerg the best posting he'd had. Four men had died during the night, including the young steward, Perkins, whose rib-cage had been stove in by the slam of the water-tight doors. Field said there was no sign of the landing craft, only bits and pieces of metal scattered among the rocks.

The wind went round that night into the north-west and the tug came close inshore. By midnight everybody had been em-barked. Everybody except my brother. It was the Doc who discovered he wasn't on board. He'd had a list made and a roll called, for the confusion on the tug was indescribable – thirty-five extra men, many of them casualties.

'Where's Major Braddock?' I heard the question passed along the deck. 'Anybody seen Major Braddock?' Voices calling in the darkness of the decks. And then the Skipper giving orders, Sergeant Wetherby piling into the boat again, the outboard motor bursting into life. I jumped in beside him and we shot away from the tug's side, slapping through the shallows over the low tide sand bar.

The outboard died as the bows grated and the boat came to a sudden halt. We scrambled out into a foot or more of water and ploughed over the sands to the beach. Wetherby thought he might have gone to check the remains of the transport that lay, battered and derelict, among the rocks behind the loading beach. He was an MT sergeant. Whilst he went towards the dim shape of the bull-dozer, now standing high and dry on the sands,

I hurried to the camp. Every now and then the wind brought me the sound of his voice calling: 'Major Braddock! Major Braddock!'

The lights were out in the camp now, the generator still. I stumbled about in the darkness, calling. At first I called his Army name, but then, because it didn't seem to matter here alone, I called: 'Iain! Iain – where are you?' I reached the hut and, fumbling in the dark, found the torch I'd used. The place was empty; the radio still there and all the mess and litter of its temporary use as a casualty clearing station. I went outside then, probing and calling.

I'd never have found him without the torch. He was standing in the lee of the cookhouse, quite still, his back turned towards me as though afraid his face might catch the light. 'What the hell are you playing at?' I demanded. 'Why didn't you answer?'

He stared at me, but didn't say anything for a moment. There was a twitch at the corner of his mouth and his face was deathly pale. 'Are you ill?' I asked.

He moved then, came closer to me and reached for my arm. 'Donald.' His voice was hoarse, little more than a whisper against the blatter of the wind. 'Go back. Go back to the ship. You haven't seen me. Understand?' The urgency of his request was almost as startling as the request itself. He jerked at my arm. 'Go – back.' Behind the hoarseness of his voice, I caught the tremor of his mood, something deep that he couldn't control. 'As you love me, Donald, go back.'

'But why? What's wrong? Is it Lane?' I asked. 'Has he been worrying you?'

'He's been on to me – twice from the mainland. But it isn't that.' His grip tightened on my arm. 'Leave me now, will you.'

'But why?'

'Damn you, Donald! Can't you do what I ask?' And then, his voice more controlled: 'Something I have to do. We left in a hurry – the tide and a change of wind. No time . . . and Leroux half dead, too weak to do anything. It was either that or be trapped.' His voice had died to a whisper.

'You mean you were here?' I asked. 'After the *Duart Castle* . . .'

'Try to understand, can't you? Just leave me here and no questions.'

I hesitated. The torch on his face showed his mouth tight-set, his eyes urgent. 'All right,' I said. 'If that's what you want . . .'

But I was too late. As I switched off the torch and turned to go, a voice spoke out of the darkness behind me: 'You've found him then?' It was Sergeant Wetherby. His jacketed figure loomed bulky from the direction of the generator. And to Iain, he said, 'Major Braddock, sir. The tug's all ready to go – everybody on board. Only yourself, sir. They're waiting for you.'

I heard Iain's muttered curse. And then in a flat voice: 'Very good, Sergeant. Sorry if I held things up – just a last check round.' He came with us then. There was nothing else he could do for he couldn't hope to persuade the sergeant to let him stay. And so we embarked and at 0115 hours on the morning of 24 October, the tug steamed out of Shelter Bay with the last remnant of the Army Detachment.

The evacuation was complete at a cost of fifty-three lives, the loss of one landing craft, a helicopter and a great deal of equipment.

PART THREE

I

WITCH-HUNT
(24 October – 28 February)

Press reaction to the news of the disaster was immediate. The first scattered fragments had begun coming through within hours of our landing craft being wrecked. Radio and TV put it out in their newscasts as it filtered through and during the day the story moved from the Stop Press of the evening papers to the front page. The main body of the Press, however, had almost twelve hours in which to build the story up; and because it involved the out-islands, ships, the sea, the weather, they knew the impact it would have on the public. All that day telephones rang continuously in the press offices of the three Services and in the Meteorological Office in Kingsway. The Admiralty and the Air Ministry were helpful; the Army less so for they were inhibited by the knowledge that a commanding officer had ordered the arrest of his second-in-command. In an attempt to avoid this becoming known to the Press, they clamped down on all comment, closed the military line to Northton to all but official calls and confined their press releases to the facts of the situation. The effect was to make the Press suspicious.

An enterprising reporter on the local Stornoway paper got hold of Fellowes. His story of the flight to Laerg and Mike Ferguson's death was scooped by a popular daily. A Reuters' man, who had flown north from Glasgow that morning, reached Northton in time to get the news of Standing's death and watch the tug leave from Leverburgh quay. His dispatches went out on the Reuters teleprint service to all newspaper offices.

By that night the full extent of the disaster was known, the presses of the national dailies were rolling out the story and reporters and photographers were hurrying north. So many took the night train to Glasgow that BEA, who had cancelled the morning flight to Stornoway, had second thoughts. The newspaper men had a rough flight, but by midday they were piling into Northton and Leverburgh. Others, mainly photographers with specially chartered planes, stood by at Stornoway from dawn onwards waiting for the weather to lift and give them an opportunity to take pictures of Laerg. Fellowes found his plane in great demand.

The fact that there were survivors gave a dramatic quality to the news and most of Britain had the story on their breakfast tables, front-paged under flaring headlines – a story of storm and disaster, of a colonel and his adjutant killed in attempts to rescue men trapped on a gale-torn rock in the North Atlantic. And to add to the drama was the suggestion that the Army had something to hide. Editors' instructions were to get at the truth.

Two reporters in search of a drink landed up at the hotel at Rodil. They got hold of Marjorie. She was in a highly emotional state and prepared to talk. If Standing had been alive, she might have blamed him on account of Mike Ferguson's death. But Standing was dead, and because she was frightened for her father, she put the blame for everything on Major Braddock, and in attacking him, she revealed that he had been placed under arrest for ordering the LCT in to the beach. For those two reporters she was worth her weight in gold.

Other reporters, casing the Northton HQ and getting no change out of the Army personnel who had all been instructed to have no contact with the Press, transferred their attention to the Met. Office. They, too, struck gold. Cliff was a story in himself and nothing would have stopped that little Welshman from talking. He gave it to them, blow by blow, as seen from the weather man's point of view. One correspondent, reporting him from a tape-recorded interview, gave his words verbatim: 'I tell you, the man must have been off his bloody nut, ordering a landing craft into the beach on a night like that. Oh yes, the wind was north then and they were under the lee of the island in Shelter Bay. But aground like that, she was at the mercy of the elements, you see, and when the wind swung into the south . . .'

There was more in the same vein and it all went south by wire and phone to the waiting presses in London. And by the following morning the public was convinced that the man responsible for this appalling loss of life was Major Braddock. They weren't told that in so many words, but it was implied, and this before he had had a chance to defend himself, when he was, in fact, still out on Laerg organizing the rescue operations.

Once the survivors had been reported safe, the excitement of the story dwindled and news-hungry reporters, looking for a fresh angle, began delving into the relations between Braddock and his Commanding Officer. What had happened at that interview in Standing's office in the early hours of the morning of 22 October? Why had he placed Braddock under arrest? Cliff was interviewed on TV and radio. So was Marjorie. Laura Standing, too, and Fellowes. The evidence piled up and all this canned material was being rushed down to London whilst the tug was still battling its way through the aftermath of the gale.

We steamed into Leverburgh just after four-thirty in the afternoon. We had been hove-to twice for the MO to carry out minor operations. The rest of the time we had managed little more than seven knots. The tug's internal accommodation was sufficient only for the serious casualties. The rest – men suffering from exposure and extreme exhaustion – had to be left out on the open deck. Anything over seven knots and the tug would have been shipping water in the heavy seas. As a result the voyage took almost fourteen hours and during all that time the men were exposed to wind and spray. One man died during the night and there were several showing symptoms of pneumonia by the time we docked.

The quay was packed as we came alongside, packed solid with men whose dress proclaimed them foreigners to the Hebrides. Army personnel in charge of the vehicles to take the survivors to Northton tried to hold them back, but as the tug's sides touched the quay they swarmed on board. They were all after one man. 'Where's Braddock? Which is Major Braddock?' A man in a bow tie and thick horn-rimmed glasses seized hold of my arm. 'I want Major Braddock. Where is he – in the Captain's cabin?'

In fact, Iain had been sleeping in the scuppers on the port side. 'I don't think he'll see anybody. He's very tired.'

'I can't help that. He's news.' He told me the paper he represented and thrust a note into my hand. 'Here's a fiver. Just point him out to me, that's all.' And when I told him to go to hell, he tried to make it a tenner.

They found him in the end, of course. They brought him to bay like a pack of hounds in a corner under the bridge housing and he stood there, facing them, his battered face grey with fatigue, his voice hoarse with shouting above the wind. They were all round him, their notebooks out, firing questions. And all he said was, 'No comment.'

He didn't realize that this was his one opportunity to defend himself – that he'd never get another. He stuck to the letter of QRs and refused to make a statement, relying on his superiors to back him up. Relying, too, on the fact that without his efforts the survivors would never have been got off Sgeir Mhor alive.

He didn't know then that his superiors were going to throw him to the wolves, that he was to be the scapegoat. How could he? For the last thirty-six hours he'd been involved in physical action, body and mind devoted to one thing alone – getting those men off. He didn't understand that these reporters couldn't visualize the circumstances. He was dead tired and his own mind was incapable at that moment of making the leap from individual effort to the broader aspects of the affair. No comment! A statement will be issued in due course. His Army training overlaid whatever personal inclination he had. He behaved, in fact, with perfect correctness and in doing so he damned himself before that most violent and blind of all judges – the public.

I saw the faces of the reporters harden. Frustration developed into anger. One man, snapping his notebook shut, seemed to speak for the rest: 'Okay, Major, have it your own way. But don't blame us if the public forms its own opinion of your evacuation order.'

Other notebooks snapped. The circle broke up and Iain stood there, tight-lipped and with a baffled look on his face, as they suddenly abandoned him to move amongst the survivors in search of personal, human interest stories. There was no shortage of these. The struggle to get the landing craft off the beach, the fight to get her out of Shelter Bay and clear of the rocks of Sgeir Mhor in the teeth of the hurricane, the failure of the engines, the scene of utter confusion as she struck with the bridge deck concertinaed against the fortress mass of Sgeir Mhor; how for a short while the up-lifted stern section had acted as a sort of ramp, enabling those that were still alive to scramble ashore, the desperate hours of waiting through that ghastly night and the rising seas and the new storm breaking over them.

There was so much of human interest. In particular, there was Field. They got the story of his climb from Sergeant Wetherby and a bunch of them crowded round him. 'Tell me, Mr Field – how did you feel? Were you scared?' He tried to tell them about Braddock's crossing of the gut between Butt of Keava and Sgeir Mhor, but they weren't interested in that now. Reporters in London, working on the background of the officers involved, had interviewed Field's wife. As a result they knew who he was. 'Could you give us your reactions please? . . . How did it feel climbing that sheer cliff face? . . . Was it as stiff as the climbs you faced in the Himalayas?' Cameras clicked, the TV men closed in.

And all the time Captain Flint with a squad of men was trying to get the injured off the ship and into the waiting vehicles.

'Get the hell out of it, you bloody blood-sucking bastards.' His Cockney humour had deserted him. The essential warmth of his nature was revolted by this spectacle of news-hungry men milling around amongst injured and exhausted survivors, fighting to get to grips with their stories. I saw him take a camera out of one photographer's hand and throw it over the side. The man had been trying to get a close-up of some poor devil with his face smashed in. 'The next one of you ghouls that tries that I'll 'eave the beggar over the side, camera an' all.'

I found Marjorie struggling to get near her father – shut out by the ring of men surrounding him. 'Oh, thank God!' she said when she saw me. 'What happened? Why are they all crowding round him?' The bloom was gone from her face, all the vitality knocked out of her. 'I can't get near him.' The pupils of those strangely blue eyes were dilated and the words came in a panic rush, almost a sob.

Briefly I told her what her father had done, and all the time she had hold of my hand, clinging to it as though I were the one stable thing left to her. But as I talked I saw a change come over her. She seemed gradually to come alive. 'Then perhaps it's all right,' she breathed. 'Perhaps this is the end of it then.' It was extraordinary – the recuperative power of youth. Her eyes were suddenly shining, bright with hope, and then she kissed me full on the mouth for no apparent reason that I could see except that she needed to express her joy, her sense of relief that her father was safe and she didn't have to worry about him any longer. 'And what about you? All those hours alone on Laerg. You must be exhausted.' And she suggested that I come up to the croft with her father. 'It'll be better than going to the camp.' And with an understanding that surprised me because I'd never had anybody who'd cared a damn how I felt, she said, 'You'll need to unwind – slowly.'

I knew she was right. I was still extraordinarily keyed up. And yet at the same time I was utterly exhausted – a state of complete nervous fatigue. I did need to unwind, and I was grateful to her.

'If you'll just try and extricate my father . . .'

And so I left with them in the little estate car and I didn't see my brother again for a long time.

The next day's papers were full of the story of the disaster, pages of it – eye-witness accounts and personal stories, timetables of the events leading up to the rescue and Field's climb. Charles Field was suddenly a hero again. There were pictures of him. Pictures of the survivors. But reading the papers with the whole story written up like a thrilling serial, the blow-by-blow account of a great storm with human courage surmounting disaster, I detected an ominous note. There were leaders implying that men had died unnecessarily. There were feature articles that showed the whole course of that intense local depression – some gave the wind speed as high as 150 knots, though they had no means of knowing since there were no anemometers to record it – and here the implication was that if the officer in charge (meaning my brother) had taken the advice of the local Met. Officer, no lives need have been lost. They completely ignored the fact that Cliff's warning had come too late, almost three hours after the order to evacuate had been given.

Throughout every paper there was the same searching, angry note of inquiry. Somebody was reponsible, and with Standing dead that man could only be Braddock. The order to evacuate, taken on his own responsibility, and his subsequent arrest, damned him utterly. There were questions asked about it in the House. The Secretary of State for War promised a full-scale inquiry.

It was a witch-hunt, nothing less, and my brother was the man they were all gunning for. The people responsible for his appointment to the Hebrides did nothing to demonstrate their confidence in him. The reverse, in fact. They relieved him of his temporary command and sent him on indefinite leave pending the results of the Inquiry. No doubt this action was intended to relieve him of the pressure of phone calls, but its effect, inevitably, was to confirm the Press in their condemnation of his conduct.

I only heard that he'd been ordered away on leave two days later when I felt sufficiently recovered to visit Northton. Marjorie drove me to the camp. With her father and myself to look after, the croft to run and reporters to keep at bay, she was out of touch with camp affairs. I went straight to the Admin. block. There was a new adjutant, a Captain Davidson, short and dapper with a little moustache. 'Major Braddock? I'm sorry, he's away on leave. Colonel Webb's in command here now.' And he added, 'I'm afraid I can't give you Braddock's address. I don't think we've been notified where he's staying.'

And that was that. I saw Rafferty and Flint. Nobody had Iain's address. The slate had been wiped clean, my brother expunged as though he'd never existed. Whether they acted under orders, I don't know. The effect, at any rate, was the same. He was gone and nobody would, or could, tell me where. I returned to Marjorie waiting in the car and all the way back to Rodil I was thinking of Iain, somewhere in the British Isles, a man condemned without a hearing. They hadn't even been able to tell me when the Inquiry would be held. 'You'll be notified in due course, Mr Ross,' the dapper little adjutant had said. 'At least, I imagine you will, since I gather you're a vital witness.'

A witness! I hadn't thought of that. A witness against my own brother. And Iain wandering lost and alone with nobody to turn to. If he hadn't been separated from his wife, if he'd been able to draw on the strength of his family . . . But life had kicked even that support from under him.

'He's alone,' I said, not realizing I was speaking aloud. 'Absolutely alone.'

Marjorie braked, glancing at me quickly. 'Who? Major Braddock?' And then, in a quiet voice, she said, 'Donald, I've been wondering – we've both been wondering . . . What is your connection with Major Braddock?' She was staring straight ahead of her then, her eyes fixed on the road. 'There is a connection, isn't there?'

So they'd noticed. I didn't say anything for a moment. 'If you don't want to talk about it . . . But I thought perhaps it might help.'

I had to think about this, about whether it was fair to Iain. But I, too, was alone. And they'd been kind to me. Friendship, understanding . . . I suppose even then I was aware of the attraction of this girl, a growing closeness between us that wasn't only physical. And to share my fears . . .

But remembering the haunted look on his face, I shook my head. 'Not now,' I said. 'Later perhaps . . .'

She touched my hand, a gesture of sympathy. 'If I'd known . . .' But then she shook her head. 'No, I'd still have felt the same. He did give the order, you know.' And she added, 'Why? Why was he so determined to get them away on that last LCT?'

Why indeed? With a woman's intuition she had hit on the real point, the basic fact that made my brother guilty. But I couldn't see it then. I was thinking only of the disaster, not of what might have gone before when he cloaked himself in another man's identity, and I said, 'It was because he knew if he didn't get them off then, they'd have been stuck there for the winter with insufficient supplies.' I was quoting Field, who'd had it from Rafferty, and all the time the thing was there, staring me in the face.

But Lane, his mind concentrated on his own monetary affairs, unclouded by all the details of the disaster, had seen it. I had a phone call from him within an hour of my return to London.

'That you, Ross? Glad to know you're back at last. Where's your brother?' I tried to deny that he was my brother, but he ignored that. 'I want a word with that guy. Now you just tell me where he is or I'm going to pass this whole story over to the Press. After what's happened, they'll just lap it up.'

'I don't think so,' I said.

'And why not?'

'In this country the law of libel is still very . . .'

'Libel!' His soft voice was suddenly tough. 'You talk about libel when the man may prove to be a murderer. Yeah, a murderer.' I thought he was referring to the men who'd been drowned. But it wasn't that. His one-track mind was making a much more specific charge. 'Have you considered, Mr Ross, what happened to the original Braddock – the young George Braddock, aged twenty and just commissioned, afloat on that life-raft with this monster of a brother of yours? Have you considered that?'

It came as a shock. And yet it had been at the back of my mind ever since I'd seen Iain standing with his finned feet in the surf, staring up at the hidden heights of Laerg; ever since that moment when I'd come ashore to find him waiting up in the camp, desperate to be left alone there. 'I think,' I said, trying to keep control of my voice, 'you'd better not repeat that. Major Braddock may be facing an Inquiry, but that doesn't mean you can make wild accusations . . .'

'Major Braddock!' There was anger and contempt in his voice. 'His name's Iain Ross. It's Iain Ross we're talking about, and you know it. Why else did you go north to the Hebrides? How else could you have managed to get on that landing craft and finish up in Laerg? Both of you, there on your own island together. Now you just tell me where I'll find the son-of-a-bitch. That's all I want from you – for the moment.' And when I told him I didn't know, he said, 'All right, Ross. You stick by him. Very admirable of you – very fraternal. But you won't fob me off as easily as that. I'll just stay on here in England. I can wait. They'll produce him when the Board of Inquiry sits. And then I'll get him. I'll get the truth out of him then, so help me God, and if it's what I think it is, I'll brand him for the goddammed murdering bastard he is. Goo'bye.' And he slammed the phone down.

I didn't see my brother again until the Board of Inquiry, which was held at Scottish Command on 2 November. He had, however, been in touch with me once, very briefly, during the intervening ten days. It was a phone call late at night, about eleven-fifteen. I recognized his voice at once for he made no pretence of concealing his natural accent. 'Donald? Is that you, Donald?'

'Where are you?' I said. 'In London?'

'Aye, in some bluidy nightclub – I forget the name. I must ha' a wee talk wi' you, Donald. Can you come down here? Right away. I must ha' a talk wi' ye.'

'Of course.' And I added, 'Are you all right, Iain?' His voice sounded thick and slurred. I thought he'd been drinking.

'Yes, I'm all right, laddie. It's just that I've made up my mind. I must talk to somebody. I'm all alone, you see. An' I thought maybe if you'd nothing better to do . . .'

'Whereabouts are you?' I said. I didn't want to lose him. 'I'll come right down. Just tell me where to meet you.'

'Aye, weel – I'm somewhere doon Curzon Street way.' The accent was very broad and getting more slurred. 'What about Cook's now, meet me outside Cook's in Berkeley Street.'

'Okay, I'll be there at midnight,' I said.

'Fine, fine, that'll do fine. We'll ha' a wee drink together, eh? Like old times. Only hurry. I canna stand my own company much longer.' And he'd hung up.

I'd just gone to bed, so that I had to dress, and then there was the problem of transport. Fortunately I had enough money in the studio for a taxi and I found one on the rank outside Aldgate East Station. I was at Cook's by five to twelve. But he wasn't there, and though I hung around until 2 a.m., he never showed up.

He didn't ring me again and that was my only contact with him until I saw him in Service dress walking out of the Conference Room where the Board of Inquiry was being held. I was shocked at the change in him. The twitch at the corner of his mouth had become much more marked, the lines of his face deeper. There were bags under his eyes, and above them the eyes themselves stared weary and lack-lustre out of darkened sockets. He'd obviously been drinking heavily. His hands were trembling. He passed me without a flicker of recognition.

Shortly afterwards I was called to give evidence. The Inquiry was being conducted by a colonel. He sat at a mahogany table with a major on one side and a captain on the other. None of these officers was connected with Northton. They were taking depositions and by the way they questioned me I was certain it was merely the prelude to a court martial.

They took my evidence under oath. To some extent it was a

cross-examination, with the Major making notes of my replies. They went over the whole sequence of events and my part in them. And when I had told them all I knew, the Major laboriously wrote out a summarized version in longhand. Then he read it through to me and when I had agreed that it was a fair statement of what I'd told them, I was asked to sign it.

I thought that was the end of it and was just getting up to leave, when the Colonel said, 'One moment, Mr Ross.' He searched through the folder in front of him and produced a letter. 'D'you know anything about a Mr Edward William Lane of Vancouver, a Canadian businessman?' I'd been expecting this and I was prepared for it. 'Yes,' I said. 'He visited me in London on 15 October. My brother Iain was among those missing when the *Duart Castle* was torpedoed in 1944. Lane had a theory that he was still alive.'

'In fact, he thought Major Braddock might be your brother. Correct?'

I nodded.

'The next day you left London for the Outer Hebrides. You landed at Rodil in the Island of Harris on 18 October and I understand you saw Major Braddock the following day.'

'Yes.'

'Had you ever visited the Outer Hebrides before?' And when I admitted I hadn't, he said, 'I take it then that you went up there for the express purpose of checking on Major Braddock's identity? In other words, you thought there was a possibility that he might be your missing brother?'

'It was partly that,' I agreed. 'Lane had convinced me that my brother could have been with Braddock on that life-raft and I thought he might be able to tell me what had happened. Also,' I added, 'there seemed a possibility that I might be able to get out to Laerg.' I started to explain to him then about my connection with the island and my desire to paint the scenes that my grandfather had described, but he cut me short.

'We are only concerned here with your visit as it affected Major Braddock. Now then, is there any truth in Lane's suggestion?'

I didn't give him a direct answer. Instead, I said, 'I understand that you've already taken evidence from the Senior Meteorological Officer at Northton. My first meeting with Major Braddock took place in the Met. Office. I imagine you have already asked Cliff Morgan whether Braddock and I recognized each other.'

He nodded.

'What did he say?' I asked.

'That as far as he can remember there was no indication that you had ever met each other before.'

It was a great weight off my mind to know that. 'Then that surely is your answer, sir,' I said. 'If Braddock had, in fact, been my brother, then I would hardly be a reliable witness. At the same time, it would have shown in our reaction to each other at that first meeting. You can have my word for it, if you like, but I think you will agree that the best evidence you have that there is no connection between us is Morgan's.' And I added, 'Perhaps you haven't appreciated this point. I don't know whether Lane explains it in that letter, but he's over here in an attempt to prove that Major Braddock is not entitled to a fortune of some quarter of a million dollars left him by his aunt. From what Lane told me, I got the impression that he was prepared to go to almost any lengths to upset the Will and get the money for his wife's family.'

'I see. No, he doesn't mention that here.' The Colonel hesitated. Finally he said, 'It puts rather a different complexion on the whole business.'

For Iain's sake I'd been prepared to lie, but after that it wasn't necessary. The Colonel was faced with an unpleasant enough task as it was. He'd no wish to become involved with something that had happened more than twenty years ago. 'Very well, I agree. That settles it. And I'm glad, for if there'd been any truth in it, then it would have raised the question of what had happened to the real George Braddock.' He gave a little sigh and pushed the letter back into the folder. 'Extraordinary what people will do for money. I'm sorry I've had to raise the matter . . . most unpleasant for you.' And he smiled his relief and said, 'That's all, Mr Ross. Thank you for coming to give evidence. I am also asked by my superiors to thank you for all you did on Laerg to assist in the rescue of the survivors.'

'I didn't do much,' I said. 'Braddock's the man to whom the survivors owe their lives. Field would never have made that climb if it hadn't been for Braddock. He organized the whole thing.'

The Colonel's sharp little eyes stared at me hard and I wondered for a moment if I'd said too much. But it was true and I was damned if I was going to leave the Inquiry without making the point. If they were going to blame him for what had happened, at least they ought to realize that without the driving force of his personality nobody would have been saved and the loss of life would have been that much greater.

Probably they knew that already. But it made no difference.

After hearing over two dozen witnesses they passed the depositions to the Director of Army Legal Services and in due course the next step towards Court Martial proceedings was taken. This was a Summary of Evidence and again I was called. Iain was present throughout the examination of witnesses, and this, more than anything else, seemed to emphasize the seriousness of his situation.

I understand he had the right to question witnesses. Whether he availed himself of this right I do not know; in my case he certainly did not, sitting tense and very still, his eyes never raised to my face. I was in the room almost two hours and all the time I was conscious of the nervous tension in him, could literally feel it. And he looked desperately ill.

I thought perhaps he would contact me afterwards, but he didn't, and though I stayed the night in Edinburgh just in case, I had no word from him. Perhaps he thought it would be unwise. In any case there was nothing I could have done – only given him moral support. Back in London I wrote him a carefully worded letter beginning *Dear Major Braddock* and inquiring whether there was anything I could do to help. I received no reply.

The waiting I knew would be hard on him, a nervous strain. The loneliness, too. This worried me as much as anything else, and in desperation I went and saw his wife.

I'd kept a newspaper cutting that gave her address and I found her living in one of the back streets of Hertford, a small woman with doe-like eyes and a will that was hard as iron. I went in the evening with the story that I was a welfare worker for SAAFA, but nothing I could say would induce her to visit her husband. She got the Army allowance, and that was all she wanted of him. And the only clue she gave as to why they had parted was when she said, 'I had five years of it.' And added, 'Nerves are one thing, but nerves and drink . . . No, I don't want to see him again.'

Yet she still had his photograph in a silver frame standing on a table beside the TV set – aged about thirty, I thought, and much as I remembered him in the Glasgow days, the lines of his face barely showing, but still that scar above the bridge of the nose. 'If it's any comfort to him in his present circumstances,' she said as she showed me to the door, 'you can tell him both the girls are well and pray for him nightly.' And she added, her lips tight and no tenderness in her eyes, 'I told them he'd been killed – and then this business with reporters coming here and the news of it on the telly, you can imagine the shock it was – how I felt.'

Christmas came and went, the New Year. Marjorie wrote from Rodil that Iain was in hospital. 'My father says they think Major Braddock is suffering from some sort of nervous breakdown. It's not serious apparently, but I thought you'd like to know. It's the waiting, of course. And now I can't help feeling sorry for him.'

There was nothing I could do about it. I couldn't very well write to him again, and if I tried to visit him the authorities would wonder at my interest. I was working all the time and so January slipped into February with news from Marjorie that he was out of hospital. The rest of her letter was about the fishing and how the solan geese were starting to come back. 'Soon there'll be all manner of birds and it'll be warmer with clear skies. Come back then and paint. It's so beautiful in the spring . . .'

And then at last the official letter notifying me that Major Braddock's Court Martial would be held in Edinburgh on 24 February, starting at 10 a.m.: – *You are, pursuant to Section 103 of the Army Act, 1955, and Rule 91 of the Rules of Procedure (Army), 1956, made thereunder, hereby summoned and required to attend at the sitting of the said court . . . and so to attend from day to day until you shall be duly discharged; whereof you shall fail at your peril.*

Four days later I got an airmail letter from Lane in Vancouver. Obviously he was paying somebody to keep him posted. 'Tell your brother that I'm flying over immediately and will be in Edinburgh on the 24th. Tell him also that I have some fresh evidence. My agents have located one of the Military Policemen acting as his escort on the *Duart Castle*. This man survived on one of the boats that reached Ireland and he is prepared to swear that Sergeant Iain Alasdair Ross was on that life-raft. He also saw Second-Lieutenant George Braddock clinging to it. Furthermore, he says he would recognize your brother . . .'

The Court Martial was held at Dreghorn Camp just outside Edinburgh. It opened prompt at ten o'clock with the swearing-in of the Court. For this ceremony the witnesses were present, all of us standing at the back of the court. It was a bare, rather bleak room, but the arrangement of the desks and tables and the grouping of the officers transformed it, and the colour of the uniforms made it impressive so that I was conscious of the atmosphere, the sense of being caught up in the Military legal machine. Instead of a judge with his wig and scarlet robes, five officers sat in judgement. And in the body of the court – the accused, the officer defending him, the Prosecuting Officer, all the various officials, even to the NCOs on duty, in full dress. The effect was overpowering and I wondered how my brother felt as the doors closed and quiet descended. The Judge Advocate, seated on the President's right hand, read the convening order.

From where I stood I could see only the back of Iain's head, hunched down into his shoulders, which sagged slightly as he sat slumped in his seat, staring down at the table in front of him. He seemed quite passive, almost dazed, and when he was asked if he objected to being tried by the President or any of the other members of the Court his reply was inaudible. And then the Judge Advocate's voice, clear and crisp: 'Everybody will stand uncovered whilst the Court is sworn.' A shuffle of chairs and the court-room rose to its feet as he faced the President. 'Please repeat after me – ' The Brigadier spoke the words he knew by heart in a clipped, very clear voice: 'I swear by Almighty God that I will well and truly try the Accused before the Court according to the evidence and that I will duly administer justice according to the Army Act, 1955, without partiality, favour or affection . . .'

The four other officers who constituted the Court were sworn and then the President swore in the Judge Advocate himself. After that the witnesses were ushered out into an adjoining room. There were altogether twenty-seven witnesses. Most of them were from Northton – Field, Rafferty, Flint, the MO, Phipps, Sergeant Wetherby and several other ranks I'd never seen before, including the Signals NCO who'd been on duty when the fatal order was given. Cliff was there and another civilian who turned out to be Fellowes, the pilot who had flown the plane from which Mike Ferguson had jumped to his death. Wentworth, too, and a young Captain whom Field told me was the Commander of L4400. Both Brigadier Matthieson and the BGS from the War Office had also been called, but their rank enabled them to avoid the tedium of waiting in the confines of that small room.

There was a Military Policeman on the door to see that we didn't discuss the case, nothing to do but sit and smoke, and I had ample opportunity to consider what my brother must be going through in the next room. Occasionally we could hear the murmur of voices, the stamp of boots as some NCO moved, the scrape of chairs, the sound of coughing.

The preliminaries took just over an hour – the reading of the charges and the Prosecuting Officer's speech in which he put his case. We could just hear the murmur of his voice. The first witness was called shortly after eleven thirty. This was the Signals NCO. He was followed by the duty driver, then Flint, then Wentworth. Wentworth was still giving evidence when the Court adjourned for lunch. The order in which the witnesses had been called was our only indication of the course the case was taking. Clearly the Prosecuting Officer was establishing the fact of the order to evacuate having been given.

Field was called during the afternoon and when the Court finally rose, he was waiting for me outside. 'Marjorie asked me to give you her love.' He smiled. He was looking younger, more buoyant, and his eyes had lost that nervous blink.

'How was Braddock?' I asked.

He hesitated, then shook his head. 'Not good, I'm afraid. Very nervy-looking; at times I wondered whether he understood what was going on. He's still a sick man, I'm afraid.'

I asked him about the nervous breakdown, but he didn't know the details. 'The strain of waiting, I imagine. Three months almost. It's a long time. Too long. But once it's over, probably he'll be all right then.'

'What are the chances?' I asked.

He shrugged. 'Hard to say. He's got a good man defending him, good enough at any rate to handle the two brigadiers. But even if he gets them to say they had every confidence in the accused, it won't outweigh the fact that Standing had him arrested. If Standing were here to be cross-examined . . .' Again that little shrug. 'But he isn't, you see, and dying like that he's something of a hero. That counts for a lot in a case like this. And there's all the publicity. The Judge Advocate may tell them what the law is, but the Court is human; they can't help being influenced by it. And the size of the disaster. Fifty-three men dead. Who's to be blamed if Braddock is acquitted? The Press will say the Army is covering up and there'll be more questions in the House.'

'So you don't think he's got a chance?'

He hesitated. And then he said, 'No. Frankly, I don't.'

I was called the following afternoon, immediately after Cliff Morgan had given evidence. When I took my place at the witness table I was shocked to see how ill Iain looked, his eyes wandering vacantly, his big, powerful hands never still – plucking at the buttons of his uniform, toying with his pencil, sometimes brushing over his face and up through his hair with a quick, nervous gesture. I don't think he once looked directly at me all the time I was being questioned. As Field had said, he still seemed a sick man – all his intense nervous energy beaten down, as though something had destroyed his will to fight back. I had that feeling very strongly, that his strength was being sapped from within, and I wondered to what extent he had been affected by the fact that Lane was in

Edinburgh. I had seen Lane that morning, just a glimpse of him as I was entering the main gate of the camp. He was sitting there in a car with another man.

'Will the witness please answer the question.' The President's voice, kindly but firm, brought me back to the stillness of the court-room and the rather bland-looking major who was defending Iain standing facing me, waiting patiently for my answer.

'I'm sorry,' I said. 'Perhaps you would repeat the question.'

'I asked you, Mr Ross, whether you could recall the time at which Major Braddock gave the order to evacuate the island?'

'Yes,' I said. 'Or rather, I can remember when the landing craft came in to the beach. She grounded at nine forty-eight.'

'And Major Braddock's order?'

'About ten minutes earlier. The landing craft was coming in to the beach as we left the hut. Say, nine-thirty.'

'Now I want the Court to understand the circumstances in which that order was given. What was the direction of the wind at that time?'

'Northerly. It had been northerly all day.'

'And no indication of a change?'

'No.'

'After the landing craft beached you went on board?'

'Yes.'

'Where were you then?'

'I was helping on the tank deck until nearly midnight. After that I went to the wardroom.'

'Where you found Lieutenant Wentworth talking to Captain Stratton?'

'Yes.'

'What were they discussing?'

'A radio message they had received from the Met. Officer at Northton.'

'Do you know when that message was received?'

'It had just come in so it would have been shortly after midnight.'

'Two and a half hours after Major Braddock had given the order.'

'Yes.'

'And the wind at Laerg was still northerly then?'

'Yes.' I saw the point he was trying to establish and I added, 'It remained northerly for another four and a half hours.'

The Major reached for his glasses and glanced at his notes. 'Mr Morgan in his evidence said that he was in contact with the *Viking Fisher* at twenty-three forty-seven. That's the trawler that was finally lost with all hands. Thirteen minutes to midnight. In your opinion was there any way in which Major Braddock could have foreseen how circumstances were going to change?'

'No,' I said. 'Definitely not.' I glanced at Iain as his Defending Officer said, 'Thank you, Mr Ross,' in a satisfied tone. I was surprised to see him running his pencil back and forth across the table in front of him, apparently taking no interest in the proceedings.

The Defending Officer turned to the President of the Court. 'That is the point I wish to establish.' And then to me: 'You have some experience of the sea, I believe. A year in the Navy and ten in the Merchant Service as a deck officer. Correct?'

'Yes.'

'You were on the bridge with Captain Stratton part of the time during the crossing to Laerg and throughout the events that led up to the loss of the ship. Would you say he was a capable seaman?'

'Very capable.'

'So that in coming in to the beach you would say, would you not, that it was the action of a capable seaman?'

'Yes,' I said. 'I'm certain Captain Stratton would never have brought his landing craft in to the beach if he had thought there was any danger.'

'And he was in a much better position than Major Braddock to assess the local weather situation?'

'I think you have made your point, Major Selkirk,' the President said.

The Major gave a nod and a quick smile. 'I just wanted to make it quite clear, sir.' He glanced down at the papers on his desk. 'Lieutenant Wentworth in his evidence has said that after the ship was unloaded Captain Pinney refused to take his men ashore. Can you confirm that?'

'Yes. I was in the wheelhouse at the time.'

'When was this?'

'Between two-thirty and three, I should say.'

'Can you recall the conversation?'

'It was hardly a conversation,' I said.

'A row?'

'No, not a row.' Briefly I told them what Pinney's attitude had been.

'So even then, somewhere between two-thirty and three, there was doubt about the wind shifting from the north?'

'Yes.'

'Not only in Pinney's mind, but in Stratton's as well?'
I nodded.

'Thank you.' He shifted his stance, glanced at my brother who was still fiddling around with that damned pencil, and then his gaze came back to me. 'You remember that Captain Stratton asked his radio operator to contact Colonel Standing. About what time would that have been?'

'Around twelve-thirty. We were in the wardroom then. He wanted to talk to Colonel Standing personally and he told the operator that the Colonel was to be got out of bed if necessary.' And I added, 'He said something about it being time the men who gave the orders lost a little sleep on our account.'

Quick as a flash he said, 'Are you implying that he knew Colonel Standing had gone up to his house, which was a mile from the camp – that he had, in fact, retired to . . .'

But the President interrupted him. 'Major Selkirk. I must remind you again that Colonel Standing is dead. References to him should be confined to facts. You must not include vague statements about him or expressions of opinion or the comments of other officers.'

'I quite understand, sir.' The Defending Officer's face was wooden and he rustled the papers in his hand as he faced the Court. 'I will endeavour to follow your ruling, but I must point out that the officer I am defending faces very serious charges and my case rests to some extent on the clash of personalities that, I submit, was the direct and inevitable result of this somewhat, shall I say, unusual appointment. You have heard the evidence this morning of two brigadiers, both of whom briefed the accused following his appointment. Both have admitted that their instructions could be interpreted as making Major Braddock directly responsible for the success of the operation. However, if Colonel Standing's behaviour is not to be referred to . . .' He flung his papers on to the desk. 'Mr Ross, you will now tell the Court what Captain Stratton said after he'd spoken to Colonel Standing.'

I hesitated, for I didn't see how this could help Iain. But the Court was waiting and I said, 'He didn't say very much – just that Colonel Standing hadn't known about the order and was angry.'

'Angry? Because he'd been got out of bed in the middle of the night?' I saw the President lean forward, but Selkirk was too quick for him. 'Or was it because he didn't know at that time, that there was a landing craft grounded on the beach in Shelter Bay?'

779

'I think it was because he didn't know about the evacuation.'

'Did he know there was a landing craft on the beach or not?'

'He couldn't have done.'

'Did he know about the Met. Officer's latest forecast?'

'I don't think so.'

'In other words, he was completely out of touch with the situation and it was Major Braddock . . .'

The Prosecuting Officer was on his feet, but the President forestalled him: 'I must insist that you confine yourself to questions of fact and refrain from putting opinions of your own into the witness's mouth.'

'Very well, sir. But I would ask the Court's indulgence. It is a little difficult to know who exactly was in command.' Again he adjusted his glasses, leaning down to check his notes. 'Now, about radio contact. In your deposition which I have here, you say you spoke to Mr Morgan yourself on R/T. What was the reception like?'

'Very poor,' I told him. 'And Stratton said it was bad when he was talking to Colonel Standing.'

'Was that the reason, do you think, that Captain Pinney wasn't given a direct order by his superiors to get his men off the ship?' And before I could reply, he went on, 'Or would you say, from your own experience, that in a situation like this Major Braddock would be fully justified in leaving any decision like that to the men on the spot?'

'I think by then,' I said, 'the situation was beyond the control of anybody at Base.'

He nodded, and after that he stood for a moment reading through his notes. I saw my brother's attention wander to the door at the back of the court. He had done that several times. Major Selkirk had stepped back from his desk, head thrown up and his eyes fixed on me again. 'Now we come to the loss of L-eight-six-one-o . . . the cause, or rather the twin causes, for there were two, weren't there?' And when I nodded, he went on, 'These were covered very fully by Lieutenant Wentworth in his evidence, but I would like to confirm one point with you – the failure of the steering. Do you remember Lieutenant Wentworth making a comment about the tiller flat? He says he told Captain Stratton that it was being flooded. Do you recall him making that report?'

'Yes.'

'And did he give a reason?'

I told them then how the stretcher party had taken McGregor's body to the tiller flat and had failed to secure the hatch on leaving. 'That was what caused the flooding.'

'And it was the failure of the steering, was it not, that threw the ship on her beam ends and made it impossible to deal with the sea water in the ready-use tank?'

'Yes.'

'And that again was something that Captain Stratton couldn't have foreseen?'

'Nobody could have foreseen it,' I said.

'And certainly not Major Braddock, back at Base?'

'No.'

And on that he sat down. There was a moment of shuffling relaxation in the court-room, and then the Prosecuting Officer rose to cross-examine me. He was a large, quiet man with a soft voice and a manner that was easy, almost friendly. 'One or two small points, Mr Ross. We know that Captain Pinney virtually refused to take his men off the ship. But later, just before you got off the beach, I think I'm right in saying that Colonel Standing spoke to him on the R/T. Am I also right in saying that the result of that talk was a direct order from his Colonel to get his men disembarked?'

'I believe so, but by then it was quite impossible.' I knew what he was after. He wanted to show that Standing had not only countermanded the order, but had come very near to saving the situation. He was going to try and show Standing as a decisive man whose subordinate had let him down and who was making a last-minute effort to rectify the damage that had been done. I glanced at my brother, but his head was again turned towards the door, which was half open. A sergeant had come in and was just closing it. I turned to the President, determined not to have this point twisted to the advantage of the Prosecution. 'The first contact Colonel Standing had with the ship was when he spoke to Captain Stratton. My impression is that he had already taken personal command; yet he gave no order for the disembarkation of the Laerg detachment. I agree he did eventually give the order to Pinney, but by then it was at least two hours too late.'

The President nodded. 'And in your view the accused officer was not responsible at that time?'

'That's my impression – that Colonel Standing was in control.'

The Prosecuting Officer continued: 'You mentioned that radio conditions were bad . . .' He was shifting his ground, but at that moment the sergeant came down the room, his footsteps loud on the bare boards. He handed the President a note. When he had read it, the President glanced quickly at me, and from me to Iain. He didn't say anything, but after consultation with the Judge Advocate he cleared the Court.

Nobody has ever told me what was in that note. But I can guess, for Lane made a statement to the Court and this was supported by the man he had brought with him. After we had been kept waiting about half an hour, it was announced that the Court was adjourned until the following day.

Knowing what Lane would have told the Court, I was expecting every moment to be called to an interview. But nothing happened. Instead a rumour circulated that Major Braddock had collapsed and had been rushed unconscious to the Medical Reception. This proved correct. A statement was issued to the Press that night and the following morning my newspaper carried the story under the headline: ACCUSED MAJOR BREAKS DOWN – LAERG COURT MARTIAL POSTPONED.

I read it over my breakfast and I was still drinking my coffee and wondering about it when the hotel receptionist came in to tell me that there was an Army officer waiting to see me. He was a young second-lieutenant and he had orders to take me to the hospital. It is not clear to me even now whether the Army had accepted the fact that Major Braddock and I were brothers. I think probably they had – privately. But the Army, like any other large organization, is a community in itself with its own code of behaviour. As such it closes its ranks and throws a protective cloak over its members when they are attacked by the outside world. I suspect that Lane's accusation was not accepted by the Court – officially, at any rate. In any case it was quite outside the scope of their proceedings.

To Lane it must have seemed nothing less than a conspiracy of silence. First the Army, and then the Press. I know he approached several newspapers, for they dug up the *Duart Castle* story, and in addition they wrote up Lane himself – not very kindly. But none of them referred to his accusations, other than obliquely. The law of libel made that too hot a story. There was another factor, too. Braddock's collapse had to some extent swung public feeling. The disaster was now past history. It had happened more than three months ago and here was this man being hounded into a nervous breakdown.

A RAMC Colonel and a psychiatrist were waiting for me at the MR Station. Possibly they thought my presence might jerk Braddock's mind back into an awareness of the world around him. In fact, he stared at me without a flicker of recognition or even interest, face and eyes quite blank. He had a room to himself and was lying in bed, propped up on pillows. The lines of his face seemed smoothed out so that he looked much younger, almost like the youth I had known. He could talk quite lucidly, but only about the things going on around him. He appeared to remember nothing of the Court Martial or of the events on Laerg. At least he didn't refer to them. 'Do I know you?' he asked me innocently. 'We've met before, I suppose, but I'm afraid I don't remember. They say I've lost my memory, you see.'

'Talk to him about Laerg,' the psychiatrist whispered to me.

But Laerg meant nothing to him. 'You were there,' I said. 'You saved the lives of twenty-three men.'

He frowned as though making an effort to remember. And then he smiled and shook his head. There was a vacant quality about that smile. 'I'll take your word for it,' he said. 'I don't remember. I don't remember a damn thing.'

I was there nearly an hour and all the time, at the back of my mind, was the question – was this a genuine brainstorm or was he pretending? There was that smoothed-out quite untroubled face, the vacant, puzzled look in his eyes. And in a case of this sort where is the borderline between genuine mental illness and the need to seek refuge from the strain of events? One leads to the other and by the time I left I was convinced that even if he had deliberately sought this refuge, there was now no doubt that he had willed himself into a state of mental blackout.

'Kind of you to come and see me,' he said as I was leaving. He spoke quite cheerfully, but his voice sounded tired as thought talking to me had been a strain.

Outside, the psychiatrist said, 'Afraid it didn't work. Perhaps in a few weeks' time when his mind's rested, eh?' No reference to the possibility that we might be related. But it was there all the same, implicit in his assumption that I'd be prepared to come all the way up from London at my own expense to visit him again.

This I did about two weeks later at their request. By then my brother had been moved to a civilian institution and he was up and dressed. On this occasion they left us alone together. But it made no difference. His mind was a blank, or it appeared to be – blank of everything he didn't want to remember. And if he recognized me, he didn't show it. 'They've got microphones in the walls,' he said. But whether they had, I don't know. The psychiatrist said no. They'd been giving him treatment, electric shock treatment. 'This place is like a brain-washing establishment.

Refinements of mental cruelty. They think I'm somebody else. They keep trying to tell me I'm somebody else. If I'll admit it, then I needn't have shock treatment. And when I say I know who I am, they put the clamps on my head and turn up their rheostats full blast. Ever had shock treatment?' And when I shook my head, he grinned and said, 'Lucky fellow! Take my advice. Don't ever let them get their hands on you. Resist and you're in a strait-jacket and down to the torture chamber.'

There was a lot more that I can't remember and all of it with a thread of truth running through the fantasy. 'They think they'll break me.' He said that several times, and then words tumbling out of his mouth again as though he were afraid I'd leave him if he didn't go on talking – as though he were desperate for my company. 'They want me to admit that I'm responsible for the death of a lot of men. Well, old man, I'll tell you. They can flay me alive with their damned machines, but I'll admit nothing. Nothing, you get me. I've even had a lawyer here. Wanted to give me some money – ten thousand dollars if I'd say I'm not George Braddock. But they won't catch me that way.' He had fixed me with his eyes and now he grabbed hold of my arm and drew me down. 'You know they've got a Court sitting, waiting to try me.'

'All right,' I said. My face was so close to his nobody could possibly overhear. 'Then why not tell them? Why not tell them what happened out there in the Atlantic? Get it over with.' All the way up in the train I'd been thinking about it, certain that this was the root of the trouble.

But all he said was, 'Somewhere in the basement I think it is. And if I admit anything . . .'

'It's a long time ago,' I said. 'If you just tell them what happened.'

But it didn't seem to get through to him. '. . . then they're waiting for me, and I'll be down there, facing a lot of filthy accusations. I tell you, there's nothing they won't do.' And so it went on, the words pouring out to reveal a mental kaleidoscope, truth and fantasy inextricably mixed.

Mad? Or just clever simulation? I wondered, and so apparently did the psychiatrist. 'What do you think?' he asked me as I was leaving. It was the same man, thick tortoise-shell glasses and the earnest, humourless air of one who believes that the mystery of his profession elevates him to a sort of priesthood. 'If we let him out, then he's fit and the Court Martial will have to sit again. He's not fit – or is he?' He stared at me, searchingly. 'No, of course – not your department. And you wouldn't admit anything yourself, would you?'

Veiled allusions like that. And the devil of it was there was nothing I could do to help Iain.

A week later they had another attempt at shock treatment – mental, not electrical this time. They brought Lane in to see him and before the wretched man had been in there five minutes, they had to rush in and rescue him. Iain had him by the throat and was choking the life out of him.

After that they left him alone.

Two days later the police came to my studio. It was just after lunch and I was working on a canvas that I was doing entirely for my own benefit – a portrait of Marjorie, painted from memory. I hadn't even a photograph of her at that time. I heard their footsteps on the bare stairboards, and when I went to the door a sergeant and a constable were standing there. 'Mr Ross?' The sergeant came in, a big man with a flattened nose and small, inquisitive eyes. 'I understand you're acquainted with a certain Major Braddock who is undergoing treatment in the James Craig Institute, Edinburgh?' And when I nodded, he said, 'Well now, would it surprise you, sir, to know that he's escaped?'

'Escaped – when?' I asked.

'Last night. He was discovered missing this morning. I've been instructed to check whether he's been seen in this neighbourhood and in particular whether he's visited you.'

'No,' I said. 'Why should he?'

'I'm given to understand you're related. They seemed to think he might try to contact you.' He stood staring at me, waiting for me to answer. 'Well, has he?'

'I'm afraid I can't help you. He certainly hasn't been here.'

I saw his eyes searching the studio as though he wasn't prepared to take my word for it. Finally he said, 'Very good, Mr Ross. I'll tell them. And if he does contact you, telephone us immediately. I should warn you that he may be dangerous.' He gave me the number of the police station and then with a jerk of his head at the constable, who had been quietly sniffing round the studio like a terrier after a bone, he left.

Their footsteps faded away down the stairs and I stood there without moving, thinking of Iain on the run with the police as well as the Army after him. Where would he go? But I knew where he'd go – knew in the same instant that I'd have to go there, too. Everything that had happened, his every action . . . all led inevitably back to Laerg.

I lit a cigarette, my hands trembling, all my fears brought suddenly to a head. Twenty-two days on a raft in the North Atlantic. Sooner or later they'd guess – guess that no man could have lasted that long, not in mid-winter; and Laerg on his direct route. They'd work it out, just as I had worked it out, and then . . . I turned to the window; drab vistas of grey slates, the mist hanging over the river, and my mind far away, wondering how to get there – how to reach Laerg on my own without anybody knowing? I hadn't the money to buy a boat, and to charter meant involving other people. But I could afford a rubber dinghy, and given twenty-four hours' calm weather . . . I thought Cliff Morgan could help me there. A radio to pick up his forecasts, a compass, an outboard motor – it ought to be possible.

I was up half the night working it out, making lists. And in the morning I drew all my cash out of the bank, booked a seat on the night train for Mallaig and began a hectic six hours, shopping for the equipment I needed.

2

LONE VOYAGE
(1–6 March)

There was news of Iain in the papers that night. It was in the Stop Press – MISSING MAJOR SEEN AT STIRLING. A motorist had given him a lift to Killin at the head of Loch Tay. And in the morning when the train pulled into Glasgow I found the Scottish papers full of it, his picture all over the front pages. He'd been seen on the railway station at Crianlarich and again at Fort William. A police watch was being kept on the quay at Mallaig in case he tried to board the steamer for the Western Isles and all the villages along the coast had been alerted. The net was closing in on him and in that sparsely populated district I didn't think he had a chance.

A man who boarded the train at Arisaig told me a stranger had been seen walking the coast towards Loch Moidart, and with Ardnamurchan so close, I toyed with the idea that he might be making for our old croft. But at Mallaig there was more definite news, a lobster boat stolen during the night from a cove in Loch Nevin. The whole town was talking about it and an old man on the quay told me it was an open boat, 30 feet long, with a single screw and a diesel engine. 'An oldish boat, ye ken, but sound, and the bluidy man will wreck her for sure.' I was certain he was wrong there; just as I was certain now that Iain was making for Laerg. He'd push across to Eigg or Rum or one of the smaller islands and lie up in the lee. But to cross The Minch and cover the eighty-odd miles of Atlantic beyond he'd need better weather than this; he'd also need fuel. By taking the steamer I'd be in the Outer Hebrides before he'd even left the mainland coast.

It was late in the afternoon of the following day, 3 March, that I reached Rodil. The passage across The Minch had been bad – the steel-grey of the sea ribbed with the white of breaking waves, the sky a pale, almost greenish-blue with mares' tails feathering across it like vapour trails. Later the black outline of the Western Isles had become blurred by rain.

I had planned to pitch my tent at the head of Loch Rodil, well away from the hotel, but the boatman refused to attempt it and landed me at the jetty instead, along with my gear and two other passengers. 'Will you be staying long this time, Mr Ross?' He eyed me doubtfully. 'Last time you were here . . .' He shook his head. 'That was a tur-rible storm.' The two passengers, Army officers in civilian clothes, regarded me with interest.

I dumped my gear and got hold of Marjorie. I was in too much of a hurry to consider how she would react to my sudden unexpected appearance. All I wanted was to contact Cliff and get away from Rodil before the Army discovered I was there.

As she drove me in to Northton, she said, 'It's true, then, that Major Braddock has stolen a Mallaig boat. That's why you're here, isn't it?'

I didn't want to be questioned and when I didn't answer she gave me a wry grin. 'For one wild moment I thought you might have come to see me.'

'I'm sorry.' I ought to have managed this meeting better, but it couldn't be helped. She was wearing the faded anarak she'd had on when I'd first seen her. Wisps of her black hair escaped the hood, glistening with moisture. She looked very attractive and at any other time . . .

'That rubber dinghy, the outboard, all that gear on the jetty – it's yours I take it.' And when I nodded, she said, 'I'm afraid you haven't chosen a very good time. It's been like this for almost a fortnight, nothing but rain and wind.' She meant it as a warning. And she added, 'It's Laerg, isn't it? You're going to Laerg.'

787

'Yes,' I said. 'I'm going to Laerg.' No point in denying it when she'd known it instinctively. 'But please don't tell anybody. I'm hoping Cliff will give me the local forecasts and then I'll get away from here just as soon as I can.'

We were driving into the camp then and she stopped at the main gate. 'I'll wait for you here. I have to pick my father up anyway.'

My luck was in. Cliff was on the afternoon shift and he was still there, standing by the sloped desk, checking through a teleprint sheet. 'Ross.' He put down the teleprint sheets. 'Damn it, man, what are you doing here?' He hadn't changed – still the same old cardigan, the open-necked shirt, the quick, volatile manner.

'I want your help,' I said. And I told him about my plan to go to Laerg.

'Good God! I should have thought you'd have had enough of the place after what you went through there.' The quick brown eyes stared at me curiously from behind their thick-lensed glasses. 'What makes you want to go back?'

'You forget I'm an artist,' I said. 'And my father was born on Laerg. Now that the Army's evacuated, it's an opportunity to be there alone. The birds will be back now. I want to paint.'

He nodded and I thought he'd accepted my explanation. But he was still looking at me curiously. 'Have you got the Army's permission?'

'No.'

'What about Nature Conservancy then?'

'I haven't got anybody's permission,' I said. 'I'm just going to go there.' And I explained what I wanted from him; a weather clearance at the first possible moment, the certainty of at least twenty-four hours of light winds; and one, preferably two, personal weather forecasts during the voyage. 'I want to sail as soon as possible and it's essential that I have calm conditions on arrival at Laerg.'

He asked then about the sort of boat I'd got, and when I told him, he reached for his cigarettes. 'You know what you're doing, I suppose.' He didn't expect an answer to that, but went on to inquire about my radio. Could I take morse? What speed?

'Fast enough,' I said.

'And you'll be on your own?'

'Yes.'

He lit his cigarette, staring thoughtfully out of the window.

'Well,' I said, 'will you do it?'

'And you need calm weather at the other end.' He seemed to be thinking aloud. 'That means you're not planning to land in Shelter Bay.' I thought he was much too shrewd where weather was concerned. But instead of pursuing the matter, he turned abruptly to the maps on the wall. 'Well, there's the situation.' The lower one showed a low pressure area south-east of Iceland and another Low coming in from the Atlantic. But it was the upper one that interested me, the one that gave his forecast for midnight. It showed that second Low just west of the Hebrides. 'A southerly air stream, you see, with the wind veering south-westerly some time during the night.' Behind the depression with its wedge-shaped lines marking the warm and cold fronts was a shallow ridge of high pressure. Beyond that, further out in the Atlantic, another Low.

'It doesn't look very promising,' I said.

He had walked over to the map and was standing there, staring up at it. 'No. Fine tomorrow with the wind falling fairly light, and after that high winds again. But it's not quite as bad as it looks. The Azores High is strengthening – I was just looking at the figures when you came in. Maybe in a couple of days . . .' And then without a change in his voice: 'You know Braddock's been seen on the mainland.' He turned abruptly and faced me. 'There's talk in the Mess that he's stolen a boat – one of those lobster boats. He could reach Laerg in a boat like that.' He was staring at me, his gaze fixed on my face. 'The last time you were in this office, Braddock came in. Remember? They questioned me about that at the Inquiry. They asked me whether you'd recognized each other. Did you know that?' And when I nodded, he added, 'I told them no.' He hesitated. 'You're not being quite frank with me now, are you? It's because of Braddock you're going to Laerg.'

It was no good denying it. I needed his help. 'Yes,' I said. 'But I'd rather not talk about it now.'

To my relief he seemed to accept that. 'Well, it's your own business, nothing to do with me. I don't give a bloody damn about Braddock. He cost a lot of men their lives and if he'd bothered to consult me first . . . However – ' He shrugged. 'It's done now and I don't like to see a man hounded out of his wits. Did you know they'd got an aircraft up looking for him?' He stood there a moment, thinking it out. 'Suppose I refuse to give you the local forecast – what then, would you still go?'

'Yes. I'd have to rely on the BBC shipping forecasts, and that wouldn't be the same as having the local weather from you. But I'd still go.'

He nodded. 'Okay. That's what I thought.' And he added, 'I don't know what your connection with Braddock is or what you hope to achieve by going to Laerg, but nobody would undertake a trip like that unless they had very strong reasons for doing so. I accept that, and I'll do what I can to help you.' He stubbed out his cigarette. 'The weather's been bloody awful these last few weeks and that Low that's coming in from the Atlantic – ' he nodded to the weather map – 'it's still intensifying. The new figures just came in over the teleprinter. Pressure at the centre is nine-seven-two falling and unless the ridge of high pressure in front of it builds up – and I don't think it will – that next Low will start coming through some time tomorrow night. After that . . . well, this is just guesswork, but we might get a fine spell. It's about time, you know.' He went back to the desk. 'I'll give you my call sign and the frequency you have to listen on.' He wrote it down for me and suggested I tuned in to his net at 2200 hours. 'Just to check that you're picking me up all right. Phone me at nine o'clock tomorrow morning here. I usually look in about that time if I'm not on the morning shift.'

I thanked him, but as I turned to go he stopped me. 'Take my advice, Ross, and keep clear of the Military. It's not only Braddock they're worried about. There's a report of a Russian trawler in the area, and this new chap, Colonel Webb – very cautious he is. Can't blame him after what's happened. And a fellow alone in a rubber dinghy, you see . . . thought I'd better warn you.'

I left him then. It was just after six-thirty. The car was waiting for me at the main gate and there was an officer leaning against it, talking to Field. It was the dapper little captain who had replaced Mike Ferguson as Adjutant. He watched as I climbed into the back of the car and I thought he recognized me.

'Marjorie tells me you're going to Laerg,' Field said as we drove off. 'Alone?'

'Yes.'

'Well, I hope Cliff Morgan was able to offer you the prospect of some better weather.' He didn't ask me why I was going.

But later that evening, sitting by the peat fire in their croft, it was obvious he had guessed. 'The air search is being stepped up tomorrow – two helicopters and a Shackleton. They'll be concentrating on The Minch and the Inner Hebrides, and every fishing vessel will be on the lookout for him.'

'He hasn't been seen then?'

'No. But it's just a matter of time.' And he added, 'I gather he was under treatment. It's possible he said things . . .' He didn't look at me, but sat staring into the fire, his long, beaked face in silhouette against the lamplight. 'These truth drugs, they quite often work, you know.' And then he gave me the same advice that Cliff had given me. 'If you don't want the Army bothering you, I should get away from here just as soon as you can. The North Ford, between North Uist and Benbecula, is as good a jumping-off place as any. Nobody will bother you there, and when you do sail you'd have the Monach Isles to land on if the wind got up.' He turned his head suddenly and looked at me. 'I wonder what makes you so certain Braddock is headed for Laerg?' And when I didn't say anything, he added, 'That night when we were leaving, he wanted the tug to go without him, didn't he?' I hadn't expected him to have guessed that. His gaze returned to the fire. 'A strange man. Quite ruthless. But a great deal of courage. And with a drive . . . I think that's what one most admired, that driving energy of his.' And after a moment he added, 'For your sake I hope the end of it all isn't – ' he hesitated – 'some ghastly tragedy.'

Marjorie came in then with supper on a tray. We ate it there by the fire. It was a cosy, pleasant meal, and for a while I was able to forget the weather and the sense of loneliness, almost of isolation, that had been growing in me ever since I'd returned to the Hebrides.

I had to leave at nine-thirty in order to be back in time to pick up Cliff's transmission and test reception. 'I'll walk down with you,' Field said. Marjorie came to the door with us. 'I'll see you in the morning,' she said. 'I hope you don't have too unpleasant a night.'

Outside the rain had ceased, but it was blowing harder than ever. Field didn't say anything until we had passed the church. 'I wanted to have a word with you alone.' His voice was hesitant. 'About Marjorie. You realize she's in love with you?' And he went on quickly. 'She's Celt – both sides. She's the sort of girl who'd break her heart over somebody.' He stopped and faced me. 'I wouldn't be talking to you like this if you were an ordinary fellow. But you're not. You're an artist. I don't know why that makes a difference, but it does.'

I didn't know what to say, for I hadn't given much thought to the way the relationship between us had been developing, and now . . . 'Probably it's just the reaction . . . I mean, she was fond of Ferguson.'

'Fond, yes. But nothing more. You're an older man . . .' He hesitated. 'Not married, are you?'

'I was – for a few months. But that finished years ago.'

'I see. Well . . .' He sounded awkward about it now. 'We're very close, Marjorie and I – always have been since her mother died. And now she's grown up . . .' He started walking again, his head down. 'Not your fault, perhaps, but don't make a fool of her. I couldn't bear that – and nor could she.' And he added, 'Well, there it is . . . just so that you understand.' He didn't give me a chance to say anything, but switched abruptly to the subject of my voyage to Laerg. 'I don't like it,' he said. 'The weather up here can change very quickly. Right now there are half-a-dozen lobster fishermen marooned on the Monachs. Been there almost a fortnight.'

'I'll be all right,' I said. 'Cliff's giving me the local forecasts.'

'If I weren't tied up here, I'd offer to come with you. I don't like the idea of your doing it alone. Nor does Marjorie.' We had reached the dip in the road that led down to the hotel and he stopped. 'Well, you know what you're doing, I suppose.' And he added, 'I'll let you know if there's any further news of Braddock.' He left me then, going back up the road, the darkness swallowing him almost at once.

I had pitched my tent on the same grass slope just beyond the small boat harbour and I got back to it just in time to pick up Cliff's transmission. He gave me his call sign first – GM3CMX, repeated several times; then the weather forecast, keyed much slower than he would normally send. Reception was good, loud and clear with no interruption. He followed the forecast with a brief message: *Your arrival commented on. Remember my advice and clear out tomorrow.* He ended his message with the letters *CL*, which meant that he was closing down his station.

I lit the pressure lamp and got out my charts, starting with 2508 which covered the whole hundred miles of the Outer Hebrides chain and included all the out-islands. Laerg stood solitary and alone on the very edge of the chart, a tiny speck surrounded by the blank white of ocean, with only scattered soundings. The shortest line from Laerg to the Hebrides touched North Uist at its westernmost point, Air-an-Runair. The distance was eighty-three nautical miles.

But now that I had disembarked my gear and contacted Cliff, I was no longer tied to Rodil and could shorten the voyage by crossing the Sound of Harris. The west coast of North Uist was too exposed, but remembering what Field had said, my eyes were drawn to the North Ford and to a straggle of islands shaped like the wings of a butterfly that lay barely a dozen miles to the west. These were marked on the chart – 'Heisker (The Monach Islands)'.

I lit a cigarette, got out chart No. 3168 and began to examine the North Ford in detail. It would be low water before I got there and I saw at a glance that the narrow channels through the sand would make it possible for me to go through whatever the tide. And at the western end, beyond the causeway that joined North Uist to Benbecula, the island of Baleshare stretched a great dune tongue down from the north, a bare waste devoid of any croft. I pencilled a circle round it, let the pressure out of the lamp and lay down with a sense of satisfaction. From Baleshare to the Monachs was about nine miles. From the Monachs to Laerg seventy-six miles. This way I should reduce the open sea passage by at least thirteen miles.

I left the following morning immediately after phoning Cliff. A cold, clear day with the wind fallen light and the clouds lifted to a thin grey film of cirrostratus high in the sky. And late that afternoon I pitched my tent against a background so utterly different that I might have been in another country. Gone were the lofty hills of Harris, the sense of being shut in, pressed against the sea's edge by sodden heights. Gone, too, was the brown of the seaweed, the sombre dark of rocks. Here all was sand, great vistas of it, golden bright and stretching flat to the distant hump of a solitary, purpling peak. My camp faced east and the tide was out. The peak was Eaval. Behind me were the dunes of Baleshare. All the rest was sky, thin mackerel scales of cloud, silver-grey and full of light. And not another soul to be seen, only the distant outline of solitary crofts, remote on islands in the Ford.

From the top of the dunes I could see the channelled entrance to the Ford, marked out for me by the white of waves breaking on the sand bars. A mile or more of broken water, and beyond that, low on the western horizon, the outline of the Monachs, the pointed finger of the disused lighthouse just visible.

The sun set and the heavens flared, a fantastic, fiery red. From horizon to horizon the sky blazed, a lurid canopy shot through with flaming wisps of cloud. It was a blood-bath of colour, and as I watched it, the red gradually darkening to purple, the whole vast expanse of sky was like a wound slowly clotting. Darkness fell and the tide rose; the dinghy floated closer until it rested just below my tent.

Cliff came through prompt at ten o'clock. The weather

pattern was unchanged. I had some food then and went to bed and lay in the dark, thinking of Laerg – out there to the westward, beyond the break of the sand bar surf, beyond the dim-seen shape of the Monachs, hidden below the horizon.

If, when I had left Rodil that morning, the engine had failed to start, or I had found an air leak in the dinghy, or anything had gone wrong, then I think I should have regarded it as an omen. But across the Sound of Harris, and all the way down the coast of North Uist, the engine had run without faltering. The speed, measured between identified islands, had been just over 3½ knots. Even in the North Ford, where it was wind against tide and quite a lop on the water, I hadn't experienced a moment's uneasiness. The craft was buoyant, despite her heavy load. She had shot the rapids under the Causeway bridge without taking any water, and though the tide was falling then and the channel tortuous, she had only twice grounded, and each time I had been able to float her off.

I was sure, lying in my tent that night, that I could make Laerg. But confidence is not easily maintained against such an elemental force as the sea. The break of the waves on the bar had been no more than a murmur in my ears when I had gone to sleep. When I woke it was a pounding roar that shook the dunes and the air was thick with the slaver of the gale; great gobs of spume, like froth, blown on the wind. Rain drove in grey sheets up the Ford and to stand on the dunes and look seaward was to face layer upon layer of rollers piling in, their creaming tops whipped landward by the wind.

It lasted a few hours, that was all, but the speed with which it had arrived and the suddenness of those big seas was disturbing.

The synopsis at the beginning of the one-forty forecast confirmed the pattern transmitted to me by Cliff the previous night; the depression centred over Scotland moving away north-eastward, and a high pressure system building up behind it and covering the Eastern Atlantic from the Azores to approximately latitude 60° North. Outlook for sea area Hebrides was wind force 6, veering north-westerly and decreasing to light variable; sea moderating, becoming calm; visibility moderate to good, but chance of fog patches locally.

I moved fast after that. The gale had lost me half the day and now the tide was falling. Where I was camped on the southern tip of Baleshare the deep water channel swung close in to the dunes, but on the other side, towards Gramisdale, the sands were already beginning to dry. My most urgent need was petrol. I had used over eight gallons coming down. I filled up the tank of the outboard, slid my ungainly craft into the water and pushed off with the two empty jerricans, following the channel north-east past the tufted grass island of Stromay towards the village of Carinish.

Beyond Stromay the deep water channel forked. I took the right fork. It was still blowing quite hard and by keeping to the roughest water I avoided the shallows. I beached just south of the village, tied the painter to a stone and hurried up the track, carrying the jerricans. There was no petrol pump at Carinish, but the chart had marked a Post Office and as I had expected it was the centre of village information. There were about half a dozen women gossiping in the little room and when I explained what I'd come for, one of them immediately said, 'There's Roddie McNeil now. He runs a car. D'ye ken the hoose?' And when I shook my head, she said, 'Och weel, I'll get it for you myself.' And she went off with my jerricans.

I asked if I could telephone then and the post mistress pushed the phone across the counter to me. 'You'll be the pairson that's camped in the dunes across the water to Eachkamish,' she said. Eachkamish was the name of the southern part of Baleshare. 'Would you be expecting somebody now?'

'No,' I said, thinking immediately of the Army.

'A lassie, maybe?' Her eyes stared at me, roguish and full of curiosity. 'Weel noo, it'll be a pleasant surprise for ye. She came in by the bus from Newton Ferry and now she's away to the Morrisons' to inquire aboot a boat.'

'Was it a Miss Field?'

She shook her head, smiling at me. 'I dinna ken the name. But she was in a turrible hurry to get to ye.' And she turned to a young woman standing there and told her to go down to the Morrisons' and bring the lassie back.

I picked up the phone and gave the exchange the number of the Met. Office at Northton. It couldn't be anyone else but Marjorie and I wondered why she'd come, for it wasn't an easy journey from Rodil. There was a click and a voice said, 'Sykes, Met. Office Northton, here.' Apparently Cliff had been called down to the camp. 'Will you give him a message for me,' I said. 'Tell him I'll be leaving first light tomorrow. If there's any change in the weather pattern he must let me know tonight.' He asked my name then and I said, 'He'll know who it is,' and hung up.

Five minutes later Marjorie arrived, flushed and out of breath. 'We'd almost got the boat down to the water when I saw the dinghy there. If I hadn't gone in for a cup of tea with the Morrisons I'd have seen you coming across.'

'How did you know where I was?'

'Daddy was sure you'd be somewhere in the North Ford and this seemed the most likely place.' She glanced round at the faces all eagerly watching us. 'Walk down the road with me, will you. We can't talk here. What with that odd craft of yours and me coming here asking for a man camped in the dunes – it'll be all over North Uist by this evening.' She gave me a quick little nervous smile. 'I didn't give your name.' And then, when we were clear of the Post Office, she said, 'The boat's been seen at Eriskay, on the east side. Colonel Webb was notified this morning and Daddy rang the hotel. He thought you'd want to know.' And she added, 'A crofter saw it there last night. They're not sure it's the one Major Braddock took, but it's a lobster boat and it doesn't belong to any of the local fishermen.'

So he'd crossed The Minch and was waiting like me for the expected break in the weather. I was quite sure it was Iain. The island of Eriskay was immediately below South Uist and right opposite Mallaig. 'What are they doing about it?' I asked.

'They've sent out a plane to investigate.'

'A helicopter?'

'No. A plane, Daddy said.'

A wild coast and no place to land. A plane wouldn't stop Iain. And for me to try and intercept him was out of the question. He'd shift to the little islands in the Sound of Barra and by tomorrow he'd be gone.

'It's what you were expecting, isn't it?' She had stopped and was standing facing me, the wind on her face.

'Yes.' And I added, 'It was good of you. To come all this way.'

'I suppose you'll go now.'

'Tomorrow morning.'

'He's got a much bigger boat than you. If anything happened . . . I mean, you ought to have somebody with you – just in case.'

'In case I fall overboard?' I smiled. 'I wouldn't have far to fall – a few inches, that's all.'

'It's nearly a hundred miles to Laerg, and that wretched little dinghy . . .' She was staring at me, her eyes wide. 'I realize you can't take anyone – anyone who wouldn't understand. But – ' she hesitated, her gaze, level and direct, fixed on me. 'I've brought cold weather clothing and oilskins. I thought if you wouldn't take anyone else . . .' Her hand touched my arm. 'Please. I want to come with you.'

I didn't know what to say, for she wasn't a fool; she knew the danger. And she meant it, of course. 'Don't be silly,' I said. 'Imagine what your father would say.'

'Oh, Daddy knows.' She said it quite gaily and I knew she really had settled it with him. And when I said, 'You know it's out of the question,' her temper flared immediately. 'I don't know anything of the sort. You can't go alone . . .'

'I've got to,' I said.

She started to argue then, but I cut her short. 'It's no good, Marjorie. You can't help me. Nobody can. In any case, there isn't room. When the stores are in it, that rubber dinghy is full – there's barely space for me.'

'That's just an excuse.'

I took her by the shoulders, but she flung me off. She was angry now and her eyes blazed. 'You're so bloody pig-headed. Just because I'm a girl . . .'

'If you'd been a man,' I told her, 'the answer would have been the same. There's no room for anybody else. And to be perfectly honest, I don't want anyone. This is something I've got to do alone.'

'But why? Why do you have to?'

'He's my brother,' I said. No point in concealing it from her now.

'Your brother?' She stared at me, and I could see her thinking it out and going over it in her mind.

'Now do you understand? This is something I've got to work out for myself. Perhaps for Iain, too.' I took her by the shoulders and this time she didn't draw away.

'It's settled then. You're going – tomorrow.'

'Yes.'

She didn't argue any more and when I drew her to me, she let me kiss her. 'Thank you,' I said. 'Thank you for coming, for offering to go with me.' Her lips were cool with the wind. 'That's something I'll always remember. And when I get back . . .' I felt her body come against me, the softness of it and her arms round my neck, her mouth on mine; and then she had drawn away. 'I'll see you off, anyway.' She was suddenly practical and we walked back in silence.

The woman who had gone off with the jerricans was waiting for me outside the Post Office. 'Ye'll find Roddie McNeil wi' your petrol doon by the landing place.' I thanked her. 'It's nae bother. And there's nae call for ye to be thanking Roddie. He'll be charging ye for his time as well as the petrol, ye ken.'

McNeil was waiting for me on the sands, a small, dour man with sandy hair. 'There's a wee bit extra for the cartage,' he said. I paid him and he helped me launch the dinghy and stow the jerricans. 'Is it long ye'll be camped over to Baleshare?' And when I told him I'd be gone in the morning if the weather were fine, he said, 'Aye, weel . . .' And he sniffed at the breeze like a sheltie. 'It'll be fine weather the noo, I'm thinking.'

He held the boat whilst I started the engine, and then I looked back at Marjorie. There was something almost boyish about her, standing there alone on the sands, the faded anarak and the green cord trousers tucked into gum boots, her head bare and her hair blown across her face. And yet not boyish; more like an island woman, I thought, her body slim and erect, her face clouded – and she'd been quite prepared to come to sea. The noise of the engine drowned all possibility of speech. I waved and she waved back, and that was that, and a feeling of sadness enveloped me as I motored down the channel. I didn't look back and in less than twenty minutes I had beached the dinghy below my tent. I was on my own again with the surface of the dune sand dried now and the wind sifting it through the wiry grass stems.

I began loading the dinghy ready for the morning. Reed's Nautical Almanac gave time of sunrise as 0643. There was no moon. I thought I should have sufficient light to cross the bar just before five. And once out beyond the bar I should be stuck at the helm hour after hour with no chance to change the stowage or search for things. Everything I needed had to be ready to hand.

There was another problem, too. At five o'clock in the morning the tide would be almost low. If I left the dinghy where it was, moored to the shore, it would be high and dry when I wanted to leave, and loaded it would be much too heavy to drag into the water. The only alternative was to anchor off in deep water and sleep aboard.

I stowed everything in its place except the tent and the radio set, and by the time I had finished the sun was shining, the wind no more than a rustle in the grasses. It was a calm, clear evening with Eaval standing out brown and smiling against the black storm clouds still piled against the mainland hills. I climbed to the top of the dunes, and all to the west the sky was clear, a pale pastel shade of blue, with the seas white on the bar, but breaking lazily now and without much force.

There was nothing more I could do and I got my sketchbook out. The two drawings I did show the loaded dinghy lying like a basking shark stranded at the water's edge, the tent snugged in its hollow against the dunes, and that flat world of sand and water stretching away to the sunken hulks of the distant hills. They set the scene, but they miss the bright calm of that suddenly cloudless sky, the curlews piping to the more anxious note of the oyster-catchers, the flight of the grey plover and the laboured strokes of a heron. The sun set, an orange ball that turned the Monachs black like a ship hull-down, and as twilight fell, the darkening world seemed hushed to a sort of sanctity so that I felt I understood what it was that had drawn the early Christians to these islands.

Cliff Morgan's transmission came through very sharp that night, with almost no interference. *Message received. Weather set fair for 24 hours at least, possibly 48. Fog your chief hazard. Future transmissions twice daily at 1330 and 0100 continuing for 3 days. Thereafter 2200 as before for 4 days. If no message received by 10 March will presume you are in trouble and take appropriate action.* He repeated the message, the speed of his key steadily increasing. Finally: *Bon voyage CL.*

I marked the times of his transmissions on the chart and checked once again the course I should have to steer. He had given me seven clear days in which to get a message through to him. Time enough to worry how I was going to do that when I reached Laerg. I wished Iain could have heard that forecast. Fog was just what he wanted now.

I checked the tides given on the chart for every hour before and after high water Stornoway, pencilling in the direction and speed for the twenty-four hours commencing 0500. I also made a note of the magnetic variation – 13° West – and my compass deviation which I found to be a further 4° West with all my gear stowed. Taking these factors into account the compass course I should have to steer after clearing the Monachs was 282°.

Having satisfied myself that all the navigational information I required was entered on the chart, and having checked through again for accuracy, I folded it and slipped it into its spray-proof case. Together with the radio, I stowed it in the dinghy within reach of the helm. Then I struck the tent and when that was loaded and the camp entirely cleared, I waded into the water, pushed off and clambered in. I moored out in the channel, a stone tied to the painter, and went to sleep under the stars, clad in my oilskins, lying crossways, my feet stuck out over the side and my head cushioned on the fat curve of the tight-blown fabric.

It was cold that night and I slept fitfully, conscious of the yawing of the dinghy, the ripple of the tide tugging at the mooring. I had no alarm clock, but it wasn't necessary. Seabirds woke me as the first glimmering of dawn showed grey in the east, silhouetting the dark outline of Eaval. I dipped my face in salt water, conscious now of a feeling of tension; eyes and head were sluggish with the night and the cold had cramped my bones. I drank the tea I had left hot in the Thermos, ate some digestive biscuits and cheese, and then I pulled up the mooring, untying the stone and letting it fall back into the water. The outboard engine started at the second pull and I was on my way, circling in the tide run and heading down the centre of the pale ribbon of water that ran between the sands towards the open sea.

The light in the east was pale and cold as steel; the stars overhead still bright. The speed of my passage made a little wind, and that too was cold, so that I shivered under my oilskins. All ahead was black darkness. I had a moment of panic that I should lose the channel and get stranded among the breakers on the bar. Passing through the narrows between Eachkamish and the northern tip of Benbecula – the channel marked on the chart as Beul an Toim – the broken water of the bar showed in a ghostly semi-circle beyond the piled-up bulk of my stores. Even when I could see the breaking waves, I could not hear them. All I heard was the powerful roar of the outboard. I steered a compass course, running the engine slow, and as the dunes slid away behind me, my craft came suddenly alive to the movement of the waves.

Breaking water right ahead and no gap visible. The light was growing steadily and I jilled around for a moment, searching the line of breakers. A darker patch, further south than I had expected . . . I felt my way towards it, conscious of the tug of the tide under the boat, noting the sideways drift. And then suddenly my eyes, grown accustomed to the light, picked out the channel, a narrow highway of dark water, growing wider as I entered it. The swell was bad here out on the bar, the waves steep but only occasionally breaking. The dinghy pitched wildly, the engine racing as the prop was lifted clear of the water.

There was a moment when I thought I'd missed the channel, the waves higher than my head and starting to curl at the top. I wanted to turn back then, but I didn't dare for fear the dinghy would overturn. The jerricans were shifting despite their lashings and I had to grip hold of the wooden slats at my feet to prevent myself from being thrown out. This lasted for perhaps a minute. Then suddenly the waves were less steep. A moment later, and I was motoring in calm water and the sea's only movement was a long, flat, oily swell. I was over the bar, and looking back I could scarcely believe that I had found a way through from landward, for all behind me was an unbroken line of white water, the confusion of the waves showing as toppling masses against the dawn sky, the low land surrounding the Ford already lost in the haze of spray that hung above the bar. I set my course by the compass, took a small nip from the flask I had kept handy and settled down to the long business of steering and keeping the engine going.

Shortly before seven the sun rose. It was broad daylight then and the Monachs clearly visible on the port bow. At 0645 I had tuned in to the BBC on 1500 metres. There was no change in the weather pattern and the forecast for sea area Hebrides was wind force 1 to 2 variable, good visibility, but fog locally. Shortly after nine the Monachs were abeam to port about two miles. They were flat as a table and at that distance the grass of the *machair* looked like a lawn. My compass was one of those which could be taken out of its holder and used as a hand-bearing compass. I took a bearing on the disused lighthouse, and another on Haskeir Island away to the north. These, together with a stern-bearing on the top of Clettraval on North Uist, gave me a three-point fix. I marked my position on the chart and checked it against my dead reckoning, which was based on course and speed, making due allowance for tide. The difference was 1.4 miles at 275°. That fix was very important to me, for thereafter I was able to base my dead reckoning on a speed of 3.8 knots.

The sun was warm now, shimmering on the water, a blinding glare that made me drowsy. The one thing I hadn't thought of was dark glasses. I had taken my oilskin jacket off some miles back. Now I removed the first of my sweaters and refilled the tank with the engine running slow. In doing so I nearly missed the only ship I was to sight that day – a trawler, hull-down on the horizon, trailing a smudge of smoke.

Every hour I wrote up my log and entered my DR position on the chart, just as I had always done back in the old days on the bridge of a freighter. The engine was my main concern, and I was sensitive to every change of note, real or imagined. All around me, the sea was alive, the movement of the swell, the flight of birds; and whenever I felt the need, there was always the radio with the Light Programme churning out endless music.

Just after eleven I ran into a school of porpoise. I thought at first it was a tidal swirl, mistaking their curving backs for the shadow cast by the lip of a small wave breaking. And then I saw one not fifty yards away, a dark body glinting in the sun and curved like the top of a wheel revolving. The pack must have numbered more than a dozen. They came out of the water three times, almost in unison and gaining momentum with each re-entry. At the final voracious plunge, the whole surface of the sea ahead of me seethed; from flat calm it was suddenly a boiling cauldron as millions of small fry skittered in panic across the surface. For an instant I seemed to be headed for a sheet of molten silver, and then the sea was oily smooth again, so that I stared, wondering whether I had imagined it.

A flash of white from the sky, the sudden splash of a projectile hitting the water . . . this new phenomenon thrilled me as something dimly remembered but not seen in a long while. The gannets had arrived.

There were a dozen or more of them, wheeling low and then hurling themselves into the sea with closed wings and out-thrust head, a spear-beaked missile diving headlong for the herring on which the porpoise were feeding and which in turn were attacking the small fry. I could remember my grandfather's words before I had ever seen a gannet dive: 'Aye,' he'd said, his thick, guttural voice burring at us, 'ye'll no' see a finer sight this side of heaven, for there's nae muckle fowl (he pronounced it the Norwegian way – *fugl*) can dive like a solan goose.'

Where the gannets came from I don't know, for until that moment I had seen none. They appeared as though by magic, coming in from all angles and all heights and the little bomb-plumes of their dives spouted in the sea all round me. My presence didn't seem to disturb them at all. Perhaps it was because the dinghy was so different in shape and appearance to any boat they had encountered before. Three of them dived in quick succession, hitting the water so close that I could almost reach out and touch the plumes of spray. They surfaced practically together, each with a herring gripped in its long beak. A vigorous washing, a quick twist to turn the fish head-first and then it was swallowed and they took off again, taxi-ing clumsily in a long run, wings and feet labouring at the surface of the water. Other birds were there – big herring gulls and black-backs; shearwaters and razor-bills too, I think, but at that time I was not so practised at bird recognition. The smooth-moving hillocks of the sea became littered with the debris of the massacre; littered, too, with porpoise excreta – small, brown aerated lumps floating light as corks.

It was over as suddenly as it had started. All at once the birds were gone and I was left alone with the noise of the engine, only then realizing how the scream of the gulls had pierced that sound. I looked at the Monachs and was surprised to find they had scarcely moved. There was nothing else in sight, not even a fishing boat, and the only aircraft I saw was the BEA flight coming into Benbecula, a silver flash of wings against the blue of the sky.

Though less than four miles long from Stockay to the lighthouse, the Monachs were with me a long time. It was not until almost midday that they began to drop out of sight astern. Visibility was still very good then. The stone of the lighthouse stood out clear and white, and though the North Ford and all the low-lying country of Benbecula and the Uists had long since disappeared, the high ground remained clearly visible; particularly the massive brown bulk of the Harris hills.

It was about this time that I thought I saw, peeping up at me over the horizon ahead, the faint outline of what looked like a solitary rock. The peak of Tarsaval on Laerg? I couldn't be certain, for though I stared and stared and blinked repeatedly to re-focus my eyes, it remained indefinite as a mirage, an ephemeral shape that might just as easily have been a reflection of my own desire; for what I wanted most to see – what any seaman wants to see – was my objective coming up right over the bows to confirm me in my navigation.

But I never had that satisfaction. It was there, I thought, for a while; then I couldn't be certain. Finally I was sure it wasn't, for by that time even the Harris hills had become blurred and indistinct.

I was conscious then of a drop in temperature. The sun had lost its warmth, the sky its brilliance, and where sky met sea, the pale, watery blue was shaded to the sepia of haze. Where I thought I had glimpsed Laerg there was soon no clear-cut horizon, only a pale blurring of the light like refraction from a shallow cloud lying on the surface of the sea.

Fog! I could feel it in my bones, and it wasn't long before I could see it. And at 1330 Cliff Morgan confirmed my fears. After giving me a weather forecast that was much the same as before, he added: *Your greatest menace now is fog. Weather ship India reports visibility at 1100 hours 50 yards.* The BBC forecast at 1340 merely referred to *Chance of fog patches.*

I had already put on my sweaters again; now I put on my oilskin jacket. Within minutes the atmosphere had chilled and thickened. A little wind sprang up, cats' paws rippling the oily surface of the swell. One moment the hills of Harris were still there, just visible, then they were gone and the only thing in sight, besides the sea, was the tower of the Monachs lighthouse iridescent in a gleam of sun. Then that, too, vanished, and I was alone in a world where the sky seemed a sponge, the air so full of moisture that the sun scarcely percolated through it.

Half an hour later I entered the fog bank proper. It came up on me imperceptibly at first, a slow darkening of the atmosphere ahead, a gradual lessening of visibility. Then, suddenly, wreathing veils of white curled smoky tendrils round me. The cats' paws merged, became a steady chilling breeze; little waves began to break against the bows, throwing spray in my face. Abruptly my world was reduced to a fifty-yard stretch of sea, a dank prison with water-vapour walls that moved with me as I advanced, an insubstantial, yet impenetrable enclosure.

After that I had no sense of progress, and not even the sound of the engine or the burble of the propeller's wake astern could convince me that I was moving, for I took my grey prison with me, captive to the inability of my eyes to penetrate the veil of moisture that enclosed me.

Time had no meaning for me then. I nursed the engine, watched the compass, stared into the fog, and thought of Laerg, wondering how I was to find the entrance to the geo – wondering, too, whether I should be able even to locate the island in this thick wet blanket of misery that shut out all sight. It would be night then, and the slightest error in navigation . . .

I checked and re-checked my course constantly, the moisture dripping from my face and hands, running down the sleeves of my oilskin jacket on to the celluloid surface of the chart case. Tired now and cold, my limbs cramped, I crouched listless at the helm, hearing again my grandfather's voice; stories of Laerg and his prowess on the crags. He had claimed he was fleeter than anyone else. Even at sixty, he said he'd been able to reach ledges no youngster dare visit. Probably he was justified in his claims. At the time the islanders left Laerg there were only five men left between the ages of fifteen and twenty-five, and remembering those long, almost ape-like arms, those huge hands and the enormous breadth of his shoulders, I could well imagine the old devil swinging down the face of a thousand-foot cliff, his grizzled beard glistening with the vapour that swirled about him as he sought some almost invisible ledge where the guillemots or solan geese were nesting.

In just such a fog as this he had gone down the face of the sheer cliffs on the north side of the island, below Tarsaval, lowering himself on the old horse-hair rope that had been part of his wife's dowry when they married at the turn of the century. Those cliffs were over 1300 feet high, the most spectacular volcanic wall in the British Isles. He was on his own and he had missed his footing. His hands had slipped on the wet rope and he had fallen fifty feet, his foot catching in the loop at the end. They had found him hanging there head-downwards in the morning. He had been like that most of the night, a total of five hours, but though he was frozen stiff as a board and his joints had seized solid, he nevertheless managed to walk down to his cottage. He had been fifty-two years old then.

These and other stories came flooding back into my mind; how when he had married my grandmother he had had to undergo the ordeal of the Lovers' Stone. That sloped crag, jutting out high over the sea where it boiled against the base of the cliffs, had made an indelible impression on my young mind. He had told us that all bridegrooms had had to pass this test, walking out along the tilted stone to stand on the knife-edge, balanced on the balls of their feet and reaching down to touch their toes. It was a test to prove that they were competent cragsmen, men enough to support a woman on an island where the ability to collect eggs and birds from their nesting places could make the difference between a full belly and starvation in winter. 'Aye, and I was fool enough to stand first on one foot and then the other, and then put my head down and stand on my hands – just to prove I wasna scared of anything at all in the whole wide wor-rld.' The old man's voice seemed to come to me again through the roar of the engine.

I was tired by then, of course, and I had the illusion that if only I could penetrate the grey curtain ahead of me, I should see the towering cliffs of Laerg rising out of the sea. At moments I even imagined there was a sudden darkening in the fog. But then I reached for the chart and a glance at it confirmed that my imagination was playing me tricks. At five o'clock the island was still almost thirty miles away. I had most of the night ahead of me before I reached it. Then, if the fog held, the first indication would not be anything seen, but the pounding of the swell at the base of the cliffs, perhaps a glint of white water.

And that was presuming my navigation was accurate.

It was just after the six o'clock weather forecast, in which the BBC admitted for the first time that the whole Eastern Atlantic was enveloped in fog, that the thing I had most feared happened. There was a change in the engine note. The revolutions fell off and it began to labour. I tried it with full throttle, but it made no difference. I adjusted the choke, giving it a richer mixture, but it still continued to labour. The water cooling outlet thinned to a trickle and finally ceased, The engine was beginning to pound as it ran hot. In the end it stopped altogether.

The sudden silence was frightening. For more than twelve hours I had had the roar of the engine in my ears to the exclusion of all other sounds. Now I could hear the slap of the waves against the flat rubberized gunnels. I could hear the little rushing hisses they made as they broke all round me. There wasn't anything of a sea running, but the swell was broken by small cross-seas. The wind was about force 3, northerly, and in the stillness I could almost hear it. Other sounds were audible, too – the slop of petrol in a half-empty jerrican, the drip of moisture from my oilskins, the rattle of tins badly stowed as the dinghy wallowed with a quick, unpredictable movement.

My first thought was that the engine had run out of fuel, but I had refilled the tank less than half an hour ago, and when I checked it was still more than half-full. I thought then that it must be water in the petrol, particularly when I discovered that the jerrican I had last used was one of those that had been filled by the crofter at Carinish. Rather than empty the tank, I disconnected the fuel lead, drained the carburettor and refilled it from another jerrican; a difficult and laborious business, cramped as I was and the motion at times quite violent.

The engine started first pull and for a moment I thought I had put my finger on the trouble. But no water came out of the cooling outlet and though it ran for a moment quite normally, the revolutions gradually fell off again and for fear of permanent damage due to overheating, I stopped it.

I knew then that something must have gone wrong with the cooling system. The outlook was grim. I was not a mechanic and I had few spares. Moreover, the light was already failing. It would soon be dark, and to strip the engine down by the light of a torch was to ask for trouble with the dinghy tossing about and all available space taken up with stores. The wind seemed to be rising, too; but perhaps that was my imagination.

I sat there for a long time wondering what to do – whether to start work on it now or to wait until morning. But to wait for morning was to risk a change in the weather conditions and at least there was still light enough for me to make a start on the job. First, I had to get the engine off its bracket and into the boat. It was a big outboard, and heavy. For safety, I tied the painter round it, and then, kneeling in the stern, I undid the clamp and with a back-breaking twist managed to heave it on to the floor at my feet.

It was immensely heavy – far heavier than I had expected. But it wasn't until it was lying on the floor at my feet that the reason became apparent. The propeller and all the lower part of the shaft, including the water-cooling inlet and the exhaust, was wrapped and choked with seaweed. I almost laughed aloud with relief. 'You silly, bloody fool.' I had begun talking to myself by then. I kept repeating, 'You bloody fool!' for I remembered now that as I had sat with the earphones on, listening to the forecast, I had motored through a patch of sea that was littered with the wrack of the recent gale – dark patches of weed that produced their own calm where the sea did not break.

Cleared of weed and refastened to its bracket, the engine resumed its purposeful note and the sound of the sea was lost again. Lost, too, was that sense of fear, which for a moment had made me wish Cliff Morgan had allowed less than seven days before presuming I was in trouble.

I switched on the compass light and immediately it became the focus of my eyes, a little oasis of brightness that revealed the fog as a stifling blanket composed of millions upon millions of tiny beads of moisture. All else was black darkness.

It became intensely cold. Surprisingly, I suffered from thirst. But the little water I had brought with me was stowed for'ard against an emergency – and in any case, relieving myself was a problem. I suffered from cramp, too. Both feet had gone dead long ago due to constriction of the blood circulation.

My eyes, mesmerized by the compass light, became droop-lidded and I began to nod. I was steering in a daze then, my thoughts wandering. 'You'll go to Laerg, and I'll go to my grave fighting for the mucking Sassenachs.' That was Iain, ages and ages ago, in a pub in Sauchiehall Street. What had made him say that, standing at that crowded bar in his new battledress? I couldn't remember now. But I could see him still, his dark hair tousled, a black look on his face. He was a little drunk and swaying slightly. Something else he'd said . . . 'That bloody old fool.' And I'd known who he meant, for the old man had both fascinated and repelled him. 'Dying of a broken heart. If he'd had any guts, he'd have stuck it out alone on the island, instead of blethering about it to the two of us.' But that wasn't what I was trying to remember. It was something he'd said after that. He'd repeated it, as though it were a great truth, slurring his words. 'Why die where you don't belong?' And then he'd clapped me on the back and ordered another drink. 'You're lucky,' he'd said. 'You're too young.' And I'd hated him as I often did.

Or was that the next time, when he'd come swaggering back, on leave after Dieppe? Too young! Always too young where he was concerned! If I hadn't been too young, I'd have taken Mavis...

The engine coughed, warning that the tank was running dry. I refilled it, still seeing Iain as I had seen him then, cocksure and getting crazy drunk. Another pub that time, his black eyes wild and lines already showing on his face, boasting of the girls he'd ploughed and me saying, 'She's going to have a baby.'

'Yours or mine?' he said with a jeering, friendly grin.

I came near to hitting him then. 'You know damn well whose it is.'

'Och well, there's a war on and there's plenty of lassies with bairns and no father to call them after.' And he'd laughed in my face and raised his glass. 'Well, here's to them. The country needs all they can produce the way this bloody war is going.' That was Iain, living for the moment, grabbing all he could and to hell with the consequences. He'd had quite a reputation even in that Glasgow factory, and God knows that was a tough place to get a reputation in. Wild, they called him – wild as a young stallion, with the girls rubbing round him and the drink in him talking big and angry.

And then that last evening we'd had together ... he'd forgotten I was growing up. It had ended in a row, with him breaking a glass and threatening to cut my face to ribbons with the jagged edge of it if I didn't have another drink with him – 'One for the road,' he'd said. 'But not the bloody road to the Isles.' And he'd laughed drunkenly. 'Donald my Donald, my wee brother Donald.' I'd always hated him when he'd called me that. 'You've no spunk in your belly, but you'll drink with me this once to show you love me and would hate to see me die.'

I'd had that last drink with him and walked with him back to his barracks. Standing there, with the sentry looking on, he'd taken hold of me by the shoulders. 'I'll make a bargain wi' ye, Donald my Donald. If ye die first, which I know bloody well ye'll never do, I'll take your body to Laerg and dump it there in a cleit to be pickled by the winds. You do the same for me, eh? Then the old bastard can lie in peace, knowing there's one of the family forever staring with sightless eyes, watching the birds copulate and produce their young and migrate and come again each year.' I had promised because he was tight and because I wanted to get away and forget about not being old enough to be a soldier.

Damn him, I thought, knowing he was out there somewhere in the fog. He wouldn't be thinking of me. He'd be thinking of the last time he was in these waters – a Carley float instead of a lobster boat and men dying of exposure. All those years ago and the memory of it like a worm eating into him. Had Lane been right, making that wild accusation? Quite ruthless, Field had said. I shivered. Alone out here in the darkness, he seemed very close.

3

ISLAND OF MY ANCESTORS
(7 March)

Thinking of him, remembering moments that I'd thought obliterated from my mind, the time passed, not quickly, but unnoticed. I got the weather forecast just after midnight – wind north-westerly force 3, backing westerly and increasing to 4. Fog. Cliff Morgan at 0100 was more specific: *Fog belt very extensive, but chance of clearance your area mid-morning.* The wind was westerly force 4 already and my problem remained – how to locate the island.

Between two and three in the morning I became very sleepy. I had been at the helm then for over twenty hours and it was almost impossible for me to keep my eyes open. The engine noise seemed to have a brain-deadening quality, the compass light a hypnotic, sleep-inducing effect. Every few moments I'd catch my head falling and jerk awake to find the compass card swinging. This happened so many times that I lost all confidence in my ability to steer a course, and as a result began to doubt my exact position.

It was a dangerous thing to do, but I took a pull at the flask then. The smell of it and the raw taste of it on my dried-up tongue, the trickle of warmth seeping down into my bowels – I was suddenly wide awake. The time was 0248. Was it my imagination, or was the movement less?

I picked up the chart, marked in my DR position for 0300 and then measured off the distance still to go with a pair of dividers.

It was 4.8 miles – about an hour and a half.

I hadn't noticed it while I had been dozing, but the wind had definitely dropped. I could, of course, already be under the lee of Laerg if my speed had been better than I'd reckoned. But I'd no means of knowing. The fog remained impenetrable. I switched off the compass light for a moment, but it made no difference – I was simply faced with darkness then, a darkness so absolute that I might have been struck blind.

With my ETA confirmed now as approximately 0430, I no longer seemed to have the slightest inclination to sleep. I could easily be an hour, an hour and a half out in my reckoning. At that very moment I might be heading straight for a wall of rock – or straight past the island, out into the Atlantic.

I topped up the tank so that there would be no danger of the engine stopping at the very moment when I needed it most, and after that I kept going. There was nothing else I could do – just sit there, staring at the compass.

Four o'clock. Four-fifteen. And nothing to be seen, nothing at all. If this had been a night like the last, the bulk of Tarsaval would be standing black against the stars. There would have been no difficulty at all then.

At four-thirty I switched off the engine and turned out the compass light. Black darkness and the boat rocking, and not a sound but the slop and movement of the sea. No bird called, no beat of waves on rock. I might have been a thousand miles from land.

I had only to sit there, of course, until the fog cleared. But a man doesn't think that rationally when he'd bobbing about in a rubber dinghy, alone in utter darkness and virtually sitting in the sea. My grandfather's voice again, telling us of fogs that had lasted a week and more. I switched on the torch and worked over my figures again, staring at the chart. Was it the tide, or an error in navigation or just that, dozing, I had steered in circles? But even a combination of all three wouldn't produce an error of more than a few miles, and Laerg was a group of islands; it covered quite a wide area. The only answer was to cast about until I found it. The search pattern I worked out was a simple rectangular box. Fifteen minutes on my original course, then south for half an hour, east for fifteen minutes, north for an hour. At four forty-five I started the engine again, holding my course until five o'clock. Stop and listen again. Steering south then, with the grey light of dawn filtering through and the sea taking shape around me, a lumpy, confused sea, with the white of waves beginning to break.

The wind was freshening now. I could feel it on my face. At five-fifteen I stopped again to listen. The waves made little rushing sounds, and away to my left, to port, I thought I heard the surge of the swell on some obstruction – thought, too, I could discern a movement in the fog.

It was getting lighter all the time, and I sat there, the minutes ticking by, straining to listen, straining to see. My eyes played tricks, pricking with fatigue. I could have sworn the clammy curtain of the mist moved; and then I was certain as a lane opened out to starboard and the fog swirled, wreathing a pattern over the broken surface of the sea. Somewhere a gull screamed, but it was a distant, insubstantial sound – impossible to tell the direction of it.

I continued then, searching all the time the shifting, wraith-like movements of the fog. A gust of wind hit me, blattering at the surface of the sea. A down-draught? I was given no time to think that out. A sudden darkness loomed ahead. A swirling uplift of the fog, and there was rock, wet, black rock ahead of me and to port.

I pulled the helm over, feeling the undertow at the same instant that I saw the waves lazily lifting and falling against a towering crag that rose vertically like a wall to disappear in white, moving tendrils of mist. Laerg, or Fladday, or one of the stacs – or was it the western outpost reef of Vallay? In the moment of discovery I didn't care. I had made my landfall, reached my destination.

I celebrated with a drink from my flask and ate some chocolate as I motored south-west, keeping the cliff-face just in sight.

It wasn't one of the stacs, that was obvious immediately. That darkening in the fog remained too long. And then it faded suddenly, as though swallowed by the mist. I steered to port, closing it again on a course that was almost due south. The wind was in front of me, behind me, all round me; the sea very confused. Then I saw waves breaking on the top of a rock close ahead. I turned to starboard. More rock. To starboard again with rocks close to port.

A glance at the compass told me that I was in a bay, for I was steering now north-west with rock close to port. The rocks became cliffs again. Four minutes on north-west and then I had to turn west to keep those cliffs in sight. I knew where I was then.

There was only one bay that would give me the courses I had steered – Strath Bay on the north side of Laerg itself.

I checked with the survey map, just to be certain. There was nowhere else I could be. Confirmation came almost immediately with a ninety degree turn to port as I rounded the headland that marked the northern end of Aird Mullaichean. Course south-west now and the sea steep and breaking. I hugged the cliffs just clear of the backwash and ten minutes later the movement became more violent.

I was in a tide-rip, the sound of the engine beating back at me from hidden rock surfaces. An islet loomed, white with the stain of guano, and as I skirted it, the wind came funnelling down from the hidden heights above, strong enough to flatten the sea; and then the down-draught turned to an up-draught, sucking the fog with it, and for an instant I glimpsed a staggering sight – two rock cliffs hemming me in and towering up on either side like the walls of a canyon.

They rose stupendous to lose themselves in vapour; dark volcanic masses of gabbro rock, high as the gates of hell, reaching up into infinity. *Sheer adamantine rock.* Wasn't that how Milton had described it? But before I could recall the exact words, I was through, spewed out by the tide, and Eileann nan Shoay had vanished astern, mist-engulfed as the fog closed in again.

I had marked the geo on the survey map, guessing at the position from the stories my grandfather told of how he had stumbled on it by accident and as a result had sometimes been able to bring in lobster when the waves were so big in Shelter Bay that nobody dared put to sea. 'I didna tell them, ye ken. A tur-rible thing that in a community as close as ours.' And his eyes had twinkled under his shaggy brows. 'For ken it was a secret and I'm telling it to ye the noo so it willna die wi' me. There'll come a day mebbe when ye'll need to know aboot that geo.'

For me, that day was now. I closed in to the cliffs, the engine ticking over just fast enough to give me steerage way. South of Eileann nan Shoay he'd said, about as far as it is from the Factor's House to the old graveyard. Measured on the map that was just over six hundred yards. The middle one of the three – he had described the other two as full of rock and very dangerous to enter.

I saw the first of the gaping holes, black with the waves slopping in the entrance. It was a huge yawning cavity. The other two were smaller and close together, like two mine adits driven into the base of the cliffs.

Geo na Cleigeann, the old man had called it. 'And a tur-rible wee place it looks from the water wi' a muckle great slab hanging over it.' I could hear his words still and there was the slab jutting out from the cliff face and the black gap below about as inviting as a rat hole with the sea slopping about in the mouth of it. It took me a moment to make up my mind, remembering the old devil's dour sense of humour. But this was no place to hang about with the wind whistling down off the crags above and the tide sweeping along the base of those fog-bound cliffs.

I picked up the torch, put the helm hard down and headed for the opening. A gull shied away from me and was whirled screaming up the face of the cliffs like a piece of wind-blown paper. The fog, torn by an up-draught, revealed crag upon crag towering over me. I had a fleeting impression of the whole great mass toppling forward; then the overhanging slab blotted it out and I was faced with the wet mouth of the cave itself, a grey gloom of rock spreading back into black darkness and rever-berating to the noise of the engine.

The hole was bigger than I had first thought – about fifteen feet wide and twenty high. The westerly swell, broken on the skerries of Shoay Sgeir that jutted south from Eileann nan Shoay, caused only a mild surge. Behind me the geo was like a tunnel blasted in the rock, the entrance a grey glimmer of daylight.

I probed ahead with the beam of my torch, expecting every moment to see the shape of the lobster boat. I was so certain Iain must be ahead of me, and if I'd been him I thought I'd make for the geo rather than Shelter Bay. The surface of the water was black and still, lifting and falling gently; rock ahead and I cut the engine. The roof was higher here, the sides further away. I was in a huge cavern, a sort of expansion chamber. No daylight ahead, no indication that there was a way out. The bows touched the rock and I reached out to it, gripping the wet surface with my fingers and hauling myself along.

In a westerly, with the waves rolling clean across the reef of Shoay Sgeir, this place would be a death trap. The rock round which I hauled myself had been torn from the roof, now so high that my torch could barely locate it. I probed with an oar. The water was still deep. Beyond the rock I paddled gently. The walls closed in again. The roof came down. And then the bows grounded on a steep-sloped beach, all boulders. I was ashore in the dark womb of those gabbro cliffs and no sign of Iain.

In the tension of the last hour I had forgotten how stiff and cramped I was. When I tried to clamber out I found I couldn't move. I drank a little whisky and then began to massage my limbs. The enforced wait made me increasingly conscious of the eeriness of the place, the slop of the sea in the entrance magnified, and everywhere the drip-drip of moisture from the roof. The place reeked of the sea's salt dampness and above me God knows how many hundred feet of rock pressed down on the geo.

As soon as I was sure my legs would support me, I eased myself over the side and into the water. It was knee-deep and bitterly cold; ashore I tied the painter to a rock, and then went on up, probing with my torch, urgent now to discover the outlet to this subterranean world. It was over thirty years since my grandfather had been here; there might have been a fall, anything.

The beach sloped up at an angle of about twenty degrees, narrowing to a point where the roof seemed split by a fault. It was a rock cleft about six feet wide. The boulders were smaller here, the slope steeper. I seemed to cross a divide with mud underfoot and I slithered down into another cave to find the bottom littered with the same big rounded boulders.

It took me a little time to find the continuation of the fault, and it wasn't the fault I found first, but a rock ledge with the remains of some old lobster pots resting on a litter of rotted feathers. On the ground below the ledge was a length of flaking chain half-buried amongst the skeletal remains of fish. All the evidence of the old man's secret fishing, all except the boat he'd built himself and had abandoned here when he'd left with the rest of the islanders. And then, probing the further recesses of the cavern, I saw a blackened circle of stones and the traces of a long-dead fire. Though the planking had all gone, the half-burnt remains of the stem and part of the keel were still identifiable, rotting now amongst a litter of charred bones.

I was too tired then, too anxious to locate the exit to the geo to concern myself about the wanton destruction of the boat, vaguely wondering who had made that fire and when, as I scrambled up the last steep slope to see a gleam of sunlight high above me. The slope was almost vertical here and slabs of stone had been let into the walls to form a primitive staircase, presumably the work of some long-dead generation of islanders.

The cleft at the top was wet and grass-choked, the crevices filled with tiny ferns; a small brown bird, a wren, went burring past me. And then I was out on a steep grass slope, out in the sunlight with the fog below me. It lay like a milk-white sea, lapping at the slopes of Strath Mhurain, writhing along the cliff-line to the north of Tarsaval, and all above was the blue of the sky – a cold, translucent blue without a single cloud. The sun had warmth and the air was scented with the smell of grass. Sheep moved, grazing on the slopes of Creag Dubh, and behind me white trails of vapour rose and fell in strange convoluted billows above the cliff-edge where fulmars wheeled in constant flight, soaring, still-winged, on the up-draughts.

I stood there a moment filling my lungs with the freshness of the air, letting the magnificence of the scene wash over me – thanking God that my grandfather hadn't lied, that the exit from the geo had remained intact. I thought it likely now that Iain had landed in Shelter Bay and because I was afraid the fog might clamp down at any moment, I stripped off my oilskins and started out across the island. I crossed the top of Strath Mhurain, skirting black edges of peat bog, and climbed to the Druim Ridge with the sun-warm hills standing islanded in fog and the only sound the incessant wailing of the birds.

From the Druim Ridge I looked down into the great horseshoe of Shelter Bay. The Military High Road was just below me, snaking down into the fog. To my left Creag Dubh, with the pill-box shape of the Army's lookout rising to Tarsaval; dark scree slopes falling to the dotted shapes of cleits and, beyond, the long ridge of Malesgair vanishing into the milk-white void. To my right the High Road spur running out towards the Butt of Keava, the rocky spine of the hills piercing the fog bank like a jagged reef. It was a strange, eerie scene with the surge of the swell on the storm beach coming faint on puffs of air; something else, too – the sound of an engine, I thought. But then it was gone and I couldn't be sure.

I hurried on then, following the road down into the fog, iridescent at first, but thickening as I descended until it was a grey blanket choked with moisture. Without the road to follow the descent would have been dangerous, for the fog was banked thick in the confines of the hills and visibility reduced to a few yards. It lifted a little as the road flattened out behind the beach. I could see the swell breaking and beyond the lazy beds the outline of the first ruined cottage, everything vague, blurred by the dankness of the atmosphere. And then a voice calling stopped me in my tracks. It came again, disembodied, weird and insubstantial. Other voices answered, the words unintelligible.

I stood listening, all my senses alert, intent on piercing the barrier of the fog. Silence and the only sounds the surge of the waves, the cries of the gulls. Somewhere a raven croaked, but I couldn't see it. Ahead of me was the dim outline of the bridge.

And then voices again, talking quietly, the sound oddly magnified. The fog swirled to a movement of air from the heights. I glimpsed the ruins of the old jetty and a boat drawn up on the beach. Two figures stood beside it, two men talking in a foreign tongue, and out beyond the break of the waves I thought I saw the dark shape of a ship; a trawler by the look of it. Two more figures joined the men by the boat. The fog came down again and I was left with only the sound of their voices. I went back then, for I was cold and tired and I'd no desire to make contact with the crew of a foreign trawler. Looting probably, and if Iain had landed in Shelter Bay he'd have hidden himself away in one of the cleits or amongst the ruins of the Old Village. Wearily I climbed the hairpin bends, back up to the Druim Ridge and the sunlight, nothing to do now but go back down into the bowels of that geo and bring up my gear. My mouth was dry and I drank from a trickle of peat water at the head of Strath Mhurain.

And then I was back on the slopes of Aird Mullaichean, walking in a daze, my mind facing again the mystery of that fire, conscious of a growing sense of uneasiness as I approached the rock outcrop that marked the entrance to that dark, subterranean fault. Had the crew of some trawler rowed into the geo and made a fire of the boat just for the hell of it? But that didn't explain the bones unless they'd killed a sheep and roasted it. And to burn the boat . . . On Laerg itself and all through the islands of the Hebrides boats were sacrosanct. No man would borrow so much as an oar without permission.

I picked up my torch and started back down the slabbed stairway. Darkness closed me in. The dank cold of it chilled the sweat on my body. I tried to tell myself it was only the strangeness of the place, my solitary stumbling in the black darkness and the cavernous sound of the sea that made me so uneasy. But who would come into that geo if he hadn't been told about it? Who would have known there was a boat there, firewood to burn? I was shivering then and, coming to the cave where the boat had been, I was suddenly reluctant, filled with a dreadful certainty. Twenty-two days. I'd had only a night at sea, a single cold night with little wind. But I knew what it was like now – knew that he couldn't possibly have survived . . . And then I was into the cave, my gaze, half-fascinated, half-appalled, following the beam of my torch, knowing what I was going to find.

Down on my knees, I reached out my hand to the bones, touched one, plucked it from the blackened heap with a feeling of sick revulsion as I recognized what it was. The end of the bone disintegrated into dust, leaving me with a knee joint in my hand. I poked around – a hip bone, femurs, pieces of the spinal column, the knuckles of human fingers. It was all there, all except the head, and that I found tucked away under a slab of rock – a human skull untouched by the fire and with traces of hair still attached.

I put it back and sat for a moment, feeling numbed; but not shocked or even disgusted now that I knew. It had to be something like this. I was thinking how it must have been for him, his life soured by what had happened here, the prospect of discovery always hanging over him. And then automatically, almost without thinking, I stripped my anarak off and began to pile the grim relics of that wartime voyage on to it. There was more than the bones – buttons like rusted coins, the melted bronze of a unit badge, a wrist watch barely recognizable, all the durable bits and pieces that made up a soldier's personal belongings. And amongst it all an identity disc – the number and the name still visible; ROSS, I. A. Pres.

A pebble rattled in the darkness behind me and I turned. But there was nothing, only the swell sloshing about in the great cavern of the geo, a faint, hollow sound coming to me from beyond the narrow defile of the fault. The last thing I did was to scatter the blackened stones about the cave, flinging them from me. Then, the pieces of wood bundled into my anarak, the last traces removed, I scrambled to my feet, and picking up my burden, started for the faulted exit that led to the geo.

I was halfway up the slope to it when the beam of my torch found him. He was standing by the exit, quite still, watching me. His face was grey, grey like the rock against which he leaned. His dark eyes gleamed in the torch beam. I stopped and we stood facing each other, neither saying a word. I remember looking to see if he were armed, thinking that if he'd killed Braddock . . . But he'd no weapon of any kind; he was empty-handed, wearing an old raincoat and shivering uncontrollably. The sound of water in the geo was louder here, but even so I could hear his teeth chattering. 'Are you all right?' I said.

'Cold, that's all.' He took a stiff step forward, reaching down with his hand. 'Give me that. I'll do my own dirty work, thank you.' He took the bundled anarak from me.

'Who was it?' I asked. 'Braddock?' My voice came in a whisper, unnatural in that place.

'Give me the torch, will you.'

But I'd stepped back. 'Who was it?' I repeated.

'Man named Piper, if you must know.'

'Then it wasn't Braddock?'

'Braddock? No – why?' He laughed; or rather he made a noise that sounded like a laugh. 'Did you think I'd killed him? Is that it?' His voice was hoarse, coming jerky through the chattering of his teeth. 'Braddock died two days before we sighted Laerg.' And he added, 'You bloody fool, Donald. You should know me better than that.' And then, his voice still matter-of-fact: 'If you won't give me the torch, just shine it through here.'

I did as he asked and he went through the narrow defile in the rock, down the slope beyond into the geo, hugging the bundle to him. The falling tide had left my dinghy high and dry. The bows of his boat were grounded just astern of it. There were sails, mast and oars in it, two rusted fuel cans, some old lobster pots; but no clothing, not even oilskins. 'Got anything to drink with you?' he asked as he dumped the bundle.

I gave him my flask. His hands were shaking as he unscrewed the cap, and then he tipped his head back, sucking the liquor down. 'How long had you been there?' I asked.

'Not long.' He finished the whisky, screwed the cap back in place and handed me the empty flask. 'Thanks. I needed that.'

'Were you watching me all the time?'

'Yes. I was coming through the fault when I saw the light of your torch. Luckily it shone on your face, otherwise . . .' Again that laugh that had no vestige of humour in it. 'You reach a certain point . . . You don't care then.' He waded into the water, swung a leg over the side of the boat and clambered wearily in. 'You wait there. I'll be back in a moment. Deep water . . . if I'd been able to do this at the time . . .' He swung the engine and it started at once, the soft beat of it pulsing against the walls. He pushed the gear lever into reverse. The engine revved and the bows grated and then he was off the beach and reversing slowly, back down that geo towards the grey light of the entrance. He backed right out and then disappeared, and I stood there in the half-darkness of the cavern's gloom, wondering whether he'd come back and if he did, what would happen then. Did he trust me? Or did he think I was like the rest of the world – against him? My own brother, and I wasn't sure; wasn't sure what he'd do, what was going on in that strange, confused mind of his – wasn't even sure whether he was sane or mad.

And all the time the drip, drip of moisture from the roof, the slop of water never still as the swell moved gently against the rock walls.

The beat of the engine again and then the boat's bows nosing into the gap below that hanging slab. It came in, black against the daylight, with him standing in the stern, a dark silhouette, his hand on the tiller. The bows grated astern of my dinghy and he clambered out, bringing the painter with him. 'Is the tide still falling?' he asked.

'For another two hours.'

He nodded, tying the rope to a rock. 'No tide table, no charts, nothing in the lockers, and bloody cold.' He straightened up, looking down at the rubber dinghy. 'How did you make out in that thing – all right?' And then he was moving towards me, his eyes fixed on my face. 'Why?' he demanded hoarsely. 'Why did you come here?'

'I knew you were headed for Laerg.' I had backed away from him.

'Did you know why?'

'No.'

'But you guessed, is that it?' He had stopped, standing motionless, his eyes still on me.

'How could I?' I was feeling uneasy now, a little scared, conscious of the strength of that thick-set body, the long arms. Standing like that, dark in silhouette, he reminded me of my grandfather – and the same crazy recklessness, the same ruthless determination. 'I just knew there was something, knew you had to come back.' And I added, 'Twenty-two days is a long time . . .'

'Yes, too long.' He seemed to relax then. He was looking about the cavern now and I could see his mind was back in the past. 'Thirteen days it took us. And then in the dawn I saw Tarsaval. God! I thought I'd never seen anything more beautiful.' He glanced about him, moving his head slowly from side to side, savouring the familiarity. 'This place – brings it back to me. We were five days . . . Yes, five, I think.'

'In here?'

He nodded, handing me back my anarak, empty now.

'How many of you?'

'Just the two of us – Leroux and myself. Alive. The other – he died during the night. We were grounded, you see. On one of the rocks of Eileann nan Shoay, out there. Hadn't the strength to get her off. It was heavy, that raft. The tide did that, some time during the night, and when the dawn came we were right under the cliffs. That dawn – there was a little breeze from the nor'-east. Cold as ice, and the stars frozen like icicles fading to the dawn sky – pale blue and full of mares' tails. We paddled along the cliffs. Just got in here in time. The wind came out of the north.

I'd never have stood that wind. We were frozen as it was, frozen stiff as boards, no heat in us – none at all. We hadn't fed for six days, a week maybe – I don't know. I'd lost count by then.' He turned his head. 'What made you come?' he asked again.

I shrugged. I didn't really know myself. 'You were in trouble...'

He laughed. But again there was no humour in that laugh. 'Been in trouble all my life, it seems. And now I'm too old,' he added, 'to start again. But I had to come back. I didn't want anybody to know – about that.' And he added, 'Not even you, Donald. I'd rather you hadn't known.'

I stared at him, wondering how much was remorse, how much pride and the fear of discovery. 'Did you have to do it?' I shouldn't have asked that, but it was out before I could stop myself, and he turned on me then in a blaze of fury.

'Have to? What would you have done? Died like Leroux, I suppose? Poor little sod. He was a Catholic. I suppose if you're a Catholic . . .' He shook his head. 'Christ, man – the chance of life and the man dead. What did it matter? Lie down and die. I'm a fighter. Always have been. To die when there was a chance . . . That isn't right. Not right at all. If everybody lay down and died when things got tough – that isn't the way man conquered his world. I did what any man with guts would have done – any man not hide-bound by convention; I had no scruples about it. Why the hell should I? And there was the boat – fuel for a fire ready to hand. I'll be honest. I couldn't have done it otherwise. But life, man – life beckoning . . . And that poor fellow Leroux. We argued about it all through the night, there in the cave with the wind whistling through that fault. God in heaven, it was cold – until I lit that fire.' He stopped then, shivering under that thin raincoat. 'Colder than last night. Colder than anything you can imagine. Cold as hell itself. Why do they always picture hell as flaming with heat? To me it's a cold place. Cold as this God-forsaken geo.' He moved, came a step nearer. 'Was the old man right? Is there a way out of here?'

'Yes,' I said. 'If you'd only tried...' I was thinking of the sheep that roamed the island wild. 'Didn't you try?'

'How could I? We only just had strength to crawl through to that cave. We were dead, man – both of us as near dead as makes no odds. You don't understand. When the ship went down . . . I wasn't going to have anything to do with the boats. I'd an escort. Did you know that? I was being brought back under escort. I saw those two damned policemen make bloody sure they got into a boat. They weren't worrying about me then. They were thinking of their own skins. I saw this Carley float hanging there, nobody doing anything about it. So I cut it adrift and jumped. Others joined me just before she sank. It was late afternoon and the sun setting, a great ball. And then she went, very suddenly, the boilers bursting in great bubbles. There were seven besides myself.' He paused then, and I didn't say anything. I didn't want to interrupt him. Nobody to confide in, nobody to share the horror of it with him; it had been bottled up inside him too long. But he was looking about the place again and I had a feeling that he had slipped away from me, his mind gone back to his memories. And then suddenly: 'You say the way out is still there – you've been up to the top, have you?'

'Yes.'

'Well, let's get out of here. Up into the fresh air.' He started to move up the beach towards the fault, and then he paused. 'What's it like up there? Fog, I suppose.'

'No, it's above the fog. The sun's shining.'

'The sun?' He was staring at me as though he didn't believe me. 'The sun. Yes, I'd like to see the sun . . . for a little longer.' I can't describe the tone in which he said that, but it was sad, full of a strange sadness. And I had a feeling then – that he'd reached the end of the road. I had that feeling very strongly as I followed him up the slope and through the fault, as thought he were a man condemned. 'Give me the torch a minute.' His hand was on it and I let him have it. For a moment he stood there, playing the beam of it on that recess, standing quite still and searching the spot with his eyes. 'Thanks,' he said. 'I couldn't bear to go, you see, with the thought that somebody would find that. It wouldn't have mattered – not so much – if I hadn't changed my identity. But taking Braddock's name . . . They'd think I'd killed the poor bastard. Whereas, in fact, I saved his life. Pulled him out of the water with his right arm ripped to pieces. Managed to fix a tourniquet. He was tough, that boy. Lasted longer than most of the others despite the blood he'd lost. Do you know, Donald – I hadn't thought of it. But when he was dying, that last night – he was in my arms, like a child, and I was trying to keep him warm. Though God knows there wasn't much warmth in me by then. The other two, they were lying frozen in a coma, and young Braddock, whispering to me – using up the last of his breath. You're about my build, Iain, he said. And his good arm fumbling at his pockets, he gave me his pay book, all his personal things and the identity disc from round his neck, and all the time whispering to me the story of his life, everything I'd need to know.'

The beam of the torch was still fastened on the recess and after a moment he said, 'When a man does that – gives you a fresh start; and he'd got such guts, never complaining, not like some of the others, and none of them with so much as a scratch. Hell! You can't just pack it in. Not after that.' And then he turned to me suddenly. 'Here. Take the torch. You lead the way and let's go up into the light of day.' But instead of moving aside, he reached out and gripped my shoulders. 'So long as you understand. Do you understand?' But then he released me and stepped back. 'Never mind. It doesn't matter. It's finished now.' And he gave me a gentle, almost affectionate push towards the cave's exit. 'We'll sit in the sun and listen to the birds. Forget the years that are gone. Just think of the old man and the way it was before he died. The island hasn't changed, has it? It still looks the way he described it to us?'

'Yes,' I said. 'It looks very beautiful.' And I climbed up through the continuation of the fault, up the slabbed stairway and out through the final cleft into the sunlight. The fog had thinned, so that it no longer looked like a sea below us, but more like the smoke of some great bush fire. It was in long streamers now, its tendrils lying against the lower slopes, fingering the rock outcrops, turning the whole world below us a dazzling white. Iain stood quite still for a moment, drinking it in, savouring the beauty of the scene just as I had done. But his eyes were questing all the time, searching the slopes of the hills and seaward where the rents in the fog were opening up to give a glimpse of the Atlantic heaving gently to the endless swell. The sunlight accentuated the greyness of his face, the lines cut deep by fatigue. He looked old beyond his years, the black hair greying and his shoulders stooped. As though conscious of my gaze he pulled himself erect. 'We'll walk,' he said gruffly. 'Some exercise – do us good.' And he started off towards the head of Strath Mhurain, not looking back to see if I were following him. He didn't talk and he kept just ahead of me as though he didn't want me to see the look on his face.

At the top of the Druim Ridge he paused, looking down into Shelter Bay where the fog was still thick. And when I joined him, he turned and started up the High Road, heading for the Lookout. He went fast, his head bent forward, and he didn't stop until he'd reached the top of Creag Dubh. Then he flung himself down on the grass, choosing the south-facing slope, so that when the fog cleared he'd be able to see down into Shelter Bay. 'Got a cigarette on you?' he asked.

I gave him one and he lit it, his hands steadier now. He smoked in silence for a while, drawing the smoke deep into his lungs, his head turned to feel the warmth of the sun, his eyes half-closed. 'Do you think they'll have guessed where I was going in that boat?' he asked suddenly.

'I don't know,' I said. 'Probably.'

He nodded. 'Well, if they have, they'll send a helicopter as soon as the fog clears. Or will they come in a ship?' I didn't answer and he said, 'It doesn't matter. From here you'll be able to watch them arrive.'

'And then?' I asked.

'Then . . .' He left the future hanging in the air. He was watching two sheep that had suddenly materialized on an outcrop below us. They were small and neatly balanced with shaggy fleeces and long, curved horns. 'It would be nice, wouldn't it,' he said, lying back with his eyes closed, 'if one could transform oneself – into a sheep, for instance, or better still a bird.' Startled by his voice, the sheep moved with incredible speed and agility, leaping sure-footed down the ledges of that outcrop and disappearing from view.

'You've nothing to worry about – now,' I said.

'No?' He raised himself on one elbow, staring at me. 'You think I should go back, do you? Tell them I'm not Braddock at all, but Sergeant Ross who deserted in North Africa. Christ! Go through all that.' He smiled, a sad, weary smile that didn't touch his eyes. 'Funny, isn't it – how the pattern repeats itself? Lieutenant Moore, Colonel Standing . . . I wonder if that little bastard Moore is still alive. Ten to one he is and ready to swear he gave the only order he could. Probably believes it by now. No,' he said, 'I'm not going back to face that.'

He was silent then, lying there, smoking his cigarette – smoking it slowly, his face, his whole body relaxed now. I thought how strange the human mind is, blank one moment and now remembering every detail. The sun, shining down into the horse-shoe curve of Shelter Bay, was eating up the fog. The whole world below us was a blinding glare. And high in the brilliant sky above an eagle rode, a towering speck turning in quiet circles. 'Well . . .' He shifted and sat up. 'I'll leave you now.' He looked around him, turning his head slowly, taking in the whole panorama of the heights. 'God! It's so beautiful.' He said it softly, to himself. Then, with a quick, decisive movement, he got to his feet. I started to rise, but he placed his hand on my shoulder, holding me there. 'No. You stay here. Stay here till they come, and then tell them . . . tell them what you damn well like.' He dropped his cigarette and put his heel on it. 'You needn't worry about me any more.'

'Where are you going?' I asked.

But he didn't answer. He was staring down into the bay where the fog had thinned to white streamers with glimpses of the sea between. 'What's that? I thought I saw a ship down there.'

'I think it's a trawler,' I said.

'Are you sure it isn't . . .'

'No,' I said. 'It's a foreign trawler.' And I told him how I'd been down into the bay and heard the crew talking in a language I couldn't recognize.

He stood for a moment, staring down into the bay. The streamers of the fog were moving to a sea breeze and through a gap I caught a glimpse of the vessel lying at anchor with a boat alongside.

'Yes. A foreigner by the look of her.' Another rent and the view clearer. I could see men moving about her decks and a lot of radar gear on her upper works. And then his hand gripped my shoulder. 'Donald my Donald,' he said, and the way he said it took me back. 'Thanks for coming – for all your help. Something to take with me. I'd rather be Iain Ross, you know, and have a brother like you, than stay friendless as George Braddock.' And with a final pat he turned and left me, walking quickly down the Druim Ridge.

I watched him until he disappeared below the ridge, not moving from my seat because there wasn't any point. A little later he came into sight again crossing the top of Strath Mhurain, walking along the slopes of Aird Mullaichean until he reached the outcrop. He paused for a moment, a small, distant figure standing motionless. And then he was gone and I sat there, seeing him still in my mind going down that subterranean fault, back to the geo and the waiting lobster boat. The bright sunlight and the warm scent of the grass, the distant clamour of the birds and that eagle still wheeling high in the vaulted blue; the whole world around me full of the breath of life, and I just sat there wishing I could have done something, and knowing in my heart there was nothing I could have done.

I watched the fog clear and the trawler lift her boat into its davits. She got her anchor up then and steamed out of the bay. She was flying a red flag, and as it streamed to the wind of her passage, I thought I could make out the hammer and sickle on it.

She rounded Sgeir Mhor, turned westward and disappeared behind the brown bulk of Keava. And later, perhaps an hour later – I had lost all track of time – a helicopter came in and landed on the flat greensward near the Factor's House. Men in khaki tumbled out, spread into a line and moved towards the camp. I got up then and started down to meet them, sad now and walking slowly, for I'd nothing to tell them – only that my brother was dead.

They found the lobster boat two days later. A trawler picked her up, empty and abandoned about eight miles north-east of Laerg. Nobody doubted what had happened. And in reporting it there was no reference to my brother. It was Major George Braddock who was dead, and I think it was the story I told them of what had really happened in North Africa that caused the various officers concerned, right up to the DRA, to be so frank in their answers to my questions. And now it is March again here on Laerg, the winter over and the birds back, my solitary vigil almost ended. Tomorrow the boat comes to take me back to Rodil.

I finished writing my brother's story almost a week ago. Every day since then I have been out painting, chiefly on Keava. And sitting up there all alone, the sun shining and spring in the air, the nesting season just begun – everything so like it was that last day when we were together on Creag Dubh – I have been wondering. A man like that, so full of a restless, boundless energy, and that trawler lying in the bay. Was he really too old to start his life again – in another country, amongst different people?

THE STRODE
VENTURER

PART ONE

I

STRODE ORIENT

March, 1963. Looking back through my diary, as I begin this account of the strange means by which the prosperity of the company I now serve was founded, I find it difficult to realize that there was a time when I had never been to the Maldives, had scarcely ever heard of Addu Atoll. The island we now call Ran-a-Maari had only recently been born the night I flew into London from Singapore. The stewardess had woken me shortly after four with a cup of coffee and through my window I could see the moon falling towards the west and a great bank of black cloud. The plane whispered softly as it lost height. The first lights showed below us, long ribbons of amber, orange, white and blue. And then the great sprawling mass of the city seen only as slashes of arterial brilliance, the blank spaces in between dotted with the pinpoints of individual street lights like thousands upon thousands of tiny perforations in a black sheet of paper. It was breathtaking, beautiful – immensely impressive; and it went on and on until the pattern of lights was spread from horizon to horizon.

By the time we landed the moon was gone and the sky was clouded over. A chill north-westerly wind blew a light drizzle across the apron and London Airport glimmered damply as we made our way into the terminal building. At that dead hour before the dawn the Customs and Immigration officers, all the night staff, moved with careful deliberation. But though they were slow, they still possessed that quiet air of politeness, even kindness, that always surprises one when coming home after a long sojourn abroad. I hadn't been back for over three years and the consideration with which they treated the passengers erased some of the weariness of the flight. 'Any watches or cameras?'

'No, only what's on the list.'

It was quite a long list for I thought I was returning to England for good, but he chalked my bags and let me through without charging me anything. He had a cold and perhaps he didn't want to be bothered. 'If you'd declared some sunshine I might have charged you,' he said with a tired smile. His face looked white

under the lights, even the dark tan of the passengers was sallowed
by the glare.

I went down the escalator and out through Channel Nine with
the man who had been my companion throughout the flight, but
we didn't talk. We had said all there was to say in the long hours
we had been cooped up in the plane together and now we were
going through the process of readjustment that is common to all
travellers at the moment of separation into individual existence.
Dawn was only just beginning to break as the coach took us into
London – a slow, reluctant dawn coming grey out of a grey sky.
The wet road surface reflected the pallid gleam of the street
lighting. There wasn't much traffic, heavy lorries mainly and the
first milk roundsmen, and in the thickening lines of semi-detached
and terraced houses a scattering of lights as London began to stir
from its sleep.

We crossed the Chiswick and Hammersmith fly-overs and were
into the area where the dual carriageway had slashed like a
sword through residential suburbs, the scars showing in the blank
ends of houses, in the dead ends of streets abruptly severed. 'I'd
forgotten how bloody big this city was,' my companion said. His
name was Hans Straker; he was half Dutch, a big florid man with
close-cropped hair bleached the colour of pale straw by the
Indonesian sun. He'd been in rubber most of his life and now, in
his late forties, he'd been forced to sell his estates and get out. His
love of Java, where he'd lived and worked in recent years, had
been soured by the difficulties of operating under the Sukarno
Government and the shifts he'd been put to to get his money out.
Between Singapore and London I'd been given his whole life
story including accounts of his early travels in the Melanesian
Islands and as far afield as Polynesia. His hobby was seismography
and he had talked a lot about the records he'd kept of submarine
disturbances, his theory that the bed of the Indian Ocean was in
process of change – a theory he expected to be confirmed by the
international hydrographic survey due to commence shortly. He
was almost as bitter about the loss of his seismometer as he was
about his estates.

But now that we had reached London he was strangely silent,
as though he, too, was overawed by the sprawl of the great city.
Which was perhaps as well since I was no longer in a mood to
listen. A dawn arrival after a long flight is not the best moment to
face up to one's prospects. I'd very little money and no job to
come back to. On my own for the first time since I'd joined the
Service at the start of the war, I was conscious of a sense of

uneasiness, a lack of confidence in myself that I'd never experienced before.

My decision to leave the Navy had been based on an assessment
of my prospects following Britain's application for membership of
the Common Market. I spoke French and German and the way
the newspapers talked at that time of the economic future of the
country I thought I'd have no difficulty in finding a job. Even so,
with two children at school in England, I'd never have left the
Service on the strength of the gratuity alone. What finally decided
me was a letter from a London firm of solicitors offering to
purchase on behalf of a client the Strode Orient shares my
mother had left me. It was so unexpected, so opportune that it
seemed like the hand of providence. And the price they offered
was well above the market value of the shares. I had accepted at
once and at the same time had applied for my discharge. And then
everything had gone wrong; France had blocked Britain's entry
into Europe and the London solicitors had written to say that the
Company's Registrar had refused transfer of the shares under the
terms of an agreement signed by my mother in 1940. They had
added that they had seen the letter of agreement and were
satisfied that it was binding on her heirs and assigns.

I could understand my mother's acceptance of the terms for I
knew her circumstances at the time, but that did not soften the
blow. Indeed, it revived all the anger and bitterness I had felt as a
kid when she had tried to explain to me what had happened to my
father and the great shipping line we had owned. The shock of the
solicitor's letter was aggravated by the fact that I had been
relying on the money to start me in civilian life, for by then I knew
the form. Not one of the firms I had written to had held out any
prospect of employment. They wanted technicians, specialists,
men with experience in their own particular field, and all I knew
about was ships and how to run them. Shipping was in a hell of a
mess and here I was in London, unemployed and damn' near
unemployable, the only capital I possessed unsaleable, and
nothing to show for my twenty-odd years in the Navy but the
gratuity and a small pension.

Something of this my companion must have gathered in the
long hours we'd spent together for he suddenly said, 'All this new
building. I haven't been here for years, but it's still the most
exciting city in the world. The sheer ramifications . . .' His small
china-blue eyes stared at me. 'I envy you. You're young enough to
get a kick out of starting all over again.'

It was all very well for him to talk; his wife was dead and he hadn't any children. 'School bills have to be paid,' I said.

That seemed to touch a loss he felt deeply for he snapped back, 'Christ, man! You talk as though it were a millstone. You don't know how lucky you are.' And he added, 'If I were your age and a family behind me, by God I'd rip this city apart to get myself the niche I wanted.' He didn't know about Barbara. I hadn't told him our marriage was just about on the rocks. He shifted angrily in his seat, his quick little eyes looking me over as though I were a stranger whose worth he was trying to assess. 'But maybe you don't want anything, just security – the same sort of security you've had in the Navy.' He hesitated as though searching for the right words, and then he said, 'All your working life you've been sheltered from the raw rough world outside, and now you're scared. That's it, isn't it? You're scared and beginning to feel you'd like nothing better than to get into some big outfit that'll recreate for you the sheltered world you've just left.' He gripped my arm, a gesture of friendliness that was meant to ease the probing bite of what he'd just said. 'Take my advice, Bailey. Find out what you want, find something you really care about. When you know what you want the rest follows. But don't just drift into something because it offers security. Security is never worth a damn. We're meant to live, and to live means living dangerously, half on the edge of trouble, half on the edge of achievement. Myself, I've never felt really alive unless I was fighting something, and here I am, more than ten years older than you and starting all over again. And I'm excited. Yes, dammit, I'm thrilled by the prospect.'

I couldn't see it then. Our circumstances were so entirely different; though the price he'd got for his plantation might be low it must still represent quite a nice amount of capital. But I was to remember his words much later and realize that they were true. We parted at the Air Terminal and he gave me his address – the Oriental Club. 'If you care for a drink sometime . . .' He left it at that and as I picked up my case and went over to Information it never occurred to me that I should see him again. I asked for a cheap hotel and the girl at the desk fixed me up at one of those small residential places off the Cromwell Road. I took a taxi there, but the room wasn't ready of course, and it was still too early for breakfast. I signed the register and had a wash, and then, leaving my bags with the night porter, I walked out into the grey loneliness of London. The traffic was still light, the clatter of milk bottles the dominant sound. A newsboy was delivering papers and across the road a lighted shop front showed two policemen in sharp relief; they stood quite still staring at a bosomy model dressed in a black brassière and matching elastic girdle. Lights were on in some of the upper windows, boarding houses and shops mingling haphazardly with still-lifeless offices, and up a side street a glimpse of trees and an old Regency square.

There is something about London at this hour of the morning, a hint of greatness past and present, the sense of a leviathan stirring, stretching itself to meet the challenge of a new day. It never failed to excite me and tired though I was, I too felt the challenge. I joined two early workers waiting for a bus and when it came, its side lights and the red bulk of it rumbling to a stop in the empty street, I climbed to the upper deck and sat in the front to watch Knightsbridge and Piccadilly, all the old, remembered, familiar façades roll by. It was only later when I switched to a bus going City-wards that I was consciously aware of a destination, and all the way down Fleet Street and up Ludgate Hill I had the sense of a pilgrimage, for the building I was going to visit was the power-symbol of the man who had broken my father.

It was a long time ago, more than thirty years, and I'd been away at school so that I'd only felt the impact of it through my mother and through our changed circumstances and the void my father left in our lives. At that age you don't feel bitterness; you accept things as they are, adapting quickly and not thinking too much. It had meant Dartmouth to me instead of an expensive school and Henry Strode was just a name, a sort of monster whom I'd get even with some day. Now, of course, he was dead, too, and when I'd met his son sitting cross-legged on the deck of a dhow beached on an island in the Persian Gulf I'd felt no hostility towards him. He wasn't that sort of a man and anyway our circumstances seemed oddly reversed – I was in command of a minelaying exercise and he was bumming a ride in a *sambuq* down to Mukalla.

We had reached the Bank and I got out at the bus stop by the Royal Exchange. The City was still dead, the rush-hour not yet begun. I walked slowly along Cornhill, staring at the still empty buildings, wondering what I was doing there. This wasn't my sort of world, which was probably why in all the years since my father's death I'd never bothered to visit the scene of the battle he'd fought and lost up here in this close-packed, money-conscious square mile. Where Bishopsgate joined Gracechurch Street I came to Leadenhall Street and five minutes later I was in the shipping quarter, looking across at the façade of Strode House. It was smaller than I had expected, but perhaps that was because I had just passed the new Lloyds building. Also it looked dirty, but then so did most of the buidings in this area of the City; shipping had been depressed for so long that the only office block that looked as though it had been cleaned in living memory was the palatial headquarters of the Cunard Company.

Somewhere behind me, in St Mary Axe, a clock struck eight. I crossed the street to stand on the pavement, looking up at Strode House with its scrolls and figures and pseudo Dutch gables all outlined in a coating of grime and pigeon droppings. It was a solid, pretentious building, unspeakably self-conscious – a merchant prince's house crying aloud the power and riches of its dead builder.

The door was open and I went in. Marble floors and a big curved staircase with oil paintings, and hanging from the centre of a cupola that didn't seem to fit the design, a magnificent Venetian chandelier. An old man in his shirt sleeves appeared from the door on my left. He was carrying a bucket and a broom with a cloth wrapped round its head. I asked him what time the staff arrived. 'Some at nine, some at nine-thirty,' he mumbled and spilled some of the dirty water from the bucket on the floor with the deliberate movements of a man who has been doing the same thing every morning for as long as he can remember. 'You wanting to see anyone in partic'lar?' There was no interest in his voice as he spread the dark water with slow sweeps of the broom.

'Mr Strode,' I said.

'Oh, one of the directors. Well, I wouldn't know when they come in. I finish at nine.'

'Mind if I look at the pictures?' There was one half-way up the stairs that had caught my eye, a head and shoulders portrait familiar even at that distance.

The broom paused in a stroke and he turned and inspected me out of old watery eyes. 'This ain't a pitcher gallery, yer know. But no 'arm in looking.' He nodded. 'Yuo go ahead.' And he added as I climbed the stairs, 'Don't often get people coming 'ere at this time o' the morning. An' nobody don't bother about the pitchers any more. They're all dead, anyway, 'cepting the two in the boardroom.'

It had come as a shock to see my father's face hanging there on the dark turn of the staircase, and as I stood in front of it the years rolled back and I was a kid again running down to greet him as he entered the house. That was when we'd lived in Eaton Square and there'd been a butler and every night people in to dinner or my parents out somewhere. I'd seen very little of him, but there was one holiday I could remember when we'd gone on a ship. I must have been about six or seven then and we'd had the ship to ourselves, no other passengers, so it must have been a freighter. He'd spent a lot of time with me then, up on the bridge, taking me round the engine-room. But something had gone wrong and he'd had to leave suddenly, and after that it hadn't been the same with only my mother and some sort of governess, though the captain had still let me come up to the bridge. It was all a long time ago, the house in Eaton Square a dim memory, and this portrait, though familiar, quite unlike the father I'd thought I could remember – more rigid, more impersonal.

It was a boardroom picture, head and shoulders painted against a symbolic background of ships seen through a window. He wore a stiff collar very high against the throat and his thin, almost ascetic face looked lined, the eyes tired. There was no date given, just the name – Sir Reginald Bailey.

I called down to the caretaker and asked him how long he'd been working here. Forty-one years, he said, and I wondered whether he'd known my father. I was still shocked at finding his portrait here, stuck on the wall like a trophy. There were other portraits above me. Were they also of men whose companies Strode had swallowed in the great depression of the thirties? 'I come 'ere when Strode 'Ouse was new-built,' the old man said. He was leaning on his broom, staring up at me, curious now.

'You knew Henry Strode, then?'

'The Ol' Man? 'Course I knew the Ol' Man. There wasn't nobody in Strode 'Ouse didn't know 'im. 'Ere every morning punctuool at eight o'clock, 'e was, right up to the day he died. 'E 'ad a stroke and died in 'arness sitting at 'is desk up there on the first floor under the big pitcher of the ss *Henry Strode*. That was the biggest ship we ever built; the 'ole staff, every man jack o' us, taken in a special train up to Glasgow to see her launched. Mr Strode, 'e was like that – did things in style.' He shook his head and gazed around him as though the place were suddenly strange to him. 'Things is different now. Never bin the same since the Ol' Man died. But then we don't breed men like 'im any more.' He hesitated, squinting up at me. 'You connected wiv the family, sir? I didn't ought to talk like this, but when you've lived through the great days – well, it's me age, yer see. I'll be sixty-five next year and then I'll 'ave the pension.' He was still staring at me, his curiosity mounting. 'You don't look like a City gent, if yer don't mind my saying so.'

'No, I'm not.' I moved back down the stairs, not wanting to

look any more at my father captive on that wall. 'Did you ever meet Sir Reginald Bailey?'

'Once.' He gave me a sidelong glance, his head at an angle, and I knew he was comparing me with the picture. 'Nineteen thirty-one, it was. I was doorman then. Livery, top 'at an' all. Like I say, we did things in style then and the Ol' Man, 'e puts on a lunch for Sir Reginald . . .' But then he stopped as though he knew he was on delicate ground. 'This was one of the first City 'ouses to 'ave a directors' dining-room,' he added lamely, and he veered away from the subject, muttering about the great days being gone. 'Seventy-three ships we 'ad at one time, vessels sailing all over the world an' this place a 'ive of activity wiv clerks dashing in an' out wiv bills an' things an' captins coming for orders an' half the bankers of the City 'ere to lunch an' do business. That room there – ' He nodded to the ornate bronze doors to the left of the entrance. 'That was the counting 'ouse as you might say. Millions, literally millions, 'ave gone through that door. Now the room's empty an' all we got left they tell me is seventeen ships. You want to see the old counting 'ouse? Got some nice pitchers. The Ol' Man, 'e 'ad a pitcher painted of every vessel 'e 'ad built.'

I shook my head. 'I'll come back later,' I said and I gave him half a crown and asked him to have a drink on me. 'What's your name?'

'Billings, sir. Any time you want ter know anything about the old days just come an' ask me.'

I thanked him and went out into the street where the traffic had thickened, piling up against the Gracechurch Street-Bishopsgate crossing in an almost solid block. I found a self-service café by Leadenhall Market and had some breakfast whilst I thought it out. But I knew the answer already. It wasn't just a matter of having met Strode. It was the sense of continuity, of following in my father's footsteps. And later perhaps – who knows? I was dreaming, dreaming of recovering what my father had lost, thinking of the little church overlooking the sea and the plaque my mother had had erected on the north wall. They had been married in that church and four years ago I had stood in the graveyard with the wind blowing in my hair and the rain on my face as they committed her to the earth. And afterwards I had gone inside and looked at that plaque: *To the Memory of Reginald Horace Baily who died at sea 21st December 1931. What he had built other men coveted.* It was the first time I had seen it and I pictured her crying over the paper as she wrote that strange line. She'd cried a lot after his death. And now here I was, her only son, going to ask Strode's son a favour. I hoped she'd understand. Pride was a luxury I couldn't afford and anyway I'd liked Strode. Enough at any rate not to reveal my connection with the old Bailey Oriental Line.

It was in the late autumn of 1955 I'd met him, sat talking with him all one night, about almost everything from birth to death and what happened afterwards. He was that sort of man. Now that his father was dead he'd presumably be on the board. I hoped it hadn't changed him. Hoped, too, that the few hours we'd spent in each other's company on Abu Musa would have made as much of an impression on him as they had on me.

But when I returned to Strode House shortly after ten and asked for Mr Strode, the commissionaire said, 'Which one? There's five of them work here.'

I hadn't expected that and the trouble was I didn't know his Christian name. 'The one I want is the son of Henry Strode, the founder.' But even that wasn't sufficient to identify him. There were apparently two sons, whereas I had got the impression that he was the only one. 'There's Mr Henry Strode,' the commissionaire said. 'He's the chairman and managing director of Strode & Company. And then there's his younger brother, Mr George Strode. He manages Strode Orient.' I chose the latter since he ran the ships and was passed on to his assistant, a small, pale man with narrow eyes and sandy hair who sat at a corner desk in a huge office on the first floor. 'I'm afraid Mr Strode isn't in today,' he snapped at me like a dog that's not sure of himself. The dark panelled walls were full of pictures of ships and the portrait of a heavily-built, vital old man hung over the fireplace. 'You haven't an appointment, have you? He never makes appointments for Thursdays.'

'No,' I said. 'I haven't an appointment. But I wrote to him.'

'He didn't mention it.' He was frowning nervously. 'Mr Geoffrey Bailey you said? I haven't seen any letter.'

'I wrote from Singapore. But perhaps it went to his brother.' And I explained about not knowing his Christian name and how we'd met in the Persian Gulf.

He shook his head. 'Mr Strode has never been in the Persian Gulf.'

'Then it must be his brother.'

'I don't think so.' He was puzzled now. 'I'm quite certain Mr Henry Strode hasn't been in the Persian Gulf either.'

'If I could have a word with Henry Strode then . . .'

'I'm sorry. He's never in on Thursdays. Neither of them are. It's their day for hunting.' He said it almost with malice as though he disliked his employer. 'You could see John Strode, if you like. He's Mr Henry's son.'

But that was no good. 'I'll come back tomorrow, then.'

He shook his head firmly. 'Tomorrow's the annual general meeting. He couldn't possibly see you tomorrow.' He bit his lip, strangely agitated. 'Would Monday do? I think Monday would be all right.' He glanced at a diary. 'Three o'clock. It's a personal matter, presumably?'

'Yes, personal,' I said and left it at that, unwilling to explain the purpose of my visit to this terrified little clerk. 'Just find the letter I wrote from Singapore, will you, and let Mr Strode see it. That explains everything.' And I added as I went to the door, 'The secretary probably has it since he acknowledged it.'

'The secretary.' He seemed suddenly confused. 'If it's Mr Whimbrill you want, then I'm sure . . .'

'No, no,' I said. 'I'll come back on Monday.' And I went out and closed the door, wondering what sort of man George Strode was that this assistant should appear to be on the verge of a nervous breakdown.

Remembering what Billings had said about the portraits in the boardroom I walked past the head of the stairs and opened the first door I came to. A young man sat alone at a big desk, smoking and staring out of the window. I asked him where the boardroom was and he told me in a bored voice that it was the second door on the right. It proved to be no bigger than the office I had just left, but the pictures on the panelling were all portraits. The same face looked down from the position of honour over the big stone fireplace – a head and shoulders this time, the hair grizzled instead of white, the eyes more vital, the mouth less sour, but still the same heavy, fleshy face, the sense of thrust and power. The pictures I had come to see were on the right and left of this portrait. Underneath were the names Henry Strode and George Strode. The faces had something of the same heaviness, but that was all; they had inherited none of the ebullient vitality, the strength, the personality of their father. And neither of them was the man I had met in the Persian Gulf clad like the nakauda of the dhow on which he was travelling.

I went back to the central portrait, trying to see in it a resemblance to the Strode I knew. But he had been small and wiry, his face thin, almost drawn, and burned black by the sun, the hair black, too, and the ears very pointed so that he had almost faunlike quality. This had been accentuated when he smiled, which he had done often, causing little lines to run away from the corners of eyes and mouth. My memory of him was blurred by time, but I thought, looking up at that portrait, that the only thing he shared with his father was the same powerful impression of vitality, that and something in the eyes, a sort of zest. Or rather it had been zest in the case of the man I knew – zest for life and a strange excitement; here I thought it looked more like greed.

I was thinking of my father again as I went down the stairs, of what he must have gone through, everything he had worked for smashed by that ruthless man whose face I had now seen for the first time. He had died shortly afterwards. It hadn't meant anything much to me at the time for I was at Dartmouth busy coping with the problem of fitting myself into a new life. It was only when I got home and saw my mother suddenly turned grey in a matter of months that I felt the impact of it. She had moved to Sheilhaugh, a little farmhouse on the Scottish border that had originally belonged to her family, and was busying herself keeping chickens . . . 'Everything all right, sir?' It was the commissionaire, polite and friendly.

'Yes. Yes, thanks.' And then on the spur of the moment, not thinking what I planned to do, I asked him where the annual general meeting would be held.

'Right here, sir.' He nodded to the bronze doors on the right of the entrance.

'What time?'

'Noon tomorrow. You're a shareholder, are you, sir?'

'Yes, I am.' I hesitated. 'You've been here some time I take it?'

'Over ten years.'

'Then perhaps you could tell me whether there's another son – son of the founder who doesn't work here.'

For a moment I thought he wasn't going to answer. But then he said, 'Well, it's not for me to discuss the family's affairs, but I believe there was a son by the Old Man's second marriage. It's just gossip, you know. I've never met him and I don't think anybody else has. Was he the one you wanted to see?'

'Do you know his name?'

But he shook his head. 'No, only that he's . . . well, a bit of a rolling stone, if you see what I mean.'

So that was it and the Strode I'd met was probably still wandering around the world. Feeling suddenly tired I went out again into Leadenhall Street, to the throb of buses and heavy lorries pumping diesel fumes into the narrow gut between the grubby buildings. I would like to have gone back to the hotel and had a bath, perhaps a short sleep. but it was a long way and there was at least one other man I knew in the City, a stockbroker in Copthall Court. The last time I had seen him had been at a party in Harwich Town Hall the night before the North Sea Race. I'd been crewing in one of the RNSA boats; he'd been racing his own yacht. That had been nearly five years ago.

I went down Bishopsgate and then turned left into Thread-needle Street, a gleam of watery sunlight softening the façade of the Bank of England. All about me were buildings that seemed to date from the massive Victorian age of greatness, richly ornate, stolid buildings grimed with dirt, their interiors permanently lit by artificial light. The people in the streets, mostly men wearing dark suits, some with bowler hats, looked pale and ill, like busy ter-mites coming out of dark holes in the grey slabs of the buildings. And when I came to Throgmorton Street and the Stock Exchange, the City seemed to swallow me, the narrow street closing in above my head. A top-hatted broker passed me, his pallid features a dyspeptic grey, his mouth a tight line. Youths jostled each other as they scurried hatless from place to place. And on every face, it seemed to me, there was a strange lack of human feeling as though the concentration on finance had bitten deep into all their souls. It was an alien world, far more alien to me than a foreign port.

Copthall Court was through an archway opposite the Stock Exchange and in a building half-way down it I found the firm I wanted listed among about a hundred others on a great board opposite the lift. Their offices were on the sixth floor, a group of poky little cubby-holes looking out on to the blank wall of the neighbouring building. To my surprise George Latham seemed as bronzed and as fit as when I had last seen him. What is more he recognized me at once. 'Come in, dear boy. Come in.' He took me into his office which he shared with two of his partners and an Exchange Telegraph tape machine that tickered away erratically. 'Excuse the mess.' There was barely room to move in the litter of desks and papers. 'Only got back the other day. Been in the Caribbean and now I'm trying to catch up.' He was a big bull of a man, broad-shouldered, with a massive square-jawed head. 'Well now, what can I do for you? No good asking me what to buy. I don't know. Market should have gone to hell with the collapse of the Common Market talks. But it hasn't, God knows why.'

'I want your advice about some Strode Orient shares I hold.'

At that he raised his eyes heavenwards and heaved a sigh. 'For God's sake, man. What price did you pay?' And when I told him

I'd inherited them from my mother who'd been given them in 1940 he seemed relieved. 'I thought for a moment you'd been caught when they were run up to over five shillings a couple of months or so back. A take-over rumour, but nothing came of it. Strode & Comapny blocked it. They own about forty-five per cent of the shares.' He reached for *The Financial Times* and checked down the list of quotations. 'They're now about two bob nominal. Just a moment. I'll get the Ex Tel card.' He went to a filing cabinet and came back with a card that gave all the details of the company. 'Yes, I remember now. Some slick outfit thought they'd make a killing. The company owns seventeen vessels standing in the balance sheet at just over a million. The scrap value alone must be all of that and even in the present depressed state of shipping there'd be a market for the five newer vessels. Say a million and a half for them and half a million for the rest. That's two million plus half a million cash. The capital is four and a half million in one pound shares which means that at five bob a share, which was what these boys were offering, they would have had the whole boiling for little more than a million.'

'They offered me ten shillings a share,' I said.

'And you didn't take it?'

I told him the whole story then, producing from my pocket the company's photostat copy of the letter of acceptance my mother had signed. He read it through and then shook his head. 'I can't advise you on this and I doubt whether your solicitors could either. You'd need to take counsel's opinion to find out whether it really was binding on you as the present owner of the shares. How many do you hold?'

'Twenty thousand.'

'Well, I can tell you this: you put twenty thousand on the market as it is at present and you wouldn't get anywhere near two bob. Probably you wouldn't get an offer. Still, it might be worth spending fifty quid for an opinion – just in case the boys who were after the company become active again. You never know. They may find a way of getting control. Let's see what the market thinks.' He reached for the telephone and in two minutes had the answer. 'Well now, this is interesting. Apparently they've switched their Campaign from Strode Orient to the parent outfit, Strode & Company. The jobbers say they can't hope to get control through the market. As with Strode Orient, the public holds less than fifty per cent of the capital, but they've pushed the shares up from around eight shillings to nine shillings and sixpence in the past month so it looks as though some of the family may have sold out. Not that it helps you.' He sat back in his chair, swivelling it round to face me. 'Pity your mother couldn't have sold her shares when old Henry Strode was alive. I remember when I first started in as a stockbroker after the war Strode Orient were virtually a blue chip and stood at over four pounds, which meant that at that time her holding was worth all of eighty thousand.' He smiled. 'But that's the Stock Exchange for you. If you know when to buy and when to sell . . .' He gave a little shrug. 'Maybe I live too close to it. I'm in and out of the market and I make a bit here and there, but as you see, I'm still working for my living.'

I wasn't really listening to him. I was thinking of what had happened to the Strode shipping empire since Henry Strode had died and what it meant to me. Eighty thousand! And now, even if I could find a way round the agreement, those shares were worth less than my gratuity. 'Any point in going to the meeting tomorrow?' I asked.

'The meeting? Oh yes, I forgot to tell you. The market is expecting the chairman to face some awkward questions. Could be some fireworks, in fact. Apparently one of the big institutions purchased a large block of Strode Orient shares when they were marked down on the death of the old chairman and they've been stuck with them ever since.' The phone rang and when he'd answered it he pushed the Ex Tel card across to me. 'Henry Strode died in 1955 and the price of the shares in that year ranged from a low of forty-two shillings to a high of fifty-eight and six. Even around the low they must have paid more than twenty times the present price. That's not a very good record for an institution.' He got to his feet. 'I've got to go and deal for a client now. But I should go to the meeting if you've nothing better to do.' And he added as he held the door open for me, 'Practically all our shipping companies are the same; they've been too bloody slow to move with the times. They've stuck to the small general-purpose tramp and let the Swedes and the Norwegians with their big specialized bulk carriers grab the much more lucrative long-term charter business. But the Strode Orient Line has been about the slowest of the lot. If you go to the meeting you'll see the sort of management you've got.

'The trouble with meetings,' he went on as we waited for the lift, 'is that the chairman doesn't have to answer any questions put to him by shareholders. It's only when shareholders get together with sufficient voting strength to push the old directors out and get their own men in that the fur really begins to fly. Directors love their salaries, you know. Or perhaps I should say in these days of high taxation that, like politicians, they love the power and advantages of their position – the chaffeur-driven car, the big office, expense accounts, the ability to make and break people, to order others about. Those they cling to like limpets.' He laughed as we went out into the street. 'So would I. And so would you if you had the chance. It's the only way to live well in a country where the State dominates. The Russians discovered it long ago, and when all's said and done the power of the State is now so great that the gap between our brand of capitalism and Russia's brand of Communism is closing all the time.' We had reached Throgmorton Street and he paused. 'Do I gather you've left the Navy?'

'In the process of leaving,' I said.

'Well, get yourself with one of the big institutions, or better still with a small one that's growing.' He glanced round, seeming to savour the bustle of the street. 'Whatever they say about the City, it's still a huge dynamo with its tentacles reaching out to every corner of the globe. If you've the right contacts . . .' He smiled and left it at that. 'Well, sorry I couldn't be of more help to you.' A quick pat on the arm and he was gone, moving quickly across the street and up the steps into the Stock Exchange.

The sun had broken through now and patches of blue sky showed between the buildings. I walked to the Bank and on down Queen Victoria Street. Here I was in an area of new office blocks and the sense of power and wealth that surrounded me was very strong. I felt suddenly alone and without purpose in a world that had its own built-in dynamic drive. I had always heard it said that a human being could feel lonelier in London than in any city in the world and now it was beginning to be true for me. It was natural, I suppose, that at that moment my thoughts should have turned to Barbara, now some eight thousand miles away. I wondered if she realized how she'd driven me to this and how much she was a part of the loneliness I felt.

When a marriage goes wrong it's difficult not to blame the other partner. You see their faults so clearly. You never see your own. How much was I to blame? Again, I didn't know. She'd been barely twenty when I'd rushed her into marriage in 1949. I hadn't stopped to consider how glamorous Ceylon must have seemed to a young and very vital girl straight from the austerity of post-war Britain. We were in love and it was so marvellous that that was all that had seemed to matter. It was only later that I began to realize that the vitality that had attracted me to her in the first place was not physical, but an expression of a furious energy that conditioned her whole mental approach to life so that she grabbed at it with both hands like a child unable to resist forbidden fruit. She wanted the stars as well as the moon. The excitement and novelty of having children had satisfied her for a time, but after that . . . God knows what she had been up to in the long periods when I was away at sea. I hadn't dared inquire too closely. The satisfaction of sexual appetite can be a useful palliative to some women when ambition is thwarted and abundant natural energy frustrated. It wasn't altogether her fault, but I couldn't help thinking with envy of some of my fellow officers. The strength they drew from a happy marriage was something I had never had. And now in a last desperate effort to deal with the problem I had abandoned a career for which I had been trained all my life. I was feeling very bitter as I walked towards Black-friars, drawn invitably towards the river, the one link in this city with the world I knew and loved. I'd see the children. That was something, at any rate. John was at prep school near Hailsham and Mary at a convent school in the same county. Hostages to the future and in a sense my only sheet anchor. Now that I was away from Barbara she didn't seem to matter so much. But these two did and I felt I couldn't fail them.

I was passing *The Times* building then and the sight of it reminded me that I had met one of their correspondents at the time of the Oman war. But when I went in and inquired for him I was told that he was in Southern Rhodesia. I had never been in a newspaper office before and seeing the copies of the day's paper spread about and people looking through them I realized that here was a world whose function was to record the news, to record it permanently in print. 'How far do your records go back?' I asked.

'You want to look something up?' the man at the desk asked. 'We've all the back issues. If you'd care to give me the date, sir?'

'I can give you the year. It was 1931.'

'And the subject?'

'Strode & Company's acquisition of the Bailey Oriental Line and anything you have on the death of Sir Reginald Bailey. That was 21 December, 1931. There might be an obituary.'

He nodded and reached for the phone. It was all much easier than I had expected and in less than quarter of an hour I was seated at a table with several bound volumes of *The Times* stacked beside me and a list of references. What precisely it was that made me want to rake over the past I don't quite know, but once started, I sat there reading on and on, fascinated by the picture conjured up by those faded columns of print. It was all there – the cut-throat competition for freight as world trade slumped, the news that two of the largest shareholders in Bailey Oriental, one of them my father's own brother, had sold out to Henry Strode, and then the long-drawn-out struggle for control with my father pledging his credit to the limit and beyond in a wild and reckless attempt to buy back control in the open market. Mostly the story was confined to the financial pages so that much of it was written in terms that were difficult to follow, but I understood enough of it to read between the lines and realize what my father must have gone through. Only in the final stages did it spread over into the general news pages. This was when Strode began to unload and the market in Bailey Oriental collapsed overnight. He had timed it so that he caught my father overextended, with short-term loans falling due and a large block of shares he couldn't pay for. The result was bankruptcy. Three months later, in the issue of 23 December, I found the obituary. He'd died at sea, in one of his own ships. He was given ten lines, that was all; ten lines written in such a way that I was reminded of the letter from Strode I had found amongst my mother's things. Both the obituary and that letter implied something that was never stated.

I returned the volumes to the desk and went out into the sunlight, down to the river where I leaned on the warm stone of the embankment parapet, staring at the barges slipping down on the ebb, feeling once again as I had felt as a child when I came home to Sheilhaugh to find my mother gone suddenly haggard. Henry Strode had been a monster, and yet even he had been touched by remorse when the bombs began to fall and with half the City in flames he had had to face up to the possibility of death.

The thick river water ran sludge-grey to the sea and clouds sailed the South Bank sky, dirty white and cold looking. But it was warm under the bare black trees where I was sheltered from the north-east wind. I walked all the way to Westminster trying to get the sour taste of what had happened out of my system. But long before I reached the shadow of Big Ben I had discovered that the sour taste belonged to the present, not the past, for if it hadn't been for Henry Strode I'd have inherited a shipping line and from what I'd seen and heard that morning I knew I could have run it a damned sight better than Strode's sons. I knew, with that inner certainty that comes of experience, that I had it in me, that it was bred in me, and the bitterness I felt didn't only arise from the fact that this would have satisfied Barbara. It stemmed from my own frustration – the same frustration that I had suffered in the Navy as I watched our ships and our power decline. Standing

in Parliament Square, looking across to the Palace of Westminster, I realized that what had happened to the Navy and in a
much smaller way to the Strode Orient Line was all part of the
same thing, part of the malaise that had gripped the country since
the war.

I turned abruptly on my heels and went into the nearest pub for
a drink.

That afternoon I saw the Employment Liaison Officer at one
of the Admiralty's outlying offices. He was sympathetic, but not
hopeful. I was a Commander TAS – Torpedo Anti-Submarine –
in mine-layers; it wasn't the sort of background to give me ready
access to employment in industry in present conditions. He
advised me to wait six months until the economy had had time to
recover. Meantime, he would put my name on the books and if
anything suitable turnd up . . . I went back to the dreary little
hotel, had a bath and after an early meal spent the evening alone
at the theatre. I had friends in London, of course, but they were
naval friends and couldn't help. Besides, I wasn't in the mood for
company and though I was tired when I finally got to bed, I still
found myself thinking of the Strode-Bailey affair, of the disparity
between the Strode I had met and the Strodes who now ran the
business. It was some time before I got to sleep and long before
that I had made up my mind to attend the meeting in the morning.

2

THE STRODE VENTURER

I ARRIVED at Strode House just before twelve. The commissionaire took my hat and coat. 'The meeting, sir?' He directed me to
the bronze doors of what Billings had called the counting house,
one of which stood open. There was a small table there and in
attendance beside it, dressed in black jacket and pin-stripe
trousers, was the man I'd seen in George Strode's office the
previous day. 'Name, please?' And then he recognized me. 'Mr
Bailey?' There was surprise, almost a note of relief in the way he
said my name. 'Your initials, please, and the address.' He wrote it
down on a single sheet of paper that contained barely half a
dozen names and as I started to move on through the door he

grabbed hold of my arm. 'After the meeting, you won't leave, will you? I'm sure the chairman . . .' He checked himself. 'If you'd just have a word with me first.'

His manner was so strange that I hesitated. But then somebody else arrived and still wondering at his agitation I passed through into a room with an ornate ceiling and marble floor that still contained the mahogany desks and counter that revealed its original function. A big table had been placed across the far end of the room below the picture of an old stern-wheeler. Seven men were seated behind it, the two Strode brothers together in the centre, and facing them was a close-packed audience of some thirty men. There were no women present and as I slipped into one of the few vacant seats I thought they had been able to guage the attendance very accurately. The list outside, presumably for unexpected shareholders, suggested that the meeting had been packed in advance by shareholders known to be friendly to the board.

I turned to the report, a copy of which had been waiting for me on the seat. It was printed on glossy paper with the House flag embossed on the cover in blue and gold, and I had just turned to the balance sheet when the man who had been on the door came hurrying down the central aisle to lean across the table and whisper to George Strode. For a moment they were both of them looking in my direction, and then the chairman nodded and his assistant went back to the door, leaving me wondering whether their interest was due to my name or to the letter I had written.

To avoid any appearance of having noticed Strode's interest I tried to concentrate on the balance sheet, but the mass of figures meant very little to me, though I did notice that the cost of the fleet was not given, only the written-down value, which as Latham had said was just over a million. The profit and loss account gave the measure of the company's difficulties with an operating deficit on voyages completed to 31 December of more than seventy thousand pounds. On the back cover were listed the ships the company owned, each name beginning with Strode – *Strode Seafarer*, *Strode Trader*, *Strode Glory*, a total of seventeen of them. Inserted in the report was the chairman's statement and I had just begun to read this when the man himself rose to start the proceedings by calling on the secretary to read the notice convening the meeting. George Strode had put on wieght since the picture of him in the boardroom had been painted. His face had thickened, become coarser, and the small, rather moist eyes now protruded from fleshy pouches. Yet there was nothing soft about him. He was a massive, broad-shouldered man with thick black hair and black eyebrows just starting to bush out, and he looked fit.

As soon as the secretary had finished he called on the auditor's representative, and all the time his eyes moved restlessly over the assembled shareholders as though searching out the opposition. If he was nervous, this was the only sign of it he gave for he had the sort of features that expressed nothing of his feelings. His voice, too, was expressionless as he got to his feet again and said, 'The report and accounts of your company, together with my review of the year, have been in your hands now for almost a month. I take it, gentlemen, that your time is as precious as mine and that you will not expect me to read them through to you. May I take them as read then?' There was no dissenting voice. 'Very well. But before I put the motion of acceptance of the accounts to the meeting it is my custom at these yearly gatherings of our share-holders to inquire if there are any questions you wish to put to your board. I may say,' he added with a disarming smile, 'that I don't necessarily undertake to answer *any* questions you put to me. It is not always in the interests of shareholders . . .'

But the opposition was already on its feet and for over ten minutes we were given a review of the decline in the company's fortunes by a man who might have been a clerk, he was so lacking in any presence and his voice so flat and monotonous. Like most of the other men present he was dressed in a city suit, white collar, blue tie, a strangely anonymous figure whose speech was so full of figures I could barely follow it as he read from a mass of papers he shuffled out of a battered brief-case. Before he had managed to give any substance to his complaint Strode, by surprised raisings of his eyebrows, by puzzled, sometimes even amused glances at his fellow directors and at the body of the hall, had managed to attract to himself the sympathy of the majority of those present. Timing it to a nicety, he rose to his feet whilst the other was still speaking. 'If you'd care to put your question, Mr Felden . . .' This was, of course, a query as to what the directors proposed to do about the deplorable state of the company, and Strode snapped back at him, 'You asked me that last year.' He was at ease now, quite confident he had the meeting with him and prepared to bull-doze his way through any opposition. 'My answer, I am afraid, must be the same. It is not in the interests of the company . . .'

'I am sorry, Mr Chairman, but I am not prepared to accept that as an adequate reply on this occasion.' The same flat monotone, but a certain hardness had crept into Felden's voice.

'Well, you'll have to.' Strode turned to the rest of us. 'I am sure you will appreciate, gentlemen, that my attitude here must be dictated by the interests of the company and the shareholders as a whole. Shipping, as you know, is going through the worst slump in its whole history. We operate in a competitive field and to reveal all the various ways in which I and my fellow directors are endeavouring to meet . . .'

But Felden cut him short. 'You have fobbed your shareholders off with this same nonsense for five years now.' His choice of words as much as the sudden lift of his voice had its impact and I felt myself warming to this dry little man who looked so inoffensive but who was doing just what I would like to have done. 'As you know,' he went on, 'I represent a considerable shareholding . . .'

'A bare seven per cent, Mr Felden.'

'I understand and I do not expect to be successful in moving a motion at this gathering.' He glanced pointedly round the room with a thin smile. 'Nevertheless it is my duty, as representing I think by far the greatest shareholding present – and that includes your directors – to sound a note of warning.' He had turned and was facing the meeting. 'The present market valuation of the company's shares is now so reduced that it represents no more than the cash in hand. In other words, anybody acquiring your company by purchase of shares at the current price of two shillings per one pound share gets the Strode Orient fleet for next to nothing. This is a classic take-over situation and still our chairman refuses to take us into his confidence and tell us how he and his board propose to improve the position of the company so that the market valuation of its shares more adequately reflects the value of its assets.'

'Those remarks, Mr Felden, would have been better addressed to me than to the body of the meeting.' Strode's voice was calm, still apparently unperturbed. 'What you have said is very much to the point and both I and my board are fully aware of the need to increase the profitability of the company and so improve the value of its shares. This will happen, never fear. The freight market is at times a very volatile one and for all you or I know the turn-round may happen this current year. But – and this I do ask you to consider very seriously – the dangers to which you refer, which in any other company might be very real, only confirm my view that it is not in the company's interests for me to reveal our intentions or to make our policy public.'

Felden nodded briefly. 'Then perhaps, Mr Chairman, you

would answer this question: Have you, or have you not, received a bid for the company?'

'I have not.' Strode said it with emphasis. And he added, 'I am glad you put that question. A rumour has been circulated by people who have not the best interest of the company at heart and I welcome this opportunity of refuting it. There has been no take-over bid for your company. And I would add that, even if there had been, there is no chance of it succeeding.'

'Because Strode & Company hold two million shares?' Felden asked.

'Exactly.'

'But that, sir, does not give Strode & Company absolute control. With four and a half million Strode Orient shares in issue, Strode & Comapny's interest is just under forty-four per cent.'

'Quite enough, Mr Felden, to ensure that any attempt to take over our company is doomed to failure. And to settle this matter once and for all I will now call on my brother Henry to make the position of Strode & Company in this matter quite clear.' He turned to the rest of us. 'As you know, gentlemen, besides being a director of your company, Henry Strode is also chairman of Strode & Company.' He nodded to his brother and sat down.

Henry Strode was a more polished, less aggressive man. But his languid, almost condescending manner was, I thought, a question of schooling rather than breeding. He was slightly stooped at the shoulders and he wore glasses which caught the light as he turned to face the audience. Perhaps it was this that gave him a slightly foxy look. 'Mr Felden. Gentlemen. Most of you here know very well that Strode & Company is essentially a family business.' He stood with his head thrown slightly back and his legs straddled and I was certain that this was not a natural stance but something he had copied from his father. Here was the manner without the substance. 'As chairman of that company I can assure you there's no question of our relinquishing control of Strode Orient, absolutely none at all.' His eyes shifted behind their glasses. He stared at Felden. 'I trust that statement is categorical enough to satisfy you, sir – and anyone else who may be interested.' And he started to sit down.

But Felden stopped him. 'I'm afraid not, Mr Strode.'

'How do you mean? Do you doubt my word?'

'No, only that I'm not convinced – '

Strode cut him short. 'Then you should be, sir, for I have given you my absolute assurance.' Outwardly he was unruffled, but I thought I detected a tremor in his voice as he added, 'These rumours – I don't know who has been putting them about, but they're quite without foundation. There is no possibility whatsoever of a take-over bid for Strode Orient being successful – not so long as I am chairman of the parent company.'

'Quite so. But I have been examining the share register of your company – '

'So I was informed, Mr Felden. But I fail to see the point.'

'No? Then let me say that I am less concerned about Strode Orient than I am about the vulnerability to a take-over of your own company.'

'Are you suggesting that the family – '

But Felden held up his hand. 'Allow me to finish, if you will be so kind. You fail to see why I took the trouble to examine the share register of Strode & Company? I will tell you. Strode & Company can be taken over tomorrow and there nothing you or the rest of the directors could do about it.'

'That's a lie.' George Strode had leapt to his feet. 'Kindly sit down, sir. You are not in order in discussing the affairs of Strode & Company here. This is a meeting of the Strode Orient Line and I must insist that we deal only with the affairs of that company.' And with a return to something of his previous bland manner he motioned his brother to resume his seat and said, 'Well now, if there are no further questions . . .'

But Felden was still standing, refusing to be silenced. 'Let us by all means deal with the affairs of our own company.' He smiled thinly. 'I was under the impression I was doing that in any case. However . . .' He gave a little shrug and reached into his brief-case, producing another sheet of paper. 'I have here – ' he put his glasses on again to peer at it – 'a list of the shareholdings of Strode & Company.'

But George Strode's voice over-rode him, echoing through the hall as he said, 'I must ask you to sit down and let us get on with the business in hand. You have my own and my brother's assurance that a take-over bid is out of the question. The matter is closed.'

'But if a member of the family were to sell Strode & Company shares – '

It was Henry Strode who answered that. 'None of the family will sell. It is contrary to family policy.'

'Is it?' And Felden added, 'I'm sorry, I cannot accept that. It certainly isn't true in the case of Strode Orient. You yourself have reduced your holding of Strode Orient from two hundred thousand shares at the time of your father's death to a mere five thousand. And the chairman of the company did precisely the same.'

'That was a long time ago,' Strode snapped. 'I'm buying now, when I can afford it.'

'It was in 1956, during the Suez crisis when there was a boom in shipping.' Felden gripped the back of the chair in front of him, leaning slightly forward. 'You say,' he said, addressing Henry Strode, 'that Strode & Company is essentially a family business. I would agree with this – with certain reservations. In your father's day the public owned only forty per cent – two hundred thousand shares out of the issued capital of half a million. That has now risen to nearly fifty per cent and the shares held by the family have been correspondingly reduced. These are as follows.' He glanced down at the paper he held in his hand and in the same dry businesslike voice read out the list: 'You yourself own forty thousand shares, so does your brother George Strode and also Mrs Roche. Your sister, Jennifer de Witt, holds fifteen thousand, your other sister, Emily Strode, four thousand, and there's over another five thousand in the names of your and your brother's children. Add to this the holdings of the three outside directors and various friends and associates . . .' But by then both the brothers were on their feet and the two other directors as well, all shouting at him to sit down, that it was nothing to do with the business in hand. All around me men were talking, whispering, and through the pandemonium I heard Felden say, 'A total of a hundred and fifty-six thousand, five hundred and twenty-three shares; less than thirty-one per cent.' He put his notes away and looked round at the shareholders, waiting. Quiet suddenly descended on the gathering. 'There is one member of the family I have not mentioned.' He faced Henry Strode again. 'I refer to your half-brother, Peter Strode. He holds one hundred and seventeen thousand shares and if he were to sell . . .' He left it at that, a slight lift of his eyebrows signifying that it was for Strode to answer the point.

Henry Strode licked his lips. But apart from that he appeared perfectly at ease as he indicated to his brother that he would deal with the matter and turned to face the meeting. 'Since Mr Felden has taken such trouble to make public to you the family holdings in Strode & Company I think it right that you should know the full facts. It is perfectly true that my father made his son, Peter, heir to what remained of his holding in the company at the time of his death. But he did so with certain safeguards. Peter Strode cannot sell a single share without the permission of the chairman of Strode & Company. In other words, when I say that the family has no intention of disposing of any shares, I am speaking for Peter Strode as well as the others.' He paused and looked over the gathering. 'I do assure you, quite categorically, that Strode & Company cannot be taken over without my acquiescence. And since I have no intention of letting that happen there is no possibility of outside interests gaining control of the Strode Orient Line and its vessels, by the back door as it were.'

'Why is your half-brother not on the board?' This from a man on my left.

'Because he knows nothing about the business.'

'But surely with such a large shareholding – '

'He not only knows nothing about the business,' Henry Strode snapped, 'but he's not interested. Never has been.' He hesitated and then added, 'Perhaps I should explain. He has spent his life travelling, mostly in remote places. I may say that at this precise moment I've no idea where he is.'

'Do you mean,' Felden asked, 'that you do not even know whether he is alive or dead?'

Again the slight hesitation. 'That's putting it rather strangely, Mr Felden.' He smiled and with the smile the charm returned to soothe the ruffled gathering. 'In reply to that I think I may say I have every confidence in Peter Strode's ability to remain alive in the most outlandish places. And now – ' He glanced at his brother.

But before he could sit down Felden had produced another point. 'I have also taken the trouble to check on the terms of your father's will. The control you have so far been able to exercise . . .'

'Please, Mr Felden. The point I think you are going to raise is one I'm not prepared to discuss here. However . . .' He leaned down and whispered quickly to his brother, who nodded. 'I think it only right in the circumstances – and my brother agrees with me – that I should inform you, in the strictest confidence of course, of a decision taken at a recent meeting of my board. At that meeting it was unanimously agreed that Mr Peter Strode be invited to become a director of Strode & Company. I may say he has nothing to offer in the way of experience, but we felt – my brother and I – that it was the right thing to do in view of his very large holding in the company. I am sure it is what my father ultimitely intended.' And he added, 'A Press release of this information will be made as soon as we have been able to obtain his formal acceptance.'

He sat down then to a murmur of approval. Felden, too, had resumed his seat. George Strode took over again, dealing rapidly with the remaining business. In five minutes it was over and the meeting broke up.

'Well, that's that, and the whole issue neatly side-tracked.' This from the man on my left who might have been a lawyer, his manner and voice were so neat and precise. 'Have you been to one of these meetings before?'

I shook my head. I was watching the directors filing out through a gap in the counter which enabled them to avoid the shareholders. All around us the meeting was splitting up into little groups, the buzz of speculation in the air. 'Well, I can tell you this,' my companion said as we walked towards the door, 'Felden got more out of them than I expected. But Strode, the clever fellow, never answered the question, did he?'

'Which question?' I was thinking of Peter Strode, wondering how he would react to this.

'He was on safe ground dealing with the Strode Orient take-over. But there's a rumour that the family has been approached to sell their Strode shares.' We were in the press by the door then and as we passed through he added, 'Do you think he really didn't know where his half-brother was?'

'Quite likely,' I said. 'I've met Peter Strode and my impression was – '

'Commander Bailey.' I felt a touch on my arm and turned to find George Strode's assistant at my elbow. 'Would you come this way, please? They're waiting for you.'

'They?'

'The directors. They'll be in the boardroom now.' Conscious that the attention of the man beside me had become suddenly riveted he plucked nervously at my sleeve. 'If you'll follow me, sir.'

He led me quickly up the great staircase and as I passed my father's portrait, wondering what the hell they wanted I had a strange feeling that all my life had been leading up to this moment. I cannot explain it even now, this feeling of inevitability, the sudden certainty that my future was linked with the Strode Orient Line. All I can say is that it was in a mood of intense expectation that I walked into the boardroom to my first meeting with the directors. 'Commander Bailey, gentlemen.' The doors closed behind me and George Strode came to greet me. 'Nice of you to join us.' He shook my hand and led me by the arm to introduce me first to his brother and then to the other four men clustered round a tray of drinks at the end of the boardroom table – Julian le Fleming, Adrian Crane, Sir Miles Everett, Colonel Jacob Hinchcliffe. They all bore the stamp of a social strata that too often depends on inherited wealth rather than ability to place them in a position of authority and their acknowledgment of my presence was distant, almost chilling. 'Well now, what can I get you? A Scotch?'

I nodded and he poured it for me whilst the others stood in a tight little huddle. Clearly my arrival had interrupted a private discussion and now they were waiting – but for what? I looked at George Strode who said, 'I gather you're a shareholder in our company, eh?' He handed me my drink. 'Very fortunate your coming to the meeting. That fool Elliot didn't take a note of your address when you were here yesterday so we'd no means of contacting you.' An awkward silence followed as I sipped my drink and waited. 'No doubt you're wondering why we've asked you up here to join us.' His manner was that adopted by some senior officers to put juniors at their ease, a sort of avuncular bonhomie. It didn't endear him to me. 'You're just out of the Navy, I believe?'

I nodded, 'On my way out.' I was trying to remember what I'd said in that letter.

'How well do you know Peter?'

So that was it and nothing to do with my name; probably they'd forgotten there ever had been a Bailey Oriental Line. 'Depends what you mean,' I said. 'Some men you can live with for years and never get to know. Others – ' But I couldn't explain to them what a night of talking could mean to two lonely men sitting under the stars on an island that was little more than a sandbank. 'Well enough,' I said, 'to know he'd never resign himself to working in a City office.'

The two brothers exchanged glances. 'We don't expect that,' Henry Strode put in quickly. And George Strode said, 'Anyway, you knew him sufficiently well to think he'd give you a job, eh? I read your letter, you see. Had to. No initials, just the name – it might have been for any one of us.' It was a lie, of course. I was certain he hadn't known of the letter's existence until that morning. And the favour to which I had referred concerned the shares, not a job. But he wasn't to know that. 'And we couldn't forward it,' he added. 'Didn't know where the beggar was. Still don't for that matter.' And then, looking directly at me, 'I suppose you've no idea where he is at the present moment?'

'None whatever,' I said.

He nodded. 'Quite. Otherwise you wouldn't have addressed that letter to him here.'

'When did you last see him?' Henry Strode asked.

I didn't answer that. No point in telling them it was six years ago when I didn't have to.

'Was it recently?' And when I still didn't answer, he said, 'Oh, come, we're not trying to pry into his private life or anything like that. In fact, as you heard at the meeting, we want him on the board – nothing else.' He put his drink down carefully, a clink of glass on silver in the stillness. 'You were in the Persian Gulf together?'

'That's where I met him.'

'If our information is correct it's some years since he was in that area. Have you been in touch since?'

But I'd had enough of questions. 'Suppose you tell me what this is all about?'

Henry Strode started to say something, but his brother stopped him. 'Please, Henry.' He turned to me. 'You don't know where he is. But could you locate him for us?'

'I don't know,' I said. 'But it shouldn't be all that difficult.'

'Ah, well, that's what we wanted to talk to you about.' He took my arm and walked me to the far end of the table out of hearing of the others. 'This is my idea, so I'm handling it. Henry's a more cautious bird.' He hesitated. Then he lifted his head, staring at me with those moist eyes that looked at close quarters like tiny oysters. 'I'll be frank with you,' he said. 'My brother and I – we never got on very well with Peter. Different generations, different upbringing, schooling, everything – different mother, that was the main reason. Like you, I think I could find him if I tried. But I'd still have to put the proposition to him and – well, I don't know – I think he'd probably tell us to go to hell. He's like that, no business sense. None at all.' He smiled at me. 'Well now, you're just out of the Navy. Shopping around for a job, eh? I'll make you a proposition. You find Peter and persuade him to come back to England and join the board and there'll be a job for you in Strode Orient. How's that?'

I tried to pin him down, but he wouldn't commit himself; all he said was, 'We'll find you something.' And whilst I was considering it I kept catching snatches of the conversation they had resumed at the other end of the room: 'If he did, we'd be out – all of us.' And then Henry Strode's voice was saying something about 'nothing but bitter reproaches.' And later, Hinchcliffe I think:

'Exactly. The fellow needs money. He'll jump at it.'

'Well?' George Strode was getting impatient.

'I've still got to reach him,' I said. 'And what I know of the man it means travelling to some distant part of the world.'

He took my point immediately. 'My dear fellow, of course. Draw on the company for all necessary expenses. I'll fix that with Elliot; and your salary, same as you were getting in the Navy, back-dated to today as soon as Peter is on board. That satisfy you?'

I nodded. 'Can I have it in writing?'

For a moment I thought he was going to refuse, but all he said was, 'Fair enough. You'll have it in the morning and also an official letter from my brother confirming Peter Strode's appointment to the board.' He took my arm again. 'Now, come and have another drink. And then I must be off.' He led me back to the others. 'Well, it's all settled. Bailey will act as our go-between.'

Henry Strode nodded as though the issue had never been in doubt. 'I don't think you'll have any difficulty persuading him. Just remind him that a seat on the board means four thousand a year in his pocket. As Hinch says, he'll jump at it, but it's still better coming from a personal friend.'

George Strode nodded. 'That's what I think.' And he added, 'I wonder what the devil he's been living on since we stopped paying dividends?'

I had another drink with them and then I left. George Strode saw me to the head of the stairs. 'When you write me that letter,' I said, 'perhaps you'd give me the names and addresses of any possible contacts. There must be somebody in England who knows where he is.'

But he shook his head. 'There's his sister, Ida – Mrs Roche; she lives in Dartmouth. And his bank, of course. We've tried them both. If he has friends in England, then we don't know of them.' And he added, 'Peter never mixed much with his own kind. Preferred bumming his way round the world. Somebody told me they'd met up with him once in the Pacific – Fiji, I think it was. He was skippering some sort of a native craft. Where was it you met him in the Persian Gulf?'

'An island called Abu Musa,' I said.

'Inhabited?'

'No.'

He laughed. 'Well, there you are. That's Peter. Desert islands, wide open spaces, lost settlements. He was in Peru at one time. Four years ago he was in San Francisco, just back from Easter

Island. We haven't had news of him since.' He glanced at his watch. 'Well, I have a lunch date now. Call in and see Elliot tommorrow.'

I nodded to my father's portrait as I went down the stairs. The chance of a foothold in the business he'd partly created, the prospect of meeting Peter Strode again, the drink, too, I suppose – I felt curiously elated. And in the entrance hall below I was waylaid by the man who had sat beside me at the meeting. 'Didn't imagine they'd give you lunch so I waited.'

'Why?'

But all he said was, 'I thought if you were free we might go to the City Club.' The sun was shining in the street outside. The world seemed suddenly bright and full of promise. Curious, I nodded my acceptance and as we walked through to Old Broad Street I didn't notice the drabness of the buildings any more, only the window-boxes, gay with the first daffodils. Spring seemed in the air.

The City Club is the lunchtime rendezvous of those men of money who are not close enough to the Establishment to belong to West End clubs and not quite big enough to have private dining-suites of their own. In its stuffy atmosphere, over a game pie lunch, I was given a glimpse of a financial jungle in which the hunter stalked his prey along tracks paved with legal documents, his methods and his code of behaviour prescribed by custom and just as rigid as those in the animal kingdom. The man I was with, whose name was Slattery, gradually emerged as a sort of procurer for certain financial interests. His quarry was Peter Strode and the hundred thousand shares he owned. He didn't put it as crudely as that, of course. It was all done very obliquely and he was so skilled at directing the conversation, so smooth in his approach, that by the end of lunch he knew my background and I was pretty certain had satisfied himself as to the role I had been asked to assume.

This was confirmed over coffee and port when he said, 'I think I'm in a position to help you. We know where Strode is.' But when I asked him where, he smiled and sipped his drink. 'You'd never guess. Nor would those two half-brothers of his. It took us weeks to ferret it out.' It was then that he put his proposition to me, but so guardedly, so indirectly that it was some time before I realized he was offering me quite a large sum of money if I could persuade Peter Strode to sell. 'Under the terms of his father's will he couldn't dispose of his holding until he was thirty. His thirtieth birthday is less than a month away. That's why

they want to make him a director. They think four thousand a
year will satisfy him. My guess is it won't.' He then went on to
outline the deal his principals had in mind – twenty thousand
down and the balance of the purchase price of ten shillings a share
in instalments as soon as the parent company had been able to
dispose of the Strode Orient assets.

'Why don't you write to him if you know where he is?' I asked.

'We've done that. Five weeks ago we cabled him our offer,
confirming it by letter and pointing out that he couldn't possibly
hope to get anything like that price for the shares if he tried to sell
them on the open market.'

'And you haven't had a reply?'

'An acknowledgment, nothing more. That's why I went to the
meeting today. I knew what Felden was going to say – in fact, I
briefed him. I wanted to see what the Strodes were going to do to
meet the situation.' And he added, 'It was a lucky chance that put
you next to me. I take it the inducement they offered you was a
job in Strode Orient?'

'Yes.'

'I'm offering you cash and that's a better proposition than a job
in a dying company.'

'I'm afraid I've already accepted the job,' I said.

He laughed. 'I shouldn't let that worry you. You've got yourself and your family to consider.' He finished his drink and got to
his feet. 'You think it over.' Before we parted in Old Broad Street
he gave me his card. 'You'll probably find you'll need me anyway
– to tell you where he is.'

He was very nearly right, but it was to take me over a week to
discover it, for I was convinced that my own line of approach
would yield results. A man as colourful and as widely travelled as
Peter Strode could hardly have passed unnoticed and Whitehall
has its own methods of keeping tabs on such people. It didn't take
me long to pick up the trail. Starting with friends in the Admiralty
I was passed to the War Office and the Air Ministry, to the Foreign
Office, to Commonwealth Relations, to Colonial Affairs, and at
each of these Ministries I found men who knew him or at least had
heard of him. Intelligence officers were particularly helpful for
some of his travels had taken him to areas that specially concerned
them. I finished up with a list of over forty places where he was
known to have been, places that ranged from the Hadhramaut to
the Society Islands and as far south as Auckland, and for most of
them I was able to get rough dates. None of the dates covered the
last three years. I tried another line of approach then, contacting

scientific and academic institutions in London, many of whom had
field workers operating in out of the way places. In this way I
established three more contacts, but again they were all prior to
1959. I did discover, however, that he was a member of the Royal
Geographical Society and had written two papers for them – one
on the dhow traffic between South-East Arabia and the East
Indies, the other on 'The Structure and Life of the Maldivian
Atolls.' These were written in 1954 and 1956 respectively, but
though I read them both they gave no indication of his future
plans, and being complete in themselves, the by-product of
voyages made, there was no suggestion that he intended to revisit
either of the areas. And I could find no reference to any other
work of his in the voluminous index in the reading room of the
British Museum.

At the end of a week of persistent inquiries my notes showed
that the most recent trace of him I had been able to discover was a
young man in the Foreign Office who had met him at a cocktail
party on board the C-in-C's 'yacht' in Malta. That was late in
1959, probably in November, but he couldn't remember the
exact date. Strode had borrowed a fiver from him. He was dead
broke and trying to hitch a ride with the RAF, he thought to the
Far East. I tried the Air Ministry and Transport Command, but
there was of course no record of their having granted him transport facilities, and a cable to the Maltese immigration authorities
yielded nothing. From Malta Peter Strode seemed to have vanished off the face of the earth and with Africa only a short boat
voyage away I'd have thought the man was dead, lost in some
desperate trek across the desert, if it hadn't been for Slattery's
confident assertion that he knew where he was – that and the fact
that his sister was still getting letters from him.

I discovered this when finally and in desperation I visited her
at her flat in Dartmouth overlooking the estuary I'd known as a
kid. I found her as curious about his whereabouts as I was myself
for he had taken trouble to conceal it even from her, the letters
undated with no address and written on cheap typing paper. She
showed me the last which she had received just over a month ago.
'I don't even get them direct,' she said. 'The solicitors forward
them to me.' That was the first I knew that he had solicitors, but
when I asked her whether they would have his address, she
laughed and said she'd tried that. 'Old Mr Turner has his
instructions and if he does know he's not revealing it.'

I suppose the unusual nature of my errand intrigued her or
perhaps it was the fact that I'd met her brother – they'd obviously

been very close; at any rate, she talked very freely to me over a drink, about him and about the atmosphere in which they had been brought up. She wasn't in the least like her brother to look at. Hers was a square, wide-mouthed face, but she had the same vitality and alertness of mind, the same quick nervous energy. The high cheekbones, the dark hair, the large, almost luminous brown eyes; there was something almost Latin about her, which was hardly surprising since their mother had been half French.

They hadn't had a very happy childhood. The mother had been a model in the days when models were much less respectable than chorus girls. She'd been almost twenty years younger than Henry Strode when he'd married her following a much-publicized divorce case. Peter had been born two months later. 'Barely legitimate, you see.' And Ida Roche smiled at me over her drink. There was a gap of three years between her brother and herself and at the age of seven, when she was just old enough to understand, their father and mother had separated. 'It had never really worked. My mother, bless her heart, was too feminine, my father too old, too much a business tycoon.' She was smoking, moving restlessly about the room which was full on antiques. She had an antique shop below which absorbed some of her energies. 'It was a hell of an atmosphere. I think Father hated us then. No man as big as he was likes being made a fool of, and Mummy blazed a trail right across the social world he'd worked his way up into. He'd no time for us after that. He got the children of his first marriage back – Henry, Emily, Jennifer and George, all four of them back in the big house in Hampstead. I remember Peter came home from school – he was twelve then – to find his room occupied by brother George and himself relegated to an attic bedroom. He walked out of the house in a silent rage and was missing for over a week before the police found him on an east coast barge.'

She ground out her cigarette and turned suddenly and faced me. 'I'm telling you this because I don't want you to have any false hopes. You're wasting your time going to Peter with a proposition like that. He'd never accept a seat on the board – never. He'd never accept anything from either Henry or George. He hates their guts and everything they stand for.'

'Then why doesn't he fight them?' I said. 'What's he running away from?'

She stared at me, her brown eyes suddenly wide. I thought for a moment she was angry. But then she shrugged her shoulders. 'Pride, I suppose. There's a lot of his father in Peter. He's not very like him to look at, but it's there all the same.' She shook her head, smiling suddenly. 'Maybe you're right. Maybe all his life he has been running away. I don't know.' She lit another cigarette. 'You tell him that and it's just possible . . .' But again she shook her head. 'He'd never sit on a board of directors run by those two. Never. There's too much bad blood, and none of it his fault. They behaved – abominably. And so did Father.'

'Yet he gave him a huge holding in the business he'd created.'

'To save death duties. At least that's what he told me when he gave me my shares.'

And when I pointed out that he could have achieved that just as easily by leaving the shares to his two sons who were in the business, she said, 'Yes, that's true. Well, maybe he'd got the measure of them by then.' And she added, 'This didn't concern me at the time. It was 1950 when he gave me my shares and I'd just got married. Now that my husband's dead, I'm much more interested.' She was standing in front of the fire now, staring down into the flames. 'Philippe died in a car crash two years ago and left nothing but debts. He was that sort of man. He'd have run through my Strode shares if he'd been able to.'

There was a sadness about her that had its appeal, a sense of frustration that matched my own. She'd no children and her loneliness was apparent. I stayed much longer than I'd intended, for I was spending the night with friends who had a cottage on the edge of Dartmoor and they were waiting for me. 'If you do get to see Peter,' she said as I was leaving, 'give him my love, won't you. And tell him if he's got the guts of a louse he'll accept their offer.' She was smiling again then as she held the door open for me. 'And you can tell him also that I'm not selling – not until I know what he's going to do.'

She had given me the solicitor's address and two days later I saw him at his office off Holborn, a dry little wisp of a man with skin like parchment. 'So they're offering him a directorship.' He smiled thinly, nodding to himself. All the time I'd been talking he'd been busy with a pencil embellishing my name which he'd written down on a blank sheet of paper. Now he looked up at me, staring at me fixedly out of pale blue eyes. 'You were at the meeting, you say. You must be a shareholder, then?' And when I nodded, he said, 'I was in correspondence with a Lady Bailey once about some Strode Orient Shares. Are you her son by any chance?'

'Yes.'

He leaned back in his chair. 'It was a long time ago,' he

murmured. 'At the beginning of the war. And now you come here saying you're a friend of Peter Strode. It's a queer world.' He laughed, a quick sour laugh that disintegrated into a fit of coughing. The thin white skin of his face mottled and he reached into a drawer for a box of pills. He took one and leaned back with his eyes closed. 'Well now, what was it I was going to say? Oh, yes. The letter. You say young Henry has written confirming the offer. If you like to give it to me – ' But he knew I wasn't going to do that, for he shook his head. 'No, you want to go out there, don't you. You want to talk to Peter. I wonder why?' He was staring across at me speculatively. 'What's your motive?' And when I told him, he shook his head, smiling gently to himself. 'The human mind is more complex than that. You say it's just the job you're after. You may even believe it, but deep down . . .' He hesitated and I could see his mind searching the dusty files of his memory. 'You wouldn't remember it, but it was a bitter struggle. I was a young man then. Young, that is, to have a man like Henry Strode for a client. I was just under forty.' He was back in the past, his thoughts withdrawn.

'Did you know my father?' I asked.

He nodded without looking up. 'I met him – twice. And I can tell you this, they weren't pleasant meetings. Your father was tough. Quite as tough as Henry Strode. But in a different way. It was the breeding, I suppose. There was always a veneer of politeness.' He peered up at me, a quick, searching look. 'How tough are you, Bailey?'

I laughed. 'I don't know.'

The pale eyes watching me remained fixed for a long time. Finally he said, 'No, you probably don't. But it's something I have to consider.'

'Damn it,' I said. 'I'm only asking you for his address.'

He nodded, still staring at me with those cold, heavy-lidded eyes. And then his hand reached out for the bell-push on his desk. 'It hasn't occurred to you, I suppose, that that's just what he doesn't want anybody to know.' He pressed the bell and I thought I'd failed. But instead of ordering his clerk to show me out he told him to bring the Strode file. 'My connection with Strode House ended when Henry Strode died. From a business that occupied a great deal of my time I was left with nothing but a young man whose only thought in life was travel.' He leaned forward, his hands clutching at the edge of the desk as though bracing himself. 'Now, before I let you have Peter's address I want you to understand and appreciate that my hopes are now centred on this young man. First, let me say that I was in on all his father's deals, all the battles that built up the Strode group, including the battle with Bailey Oriental. We weren't always in agreement, for he sailed very close to the wind at times, but he was one of the most exciting men in the City at a time when the City lacked personalities and had become almost moribund. I'm talking now of the period between the wars. I don't think we were conscious then that the Empire was slipping from our grasp, but the smell of decay was in the air, all the life blood of the country poured out in the trenches of that First World War and the men that were left, most of them of poor quality. In a world of mediocrity and sloth Henry's drive and ability stood out, and I'm proud to have been associated with him. I helped him build a great merchant adventuring business at a time when safety first and security was the dominent mood; and I've lived to see it virtually destroyed in less than a decade.' He leaned back, exhausted as much by the emotions his thoughts had evoked as by the effort of putting them into words.

The clerk came in and he reached out a skinny hand for the file. 'Peter is a different sort of man.' He was a little breathless now, dabbing at his lips with his handkerchief. 'He's travelled, whereas his father was essentially a City man. He's educated, too. But he's still his father's son and I have hopes – great hopes. That's what I want you to understand.' He had spread the file open on his desk. 'Four years ago I was resigned to the fact that he'd sell his Strode shares as soon as he was thirty and entitled so to do. Now – ' He took a cable from the pile and passed it across to me. 'Perhaps you'd read that.'

It was the usual tape pasted on a Cable and Wireless form. *Have received cable offering ten shillings a share signed Slattery stop whos behind him and whats the game – Peter.* 'And here's what I replied.' He handed me a typewritten sheet, which in addition to the motive for the offer, which I already knew, gave the name of the man behind it: *Slattery's principals are property dealer Joseph Lingrose and his associates.* The cable concluded with these words: *These are very slick operators with no other interest but a quick profit. If you sell to them they will dispose of what remains of your heritage and you will regret it to your dying day.*

When I had read it the old lawyer said, 'You're a naval man and I don't expect you to understand what all this is about. But I think you may understand this much. These men are bloodsuckers, and they smell money. Peter will be subjected to very great pressure. I don't want him to yield to that pressure. I'd rather he made peace with his half-brothers and joined the board of Strode & Company. That's why I'm going to ignore my instructions and give you his address. Now listen carefully please –' And for the next ten minutes he gave me a detailed and very lucid analysis of the financial position and future prospects of the Strode Orient Line, finishing up with these words: 'As a director of Strode & Company he will be on the inside, which will mean that he will be in a position not so much to dictate as to influence decisions. And time is on his side. He'll be the youngest member of the board by more than ten years.' He picked up his pen and reached for a sheet of paper. 'I've been waiting for them to make a move like this, and I think Peter has, too. At any rate, he's done his best these last three years to groom himself for the job.' He wrote down the address for me and then sat for a moment, quite still, staring at it. 'I'd like to think that in bringing the two of you together . . .' But then he sighed and shook his head. 'It's too late for that now.' He folded the sheet of paper, slipped it into an envelope and handed it to me. Then he pressed the bell again. He didn't say anything more and glancing back from the doorway I saw he had turned his swivel chair to the window and was leaning back in it, staring up at the sky.

The address he had given me was Guthrie & Coy. (Singapore) Ltd., 24 Battery Road, Singapore 1. And underneath he had written: Ask for Charles Legrand. I knew Guthrie's of course; everybody does who has been stationed in Singapore. Their offices in Bank Chambers look out over the Singapore river and when I rang Latham for details it was apparent why Strode had chosen that particular firm. It had been founded in 1821, but though a relic of the great days of the East India Company it had adjusted its merchanting techniques to the changed conditions of the Far East and now had some twenty offices and godowns in Malaysia alone. 'Same sort of business as Strode & Company,' he said. 'Except that Guthrie's have moved with the times. Strodes haven't – not in recent years.' The name Legrand was also a natural choice, for Ida Roche had told me that her mother had been known as Marie Legrand when she was a model, before her marriage to their father. But why had he felt it necessary to change his name?

I had two days to spare whilst waiting for the plane and I used them to see the children. Those two days made my whole trip – John bubbling over with the news that next term, his last before going to public school, he'd be captaining the cricket team, and Mary already losing her puppy fat and showing obvious signs of girlhood. She already had something of her mother's looks, the same sparkling vitality, but she was darker and there was a seriousness about her that touched a chord in me. I had to break it to them that they wouldn't be coming out to Singapore any more for the holidays. They were old enough to be told the facts of the situation and they seemed to understand. But their questions were disconcerting in the circumstances: Will we have a London flat? Will you buy a house in Sussex? You'll be a director or something like that, won't you?

How do you answer the questions of youth when they leap-frog all the difficulties? It saddened me, and at the same time it bolstered my courage. Whether I was a civilian or a naval officer made no difference to them – they looked up to me with the same absolute confidence.

It was on the Saturday evening that I arrived back in Singapore. I should have cabled Barbara, of course. But I hadn't. It wasn't a conscious attempt to catch her out, though she naturally accused me of that. The truth was that I just didn't think of it. My mind was full of other things. The result was that my unexpected arrival precipitated the crisis that had long been inevitable. The two chairs drawn up close on the veranda, the two glasses on the table were a warning. Inside the pattern was repeated, dinner for two and a man's jacket thrown carelessly over the back of a chair. Our house was of the bungalow type and before I had started to move hesitantly and with great reluctance towards the bedroom, Barbara appeared. She was flushed and slightly dishevelled, but with a bloom on her that still had the power to make me catch my breath even though the bloom wasn't of my getting.

It was a hopeless situation and it was only later that she found her voice and began to upbraid me. For the moment she was as aghast as I was and let me pass without a word. At least he hadn't tried to hide or anything stupid like that. 'You'd better get dressed and then we'll discuss this over a drink,' I told him. What else could I say? It wasn't altogether his fault and my appearance must have come as a shock to the poor devil. He was an American businessman.

There are no rules for a situation like this. A combative mood is the prerogative of those who feel that a theft has been committed, but Barbara hadn't really belonged to me for a long time. There was no anger as I surveyed the final wreck of my family. Bitterness, yes. You can't help feeling bitter when the evidence that you've been cuckolded is forced on you. It's a slap in the face to your male pride so that the desire to hurt is very strong. For a moment I felt I could have strangled Barbara with my bare hands. But I kept a hold on my temper and gradually the mood passed, leaving me drained of all emotion and with a feeling of icy coldness. I gave him a drink whilst I explained that my lawyers would be in touch with him in due course and then I took the car and drove into Singapore. I spent the night at a hotel, lying awake for hours, remembering every one of Barbara's vicious, frightened words, the way she'd pleaded, using the children as the basis of her argument, and how she'd finally assumed a sullen victimized air.

There's no point in dwelling on this or giving the name of the man I cited as co-respondent. I knew him quite well and even liked him. The only reason I have referred to my personal affairs at all is because my break with Barbara had a considerable influence on my subsequent actions. For one thing it left me entirely free of any encumbrance. The children were taken care of – they would spend the holidays with my sister in Scotland as they did whenever they couldn't come out to join us. Barbara could now fend for herself. For another, it induced in me an urgent desire to involve myself in something that would effectively take my mind off my own affairs. In other words, I was in the right frame of mind to give myself whole-heartedly to any project, however outlandish or fantastic. Such a project was ready to hand.

Charles Legrand was in the phone book, but when I rang him from the hotel on Sunday morning his house-boy told me he was away. I spent part of the day clearing my own personal belongings out of the hose. The Symingtons – Alec was an old friend from destroyer days – put a room at my disposal and I moved in with them that evening. On the Monday morning I phoned Guthrie's. I had presumed 'Legrand' was merely away for the weekend. Instead, I discovered he had been gone over a week.

I drove into town then. Battery Road is on the waterfront and as usual the river was thronged with tongkangs lightering goods out to the ships in the Roads. Peter Strode was on the general imports side of the business and I was passed to his boss, a man named Ferguson whose office looked across the river to the go-downs on the North Boat Quay. He told me Charles Legrand was on indefinite leave.

'Did he say where he was going?'

'No, and I didn't ask him. But he mentioned something about it being quite a long voyage so I imagine it was by sea. He was due for a long leave anyway.'

'When exactly did he go?'

'As far as we're concerned the Friday before last. Would you like me to check for you?' He reached for the phone and rang Legrand's house. Ferguson was a very thorough individual. He not only produced the time at which Legrand had left – shortly after ten on the Sunday morning – but also the fact that his car was still at the house. He'd left in a taxi with almost no luggage, just an old bed-roll, a cardboard box containing some books, sextant and chronometer and a roll of charts. 'Not unnaturally the house-boy didn't take the number of the taxi and I'm afraid he doesn't know the driver. My guess is that Charles was planning a trip up the coast on a native boat.'

It was a shrewd guess on his part and entirely in keeping with what I knew of the man. If he'd gone on a native craft he might be anywhere – on the Malay coast or Burma or up the east side of the archipelago to Siam, even China. And there were all the Indonesian islands. It seemed hopeless. 'Have you got a list of sailings?' I asked.

He rang for his clerk and a few minutes later the list was in my hands. The ss *Montrose* and the mv *Nagasaki* – those were the only two ships that had sailed on Sunday, 17 March. Four had left on the Monday and suddenly my quest seemed less hopeless, for one of them was a Strode ship. 'Do you happen to know where the *Strode Venturer* was bound for?' I asked.

'She's on a regular run. From here she normally goes to the Maldives – to Addu Atoll. Provided, of course, she's got cargo on board for RAF Gan. It's a somewhat irregular service, but still a service.'

'Who are the agents?'

'Strode & Company. But she's under charter to a Chinese outfit, the Tai Wan Shipping Company.'

A Strode ship and her destination the Maldives. Remembering the paper he had written for the RGS, I felt certain he was on board. 'And she sails direct for Addu Atoll – no stops between?'

'Aye, direct. It usually takes her about a week. She should be there this evening or tomorrow morning at the latest.' And he added, 'Since it's urgent the best thing for you to do is cable her.'

But a cable wouldn't be any use if he didn't want anybody to know he was on board. 'How long will the ship stay at Addu Atoll?' It was now 25 March and I was thinking that if I could get a flight tomorrow I might still catch up with him. Gan was the first stage on Transport Command's Singapore-UK run.

But he couldn't tell me that. 'You'd better ask Strode &

Company. It depends how much cargo she's got on board or Gan.'

I thanked him and went out again into the torrid heat of Battery Road. The Strode offices were only a short distance away and I had to be certain before I committed myself to Transport Command, for I didn't think they'd fly me back to Singapore. It would be Gan and on to the UK. But at Strode & Company I came up against a blank wall. The manager, a man named Alexander who looked half Chinese, assured me that no passengers were carried on the *Strode Venturer*. He was far less helpful than Ferguson and when I suggested he telephone the charterers he simply said, 'The *Strode Venturer* is a cargo vessel.'

'My information is that Legrand joined the ship on the morning of Sunday, 17 March – the day before she sailed,' I told him. But it was only after I'd informed him that I was acting on the direct instructions of Mr George Strode that he reluctantly picked up the phone. The conversation was in Chinese and I sat in the worn leather chair facing the desk and waited. The office was a large panelled room hung with pictures of Strode Orient ships that had long since gone to the breaker's yard. Models of two of them stood under glass cases in the window recesses. The room looked dusty and neglected. So did the frail, dried-up little man behind the desk. 'I spoke with Mr Chu Soong personally,' he said as he put the phone down. 'He is manager of the Tai Wan Shipping Company. He assured me that Mr Legrand is not a passenger on the ship. There are no passengers on board.'

'He may be on board as a guest of the captain,' I suggested.

The sallow face seemed to reflect a momentary glint of humour; it flickered for an instant in the brown eyes, touched the corners of his colourless lips, and then was gone. 'Captain Deacon is not the sort of man to encourage guests,' he said, his voice expressionless.

I hesitated. There was only one other possibility. 'He may have shipped as a member of the crew.'

The manager shook his head. 'There is nobody of that name amongst the crew.'

'May I see the list please?' I should have asked him for it in the first place. Although there was no change in the impassivity of his features I sensed his reluctance to produce it. Finally he got to his feet and went to the filing cabinet in the corner. The list he produced showed the vessel to be manned on the usual scale for a British ship with a Chinese crew. His name did not appear among the twelve Europeans. But then it was unlikely he'd be qualified to ship as an officer. I glanced at the names of the Chinese crew and nearly missed it because I was looking for the name Legrand. He was down as an ordinary sailor – Strode, Peter Charles. I looked up at the manager. 'You knew Mr Strode was on board?'

He stared at me without any change of expression in his eyes. 'One of my staff engaged the crew – in the presence of the Mercantile Marine Officer.'

'Of course. But you know very well who he engages.' The list here on his files and the name Strode – he must have known it was one of the family. I got to my feet. 'I understand the ship is sailing direct to Gan and that the voyage takes about a week. Is that correct?'

He nodded.

'Exactly when is she due to arrive?'

'This evening.'

'And she leaves when?'

'That depends on the RAF – how quickly they unload her.'

I thanked him and he rose from his chair and gave a little bow as I made for the door. 'If there's any message you'd like sent?'

'No, no message.' But I thought he'd send one all the same and I wondered what Strode would make of the information that I was inquiring about him. But the thing that really puzzled me was the reason for his visit to Addu Atoll. Why would a man who had been offered a large cash sum for his share in the family business suddenly go rushing off to a coral atoll in the middle of the Indian Ocean? I was thinking about this all the way out to Changi, the RAF base. But thinking about it produced no obvious answer. That he'd been forced to use his own name because it was the name on his passport didn't alter the fact that there was an element of secrecy about his movements. In fact, everything about the man had a curious twist to it, as though he were impelled by some strange inner urge. But at least I'd traced him and since I was still officially a serving officer I had access to a means of transportation which would enable me to catch up with him.

At Changi I saw the Senior Movements Officer. 'Gan? Well, yes, I expect it could be arranged . . . We usually keep a certain number of seats open for men getting on there. But I'll have to contact the CO at Gan. How long do you want to stay?'

'Two days, that's all.'

'And then home to the UK?'

'If that's possible.'

He nodded. 'It'll be an indulgence passage, of course, and on a space available basis. I'll give you a buzz tomorrow morning. Okay?'

I gave him the Symingtons' telephone number and drove back to their house for lunch. There was the business then of clearing up my personal affairs. The bank, lawyers, Naval HQ – it wasn't until after dinner that I could settle down to the most important job of the lot – explaning it all to the children. Those two letters were just about the most difficult I had ever had to write and it was almost midnight before I had finished. Alec gave me a drink then. He also gave me my first briefing on Addu Atoll. I had never been there. All I knew of it was a description given me by one of the Britannia pilots – 'Like a huge aircraft carrier stranded on a coral reef.' But that was just the island of Gan, not the whole atoll. Alec, on the other hand, had been on a destroyer that had refuelled there during the war when it was known as Port 'T.' 'It's the finest natural harbour I've ever seen – a hundred square miles of water entirely protected by reefs and only four navigable channels between them.' He hadn't been there since, but without my asking he had borrowed from a destroyer the Admiralty Pilot for the West Coast of India which includes the Maldives. He had also borrowed charts 2898 and 2067 – the first a general chart of the whole 500 mile chain of islands, the second a large-scale chart of Addu Atoll itself.

These I took up to bed with me and since it might be the last opportunity I had of studying them I worked at them for almost an hour. The charts were like no charts I had ever seen, for the Maldives are not islands in the normal sense, but groups of coral growth forming lace-like fringes around shallow seas dotted with islets. There were altogether nineteen groups extending from Addu Atoll, which was almost on the equator, 470 miles north to a position west of Ceylon. Some of these groups were over a hundred miles in circumference. It was a great barrier reef with only a few deep-water channels through it – the Equatorial Channel, the One and a Half Degree Channel, the Eight Degree Channel.

But neither the charts nor the Pilot, which as usual went into considerable detail about the topography and inhabitants of the islands, gave me the slightest clue to Peter Strode's interest in the area. The Adduans were described as 'great navigators and traders,' but the only things they exported were dried fish and cowrie shells, their existence dependent on what they harvested from the sea and from the soil of pitifully small islands that were nowhere more than five or six feet above sea level. There was nothing there to attract the attention of a trading concern like

Guthrie's – the islands were far too poor, far too remote. And if he had been going there for purely scientific reasons why ship as crew in circumstances that suggested a desire for secrecy?

The element of mystery surrounding his journey distracted me from my personal problems. The man was beginning to fascinate me and this mood of fascination was still with me in the morning when Movements rang up shortly after ten to say that a seat would be available for me on the flight leaving at 1600 hours. Jilly Symington very kindly drove me out to Changi after lunch and an hour later I was in the air.

The flight from Singapore to Gan crosses Sumatra and the off-lying islands; after that there is nothing but sea. At first the sky was clear. But as the sun set in a blaze of flaming red, thunder-heads of cu-nim began to appear black like anvils along the horizon ahead. Darkness closed in on us and the oil-flat surface of the sea below faded as wisps of cloud swept across the wings, obscuring the blink of the navigation lights.

My first sight of Addu Atoll was a cluster of red lights in the blackness of the night. These marked the radio masts of the trans-mitter on Hittadu, the largest island of the group. The lights vanished abruptly, obscured by rain. We were over the lagoon then, but though I strained my eyes into the darkness I could see no sign of the *Strode Venturer*. There wasn't a glimmer of a light visible anywhere. The plane tilted, the angle of descent steepening. The runway lights appeared, fuzzed by rain. It was sheeting down and as our wheels touched a great burst of spray shot up into the glare of the landing lights. The humid, earthy smell of that tropical downpour had seeped into the fuselage before we finished taxi-ing and when the doors were finally opened we were swamped by the equatorial warmth of it. And then suddenly the rain stopped as though a tap had been turned off and as I went down the steps to be greeted by Jack Easton, the station adjutant, I was overwhelmingly conscious of two things – the isolation of the place and the feel of the sea all about me. A breeze had come up behind the rain, salt-laden and full of the smell of exposed reefs.

'Is the *Strode Venturer* still here?' I asked.

'Yes, she's still here.' He had an RAF Land-Rover waiting and as we drove off, he said, 'Would you like to go out to her straight away?'

I nodded. 'If that's possible?'

The control tower loomed up in the lights. The road was tarmac, everything neat and ordered; it might have been an aerodrome anywhere – except for the equatorial warmth and the smell of the sea. 'I arranged for Corporal Slinger to stand by with the launch – just in case.' Easton glanced at me curiously. 'I think the CO would appreciate it if I could give him some idea of why you're here. All we've had so far is a signal saying you're interested in somebody on board the vessel.'

'That's all I can tell you at the moment.'

He nodded as though he had expected that. 'We feel a little isolated here sometimes. Hence our curiosity. Anything out of the ordinary has an exaggerated importance for us.' We swung left and then right; long, low buildings and the green of well-kept grass. 'Do you know the *Strode Venturer*?' he asked.

'No.'

'She's an odd vessel. Damned odd.'

'How do you mean?'

He laughed. 'Oh, I wouldn't like to spoil your first vivid impression of her. But when you've been on board I think you'll understand our curiosity.'

PART TWO

ADDU ATOLL

The *Strode Venturer* lay anchored about half a mile out from the jetty. Beyond her were the lights of another vessel – the *Wave Victor*, a derelict old tanker used by the Navy as a floating bunker for ships in the Indian Ocean. Far away across the blackness of the lagoon the red warning lights of the Hittadu transmitter hung like rubies in the sky. The air was remarkably clear after the rain, the clouds all gone and the night sky brilliant with stars. 'Ugly old bitch, ain't she, sir?' Slinger shouted in my ear as we roared out across the slight chop produced by the breeze.

The shape of the *Strode Venturer* was standing out now against the horizon and I could see that she was a typical 'three-islander' of pre-war vintage. She looked about five thousand tons and her outline, with the single vertical smoke stack set amidships, was uncompromisingly utilitarian. She came of a long line of economical vessels designed and built by British yards for tramping cargoes in and out of a far-flung empire's more primitive ports. 'When was she built?' I asked.

'God knows, sir,' the corporal replied. 'Before my time anyway.' And he grinned as he swung the launch under the rounded counter and came up alongside under her lee. There was no gangway down. The black-painted hull was blotched with rust which shone redly in the launch's port navigation light. We shouted and eventually one of the crew, a Chinese, put his head over the side. 'Take my advice, sir,' Slinger said. 'See the Chinese steward. He just about runs the ship as far as we can see. Calls himself the purser. You won't get much sense out of the captain. He an' his first officer are just there for decoration as you might say.' A rope ladder hit the deck with a thud. 'All right if I leave you for half an hour? I got to check the barges and landing craft.'

I told him half an hour would do fine and climbed the rusting sides of the ship. The deck above was cluttered with stores, the hatches open, the cargo booms not properly stowed. The ship looked a mess. From somewhere deep in the bowels of her a radio was blaring forth Eastern music. It was the only sound, the only sign of life – that and the man who had thrown me the rope

874

ladder. He appeared to be some sort of steward dressed in cotton trousers and jacket. But when I asked for Captain Deacon he grinned at me and said, 'Yessah, Capting not seeing anybody.'

It was a good start. But these ships are all roughly alike and I pushed past him and made for the captain's cabin which was in the usual place, below the wheelhouse. I knocked. There was no answer so I pushed open the door. The cabin was dark, the curtain drawn and the portholes closed; it reeked a sour smell of whisky and sweat. I switched on the light. He was lying on his bunk, the waistband of his trousers undone and his shirt open. He was a big man and the great barrel of his chest, covered with a mat of black hair, rose and fell with quiet regularity. He wasn't asleep, nor was he in a stupor, for I could see his eyes watching me. 'Captain Deacon?'

He didn't say anything. He just lay there staring up at me with his head twisted a little on one side whilst I told him who I was and why I'd come. It was a very strangely-shaped head, almost bald, with a high bulging forehead. 'Strode, you say.' His voice was no more than a whisper as though all his life he'd had to keep it in check.

'Yes, Peter Strode. He's on board and . . .'

'What d'you want with him?' The big hooked nose, slightly bent to one side, lifted as though to sniff a scent, and the small eyes, still staring at me from under the shaggy brows, glinted suspiciously in the glare of the unshaded light.

'I want a word with him, that's all,' I said.

'A word with him.' He repeated it to himself as though chewing on a lean piece of meat. 'And you say you're from the London Office. Well, it's got nothing to do with London who I ship as crew.'

'A member of the Strode family,' I said. 'Surely you must have realized . . .'

He shifted angrily in his bunk. 'If a man wants to lead his own life, well, Christ, he's entitled to, isn't he? I'd have given him my own cabin if he'd wanted it. Did it once before when he came on board half-dead with fever. What the hell's it got to do with London if he insists on shipping as crew?'

'Nothing,' I said. 'They don't even know he's here.'

'Well, what are you here for then?' He reached up a hand and twitched the curtain back from one of the port-holes as though he thought it might still be daylight outside. Then he grunted and heaved himself up on one elbow, peering at me closely. 'What's your position with the company?'

'I'm acting for the chairman of the board,' I said. 'I've full authority . . .'

'Oh, I don't doubt that. But there's something about you . . .' That bulging, bony forehead of his was creased in a frown. He shook his head, still with that puzzled frown, so that he looked like a great bloodhound. 'Queer. My memory – ' He passed his hand up over his face and swung his legs off the bunk. 'Plays me tricks now and then. I've met so many men – all types – but seeing you . . .' His bloodshot eyes were still staring at me and there was a sort of shocked expression in them as he reached automatically for his glass, which was empty, and felt the floor with his stockinged feet. 'Time passes,' he mumbled.

'I'm waiting to see Strode,' I reminded him.

He sat quite still, staring down at his empty glass. He seemed to be thinking it over and it was a process that took time. Finally he nodded his big head slowly. 'Well, it's up to him, I suppose.' And he suddenly threw back his head and let out a great bellow. 'Mr Fields! Mr Fields!' There was the sound of movement from the deck below and then a door banged and a small man with sandy hair and a long, drooping face appeared. 'This is my first officer,' Deacon said. And he asked where Strode was. 'Is he still on board?'

The mate's eyes shifted uneasily between the two of us. 'I dunno. I think so.'

'Well, find out.' Deacon turned to me. 'What did you say your name was?'

'Bailey.'

He nodded. 'Tell him there's a Commander Bailey from the London office wants a word with him.'

The mate hesitated. Curiosity flickered in his eyes. 'He'll want to know what it's about, won't he?'

'Just tell him I'd like to see him for a moment – in private,' I said.

Deacon rumbled something that sounded like a cross between a belch and the words 'Get out,' and the mate hurried away, closing the door behind him. There was a long silence then, the cabin sealed and completely airless. Sweat began to trickle down behind my ears. 'So your name's Bailey?'

'Yes.'

Deacon stared at me, not saying anything more, his heavy cheeks, covered with stubble, giving him a grey, ghostly look. He moved his head from side to side; finally he lumbered to his feet. 'Drink?'

'No, thanks.'

He poured himself a Scotch from the half-empty bottle on the rack above his bunk and then he subsided into the only chair, watching me covertly out of the corners of his eyes. 'You wouldn't remember the old Waverleys, I suppose?' And then I shook my head he nodded. 'It's a long time ago now. Before you were born almost. Christ, it's bloody years and I was the youngest first officer in the Line.' He was staring down at his drink, smiling to himself and that smile seemed to change his face so that for a moment I caught a glimpse of the young man he'd once been. 'It's like I was saying. Time passes. Time and people – opportunity, too.' He told me how he'd been offered the post of third officer on one of the crack P. & O. ships and had turned it down out of a misguided sense of loyalty, and then he was rambling on about some Court of Inquiry in which he'd been wrongly blamed for endangering his ship. 'I'd the wrong owners then, nobody to back me up.' And he fell suddenly silent, sitting there, huge and hairy, with great sweat patches under his arms, staring morosely up at me out of those veined, bloodshot eyes.

The heat in that cabin was stifling. I wished Strode would come. 'Have you been at sea all your life?' I asked him, not because I was interested, but because there was something uncomfortable in the silence and the way he stared at me.

'Thirty-seven years,' he said. 'Thirty-seven bloody years and I end up working for a bunch of Chinamen.' And then he was back in the past again, to some old ship – the *Lammermuir* I think he said; not a Strode ship at all. 'Another year and I'd have been captain of her. But she was torpedoed in the Malacca Strait with two hundred women and children on board. I beached her on the Oostkust – Sumatra – and spent nearly four years in a Jap prison camp, and afterwards – ' He was staring down at his drink. 'Afterwards everything was different – new ships, new men, new countries, too, and the trade all gone to hell, and I was suddenly too old.' He swirled the whisky round in his glass. 'And the ship – a scrapheap relic of the war . . . I was given the same bloody ship. What do you think of that now?' He looked up at me with a bitter, twisted smile and a gleam of hostility in his eyes. 'Didn't they teach you to drink in the Navy?' The way he said it I knew he hated the Navy.

'It's too hot,' I said.

He laughed, an almost silent movement of his great belly. 'You tell that to the directors sitting on their fat arses in London. There are ships now with air conditioning, quarters for the crew got up all airy-fairy like a tart's boudoir. Jesus Christ! They should make a voyage in some of their own ships once in a while. And I'll tell you something else.' There was a sudden gleam in his eyes. 'One of these days this old bitch is going to lie down and die on me. Christ knows how she passed her last survey. She's patched in a dozen different places and in a sea we have to keep the pumps going. If we ever hit a real storm – '

The door opened and the mate put his head in. 'He says he doesn't wish to see you.'

I hadn't expected that. 'Did you give him my name?'

'Oh, yes.' And the way he said it, with a glint of malice, revealed him as one of those who resent authority.

'Where is he?' I asked.

He hesitated, glancing quickly at Deacon. 'In the crew's quarters aft.'

It wasn't the place I'd have chosen to see him, for I knew the interview was going to be a difficult one, and as I made my way aft I was thinking of our previous meeting. That had been difficult, too, at first. For the purposes of an exercise the anchorage at Abu Musa Island was being regarded as a submarine base from which the enemy was endeavouring to stop our oil shipments through the Strait of Hormuz. Our orders were to lay mines off the anchorage and endeavour to destroy any submarines returning to base. We had the co-operation of one submarine, which like ourselves was on passage to Trincomalee, and as certain special A/S equipment was involved the presence of an Arab dhow was quite unacceptable. I therefore, went ashore to clear the dhow out of the anchorage, but instead of an Arab nakauda I was faced with Strode who calmly informed me that since the dhow was there first the Navy should shift their exercise to another island if they wanted the place to themselves. The fact that he was dressed in little more than a loin-cloth and that I was there as representative of one of HM ships didn't apparently strike him as being in the least incongruous. We had argued for nearly half an hour and by the time I had decided that there was no hope of budging him a shamal was blowing and I had had to spend the night there.

I was still thinking about this, remembering the absurdity of the situation and my complete impotence in the face of it, when I reached the after deck. I pushed open the door of the crew's quarters to find myself in a sort of mess room slung with hammocks and crowded with Chinese. I didn't see him at first for he was squatting on the floor with three others, dressed in a coloured

sarong and a faded khaki shirt, engrossed in a game of Mah Jong.
He looked less emaciated than when I'd seen him last. Also he had
grown a beard, one of those little French beards that fringe the
line of the jaw. It altered the whole appearance of his face so that I
barely recognized him. He looked up as the chatter and the
laughter died, the 'tile' he had just drawn still gripped in his hand.
He recognized me all right. But there was no welcoming smile.
Instead, his eyes had a wary look and there was a tenseness about
him, an air almost of suspicion that somehow communicated
itself to me. It was an odd feeling, standing there amongst those
yellow-skinned men, and no word of greeting from him, only that
flat, near-hostile stare; and when I suggested he came outside
so that we could talk in private, all he said was, 'I'm not prepared
to discuss my affairs – with you or anybody else from London.' He
glanced down at the ivory-and-bamboo piece in his hand and
then discarded it. One of the others said 'kong' and took it up.

The 'wall' was still virtually complete, the game only just
begun, so that I knew very well his absorption in it was a deliberate attempt to freeze me out, and I wondered why as I stood
there watching him. The Chinese seamen, quick to catch a mood,
were silent. The only sound was the click of the 'tiles' and the
blare of a radio. It was a strange meeting after all these years and
in the end I took Henry Strode's letter from my wallet and
dropped it, open, in front of him. It wasn't easy to see his eyes
in that dim light, but as he took it up and read it through I
thought I caught a gleam of satisfaction. He sat for a long time
with the letter in his lap. Finally he looked up at me. 'Where do
you come into this?'

The suddenness of the question took me by surprise – that and
the hardness of his tone, the look of distrust back in his eyes as he
stared straight up at me.

'And how the devil did you know where to find me?'

I hesitated, for I saw immediately what was in his mind – the
connection between my visit and the cabled offer he'd had from
Slattery. He handed the letter back to me, not waiting for me to
formulate a reply. 'You can tell my brothers I'll consider their
proposition when I get back to Singapore.' The finality of his
tone and the way he consciously turned back to the game made it a
dismissal. It was his turn and he reached out his hand for a 'tile.'
He drew one of the Seasons and cracked some joke to the others
in their native tongue as he laid it down.

I tried to talk to him, but it was no use. The whole atmosphere
of the crowded quarters was against me. And there was some-

thing else, I felt, something that stood between us, blocking all communication. The old lawyer's advice, his own sister's words made no impression. I even told him how I'd come into it, but it was like talking to a brick wall. And yet I knew his mind wasn't on the game, for he missed two 'kongs' in succession.

I'd come six thousand miles to offer him a directorship and fees of four thousand a year and all he did was sit there on the floor in a dirty sarong pretending to be engrossed in a Chinese game and waiting anxiously for me to go. It didn't make sense – unless . . . unless he had some objective, some secret objective so immediate and all-absorbing that my arguments touched only the outer fringes of his consciousness. At what point I became certain of this I don't quite know. Nor do I know how it was communicated to me, whether by some form of thought-transference, or by the more reasonable processes of observation and deduction. All I know is that I was suddenly convinced of it. 'You wrote a paper on the Maldives.'

He looked up at me then and even in that dim light I couldn't miss the look of sudden animal wariness.

'And now you're here in Addu Atoll,' I said. 'Why? What's so important to you about . . .'

It was as though I had touched a spring or flicked the raw edge of a nerve. 'What are you after, Bailey?' He flung down his 'tiles' and came to his feet in one flowing Arab movement. 'Do you think I don't know who you are? I know the company's history as well as you do. As soon as I had Alexander's cable I guessed – '

He stopped there, a conscious effort to get a grip on himself for he was actually trembling. And then in a quieter voice he said, 'I know how you feel. The sins of the father . . .' The trace of a smile flitted across his faun-like face. 'I've been through it all myself and even if Alexander hadn't cabled . . .' He stepped over the Mah Jong pieces and came across to me, taking hold of my arm and leading me outside into the quiet stillness of the night. 'Now, what are you after – what's behind this?' He tapped the letter I still held in my hand. 'They're worried, aren't they – about the future of the company?'

'They'd rather have you on the board,' I said, 'than run the risk of being taken over.'

'Did you know somebody was after my shares?'

'Yes.'

'And if I sell they'll liquidate the company. Is that right?'

I nodded.

'And where do you come into it? What do you get out of it?'

He was staring at me angrily. 'Are you trying to play off one against the other? Do you want to smash the company – is that it?'

'Don't be absurd.'

'Well, what then?'

'I've told you already – a job.'

'Sir Reginald Bailey's son – in Strode House? Balls. You've got more guts than that.'

'If I wanted to smash the company,' I said, 'I'd be trying to get you to sell your shares instead of pressing you to accept a directorship.' And I told him about the lunch I'd had with Slattery.

'And you turned him down – why?'

'I can't think,' I said. And I added, 'You've got a choice now – either you stop running away and join your brothers on the board or you sell your shares.'

'I don't have to do either.'

'No, but it's time you made up your mind.'

'I see. And I'm running away, am I?'

I shrugged. I was remembering his sister then – seeing again the firelight glinting on the bone structure of her face, on the dark eyes and the jet black hair. 'I think you've been running away all your life.'

I thought he was going to hit me then for his face went suddenly white and all his body seemed to contract with tension. 'My father said that to me once.' There was a strange mixture of hate and sadness in his voice. And then suddenly the tension was gone and he was smiling. 'I should have remembered the sort of person you were. But it was several years ago that we met and – ' His head jerked up at the sound of a voice hailing out of the darkness. It came floating across the water, strangely disembodied like the call of a muezzin.

He glanced at his watch and then at me as though uncertain what to do. And then he called back in a language which took me back to the years I had had at Trincomalee. 'Would you like to come?' he asked.

'Where?'

'One of the islands.' He didn't wait for an answer but dived back into the crew's quarters. The white glimmer of a sail emerged out of the night. It was there for a moment and then it was struck and the dark shape of a boat glided in to where the rope ladder still hung over the ship's side.

By the time it was alongside Strode was back, a kit-bag slung over his shoulder and a valise in his hand. He dropped the kit-bag carelessly down to the natives in the boat, but the valise he lowered carefully on a length of nylon cord. 'Well, are you coming?'

'There's a launch picking me up – '

'Let it wait. Once you're on Gan you'll be stuck there. The islands are out of bounds to service personnel.' He hesitated, peering at me in the starlight. 'Also there's something I want to show you – something I'd like you to see.'

The way he said it, there was a sort of urgency that compelled me to go with him though I knew that I was being grossly discourteous to the Commanding Officer at Gan.

As I went down the ladder the shape of the boat showed long and slender with a curved-up prow like a Viking longship. Hands reached out to steady me. I saw the mast against the stars and below me dark faces with eyes glinting in the light from an open porthole, the gleam of teeth. And then my feet were on the thwart and as Strode jumped nimbly down beside me, the bows were pushed clear, the oars dipped and the rusty plates of the old tramp were sliding away from us.

Nobody spoke. The sail was hoisted without a sound, the clew-end sheeted hard home. It was a square-sail, but by thrusting a long pole into the upper of two cringles in the luff the vessel was converted to the semblance of a fore and aft rig. She heeled as she came on to the wind and the rowers shipped their neat home-made oars, the water hissing quietly along the lee gunn'l.

'This is one of their big inshore boats – a bondo-dhoni,' Strode said. 'With a good sailing breeze like this we'll be there in under the hour.'

The wind on my face, the surge of water at the bows creaming white to leeward – and when I turned my head the *Strode Venturer* was already merging with the dark treed island of Fedu and the lights of Gan itself were far away. I couldn't see the men around me. They were no more than dark shapes, unidentifiable. But aft, standing high above us on the little stern platform, the helmsman stood outlined against the radiance of the Milky Way. There was a timeless quality about him. He stood with one hand gripping the stern post, his right foot curled round the graceful curve of the tiller, a tall, thin old man in a shapeless bundle of clothes. He wore them with the dignity of a toga and the tatters of rag that did for a turban streamed in the wind. Age and his command of the elements lent him authority. So might Charon have looked, master of the black waters as he steered his craft along the edge of coral reefs.

882

The boat itself was quite different from any I had ever sailed in before. It was home-made, of course, but running my hand curiously over the rough, sun-worn surface of the wood, I found each morticed joint as tight as any boatyard could have made them, the planking copper-fastened and neatly stopped below the paint. The oars consisted of a bent blade of wood with the shaft socketed into a hole in the middle and bound with coir rope through two small holes. The thole pins were of wood, too, and the oars were strapped to them with fastenings of twisted rushes. In a matter of moments, it seemed, I had been transported back in time to another age where men existed by what they could make with their own hands. It was primitive and yet, glimpsing the line of coral islands ringing the horizon, conscious of their remoteness, their isolation in the enormous wastes of the Indian Ocean, everything about me in the boat seemed essentially right, a part of man's creative genius, his ability to survive.

At an order from the helmsman the starboard rowers took their places and five oars dipped as one, the men taking up a tireless rhythm that balanced the sail as it was sheeted still farther in. 'Wind's shifted,' Strode said. 'There'll be some spray flying as we get the sea coming in through the Wilingili Channel.'

We were close-hauled now, the boat going very fast to windward under sail and oar with the sea lipping the gunn'l. 'Where are we making for?' I asked.

'Midu.'

From the chart I knew this was the island farthest from Gan, straight across the lagoon in the north-east corner of Addu Atoll. 'And when we get there – what are you going to do?' His kit piled at our feet and the boat sent to fetch him . . . 'You're staying there – why?'

But he had turned his head, his attention distracted by the distant sound of an aircraft. It was coming in from the north and peering under the sail I caught the blink of its navigation lights far out across the lagoon. It passed to the west of us, flying low, a dark bat shape moving across the sky. 'Do you know anything about the political situation here?' he asked suddenly. 'Do you realize we're going to sell these people down the river, destroy their independence?'

I didn't say anything and we watched in silence as that tenuous link with the outside world made a wide sweep in the starlit night, and then it slowed, nosing down far astern of us to touch the runway end and shatter the quiet with the scream of its jets. 'No, of course, you don't. You've only just arrived and you know nothing about these people – how they've always been different from the rest of the Maldives, how the little they're able to produce for export has always had to be sold through Malé. That's the Sultan's capital. It's nearly three hundred miles north of here and the Malé Government doesn't give a damn for the welfare of the Adduans. Exploited, living near the edge of starvation, TB and elephantiasis rife – you've only got to look at the size of them. You see what you think is a ten-year-old boy and you find he's eighteen, possibly twenty. It's pathetic.'

'What do you think you can do about it?' I asked.

He shrugged and gave a little sigh. 'Maybe nothing. I don't know. The RAF have done a good job. Things are a lot better here than when I first came. But these people need trade, something permanent that they can rely on.' He stopped then, sitting silent, his face immobile.

'Is that why you're here?' I asked.

But he didn't answer.

I could see the shore-line ahead quite plainly now and the sea was rough, spray coming aft and an occasional wave-top spilling over into the boat. The sheets were eased and the helmsman steered a little freer. The oars were shipped. Water creamed along the gunn'l so that it felt as though we were doing at least ten knots. 'The Gan base must have made a big difference to them,' I said.

'Oh, yes.' He nodded. 'It provides employment for about seven hundred men. And the RAF have hygiene squads going round the islands keeping down mosquitoes. The MOs make regular visits. The standard of living is better, the people healthier, but . . .' He turned and stared at me. 'What happens when the RAF go?'

'There no question of that,' I said.

'Not yet. But some transport aircraft are already overflying Gan. And even if Gan never becomes redundant, we could still be pushed out. We've been pushed out of so many places. What happens then?' he repeated, leaning forward, his eyes gleaming strangely bright as we passed through a patch of phosphorescence. 'Two years ago the Adduans set up an independent People's Republic. A couple of gunboats were sent down from Malé and if it hadn't been for the RAF there'd have been a bloody massacre. The island group to the north was brought to heel, but these boys still have their own government. They're free. But they've had to pay a high price for their freedom. You'll see when we land. I'll show you something that as a sailor will make your heart bleed.'

The wind was freeing, veering towards south-east and rising.

The sheets were eased still further and the boat flew with the dark line of the shore paralleling our course to starboard. It was not high enough to blanket the wind, but it gave us a lee so that the sea became smooth and the hiss of the hull friction on the water was very loud. In less than half an hour I could see the land curving round ahead of us. The dark blur became steadily blacker, more pronounced. Suddenly there were palm trees, the dark outline of thatched houses, and then the shadow of a coral reef was slipping by and the crew were lowering sail as we glided into a white sand beach where men stood in the shallows waiting for us. Strode touched my arm and pointed. 'See those?'

'What are they?' I asked. 'Some kind of long house?' They were built just back from the water's edge, big thatched buildings not unlike the communal long houses of the Malay villages.

'No,' he said. 'They're not houses.'

There was a bump as our dhoni touched a nigger-head of coral. Thin wiry hands reached for the gunn'l and a dozen men guided her in to the beach, not caring that they were up to their waists in water, all talking at once, and laughing with their teeth showing white in the soft half-light. They carried us ashore and on the coral strand Strode was greeted by a man who wore a linen jacket as a sign of his authority. The rest clustered round, touching him, reaching to shake his hand. They knew him for they called his name in their high guttural tongue and there was something more than the pleasure of greeting an old friend – a strange aura of excitement in the air.

Strode turned at last and called to me so that I, too, was drawn into the circle of animated faces. 'I want you to meet Don Mansoor.' The man in the linen jacket shook my hand. 'I am very pleased to meet you,' he said in precise English. 'Happy to be welcoming you to the island of Midu.' There was dignity and an old-world charm in the manner of his welcome, but his gaze was shrewd and his hand, though small, had a powerful grip.

'Don Mansoor is a great navigator,' Strode added. 'Probably the greatest in Addu.'

The long, rather sad face broke into a smile that sent little lines running out from the corners of the eyes. 'I am sailing very many times to Ceylon.'

'And other places,' Strode said.

They looked at each other, smiling. 'That's right. Some other places also.' And I wondered where else this strange little man with the sad face had been. Zanzibar perhaps or the Nicobar Islands to the east or north to Arabia.

'But there's no voyaging now. Not for two years.' Strode's voice was suddenly harsh. 'Come on. I'll show you.' He turned to Don Mansoor. 'I want him to see one of the vedis.'

'Tomorrow he can see.'

'No, not tomorrow. And not that one. He has to go back to Gan.'

'But we have to talk about it now, Peter.' A note of urgency had crept into Don Mansoor's voice and he pointed along the beach to where a small boat lay on the sand with an attendant sitting cross-legged beside it.

'So he's come to meet me here?' Strode sounded pleased.

'He is coming more than an hour ago. Now you are here we should not keep him waiting.'

'Don't worry. He'll understand.' He nodded to me and we started off along the beach towards the first of the long houses. Everybody followed us, a retinue almost fifty strong, their bare feet scuffing the fine coral sand, churning up the water of the shallows. We passed the little boat with its attendant. It proved to be an imported British sailing dinghy, one of the GP14s. The mast was in, but no sign of any sails; instead, an outboard motor was strapped incongruously to the stern. Ahead of us palms stood against the stars, dark frond-fingers stirring in the breeze, and below them the bulk of the first thatched building loomed black. 'You said something about a vedi?' I said.

'Bugaloe, hodi – it's all the same. Vedi is the local word.'

Bugaloe I knew. Bugaloe was Sinhalese for a certain type of sailing craft. And now I could just see the clipper-type bow of a boat poking out of the seaward end of the thatch. 'Two years,' Strode said as he led the way over the wrack of reef weed until we stood together right under the bows. 'A little over two years. That's how long it's since they've traded with Ceylon. And all the time these boats have lain hauled out on the beaches rotting in the tropical heat.'

It was a beamy-looking boat and though it was difficult to estimate size in that dim light, it looked about two or three hundred tons. The keel was long and straight, still resting on the palm bole rollers on which they'd hauled it up the beach. I passed my hand over the wood of the stern post. The surface was rough and tired, the wood exhausted with the sun's heat. Strode guessed what I was thinking. 'Another few years and they'll never go to sea again.' It was a pity for they had done their best to preserve their ships, moth-balling them the only way they could, under thatchings of palm fronds with the ends left open to allow air to circulate. 'What stops you trading with Ceylon?' I asked Don Mansoor.

'Piracy,' he said, pronouncing it pir-rassy. 'All Adduan peoples fear piracy of Maldivian Government.' And he added with sudden vehemence: 'Sultan's men have motor launches, machine-guns. Our ships are sail and we have no guns. I am going once to Ceylon and I lose my ship. So, we can do nothing – only lay up our vedis and pray to Allah.' He glanced at Strode and again I was conscious of their closeness, the sense of communion between them.

We moved slowly down the plaited palm frond walls and stood for a moment by the stern, which was shaped not unlike some of the smaller trading dhows. A little group of children pressed close, staring up at us with wide eyes. Chains of gold coins gleamed against the satin dark of young flesh. 'They still use a variation of the calabash with its water horizon as a sextant,' Strode said. 'And they've no engines in these boats. Just sail.'

I nodded, thinking what it must be like sailing these heavy, beamy boats loaded with dried fish in equatorial waters. The monsoons didn't reach down here; light trade winds, that's all, and an occasional storm. Conditions couldn't be very different from the doldrums of the Pacific. 'Why did you bring me here?'

'I thought you'd be interested.'

But there was more to it than that, for he was watching me closely. Here I felt was the key to his presence on the island. It was the ships and this man Don Mansoor that had brought him back. But why?

I think if we'd been alone he might have told me. The velvet night and the shadow of that sun-dried vessel – it had still, sad magic that invited confidence. But then Don Mansoor was talking to him. 'You're invited up to his house,' Strode said. It was already past nine, but he made it clear the man would be offended if I refused. 'It won't take long and the dhoni will be waiting. You'll have a fair wind back to Gan.'

We moved off along a path that wound beneath a jungle growth of palms and other thick-leaved trees. The sky was blotted out, the breeze killed. The air was still and heavy with the day's heat trapped. And then suddenly the stars above again and a broad straight street of coral sand glimmering white and walled by dense plantations. Don Mansoor's gai or house was built like the rest of coral cement with a palm-thatched roof. There was a well in the forecourt and the interior was lit by a roaring pressure lamp that cast giant shadows with every movement of the occupants. There was a table, chairs and a big, ornate mirror, a dresser with cheap English china displayed. But the thing I remember most clearly was a great swinging bed slung by ropes from the palm bole roof beams.

His wife greeted us, slight and dark with doe-like eyes and a beauty that was clearly derived from Ceylon. There were other, older women in the background, and as I sat down a young girl brought me a glass of some pale, amber-coloured liquid. Her soft nubile features smiled at me shyly as she moved back into the shadows with a glint of gold at waist and throat.

'It is a drink we make from faan – from the palm trees,' Don Mansoor said. And Peter Strode added, 'They tie the stamen down and collect the sap. This has been allowed to ferment and is slightly alcoholic.' He was watching me curiously. 'I wanted you to see the inside of one of their houses – the sort of people they are.' But he didn't say why.

The family atmosphere, the sense of order and neatness, of a culture and a way of life nurtured and maintained in absolute isolation; it was impressive and strangely attractive so that I felt relaxed and at ease, and as I sipped my drink I found myself falling under the spell of the island. Was that what he had intended? The drink was smooth and gentle like saké, refreshing in the sultry heat. I passed a packet of cigarettes round and they disappeared like manna in the desert. Talk flowed in a haze of smoke until a bright, wiry boy, one of Don Mansoor's sons, came in with a message, his bare chest gleaming dark in the lamplight.

Strode finished his drink and got to his feet. 'I have to go now.' He spoke to the boy. 'Ali will see you down to the boat.'

I said my good-byes and we went out into the night. 'You're staying here, are you?' I asked him.

'I think so. I have a meeting now. If I get their agreement, then yes – I'll stay.'

I wanted to question him further, but I knew by the look on his face he wouldn't tell me more than that. 'What answer do I take back to your brothers?'

He stared at me and I had a feeling that the purpose of my seeking him out had been completely wiped from his mind. 'Are you flying back to England?'

'Yes.'

'When?'

It seemed strange to be talking about flying in the shade of the palms on a remote coral island. 'I don't know yet. Thursday, perhaps.'

He was silent for a moment. Finally, he said, 'Tell them I'll discuss it with them when I get back to London.'

'When will that be?'

'A month – maybe two.'

He sounded very vague and I knew it wouldn't satisfy the Strodes. It didn't satisfy me. 'The *Strode Venturer*'s bound for Aden next. From Aden you could fly to London and be there in little more than a week.' But I knew he wasn't going to do that. Exasperated, I said, 'What is there on this atoll that's more important to you than the thing you've been working towards for three years?'

He looked at me and smiled. 'People,' he said. 'I've spent nearly all my life roaming the world looking for some place to put down roots.'

'And you've found it here?'

He didn't answer that. All he said was, 'You'd better get down to the boat now or Gan will be wondering what's happened to you.' He gripped my hand. 'Just remember, Bailey, what you've seen tonight. There's an opportunity here – a chance to build something for the future.' There was a touch of the fanatic in the bright gleam of his eyes. 'And if George and Henry don't take it . . .' He let go my hand. 'Well, I'll face that one when I come to it.' And he said something to the boy who tugged at my arm.

I left him then standing like an Adduan in his sarong outside Don Mansoor's hut and the boy led me down the long pale street of cleanly swept coral to the beach at the northern end. The dhoni was manned and waiting, and as soon as they'd carried me on board, they rowed her out through the reef and hoisted sail. In a moment it seemed the island of Midu was no more than a dark line astern. The wind was free, the squaresail bellied out; the rowers squatted idle on the thwarts and only the helmsman had work to do as the long lean hull clove through calm water with a hiss like steam.

There was a Land-Rover parked on the jetty end and an officer waiting for me who wasn't Easton but a Lieutenant Goodwin of the RAF Police. 'Thought we'd lost you.' He said it cheerfully, but it was a question nevertheless.

'Yes, I'm sorry,' I said. 'I was delayed.'

He stared at me a moment, his eyes slightly narrowed. Then he walked to the edge of the jetty. 'You dhoni-men,' he called down. 'Where you from?' Nobody answered him and the dark shape of the boat shied away from the jetty. 'They're not supposed to come in here after dark.' He stood there watching as the sail was hoisted and the pale glimmer of it ghosted out to lose itself in the dark waters of the lagoon. 'Well, I hope you got what you wanted.' He took me over to the Land-Rover. 'I'll drive you down to the Mess now. The CO wants to meet you.'

We drove off down the jetty and as we came out on to the tarmac road beside the airfield he said, 'I understand you were questioning one of the crew.' He had clearly visited the *Strode Venturer*. And since I had come back in a dhoni he must know I had been out to the islands. 'As the policeman here I'd like to put you in the picture.' He glanced at me curiously. 'A Chinese crew is always a risk in the sort of situation we have here. But if it's arms you were after I could have told you straight off you wouldn't find any. I was in the Cyprus business and I'm not such a fool as to have ignored that possibility. Not that I wouldn't be glad,' he added, 'to see the Adduans with the means to defend themselves. But I've got my orders.'

'I'm not interested in arms,' I said.

'No?' He forked right past the camp church. Ahead were a few palm trees, last relics of the jungle growth they had bull-dozed flat when they made the airfield. 'I warned the CO your visit might be political. Is the Admiralty thinking of re-creating Port T?'

'My visit is entirely unofficial.'

'Naturally.' He nodded with a sly grin. 'Okay. I know when to keep my big trap shut. But I think the CO will want some explanation.' And after that he didn't say anything more so that I was left wondering what the hell he thought I was.

Tennis courts showed in the headlights, a sweep of lawns and palm trees edging the shore. We drew up at a long low building and he took me through into the bar, which was crowded with men all dressed alike in civilian rig of dark trousers and cream or white shirts and ties. Their barrage of talk came to me in snatches: 'Mushy – very mushy it was, man . . . You silly bugger, didn't you see the marks on the runway?' The same talk you get in any RAF Mess. The islands were gone. I was in another world – an RAF world shut in on itself with only the Adduan serving behind the bar to remind me that this was one of the last lost outposts of empire, a small dot on the map surrounded by the Indian Ocean.

The average age seemed about twenty-five. But there was an older group at the far end of the bar, among them Canning, the Station Commander. 'Sorry I couldn't meet you myself,' he said as he shook my hand. And then he was introducing me to the others in the group, Wilcox, the Marine Craft Officer, Ronald

Phelps, Supplies and Services, the NAAFI Manager, and a pot-bellied little man with an enormous handlebar moustache that made him look like a caricature of a Spitfire pilot of the last war. This was Mac, his Senior Administration Officer, who said, 'I'm in the chair. What are you having?'

'Beer, please,' I said.

'One Slops for the Navy, Ali,' he boomed and the boy behind the bar grinned, a flash of white teeth in a laughing brown face. As he handed me the pint glass tankard I was conscious that Goodwin had drawn his CO to one side.

Canning was not a man to rush his fences. He let me finish my drink and ordered me another before he broached the subject of my presence on Gan. 'You've been out to the ship, I gather. Did you contact your man all right?'

'Yes, thank you.' And I apologized for not making my number to him first.

'Oh, that's all right – so long as you got what you came for.' He had drawn me to one side and his gaze was very direct as he said, 'Anything I should know about?'

'A purely private matter.'

He nodded and sipped his beer, letting the silence between us run on. Finally he said, 'As Commander of this base, a great deal of my time is taken up with political questions. No doubt you've been thoroughly briefed on the situation so I don't need to tell you that I have what the Malé Government regard as a rebel president on my hands. I am also responsible for defending the whole island group without, of course, stirring up any political mud that can be flung at us in the United Nations. As things stand the Adduan problem is an RAF responsibility. If the Navy wishes to investigate the islands – either officially or unofficially – then the RAF should be informed. You understand my position, I hope.'

'Of course,' I said. 'But as this was a purely private matter . . .'

'I don't accept that, Commander Bailey. If you go visiting the islands – ' He gave a little shrug and then smiled. He had great charm when he smiled. 'Well, don't leave me in the dark too long. Sometime tomorrow I shall probably feel it incumbent on me to contact Whitehall about your visit.'

It was no good protesting again that my visit here had no connection with the Navy. He didn't believe it.

'Meantime,' he added, 'I have instructed Goodwin to see that you don't go out to the islands again without my authority.' And then in a more friendly tone he offered me the use of a helicopter. 'It's much the best way to see the islands. I'll lay it on with our chopper-man for tomorrow. All right?' He turned to the Marine Craft Officer. 'When is that hell-ship of yours due to leave?'

'About noon tomorrow,' Wilcox replied. 'We haven't much more to off-load.'

Canning glanced at me. 'Well, it's up to you. If you want to go on board the *Strode Venturer* again – '

'No,' I said, 'I've done what I came to do.'

A flicker of interest showed in his eyes and was instantly suppressed. 'It hasn't taken you long.' I think he would have liked to probe the matter further, but to my relief the Movements Officer arrived with a problem requiring his immediate attention. The flight due at 23.30 had an oil pressure drop on Number Three and it was a question of whether passengers were to be kept waiting in the Transit Mess whilst SAS coped with the trouble or billeted for the night. 'Sorry about this, Bailey. We'll have another chat tomorrow – after you've flown round the islands.' He called to Goodwin and then went out, moving with a quick purposeful stride, the police officer at his heels.

Shortly after that I asked Easton to show me my room. It was in the centre of a long verandahed block only a short distance from the Mess and my bags were there waiting for me. I stripped, washed and flung myself naked on the bed. The big ceiling fan stirred the air, but the room was hot and I was tired, exhausted as much by lack of food as by long hours of travelling. I turned out the light and lay listening to the whirring of the fan, the croak of the frogs outside in the grass that wasn't grass but some exotic creeping vegetation clipped to the semblance of a lawn.

A chance to build something, he'd said. And the way he'd said it, as though it were a challenge, his voice vibrant, his eyes over-bright. Did he think he could fight George and Henry Strode on their own ground? I tried to picture him in a City suit instead of a sarong seated at the boardroom table in Strode House with his tanned face and that little French beard, but the picture didn't fit. He'd no experience of the City. Three years in Guthrie's didn't mean he could hold his own in that jungle. They'd cut him to pieces.

At least, that's what I thought as I drifted off to sleep, still wondering what he hoped to achieve by stopping a month or so on Addu Atoll.

At six-thirty my room boy produced a cup of thick sweet tea. 'What time's breakfast?' I asked him, but he shook his head, smiling shyly. His face was long and pointed with large ears and straight black hair. He might almost have been an Arab. 'Do you understand English?'

'Me speaking little bit, sah.' The brown eyes stared at me, serious and gentle, almost dog-like. His name was Hassan and he was from the island of Midu, which he pronounced Maydoo. I sent him off to clean my shoes and had a cold shower whilst the public address system played soft music interspersed with time checks. I was back in my room dressing when there was a knock at the door and Easton came in. 'The CO would like a word with you.'

'What about?'

But all he said was, 'When you're ready I'll take you over. He's in his house.'

Outside the sunlight was very bright, the air already hot. A slight breeze rustled the palms and along the shore-line of the lagoon the sails of dhonis moved in stately procession against the clear blue of the sky. Work on the station began at seven and the dhonis were bringing in men from the neighbouring islands of Fedu and Maradu. It was a bus service, but the effect was incredibly theatrical. Like the Adduans themselves, the dhonis were part of the magic of the place. It was only when we reached the CO's house, which stood facing the Mess, that I could see the jetty and the ugly landing-craft and barges clustered round the *Strode Venturer*.

The CO was waiting for me in the shade of the verandah dressed in khaki drill shirt and shorts. He had the police lieutenant with him. 'About your visit to the *Strode Venturer* last night. Goodwin tells me there's a white man amongst the crew – a fellow named Strode. Was it Strode you went to see?'

'Yes.' There was no point in denying it, but I didn't like the way Goodwin was treating it as a police matter. 'Did you go out to the ship again after I'd gone to bed?' I asked him.

'On my instructions,' Canning said quickly.

Goodwin nodded. 'I got the crew list from that Chinese purser fellow. He couldn't produce Strode for me and when I saw the captain he refused to let me talk to him. Told me to go to hell. He was drunk, of course.'

'Come inside a minute.' Canning obviously felt he wasn't going to get anywhere unless we were alone. He took me through into his sitting-room and closed the door. 'Now then, what's this man Strode doing here – do you know?'

'No, I don't,' I said.

He stared at me hard, but it was so dark after the glare outside that even without my sun glasses I couldn't see the expression of his eyes. 'I met a Peter Strode once on the Trucial coast,' he said. 'I was at Sharjah for a time and he came in on an Arab dhow and joined a caravan bound for Buraimi. The political boys got very upset about it.' He reached for a packet of cigarettes that lay on a table beside the model of a vedi complete with sails. There were models of dhonis too, all in the same satin-pale wood and shells that gleamed a high gloss orange. He held the packet out to me. 'That boat's going to Aden and God knows there's trouble enough brewing there. If he thinks he's going to slip across into the Yemen . . .' He tossed the packet back on to the table. 'Do you think that's what he's planning? Because if so, I'll have to warn our people.'

'No,' I said, 'I don't think he's planning to go into the Yemen.'

'Then where is he going?'

I shrugged. 'Your guess is as good as mine.'

'I see.' He lit his cigarette and put the match down carefully in the ash tray. 'Have you any reason to regard him as a political risk?'

I started to explain again that my interest in him was a purely personal matter, but he brushed that aside. Like his police officer, he seemed convinced that my visit had some special significance. 'I don't want any repetition here of the trouble we had at Sharjah,' he said, thrusting his jaw out at me. 'By the time we'd finished we had a file on him an inch thick. The Buraimi crisis was still on the boil and he took off with that Bedou caravan and just disappeared into the blue. God knows where he got to. We had search planes out, the works.'

'He finished up in the Hadhramaut.'

'I don't care where he finished up. He caused one hell of a flap. And the situation here is almost as tricky. As you know, the Maldivian Government had the question of Addu Atoll raised in the United Nations. Contrary to what they claim, we did nothing to encourage the Adduans to form a break-away republic. One may sympathize with them privately, but officially it's been a damned nuisance.'

He went over to the window and stood staring out, drawing on his cigarette, lost in thought. 'No man ships as crew with a bunch of Chinese just for the pleasure of their company,' he murmured. 'Or does he?' He turned then and began questioning me about Strode again; he guessed, of course, that he was connected in some way with the owners of the *Strode Venturer*. 'Makes it all the more odd, doesn't it? Even if he is, as you say, just a rolling stone, a sort of black sheep of the family . . .' He hesitated, standing there, legs slightly apart, his right hand joggling some keys in the pocket of his shorts. Finally he said, 'Well, there's no record of his having stirred up trouble anywhere, as far as I know.' And he added, 'I'm an Air Force man, not a politician. But Whitehall expects me to handle this situation – and if anything goes wrong I carry the can. Kindly remember that.' He reached for his cap then and we went out to where his staff car stood in the blazing sun. 'I've laid on the helicopter for you. Beardmoor does a daily flip round the islands – just to show the RAF is watching over them. He'll meet you in the Mess at nine-thirty.' He smiled at me, a touch of his natural charm returning. 'We'll have a drink together before lunch. I'll be in a better frame of mind then – with that ship gone.' He drove off then with Goodwin beside him and the RAF pennant streaming from the bonnet, and I went into the Mess for breakfast.

I hadn't asked for that helicopter flight, but as the machine lifted me up over the hangars, crabbing sideways towards the reefs, my interest quickened with the thought that somewhere along the fringes of that huge lagoon there must exist some indication of the purpose of Peter Strode's visit.

'Anything you particularly want to see?' Beardmoor's voice crackled in my helmet.

'The vedis,' I said.

'Vedis? Oh, you mean the old trading vessels. Can't show you much of them – all battened down, you know. The dhonis now . . .' I lost the rest and realized he had switched channels and was talking to the tower. We had already crossed the Gan Channel and were over Wilingili. 'That's where the bad boys go.' It was used as a sort of penal settlement and all along the shore the undergrowth was beaten flat, discoloured by salt. Apparently the southern shores of Addu Atoll had been swept by a tidal wave some six months before. 'They say the runway was a foot deep in water. It just about ruined the golf course.' We were swinging back now towards the bare flat bull-dozed expanse of Gan and as we crossed the runway end I saw some wag of a matelot had painted in enormous white letters – YOU ARE NOW UNDER THE PROTECTION OF THE ROYAL NAVY.

He took me low along the lagoon shore and hung poised in the bright air to show me dhonis laid up in palm-thatched boat-houses just back of the beach the way the vedis had been on Midu. 'Now the most of the men work on Gan about half the dhonis are surplus to requirements,' he said. 'They've dealt with the vedis the same way. Only the battelis – the fishing boats – are in constant use.'

'Are all the vedis laid up?'

'Yes. Or at least they were. If they haven't hauled it out again I'll be able to show you one in the water.' I asked him when they had launched it and he said, 'Yesterday morning, I imagine. When I came over about this time Monday they were stripping the palm thatch off her and had started work on recaulking the seams.'

And Monday was the day the *Strode Venturer* had arrived. 'Are they preparing for a voyage, d'you think?'

We had passed now from the jungle green of Fedu to the jungle green of Maradu. 'No, I should imagine it's just a question of maintenance.' He held the machine stationary to show me a mosque built of coral with white flags hung out for the dead so that it looked like washing day. There were children flying a kite and white teeth flashed in their dark little upturned faces as they laughed and waved. 'But that vedi was quite a sight. There must have been at least fifty men working on her.'

We slashed our way over the treetops to look down on a broad street of coral chips that ran ruler-straight almost the length of Maradu. The houses, each with their well for washing and another for drinking, were neat and ordered, the street immaculate. The whole impression was of a highly civilized, highly organized community, and I wondered that they had been content with a life so near to subsistence. Maybe it was the climate. The islands were as near to paradise as you could get on earth. And yet they were obviously not an enervated people for the evidence of their energy and vitality lay below me.

Maradu, Abuhera, the flat bare area of the transmitting station on the southern tip of Hittadu, and then we were hovering over a long thatched roof. 'There you are, sir, that's one of them.' Alone or in groups there were nearly a dozen vedis cocooned on the beach at Hittadu and the water of the lagoon was a livid green, slashed with the white of the deep-water channel they had cleared through the reefs. 'Where's the one that's in the water?' I asked him.

'On Midu.'

Inevitably, I thought, and fretted whilst he showed me the Government building, the house of the man who had styled himself President of the Adduan People's Republic, the neat ordered streets of the capital; and then we were whirring low over the reefs, heading east. There was a batteli fishing in the Kudu Kanda Channel, the curve of its white sail like the wing of a bird, and shoals of big fish – bonito – just beyond Bushy Island;

and on the far side of the Man Kanda Channel he came down low to follow four big rays winging their way with slow beats across reef shallows that were shot with all the hues of coral growth.

'There she is, sir. And by God they've got the masts in. That's quick work.'

The vedi lay in the little coral harbour at the end of Midu's main street, her two masts and her topsides mirrored in the pool's still surface. There were dhonis alongside and men working on her deck. 'Looks as though she is preparing to put to sea.' Beard-moor sounded excited. 'I wonder if she's going to try and run the blockade.'

It was absolute confirmation – the ships and that Adduan navigator, Don Mansoor, were what had brought Peter Strode back to the islands. But why? What reason had he given them to get one of their ships ready? 'Take me as close as you can,' I told the pilot.

'Okay.' His mind, his whole body, was concentrated on the vibrating control column as the helicopter descended to hover just clear of the masts, the wind of the rotors beating at the flat surface of the water, shattering the ship's reflection. She wasn't particularly beautiful – a trading vessel, broad-beamed like a barge with a short bowsprit and a high square stern. Yet she had a certain grace and the unpainted hull and decks had the dull, silver-grey sheen of wood that has been aged and bleached in the sun. The men working on her had all stopped to stare up at us. I counted twenty of them. Some were caulking the decks, others working on the topsides, and stores were being got aboard from one of the dhonis.

Beardmoor angled the machine round the stern so that we could see the dhoni on the far side. There were another dozen men there getting the sails on board and I could have sworn that one of them was Peter Strode. He looked up for a moment and then turned away, bending over the great fabric mass of the mainsail.

'They're going to sea all right,' Beardmoor said. And he added, 'I'll have to report this to the CO.' The helicopter lifted and slipped sideways towards the beach. The whole village seemed to be gathered there, a gaily-coloured mass of women and children who laughed and waved to us as they crowded the coral sand or stood in the shadows by the palm-thatched houses of vedis still laid up. 'Seen all you want, sir?' And without waiting for my reply he lifted the machine vertically and headed back towards Gan, ten miles across the lagoon. 'You were expecting that, weren't you?' he asked.

'Something like that – yes.' I heard the click as he switched to the transmitting channel and then he was talking to Control, reporting what he'd seen, and I wondered what Canning would do when he heard.

I hadn't long to wait. As we approached the rusting hulk of the *Wave Victor* I saw the big high-speed launch ploughing towards us. It was doing about forty knots and headed out towards Midu, the RAF ensign streaming taut and a great arrow of churned-up water spreading out astern. 'They were quick off the mark,' I said.

'A little too quick,' Beardmoor answered. 'They must have had their orders before I got through to Control.' And he added, 'Our local President's no fool. He has his own intelligence network and he's not looking for trouble. A head-on clash with the Malé Government is the last thing he wants.'

A few minutes later we passed right over the *Strode Venturer*. The barges were gone, the booms stowed, the hatch covers on. She was all ready for sea, yet the anchor was still down and no sign of life on board. She hadn't even got steam up as far as I could see.

Back at Gan I went straight to Station HQ. But Canning wasn't there. 'He's down at the trading post discussing the situation with the President,' Easton said. 'And you're not very popular at the moment. He feels you should have warned him.'

'About the vedi? I didn't know.'

'But you knew this man Strode was going to jump ship.'

'So did Canning,' I said. 'Or at least he'd a pretty shrewd idea after our talk this morning.'

'Did you know there were two Adduans on the *Venturer*?'

'No.'

I don't think he believed me, but when I asked for the details he went to his desk and picked up a sheet of paper. 'Don Mansoor and Ali Raza. They're both from Midu. Goodwin went on board this morning to have a word with Strode. When he couldn't find him he had the whole crew lined up. That was how he found two more were missing. We're holding the ship until we find out what it's all about.'

'What are you going to do with Strode?'

'Ship him out. The Adduans are another matter. They signed on for the voyage and in theory they should be returned to the ship to complete it. But that's for the President to decide, presuming that the captain is willing to release them.'

I went down to the jetty then, but though I waited there for an hour the high-speed launch did not return. There was no breeze, the lagoon flat calm and the *Strode Venturer* quivering in the sultry heat. Canning didn't come into the bar that morning. He arrived late for lunch, had a quick meal and left immediately afterwards. In theory nobody worked in the afternoon, but the demands of the station made few concessions to climate. Shortly before three he sent for me. He was alone in his office.

'Where's Strode?' I asked him.

'Still on Midu, and I've spent half the day arguing with our local President about him. As soon as Goodwin reported he was missing and two Adduans with him I sent the launch out there, but the people wouldn't let Wilcox land. My jurisdiction doesn't extend to the islands and the queer thing is I got the impression the President not only knew about Strode but approved whatever it is he's trying to do.' He was smoking a cigarette and he seemed ill-at-ease. 'However, that isn't the reason I sent for you. I'm afraid I've got some bad news.' He reached for a message form that lay on the desk. 'Com. Cen. have just sent this over.' He glanced at it and then handed it to me. 'I'm sorry, Bailey.'

The message read: *Please infrom Cdr. Bailey that his wife Barbara was found unconscious in their bungalow this morning. She died in hospital about an hour later. Cause of death is believed to have been an overdose of sleeping pills. Also convey our sympathy.* It was signed *Alec*.

'If there's anything I can do?' Canning said. 'Anything you want?'

'Nothing, thanks.'

I stumbled out of his office and the brilliance of the sun outside seemed to mock. Its tropical warmth held the promise of life and what I held in my hand was the death of all the years we'd had together. I couldn't believe she was gone. All that vitality, that desperate energy – wasted. To sorrow was added guilt, the feeling that somehow I ought to have done something to prevent it. I hadn't loved her – not for several years. It hadn't been possible, yet now I felt the loss of the love that had once been between us, and it hurt. It hurt like hell to think she'd found it necessary to go like this.

I don't remember walking through the camp. I don't remember much of what I thought, even. I heard the sound of the sea and have a vague impression of coral sand. In the end I went back to HQ, to the adjutant's office. There were messages I had to send – to Barbara's parents, to various relatives and friends in different parts of the world. Hers was a Service family and very scattered. 'There'll be a flight through from the UK tomorrow morning,' Easton said. 'The CO has told Movements to make a seat available for you on it to Singapore. Take-off will be around nine o'clock.'

I thanked him and walked back to my billet. It was the end of the day now and the dhonis were taking the Adduans back to their islands, the palms turning black against the setting sun and the sky to the west taking on that violent synthetic hue. Four men in white shorts were playing tennis in the fading light and the first of the fruit bats, the flying foxes, was coming in from Fedu, the beat of its wings slow as a raven. I went into my room and shut the door. The soft hiss of the fan revolving, the liquid murmur of the two house-boys talking on the verandah outside, the sound of tennis balls – how often had Barbara and I shared such sounds. I wrote some letters, then stretched myself out on the bed, my mind numb, my body drained. It was over now, finished, done with. She had been my first love and it would never be quite the same for me again. My tired mind groped for some consolation and finding none produced its own remedy. I slept, and when I woke the light was on and Hassan was standing over me. He was holding out a piece of paper.

It was from Strode: *All my plans have been upset by the authorities here and it's urgent I discuss the position with you. Can you come at once? There will be a dhoni waiting for you off the jetty. Hassan will take you to it.* He had signed it *Peter S.*

I looked up at the dark figure standing over me. 'Have you come from Midu?'

'Midu.' He nodded.

I hesitated. But what the hell – anything was better than just lying here with all the night before me. 'Okay,' I said. And he waited whilst I put on my shoes. I took a sweater with me, but outside the night was still warm. Ten minutes later we were on the end of the jetty. There was no moon, but it didn't matter; the sky was all stars, only the water was black. 'You give me cigarette please.' I handed him one and he lit it, letting the match flare against his face. A white glimmer showed suddenly against the black darkness of the water and in an instant it became identifiable as a sail filled by the light breeze coming in from the north. I heard the gurgle of the water at the dhoni's bow, but no human sound as the square of white was abruptly snuffed out. Then the dark shape of the boat itself glided alongside. Hands reached out to grasp the concrete and fend her off, a mast against the stars and dark faces, almost invisible, eyes glinting in the starlight. A thin hand reached out to draw me on board, and as Hassan jumped to the thwart beside me the bows were pushed clear, the oars dipped and the long black line of the jetty slid away.

They sailed out as far as the *Wave Victor* and then they began to row, keeping up a steady tireless rhythm and heading straight into the wind. It took them over two hours to reach Midu and closing the shore we passed the high-speed launch lying like a watch-dog chained to its anchor. Peter Strode was waiting for me at Don Mansoor's house.

'Sorry to drag you out here, but it's important. You saw that launch as you came in?' I nodded and he hitched his chair forward, his face urgent in the harsh light of the pressure lamp. 'What the hell are they so worried about – that I'll try and run a cargo to Ceylon?'

'Canning doesn't want any trouble,' I said.

'There isn't going to be any trouble. I'm going south, not north.'

'He doesn't know that.'

'Exactly. That's why I asked you to come out here. If I give you my word that I'm not going north . . .' He wanted me to persuade Canning to call off his watchdogs.

But I knew it wasn't as simple as that. 'Suppose you tell me where you are going?'

'No.' His refusal was immediate and final. And he added quickly, 'You must know by now that I have the local President's agreement – his support, in fact.'

'It's no use,' I said. 'Canning's worried about the political implications.'

'Then he's a bloody old woman. What the hell's it got to do with him?'

'Only that he's answerable to Whitehall. You can't blame him.'

'You won't help me, then?'

'I can't unless I know what you're up to.'

He was silent then and I waited, listening to the liquid sound of the Adduans talking amongst themselves. In the end it was Don Mansoor who answered. 'You must understand that we are very poor peoples here on Addu. Very poor indeed before the RAF are coming to the island.' His voice was soft and gentle, his English nearly fluent. Later I discovered he had been educated at Bombay University. 'We are always very distant from Malé and the government of the Sultan. Now we have our own government. But we have nothing but fish and cowrie shells to sell to the world outside. We wish to be less dependent upon the RAF. They are our friends. They have been very welcome to us. They raise our conditions of living so that we have lamps and oil to put in them, flour and cigarettes, even radios. But what happens next year or the year after? We do not know. We want independence for all times, but we are not being certain of our independence if we are not having – if we do not have . . .'

'Resources,' Peter Strode said. 'What he is saying is that they will never be truly independent until they have resources of their own quite apart from what they get out of the RAF's presence on Gan. In other words, they don't trust the British to support their separatist movement.'

'This is political, then?' I was thinking of the launch anchored out in the lagoon and how right Canning was from his point of view to station it there.

A silence had descended on the room. 'You want me to join the board of Strode & Company – so that you can get your foot in the door of what's left of your father's shipping line. Correct?' Peter Strode's voice was urgent, so tense that it trembled slightly. 'Well, I can tell you this, Bailey, unless I can get out of here, free to sail where I want, I won't do it. I'll sell my shares in the company and you can go to hell. Understand?' I could almost hear his teeth grate, the frustration he felt was so violent.

'Yes, I understand,' I said. 'But trying to blackmail me won't help you, and what you do with your shares is your own affair. I can only help if I know what your intentions are.'

His fist came down on the table. 'You stupid bastard – why don't you stay in the Navy if you're not prepared to take a chance and back your own judgement?' He was leaning towards me across the table, in silhouette against the lamp, the pointed ears standing out on either side of the black shape of his head. 'Can't you understand what it means to these people? Can't you trust me?'

'You're wasting your breath,' I told him. 'It's not me you've got to convince. It's Canning.'

'But I'm not talking to Canning. I'm talking to you. I'm asking you to help me.' His voice was quieter now. He seemed to have got a grip on himself. 'All right. It seems I have to convince you first that I'm not some bloody crackpot.' He jumped from his seat and went to a wooden seaman's chest that stood against the wall. A moment later he was back. 'Know anything about minerals?' He dropped what looked like several knobbly black potatoes on to the table in front of me. 'Take a look at those.' I picked one up and carried it over to the lamp. It was heavy – heavy and hard, with a metallic gleam. 'Lava?' I asked, thinking of a visit I had once paid to the island of Stromboli.

'No. They're manganese. Manganese nodules to use the

geological term.' He sat down again facing me. 'Listen,' he said.
'I'm not telling you where they came from. All I'll tell you is
this: When I came out of the Hadhramaut I found Don Mansoor
at Mukalla just about to sail. He was bound for Addu Atoll on the
monsoon. That was how I came to visit the Maldives and write
that paper for the Royal Geographical Society. That's how Don
Mansoor and I became friends. He's not only a damn' fine
navigator – he's a very brave man. Last year he had a crack at
running the blockade. Down here on the equator the monsoon
winds are light, mere trade winds. Storms aren't very common –
not storms of any duration. But he hit one and it carried him into
an area that he'd never been in before. Probably no one has. It's
right off the track of any shipping, away from any route that
aircraft take, even RAF planes.' He paused there. I think he was
afraid that he was being betrayed into telling me too much.

'An undiscovered island?' I asked.

'Perhaps.' He picked up one of the lumps of ore and held it in
his hand, staring at it as though it contained some magical
property. 'Strange, isn't it? Here's a people desperate for independence and this little fragment could be the answer – for
them and for me. For you, too, perhaps.' He set it down on the
table carefully. 'But I was telling you about Don Mansoor. In the
end he did reach Ceylon. He sold his cargo of dried fish privately
instead of doing it through the Malé Governemnt representative.
As a result his ship was impounded and his crew sent back to the
Maldives. Don Mansoor and another interpid character, Ali
Raza – he's over there.' He pointed to a small, wrinkled old man
standing in the shadows. 'They worked their passage to Singapore
knowing that at Singapore they could catch the *Strode Venturer*
back to Addu. I was down at Strode House the day they applied
to ship as crew. That's how I learned what had happened to them
– that's how I got hold of these. They'd kept them as souvenirs to
prove that they really had seen something strange. Do you know
anything about seismology? Did you know a tidal wave had
struck this atoll, that there has been evidence for several years of
submarine volcanic activity in the Indian Ocean?'

I nodded, my mind going back to Hans Straker and what he
had told me on the plane between Singapore and London. 'Isn't
there a plan for a proper hydrographical survey of the Indian
Ocean this year? If you wait a few months you'd probably
get . . .'

'Wait? I'm not waiting a day longer than I have to. The
International Indian Ocean Survey – the IIOS they call it –

includes the Russians as well as ourselves. It's a fully international survey and if I wait for them to confirm whatever it was that Don Mansoor saw, then I'll have missed the chance of a lifetime.' His fingers reached out, toying with the metallic nodules on the table between us. 'I've had this analysed. It's high-grade manganese, about forty-five percent. There's a ready market for it – in Britain, in Germany, in any of half a dozen industrialized countries. Now do you understand?' And he added, pounding the table, 'But I must have confirmation. I must know it's there in quantity and not part of a blazing ash heap that can't be worked. And I've got to find that out ahead of the International Survey. Now then – are you going to help me or not?'

Somebody had moved the pressure lamp to the table and I could see the excitement blazing in his eyes. He was like a prospector who has come upon a pile of nuggets. The ore-black lumps gleamed balefully. But my service-trained mind saw it from Canning's point of view, not his. Canning would never let him sail. I tried to explain this, but he wouldn't listen. He was one of those men who refuse to accept defeat once they have got an idea into their heads. 'I'm going,' he said. 'With your help or without it, I'm going. Tell Canning that, and if he tries to sink the ship . . .'

'Don't be a fool,' I said. 'He's not going to sink a vedi.'

'Then what is he going to do?'

'Arrest you and ship you out to Aden. Why else do you think he's holding the *Strode Venturer*?'

'The *Strode Venturer* . . . Yes, I'd forgotten she was still in the lagoon. So that's what he's going to do.' He sat there, thinking about it, suddenly much quieter. 'Have you got that letter on you? The one Henry wrote?' I took my wallet out and handed him the letter. He held it to the lamp, reading it through carefully. Finally he folded it and placed it on the table, using a manganese nodule as a paperweight. 'When will you be in London?'

'I'm leaving for Singapore in the morning.' I started to explain the reasons, but he wasn't interested in my personal affairs. 'When you get to Singapore you can cable them that I accept their offer.'

His change of front was so abrupt it was almost disconcerting. His mood had changed, too. He seemed suddenly relaxed. At the time I accepted it as confirming a certain instability in his make-up. Some men have an unpredictable quality that is not very easy for more disciplined minds to understand. It didn't occur to me then that what I was witnessing was the behaviour of a man who could change his plans in the face of necessity with lightning rapidity.

After that he talked about other things, relaxed and at ease as though everything were now settled to his satisfaction. He insisted I had another drink and even talked about his sister. 'Ida and I were always very close. It will be good to see her again. Give her a ring, will you, and tell her I'll be back soon.' When I left he accompanied me to the beach. The coral surface of Midu's main street glimmered white between the black walls of tropical growth and the stars above showed through the dark fingers of the palms. The sense of peace was absolute for no breeze penetrated the densness of the trees. The dhoni was waiting, the crew squatting on the coral strand beside it, and as he saw me into it, he said, 'What I told you tonight is in confidence. I want your word that you won't repeat it – to anybody, do you understand?'

'Of course,' I said.

His eyes were fixed on me, luminous in the starlight. He seemed to accept my assurance for he nodded slightly. 'And when you get to Singapore I'd be glad if you'd phone Alexander. Tell him I'm now a director. He'd like to know that.' I said I would and climbed into the dhoni, and in a moment the beach was gone and we were out in the lagoon with the sail up and the water creaming past as the night breeze took us south towards Gan.

I saw him once again, briefly, before I left. I had gone in to say good-bye to Canning and he was there in the CO's office, still in sarong and khaki shirt, smoking a cigarette. 'Strode understands the situation now,' Canning said. 'He's leaving for Aden in the *Strode Venturer* and then flying to London. He tells me he's been invited to join the board.' That settled it as far as Canning was concerned. A directorship was something he could understand. But looking at Strode, remembering all the things he'd told me the previous evening, I knew damn' well he wasn't going to Aden.

PART THREE

STRODE HOUSE

It was a week later that the first of George Strode's angry cables caught up with me in Singapore. *Strode Venturer overdue Aden. Cable immediately exact whereabouts also explanation Peter Strode's extraordinary behaviour.* But I was in no state then to worry about the *Strode Venturer*, for that was the day of the funeral. Barbara's parents were there, tight-lipped and appalled, for there had been an inquest, of course, following the post-mortem. And after the funeral her father saw me. Perhaps he understood. I don't know. If he blamed me, at least he didn't say so. We were both of us in a state of shock.

Other cables followed, and later, when I had begun the business of clearing up Barbara's affairs, sorting out our things and arranging for them to be shipped home, it was easier to cope with this flood of queries from the London office. What Peter Strode had done, of course, was to use his position as director to persuade Deacon to take the ship off in search of his island. I had it all from Alexander, who for all his impassivity was obviously thoroughly alarmed; it was he who had arranged with the Tai Wan Shipping Company the terms under which they would agree to the owners breaking the charter agreement.

In the end I cabled George Strode that this was a matter that couldn't be dealt with by an exchange of cables. By then I had booked air passage back and was able to give him my date of departure and flight number. I was not surprised, therefore, to find a message waiting for me on arrival at London Airport. He had sent his car and the chauffeur had instructions to drive me straight to Strode House.

He was waiting for me in his office and in no mood to thank me for finding Peter Strode and getting him on to the board. 'I expected you back sooner. What the devil have you been doing all this time?' But his mind was on the *Strode Venturer* and he didn't wait for me to explain. 'She was due at Aden on 3 April. It's now 10 April. She's still not arrived. Where is she – do you know?'

'I've no idea.'

'You saw Peter. You talked to him. You must have some idea.'

I didn't say anything. I had been awake half the night. I was tired after the long flight and anyway I didn't like his manner.

He had a sheaf of cables on his desk. He picked up the top one and handed it to me. 'That was the first we heard that something was wrong.' It was from their Aden agent, dated 5 April, announcing that the *Strode Venturer* was overdue. 'And this from the RAF – ' He read it out to me: 'Re your inquiry etc., we have contacted the Commanding Officer RAF Gan and he informs us that your vessel, *Strode Venturer*, sailed at 11.30 approx. on 28 March bound direct for Aden. Peter Strode was on board. No further information is available.'

He slammed it down on his desk. 'Immediately on receipt of our agent's message we asked Cable & Wireless to try and contact the ship. Here's our message and the *Strode Venturer*'s reply.' He thrust a typewritten sheet across the desk to me: *Please inform us expected date of arrival Aden and reasons for delay.* The reply, also dated 5 April, read: *Date of arrival Aden not yet certain. Will inform you later. Charterers have agreed interruption of time charter by sub-chartering vessel to us for maximum period one month. Am engaged vital exploration little known area Indian Ocean. Will explain on arrival London.* It was signed – *Peter Strode.*

'We've now got the rate for the sub-charter from the Singapore manager. It's half as much again as the rate we were getting for the charter and Alexander says he only agreed to their terms because you'd informed him that Peter was now a director. Did you tell him that?'

'Yes.'

'Why?'

'There was nothing confidential about it. You had already announced his appointment at the meeting.'

He grunted. 'Well, that's the lot.' He clipped the cables together again. 'That's all we know. Just that one message from him.'

'Have you wirelessed the ship since?' I asked.

'Of course I have. I've sent damn' near a dozen messages – to Deacon as well as Peter. But no answer. For all I know the ship may be at the bottom of the sea.' He stared at me angrily. 'Now then, what is all this exploration nonsense? What's he doing out there?'

'I think you'll have to ask him that.'

'I'm asking you.'

I didn't say anything and he sat there, his small moist eyes watching me across the desk. The silence between us seemed to last a long time. Finally he said, 'I've ordered Deacon to turn his ship round and make for Aden at once. If he doesn't obey he's fired. And I've cabled Peter that he's a director of Strode & Company, not of Strode Orient and that he's personally liable for the amount of the sub-charter.' He got to his feet. 'In all the years I've been in shipping I've never heard of such monstrous behaviour. And if I thought you'd encouraged him . . .' He stared at me for a moment and then he gave a little shrug. 'Well, you found him, that's something. You've done what we asked.' He came round the desk then, his manner suddenly more friendly. 'Now, when he gets here – ' He was frowning as though he didn't look forward to the prospect. 'You're on friendly terms with him, I presume? The point is, I want to know what's in his mind. Are you married?'

'Not now.'

'Well, that makes it easier. See as much of him as you can. And keep me informed. Understand? Meantime,' he added, 'get yourself somewhere to stay and tomorrow report to Dick Whimbrill. He's secretary to both companies and a director of Strode's. I'll tell him to give you an office and find you something to do.'

In his younger days Whimbrill had been a fine athlete – a rugger blue at Oxford and one of the fastest milers of his day. He had been badly shot up in the war and when I met him he was a rather tragic figure, old before his time, his face slightly disfigured and the air of a man with nothing much to live for but his job. His wife was supposed to be bedridden, dying slowly of some incurable bone disease, but nobody had ever seen her and he never talked about it. Later, when he risked everything by giving us his unqualified support, I came to respect him for his courage and integrity. But I cannot say I ever got to know him. He was a Roman Catholic and he had built such a wall around himself against the world that I don't think any man who was not a priest could have penetrated it.

His association with Strode House went back to the early days and though he did not comment on it at that first meeting, I knew instinctively that he had linked my name with the events of 1931 and had confirmed the link by inquiries. He had been told to find me a job and he gave me the run of a technical file that was his own particular baby. 'Five years ago I commissioned the design of a bulk carrier of fifty thousand tons.' His voice was toneless, dry and quite untouched by any shade of feeling. 'I was a little ahead of my time and anyway the board turned it down. Too costly.' He pushed the fat folder across to me. 'I'd be glad to have your

comments and any suggestions in the light of modern developments and experience. We'll never build it, but I like to keep the
file up-to-date – just in case.' There was something almost
conspiratorial in the way he smiled at me, a slight movement of the
left side of his mouth that gave a lop-sided look to his damaged
face. I left his office with the feeling that there was at least one man
in Strode House with whom I could get on.

There were others, too, of course, and I soon got to know them.
I was the only member of the staff who had had any direct contact
with Peter Strode and this broke down the barriers that normally
separate the newcomer. They were curious about their new
director: curious, too, about the *Strode Venturer*. One by one, on
one pretext or another, they sought me out.

Their reactions varied. Some were instinctively hostile to him,
particularly the older men like Phillipson – he was Marine
Superintendent, a one-time master with flabby stomach muscles
and the look of a heavy beer drinker. They were the real hard core
of the shipping side of the business, complacent, conservative.
They regarded him as a threat to the even tenor of their lives.
The younger ones, their imaginations not yet stultified by routine
and the pressures of life, responded more freely to the aura of
excitement he had already created, and the little that I was able
to tell them increased their fascination. The mystery surrounding
the movements of the *Strode Venturer* had given them a glimpse of
the world beyond bills of lading, invoices, accounts – the world
where ships actually moved across the oceans. But it was the
women mostly who saw beyond the event to the man himself. A
young typist in the freight department stopped me on the stairs
the second day I was there. 'Did you really meet him?' she asked
breathlessly. 'What's he like? To go off with one of our ships like
that – it's so terribly thrilling.' And there was the grey-haired
woman who worked with the P & I man; she came to my office
to ask whether I thought there was anything in the affair that
would have to be covered by the Club – the association to which
Strode Orient contributed on a tonnage basis for protection and
indemnity. 'I've been with Mr Fripp in P & I since my husband
was killed in 1943. Nothing like this has happened since the war
years. Is he really coming to work here?'

They seemed to have a desperate need of excitement and some
of them, like Mrs Frayne, sensed that Peter would provide them
with it.

The directors, of course, didn't see it in quite the same light.
Only those possessed of imagination and abundant vitality

dedicated to the service of the companies they direct thrive on excitement. Strode House did not possess such men. They held a post-mortem the following day and half-way through it they sent for me.

I had been allocated an office at the top of the building, a bare, dusty-looking place with a desk, two chairs, a cabinet full of old files and an obsolete Underwood typewriter. There was a hat-stand in the corner and the windows were filthy. There was nobody else on this top floor for the staff was very much smaller than it had been in the Old Man's day. It was Elliot who brought me the summons, slightly out of breath after climbing three flights. He regarded my room with distaste as he said in his old-womanish voice, 'They're discussing this business of the *Strode Venturer*. I'm afraid you'll find the atmosphere a little strained this morning.'

The relationship between George and Henry Strode is not easy to define. In the physical sense it was close; they had been to the same school, the same college at Cambridge, their estates in Sussex were only a few miles apart, they hunted and shot together. But their temperaments were widely different. Henry was quiet, withdrawn, very conservative in his outlook, a man who waited upon events and never ventured a decision until he was assured of the support of others. As the elder of the two he had probably borne the brunt of his father's overbearing temperament and reacted accordingly. George was much more volatile priding himself on his bluntness. He was a difficult man, too, for he had some of his father's qualities, and vanity was one of them. This made him obstinate. Once he had stated his position it was very difficult to get him to retract or agree to a compromise.

The post-mortem was being held in George Strode's office. Most conferences of any importance at Strode House seemed to happen there. Hinchcliffe, the only outsider who was an executive director, had been called in and the point at issue was the be-haviour of their Singapore manager. George Strode, sitting squat and solid behind his desk, had worked himself up into a towering rage and the atmosphere was tense. 'You admitted to me yester-day that you'd notified Alexander of Peter's appointment to the board. Why did you do that? Was it at Peter's request?'

'Yes. I phoned Alexander the day after I got back to Singapore.'

He glanced at his brother, a gleam of triumph in his eyes. 'You see – I was right. And he took your word for it, just like that, over the phone?' He was glowering at me then as though I were responsible for what happened.

'At the time,' I said. 'Later he asked to see me about it. I was staying with friends and he made an appointment and drove out to the house.'

'What did he want?'

'Confirmation. I showed him your letter to me and that seemed to satisfy him.'

'Well, there you are, George.' Henry Strode's voice sounded weary as though he had spent a lifetime trying to cope with his brother's temper. 'This isn't Alexander's fault. It's ours. We made Peter a director. We knew the sort of man he was.'

'We made him a director of Strode & Company.'

'It's all the same to a man who's been – '

'It's not the same at all, Henry, and you know it.' George Strode was jabbing angrily at his blotter with a paper-knife. 'So does Alexander. He's not that much of a fool.'

'Alexander's half Chinese.'

'What the hell's that got to do with it?'

'He's been with us since 1936 and to him the family is the family. Father dinned that into his head years ago.'

'You're just making excuses for him.' The two brothers sat facing each other and an ugly silence hung over the panelled and gilded room. Finally George Strode said, 'There's something more to it than that.' His little oyster eyes switched to me. 'As I understand it, Peter was already a member of the crew of the *Strode Venturer* when you finally tracked him down. Did you get the crew list from Alexander?'

'Yes.'

'And his name was on it?'

I nodded.

'In other words Alexander knew who he was, had in fact connived at his becoming a member of the *Strode Venturer*'s crew?'

'His name was on the crew list,' I said. 'That was all that interested me at the time.'

'At the time?' He leaned towards me across the big mahogany desk, a gleam of triumph in his eyes. 'But later – didn't it strike you as curious?'

It was Colonel Hinchcliffe who saved me answering that one. 'What are you suggesting, George – that there was some sort of collusion between the two of them?'

'Yes, that's exactly what I am suggesting. I think Alexander was in this thing from the beginning.' He looked across at his brother. 'Well, Henry?' And when his brother didn't say anything, he pointed the paper-knife at him. 'You cable your manager and find out what he's got to say about it. I'm firing Deacon as soon as his ship gets to Aden.'

'Are you suggesting I suspend Alexander?' Henry Strode shook his head. 'I can't do that. Business is bad enough . . .' He glanced up at me. 'I don't think we need Commander Bailey any more, do we?'

George Strode hesitated. Then he gave me a brief nod of dismissal. As I went out I heard Henry Strode say, 'Well, it's taught us a lesson. But once he's here . . .' He was switching the argument away from Alexander. But I thought George Strode was probably right. During the three years Peter Strode had been with Guthrie's he would have had ample opportunity to cultivate Alexander. It was even possible he had taken him into his confidence. As for Deacon . . . he might be a drunkard, but he wouldn't have jeopardized his position, risked what remained of his career, if Peter hadn't been able to convince him it would be to his advantage. To charm two such different birds as Alexander and Deacon . . . My thoughts were interrupted by the phone. It was West, Wright, Turner & Company, the solicitors. Somehow Turner had heard I was back. He wanted to see me. I made an appointment for Monday morning and shortly afterwards I left to take the train north.

The school holidays had started and the children were staying with my sister at Sheilhaugh, the 300-acre farm on the edge of the Lammermuirs that was all that was left of my family's Border estates. I hadn't been there since my mother's death.

Agnes and her husband met me at the station and late though it was they had John and Mary with them. Strange how matter-of-fact children are about death. They asked questions, of course – some of them questions I found difficult to answer. But at that age the excitement of living is a moment-to-moment affair and death, like life, a natural thing to be accepted as an inevitable part of a world that is still fresh and new.

It was glorious weather all that week-end with spring in the air and the grass sweet on the moors where sheep grazed with their growing lambs. And when I took the train south on the Sunday evening I felt I had stolen a moment of time that belonged to childhood days. For the first time in years, it seemed, I had been happy – completely and absolutely happy.

I had not realized that the background of the company for which I was now working had registered with the children. But as we stood on the platform waiting for the train John suddenly said with great seriousness, 'Will we have ships of our own again now?' His small face was alight with eagerness. 'I'm going to sea like you.

Only I'd like it to be in one of our ships.' God knows what Agnes's husband, Jock McLeod, had told him. He was a marine engineering consultant in Glasgow and he'd no use for Strode Orient. He'd made that very clear over a drink the previous night. 'Their maintenance record is poor and so are the conditions of service. It's a bad line to work for and a man like you should either get out or do something about it.'

'When we build a ship,' Mary said, 'can I launch her? You know, champagne on the bows and everything.' They had it all worked out for me and as the train pulled out I wondered how any father could ever measure up to the hopes of his offspring. What they had in their eager little minds was an absurd, impossible idea; or was it? At least I had taken the first tentative step. I was in Strode House. And next morning, in Turner's office, I was given a fleeting glimpse of a larger prospect.

The old man looked even frailer than when I had seen him three weeks before. 'So you found Peter and he's accepted the directorship.' He knew all about the *Strode Venturer* and for several minutes he questioned me closely. He was very short of breath, but though his body was ailing, there was nothing wrong with his mind, which was clear and very active. 'If Peter wants to rebuild his father's empire he must do it within the framework of the existing companies. I hope he realizes that.' And he added, 'He'll have a tough fight on his hands. Is he prepared for that?'

'I think so,' I said. But I wasn't sure. 'His chief interest seems to be in helping the people of Addu Atoll.' And I told him about Don Mansoor and the vedis. I thought he had a right to know what Peter Strode's real motives were. He listened in silence, without comment, as I gave him the gist of the two conversations I had had with him on the island of Midu. And as I talked I couldn't help feeling that his reference to building something for the future applied just as much to the Adduans as to Strode Orient. 'He seems to have identified himself with the people there.' I was remembering what he had said about his search for a place to put down roots.

But it didn't seem to worry Turner. 'It was never money that interested Peter.' He was smiling quietly to himself. 'What you have told me only confirms my assessment of him. Now that I have reached the end of my life I am better able to appreciate real values. Money must always be the servant, the means to something you really believe in. Since he has learned that so early in life he may well prove to be a more formidable person than his father. This business of the *Strode Venturer*, for instance. You met

Deacon, did you?'

'Yes.'

'Deacon would never have agreed to do it for money. You can't buy men like that.' And he added, 'Deacon was one of your father's officers. Did you know that?'

I didn't know it, but I had had a feeling he was. 'And the *Lammermuir* – was that one of our ships?'

'Yes.' He nodded his head slowly. 'Bailey Oriental tramps were all named after characters or places in Scott's novels. The Waverleys they were known as when we took them over. I think the *Lammermuir* was one of the first. There were things about her, the accommodation and loading gear in particular, that made her somewhat revolutionary at that time.' He was doodling and I saw the name Deacon emerge in flowery script on the pad in front of him. 'He took to drink, I believe. But you can't blame him – he had a rough deal.' He looked up at me then, his watery eyes strangely bright. 'I don't pretend to understand what Peter is up to. What you have told me helps, but at this distance I cannot see into his mind. When do you expect him back?' And when I said two weeks, a month at the outside, he sighed. 'Even that may be too late. My doctor – ' He gave a little smile. 'The body is only a mechanism and I've worked mine pretty hard. It tires eventually.'

He paused then and it was such a long pause I thought the interview was over. I started to get to my feet, but he waved me back and pressed the bell-push on his desk. 'Ask Mrs Roche to come in,' he told his clerk.

A moment later Peter Strode's sister was shown into the office. The old man didn't rise, but he took her hand in both of his and held it for a moment. 'Sorry to keep you waiting, my dear, but I wanted a word with this young man first.' The clerk pulled up a chair for her and she gave me a fleeting smile as she sat down. 'You've met, I think.' The old man had picked up his pencil again and was drawing, his head bent, and I could have sworn there were tears in his eyes. 'I've no children of my own. I've always thought of you, Ida – and Peter . . .' He dropped the pencil and looked up at me. 'Have you told her about your meeting with Peter?'

I nodded and Ida Roche said, 'He phoned me when he got back.'

'Good. Then I needn't go over that.' He put his thin hands on the desk as though bracing himself for a long speech. 'I don't get about and meet people the way I used to, but I still have contacts in the City and there is always the telephone. And I still know where to go for information about Strode affairs.' He was talking to Ida Roche now. 'When your father died I lost interest, of course, and my interest didn't revive until Peter made his decision to go into Guthrie & Company. When I realized he was serious I got a merchant banking friend to make a detailed analysis for me of the finances and trading prospects of Strode Orient together with the share distribution of the company and that of the parent concern. From that analysis two things emerged. One, that Strode Orient had become a plum ready to fall into a clever man's hands. The other, that the key to any take-over was not the obvious one, Strode Orient, but Strode & Company. If this bores you, my dear, I must ask you to bear with me because it's important, and as you will see in a moment I have taken action to avoid a certain possibility that might otherwise stop Peter in his tracks.'

Ida Roche shook her dark head, smiling. 'No. On the contrary, I find it fascinating. Anything concerning Peter has always fascinated me. He's that sort of person. Do you mind if I smoke?'

'No, no. I'm past caring about the effects of tobacco smoke.'

She had already taken a small gold case from her bag. I lit her cigarette, and her eyes, glancing at me over the flame, had a speculative expression as though she were seeing me for the first time and wondering what sort of person I was. It may be that intuitively she had guessed what was coming, though she denied it later.

'This is a little technical,' the old man continued, 'but I will try and explain it to you in simple terms. I have told you that the key to any take-over of the Strode Orient Line is control of the parent company. But Peter does not have control of Strode & Company. He has a hundred and seventeen thousand of the half million shares in issue, and now that he's a director he can't sell without the agreement of the majority of the board. No director can. We wrote that into the Articles of Association as a safeguard. At the moment I am quite sure that the other directors do not intend to sell and are anxious that he should not sell either. But what if his behaviour – once on the board – made them change their minds? Suppose they decide to sell? In that case it is just possible control of Strode & Company – might pass into – other hands.' He had become very breathless and he paused, dabbing at his lips with his handkerchief.

Ida Roche leaned forward, a little movement of sympathy. 'Please, you don't have to explain your reasons. Just tell us what you've decided.'

'No, Ida. You're entitled to know, not only – what I've done, but why.' There was silence then whilst he gathered his reserves of strength. 'All my life I have been concerned with the tortuous minds of men who deal in finance. I could see what the line of attack must be and over the last few months I have set out to block it. I am a fairly rich man, but to buy control of a shipping line was quite beyond my means. What I did was to buy Strode shares. I now hold over sixty thousand of them. With Peter's holding and yours, Ida, we control between us over forty per cent of the equity. It does not give us absolute control, but it is a strong position and will I hope be sufficient, since the rest of the family, plus the outside directors, hold no more than a hundred and sixteen thousand. It will depend on how many shares can still be bought in the market.'

He paused again and now his eyes were directed at me. 'I have only seen you once before and my contacts with your mother and father were in somewhat trying circumstances. Since you came here a few weeks ago I have instituted inquiries. I have what amounts to a complete dossier on you right here.' And he tapped a folder on his desk. 'My opinion is that you have inherited some, but not all, of your father's qualities. I am not in a position to make an exact assessment of your potentialities. But at least you have been bred to the sea and though there is nothing in your record to suggest that you are possessed of originality or more than average initiative, you appear honest, hard-working – in fact, a thoroughly reliable man. It was this last characteristic that decided me – that and a certain sense of justice – in what I now propose.'

He let go of his desk and sagged back in his chair as though, now that the decision was taken, he could relax. 'I have today added a codicil to my Will. The shares I hold in Strode & Company will pass to you at my death and they are protected from sale by my executors for the purpose of estate duty. You understand? I'm giving you what I hope amounts to final control of Strode & Company in the event of a showdown between Peter and the others.' And he added, 'The market price this morning is fifteen and six. They have risen six shillings in a fortnight and the inference I draw from that is that Lingrose and his friends are mopping up the last few shares still held in public hands. I have seen this sort of thing happen before and I know what it means. The heat is on and they are pressing for control by one means or another.'

He put his handkerchief to his lips again, his face darkly

mottled, his body slumped. 'I think I must ask you both – to leave now. I just wanted you – to understand, Ida.'

'Of course.' Her voice was very quiet and restrained, the huskiness reduced almost to a whisper. 'It was kind of you to explain.' She had got to her feet and she went round the desk and took his hands. 'Is there anything we can do for you?'

'No, my dear. Nothing. Nothing at all. Just remember me once in a while when I'm gone.' He smiled faintly. 'I'm not certain – not yet – but I think perhaps it helps to be remembered sometimes.'

'Of course.' She smiled. 'Often. But it's not yet.'

'Very soon now, I fear.'

I, too, had got to my feet. It was difficult to explain how I felt. It was a lot of money to be handed by a stranger, a man I hadn't known existed until a few weeks before. I didn't think of it like that, of course. It was the obligation that hit me, the realization that with the lawyer's knowledge of human reactions he'd tied me to Strode House for life. What he had done was to give me back part of the responsibility and power that should have been mine by birth and he'd done it in a way that had made me both a check and a prop to the man in whom he was really interested.

'Are you sure this is really what you want?' I asked him. I was still a little dazed or I would have realized he wasn't the sort of man who didn't know his own mind.

'Quite sure,' he snapped. And it wasn't until Ida and I were going down the dark stone stairway together that I realized I hadn't thanked him, hadn't even said good-bye. I'd walked out of his office, leaving her alone with him, and had waited outside, my mind full of the future, realizing gradually the full extent of the obligation – and the challenge – I had had thrust upon me. And then she came out, dry-eyed but emotionally upset, and we walked down the stairway together without saying a word, out into the spring sunshine.

We walked through Lincoln's Inn and across Kingsway and came to Covent Garden, neither of us having thought of taking a taxi or of going our separate ways. Once she said, 'He knows he's dying.' And later: 'He's been in our lives always – a sort of rock, something solid to cling to when we were in trouble.' She wasn't upset about it any more, but the break in her voice showed the depth of her feeling. 'I shall miss him.' And, after that she didn't say anything until we crossed the Market and came to the Round House pub by Moss Bros. 'I think I'd like a drink,' she said then.

In the end we had lunch together for we were still under the old man's spell, feeling ourselves drawn together by the web of circumstance.

'Where's Peter now, do you think?'

'God knows!' For all I knew the *Strode Ventruer* might be lying broken against the laval side of some newly-erupted island. But I couldn't help feeling that Peter was too live, too vital a man to get sunk without trace before he'd had time to get to grips with the world his father had bequeathed him. She must have felt this, too, for all she said was, 'I hope he doesn't make a fool of himself.' We had finished the meal and she was sitting facing me, smoking a cigarette and sipping her coffee. 'I want you to promise me something. See that he doesn't do just that. Like me, he can be terribly impulsive. He does things on the spur of the moment. He once told me all his travelling was on the spur of the moment. Somebody in a bar, a ship in a harbour, the signpost beckoning. He doesn't plan. He acts. That's why you've been left those shares. The old dear knows Peter's weakness.' She smiled at me, a humorous gleam in her eyes. 'You're my brother's keeper now. D'you realize that?'

I didn't, of course – not then. I didn't know him well enough to realize he needed one. But she did, and so did the old lawyer. It was only later, much later, that I came to understand the crazy streak in him. It wasn't a question of instability so much as a certain theatrical quality in his make-up. His was a volatile, flamboyant nature feeding on excitement, carried away by his enthusiasm, his delight in the grand gesture. I was cast in the role of ground tackle, an anchor to keep him from wrecking himself.

'Read that,' George Strode said, reaching across his desk to hand me a letter. It was the following morning and the letter was from the Admiralty. The *Strode Venturer* was apparently safe. She had returned to Addu Atoll on 14 April short of fuel and had requested permission from the naval officer in charge of the *Wave Victor* to bunker for the voyage to Aden. *In the circumstances there appeared no alternative but to accede to the request, particularly as it was made by a director of Strode & Coy. We would point out, however, that the* Wave Victor *is anchored at Addu Atoll for the refuelling of naval vessels. It is not to be regarded as providing a bunkering service for commercial vessels and you are warned that in the future* . . . The final paragraph read: *In view of the threat to life constituted by your failure to provide sufficient fuel for this vessel kindly forward by return a full report as to the reasons why the* Strode Venturer *could not make Aden without recourse to Admiralty bunkering facilities.*

'Well, what do I say to that?' George Strode demanded. 'Is Peter quite out of his mind? The chief engineer, Brady, must have warned him about the fuel situation. To sub-charter the ship and take her off for a joy-ride round the Indian Ocean knowing damn' well he couldn't reach Aden . . .' His words, tumbling over themselves, were choked by anger. 'Do you know the man who wrote that letter?'

I glanced at the signature. 'No, I'm afraid not.'

'Well, you know the form. Draft a reply – the usual thing, full inquiry, disciplinary action, and bring it down to me for signature. That should satisfy them.' And he added, 'The *Strode Venturer* is due in Aden on Saturday. And I've just had confirmation that Peter's still on board. I've cabled Simpkin to get him on a plane the moment the ship docks. I'd like a full report on his activities from you before I see him on Monday morning.'

But it wasn't until the Tuesday that he arrived, and then quite unexpectedly. About four in the afternoon he came bursting into my office lugging an old duffel-bag. He heaved it up on to my desk and the mouth of it fell open, pouring a cascade of those manganese nodules into my lap. 'Well, there you are – the first consignment.' He glanced round my office. 'Why did they shove you up here? I barged in on a languid young man downstairs – acres of carpet and about a dozen pictures all to himself.'

'That's John,' I said. 'Henry Strode's son. He acts as PA to his father.' I had moved the duffel-bag on to the floor and was clearing the stuff from my desk. 'So you found the island.'

'I suppose you could call it an island, yes. It was the bed of the Indian Ocean really.' He'd come straight from the airport, his tropical suit still rumpled from the journey, but he didn't seem tired and he wanted to talk. 'Never seen anything like it. All grey slime and weed and the empty cases of shellfish, and stinking like a dirty harbour at low water.' The description, the atmosphere of the place came pouring out of him compulsively, leaving me with the impression of a dark whale shape about three miles by two, a dead decaying mass from the ocean depths lying stranded in a flat calm oily swell a thousand miles from anywhere. He had seen the manganese lying exposed in drifts like banks of black metallic shingle. And here and there were outcrops of the basalt from which the nodules had been leached by the sea's action. But most of the island was overlaid by sediment, a grey slime baking under a blazing hot sun. He wouldn't tell me where the island was. 'It's way off any steamer track, clear of the flight path of any plane.'

'Volcanic?' I asked.

He shrugged. 'In origin – yes, I suppose so. Sometimes, when the wind was southerly, the air became sulphurous as though gases were seeping out of some submarine rectum. But there was no vent on the island. I haven't walked it all, but you can see most of it for it's nowhere more than fifty feet high and damned difficult to approach, though we found deep water on the western side.'

'Any picture of it?' I was thinking it would help when it came to putting a scheme up to his fellow directors. But he hadn't had a camera with him. Nor had any of the crew. 'Just as well,' he said. 'We don't want anyone else out there searching for it.' He seemed to have forgotten about the ship's officers.

'They must have known what you were up to, bringing off samples.'

He laughed. 'They were scared stiff, most of them. There's a damned queer atmosphere about a hunk of land that's just emerged from the sea. Geology isn't their business and anyway they thought I was crazy.'

'But they know where it is and they'll talk.'

'They'll talk, yes. But you're wrong – they don't know where it is. There were only two sextants on board besides my own and I got hold of those before we sailed. As soon as we were in the area – I had Don Mansoor with me and his reckoning of its position was a little vague – I started a square search. You know how confusing that can be unless you're plotting it yourself. And I saw to it that nobody else kept a track chart.' He had seated himself on the edge of my desk and was toying with one of the ore pieces. A strange smell of the sea and of decay had invaded my office. 'If we follow this up – get out there quick . . .' He stared down at the lava-like substance he held in his hand. 'There's shiploads of this stuff there – millions of tons of it for the taking. With a surplus of shipping and the eastern countries taking over our traditional cargoes it'd make a difference to have our own freight source, wouldn't it? And nobody owns the island. An opportunity like this comes only once in a lifetime . . .'

He was still sporting that little French beard and with his skin tanned to the colour of old teak and his eyes alight with excitement he looked very strange indeed. I thought of the other times I had met him, how on each occasion he had seemed in his element. But here in the City, dressed in a tropical suit . . . It was one thing to dream of resuscitating Strode Orient, quite another to convince the directors. Dreams and company balance sheets, the hard facts of money, don't go easily together.

I started to tell him this, but he brushed the difficulties aside.

'Even my brothers must see the possibilities. It's so damned obvious.' And he went on: 'I didn't just bring back a bag of ore. I had Number Four hold half-filled with the stuff. We were digging it up with shovels and bringing it off in the boats for two solid days.' He laughed. 'When we got to Aden, there was our little agent, Simpkins, running up the wall because he'd been told to rush me off by plane and I wouldn't leave till I'd got samples away to a long list of industrial concerns I'd had prepared back in Singapore. He sacked Deacon, by the way. Did you know that?'

I nodded. 'The instructions were sent over a week ago.'

'Well, that's soon put right. And after I'd got the samples off, I had the rest of it transhipped to a freighter bound for the Tyne. Wouldn't be surprised if I make enough to cover the fuel bills.'

'That would help,' I said. And I tried to explain to him what the reaction had been at this end. But he was so full of his own plans that he couldn't conceive of any opposition to them.

There was a knock at the door and Elliot came in. He stood there for a moment, staring. 'Are you Mr Peter Strode?' He said it with the air of a man forced to make friends with a rattlesnake. And then he added hastily, 'Mr George would like to see you.' He held the door open. 'If you'll follow me, sir.'

That first meeting with his brother must have opened his eyes to the position, for he came back to my office half an hour later in quite a different mood. 'Let's for God's sake go and have a drink.'

'They're not open yet,' I said. 'Not in the City.'

'To hell with the City. We'll go down West.'

He left the duffel-bag in my office and we went down the stairs together. 'Only been in this place twice before. Always hated it.' He stopped at the head of the main staircase, looking down at the ornate entrance with its glistening chandeliers and marble floor. 'Incredible, isn't it? Modelled on a palazzo in Milan. My father was very fond of baroque. It appealed to the flamboyant side of his nature.' He smiled. 'Italian palazzi, Haussman's Champs-Élysées, the Escorial – anything really big. You never met him, I suppose?'

'No.'

He nodded, still smiling. 'Just as well, perhaps, you wouldn't have liked him. He was a man of enormous appetite, egotistical, ruthless – anything he saw he wanted to own. Another twenty years and he'd have got his hands on half the ships in the country.' He gave a little shrug. 'I hated him, of course, but that was years ago. Now I understand him better, can appreciate that driving energy of his, that acquisitive, expansive lust for the power that money gives.' His dark hand tightened its grip on the smooth wood of the staircase rail. 'This is the first time in my life I ever felt the need of him. He'd have known how to make a thing like this come to life, and he'd have backed me . . . I'm damned sure he would.'

'Well, he's dead now,' I said and there wasn't much kindness in the way I said it.

He nodded and started down the stairs. 'Yes, he's dead and brother Henry sits at the desk where he used to sit.' One of the freight department clerks went past us, his eyes almost popping out of his head as he stared at my companion. We reached the portrait of my father and Peter Strode hesitated, glancing at me. Was he checking the likeness or was he considering how I must feel working in this building? I couldn't be certain, for his eyes were without expression and he didn't say anything.

He took me to a little drinking-club off Curzon Street owned by a man who had been at Rugby with him. But he didn't really want to drink. He wanted to talk – about his brothers and Strode Orient and what he would do if he were in control of boardroom policy. The idea that he could dictate policy to men who had lived and worked in the City all their lives seemed distinctly naïve. But when I pointed this out to him, he laughed and said, 'Why the hell do you think my father left me the shares if he didn't want me to use them?' And he added, 'I've a darned good mind to sell them – start a new company from scratch.' He didn't seem to realize that he couldn't sell them now without the assent of the majority of the board. 'Who told you that?'

'Turner. It's just to prevent you selling your shares that you've been elected to the board.'

'I see. Then I'd better go and have a talk with the old boy in the morning. He'll know what I ought to do. There's a board meeting tomorrow afternoon – specially called on my account.' He laughed and downed the rest of his drink. 'Come on. Let's go and feed.'

We had dinner together, and then, since he'd nowhere to go and no kit, I took him back to the little furnished flat I'd rented off the King's Road, Chelsea. In the morning he rushed off after a quick cup of coffee to buy some clothes and see his sister who had come up on the night train and was waiting for him at a friend's flat.

I didn't see him again until he came into my office about four when the board meeting was finally over. He'd got himself a dark suit, but it didn't go with the sun-tanned face or the fringe of beard and he had a wild look in his eyes. 'They accept the fact that I was acting in the interests of the company. That's the only concession I got out of them.' He was laughing, but not with humour. 'Impetuous and misguided. That was how Henry put it. George used stronger words.' He was pacing up and down, the poky little office caging him like an animal that has been stirred to fury. 'Five of them, all sitting there at the table solemn as judges, and it took them the best part of half an hour to reach that conclusion. Talk, talk – nothing but talk. And after that they discussed the line Henry would take at the annual general meeting in June. I got them to listen to me in the end, but they didn't want to and all the time I was talking there was a sort of frozen silence. And when I'd finished that old fox Henry washed his hands of the whole matter by telling me to take it up with his brother since the operation of the ships was Strode Orient's business. Well, I grabbed George afterwards, but he wasn't interested. Said it would be a costly operation and he'd no money to spare for harebrained schemes like that. And when I told him it would cost less than one year's directors' fees and I was prepared to waive mine for a start, he wriggled out of it by saying that his company hadn't the equipment or the know-how – "You go and sell your idea to one of the big mining companies, then we might be interested".' He leaned his hands on my desk. 'Here's a chance of grabbing something before others get hold of it – a chance to build something big.' He was glaring down at me. 'But they've no imagination. They can't see it.' He flung away from the desk and began pacing up and down again.

His feeling of frustration was painful to watch. I had expected this, had even tried to warn him the previous night, but that didn't make it any pleasanter for him. And there was his pride, too. He was standing by the window, his hands clenching and unclenching, his gaze on the thin line of sky above the rooftop of the neighbouring building. 'There must be some way . . .' He swung round on me suddenly. 'Do you know anything about company law?' But he knew I didn't and he turned back again to the window, staring up at the sky. 'This damned place – ' He understood what he was up against now – vested interests and the entrenched power of men who have dug themselves in over the years. They knew all the ropes of this financial labyrinth. They had the contacts, the solidity of being a part of the City. He was a newcomer, friendless and alone; a rebel with a cause, his mind seething with ideas, but no means of implementing them. 'Damn old man Turner,' he said suddenly. 'Going sick on me just when I need him.' He swung round on me. 'I've got to fight them – their way, with their own weapons. Turner's the only man who could have told me how to do it.'

'Have you seen him?' I asked.

He shook his head. 'I can't worry him with my troubles now. A man has a right to die in peace.' And he added, 'They carted him off to a nursing home last Friday. It seems it's just a question of time.'

'I'm sorry,' I said. But it didn't surprise me, remembering how breathless and exhausted he had been at that long interview with Ida and myself. 'Nevertheless, if he's conscious I think he'd want to see you. He thinks a lot of you and . . .' I hesitated. But whether it had been in confidence or not I felt he should know. 'He's been buying Strode shares. Did Ida tell you?'

'No. What for?'

'I think that's something he'd want to explain to you himself.'

He nodded. 'Funny, isn't it – the way life goes in circles. Father relied on him for advice . . . all his trickiest deals. And now when he's dying – ' He turned back to the window. 'I wish to God he hadn't chosen this moment. With him to guide me – ' He let it go at that. 'Can you lend me some money?'

He didn't get back to the flat until after seven-thirty. By then Ida had come to pick him up, but he barely glanced at her. He was too obsessed with his own feelings. 'The last time I saw him I thought he'd live to be a hundred, he was so full of life. And now to see him like that, slumped down under a pile of blankets complaining of the cold, just his head showing and his eyes staring up at me with that faraway look as though he could already see what was on the other side . . . And he looked so bloody small – ' He asked for a drink then and I poured him a Scotch. 'My God! When I go I hope it isn't like that – fading slowly away in a nursing home.' He gulped at his drink. 'It was only his body, you see. His mind was clear. Clear as a bell.'

He wouldn't tell us what advice the old man had given him. All he'd say was, 'I had an idea and he told me how to make it work.'

It was very simple really; at least it seemed so to me when I heard he'd contacted Lingrose. He did it through Slattery and the three of them lunched together on the Friday. He made no attempt to conceal what he was doing and the significance of it was not lost on his fellow directors, particularly George Strode and Colonel Hinchcliffe, the two directors retiring by rotation. They were, of course, offering themselves for re-election and normally this would have been automatic, a mere formality. Now suddenly their whole future was threatened, for though Peter couldn't sell his shares, they still carried voting rights, and the annual general meeting of Strode & Company was by then less than six weeks away.

George Strode called me down, wanting to know what the hell it was all about. I couldn't tell him much that he didn't already know, for I could see by his face and the questions he asked that he was well aware that the ground was being cut from under his feet. 'If he thinks he's going to blackmail me into supporting his scheme . . .' He was angry and a little confused.

I think they all were for a special meeting of the board was hurriedly called for Tuesday morning. That was on the Monday after they'd had an opportunity of talking it over during the week-end and Whimbrill took me out to lunch in the hope that I would use my influence with Peter to avoid a head-on collision between him and the rest of the board. 'I don't think he realizes how deeply George resented his action over the *Strode Venturer*. And then to hold a pistol to their heads like this.' His hand went up to the skin-grafted ear and the side of his head where no hair grew. It was a habit of his when he was nervous or ill-at-ease. 'Was this Lawrence Turner's idea?' And when I didn't answer, he said, 'Turner's very clever – always was.'

He must have worked very closely with Turner in the old days and I thought he was probably the source of the old man's information about the company. 'I only hope,' he murmured to himself, 'that he isn't too ill to have thought this thing through properly. George isn't going to like it – and he can be awkward, very awkward indeed when he's cornered.' Back in his office after lunch he lit a cigarette and reached for a folder lying in one of the trays on his desk. 'The day after Peter contacted Lingrose I received letters of nomination proposing two further names for election to the board. Slattery I think you know?'

I nodded.

'The other is a man named Benjamin Wolfe. Both are directors of Liass Securities, close associates of Lingrose, and checking the share register I find that over the last three months more than a hundred and sixty-four thousand shares have changed hands, about thirty-four thousand being purchased in the names of these two gentlemen. I've been in the market for some myself and Turner purchased a further twenty-nine thousand odd. All the rest, some eighty-six thousand shares, have been bought on behalf of nominees. Presuming that these were acquired by Lingrose's investment company, Liass Securities, which already held over thirteen thousand, then I think we must reckon on Lingrose controlling a minimum of a hundred and thirty-three thousand shares. If Peter supports him, then control of the company will undoubtedly pass out of the hands of the present directors. Even if they got Turner's backing it still wouldn't be enough.' His face was bleak as he reached for the house phone. 'Since you're certain Peter won't change his mind I'll have to see whether I can't persuade George.'

He went down to see him a few minutes later. What he had to say must have come as a shock for shortly afterwards I ran into Elliot and he told me Henry Strode was in there and Hinchcliffe too, and they had sent for le Fleming and Crane. The meeting was still going on when I left at five-thirty to pick Ida up. Peter was out with some fellow he knew in the Foreign Office and we spent most of the evening discussing what would happen if he did go in with Lingrose.

But it never came to that for George Strode called him down to his office first thing next morning and told him that Strode Orient would accept responsibility for a pilot operation in the Indian Ocean. He offered him the *Strode Trader* just laying up in Bombay at the end of a charter, and in addition to the ship and her crew, financial support to a maximum of £10,000. 'Turner was right,' Peter said to me afterwards. 'You can plead a cause till you drop dead in your tracks. Nobody cares a damn in a place like this. But threaten to vote them off the board, frighten them with the thought they may lose their directors' fees – ' He smiled at me sourly. 'It's human nature, I suppose. But I'll be glad to get back to a world I know, to people I understand.'

As a result, the board meeting that afternoon was a mere formality. Henry expressed his satisfaction that, after a closer examination of what he called 'our Indian Ocean venture,' his brother had decided to give it the full backing of Strode Orient's resources. Nobody was fooled, but it sounded good, and there was more in a like vein from the other directors and from George Strode himself. It was only at the end that the true purpose of the meeting was revealed when Henry Strode suggested, almost diffidently, that as Peter would be away he might like to sign a proxy in favour of one of his co-directors so that they would have the support of his votes at the annual general meeting.

'They weren't taking any chances,' Peter said. 'They wanted it signed then and there. But I was damned if I'd give my votes to Henry.' He had made the proxy out in favour of Whimbrill.

We celebrated expensively that night, dining at L'Ecû de France with Ida and the girl she was staying with. For them it can't have been a very gay evening, for Peter spent most of the time discussing stores and equipment, the basic essentials he needed to get the stuff out to the ship. Later he hoped to establish a proper loading quay and blast a deep water channel into it, but at present the nearest he could get the ship was about two cables off. That meant barges, all the paraphernalia of beach loading. And he'd want mechanical diggers, loaders, transporters, a portable drilling rig, huts for the men ashore, an electric generator, refrigerator, cooking stove, fuel, food, stores. The list was almost endless. If the girls were bored by it all, they didn't show it. Peter's enthusiasm, his single-purposed concentration was infectious.

Next morning George Strode rang me on the house phone. I was to put myself entirely at Peter's disposal, give him all the help I could. 'And we're throwing a little party for him tonight at the Dorchester. I'd like you to be there.'

The object of the party was a public demonstration of family solidarity. When Ida and I arrived there must have been at least two hundred people in the room – ship-owners, bankers, financiers, stockbrokers, a sort of cross-section of the City and their wives, together with a sprinkling of journalists, mainly from the City offices. Henry Strode was acting as host, taking Peter round, introducing him to everybody. Then about eight o'clock he thumped on a table for silence and made a little speech welcoming him to the board. It was the usual thing – a couple of funny stories, a few platitudes and then champagne glasses raised, his health toasted.

Somebody called out 'Speech' and the next moment Peter had leapt on to a table. 'Ladies and Gentlemen – Strode Orient have allocated me a ship and the necessary finance and I am leaving in a few days' time for an unknown destination. This is a new venture, the sort of venture my father would have revelled in. I want you to drink to its success.' He raised his glass, standing there, high above that crowd of sober, calculating men, his dark faun face flushed, his eyes glinting in the light from the chandeliers.

There was a moment of stunned silence. Then a murmur that rose to a roar as, having drunk the toast, they began to speculate.

'The idiot!' Ida said. And I watched as the journalists closed in on him.

'Commander Bailey.' Slattery was at my elbow. He had a square, paunchy, rather truculent-looking man with him. 'This is Mr Lingrose.' Bright, bird-like eyes, sharp as a magpie's, stared at me out of a Jewish face that had the high colouring of blood pressure. But it was Slattery who said, 'What is this venture?'

I didn't answer him and there was an awkward silence. Finally Lingrose said, 'Never mind. It's not important. What I wanted to say to you was this. Young men full of fire and vision make uneasy bedfellows.' He smiled, thin-lipped. 'What happens when the honeymoon is over, eh?' The smile was gone, the thin lips hard, and deep, downward lines at the corners of the mouth. 'He's a fool.'

'He believes in what he's doing,' I said.

His dark brows lifted slightly. 'I see. Then you're a fool, too, if you think faith alone suffices in this wicked world. You should have persuaded him to sell.'

'Why?'

He looked at me hard. 'Because I was prepared to pay you for your good offices then. Now it's only a matter of waiting.' And he jerked his head at his minion and waddled off to join another group.

'I couldn't help it,' Peter said afterwards. 'That unimaginative tiresome little speech Henry made and all those smug bastards thinking I was being elected to the board because I was a member of the family and owned a lot of shares – a mere cipher. Besides,' he added, 'if you're going to try and rebuild something it's no good keeping quiet about it.'

STRODE STRIDES OUT: That was the flashy headline in the City page of one popular paper. His secretiveness, his personality, above all his background, had just that touch of the unexpected that appealed to all papers, even the staidest. 'This brilliant young expert on Far Eastern trade . . . much needed dynamism in the direction of the company's affairs . . . may herald a new era of prosperity for the long-suffering owners of Strode shares . . . a true son of his father, the man who built Strode's.'

There was more of it in other papers, all in a similar vein, and all of them mentioned that he'd worked for Guthrie's. 'Did you tell them that?' I asked him.

'No.'

It could only have come from Slattery then. And there were other items – in particular a reference to his refusal to sell his shares. I was thinking of Lingrose and what he had said about it being only a matter of waiting. Were they trying to give him enough rope to hang himself?

But Peter was oblivious of manœuvrings of this sort. He was interested only in one thing – getting the expedition under way.

Two days later he left for Bombay. I was to follow him as soon as I had dealt with all those organizational details that could only be handled in London, including the contract for sale of the first cargo of ore. There was also the question of who should command the *Strode Trader*, the captain having been invalided home with jaundice. Peter had had a letter from Deacon and this he handed to me at the airport. 'Do what you can for the poor devil. I'd as soon have him as somebody I don't know. But at least try and get George to reinstate him.'

It was a pathetic letter. Aden is a refinery terminal for tankers mainly and no place for a man of Deacon's age to pick up a ship. Since his dismissal he had been virtually destitute. I saw George Strode about it next day. He showed not the slightest interest. 'He has only himself to blame.' There was no glimmer of sympathy in his voice. And when I reminded him that Deacon had served Strode Orient for almost thirty years, he said, 'You mean we've put up with him for thirty years. He came to us as part of the Bailey Oriental deal – a legacy we could well have done without. The man's a drunkard and you know it.' There was something in his tone, a suggestion of vindictiveness, as though in Deacon he saw a means of getting at me personally, for he knew by then that Bailey Oriental had been my father's company.

'When Deacon came to Strode Orient,' I said, 'he was second-in-command of the *Lammermuir*, a brilliant young officer with a fine career ahead of him.' Before the interview I had checked his records from the files in Phillipson's office. 'He didn't start drinking until 1953 when his ship was in collision with a tanker in the English Channel.'

It had still been the same ship, the *Lammermuir*, renamed the *Strode Venturer*. She had been feeling her way through thick fog for three days. She had no radar and all that time Deacon had been on the bridge. He had finally handed over to his second officer a bare two hours before the collision. 'I don't think you've any idea how he must have felt. The tanker burst into flames and he had to watch, helpless, because his steering gear was out of action, whilst twenty-two men died a horrible death in a sea of blazing oil.'

'He was exonerated at the Court of Inquiry.'

'I've read the evidence of that Inquiry.'

His head jerked up. 'What am I to infer from that?'

He knew damned well. Strode Orient had made no attempt to support their captain. Quite the reverse, in fact; their counsel had gone out of his way to shift the blame on to the officers and so avoid condemnation of the company for its failure to install radar equipment. He had partly succeeded for the second officer had had his ticket suspended for a year and though Deacon was exonerated from any direct responsibility, he had been censured for not ensuring that his relief had definite instructions to proceed with due caution. This followed his admission under cross-examination that he'd been under great pressure to make good lost time due to an engine failure in the Bay of Biscay, an implication which the company's counsel had flatly denied.

'All I'm saying,' I told him, 'is that I think Deacon deserves better of the company than to be left to rot on the beach at Aden.'

'You do, do you?' He gazed at me, silent – a blank wall of indifference. And when I suggested his re-engagement as master of the *Strode Trader*, all he said was, 'The appointment of ship's officers is a matter for the Marine Superintendent. I think you will find that that particular vacancy has already been filled.' I left his office feeling that all the Strodes, Peter included, had in them a streak of their father's ruthlessness.

The man Phillipson had chosen to command the *Strode Trader* was Reece, first officer of the *Strode Wayfarer* now in the Clyde for refit. He was twenty-nine and had held his master's certificate for barely two years. I thought it an odd choice for what might prove to be a tricky operation.

'He's a very good man,' Phillipson said, nodding his head decisively. 'Very keen. We'll not be having any trouble with him in command.' What he meant was that as a young man promoted to his first command Reece would be very amenable to orders from head office – particularly from the company's chairman. In the circumstances, and from George Strode's point of view, it was not unreasonable, and though I would have preferred a more experienced captain I didn't press the matter. Anyway, it wouldn't have been any use. Phillipson was one of the old guard at Strode House, a Scot with his pension to consider. I had some difficulty even in persuading him to let me have sight of Reece's personal file.

He had been born David Llewellyn Reece at Swansea in 1934. His father had been killed in the St Nazaire raid in 1942, his mother had died in London two years later when the clothing factory in which she worked had been bombed. He had been brought up by his eldest sister and had gone to sea at the age of fourteen, sailing out of London in coasters. In 1949 he had been arrested for smuggling. The two men charged with him had been given prison sentences. He had been bound over for two years. He had joined Strode Orient in 1952 and had been involved in a curious incident the following year when his ship had been boarded whilst anchored off the Java coast. There was a cutting from a Singapore newspaper showing an attractive, fair-haired youth standing at the head of a gangway with a drawn cutlass. It was captioned: *Strode Apprentice Routs Pirates*. He had become third officer on the *Strode Glory* in 1957, promoted second officer in 1958 and two years later had been transferred to the *Wayfarer* as first officer. On the basis of that rather unusual record I thought he was probably as good a choice as any for the task in hand. He obviously had drive and energy, and the indications of lawlessness were not unexpected in view of his background.

Perhaps if I hadn't been so pressed I would have probed his background further. At least I should have insisted on inter-viewing him when he passed through London on his way out to Bombay, for it was undoubtedly Reece I saw by chance in the pub I frequented near Leadenhall Market. I had gone in for a quick beer and a sandwich lunch and in the mirror behind the bar I caught a glimpse of Phillipson standing with his face buried in a tankard and beside him a broad-shouldered, well-built man with a pleasant open face and fair crinkly hair. Though he was older now, his face still had the attractive boyish look of the young man with the cutlass in that newspaper cutting. I was being served at the time and when I turned round they were gone. I rang Phillip-son as soon as I got back to the office and he not only denied having seen Reece, but said he hadn't visited the pub at all that day. It was a lie and such a silly one that it magnified the whole episode so that it stuck in my mind.

But whatever instructions Reece had been given privately I didn't see that it could have any bearing on the success or other-wise of the expedition. In any case, I was faced with many other, and more pressing, problems. In particular, the location of the necessary equipment. The loading of it and the engagement of mechanics, drivers and labourers was Peter's responsibility and he had the help of Strode Orient's Bombay agent. But things like bull-dozers, crawler trucks, conveyor belts, all the machinery for shifting ore, could only be found by spending hours on the tele-phone ringing companies who had interests in India, for there was no time to ship the stuff out there. It had to be on the spot, and available. In this way I managed to lay my hands on two war surplus infantry landing craft and an old coaling barge for the transport of ore from shore to ship, and one brand-new piece of American equipment, a tumble-bug. But the stuff was hard to find and it took time.

Ida had stayed on in London and this made a great difference to me. She had Peter's ability to become involved in an idea to the exclusion of everything else and this did much to offset the very apparent lack of enthusiasm for the project at Strode House. She had his vitality, too, his essential feeling of the excitement of life, and also a certain feminine acquisitiveness that made it fun each time I managed to lay my hands on a fresh piece of equipment. I had never had this sort of companionship from a woman before. It was an exhilarating experience and I only realized very gradually that I was becoming emotionally involved.

Meantime, Whimbrill was dealing with the matter of contracts for the sale of the ore. The Tyneside firm that had taken the first small consignment had done it more or less as a favour – they had been associated with old Henry Strode and Peter had been at school with the son who now ran the business. Long-term contracts covered their requirements and this applied to most British companies. In the end Whimbrill had to turn to the European market which had no Commonwealth ties and he finally negotiated a contract through Dutch agents for monthly deliveries in Rotterdam starting 1 August. As it involved a penalty clause I telephoned Peter about it and at the end of our conversation I asked how Reece was making out. The line to Bombay was very clear and there was no mistaking his slight hesitation. 'Fine,' he said. 'Without his drive we wouldn't be anywhere near as ready as we are.'

'What's the trouble, then?'

'Nothing. I don't know. Maybe it's the heat. He's so damned efficient.' That was all he would say, except that the way things were going he thought we could leave within the week. It was time I went out.

I told Ida that evening and had some difficulty in convincing her that an old freighter bound for a volcanic island in the Indian Ocean was no place for a woman. By then she had fallen into the habit of waiting for me at my flat. We'd have a drink there, talk over the day's progress and then go out for dinner. But sometimes she'd have a meal prepared and we'd spend the evening in the flat. We were so involved in the venture that we were more like business partners than two people in the process of falling in love. We didn't talk about it. We'd been through it all before, both of us, and I think we were a little suspicious of our feeling for each other, even a little guilty about our need for physical contact.

That day she had been down to Redhill, to the nursing home. She had been down several times to see the old man. 'He was very low,' she said. 'I don't think he can last much longer.' And she added, 'Has the transfer of those shares gone through yet? He's very worried that he'll die before they're registered in your name.'

'No,' I said. 'I haven't heard anything further.' It was nearly a fortnight since I had received a letter from West, Wright, Turner & Coy. *My partner*, West had written, *has instructed me to make arrangements for the immediate transfer of the 67,215 Strode & Coy. Ordinary £1 shares he had already bequeathed to you in his Will. He gave me to understand when I saw him this morning that he thought you might need them sooner than he had originally anticipated.*

The shares were, in fact, registered in my name two days later. This brought Whimbrill into it as secretary of the company and he called me down to his office. 'I knew, of course, that Lawrence Turner had been a persistent buyer during the last year and more. Latterly, as you know, I have been watching the situation very closely and I was becoming increasingly concerned about the future of these shares.' His hand had gone up to the left side of his face. 'It's a big block and faced with the necessity of providing for death duties his executors might well have decided to sell. I am relieved to know that he has taken this step and placed them beyond his executors' reach.' He lit a cigarette and passed me the packet. 'I take it you do not intend to sell?'

'No.'

He nodded, sitting hunched in his chair, jotting figures on a slip of paper. 'You realize that you are now one of the biggest shareholders in the company?' The point of his silver pencil moved quickly as he added up three separate columns. 'It will be tight, very tight – but the public still holds some. And there's Mrs de Witt. I think she might support us.' He dropped the pencil and sat back. 'Lingrose hasn't withdrawn his nominations and the meeting is next month. You won't be back by then.'

'It's the equipment,' I said. 'It's taken a little longer than we thought.'

He nodded. 'When do you leave?'

'The day after tomorrow.'

'You know Peter signed a proxy in my favour. Would you be willing to do the same?' He was worried about something. But when I asked him what it was he seemed reluctant to put it into words. 'It's just a feeling I have – no more. It's all been too easy and as an accountant I am by nature a pessimist.' He sat silent for a moment, frowning. Finally he said, 'Lingrose is a dangerous man to fool around with. Peter used him as a lever to get what he wanted, and when he got it he dropped him flat. And there's

933

George to consider. George didn't like it, and neither did Henry. And if this expedition of yours were a success . . .' He leaned forward and flicked the ash from his cigarette. 'They know where they are with Lingrose. But Peter's different. He's not interested in money. He's doing this for quite other reasons. That makes him unpredictable. They don't understand him or the motives that are driving him.'

I wondered whether Whimbrill did. 'What are you suggesting?'

He looked away to the far corner of the room, sightless, his whole mind, all his senses concentrated on his thoughts. 'I think the two parties will finally come together and reach agreement. Lingrose will probably make the first move. In fact, if my information is correct he has already done so. The nature of his proposition might well be the liquidation of both companies and the formation of an investment company or trust based on Strode House with some of the same directors.'

'Would you support that?' I asked.

'No.' He gave me a tired little smile. 'I doubt whether I should be given the opportunity. I think I'd be left out in the cold, and so would a lot of others – ships' officers, superintendents, clerks, men who have given most of their lives to one or other of the two companies.' He pulled open a drawer and took out a proxy form already made out in my name. 'I don't think they'll try to push anything through at the annual general meeting, but I'm doing what I can to counter it, just in case.'

I signed the proxy and left him with the uneasy feeling that things were moving to some sort of climax. It was less than three months since I had first set foot in Strode House. Now I owned the third largest block of shares in the parent company. I went out, past the portrait of my father, out into the sunshine and walked up Leadenhall Street, past Lloyds to the pub in the Market where I had seen Reece. It was almost the last day of May and a heat wave. The doors were blocked open. I ordered a beer and stood drinking it in a shaft of sunlight, feeling warm and slightly dazed, thinking of the children – that perhaps after all I'd be able to match the measure of their expectations, thinking, too, of the Maldives and the new world into which I would be flying in two days' time.

That evening, as though she had known I wouldn't want to go out, Ida had cooked some salmon and made a mayonnaise and there was a bottle of Pouilly Fumé to go with it. And afterwards we sat by the open windows watching the lights go on and the sky darken and talking, not about ourselves, but about Strode House and how our lives were being shaped by events beyond our control. The women I had met before had none of them been interested in finance, nor the men either, for City intrigue and the intricacies of financial battles are not spotlighted in headlines the way political struggles are. They are for the most part fought out in secret behind closed doors and so are unfamiliar to the majority of people. But Ida was interested. She had been brought up with it and she understood very well that they were about the same thing – Power. 'If Dick Whimbrill is right – ' The pucker of a frown showed below the black line of her hair. 'I don't like the idea of your both being away for the annual general meeting.'

'Whimbrill holds our proxies.'

'That's what's worrying me. I don't know him very well, but he doesn't strike me as a very forceful man.'

'He believes his own future is at stake.'

But I could see she wasn't sure of him. 'That's not quite the same thing, is it? And if they made him an offer – ' She hesitated. 'He's an accountant, you see. They have a different way of looking at things.'

'Well, there's nothing we can do about it now,' I said.

'No.' She nodded reluctantly. 'He's a strange man. He doesn't seem to have anything to live for outside Strode House. That makes him very vulnerable. But you're probably right. If they liquidate both companies, then they destroy him, and that's something that puts fight into the mildest of men.' She was silent for a moment, and then she said, 'All this wouldn't have happened if there'd been anybody at Strode House to succeed Father – a man with real drive. When he died the guts went out of the organization. It had been slipping for some time and it needed somebody with a fresh outlook, new horizons.' Her hand was in mine and the night was warm, the sound of London's traffic a muffled roar. 'I often wonder what would have happened if I had married Hans de Witt,' she murmured. And she went on to talk about the obligations of members of the family in a family business. 'I didn't understand this at the time. I was only a kid.'

I asked her who Hans de Witt was and she said, 'The son of a Dutch shipowner.' She was smiling gently and her fingers tightened on mine. 'It's a long time ago now. He was much older than I was, but Father was interested in a merger. He was looking to the future and he threw Hans at me. But I was having my first love affair and Jennifer grabbed him before I had recovered my senses.' Her voice betrayed an enviousness she didn't bother to conceal. 'Jennifer is a great big woman; she's quite content to be a Dutch hausfrau.'

'So the merger never went through.'

'Oh, it wasn't Jennifer's fault. Not then. Hans inherited from his father just after the war when the de Witt cargo line was crippled by Holland's loss of the Dutch East Indies. He switched to passenger carrying, running emigrants to North America. He's very successful now and if I'd married him . . .' She looked at me, smiling. 'Well, I didn't, and that's that. But I wanted you to know why I feel as I do. As a member of the family I had an obligation and I failed to see it as such. Father was right, of course. Hans has the nerve, the drive, the energy, all the things that Henry and George lack. He'd have made a big company of it – a rival to P & O perhaps.' She sighed. 'I've been paying for my selfishness ever since. And now if Peter fails – '

She was silent then and when I glanced at her I saw that her eyes were closed. The glow of the lights picked out the bone formation of her face, glimmered on her raven black hair. It was a strong face and her small body tight-packed with energy so that I felt myself in the grip of something stronger than myself. 'Never mind,' she said softly. 'Don't let my conscience spoil our last evening.' I knew then that her need was as great as mine. I lit a cigarette and my hand was trembling for there is a luminosity about London at that time of the year, the promise of full summer just ahead, and tomorrow I was seeing the children. The feeling of longing had become an ache deep down in the life-stream of my blood. Her hand slipped from mine and without a word she got to her feet and went into the bedroom, the rustle of her dress a silken sound in the quiet stillness of the room.

And later as I lay beside her in the dark, relaxed and smoking a cigarette, listening to the sounds of a great city falling silent into slumber, I found myself thinking over the things she had said to me that evening. Never having had money I had not given a thought to its obligations. She had not only made me realize that a company, like a ship, is only as big as the men who run it, but also that the direction of it must have an impulse greater than money. A fresh outlook, new horizons, she had said – it was this I had been groping towards when I had stood staring at the Palace of Westminster on my first day back in London. This was the malaise that had spread through all sections of the country and the thought bolstered my determination to back Peter with everything that was in me. To build something for the future, that was it, and my thoughts turned to the great days of our mercantile expansion, to the East India Company and men like Alexander Guthrie who had opened up new territory with nothing but their wits and determination to sustain them. I was thinking of an island in the Indian Ocean and dreaming dreams and falling gently into sleep.

PART FOUR

I

THE ISLAND

'STEER ONE-TWO-ZERO.' Reece's voice was sharp, almost staccato, and he stared straight ahead at the flat, calm, oily sea that reflected a blinding dazzle of light. White shirt, white shorts, white stockings and shoes, his head bare and the crinkly fair hair bleached almost white by the sun – he looked cool and immaculate, very slim, very good-looking, with a certain air about him, not cocky quite, but ambitious – certainly ambitious. And that puzzled me, for an ambitious man you would have thought would be at pains to cultivate a member of the family who was not only the mainspring of the whole venture but also a man about his own age who could be expected to be a power in the company when older directors had retured.

The wheel moved under the lascar helmsman's hands and the *Strode Trader* swung slowly on to her new course. It was a twenty-degree turn, but apart from the compass there was nothing to show that the ship's head had altered, for there was nothing anywhere but the eye-searing blink of flat water, an empty heat-hazed void with sea and sky all one great refraction of light and no horizon.

'That do you?'

'Yes.'

Peter was standing behind the helmsman wearing a sarong and nothing else, his bare chest smooth and brown. The lascar wore khaki shirt and shorts. The time was 1420 hours and the heat in the wheelhouse intense, no air stirring except that made by our passage through the water – a hot, humid current of air coming in through the open doors to the bridge wings. This was the third change of course in twenty-four hours, each course dictated by Peter and given by Reece himself direct to the helmsman. And each time he had given it standing in front of the empty mahogany expanse of the wheelhouse chart table. Chart 748b – the one that covered the northern half of the Indian Ocean – was locked away in Peter's cabin, as were the ship's three sextants, the chronometer and the navigation tables. He had commandeered them late at night on the second day out from Bombay. Since then he had twice insisted on steering the ship himself, shut up alone in the wheelhouse with nobody else present. Reece had objected, of course, but had finally agreed after an exchange of wireless messages with head office. Now after six days at sea nobody but Peter knew within a hundred miles where we were.

'Have you worked out an ETA?' Reece was still staring straight in front of him. His voice was tense.

'Not yet.'

'When can I have it?' He turned suddenly. 'I'm not sailing my ship blind into an uncharted area. Not for you or anybody else. All this secrecy – it's bloody stupid, man.' He was on edge and I thought a little scared. It was only when you saw him full face that you noticed the little pouches under his eyes, the suggestion of dissipation, of a flaw in the boyish good looks.

'I'll let you have it tomorrow,' Peter said.

Reece hesitated. He wanted it now. But he wasn't prepared to make an issue of it. 'Tomorrow by sundown then. Otherwise I stop engines. You're not a qualified navigator and steaming through the night – '

'Experience is more important than qualifications,' Peter said quietly. 'I've navigated boats all over the South Pacific, in and out of more islands than you've ever set eyes on. And I've more at stake than just this ship, so you needn't be afraid I'll put her aground.'

An awkward silence followed, the only sounds the hum of the engines, the surge of the bow wave. Finally Reece said, 'To-morrow then,' and he walked past us, back to his cabin.

'He's getting scared,' I said. 'Sailing blind like this – '

'He's not as ignorant of our position as he pretends.'

He was referring to the fact that the wireless operator had picked up Gan aircraft beacon on his DF. 'That was two nights ago,' I said.

'It gave him a position line.' His voice was irritable. He, too, was on edge, the heat and humidity eating into his last reserves. His face had a closed, tight-set look. It was like the face of a man in a trance, the eyes staring, seeing nothing, only what was in the mind, and the body taut.

'What's the point of all this secrecy?' I asked. It seemed to have become an obsession with him and the heat was affecting me, too. 'If you'd just let Reece navigate his own ship – '

'You've met them, you've talked to them, been in their houses, seen those vedis.' He had turned on me with quite extraordinary violence. 'Surely to God you understand? That island belongs to

939

Don Mansoor, to the Adduans. It's their one hope of survival in the twentieth century that's now broken in upon them and I'll do anything, anything at all, to keep its position a secret until they have established a settlement on it and claimed it for their own.'

He drew me out on to the wing of the bridge where the surge of the water creaming past was louder, the breeze of our passage hot on my face. 'One more day,' he said. 'That's all, thank God. I'll get star sights tomorrow night and we'll close the island at dawn.'

'Then why didn't you tell Reece that?'

'I don't know.' He shrugged peevishly. 'I suppose because I don't trust him. He's George's man.' He stared at me hard with his eyes narrowed against the sunlight so that he seemed to be considering whether he could trust even me. Then he turned and left, silently on bare feet.

I leaned on the rail, staring down into the water boiling along the ship's side. Probably he was right. Probably Reece was George Strode's man. But I could still see it from his point of view, newly appointed to command and responsible for the safety of his ship. This wasn't the *Strode Venturer* and the man himself was a very different proposition from Deacon; he ran a disciplined, efficient ship, with everything neat and ordered and as clean as paint and hard work could make it. And he was very conscious of his new position. To have his navigational instruments confiscated, his courses dictated, even his bridge commandeered, these were blows to his pride, for once we were at sea he had naturally looked upon Peter and myself as little more than supercargoes.

But the trouble went deeper than that, a question of temperament. They were entirely different in every way. I hadn't noticed it in Bombay, chiefly because I hardly ever saw them together, Peter having been entirely immersed in the problems of acquiring adequate stores and equipment in the face of the petty restrictions and prevarications of modern India, Reece in seeing to the re-fitting, storing and fuelling of the ship and personally supervising the loading of the heavy equipment, much of which had to be carried as deck cargo. It was only after we had sailed, when they were cooped up together within the small confines of the ship, that their temperaments had clashed.

'Did he tell you when we'd get there?' It was the second officer's watch and he was standing in the doorway behind me, the cigarette he'd just rolled hanging unlit from the corner of his mouth.

'Yes,' I said.

'In confidence like.' His leathery, sun-creased face cracked in a grin. 'Well, that's all right by me. Always did like surprises. But there's others that don't.'

Lennie Porter was a cockney. He could see the funny side of things even after six days of torrid heat. But as he said, there were others who couldn't, particularly the first officer, Blake, an elderly, grey-haired man with a sour face and a sour disposition made sourer by his bitterness at being passed over for promotion again.

'It won't be long now,' I said.

'I should hope not. All these changes of course – you'd think Mr Strode was trying to teach the old girl the twist.' He winked at me and little creases of laughter crinkled the corners of his eyes. 'Another flipping week of this an' we'd be slitting each other's throats to pass the time as you might say.' He turned his head. 'Ah – re-freshment. What should we do without you, Gunga Din?' There was the welcome clink of ice and the steward appeared with a tray of lemonade.

I took mine to my cabin and lay on my bunk, stripped and wishing I were back in London, anywhere but in the Indian Ocean. It was the monotony of it I found exhausting. The first few days hadn't been so bad. The conveyor belt and the bulldozer had kept me occupied. They had been lying unused for a long time and the Pakistani mechanics had to be drilled in their operation and maintenance. We had spent two sweltering, exhausting days stripping the conveyor belt right down with the help of the ship's engineers. Now both machines were running, the engines of the two landing craft lashed on the after hatches had been checked and the small launch on the poop, which had had a hole knocked in its bottom, had been repaired. I had even had the ship stopped so that I could get aboard the barge we were towing. It had shipped a lot of water in a bit of a blow we had had four days back and we had rigged a small mobile pump and got it cleared so that she was now riding high with less strain on the towing hawser. Now there was nothing else for me to do until we got ashore and I lay on my bunk, listening to the beat of the engines and trying to read a dog-eared paperback I had borrowed. But even that seemed too much of an effort. There was no fan in the cabin and the air was stifling. The sounds of the ship drifted soporifically in to me, the open porthole breathing the hot spice smell of curry in my face. Even the flies we'd brought with us from Bombay moved sluggishly. I dozed, thinking about the island, wondering what it would be like working close inshore to a slice of the sea bed only recently emerged.

That evening there was no sunset flaming in the west. The light just faded damply from the sodden air. One minute we were in a pale milky void, the next it was dark and all the steelwork suddenly wet to the touch. Yet the temperature seemed hardly to have dropped. The night was very oppressive.

Reece didn't appear at the evening meal. He had his curry served in the wheelhouse and all that evening he paced nervously up and down between the empty chart table and the port bridge wing, peering into the pitch black darkness as though he expected at any moment the island to rear up in front of the ship's bows. Once he sent for Peter. 'Was it like this before?' he asked him. 'When you came here with the *Venturer*?'

Peter went out on to the wing of the bridge and stood there sniffing the atmosphere. 'No,' he said. 'It was hot and humid, but not like this. There's a lot of electricity in the air tonight.'

'Well, I don't like it,' Reece said. 'There's no moon. We can't see a thing. It's like steaming through thick fog. What do you think, Mr Blake?'

It was the first officer's watch and he was standing by the chart table sucking at an empty pipe. His short grey hair seemed to stand out on his head like a wire brush. 'I think there's going to be a storm,' he said.

'Storms are very rare in this area.' There was a note of exasperation in Peter's voice. 'If you check the meteorological charts – '

'To hell with the Met charts. They don't mean a damn' thing out here.'

Reece nodded. 'Blake's right. They're generalizations. They're not specific to this area. They can't be. Hardly anybody has ever been here.' The Welsh intonation was suddenly very marked. 'I think we should heave-to till dawn.'

Peter stared at him. 'Whatever for? You've empty sea for miles ahead of you.'

'How do you know? You've found one new island. There may be others.'

Peter shrugged. 'If you're worried, why don't you put a lookout in the bows and keep the echo-sounder going through the night?' He crossed to the wall behind the helmsman and switched the instrument on, standing in front of it, watching as the trace arm clicked back and forth like a metronome. 'Nothing,' he said. 'Too deep. You're in more than two thousand fathoms here and you'll be in that depth all night and all tomorrow too.' He was looking straight at Reece. 'You'd be recording bottom all right if the sea bed were coming up to meet you.' And with that he turned on his heel and left the wheelhouse.

Reece watched him go and then abruptly turned and stared ahead through the glass of the wheelhouse window. The foremast steaming light cast a faint glow as far as the bows, a ghostly radiance that was a refraction of light from millions of droplets of water as the ship thrust its blunt nose into the hot blanket of humidity that covered the sea. In that strange light the *Strode Trader* looked much bigger than her 6000 tons. She had been built during the Second World War to the old three-island design, but the changes of deck level were hidden by the equipment she was carrying and this enhanced the effect of size. Immediately below the bridge the tumble-bug was a bright splash of yellow in the dark. This was an American-type scraper truck with floor doors for dumping its load and it had been lashed athwartships across No. 2 hatch cover. For'ard of that the ungainly bulk of the conveyor belt sprawled over No. 1 hatch flanked by the bulldozer on one side and the big crawler tractor on the other. Right as far as the bows the whole fore part of the ship looked like a cross between a scrap yard and a war surplus stores.

'Very well, Mr Blake. A look-out in the bows and keep your eye on the echo-sounder. I'll take over from you at the change of watch.' He walked past me then, his eyes avoiding mine. He didn't like it, but with the older man there he hadn't quite the self-confidence to order the engines stopped and the ship hove-to.

I stayed with Blake for a time, not because I enjoyed his company, but it was cooler on the bridge than in my cabin. It was shortly after eleven when I turned in. I couldn't sleep for a while. The air in the cabin was stifling and there was a queer singing in my ears. My head ached, too. I put it down to the atmosphere, which seemed to press down on me. The sweat on my naked body tingled. I must have dropped off into a deep sleep, for I woke suddenly with a start to the certainty that something was wrong. I couldn't place it at first, but then I became conscious of the silence and realized the engines were stopped.

I jumped out of bed, pulled on my shorts and padded down the alleyway and up the ladder to the wheelhouse. Peter was just ahead of me. 'What is it?' I heard him ask anxiously. 'What's happened?' And then Reece's voice: 'Breakers ahead. The look-out spotted them.'

'Breakers? How can there be breakers?'

The ship was steady as a rock, the sea flat calm.

They were out on the starboard bridge wing, their figures two black silhouettes against the peculiar luminosity. 'There, man. There. Do you see them? Straight over the bows.' Reece's voice was pitched high on a note of tension as he turned and called to the helmsman, 'Slow astern.' The engine-room telegraph rang and the bridge wing juddered as the shaft turned and the screw threshed the water. There was no other sound; no sound of breakers, and yet there they were, straight over the bows, a long line of white water that made my eyeballs blink with the strain of watching the waves bursting against – what? Against coral reefs? Against some laval heap that had suddenly reared itself up?

'Full astern. Starboard helm. Hard over, man.' The ring of the telegraph, the wheel turning, and then the bows began to swing. 'Christ!' It was Lennie Porter breathing down my neck. 'She's being sucked in.' The ship was broadside now to the white-fanged line of the breakers and they were much nearer, a leaping, plunging cataract of surf.

It was Blake who said quietly – 'The white water.'

'What's that? What did you say?' Reece was shouting, though there wasn't another sound in the wheelhouse.

'Christ!' Lennie said again and there was a pain in my head and behind my eyeballs as the white line of the breakers engulfed us.

They caught us broadside, great waves of broken water, great combers bursting on all sides, their tops high as the mast and all shot with blinding streaks of light. And not a sound. No hiss of surf, no growl of combers spilling, no crash of breakers thundering aboard, and the ship steady as a rock.

'He is saying' – Peter's voice was startlingly clear considering that the sea all round us appeared to be violently agitated and boiling like a cauldron ' – that this is the white water.'

'What are you saying? What is it, man?' Reece's face looked ghastly white in the frightful luminosity. Everybody in the wheelhouse had a deathly pallor and his voice, sunk to a whisper, was still clearly audible, for the only sound was the hum of the engines and the click-click-click of the echo-sounder.

'An optical illusion,' Peter said. 'I've never seen it, but I've heard about it.'

'I saw it once,' Blake said. 'Off the Konkan coast. Let me see – it was wartime – '44 I think. We ploughed straight into a line of breakers. The Old Man knew what he was about. He knew there weren't any reefs ahead of him, and as we ploughed into it there was a sort of white mist across the bows and then it was gone and all we saw after that was streaks of light and a lot of phosphorescence.' He asked permission then to turn back on to course and Reece gave it to him in a strained voice. 'You'll find it in the Pilot,' Blake said as he gave the necessary orders. 'There's quite a bit about it in the West Coast of India volume under "Luminosity of the Sea", including an eye-witness report by the master of a merchant ship.'

We were back on course and coming up to our usual eight knots and still the night was stabbed with lines of light and the sea boiled, the waves all moving with the light so that the effect was hypnotic and painful to the eyes. And then suddenly it was gone, the night clear, no humidity and the stars bright overhead.

Nobody said anything. We just stood there, too dazed, too mesmerized by what we had seen to speak. Lennie Porter was the first to find his voice. 'What was it? What the hell was it?'

But nobody could explain it. We looked it up in the Pilot. The master of the *Ariosto* had seen very much what we had seen, but off the coast of Kutch in India more than fifty years ago. In his case the phenomenon had lasted twenty minutes with the appearance of very high seas. He had described them as so agitated that they appeared 'like a boiling pot, giving one a most curious feeling – the ship being perfectly still, and expecting her to lurch and roll every instant.' And his report added, 'It turned me dizzy watching the moving flashes of light, so that I had to close my eyes from time to time.' On leaving it the line of light had presented the same appearance as on entering, as of breakers on a low beach, and after steaming through a bright, clear cloudless night for a further twenty minutes, the whole thing had been repeated, but if anything slightly worse. The Pilot recorded two other instances, both reported by naval vessels – in 1928 and 1933. But it offered no explanation, merely observing that the phenomenon could occur in the open sea as well as near land and either in calm or stormy water and that it might be caused by 'the presence of confervæ or other organic matter in the water.'

Peter had heard about the 'white water' from Don Mansoor during his voyage from Mukalla to Addu Atoll. 'He told me he had seen it twice and each time his crew had been very frightened, thinking it was Ran-a-Maari.' Ran-a-Maari, he explained, was apparently some sort of a jinn or devil, and he added, 'The first man the Adduans recognize is Adam, the second Noah and the third Solomon, whom they call Suleiman. According to legend, Suleiman made a copper ball and confined Ran-a-Maari inside

it, but it wasn't big enough to encase the jinn's legs.' He smiled,
the lines at the corners of his eyes deepening. 'Suleiman threw the
copper ball with Ran-a-Maari inside it into the sea and it's their
belief that the white water is the threshing of the jinn's legs as he
struggles to release himself.'

A pleasant enough story to chuckle over beside a winter fire
back in England. But out there in the Indian Ocean, in seas that
were virtually uncharted, the superstitions of a primitive people
seemed less absurd. Whatever the cause of the white water, our
sighting of it had an unsettling effect on the ship's company. At
least half the crew had been up on deck and had seen it with their
own eyes, and for those who had remained in their bunks or been
on duty in the engine-room it was even more frightening since
they had it second-hand from their companions and it was much
exaggerated in the telling. And it wasn't only the lascar crew that
felt uneasy; the Europeans were affected, too, for it emphasized
the uncertainty of the venture, the fact that we were steaming into
a little-known area and only one man who knew where we were or
where we were going or what to expect when we got there. Uncertainty of that sort can play the devil with a group of men
cooped up in a ship and in the morning everybody was very quiet,
not sullen exactly, but shut in with their thoughts, and the feeling
of tension mounted as the sun rose and the heat increased.

As on the previous day we were steaming through an opaque
void, the sea flat calm, not even any swell, and the sun's heat
drawing moisture up from the surface of the water so that there
was no horizon, nothing ahead of us but a blinding haze. I
couldn't read. I couldn't think even and the solitude of my cabin
was oppressive. I spent most of the morning on the bridge, not
talking and my clothes sticking to my body. The second officer
had the watch and even Lennie was silent. Reece came in several
times, pacing up and down for a while and then returning to his
cabin. The little pouches under his eyes were more marked and I
could feel the nervous tension in him building up.

And then, just at the change of the watch, something happened
to bring things to a head. The sea ahead was suddenly different.
Strange patches appeared in the haze, as though the flat surface
of it had been paved here and there with cobblestones. Lennie had
just handed over to Reece. The course, changed again during the
night, was now 145° and Reece had just said something about the
chance of a breeze soon, the wireless operator having got a Met
forecast from Gan. His body stiffened suddenly as he peered
ahead, his eyes narrowed against the glare. I think we all saw it

946

at about the same time.

Nobody spoke. Nobody moved. The beat of the engines, the hiss of water as the bows ploughed into the sea's unending flatness, these were sounds that had been with us day and night for just on a week. Nothing had changed and yet suddenly the mood was different. We had sighted something. It came at us out of the haze, like huge plates at first, as though a painter's brush had tried to break the monotony of calm water by stippling it, the way Seurat painted shingle beaches. The effect was of a sea suddenly become diseased, the skin of it blotched with the grey of some fungus growth.

The engines were slowed and soon we were steaming slowly into great patches of pumice, and ahead of us the patches were closing up so that the whole surface of the sea was a solid grey sheet of the stuff. How we knew it was pumice I don't know. The look of it, I suppose, though none of us had seen the aftermath of a submarine eruption before. It was all sizes, from mere dust to what looked like rough pieces of rock the size of dinner plates. And it was many hued, from buff through orange and brick-red to grey and near-black, all light aerated stuff that floated like cork and danced in the bow wave.

The change in the engine beat had brought Peter to the wheelhouse and Reece faced him, demanding to know how far we were from the island, how much longer he was expected to drive his ship into an area that was demonstrably volcanic?

'We'll discuss it in your cabin,' Peter said.

The lunch gong was sounding as they disappeared and all through the meal the ship was held on her course at reduced speed. There was a lot of talk as we ate about the origins of pumice and the effects of shock waves. Evans, the wireless operator, had been in a Japanese port when it was swept by the shock wave of a distant earthquake and Robbins, the chief engineer, had once steamed through a sea of dead fish. But none of us knew very much about submarine disturbances. 'All I can say,' Lennie observed, 'is that I hope to Christ we're not anchored off this island when the whole flipping lot goes up.' As usual his words were the echo to our inner thoughts, for the pumice, coming so soon after our experience of the white water, had greatly increased the sense of uneasiness, and uneasiness in the face of the unknown can so easily lead to fear and even panic.

When I went up into the wheelhouse after lunch we were still steaming through a sea of pumice and the ship's speed was back again to normal. By then it was so thick it looked like loose pack-ice. We ran out of it about an hour later, but I was resting on my bunk then, for I thought there wouldn't be much sleep that night.

As the sun set and darkness closed in on us the nervous tension that had been building up in the ship all day seemed suddenly a physical thing, so strong you could almost smell it. During the afternoon several of the crew had been fishing with buckets and home-made nets and now there was hardly a soul on board who didn't have a piece of pumice to prove that he'd sailed through the debris of some underwater upheaval. And somehow they all seemed aware that we were within a few hours' steaming of our destination.

There was some cloud around at dusk, but it soon cleared and after that it was cooler for a light breeze came in from the west, darkening the sea. Between nine-thirty and ten Peter took a whole series of star sights. I handled the stop watch for him and jotted down the sextant readings as he called them to me. Afterwards he locked himself in his cabin to work them out and about eleven o'clock came back on to the bridge with Reece and course was altered to 012°.

That last course – the one that took us to within a few miles of the island – I do remember. It has stayed in my mind all these months. But the star sights, no. That would have meant remembering the stars he had selected, the sextant elevation for each shot and the stop-watch time at which it was taken. If I could have remembered all that, accurately, then things might have been different. I tried to when they asked me; that was when they were still desperately searching, before they gave up. But the names of stars and a string of figures and times – it isn't humanly possible to remember all that. I wasn't a navigator. I'd never piloted a ship in my life. As a TAS officer I hadn't been trained to absorb that sort of thing automatically.

A look-out was posted and speed reduced to six knots. 'How long on this course?' Reece asked.

'Until three o'clock, say, when you should be about ten miles south of the island.' And Peter added, 'I think we should stop engines then and wait for daylight to make the final run in.' He asked to be called at three.

Later he came to my cabin. By then he had been the rounds of the shore party, giving them a final briefing on their duties. There were sixteen of them, including the two Europeans and six Pakistani mechanics who had been engaged to drive and service the heavy equipment. The rest were labourers. 'You'll come in with me in the first boat.' He wanted me to act as a sort of beach master and for half an hour we went over all the stores and equipment. Everything that had to be got ashore was allocated a priority. We listed it all and when we had finished it was past midnight. 'You'd better get some sleep,' I said. Besides navigating, he had been working with three of the Pakistanis on the tumble-bug as well as helping our two European mechanics, Ford and Haines, to get the electric generator ready for use. And all the time he had kept an eye on the rest of the shore party, looking after their welfare and seeing that they were occupied so that inactivity didn't make them a prey to fear. He was quite extraordinarily good with men of a different race, but it had taken a lot out of him and now there were dark shadows round his eyes.

'You'll knock yourself up if you're not careful.'

He nodded. But he made no move to go. Instead he stayed talking until almost one o'clock. He wanted company, for the fear that the island might not be there any more was nagging at his mind. 'All that pumice around – something's been going on, some sort of submarine activity. Suppose it's disappeared? I'd look bloody stupid, wouldn't I? And the Adduans – God knows, they may have sailed by now. I got a message through to Don Mansoor.'

Dimly in the dark hours I was conscious of an unnatural stillness as the engines were stopped and we lay drifting. The ship slept then, quiet as the grave. But at first light it stirred, the padding of feet, the banging of doors, and as dawn broke it came to life with the beat of the engines throbbing at the deck. I dressed and went to the wheelhouse; a grey, milky light, the sun not yet risen, and the sea ruffled by a slight breeze. Reece was there, and Peter, all the watch-keeping officers – quite a crowd. And nothing visible, nothing at all. The steward brought coffee and we drank it, peering at that pale horizon, not speaking, each of us in that cold, half-empty state that is midway between the loneliness of sleep and the community of the day's beginning.

And then suddenly a voice from the port bridge wing – one of the lascar crew. 'Starboard bow, Captain Reece, sahib.' The dark face was suddenly animated as he pointed. 'Fine on starboard bow.' We all saw it then, a faint smudge as though the line of the horizon had been scored by the point of a black chinagraph pencil. 'Starboard a little.' Reece gave the order quietly and steadied the ship as the bows swung to that distant smudge, dipping slightly to the movement of the sea. He stepped back and glanced at the echo-sounder. 'When do you reckon we'll start picking up soundings?'

'About two miles off,' Peter answered. 'You should be recording 300 fathoms. After that it gradually shallows. A bit irregularly at times, but you should be able to anchor two cables off in ten fathoms.'

Reece didn't say anything. He was leaning against the door of the starboard bridge wing and he had the ship's binoculars pressed to his eyes. 'Land all right, and black – nothing growing at all.' He handed Peter the glasses. 'Bleak enough – like the back of a whale at this distance.'

Peter took a quick look at it through the glasses. 'Yes, that's it all right.' He said it flatly so that everyone in the wheelhouse should feel that this was a routine sighting, something about which there had never been the slightest doubt in his mind. But though his voice didn't betray him, his eyes and the quick spring of his movements did, his relief and his sense of satisfaction obvious to all as he crossed to the compass and took a bearing. A few quick pencil jottings on a piece of paper and then he requested an alteration of course to port. 'There's a shallow bay on the western side giving some shelter and reasonable holding. I'd like us to run in with the island bearing 034°. On that course it's all clear, no obstructions.'

Reece nodded and gave the order. The ship's head swung and settled to the new course with the dark smudge of the island now broad on the starboard bow. The sun's rim lipped the horizon, a shaft of bright light turning the sea to molten gold as the burnished disc rose, gathering strength, flooding our world with heat. And as though the sunrise had loosened their tongues everyone was suddenly talking, a flood of speculation, a barrage of questions flung at Peter's head, and in a moment he had taken the floor like an actor, all his sense of the dramatic pouring out of him as he described to us how they had come upon the island that first time in the *Strode Venturer* – at night, feeling their way in on the echo-sounder and seeing it suddenly in the moonlight. 'It really did look like a whale then, like the blue-black back of a monstrous cetacean.'

The call to breakfast came, but nobody moved. We stood there watching as gradually the bearing changed until at last it was 034° and we altered course and headed straight for the island. It was nearer now and every minute getting perceptibly larger. The night breeze had died, killed by the heat, and the sea was flat again so that the island seemed to be floating in the sky.

About two and a half miles off we found bottom in 328 fathoms and thereafter the soundings decreased fairly steadily. The bridge was silent now. Everyone except the helmsman had one eye on the echo-sounder as though mesmerized by the click-clicking of the trace arm, and gradually the recordings fell until we were in less than 100 fathoms.

'Stop engines.' The telegraph rang to Reece's command and the engines died under our feet, the ship continuing under her own momentum, silent except for the soft hiss of the water she displaced.

The island was then about a mile away, not floating in the sky any more, but like a black reef exposed by the tide. It had the naked ugliness of slag straight from the furnace, nothing growing and not a vestige of colour, only the texture varied, so that there were shades of black – the light grey of the dust drifts merging to darkest jet where drifts of exposed ore were like clinker and shadowed from the sun. The bottom was uneven now and the flat surface of the sea pocked with little whorls caused by the current.

'Engines half astern.'

Almost everyone except the engine-room staff was on deck now and the anchor watch was closed up with Blake standing in the bows waiting for the word to let go. 'And during the cruise we stop at the world's most beautiful, most exclusive beach . . .' Nobody laughed. Nobody even smiled at Lennie's attempt to relieve the tension. The lonely deadness of the place held us awed and a little dismayed.

'You'll need to get closer than this.'

Reece hesitated, glancing at the echo-sounder. It was now recording depths of less than fifty fathoms. 'No.' He shook his head. 'I'm not going any nearer.'

To my surprise Peter accepted this. He was standing very still, his head thrust forward, peering through one of the open windows of the wheelhouse at the long black shore of the island. His face was pale under the tan, his eyes almost luminous with fatigue. Again I was conscious of a trance-like quality, a mood of tension, his body taut. 'What's wrong?' I asked.

'Nothing,' he snapped and reached for the glasses.

The way was off the ship now and Reece came back into the wheelhouse and ordered the engines stopped. 'I thought you said there were depths of ten fathoms within two cables of the shore.'

Peter didn't answer. He didn't turn or shift his position. His whole attention was concentrated on the island. But even without glasses we could all see that there were shallows extending at least a quarter of a mile from the shore. It showed in the colour of the sea, for the water was very clear, and here and there a shoal awash pushed its black gritty back above the surface.

Reece stood for a moment undecided. Then he picked up the bow telephone and gave the order to let go the anchor. It fell with a splash into the still water and the cable rattled out, a plume of red dust rising from the rusty hawse-hole. Lennie reached for the telegraph and at a nod from Reece rang down 'finished with engines'. We had arrived.

But nobody looked happy about it, not even Peter. He was still standing there at the open window, the binoculars pressed to his eyes. The intensity with which he was examining the island increased my feeling of uneasiness, for this wasn't an island three miles by two; it stretched a good six miles north and south and the sea at either end was bright green, indicating extensive shallows.

'You're sure this is the same island?' Reece's question expressed the doubt in all our minds. If one island had emerged from the depths, there could be others.

'Quite sure.'

'But it's changed.'

'Yes, it's changed.' Peter put the glasses down and swung away from the window, facing Reece, his voice harsh: 'What the hell did you expect after yesterday? It's larger, that's all. There's more of it. You should be pleased,' he almost snarled. 'You'll get a bigger ship, bigger cargoes.' They faced each other across the wheelhouse, the atmosphere electric, the rift between them wide open. 'If you don't like it – if you're scared . . .' But he stopped himself in time and suddenly he was smiling, all the tension wiped from his face. It was a conscious, controlled relaxation of every muscle of his body. 'Let's go and have breakfast. We're at anchor and there's nothing to worry about.'

It was sausages and bacon and fried onions, not the most suitable meal for a blistering morning on the equator, but I remember I had two helpings and so did most of the others. We were all damned hungry. I must have had four or five cups of coffee, all of us sitting there smoking, as though by lingering in the familiar surroundings of the saloon we could obliterate the island from our minds. I think perhaps we succeeded for those few minutes, but as soon as we went on deck there it lay, black and sinister-looking against the sun's glare, separated from us by no more than a mile of flat calm shoaling water.

Work had already started. The cargo booms were being rigged, the barge alongside and the lashings being cleared from the deck cargo. The little runabout we had stowed on the after end of the boat deck was manhandled to davits and lowered into the water.

The winches clattered, the first of the landing craft was lifted clear of No. 4 hatch and swung over the side. The ship seethed with activity and a message was wirelessed to Gan for onward transmission to Strode House to say we were anchored off the island and were proceeding to offload stores and equipment for the establishment of the shore base. Whimbrill, at any rate, would be glad to know, and so would Ida. No reference was made in the message to the fact that the island had increased in size or that we had seen evidence of submarine volcanic disturbance.

By eleven o'clock Peter and I were in the runabout and headed for the shore. We took Ford with us and also Amjad Ali, the Pakistani foreman. Reece stayed on board. He wasn't interested in the island. All that concerned him was the safety of the ship. He had made that perfectly clear to us and he wanted to get away from the place just as soon as he could. A light breeze blew spray in our faces and the wavelets glittered in the burning sun, blinding us with reflected light. But as we approached the first shoal we came under the lee of the island. The water was smooth then and we could see the bottom dark with weed growth.

Ahead of us were patches of emerald-coloured water and after skirting the dark back of the second shoal, the bottom changed to sand of a coarse grey texture. The water here was so clear and still that our shadow followed us, gliding across the flat sands four fathoms deep. We were in a small bay then, its shores a dark sweep of sediment, grey slopes streaked with black and the metallic glints of cuprous green. Smooth rock outcropped on the southern shore and at the extremities of the bay's two arms, which were about half a mile apart, the breaking swell had sucked away the overlying sediment, leaving the nodules exposed in black shingle banks of naked ore. 'It was about here we anchored in the *Strode Venturer*,' Peter said.

His statement came as a shock for I knew the *Strode Venturer* had anchored in ten fathoms. In the short space of two months the earth's crust had been lifted almost forty feet.

We landed on the north side of the bay, where beaches of coarse-grained sand ran up like ramps to merge with the caked debris of sun-dried slime and weed. All this shore was ideal for beaching landing craft. But for the barge, which would be ferrying the heavy equipment in on its hatch covers, we needed some sort of a natural quay so that it could be brought alongside. Then when the tide fell and it took the ground the big stuff could be driven straight ashore. We needed a camp site, too, and all this had to be considered in relation to what looked like being the most promising area for open cast working of the ore deposits.

Back of the beach there was a shallow ridge. It was easy walking, the sediment baked hard by the sun, the weed all dead. There were no birds, no sign of any living thing. But shells crunched under our feet and the smell of the dried weed was very strong. The ridge was about thirty feet high and from the top of it we had the beginnings of a view across the island. It was fairly narrow, shaped like the inverted shell of a mussel, the high point towards the south, and it was dark and bare – a lunar landscape. But not hostile; only the neutrality of a dead place.

It was a relief then to turn and face the sea. The *Strode Trader* looked very small at that distance and only the runabout lying beached below to link this barren island with the cosy familiarity of my cabin on board. I tried to analyse my feelings about the place as I followed Peter along the top of the ridge. I'd seen the bed of the sea before, for I had done a lot of underwater fishing. But it had been alive then, a wet, live world where fish swam and sea grasses grew and there were shells that moved with the purposiveness of living creatures. Here nothing moved. All was dead. No life, no growing thing, nothing – only the skeletal shells of things that had died in the sun and the smell of their death and decay still hanging in the air.

A sudden almost vertical drop and we were on sand, the grain smaller, but sand that was caked and salt-crusted, filmed in places with a filthy livid green as though the whole pan of it was diseased. And then up again, climbing a little higher now, above the tide mark of the last upheaval, clear of the decayed weed growth. We were on the old island then, the place where Peter had landed two months earlier, and here the receding ocean had left the sediment in great banks with exposed ore lying between them in drifts of black cobbles. Wind and rain had carved the sedimental dunes into fantastic shapes and the sun had baked them hard so that they looked like crumbling castles of grey sandstone. Black and grey, this moon-mad landscape lay tumbled about us. All the weed that had once covered it was burned to dust. It was naked now and hot to the touch in the shadeless sun. Here and there streaks of chemical greens and yellows showed the trace of copper and sulphur and in small pockets there were pans of sea salt shining white. From this height we had a view over many hundreds of acres of newly-emerged land, a desert island shimmering in the heat.

'I'll show you something,' Peter said, and for ten minutes we scrambled inland towards the centre of the island. Suddenly a leaf stirred, the soft live green of chlorophyll bright in the sun. We clawed our way up a fine drift of dark grit and at the top we were looking down into a hollow about fifty yards across. Three palm seedlings grew there, close together and about five feet high. Three coconut palms. And under them a matter growth of lesser vegetation, the soil there dark with moisture. 'A natural rain trap – ' Peter stopped and picked up a handful of the wind-blown sediment on which we stood. 'It's like the desert, this stuff,' he said, sifting it through his fingers. 'In the high dunes of the Empty Quarter – you'd think nothing could live – and then you come on a Bedou encampment and the sudden green of vegetation.' He trailed the last of the grit through his fingers, watching it fall. 'It's incredible what water can do. The most barren place on earth transformed almost overnight by a single rain storm.' He lifted his head, his eyes on the coconut palms. 'And here, on the equator with the sea all around, there is more rain, much more rain – eighty, perhaps ninety inches a year. When I was here last I saw about half a dozen pockets of vegetation like this, but as the surface weathers and the roots of trees get a grip on it, the pockets will spread. A few years and much of the island will be covered by a lush tropical growth.' He was looking around him now, seeing it as it would be then. 'With the right seeds introduced at this early stage, it will be like Addu Atoll, it will be capable of sup-porting human life.'

He was a visionary, standing there, his dark hair blowing in the breeze, his eyes bright in the sun's harsh glare, seeing the island as he wanted it to be, a dream place, a sort of Promised Land, an equitorial Garden of Eden for the people he had made his own. I thought of Strode House then, how remote this was from the City of London, how utterly different his outlook from that of Henry and George Strode. No wonder they hadn't understood him. I barely did myself, for this little pocket of green was an oasis in a brutal, hostile landscape and the picture he had conjured seemed born of wishful thinking. 'What happens,' I said, 'if it sinks below the surface of the sea again?'

He looked at me, a little surprised. 'You think it will?'

'It's happened before with newly-emerged islands.' And I quoted the classic case of Graham's Reef, a shallow bank in the Malta Channel south of Sicily.

'Quite different,' he said. 'This is part of a much bigger, much more prolonged process of readjustment. I talked to several vulcanologists in London. They were all agreed – if an island emerged in this area, then it would continue to grow, or at least it would remain above the surface of the sea. The movement here is a slow one. Nothing dramatic.' He gave a little shrug. 'Anyway, danger has never deterred the human race. Man has established himself on the slopes of half the volcanoes of the world, attracted by the fertility of the ash. Here there is not only fertility, but natural resources that can be marketed and exchanged for the products of the outside world.' He had turned and was starting back towards the bay where Ford and Amjad Ali were waiting for us.

'Do you really imagine they can survive in this desolation?' He didn't answer and I was angry then, for it seemed to me he was sentencing them to a living hell to fulfil a dream that was quite unreal. 'You must be mad,' I said. 'To encourage such helpless people – '

'They're not helpless.' He turned on me furiously, his eyes glittering in the sun so that for a moment he really did look mad. And then in an even tone he said, 'They're an intelligent, highly civilized people, an island race that understands the sea. And they're tough.'

'They'll need to be,' I told him. 'Even if they can survive, what do you imagine the effect on them will be?' It seemed to me he was ignoring the psychological impact of such desolation. 'It isn't only that it's bleak. It has an atmosphere, a soul-destroying sense of deadness.'

'To you maybe. Not to them.' And he added, 'You wouldn't have said that if you'd seen Don Mansoor. He stood looking down into that little oasis of green, muttering to himself, his eyes alight. And then he picked up a handful of that coarse gritty soil, putting it to his mouth to taste, smelling it, crooning over it. Finally he stood there, a little of it tightly gripped in his brown hand, gazing about him as excited as a child . . . no, more like Cortes. If you'd seen him you'd know that I didn't need to encourage him. In fact, when we got back to Addu Atoll I had the greatest difficulty in persuading him to wait until I had had time to get the ore samples analysed.'

'When are they coming?' I asked.

'God knows. I managed to get a message to him through a Sergeant-Tech on Gan who's a ham radio operator. But when they'll actually sail – ' He shrugged. 'It depends on Canning, on the President of their Republic – on the verdis and the wind. I don't know when they'll get here. But whenever it is, they'll now find proof that I haven't let them down. They'll find a camp, stores

and equipment – the beginnings of the miracle they've been praying for.'

He was the visionary again, standing there, his eyes shining,
with the ship behind him to prove he had kept faith. He had given
me a picture of Don Mansoor, the hero of his people, the Dis-
coverer. It was also a picture of himself, for he had identified himself with the Adduan, had seen the same vision and had dedicated
his life to its fulfilment. And as I followed him down to the bay to
choose a site for the shore camp I knew that nothing – only death
– would deflect him from his purpose.

2

THE BOILING WATER

IT TOOK three days to get the equipment and all the stores ashore,
and whilst we were doing that, Haines drilled a series of test bore-
holes, using a small portable drill. They were all shallow bore-
holes and two of them, drilled a mile apart, inland from the
northern arm of the bay, came up against solid rock at less than
100 feet. But further south, near the high point of the island, the
drill probed over 250 feet and it was all manganese. We established
our field of operations in this area, on a flat shelf not unlike a
raised beach. Here the nodules outcropped on to the surface and
the shelf itself provided a good working platform with the slope
of the island running gently towards the southern arm of the bay
so that roading presented no problems. Moreover, the rock outcrop on this arm made a satisfactory loading quay. It was basalt,
very smooth, and steep-to on the seaward side so that it was like a
natural dock. Some blasting was necessary, but when that was
done there was a solid base for our road terminal and the barge
was able to lie alongside in water deep enough for it to remain
afloat at low tide, protected from the swell by the off-lying shoals.
The camp was sited about half a mile back up the line of the road.
Here there was another shelf backed by a high dune of sediment
that would shelter it from the south-east wind. It faced the bay
and was about forty feet above sea level which gave some margin
of safety in the event of a subsidence.

My diary covering this period is incomplete, of course. That I still have it is due to the fact that once the base hut was up I left it there with Peter's papers. The last entry, that for 8 June, reads: 'Road completed during night and at 10.38 this morning tumble-bug dumped first load of ore on the loading quay. Six Pakistanis feeding the conveyor belt with shovels got this first load into the barge in 1 hr 35 mins. Sun very intense, no wind. Rate of delivery by tumble-bug approximately one load every fifty minutes. Bunk and cookhouse huts completed midday. Electric generator working. From loading terminal right up to mine-working whole area beginning to look like invasion beach – vehicles, oil drums, crates, bits and pieces of mechanical equipment, all the para-phernalia of a seaborne landing. First barge load away shortly after 15.00. Both landing craft brought in to quay. Reece came ashore. His crew are man-handling stores, loading them into our two trucks for transportation to camp. He drives them very hard. Obviously anxious to get loaded and away as soon as possible. Glad when sun went down. A hard day. Good to be back on board and have a shower. After evening meal had a few beers with Evans in the wireless room. Discovered Reece had signalled George Strode our DR position. He gave it as Lat.: 08° 54′ S; Long.: 88° 08′ E. But do not think his dead reckoning can be very accurate. Air very humid tonight and just before turning in there was a tropical storm – strong wind and torrential rain. Lasted about quarter of an hour, the sound of it all over the ship like a waterfall as it hammered at the plating and streamed like a cataract down the sides. At least it laid the dust. Now we are loading everything is becoming filmed with the black grit from the island. The bloody place gets more pervasive every day!'

So far we had had good weather with almost no wind, clear skies and very little humidity. All that was changed now. Several times I woke during the night to the lash of rain on the deck beyond the porthole and in the morning the sky was heavy and louring, full of low cloud that hung over us quite stationary. There was still no wind and the air was hot like a Turkish bath. Around ten o'clock the atmosphere gave up. It was like a sponge, heavy with water, which it couldn't contain any longer. It fell – solid, breath-stopping water – and suddenly visibility was barely a hundred yards.

I was ashore at the time and it caught me half-way between the quay and the camp. There was no cover at all and I just stood there, my head bowed, gasping for air, whilst at the edge of the road a rivulet thickened to a blackened flood that poured down a gully into the bay. After ten minutes the rain stopped like a tap turned off. A shaft of sunlight showed the island gleaming bright and every crevice running water.

It was like that all day, the air filling up with moisture and then dropping its load and starting the process all over again. It was so oppressive you could hardly breathe. The barge was towed out to the ship with more water in it than ore. The work went slowly and tempers frayed. Reece was ashore again in the afternoon. I had driven a truckload down to the loading quay and I stepped out of the cab almost on top of him. '. . . Number Two about a third full and the other two empty. At this rate it'll take the better part of a fortnight before all four holds are loaded.' He was facing Peter, his cap at its usual rakish angle. What he wanted was night shifts.

'You try a day's work shovelling ore on to the conveyor belt in this heat,' Peter told him sharply. 'You wouldn't talk about night shifts after that.'

The line of Reece's mouth tightened, the muscles at the side of his jaws knotting slightly. Right in front of us the conveyor belt leaned over the barge dribbling a small stream of ore. He let the silence run on, making no comment. Finally he turned to me and said I could have six of his crew to work through the night if I'd supervise them.

'All right,' I said. 'But you put one of your officers in charge of them tonight.' I was as anxious as he was to speed our departure, but I was tired now and very dirty. 'We can work it on a roster.' But he didn't seem to like that. His eyes hardened and his face went wooden. 'Thought it would help you, that's all.' And then suddenly he was smiling. 'I'll talk to Blake about it.' And he left us then, the boyish debonair look back in his face. He was whistling through his teeth as he leapt a pile of ore and went with jaunty stride down to the sea's edge where he bawled one of his lascars out for not keeping his boat properly fended off. We watched him as he went puttering out between the shoals and headed for the ship, the jolly boat cutting a sharp V in the still waters of the bay.

'Why is it,' Peter said, 'that every time that man suggests something I start wondering what's behind it?'

I didn't say anything for I thought it was the heat, the dreadful oppressiveness. As we walked together up the wet track of the road and across the hump of the island the next storm was already looming, a dark anvil-headed column of cu-nim. Flashes of lightning forked across its black belly, but as yet there was no sound of thunder. All about us the sea was flattened by the weight of the atmosphere, so still and leaden it might have been metal just congealed. It lay against the sides of the bay and around the shoal backs, torpid and listless, without even enough energy to suck at the land.

'It'll be bad tonight,' I said, and Peter nodded. 'The Pakistanis hate it here. I'll be glad when the loading is done by Adduans.'

We had a cup of tea in the base camp canteen, standing at a trestle table. One of the Pakistanis was seated on a bench, his head in his hands, rocking back and forth and moaning to himself. Another was rewinding his turban. He had short, grizzled hair and it seemed literally to be standing on end. 'Electricity,' Peter said. 'The air's full of it.'

I ran my hand through my own hair and it crackled like nylon. We had moved to the open doorway then for the canteen was cramped, just an annexe to the main body of the hut which was a bunkhouse. A shaft of sunlight picked out the *Strode Trader* lying broadside-on to us. The barge was alongside and the crew were loading into No. 3 hold. One of the landing craft was waiting by No. 2 and the other was nosing its way out through the shoals, a grey box of a vessel following the channel we had marked with dan buoys.

The shaft of sunlight was suddenly snuffed out. The sky darkened. We stood there listening to the grumbling and growling of the storm. And then with a crackling stab of lightning it was on top of us. The sky opened and ship and landing craft disappeared, engulfed in the downpour. There was wind this time and it took the surface clean off the bay, turning the sea at the edge of visibility into a seething foam of white. Lightning forked and stabbed and the thunder reverberated. Men joined us, running for shelter, their clothes clinging to their bodies and streaming water. The whites of their eyes showed in fear and they echoed the moaning of the man on the bench as the hut shook to the onslaught of the wind.

It lasted longer this time, and even after the rain had ceased, the sky remained dark and lightning flashed incessantly to the accompaniment of great claps of thunder. And then at last it was over, the black cloud rolling seawards, and the sunset blazed on the back of it like the reflection of a great conflagration. But only for a moment and then the fire burned itself out and the sky had a livid sick look. It was past six and the vanished sun already setting, night was closing in. 'Time you got back to the ship,' Peter said.

I toyed with the idea of staying ashore, but he wouldn't hear of it. 'I've got to stay – otherwise these poor sods would go crazed with fear.' He gave a wry smile. 'We should have shipped a sociologist. A place like this soon shows just how deep most men's religion goes. For instance, only three of these men really believe in Mohammed. The rest have a whole series of devils and hob-goblins they fall back upon when all hell breaks loose as it did during the night. It's a breakdown of the intellect in the face of conditions that promote more instinctive reactions and the result is pretty shattering.'

'It'll be worse tonight,' I told him. 'Wouldn't it be better if I stayed ashore with you?'

'No. I'd rather you were on the ship. I like to think my line of retreat is absolutely secured.' It was the only time he admitted to any fear of the island.

It wasn't until I got down to the loading terminal that I re-membered I had seen the second landing craft leaving for the ship. That left only the runabout which had been holed the previous day when some fool of a mechanic, testing it after repairing a broken fuel line, had run it at full throttle on to a shoal. It was beached at the head of the bay. I looked round for somebody to help me launch it, but the terminal was completely deserted, not a soul in sight. An engine roared up at the workings and the tumble-bug moved on the sky-line like some prehistoric monster. But night was closing in fast and I hurried scrambling round the shore of the bay, hoping I would be able to manage it on my own.

By the time I reached the boat it was almost dark, and yet not really dark for everything seemed limned in a curious luminosity. The air was very thick and charged with electricity. The runabout had been dragged up clear of the tide mark, stern to the sea, and it was half full of water. I manged to tip most of it out, but it was a heavy boat and it took me some time to drag it down the beach. Once it was afloat I could feel where the damage was – one of the planks had been stove in close up by the bows. I rammed a piece of cotton waste into the crack and started the engine. Lightning sizzled beyond the back of the island, but when my eyes had readjusted themselves to the dark that followed the flash I could see the lights of the *Strode Trader* again, clear and bright as she lay to her anchor a mile off-shore. I was thinking of a cold shower and the evening meal as I headed out to the first shoal. It never occurred to me that I might not reach the ship.

I got to the first shoal all right and the slender stick of the dan buoy slid past the bows, illumined in a triple flash of lightning. The flag was fluttering, the end of it already badly frayed. The sound of the thunder came to me only faintly above the noise of the engine. More lightning and in its photographic flash I saw the cotton waste was doing its job. There was very little water in the boat.

The wind came up from astern so that I didn't notice it at first. And straight ahead were the lights of the ship, nearer now and brighter. Lightning struck again, a jagged fork splitting the blackness of the sky, stabbing at the dark line of the bay's southern arm. I heard it strike and in the same instant the shock wave of cloud meeting cloud rammed against my ear-drums like the broadside of a battleship. Then the wind came in full fury, hitting me like a blow between the shoulder blades, lifting the surface of the sea so that the air was full of spray and I could hardly breathe. The lights of the ship were gone, engulfed in the curtain of wind-blown water.

I was close to the second shoal then and I only saw it because of the line of foam where the waves broke. And then suddenly even that was gone, drowned by the rain. It was as though a torrent flooding through the sky had reached a point where there was no bottom. It was a cataract so violent that it killed all sound, even the sound of thunder, and the lightning flickered only dimly. I held my course as best I could, crouched low, half-flattened by the weight of water pouring down on me. And then the deluge ceased abruptly and lightning flashes showed me the clouds whirling in convoluted masses overhead.

The ship was nearer now. I could see her quite plainly. But astern of me there was nothing, only black darkness – the next rainstorm coming in. I began to bale then, for it never occurred to me to turn back. I was intent only on reaching the ship, which was now showing the red and green of her navigation lights. She had her steaming lights on, too, but I had no time to think about that for the next storm was on me with a roar of wind and the flash of lightning. I was clear of the shoals now, in the open sea, and I kept on running with the spray driving past me and the waves building up. The lightning was almost incessant again and seen like that, in the flashes through a murk of spray, the *Strode Trader* looked a grey ghost of a ship. She was lying bows to the wind, facing straight towards me, and I came down on her fast. But not fast enough, for she began to swing, presenting her starboard side with the barge lying alongside, butting at her flank like a whale calf seeking its mother's milk. And then, when she was broadside-on, she seemed to hold her distance.

A great ball of fire burned for an instant in the clouds behind her. She was a black silhouette then with the tiny figures of men moving on her bows. They were fetching her anchor, and in the next flash of lightning I saw it was already up and down. I knew then why it was taking me so long to reach her. She was broadside to the wind and drifting with it. In the jet darkness that followed the flash I was suddenly afraid, for there was no turning back to the island now. Out here the waves were steep and breaking, the runabout little better than a cockleshell.

My whole mind, my every nerve became instantly concentrated on driving the boat forward, intent on reaching the ship before she got under way. I had the throttle wide open, leaning forward over the engine casing as though I could by sheer willpower drive her faster. The stern sank in a trough and I heard the break of the wave almost at the moment it thumped me in the back, spilling across the stern, flooding over the gunn'ls as it carried the boat forward like a surf-board. And at the same moment lightning forked across the ship, showing it very near now, so that I could see the prop beginning to thresh the water. The thunder crashed. The barge was swinging away from the ship's side and it was the barge I hit. And as the bows splintered and the boat began to sink under me I jumped, caught the steel edge of the barge's side and hauled myself aboard. Lying there, panting on the grit-grimed plating, I could feel the strong pulsing beat of the *Strode Trader*'s engines transmitted through the barge's hull every time it rammed its blunt nose against the ship's side.

I tried to attract their attention, of course, but no human voice could be heard above the turmoil of the storm. A wave broke and then another. The barge's flank was like a breakwater, the waves pouring over the side and cascading down into the half-empty hold. I struggled to my feet, balancing myself to the pitch and roll of the ungainly hulk and in the next flash of lightning waved my hands. But there was nobody on deck. There was a shuddering jar, the clank of steel on steel, and beyond the open cavern of the barge's hold I could see the dark side of the ship towering above me. Food and warmth, the cosy familiarity of my cabin all so near, but nobody to tell Reece to stop his bloody engines and get me off the barge.

The ship was gathering way fast now. She had turned her fat stern to the island and was running down wind. The barge yawed, grinding its bows. I stood and waved and shouted, and still nobody answered.

I began working my way for'ard then. I had almost reached the broader platform of the bows when the stern of the barge was lifted and flung sideways. She lay wallowing for an instant, rolling her topsides into the waves, water pouring over me. Then the bow line tautened with a jerk. It steadied her and I started forward again. It was a mistake, for the bows swung in, both vessels rolling towards each other. The crash as they met caught me off balance. I can remember falling, but that's all.

I came to, gasping and sobbing for breath, a great roaring in my ears. I knew I was drowning and I fought with all my strength, clawing and kicking, with the water gurgling in my lungs and throat and one little horrified corner of my brain aware that my hands and feet were motionless as in a nightmare where the struggle is in the mind and not transmitted into physical action. My brain, groping towards full consciousness, recorded sluggishly – the feel of grit under the palms of my hands, the hardness of solid steel beneath my body, the slosh of water resounding loud as in a tank.

I lay still a moment. Then I was gulping air, my mouth filled with grit and the sickening salinity of sea water. Somewhere my head was hurting, a raw burn of pain, and I retched, vomiting nothing but grit and slime. A blinding jar, the crash of steel, a great swooping movement. I was riding a roller-coaster and the water was back. I was afloat in a great sea and being battered to death against a shingle beach. It changed to a sea wall; I could feel its vertical sides as I clawed at it, calling for help, conscious that however hard I called nobody would come to save me since no sound was coming out of my mouth. Another jar and the tide receding – or was I trapped in the engine-room of a sinking ship? Steel under my hands – cold steel, pitted with rust and filmed with grit. A great searing flash and my smarting eyes saw the rusty pit with its vertical steel walls, the pile of ore awash, and the water flooding back at me as the stern lifted, a wall of black filthy water that spilled over me.

This time my muscles responded to the call of my brain. I struggled to my feet and the water broke, knocking me backwards and forcing me to my knees, and as it receded I was sick again. I felt better then and when the water trapped in the bottom of the barge came back at me I was ready for it, my body braced against the steel side. It broke harmlessly against me, surging round my knees, reaching finally to my waist before it receded, sucking at the heap of unloaded ore. The barge was close against the ship's side then, grinding at the steel, and the faint throb that was transmitted to my body told me that the *Strode Trader* was still under way.

The clouds overhead were low, and in the stabs of lightning I could see dark bellying masses constantly on the move, a pattern of suspended vapour that was never still. I could also see that there was no way out of the hold in which I was trapped. It was like a tank, sheer-sided, and roofed at the edges by the overhang of the side decks, and the water inside it rolled back and forth with the movement of the waves; each time I braced myself to withstand the surge and suck of it and each time the effort sapped a little more of my strength. The ship was steaming broadside to the storm now. Her side was a steel wall, rolling and toppling above me, the seas breaking against it. How long before Reece stopped his engines, or would he steam all night? He couldn't anchor now. It was too deep. I looked at my wrist-watch, but my eye were tired and all I could see in the flickering lightning was the pale disc of it spattered red with the blood dripping from my head. There was a gash somewhere in my scalp below the hair. In fact, the glass was broken and the watch had stopped. Dawn was a long way off.

Ten hours! I wondered whether I could last that long. I felt light-headed and I was shivering, but not with cold for sea and air were both warm; it was exhaustion. The water came and went, rolling nodules of ore. The noise of it sloshing back and forth along the empty barge walls was constant, unending, and behind it were other sounds, the surge of the ship's bow wave, the growl of thunder, the crackle of lightning. It was a wild night and we seemed to be travelling with the storm for it stayed with us, the clouds hanging in great masses so low they seemed pressing down against the high glimmer of the mast-head lights. And then the rain came as it had before in a solid downpour of water, the roar of it drowning out all other sounds.

Time passed and the rain stopped. As before it had flattened the sea so that I no longer had to fight the surge of the water. The wind had gone, too, and the barge lay snugged against the ship's side, not bumping now nor even grinding at the plates, but steady, and the water lapped around my knees. My eyelids drooped and closed, the eyeballs strained by the violent contrasts of million-voltage light and pitch darkness, seared with salt. I dozed standing, never quite losing consciousness, but relaxed now that I didn't have to fight the water. I could survive till dawn. Drowsily I wondered how Peter was faring, what it was like shut up in that small hut with fourteen frightened Pakistanis, and then I was thinking of Reece, wondering what the hell he was playing at. To up anchor and put to sea, that was reasonable enough. He was responsible for the safety of his ship and any captain might reasonably have thought his position insecure. But to go on steaming away from the island . . .

I became conscious then of a change in the beat of the engines. The drowsiness vanished and I was suddenly wide awake. The ship's engines had slowed. The surge of the bow wave died to a murmur. In a brief pause in the thunder I thought I heard the slow threshing of the screw. Then that ceased and I sensed the ship was losing way. I moved out from the side of the barge, climbing the heap of ore so that I could see the ship in the lightning. But of course nothing had changed, it was only that sounds which had become familiar had now ceased. The storm alone remained, thunderous and crackling. It was all forked lightning now. It stabbed and banged around us, the ship's superstructure lit by flashes so that the effect was of a vessel going in with the first wave of a seaborne landing.

Somebody shouted then. I remember it very clearly because it was the first human voice I had heard for what seemed a very long time. He must have been out on the starboard bridge wing for the sound of his voice was clear and distinct. 'Full astern! Full . . .' The thunder cracked and lightning stabbed, obliterating the rest of it. I think it was Reece and in the momentary silence that followed the thunder I heard the beat of the engines, the thresh of the screw. There was a visual change, too. The ship slid away from me. For one ghastly moment I thought the bow line had been let go and the barge set adrift, but it wasn't that; it was just that the barge was swinging as the ship went astern.

I waited, my head bent back, watching as the side of the ship moved away from me, its position changing. The barge checked at the end of its securing wire. Soon it would swing in again, port side on as the ship gathered stern way. But it didn't. It stayed like that, bows-on to the *Strode Trader*. A figure came out on to the bridge wing. A torch glimmered palely in the flash brilliance of a fork of lightning. The man was peering down. His hand waved. Still nothing happened, the barge bows-on and steady at the end of the bow line, which was taut – a single, slender strand of wire.

It was a strange sight, the ship standing there, the lights bright in the darkness, dim as glow-worms when the lightning banged, and not moving though I could hear the engines and the frenzied turning of the screw. A flash, brighter still and close behind me, and in the succeeding blackness the mast, the bridge, the whole superstructure limned with a blue-green light, the ship's whole outline traced in a sort of St Elmo's fire. And then it happened.

There was a flash, a great sizzling firework fork of electricity – a thousand million volts stabbing down, striking straight at the foremast. I heard it hit. There was a crack as the full blast of power touched the mast top, a crackling and a sizzling, and then the ear-splitting unbelievable sound of the cloud-clash that had sparked it. And with the sound the mast crumpled, falling slowly to lean in drunken nonchalance against the bridge before the heat of that great charge of electricity burned the metal to a molten white. Flames burst like bright orange flowers as the woodwork caught, and then the whole bridge went up, a shower of sparks, a soft whoof of heat rising. It was spectacular, fantastic, beautiful but deadly. *Tiger, tiger, burning bright* . . . My God! I thought. This is it – the ship on fire a thousand miles from any help. And something else – something even more appalling. It had been nagging at my brain, and now suddenly the position of the barge, the man peering down at the water, the call for full astern – it all came together in my mind. The ship was aground.

Aground and on fire, and myself imprisoned in that barge, a helpless spectator as the flames licked higher and higher and figures lit by the glare and the forked flashes ran shouting about the decks. Lightning stabbed again, struck with a blue flash. A lascar seaman caught on the bridge deck was withered instantly, a blackened rag doll dying with a piercing shriek. Hoses were being run out and a jet of water sprang from a nozzle, insignificant against the flames licking up from the bridge superstructure. And where the jet struck the heat of the fire it sent up a little puff of steam that was instantly burned out in the heat. Two more jets and then another bolt of lightning. The ship, with her steel bottom firmly stranded on the sea bed, was earthed; she was acting as a huge lightning conductor.

The flames, the lightning, the ship aground where no land should be – my mind reeled before the extent of the disaster, dazed and unable in that moment to comprehend it. The flames licked the humidity out of the night air and a red glow lit the storm clouds overhead. The heat was intense. My clothes dried on me, became stiff with salt and sweat and the darker streaks of my own blood. I watched for a time, held stupefied by the roaring holocaust of fire, by the sheer fascination of it as a spectacle, not conscious then of any fear, only of the childlike need to gape. But the bow line was not more than fifty or sixty feet long and soon the heat forced me to crouch, seeking the protection of the barge's steel plates. By then my eyeballs were burned dry, my skin parched, my hair like grass. I was glad then of the water in the bottom. I bathed my face and finally lay full-length in it, floating and watching the storm flickering and banging in the red inferno of the clouds.

It was no longer immediately overhead. In fact, that third lightning stab proved to be the last. But lying there in the bottom of the barge with the water buoying me up I wondered whether perhaps the poor wretch who had been fried by that second bolt of lightning wasn't the lucky one. I could hear the roar of the flames, could see the leap and glow of them reflected in the sky, but no longer distracted by the visual excitement of them, my mind groped towards an appreciation of my situation, and the result was frightening. I was like a rat trapped in a giant bath, the heat increasing all the time, the water getting warmer, and if I survived till the fire burned itself out – what then? A lingering death, for I'd no fresh water, no food, no prospect of being rescued. I was tied to a ship that would never move again in seas that were unvisited and in an area that was in the process of volcanic change.

Sparks flew in the night, some burning embers fell with a hiss into the water close by my feet. My left shoulder was beginning to stiffen. My whole body ached from my fall and I wished to God I had never recovered consciousness. I closed my eyes, wearied to death with the glare and the flicker. I pretended then that I was back in London, in the little flat I'd rented, lying in a hot bath. God! I was tired. Would Ida still be in London, or was she back in Dartmouth now, in the room above the antique shop where I had first met her? With my eyes closed, the red glare through my eyelids was like the light of the maroon lamp-shade in the bedroom. I saw her then as I had seen her that last night we had spent together, her slim, warm, golden body emerging and then the closeness and the warmth, the soft yielding, the sense of being one. Would she have a child, or had she taken precautions? I didn't know. Strangely, I found myself hoping it was the former, hoping that between us we had found new life to replace the old that would die here in this filthy steel tank. The thought of that, of life reproducing itself, switched my mind to John and Mary. All their hopes, and now this. How would they view my death? Would they feel I had let them down? I felt my mind recoil from their contempt, seeking to obliterate the thought of how they'd feel. For their sake, if not for my own, I must struggle for survival. I knew that. But I was drifting now, drifting away from the thought of the effort, the terrible ghastly effort that is involved in dying slowly.

I slept, pretending to myself as I dozed off that I was lying in my bath, having a little nap, and that soon I'd get up and dry myself and put on my pyjamas and go to a soft, cool bed. And Ida was there, her dark eyes looking straight into mine, her cheek pressed against me, her hair falling about her and her hand was holding me tight, not letting me go, refusing to let me slip away, but keeping me just on the edge of consciousness. Was this the knife-edge between life and death? Somewhere there was a rending crash, the splash and hiss of flaming debris quenched in water. The thunder died, the lightning, too. The world became deathly still, only the roar of the fire in the grate, and then that died down and there were distant shouts from the pavement below and a fire engine playing water on a gutted ship across the street.

So my mind recorded things, blurring them with the desire for an ordinary setting, an ordinary explanation, whilst I drifted half unconscious. And suddenly the glow was gone and a grey light filtered through my closed eyelids. Dawn was breaking.

I had floated against the remains of the barge's load of ore and was reclining against the piled-up heap. My body ached and my skin was crinkled white with long immersion. It was an effort even to shift my position and I lay there with my eyes open, staring at the rusty interior of the barge, at the water, black and filthy and quite inert. Nothing stirred. There was no sound of the sea. I might have been lying in a tank on dry land for all the movement. The sun came up, a rosy glow for a moment, but then a bright, hard light casting dark shadows. When I stirred – when I made the awful effort of struggling to my feet . . . what should I find? A gutted ship, the crew all gone? Would I be the only living thing? I called out. But my voice was weak. I did not want to call too loudly for then I could continue to lie there, fooling myself that they had not heard. The sun climbed quickly till it touched my body with its warmth, and then the full heat of it was shining directly on me and I knew I had to move, for the sun's heat meant thirst.

I forced myself to my feet and standing on the shingle heap of ore turned and faced the ship. The barge still lay bows-on to it at the full extent of its securing line, held apparently in the grip of some current. The *Strode Trader* was an appalling sight. All the bridge was gone, the whole superstructure a twisted heap of blackened, tortured metal, with here and there charred fragments of wood still clinging like rags of flesh to a burned carcass. The timbers of the hatch covers were scorched but not consumed. The cargo booms, too, though scorched, were still identifiable in the contorted wreckage of the masts. The only structure to escape the fire was the deck housing on the poop aft and as I stood there the sound of Eastern music came faint on the still morning air.

At first I refused to believe it. I was afraid it was in my head, for it was a singing sound – a siren song in the midst of desolation. The minutes passed and I stood rooted. But still that music floated in the stillness, something live and real and unbelievable. It was pipes and drums and a girl's voice singing sweetly, and all so soft, so insubstantial, so impossible in the midst of chaos and ruin.

It was a radio, of course. Some poor devil had been listening in as the lightning struck, one of the lascar crew in the quarters aft, and he had run, leaving his little portable radio still switched on. I turned, dejected, but still glad of the sound, and as I turned to find a means of reaching the barge's deck, I caught a glimpse of something moving, and then a voice called, giving an order. He was on the poop, looking over the stern, a man in a rag of a shirt and clean white trousers neatly creased, all the hair scorched from his head. It was the second officer – Lennie – and before I knew it I was on the deck of the barge, scrambling to the bows and shouting to him. 'Lennie! Lennie!'

He turned and I can still see him, standing shocked and un-believing as though he thought I were a ghost. And then he called back, dived limping to the deck house, and a moment later half a dozen lascars like demon beggars dressed in rags and black as sweeps came slowly, wearily along the deck to pull on the bow line and bring the barge alongside.

'I didn't know,' Lennie said as they hauled me up at the end of a rope to what had once been a white scrubbed deck of laid pine and was now black charcoal with the plates all showing, buckled by the heat. 'Nobody knew you were there.' And then Reece arrived and Blake, their eyes red-rimmed and sunk deep in their sockets, all moving and speaking slow with the dazed look of men who have gazed into the mouth of hell and do not yet believe that they are still alive.

'What happened?' I asked. 'Why is the ship aground?' But it was no good asking questions of men so tired they could hardly stand. In any case, they didn't know, they barely cared. They'd fought a fire all night and somehow they had won. That was enough – for the moment.

The crew's galley was still functioning. It produced breakfast and afterwards we cleaned ourselves up, got some sort of an awn-ing rigged and slept, huddled together right at the stern. Three men had died, including the third officer, Cummins, and there were four seriously injured. Most of the rest were suffering from burns and there were few whose hair hadn't been scorched, some with no eyebrows, no eyelashes even; all were in a state of shock.

There was no breeze that day and by noon the heat was intense. Sleep was no longer possible and Reece called a conference. He had had another bit of awning rigged just for'ard of the deck house. From this position we all had a clear view of the length of the ship. She was in a desperate state. Above decks there was nothing left, just a contorted heap of blackened steel. Below decks the situation was better. The engine-room had suffered some damage due to falling debris, but on a cursory inspection Robbins thought it largely superficial. 'We're fortunate that this is an old ship. If she'd been a motor vessel the blazing debris from the deck above might have smashed the fuel lines, then the whole ship would have gone up.' He reckoned a day's work might see the main engines functioning, though it was impossible to say until they were on test whether there had been any heat distortion. The electrical installation, however, was all burned out and beyond repair.

There was no question of taking to the boats. The quartermaster had saved one of the ship's lifeboats by having it cut from its davits and moored astern just after the bridge caught fire, but the rest were gone. The two landing craft had been swamped and had snapped their mooring lines and sunk. Only the barge would accommodate all the crew and that had no means of propulsion. The question of search and rescue was discussed, but nobody was optimistic. There was no arrangement for regular wireless reports to head office and it might be a week before they tried to contact us. And then there was the question of our position. Reece admitted that his estimate of it might be anything up to 200 miles out. 'Navigating blind like that – only one man knowing where we were . . .' His voice was high-pitched, querulous. 'I should never have agreed to it.'

'Well, you did,' Blake snapped. 'So it's no good belly-aching about it.'

But Reece seemed driven now by a compulsion for self-justification. 'It's Strode's fault. All that secrecy – I knew it was a mistake and now we may have to pay for it with our lives.'

'It's not only us,' I said. 'There's Strode and the men with him.' My head hurt and I was in no mood to care about his susceptibility to criticism. 'You made no attempt to get them off . . .'

'There wasn't time, man.' He stared at me, pale and angry. A little frightened, I thought, and his boyish good looks marred now, for his hair was burned short and his eyebrows gone. 'You don't seem to realize . . . we were dragging.'

'The wind was from the east,' I said. 'It was blowing off the island.'

'We were dragging, I tell you. Cummins was on anchor watch and when he called me we were being blown down-wind fast. The fact that we were under the lee of the island didn't mean a bloody thing. Small, intense storms like that – down here on the equator – they're circular, you see. Once you're through the eye of it, then the wind comes in from the opposite direction.' There was something more to it than resentment of my criticism. He was trying to convince himself that what he'd done was right. 'When that happened we'd have piled up on that damned island.'

'I was out in that sea,' I told him. 'You could have sent one of the landing craft in.' I was thinking of what Peter must be feeling now, the ship gone and himself and the sixteen men with him marooned there with supplies for less than a month. 'You could have got them off.'

'Why? Why should I risk men's lives sending in a boat for them? They were perfectly safe where they were. Christ, man! It wasn't they who were in danger. It was us.'

I thought of the night I had spent in the barge and what had happened to the ship, wondering why the hell he'd found it necessary to keep steaming for four solid hours. He seemed to guess what was in my mind for he said, 'There was the current to consider then. If I'd hove-to a few miles off, we might have drifted anywhere. I couldn't be sure of either its direction or its rate. I still can't. I thought it better to steam a set course – so many hours out, so many hours back.'

It was reasonable. So reasonable that I thought a Court of Inquiry would accept it. I glanced at Blake. His quiet grey eyes met mine and I knew he was thinking the same thing, that the man had panicked and this was no more than a plausible excuse. But he didn't say anything and I didn't pursue the matter. There was no point, for it was the future that mattered.

This it was finally agreed rested on our own efforts. If we could get the ship re-floated and the main engines working, then with jury-rigged steering from the tiller flat we had a chance. Navigation would have to be by the stars at night and the sun by day, for the compass, all the normal means of steering a course, had been destroyed. However, Evans thought he might be able to produce some sort of a DF set by cannibalizing the radio sets belong-

ing to various members of the crew. If so, we could home on the
Gan aircraft beacon. Alternatively, we would have to give the
Maldives a wide berth and head north for the coast of India.

The discussion switched to tides then. We had no tide tables
now, but Blake reckoned the ship had gone aground about an
hour or at the most two hours after low water. With all efforts
concentrated on fighting the fire and no anchor put down, the
ship would have drifted as the tide lifted her until she finally
grounded at high water. Our hope was, therefore, that she was
only lightly resting on the bottom. There was the moon, too.
When it was at the full in a few days' time sun and moon would be
pulling together to give us spring tides. It would mean an increased lift of a few inches at high water.

Lunch arrived and we ate it sitting cross-legged on the deck.
It was a curry and I cannot remember ever having a finer one.
It put new heart into all of us. If the cook could produce a meal
like that in such difficult circumstances, then surely to God we
could get the ship re-floated. Work started on this immediately
after we had fed.

But it is one thing to unload a vessel when she is fully equipped
with cargo booms and power to the winches; quite another when
tons of materials have to be loaded in sacks and each sack hauled
up by hand and carried to the ship's side. At the back of our minds
was the nagging thought that when this Herculean task had been
completed, it still might not be enough to raise the ship's bottom
off the sea bed. Three barge and seven landing craft loads of ore
had been delivered into her holds, a total of little more than
400 tons. Jettisoning this would gain us less than a foot on the
Plimsoll line. The third engineer with three of his men had started
clearing the remains of the bridge deck, all the wreckage of mast,
booms and smoke stack. There was probably another 100 tons to
be gained by pitching this over the side – three more inches perhaps out of the water.

With Reece's agreement I took the lifeboat and began sounding
round the ship with a lead. There was an easterly current running
one and a half to two knots and with only one to help me it was
slow, exhausting work for the boat was heavy and the heat
intense with the sun's rays reflected from the sea's calm surface.
The water was very clear and most of the time we could see the
bottom. By sunset I had pencilled a rough chart of the sea bed
up to a distance of a quarter of a mile from the ship. There were
no rocks, no sign of coral. We were on a flat plateau of sand with
occasional patches of some darker sediment. There was a slight

increase of depth towards the north, a matter of a foot or so, and in one place off the starboard quarter a hole in the sea bed that took all fifty fathoms of the lead line without recording bottom.

When I showed Reece the pattern of the soundings he nodded and said that was what he had expected, the deep water towards the north. 'We were steaming south – one nine two degrees to be exact.'

'You mean you were back-tracking the route by which we approached the island?'

He nodded, his mouth set in a tight line. 'I thought it safer.'

'How long for?' I asked, hoping to God he'd say he'd changed course.

'Four hours – a little over. We fetched the anchor just after seven – I think it was 19.08 we got under way. We grounded about 11.20. I remember that because I had just glanced at the chronometer when the lightning struck.'

'What about the echo-sounder? Did you have that on?'

'Of course I did. But I wasn't paying much attention to it. There didn't seem any point, you see. It had been recording no bottom ever since we cleared the vicinity of the island.'

Four hours along the same track; and when we had approached the island it had been all deep water. I stared at him, but he made no comment. There was no need. We both of us knew what it meant.

'The sooner we get out of here the better,' I said.

He nodded and his face looked grey.

I left him then and went in search of Blake who was directing work up for'ard in No. 1 hold. He had already arrived at the same conclusion. 'Ay, it's not a very nice thought, is it? The bed of the ocean come up a thousand fathoms and us sitting on the very top of a mountain as you might say.' He smiled. 'You must just put your trust in the Lord.' He was from the islands of the Outer Hebrides and he believed in God with the same absolute faith as the men who wrote the Scriptures. The strange thing is that his simple statement seemed to help me to accept the situation. We stood together for a while, not saying anything and watching the sunset flame on the horizon, slowly deepening to purple as night spread like a canopy across the sky, shutting us in with the stars. The work went on without a break for there was a half moon cutting a silver swathe across the flat desert of ocean.

We worked in shifts and when the dawn came men and officers fed in relays. A short rest and then back into the holds, shovelling ore into sacks, hoisting them up to the deck and emptying the contents over the side, and the ship rang to the axe and hammer blows of the demolition gang. By evening the whole appearance of the vessel had changed. I was working the pulley they had rigged over No. 1 hatch then and shortly after the moon rose I was conscious of an anxious twitter of voices. I turned as I swung the next sackload on to the deck. The lascar who was working with me had also turned. Four or five of the crew were clustered by the remains of the port winch, their quick, high voices sounding for all the world like birds in the sudden stillness that had descended upon the ship.

The lascar beside me seized my elbow. 'There, sahib. You look, please.'

It was in the moon's path, a flurry in the water, a disturbance of the surface and something spouting. A whale? I heard Reece's voice driving at the crew and then the ship seemed suddenly to come alive so that I thought for a moment she was afloat. But it wasn't a gentle movement, more of a shiver, and far away a deep growling sound. The gasp that went up from the huddle of the crew was an audible reflection of my own sudden sense of insecurity. It was as though my brain were poised on the edge of some deep unknown. Three of the crew had prostrated themselves, bowing their heads to the buckled deck plates, and far out on the horizon something stirred, shattering the still path of the moon. The crew gasped out an audible expression of their fear. And then silence, an utter stillness, and I knew the danger, whatever it was, had receded. Slowly the men relaxed, the stillness broken by that same bird-like twitter as they found their voices, all speaking at once, and the cook on deck telling us how his pots had gone mad and all the ship full of jinns and devils making them dance on their hooks. And Lennie saying in a carefully casual voice, 'Real friendly, ennit? We should come here more often.'

We worked through the night in a frenzied, driven haste till the moon set and we could no longer see. We were dead on our feet then and when the dawn came we found the sea littered with pumice. It lay all round, grey cobbles to the horizon, and when the sun rose the paved surface of the ocean was patched with all the colours of primeval earth. It undulated strangely to the movement of a shallow swell. About midday there was clear water to the west of us. By sunset the pumice had all gone, drifted eastward by the current. But by then we had experienced something much more startling – a boiling of the sea.

It occurred just as Robbins was testing the main engine. It was a wonderfully hopeful sensation to feel the deck alive again under our feet and then to hear the threshing noise of the prop turning, the beat of the engines rising as power was increased to drive the shaft. We were most of us on deck, peering over the side, watching the turgid water being thrust forward along the hull as the screw drove full astern. Nothing happened, of course, except that a lot of sand was kicked up from the bottom, for there was still an hour to go to high water and the anchor was down.

We didn't notice it at first; the reek of sulphur, that was all. I thought something was wrong with the engines, something burning, until two lascar seamen on the far side of the ship called to me. I caught the note of urgency in their voices and crossed to the starboard side. About three cables off on the quarter the sea was boiling like a cauldron, bubbles of hot gas bursting and every thirty seconds or so the surface of the water lifted as though under pressure from below.

It came from the place where our lead had found that hole in the bottom of the sea bed. I hadn't liked it at the time. I liked it less now that I knew what it was; and there were other disturbances further away, to the south mainly, like blisters bubbling on the sea's surface. Then suddenly they were gone, all stopped together, and the water resumed its flat oily calm, only the smell of sulphur hanging on the air to remind us that we were aground on a submarine volcano that was fissured with gas vents like a colander.

Living in an area of volcanic instability is disturbing enough on land, but living with it at sea, your ship stranded in the vicinity of one of the vents, is infinitely worse, for you have no means of fleeing the area. This boiling of the sea happened not just that once but several times, and each time it wasn't only our own vent that blew off, but all the others to the south of us – all starting and stopping at the same time. It was a very strange thing to watch, not frightening, for the forces that produced it were too remote. Fear is the instinctive preparation for resistance. Here we were faced with a power beyond our control and we accepted it as something that if it came would be inevitable.

There was nothing frenzied now about the way in which we went about the work of lightening the ship. We moved with a steady concentrated purpose, conserving our energies and not talking much, but unusually sensitive of each other, conscious that what strength we had we drew from the community of our fellows. European and lascar alike, there was no difference. We slept and ate and worked together, treating each other with the consideration of men whose lives are forfeit, and even Reece and Blake seemed to have forgotten, or at least set aside, their differences.

On the morning of the third day, with the decks all cleared of debris and half the ore emptied from the holds, we gathered at the side of the ship as the time of high water approached – waiting, hoping. There was a breeze from the west, the surface of the sea aglint with small waves breaking and the lead showed the depth of water the same as our draft. At 10.48 I felt the first stirring of the ship, a barely perceptible movement under my feet. Ten minutes later she began to swing, slowly at first, but then, as though suddenly freed, she moved to the joint thrust of wind and current until checked by the anchor. She swung then, steadily and easily, until she was head to wind, her bows pointing west. Twenty minutes later we were aground again.

Blake took the lifeboat then with a full crew at the oars and a leadsman in the bows, sounding northwards to the limit of the shallows. They extended for just over a mile and then fell away rapidly into deep water. There were no obstacles and all the way out to the edge the sea bed sloped very gradually downwards.

We saw the boiling water once more that afternoon, shortly after four, but we scarcely glanced at it, accepting it now as a part of our predicament. In any case, we were too tired, too dazed to care, working like automatons through the blazing heat, intent only on shifting sufficient ore in the twelve hours between tides to ensure our escape that night. We didn't stop for food. We kept right on as the sun fell into the sea and the cloudless sky blazed a flame-red orange that quickly faded to an incredible green. The stars and the moon were suddenly with us and the sacks came up and were emptied over the side in the pale spectral light.

The engineers had steam up then, smoke pouring from the gaping hole in the deck where the funnel had been. At ten-thirty Reece gave the order for work to cease. Already we could sense that the ship was barely touching bottom. Three-quarters of an hour to go to high water. At eleven o'clock the anchor cable, already severed behind the bits, was let go. It fell with a rattle and a splash and word was passed along the chain of men to the engine-room. The screw bit into the water and from the top of the poop deckhouse, which had now become the bridge, we watched breathless, waiting for the moment when she would answer her helm which was hard over.

It seemed an age, the minutes dragging endlessly. At last there was a grating shiver. The sound continued for a moment and then there was silence, only the beat of the engines, and for'ard the bows swung against the stars – turning, turning steadily towards the north, the shadow of the deckhouse changing shape as the moon's position changed. 'Helm amidships.' Reece's voice was clear and sharp against the rhythmic thump of the screw immediately below us.

'Helm amidships.' The order passed down the chain of men to the tiller flat. The bows stopped swinging, steadied on a star, and now we saw the sea beginning to move past us. Twice the grating sound deep under our keel sent our hearts into our mouths. But the ship had way now and though we could feel her check she did not stop. Astern the sea was lifted into great waves as the water we had displaced flooded in behind us, dredged up by the shallows. But these stern waves gradually diminished. By eleven-twenty they were gone and the wake was a normal wake, frothing a white line back across the moonlit sea as we thumped our way into deep water.

The cook had produced another curry, but most of us were too tired, too nervously exhausted to eat. Two bottles of Scotch were conjured up and we drank them fast, pouring the liquor urgently down our throats. I fell asleep where I was, lying on the hard deck, the sound of the engines, the sense of movement acting like a lullaby. And the next moment I was being shaken violently and a voice was saying, 'Wake up, Bailey. Wake up.'

It was Blake bending over me and shaking me violently. 'Are you awake now?'

I nodded, staring up at him, my brain still numb. 'What is it? What's happened? What's the time?'

'Midnight and Reece has altered course.'

'Altered course?' I stared at him stupidly, not understanding what he was trying to tell me.

'To the north-west – towards Gan.'

It took a moment for the implication of that to sink in. 'Towards Gan?' I started up. 'But the island . . .' He couldn't head for Gan, not yet – not without getting Peter and the others off that island.

'I thought you'd like to know,' Blake said.

'But didn't you tell him? He can't just leave them . . .'

'I've been arguing with the bugger for the last ten minutes. Finally I told him I'd call you.'

'Thanks.' I scrambled to my feet and up the ladder to the top of the deckhouse. Reece was there, sitting with his legs dangling over the for'ard edge of the roofing, a lascar at his side ready to pass his orders to tiller flat or engine-room. He turned as I stepped on to the roof, Blake close behind me. He knew why I was there and his face had a blank obstinate look. I sat down beside him. 'You've altered course I see.'

'My concern is for the safety of the ship.' He said it flatly as though repeating something he had learned by heart, his eyes deep-sunk in their sockets, his voice tired.

'You're headed for Gan, then?' He nodded. I asked Blake to leave us then. I knew Reece wouldn't give way in front of the older man. 'Now,' I said as the grey head of the first officer disappeared down the ladder, 'let's get this quite clear. If you abandon Strode and the rest of the men on the island it won't look good.'

'My instructions are that the safety of the ship is paramount,' he said woodenly.

'You had specific instructions to that effect?'

He nodded.

'From George Strode?'

'From Phillipson – though it's the same thing.'

'Specific instructions – in writing?' My brain was working painfully slowly.

'Yes.'

'Such instructions,' I said, 'only restate a responsibility vested in every captain. It extends to the crew and also to any passengers. There'll be an inquiry – you realize that?' He didn't say anything. 'It won't look good at an inquiry if you abandon these men.'

'I'm not abandoning them. They're ashore there, and they've food for a month.' And he added, 'We're taking in water. Did you know that? Robbins says some rivets have gone, midships on the starb'd side. The heat, he thinks.'

'Are the pumps holding it?'

'At present, yes.'

'You're at least three days' steaming from Gan,' I said. 'Two or three hours isn't going to make all that difference.'

'How do you know?' His face remained set and I wondered what was behind his obstinacy, for I was certain this was something he'd made up his mind to some time back.

I was ten minutes sitting there arguing with him. Finally I said, 'All right. You have one view. I have another. But I would remind you that I'm an executive of Strode Orient. I'm ordering you now, Reece. Head the ship back to the island and get those men off.'

He shook his head. 'You have no power to give me orders on my own ship.'

He was right there, of course, but there was always the question of fitness to command. And when I told him that if he refused to head for the island I would gather the ship's officers together and put it to them that he was no longer fit to captain the vessel, he sat for a long time without speaking. He knew it would finish his career coming on top of the stranding. Finally he said, 'Will you give it to me in writing – a written order? Then, you see, man, if there's any question – ' His voice trailed away, broken and tired. Now that the ship was afloat and under way every turn of the screw brought the hour of reckoning nearer. And this was his first command. I felt sorry for him then. 'Yes, of course,' I said. 'You can have it in writing.'

'Now?' he asked, almost eagerly. 'Now, please, before I change course?'

I went below and borrowed a pen and a sheet of paper and wrote it out for him and when I'd handed it to him he read it slowly, carefully, by the light of the moon. And then he gave the order to change course and the bows swung north, back on to the track we'd steamed from the island to the point of stranding.

Shortly after four that morning the engines were stopped and we lay hove-to till dawn, when we got under way again, with a leadsman sounding regularly. But there was no bottom and no sign of the island.

As the sun rose we turned east, searching all the time, but there was nothing, nothing but the empty sea. We searched till noon, steering a pattern that even with the reduced vision from our improvised bridge must have covered 500 square miles. We saw no vestige of the island and the insistent cry of 'No bottom' from the leadsman seemed constantly drumming home to me the fact that it had gone again, submerged beneath the steaming surface of the Indian Ocean.

'Have we been searching the right spot?' I asked Blake. And he shrugged and said, 'As far as we can tell, yes.' His dour voice had a grim finality about it and when Reece finally gave the order to turn the ship towards Gan again I didn't try to stop him. The midday heat was steadily reducing visibility. 'It's gone,' Reece said and there was something in his voice, in the look of his eyes – an agonized despair as though he were somehow responsible. And I wondered again why he'd left them there.

The following day it was cloudy with a fresh breeze. The old ship rolled as she ploughed her way nor'-westwards as near as we could guess. And after that the sea was calm again, the sky clear, and nothing to relieve the monotony. On the third day Evans

raised Gan beacon on an improvised DF set. We were much
further to the east than we had expected and course was altered
accordingly. Just about sunset a plane flew over us. It was a
Comet and we knew then that we were on the direct line between
Singapore and Gan. The pilot must have spotted us for at dawn a
Shackleton appeared, circling low. After making several runs over
us at what would have been mast-head height, it headed back for
Gan. It returned shortly after noon and stayed with us for nearly
an hour to guide the high-speed launch to us.

Wilcox had come out himself to pilot us in and he told us that
the search had been on for three days now with another Shackleton flown in from Changi to relieve the one operating from Gan.
'They've been working seventeen hours at a stretch, the maximum,
and not a sign of you or that island. Every report negative.'

'Not even any shallows?' I asked.

'No, nothing.' He turned to Reece. 'Either your position was
way out, old man, or else . . .' He gave a quick little shrug.

A Shackleton has a cruising speed of about 150 knots. It would
be flying at a height of say 1000 feet. In three days they
would have covered thousands of square miles. If Reece had made
an error it would have to be an enormous one. I turned to Wilcox.
'Did they report any sign of volcanic activity – gas vents, pumice,
anything like that?'

He shook his head. 'No. I told you, the reports were negative.
Nothing sighted at all. Oh, yes, two whales.' He grinned, but the
grin vanished when I told him there were seventeen men on the
island. 'My God!' he said. 'And you left them there?' The note
of accusation in his voice made it obvious that he regarded the
island as gone, vanished without trace. I turned away, the feeling
of hopelessness that had been with me for three days now crystal-
lized into certainty. The island was gone, and the shallows where
we had stranded must have dropped back into the depths a
matter of hours after we had got clear of them.

PART FIVE

STRODE & COMPANY

'I DON'T BELIEVE IT.' Ida's tone was one of absolute conviction. 'If Peter were dead I'd know about it. I'm certain I would.' She had come out to the airport to meet me and all the way in to London she had been questioning me, listening to my account of what had happened. Now we were back at the flat and her final comment was that I was wrong, everybody was wrong, that Peter was still there, on an island that couldn't be found.

She accepted everything I had told her – the white water, the pumice, the stranding, the fire, even the sulphurous boiling of the sea around us – all the surprising, the unusual things, but not that the island had vanished. It made no difference that I had actually flown one of the searches; I'd probably have flown others if it hadn't been for the urgency of her message. 'I'm sorry,' I said, 'but you'll have to accept the facts as we know them. The island's just not there any more, neither the island nor the shallows on which we stranded.'

'Balls! You just haven't searched in the right place, that's all.' It could almost have been her father speaking – rude, obstinate, determined.

'Suppose you tell me where we should have searched?' It was the nearest we had come to a row since we first met.

She smiled, a little gesture of appeasement that didn't reach to her eyes. 'I can't do that. All I can tell you is that he's alive.'

'Then either you're daft or Peter's capable of performing miracles. There's nothing there but sea.' And once more I told her about the flight I'd made, but this time in greater detail. I thought if she could see it through my eyes it would help her to accept the truth.

It was Canning's idea. He came down to the transit Mess the day Reece had run the *Strode Trader* aground east of the oil jetty. It was just after sundown and we had a beer together. Canning had been extremely helpful – billeting us ashore, the lascars in the Pak camp, the Europeans in the transit quarters, sending engineers out to the ship to see if they could patch the leaking plates, allowing Reece and myself to be present when the Shackleton skippers made their search reports. 'Would you like to fly tomorrow's search? I've had a word with Freddie Landor. He'd be happy to take you along.'

I guessed what was behind the offer. He wanted to prepare me for the moment when the search would be called off, to convince me that the RAF had done everything possible. 'Is tomorrow your last attempt to find them?' I asked.

'No. But two more flights will complete the pattern. We'll then have had sight of a quarter of a million square miles of ocean. Anyway,' he added, 'I thought it would help if you saw for yourself.'

'Is tomorrow's flight part of the pattern?' I asked.

He hesitated. 'You think they've overflown the island without seeing it?'

'They've put in a hell of a lot of flying hours,' I said. 'And it gets pretty hazy after midday.' I wasn't happy about putting it like that, but I'd seen the crews when they came in. It was three hours out to the search area, three hours back and ten hours flying patterns – a long day.

He thought about it for a moment. 'You could be right.' He took a pull at his beer. 'Okay. Talk it over with Reece. I'll tell Freddie he's to fly you anywhere you like.'

Take-off was at 03.00 hours. The crew truck picked me up at two-fifteen in the morning. There were nine of them for a Shackleton carries an extra navigator, an air electronics officer and up to four signals personnel as well as two pilots and an engineer. Nobody spoke very much as we trundled out to the apron where the Shackleton's bulk cast a dark moon shadow. Somebody gave me a spare flying suit and a helmet and when finally we took off I was told to sit braced on the floor just aft of the flight deck. The noise was deafening. Airborne, I was given the co-pilot's seat and with my intercom plugged in could listen to the reports of the crew. We flew at 4000 feet, nothing to see but the pale expanse of ocean below and the stars above. Sandwiches and coffee were handed round as dawn began to break in the east. Afterwards Landor called me to the navigator's table.

He was a skipper navigator, an arrangement peculiar to some Shackletons, and he had our position marked on the air charts. 'In seventeen minutes we'll be bang over the target.' I had discussed it with Reece and we had agreed that the day's search should start from his estimated position and that I would then fly a circular pattern outwards. In one day it ought to be possible to cover an area big enough to take in any possible error. 'If the position is correct and the island's there, then it should be on the radar now.' We had come down to 1000 feet, but the scanner was empty, nothing showing.

The sun came up as we started to turn, beginning the ring pattern that would spread further and further out from the target as the day progressed. I was taken for'ard then, beyond the flight deck to the gun position in the nose. Here I stayed the whole day, searching and searching with my eyes and seeing nothing but the flat unending expanse of the sea below. The nose-gunner's position had a Perspex hood and as the day wore on it became a hothouse, the sun blazing on my hands, burning through the rough denim of the flying suit. The sweat poured off me to be replaced every hour or so by the iced lemonade which they brought round.

Hour after heat-searing hour and the sea empty of anything. The monotony and the noise dug into my brain. More sandwiches and afterwards my head nodding and all my will-power concentrated on keeping my eyes open. Haze was forming, visibility decreasing and the plane flew on and on, the circles much bigger now so that the position of the sun changed only gradually. Coffee and still I had to fight to keep awake in the blazing heat. 'Captain to Bailey – are you all right there or would you like to sit in on the radar?'

'Bailey answering. No, I'm fine, thanks.'

They'd been flying this monotonous, soul-destroying routine every other day for almost a week. I wasn't admitting that I couldn't take it though it was like being roasted alive. Somehow I kept awake, regarding it as a sort of penance for being the cause of their having to go over the same ground again. Then the sun was going down, the heat lessening. At sunset we turned for home and that was that – nothing seen, and nothing to report. All that time and energy and fuel wasted.

And when we landed Canning met me. A lift of his eyebrows, but he didn't need to be told. He knew from the look on my face. 'Well, no good worrying,' he said. 'We'll keep at it until we're ordered to stop.' And he handed me the telex with Ida's message.

I looked across at her. She had her eyes closed and the lines of strain showed on her face. 'Why the urgency?' I asked.

'The annual general meeting is the day after tomorrow.'

'I know that. But what's the trouble? It was just luck that there was a spare seat in a Britannia that night to Aden. Whimbrill has my proxy.'

'I think I'd better leave him to tell you. I rang him at his home this evening to say you'd be in the office in the morning. The shares have slumped, of course.' She opened her eyes, staring straight at me. 'This wretched business has brought things to a head. But he'll explain it to you better than I can.' She reached to the table behind her where she'd put her bag and gloves. There was a copy of the evening paper there and she passed it to me. 'I didn't tell you before. They've called off the search. You'll find it in the Stop Press.'

It was on the back page. *An Air Ministry spokesman stated that they had now abandoned all hope for the men still missing on a volcanic island in the Indian Ocean.* It gave the names of the three Europeans. The decision was inevitable, of course, but it still came as a shock. 'I'm sorry,' I murmured.

'No good being sorry,' she said sharply. 'It's a question of what we do now.'

'What the hell can we do?' I said angrily. 'The island's gone and Peter's dead.' I didn't mean to put it as brutally as that, but I was tired and it worried me that she was still refusing to accept the truth of it.

An uneasy silence hung over the room. Finally she got to her feet. 'I'm going to make coffee. And there's some eggs and bacon in the fridge – will that do?'

I nodded. Sitting there, listening to her moving about in the tiny kitchen, I was thinking of Peter, wondering what it had been like at the end, trying to visualize it. All his hopes, all his plans vanished in one cataclysmic upheaval. And the Adduans – Canning hadn't mentioned any vedis sailing. I wished now I had tried to visit Midu.

It was after we had fed, when we were sitting over our coffee, smoking, that Ida mentioned Deacon. 'When Peter first went to the island it was in the *Strode Venturer,* and Deacon was in command. George sacked, him didn't he?'

'Yes.'

'Where is he now?'

'Still at Aden, I imagine.'

She finished her coffee and stubbed out her cigarette. 'It's late,' she said. 'I'm going now. But I think it might be worth having a talk with Deacon. Could we get him to London?'

'What's the point?' I said. 'Peter was just as secretive about the position of the island when he made the voyage in the *Strode Venturer.*'

'But Deacon is an older man than Reece – more experienced.'

'He's also an alcoholic.'

'I know that. But drunk or sober a man who's been to sea as

long as he has ought to have some idea where his ship was.' She got to her feet. 'Think about it, will you? I'm not accepting the situation until we have some sort of a check on Reece's position.' She left it at that and I saw her to her car. And afterwards, when I was in bed, I lay thinking about it. In this she didn't seem any different from the other women I had known – logic abandoned as soon as the emotions were involved. For the island to be outside the area of search the real position would need to be five or six hundred miles at least from Reece's DR position. He couldn't possibly have made an error of such staggering proportions unless he'd done it deliberately. And there was no question of that, for Blake had also kept a note of the course and his estimate of the position had differed by less than 50 miles.

But doubt, once planted with sufficient forcefulness, is an insidious thing. It was still with me when I woke in the morning and I knew that for the sake of my own peace of mind I would have to try and see Deacon. And there was Hans Straker, the man who had sat with me all the way from Singapore when I'd flown back to London that first time. It seemed years ago now, but I remembered his interest in the Indian Ocean. He would know who to contact and even at this distance a seismograph would surely record volcanic activity large enough to cause a subsidence in the area?

But when I arrived at Strode House I was plunged back into a world where catastrophe was seen as something affecting a balance sheet, not in terms of human suffering. 'We are naturally very upset at this news, both my brother and I – indeed everyone who knew him here in Strode House.' George Strode had risen on my entrance and the palms of his hands were pressed flat against the top of his desk as he leaned earnestly towards me. 'Believe me, Bailey, we shall miss him – his energy, his cheerful optimism. And the men with him. It's all very tragic.' He stared at me a moment like a frog with his protuberant eyes, as though expecting me to thank him for his little funeral oration. Finally he straightened up. 'Well, no good grieving over it. He's dead and the whole venture with him. It's for us to pick up the pieces.' He reached for a fat envelope on his desk. 'Reece has sent in a full report. I'd like you to read it through and add anything to it you think relevant.' He wanted it back in time for a press hand-out the following day. 'It's come at a bad time, just ahead of the meeting. Henry will have to make a statement for the Strode shareholders and in the circumstances I think it would be as well if you were present.'

Reece's report had been sent by telex from Gan and the final paragraph made it clear that it had been written after he knew the search was being abandoned. 'The search pattern has been completed and they have not found any trace of the island. There is, therefore, no doubt that the re-submergence of the island . . .' I put it away in the drawer of my desk. Somehow I couldn't face going over it all again – not then.

There was a strange feeling about Strode House that morning, a sort of hush, as though the abandonment of the search touched the members of the staff personally. They stood in little huddles at the end of corridors or in their offices, talking in whispers that ceased abruptly on my approach. The quick, furtive glances, the sudden silences more expressive than words; the ghost of Peter Strode seemed to haunt the building. 'They feel his loss very deeply,' Whimbrill said. 'It's as though the spark that might have set this place alight with a new spirit of adventure had suddenly been snuffed out.' I think he was speaking for himself as much as for the staff, for at once stage, when they had received Peter's message announcing the establishment of the shore base on the island, he said he thought the boards of both companies were beginning to swing towards wholehearted support of the venture. 'Not George, perhaps. But le Fleming certainly, and also Crane, possibly Everett. Even Henry was becoming convinced of the need to go along with it. That was when the shares were still going up.' He smiled a little sourly. 'The mood has changed, now of course.'

'You mean they're going to sell out?'

He shrugged. 'The Lingrose nominations still stand, but I think perhaps they'll wait until all the publicity has died down.'

'And then?'

'Presumably they'll call an extraordinary general meeting – do it that way.' He sounded depressed, all the fight knocked out of him.

I left him shortly afterwards, feeling depressed myself. All the plans, all the energy and enthusiasm we had expended – gone, wasted. I went down the main stair, out into Leadenhall Street. I felt I couldn't stand the atmosphere of Strode House any more. I needed a drink and it was in the pub by Leadenhall Market, standing alone with a large Scotch in my hand, that I remembered how I had seen Phillipson there with Reece. Why had he denied it? And Reece himself, that night we had re-floated the *Strode Trader* on the tide, so strangely reluctant to return to the island, so insistent that they had stores for a month. Was this a case of 'Who will rid me of this turbulent priest?'

I drank the rest of my whisky and walked slowly back to Strode House, and by the time I got there I knew it was no good talking to George Strode or even to Phillipson. Instead, I went straight up to my office and began a close study of Reece's report. He had obviously given a great deal of thought to it, for it was very carefully phrased to put his own decisions in the best possible light. 'Bearing in mind the volcanic nature of this uncharted area and my owner's instructions – with which I was in entire agreement – to regard the safety of the ship and her crew as of paramount importance, I decided shortly after 19.00 hours on 9 June to up-anchor and steam southwards to the safety of what had been deep water when we had approached the island only four days before.' This was half-way down the second page and he went on to explain that the wind being off the island strong in the gusts he was of the opinion that it would be a needless risk of life to send boats in to bring off the shore part. 'I did not consider them in danger. This was a tropical storm. I could not know that within a few days the island would disintegrate and disappear below the surface of the sea.'

I sat for a long time staring at that passage – so natural, so convincing. And I kept on hearing Ida's voice: 'I don't believe it.' And if Peter wasn't dead, then the island hadn't disappeared, and from that it followed inevitably that we had been searching in the wrong place. I went all through the report, but in the end it was to those two passages that my mind kept returning. Finally, I phoned the Oriental Club. I wanted an expert's opinion on whether the island could have disappeared like that, so quietly, so unobtrusively. We had felt no shock, seen no tidal wave.

But Hans Straker had left. They gave me the address of the farm he had taken in Wiltshire and also his telephone number. After some delay I got his housekeeper. He was out, but would be back for lunch. I left a message that he could expect me some time that afternoon.

I am not quite certain now of my motive in suddenly deciding to go down to Wiltshire. I think it was partly the need to do something positive, partly a reluctance to face Ida that evening. I marked the report 'No comment,' handed it to Elliot and caught the next train to Swindon. The farm was some way beyond Ogbourne St George, a big, mellow, brick house built on the slope of a chalk down. The wheat was coming up in the bottom fields, a sea of green in the still bright air, and looking at that quiet rural scene as my taxi climbed the hill, the Indian Ocean seemed a million miles away. But a man's interests are not changed by his immediate surroundings.

Hans Straker looked even bigger and more florid than when I had last seen him, his fair hair bleached almost white so that the greying of his years barely showed. He gave me a whisky whilst I explained the purpose of my visit. 'Strode Orient, eh? So you took my advice.' He was smiling as though it really did give him satisfaction that I had got myself a job that meant something to me. And then he took me through into a room full of seismographical equipment and gave me a short lecture on the general principles of submarine volcanic action.

His voice was thick and guttural, his English very precise, as he explained to me that an island such as I had described must have originated from the bed of the ocean itself – in this case probably from a depth of around 2000 fathoms. 'The wrinkling of the earth's crust as it gradually shrinks over the millennia produces fissures and lines of weakness much as clay soil does in a drought. This process goes on under the sea exactly as it does on land. The difference is that two thousand fathoms of water acts as a gigantic damper so that unless the eruption is a very major one it has little effect except to produce shock waves in the water. The surface speed of these shock waves is around three hundred miles per hour and in a big volcanic disturbance such as Krakatoa these hills of surface water will travel round the entire globe. However,' he added, 'a thing like Krakatoa happens only once in a lifetime – at least one hopes so.'

He stood with his glass gripped in his big hand, staring at the trace of the recording needle. 'You have to remember that the earth's crust is only about fifty miles thick. It is like a thin skin. The wrinkles and weaknesses in it are formed by the stresses of contraction through cooling. It is only when the tension breaks that you get a major earthquake or an eruption.'

'And you don't think that could have happened in this case?'

'About a fortnight ago? And you say you flew over the area and saw nothing?' He shook his big head. 'Definitely not. For an island and adjacent shallows to disappear so completely in a matter of days would constitute a major disturbance. My new instruments are very good. If there had been such a disturbance they would have recorded it.'

'Even at this distance?'

'Ja. Even at this distance. That is quite definite.' He downed his drink. 'Now, about this island of yours. It interests me very much. That area of the Indian Ocean is known to be weak. But it is not regarded as dangerous. At least, not as far as we know. The trouble is we are very short on information. The seismographic stations are a long way from it and we know almost nothing about the sea bed stratas.' He stood, feet slightly straddled, staring thoughtfully at his instruments. 'However, I did record a very considerable number of small tremors during the period I was taking readings at my place in Java.' He took a great sheaf of recordings from a drawer. 'I'm afraid these won't mean anything to you, but I had the very latest equipment – it was probably the most sensitive in the area.' He paused at a sheet. 'See that?' He showed it to me, a barely perceptible movement of the inked trace. 'This is quite a pronounced tremor in the area of the Chagos Archipelago – south of Addu Atoll.' He pointed to the date. 'April last year.' He tossed the sheaf of recordings on to the table. 'No point in going through them with you. Simpler for you to take my word for it that it was one of the many indicating a persistent process of adjustment of the earth's crust in that area.' And he went on to consider the significance of manganese nodules, confirming that this would normally be associated with the sea bed, indicating that the island was the result of a protracted upward movement of the earth's crust.

'But all that debris,' I said.

'Pumice. Aerated laval debris.' He nodded. 'It would point to some submarine vent or fissure.'

'And the water round us boiling like that?'

'That is, of course, an indication of volcanic action, but not I think severe.' And he explained that eruptions of any magnitude only occurred when the increase in tension of the earth's crust became insupportable and was suddenly released. 'Then you get a really big tremor, an earthquake of shattering proportions.'

'And you don't think it possible – '

'I tell you – I have recorded nothing of any magnitude.' He reached for the file containing his records. 'See for yourself. There is the trace covering that week.'

It showed nothing, absolutely nothing of note. I asked him then what the effect would have been if the movement had been too slight for his seismograph to record it. I was thinking of the island as I had last seen it, the lonely hut lashed by wind and rain, the lightning stabbing. 'Would it have been a quick death?' But he couldn't tell me that. He wasn't an imaginative man and he only knew the theory of it. He had never seen an eruption, never experienced an earthquake. To him it was a game played on graph paper, an ink trace wavering as the thin skin of the globe on which humanity dwelt made its small local adjustments. He had never been present. He had only read about it. It wasn't the same thing. 'To my knowledge it has been going on for three years and all the tremors have been slight. I see no reason why such a slow, steady movement should suddenly snap and the whole thing explode. Volcanic action of that sort is mercifully rare.'

He took me back into the other room and refilled my glass. He was talking about Fayal in the Azores where a new island had been born in 1957, but I was puzzling over the disparity between his categorical assurance that the island could not have disappeared and the evidence of my own eyes. 'Do your instruments give you the exact location of tremors?'

'No.' He shook his head. 'For that you need recordings from a number of stations and my inquiries at the time showed only one other seismographer who had recorded it – in India. We had quite a correspondence about it, but failed to develop any definite theory as to what exactly was going on or where precisely the centre of activity was. Then, of course, my work was interrupted so that I never did get to the bottom of it.'

He insisted that I stayed to dinner, and all the time he talked about eruptions and volcanic islands, his mind roving the vulcanologists' world in search of parallel cases, constantly referring to the books in his library to check on details that had escaped his memory. The situation fascinated him, and he kept on questioning me – about the analysis of the island's ore deposits, the sea temperatures at various distances off, the nature of the pumice we had steamed through. He was like a detective of the geophysical searching for clues in a new and absorbing case.

Afterwards he drove me into Swindon, and as we parted at the railway station, he said 'I shall cable my Indian contact and also make some inquiries here in England. Whether your friend Strode is still alive or not, I cannot say, but I think you must proceed on the premise that you have been searching the wrong area.' And when I reminded him that the area already searched was a quarter of a million square miles, he said obstinately, 'Then your island must be outside of that area.' And he added, 'Have you considered, for instance, that it may have contained other minerals besides manganese, minerals that might affect a ship's compass? Even aircraft, I believe, can be thrown off course by large iron ore deposits when flying low.'

How near, how desperately near, he had got to the truth, and I dismissed it without giving it another thought. There was no iron in the ore samples – we knew that. And Shackletons are fitted with gyro compasses. But his conviction that the island could not have disappeared suddenly without trace, that was a different matter, and it occupied my mind all the way back to London. He had been so certain of it, so categorical that I found myself, against all the evidence, swinging to Ida's view.

I rang her as soon as I got back to the flat, but she was out, and in the morning her friend told me that she still hadn't returned. She had been away all night and I might have worried about it if I hadn't had something more immediate to occupy my mind. Under the headline STRODE BUBBLE PRICKED the City page of my newspaper carried a long piece on the future of the Strode companies. It described the Indian Ocean venture as the brainchild of an inexperienced young man who should never have been elected to the board. 'Whilst everybody must regret his death in such circumstances, and the deaths of those with him on the island, it is some consolation to the management and shareholders of Strode Orient that the prompt action of Captain Reece in saving his ship prevented what might have been a much greater loss of life.' It went on to consider plans for the reorganization of the two companies and finished up by advising any members of the public who still held shares in Strode & Company to attend the meeting and support those directors who were in favour of strengthening the board and reorganizing the companies.

The piece was so obviously inspired that I knew Whimbrill was wrong; the show-down was going to be now, today, at the annual general meeting. I had a quick cup of coffee and left immediately for Strode House. But though I arrived there shortly after nine Whimbrill was already in the boardroom with the rest of the directors. The meeting was a long one and I spent a frustrating morning, not knowing what was going on. I had the papers brought up to me and several other City editors had the same sort of story and took the same line, and when I rang Latham he told me the shares were down to a nominal seven shillings. The outlook was grim. I couldn't trust Whimbrill any longer and once Slattery and Wolfe were on the board and the reorganization of the companies under way I knew I wouldn't have a hope of getting the co-operation I needed from Strode Orient. We had come so far – all our hopes so nearly fulfilled – and now to end like this, blocked by men in pursuit of money. And as I sat there in my office, alone and waiting, there was the thought nagging at my mind – that the island might still be there and Peter alive. The minutes ticked slowly by, the time of the meeting steadily approaching, and still I couldn't get at Whimbrill, find out what he intended to do.

I was in a mood of complete depression when, shortly after eleven-thirty, Ida came in. She was dressed in a coat and skirt and looked deathly pale. 'Have you seen this?' She had a copy of one of the papers with her, open at the City page. 'How did they get hold of all this information?'

'Lingrose, I imagine,' I said.

'What's Dick Whimbrill going to do? Have you discussed it with him?'

'No. He was at a board meeting when I arrived. It's been going on ever since.'

'Arguing over the terms, I suppose – who gets what.' Her voice trembled. 'Father would kill them if he knew. What are you going to do about it? If even a few outside shareholders support them – '

'What can I do?' I said wearily.

'For God's sake – something. You can't just sit there.' She was staring at me wide-eyed, her face blank. 'Haven't you any fight in you?' There was a violence about her I could literally feel. It hung quivering in the air. 'That man Reece,' she said suddenly. 'Abandoning Peter like that. It was all part of a plan. You realize that? And they're down in the boardroom, carving up the remains. If you'd any guts you'd have gone down there and told them what you thought of them.'

I tried to calm her, but she was quite beside herself. 'George hated Peter – always did.' She drew a deep breath. 'If you won't break in on them, then I will.' And she turned abruptly, making for the door.

'Ida! Just a minute.' I jumped to my feet. This wasn't the moment to make wild accusations, not until we knew what they had decided. I needed George Strode, needed his co-operation. 'Ida!' I caught up with her as she was opening the door and gripped her arm.

She didn't attempt to get free of me. She just stood there, staring up at me and the expression of her eyes shocked me. It wasn't anger. It wasn't hate even. It was something more deadly – absolute contempt. And in an ice-cold voice she said, 'That story was leaked – for a purpose. It's an old game. You build up a company's prospects, get the small investor in, then you arrange for something to go wrong, leak it as a rumour that frightens all the rabbits, and when the crash comes you step in and pick up the bits. Father told me how it was done. That was after he'd destroyed a wretched little company that owned some godowns out East he wanted . . . He was a devil at that sort of thing.'

'This has got nothing to do with your father,' I said. 'This

993

is quite different.'

'An absolute devil,' she breathed, her lips drawn back and her teeth showing, so that I glimpsed for an instant the love-hate relationship that had existed between them.

I closed the door firmly, suddenly realizing there was a side of her that was attracted by her father's ruthlessness. 'George isn't in his class,' I said.

'No? Then why was that man Reece appointed? He was brought in for a definite purpose.'

I wasn't prepared to argue about that, but Reece was a professional seaman and I had seen his face when he realized the island wasn't there any more. 'Whatever his instructions,' I said, 'it never occurred to him that they would involve loss of life. As the man responsible for not having brought them off to the ship he took it very hard.'

'Naturally. It had become something different then. Not just an accident, an error of judgement.' She was standing, dry-eyed and rigid, her hands quite cold. 'It had become murder.' She said it in a flat, tired voice, and having made that appalling statement all the violence seemed drained out of her.

'We don't know Peter is dead. Not yet.' But she didn't seem to hear and I realized that something had happened since I had seen her last to make her change her mind; she no longer believed he was alive. I told her then about my visit to Hans Straker. 'I tried to phone you last night and again this morning.' But though I went over all he had said to me, all his arguments, I don't think she took it in. 'You were right,' I said finally. 'I must see Deacon, and there's the *Strode Venturer* herself. She'll be in Aden at the end of this week and there'll be entries in her log covering that first voyage to the island.'

She nodded, her face blank, her eyes empty, her hand in mine entirely limp. And then in a dull voice she said, 'I've been up most of the night. Old Mr Turner died this morning. That's why you couldn't get me. I was at the nursing home. They rang me shortly after eight yesterday evening. I was with him when he died.'

'I'm sorry,' I said. 'I hope it wasn't – ' I was going to say 'too painful an end', but I let it go and she smiled wanly and shook her head.

'He was under drugs. It was quite easy – for him, I think. Not for me. He was conscious for a while.' Her face had softened at the recollection and I asked whether he'd said anything. She nodded and her eyes came suddenly alive, a glint of amusement though she was very near to tears. 'He asked me whether I was going to marry you. And when I admitted that we had discussed it, he seemed pleased; gave us his blessing and some advice. He always liked to give me the benefit of his advice. He's been doing it since I could crawl.'

The phone rang then and I took it off its cradle and laid it on the desk. 'What was his advice?'

She shook her head. 'I'm not telling you what he advised me. It was much to much to the point. But he had some advice for you.' She looked up at me, a long questioning look.

'Well?' I asked.

'It was to cultivate toughness. He said to warn you that nobody could direct the affairs of a company and survive in the City unless he had bounce as well as energy. He thought you had the vitality, but not the bounce, and that if you were going to get back what your father had lost you'd need to be tougher than he was – and you'd need luck as well.' She was still looking straight at me. 'He died just as it was getting light. I had breakfast at the nursing home and when I got to the station I bought that newspaper. His advice seemed suddenly very apt.' And she added, the harshness back in her voice, 'It's not George and Henry we're up against now. It's these new men and somebody will have to be cleverer as well as tough to beat them at their own game.'

I stared at her, my eyes suddenly opened to the sort of person I was thinking of marrying. She had spent the night by the bedside of a dying man, gradually convincing herself that her brother had died a ghastly death on the other side of the world, and now dry-eyed and cold as ice she was bolstering up my courage and telling me how tough I'd got to be if we were to hold on to Strode & Company. 'You take after your father,' I said.

'So I've been told,' she replied tersely. And then with a little smile – 'Fortunately my mother also contributed.'

That glint of humour, the fact that she could smile – it's often the little things that give one confidence. And when I put the phone back on its cradle Elliot rang to remind me that George Strode expected me to attend the meeting. It meant that they had no idea I was a Strode shareholder in my own right. I had an edge on them then, the chance of springing a surprise, and when Whimbrill came through just as we were leaving to say that the directors had finally decided to support the Lingrose nominations, I was no longer in the mood to accept it as inevitable. Indeed, I was suddenly glad it had come to a head. 'You opposed it, of course.'

There was silence at the other end of the line and I knew that he hadn't. He hadn't dared. 'Well, it doesn't matter what you do yourself,' I said, 'but see that you use Peter's proxy to vote the way he would have voted had he been here.' He started to argue that the proxy was invalid now that Peter was dead, but I told him that was nonsense. It would only be true when his death was proved beyond any doubt. And in any case . . . 'Surely it's the intention at the time he signed the proxy that counts.' And I told him to get on to Turner's partner and find out what the legal position was. 'I'm not at all certain Peter is dead,' I said and put the phone down.

It was time to go to the meeting then and as we went down the stairs together I was thinking of the haphazard way it had all started – that pilgrimage to the City on the top of a bus in the early morning. And now the dream was ended. It was all very well to talk like that to Whimbrill, but I wasn't at all sure he would use that proxy the way Peter had intended. I wasn't even sure that if he did we had enough shares to block them. I'd no confidence in myself or anybody else as we reached the main entrance under the cupola and the great chandelier.

The annual general meeting of Strode & Company was an even smaller gathering than the Strode Orient meeting I had attended three months previously. It was almost entirely a family affair with a few friends and members of the staff to help fill it out. I doubt whether the shareholders present included more than three members of the general public. The directors were already seated at the top table when we came in, all except Whimbrill. The proceedings started prompt at twelve o'clock with the same formal reading of the notice convening the meeting. Ida's hand touched mine, a quick grip of the fingers. She was keyed up, leaning slightly forward, her face very tense. Something of her mood must have communicated itself to me for as Henry Strode rose from his seat I found myself suddenly calm, the sort of calm you feel when the battle klaxons have gone and the guns' crews closed up.

His conduct of the proceedings was easy, almost casual. He had the air of a man who had done this so many times before that his words were quite automatic. The accounts were passed, his speech taken as read, and then there was a pause, everybody waiting. Whimbrill slid into his seat, not looking at anyone, his eyes on the table and his face very pale, the burn scars showing livid. The traffic in the street outside was loud in the stillness as Henry Strode picked up the agenda, glanced at it, tossed it down and then removed his glasses to face the hall. 'This year two of our directors retire by rotation. My brother, George Strode, has served on the board for seventeen years; Colonel Hinchcliffe for fourteen. In the interests of the company's future they are not offering themselves for re-election and I am sure you will wish me to express your thanks to them for the long years of service . . .'

Whimbrill was staring up at his chairman with the set expression of a man under sentence, his hands clenched round each end of the ball-point pen he held. The snap of the plastic as it broke was loud against the quiet monotone of Henry Strode's voice. 'In their place your company has been offered the services of two very able and experienced men.' As he named Slattery and Wolfe and spoke of their connection with Liass Securities – 'a powerful and very go-ahead investment group who already have a big stake in your company' – Ida leaned towards me and whispered, 'Those two smug bastards.' She said it elegantly, with a little smile, but the light of battle was in her eyes as she nodded to where Slattery and Wolfe sat together just across the aisle from us.

Henry Strode was now proposing their election to the board. He was seconded by le Fleming and it was then put to the meeting. He nodded as hands were dutifully raised. 'Against?' Except for Ida and myself there wasn't a soul left in that small gathering to raise their hands in opposition and he didn't even glance at the directors' table where Whimbrill sat, taut-faced and still, fingering that damaged ear. 'Motion carried.'

I glanced at Whimbrill, waiting. But he sat quite still, his eyes on the table, making no move. I knew then that it was up to me and I got slowly to my feet. 'This is a very vital decision, Mr Chairman. It affects the whole future of the company. In the circumstances I think it right to request that votes be counted.'

George Strode tugged at his brother's sleeve and I had scarcely resumed my seat when Henry Strode said on a note of cold severity: 'I understand you are here solely as an employee of Strode Orient to answer certain questions that may be raised later. You are, therefore, out of order – '

'I am here as a shareholder,' I said.

He hesitated and then glanced at Whimbrill who, almost reluctantly it seemed, nodded his head. 'Well, it doesn't really matter,' Henry Strode went on suavely. 'Since the number voting in favour of the motion is so overwhelming I see no real necessity – '

'Well, I do.' Ida had risen to her feet. 'I hold forty thousand shares and I'm not going to stand by and see the company my father built – '

'Kindly sit town, Ida. And remember please that he was my father also.' And in a quieter tone, facing the body of the hall again, Henry Strode said, 'I think you should know that the votes supporting the motion total over two hundred and thirty thousand – nearly half the capital of the company.'

'Nevertheless, sir, since it has been challenged' – Whimbrill had at last decided to intervene. His tone was diffident but firm. 'It would be advisable to count votes – for the record.'

Henry Strode hesitated. Then he nodded. 'As you please.' He sounded indifferent. But his eyes followed closely as each raised hand giving his name whilst the auditor, acting as teller, checked his shareholding. Even in such a small meeting it took time. When it came to those against the motion there was only Ida and myself. The figures were totted up, secretary and auditor conferring as the directors' proxies were added. At last it was done and Whimbrill rose slowly to his feet, still pale, still diffident, his voice betraying his nervousness. 'The motion is lost.'

'Lost!' George Strode was on his feet. Several others, too. 'Read out the figures,' somebody demanded.

'For the motion – 232,816; against – 241,265.'

George Strode sat down again, a look of bewilderment on his face. His brother said something to him and their eyes fastened on Ida and then on me, puzzled, uneasy, anxious to know where the attack had come from. Finally George Strode turned to the auditor. 'Only two hands were raised against the motion.' He stared at the man, his head thrust angrily forward like a bull searching for his adversary.

It was Whimbrill who answered him. 'Mrs Roche, as you know, owns forty thousand shares, and Commander Bailey – ' he glanced at a slip of paper in front of him ' – holds sixty-seven thousand, two hundred and – '

'Bailey, you say – but this morning, when you produced that list for us . . .'

'This isn't a recent purchase.'

'How long has he had them then?'

'These shares were purchased over a long period by Mr Lawrence Turner. He gave them to Commander Bailey a few weeks ago.'

'Gave them to him?'

They were all staring at me and if he could have been there I am certain old Turner would have enjoyed that moment. I got to my feet. 'You will know better than I,' I said, speaking directly to Henry Strode, 'how closely Mr Turner was associated with your father. He gave me these shares, in trust as it were for the future of this company, to be used in just such an eventuality as this. He died this morning,' I added, a feeling of contempt rising in me, 'and it can have been cold comfort to him knowing as he did what you were planning to do. The gift of these shares to me is the measure of his determination to do what he could to prevent the company falling into the hands of a group of unscrupulous men bent on wrecking what he had helped to build.'

The room was very still as I sat down. Henry Strode gave a little cough. 'I think you should withdraw that last remark.' And when I didn't answer, he said with emphasis, 'In reaching our decision this morning about the future we all of us had the best interests of the two companies in mind.' He turned to Whimbrill again. 'I take it that the balance of the shares against the motion was in the form of proxies?'

'I hold one proxy only. It's for a hundred and seventeen thousand shares – signed by Peter Strode.'

I saw Henry Strode make a quick mental calculation. 'And you have no other proxy. My sister, Jennifer de Witt didn't – '

'No. She decided that as a Dutch resident she would prefer not to vote. The balance – ' Whimbrill hesitated, looking up at his chairman, a small, tired, disfigured man who, now that he had decided to fight, suddenly had stature. 'The balance is made up of my own shares. I own seventeen thousand and fifty and I voted against the motion.'

'I see.' Henry Strode removed his glasses and stooped towards Whimbrill. 'And you voted against us.' His tone was magisterial, the threat of dismissal there for all to see. 'You realize, of course, Mr Whimbrill, that with Peter Strode's death – '

'He's reported missing, that's all.'

'My information leads me to fear that it's more definite than that.' And in support of his brother, George Strode said, 'They've been searching for him for a week – and for that damned island of his. And now the search has been called off.'

'That's not conclusive,' Whimbrill said obstinately. 'And in any case, I have taken legal opinion on this. Until a coroner or some other court has confirmed his death the proxy he signed is perfectly valid.'

'Dammit, man, what more do you want? The whole resources of the RAF – '

George Strode was on his feet again, and so was I. 'That would mean nothing,' I said, 'if it is proved that Reece has deliberately

999

given them the wrong position.' It was a shot in the dark, the use of the word deliberately quite unjustified, but by then I was past choosing my words. I was so angry I didn't care what I said and as I stood there, staring at George Strode, I saw him wilt and his eyes dart quickly round the room as though afraid others would make the same accusation. The man was suddenly scared. He sat down abruptly and an awkward silence hung over the room, broken by the scrape of Slattery's chair as he left. Henry Strode stood there a moment, undecided. To press the matter was to appear to be wanting his own half-brother dead. Finally he said, 'I think in the circumstances it would be best to adjourn this meeting *sine die*.'

I would have been prepared to accept that, but to my surprise Whimbrill demanded that the question of adjournment should be put to the meeting in the form of a motion. As sometimes happens when a man has his back to the wall and is forced to fight, he was a different person entirely. He seemed suddenly in command of the situation. Henry Strode sensed this and after a hurried con- sultation he proposed instead the re-election of his brother and Hinchcliffe. We followed Whimbrill's lead and voted against it. With Lingrose's support withdrawn the motion was lost by a huge margin.

'I think, Mr Chairman,' – Whimbrill had risen to his feet – 'there is really only one solution to the present difficulty.' And he then proposed that Ida and I should be elected to fill the vacancies on the board. 'Mrs Roche is, of course, a member of the family. Commander Bailey, who is now one of the largest share- holders, has also been closely connected . . .' I don't think anybody heard him refer to my connection with Bailey Oriental for the sudden outbreak of conversation almost drowned his voice. He put the motion and to my astonishment it was seconded by Elliot from the body of the hall. There was no need to count the votes and Henry Strode, his voice trembling, all his casual ease of manner gone, said, 'I shall, of course, take legal opinion myself. In the meantime, I must make it plain that I propose calling a further meeting as soon as Peter Strode's unhappy death is con- firmed.' He then concluded the formalities by proposing the re- election of the auditors and after that the meeting broke up.

An air of shock hung over the big, ornate room, and as the members of the family and their friends filed out they stared at us curiously. At the directors' table Whimbrill was as isolated as we were. 'You won't get away with this.' It was John Strode. He had occupied the big office next to his father ever since he had come

down from Cambridge and his face was white with rage. Then a
reporter was at my side asking me to fill in for him on what Whimbrill had said about my connection with the company. He looked
barely twenty and he had never heard of Bailey Oriental. And
then he was asking Ida how she felt as the only woman on the
board. 'I've no idea,' she said sharply. 'I'm more concerned about
my brother at the moment.'

By the time we'd got rid of him the place was empty, only
Whimbrill and ourselves left. 'What happens now?' Ida inquired.

'You may well ask, Mrs Roche.' Whimbrill gave her a lop-sided
smile. 'To comply with the Companies Act you both have to write
me letters expressing your willingness to serve as directors. Ante-
dated, of course. But that can wait. Right now I think a drink, perhaps.' He was in that mood of elation that follows upon the
success of a desperate decision and as we went out through the
main doors I was wondering whether Turner had envisaged this.
Had he planned it all, thinking it through like a game of chess –
right through to the point where Whimbrill would be forced to
propose Ida and myself for election to the board? But I didn't
think so, for nothing had been solved. All we had done was gain
time.

We lunched together, but though we discussed it from every
possible angle we always came back to the same thing in the end
– everything depended on Peter being alive, the island still there.
Back at the office I rang George Strode. I thought he might refuse
to see me after what had happened, but instead he told me to
come straight down so that I had the feeling he had been expecting me. 'I want you to understand, Bailey, that the full resources
of Strode Orient are at your disposal so long as you think there's
a chance those men may still be alive.' He seemed almost relieved
when I told him what I wanted – Deacon reinstated and authority
to question the crew of the *Strode Venturer*.

'You're planning to go out there yourself, are you?'

'Yes. If I catch tomorrow's flight to Cairo I can be in Aden at
ten-thirty on Thursday.'

'Very well. I'll tell Simpkin to be at Khormaksar to meet you.'
And he drafted a cable to his agent and had it sent off straight
away. 'If there's anything else . . .' His manner was strangely
affable, quite at variance with the attitude he and his brother had
taken at the meeting. But I didn't have time to consider the
implications of this. In less than twenty-four hours I was in a
Comet being lifted over the huge sprawl of London on a journey
that would take me back again to the Indian Ocean.

PART SIX

I

DEACON

THE *Strode Venturer* was already at Aden when I arrived. I had seen her, anchored off Steamer Point, through the plane windows as we came in to land at Khormaksar. Deacon was not there to meet me, only Simpkin, a neat, dapper man in a tropical suit. He had pale eyes and a little brushed-up moustache and he kept me standing in the blazing sun whilst he told me how he'd found Deacon in the Arab town of Crater, dead broke and living in absolute squalor. He had got him into a hotel for the night, but in the morning he had vanished.

'Did you give him any money?' I asked.

'I had to. He had nothing and Mr Strode's cable – '

'Then what the hell did you expect?' I was hot and tired and very angry. I had expected Deacon to be waiting so that we could go straight on board the *Strode Venturer* and try to work out the courses Peter had steered with the charts in front of us. Now I'd have to waste time searching for him, and when I found him he'd undoubtedly be drunk.

It was a long time since I had been in Aden, but it hadn't changed much and down by the harbour at Steamer Point we picked up one of those Arab pimps that lie in wait for seamen coming ashore. He was a fat, fawning man with a pock-marked face and greedy eyes, but he knew the grog shops, all the dives. What's more he knew Deacon. No doubt half the riff-raff of the waterfront knew him by now, which was why I hadn't gone to the police.

Three hours we wasted, along the waterfront of Ma'alla wharf where the dhows lay and all up through the back streets of Crater. Finally, exhausted with the heat and the aimless futility of the search, I threatened to kick our Adeni guide out of the car and go to the police. A panic flash of gold teeth in the pock-marked face and he was pleading for us to drive back to Steamer Point and the port. 'I talk to boatmen, sah. Captain Deacon, he have Ingleesh friends, eh? Drinks all free on Ingleesh sheep.'

It was obvious then that he'd known where Deacon was all the time. The hours of searching had been a charade to demonstrate that he'd earned the five pounds I'd offered him. I cursed him wearily and we drove back to Steamer Point. 'When were you last on board the *Strode Venturer*?' I asked Simpkin.

'This morning.'

'Did you inquire whether Deacon was there?'

'Of course.' But he had only inquired of Captain Jones. He hadn't inquired of the first officer and he certainly hadn't searched the cabins. I was remembering that long, lugubrious face, the shifty, foxy eyes. Fields. That was the name. Arthur Fields. And he'd been with Deacon a long time; at least that was my impression. 'I think we'll find he spent the night on board.'

They had, in fact, gone on board in the early hours of the morning. The boatman who had rowed them out to the ship, produced now with great alacrity by our guide, said that the big man had been very drunk and had had to be helped up the gangway.

It was blowing a hot wind off the volcanic heights as we took a launch out to the *Strode Venturer*. There were lighters alongside and she was loading cargo into No. 2 hold, some of it RAF stores for Gan. The first officer could hardly be said to be in charge of the loading, but he was there, his face grey under the peaked cap, his eyes slitted against the glare of the sun now falling towards the west. 'Mr Fields!' I called and his eyes flicked open lizard-like in the sun. The winch clattered close behind him and as though that provided him with a working excuse he turned deliberately away to watch the Chinaman at the controls.

I swung myself up the ladder to the deck where he was standing. He must have heard me coming, but he didn't turn until I tapped him on the shoulder. 'I called to you,' I said. The tired, bloodshot eyes faced me for a moment, long enough for me to realize that dislike was mutual. Then they shifted uneasily away and he reached into his pocket for his cigarettes. 'Where's Deacon?' I asked him.

'How would I know?'

'You brought him on board – some time in the early hours.'

He lit his cigarette and puffed a cloud of smoke. 'You caused enough trouble,' he said. 'You and that fellow Strode. Soon as you came on board at Gan – '

'Would you mind taking me to his cabin?' I said.

'Why should I?' The sour cockney face looked suddenly full of hate. 'You get him sacked and thrown on the beach and the agent comes on board this morning and tells Jones he can pack his bags and go ashore 'cause Harry Deacon's reinstated.' There was something almost vicious in the way he'd turned and snapped at me – like a vixen defending its mate. 'What're you trying to do – crucify him? A man needs warning after that sort of treatment. He needs an hour or two to get used to the idea he's taking command again.' The thin, sensitive mouth, the lank hair under the dirty white cap . . . I was beginning to understand as he spat out, 'You educated bastards think other men haven't got any feelings. What do you want with him, anyway?' The foxy eyes peered up at me. 'Either he's reappointed or he isn't.'

'Don't you listen to the BBC news bulletins?'

'Why should I?' And he added sourly, 'If you'd been on this ship as long as I have, the same ports, the same dead, hell-hot sea . . .'

'If you hate it so,' I snapped, 'why don't you get another job?' But I knew why, of course. He couldn't face the world outside. He was a failure, relying on Deacon's friendship and afraid to stand on his own feet. This was his escape, this battered ship, and he was a prisoner serving a life sentence. I told him what had happened, but it didn't register. Nothing would ever register with him but what directly concerned himself. 'So that's why he's reinstated – just so that he can find the island for you.' And he added, 'Serves Strode right if he has killed himself on that filthy heap of volcanic slag. He went to enough trouble to see that we wouldn't be able to tell anyone where the hell it was.' He looked up at me out of the corners of his eyes, greed glimmering through the shiftiness. 'What's there, anyway? Gold? Diamonds?'

'Manganese,' I said. 'And now I want to talk to Deacon.' No good asking him where the island was. He might be capable of navigating according to the book, but he'd no feeling for the sea. I gripped his arm and turned him towards the bridge accommodation. 'Don't let's waste any more time,' I said.

'He's tired, you know.' The voice was almost a whine, for he'd caught my mood and was suddenly scared.

'Drunk, you mean.'

He shook my hand off. 'He was in a Jap prison camp for three and a half years. We both of us were. But it wasn't the Japs that beat him.' He had a sort of dignity then as he faced me, defending his friend. 'It was afterwards. They never gave him a chance. The Strodes, I mean.' The foxy face peered up at me, the thin lips drawn back from his long discoloured teeth. 'He worked for your father. Did you know that? The Bailey Oriental Line.' I nodded. 'They never forgave him for that. And did you know this – ' He gave me a long-toothed vicious smile. 'Your father committed suicide on this ship.'

I grabbed him without thinking, grabbed him with both hands and shook him till his long teeth rattled in his head. And through the rattle of them I heard the little rat say gleefully, 'Didn't you know? Walked off the stern in the middle of the night.'

'You're lying,' I said. 'He died at sea – a natural death.'

'He drowned himself. In the Bay of Biscay it was and Harry Deacon swore the crew to secrecy.'

I let him go. It could be true. It would explain the shortness of *The Times* obituary, old Henry Strode's sense of remorse, the strange nature of that letter. The sudden wave of anger that had gripped me drained away. If it were true, then what difference did it make now, after all these years? I glanced over my shoulder, but fortunately the agent hadn't followed us. 'Why did you tell me that?' But I knew why. He wanted to make certain I wouldn't have Deacon thrown off the ship again.

He had tucked him away in a little cubby-hole of a cabin two decks down and as he unlocked the door the smell of vomit and diarrhœa hit me in a nauseating wave. Deacon wasn't just drunk. He was dead drunk, and I knew at a glance I wouldn't get any sense out of him for twenty-four hours at least. He was lying half-naked on a pipe-cot that was too small for him and his huge body, glistening with sweat in the light of the unshaded bulb, seemed to fill the place, a bloated, hairy carcass. His mouth was a gaping hole in the stubble of his face and his skin the colour of lead. He looked ghastly. 'Have you had a doctor?'

'He'll be all right,' Fields said quickly. He hadn't dared risk a doctor. 'Some bad liquor he was given, that's all.'

'Too much of it more likely,' I said angrily. 'And no food. He doesn't look after himself.' I wondered if I dared call a doctor. If Deacon were whipped into hospital and the *Strode Venturer* sailed he'd be no good to me. 'Get him up to his old cabin,' I said. 'And see that the portholes are open. He needs air.'

I went in search of Simpkin then. The agent ought to be able to produce a doctor who would do what was necessary and keep his mouth shut. Out on the deck again I found the winches silent, the crew sweating at the hatch covers. Loading seemed to have finished, one of the lighters already pulling away from the ship's side. There was no sign of Simpkin. I went up to the bridge. It was empty – the chartroom, too. And then I heard the sound of a voice coming from behind a door marked 'W. R. Weston, Wireless Operator.' I pushed through it and the voice was the voice of a BBC announcer. The wireless operator was sitting in his shirt sleeves, a glass of beer at his elbow, a small, pale man with tired eyes and a sallow skin. Simpkin was leaning against the white-painted wall behind him, smoking a cigarette. He tapped the wireless operator on the shoulder. 'Commander Bailey,' he said.

Weston looked up at me, at the same time reaching out long, tobacco-stained fingers to the control panel in front of him. The announcer's voice faded and the wireless operator said, 'I have a cable for you.' And he passed me a typed sheet. It was from Ida. *This morning Dick was instructed to post notices to Strode Orient shareholders giving statutory three weeks' notice of extraordinary general meeting. You have until July 24.* So that was the reason George Strode had been so co-operative. I folded it and put it away in my pocket. 'When is the *Strode Venturer* due to sail?' I asked Simpkin.

'Tomorrow morning.'

'You've finished loading. Why not tonight?'

Simpkin hesitated. 'I suppose it could be arranged. She's due to take on fuel at 21.30 hours. If you like I'll try and arrange for you to sail direct from the bunkering wharf.'

He got us away just before midnight and by then I knew what was wrong with Deacon. It wasn't just alcohol. He had picked up some sort of a virus and his liver, weakened by bad liquor, had temporarily packed up. 'If it wasn't that he has the constitution of a bloody ox,' the doctor said, 'I'd have him into hospital right away.' He was an oil company doctor, a florid, big-boned Scot who looked after the tanker crews as well as the refinery personnel. He understood men like Deacon. 'See that you have some Scotch on board,' he advised as I saw him to the gangway. 'Simple food, of course, but ye canna change a man's basic diet just because he's been pumped full of antibiotics.' He thought Deacon would be conscious within twenty-four hours and might have enough energy to start working on my problem in two or three days' time. 'But go easy,' he said. 'By rights I should have moved him ashore. I'm taking a chance and I've only done it because of what you've told me.' He wished me luck and left me with a list of instructions and a whole bagful of pills.

I had the Chinese steward sit up with him all night, but Deacon never stirred, and when I saw him in the morning the only change was that his face seemed to have more colour beneath the black stubble of his growing beard and his breathing was stronger and more regular. He was no longer in a coma, but in a deep, drugged sleep. I sat with him for a time, listening to the steady juddering sound of the ship's engines, the swish of the bow wave through the open porthole. I felt relaxed now, the worries of the last few days set aside by the deep satisfaction I always felt at being at sea.

I must have dozed off for I suddenly woke to find the first officer in the cabin. He was hovering over me and there was something in the expression of his eyes that I didn't like. 'Everything all right, Mr Fields?' It was noon and he'd just come off watch.

'What you doing here?' he asked. 'You waiting to interrogate him?' And he added, 'Can't you realize he's sick? He oughter be in hospital.'

'In that case,' I said, 'Captain Jones would have sailed as master of the *Strode Venturer*.' I got to my feet. 'Come up to the chartroom,' I told him. 'If you don't want me to worry Deacon with my questions then the remedy is in your hands.'

'How do you mean?' He was suddenly suspicious, his eyes uneasy, shifting round the cabin as though for a way of escaping me.

'You tell me where that island really is and I won't have to sit here waiting for Deacon to surface.'

'I don't know where it is.' His voice had changed to that familiar, affronted whine. 'I told you before. Strode hid the ship's sextants. It was he who directed the courses and plotted them, and he wouldn't let anyone near him while he was doing it.'

'And you never managed to get even a glimpse of it over his shoulder?'

'Yes, but it didn't help. There was nothing marked on the chart. He was using a Baker plotting sheet, you see.'

'But you must know what course you were on when you sailed from Addu Atoll.'

'The usual one. You'll find that in the log. And then after dark we turned south. After that I lost track, for he kept on changing the course. He changed the helmsmen, too. Sometimes he'd clear the bridge and steer the ship himself.'

'What about Deacon – where was he?' The pale eyes slid away from me. 'In his cabin?'

'No, he came up to the bridge every now and then, same as he always did.' And he added belligerently, 'No reason why he should change his habits just because one of the Strodes was on board.'

'You mean he was drunk?'

'No, he wasn't drunk. You couldn't ever accuse him of being drunk, not when we were at sea. But the captain doesn't have to be on the bridge all the time.'

I looked at Deacon, lying there, his thick, hairy arms black against the sheets, his eyes closed and his forehead like a great bald dome shining with sweat. Was it really there, the information I wanted, locked behind the gleaming bone? It was hard to believe after what Fields had told me, and my hopes fading, I turned towards the door. 'I'd like to see the ship's log,' I said, and I took him, protesting, up to the chartroom.

But the log didn't help. Thursday, 28 March: Anchor up at 13.56: steamed out of Addu Atoll by the Kudu Kanda Channel, log streamed at the outer buoy 15.07; course 350°, wind NW 7–10 knots, sea calm, visibility five miles approx., haze. At 16.30 hours, having cleared Hittadu, which juts some ten miles to the north, course had been altered to 298°. This was the course for Aden. But at 19.20 there had been a further alteration of course – this time on to 160°. 'It was dark then, I suppose?'

Fields nodded. 'He didn't want the RAF to know he'd turned south. At least, I presume it was that. We were about twenty miles off the island, but he still had the navigation lights switched off.'

'And Deacon agreed to that?'

'I suppose so. I don't know. All I know,' he added venomously, 'was that from then on Strode gave orders around the ship as though he were the captain, not Deacon.'

At 23.00 hours the course had still been 160°, but when I turned the page the continuity was gone. Several pages had been torn from the log and the next entry was dated Sunday, 14 April. It simply recorded that the *Strode Venturer* had dropped anchor off Gan at 17.15 hours. Thereafter the ship's log gave absolutely no indication of where the vessel had been during that crucial fortnight, 29 March to 13 April. And chart No. 748b, which covers the whole northern half of the Indian Ocean, was equally unhelpful. It was grubby, drink-stained and obviously a veteran of many voyages from Singapore to Gan and Gan to Aden, but there was no trace of any pencil markings below 0° 42' South, which is the latitude of the southern end of Addu Atoll.

'Is there any other chart he could have used?' But Fields shook his head and when I checked the *Catalogue of Admiralty Charts*, which he produced from a drawer full of Admiralty publications, it confirmed that there was only this one small-scale chart covering the whole enormous area from the African coast right across to Indonesia. Looking at it in detail with the aid of the chartroom magnifying glass, and in particular the area to the south and east of Addu Atoll and the Chagos Archipelago, I couldn't help thinking that an international survey was long overdue. The paucity of soundings demonstrated all too clearly how little attention hydrographers had paid to the Indian Ocean.

With both log and chart barren of any information as to courses steered I could hardly blame Fields for his failure to help me. However, I did get something out of the hour I spent with him, a clear and surprisingly vivid account of that first expedition to the island. They had sighted it late in the afternoon. 'Just a line against the westering sun,' he described it, and the line so thin at first they had thought it some local squall ruffling the oily swell. It was only gradually, as they steamed steadily towards it, that they had realized it was not the darkening effect of waves, but the low-lying shore of an island. 'Like a coral reef, like an atoll,' he said. 'But as we got nearer we knew it couldn't be an atoll. Least, it wasn't like the atolls of the Maldives. The sun was setting then, the usual tropical blaze, and this filthy island floating there, black and bare like somebody had just raked it out of the fire. There wasn't nothing growing on it – nothing at all. Just a bit of the sea bed.'

'You were approaching from the east then?'

He nodded. 'I can remember the course – so can Deacon, I expect. It was two-seven-o degrees near as makes no odds. But that won't tell you anything. We'd been on all sorts of courses, just about boxing the compass day after day for almost five days, searching all the time.' They had had the echo-sounder on, of course, but the ocean depth was too great for it to record anything until they were within two miles of the island and then suddenly it was reading around 150 fathoms. They went in very slowly, feeling their way, with the water shoaling all the time. They had anchored about a mile off in seventy fathoms. 'We couldn't see very much of the island then. The sun had set right behind it, but what we could see it looked a hell of a place, and there was a strange smell about it. Strode had one of the crew plumb the bottom with the lead and the tallow arming came up covered with a lot of black grit as though we were sitting on a bed of cinders.'

'Was there any volcanic debris floating around?' I asked. 'Pumice, anything like that?'

But he shook his head. There had been no indication at all of volcanic activity and in the morning they had steamed round the island, finally moving the ship into a bay on the western side, leading with the boats and anchoring about two cables off-shore in sixty-four feet. They had worked like blacks all that day and most of the next ferrying boatloads of ore nodules out to the ship until they had the after-hold half full of the stuff and then they had sailed.

'What day was that, do you remember?' I asked him.

He thought for a moment. 'April ninth, I think.' He nodded. 'Yes, it must have been the ninth 'cause I remember it was the night of seventh we'd first sighted it.' And they had been back at Gan the evening of the 13th. Four days' steaming at, say, ten knots. That would be just over 900 miles. 'Did you return to Addu Atoll direct – the same course all the time?' But I knew Peter wouldn't have done that. 'I don't know what course we steered,' Fields said. 'Nor does anyone, not even Deacon. For the first twenty-four hours after we left Strode wouldn't allow any-one in the wheelhouse. He steered the ship himself.'

'Right through the twenty-four hours?'

'Right through the night and all the next day.'

'You had the stars,' I said. 'And the sun during the day. You must have some idea what point of the compass you were steam-ing.'

His eyes shifted uneasily. 'Why should I worry what direction we were steaming? We were getting away from that hell-hole of an island. That's all I cared about. And if one of the directors wants to keep the course secret, it's no concern of mine. Let him get on with it, that's what I thought.'

'You weren't curious?'

'No, I was bloody tired, sick to death of the whole mucking expedition. I'd had a basinful of it, driving those Chinese to quarry the stuff out with picks and shovels, load it into the boats and then get it off-loaded on to the ship. You try filling half a hold with dirty muck like that under a blazing tropical sun. You'd be tired by the end of it. I was just glad I didn't have to stand any watches. I had a few drinks and took to my sack.'

'And Deacon – was he drinking with you?'

His eyes shifted nervously, staring at the sea beyond the chart-room window. 'What if he was? Strode taking over his ship like that, what the hell else was there for him to do?'

So they'd both of them stumbled into their bunks with a skinful of liquor and not a care in the world. I began to doubt whether Deacon would be able to give me any more information than Fields had given me. But at least I had something. I knew the outer limit of the island's distance from Gan was about 900 miles. 'How was we to know the position of that bloody island was going to be important?' The whine was back in his voice.

'No, you weren't to know,' I said. I had got a pair of compasses out of the chart table drawer and was marking a circle in on the chart with a radius of 900 miles from Addu Atoll. The next thing was to interview Brady, the chief engineer.

I saw him after lunch, a thick-set, paunchy little man with red-rimmed eyes whose breath smelt of stale whisky. Yes, they had been short of fuel. In fact, he had raised the matter with Deacon and also with Strode at the time the ship had been turned south in the night past Addu Atoll. They had been due to bunker at Aden and as a result had fuel for rather less than 3000 miles at normal speed. Normal speed was a little over nine knots.

'And economical speed?' I asked him.

The economical speed was nearer seven knots. He had raised the question of fuel again only the day before they had sighted the island. There was then no question of being able to reach Aden; the danger facing them was that they wouldn't have enough fuel to get back to Addu Atoll. 'Did you discuss the fuel situation with Mr Strode at all before you sailed from the island?' I asked.

'Aye. He was aware of the danger.' He had a slow, north country voice.

'So that you had to keep engine revolutions down to the most economical speed all the way back to Gan.'

'We were doing between seven an' eight knots most of the time.'

The circle had narrowed to under 800 miles. It narrowed still further as I began to question the crew, for Peter hadn't steered direct for Gan in those first twenty-four hours. I had no hope of reconstructing the ship's exact course, but at sea most men have some general idea of the direction they are headed – a star seen through a porthole, sunrise, sunset and the heat of the sun during the day, the side of the ship in shade, the dazzle of its reflection in the sea.

Gradually the picture built up – first southerly, then westerly for the first day, the final approach to Addu Atoll from the south, the intermediate variations of course always between 180° and 360°. It was slow work, particularly with the Chinese where I had to depend on an interpreter, mostly the chief steward. But strangely enough it was from the Chinese that I obtained most of my information. They had been scared by the island and not knowing where they were going when they left it, they had been unusually alert to the ship's general direction. I saw most of them twice, some of them three times, checking and cross-checking each observation. It was a process of elimination and when I finally plotted the result on the chart it all added up to an area of probability centred on 03° South, 84° East.

This position was roughly 600 miles east-south-east of Gan and nearly 250 miles north-east of the line the Shackletons had flown on their way to and from the search area. I marked in the position Reece had given. The distance between the two was just over 500 miles.

It was evening of the second day out and the sun was setting by the time I had worked it all out to my satisfaction. I picked up the chart and went through into the wheelhouse. The second officer, Taylor, was on watch, sprawled drowsily in the chair, his eyes half closed. We had just cleared Socotra and the Chinaman at the wheel was steering 118°. Away on the starboard quarter where the sun had just gone down the sky flamed a searing brilliant orange with isolated patches of cu-nim thrusting up black anvil shapes, sure sign that we were getting near the equator. 'What speed are we making?' I asked.

'Eleven knots,' Taylor replied. 'Chief's been on the blower twice.'

I could guess what Brady had said. It wasn't that he loved his engines. It was just that the mountings were so rotten, the hull so strained, he was scared they would shake themselves out through the bottom of the ship. I went along to Deacon's cabin, taking the chart and the parallel rule with me. I had had a talk with him that morning. Now he had had a whole day to think it out and note down all the courses he could remember.

I found him propped up in his bunk, a glass of whisky on the locker beside him and the notebook I had left with him scrawled full of courses, dates and times. I spread the chart on the table and whilst he read the courses and distances out to me I plotted them. There were many gaps, for this was one man's observation covering nearly a fortnight and reproduced from memory nearly three months later when he was ill and suffering from the after-effects of great mental strain.

He gave me the notes on the voyage out from Gan first. The period covered was more than a week, including nearly five days of searching. The search courses could only be guessed at since they had been changed at increasing intervals as the area covered increased. He had, however, been able to reconstruct, with what he thought was a reasonable degree of accuracy, the voyage out to the search area. Plotted on the chart this indicated a position of little over 200 miles north-west of the area of probability I had already arrived at.

I then plotted on a piece of tracing paper the courses he'd noted of the voyage back. The overall course for the first twenty-four hours he reckoned at between SSW and WSW, confirming what I had already learned from the crew. The result of the trace when the final point of it was laid on Gan and the sheet aligned with the chart gave a position south-south-east of his previous position – a difference this time of only 100 miles from my area of probability.

'Well, what's the answer?' His voice sounded tired, a low, rumbling whisper, and he fumbled for his glass. 'Does it add up to anything?' Whisky ran down the stubble of his chin and he didn't bother to wipe it away. 'It seems a long time ago. Too damned long, and my mind's not all that clear . . .' His voice trailed away and his eyes closed.

I gave him the results and he nodded slowly. 'A big area to cover.' I could see him working it out, the island little more than sixty feet high, its range of visibility barely fifteen miles and even that reduced by haze. But he was thinking of it as a sea-level search, whereas a Shackleton would probably be able to cover it in a single day. I drew in a square on the chart, noted the latitude and longitude of the four corners and got to my feet. 'I'll wireless Gan.'

It was almost twenty-four hours before I got Canning's reply: *Regret little likelihood of resumed search being authorized unless you can give me clearer justification. Reece satisfied areas already searched covered the island's last known position. In the circumstances volcanic action still seems most likely explanation of our failure to locate it, but we can discuss it further on your arrival.*

When I showed this to Deacon, he read it through slowly, his steel-rimmed spectacles perched on his big nose. 'Volcanic action,' he growled. 'Submarine pressures, yes. But that island wasn't a bloody volcano. It was a bit of the sea bed, nothing more.' And he added, 'I never did trust Welshmen.' The message-sheet slipped from his fingers and he leaned back with a sigh. 'Justification, he says. What's he mean by that?' His bloodshot eyes stared at me, strangely magnified by the glasses. 'The opinion of an Adduan – a serving officer who's never had anything to do with them.'

'You're thinking of Don Mansoor, are you?'

He nodded. 'He's been there twice, once on his own and once with me, and he shared some of Peter Strode's watches with him.'

'Could he mark the position in on a chart?'

The laugh was thick with phlegm. ' 'Course not. He'd barely seen a chart before he sailed with me. But he knows about the stars, and in his own way he's a good navigator.'

'Canning has had a great deal to do with the Adduans,' I said. He respected them, even admired them. And remembering how those working on the base came in from the other islands each morning sailing their dhonis, I thought perhaps Gan was the one RAF station where the view of the local inhabitants on a matter of navigation might carry weight. At any rate, it was worth trying.

It was the afternoon of 10 July that we reached Addu Atoll, steaming in by the Kudu Kanda Channel. But instead of continuing south across the lagoon to Gan, I ordered Fields to turn the ship to port and anchor just clear of the reefs off Midu. The breeze was fresh on my face as I rowed in to the beach, the palm fronds rattling with a noise like surf and the hot sun glistening on the broken tops of the waves. Inside the reef five vedis lay afloat with their masts already stepped. The palm-thatched boathouses along the beach all stood empty.

The *Strode Venturer*, anchored so close, seemed to have drawn the whole island from its green jungle shell, a great crowd that hemmed me in as I stepped ashore, a circle of brown faces bright with curiosity. An old man came forward, bade me welcome in halting English. But when I asked him for Don Mansoor he swept his arm towards the open sea and said, 'Him leaving on great journey. Looking to island, all men looking to your friend.'

I remembered him then, this old man in the ragged turban, his clothes bunched tight around his thin shanks; he had steered the dhoni that night they brought me secretly to Midu. I asked him when Don Mansoor had left and he said he was leaving now four days. 'And these?' I pointed to the vedis lying in the shelter of the reef. He thought they would leave next day or perhaps the day after. 'All strong men now leaving Midu.' Without their sails the vedis looked lifeless, their fat hulls listless in the still water, the wood tired after the years ashore in the hot sun. I asked him whether they were not afraid to make such a voyage in ships that had been laid up so long.

Yes, he said, they were very much afraid. 'All women fearing their men drown.' He smiled, adding that the fears of their womenfolk wouldn't stop the men of Midu from following Don Mansoor – the Malimi, he called him. 'We Adduans hoping for new life now.' And as we went up to his house he began telling me a rambling story about some monster long ago that used to come in from the sea at night to devour human tribute and how the malimi, the captain of a foreign ship, who believed in a greater god had stood in for the sacrifice and had defeated the monster by his fearless demeanour and by reading the Koran. It was a mythological story, a Maldivian version of St George and the Dragon that represented the islanders' conversion to the Muslim faith, and long before he had finished it I was seated in his house with a drink of palm juice in my hand. It made a very strong impression on me sitting there, conscious of the bed at the far end of the room swaying on its cords, dark feminine eyes limpid in the shadows and the old man talking as the sun went down and the dhonis came in with the men from Gan.

The point of the story was to explain to me that men were not afraid to die if they believed in something. 'Now Ali Raza is making all Midu vedi ready and we are sailing to find your friend and the new land. If Allah wills it,' he added, and the old eyes stared at me, the whites yellowed with age. One of the vedis now afloat was apparently his. 'I am not sailing my vedi for three years now because those Malé men making piracy on the sea. But now I am going for I am – how you saying – *odi vari meeka*, and wishing to see this new land.' The words *odi vari meeka* mean owner rather than captain. There is no word for captain in Adduan, doubtless because they are a seafaring race and any owner would automatically sail his own boat.

A pressure lamp had been lit and the glare of it showed a crowd of men in the open doorway. Others were arriving all the time and soon Ali Raza came in and with him his son who spoke good English and wore a khaki shirt and an aircraftsman's beret.

When I left I took both back to the ship with me. Even if he couldn't point the island's position out on the chart, I thought his determination to sail his vedi in support of Don Mansoor's expedition might spur Canning into flying a new search.

The wind had dropped away and the warm night air was still, not a ripple on the surface of the water as the *Strode Venturer* ploughed south across the black lagoon. The sky was clear, a bright canopy of stars, and standing with Ali Raza on the open wing of the bridge I could see the palm treed fringe of the islands away to port gradually closing in on us. The beauty of the night, the warmth, the absolute tranquillity – it was an island paradise and it seemed tragic to me that these people should have such a desperate longing for something different, all because we had broken in upon their centuries of solitude with our flying machines, our parade of wealth and mechanical power.

We dropped anchor off the Gan jetty and as our engines stopped the scream of a jet tore the stillness of the night apart. The runway lights were on and I could see the *Strode Trader* grounded on the foreshore only a few cables away. Seen like that, black and sharp against the runway glare, she looked a complete wreck, and clear in my mind I saw the island again and the lightning stabbing.

The plane took off, the wink of its navigation lights arcing against the stars as it swung eastwards for Singapore. The marine craft officer arrived. I heard his voice immediately below the starboard bridge wing. He was talking to Fields and shortly afterwards the crew began clearing the hatch covers from No. 2 hold. One of the RAF barges was being manœuvred alongside, the winches were manned and by the time Canning came out in a launch from the jetty the first of the stores was being off-loaded. I met him at the head of the gangway. He had Reece with him and the police officer, Goodwin. 'I'd have been out before,' he said as he shook my hand, 'but I had an Air Vice-Marshal passing through.' He reached into his pocket and handed me a letter. 'This arrived for you two days ago.' It was from Ida and the fact that he had remembered to bring it out with him reminded me how isolated Gan was, how important to them the mail from home.

I took him up to the bridge, and when he saw Ali Raza and his son waiting there he said, 'I've done my best to stop them sailing their vedis off into the blue.' He knew about my visit to Midu and he added, 'I hope you've not been encouraging them. I'm very concerned that they're risking their lives unnecessarily.'

'They don't need encouragement,' I said. 'They've made up their minds.' His concern was genuine. I knew that. But I couldn't help feeling that the organized routine of an RAF station made it difficult for him to understand the urgent emotional forces that were driving them. 'You're faced here with something as inevitable as the suicidal migration of a bunch of lemmings,' I told him. 'That island is important to them. And so is Peter Strode.' I spread the Indian Ocean chart out in front of him. I had ringed my area of probability in red and I was watching Reece as I explained how it had been arrived at. His eyes looked tired, the skin below them puffy. Like all Celts he was gifted with imagination, and imagination can play the devil with a man in moments of stress. I wondered how near he was to cracking up. Very near, I thought, for he didn't let me finish, but leapt at once to his own defence.

'I kept a note of all courses steered. Compass courses, you understand.' He turned to Canning. 'This position is based on nothing more solid than the random observations of a bunch of Chinese seamen.'

'It's confirmed by Captain Deacon,' I said.

'Deacon!' He put his hand to his head. 'My God, man! Are you serious?' He gave a quick little laugh. 'Deacon wouldn't have had a clue where he was. Nor would the crew.' He had become very excited and when I reminded him that what we were discussing might mean the difference between life and death to the men on that island, he stared at me, the muscles of his jaw bunching. 'They're dead,' he said. 'And the island's gone.' And I knew by the way he said it that he had convinced himself that it was true.

'Then why have those two vedis sailed?'

'Natives. They know nothing about navigation.'

'Excuse please.'

Ali Raza moved forward, but Reece brushed him aside. 'Do you think I'd make an error of navigation of over 500 miles? If they want to kill themselves, that's their affair. It proves nothing. The shallows on which we grounded were volcanic. You know that as well as I do. So was the island in my opinion – all part of a volcanic instability.'

'Then why didn't you make an attempt to get the shore party off?'

It pulled him up short and the sweat burst out on his forehead. 'I have explained all that in my report. My first consideration was for the safety of the ship.'

'Yes,' I said. 'I've read your report. It's very convincing, but if you thought the island – '

'You're trying to blame me for what's happened. It's not my fault – it's Strode's. Taking the ship into an area like that, anchoring her on top of a submarine volcano – he must have been crazy. If it hadn't been for me – '

'You dirty little Welsh bastard!' A great paw of a hand reached out and gripped him by the shoulder. 'You left them there to rot.' Deacon's voice, solid, angry, with an edge of violence in it, held us all rooted, whilst Reece squirmed in his grasp.

How long he'd been there, how much he'd heard I don't know. He had entered without a sound and now he stood like an enormous bear, his black, matted chest of hair showing through the open front of his pyjama jacket. He wore an old pair of blue serge trousers, worn-out carpet slippers, and the bald dome of his head shone in the light. 'Well?' The grip of his hand on Reece's shoulder tightened, thick hairy fingers digging into the man's flesh. 'Why did you do it? Why did you leave them there if you were so bloody sure the place was going to erupt in your face?'

'I didn't think there was any immediate danger.' The words came in a rush – quick, almost glib. 'It was the storm that concerned me then, you see. I had to think of the ship.'

'Come here.' Deacon lumbered to the chart table, dragging Reece with him. 'You went aground somewhere there – that's what you claim, isn't it?' His thick finger pointed to the position Reece had given and which I had pencilled in on the chart. 'On the northern tip of a big area of shallows. Are you telling me those shallows wouldn't be visible from the air?'

'It's quite possible,' Canning interjected. 'The light out here can be very difficult, especially in the afternoon heat.'

'What about the ship then?' Deacon had swung his big head, his bloodshot eyes seeming to stare as he faced Canning. 'The *Strode Trader* must have been about half-way between the island and Gan when you began your search.'

'The crews went out before dawn and returned after dark. There was no possibility of their sighting the ship.'

'All right. They couldn't see the ship because it was dark and they missed the shallows because of the midday haze. But Christ! There's no excuse for missing a bloody island, not with radar.'

Canning didn't say anything and his silence was more expressive than words.

'It's disappeared. That's your point, is it? Bloody convenient!' Deacon growled. 'Since your aircrews have failed to sight it you say it isn't there any more. Christ Almighty, man! Why can't you admit you've been searching the wrong area?' He stared at Canning, and when the CO made no comment, he swung round on Reece again, his eyes blazing with anger. 'Who told you to fix it so that they were left to fend for themselves?'

Reece looked up, a quick movement of his head. He was scared then. 'Nobody,' he said quickly, and the way he said it, the sudden shiftiness of his eyes – it made me want to take hold of him and shake the truth out of him.

Deacon's hand reached out, gripped his shoulder again. 'You're lying.' Canning started to say that accusations of that sort didn't help, but Deacon turned on him furiously. 'I know when a man's lying. Somebody's got at him.'

There was a heavy silence. Finally Deacon let go of Reece. 'It doesn't matter,' he said. 'It's not important at the moment. What worries Bailey and myself is those men – out there in the middle of the Indian Ocean with nobody bothering to look for them any more.' He turned back to the chart, ignoring Reece, his eyes on Canning. 'You've searched one area and found nothing. What's your objection to searching there?' And he jabbed at the chart with his finger. 'Don't forget, I've been to this island, too. And I say it's there – somewhere in that area. Hm?' The phlegm sounded in his throat as he stared belligerently. 'Well, what do you say to that?'

Canning gave a little shrug. 'There's nothing I can say. A resumption of the search requires Air Ministry authority. Of course, if Captain Reece were in any doubt about his position . . .'

'I have no doubts,' Reece said quickly. 'No doubts whatever.' He reached for the dividers and measured the distance against degrees and minutes at the side of the chart. 'There's just on six hundred miles between his position and mine.' He turned to Deacon. 'Are you accusing me of deliberately giving a false position?' Even Deacon wasn't prepared to go that far and Reece was suddenly sure of himself as he faced Canning. 'I've said this to you before and I'll say it again in front of these two gentlemen: the position I have given is not exact, but it is reasonably correct. That I will swear to.' It was said firmly, confidently, and I could see Canning comparing the two of them and settling irrevocably for the neat, tidy, reasonable Reece who probably didn't drink and was ambitious. I couldn't blame him. Reece had brought his ship in leaking like a sieve and gutted by fire. He was, therefore, the sort of man you could rely on. Not like Deacon whose reputation in Gan was that of a drunk who let his ship be run by a Chinese steward and who was now standing there, baffled and sullen, a great fat slob of a man looking like a brewers' drayman, half-clothed and with the black stubble of a beard accentuating the ill pallor of his skin.

Deacon must have sensed the comparison that was being made for he turned to Canning and said, 'So you've made up your mind. You won't fly a search in that area?' He pointed to the red circle on the chart.

'I'm afraid it's out of my hands now. If you can put up a convincing case, then I'll be happy to pass it on to Air Ministry.' The matter was closed as far as Canning was concerned.

Deacon stared at him for a moment, then at Reece. Finally he seemed to brace himself. 'Mr Fields!' The first officer materialized in the doorway as though he had been waiting upon his cue. 'Clear the ship and prepare for sea.'

'Aye, aye, sir.'

'If you're thinking of taking your ship into that area I must warn you . . .'

'You can't stop me.'

'No. But you do so at your own risk. You understand that?'

'What risk? What the hell are you talking about? I'm going five hundred miles away from where Reece says he was.'

An awkward silence followed, the two of them standing there facing each other. But Canning was too experienced an officer to let his personal feelings over-ride his duty. Quietly he reminded Deacon that air-sea rescue in the Indian Ocean was his responsibility, that his air crews had already pressed one search to the point of exhaustion. 'I don't want any more trouble.' And he added, 'You don't seem to understand what Captain Reece has been telling you. The shallows where his ship stranded were volcanically active. That activity may be just local or it may extend over a wide area.'

And Reece, still following his own train of thought, said, 'They'd no boats, you see – no means of getting away from the place.'

'What's that got to do with it if the position you've given is the wrong one?' Deacon spoke slowly, a hoarse whisper, and a little runnel of sweat ran down the side of his face as he swung his head to stare at Reece. 'You little bastard!' he said in that same hoarse whisper. 'You're lying – about something; but I don't know what it is.' He looked sick and tired and his eyes had a baffled look. Canning had turned towards the door, Goodwin at his heels. Reece started to follow him, but Deacon gripped him by the shoulder again. 'You're coming with us,' he said. 'We'll see who's bloody right, you or me.'

I saw Reece's fist clench and I moved just ahead of Goodwin. 'Let him go,' I said. 'You'll find out the truth, whether he's with you or not.'

Deacon hesitated. Then slowly his hand relaxed its grip. 'Perhaps,' he murmured. 'But truth is not an absolute and the events that lead to a man's death can be very devious.' He was looking at me then and I knew he was referring to my father. But what surprised me was his choice of words, the remnants of a good education glimpsed through the rags of life's hard schooling. He turned abruptly and went out on to the wing of the bridge, his voice bawling at the mate to get a man on the helm.

'Are you coming ashore?' Canning asked me.

'No,' I said.

He nodded, his mouth a tight line, his eyes cold and unsmiling. Isolated here in the middle of a big ocean he carried a heavy load on his shoulders and I was glad I didn't have his burden of responsibility. 'I'll instruct my people to maintain wireless contact. And I'll notify Air Ministry, of course.' At the head of the gangway he turned to me again. 'I'm sorry, Bailey. It's the best I can do in the circumstances.'

'I understand,' I said, and I stood there and watched them go, the launch cutting a broad V of white in the darkness as it headed in towards the jetty. I was thinking of the broken line of the palms on Wilingili that I had seen from the helicopter and my gaze turned involuntarily to the beached hulk of the *Strode Trader* standing black against the low shore line, remembering how it had happened. Now that I was back in the islands it all seemed to add up to one thing. And if Canning were right, if the whole area were unstable . . .

'Can't you persuade him to hold off till morning, sir?' It was Wilcox, angry at being told to get his men off the ship when unloading had only just begun.

'No,' I said. 'And I don't intend to try.'

The anchor was coming up, the hatch cover going on, the cargo booms already lowered; a hiss of steam from for'ard of the funnel, a white plume against the stars, and then the boom of the siren, brazen in the quiet of the night. I sent Ali Raza ashore with the marine craft officer, and when he had gone I felt suddenly depressed, cut off from the world I knew, the future full of uncertainty. The bridge was manned now, the deck alive under my feet. The engine-room telegraph rang; the screw threshed the water. The *Strode Venturer* gathered way, throwing off the last of the barge warps as she swung her bows towards the Wilingili Channel. And as we steamed through it and the dark line of Addu Atoll was swallowed up astern, I knew there was no escape. I was committed now. The night air was warm on my face and ahead of me the Indian Ocean lay stretched out under the stars. But all I saw was what was in my mind – the water boiling on those shallows, the pumice and the smell of sulphur, the ship stranded. I didn't think I could expect to get away with it a second time.

2

RAN-A-MAARI

Two DAYS OUT from Addu Atoll and the day dawning like all the other days I had spent on that strange ship. I woke to the surge of the bow wave and a flat calm sea that was like the beaten surface of a bronze shield. Then suddenly the sun was up and it was hot, the sea a mirror so full of light it hurt the eyes. A knock at the door, and one of the Chinese crew came in with a wireless message. It was from George Strode ordering the ship to return to Gan immediately to complete the unloading of RAF stores. It was a terse, angry message, demanding an explanation of the ship's failure to deliver the cargo and threatening legal action.

I lay there listening to the sound of the sea and thinking about the future, my naked body sweating under the coarse cotton sheet; thinking, too, of what Ida had said in that letter, the Strode Orient meeting only a fortnight away and Felden now prepared to vote for the liquidation of the company. We couldn't even rely on Whimbrill any more. *They have made him an offer and he is under great pressure.* And Ida had added, *I have done my best. I am at Strode House almost every day. But unless you find the island – and Peter – the situation is hopeless.*

I stared out of the open porthole. Nothing but sea – endless, flat and torpid with the heat. The horizon was already hazed, a blurred line shimmering. London seemed a long way away, so remote that I thought it hardly worth the effort of replying to Ida's letter. The knowledge that tomorrow we would start searching did nothing to lift my spirits. The chances of success appeared very slight indeed. I dressed and went up on to the bridge. The Chinese quartermaster was there. Nobody else, except the helmsman. And the ship ploughing steadily on into the blinding dazzle of the sun's reflected light. I had scarcely seen Deacon since we'd sailed. Once we were through the Wilingili Channel he had retired to his cabin. And yet in some strange way the personality of the man seemed to dominate the ship so that in spite of everything it was an entity that worked. Nobody questioned his decision to sail in search of the island, not even Fields whom I knew to be scared, or Brady who was worrying about his engines which had been running now for almost sixty hours at near maximum revolutions. They were both of them at breakfast when I went into the stuffy little dining-saloon just aft of the galley, Fields shifty-eyed and nervous, snapping at the steward, the smell of whisky stale on his breath. And then Weston came in with the news that the Met officer at Gan had warned of a deterioration in the weather.

'Coom off it, lad,' Brady said. 'Tha's trying to scare us.'

Weston helped himself from the greasy plate of liver and sausages. 'The usual tropical storms, that's all. Cu-nim building up, wind strength forty knots plus in centres of disturbance, bad vis.' He was a solitary, a man whose world was the ether. It was a long speech for him and he added, 'Nothing to worry about, Chief. Those tropical storms are always short-lived.'

'Nowt to worry aboot, eh?' Brady growled. 'At this rate t'engines'll shake the bloody bottom out of her wi'oot the aid of a storm.' He had had the pumps going ever since we left Addu Atoll and I remembered what Deacon had said that first time I'd set foot on the *Strode Venturer*, that some day the old bitch would lie down and die on him. I looked at Fields. His face was putty-coloured.

'I'll tell the Captain,' he said.

Brady belched. 'No good you running to Daddy. The Old Man's dead to the world. A whole bottle he's had.'

Fields had half risen, but now he sat down again, his thin lips working. 'We should alter course for Singapore,' he mumbled.

'Aye, and reduce speed.'

Fields's eyes shifted to me. 'This bloody island,' he said, the whine back in his voice. 'It's caused nothing but trouble.'

'Aye, it 'as that.' Brady stared at me accusingly, but I knew that neither of them was capable of acting on his own responsibility.

'And supposing we hit that area of shallows when visibility is bad.' Fields's mouth was trembling. 'The *Trader* was lucky, she had cargo she could jettison. We're empty except for Number Two.'

'There's no danger of our going aground until dawn tomorrow,' I said. But I could see he didn't believe me. Like Reece he was cursed with too much imagination; he was scared out of his wits.

I finished my breakfast quickly and went to Deacon's cabin. I thought it was time he made an appearance, but when I went in I found Brady had understated the situation. Deacon was lying sprawled across his bunk, the whisky bottle on the floor, the glass lying amongst the bedclothes where it had slipped from his nerve-less grasp. His head was pillowed on his bare arm and when I peered at his face I saw that it was unnaturally dark, the blood vessels standing out under pressure like an intricate pattern inked in red. He was dead to the world, and yet as I stood there one eye opened, bloodshot and swimming. 'Get out!' he breathed.

I hesitated. 'There's a report of bad weather ahead,' I said.

'I'm in command si'uation, so get out.' The eye closed, the coarse mottled face relaxed from the effort of speech and his body sagged into sleep again.

I opened the portholes which were tightly closed and then I left him and started on a tour of the ship. I went all over her – the engine-room, the holds, even the tiller flat, making a point of speaking to as many of the Chinese crew as I could find. It wasn't that I didn't trust them. They seemed a competent, hard-working lot, but I wouldn't trust any bunch of men not to panic if things got bad and their officers failed them. As for the ship, you could see the water seeping in between the plates. But in old riveted ships this isn't all that uncommon. I'd seen naval vessels whose plates weeped just as much. I had the carpenter sound all the wells and in the engine-room I asked Brady to give me the times at which he ran the pumps and the duration in various weather conditions. They didn't like it, but none of them questioned my authority.

By the time I reached the bridge again it was past eleven. The south-west breeze was blowing stronger now. 'Little piece monsoon wind,' the quartermaster described it. The sea glinted with rushes of broken water, but there was no sign of the swell increasing.

I stood there for a while thinking of George Strode and his arrogant assumption that we'd turn the ship round and go back to Gan, leaving Peter and the rest to rot on an island that was supposed not to be there any more. A fine, slow death if they were still alive. Finally I went to the wireless room and had Weston send him a message – *My information Reece's position so inaccurate may call for full investigation. Expect reach island next few days. Please do utmost to obtain further co-operation RAF. In any case rely on you not to obstruct final effort to rescue these men.* I thought it would worry him. Anyway, I didn't care. I'd nothing to lose now.

I went back to the wheelhouse. The breeze had changed. It had swung round into the north, a hot breath from the vastness of Asia where the great deserts and arid wastes of the interior were like a burning glass, raising the temperature of the air masses to furnace heat. Little cross seas broke and sparkled.

We were steaming into an area where the Pilot's thirty-year observation tables give the number of days with wind speeds over Force 8 as nil, but freak weather conditions are always possible. All morning clouds had been building up to the south of us, great convoluting mushroom growths standing like stacs along the horizon and constantly changing shape. Shortly after lunch the northerly breeze died away. It became suddenly very humid, and standing in the doorway leading to the foredeck, I could see a great toppling mass of cloud leaning over us. The sun vanished, huge raindrops fell singly, large as coins, and the surface of the sea began to dance as though struggling to reach up to the water still prisoned in the cloud above. Lightning stabbed and instantaneous thunder clapped a great peal of noise on to the stillness; and then suddenly white water below the blackness of the cloud, a tooth-white line that grew broader and broader as it bore down on us until it stretched from horizon to horizon with the sea behind it all boiling. Then the wind hit us with screaming force and the ship heeled.

It was a line squall – but what was behind it? The time was 14.28. I turned, my natural instinct to head for the bridge, and as I turned I saw the mate come out of his cabin like a startled rabbit bolting from its burrow. I know fear when I see it – most men do – and it was there in his face, in his shiftless eyes and the frantic haste with which he flung past me, out into the open and up the ladder to where the boats were.

I hesitated only a moment, and then I followed him. I caught up with him by the boat on the starboard side as he stood ir-resolute and half-dazed, his clothes wrapped tight against his thin body by the force of the wind howling through the gap between the funnel and the bridge. I grabbed hold of his arm. 'Fields!' I yelled. But he showed no sign of having heard me; his pale eyes had a vacant stare, the whites showing a jaundiced yellow and his teeth chattering. I could smell the liquor on his breath as I shook him. 'Fields! Pull yourself together, man!' I could damn' near smell his fear. And then suddenly he was struggling, fighting to get free of me, and the heel of the deck carried us against the winch gear of the davits. I hit him then, a sharp jab to the midriff that knocked the wind out of him, and as he sagged, his breath whistling through his teeth, gulping for air, I got a grip on him and dragged him back to the ladder. 'Your place is on the bridge,' I told him. 'And you're going to stay there till we're out of this.'

He stared down at the wet steel deck below and I felt him cringe. I think he was afraid I was going to pitch him down the ladder. He was trembling and the skin of his face was a muddy grey. He looked as though he were going to be sick. I let go of him then, feeling suddenly sorry for him; he was one of those poor wretches that need the support of a man stronger than themselves in order to face the world, resenting that need and hating them-selves and others because of it. 'I'm – all right – now.' His long, weak features shone with sweat and he looked ghastly as he went slowly down the ladder, back past his cabin and up into the wheel-house.

I followed him. I don't know what I expected to find there – certainly not Deacon. But there he was, standing magnificent and indomitable, his legs straddled to the increasing movement of the sea, doing automatically, almost unconsciously, what he'd done all his seagoing life – helping his ship to face the elements. His face was unshaven and the sag of his stubbled cheeks, the drawn-down look of his puffy bloodshot eyes reminded me again of a grizzled old bloodhound. He had slung a reefer jacket, green with age and sea mould, over the dirty pyjama jacket and he stood there, huge in the half light of that sudden storm, sniffing the weather with his big nose, not saying a word, but by his mere presence giving support to the helmsman, a feeling of stability to the whole ship.

'Is everything – all right?' Fields's voice, hesitant, doubtful, was in itself a plea for strength.

The big high-domed head turned. 'Ah, it's you, Arthur. A squall, that's all. Very sudden.' And he added with surprising gentleness, 'Nothing to worry about.' The strength of the man at that moment, the absolute sense of command!

He swung his head back to face the sea and I wondered again about the relationship between these two. Had it been physical as well as psychological at one time? They made a pair, there was no doubt of that – this poor little undersized runt, as yellow as a cur, and this towering, soft-bellied, sodden man who could rise out of a stupor of drink to take command of his ship the instant she needed him. I watched him as he hunched his half-bald head down into the upturned collar of his jacket the way I did myself, the way all sailors do, his eyes cocked to the weather side where the horizon was white against the ink-black cloud and the seas broke in long streamers of spray, beaten almost flat by the weight of the wind. I didn't mind about his alcoholism then or his relationship with the wretched mate whom he'd probably ruined as much as he'd helped. I recognized him for what he was, a born seaman, and my heart warmed to him.

'See that all the pumps are working, will you? And have them reduce speed to six knots.'

Fields went to the engine-room telephone. He seemed in command of himself now. The sweat had dried on his face and the skin no longer had that muddy look. 'All pumps working. Reducing speed now.'

'Check the holds. See how much water she's making.' And as the mate left the wheelhouse Deacon turned to me. 'Where did you find him?'

'Beside Number One boat.'

He nodded. 'It's his nerves. You can't blame him.'

That was all. He knew his man all right. Knew himself, too, probably. And as though he wanted to wipe that subject from his mind he said in a quiet, level voice: 'Be a bad sea when the wind eases, I shouldn't wonder.' And after that he didn't say anything.

The wind began to ease about half an hour later. In the shelter of the wheelhouse we couldn't feel it, of course, and we couldn't hear it either for the noise of the sea was too great. But we could see it in the changed pattern of the waves. Now, instead of the break of each comber being laid flat, the seas were free to build up so that the ship wallowed in the troughs and as she rose the crests broke against her sides with the thrust and drive of hundreds of tons of water flung forward with a mighty surge. The waves were rolling green across the for'ard hatch covers and in those moments the high, old-fashioned fo'c'sle looked like a rock awash with spray driving across it and white water cascading off its steel sides. I could feel the old boat straining, hear the creak of her woodwork as the steel-plated hull changed its shape fractionally to the pressure of the seas.

When Fields returned to the bridge the scared look was back in his eyes. 'The water's beginning to make in Number One hold and the pumps are only just holding their own in the others.'

Deacon half turned and his eyes met mine as he gave the order to turn south and run before it. 'Makes you laugh, doesn't it?' There was an ugly look on his face, frustration and bitterness needling his half-sunk pride. 'A piddling little blow like this and I have to lift up my tail and show my arse. Like a greenhorn,' he snarled, 'mucking my trousers at the first glimpse of a big sea.'

I looked out over the bows, now riding high and free of spray, the paintwork gleaming black, out to where the seas rolled white. I was thinking of what Fields had said at breakfast. If we were right, then we were getting very close to the area of shallows where the *Strode Trader* had grounded. How quickly the mental picture conjures fear when the body is starved of action! My mouth felt suddenly dry, for in that turmoil of broken water there was no chance of any warning. I turned to the echo-sounder clicking metronomically on the wall behind me. But the fact that it was recording no bottom meant very little. For all I knew those shallows might rise up sheer out of 2000 fathoms. 'It was in conditions like these – a sudden storm – that Sir Reginald went.' Deacon's voice was barely audible above the sound of the seas, and for a moment I didn't grasp what he was saying. 'You knew he died at sea?'

I turned then. 'My father, you mean?'

He was staring ahead at the rise and fall of the bows and the tumbled water beyond, his mind going back into the past. 'It was in Biscay, just after we'd passed the Ar Men buoy. About mid-night. It came up very fast as it often does round Ushant. There was a full moon, but the murk had covered it so that there was a weird half-light.'

'Are you talking about my father?' I asked him again.

He nodded his head slowly. 'I'd just come down from the bridge. He was alone in the saloon and I said I'd see him to his cabin. He'd been drinking a bit heavy, you know, for several days and he'd got a bottle of whisky under his arm. But he waved me off. "Kind of you," he said, standing very straight. "But I'm on my own now. And Harry," he added. "Don't stop – not for anything. Understand?" ' Deacon turned and looked at me then and there were tears in his bloodshot eyes. 'That was the last I saw of him.'

'What happened?' I asked.

He shrugged. 'I never knew for certain. One of the crew said he saw him leaning on the stern rail staring down into the wake. My guess is he just drank the bottle and let himself go over.' The swollen red eyes stared at me a moment and then he turned abruptly away. He was crying – but whether for my father or for the past that was lost I didn't know. And after that he wouldn't say anything more but stared fixedly ahead.

We steamed south for a little over an hour and then south-east while the storm blew itself out behind us. At 16.44 Deacon ordered the helmsman back to the original course, told Fields to take over and went below to his cabin. I went aft to the stern rail and stood there watching the ship's broad wake as my father had done all those years ago, wondering about his end and how Henry Strode had known. The sun was falling now towards the west and I stayed there, watching the sparkle of it on the water until it sank into the sea and the sky turned fiery red, a flaming furnace glow dyed purple at the edges. Three pillars of cu-nim burned for a while, anvil-headed; the glow faded to a hard duck's egg green and the first stars appeared. Then, suddenly it was night. So long ago and my memory of him a vague shadow, elusive as all my childhood recollections were. The portrait on the stairs, the reports in *The Times*, even those words composed by my mother, they all obtruded, overlaying my recollection of the man himself. And yet there were moments as I stood there watching the wake white in the stern light when I felt so close to him. I could have sworn he was standing there beside me. No doubt it was all in my own mind, but I know this, that when I finally returned to the bridge I had a feeling of most extraordinary confidence.

Speed had been reduced to six knots again and all through the night the ship wallowed slowly eastwards, a look-out in the bows. And at dawn we were in the search area. The sun came up and I went into the wheelhouse in pyjamas to find Deacon there, slumped in his chair, his eyes half closed. He didn't say anything, but I could see by the position of the sun that we were steaming north now. We were on the first leg of our search pattern and when I went out to the bridge wing I saw that one of the crew had been hoisted to the foremast on a bos'n's chair.

Nothing to do now but wait, and hope. There was a swell still running and the wind was back into the south-west where it had been most of the time since we had sailed from Gan. Blue sky, blue sea, the sun blazing down, and the *Strode Venturer* ploughing her way across the endless expanse of ocean. Time passed slowly. There might be days and days of this, but still I was possessed by that same strange feeling of confidence. It was so strong that twice I went out and called to the masthead look-out, but each time he shook his head and shouted that he could see nothing.

The steward brought the mid-morning coffee and we drank it silently. An air of torpor had settled on the bridge, Deacon dozing in his chair, the officer of the watch half asleep, the helmsman's hands motionless on the wheel, the ship steady as a rock, only the beat of the engines against the soles of my feet and the surge of the water at the bows to indicate that we were moving across the sea.

Weston entered from the chartroom and stood looking at the sea a moment, his watery blue eyes blinking in the glare. 'This message just came in.' He thrust a sheet of paper at Deacon, but the big man didn't stir. 'A message for you. From Gan.' And he added, 'You might be interested to know I've been in contact with an Australian ship bound from Colombo to Perth. She reports steaming through scattered areas of pumice for the past two hours.'

Deacon's eyes opened slowly and he dragged himself to his feet, fumbling for his glasses in the litter of the chart table. 'Bound for Perth, eh? She's to the east of us, then?' Weston gave him her position and he reached for the parallel rule and marked it on the chart. 'Bearing one-o-four degrees from us and almost four hundred miles away.' He swung his head in that slow, bear-like movement, staring at me over his glasses. 'The equatorial counter-current is east-going, say just over two knots – fifty miles a day. If that pumice originated from a disturbance in this area, it happened at least eight days ago.'

'What's the message from Gan?' I asked.

He read it through and pushed it across to me. It was from Canning. The support Shackleton, the one I had flown in, was being withdrawn from Gan. It was leaving for Changi in the morning and Canning was offering to divert it *en route*. *Fuel would limit the time it could spend over your area to five hours, but if it would be of help to you the crew are willing to put in the extra flying time.*

Five hours wasn't much, but it was better than nothing, and if we asked them to fly the northern part of the area it would be closer to their direct flight path to Singapore. They might manage more than five hours. But when I suggested this to Deacon he simply said, 'Do what you like.' He wasn't interested. Aircraft meant nothing to him. All he understood was ships and he was poring over the chart again. I drafted a reply and handed it to Weston. Deacon was back in his chair, then his eyes closed. 'I've only once seen pumice floating on the surface of the sea,' he murmured thickly. 'That was off the China coast. I forget the year now – a long time ago.' He shifted slowly in his seat and opened his eyes, staring at me. They were very bloodshot in the sun's glare. 'You said something about pumice – when you came here before, in the *Trader*. That was before you sighted the island, hm?'

'The day before,' I said.

'You were to the west of it, then?'

I nodded. 'Eighty miles at least.'

He sighed. 'Have to be careful tonight.' He closed his eyes again, relapsing into silence. I think he slept for a while. He looked very tired and later, when Fields took over, he went to his cabin. He didn't come down to lunch. At two o'clock we altered course to the east again. The haze was thickening, visibility not more than five miles. Two hours and then we'd turn south and when we'd steamed 50 miles we'd turn east for two hours, then north. In this way our search pattern would be a broad fifty-mile band across the southern half of the probable area, and if the Shackleton could cover the northern half . . .

I was lying on my bunk then, drowsy with the heat and sweating. Through the porthole I could see the sea ruffled by the breeze, but it was still from the west and we were going with it so that the ship seemed lifeless, without air. Flies moved lazily and where they touched my skin they stayed until I roused myself to brush them off. It was better when we altered course at four. My cabin was on the starboard side and the breeze came gently in through the open porthole. I was thinking of Ali Raza and those five vedis with their masts stepped. Apart from the storm they would have had a steady following wind. Or had Canning stopped them from sailing? The sun was slipping down the sky now, the cabin a blaze of light. I dressed and went up to the bridge where Fields was lolling in Deacon's chair, the cigarette dangling from the corner of his mouth stained a damp brown. Nothing had happened, nothing had been sighted, but visibility was improving now, the sea a deeper blue stretching out in a great circle to the hard line of the horizon.

Tea came and Fields stirred from his lethargy. 'How long're we going on like this? It seems bloody years since we saw a real port.' I took my tea out on to the starboard bridge wing. It was cooler there and I stayed watching as the sun sank, flattening its lower rim against the horizon and then dropping quickly. The whole world was suddenly ablaze, the mackerel sky overhead flaming to a surrealist pattern. I went into the wheelhouse to put my cup down and at that moment the masthead look-out called. But all he had seen was a whale. A whale spouting, he said; but he wasn't very sure. It had been a long way away on the port bow. We searched through the glasses but could see nothing; the sky was fading, the surface of the sea darkening. Night was falling and the echo-sounder showed no trace. The second officer came up to relieve Fields and I left them talking together by the open bridge wing door and went to my cabin.

I had just stretched myself out on my bunk with a paperback I had borrowed from Weston when the faint sound of the telegraph brought me to my feet. The beat of the engines died away as I slipped into my sandals and hurried back to the wheelhouse. The lights had been switched on and outside the sea was dark. Fields and Taylor were standing staring at the echo-sounder. The trace showed eighty-two fathoms. It had picked up bottom at 200 and had come down with a rush, in a matter of five or ten minutes.

Nobody spoke. The echo-sounder held us riveted. Eighty. Seventy-five. Seventy-three. The ship was losing way, the fall in depth slowing down. There seemed no other sound in the wheelhouse as the three of us stood and stared. And then suddenly the depths were increasing. Seventy-five again. Seventy-seven. Seventy-eight.

A smell of stale sweat and Deacon was there, his cheap, steel-rimmed glasses perched on his nose, his heavy face thrust forward as he stared at the trace. And then his voice, solid, decisive: 'Slow ahead. And hold your course – due south.' He stood, his feet slightly apart, his head thrust forward, watching as the beat of the engines responded to the call of the telegraph. The trace changed slowly, the depths gradually increasing. At two hundred fathoms he ordered full starboard wheel. There were stars now and we could see the ship's bows swinging. He swung her through 180° and at slow ahead took her back over the same track, watching as the trace repeated itself. At 200 fathoms he ordered the engines stopped.

'What's up? What're you doing?' Fields's voice was sharp with an edge of panic to it. 'We can't stop here.'

'We'll have to.' Deacon let his arm rest for a moment on the thin shoulders. 'You've found bottom. That's the main thing. Whatever it is – shoal or island – we're all right here.' A quick pat and he let his hand drop, turning away to the chart table. Fields followed him, the sweat still shining on his face, but eager to please now. He was telling him about the look-out sighting a whale. Deacon sent for the man, but the Chinese seaman couldn't tell us any more than he'd called down to us at the time. He hadn't seen the whale – just a disturbance in the sea, something that looked like a whale venting. 'Off the port bow, eh?' Deacon stared at the trace he'd ripped from the depth indicator. I knew what he was thinking. If it wasn't a whale, if it was the venting of gases . . . 'Get out!' he bellowed irritably and he shook his head, staring down at the chart. But the chart didn't help. There wasn't a single line of soundings within a hundred miles of us. He got his sextant out of its box and for the next half-hour he was engrossed in taking star sights and working out our position. Finally he marked it in on the chart.

'Sights every two hours and maintain depth at two hundred fathoms. What's the reading now?' he asked Fields. It had fallen to one-nine-three and he ordered slow ahead with the ship's bows pointing west until we'd made good the drift of the current and the echo-sounder was showing 200 fathoms again. He left the wheelhouse then. When he came back he had a fresh bottle of whisky tucked under his arm and the tooth glass from his cabin. Automatically he took in the details of the bridge the way a man does when he comes on watch. He nodded to himself, his great dome glinting in the light. Then he settled himself in his chair. He had swung it round so that it faced the echo-sounder and now he reached for the bottle which he had placed carefully on the deck, peering up at me at the same time over the rim of his glasses. 'Going to be a long night,' he growled and his hands were trembling slightly as he slopped whisky into the glass. They had been perfectly steady when he had been taking his star sights.

I stayed with him most of the night and by dawn he had finished the bottle. But though he cat-napped he never had to be roused to take his sights and always seemed to know when we had drifted out of position and the depth under our keel was decreasing. He didn't talk much, though in the early hours, when he had drunk most of the whisky, he told me a bit about his early life. He had been to a private school for a time, but then his father, who had been a draper in Camden Town, had gone bankrupt and he had had to start earning a living. He was older than I had expected, for that had been during the First World War and after his father had been killed at Passchendaele he had enlisted and had been with Ironside's troops fighting in Russia. And after that he'd bummed his way around the world, finishing up in Karachi where he had signed on as cook on an old tramp steamer. How he'd come to be first officer on the *Lammermuir* when my father died he didn't say, for by then he had withdrawn again into his shell. Once I woke to hear him gasping, his big hands clutching at his stomach. But whatever it was it seemed to pass for I heard the clink of the bottle as I dozed off again. He took sights again at four and after that he didn't bother any more, leaving it to Fields whose watch it was to keep the ship on the 200-fathom mark. Even when dawn came he didn't stir.

I was out on the bridge wing then, watching as the light strengthened in the east. But there was nothing there – no island, no sign of a reef, nothing; just the sea with a westerly breeze chasing little waves across the swell. It wasn't until after breakfast that Deacon took over and we got under way, proceeding south to the point of least depth, and then, with the echo-sounder reading less than eighty fathoms, heading east and feeling our way. Almost immediately the foremast look-out called that there were shoals ahead. The depth was then sixty fathoms, decreasing rapidly. The engines were stopped and before the way was off the ship we could see the changed colour of the sea from the bridge. From blue it changed to green and beyond that to a lighter green that was almost white in the sunlight.

'Full astern!' The screw thrashed and the old ship juddered as Deacon turned her round and headed back to the west, the depth increasing rapidly until it was too deep for us to record. We swung north then on to 012°. The time was ten-seventeen. Reece had steamed south from the island on a course of 192° for just over four hours before his ship had struck the shoals. Assuming that we had been on the western edge of the same shoals we could expect to sight the island about one o'clock.

But one o'clock came and one-thirty and still nothing ahead of us but the dim line of the horizon blurred with heat haze. A hundred miles to the north of us the Shakleton was flying her own search pattern. Weston had been in wireless contact with Landor since nine-thirty, but Deacon had obstinately refused to let him call the plane south to search our area. He hadn't come all this way, he said, to have the bloody RAF locate the island. Three years in a Jap prison camp had bitten deep. He couldn't forgive the Services for letting Singapore be over-run, for the shambles of the evacuation. He hated the lot of them.

At one-forty-five there was still no sign of the island. For the Shackleton time and fuel were both running out, and when I told Deacon I was going to call the plane south he didn't argue. 'Just as you like,' he said, staring at me morosely. I don't think he understood the limitations of an aircraft any more than he understood the equipment that made the Shackleton such a formidable search weapon.

The aircraft had been working steadily south and it was now less than sixty miles away. I lit a cigarette whilst Weston fiddled with his controls and suddenly Landor's voice came in very clear. I gave him our position and also the position of the shoal and suggested he fly a pattern to the east and west of both positions. 'Roger. But we'll only be able to stay about half an hour in your area.' There was a short pause and then he added, 'We already have you in radar sight. Bearing one-six-three, fifty-five miles. Be with you inside of twenty minutes.'

I had some lunch brought up to the radio shack and just after two Landor was back on the air again. 'There's a blip on my screen – quite a big one – almost due east of you. Hold on while I work it out. From you it bears about one-one-o degrees, thirty miles. Can you see it from where you are? Over.' But of course I couldn't. Our radar was out of action and visibility, even from the lookout's position at the foremast, was little more than five miles. There was a good deal of cloud about. I passed the information on to Deacon and he immediately altered course to the east. 'If that's the island,' he growled, 'then the shoal bears about two-thirty degrees, not one-nine-two, which was the course Reece said he steered.'

The truth was staring us in the face then. 'And when we steamed north again after the fire it was a true course. We'd nothing to steer by – only the stars.'

'That's what I mean. His compass must have been out – badly out.' He was staring at me and the same thought was in both our minds. 'Christ!' he said. 'What a thing to have done to you. And I accused him of lying.'

'You weren't to know,' I said. 'And anyway, if he wasn't lying, he was certainly holding something back.' I was thinking of the report he had written on the stranding. 'I'm quite sure he had his instructions – to use a storm, something – any excuse to get clear of the island and leave us there, isolated for a few weeks. George Strode needed time.'

'I see.' And he sat there with troubled eyes, his head hunched into his shoulders, thinking about it. He didn't say anything for some time and I knew he was seeing it from Reece's point of view, knowing what it was like to be under pressure from owners who were prepared to sacrifice their captains. At length I heard him mutter to himself, 'Poor sod!' And then he leaned back and closed his eyes, his face grey and drawn under the stubble.

We heard the plane pass to the north of us, but it was hidden by a rain-storm. Landor came on the air to say it was definitely an island. He began to describe its appearance on the radar screen – about six miles by three, a bay on the western side. And then he was shouting that the pilot could see it, a bare island with nothing growing. 'We're over it now – flying very low – two-three hundred feet. There's a hut – some sort of road – yes, and equipment. It's your island all right. And we can see men – about half a dozen – waving to us.'

I sat down then, suddenly tired as the tension drained out of me. I was trembling slightly, my body damp with sweat. Rain beat against the deck outside and it was suddenly much darker. To the east of us the Shackleton was clear of the rain and climbing to 4000 feet heading south-west. Soon they could see the area of shallows where the *Strode Trader* had grounded. 'A big oval patch about fifteen miles by ten.'

'What's it bear from the island?' I asked.

'Bearing two-two-seven degrees.'

I told Deacon and he nodded his big head, slowly, almost sadly. 'A compass error as big as that doesn't happen by chance.' It was what he had expected – what we had both expected. 'He's like his father. No consideration for anybody once he's made up his mind to a thing. And he'll get more and more like him as time goes on,' he added in a grim, tired voice.

Forty miles to the south of us the Shackleton plotted the shallows and then made a wide sweep searching for others. But Landor reported nothing – all deep water and the sea empty except for a couple of native boats some twenty miles west-south-west of the shoal, both under sail. 'Vedis?' I asked, and he said he thought so. He had taken the Shackleton in low, trying to head them off from the danger area and direct them towards the island. Now he was coming back. He couldn't stay any longer because of his fuel situation. A few minutes later the big, clumsy-looking aircraft bumbled over us at masthead height. A great roar of engines, an old-maidish waggle of the wings and it was gone, lost in a rain cloud and heading for Singapore over a thousand miles away.

Three hours later we found bottom in just over 290 fathoms. The island was hidden by rain and we stopped engines and lay to. Shortly after six we had a brief glimpse of it, a blurred line seen through a mist of rain at a distance of about three miles. It looked like a great sandbank, bare and glistening wetly. Deacon roused himself from his chair and came out on to the bridge wing to look at it. And as the rain closed in again and the dim outline of it faded he said, 'Well, he's got what he wanted; an island, a people of his own. He'll get Strode Orient, too. Or he'll build another company. He'll finish up with more power than his father had.' His eyes were staring blankly into the rain. 'New men, new ships . . .' His voice died, his big head sagging between the massive shoulders. He was an old man, lonely now and filled with misgivings about the future. 'There was a time,' he murmured, 'when I'd have enjoyed a fight.' He shook his head. 'Not now, not any . . .' A fresh downpour drowned his voice and we ducked inside the wheelhouse.

The sun set, but we saw it only as a darkening of the rain clouds. Night closed quickly in on us. Another twelve hours to spend keeping the ship to a depth position. Deacon had drinks served in the saloon. He had shaved and put on a clean khaki shirt and trousers. Like the rest of his clothes they had been run up for him by one of the Chinese seamen. He even stayed for the evening meal, a massive, almost paternal, figure at the head of the small table. And afterwards he insisted on standing a watch, sitting alone in the wheelhouse watching the echo-sounder, giving the necessary orders. I went up there just after eleven and stayed with him until the second officer took over. He didn't talk much, just sat looking about him, his eyes surprisingly alert as though every detail of the bridge was new to him. I put it down to the fact that he was sober. I don't think I had seen him properly sober before. As soon as he was relieved he got to his feet. 'Just hold her here

on the three-hundred-fathom mark,' he told Taylor. He stood
there a moment, looking uncertainly round the wheelhouse as
though reluctant to leave it. 'Who's relieving you?' he asked.

'Fields.'

He nodded. 'Good. Tell him to get under way as soon as there's
light enough. He's to make straight for the anchorage. He's not to
delay – not under any circumstances.' He nodded good night to
us and then he turned very slowly and walked out of the wheelhouse, his head high, his shoulders no longer stooped – walking
with a steady, purposeful gait.

Shortly afterwards I went to my cabin. The rain had stopped,
but it was still overcast, the air very oppressive, and I couldn't
sleep. I was thinking of Deacon, wishing there was something I
could have said, something I could do to relieve his desperate sense
of hopelessness. It wasn't just the despair of the alcoholic. It was
much deeper than that. All those years, all the post-war years
nursing an old tramp whilst younger men driving bigger and
faster ships passed him on the sea lanes of the world. The bottle
helps, but it isn't the answer, not when you're a born seaman and
living in a world that has no use for you. There comes a time when
you don't fight any more. You give up then.

In the end I got out of my bunk and went along to his cabin. It
was just after one. I pushed open his door and stood there listening.
There was no sound, the portholes open and a feeling of emptiness.
I switched on the light. He wasn't there and his bunk hadn't been
slept in. It was all tidied up, the few clothes he possessed folded
neatly. Two letters had been placed carefully on his pillow. One
was addressed to Fields, the other to a Mrs Chester in England. I
hurried aft, across the well deck and up on to the poop. But there
was nobody there. I stood for a moment leaning on the stern rail,
looking down into the still, dark water below, wondering what to
do. In the end I went back to my bunk without telling anybody.
He wouldn't have wanted them to launch a boat and start searching any more than my father had. I only wished I had known him
earlier, before he took to drink. To go like that, so quietly, so
unobtrusively – and cold sober.

I was up again at five. The third officer was on watch, but
Fields was still there and we watched together as dawn broke and
the shape of the island appeared like a ghost against the fading
stars. As soon as there was enough visibility he got under way,
steaming north along the 300-fathom line. The light was increasing all the time, a hot glow in the east that silhouetted the island
so that it was a black shape without detail. Only the glint of water

beyond the nearest land identified it as the southern arm of the bay. As soon as we had opened up the anchorage he stopped the engines and went to call Deacon. He came back a few minutes later, very white and the letter crumpled in his hand. 'He's gone,' he said, a shocked look in his eyes. He stood there in a sort of daze, smoothing the letter out and staring at the words he'd already read. 'The end of the road. That's what he says. I don't understand.' He shook his head, tears welling up in his eyes and trickling down his sallow cheeks.

There was nothing I could say. They'd been together so long, and now he was on his own. The depth was decreasing, the anchorage opening up. 'You'll have to take her in yourself,' I told him.

He nodded slowly and his thin body stiffened as though he were bracing himself. 'Starboard wheel. Engines slow ahead.' We could see the backs of the shoals gleaming in the sunrise, a great heap of ore stockpiled on the quay and the bulldozer looking small as a beetle on the shelf where the ore had been excavated. The bows swung in towards the anchorage and Fields sent the second officer to get the anchor ready whilst he conned the ship from the starboard bridge wing.

He took her in much closer than Reece had taken the *Strode Trader* and the sweat shone on his face as the depths decreased and the nervous tension built up in him. When he finally gave the order to let go the anchor the echo-sounder was reading eighteen fathoms. He had done what Deacon would have done and from that moment my opinion of the man began to change.

A boat had already been swung out and I left immediately for the shore. Peter met me at the loading quay where most of the shore party were already gathered. He was wearing nothing but a sarong and sandals, his bare torso burned black by the sun and so thin every bone and sinew showed. Standing there on that desolate shore in the bright morning light he looked native to the place, a wild, strange figure with his beard unkempt and his black hair grown down over his ears. 'Where the hell have you been?' His teeth showed in his beard and the whites of his eyes shone in the dark tan of his face. He was angry, a driven bundle of nervous energy that had been badly frightened by lack of contact with the outside world. 'What's Reece think he's playing at?'

'Did you monkey around with the compass?' I asked him.

'The compass?' I saw his eyes go blank. 'What's the compass got to do with it? We're half starved, food rationed, the fuel almost exhausted. You've been gone damned near a month and – '

'Well, did you?' I demanded, remembering the shallows and how the lightning had struck, that poor devil burning like a torch.

His eyes slid away from me and I knew then that we'd been right. It wasn't Reece's fault. 'You stupid fool!' I said. 'You nearly cost us all our lives.' I was remembering what Deacon had said, that he'd get more and more like his father. Despite the growing heat my body was cold with anger. 'You've only yourself to blame.'

'Never mind about that,' he said. 'Where the hell has the *Strode Trader* been all this time?'

'That isn't the *Strode Trader* out there,' I said. 'It's the *Strode Venturer*.' And I told him briefly what had happened. But it didn't seem to register, his mind half unbalanced by lack of food and the solitude of this lonely island. 'You must have been crazy,' I said, 'to fool around with the magnetic field of a ship's compass. Three men dead, four injured and the ship gutted by fire.'

He had the grace to say he was sorry then. 'But it can't be helped. It seemed the only thing to do – at the time. I didn't trust Reece and to have the position of the island – ' He shrugged his shoulders. 'Well, everyone knows where it is now, I suppose. That Shackleton – ' He leaned towards me, his eyes staring and luminous in the hard light. 'Did you see Don Mansoor? Did he tell you when he was sailing?' There was a nervous urgency in his voice.

'The Shackleton reported two native craft twenty miles to the west of the shoal area,' I said. 'I imagine they're Don Mansoor's vedis.' The creak of oars sounded behind me and I turned. It was Fields coming ashore in the other boat.

'Where's Deacon?' Peter asked. 'Is he on board?'

'Deacon's dead,' I said. 'Suicide.'

He stared at me, shocked. That at least meant something to him. 'I'm sorry,' he said. And then again, 'I'm sorry.' The anger, the nervous energy, all the driving vitality seemed to leave him then. He looked suddenly very tired. 'And the *Strode Trader* a wreck, you say?' He passed his hand wearily over his face.

And then Fields was ashore and facing us, his body tense, his mouth trembling. 'You knew he'd gone, didn't you?' He was staring at me, his long, sallow face reflecting a personal tragedy. 'On the bridge, when I told you – you weren't surprised. You knew.'

'Yes,' I said. 'I knew.'

I thought he was going to hit out at me, blame me for what had happened. But all he said was, 'Why? Why did he do it? I don't understand.'

The tears were coming back into his eyes and I felt sorry for the poor devil. 'He couldn't go on, that's all. Like my father,' I said.

He nodded slowly as though the mention of my father helped.

'It's your ship now,' I said and he stared at me, his eyes wide and the tears running unashamedly down his face. Finally he turned away, still crying, and stumbled blindly back to the boat. I called to him to take as many as he could of the shore party off to the ship and send the boat back for the rest. My own boat was already pulling away with about half a dozen Pakistanis in her. 'So they may be here today?' Peter said and I realized his mind was still on those two vedis.

I looked at the sea, shining blue to the horizon. The zephyr of a breeze touched my face, scattering cat's paws over the bay's calm surface. 'With luck,' I said and we walked slowly up the road together towards the hut. It was then that he explained his urgency, his desperate need for them to arrive before anybody else from the outside world.

It was a question of the future of the island under international law. At the moment it was *terra nullius* in the sense that it was newly emerged and open to occupation by anybody. He couldn't claim it as an individual or on behalf of Strode & Company – the days for that sort of thing were long since past. In any case, to effectively establish title in international law the claimant must satisfy two requirements: first, the intention to occupy, signified by some formal act of declaration such as the planting of the national flag to give other powers notice that the territory is no longer *terra nullius*; and secondly, a continuing and effective occupation. As an Englishman, the correct procedure, according to a friend he had contacted in the Foreign Office, was for him to notify the British Government of the island's location and ask them to take formal occupation. 'It would then have the status of a British olony.' He said it without enthusiasm.

'And you want it for the Adduans?'

'Yes. Don Mansoor discovered it. It's their island. Besides,' he added, 'in view of the behaviour of the Malé Government over the Gan lease I don't think there's any doubt that if this place were annexed by Britain it would be for strategic purposes.'

I knew he was right there. An uninhabited island belonging to nobody – it was the dream of every major power. If we got hold of it, we'd undoubtedly establish a base and clamp a security guard on the place.

'I doubt whether we'd even be allowed to exploit the manganese. Certainly no Adduans would be permitted to land.' We had reached the hut now and he paused before going in, looking round him at the long, bare sprawl of the island. The sun was rising over the back of it so that it had a warm glow. 'That's why I made sure Reece wouldn't be able to report its real position. All these months – it's been like sitting on a time bomb. At any moment a stray ship – the Navy, for instance, or an aircraft like that Shackleton – worse still, a Russian trawler – ' He had turned and was looking towards the bay where the *Strode Venturer* lay reflected in the calm waters. 'So you think they could be here today?'

'The Adduans? Yes,' I said, 'if the breeze gets up with the sun.' But I was more concerned now with what was happening back in London, and I told him about the extraordinary general meeting called by Strode Orient and what Ida had told me in that letter. 'Somehow we've got to find the means of reaching London before the twenty-fourth.'

But though we discussed it for almost an hour in the stuffy, sweat-rancid atmosphere of that hut, we could think of no form of transport that would get us there in time. The only aircraft that could pick us up was a flying boat and we knew of none that we could charter. The only ship we had was the *Strode Venturer*. To use her was out of the question if we were to deliver our first consignment of ore on time. Even the voyage back to Gan would cost her nearly a week and she would then be short of fuel. In any case, there was no certainty that Canning would be able to get us on a Transport Command flight. Finally Peter said, 'Well, we'll just have to play it from here and hope for the best.' But he knew as well as I did that wireless contact was no substitute for our physical presence at Strode House.

It was in a sombre frame of mind that we went back down the road to join the last of the shore party going out to the ship. Our only hope was that the news that the island still existed would have its impact and enable Whimbrill to support us, possibly Felden, too.

There was nothing to do then but wait as the sun climbed to its zenith and the sea took on the brassy glare of midday heat. The shore party were fed and stayed on board, cluttering up the deck. The breeze was very light and Peter became more and more morose as the hours ticked slowly by. No point now in stockpiling ore for without the barge and the landing craft we had no means of ferrying it out to the ship.

Fields, in command now of a vessel that had no purpose, stayed in his cabin and drank alone. The only man who had anything to do was Weston, who sent out a stream of messages as we drafted them – to Whimbrill, to the Strodes, to Ida, Felden, the Dutch agent who had negotiated the contract for the sale of the ore, and also to Canning to thank him for diverting the Shackleton on his own responsibility. Finally we sent out a report on the situation and prospects for Whimbrill to circulate to all Strode Orient shareholders. Later, messages from the outside world began coming in, messages of congratulation, replies to our own communications, and then shortly after lunch a stream of cables from newspapers, not only in London, but all over the world.

We were news and I took full advantage of it, sitting in my cabin, the sweat rolling off my naked body, as I wrote eyewitness accounts of my return to the island, of what it looked like, what the shore party had been doing, the glowing future of the place as a major source of manganese. And all the time Peter stayed on the bridge, searching the hazed horizon to the west. But there was no sign of the vedis. About three o'clock in the afternoon he burst into my cabin. 'This has just come through.' It was from one of HM ships – a frigate. It asked for confirmation of the position of the isalnd as given by the Shackleton and added: *Our instructions are to take formal possession. We are now approximately 250 miles away. Expect arrive 16.00 hours tomorrow.*

'I have told them to save their fuel, that the island belongs to the Adduan People's Republic. But that won't stop them.' And he added, 'It's just what I feared – a land grab that will cut the Adduans out and possibly ourselves, too. Your bloody Navy would have a ship in the vicinity.'

Just twenty-four hours. Tea was served. The sun sank. The air was deathly still and I could picture those two vedis lying just below the wild glow of the horizon, motionless, their sails limp, their reflections mirrored in the long Indian Ocean swell. With night coming on it was pointless taking the *Strode Venturer* to sea in search of them. 'We'll leave at dawn.' But I could see Peter thought the chances of finding them and towing them into the anchorage before the frigate arrived were remote. For all we knew they might now be aground on the shallows where the *Strode Trader* had struck.

The waiting was bad for all of us, a sense of anti-climax, of life temporarily suspended. Sunset faded into night, with Peter pacing the narrow confines of my cabin like a man jailed. I got out a fresh bottle of Scotch and gave him a drink, and once he'd started he didn't stop. Yet it made no difference to him. His nerves burned up the alcohol as fast as he swallowed it.

By midnight we had finished the bottle. He was sharing my

cabin and he had just curled up like a dog on the floor when the watch we had set knocked at the door. 'Plenty wind coming now, sah.' We went up on deck. There was a wrack of cloud to the south of us, very black and stormy looking against the moon riding the ragged gap. It was blowing fresh from the south-west and in the pale light we could see the waves breaking on the shoals. The ship was beginning to come alive under our feet, a slow, trembling movement as she tugged at her cable. We stayed on the bridge about an hour, the sweat drying cold on our bodies as we strained our eyes seaward. But though the cloud gradually drifted away southward and the moon was bright we saw no sail, only the sea flickering white as the waves broke.

It was still blowing fresh when we went below about one-thirty. It was pointless standing there for there was nothing we could do till dawn broke. I fell asleep as soon as my head touched the pillow and the next moment the light was on and Peter was shaking me. 'They've seen something – a sail, they think.'

The time was 04.55. Out on deck the moon was falling to the west, still bright, but in the east, beyond the dark back of the island, there was the first greying of the light before the coming dawn and the stars were beginning to lose their brightness. At first I couldn't see it, only the dead line of the horizon on to which my eyes, straining into that strange ghostlight, superimposed imagined shapes, even the glimmer of lights which were too ephemeral to be real. Peter handed me the glasses. 'I think it's a sail, but I can't be sure.' The horizon seen through the glasses was both clearer and less distinct, blurred by magnification. I swept the area slowly, gradually fastening on a pale blotch that might have been a trick of the light except that it was there each time I searched that section of the sea. 'We won't know for certain till dawn breaks,' I said. 'Another hour, probably.'

The wind had fallen, light to moderate now, but still strong enough to drive a ship under sail. We stood there watching through the glasses, neither of us feeling like going back to bed, and as the sky paled in the east and the moon's light dimmed we lost sight of even that vague blur. Our tired eyes played us tricks and soon we were no longer certain that we had seen anything at all.

Dawn came milky white, a pale glimmer that grew imperceptibly. The island, at first a remote silhouette, gradually came closer as details became visible – the gleam of a crevice, the shape of the road, the ore pile and the machines stationary on the plateau. Finally we could see it all, the familiar pattern of it clear, and the sky behind it taking on the first tints of the sun's spectrum. In contrast, the west had dimmed, the stars, even the moon, pallid now, the horizon gone.

Coffee was brought to us and we leaned against the steel of the bridge housing, smoking, our eyes drawn to the east where colours were beginning to flare. The blaze of that tropical dawn had us mesmerized so that it was some minutes before we looked again towards the west. And suddenly they were there, clear and distinct, a splash of white canvas – not one ship, but two, sailing so close their spars and sails seemed one. It seemed incredible to us that we hadn't seen them before, for they were quite close, barely a mile off. And as the sun thrust its red rim over the horizon beyond the island, their sails took on a rosy glow and every detail of the vessels was suddenly clear.

They were vedis all right. The snub-nosed stems with the blunt attempt at the clipper bow where it was shaped to take the bowsprit, the fat buxom hulls and the squares'l yard trimmed to the quartering wind. They came on steadily under their full press of canvas, bright now in the blinding glare of the newly-risen sun – a rare, proud sight as they stood in to the island that was to be their home.

Peter reached for the siren cord and gave them three long blasts, and then we hurried aft as the deck of the *Strode Venturer* became alive with men tumbling from their sleep. The vedis were bearing down to pass astern of us, the windward gunn'ls crowded with Adduans. They were almost naked, teeth and eyes agleam with the excitement of their landfall. There was no shortening of canvas. The vedis came down on us under full sail, heeling to the breeze and the water bone-white in front of their blunt bows. They were doing a good six knots and as they came abreast of us, so close we could have tossed a coin on to their decks, their crews began to sing – a sad, strange chant. Both ships were flying the blue, green and red flag of the Adduan People's Republic and when they were past and showing us their blunt, dhow-like sterns, the crews moved to their stations. They stood in as far as the first shoal, and just beyond it they turned as one with their bows facing into the wind and the sails came down with a run as the anchors were let go.

I shall never forget the arrival of those first two vedis. It wasn't just that they looked so magnificent, coming in like that without engines, their decks littered with the bits and pieces of the boats they had brought with them. It was the behaviour of their crews· After such a long and dangerous voyage they might have been expected to rest or embark on a leisurely exploration of the island. Instead, they went to work at once unloading gear and stores, getting their dhonis launched. Their urgency and enthusiasm was so immediate that we just stood there, watching spellbound, so that it was some time before we got into a boat and went across to them.

A gangway had been lowered on the leading vedi and Don Mansoor met us at the head of it, immaculate in a clean sarong and a kahki shirt, a cheerful smile on his face. 'Nine days we are sailing here – no very bad, uh?' Then he turned to the island with a wave of his hand: 'Is changing very much.'

'It's grown a bit, that's all,' Peter said. 'But there's nothing to worry about.'

Don Mansoor nodded, still smiling broadly. 'All men having more land now.' Cans of grapejuice were opened, a celebration, with Don Mansoor talking of the voyage, of the storm that had driven them too far south. 'The aircraft from Gan very kind. Is flying over us some time to show us what course we must steer.'

All the time he was talking I could feel Peter's impatience growing. Finally he told him about the frigate. And as soon as Don Mansoor understood what was involved he had an extra spar they were carrying lowered into our boat and we took it ashore and erected it as a flag pole just back of the quay.

The ceremony took place at ten-thirty in the presence of the Adduans, the shore party and most of the crew of the *Strode Venturer*. Peter addressed the gathering, first in English and then briefly in Adduan. He was followed by Don Mansoor who named the island Ran-a-Maari because he said it was born of the white water, of the struggle of the imprisoned land against the power of the great ocean – good emerging out of evil. The Adduan flag was then run up on the spar they had brought from Midu. It was an impressive, very colourful flag – blue, green and red in horizontal stripes with white stars in opposite corners and a white star and crescent in the centre. Peter then produced a new ship's log book and everybody signed their name in it as witness to the formal annexation of the island by the Adduan People's Republic.

As soon as the ceremony was over Peter went back to the ship and drafted messages to the outside world. The first, sent out by Weston at eleven-fifteen and addressed to Reuter, simply announced the formal occupation of the island and gave its name and location. This was followed by a fuller account, including passages from the speeches that he and Don Mansoor had made. Finally, messages were sent to *The Times*, The *Daily Telegraph*, the

New York Times, Tass and *Paris Match.*

Two things I particularly remember that afternoon: the first was a tour of the island we made with Don Mansoor. He was tired and his first enthusiasm had worn off. He was looking at the island then with a critical eye, facing the problem of establishing his people in an area that to my mind was distinctly inhospitable. We went first to the hollow where the palm tree seedlings had established themselves and I was amazed to see how lush the growth of vegetation had become in the short time since I had last seen it. He went down on his hands and knees, tearing at the soil with his dark fingers, examining the roots. Finally he stood up. 'We are bringing with us many little plants. Everything growing on Midu. Is okay. All making good in this soil.' He was smiling happily. And then we went out to the north end of the island where the shallows were. There were drifts of dark, rich sand and already here and there the first green of vegetation, the growth of seeds carried on the wind from distant shores. And there were terns, the first wild life I had seen. 'Is good,' he said. 'Is very good. A year, two years – all is green.'

The second thing I shall always remember occurred just after we had returned to the quay. The Adduans had been checking on the fishing, using one of the dhonis since it would be several days before the batteli could be reassembled. The breeze had held all day and the dhoni came roaring in through the shallows, its squares'l sheeted hard in and the men in her shouting and waving. In little over an hour, using their bent metal nails and long bamboo rods, they had half-filled the boat with fish, mainly bonito.

They would still need sugar, rice, implements, but they knew now that the island was viable. They had the illusion, if not the actuality, of independence. And in the stockpile of ore on the quay they had the assurance that here was something else besides cowrie shells and dried fish that they could trade to the outside world. They were in great spirits and their morale was high when shortly after four the frigate was sighted, steaming in from the north-west.

She came into the anchorage, feeling her way carefully, and let go just astern of the *Strode Venturer*. A few minutes later a boat put off from her side. It was a lieutenant-commander who came ashore, a strange contrast in his immaculate white uniform to the motley crowd awaiting him on the quay. Don Mansoor stepped forward to greet him. 'Welcome, sir, to Ran-a-Maari. Me commanding expedition of the Adduan People's Republic.' It was said gravely, courteously.

The lieutenant-commander saluted him, equally grave, equally courteous as he shook hands. 'My name is Wainwright.' He glanced at the flag now hanging limp from its improvised pole. 'I am instructed to offer you any assistance you may need and for your protection to put a naval party ashore on the island.'

No doubt in international law the occupation of the island by the Adduans posed a nice problem, since they were regarded as rebels by the Malé Government and the People's Republic was not recognized by any of the powers. But by establishing a naval party ashore, ostensibly for the protection of the Adduan settlers, the British Government had reserved its rights without committing itself in any way. The presence of the frigate certainly pleased Don Mansoor. It gave strong backing to his occupation of the island. And now that the Adduans had arrived it pleased Peter too, since it had the effect of endorsing our claim for the exploitation of the mineral rights. It also solved our transport problem, the frigate having been *en route* for Singapore when it had been diverted.

A party of us, including Don Mansoor, were entertained on board that night. And in the morning Wainwright started setting up his shore base. The Adduans were also establishing themselves ashore, erecting huts of palm matting on spars and planks brought off from the vedis. The masts were taken out and the vessels stripped of their decks and all superstructure so that they could be used as ore-carriers. The *Strode Venturer* was manœuvred into the deep-water channel by the first shoal and hawsers run out between the vessel and the quay so that the loaded vedis could be winched out to the ship. And that evening as the sun set sails were sighted to the west – five ships in silhouette against the flaming sky.

It was Ali Raza with the rest of the fleet, his vedis spread out in a line, their sails filled by a gentle westerly. Slowly the sky's glow faded, darkness fell and they came in gliding like ghosts on the last of the breeze. The sea was calm, a lake across which every sound was magnified, and the quiet of Ran-a-Maari was broken by the high, wild cries of the people of Midu greeting each other.

We were already embarked on the frigate, having left Ford and Haines in charge of loading. The anchor was coming up, the engines vibrating under our feet, and as the bows swung to the open sea the siren blared. 'A pity George can't see this,' Peter said. We were standing on the upper bridge and as the frigate steamed out of the anchorage bound for Singapore, the vedis were coming to rest, the sails falling to the decks like five fat women shedding their clothing. The dhonis were putting off from the quay, four men rowing, and ashore, in a blaze of lights from the generator, we could see small figures shovelling ore from the stockpile on to the conveyor belt and the black nodules falling steadily into the vedi lying alongside. The dark bulk of the island, the stars bright as diamonds and the *Strode Venturer* huge in the night with her deck lights blazing and the hatch covers off, the cargo booms swung out ready; it was a strange, almost beautiful sight. And the man whose dream it was stood tense beside me. He did not move or utter a word until we had turned the northern end of the island and the great expanse of ocean had closed us in. Then he murmured something in Adduan, the word Ran-a-Maari rolling off his tongue. It might have been a prayer the way he said it. And after staring for a moment longer at the blackness of the sea ahead, he turned without another word and left me, his shoulders drooped, his feet dragging, a man exhausted with the effort of turning a dream into reality.

PART SEVEN

BOARDROOM POSTSCRIPT

THE EXTRAORDINARY general meeting of Strode Orient share-holders had been convened for one purpose and one purpose only – the voluntary liquidation of the company. This proposal had the backing of the entire board of directors and was supported by Strode & Company as well as Lingrose and his associates. The meeting was held at noon on 24 July. At that time we were off the coast of Sumatra, the frigate having proved slower than we had expected. We didn't reach London until two days later and it was only then that we heard from Ida what had happened.

The resolution had been carried on a show of hands. A vote had then been demanded and at that point Felden had intervened, stating that his clients had not been given the statutory twenty-one days' notice. This was confirmed by Whimbrill who said that owing to an oversight several shareholders, among them Moss-bacher Fayle & Co., the merchant bankers acting for the in-surance company's interests, had not been given notice of the meeting. The oversight had, of course, been deliberate. Whimbrill was playing for time. So was Felden by then. Merchant bankers don't like to have their clients accept a big loss when by holding on they could come out of it with a profit. He had demanded a postal vote and at least ten days' grace.

It was a technicality, of course, and the Strode Orient board already had overwhelming support for their resolution. But half of it was represented by the forty-four per cent Strode & Com-pany holding and the board's decision to vote in favour had been taken at a meeting attended only by Henry Strode, le Fleming, Crane and Whimbrill. Ida had not been present and once it was known that Peter was alive the validity of that decision was in doubt. Felden's support had then become crucial.

'So we have ten days,' Peter said. 'Ten days in which to tear this resolution to shreds.' The excitement in his voice, the under-lying note of violence brought a cautionary glance from Ida.

'You have seven days as from tomorrow,' she said quietly. 'And you still have to convince Felden that his clients will make more by backing you than they would out of the carving up of Strode Orient.'

Prior to that, of course, the Strode & Company decision to support the winding-up had to be reversed. Peter had cabled Whimbrill from Singapore and now Ida told us that a meeting of the board had been called for nine o'clock next morning. Peter refused to discuss the line he would take and this worried her. She was also worried about Henry Strode's attitude to our appointment as directors. It was the first board meeting either of us had attended and I think we were both a little nervous – so much depended on it.

It was raining when we left the flat in the morning, a warm summer rain that reminded me of Ran-a-Maari, but softer, more gentle. By the time we got to the Embankment it had stopped. The flooding river gleamed mistily in shafts of watery sunlight and the churches and office towers of the City had a soft, Turneresque glow. We didn't talk. We had said all there was to say. But as our taxi stopped in the traffic at the Bank Ida's hand sought mine and held it a moment – a gesture that was part affection, part encouragement.

I was thinking of that time I had stood alone on the Embankment in the bitter cold after having read the account of my father's crash. It seemed a long time ago now, and this the end of a long journey. I glanced at Ida and her eyes met mine – warm and alive. She was dressed in a dark blue suit, silk by the sheen of it, and she wore an antique gold necklace, a gold fob. The effect was businesslike and at the same time very feminine, her dark hair framing her face.

And then our taxi pulled up at Strode House and we went in together, up the big staircase with the portrait of Sir Reginald Bailey. It no longer seemed to me like a trophy hung on the wall, rather the ghost of my father welcoming me into the world he had helped to create. Peter was waiting for us at the head of the stairs, his tanned face gaunt under its fringe of beard. The tightness of his mouth, the hard, tense look in his eyes, should have warned me. It was the face of a man who had worked himself up to a point where he would destroy anybody who stood between him and his objective. I think Ida understood his mood for she put her hand on his arm as though to restrain him. But she didn't say anything. Whimbrill was there. By contrast his face looked very pale, almost scared.

We went into the boardroom then. Henry Strode was already there, seated at the head of the big table talking to Crane. Behind him loomed the portrait of his father. The atmosphere of the room with its panelling, its pictures, its heavy chandeliers, was solid, almost Victorian. It had the air of established power that belonged to a past age. Le Fleming arrived a moment later. Whimbrill closed the door behind him and a heavy silence settled on the room. It was broken by Henry Strode. 'If you'll sit down, gentlemen . . .' And when we were settled he opened the meeting by formally welcoming Ida and myself to the board. He did it without enthusiasm, his eyes fixed coldly on Ida's handbag as though the polished surface of the boardroom table had been somehow desecrated. He then turned to Peter and in the same flat, formal voice congratulated him on what he described as his miraculous escape. 'And now, since I gather from Whimbrill that it is at your instance we have all foregathered here, perhaps you would care to address the meeting.'

I naturally assumed that Peter would take this opportunity to enlarge on the potentiality of the island in an endeavour to persuade them that this was not the time to wind up the shipping side of the business. I think the others expected it, too, for there was a general settling back into the big, comfortable chairs. But he didn't bother about that. He was intent only on destroying all opposition. 'I have been looking at the Memorandum and Articles of Association of the Strode companies and I find we have the right to nominate two directors to serve on the Strode Orient board. Our two nominees at the present time are yourself – ' He was looking straight at Henry Strode – 'and your brother George. I propose that you both be instructed to resign as directors of Strode Orient and that in your place we nominate Geoffrey Bailey here and a man of some standing from outside the organization who has an interest in Strode Orient – I think Felden would be a good choice and suggest that he be approached.'

There was a moment of stunned silence. Nobody was leaning back in their chairs any more. They were all staring at Peter. And the stillness in the room was absolute so that I became conscious of the ormolu clock on the mantelpiece. The ticking of it was very loud, and above it the face of old Henry Strode glowered down at us from its ornate frame.

Peter looked across the table at Whimbrill. 'Will you second that?'

'Just a moment.' Henry Strode leaned quickly forward. His eyes gleamed behind his glasses, two angry spots of colour showing on his sallow cheeks. 'Your proposal has not yet been formally put before the meeting. And I think I should tell you that as long as I am in the chair here it will not be put. It's the most outrageous – '

'I quite understand your reluctance.' Peter's voice was tense and hard. 'To save you that embarrassment perhaps I should tell you that I have a further proposal to put to this meeting.' I saw Ida's hand reach out to restrain him, but he ignored it. ' You've forced me to this – you and George between you. Now there is no alternative. I propose that you be removed from the chairmanship of this board and also from the position of managing director and that a new chairman and managing director be elected from among the directors present at this meeting.'

The directness of the attack, the personal nature of it took Henry Strode completely by surprise. There was a shocked look on his face – on the faces of the others, too. Whimbrill's breath expelled in an audible hiss.

'Perhaps you would have the motion read out and put to the meeting,' Peter said quietly.

It was a moment before Henry Strode found his voice. 'I think I am entitled to say a few words before I do that.' He hesitated, his hands gripped on the arms of his chair so that he seemed to be bracing himself. He was literally trembling, dominated now by the family feud that had soured their relationship for years. 'I've worked in the City for over thirty years, and so has George, whilst you've been travelling the world on the money we made for you. You know nothing about the problems we've had to face; yet now, after only three years' business experience – and that in quite a junior capacity – you want to run this company, and Strode Orient as well.' The heavy eyelids flicked open and he stared stonily round the table. Finally his gaze settled on Whimbrill. He knew he had to have Whimbrill's support or he would be out. 'I think you should understand – all of you – what is involved here. I have a service agreement with this company and it was only renewed last year. If you break it I shall certainly sue. Further, I think I should make it clear that if this motion were to succeed my immediate reaction would be to resign from the board.' He stared at Whimbrill a moment longer and then his head turned and he was facing the rest of us. 'I hope, gentlemen, I have made my position clear.'

Nobody spoke after that and in the end Whimbrill read out the motion. At Peter's request – and somewhat reluctantly – I seconded it. Henry Strode had no alternative then but to put it to the meeting. For a moment there were only our three hands raised. We were all of us staring at Whimbrill and he sat there very still and pale, angry at being placed in such a position. Finally, he faced his chairman. 'It was your father who brought me into the business. I admired him greatly and since his death I have seen the organization he built up go steadily downhill. Now we are faced with a challenge, a new opportunity – '

'You're voting for the motion, is that it?' Henry Strode's voice was bleak.

Whimbrill hesitated. Then he nodded. 'Yes,' he said and raised his hand.

Henry Strode sat without moving for a moment. He had lost and there was an expression almost of disbelief on his face as he stared round the table. Finally his gaze fastened on me and his face contracted, a spasm of quite uncontrolled rage. 'First you talk my brother into giving you a job in Strode House. Then you persuade an old dotard to give you his shares, get yourself appointed to the board. You're the real instigator of these – these shoddy manœuvres.' He took a deep breath, struggling to control himself. 'Now we know your background I can promise you this,' he said, his voice trembling. 'Strode Orient will be placed beyond your reach.' And then he got to his feet and stood for a moment looking vaguely round the room, much as Deacon had done that last time he had left the wheelhouse. 'Are you coming, Adrian?' Crane nodded, pushing back his chair. 'Julian?' Henry Strode was looking down at le Fleming. But like Whimbrill, le Fleming had been brought into the business by old Henry Strode. He held other directorships in the City and he liked to be on the winning side. He didn't answer, and after staring at him a moment longer, Henry Strode walked out of the room followed by Crane.

There was a moment of complete silence as the door closed behind them. Then Whimbrill turned to Peter. 'I assume you wish to take over the chair and the office of managing director?' His voice sounded tired and strained.

But Peter shook his head. 'I know far too little about the day-to-day management of the company and if things go as I hope I shall be out of the country most of the time.' Instead, he proposed that le Fleming be elected chairman and Whimbrill managing director. It was a shrewd move, particularly the appointment of le Fleming as chairman. He then put his original proposal to the meeting. But I was against it. So were Whimbrill and le Fleming; Ida, too. This wasn't the moment to drive the Strodes into a corner. They had too many friends in the City. And with all his faults George Strode at least had energy and drive. Given something to get his teeth into I thought he might serve us very well. Moreover, there was the matter of the *Strode Trader*. 'There's no point in alienating George Strode,' I said. 'If we can get his co-operation – and I think ultimately he might be persuaded – then the whole venture becomes much simpler, particularly the organization of the shipping side of it.' This was the first of many occasions that I was to find myself in disagreement with Peter, forced to counter his impetuosity and seek a compromise to avoid creating enemies. It was just one more thing that Turner had foreseen. In the end it was agreed to shelve the matter and Peter sat there, furious at being balked, whilst we went on to consider a proposal from Whimbrill for the formation of a new operating company. This was in case we failed to get Felden's support and lost control of Strode Orient. Whimbrill also wanted authority to place an order with a Japanese yard for a 60,000-ton ore carrier.

We were still discussing these points when George Strode burst into the room, his heavy face blazing with anger. 'I was out or I'd have been in to see you before. My brother has just told me.' He stared at le Fleming. 'You've taken over the chair, have you?'

Le Fleming was momentarily caught off balance. He looked embarrassed. 'I'm sorry, George. Henry had a majority against him.'

'So I understand. After all these years . . .' George Strode's eyes fastened on Peter. 'You won't get away with this,' he said. 'Not if I can help it. And let me tell you this, all of you. You take any decision affecting the operation of this company without Henry present and we'll sue you for damages on the grounds of mis-management.'

'Henry resigned,' le Fleming said.

'He may have threatened to resign. He certainly walked out. I'd have walked out myself. But he didn't resign.' He hunched his shoulders aggressively. 'Until you have a letter of resignation from him Henry is still a director. Meantime, if you take any decision materially affecting the company or its shareholders we'll sue you each and individually. This we're entitled to do. Henry's been on to our lawyers. He's also been on to Jacob Hinchcliffe. He's with us and so is Adrian Crane.' And with that he turned and stamped out of the room.

It was almost lunchtime before le Fleming declared the meeting closed. Nothing had been decided. George Strode's threat of court action had effectively killed all initiative. 'Culpable negligence on the part of a director or the directors of a company isn't an easy

thing to prove,' le Fleming said. 'But the position of a new board taking over is never a strong one and in the circumstances . . .' In the circumstances he thought it best to wait until after the meeting with Felden, and to that Whimbrill agreed.

Le Fleming went with Peter to that meeting. It was inconclusive. Felden listened to what they had to say, asked a few questions and agreed to consult his clients. Meantime, I had seen George Strode. I had to, for he had called a Press conference for the following morning. As I had expected Reece, now back in England, had reached the same conclusion about his navigational error that Deacon and I had – a faulty compass. 'You can't prove that,' I said, 'any more than I can prove Reece was given instructions to leave us stranded on the island.' George Strode didn't say anything, but I knew he had taken the point.

Neither of the Strodes had any experience of dealing with the Press. Publicity to them meant telling the public what they wanted it to know and that usually through the medium of a chairman's speech advertised in the more sober papers. To hold a Press conference so soon after the *Strode Venturer*'s re-discovery of the island was a fatal mistake. It merely drew attention to Peter's return, adding fuel to the fire already smouldering under them. Instead of City correspondents they were faced with a large number of Fleet Street journalists and broadcasting men, all of them interested in a much wider story and in the personalities involved. They listened politely to what the Strode brothers had to say and then sought Peter out. TV cameras rolled, the pencils flew, and women reporters got hold of Ida, intrigued by the fact that one of their own sex had become involved in a boardroom squabble. The result was a great deal of publicity for Ran-a-Maari and the venture on which we were embarked, all within the framework of the story of a brother and sister fighting for their rights against the entrenched power of the older generation of Strodes. And I came into it, too – the story of the Bailey Oriental crash dredged from the files.

Felden came to us two days later. He wanted an undertaking that we would not form a new operating company. 'My clients,' he said in his prim, careful voice, 'are holders of Strode Orient shares and their interest is, therefore, limited solely to that company. So long as it is understood that the transport of all ore from the island is in the hands of Strode Orient I am instructed to tell you that you have their support.'

We had an effective majority then and the resolution that would have meant the end of Strode Orient was defeated. We were free to go ahead. We had an operating company with ships to transport the ore and the cash to finance the mining of it. Henry Strode retired, a golden handshake that was in effect a pension for life. George stayed on as chairman of Strode Orient whilst I took over the management of the company.

Nine months later Ida and I took the two children half across the world, and in a foreign yard, with Dick Whimbrill beside her, Mary stood in a drizzle of rain facing the towering bows of a new ore carrier. In a small, clear, English voice she said, 'I name this ship the *Strode Venturer* – and I wish her and all who sail in her good fortune.' And then she pulled the lever and the high bows slid away from us.

The old *Strode Venturer* – Deacon's ship – had been sold for scrap six months before.